Jeeves and Psmith Collection

By

P G Wodehouse

Cover Photograph: Paul Stephenson

ISBN: 978-1-78139-291-1

Contents

MIKE

Psmith in the City

Psmith, Journalist

THE MAN WITH TWO LEFT FEET

MY MAN JEEVES

RIGHT HO, JEEVES

MIKE

A PUBLIC SCHOOL STORY

CONTAINING TWELVE
ILLUSTRATIONS BY
T. M. R. WHITWELL

TO
ALAN DURAND

"ARE YOU THE M. JACKSON, THEN, WHO HAD AN AVERAGE OF FIFTY-ONE POINT NOUGHT THREE LAST YEAR?"

p. 225

CHAPTER I MIKE

It was a morning in the middle of April, and the Jackson family were consequently breakfasting in comparative silence. The cricket season had not begun, and except during the cricket season they were in the habit of devoting their powerful minds at breakfast almost exclusively to the task of victualling against the labours of the day. In May, June, July, and August the silence was broken. The three grown-up Jacksons played regularly in first-class cricket, and there was always keen competition among their brothers and sisters for the copy of the *Sportsman* which was to be found on the hall table with the letters. Whoever got it usually gloated over it in silence till urged wrathfully by the multitude to let them know what had happened; when it would appear that Joe had notched his seventh century, or that Reggie had been run out when he was just getting set, or, as sometimes occurred, that that ass Frank had dropped Fry or Hayward in the slips before he had scored, with the result that the spared expert had made a couple of hundred and was still going strong.

In such a case the criticisms of the family circle, particularly of the smaller Jackson sisters, were so breezy and unrestrained that Mrs. Jackson generally felt it necessary to apply the closure. Indeed, Marjory Jackson, aged fourteen, had on three several occasions been fined pudding at lunch for her caustic comments on the batting of her brother Reggie in important fixtures. Cricket was a tradition in the family, and the ladies, unable to their sorrow to play the game themselves, were resolved that it should not be their fault if the standard was not kept up.

On this particular morning silence reigned. A deep gasp from some small Jackson, wrestling with bread-and-milk, and an occasional remark from Mr. Jackson on the letters he was reading, alone broke it.

"Mike's late again," said Mrs. Jackson plaintively, at last.

"He's getting up," said Marjory. "I went in to see what he was doing, and he was asleep. So," she added with a satanic chuckle, "I squeezed a sponge over him. He swallowed an awful lot, and then he woke up, and tried to catch me, so he's certain to be down soon."

"Marjory!"

"Well, he was on his back with his mouth wide open. I had to. He was snoring like anything."

"You might have choked him."

"I did," said Marjory with satisfaction. "Jam, please, Phyllis, you pig."

Mr. Jackson looked up.

"Mike will have to be more punctual when he goes to Wrykyn," he said.

"Oh, father, is Mike going to Wrykyn?" asked Marjory. "When?"

"Next term," said Mr. Jackson. "I've just heard from Mr. Wain," he added across the table to Mrs. Jackson. "The house is full, but he is turning a small room into an extra dormitory, so he can take Mike after all."

The first comment on this momentous piece of news came from Bob Jackson. Bob was eighteen. The following term would be his last at Wrykyn, and, having won through so far without the infliction of a small brother, he disliked the prospect of not being allowed to finish as he had begun.

"I say!" he said. "What?"

"He ought to have gone before," said Mr. Jackson. "He's fifteen. Much too old for that private school. He has had it all his own way there, and it isn't good for him."

"He's got cheek enough for ten," agreed Bob.

"Wrykyn will do him a world of good."

"We aren't in the same house. That's one comfort."

Bob was in Donaldson's. It softened the blow to a certain extent that Mike should be going to Wain's. He had the same feeling for Mike that most boys of eighteen have for their fifteen-year-old brothers. He was fond of him in the abstract, but preferred him at a distance.

Marjory gave tongue again. She had rescued the jam from Phyllis, who had shown signs of finishing it, and was now at liberty to turn her mind to less pressing matters. Mike was her special ally, and anything that affected his fortunes affected her.

"Hooray! Mike's going to Wrykyn. I bet he gets into the first eleven his first term."

"Considering there are eight old colours left," said Bob loftily, "besides heaps of last year's seconds, it's hardly likely that a kid like Mike'll get a look in. He might get his third, if he sweats."

The aspersion stung Marjory.

"I bet he gets in before you, anyway," she said.

Bob disdained to reply. He was among those heaps of last year's seconds to whom he had referred. He was a sound bat, though lacking the brilliance of his elder brothers, and he fancied that his cap was a certainty this season. Last year he had been tried once or twice. This year it should be all right.

Mrs. Jackson intervened.

"Go on with your breakfast, Marjory," she said. "You mustn't say 'I bet' so much."

Marjory bit off a section of her slice of bread-and-jam.

"Anyhow, I bet he does," she muttered truculently through it.

There was a sound of footsteps in the passage outside. The door opened, and the missing member of the family appeared. Mike Jackson was tall for his age.

His figure was thin and wiry. His arms and legs looked a shade too long for his body. He was evidently going to be very tall some day. In face, he was curiously like his brother Joe, whose appearance is familiar to every one who takes an interest in first-class cricket. The resemblance was even more marked on the cricket field. Mike had Joe's batting style to the last detail. He was a pocket edition of his century-making brother. "Hullo," he said, "sorry I'm late."

This was mere stereo. He had made the same remark nearly every morning since the beginning of the holidays.

"All right, Marjory, you little beast," was his reference to the sponge incident.

His third remark was of a practical nature.

"I say, what's under that dish?"

"Mike," began Mr. Jackson—-this again was stereo—-"you really must learn to be more punctual——-"

He was interrupted by a chorus.

"Mike, you're going to Wrykyn next term," shouted Marjory.

"Mike, father's just had a letter to say you're going to Wrykyn next term." From Phyllis.

"Mike, you're going to Wrykyn." From Ella.

Gladys Maud Evangeline, aged three, obliged with a solo of her own composition, in six-eight time, as follows: "Mike Wryky. Mike Wryky. Mike Wryke Wryke Wryke Mike Wryke Wryke Mike Wryke Mike Wryke."

"Oh, put a green baize cloth over that kid, somebody," groaned Bob.

Whereat Gladys Maud, having fixed him with a chilly stare for some seconds, suddenly drew a long breath, and squealed deafeningly for more milk.

Mike looked round the table. It was a great moment. He rose to it with the utmost dignity.

"Good," he said. "I say, what's under that dish?"

After breakfast, Mike and Marjory went off together to the meadow at the end of the garden. Saunders, the professional, assisted by the gardener's boy, was engaged in putting up the net. Mr. Jackson believed in private coaching; and every spring since Joe, the eldest of the family, had been able to use a bat a man had come down from the Oval to teach him the best way to do so. Each of the boys in turn had passed from spectators to active participants in the net practice in the meadow. For several years now Saunders had been the chosen man, and his attitude towards the Jacksons was that of the Faithful Old Retainer in melodrama. Mike was his special favourite. He felt that in him he had material of the finest order to work upon. There was nothing the matter with Bob. In Bob he would turn out a good, sound article. Bob would be a Blue in his third or fourth year, and probably a creditable performer among the rank and file of a county team later on. But he was not a cricket genius, like Mike. Saunders would lie awake at night sometimes thinking of the possibilities that were in Mike. The strength could only come with years, but the style was there already. Joe's style, with improvements.

Mike put on his pads; and Marjory walked with the professional to the bowling crease.

"Mike's going to Wrykyn next term, Saunders," she said. "All the boys were there, you know. So was father, ages ago."

"Is he, miss? I was thinking he would be soon."

"Do you think he'll get into the school team?"

"School team, miss! Master Mike get into a school team! He'll be playing for England in another eight years. That's what he'll be playing for."

"Yes, but I meant next term. It would be a record if he did. Even Joe only got in after he'd been at school two years. Don't you think he might, Saunders? He's awfully good, isn't he? He's better than Bob, isn't he? And Bob's almost certain to get in this term."

Saunders looked a little doubtful.

"Next term!" he said. "Well, you see, miss, it's this way. It's all there, in a manner of speaking, with Master Mike. He's got as much style as Mr. Joe's got, every bit. The whole thing is, you see, miss, you get these young gentlemen of eighteen, and nineteen perhaps, and it stands to reason they're stronger. There's a young gentleman, perhaps, doesn't know as much about what I call real playing as Master Mike's forgotten; but then he can hit 'em harder when he does hit 'em, and that's where the runs come in. They aren't going to play Master Mike because he'll be in the England team when he leaves school. They'll give the cap to somebody that can make a few then and there."

"But Mike's jolly strong."

"Ah, I'm not saying it mightn't be, miss. I was only saying don't count on it, so you won't be disappointed if it doesn't happen. It's quite likely that it will, only all I say is don't count on it. I only hope that they won't knock all the style out of him before they're done with him. You know these school professionals, miss."

"No, I don't, Saunders. What are they like?"

"Well, there's too much of the come-right-out-at-everything about 'em for my taste. Seem to think playing forward the alpha and omugger of batting. They'll make him pat balls back to the bowler which he'd cut for twos and threes if he was left to himself. Still, we'll hope for the best, miss. Ready, Master Mike? Play."

As Saunders had said, it was all there. Of Mike's style there could be no doubt. To-day, too, he was playing more strongly than usual. Marjory had to run to the end of the meadow to fetch one straight drive. "He hit that hard enough, didn't he, Saunders?" she asked, as she returned the ball.

"If he could keep on doing ones like that, miss," said the professional, "they'd have him in the team before you could say knife."

Marjory sat down again beside the net, and watched more hopefully.

CHAPTER II THE JOURNEY DOWN

The seeing off of Mike on the last day of the holidays was an imposing spectacle, a sort of pageant. Going to a public school, especially at the beginning of the summer term, is no great hardship, more particularly when the departing hero has a brother on the verge of the school eleven and three other brothers playing for counties; and Mike seemed in no way disturbed by the prospect. Mothers, however, to the end of time will foster a secret fear that their sons will be bullied at a big school, and Mrs. Jackson's anxious look lent a fine solemnity to the proceedings.

And as Marjory, Phyllis, and Ella invariably broke down when the time of separation arrived, and made no exception to their rule on the present occasion, a suitable gloom was the keynote of the gathering. Mr. Jackson seemed to bear the parting with fortitude, as did Mike's Uncle John (providentially roped in at the eleventh hour on his way to Scotland, in time to come down with a handsome tip). To their coarse-fibred minds there was nothing pathetic or tragic about the affair at all. (At the very moment when the train began to glide out of the station Uncle John was heard to remark that, in his opinion, these Bocks weren't a patch on the old shaped Larranaga.) Among others present might have been noticed Saunders, practising late cuts rather coyly with a walking-stick in the background; the village idiot, who had rolled up on the chance of a dole; Gladys Maud Evangeline's nurse, smiling vaguely; and Gladys Maud Evangeline herself, frankly bored with the whole business.

The train gathered speed. The air was full of last messages. Uncle John said on second thoughts he wasn't sure these Bocks weren't half a bad smoke after all. Gladys Maud cried, because she had taken a sudden dislike to the village idiot; and Mike settled himself in the corner and opened a magazine.

He was alone in the carriage. Bob, who had been spending the last week of the holidays with an aunt further down the line, was to board the train at East Wobsley, and the brothers were to make a state entry into Wrykyn together. Meanwhile, Mike was left to his milk chocolate, his magazines, and his reflections.

The latter were not numerous, nor profound. He was excited. He had been petitioning the home authorities for the past year to be allowed to leave his private school and go to Wrykyn, and now the thing had come about. He wondered what sort of a house Wain's was, and whether they had any chance of the cricket cup. According to Bob they had no earthly; but then Bob only recognised one house, Donaldson's. He wondered if Bob would get his first eleven cap this year, and if he himself were likely to do anything at cricket. Marjory had faithfully reported every word Saunders had said on the subject, but Bob had been so careful to point out his insignificance when compared with the humblest Wrykynian that the professional's glowing prophecies had not had much effect. It might be true that some day he would play for England, but just at present he felt he would exchange his place in the team for one in the Wrykyn third eleven. A sort of mist enveloped everything Wrykynian. It seemed almost hopeless to try and compete with these unknown experts. On the other hand, there was Bob. Bob, by all accounts, was on the verge of the first eleven, and he was nothing special.

While he was engaged on these reflections, the train drew up at a small station. Opposite the door of Mike's compartment was standing a boy of about Mike's size, though evidently some years older. He had a sharp face, with rather a prominent nose; and a pair of pince-nez gave him a supercilious look. He wore a bowler hat, and carried a small portmanteau.

He opened the door, and took the seat opposite to Mike, whom he scrutinised for a moment rather after the fashion of a naturalist examining some new and unpleasant variety of beetle. He seemed about to make some remark, but, instead, got up and looked through the open window.

"Where's that porter?" Mike heard him say.

The porter came skimming down the platform at that moment.

"Porter."

"Sir?"

"Are those frightful boxes of mine in all right?"

"Yes, sir."

"Because, you know, there'll be a frightful row if any of them get lost."

"No chance of that, sir."

"Here you are, then."

"Thank you, sir."

The youth drew his head and shoulders in, stared at Mike again, and finally sat down. Mike noticed that he had nothing to read, and wondered if he wanted anything; but he did not feel equal to offering him one of his magazines. He did not like the looks of him particularly. Judging by appearances, he seemed to carry enough side for three. If he wanted a magazine, thought Mike, let him ask for it.

The other made no overtures, and at the next stop got out. That explained his magazineless condition. He was only travelling a short way.

"Good business," said Mike to himself. He had all the Englishman's love of a carriage to himself.

The train was just moving out of the station when his eye was suddenly caught by the stranger's bag, lying snugly in the rack.

And here, I regret to say, Mike acted from the best motives, which is always fatal.

He realised in an instant what had happened. The fellow had forgotten his bag.

Mike had not been greatly fascinated by the stranger's looks; but, after all, the most supercilious person on earth has a right to his own property. Besides, he might have been quite a nice fellow when you got to know him. Anyhow, the bag had better be returned at once. The train was already moving quite fast, and Mike's compartment was nearing the end of the platform.

He snatched the bag from the rack and hurled it out of the window. (Porter Robinson, who happened to be in the line of fire, escaped with a flesh wound.) Then he sat down again with the inward glow of satisfaction which comes to one when one has risen successfully to a sudden emergency.

The glow lasted till the next stoppage, which did not occur for a good many miles. Then it ceased abruptly, for the train had scarcely come to a standstill when the opening above the door was darkened by a head and shoulders. The head was surmounted by a bowler, and a pair of pince-nez gleamed from the shadow.

"Hullo, I say," said the stranger. "Have you changed carriages, or what?"

"No," said Mike.

"Then, dash it, where's my frightful bag?"

Life teems with embarrassing situations. This was one of them.

"The fact is," said Mike, "I chucked it out."

"Chucked it out! what do you mean? When?"

"At the last station."

The guard blew his whistle, and the other jumped into the carriage.

"I thought you'd got out there for good," explained Mike. "I'm awfully sorry."

"Where *is* the bag?"

"On the platform at the last station. It hit a porter."

Against his will, for he wished to treat the matter with fitting solemnity, Mike grinned at the recollection. The look on Porter Robinson's face as the bag took him in the small of the back had been funny, though not intentionally so.

The bereaved owner disapproved of this levity; and said as much.

"Don't *grin*, you little beast," he shouted. "There's nothing to laugh at. You go chucking bags that don't belong to you out of the window, and then you have the frightful cheek to grin about it."

"It wasn't that," said Mike hurriedly. "Only the porter looked awfully funny when it hit him."

"Dash the porter! What's going to happen about my bag? I can't get out for half a second to buy a magazine without your flinging my things about the platform. What you want is a frightful kicking."

The situation was becoming difficult. But fortunately at this moment the train stopped once again; and, looking out of the window, Mike saw a board with East Wobsley upon it in large letters. A moment later Bob's head appeared in the doorway.

"Hullo, there you are," said Bob.

His eye fell upon Mike's companion.

"Hullo, Gazeka!" he exclaimed. "Where did you spring from? Do you know my brother? He's coming to Wrykyn this term. By the way, rather lucky you've met. He's in your house. Firby-Smith's head of Wain's, Mike."

Mike gathered that Gazeka and Firby-Smith were one and the same person. He grinned again. Firby-Smith continued to look ruffled, though not aggressive.

"Oh, are you in Wain's?" he said.

"I say, Bob," said Mike, "I've made rather an ass of myself."

"Naturally."

"I mean, what happened was this. I chucked Firby-Smith's portmanteau out of the window, thinking he'd got out, only he hadn't really, and it's at a station miles back."

"You're a bit of a rotter, aren't you? Had it got your name and address on it, Gazeka?"

"Yes."

"Oh, then it's certain to be all right. It's bound to turn up some time. They'll send it on by the next train, and you'll get it either to-night or to-morrow."

"Frightful nuisance, all the same. Lots of things in it I wanted."

"Oh, never mind, it's all right. I say, what have you been doing in the holidays? I didn't know you lived on this line at all."

From this point onwards Mike was out of the conversation altogether. Bob and Firby-Smith talked of Wrykyn, discussing events of the previous term of which Mike had never heard. Names came into their conversation which were entirely new to him. He realised that school politics were being talked, and that contributions from him to the dialogue were not required. He took up his magazine again, listening the while. They were discussing Wain's now. The name Wyatt cropped up with some frequency. Wyatt was apparently something of a character. Mention was made of rows in which he had played a part in the past.

"It must be pretty rotten for him," said Bob. "He and Wain never get on very well, and yet they have to be together, holidays as well as term. Pretty bad having a step-father at all—I shouldn't care to—and when your house-master and your step-father are the same man, it's a bit thick."

"Frightful," agreed Firby-Smith.

"I swear, if I were in Wyatt's place, I should rot about like anything. It isn't as if he'd anything to look forward to when he leaves. He told me last term that Wain had got a nomination for him in some beastly bank, and that he was going into it directly after the end of this term. Rather rough on a chap like Wyatt. Good cricketer and footballer, I mean, and all that sort of thing. It's just the sort of life he'll hate most. Hullo, here we are."

Mike looked out of the window. It was Wrykyn at last.

CHAPTER III MIKE FINDS A FRIENDLY NATIVE

Mike was surprised to find, on alighting, that the platform was entirely free from Wrykynians. In all the stories he had read the whole school came back by the same train, and, having smashed in one another's hats and chaffed the porters, made their way to the school buildings in a solid column. But here they were alone.

A remark of Bob's to Firby-Smith explained this. "Can't make out why none of the fellows came back by this train," he said. "Heaps of them must come by this line, and it's the only Christian train they run,"

"Don't want to get here before the last minute they can possibly manage. Silly idea. I suppose they think there'd be nothing to do."

"What shall *we* do?" said Bob. "Come and have some tea at Cook's?"

"All right."

Bob looked at Mike. There was no disguising the fact that he would be in the way; but how convey this fact delicately to him?

"Look here, Mike," he said, with a happy inspiration, "Firby-Smith and I are just going to get some tea. I think you'd better nip up to the school. Probably Wain will want to see you, and tell you all about things, which is your dorm. and so on. See you later," he concluded airily. "Any one'll tell you the way to the school. Go straight on. They'll send your luggage on later. So long." And his sole prop in this world of strangers departed, leaving him to find his way for himself.

There is no subject on which opinions differ so widely as this matter of finding the way to a place. To the man who knows, it is simplicity itself. Probably he really does imagine that he goes straight on, ignoring the fact that for him the choice of three roads, all more or less straight, has no perplexities. The man who does not know feels as if he were in a maze.

Mike started out boldly, and lost his way. Go in which direction he would, he always seemed to arrive at a square with a fountain and an equestrian statue in its centre. On the fourth repetition of this feat he stopped in a disheartened way, and looked about him. He was beginning to feel bitter towards Bob. The man might at least have shown him where to get some tea.

At this moment a ray of hope shone through the gloom. Crossing the square was a short, thick-set figure clad in grey flannel trousers, a blue blazer, and a straw hat with a coloured band. Plainly a Wrykynian. Mike made for him.

"Can you tell me the way to the school, please," he said.

"Oh, you're going to the school," said the other. He had a pleasant, square-jawed face, reminiscent of a good-tempered bull-dog, and a pair of very deep-set grey eyes which somehow put Mike at his ease. There was something singularly cool and genial about them. He felt that they saw the humour in things, and that their owner was a person who liked most people and whom most people liked.

"You look rather lost," said the stranger. "Been hunting for it long?"

"Yes," said Mike.

"Which house do you want?"

"Wain's."

"Wain's? Then you've come to the right man this time. What I don't know about Wain's isn't worth knowing."

"Are you there, too?"

"Am I not! Term *and* holidays. There's no close season for me."

"Oh, are you Wyatt, then?" asked Mike.

"Hullo, this is fame. How did you know my name, as the ass in the detective story always says to the detective, who's seen it in the lining of his hat? Who's been talking about me?"

"I heard my brother saying something about you in the train."

"Who's your brother?"

"Jackson. He's in Donaldson's."

"I know. A stout fellow. So you're the newest make of Jackson, latest model, with all the modern improvements? Are there any more of you?"

"Not brothers," said Mike.

"Pity. You can't quite raise a team, then? Are you a sort of young Tyldesley, too?"

"I played a bit at my last school. Only a private school, you know," added Mike modestly.

"Make any runs? What was your best score?"

"Hundred and twenty-three," said Mike awkwardly. "It was only against kids, you know." He was in terror lest he should seem to be bragging.

"That's pretty useful. Any more centuries?"

"Yes," said Mike, shuffling.

"How many?"

"Seven altogether. You know, it was really awfully rotten bowling. And I was a good bit bigger than most of the chaps there. And my pater always has a pro. down in the Easter holidays, which gave me a bit of an advantage."

"All the same, seven centuries isn't so dusty against any bowling. We shall want some batting in the house this term. Look here, I was just going to have some tea. You come along, too."

CHAPTER III MIKE FINDS A FRIENDLY NATIVE

"Oh, thanks awfully," said Mike. "My brother and Firby-Smith have gone to a place called Cook's."

"The old Gazeka? I didn't know he lived in your part of the world. He's head of Wain's."

"Yes, I know," said Mike. "Why is he called Gazeka?" he asked after a pause.

"Don't you think he looks like one? What did you think of him?"

"I didn't speak to him much," said Mike cautiously. It is always delicate work answering a question like this unless one has some sort of an inkling as to the views of the questioner.

"He's all right," said Wyatt, answering for himself. "He's got a habit of talking to one as if he were a prince of the blood dropping a gracious word to one of the three Small-Heads at the Hippodrome, but that's his misfortune. We all have our troubles. That's his. Let's go in here. It's too far to sweat to Cook's."

It was about a mile from the tea-shop to the school. Mike's first impression on arriving at the school grounds was of his smallness and insignificance. Everything looked so big—-the buildings, the grounds, everything. He felt out of the picture. He was glad that he had met Wyatt. To make his entrance into this strange land alone would have been more of an ordeal than he would have cared to face.

"That's Wain's," said Wyatt, pointing to one of half a dozen large houses which lined the road on the south side of the cricket field. Mike followed his finger, and took in the size of his new home.

"I say, it's jolly big," he said. "How many fellows are there in it?"

"Thirty-one this term, I believe."

"That's more than there were at King-Hall's."

"What's King-Hall's?"

"The private school I was at. At Emsworth."

Emsworth seemed very remote and unreal to him as he spoke.

They skirted the cricket field, walking along the path that divided the two terraces. The Wrykyn playing-fields were formed of a series of huge steps, cut out of the hill. At the top of the hill came the school. On the first terrace was a sort of informal practice ground, where, though no games were played on it, there was a good deal of punting and drop-kicking in the winter and fielding-practice in the summer. The next terrace was the biggest of all, and formed the first eleven cricket ground, a beautiful piece of turf, a shade too narrow for its length, bounded on the terrace side by a sharply sloping bank, some fifteen feet deep, and on the other by the precipice leading to the next terrace. At the far end of the ground stood the pavilion, and beside it a little ivy-covered rabbit-hutch for the scorers. Old Wrykynians always claimed that it was the prettiest school ground in England. It certainly had the finest view. From the verandah of the pavilion you could look over three counties.

Wain's house wore an empty and desolate appearance. There were signs of activity, however, inside; and a smell of soap and warm water told of preparations recently completed.

Wyatt took Mike into the matron's room, a small room opening out of the main passage.

"This is Jackson," he said. "Which dormitory is he in, Miss Payne?"

The matron consulted a paper.

"He's in yours, Wyatt."

"Good business. Who's in the other bed? There are going to be three of us, aren't there?"

"Fereira was to have slept there, but we have just heard that he is not coming back this term. He has had to go on a sea-voyage for his health."

"Seems queer any one actually taking the trouble to keep Fereira in the world," said Wyatt. "I've often thought of giving him Rough On Rats myself. Come along, Jackson, and I'll show you the room."

They went along the passage, and up a flight of stairs.

"Here you are," said Wyatt.

It was a fair-sized room. The window, heavily barred, looked out over a large garden.

"I used to sleep here alone last term," said Wyatt, "but the house is so full now they've turned it into a dormitory."

"I say, I wish these bars weren't here. It would be rather a rag to get out of the window on to that wall at night, and hop down into the garden and explore," said Mike.

Wyatt looked at him curiously, and moved to the window.

"I'm not going to let you do it, of course," he said, "because you'd go getting caught, and dropped on, which isn't good for one in one's first term; but just to amuse you——-"

He jerked at the middle bar, and the next moment he was standing with it in his hand, and the way to the garden was clear.

"By Jove!" said Mike.

"That's simply an object-lesson, you know," said Wyatt, replacing the bar, and pushing the screws back into their putty. "I get out at night myself because I think my health needs it. Besides, it's my last term, anyhow, so it doesn't matter what I do. But if I find you trying to cut out in the small hours, there'll be trouble. See?"

"All right," said Mike, reluctantly. "But I wish you'd let me."

"Not if I know it. Promise you won't try it on."

"All right. But, I say, what do you do out there?"

"I shoot at cats with an air-pistol, the beauty of which is that even if you hit them it doesn't hurt—-simply keeps them bright and interested in life; and if you miss you've had all the fun anyhow. Have you ever shot at a rocketing cat? Finest mark you can have. Society's latest craze. Buy a pistol and see life."

"I wish you'd let me come."

"I daresay you do. Not much, however. Now, if you like, I'll take you over the rest of the school. You'll have to see it sooner or later, so you may as well get it over at once."

CHAPTER IV AT THE NETS

There are few better things in life than a public school summer term. The winter term is good, especially towards the end, and there are points, though not many, about the Easter term: but it is in the summer that one really appreciates public school life. The freedom of it, after the restrictions of even the most easy-going private school, is intoxicating. The change is almost as great as that from public school to 'Varsity.

For Mike the path was made particularly easy. The only drawback to going to a big school for the first time is the fact that one is made to feel so very small and inconspicuous. New boys who have been leading lights at their private schools feel it acutely for the first week. At one time it was the custom, if we may believe writers of a generation or so back, for boys to take quite an embarrassing interest in the newcomer. He was asked a rain of questions, and was, generally, in the very centre of the stage. Nowadays an absolute lack of interest is the fashion. A new boy arrives, and there he is, one of a crowd.

Mike was saved this salutary treatment to a large extent, at first by virtue of the greatness of his family, and, later, by his own performances on the cricket field. His three elder brothers were objects of veneration to most Wrykynians, and Mike got a certain amount of reflected glory from them. The brother of first-class cricketers has a dignity of his own. Then Bob was a help. He was on the verge of the cricket team and had been the school full-back for two seasons. Mike found that people came up and spoke to him, anxious to know if he were Jackson's brother; and became friendly when he replied in the affirmative. Influential relations are a help in every stage of life.

It was Wyatt who gave him his first chance at cricket. There were nets on the first afternoon of term for all old colours of the three teams and a dozen or so of those most likely to fill the vacant places. Wyatt was there, of course. He had got his first eleven cap in the previous season as a mighty hitter and a fair slow bowler. Mike met him crossing the field with his cricket bag.

"Hullo, where are you off to?" asked Wyatt. "Coming to watch the nets?"

Mike had no particular programme for the afternoon. Junior cricket had not begun, and it was a little difficult to know how to fill in the time.

"I tell you what," said Wyatt, "nip into the house and shove on some things, and I'll try and get Burgess to let you have a knock later on."

This suited Mike admirably. A quarter of an hour later he was sitting at the back of the first eleven net, watching the practice.

Burgess, the captain of the Wrykyn team, made no pretence of being a bat. He was the school fast bowler and concentrated his energies on that department of the game. He sometimes took ten minutes at the wicket after everybody else had had an innings, but it was to bowl that he came to the nets.

He was bowling now to one of the old colours whose name Mike did not know. Wyatt and one of the professionals were the other two bowlers. Two nets away Firby-Smith, who had changed his pince-nez for a pair of huge spectacles, was performing rather ineffectively against some very bad bowling. Mike fixed his attention on the first eleven man.

He was evidently a good bat. There was style and power in his batting. He had a way of gliding Burgess's fastest to leg which Mike admired greatly. He was succeeded at the end of a quarter of an hour by another eleven man, and then Bob appeared.

It was soon made evident that this was not Bob's day. Nobody is at his best on the first day of term; but Bob was worse than he had any right to be. He scratched forward at nearly everything, and when Burgess, who had been resting, took up the ball again, he had each stump uprooted in a regular series in seven balls. Once he skied one of Wyatt's slows over the net behind the wicket; and Mike, jumping up, caught him neatly.

"Thanks," said Bob austerely, as Mike returned the ball to him. He seemed depressed.

Towards the end of the afternoon, Wyatt went up to Burgess.

"Burgess," he said, "see that kid sitting behind the net?"

"With the naked eye," said Burgess. "Why?"

"He's just come to Wain's. He's Bob Jackson's brother, and I've a sort of idea that he's a bit of a bat. I told him I'd ask you if he could have a knock. Why not send him in at the end net? There's nobody there now."

Burgess's amiability off the field equalled his ruthlessness when bowling.

"All right," he said. "Only if you think that I'm going to sweat to bowl to him, you're making a fatal error."

"You needn't do a thing. Just sit and watch. I rather fancy this kid's something special."

Mike put on Wyatt's pads and gloves, borrowed his bat, and walked round into the net.

"Not in a funk, are you?" asked Wyatt, as he passed.

Mike grinned. The fact was that he had far too good an opinion of himself to be nervous. An entirely modest person seldom makes a good batsman. Batting is one of those things which demand first and foremost a thorough belief in oneself. It need not be aggressive, but it must be there.

Wyatt and the professional were the bowlers. Mike had seen enough of Wyatt's bowling to know that it was merely ordinary "slow tosh," and the professional did not look as difficult as Saunders. The first half-dozen balls he played carefully. He was on trial, and he meant to take no risks. Then the professional over-pitched one slightly on the off. Mike jumped out, and got the full face of the bat on to it. The ball hit one of the ropes of the net, and nearly broke it.

"How's that?" said Wyatt, with the smile of an impresario on the first night of a successful piece.

"Not bad," admitted Burgess.

A few moments later he was still more complimentary. He got up and took a ball himself.

Mike braced himself up as Burgess began his run. This time he was more than a trifle nervous. The bowling he had had so far had been tame. This would be the real ordeal.

As the ball left Burgess's hand he began instinctively to shape for a forward stroke. Then suddenly he realised that the thing was going to be a yorker, and banged his bat down in the block just as the ball arrived. An unpleasant sensation as of having been struck by a thunderbolt was succeeded by a feeling of relief that he had kept the ball out of his wicket. There are easier things in the world than stopping a fast yorker.

"Well played," said Burgess.

Mike felt like a successful general receiving the thanks of the nation.

The fact that Burgess's next ball knocked middle and off stumps out of the ground saddened him somewhat; but this was the last tragedy that occurred. He could not do much with the bowling beyond stopping it and feeling repetitions of the thunderbolt experience, but he kept up his end; and a short conversation which he had with Burgess at the end of his innings was full of encouragement to one skilled in reading between the lines.

"Thanks awfully," said Mike, referring to the square manner in which the captain had behaved in letting him bat.

"What school were you at before you came here?" asked Burgess.

"A private school in Hampshire," said Mike. "King-Hall's. At a place called Emsworth."

"Get much cricket there?"

"Yes, a good lot. One of the masters, a chap called Westbrook, was an awfully good slow bowler."

Burgess nodded.

"You don't run away, which is something," he said.

Mike turned purple with pleasure at this stately compliment. Then, having waited for further remarks, but gathering from the captain's silence that the audience was at an end, he proceeded to unbuckle his pads. Wyatt overtook him on his way to the house.

"Well played," he said. "I'd no idea you were such hot stuff. You're a regular pro."

"I say," said Mike gratefully, "it was most awfully decent of you getting Burgess to let me go in. It was simply ripping of you."

"Oh, that's all right. If you don't get pushed a bit here you stay for ages in the hundredth game with the cripples and the kids. Now you've shown them what you can do you ought to get into the Under Sixteen team straight away. Probably into the third, too."

"By Jove, that would be all right."

"I asked Burgess afterwards what he thought of your batting, and he said, 'Not bad.' But he says that about everything. It's his highest form of praise. He says it when he wants to let himself go and simply butter up a thing. If you took him to see N. A. Knox bowl, he'd say he wasn't bad. What he meant was that he was jolly struck with your batting, and is going to play you for the Under Sixteen."

"I hope so," said Mike.

The prophecy was fulfilled. On the following Wednesday there was a match between the Under Sixteen and a scratch side. Mike's name was among the Under Sixteen. And on the Saturday he was playing for the third eleven in a trial game.

"This place is ripping," he said to himself, as he saw his name on the list. "Thought I should like it."

And that night he wrote a letter to his father, notifying him of the fact.

CHAPTER V REVELRY BY NIGHT

A succession of events combined to upset Mike during his first fortnight at school. He was far more successful than he had any right to be at his age. There is nothing more heady than success, and if it comes before we are prepared for it, it is apt to throw us off our balance. As a rule, at school, years of wholesome obscurity make us ready for any small triumphs we may achieve at the end of our time there. Mike had skipped these years. He was older than the average new boy, and his batting was undeniable. He knew quite well that he was regarded as a find by the cricket authorities; and the knowledge was not particularly good for him. It did not make him conceited, for his was not a nature at all addicted to conceit. The effect it had on him was to make him excessively pleased with life. And when Mike was pleased with life he always found a difficulty in obeying Authority and its rules. His state of mind was not improved by an interview with Bob.

Some evil genius put it into Bob's mind that it was his duty to be, if only for one performance, the Heavy Elder Brother to Mike; to give him good advice. It is never the smallest use for an elder brother to attempt to do anything for the good of a younger brother at school, for the latter rebels automatically against such interference in his concerns; but Bob did not know this. He only knew that he had received a letter from home, in which his mother had assumed without evidence that he was leading Mike by the hand round the pitfalls of life at Wrykyn; and his conscience smote him. Beyond asking him occasionally, when they met, how he was getting on (a question to which Mike invariably replied, "Oh, all right"), he was not aware of having done anything brotherly towards the youngster. So he asked Mike to tea in his study one afternoon before going to the nets.

Mike arrived, sidling into the study in the half-sheepish, half-defiant manner peculiar to small brothers in the presence of their elders, and stared in silence at the photographs on the walls. Bob was changing into his cricket things. The atmosphere was one of constraint and awkwardness.

The arrival of tea was the cue for conversation.

"Well, how are you getting on?" asked Bob.

"Oh, all right," said Mike.

Silence.

"Sugar?" asked Bob.

"Thanks," said Mike.

"How many lumps?"

"Two, please."

"Cake?"

"Thanks."

Silence.

Bob pulled himself together.

"Like Wain's?"

"Ripping."

"I asked Firby-Smith to keep an eye on you," said Bob.

"What!" said Mike.

The mere idea of a worm like the Gazeka being told to keep an eye on *him* was degrading.

"He said he'd look after you," added Bob, making things worse.

Look after him! Him!! M. Jackson, of the third eleven!!!

Mike helped himself to another chunk of cake, and spoke crushingly.

"He needn't trouble," he said. "I can look after myself all right, thanks."

Bob saw an opening for the entry of the Heavy Elder Brother.

"Look here, Mike," he said, "I'm only saying it for your good——-"

I should like to state here that it was not Bob's habit to go about the world telling people things solely for their good. He was only doing it now to ease his conscience.

"Yes?" said Mike coldly.

"It's only this. You know, I should keep an eye on myself if I were you. There's nothing that gets a chap so barred here as side."

"What do you mean?" said Mike, outraged.

"Oh, I'm not saying anything against you so far," said Bob. "You've been all right up to now. What I mean to say is, you've got on so well at cricket, in the third and so on, there's just a chance you might start to side about a bit soon, if you don't watch yourself. I'm not saying a word against you so far, of course. Only you see what I mean."

Mike's feelings were too deep for words. In sombre silence he reached out for the jam; while Bob, satisfied that he had delivered his message in a pleasant and tactful manner, filled his cup, and cast about him for further words of wisdom.

"Seen you about with Wyatt a good deal," he said at length.

"Yes," said Mike.

"Like him?"

"Yes," said Mike cautiously.

"You know," said Bob, "I shouldn't—-I mean, I should take care what you're doing with Wyatt."

"What do you mean?"

"Well, he's an awfully good chap, of course, but still——-"

"Still what?"

"Well, I mean, he's the sort of chap who'll probably get into some thundering row before he leaves. He doesn't care a hang what he does. He's that sort of chap. He's never been dropped on yet, but if you go on breaking rules you're bound to be sooner or later. Thing is, it doesn't matter much for him, because he's leaving at the end of the term. But don't let him drag you into anything. Not that he would try to. But you might think it was the blood thing to do to imitate him, and the first thing you knew you'd be dropped on by Wain or somebody. See what I mean?"

Bob was well-intentioned, but tact did not enter greatly into his composition.

"What rot!" said Mike.

"All right. But don't you go doing it. I'm going over to the nets. I see Burgess has shoved you down for them. You'd better be going and changing. Stick on here a bit, though, if you want any more tea. I've got to be off myself."

Mike changed for net-practice in a ferment of spiritual injury. It was maddening to be treated as an infant who had to be looked after. He felt very sore against Bob.

A good innings at the third eleven net, followed by some strenuous fielding in the deep, soothed his ruffled feelings to a large extent; and all might have been well but for the intervention of Firby-Smith.

That youth, all spectacles and front teeth, met Mike at the door of Wain's.

"Ah, I wanted to see you, young man," he said. (Mike disliked being called "young man.") "Come up to my study."

Mike followed him in silence to his study, and preserved his silence till Firby-Smith, having deposited his cricket-bag in a corner of the room and examined himself carefully in a looking-glass that hung over the mantelpiece, spoke again.

"I've been hearing all about you, young man." Mike shuffled.

"You're a frightful character from all accounts." Mike could not think of anything to say that was not rude, so said nothing.

"Your brother has asked me to keep an eye on you."

Mike's soul began to tie itself into knots again. He was just at the age when one is most sensitive to patronage and most resentful of it.

"I promised I would," said the Gazeka, turning round and examining himself in the mirror again. "You'll get on all right if you behave yourself. Don't make a frightful row in the house. Don't cheek your elders and betters. Wash. That's all. Cut along."

Mike had a vague idea of sacrificing his career to the momentary pleasure of flinging a chair at the head of the house. Overcoming this feeling, he walked out of the room, and up to his dormitory to change.

In the dormitory that night the feeling of revolt, of wanting to do something actively illegal, increased. Like Eric, he burned, not with shame and remorse, but with rage and all that sort of thing. He dropped off to sleep full of half-formed plans for asserting himself. He was awakened from a dream in which he was batting against Firby-Smith's bowling, and hitting it into space every time, by a slight sound. He opened his eyes, and saw a dark figure silhouetted against the light of the window. He sat up in bed.

"Hullo," he said. "Is that you, Wyatt?"

"Are you awake?" said Wyatt. "Sorry if I've spoiled your beauty sleep."

"Are you going out?"

"I am," said Wyatt. "The cats are particularly strong on the wing just now. Mustn't miss a chance like this. Specially as there's a good moon, too. I shall be deadly."

"I say, can't I come too?"

A moonlight prowl, with or without an air-pistol, would just have suited Mike's mood.

"No, you can't," said Wyatt. "When I'm caught, as I'm morally certain to be some day, or night rather, they're bound to ask if you've ever been out as well as me. Then you'll be able to put your hand on your little heart and do a big George Washington act. You'll find that useful when the time comes."

"Do you think you will be caught?"

"Shouldn't be surprised. Anyhow, you stay where you are. Go to sleep and dream that you're playing for the school against Ripton. So long."

And Wyatt, laying the bar he had extracted on the window-sill, wriggled out. Mike saw him disappearing along the wall.

It was all very well for Wyatt to tell him to go to sleep, but it was not so easy to do it. The room was almost light; and Mike always found it difficult to sleep unless it was dark. He turned over on his side and shut his eyes, but he had never felt wider awake. Twice he heard the quarters chime from the school clock; and the second time he gave up the struggle. He got out of bed and went to the window. It was a lovely night, just the sort of night on which, if he had been at home, he would have been out after moths with a lantern.

A sharp yowl from an unseen cat told of Wyatt's presence somewhere in the big garden. He would have given much to be with him, but he realised that he was on parole. He had promised not to leave the house, and there was an end of it.

He turned away from the window and sat down on his bed. Then a beautiful, consoling thought came to him. He had given his word that he would not go into the garden, but nothing had been said about exploring inside the house. It was quite late now. Everybody would be in bed. It would be quite safe. And there must be all sorts of things to interest the visitor in Wain's part of the house. Food, perhaps. Mike felt that he could just do with a biscuit. And there were bound to be biscuits on the sideboard in Wain's dining-room.

He crept quietly out of the dormitory.

He had been long enough in the house to know the way, in spite of the fact that all was darkness. Down the stairs, along the passage to the left, and up a few more stairs at the end The beauty of the position was that the dining-room had two doors, one leading into Wain's part of the house, the other into the boys' section. Any interruption that there might be would come from the further door.

To make himself more secure he locked that door; then, turning up the incandescent light, he proceeded to look about him.

Mr. Wain's dining-room repaid inspection. There were the remains of supper on the table. Mike cut himself some cheese and took some biscuits from the box, feeling that he was doing himself well. This was Life. There was a little soda-water in the syphon. He finished it. As it swished into the glass, it made a noise that seemed to him like three hundred Niagaras; but nobody else in the house appeared to have noticed it.

He took some more biscuits, and an apple.

After which, feeling a new man, he examined the room.

And this was where the trouble began.

On a table in one corner stood a small gramophone. And gramophones happened to be Mike's particular craze.

All thought of risk left him. The soda-water may have got into his head, or he may have been in a particularly reckless mood, as indeed he was. The fact remains that *he* inserted the first record that came to hand, wound the machine up, and set it going.

The next moment, very loud and nasal, a voice from the machine announced that Mr. Godfrey Field would sing "The Quaint Old Bird." And, after a few preliminary chords, Mr. Field actually did so.

"Auntie went to Aldershot in a Paris pom-pom hat."

Mike stood and drained it in.

"... Good gracious (sang Mr. Field), *what was that?"*

It was a rattling at the handle of the door. A rattling that turned almost immediately into a spirited banging. A voice accompanied the banging. "Who is there?" inquired the voice. Mike recognised it as Mr. Wain's. He was not alarmed. The man who holds the ace of trumps has no need to be alarmed. His position was impregnable. The enemy was held in check by the locked door, while the other door offered an admirable and instantaneous way of escape.

Mike crept across the room on tip-toe and opened the window. It had occurred to him, just in time, that if Mr. Wain, on entering the room, found that the occupant had retired by way of the boys' part of the house, he might possibly obtain a clue to his identity. If, on the other hand, he opened the window, suspicion would be diverted. Mike had not read his "Raffles" for nothing.

The handle-rattling was resumed. This was good. So long as the frontal attack was kept up, there was no chance of his being taken in the rear—-his only danger.

He stopped the gramophone, which had been pegging away patiently at "The Quaint Old Bird" all the time, and reflected. It seemed a pity to evacuate the position and ring down the curtain on what was, to date, the most exciting episode of his life; but he must not overdo the thing, and get caught. At any moment the noise might bring reinforcements to the besieging force, though it was not likely, for the dining-room was a long way from the dormitories; and it might flash upon their minds that there were two entrances to the room. Or the same bright thought might come to Wain himself.

"Now what," pondered Mike, "would A. J. Raffles have done in a case like this? Suppose he'd been after somebody's jewels, and found that they were after him, and he'd locked one door, and could get away by the other."

The answer was simple.

"He'd clear out," thought Mike.

Two minutes later he was in bed.

He lay there, tingling all over with the consciousness of having played a masterly game, when suddenly a gruesome idea came to him, and he sat up, breathless. Suppose Wain took it into his head to make a tour of the dormitories, to see that all was well! Wyatt was still in the garden somewhere, blissfully unconscious of what was going on indoors. He would be caught for a certainty!

CHAPTER VI IN WHICH A TIGHT CORNER IS EVADED

For a moment the situation paralysed Mike. Then he began to be equal to it. In times of excitement one thinks rapidly and clearly. The main point, the kernel of the whole thing, was that he must get into the garden somehow, and warn Wyatt. And at the same time, he must keep Mr. Wain from coming to the dormitory. He jumped out of bed, and dashed down the dark stairs.

He had taken care to close the dining-room door after him. It was open now, and he could hear somebody moving inside the room. Evidently his retreat had been made just in time.

He knocked at the door, and went in.

Mr. Wain was standing at the window, looking out. He spun round at the knock, and stared in astonishment at Mike's pyjama-clad figure. Mike, in spite of his anxiety, could barely check a laugh. Mr. Wain was a tall, thin man, with a serious face partially obscured by a grizzled beard. He wore spectacles, through which he peered owlishly at Mike. His body was wrapped in a brown dressing-gown. His hair was ruffled. He looked like some weird bird.

"Please, sir, I thought I heard a noise," said Mike.

Mr. Wain continued to stare.

"What are you doing here?" said he at last.

"Thought I heard a noise, please, sir."

"A noise?"

"Please, sir, a row."

"You thought you heard——!"

The thing seemed to be worrying Mr. Wain.

"So I came down, sir," said Mike.

The house-master's giant brain still appeared to be somewhat clouded. He looked about him, and, catching sight of the gramophone, drew inspiration from it.

"Did you turn on the gramophone?" he asked.

"*Me*, sir!" said Mike, with the air of a bishop accused of contributing to the *Police News*.

"Of course not, of course not," said Mr. Wain hurriedly. "Of course not. I don't know why I asked. All this is very unsettling. What are you doing here?"

"Thought I heard a noise, please, sir."

"A noise?"

"A row, sir."

If it was Mr. Wain's wish that he should spend the night playing Massa Tambo to his Massa Bones, it was not for him to baulk the house-master's innocent pleasure. He was prepared to continue the snappy dialogue till breakfast time.

"I think there must have been a burglar in here, Jackson."

"Looks like it, sir."

"I found the window open."

"He's probably in the garden, sir."

Mr. Wain looked out into the garden with an annoyed expression, as if its behaviour in letting burglars be in it struck him as unworthy of a respectable garden.

"He might be still in the house," said Mr. Wain, ruminatively.

"Not likely, sir."

"You think not?"

"Wouldn't be such a fool, sir. I mean, such an ass, sir."

"Perhaps you are right, Jackson."

"I shouldn't wonder if he was hiding in the shrubbery, sir."

Mr. Wain looked at the shrubbery, as who should say, *"Et tu, Brute!"*

"By Jove! I think I see him," cried Mike. He ran to the window, and vaulted through it on to the lawn. An inarticulate protest from Mr. Wain, rendered speechless by this move just as he had been beginning to recover his faculties, and he was running across the lawn into the shrubbery. He felt that all was well. There might be a bit of a row on his return, but he could always plead overwhelming excitement.

Wyatt was round at the back somewhere, and the problem was how to get back without being seen from the dining-room window. Fortunately a belt of evergreens ran along the path right up to the house. Mike worked his way cautiously through these till he was out of sight, then tore for the regions at the back.

The moon had gone behind the clouds, and it was not easy to find a way through the bushes. Twice branches sprang out from nowhere, and hit Mike smartly over the shins, eliciting sharp howls of pain.

On the second of these occasions a low voice spoke from somewhere on his right.

"Who on earth's that?" it said.

Mike stopped.

"Is that you, Wyatt? I say——"

"Jackson!"

The moon came out again, and Mike saw Wyatt clearly. His knees were covered with mould. He had evidently been crouching in the bushes on all fours.

"You young ass," said Wyatt. "You promised me that you wouldn't get out."

"Yes, I know, but——"

"I heard you crashing through the shrubbery like a hundred elephants. If you *must* get out at night and chance being sacked, you might at least have the sense to walk quietly."

"Yes, but you don't understand."

And Mike rapidly explained the situation.

"But how the dickens did he hear you, if you were in the dining-room?" asked Wyatt. "It's miles from his bedroom. You must tread like a policeman."

"It wasn't that. The thing was, you see, it was rather a rotten thing to do, I suppose, but I turned on the gramophone."

"You—-*what?*"

"The gramophone. It started playing 'The Quaint Old Bird.' Ripping it was, till Wain came along."

Wyatt doubled up with noiseless laughter.

"You're a genius," he said. "I never saw such a man. Well, what's the game now? What's the idea?"

"I think you'd better nip back along the wall and in through the window, and I'll go back to the dining-room. Then it'll be all right if Wain comes and looks into the dorm. Or, if you like, you might come down too, as if you'd just woke up and thought you'd heard a row."

"That's not a bad idea. All right. You dash along then. I'll get back."

Mr. Wain was still in the dining-room, drinking in the beauties of the summer night through the open window. He gibbered slightly when Mike reappeared.

"Jackson! What do you mean by running about outside the house in this way! I shall punish you very heavily. I shall certainly report the matter to the headmaster. I will not have boys rushing about the garden in their pyjamas. You will catch an exceedingly bad cold. You will do me two hundred lines, Latin and English. Exceedingly so. I will not have it. Did you not hear me call to you?"

"Please, sir, so excited," said Mike, standing outside with his hands on the sill.

"You have no business to be excited. I will not have it. It is exceedingly impertinent of you."

"Please, sir, may I come in?"

"Come in! Of course, come in. Have you no sense, boy? You are laying the seeds of a bad cold. Come in at once."

Mike clambered through the window.

"I couldn't find him, sir. He must have got out of the garden."

"Undoubtedly," said Mr. Wain. "Undoubtedly so. It was very wrong of you to search for him. You have been seriously injured. Exceedingly so."

He was about to say more on the subject when Wyatt strolled into the room. Wyatt wore the rather dazed expression of one who has been aroused from deep sleep. He yawned before he spoke.

"I thought I heard a noise, sir," he said.

He called Mr. Wain "father" in private, "sir" in public. The presence of Mike made this a public occasion.

"Has there been a burglary?"

"Yes," said Mike, "only he has got away."

"Shall I go out into the garden, and have a look round, sir?" asked Wyatt helpfully.

The question stung Mr. Wain into active eruption once more.

"Under no circumstances whatever," he said excitedly. "Stay where you are, James. I will not have boys running about my garden at night. It is preposterous. Inordinately so. Both of you go to bed immediately. I shall not speak to you again on this subject. I must be obeyed instantly. You hear me, Jackson? James, you understand me? To bed at once. And, if I find you outside your dormitory again to-night, you will both be punished with extreme severity. I will not have this lax and reckless behaviour."

"But the burglar, sir?" said Wyatt.

"We might catch him, sir," said Mike.

Mr. Wain's manner changed to a slow and stately sarcasm, in much the same way as a motor-car changes from the top speed to its first.

"I was under the impression," he said, in the heavy way almost invariably affected by weak masters in their dealings with the obstreperous, "I was distinctly under the impression that I had ordered you to retire immediately to your dormitory. It is possible that you mistook my meaning. In that case I shall be happy to repeat what I said. It is also in my mind that I threatened to punish you with the utmost severity if you did not retire at once. In these circumstances, James—-and you, Jackson—-you will doubtless see the necessity of complying with my wishes."

They made it so.

CHAPTER VII IN WHICH MIKE IS DISCUSSED

Trevor and Clowes, of Donaldson's, were sitting in their study a week after the gramophone incident, preparatory to going on the river. At least Trevor was in the study, getting tea ready. Clowes was on the window-sill, one leg in the room, the other outside, hanging over space. He loved to sit in this attitude, watching some one else work, and giving his views on life to whoever would listen to them. Clowes was tall, and looked sad, which he was not. Trevor was shorter, and very much in earnest over all that he did. On the present occasion he was measuring out tea with a concentration worthy of a general planning a campaign.

"One for the pot," said Clowes.

"All right," breathed Trevor. "Come and help, you slacker."

"Too busy."

"You aren't doing a stroke."

"My lad, I'm thinking of Life. That's a thing you couldn't do. I often say to people, 'Good chap, Trevor, but can't think of Life. Give him a tea-pot and half a pound of butter to mess about with,' I say, 'and he's all right. But when it comes to deep thought, where is he? Among the also-rans.' That's what I say."

"Silly ass," said Trevor, slicing bread. "What particular rot were you thinking about just then? What fun it was sitting back and watching other fellows work, I should think."

"My mind at the moment," said Clowes, "was tensely occupied with the problem of brothers at school. Have you got any brothers, Trevor?"

"One. Couple of years younger than me. I say, we shall want some more jam to-morrow. Better order it to-day."

"See it done, Tigellinus, as our old pal Nero used to remark. Where is he? Your brother, I mean."

"Marlborough."

"That shows your sense. I have always had a high opinion of your sense, Trevor. If you'd been a silly ass, you'd have let your people send him here."

"Why not? Shouldn't have minded."

"I withdraw what I said about your sense. Consider it unsaid. I have a brother myself. Aged fifteen. Not a bad chap in his way. Like the heroes of the school stories. 'Big blue eyes literally bubbling over with fun.' At least, I suppose it's fun to him. Cheek's what I call it. My people wanted to send him here. I lodged a protest. I said, 'One Clowes is ample for any public school.'"

"You were right there," said Trevor.

"I said, 'One Clowes is luxury, two excess.' I pointed out that I was just on the verge of becoming rather a blood at Wrykyn, and that I didn't want the work of years spoiled by a brother who would think it a rag to tell fellows who respected and admired me——-"

"Such as who?"

"——-Anecdotes of a chequered infancy. There are stories about me which only my brother knows. Did I want them spread about the school? No, laddie, I did not. Hence, we see my brother two terms ago, packing up his little box, and tooling off to Rugby. And here am I at Wrykyn, with an unstained reputation, loved by all who know me, revered by all who don't; courted by boys, fawned upon by masters. People's faces brighten when I throw them a nod. If I frown——-"

"Oh, come on," said Trevor.

Bread and jam and cake monopolised Clowes's attention for the next quarter of an hour. At the end of that period, however, he returned to his subject.

"After the serious business of the meal was concluded, and a simple hymn had been sung by those present," he said, "Mr. Clowes resumed his very interesting remarks. We were on the subject of brothers at school. Now, take the melancholy case of Jackson Brothers. My heart bleeds for Bob."

"Jackson's all right. What's wrong with him? Besides, naturally, young Jackson came to Wrykyn when all his brothers had been here."

"What a rotten argument. It's just the one used by chaps' people, too. They think how nice it will be for all the sons to have been at the same school. It may be all right after they're left, but while they're there, it's the limit. You say Jackson's all right. At present, perhaps, he is. But the term's hardly started yet."

"Well?"

"Look here, what's at the bottom of this sending young brothers to the same school as elder brothers?"

"Elder brother can keep an eye on him, I suppose."

"That's just it. For once in your life you've touched the spot. In other words, Bob Jackson is practically responsible for the kid. That's where the whole rotten trouble starts."

"Why?"

"Well, what happens? He either lets the kid rip, in which case he may find himself any morning in the pleasant position of having to explain to his people exactly why it is that little Willie has just received the boot, and why he didn't look after him better: or he spends all his spare time shadowing him to see that he doesn't get into trouble. He feels that his reputation hangs on the kid's conduct, so he broods over him like a policeman, which is pretty rotten for him and maddens the kid, who looks on him as no sportsman. Bob seems to be trying the first way, which is what I should do myself. It's all right, so far, but, as I said, the term's only just started."

"Young Jackson seems all right. What's wrong with him? He doesn't stick on side any way, which he might easily do, considering his cricket."

"There's nothing wrong with him in that way. I've talked to him several times at the nets, and he's very decent. But his getting into trouble hasn't anything to do with us. It's the masters you've got to consider."

"What's up? Does he rag?"

"From what I gather from fellows in his form he's got a genius for ragging. Thinks of things that don't occur to anybody else, and does them, too."

"He never seems to be in extra. One always sees him about on half-holidays."

"That's always the way with that sort of chap. He keeps on wriggling out of small rows till he thinks he can do anything he likes without being dropped on, and then all of a sudden he finds himself up to the eyebrows in a record smash. I don't say young Jackson will land himself like that. All I say is that he's just the sort who does. He's asking for trouble. Besides, who do you see him about with all the time?"

"He's generally with Wyatt when I meet him."

"Yes. Well, then!"

"What's wrong with Wyatt? He's one of the decentest men in the school."

"I know. But he's working up for a tremendous row one of these days, unless he leaves before it comes off. The odds are, if Jackson's so thick with him, that he'll be roped into it too. Wyatt wouldn't land him if he could help it, but he probably wouldn't realise what he was letting the kid in for. For instance, I happen to know that Wyatt breaks out of his dorm. every other night. I don't know if he takes Jackson with him. I shouldn't think so. But there's nothing to prevent Jackson following him on his own. And if you're caught at that game, it's the boot every time."

Trevor looked disturbed.

"Somebody ought to speak to Bob."

"What's the good? Why worry him? Bob couldn't do anything. You'd only make him do the policeman business, which he hasn't time for, and which is bound to make rows between them. Better leave him alone."

"I don't know. It would be a beastly thing for Bob if the kid did get into a really bad row."

"If you must tell anybody, tell the Gazeka. He's head of Wain's, and has got far more chance of keeping an eye on Jackson than Bob has."

"The Gazeka is a fool."

"All front teeth and side. Still, he's on the spot. But what's the good of worrying. It's nothing to do with us, anyhow. Let's stagger out, shall we?"

Trevor's conscientious nature, however, made it impossible for him to drop the matter. It disturbed him all the time that he and Clowes were on the river; and, walking back to the house, he resolved to see Bob about it during preparation.

He found him in his study, oiling a bat.

"I say, Bob," he said, "look here. Are you busy?"

"No. Why?"

"It's this way. Clowes and I were talking——"

"If Clowes was there he was probably talking. Well?"

"About your brother."

"Oh, by Jove," said Bob, sitting up. "That reminds me. I forgot to get the evening paper. Did he get his century all right?"

"Who?" asked Trevor, bewildered.

"My brother, J. W. He'd made sixty-three not out against Kent in this morning's paper. What happened?"

"I didn't get a paper either. I didn't mean that brother. I meant the one here."

"Oh, Mike? What's Mike been up to?"

"Nothing as yet, that I know of; but, I say, you know, he seems a great pal of Wyatt's."

"I know. I spoke to him about it."

"Oh, you did? That's all right, then."

"Not that there's anything wrong with Wyatt."

"Not a bit. Only he is rather mucking about this term, I hear. It's his last, so I suppose he wants to have a rag."

"Don't blame him."

"Nor do I. Rather rot, though, if he lugged your brother into a row by accident."

"I should get blamed. I think I'll speak to him again."

"I should, I think."

"I hope he isn't idiot enough to go out at night with Wyatt. If Wyatt likes to risk it, all right. That's his look out. But it won't do for Mike to go playing the goat too."

"Clowes suggested putting Firby-Smith on to him. He'd have more chance, being in the same house, of seeing that he didn't come a mucker than you would."

"I've done that. Smith said he'd speak to him."

"That's all right then. Is that a new bat?"

"Got it to-day. Smashed my other yesterday—against the school house."

Donaldson's had played a friendly with the school house during the last two days, and had beaten them.

"I thought I heard it go. You were rather in form."

"Better than at the beginning of the term, anyhow. I simply couldn't do a thing then. But my last three innings have been 33 not out, 18, and 51.

"I should think you're bound to get your first all right."

"Hope so. I see Mike's playing for the second against the O.W.s."

"Yes. Pretty good for his first term. You have a pro. to coach you in the holidays, don't you?"

"Yes. I didn't go to him much this last time. I was away a lot. But Mike fairly lived inside the net."

"Well, it's not been chucked away. I suppose he'll get his first next year. There'll be a big clearing-out of colours at the end of this term. Nearly all the first are leaving. Henfrey'll be captain, I expect."

"Saunders, the pro. at home, always says that Mike's going to be the star cricketer of the family. Better than J. W. even, he thinks. I asked him what he thought of me, and he said, 'You'll be making a lot of runs some day, Mr. Bob.' There's a subtle difference, isn't there? I shall have Mike cutting me out before I leave school if I'm not careful."

"Sort of infant prodigy," said Trevor. "Don't think he's quite up to it yet, though."

He went back to his study, and Bob, having finished his oiling and washed his hands, started on his Thucydides. And, in the stress of wrestling with the speech of an apparently delirious Athenian general, whose remarks seemed to contain nothing even remotely resembling sense and coherence, he allowed the question of Mike's welfare to fade from his mind like a dissolving view.

CHAPTER VIII A ROW WITH THE TOWN

The beginning of a big row, one of those rows which turn a school upside down like a volcanic eruption and provide old boys with something to talk about, when they meet, for years, is not unlike the beginning of a thunderstorm.

You are walking along one seemingly fine day, when suddenly there is a hush, and there falls on you from space one big drop. The next moment the thing has begun, and you are standing in a shower-bath. It is just the same with a row. Some trivial episode occurs, and in an instant the place is in a ferment. It was so with the great picnic at Wrykyn.

The bare outlines of the beginning of this affair are included in a letter which Mike wrote to his father on the Sunday following the Old Wrykynian matches.

This was the letter:

> "DEAR FATHER,—Thanks awfully for your letter. I hope you are quite well. I have been getting on all right at cricket lately. My scores since I wrote last have been 0 in a scratch game (the sun got in my eyes just as I played, and I got bowled); 15 for the third against an eleven of masters (without G. B. Jones, the Surrey man, and Spence); 28 not out in the Under Sixteen game; and 30 in a form match. Rather decent. Yesterday one of the men put down for the second against the O.W.'s second couldn't play because his father was very ill, so I played. Wasn't it luck? It's the first time I've played for the second. I didn't do much, because I didn't get an innings. They stop the cricket on O.W. matches day because they have a lot of rotten Greek plays and things which take up a frightful time, and half the chaps are acting, so we stop from lunch to four. Rot I call it. So I didn't go in, because they won the toss and made 215, and by the time we'd made 140 for 6 it was close of play. They'd stuck me in eighth wicket. Rather rot. Still, I may get another shot. And I made rather a decent catch at mid-on. Low down. I had to dive for it. Bob played for the first, but didn't do much. He was run out after he'd got ten. I believe he's rather sick about it.
>
> "Rather a rummy thing happened after lock-up. I wasn't in it, but a fellow called Wyatt (awfully decent chap. He's Wain's step-son,

> only they bar one another) told me about it. He was in it all right. There's a dinner after the matches on O.W. day, and some of the chaps were going back to their houses after it when they got into a row with a lot of brickies from the town, and there was rather a row. There was a policeman mixed up in it somehow, only I don't quite know where he comes in. I'll find out and tell you next time I write. Love to everybody. Tell Marjory I'll write to her in a day or two.

"Your loving son,
"MIKE.

> "P.S.—-I say, I suppose you couldn't send me five bob, could you? I'm rather broke.
>
> "P.P.S.—-Half-a-crown would do, only I'd rather it was five bob."

And, on the back of the envelope, these words: "Or a bob would be better than nothing."

The outline of the case was as Mike had stated. But there were certain details of some importance which had not come to his notice when he sent the letter. On the Monday they were public property.

The thing had happened after this fashion. At the conclusion of the day's cricket, all those who had been playing in the four elevens which the school put into the field against the old boys, together with the school choir, were entertained by the headmaster to supper in the Great Hall. The banquet, lengthened by speeches, songs, and recitations which the reciters imagined to be songs, lasted, as a rule, till about ten o'clock, when the revellers were supposed to go back to their houses by the nearest route, and turn in. This was the official programme. The school usually performed it with certain modifications and improvements.

About midway between Wrykyn, the school, and Wrykyn, the town, there stands on an island in the centre of the road a solitary lamp-post. It was the custom, and had been the custom for generations back, for the diners to trudge off to this lamp-post, dance round it for some minutes singing the school song or whatever happened to be the popular song of the moment, and then race back to their houses. Antiquity had given the custom a sort of sanctity, and the authorities, if they knew—-which they must have done—-never interfered.

But there were others.

Wrykyn, the town, was peculiarly rich in "gangs of youths." Like the vast majority of the inhabitants of the place, they seemed to have no work of any kind whatsoever to occupy their time, which they used, accordingly, to spend prowling about and indulging in a mild, brainless, rural type of hooliganism. They seldom proceeded to practical rowdyism and never except with the school. As a rule, they amused themselves by shouting rude chaff. The school regarded them with a lofty contempt, much as an Oxford man regards the townee. The school was always anxious for a row, but it was the unwritten law that only in special circumstances should they proceed to active measures. A curious dislike for school-and-town rows and most misplaced severity in dealing with the offenders when they took place, were among the few flaws in the otherwise admirable character of the headmaster of Wrykyn. It was understood that one scragged bargees at one's own risk, and, as a rule, it was not considered worth it.

But after an excellent supper and much singing and joviality, one's views are apt to alter. Risks which before supper seemed great, show a tendency to dwindle.

When, therefore, the twenty or so Wrykynians who were dancing round the lamp-post were aware, in the midst of their festivities, that they were being observed and criticised by an equal number of townees, and that the criticisms were, as usual, essentially candid and personal, they found themselves forgetting the headmaster's prejudices and feeling only that these outsiders must be put to the sword as speedily as possible, for the honour of the school.

Possibly, if the town brigade had stuck to a purely verbal form of attack, all might yet have been peace. Words can be overlooked.

But tomatoes cannot.

No man of spirit can bear to be pelted with over-ripe tomatoes for any length of time without feeling that if the thing goes on much longer he will be reluctantly compelled to take steps.

In the present crisis, the first tomato was enough to set matters moving.

As the two armies stood facing each other in silence under the dim and mysterious rays of the lamp, it suddenly whizzed out from the enemy's ranks, and hit Wyatt on the right ear.

There was a moment of suspense. Wyatt took out his handkerchief and wiped his face, over which the succulent vegetable had spread itself.

"I don't know how you fellows are going to pass the evening," he said quietly. "My idea of a good after-dinner game is to try and find the chap who threw that. Anybody coming?"

For the first five minutes it was as even a fight as one could have wished to see. It raged up and down the road without a pause, now in a solid mass, now splitting up into little groups. The science was on the side of the school. Most Wrykynians knew how to box to a certain extent. But, at any rate at first, it was no time for science. To be scientific one must have an opponent who observes at least the more important rules of the ring. It is impossible to do the latest ducks and hooks taught you by the instructor if your antagonist butts you in the chest, and then kicks your shins, while some dear friend of his, of whose presence you had no idea, hits you at the same time on the back of the head. The greatest expert would lose his science in such circumstances.

Probably what gave the school the victory in the end was the righteousness of their cause. They were smarting under a sense of injury, and there is nothing that adds a force to one's blows and a recklessness to one's style of delivering them more than a sense of injury.

CHAPTER VIII A ROW WITH THE TOWN

Wyatt, one side of his face still showing traces of the tomato, led the school with a vigour that could not be resisted. He very seldom lost his temper, but he did draw the line at bad tomatoes.

Presently the school noticed that the enemy were vanishing little by little into the darkness which concealed the town. Barely a dozen remained. And their lonely condition seemed to be borne in upon these by a simultaneous brain-wave, for they suddenly gave the fight up, and stampeded as one man.

The leaders were beyond recall, but two remained, tackled low by Wyatt and Clowes after the fashion of the football-field.

The school gathered round its prisoners, panting. The scene of the conflict had shifted little by little to a spot some fifty yards from where it had started. By the side of the road at this point was a green, depressed looking pond. Gloomy in the daytime, it looked unspeakable at night. It struck Wyatt, whose finer feelings had been entirely blotted out by tomato, as an ideal place in which to bestow the captives.

"Let's chuck 'em in there," he said.

The idea was welcomed gladly by all, except the prisoners. A move was made towards the pond, and the procession had halted on the brink, when a new voice made itself heard.

"Now then," it said, "what's all this?"

A stout figure in policeman's uniform was standing surveying them with the aid of a small bull's-eye lantern.

"What's all this?"

"It's all right," said Wyatt.

"All right, is it? What's on?"

One of the prisoners spoke.

"Make 'em leave hold of us, Mr. Butt. They're a-going to chuck us in the pond."

"Ho!" said the policeman, with a change in his voice. "Ho, are they? Come now, young gentleman, a lark's a lark, but you ought to know where to stop."

"It's anything but a lark," said Wyatt in the creamy voice he used when feeling particularly savage. "We're the Strong Right Arm of Justice. That's what we are. This isn't a lark, it's an execution."

"I don't want none of your lip, whoever you are," said Mr. Butt, understanding but dimly, and suspecting impudence by instinct.

"This is quite a private matter," said Wyatt. "You run along on your beat. You can't do anything here."

"Ho!"

"Shove 'em in, you chaps."

"Stop!" From Mr. Butt.

"Oo-er!" From prisoner number one.

There was a sounding splash as willing hands urged the first of the captives into the depths. He ploughed his way to the bank, scrambled out, and vanished.

Wyatt turned to the other prisoner.

"You'll have the worst of it, going in second. He'll have churned up the mud a bit. Don't swallow more than you can help, or you'll go getting typhoid. I expect there are leeches and things there, but if you nip out quick they may not get on to you. Carry on, you chaps."

It was here that the regrettable incident occurred. Just as the second prisoner was being launched, Constable Butt, determined to assert himself even at the eleventh hour, sprang forward, and seized the captive by the arm. A drowning man will clutch at a straw. A man about to be hurled into an excessively dirty pond will clutch at a stout policeman. The prisoner did.

Constable Butt represented his one link with dry land. As he came within reach he attached himself to his tunic with the vigour and concentration of a limpet.

At the same moment the executioners gave their man the final heave. The policeman realised his peril too late. A medley of noises made the peaceful night hideous. A howl from the townee, a yell from the policeman, a cheer from the launching party, a frightened squawk from some birds in a neighbouring tree, and a splash compared with which the first had been as nothing, and all was over.

The dark waters were lashed into a maelstrom; and then two streaming figures squelched up the further bank.

The school stood in silent consternation. It was no occasion for light apologies.

"Do you know," said Wyatt, as he watched the Law shaking the water from itself on the other side of the pond, "I'm not half sure that we hadn't better be moving!"

CHAPTER VIII A ROW WITH THE TOWN

THE DARK WATERS WERE LASHED INTO A MAELSTROM

CHAPTER IX BEFORE THE STORM

Your real, devastating row has many points of resemblance with a prairie fire. A man on a prairie lights his pipe, and throws away the match. The flame catches a bunch of dry grass, and, before any one can realise what is happening, sheets of fire are racing over the country; and the interested neighbours are following their example. (I have already compared a row with a thunderstorm; but both comparisons may stand. In dealing with so vast a matter as a row there must be no stint.)

The tomato which hit Wyatt in the face was the thrown-away match. But for the unerring aim of the town marksman great events would never have happened. A tomato is a trivial thing (though it is possible that the man whom it hits may not think so), but in the present case, it was the direct cause of epoch-making trouble.

The tomato hit Wyatt. Wyatt, with others, went to look for the thrower. The remnants of the thrower's friends were placed in the pond, and "with them," as they say in the courts of law, Police Constable Alfred Butt.

Following the chain of events, we find Mr. Butt, having prudently changed his clothes, calling upon the headmaster.

The headmaster was grave and sympathetic; Mr. Butt fierce and revengeful.

The imagination of the force is proverbial. Nurtured on motor-cars and fed with stop-watches, it has become world-famous. Mr. Butt gave free rein to it.

"Threw me in, they did, sir. Yes, sir."

"Threw you in!"

"Yes, sir. *Plop*!" said Mr. Butt, with a certain sad relish.

"Really, really!" said the headmaster. "Indeed! This is—dear me! I shall certainly—They threw you in!—Yes, I shall—certainly——"

Encouraged by this appreciative reception of his story, Mr. Butt started it again, right from the beginning.

"I was on my beat, sir, and I thought I heard a disturbance. I says to myself, ''Allo,' I says, 'a frakkus. Lots of them all gathered together, and fighting.' I says, beginning to suspect something, 'Wot's this all about, I wonder?' I says. 'Blow me if I don't think it's a frakkus.' And," concluded Mr. Butt, with the air of one confiding a secret, "and it *was* a frakkus!"

"And these boys actually threw you into the pond?"

"*Plop*, sir! Mrs. Butt is drying my uniform at home at this very moment as we sit talking here, sir. She says to me, 'Why, whatever *'ave* you been a-doing?

You're all wet.' And," he added, again with the confidential air, "I *was* wet, too. Wringin' wet."

The headmaster's frown deepened.

"And you are certain that your assailants were boys from the school?"

"Sure as I am that I'm sitting here, sir. They all 'ad their caps on their heads, sir."

"I have never heard of such a thing. I can hardly believe that it is possible. They actually seized you, and threw you into the water——"

"*Splish*, sir!" said the policeman, with a vividness of imagery both surprising and gratifying.

The headmaster tapped restlessly on the floor with his foot.

"How many boys were there?" he asked.

"Couple of 'undred, sir," said Mr. Butt promptly.

"Two hundred!"

"It was dark, sir, and I couldn't see not to say properly; but if you ask me my frank and private opinion I should say couple of 'undred."

"H'm—Well, I will look into the matter at once. They shall be punished."

"Yes, sir."

"Ye-e-s—H'm—Yes—Most severely."

"Yes, sir."

"Yes—Thank you, constable. Good-night."

"Good-night, sir."

The headmaster of Wrykyn was not a motorist. Owing to this disadvantage he made a mistake. Had he been a motorist, he would have known that statements by the police in the matter of figures must be divided by any number from two to ten, according to discretion. As it was, he accepted Constable Butt's report almost as it stood. He thought that he might possibly have been mistaken as to the exact numbers of those concerned in his immersion; but he accepted the statement in so far as it indicated that the thing had been the work of a considerable section of the school, and not of only one or two individuals. And this made all the difference to his method of dealing with the affair. Had he known how few were the numbers of those responsible for the cold in the head which subsequently attacked Constable Butt, he would have asked for their names, and an extra lesson would have settled the entire matter.

As it was, however, he got the impression that the school, as a whole, was culpable, and he proceeded to punish the school as a whole.

It happened that, about a week before the pond episode, a certain member of the Royal Family had recovered from a dangerous illness, which at one time had looked like being fatal. No official holiday had been given to the schools in honour of the recovery, but Eton and Harrow had set the example, which was followed throughout the kingdom, and Wrykyn had come into line with the rest. Only two days before the O.W.'s matches the headmaster had given out a notice in the hall that the following Friday would be a whole holiday; and the school, always ready to stop work, had approved of the announcement exceedingly.

The step which the headmaster decided to take by way of avenging Mr. Butt's wrongs was to stop this holiday.

He gave out a notice to that effect on the Monday.

The school was thunderstruck. It could not understand it. The pond affair had, of course, become public property; and those who had had nothing to do with it had been much amused. "There'll be a frightful row about it," they had said, thrilled with the pleasant excitement of those who see trouble approaching and themselves looking on from a comfortable distance without risk or uneasiness. They were not malicious. They did not want to see their friends in difficulties. But there is no denying that a row does break the monotony of a school term. The thrilling feeling that something is going to happen is the salt of life....

And here they were, right in it after all. The blow had fallen, and crushed guilty and innocent alike.

The school's attitude can be summed up in three words. It was one vast, blank, astounded "Here, I say!"

Everybody was saying it, though not always in those words. When condensed, everybody's comment on the situation came to that.

There is something rather pathetic in the indignation of a school. It must always, or nearly always, expend itself in words, and in private at that. Even the consolation of getting on to platforms and shouting at itself is denied to it. A public school has no Hyde Park.

There is every probability—-in fact, it is certain—-that, but for one malcontent, the school's indignation would have been allowed to simmer down in the usual way, and finally become a mere vague memory.

The malcontent was Wyatt. He had been responsible for the starting of the matter, and he proceeded now to carry it on till it blazed up into the biggest thing of its kind ever known at Wrykyn—-the Great Picnic.

Any one who knows the public schools, their ironbound conservatism, and, as a whole, intense respect for order and authority, will appreciate the magnitude of his feat, even though he may not approve of it. Leaders of men are rare. Leaders of boys are almost unknown. It requires genius to sway a school.

It would be an absorbing task for a psychologist to trace the various stages by which an impossibility was changed into a reality. Wyatt's coolness and matter-of-fact determination were his chief weapons. His popularity and reputation for lawlessness helped him. A conversation which he had with Neville-Smith, a day-boy, is typical of the way in which he forced his point of view on the school.

Neville-Smith was thoroughly representative of the average Wrykynian. He could play his part in any minor "rag" which interested him, and probably considered himself, on the whole, a daring sort of person. But at heart he had an enormous respect for authority. Before he came to Wyatt, he would not have dreamed of proceeding beyond words in his revolt. Wyatt acted on him like some drug.

Neville-Smith came upon Wyatt on his way to the nets. The notice concerning the holiday had only been given out that morning, and he was full of it. He expressed his opinion of the headmaster freely and in well-chosen words. He said it was a swindle, that it was all rot, and that it was a beastly shame. He added that something ought to be done about it.

"What are you going to do?" asked Wyatt.

"Well," said Neville-Smith a little awkwardly, guiltily conscious that he had been frothing, and scenting sarcasm, "I don't suppose one can actually *do* anything."

"Why not?" said Wyatt.

"What do you mean?"

"Why don't you take the holiday?"

"What? Not turn up on Friday!"

"Yes. I'm not going to."

Neville-Smith stopped and stared. Wyatt was unmoved.

"You're what?"

"I simply sha'n't go to school."

"You're rotting."

"All right."

"No, but, I say, ragging barred. Are you just going to cut off, though the holiday's been stopped?"

"That's the idea."

"You'll get sacked."

"I suppose so. But only because I shall be the only one to do it. If the whole school took Friday off, they couldn't do much. They couldn't sack the whole school."

"By Jove, nor could they! I say!"

They walked on, Neville-Smith's mind in a whirl, Wyatt whistling.

"I say," said Neville-Smith after a pause. "It would be a bit of a rag."

"Not bad."

"Do you think the chaps would do it?"

"If they understood they wouldn't be alone."

Another pause.

"Shall I ask some of them?" said Neville-Smith.

"Do."

"I could get quite a lot, I believe."

"That would be a start, wouldn't it? I could get a couple of dozen from Wain's. We should be forty or fifty strong to start with."

"I say, what a score, wouldn't it be?"

"Yes."

"I'll speak to the chaps to-night, and let you know."

"All right," said Wyatt. "Tell them that I shall be going anyhow. I should be glad of a little company."

The school turned in on the Thursday night in a restless, excited way. There were mysterious whisperings and gigglings. Groups kept forming in corners apart, to disperse casually and innocently on the approach of some person in authority.

An air of expectancy permeated each of the houses.

CHAPTER X THE GREAT PICNIC

Morning school at Wrykyn started at nine o'clock. At that hour there was a call-over in each of the form-rooms. After call-over the forms proceeded to the Great Hall for prayers.

A strangely desolate feeling was in the air at nine o'clock on the Friday morning. Sit in the grounds of a public school any afternoon in the summer holidays, and you will get exactly the same sensation of being alone in the world as came to the dozen or so day-boys who bicycled through the gates that morning. Wrykyn was a boarding-school for the most part, but it had its leaven of day-boys. The majority of these lived in the town, and walked to school. A few, however, whose homes were farther away, came on bicycles. One plutocrat did the journey in a motor-car, rather to the scandal of the authorities, who, though unable to interfere, looked askance when compelled by the warning toot of the horn to skip from road to pavement. A form-master has the strongest objection to being made to skip like a young ram by a boy to whom he has only the day before given a hundred lines for shuffling his feet in form.

It seemed curious to these cyclists that there should be nobody about. Punctuality is the politeness of princes, but it was not a leading characteristic of the school; and at three minutes to nine, as a general rule, you might see the gravel in front of the buildings freely dotted with sprinters, trying to get in in time to answer their names.

It was curious that there should be nobody about to-day. A wave of reform could scarcely have swept through the houses during the night.

And yet—-where was everybody?

Time only deepened the mystery. The form-rooms, like the gravel, were empty.

The cyclists looked at one another in astonishment. What could it mean?

It was an occasion on which sane people wonder if their brains are not playing them some unaccountable trick.

"I say," said Willoughby, of the Lower Fifth, to Brown, the only other occupant of the form-room, "the old man *did* stop the holiday to-day, didn't he?"

"Just what I was going to ask you," said Brown. "It's jolly rum. I distinctly remember him giving it out in hall that it was going to be stopped because of the O.W.'s day row."

"So do I. I can't make it out. Where *is* everybody?"

"They can't *all* be late."

"Somebody would have turned up by now. Why, it's just striking."

"Perhaps he sent another notice round the houses late last night, saying it was on again all right. I say, what a swindle if he did. Some one might have let us know. I should have got up an hour later."

"So should I."

"Hullo, here *is* somebody."

It was the master of the Lower Fifth, Mr. Spence. He walked briskly into the room, as was his habit. Seeing the obvious void, he stopped in his stride, and looked puzzled.

"Willoughby. Brown. Are you the only two here? Where is everybody?"

"Please, sir, we don't know. We were just wondering."

"Have you seen nobody?"

"No, sir."

"We were just wondering, sir, if the holiday had been put on again, after all."

"I've heard nothing about it. I should have received some sort of intimation if it had been."

"Yes, sir."

"Do you mean to say that you have seen *nobody*, Brown?"

"Only about a dozen fellows, sir. The usual lot who come on bikes, sir."

"None of the boarders?"

"No, sir. Not a single one."

"This is extraordinary."

Mr. Spence pondered.

"Well," he said, "you two fellows had better go along up to Hall. I shall go to the Common Room and make inquiries. Perhaps, as you say, there is a holiday to-day, and the notice was not brought to me."

Mr. Spence told himself, as he walked to the Common Room, that this might be a possible solution of the difficulty. He was not a house-master, and lived by himself in rooms in the town. It was just conceivable that they might have forgotten to tell him of the change in the arrangements.

But in the Common Room the same perplexity reigned. Half a dozen masters were seated round the room, and a few more were standing. And they were all very puzzled.

A brisk conversation was going on. Several voices hailed Mr. Spence as he entered.

"Hullo, Spence. Are you alone in the world too?"

"Any of your boys turned up, Spence?"

"You in the same condition as we are, Spence?"

Mr. Spence seated himself on the table.

"Haven't any of your fellows turned up, either?" he said.

"When I accepted the honourable post of Lower Fourth master in this abode of sin," said Mr. Seymour, "it was on the distinct understanding that there was going to *be* a Lower Fourth. Yet I go into my form-room this morning, and what do I find? Simply Emptiness, and Pickersgill II. whistling 'The Church Parade,' all flat. I consider I have been hardly treated."

"I have no complaint to make against Brown and Willoughby, as individuals," said Mr. Spence; "but, considered as a form, I call them short measure."

"I confess that I am entirely at a loss," said Mr. Shields precisely. "I have never been confronted with a situation like this since I became a schoolmaster."

"It is most mysterious," agreed Mr. Wain, plucking at his beard. "Exceedingly so."

The younger masters, notably Mr. Spence and Mr. Seymour, had begun to look on the thing as a huge jest.

"We had better teach ourselves," said Mr. Seymour. "Spence, do a hundred lines for laughing in form."

The door burst open.

"Hullo, here's another scholastic Little Bo-Peep," said Mr. Seymour. "Well, Appleby, have you lost your sheep, too?"

"You don't mean to tell me——" began Mr. Appleby.

"I do," said Mr. Seymour. "Here we are, fifteen of us, all good men and true, graduates of our Universities, and, as far as I can see, if we divide up the boys who have come to school this morning on fair share-and-share-alike lines, it will work out at about two-thirds of a boy each. Spence, will you take a third of Pickersgill II.?"

"I want none of your charity," said Mr. Spence loftily. "You don't seem to realise that I'm the best off of you all. I've got two in my form. It's no good offering me your Pickersgills. I simply haven't room for them."

"What does it all mean?" exclaimed Mr. Appleby.

"If you ask me," said Mr. Seymour, "I should say that it meant that the school, holding the sensible view that first thoughts are best, have ignored the head's change of mind, and are taking their holiday as per original programme."

"They surely cannot——!"

"Well, where are they then?"

"Do you seriously mean that the entire school has—has *rebelled*?"

"'Nay, sire,'" quoted Mr. Spence, "'a revolution!'"

"I never heard of such a thing!"

"We're making history," said Mr. Seymour.

"It will be rather interesting," said Mr. Spence, "to see how the head will deal with a situation like this. One can rely on him to do the statesman-like thing, but I'm bound to say I shouldn't care to be in his place. It seems to me these boys hold all the cards. You can't expel a whole school. There's safety in numbers. The thing is colossal."

"It is deplorable," said Mr. Wain, with austerity. "Exceedingly so."

"I try to think so," said Mr. Spence, "but it's a struggle. There's a Napoleonic touch about the business that appeals to one. Disorder on a small scale is bad, but this is immense. I've never heard of anything like it at any public school. When I was at Winchester, my last year there, there was pretty nearly a revolution because the captain of cricket was expelled on the eve of the Eton match. I remember making inflammatory speeches myself on that occasion. But we stopped on the right side of the line. We were satisfied with growling. But this——!"

Mr. Seymour got up.

"It's an ill wind," he said. "With any luck we ought to get the day off, and it's ideal weather for a holiday. The head can hardly ask us to sit indoors, teaching nobody. If I have to stew in my form-room all day, instructing Pickersgill II., I shall make things exceedingly sultry for that youth. He will wish that the Pickersgill progeny had stopped short at his elder brother. He will not value life. In the meantime, as it's already ten past, hadn't we better be going up to Hall to see what the orders of the day *are*?"

"Look at Shields," said Mr. Spence. "He might be posing for a statue to be called 'Despair!' He reminds me of Macduff. *Macbeth*, Act iv., somewhere near the end. 'What, all my pretty chickens, at one fell swoop?' That's what Shields is saying to himself."

"It's all very well to make a joke of it, Spence," said Mr. Shields querulously, "but it is most disturbing. Most."

"Exceedingly," agreed Mr. Wain.

The bereaved company of masters walked on up the stairs that led to the Great Hall.

CHAPTER XI THE CONCLUSION OF THE PICNIC

If the form-rooms had been lonely, the Great Hall was doubly, trebly, so. It was a vast room, stretching from side to side of the middle block, and its ceiling soared up into a distant dome. At one end was a dais and an organ, and at intervals down the room stood long tables. The panels were covered with the names of Wrykynians who had won scholarships at Oxford and Cambridge, and of Old Wrykynians who had taken first in Mods or Greats, or achieved any other recognised success, such as a place in the Indian Civil Service list. A silent testimony, these panels, to the work the school had done in the world.

Nobody knew exactly how many the Hall could hold, when packed to its fullest capacity. The six hundred odd boys at the school seemed to leave large gaps unfilled.

This morning there was a mere handful, and the place looked worse than empty.

The Sixth Form were there, and the school prefects. The Great Picnic had not affected their numbers. The Sixth stood by their table in a solid group. The other tables were occupied by ones and twos. A buzz of conversation was going on, which did not cease when the masters filed into the room and took their places. Every one realised by this time that the biggest row in Wrykyn history was well under way; and the thing had to be discussed.

In the Masters' library Mr. Wain and Mr. Shields, the spokesmen of the Common Room, were breaking the news to the headmaster.

The headmaster was a man who rarely betrayed emotion in his public capacity. He heard Mr. Shields's rambling remarks, punctuated by Mr. Wain's "Exceedinglys," to an end. Then he gathered up his cap and gown.

"You say that the whole school is absent?" he remarked quietly.

Mr. Shields, in a long-winded flow of words, replied that that was what he did say.

"Ah!" said the headmaster.

There was a silence.

"'M!" said the headmaster.

There was another silence.

"Ye—-e—-s!" said the headmaster.

He then led the way into the Hall.

Conversation ceased abruptly as he entered. The school, like an audience at a theatre when the hero has just appeared on the stage, felt that the serious interest of the drama had begun. There was a dead silence at every table as he strode up the room and on to the dais.

There was something Titanic in his calmness. Every eye was on his face as he passed up the Hall, but not a sign of perturbation could the school read. To judge from his expression, he might have been unaware of the emptiness around him.

The master who looked after the music of the school, and incidentally accompanied the hymn with which prayers at Wrykyn opened, was waiting, puzzled, at the foot of the dais. It seemed improbable that things would go on as usual, and he did not know whether he was expected to be at the organ, or not. The headmaster's placid face reassured him. He went to his post.

The hymn began. It was a long hymn, and one which the school liked for its swing and noise. As a rule, when it was sung, the Hall re-echoed. To-day, the thin sound of the voices had quite an uncanny effect. The organ boomed through the deserted room.

The school, or the remnants of it, waited impatiently while the prefect whose turn it was to read stammered nervously through the lesson. They were anxious to get on to what the Head was going to say at the end of prayers. At last it was over. The school waited, all ears.

The headmaster bent down from the dais and called to Firby-Smith, who was standing in his place with the Sixth.

The Gazeka, blushing warmly, stepped forward.

"Bring me a school list, Firby-Smith," said the headmaster.

The Gazeka was wearing a pair of very squeaky boots that morning. They sounded deafening as he walked out of the room.

The school waited.

Presently a distant squeaking was heard, and Firby-Smith returned, bearing a large sheet of paper.

The headmaster thanked him, and spread it out on the reading-desk.

Then, calmly, as if it were an occurrence of every day, he began to call the roll.

"Abney."

No answer.

"Adams."

No answer.

"Allenby."

"Here, sir," from a table at the end of the room. Allenby was a prefect, in the Science Sixth.

The headmaster made a mark against his name with a pencil.

"Arkwright."

No answer.

He began to call the names more rapidly.

"Arlington. Arthur. Ashe. Aston."

"Here, sir," in a shrill treble from the rider in motorcars.

The headmaster made another tick.

The list came to an end after what seemed to the school an unconscionable time, and he rolled up the paper again, and stepped to the edge of the dais.

"All boys not in the Sixth Form," he said, "will go to their form-rooms and get their books and writing-materials, and return to the Hall."

("Good work," murmured Mr. Seymour to himself. "Looks as if we should get that holiday after all.")

"The Sixth Form will go to their form-room as usual. I should like to speak to the masters for a moment."

He nodded dismissal to the school.

The masters collected on the daïs.

"I find that I shall not require your services to-day," said the headmaster. "If you will kindly set the boys in your forms some work that will keep them occupied, I will look after them here. It is a lovely day," he added, with a smile, "and I am sure you will all enjoy yourselves a great deal more in the open air."

"That," said Mr. Seymour to Mr. Spence, as they went downstairs, "is what I call a genuine sportsman."

"My opinion neatly expressed," said Mr. Spence. "Come on the river. Or shall we put up a net, and have a knock?"

"River, I think. Meet you at the boat-house."

"All right. Don't be long."

"If every day were run on these lines, school-mastering wouldn't be such a bad profession. I wonder if one could persuade one's form to run amuck as a regular thing."

"Pity one can't. It seems to me the ideal state of things. Ensures the greatest happiness of the greatest number."

"I say! Suppose the school has gone up the river, too, and we meet them! What shall we do?"

"Thank them," said Mr. Spence, "most kindly. They've done us well."

The school had not gone up the river. They had marched in a solid body, with the school band at their head playing Sousa, in the direction of Worfield, a market town of some importance, distant about five miles. Of what they did and what the natives thought of it all, no very distinct records remain. The thing is a tradition on the countryside now, an event colossal and heroic, to be talked about in the tap-room of the village inn during the long winter evenings. The papers got hold of it, but were curiously misled as to the nature of the demonstration. This was the fault of the reporter on the staff of the *Worfield Intelligencer and Farmers' Guide*, who saw in the thing a legitimate "march-out," and, questioning a straggler as to the reason for the expedition and gathering foggily that the restoration to health of the Eminent Person was at the bottom of it, said so in his paper. And two days later, at about the time when Retribution had got seriously to work, the

Daily Mail reprinted the account, with comments and elaborations, and headed it "Loyal Schoolboys." The writer said that great credit was due to the headmaster of Wrykyn for his ingenuity in devising and organising so novel a thanksgiving celebration. And there was the usual conversation between "a rosy-cheeked lad of some sixteen summers" and "our representative," in which the rosy-cheeked one spoke most kindly of the head-master, who seemed to be a warm personal friend of his.

The remarkable thing about the Great Picnic was its orderliness. Considering that five hundred and fifty boys were ranging the country in a compact mass, there was wonderfully little damage done to property. Wyatt's genius did not stop short at organising the march. In addition, he arranged a system of officers which effectually controlled the animal spirits of the rank and file. The prompt and decisive way in which rioters were dealt with during the earlier stages of the business proved a wholesome lesson to others who would have wished to have gone and done likewise. A spirit of martial law reigned over the Great Picnic. And towards the end of the day fatigue kept the rowdy-minded quiet.

At Worfield the expedition lunched. It was not a market-day, fortunately, or the confusion in the narrow streets would have been hopeless. On ordinary days Worfield was more or less deserted. It is astonishing that the resources of the little town were equal to satisfying the needs of the picnickers. They descended on the place like an army of locusts.

Wyatt, as generalissimo of the expedition, walked into the "Grasshopper and Ant," the leading inn of the town.

"Anything I can do for you, sir?" inquired the landlord politely.

"Yes, please," said Wyatt, "I want lunch for five hundred and fifty."

That was the supreme moment in mine host's life. It was his big subject of conversation ever afterwards. He always told that as his best story, and he always ended with the words, "You could ha' knocked me down with a feather!"

The first shock over, the staff of the "Grasshopper and Ant" bustled about. Other inns were called upon for help. Private citizens rallied round with bread, jam, and apples. And the army lunched sumptuously.

In the early afternoon they rested, and as evening began to fall, the march home was started.

At the school, net practice was just coming to an end when, faintly, as the garrison of Lucknow heard the first skirl of the pipes of the relieving force, those on the grounds heard the strains of the school band and a murmur of many voices. Presently the sounds grew more distinct, and up the Wrykyn road came marching the vanguard of the column, singing the school song. They looked weary but cheerful.

As the army drew near to the school, it melted away little by little, each house claiming its representatives. At the school gates only a handful were left.

Bob Jackson, walking back to Donaldson's, met Wyatt at the gate, and gazed at him, speechless.

CHAPTER XI THE CONCLUSION OF THE PICNIC

"Hullo," said Wyatt, "been to the nets? I wonder if there's time for a ginger-beer before the shop shuts."

CHAPTER XII MIKE GETS HIS CHANCE

The headmaster was quite bland and business-like about it all. There were no impassioned addresses from the dais. He did not tell the school that it ought to be ashamed of itself. Nor did he say that he should never have thought it of them. Prayers on the Saturday morning were marked by no unusual features. There was, indeed, a stir of excitement when he came to the edge of the dais, and cleared his throat as a preliminary to making an announcement. Now for it, thought the school.

This was the announcement.

"There has been an outbreak of chicken-pox in the town. All streets except the High Street will in consequence be out of bounds till further notice."

He then gave the nod of dismissal.

The school streamed downstairs, marvelling.

The less astute of the picnickers, unmindful of the homely proverb about hallooing before leaving the wood, were openly exulting. It seemed plain to them that the headmaster, baffled by the magnitude of the thing, had resolved to pursue the safe course of ignoring it altogether. To lie low is always a shrewd piece of tactics, and there seemed no reason why the Head should not have decided on it in the present instance.

Neville-Smith was among these premature rejoicers.

"I say," he chuckled, overtaking Wyatt in the cloisters, "this is all right, isn't it! He's funked it. I thought he would. Finds the job too big to tackle."

Wyatt was damping.

"My dear chap," he said, "it's not over yet by a long chalk. It hasn't started yet."

"What do you mean? Why didn't he say anything about it in Hall, then?"

"Why should he? Have you ever had tick at a shop?"

"Of course I have. What do you mean? Why?"

"Well, they didn't send in the bill right away. But it came all right."

"Do you think he's going to do something, then?"

"Rather. You wait."

Wyatt was right.

Between ten and eleven on Wednesdays and Saturdays old Bates, the school sergeant, used to copy out the names of those who were in extra lesson, and post them outside the school shop. The school inspected the list during the quarter to eleven interval.

To-day, rushing to the shop for its midday bun, the school was aware of a vast sheet of paper where usually there was but a small one. They surged round it. Buns were forgotten. What was it?

Then the meaning of the notice flashed upon them. The headmaster had acted. This bloated document was the extra lesson list, swollen with names as a stream swells with rain. It was a comprehensive document. It left out little.

"The following boys will go in to extra lesson this afternoon and next Wednesday," it began. And "the following boys" numbered four hundred.

"Bates must have got writer's cramp," said Clowes, as he read the huge scroll.

Wyatt met Mike after school, as they went back to the house.

"Seen the 'extra' list?" he remarked. "None of the kids are in it, I notice. Only the bigger fellows. Rather a good thing. I'm glad you got off."

"Thanks," said Mike, who was walking a little stiffly. "I don't know what you call getting off. It seems to me you're the chaps who got off."

"How do you mean?"

"We got tanned," said Mike ruefully.

"What!"

"Yes. Everybody below the Upper Fourth."

Wyatt roared with laughter.

"By Gad," he said, "he is an old sportsman. I never saw such a man. He lowers all records."

"Glad you think it funny. You wouldn't have if you'd been me. I was one of the first to get it. He was quite fresh."

"Sting?"

"Should think it did."

"Well, buck up. Don't break down."

"I'm not breaking down," said Mike indignantly.

"All right, I thought you weren't. Anyhow, you're better off than I am."

"An extra's nothing much," said Mike.

"It is when it happens to come on the same day as the M.C.C. match."

"Oh, by Jove! I forgot. That's next Wednesday, isn't it? You won't be able to play!"

"No."

"I say, what rot!"

"It is, rather. Still, nobody can say I didn't ask for it. If one goes out of one's way to beg and beseech the Old Man to put one in extra, it would be a little rough on him to curse him when he does it."

"I should be awfully sick, if it were me."

"Well, it isn't you, so you're all right. You'll probably get my place in the team."

Mike smiled dutifully at what he supposed to be a humorous sally.

"Or, rather, one of the places," continued Wyatt, who seemed to be sufficiently in earnest. "They'll put a bowler in instead of me. Probably Druce. But there'll be several vacancies. Let's see. Me. Adams. Ashe. Any more? No, that's the lot. I should think they'd give you a chance."

"You needn't rot," said Mike uncomfortably. He had his day-dreams, like everybody else, and they always took the form of playing for the first eleven (and, incidentally, making a century in record time). To have to listen while the subject was talked about lightly made him hot and prickly all over.

"I'm not rotting," said Wyatt seriously, "I'll suggest it to Burgess to-night."

"You don't think there's any chance of it, really, do you?" said Mike awkwardly.

"I don't see why not? Buck up in the scratch game this afternoon. Fielding especially. Burgess is simply mad on fielding. I don't blame him either, especially as he's a bowler himself. He'd shove a man into the team like a shot, whatever his batting was like, if his fielding was something extra special. So you field like a demon this afternoon, and I'll carry on the good work in the evening."

"I say," said Mike, overcome, "it's awfully decent of you, Wyatt."

Billy Burgess, captain of Wrykyn cricket, was a genial giant, who seldom allowed himself to be ruffled. The present was one of the rare occasions on which he permitted himself that luxury. Wyatt found him in his study, shortly before lock-up, full of strange oaths, like the soldier in Shakespeare.

"You rotter! You rotter! You *worm*!" he observed crisply, as Wyatt appeared.

"Dear old Billy!" said Wyatt. "Come on, give me a kiss, and let's be friends."

"You——!"

"William! William!"

"If it wasn't illegal, I'd like to tie you and Ashe and that blackguard Adams up in a big sack, and drop you into the river. And I'd jump on the sack first. What do you mean by letting the team down like this? I know you were at the bottom of it all."

He struggled into his shirt—-he was changing after a bath—-and his face popped wrathfully out at the other end.

"I'm awfully sorry, Bill," said Wyatt. "The fact is, in the excitement of the moment the M.C.C. match went clean out of my mind."

"You haven't got a mind," grumbled Burgess. "You've got a cheap brown paper substitute. That's your trouble."

Wyatt turned the conversation tactfully.

"How many wickets did you get to-day?" he asked.

"Eight. For a hundred and three. I was on the spot. Young Jackson caught a hot one off me at third man. That kid's good."

"Why don't you play him against the M.C.C. on Wednesday?" said Wyatt, jumping at his opportunity.

"What? Are you sitting on my left shoe?"

"No. There it is in the corner."

"Right ho!... What were you saying?"

CHAPTER XII MIKE GETS HIS CHANCE

"Why not play young Jackson for the first?"

"Too small."

"Rot. What does size matter? Cricket isn't footer. Besides, he isn't small. He's as tall as I am."

"I suppose he is. Dash, I've dropped my stud."

Wyatt waited patiently till he had retrieved it. Then he returned to the attack.

"He's as good a bat as his brother, and a better field."

"Old Bob can't field for toffee. I will say that for him. Dropped a sitter off me to-day. Why the deuce fellows can't hold catches when they drop slowly into their mouths I'm hanged if I can see."

"You play him," said Wyatt. "Just give him a trial. That kid's a genius at cricket. He's going to be better than any of his brothers, even Joe. Give him a shot."

Burgess hesitated.

"You know, it's a bit risky," he said. "With you three lunatics out of the team we can't afford to try many experiments. Better stick to the men at the top of the second."

Wyatt got up, and kicked the wall as a vent for his feelings.

"You rotter," he said. "Can't you *see* when you've got a good man? Here's this kid waiting for you ready made with a style like Trumper's, and you rave about top men in the second, chaps who play forward at everything, and pat half-volleys back to the bowler! Do you realise that your only chance of being known to Posterity is as the man who gave M. Jackson his colours at Wrykyn? In a few years he'll be playing for England, and you'll think it a favour if he nods to you in the pav. at Lord's. When you're a white-haired old man you'll go doddering about, gassing to your grandchildren, poor kids, how you 'discovered' M. Jackson. It'll be the only thing they'll respect you for."

Wyatt stopped for breath.

"All right," said Burgess, "I'll think it over. Frightful gift of the gab you've got, Wyatt."

"Good," said Wyatt. "Think it over. And don't forget what I said about the grandchildren. You would like little Wyatt Burgess and the other little Burgesses to respect you in your old age, wouldn't you? Very well, then. So long. The bell went ages ago. I shall be locked out."

On the Monday morning Mike passed the notice-board just as Burgess turned away from pinning up the list of the team to play the M.C.C. He read it, and his heart missed a beat. For, bottom but one, just above the W. B. Burgess, was a name that leaped from the paper at him. His own name.

CHAPTER XIII THE M.C.C. MATCH

If the day happens to be fine, there is a curious, dream-like atmosphere about the opening stages of a first eleven match. Everything seems hushed and expectant. The rest of the school have gone in after the interval at eleven o'clock, and you are alone on the grounds with a cricket-bag. The only signs of life are a few pedestrians on the road beyond the railings and one or two blazer and flannel-clad forms in the pavilion. The sense of isolation is trying to the nerves, and a school team usually bats 25 per cent. better after lunch, when the strangeness has worn off.

Mike walked across from Wain's, where he had changed, feeling quite hollow. He could almost have cried with pure fright. Bob had shouted after him from a window as he passed Donaldson's, to wait, so that they could walk over together; but conversation was the last thing Mike desired at that moment.

He had almost reached the pavilion when one of the M.C.C. team came down the steps, saw him, and stopped dead.

"By Jove, Saunders!" cried Mike.

"Why, Master Mike!"

The professional beamed, and quite suddenly, the lost, hopeless feeling left Mike. He felt as cheerful as if he and Saunders had met in the meadow at home, and were just going to begin a little quiet net-practice.

"Why, Master Mike, you don't mean to say you're playing for the school already?"

Mike nodded happily.

"Isn't it ripping," he said.

Saunders slapped his leg in a sort of ecstasy.

"Didn't I always say it, sir," he chuckled. "Wasn't I right? I used to say to myself it 'ud be a pretty good school team that 'ud leave you out."

"Of course, I'm only playing as a sub., you know. Three chaps are in extra, and I got one of the places."

"Well, you'll make a hundred to-day, Master Mike, and then they'll have to put you in."

"Wish I could!"

"Master Joe's come down with the Club," said Saunders.

"Joe! Has he really? How ripping! Hullo, here he is. Hullo, Joe?"

CHAPTER XIII THE M.C.C. MATCH

The greatest of all the Jacksons was descending the pavilion steps with the gravity befitting an All England batsman. He stopped short, as Saunders had done.

"Mike! You aren't playing!"

"Yes."

"Well, I'm hanged! Young marvel, isn't he, Saunders?"

"He is, sir," said Saunders. "Got all the strokes. I always said it, Master Joe. Only wants the strength."

Joe took Mike by the shoulder, and walked him off in the direction of a man in a Zingari blazer who was bowling slows to another of the M.C.C. team. Mike recognised him with awe as one of the three best amateur wicket-keepers in the country.

"What do you think of this?" said Joe, exhibiting Mike, who grinned bashfully. "Aged ten last birthday, and playing for the school. You are only ten, aren't you, Mike?"

"Brother of yours?" asked the wicket-keeper.

"Probably too proud to own the relationship, but he is."

"Isn't there any end to you Jacksons?" demanded the wicket-keeper in an aggrieved tone. "I never saw such a family."

"This is our star. You wait till he gets at us to-day. Saunders is our only bowler, and Mike's been brought up on Saunders. You'd better win the toss if you want a chance of getting a knock and lifting your average out of the minuses."

"I *have* won the toss," said the other with dignity. "Do you think I don't know the elementary duties of a captain?"

The school went out to field with mixed feelings. The wicket was hard and true, which would have made it pleasant to be going in first. On the other hand, they would feel decidedly better and fitter for centuries after the game had been in progress an hour or so. Burgess was glad as a private individual, sorry as a captain. For himself, the sooner he got hold of the ball and began to bowl the better he liked it. As a captain, he realised that a side with Joe Jackson on it, not to mention the other first-class men, was not a side to which he would have preferred to give away an advantage. Mike was feeling that by no possibility could he hold the simplest catch, and hoping that nothing would come his way. Bob, conscious of being an uncertain field, was feeling just the same.

The M.C.C. opened with Joe and a man in an Oxford Authentic cap. The beginning of the game was quiet. Burgess's yorker was nearly too much for the latter in the first over, but he contrived to chop it away, and the pair gradually settled down. At twenty, Joe began to open his shoulders. Twenty became forty with disturbing swiftness, and Burgess tried a change of bowling.

It seemed for one instant as if the move had been a success, for Joe, still taking risks, tried to late-cut a rising ball, and snicked it straight into Bob's hands at second slip. It was the easiest of slip-catches, but Bob fumbled it, dropped it, almost held it a second time, and finally let it fall miserably to the ground. It was a moment too painful for words. He rolled the ball back to the bowler in silence.

One of those weary periods followed when the batsman's defence seems to the fieldsmen absolutely impregnable. There was a sickening inevitableness in the way in which every ball was played with the very centre of the bat. And, as usual, just when things seemed most hopeless, relief came. The Authentic, getting in front of his wicket, to pull one of the simplest long-hops ever seen on a cricket field, missed it, and was l.b.w. And the next ball upset the newcomer's leg stump.

The school revived. Bowlers and field were infused with a new life. Another wicket—-two stumps knocked out of the ground by Burgess—-helped the thing on. When the bell rang for the end of morning school, five wickets were down for a hundred and thirteen.

But from the end of school till lunch things went very wrong indeed. Joe was still in at one end, invincible; and at the other was the great wicket-keeper. And the pair of them suddenly began to force the pace till the bowling was in a tangled knot. Four after four, all round the wicket, with never a chance or a mishit to vary the monotony. Two hundred went up, and two hundred and fifty. Then Joe reached his century, and was stumped next ball. Then came lunch.

The rest of the innings was like the gentle rain after the thunderstorm. Runs came with fair regularity, but wickets fell at intervals, and when the wicket-keeper was run out at length for a lively sixty-three, the end was very near. Saunders, coming in last, hit two boundaries, and was then caught by Mike. His second hit had just lifted the M.C.C. total over the three hundred.

Three hundred is a score that takes some making on any ground, but on a fine day it was not an unusual total for the Wrykyn eleven. Some years before, against Ripton, they had run up four hundred and sixteen; and only last season had massacred a very weak team of Old Wrykynians with a score that only just missed the fourth hundred.

Unfortunately, on the present occasion, there was scarcely time, unless the bowling happened to get completely collared, to make the runs. It was a quarter to four when the innings began, and stumps were to be drawn at a quarter to seven. A hundred an hour is quick work.

Burgess, however, was optimistic, as usual. "Better have a go for them," he said to Berridge and Marsh, the school first pair.

Following out this courageous advice, Berridge, after hitting three boundaries in his first two overs, was stumped half-way through the third.

After this, things settled down. Morris, the first-wicket man, was a thoroughly sound bat, a little on the slow side, but exceedingly hard to shift. He and Marsh proceeded to play themselves in, until it looked as if they were likely to stay till the drawing of stumps.

A comfortable, rather somnolent feeling settled upon the school. A long stand at cricket is a soothing sight to watch. There was an absence of hurry about the batsmen which harmonised well with the drowsy summer afternoon. And yet runs were coming at a fair pace. The hundred went up at five o'clock, the hundred and fifty at half-past. Both batsmen were completely at home, and the M.C.C. third-change bowlers had been put on.

Then the great wicket-keeper took off the pads and gloves, and the fieldsmen retired to posts at the extreme edge of the ground.

"Lobs," said Burgess. "By Jove, I wish I was in."

It seemed to be the general opinion among the members of the Wrykyn eleven on the pavilion balcony that Morris and Marsh were in luck. The team did not grudge them their good fortune, because they had earned it; but they were distinctly envious.

Lobs are the most dangerous, insinuating things in the world. Everybody knows in theory the right way to treat them. Everybody knows that the man who is content not to try to score more than a single cannot get out to them. Yet nearly everybody does get out to them.

It was the same story to-day. The first over yielded six runs, all through gentle taps along the ground. In the second, Marsh hit an over-pitched one along the ground to the terrace bank. The next ball he swept round to the leg boundary. And that was the end of Marsh. He saw himself scoring at the rate of twenty-four an over. Off the last ball he was stumped by several feet, having done himself credit by scoring seventy.

The long stand was followed, as usual, by a series of disasters. Marsh's wicket had fallen at a hundred and eighty. Ellerby left at a hundred and eighty-six. By the time the scoring-board registered two hundred, five wickets were down, three of them victims to the lobs. Morris was still in at one end. He had refused to be tempted. He was jogging on steadily to his century.

Bob Jackson went in next, with instructions to keep his eye on the lob-man.

For a time things went well. Saunders, who had gone on to bowl again after a rest, seemed to give Morris no trouble, and Bob put him through the slips with apparent ease. Twenty runs were added, when the lob-bowler once more got in his deadly work. Bob, letting alone a ball wide of the off-stump under the impression that it was going to break away, was disagreeably surprised to find it break in instead, and hit the wicket. The bowler smiled sadly, as if he hated to have to do these things.

Mike's heart jumped as he saw the bails go. It was his turn next.

"Two hundred and twenty-nine," said Burgess, "and it's ten past six. No good trying for the runs now. Stick in," he added to Mike. "That's all you've got to do."

All!... Mike felt as if he was being strangled. His heart was racing like the engines of a motor. He knew his teeth were chattering. He wished he could stop them. What a time Bob was taking to get back to the pavilion! He wanted to rush out, and get the thing over.

At last he arrived, and Mike, fumbling at a glove, tottered out into the sunshine. He heard miles and miles away a sound of clapping, and a thin, shrill noise as if somebody were screaming in the distance. As a matter of fact, several members of his form and of the junior day-room at Wain's nearly burst themselves at that moment.

At the wickets, he felt better. Bob had fallen to the last ball of the over, and Morris, standing ready for Saunders's delivery, looked so calm and certain of himself that it was impossible to feel entirely without hope and self-confidence. Mike knew that Morris had made ninety-eight, and he supposed that Morris knew that he was very near his century; yet he seemed to be absolutely undisturbed. Mike drew courage from his attitude.

Morris pushed the first ball away to leg. Mike would have liked to have run two, but short leg had retrieved the ball as he reached the crease.

The moment had come, the moment which he had experienced only in dreams. And in the dreams he was always full of confidence, and invariably hit a boundary. Sometimes a drive, sometimes a cut, but always a boundary.

"To leg, sir," said the umpire.

"Don't be in a funk," said a voice. "Play straight, and you can't get out."

It was Joe, who had taken the gloves when the wicket-keeper went on to bowl.

Mike grinned, wryly but gratefully.

Saunders was beginning his run. It was all so home-like that for a moment Mike felt himself again. How often he had seen those two little skips and the jump. It was like being in the paddock again, with Marjory and the dogs waiting by the railings to fetch the ball if he made a drive.

Saunders ran to the crease, and bowled.

Now, Saunders was a conscientious man, and, doubtless, bowled the very best ball that he possibly could. On the other hand, it was Mike's first appearance for the school, and Saunders, besides being conscientious, was undoubtedly kind-hearted. It is useless to speculate as to whether he was trying to bowl his best that ball. If so, he failed signally. It was a half-volley, just the right distance away from the off-stump; the sort of ball Mike was wont to send nearly through the net at home....

The next moment the dreams had come true. The umpire was signalling to the scoring-box, the school was shouting, extra-cover was trotting to the boundary to fetch the ball, and Mike was blushing and wondering whether it was bad form to grin.

From that ball onwards all was for the best in this best of all possible worlds. Saunders bowled no more half-volleys; but Mike played everything that he did bowl. He met the lobs with a bat like a barn-door. Even the departure of Morris, caught in the slips off Saunders's next over for a chanceless hundred and five, did not disturb him. All nervousness had left him. He felt equal to the situation. Burgess came in, and began to hit out as if he meant to knock off the runs. The bowling became a shade loose. Twice he was given full tosses to leg, which he hit to the terrace bank. Half-past six chimed, and two hundred and fifty went up on the telegraph board. Burgess continued to hit. Mike's whole soul was concentrated on keeping up his wicket. There was only Reeves to follow him, and Reeves was a victim to the first straight ball. Burgess had to hit because it was the only game he knew; but he himself must simply stay in.

The hands of the clock seemed to have stopped. Then suddenly he heard the umpire say "Last over," and he settled down to keep those six balls out of his wicket.

The lob bowler had taken himself off, and the Oxford Authentic had gone on, fast left-hand.

The first ball was short and wide of the off-stump. Mike let it alone. Number two: yorker. Got him! Three: straight half-volley. Mike played it back to the bowler. Four: beat him, and missed the wicket by an inch. Five: another yorker. Down on it again in the old familiar way.

All was well. The match was a draw now whatever happened to him. He hit out, almost at a venture, at the last ball, and mid-off, jumping, just failed to reach it. It hummed over his head, and ran like a streak along the turf and up the bank, and a great howl of delight went up from the school as the umpire took off the bails.

Mike walked away from the wickets with Joe and the wicket-keeper.

"I'm sorry about your nose, Joe," said the wicket-keeper in tones of grave solicitude.

"What's wrong with it?"

"At present," said the wicket-keeper, "nothing. But in a few years I'm afraid it's going to be put badly out of joint."

CHAPTER XIV A SLIGHT IMBROGLIO

Mike got his third eleven colours after the M.C.C. match. As he had made twenty-three not out in a crisis in a first eleven match, this may not seem an excessive reward. But it was all that he expected. One had to take the rungs of the ladder singly at Wrykyn. First one was given one's third eleven cap. That meant, "You are a promising man, and we have our eye on you." Then came the second colours. They might mean anything from "Well, here you *are*. You won't get any higher, so you may as well have the thing now," to "This is just to show that we still have our eye on you."

Mike was a certainty now for the second. But it needed more than one performance to secure the first cap.

"I told you so," said Wyatt, naturally, to Burgess after the match.

"He's not bad," said Burgess. "I'll give him another shot."

But Burgess, as has been pointed out, was not a person who ever became gushing with enthusiasm.

So Wilkins, of the School House, who had played twice for the first eleven, dropped down into the second, as many a good man had done before him, and Mike got his place in the next match, against the Gentlemen of the County. Unfortunately for him, the visiting team, however gentlemanly, were not brilliant cricketers, at any rate as far as bowling was concerned. The school won the toss, went in first, and made three hundred and sixteen for five wickets, Morris making another placid century. The innings was declared closed before Mike had a chance of distinguishing himself. In an innings which lasted for one over he made two runs, not out; and had to console himself for the cutting short of his performance by the fact that his average for the school was still infinity. Bob, who was one of those lucky enough to have an unabridged innings, did better in this match, making twenty-five. But with Morris making a hundred and seventeen, and Berridge, Ellerby, and Marsh all passing the half-century, this score did not show up excessively.

We now come to what was practically a turning-point in Mike's career at Wrykyn. There is no doubt that his meteor-like flights at cricket had an unsettling effect on him. He was enjoying life amazingly, and, as is not uncommon with the prosperous, he waxed fat and kicked. Fortunately for him—-though he did not look upon it in that light at the time—-he kicked the one person it was most imprudent to kick. The person he selected was Firby-Smith. With anybody else the thing might have blown over, to the detriment of Mike's character; but Firby-Smith, having the most tender affection for his dignity, made a fuss.

It happened in this way. The immediate cause of the disturbance was a remark of Mike's, but the indirect cause was the unbearably patronising manner which the head of Wain's chose to adopt towards him. The fact that he was playing for the school seemed to make no difference at all. Firby-Smith continued to address Mike merely as the small boy.

The following, *verbatim*, was the tactful speech which he addressed to him on the evening of the M.C.C. match, having summoned him to his study for the purpose.

"Well," he said, "you played a very decent innings this afternoon, and I suppose you're frightfully pleased with yourself, eh? Well, mind you don't go getting swelled head. See? That's all. Run along."

Mike departed, bursting with fury.

The next link in the chain was forged a week after the Gentlemen of the County match. House matches had begun, and Wain's were playing Appleby's. Appleby's made a hundred and fifty odd, shaping badly for the most part against Wyatt's slows. Then Wain's opened their innings. The Gazeka, as head of the house, was captain of the side, and he and Wyatt went in first. Wyatt made a few mighty hits, and was then caught at cover. Mike went in first wicket.

For some ten minutes all was peace. Firby-Smith scratched away at his end, getting here and there a single and now and then a two, and Mike settled down at once to play what he felt was going to be the innings of a lifetime. Appleby's bowling was on the feeble side, with Raikes, of the third eleven, as the star, supported by some small change. Mike pounded it vigorously. To one who had been brought up on Saunders, Raikes possessed few subtleties. He had made seventeen, and was thoroughly set, when the Gazeka, who had the bowling, hit one in the direction of cover-point. With a certain type of batsman a single is a thing to take big risks for. And the Gazeka badly wanted that single.

"Come on," he shouted, prancing down the pitch.

Mike, who had remained in his crease with the idea that nobody even moderately sane would attempt a run for a hit like that, moved forward in a startled and irresolute manner. Firby-Smith arrived, shouting "Run!" and, cover having thrown the ball in, the wicket-keeper removed the bails.

These are solemn moments.

The only possible way of smoothing over an episode of this kind is for the guilty man to grovel.

Firby-Smith did not grovel.

"Easy run there, you know," he said reprovingly.

The world swam before Mike's eyes. Through the red mist he could see Firby-Smith's face. The sun glinted on his rather prominent teeth. To Mike's distorted vision it seemed that the criminal was amused.

"Don't *laugh*, you grinning ape!" he cried. "It isn't funny."

"DON'T *LAUGH*, YOU GRINNING APE!"

He then made for the trees where the rest of the team were sitting.

Now Firby-Smith not only possessed rather prominent teeth; he was also sensitive on the subject. Mike's shaft sank in deeply. The fact that emotion caused him to swipe at a straight half-volley, miss it, and be bowled next ball made the wound rankle.

He avoided Mike on his return to the trees. And Mike, feeling now a little apprehensive, avoided him.

CHAPTER XIV A SLIGHT IMBROGLIO

The Gazeka brooded apart for the rest of the afternoon, chewing the insult. At close of play he sought Burgess.

Burgess, besides being captain of the eleven, was also head of the school. He was the man who arranged prefects' meetings. And only a prefects' meeting, thought Firby-Smith, could adequately avenge his lacerated dignity.

"I want to speak to you, Burgess," he said.

"What's up?" said Burgess.

"You know young Jackson in our house."

"What about him?"

"He's been frightfully insolent."

"Cheeked you?" said Burgess, a man of simple speech.

"I want you to call a prefects' meeting, and lick him."

Burgess looked incredulous.

"Rather a large order, a prefects' meeting," he said. "It has to be a pretty serious sort of thing for that."

"Frightful cheek to a school prefect is a serious thing," said Firby-Smith, with the air of one uttering an epigram.

"Well, I suppose—-What did he say to you?"

Firby-Smith related the painful details.

Burgess started to laugh, but turned the laugh into a cough.

"Yes," he said meditatively. "Rather thick. Still, I mean—-A prefects' meeting. Rather like crushing a thingummy with a what-d'you-call-it. Besides, he's a decent kid."

"He's frightfully conceited."

"Oh, well—-Well, anyhow, look here, I'll think it over, and let you know tomorrow. It's not the sort of thing to rush through without thinking about it."

And the matter was left temporarily at that.

CHAPTER XV MIKE CREATES A VACANCY

Burgess walked off the ground feeling that fate was not using him well.

Here was he, a well-meaning youth who wanted to be on good terms with all the world, being jockeyed into slaughtering a kid whose batting he admired and whom personally he liked. And the worst of it was that he sympathised with Mike. He knew what it felt like to be run out just when one had got set, and he knew exactly how maddening the Gazeka's manner would be on such an occasion. On the other hand, officially he was bound to support the head of Wain's. Prefects must stand together or chaos will come.

He thought he would talk it over with somebody. Bob occurred to him. It was only fair that Bob should be told, as the nearest of kin.

And here was another grievance against fate. Bob was a person he did not particularly wish to see just then. For that morning he had posted up the list of the team to play for the school against Geddington, one of the four schools which Wrykyn met at cricket; and Bob's name did not appear on that list. Several things had contributed to that melancholy omission. In the first place, Geddington, to judge from the weekly reports in the *Sportsman* and *Field*, were strong this year at batting. In the second place, the results of the last few matches, and particularly the M.C.C. match, had given Burgess the idea that Wrykyn was weak at bowling. It became necessary, therefore, to drop a batsman out of the team in favour of a bowler. And either Mike or Bob must be the man.

Burgess was as rigidly conscientious as the captain of a school eleven should be. Bob was one of his best friends, and he would have given much to be able to put him in the team; but he thought the thing over, and put the temptation sturdily behind him. At batting there was not much to choose between the two, but in fielding there was a great deal. Mike was good. Bob was bad. So out Bob had gone, and Neville-Smith, a fair fast bowler at all times and on his day dangerous, took his place.

These clashings of public duty with private inclination are the drawbacks to the despotic position of captain of cricket at a public school. It is awkward having to meet your best friend after you have dropped him from the team, and it is difficult to talk to him as if nothing had happened.

Burgess felt very self-conscious as he entered Bob's study, and was rather glad that he had a topic of conversation ready to hand.

"Busy, Bob?" he asked.

"Hullo," said Bob, with a cheerfulness rather over-done in his anxiety to show Burgess, the man, that he did not hold him responsible in any way for the distressing acts of Burgess, the captain. "Take a pew. Don't these studies get beastly hot this weather. There's some ginger-beer in the cupboard. Have some?"

"No, thanks. I say, Bob, look here, I want to see you."

"Well, you can, can't you? This is me, sitting over here. The tall, dark, handsome chap."

"It's awfully awkward, you know," continued Burgess gloomily; "that ass of a young brother of yours—-Sorry, but he *is* an ass, though he's your brother——-"

"Thanks for the 'though,' Billy. You know how to put a thing nicely. What's Mike been up to?"

"It's that old fool the Gazeka. He came to me frothing with rage, and wanted me to call a prefects' meeting and touch young Mike up."

Bob displayed interest and excitement for the first time.

"Prefects' meeting! What the dickens is up? What's he been doing? Smith must be drunk. What's all the row about?"

Burgess repeated the main facts of the case as he had them from Firby-Smith.

"Personally, I sympathise with the kid," he added, "Still, the Gazeka *is* a prefect——-"

Bob gnawed a pen-holder morosely.

"Silly young idiot," he said.

"Sickening thing being run out," suggested Burgess.

"Still——-"

"I know. It's rather hard to see what to do. I suppose if the Gazeka insists, one's bound to support him."

"I suppose so."

"Awful rot. Prefects' lickings aren't meant for that sort of thing. They're supposed to be for kids who steal buns at the shop or muck about generally. Not for a chap who curses a fellow who runs him out. I tell you what, there's just a chance Firby-Smith won't press the thing. He hadn't had time to get over it when he saw me. By now he'll have simmered down a bit. Look here, you're a pal of his, aren't you? Well, go and ask him to drop the business. Say you'll curse your brother and make him apologise, and that I'll kick him out of the team for the Geddington match."

It was a difficult moment for Bob. One cannot help one's thoughts, and for an instant the idea of going to Geddington with the team, as he would certainly do if Mike did not play, made him waver. But he recovered himself.

"Don't do that," he said. "I don't see there's a need for anything of that sort. You must play the best side you've got. I can easily talk the old Gazeka over. He gets all right in a second if he's treated the right way. I'll go and do it now."

Burgess looked miserable.

"I say, Bob," he said.

"Yes?"

"Oh, nothing—-I mean, you're not a bad sort." With which glowing eulogy he dashed out of the room, thanking his stars that he had won through a confoundedly awkward business.

Bob went across to Wain's to interview and soothe Firby-Smith.

He found that outraged hero sitting moodily in his study like Achilles in his tent.

Seeing Bob, he became all animation.

"Look here," he said, "I wanted to see you. You know, that frightful young brother of yours——-"

"I know, I know," said Bob. "Burgess was telling me. He wants kicking."

"He wants a frightful licking from the prefects," emended the aggrieved party.

"Well, I don't know, you know. Not much good lugging the prefects into it, is there? I mean, apart from everything else, not much of a catch for me, would it be, having to sit there and look on. I'm a prefect, too, you know."

Firby-Smith looked a little blank at this. He had a great admiration for Bob.

"I didn't think of you," he said.

"I thought you hadn't," said Bob. "You see it now, though, don't you?"

Firby-Smith returned to the original grievance.

"Well, you know, it was frightful cheek."

"Of course it was. Still, I think if I saw him and cursed him, and sent him up to you to apologise—-How would that do?"

"All right. After all, I did run him out."

"Yes, there's that, of course. Mike's all right, really. It isn't as if he did that sort of thing as a habit."

"No. All right then."

"Thanks," said Bob, and went to find Mike.

The lecture on deportment which he read that future All-England batsman in a secluded passage near the junior day-room left the latter rather limp and exceedingly meek. For the moment all the jauntiness and exuberance had been drained out of him. He was a punctured balloon. Reflection, and the distinctly discouraging replies of those experts in school law to whom he had put the question, "What d'you think he'll do?" had induced a very chastened frame of mind.

He perceived that he had walked very nearly into a hornets' nest, and the realisation of his escape made him agree readily to all the conditions imposed. The apology to the Gazeka was made without reserve, and the offensively forgiving, say-no-more-about-it-but-take-care-in-future air of the head of the house roused no spark of resentment in him, so subdued was his fighting spirit. All he wanted was to get the thing done with. He was not inclined to be critical.

And, most of all, he felt grateful to Bob. Firby-Smith, in the course of his address, had not omitted to lay stress on the importance of Bob's intervention. But for Bob, he gave him to understand, he, Mike, would have been prosecuted with the utmost rigour of the law. Mike came away with a confused picture in his mind of a horde of furious prefects bent on his slaughter, after the manner of a stage "excited crowd," and Bob waving them back. He realised that Bob had done him a good turn. He wished he could find some way of repaying him.

Curiously enough, it was an enemy of Bob's who suggested the way—-Burton, of Donaldson's. Burton was a slippery young gentleman, fourteen years of age, who had frequently come into contact with Bob in the house, and owed him many grudges. With Mike he had always tried to form an alliance, though without success.

He happened to meet Mike going to school next morning, and unburdened his soul to him. It chanced that Bob and he had had another small encounter immediately after breakfast, and Burton felt revengeful.

"I say," said Burton, "I'm jolly glad you're playing for the first against Geddington."

"Thanks," said Mike.

"I'm specially glad for one reason."

"What's that?" inquired Mike, without interest.

"Because your beast of a brother has been chucked out. He'd have been playing but for you."

At any other time Mike would have heard Bob called a beast without active protest. He would have felt that it was no business of his to fight his brother's battles for him. But on this occasion he deviated from his rule.

He kicked Burton. Not once or twice, but several times, so that Burton, retiring hurriedly, came to the conclusion that it must be something in the Jackson blood, some taint, as it were. They were *all* beasts.

Mike walked on, weighing this remark, and gradually made up his mind. It must be remembered that he was in a confused mental condition, and that the only thing he realised clearly was that Bob had pulled him out of an uncommonly nasty hole. It seemed to him that it was necessary to repay Bob. He thought the thing over more fully during school, and his decision remained unaltered.

On the evening before the Geddington match, just before lock-up, Mike tapped at Burgess's study door. He tapped with his right hand, for his left was in a sling.

"Come in!" yelled the captain. "Hullo!"

"I'm awfully sorry, Burgess," said Mike. "I've crocked my wrist a bit."

"How did you do that? You were all right at the nets?"

"Slipped as I was changing," said Mike stolidly.

"Is it bad?"

"Nothing much. I'm afraid I shan't be able to play to-morrow."

"I say, that's bad luck. Beastly bad luck. We wanted your batting, too. Be all right, though, in a day or two, I suppose?"

"Oh, yes, rather."

"Hope so, anyway."

"Thanks. Good-night."

"Good-night."

And Burgess, with the comfortable feeling that he had managed to combine duty and pleasure after all, wrote a note to Bob at Donaldson's, telling him to be ready to start with the team for Geddington by the 8.54 next morning.

CHAPTER XVI AN EXPERT EXAMINATION

Mike's Uncle John was a wanderer on the face of the earth. He had been an army surgeon in the days of his youth, and, after an adventurous career, mainly in Afghanistan, had inherited enough money to keep him in comfort for the rest of his life. He had thereupon left the service, and now spent most of his time flitting from one spot of Europe to another. He had been dashing up to Scotland on the day when Mike first became a Wrykynian, but a few weeks in an uncomfortable hotel in Skye and a few days in a comfortable one in Edinburgh had left him with the impression that he had now seen all that there was to be seen in North Britain and might reasonably shift his camp again.

Coming south, he had looked in on Mike's people for a brief space, and, at the request of Mike's mother, took the early express to Wrykyn in order to pay a visit of inspection.

His telegram arrived during morning school. Mike went down to the station to meet him after lunch.

Uncle John took command of the situation at once.

"School playing anybody to-day, Mike? I want to see a match."

"They're playing Geddington. Only it's away. There's a second match on."

"Why aren't you—-Hullo, I didn't see. What have you been doing to yourself?"

"Crocked my wrist a bit. It's nothing much."

"How did you do that?"

"Slipped while I was changing after cricket."

"Hurt?"

"Not much, thanks."

"Doctor seen it?"

"No. But it's really nothing. Be all right by Monday."

"H'm. Somebody ought to look at it. I'll have a look later on."

Mike did not appear to relish this prospect.

"It isn't anything, Uncle John, really. It doesn't matter a bit."

"Never mind. It won't do any harm having somebody examine it who knows a bit about these things. Now, what shall we do. Go on the river?"

"I shouldn't be able to steer."

"I could manage about that. Still, I think I should like to see the place first. Your mother's sure to ask me if you showed me round. It's like going over the stables when you're stopping at a country-house. Got to be done, and better do it as soon as possible."

It is never very interesting playing the part of showman at school. Both Mike and his uncle were inclined to scamp the business. Mike pointed out the various landmarks without much enthusiasm—-it is only after one has left a few years that the school buildings take to themselves romance—-and Uncle John said, "Ah yes, I see. Very nice," two or three times in an absent voice; and they passed on to the cricket field, where the second eleven were playing a neighbouring engineering school. It was a glorious day. The sun had never seemed to Mike so bright or the grass so green. It was one of those days when the ball looks like a large vermilion-coloured football as it leaves the bowler's hand. If ever there was a day when it seemed to Mike that a century would have been a certainty, it was this Saturday. A sudden, bitter realisation of all he had given up swept over him, but he choked the feeling down. The thing was done, and it was no good brooding over the might-have-beens now. Still—-And the Geddington ground was supposed to be one of the easiest scoring grounds of all the public schools!

"Well hit, by George!" remarked Uncle John, as Trevor, who had gone in first wicket for the second eleven, swept a half-volley to leg round to the bank where they were sitting.

"That's Trevor," said Mike. "Chap in Donaldson's. The fellow at the other end is Wilkins. He's in the School House. They look as if they were getting set. By Jove," he said enviously, "pretty good fun batting on a day like this."

Uncle John detected the envious note.

"I suppose you would have been playing here but for your wrist?"

"No, I was playing for the first."

"For the first? For the school! My word, Mike, I didn't know that. No wonder you're feeling badly treated. Of course, I remember your father saying you had played once for the school, and done well; but I thought that was only as a substitute. I didn't know you were a regular member of the team. What bad luck. Will you get another chance?"

"Depends on Bob."

"Has Bob got your place?"

Mike nodded.

"If he does well to-day, they'll probably keep him in."

"Isn't there room for both of you?"

"Such a lot of old colours. There are only three vacancies, and Henfrey got one of those a week ago. I expect they'll give one of the other two to a bowler, Neville-Smith, I should think, if he does well against Geddington. Then there'll be only the last place left."

"Rather awkward, that."

"Still, it's Bob's last year. I've got plenty of time. But I wish I could get in this year."

CHAPTER XVI AN EXPERT EXAMINATION

After they had watched the match for an hour, Uncle John's restless nature asserted itself.

"Suppose we go for a pull on the river now?" he suggested.

They got up.

"Let's just call at the shop," said Mike. "There ought to be a telegram from Geddington by this time. I wonder how Bob's got on."

Apparently Bob had not had a chance yet of distinguishing himself. The telegram read, "Geddington 151 for four. Lunch."

"Not bad that," said Mike. "But I believe they're weak in bowling."

They walked down the road towards the school landing-stage.

"The worst of a school," said Uncle John, as he pulled up-stream with strong, unskilful stroke, "is that one isn't allowed to smoke on the grounds. I badly want a pipe. The next piece of shade that you see, sing out, and we'll put in there."

"Pull your left," said Mike. "That willow's what you want."

Uncle John looked over his shoulder, caught a crab, recovered himself, and steered the boat in under the shade of the branches.

"Put the rope over that stump. Can you manage with one hand? Here, let me—-Done it? Good. A-ah!"

He blew a great cloud of smoke into the air, and sighed contentedly.

"I hope you don't smoke, Mike?"

"No."

"Rotten trick for a boy. When you get to my age you need it. Boys ought to be thinking about keeping themselves fit and being good at games. Which reminds me. Let's have a look at the wrist."

A hunted expression came into Mike's eyes.

"It's really nothing," he began, but his uncle had already removed the sling, and was examining the arm with the neat rapidity of one who has been brought up to such things.

To Mike it seemed as if everything in the world was standing still and waiting. He could hear nothing but his own breathing.

His uncle pressed the wrist gingerly once or twice, then gave it a little twist.

"That hurt?" he asked.

"Ye—-no," stammered Mike.

Uncle John looked up sharply. Mike was crimson.

"What's the game?" inquired Uncle John.

Mike said nothing.

There was a twinkle in his uncle's eyes.

"May as well tell me. I won't give you away. Why this wounded warrior business when you've no more the matter with you than I have?"

Mike hesitated.

"I only wanted to get out of having to write this morning. There was an exam. on."

The idea had occurred to him just before he spoke. It had struck him as neat and plausible.

To Uncle John it did not appear in the same light.

"Do you always write with your left hand? And if you had gone with the first eleven to Geddington, wouldn't that have got you out of your exam? Try again."

When in doubt, one may as well tell the truth. Mike told it.

"I know. It wasn't that, really. Only——"

"Well?"

"Oh, well, dash it all then. Old Bob got me out of an awful row the day before yesterday, and he seemed a bit sick at not playing for the first, so I thought I might as well let him. That's how it was. Look here, swear you won't tell him."

Uncle John was silent. Inwardly he was deciding that the five shillings which he had intended to bestow on Mike on his departure should become a sovereign. (This, it may be mentioned as an interesting biographical fact, was the only occasion in his life on which Mike earned money at the rate of fifteen shillings a half-minute.)

"Swear you won't tell him. He'd be most frightfully sick if he knew."

"I won't tell him."

Conversation dwindled to vanishing-point. Uncle John smoked on in weighty silence, while Mike, staring up at the blue sky through the branches of the willow, let his mind wander to Geddington, where his fate was even now being sealed. How had the school got on? What had Bob done? If he made about twenty, would they give him his cap? Supposing....

A faint snore from Uncle John broke in on his meditations. Then there was a clatter as a briar pipe dropped on to the floor of the boat, and his uncle sat up, gaping.

"Jove, I was nearly asleep. What's the time? Just on six? Didn't know it was so late."

"I ought to be getting back soon, I think. Lock-up's at half-past."

"Up with the anchor, then. You can tackle that rope with two hands now, eh? We are not observed. Don't fall overboard. I'm going to shove her off."

"There'll be another telegram, I should think," said Mike, as they reached the school gates.

"Shall we go and look?"

They walked to the shop.

A second piece of grey paper had been pinned up under the first. Mike pushed his way through the crowd. It was a longer message this time.

It ran as follows:

"Geddington 247 (Burgess six wickets, Neville-Smith four).
Wrykyn 270 for nine (Berridge 86, Marsh 58, Jackson 48)."

Mike worked his way back through the throng, and rejoined his uncle.

"Well?" said Uncle John.

"We won."

He paused for a moment.

"Bob made forty-eight," he added carelessly.

Uncle John felt in his pocket, and silently slid a sovereign into Mike's hand.

It was the only possible reply.

CHAPTER XVII ANOTHER VACANCY

Wyatt got back late that night, arriving at the dormitory as Mike was going to bed.

"By Jove, I'm done," he said. "It was simply baking at Geddington. And I came back in a carriage with Neville-Smith and Ellerby, and they ragged the whole time. I wanted to go to sleep, only they wouldn't let me. Old Smith was awfully bucked because he'd taken four wickets. I should think he'd go off his nut if he took eight ever. He was singing comic songs when he wasn't trying to put Ellerby under the seat. How's your wrist?"

"Oh, better, thanks."

Wyatt began to undress.

"Any colours?" asked Mike after a pause. First eleven colours were generally given in the pavilion after a match or on the journey home.

"No. Only one or two thirds. Jenkins and Clephane, and another chap, can't remember who. No first, though."

"What was Bob's innings like?"

"Not bad. A bit lucky. He ought to have been out before he'd scored, and he was out when he'd made about sixteen, only the umpire didn't seem to know that it's l-b-w when you get your leg right in front of the wicket and the ball hits it. Never saw a clearer case in my life. I was in at the other end. Bit rotten for the Geddington chaps. Just lost them the match. Their umpire, too. Bit of luck for Bob. He didn't give the ghost of a chance after that."

"I should have thought they'd have given him his colours."

"Most captains would have done, only Burgess is so keen on fielding that he rather keeps off it."

"Why, did he field badly?"

"Rottenly. And the man always will choose Billy's bowling to drop catches off. And Billy would cut his rich uncle from Australia if he kept on dropping them off him. Bob's fielding's perfectly sinful. He was pretty bad at the beginning of the season, but now he's got so nervous that he's a dozen times worse. He turns a delicate green when he sees a catch coming. He let their best man off twice in one over, off Billy, to-day; and the chap went on and made a hundred odd. Ripping innings bar those two chances. I hear he's got an average of eighty in school matches this season. Beastly man to bowl to. Knocked me off in half a dozen overs. And, when he does give a couple of easy chances, Bob puts them both on the floor. Billy wouldn't have given him his cap after the match if he'd made a hundred. Bob's the sort of man who wouldn't catch a ball if you handed it to him on a plate, with watercress round it."

Burgess, reviewing the match that night, as he lay awake in his cubicle, had come to much the same conclusion. He was very fond of Bob, but two missed catches in one over was straining the bonds of human affection too far. There would have been serious trouble between David and Jonathan if either had persisted in dropping catches off the other's bowling. He writhed in bed as he re-remembered the second of the two chances which the wretched Bob had refused. The scene was indelibly printed on his mind. Chap had got a late cut which he fancied rather. With great guile he had fed this late cut. Sent down a couple which he put to the boundary. Then fired a third much faster and a bit shorter. Chap had a go at it, just as he had expected: and he felt that life was a good thing after all when the ball just touched the corner of the bat and flew into Bob's hands. And Bob dropped it!

The memory was too bitter. If he dwelt on it, he felt, he would get insomnia. So he turned to pleasanter reflections: the yorker which had shattered the second-wicket man, and the slow head-ball which had led to a big hitter being caught on the boundary. Soothed by these memories, he fell asleep.

Next morning he found himself in a softened frame of mind. He thought of Bob's iniquities with sorrow rather than wrath. He felt towards him much as a father feels towards a prodigal son whom there is still a chance of reforming. He overtook Bob on his way to chapel.

Directness was always one of Burgess's leading qualities.

"Look here, Bob. About your fielding. It's simply awful."

Bob was all remorse.

"It's those beastly slip catches. I can't time them."

"That one yesterday was right into your hands. Both of them were."

"I know. I'm frightfully sorry."

"Well, but I mean, why *can't* you hold them? It's no good being a good bat—-you're that all right—-if you're going to give away runs in the field."

"Do you know, I believe I should do better in the deep. I could get time to watch them there. I wish you'd give me a shot in the deep—-for the second."

"Second be blowed! I want your batting in the first. Do you think you'd really do better in the deep?"

"I'm almost certain I should. I'll practise like mad. Trevor'll hit me up catches. I hate the slips. I get in the dickens of a funk directly the bowler starts his run now. I know that if a catch does come, I shall miss it. I'm certain the deep would be much better."

"All right then. Try it."

The conversation turned to less pressing topics.

In the next two matches, accordingly, Bob figured on the boundary, where he had not much to do except throw the ball back to the bowler, and stop an occasional drive along the carpet. The beauty of fielding in the deep is that no unpleasant surprises can be sprung upon one. There is just that moment or two for collecting one's thoughts which makes the whole difference. Bob, as he stood regarding the game from afar, found his self-confidence returning slowly, drop by drop.

As for Mike, he played for the second, and hoped for the day.

His opportunity came at last. It will be remembered that on the morning after the Great Picnic the headmaster made an announcement in Hall to the effect that, owing to an outbreak of chicken-pox in the town, all streets except the High Street would be out of bounds. This did not affect the bulk of the school, for most of the shops to which any one ever thought of going were in the High Street. But there were certain inquiring minds who liked to ferret about in odd corners.

Among these was one Leather-Twigg, of Seymour's, better known in criminal circles as Shoeblossom.

Shoeblossom was a curious mixture of the Energetic Ragger and the Quiet Student. On a Monday evening you would hear a hideous uproar proceeding from Seymour's junior day-room; and, going down with a swagger-stick to investigate, you would find a tangled heap of squealing humanity on the floor, and at the bottom of the heap, squealing louder than any two others, would be Shoeblossom, his collar burst and blackened and his face apoplectically crimson. On the Tuesday afternoon, strolling in some shady corner of the grounds you would come upon him lying on his chest, deep in some work of fiction and resentful of interruption. On the Wednesday morning he would be in receipt of four hundred lines from his housemaster for breaking three windows and a gas-globe. Essentially a man of moods, Shoeblossom.

It happened about the date of the Geddington match that he took out from the school library a copy of "The Iron Pirate," and for the next day or two he wandered about like a lost spirit trying to find a sequestered spot in which to read it. His inability to hit on such a spot was rendered more irritating by the fact that, to judge from the first few chapters (which he had managed to get through during prep. one night under the eye of a short-sighted master), the book was obviously the last word in hot stuff. He tried the junior day-room, but people threw cushions at him. He tried out of doors, and a ball hit from a neighbouring net nearly scalped him. Anything in the nature of concentration became impossible in these circumstances.

Then he recollected that in a quiet backwater off the High Street there was a little confectioner's shop, where tea might be had at a reasonable sum, and also, what was more important, peace.

He made his way there, and in the dingy back shop, all amongst the dust and bluebottles, settled down to a thoughtful perusal of chapter six.

Upstairs, at the same moment, the doctor was recommending that Master John George, the son of the house, be kept warm and out of draughts and not permitted to scratch himself, however necessary such an action might seem to him. In brief, he was attending J. G. for chicken-pox.

CHAPTER XVII ANOTHER VACANCY

Shoeblossom came away, entering the High Street furtively, lest Authority should see him out of bounds, and returned to the school, where he went about his lawful occasions as if there were no such thing as chicken-pox in the world.

But all the while the microbe was getting in some unostentatious but clever work. A week later Shoeblossom began to feel queer. He had occasional headaches, and found himself oppressed by a queer distaste for food. The professional advice of Dr. Oakes, the school doctor, was called for, and Shoeblossom took up his abode in the Infirmary, where he read *Punch*, sucked oranges, and thought of Life.

Two days later Barry felt queer. He, too, disappeared from Society.

Chicken-pox is no respecter of persons. The next victim was Marsh, of the first eleven. Marsh, who was top of the school averages. Where were his drives now, his late cuts that were wont to set the pavilion in a roar. Wrapped in a blanket, and looking like the spotted marvel of a travelling circus, he was driven across to the Infirmary in a four-wheeler, and it became incumbent upon Burgess to select a substitute for him.

And so it came about that Mike soared once again into the ranks of the elect, and found his name down in the team to play against the Incogniti.

CHAPTER XVIII BOB HAS NEWS TO IMPART

Wrykyn went down badly before the Incogs. It generally happens at least once in a school cricket season that the team collapses hopelessly, for no apparent reason. Some schools do it in nearly every match, but Wrykyn so far had been particularly fortunate this year. They had only been beaten once, and that by a mere twenty odd runs in a hard-fought game. But on this particular day, against a not overwhelmingly strong side, they failed miserably. The weather may have had something to do with it, for rain fell early in the morning, and the school, batting first on the drying wicket, found themselves considerably puzzled by a slow left-hander. Morris and Berridge left with the score still short of ten, and after that the rout began. Bob, going in fourth wicket, made a dozen, and Mike kept his end up, and was not out eleven; but nobody except Wyatt, who hit out at everything and knocked up thirty before he was stumped, did anything to distinguish himself. The total was a hundred and seven, and the Incogniti, batting when the wicket was easier, doubled this.

The general opinion of the school after this match was that either Mike or Bob would have to stand down from the team when it was definitely filled up, for Neville-Smith, by showing up well with the ball against the Incogniti when the others failed with the bat, made it practically certain that he would get one of the two vacancies.

"If I do" he said to Wyatt, "there will be the biggest bust of modern times at my place. My pater is away for a holiday in Norway, and I'm alone, bar the servants. And I can square them. Will you come?"

"Tea?"

"Tea!" said Neville-Smith scornfully.

"Well, what then?"

"Don't you ever have feeds in the dorms. after lights-out in the houses?"

"Used to when I was a kid. Too old now. Have to look after my digestion. I remember, three years ago, when Wain's won the footer cup, we got up and fed at about two in the morning. All sorts of luxuries. Sardines on sugar-biscuits. I've got the taste in my mouth still. Do you remember Macpherson? Left a couple of years ago. His food ran out, so he spread brown-boot polish on bread, and ate that. Got through a slice, too. Wonderful chap! But what about this thing of yours? What time's it going to be?"

"Eleven suit you?"

"All right."

"How about getting out?"

"I'll do it as quickly as the team did to-day. I can't say more than that."

"You were all right."

"I'm an exceptional sort of chap."

"What about the Jacksons?"

"It's going to be a close thing. If Bob's fielding were to improve suddenly, he would just do it. But young Mike's all over him as a bat. In a year or two that kid'll be a marvel. He's bound to get in next year, of course, so perhaps it would be better if Bob got the place as it's his last season. Still, one wants the best man, of course."

Mike avoided Bob as much as possible during this anxious period; and he privately thought it rather tactless of the latter when, meeting him one day outside Donaldson's, he insisted on his coming in and having some tea.

Mike shuffled uncomfortably as his brother filled the kettle and lit the Etna. It required more tact than he had at his disposal to carry off a situation like this.

Bob, being older, was more at his ease. He got tea ready, making desultory conversation the while, as if there were no particular reason why either of them should feel uncomfortable in the other's presence. When he had finished, he poured Mike out a cup, passed him the bread, and sat down.

"Not seen much of each other lately, Mike, what?"

Mike murmured unintelligibly through a mouthful of bread-and-jam.

"It's no good pretending it isn't an awkward situation," continued Bob, "because it is. Beastly awkward."

"Awful rot the pater sending us to the same school."

"Oh, I don't know. We've all been at Wrykyn. Pity to spoil the record. It's your fault for being such a young Infant Prodigy, and mine for not being able to field like an ordinary human being."

"You get on much better in the deep."

"Bit better, yes. Liable at any moment to miss a sitter, though. Not that it matters much really whether I do now."

Mike stared.

"What! Why?"

"That's what I wanted to see you about. Has Burgess said anything to you yet?"

"No. Why? What about?"

"Well, I've a sort of idea our little race is over. I fancy you've won."

"I've not heard a word——"

"I have. I'll tell you what makes me think the thing's settled. I was in the pav. just now, in the First room, trying to find a batting-glove I'd mislaid. There was a copy of the *Wrykynian* lying on the mantelpiece, and I picked it up and started reading it. So there wasn't any noise to show anybody outside that there was some one in the room. And then I heard Burgess and Spence jawing on the steps.

They thought the place was empty, of course. I couldn't help hearing what they said. The pav.'s like a sounding-board. I heard every word. Spence said, 'Well, it's about as difficult a problem as any captain of cricket at Wrykyn has ever had to tackle.' I had a sort of idea that old Billy liked to boss things all on his own, but apparently he does consult Spence sometimes. After all, he's cricket-master, and that's what he's there for. Well, Billy said, 'I don't know what to do. What do you think, sir?' Spence said, 'Well, I'll give you my opinion, Burgess, but don't feel bound to act on it. I'm simply saying what I think.' 'Yes, sir,' said old Bill, doing a big Young Disciple with Wise Master act. '*I* think M.,' said Spence. 'Decidedly M. He's a shade better than R. now, and in a year or two, of course, there'll be no comparison.'"

"Oh, rot," muttered Mike, wiping the sweat off his forehead. This was one of the most harrowing interviews he had ever been through.

"Not at all. Billy agreed with him. 'That's just what I think, sir,' he said. 'It's rough on Bob, but still——' And then they walked down the steps. I waited a bit to give them a good start, and then sheered off myself. And so home."

Mike looked at the floor, and said nothing.

There was nothing much to *be* said.

"Well, what I wanted to see you about was this," resumed Bob. "I don't propose to kiss you or anything; but, on the other hand, don't let's go to the other extreme. I'm not saying that it isn't a bit of a brick just missing my cap like this, but it would have been just as bad for you if you'd been the one dropped. It's the fortune of war. I don't want you to go about feeling that you've blighted my life, and so on, and dashing up side-streets to avoid me because you think the sight of you will be painful. As it isn't me, I'm jolly glad it's you; and I shall cadge a seat in the pavilion from you when you're playing for England at the Oval. Congratulate you."

It was the custom at Wrykyn, when you congratulated a man on getting colours, to shake his hand. They shook hands.

"Thanks, awfully, Bob," said Mike. And after that there seemed to be nothing much to talk about. So Mike edged out of the room, and tore across to Wain's.

He was sorry for Bob, but he would not have been human (which he certainly was) if the triumph of having won through at last into the first eleven had not dwarfed commiseration. It had been his one ambition, and now he had achieved it.

The annoying part of the thing was that he had nobody to talk to about it. Until the news was official he could not mention it to the common herd. It wouldn't do. The only possible confidant was Wyatt. And Wyatt was at Bisley, shooting with the School Eight for the Ashburton. For bull's-eyes as well as cats came within Wyatt's range as a marksman. Cricket took up too much of his time for him to be captain of the Eight and the man chosen to shoot for the Spencer, as he would otherwise almost certainly have been; but even though short of practice he was well up in the team.

Until he returned, Mike could tell nobody. And by the time he returned the notice would probably be up in the Senior Block with the other cricket notices.

In this fermenting state Mike went into the house.

The list of the team to play for Wain's *v.* Seymour's on the following Monday was on the board. As he passed it, a few words scrawled in pencil at the bottom caught his eye.

"All the above will turn out for house-fielding at 6.30 to-morrow morning.—-W. F.-S."

"Oh, dash it," said Mike, "what rot! Why on earth can't he leave us alone!"

For getting up an hour before his customary time for rising was not among Mike's favourite pastimes. Still, orders were orders, he felt. It would have to be done.

CHAPTER XIX MIKE GOES TO SLEEP AGAIN

Mike was a stout supporter of the view that sleep in large quantities is good for one. He belonged to the school of thought which holds that a man becomes plain and pasty if deprived of his full spell in bed. He aimed at the peach-bloom complexion.

To be routed out of bed a clear hour before the proper time, even on a summer morning, was not, therefore, a prospect that appealed to him.

When he woke it seemed even less attractive than it had done when he went to sleep. He had banged his head on the pillow six times over-night, and this silent alarm proved effective, as it always does. Reaching out a hand for his watch, he found that it was five minutes past six.

This was to the good. He could manage another quarter of an hour between the sheets. It would only take him ten minutes to wash and get into his flannels.

He took his quarter of an hour, and a little more. He woke from a sort of doze to find that it was twenty-five past.

Man's inability to get out of bed in the morning is a curious thing. One may reason with oneself clearly and forcibly without the slightest effect. One knows that delay means inconvenience. Perhaps it may spoil one's whole day. And one also knows that a single resolute heave will do the trick. But logic is of no use. One simply lies there.

Mike thought he would take another minute.

And during that minute there floated into his mind the question, Who *was* Firby-Smith? That was the point. Who *was* he, after all?

This started quite a new train of thought. Previously Mike had firmly intended to get up—-some time. Now he began to waver.

The more he considered the Gazeka's insignificance and futility and his own magnificence, the more outrageous did it seem that he should be dragged out of bed to please Firby-Smith's vapid mind. Here was he, about to receive his first eleven colours on this very day probably, being ordered about, inconvenienced—-in short, put upon by a worm who had only just scraped into the third.

Was this right, he asked himself. Was this proper?

And the hands of the watch moved round to twenty to.

What was the matter with his fielding? *It* was all right. Make the rest of the team fag about, yes. But not a chap who, dash it all, had got his first *for* fielding!

CHAPTER XIX MIKE GOES TO SLEEP AGAIN

It was with almost a feeling of self-righteousness that Mike turned over on his side and went to sleep again.

And outside in the cricket-field, the massive mind of the Gazeka was filled with rage, as it was gradually borne in upon him that this was not a question of mere lateness—-which, he felt, would be bad enough, for when he said six-thirty he meant six-thirty—-but of actual desertion. It was time, he said to himself, that the foot of Authority was set firmly down, and the strong right hand of Justice allowed to put in some energetic work. His comments on the team's fielding that morning were bitter and sarcastic. His eyes gleamed behind their pince-nez.

The painful interview took place after breakfast. The head of the house despatched his fag in search of Mike, and waited. He paced up and down the room like a hungry lion, adjusting his pince-nez (a thing, by the way, which lions seldom do) and behaving in other respects like a monarch of the desert. One would have felt, looking at him, that Mike, in coming to his den, was doing a deed which would make the achievement of Daniel seem in comparison like the tentative effort of some timid novice.

And certainly Mike was not without qualms as he knocked at the door, and went in in response to the hoarse roar from the other side of it.

Firby-Smith straightened his tie, and glared.

"Young Jackson," he said, "look here, I want to know what it all means, and jolly quick. You weren't at house-fielding this morning. Didn't you see the notice?"

Mike admitted that he had seen the notice.

"Then you frightful kid, what do you mean by it? What?"

Mike hesitated. Awfully embarrassing, this. His real reason for not turning up to house-fielding was that he considered himself above such things, and Firby-Smith a toothy weed. Could he give this excuse? He had not his Book of Etiquette by him at the moment, but he rather fancied not. There was no arguing against the fact that the head of the house *was* a toothy weed; but he felt a firm conviction that it would not be politic to say so.

Happy thought: over-slept himself.

He mentioned this.

"Over-slept yourself! You must jolly well not over-sleep yourself. What do you mean by over-sleeping yourself?"

Very trying this sort of thing.

"What time did you wake up?"

"Six," said Mike.

It was not according to his complicated, yet intelligible code of morality to tell lies to save himself. When others were concerned he could suppress the true and suggest the false with a face of brass.

"Six!"

"Five past."

"Why didn't you get up then?"

"I went to sleep again."

"DO—YOU—SEE, YOU FRIGHTFUL KID?"

"Oh, you went to sleep again, did you? Well, just listen to me. I've had my eye on you for some time, and I've seen it coming on. You've got swelled head, young man. That's what you've got. Frightful swelled head. You think the place belongs to you."

"I don't," said Mike indignantly.

"Yes, you do," said the Gazeka shrilly. "You think the whole frightful place belongs to you. You go siding about as if you'd bought it. Just because you've got your second, you think you can do what you like; turn up or not, as you please. It doesn't matter whether I'm only in the third and you're in the first. That's got nothing to do with it. The point is that you're one of the house team, and I'm captain of it, so you've jolly well got to turn out for fielding with the others when I think it necessary. See?"

Mike said nothing.

"Do—-you—-see, you frightful kid?"

Mike remained stonily silent. The rather large grain of truth in what Firby-Smith had said had gone home, as the unpleasant truth about ourselves is apt to do; and his feelings were hurt. He was determined not to give in and say that he saw even if the head of the house invoked all the majesty of the prefects' room to help him, as he had nearly done once before. He set his teeth, and stared at a photograph on the wall.

Firby-Smith's manner became ominously calm. He produced a swagger-stick from a corner.

"Do you see?" he asked again.

Mike's jaw set more tightly.

What one really wants here is a row of stars.

Mike was still full of his injuries when Wyatt came back. Wyatt was worn out, but cheerful. The school had finished sixth for the Ashburton, which was an improvement of eight places on their last year's form, and he himself had scored thirty at the two hundred and twenty-seven at the five hundred totals, which had put him in a very good humour with the world.

"Me ancient skill has not deserted me," he said, "That's the cats. The man who can wing a cat by moonlight can put a bullet where he likes on a target. I didn't hit the bull every time, but that was to give the other fellows a chance. My fatal modesty has always been a hindrance to me in life, and I suppose it always will be. Well, well! And what of the old homestead? Anything happened since I went away? Me old father, is he well? Has the lost will been discovered, or is there a mortgage on the family estates? By Jove, I could do with a stoup of Malvoisie. I wonder if the moke's gone to bed yet. I'll go down and look. A jug of water drawn from the well in the old courtyard where my ancestors have played as children for centuries back would just about save my life."

He left the dormitory, and Mike began to brood over his wrongs once more.

Wyatt came back, brandishing a jug of water and a glass.

"Oh, for a beaker full of the warm south, full of the true, the blushful Hippocrene! Have you ever tasted Hippocrene, young Jackson? Rather like ginger-beer, with a dash of raspberry-vinegar. Very heady. Failing that, water will do. A-ah!"

He put down the glass, and surveyed Mike, who had maintained a moody silence throughout this speech.

"What's your trouble?" he asked. "For pains in the back try Ju-jar. If it's a broken heart, Zam-buk's what you want. Who's been quarrelling with you?"

"It's only that ass Firby-Smith."

"Again! I never saw such chaps as you two. Always at it. What was the trouble this time? Call him a grinning ape again? Your passion for the truth'll be getting you into trouble one of these days."

"He said I stuck on side."

"Why?"

"I don't know."

"I mean, did he buttonhole you on your way to school, and say, 'Jackson, a word in your ear. You stick on side.' Or did he lead up to it in any way? Did he say, 'Talking of side, you stick it on.' What had you been doing to him?"

"It was the house-fielding."

"But you can't stick on side at house-fielding. I defy any one to. It's too early in the morning."

"I didn't turn up."

"What! Why?"

"Oh, I don't know."

"No, but, look here, really. Did you simply bunk it?"

"Yes."

Wyatt leaned on the end of Mike's bed, and, having observed its occupant thoughtfully for a moment, proceeded to speak wisdom for the good of his soul.

"I say, I don't want to jaw—-I'm one of those quiet chaps with strong, silent natures; you may have noticed it—-but I must put in a well-chosen word at this juncture. Don't pretend to be dropping off to sleep. Sit up and listen to what your kind old uncle's got to say to you about manners and deportment. Otherwise, blood as you are at cricket, you'll have a rotten time here. There are some things you simply can't do; and one of them is bunking a thing when you're put down for it. It doesn't matter who it is puts you down. If he's captain, you've got to obey him. That's discipline, that 'ere is. The speaker then paused, and took a sip of water from the carafe which stood at his elbow. Cheers from the audience, and a voice 'Hear! Hear!'"

Mike rolled over in bed and glared up at the orator. Most of his face was covered by the water-jug, but his eyes stared fixedly from above it. He winked in a friendly way, and, putting down the jug, drew a deep breath.

"Nothing like this old '87 water," he said. "Such body."

"I like you jawing about discipline," said Mike morosely.

"And why, my gentle che-ild, should I not talk about discipline?"

"Considering you break out of the house nearly every night."

"In passing, rather rum when you think that a burglar would get it hot for breaking in, while I get dropped on if I break out. Why should there be one law for the burglar and one for me? But you were saying—-just so. I thank you. About my breaking out. When you're a white-haired old man like me, young Jackson, you'll see that there are two sorts of discipline at school. One you can break if you feel like taking the risks; the other you mustn't ever break. I don't know why, but it isn't done. Until you learn that, you can never hope to become the Perfect Wrykynian like," he concluded modestly, "me."

Mike made no reply. He would have perished rather than admit it, but Wyatt's words had sunk in. That moment marked a distinct epoch in his career. His feelings were curiously mixed. He was still furious with Firby-Smith, yet at the same time he could not help acknowledging to himself that the latter had had the right on his side. He saw and approved of Wyatt's point of view, which was the more impressive to him from his knowledge of his friend's contempt for, or, rather, cheerful disregard of, most forms of law and order. If Wyatt, reckless though he was as regarded written school rules, held so rigid a respect for those that were unwritten, these last must be things which could not be treated lightly. That night, for the first time in his life, Mike went to sleep with a clear idea of what the public school spirit, of which so much is talked and written, really meant.

CHAPTER XX THE TEAM IS FILLED UP

When Burgess, at the end of the conversation in the pavilion with Mr. Spence which Bob Jackson had overheard, accompanied the cricket-master across the field to the boarding-houses, he had distinctly made up his mind to give Mike his first eleven colours next day. There was only one more match to be played before the school fixture-list was finished. That was the match with Ripton. Both at cricket and football Ripton was the school that mattered most. Wrykyn did not always win its other school matches; but it generally did. The public schools of England divide themselves naturally into little groups, as far as games are concerned. Harrow, Eton, and Winchester are one group: Westminster and Charterhouse another: Bedford, Tonbridge, Dulwich, Haileybury, and St. Paul's are a third. In this way, Wrykyn, Ripton, Geddington, and Wilborough formed a group. There was no actual championship competition, but each played each, and by the end of the season it was easy to see which was entitled to first place. This nearly always lay between Ripton and Wrykyn. Sometimes an exceptional Geddington team would sweep the board, or Wrykyn, having beaten Ripton, would go down before Wilborough. But this did not happen often. Usually Wilborough and Geddington were left to scramble for the wooden spoon.

Secretaries of cricket at Ripton and Wrykyn always liked to arrange the date of the match towards the end of the term, so that they might take the field with representative and not experimental teams. By July the weeding-out process had generally finished. Besides which the members of the teams had had time to get into form.

At Wrykyn it was the custom to fill up the team, if possible, before the Ripton match. A player is likely to show better form if he has got his colours than if his fate depends on what he does in that particular match.

Burgess, accordingly, had resolved to fill up the first eleven just a week before Ripton visited Wrykyn. There were two vacancies. One gave him no trouble. Neville-Smith was not a great bowler, but he was steady, and he had done well in the earlier matches. He had fairly earned his place. But the choice between Bob and Mike had kept him awake into the small hours two nights in succession. Finally he had consulted Mr. Spence, and Mr. Spence had voted for Mike.

Burgess was glad the thing was settled. The temptation to allow sentiment to interfere with business might have become too strong if he had waited much longer. He knew that it would be a wrench definitely excluding Bob from the team, and he hated to have to do it. The more he thought of it, the sorrier he was for him. If he could have pleased himself, he would have kept Bob In. But, as the poet has it, "Pleasure is pleasure, and biz is biz, and kep' in a sepyrit jug." The first duty of a captain is to have no friends.

From small causes great events do spring. If Burgess had not picked up a particularly interesting novel after breakfast on the morning of Mike's interview with Firby-Smith in the study, the list would have gone up on the notice-board after prayers. As it was, engrossed in his book, he let the moments go by till the sound on the bell startled him into movement. And then there was only time to gather up his cap, and sprint. The paper on which he had intended to write the list and the pen he had laid out to write it with lay untouched on the table.

And, as it was not his habit to put up notices except during the morning, he postponed the thing. He could write it after tea. After all, there was a week before the match.

When school was over, he went across to the Infirmary to inquire about Marsh. The report was more than favourable. Marsh had better not see any one just yet, In case of accident, but he was certain to be out in time to play against Ripton.

"Doctor Oakes thinks he will be back in school on Tuesday."

"Banzai!" said Burgess, feeling that life was good. To take the field against Ripton without Marsh would have been to court disaster. Marsh's fielding alone was worth the money. With him at short slip, Burgess felt safe when he bowled.

The uncomfortable burden of the knowledge that he was about temporarily to sour Bob Jackson's life ceased for the moment to trouble him. He crooned extracts from musical comedy as he walked towards the nets.

Recollection of Bob's hard case was brought to him by the sight of that about-to-be-soured sportsman tearing across the ground in the middle distance in an effort to get to a high catch which Trevor had hit up to him. It was a difficult catch, and Burgess waited to see if he would bring it off.

Bob got to it with one hand, and held it. His impetus carried him on almost to where Burgess was standing.

"Well held," said Burgess.

"Hullo," said Bob awkwardly. A gruesome thought had flashed across his mind that the captain might think that this gallery-work was an organised advertisement.

"I couldn't get both hands to it," he explained.

"You're hot stuff in the deep."

"Easy when you're only practising."

"I've just been to the Infirmary."

"Oh. How's Marsh?"

"They wouldn't let me see him, but it's all right. He'll be able to play on Saturday."

"Good," said Bob, hoping he had said it as if he meant it. It was decidedly a blow. He was glad for the sake of the school, of course, but one has one's personal ambitions. To the fact that Mike and not himself was the eleventh cap he had become partially resigned: but he had wanted rather badly to play against Ripton.

Burgess passed on, his mind full of Bob once more. What hard luck it was! There was he, dashing about in the sun to improve his fielding, and all the time the team was filled up. He felt as if he were playing some low trick on a pal.

Then the Jekyll and Hyde business completed itself. He suppressed his personal feelings, and became the cricket captain again.

It was the cricket captain who, towards the end of the evening, came upon Firby-Smith and Mike parting at the conclusion of a conversation. That it had not been a friendly conversation would have been evident to the most casual observer from the manner in which Mike stumped off, swinging his cricket-bag as if it were a weapon of offence. There are many kinds of walk. Mike's was the walk of the Overwrought Soul.

"What's up?" inquired Burgess.

"Young Jackson, do you mean? Oh, nothing. I was only telling him that there was going to be house-fielding to-morrow before breakfast."

"Didn't he like the idea?"

"He's jolly well got to like it," said the Gazeka, as who should say, "This way for Iron Wills." "The frightful kid cut it this morning. There'll be worse trouble if he does it again."

There was, it may be mentioned, not an ounce of malice in the head of Wain's house. That by telling the captain of cricket that Mike had shirked fielding-practice he might injure the latter's prospects of a first eleven cap simply did not occur to him. That Burgess would feel, on being told of Mike's slackness, much as a bishop might feel if he heard that a favourite curate had become a Mahometan or a Mumbo-Jumboist, did not enter his mind. All he considered was that the story of his dealings with Mike showed him, Firby-Smith, in the favourable and dashing character of the fellow-who-will-stand-no-nonsense, a sort of Captain Kettle on dry land, in fact; and so he proceeded to tell it in detail.

Burgess parted with him with the firm conviction that Mike was a young slacker. Keenness in fielding was a fetish with him; and to cut practice struck him as a crime.

He felt that he had been deceived in Mike.

When, therefore, one takes into consideration his private bias in favour of Bob, and adds to it the reaction caused by this sudden unmasking of Mike, it is not surprising that the list Burgess made out that night before he went to bed differed in an important respect from the one he had intended to write before school.

Mike happened to be near the notice-board when he pinned it up. It was only the pleasure of seeing his name down in black-and-white that made him trouble to look at the list. Bob's news of the day before yesterday had made it clear how that list would run.

CHAPTER XX THE TEAM IS FILLED UP

The crowd that collected the moment Burgess had walked off carried him right up to the board.

He looked at the paper.

"Hard luck!" said somebody.

Mike scarcely heard him.

He felt physically sick with the shock of the disappointment. For the initial before the name Jackson was R.

There was no possibility of mistake. Since writing was invented, there had never been an R. that looked less like an M. than the one on that list.

Bob had beaten him on the tape.

CHAPTER XXI MARJORY THE FRANK

At the door of the senior block Burgess, going out, met Bob coming in, hurrying, as he was rather late.

"Congratulate you, Bob," he said; and passed on.

Bob stared after him. As he stared, Trevor came out of the block.

"Congratulate you, Bob."

"What's the matter now?"

"Haven't you seen?"

"Seen what?"

"Why the list. You've got your first."

"My—-what? you're rotting."

"No, I'm not. Go and look."

The thing seemed incredible. Had he dreamed that conversation between Spence and Burgess on the pavilion steps? Had he mixed up the names? He was certain that he had heard Spence give his verdict for Mike, and Burgess agree with him.

Just then, Mike, feeling very ill, came down the steps. He caught sight of Bob and was passing with a feeble grin, when something told him that this was one of those occasions on which one has to show a Red Indian fortitude and stifle one's private feelings.

"Congratulate you, Bob," he said awkwardly.

"Thanks awfully," said Bob, with equal awkwardness. Trevor moved on, delicately. This was no place for him. Bob's face was looking like a stuffed frog's, which was Bob's way of trying to appear unconcerned and at his ease, while Mike seemed as if at any moment he might burst into tears. Spectators are not wanted at these awkward interviews.

There was a short silence.

"Jolly glad you've got it," said Mike.

"I believe there's a mistake. I swear I heard Burgess say to Spence——-"

"He changed his mind probably. No reason why he shouldn't."

"Well, it's jolly rummy."

Bob endeavoured to find consolation.

"Anyhow, you'll have three years in the first. You're a cert. for next year."

"Hope so," said Mike, with such manifest lack of enthusiasm that Bob abandoned this line of argument. When one has missed one's colours, next year seems a very, very long way off.

They moved slowly through the cloisters, neither speaking, and up the stairs that led to the Great Hall. Each was gratefully conscious of the fact that prayers would be beginning in another minute, putting an end to an uncomfortable situation.

"Heard from home lately?" inquired Mike.

Bob snatched gladly at the subject.

"Got a letter from mother this morning. I showed you the last one, didn't I? I've only just had time to skim through this one, as the post was late, and I only got it just as I was going to dash across to school. Not much in it. Here it is, if you want to read it."

"Thanks. It'll be something to do during Math."

"Marjory wrote, too, for the first time in her life. Haven't had time to look at it yet."

"After you. Sure it isn't meant for me? She owes me a letter."

"No, it's for me all right. I'll give it you in the interval."

The arrival of the headmaster put an end to the conversation.

By a quarter to eleven Mike had begun to grow reconciled to his fate. The disappointment was still there, but it was lessened. These things are like kicks on the shin. A brief spell of agony, and then a dull pain of which we are not always conscious unless our attention is directed to it, and which in time disappears altogether. When the bell rang for the interval that morning, Mike was, as it were, sitting up and taking nourishment.

He was doing this in a literal as well as in a figurative sense when Bob entered the school shop.

Bob appeared curiously agitated. He looked round, and, seeing Mike, pushed his way towards him through the crowd. Most of those present congratulated him as he passed; and Mike noticed, with some surprise, that, in place of the blushful grin which custom demands from the man who is being congratulated on receipt of colours, there appeared on his face a worried, even an irritated look. He seemed to have something on his mind.

"Hullo," said Mike amiably. "Got that letter?"

"Yes. I'll show it you outside."

"Why not here?"

"Come on."

Mike resented the tone, but followed. Evidently something had happened to upset Bob seriously. As they went out on the gravel, somebody congratulated Bob again, and again Bob hardly seemed to appreciate it.'

Bob led the way across the gravel and on to the first terrace. When they had left the crowd behind, he stopped.

"What's up?" asked Mike.

"I want you to read——"

"Jackson!"

They both turned. The headmaster was standing on the edge of the gravel.

Bob pushed the letter into Mike's hands.

"Read that," he said, and went up to the headmaster. Mike heard the words "English Essay," and, seeing that the conversation was apparently going to be one of some length, capped the headmaster and walked off. He was just going to read the letter when the bell rang. He put the missive in his pocket, and went to his form-room wondering what Marjory could have found to say to Bob to touch him on the raw to such an extent. She was a breezy correspondent, with a style of her own, but usually she entertained rather than upset people. No suspicion of the actual contents of the letter crossed his mind.

He read it during school, under the desk; and ceased to wonder. Bob had had cause to look worried. For the thousand and first time in her career of crime Marjory had been and done it! With a strong hand she had shaken the cat out of the bag, and exhibited it plainly to all whom it might concern.

There was a curious absence of construction about the letter. Most authors of sensational matter nurse their bomb-shell, lead up to it, and display it to the best advantage. Marjory dropped hers into the body of the letter, and let it take its chance with the other news-items.

"DEAR BOB" (the letter ran),—-

> "I hope you are quite well. I am quite well. Phyllis has a cold, Ella cheeked Mademoiselle yesterday, and had to write out 'Little Girls must be polite and obedient' a hundred times in French. She was jolly sick about it. I told her it served her right. Joe made eighty-three against Lancashire. Reggie made a duck. Have you got your first? If you have, it will be all through Mike. Uncle John told Father that Mike pretended to hurt his wrist so that you could play instead of him for the school, and Father said it was very sporting of Mike but nobody must tell you because it wouldn't be fair if you got your first for you to know that you owed it to Mike and I wasn't supposed to hear but I did because I was in the room only they didn't know I was (we were playing hide-and-seek and I was hiding) so I'm writing to tell you,

"From your affectionate sister

"Marjory."

There followed a P.S.

> "I'll tell you what you ought to do. I've been reading a jolly good book called 'The Boys of Dormitory Two,' and the hero's an awfully nice boy named Lionel Tremayne, and his friend Jack Langdale saves his life when a beast of a boatman who's really employed by Lionel's cousin who wants the money that Lionel's going to have when he grows up stuns him and leaves him on the beach to drown. Well, Lionel is going to play for the school against Loamshire, and

it's *the* match of the season, but he goes to the headmaster and says he wants Jack to play instead of him. Why don't you do that?

"M.

"P.P.S.—-This has been a frightful fag to write."

For the life of him Mike could not help giggling as he pictured what Bob's expression must have been when his brother read this document. But the humorous side of the thing did not appeal to him for long. What should he say to Bob? What would Bob say to him? Dash it all, it made him look such an awful *ass*! Anyhow, Bob couldn't do much. In fact he didn't see that he could do anything. The team was filled up, and Burgess was not likely to alter it. Besides, why should he alter it? Probably he would have given Bob his colours anyhow. Still, it was beastly awkward. Marjory meant well, but she had put her foot right in it. Girls oughtn't to meddle with these things. No girl ought to be taught to write till she came of age. And Uncle John had behaved in many respects like the Complete Rotter. If he was going to let out things like that, he might at least have whispered them, or looked behind the curtains to see that the place wasn't chock-full of female kids. Confound Uncle John!

Throughout the dinner-hour Mike kept out of Bob's way. But in a small community like a school it is impossible to avoid a man for ever. They met at the nets.

"Well?" said Bob.

"How do you mean?" said Mike.

"Did you read it?"

"Yes."

"Well, is it all rot, or did you—-you know what I mean—-sham a crocked wrist?"

"Yes," said Mike, "I did."

Bob stared gloomily at his toes.

"I mean," he said at last, apparently putting the finishing-touch to some train of thought, "I know I ought to be grateful, and all that. I suppose I am. I mean it was jolly good of you—-Dash it all," he broke off hotly, as if the putting his position into words had suddenly showed him how inglorious it was, "what did you want to do it *for*? What was the idea? What right have you got to go about playing Providence over me? Dash it all, it's like giving a fellow money without consulting him."

"I didn't think you'd ever know. You wouldn't have if only that ass Uncle John hadn't let it out."

"How did he get to know? Why did you tell him?"

"He got it out of me. I couldn't choke him off. He came down when you were away at Geddington, and would insist on having a look at my arm, and naturally he spotted right away there was nothing the matter with it. So it came out; that's how it was."

Bob scratched thoughtfully at the turf with a spike of his boot.

"Of course, it was awfully decent——-"

Then again the monstrous nature of the affair came home to him.

"But what did you do it *for*? Why should you rot up your own chances to give me a look in?"

"Oh, I don't know.... You know, you did *me* a jolly good turn."

"I don't remember. When?"

"That Firby-Smith business."

"What about it?"

"Well, you got me out of a jolly bad hole."

"Oh, rot! And do you mean to tell me it was simply because of that——?"

Mike appeared to him in a totally new light. He stared at him as if he were some strange creature hitherto unknown to the human race. Mike shuffled uneasily beneath the scrutiny.

"Anyhow, it's all over now," Mike said, "so I don't see what's the point of talking about it."

"I'm hanged if it is. You don't think I'm going to sit tight and take my first as if nothing had happened?"

"What can you do? The list's up. Are you going to the Old Man to ask him if I can play, like Lionel Tremayne?"

The hopelessness of the situation came over Bob like a wave. He looked helplessly at Mike.

"Besides," added Mike, "I shall get in next year all right. Half a second, I just want to speak to Wyatt about something."

He sidled off.

"Well, anyhow," said Bob to himself, "I must see Burgess about it."

CHAPTER XXII WYATT IS REMINDED OF AN ENGAGEMENT

There are situations in life which are beyond one. The sensible man realises this, and slides out of such situations, admitting himself beaten. Others try to grapple with them, but it never does any good. When affairs get into a real tangle, it is best to sit still and let them straighten themselves out. Or, if one does not do that, simply to think no more about them. This is Philosophy. The true philosopher is the man who says "All right," and goes to sleep in his arm-chair. One's attitude towards Life's Little Difficulties should be that of the gentleman in the fable, who sat down on an acorn one day, and happened to doze. The warmth of his body caused the acorn to germinate, and it grew so rapidly that, when he awoke, he found himself sitting in the fork of an oak, sixty feet from the ground. He thought he would go home, but, finding this impossible, he altered his plans. "Well, well," he said, "if I cannot compel circumstances to my will, I can at least adapt my will to circumstances. I decide to remain here." Which he did, and had a not unpleasant time. The oak lacked some of the comforts of home, but the air was splendid and the view excellent.

To-day's Great Thought for Young Readers. Imitate this man.

Bob should have done so, but he had not the necessary amount of philosophy. He still clung to the idea that he and Burgess, in council, might find some way of making things right for everybody. Though, at the moment, he did not see how eleven caps were to be divided amongst twelve candidates in such a way that each should have one.

And Burgess, consulted on the point, confessed to the same inability to solve the problem. It took Bob at least a quarter of an hour to get the facts of the case into the captain's head, but at last Burgess grasped the idea of the thing. At which period he remarked that it was a rum business.

"Very rum," Bob agreed. "Still, what you say doesn't help us out much, seeing that the point is, what's to be done?"

"Why do anything?"

Burgess was a philosopher, and took the line of least resistance, like the man in the oak-tree.

"But I must do something," said Bob. "Can't you see how rotten it is for me?"

"I don't see why. It's not your fault. Very sporting of your brother and all that, of course, though I'm blowed if I'd have done it myself; but why should you do anything? You're all right. Your brother stood out of the team to let you in it, and here you *are*, in it. What's he got to grumble about?"

"He's not grumbling. It's me."

"What's the matter with you? Don't you want your first?"

"Not like this. Can't you see what a rotten position it is for me?"

"Don't you worry. You simply keep on saying you're all right. Besides, what do you want me to do? Alter the list?"

But for the thought of those unspeakable outsiders, Lionel Tremayne and his headmaster, Bob might have answered this question in the affirmative; but he had the public-school boy's terror of seeming to pose or do anything theatrical. He would have done a good deal to put matters right, but he could *not* do the self-sacrificing young hero business. It would not be in the picture. These things, if they are to be done at school, have to be carried through stealthily, after Mike's fashion.

"I suppose you can't very well, now it's up. Tell you what, though, I don't see why I shouldn't stand out of the team for the Ripton match. I could easily fake up some excuse."

"I do. I don't know if it's occurred to you, but the idea is rather to win the Ripton match, if possible. So that I'm a lot keen on putting the best team into the field. Sorry if it upsets your arrangements in any way."

"You know perfectly well Mike's every bit as good as me."

"He isn't so keen."

"What do you mean?"

"Fielding. He's a young slacker."

When Burgess had once labelled a man as that, he did not readily let the idea out of his mind.

"Slacker? What rot! He's as keen as anything."

"Anyhow, his keenness isn't enough to make him turn out for house-fielding. If you really want to know, that's why you've got your first instead of him. You sweated away, and improved your fielding twenty per cent.; and I happened to be talking to Firby-Smith and found that young Mike had been shirking his, so out he went. A bad field's bad enough, but a slack field wants skinning."

"Smith oughtn't to have told you."

"Well, he did tell me. So you see how it is. There won't be any changes from the team I've put up on the board."

"Oh, all right," said Bob. "I was afraid you mightn't be able to do anything. So long."

"Mind the step," said Burgess.

At about the time when this conversation was in progress, Wyatt, crossing the cricket-field towards the school shop in search of something fizzy that might correct a burning thirst acquired at the nets, espied on the horizon a suit of cricket flannels surmounted by a huge, expansive grin. As the distance between them lessened, he discovered that inside the flannels was Neville-Smith's body and behind the grin the rest of Neville-Smith's face. Their visit to the nets not having coincided in point of time, as the Greek exercise books say, Wyatt had not seen his friend since the list of the team had been posted on the board, so he proceeded to congratulate him on his colours.

"Thanks," said Neville-Smith, with a brilliant display of front teeth.

"Feeling good?"

"Not the word for it. I feel like—-I don't know what."

"I'll tell you what you look like, if that's any good to you. That slight smile of yours will meet behind, if you don't look out, and then the top of your head'll come off."

"I don't care. I've got my first, whatever happens. Little Willie's going to buy a nice new cap and a pretty striped jacket all for his own self! I say, thanks for reminding me. Not that you did, but supposing you had. At any rate, I remember what it was I wanted to say to you. You know what I was saying to you about the bust I meant to have at home in honour of my getting my first, if I did, which I have—-well, anyhow it's to-night. You can roll up, can't you?"

"Delighted. Anything for a free feed in these hard times. What time did you say it was?"

"Eleven. Make it a bit earlier, if you like."

"No, eleven'll do me all right."

"How are you going to get out?"

"'Stone walls do not a prison make, nor iron bars a cage.' That's what the man said who wrote the libretto for the last set of Latin Verses we had to do. I shall manage it."

"They ought to allow you a latch-key."

"Yes, I've often thought of asking my pater for one. Still, I get on very well. Who are coming besides me?"

"No boarders. They all funked it."

"The race is degenerating."

"Said it wasn't good enough."

"The school is going to the dogs. Who did you ask?"

"Clowes was one. Said he didn't want to miss his beauty-sleep. And Henfrey backed out because he thought the risk of being sacked wasn't good enough."

"That's an aspect of the thing that might occur to some people. I don't blame him—-I might feel like that myself if I'd got another couple of years at school."

"But one or two day-boys are coming. Clephane is, for one. And Beverley. We shall have rather a rag. I'm going to get the things now."

"When I get to your place—-I don't believe I know the way, now I come to think of it—-what do I do? Ring the bell and send in my card? or smash the nearest window and climb in?"

"Don't make too much row, for goodness sake. All the servants'll have gone to bed. You'll see the window of my room. It's just above the porch. It'll be the only one lighted up. Heave a pebble at it, and I'll come down."

"So will the glass—-with a run, I expect. Still, I'll try to do as little damage as possible. After all, I needn't throw a brick."

"You *will* turn up, won't you?"

"Nothing shall stop me."

"Good man."

As Wyatt was turning away, a sudden compunction seized upon Neville-Smith. He called him back.

"I say, you don't think it's too risky, do you? I mean, you always are breaking out at night, aren't you? I don't want to get you into a row."

"Oh, that's all right," said Wyatt. "Don't you worry about me. I should have gone out anyhow to-night."

CHAPTER XXIII A SURPRISE FOR MR. APPLEBY

"You may not know it," said Wyatt to Mike in the dormitory that night, "but this is the maddest, merriest day of all the glad New Year."

Mike could not help thinking that for himself it was the very reverse, but he did not state his view of the case.

"What's up?" he asked.

"Neville-Smith's giving a meal at his place in honour of his getting his first. I understand the preparations are on a scale of the utmost magnificence. No expense has been spared. Ginger-beer will flow like water. The oldest cask of lemonade has been broached; and a sardine is roasting whole in the market-place."

"Are you going?"

"If I can tear myself away from your delightful society. The kick-off is fixed for eleven sharp. I am to stand underneath his window and heave bricks till something happens. I don't know if he keeps a dog. If so, I shall probably get bitten to the bone."

"When are you going to start?"

"About five minutes after Wain has been round the dormitories to see that all's well. That ought to be somewhere about half-past ten."

"Don't go getting caught."

"I shall do my little best not to be. Rather tricky work, though, getting back. I've got to climb two garden walls, and I shall probably be so full of Malvoisie that you'll be able to hear it swishing about inside me. No catch steeple-chasing if you're like that. They've no thought for people's convenience here. Now at Bradford they've got studies on the ground floor, the windows looking out over the boundless prairie. No climbing or steeple-chasing needed at all. All you have to do is to open the window and step out. Still, we must make the best of things. Push us over a pinch of that tooth-powder of yours. I've used all mine."

Wyatt very seldom penetrated further than his own garden on the occasions when he roamed abroad at night. For cat-shooting the Wain spinneys were unsurpassed. There was one particular dustbin where one might be certain of flushing a covey any night; and the wall by the potting-shed was a feline club-house.

But when he did wish to get out into the open country he had a special route which he always took. He climbed down from the wall that ran beneath the dormitory window into the garden belonging to Mr. Appleby, the master who had the house next to Mr. Wain's. Crossing this, he climbed another wall, and dropped from it into a small lane which ended in the main road leading to Wrykyn town.

This was the route which he took to-night. It was a glorious July night, and the scent of the flowers came to him with a curious distinctness as he let himself down from the dormitory window. At any other time he might have made a lengthy halt, and enjoyed the scents and small summer noises, but now he felt that it would be better not to delay. There was a full moon, and where he stood he could be seen distinctly from the windows of both houses. They were all dark, it is true, but on these occasions it was best to take no risks.

He dropped cautiously into Appleby's garden, ran lightly across it, and was in the lane within a minute.

There he paused, dusted his trousers, which had suffered on the two walls, and strolled meditatively in the direction of the town. Half-past ten had just chimed from the school clock. He was in plenty of time.

"What a night!" he said to himself, sniffing as he walked.

Now it happened that he was not alone in admiring the beauty of that particular night. At ten-fifteen it had struck Mr. Appleby, looking out of his study into the moonlit school grounds, that a pipe in the open would make an excellent break in his night's work. He had acquired a slight headache as the result of correcting a batch of examination papers, and he thought that an interval of an hour in the open air before approaching the half-dozen or so papers which still remained to be looked at might do him good. The window of his study was open, but the room had got hot and stuffy. Nothing like a little fresh air for putting him right.

For a few moments he debated the rival claims of a stroll in the cricket-field and a seat in the garden. Then he decided on the latter. The little gate in the railings opposite his house might not be open, and it was a long way round to the main entrance. So he took a deck-chair which leaned against the wall, and let himself out of the back door.

He took up his position in the shadow of a fir-tree with his back to the house. From here he could see the long garden. He was fond of his garden, and spent what few moments he could spare from work and games pottering about it. He had his views as to what the ideal garden should be, and he hoped in time to tinker his own three acres up to the desired standard. At present there remained much to be done. Why not, for instance, take away those laurels at the end of the lawn, and have a flower-bed there instead? Laurels lasted all the year round, true, whereas flowers died and left an empty brown bed in the winter, but then laurels were nothing much to look at at any time, and a garden always had a beastly appearance in winter, whatever you did to it. Much better have flowers, and get a decent show for one's money in summer at any rate.

CHAPTER XXIII A SURPRISE FOR MR. APPLEBY

The problem of the bed at the end of the lawn occupied his complete attention for more than a quarter of an hour, at the end of which period he discovered that his pipe had gone out.

He was just feeling for his matches to relight it when Wyatt dropped with a slight thud into his favourite herbaceous border.

The surprise, and the agony of feeling that large boots were trampling among his treasures kept him transfixed for just the length of time necessary for Wyatt to cross the garden and climb the opposite wall. As he dropped into the lane, Mr. Appleby recovered himself sufficiently to emit a sort of strangled croak, but the sound was too slight to reach Wyatt. That reveller was walking down the Wrykyn road before Mr. Appleby had left his chair.

It is an interesting point that it was the gardener rather than the schoolmaster in Mr. Appleby that first awoke to action. It was not the idea of a boy breaking out of his house at night that occurred to him first as particularly heinous; it was the fact that the boy had broken out *via* his herbaceous border. In four strides he was on the scene of the outrage, examining, on hands and knees, with the aid of the moonlight, the extent of the damage done.

As far as he could see, it was not serious. By a happy accident Wyatt's boots had gone home to right and left of precious plants but not on them. With a sigh of relief Mr. Appleby smoothed over the cavities, and rose to his feet.

At this point it began to strike him that the episode affected him as a schoolmaster also.

In that startled moment when Wyatt had suddenly crossed his line of vision, he had recognised him. The moon had shone full on his face as he left the flower-bed. There was no doubt in his mind as to the identity of the intruder.

He paused, wondering how he should act. It was not an easy question. There was nothing of the spy about Mr. Appleby. He went his way openly, liked and respected by boys and masters. He always played the game. The difficulty here was to say exactly what the game was. Sentiment, of course, bade him forget the episode, treat it as if it had never happened. That was the simple way out of the difficulty. There was nothing unsporting about Mr. Appleby. He knew that there were times when a master might, without blame, close his eyes or look the other way. If he had met Wyatt out of bounds in the day-time, and it had been possible to convey the impression that he had not seen him, he would have done so. To be out of bounds is not a particularly deadly sin. A master must check it if it occurs too frequently, but he may use his discretion.

Breaking out at night, however, was a different thing altogether. It was on another plane. There are times when a master must waive sentiment, and remember that he is in a position of trust, and owes a duty directly to his headmaster, and indirectly, through the headmaster, to the parents. He receives a salary for doing this duty, and, if he feels that sentiment is too strong for him, he should resign in favour of some one of tougher fibre.

This was the conclusion to which Mr. Appleby came over his relighted pipe. He could not let the matter rest where it was.

In ordinary circumstances it would have been his duty to report the affair to the headmaster but in the present case he thought that a slightly different course might be pursued. He would lay the whole thing before Mr. Wain, and leave him to deal with it as he thought best. It was one of the few cases where it was possible for an assistant master to fulfil his duty to a parent directly, instead of through the agency of the headmaster.

Knocking out the ashes of his pipe against a tree, he folded his deck-chair and went into the house. The examination papers were spread invitingly on the table, but they would have to wait. He turned down his lamp, and walked round to Wain's.

There was a light in one of the ground-floor windows. He tapped on the window, and the sound of a chair being pushed back told him that he had been heard. The blind shot up, and he had a view of a room littered with books and papers, in the middle of which stood Mr. Wain, like a sea-beast among rocks.

Mr. Wain recognised his visitor and opened the window. Mr. Appleby could not help feeling how like Wain it was to work on a warm summer's night in a hermetically sealed room. There was always something queer and eccentric about Wyatt's step-father.

"Can I have a word with you, Wain?" he said.

"Appleby! Is there anything the matter? I was startled when you tapped. Exceedingly so."

"Sorry," said Mr. Appleby. "Wouldn't have disturbed you, only it's something important. I'll climb in through here, shall I? No need to unlock the door." And, greatly to Mr. Wain's surprise and rather to his disapproval, Mr. Appleby vaulted on to the window-sill, and squeezed through into the room.

CHAPTER XXIV CAUGHT

"Got some rather bad news for you, I'm afraid," began Mr. Appleby. "I'll smoke, if you don't mind. About Wyatt."

"James!"

"I was sitting in my garden a few minutes ago, having a pipe before finishing the rest of my papers, and Wyatt dropped from the wall on to my herbaceous border."

Mr. Appleby said this with a tinge of bitterness. The thing still rankled.

"James! In your garden! Impossible. Why, it is not a quarter of an hour since I left him in his dormitory."

"He's not there now."

"You astound me, Appleby. I am astonished."

"So was I."

"How is such a thing possible? His window is heavily barred."

"Bars can be removed."

"You must have been mistaken."

"Possibly," said Mr. Appleby, a little nettled. Gaping astonishment is always apt to be irritating. "Let's leave it at that, then. Sorry to have disturbed you."

"No, sit down, Appleby. Dear me, this is most extraordinary. Exceedingly so. You are certain it was James?"

"Perfectly. It's like daylight out of doors."

Mr. Wain drummed on the table with his fingers.

"What shall I do?"

Mr. Appleby offered no suggestion.

"I ought to report it to the headmaster. That is certainly the course I should pursue."

"I don't see why. It isn't like an ordinary case. You're the parent. You can deal with the thing directly. If you come to think of it, a headmaster's only a sort of middleman between boys and parents. He plays substitute for the parent in his absence. I don't see why you should drag in the master at all here."

"There is certainly something in what you say," said Mr. Wain on reflection.

"A good deal. Tackle the boy when he comes in, and have it out with him. Remember that it must mean expulsion if you report him to the headmaster. He would have no choice. Everybody who has ever broken out of his house here and been caught has been expelled. I should strongly advise you to deal with the thing yourself."

"I will. Yes. You are quite right, Appleby. That is a very good idea of yours. You are not going?"

"Must. Got a pile of examination papers to look over. Good-night."

"Good-night."

Mr. Appleby made his way out of the window and through the gate into his own territory in a pensive frame of mind. He was wondering what would happen. He had taken the only possible course, and, if only Wain kept his head and did not let the matter get through officially to the headmaster, things might not be so bad for Wyatt after all. He hoped they would not. He liked Wyatt. It would be a thousand pities, he felt, if he were to be expelled. What would Wain do? What would *he* do in a similar case? It was difficult to say. Probably talk violently for as long as he could keep it up, and then consider the episode closed. He doubted whether Wain would have the common sense to do this. Altogether it was very painful and disturbing, and he was taking a rather gloomy view of the assistant master's lot as he sat down to finish off the rest of his examination papers. It was not all roses, the life of an assistant master at a public school. He had continually to be sinking his own individual sympathies in the claims of his duty. Mr. Appleby was the last man who would willingly have reported a boy for enjoying a midnight ramble. But he was the last man to shirk the duty of reporting him, merely because it was one decidedly not to his taste.

Mr. Wain sat on for some minutes after his companion had left, pondering over the news he had heard. Even now he clung to the idea that Appleby had made some extraordinary mistake. Gradually he began to convince himself of this. He had seen Wyatt actually in bed a quarter of an hour before—-not asleep, it was true, but apparently on the verge of dropping off. And the bars across the window had looked so solid.... Could Appleby have been dreaming? Something of the kind might easily have happened. He had been working hard, and the night was warm....

Then it occurred to him that he could easily prove or disprove the truth of his colleague's statement by going to the dormitory and seeing if Wyatt were there or not. If he had gone out, he would hardly have returned yet.

He took a candle, and walked quietly upstairs.

Arrived at his step-son's dormitory, he turned the door-handle softly and went in. The light of the candle fell on both beds. Mike was there, asleep. He grunted, and turned over with his face to the wall as the light shone on his eyes. But the other bed was empty. Appleby had been right.

If further proof had been needed, one of the bars was missing from the window. The moon shone in through the empty space.

The house-master sat down quietly on the vacant bed. He blew the candle out, and waited there in the semi-darkness, thinking. For years he and Wyatt had lived in a state of armed neutrality, broken by various small encounters. Lately, by silent but mutual agreement, they had kept out of each other's way as much as possible, and it had become rare for the house-master to have to find fault officially with his step-son. But there had never been anything even remotely approaching friendship between them. Mr. Wain was not a man who inspired affection readily, least of all in those many years younger than himself. Nor did he easily grow fond of others. Wyatt he had regarded, from the moment when the threads of their lives became entangled, as a complete nuisance.

It was not, therefore, a sorrowful, so much as an exasperated, vigil that he kept in the dormitory. There was nothing of the sorrowing father about his frame of mind. He was the house-master about to deal with a mutineer, and nothing else.

This breaking-out, he reflected wrathfully, was the last straw. Wyatt's presence had been a nervous inconvenience to him for years. The time had come to put an end to it. It was with a comfortable feeling of magnanimity that he resolved not to report the breach of discipline to the headmaster. Wyatt should not be expelled. But he should leave, and that immediately. He would write to the bank before he went to bed, asking them to receive his step-son at once; and the letter should go by the first post next day. The discipline of the bank would be salutary and steadying. And—-this was a particularly grateful reflection—-a fortnight annually was the limit of the holiday allowed by the management to its junior employees.

Mr. Wain had arrived at this conclusion, and was beginning to feel a little cramped, when Mike Jackson suddenly sat up.

"Hullo!" said Mike.

"Go to sleep, Jackson, immediately," snapped the house-master.

Mike had often heard and read of people's hearts leaping to their mouths, but he had never before experienced that sensation of something hot and dry springing in the throat, which is what really happens to us on receipt of a bad shock. A sickening feeling that the game was up beyond all hope of salvation came to him. He lay down again without a word.

What a frightful thing to happen! How on earth had this come about? What in the world had brought Wain to the dormitory at that hour? Poor old Wyatt! If it had upset *him* (Mike) to see the house-master in the room, what would be the effect of such a sight on Wyatt, returning from the revels at Neville-Smith's!

And what could he do? Nothing. There was literally no way out. His mind went back to the night when he had saved Wyatt by a brilliant *coup*. The most brilliant of *coups* could effect nothing now. Absolutely and entirely the game was up.

Every minute that passed seemed like an hour to Mike. Dead silence reigned in the dormitory, broken every now and then by the creak of the other bed, as the house-master shifted his position. Twelve boomed across the field from the school clock. Mike could not help thinking what a perfect night it must be for him to be able to hear the strokes so plainly. He strained his ears for any indication of Wyatt's approach, but could hear nothing. Then a very faint scraping noise broke the stillness, and presently the patch of moonlight on the floor was darkened.

At that moment Mr. Wain relit his candle.

The unexpected glare took Wyatt momentarily aback. Mike saw him start. Then he seemed to recover himself. In a calm and leisurely manner he climbed into the room.

"James!" said Mr. Wain. His voice sounded ominously hollow.

Wyatt dusted his knees, and rubbed his hands together. "Hullo, is that you, father!" he said pleasantly.

CHAPTER XXV MARCHING ORDERS

A silence followed. To Mike, lying in bed, holding his breath, it seemed a long silence. As a matter of fact it lasted for perhaps ten seconds. Then Mr. Wain spoke.

"You have been out, James?"

It is curious how in the more dramatic moments of life the inane remark is the first that comes to us.

"Yes, sir," said Wyatt.

"I am astonished. Exceedingly astonished."

"I got a bit of a start myself," said Wyatt.

"I shall talk to you in my study. Follow me there."

"Yes, sir."

He left the room, and Wyatt suddenly began to chuckle.

"I say, Wyatt!" said Mike, completely thrown off his balance by the events of the night.

Wyatt continued to giggle helplessly. He flung himself down on his bed, rolling with laughter. Mike began to get alarmed.

"It's all right," said Wyatt at last, speaking with difficulty. "But, I say, how long had he been sitting there?"

"It seemed hours. About an hour, I suppose, really."

"It's the funniest thing I've ever struck. Me sweating to get in quietly, and all the time him camping out on my bed!"

"But look here, what'll happen?"

Wyatt sat up.

"That reminds me. Suppose I'd better go down."

"What'll he do, do you think?"

"Ah, now, what!"

"But, I say, it's awful. What'll happen?"

"That's for him to decide. Speaking at a venture, I should say——"

"You don't think——?"

"The boot. The swift and sudden boot. I shall be sorry to part with you, but I'm afraid it's a case of 'Au revoir, my little Hyacinth.' We shall meet at Philippi. This is my Moscow. To-morrow I shall go out into the night with one long, choking sob. Years hence a white-haired bank-clerk will tap at your door when you're a prosperous professional cricketer with your photograph in *Wisden*. That'll be me. Well, I suppose I'd better go down. We'd better all get to bed *some* time to-night. Don't go to sleep."

"Not likely."

"I'll tell you all the latest news when I come back. Where are me slippers? Ha, 'tis well! Lead on, then, minions. I follow."

In the study Mr. Wain was fumbling restlessly with his papers when Wyatt appeared.

"Sit down, James," he said.

Wyatt sat down. One of his slippers fell off with a clatter. Mr. Wain jumped nervously.

"Only my slipper," explained Wyatt. "It slipped."

Mr. Wain took up a pen, and began to tap the table.

"Well, James?"

Wyatt said nothing.

"I should be glad to hear your explanation of this disgraceful matter."

"The fact is——" said Wyatt.

"Well?"

"I haven't one, sir."

"What were you doing out of your dormitory, out of the house, at that hour?"

"I went for a walk, sir."

"And, may I inquire, are you in the habit of violating the strictest school rules by absenting yourself from the house during the night?"

"Yes, sir."

"What?"

"Yes, sir."

"This is an exceedingly serious matter."

Wyatt nodded agreement with this view.

"Exceedingly."

The pen rose and fell with the rapidity of the cylinder of a motor-car. Wyatt, watching it, became suddenly aware that the thing was hypnotising him. In a minute or two he would be asleep.

"I wish you wouldn't do that, father. Tap like that, I mean. It's sending me to sleep."

"James!"

"It's like a woodpecker."

"Studied impertinence——"

"I'm very sorry. Only it *was* sending me off."

Mr. Wain suspended tapping operations, and resumed the thread of his discourse.

"I am sorry, exceedingly, to see this attitude in you, James. It is not fitting. It is in keeping with your behaviour throughout. Your conduct has been lax and reckless in the extreme. It is possible that you imagine that the peculiar circumstances of our relationship secure you from the penalties to which the ordinary boy——"

"No, sir."

"I need hardly say," continued Mr. Wain, ignoring the interruption, "that I shall treat you exactly as I should treat any other member of my house whom I had detected in the same misdemeanour."

"Of course," said Wyatt, approvingly.

"I must ask you not to interrupt me when I am speaking to you, James. I say that your punishment will be no whit less severe than would be that of any other boy. You have repeatedly proved yourself lacking in ballast and a respect for discipline in smaller ways, but this is a far more serious matter. Exceedingly so. It is impossible for me to overlook it, even were I disposed to do so. You are aware of the penalty for such an action as yours?"

"The sack," said Wyatt laconically.

"It is expulsion. You must leave the school. At once."

Wyatt nodded.

"As you know, I have already secured a nomination for you in the London and Oriental Bank. I shall write to-morrow to the manager asking him to receive you at once——"

"After all, they only gain an extra fortnight of me."

"You will leave directly I receive his letter. I shall arrange with the headmaster that you are withdrawn privately——"

"*Not* the sack?"

"Withdrawn privately. You will not go to school to-morrow. Do you understand? That is all. Have you anything to say?"

Wyatt reflected.

"No, I don't think——"

His eye fell on a tray bearing a decanter and a syphon.

"Oh, yes," he said. "Can't I mix you a whisky and soda, father, before I go off to bed?"

"Well?" said Mike.

Wyatt kicked off his slippers, and began to undress.

"What happened?"

"We chatted."

"Has he let you off?"

"Like a gun. I shoot off almost immediately. To-morrow I take a well-earned rest away from school, and the day after I become the gay young bank-clerk, all amongst the ink and ledgers."

Mike was miserably silent.

"Buck up," said Wyatt cheerfully. "It would have happened anyhow in another fortnight. So why worry?"

Mike was still silent. The reflection was doubtless philosophic, but it failed to comfort him.

CHAPTER XXVI THE AFTERMATH

Bad news spreads quickly. By the quarter to eleven interval next day the facts concerning Wyatt and Mr. Wain were public property. Mike, as an actual spectator of the drama, was in great request as an informant. As he told the story to a group of sympathisers outside the school shop, Burgess came up, his eyes rolling in a fine frenzy.

"Anybody seen young—-oh, here you are. What's all this about Jimmy Wyatt? They're saying he's been sacked, or some rot."

"So he has—-at least, he's got to leave."

"What? When?"

"He's left already. He isn't coming to school again."

Burgess's first thought, as befitted a good cricket captain, was for his team.

"And the Ripton match on Saturday!"

Nobody seemed to have anything except silent sympathy at his command.

"Dash the man! Silly ass! What did he want to do it for! Poor old Jimmy, though!" he added after a pause. "What rot for him!"

"Beastly," agreed Mike.

"All the same," continued Burgess, with a return to the austere manner of the captain of cricket, "he might have chucked playing the goat till after the Ripton match. Look here, young Jackson, you'll turn out for fielding with the first this afternoon. You'll play on Saturday."

"All right," said Mike, without enthusiasm. The Wyatt disaster was too recent for him to feel much pleasure at playing against Ripton *vice* his friend, withdrawn.

Bob was the next to interview him. They met in the cloisters.

"Hullo, Mike!" said Bob. "I say, what's all this about Wyatt?"

"Wain caught him getting back into the dorm. last night after Neville-Smith's, and he's taken him away from the school."

"What's he going to do? Going into that bank straight away?"

"Yes. You know, that's the part he bars most. He'd have been leaving anyhow in a fortnight, you see; only it's awful rot for a chap like Wyatt to have to go and froust in a bank for the rest of his life."

"He'll find it rather a change, I expect. I suppose you won't be seeing him before he goes?"

CHAPTER XXVI THE AFTERMATH

"WHAT'S ALL THIS ABOUT JIMMY WYATT?

"I shouldn't think so. Not unless he comes to the dorm. during the night. He's sleeping over in Wain's part of the house, but I shouldn't be surprised if he nipped out after Wain has gone to bed. Hope he does, anyway."

"I should like to say good-bye. But I don't suppose it'll be possible."

They separated in the direction of their respective form-rooms. Mike felt bitter and disappointed at the way the news had been received. Wyatt was his best friend, his pal; and it offended him that the school should take the tidings of his departure as they had done. Most of them who had come to him for information had expressed a sort of sympathy with the absent hero of his story, but the chief sensation seemed to be one of pleasurable excitement at the fact that something big had happened to break the monotony of school routine. They treated the thing much as they would have treated the announcement that a record score had been made in first-class cricket. The school was not so much regretful as comfortably thrilled. And Burgess had actually cursed before sympathising. Mike felt resentful towards Burgess. As a matter of fact, the cricket captain wrote a letter to Wyatt during preparation that night which would have satisfied even Mike's sense of what was fit. But Mike had no opportunity of learning this.

There was, however, one exception to the general rule, one member of the school who did not treat the episode as if it were merely an interesting and impersonal item of sensational news. Neville-Smith heard of what had happened towards the end of the interval, and rushed off instantly in search of Mike. He was too late to catch him before he went to his form-room, so he waited for him at half-past twelve, when the bell rang for the end of morning school.

"I say, Jackson, is this true about old Wyatt?"

Mike nodded.

"What happened?"

Mike related the story for the sixteenth time. It was a melancholy pleasure to have found a listener who heard the tale in the right spirit. There was no doubt about Neville-Smith's interest and sympathy. He was silent for a moment after Mike had finished.

"It was all my fault," he said at length. "If it hadn't been for me, this wouldn't have happened. What a fool I was to ask him to my place! I might have known he would be caught."

"Oh, I don't know," said Mike.

"It was absolutely my fault."

Mike was not equal to the task of soothing Neville-Smith's wounded conscience. He did not attempt it. They walked on without further conversation till they reached Wain's gate, where Mike left him. Neville-Smith proceeded on his way, plunged in meditation.

The result of which meditation was that Burgess got a second shock before the day was out. Bob, going over to the nets rather late in the afternoon, came upon the captain of cricket standing apart from his fellow men with an expression on his face that spoke of mental upheavals on a vast scale.

"What's up?" asked Bob.

"Nothing much," said Burgess, with a forced and grisly calm. "Only that, as far as I can see, we shall play Ripton on Saturday with a sort of second eleven. You don't happen to have got sacked or anything, by the way, do you?"

"What's happened now?"

"Neville-Smith. In extra on Saturday. That's all. Only our first- and second-change bowlers out of the team for the Ripton match in one day. I suppose by to-morrow half the others'll have gone, and we shall take the field on Saturday with a scratch side of kids from the Junior School."

"Neville-Smith! Why, what's he been doing?"

"Apparently he gave a sort of supper to celebrate his getting his first, and it was while coming back from that that Wyatt got collared. Well, I'm blowed if Neville-Smith doesn't toddle off to the Old Man after school to-day and tell him the whole yarn! Said it was all his fault. What rot! Sort of thing that might have happened to any one. If Wyatt hadn't gone to him, he'd probably have gone out somewhere else."

"And the Old Man shoved him in extra?"

"Next two Saturdays."

"Are Ripton strong this year?" asked Bob, for lack of anything better to say.

"Very, from all accounts. They whacked the M.C.C. Jolly hot team of M.C.C. too. Stronger than the one we drew with."

"Oh, well, you never know what's going to happen at cricket. I may hold a catch for a change."

Burgess grunted.

Bob went on his way to the nets. Mike was just putting on his pads.

"I say, Mike," said Bob. "I wanted to see you. It's about Wyatt. I've thought of something."

"What's that?"

"A way of getting him out of that bank. If it comes off, that's to say."

"By Jove, he'd jump at anything. What's the idea?"

"Why shouldn't he get a job of sorts out in the Argentine? There ought to be heaps of sound jobs going there for a chap like Wyatt. He's a jolly good shot, to start with. I shouldn't wonder if it wasn't rather a score to be able to shoot out there. And he can ride, I know."

"By Jove, I'll write to father to-night. He must be able to work it, I should think. He never chucked the show altogether, did he?"

Mike, as most other boys of his age would have been, was profoundly ignorant as to the details by which his father's money had been, or was being, made. He only knew vaguely that the source of revenue had something to do with the Argentine. His brother Joe had been born in Buenos Ayres; and once, three years ago, his father had gone over there for a visit, presumably on business. All these things seemed to show that Mr. Jackson senior was a useful man to have about if you wanted a job in that Eldorado, the Argentine Republic.

As a matter of fact, Mike's father owned vast tracts of land up country, where countless sheep lived and had their being. He had long retired from active superintendence of his estate. Like Mr. Spenlow, he had a partner, a stout fellow with the work-taint highly developed, who asked nothing better than to be left in charge. So Mr. Jackson had returned to the home of his fathers, glad to be there again. But he still had a decided voice in the ordering of affairs on the ranches, and Mike was going to the fountain-head of things when he wrote to his father that night, putting forward Wyatt's claims to attention and ability to perform any sort of job with which he might be presented.

The reflection that he had done all that could be done tended to console him for the non-appearance of Wyatt either that night or next morning—-a non-appearance which was due to the simple fact that he passed that night in a bed in Mr. Wain's dressing-room, the door of which that cautious pedagogue, who believed in taking no chances, locked from the outside on retiring to rest.

CHAPTER XXVII THE RIPTON MATCH

Mike got an answer from his father on the morning of the Ripton match. A letter from Wyatt also lay on his plate when he came down to breakfast.

Mr. Jackson's letter was short, but to the point. He said he would go and see Wyatt early in the next week. He added that being expelled from a public school was not the only qualification for success as a sheep-farmer, but that, if Mike's friend added to this a general intelligence and amiability, and a skill for picking off cats with an air-pistol and bull's-eyes with a Lee-Enfield, there was no reason why something should not be done for him. In any case he would buy him a lunch, so that Wyatt would extract at least some profit from his visit. He said that he hoped something could be managed. It was a pity that a boy accustomed to shoot cats should be condemned for the rest of his life to shoot nothing more exciting than his cuffs.

Wyatt's letter was longer. It might have been published under the title "My First Day in a Bank, by a Beginner." His advent had apparently caused little sensation. He had first had a brief conversation with the manager, which had run as follows:

"Mr. Wyatt?"

"Yes, sir."

"H'm ... Sportsman?"

"Yes, sir."

"Cricketer?"

"Yes, sir."

"Play football?"

"Yes, sir."

"H'm ... Racquets?"

"Yes, sir."

"Everything?"

"Yes, sir."

"H'm ... Well, you won't get any more of it now."

After which a Mr. Blenkinsop had led him up to a vast ledger, in which he was to inscribe the addresses of all out-going letters. These letters he would then stamp, and subsequently take in bundles to the post office. Once a week he would be required to buy stamps. "If I were one of those Napoleons of Finance," wrote

Wyatt, "I should cook the accounts, I suppose, and embezzle stamps to an incredible amount. But it doesn't seem in my line. I'm afraid I wasn't cut out for a business career. Still, I have stamped this letter at the expense of the office, and entered it up under the heading 'Sundries,' which is a sort of start. Look out for an article in the *Wrykynian*, 'Hints for Young Criminals, by J. Wyatt, champion catch-as-catch-can stamp-stealer of the British Isles.' So long. I suppose you are playing against Ripton, now that the world of commerce has found that it can't get on without me. Mind you make a century, and then perhaps Burgess'll give you your first after all. There were twelve colours given three years ago, because one chap left at half-term and the man who played instead of him came off against Ripton."

This had occurred to Mike independently. The Ripton match was a special event, and the man who performed any outstanding feat against that school was treated as a sort of Horatius. Honours were heaped upon him. If he could only make a century! or even fifty. Even twenty, if it got the school out of a tight place. He was as nervous on the Saturday morning as he had been on the morning of the M.C.C. match. It was Victory or Westminster Abbey now. To do only averagely well, to be among the ruck, would be as useless as not playing at all, as far as his chance of his first was concerned.

It was evident to those who woke early on the Saturday morning that this Ripton match was not likely to end in a draw. During the Friday rain had fallen almost incessantly in a steady drizzle. It had stopped late at night; and at six in the morning there was every prospect of another hot day. There was that feeling in the air which shows that the sun is trying to get through the clouds. The sky was a dull grey at breakfast time, except where a flush of deeper colour gave a hint of the sun. It was a day on which to win the toss, and go in first. At eleven-thirty, when the match was timed to begin, the wicket would be too wet to be difficult. Runs would come easily till the sun came out and began to dry the ground. When that happened there would be trouble for the side that was batting.

Burgess, inspecting the wicket with Mr. Spence during the quarter to eleven interval, was not slow to recognise this fact.

"I should win the toss to-day, if I were you, Burgess," said Mr. Spence.

"Just what I was thinking, sir."

"That wicket's going to get nasty after lunch, if the sun comes out. A regular Rhodes wicket it's going to be."

"I wish we *had* Rhodes," said Burgess. "Or even Wyatt. It would just suit him, this."

Mr. Spence, as a member of the staff, was not going to be drawn into discussing Wyatt and his premature departure, so he diverted the conversation on to the subject of the general aspect of the school's attack.

"Who will go on first with you, Burgess?"

"Who do you think, sir? Ellerby? It might be his wicket."

Ellerby bowled medium inclining to slow. On a pitch that suited him he was apt to turn from leg and get people out caught at the wicket or short slip.

"Certainly, Ellerby. This end, I think. The other's yours, though I'm afraid you'll have a poor time bowling fast to-day. Even with plenty of sawdust I doubt if it will be possible to get a decent foothold till after lunch."

"I must win the toss," said Burgess. "It's a nuisance too, about our batting. Marsh will probably be dead out of form after being in the Infirmary so long. If he'd had a chance of getting a bit of practice yesterday, it might have been all right."

"That rain will have a lot to answer for if we lose. On a dry, hard wicket I'm certain we should beat them four times out of six. I was talking to a man who played against them for the Nomads. He said that on a true wicket there was not a great deal of sting in their bowling, but that they've got a slow leg-break man who might be dangerous on a day like this. A boy called de Freece. I don't know of him. He wasn't in the team last year."

"I know the chap. He played wing three for them at footer against us this year on their ground. He was crocked when they came here. He's a pretty useful chap all round, I believe. Plays racquets for them too."

"Well, my friend said he had one very dangerous ball, of the Bosanquet type. Looks as if it were going away, and comes in instead."

"I don't think a lot of that," said Burgess ruefully. "One consolation is, though, that that sort of ball is easier to watch on a slow wicket. I must tell the fellows to look out for it."

"I should. And, above all, win the toss."

Burgess and Maclaine, the Ripton captain, were old acquaintances. They had been at the same private school, and they had played against one another at football and cricket for two years now.

"We'll go in first, Mac," said Burgess, as they met on the pavilion steps after they had changed.

"It's awfully good of you to suggest it," said Maclaine. "but I think we'll toss. It's a hobby of mine. You call."

"Heads."

"Tails it is. I ought to have warned you that you hadn't a chance. I've lost the toss five times running, so I was bound to win to-day."

"You'll put us in, I suppose?"

"Yes—-after us."

"Oh, well, we sha'n't have long to wait for our knock, that's a comfort. Buck up and send some one in, and let's get at you."

And Burgess went off to tell the ground-man to have plenty of sawdust ready, as he would want the field paved with it.

The policy of the Ripton team was obvious from the first over. They meant to force the game. Already the sun was beginning to peep through the haze. For about an hour run-getting ought to be a tolerably simple process; but after that hour singles would be as valuable as threes and boundaries an almost unheard-of luxury.

So Ripton went in to hit.

The policy proved successful for a time, as it generally does. Burgess, who relied on a run that was a series of tiger-like leaps culminating in a spring that suggested that he meant to lower the long jump record, found himself badly handicapped by the state of the ground. In spite of frequent libations of sawdust, he was compelled to tread cautiously, and this robbed his bowling of much of its pace. The score mounted rapidly. Twenty came in ten minutes. At thirty-five the first wicket fell, run out.

At sixty Ellerby, who had found the pitch too soft for him and had been expensive, gave place to Grant. Grant bowled what were supposed to be slow leg-breaks, but which did not always break. The change worked.

Maclaine, after hitting the first two balls to the boundary, skied the third to Bob Jackson in the deep, and Bob, for whom constant practice had robbed this sort of catch of its terrors, held it.

A yorker from Burgess disposed of the next man before he could settle down; but the score, seventy-four for three wickets, was large enough in view of the fact that the pitch was already becoming more difficult, and was certain to get worse, to make Ripton feel that the advantage was with them. Another hour of play remained before lunch. The deterioration of the wicket would be slow during that period. The sun, which was now shining brightly, would put in its deadliest work from two o'clock onwards. Maclaine's instructions to his men were to go on hitting.

A too liberal interpretation of the meaning of the verb "to hit" led to the departure of two more Riptonians in the course of the next two overs. There is a certain type of school batsman who considers that to force the game means to swipe blindly at every ball on the chance of taking it half-volley. This policy sometimes leads to a boundary or two, as it did on this occasion, but it means that wickets will fall, as also happened now. Seventy-four for three became eighty-six for five. Burgess began to look happier.

His contentment increased when he got the next man leg-before-wicket with the total unaltered. At this rate Ripton would be out before lunch for under a hundred.

But the rot stopped with the fall of that wicket. Dashing tactics were laid aside. The pitch had begun to play tricks, and the pair now in settled down to watch the ball. They plodded on, scoring slowly and jerkily till the hands of the clock stood at half-past one. Then Ellerby, who had gone on again instead of Grant, beat the less steady of the pair with a ball that pitched on the middle stump and shot into the base of the off. A hundred and twenty had gone up on the board at the beginning of the over.

That period which is always so dangerous, when the wicket is bad, the ten minutes before lunch, proved fatal to two more of the enemy. The last man had just gone to the wickets, with the score at a hundred and thirty-one, when a quarter to two arrived, and with it the luncheon interval.

So far it was anybody's game.

CHAPTER XXVIII MIKE WINS HOME

The Ripton last-wicket man was de Freece, the slow bowler. He was apparently a young gentleman wholly free from the curse of nervousness. He wore a cheerful smile as he took guard before receiving the first ball after lunch, and Wrykyn had plenty of opportunity of seeing that that was his normal expression when at the wickets. There is often a certain looseness about the attack after lunch, and the bowler of googlies took advantage of it now. He seemed to be a batsman with only one hit; but he had also a very accurate eye, and his one hit, a semicircular stroke, which suggested the golf links rather than the cricket field, came off with distressing frequency. He mowed Burgess's first ball to the square-leg boundary, missed his second, and snicked the third for three over long-slip's head. The other batsman played out the over, and de Freece proceeded to treat Ellerby's bowling with equal familiarity. The scoring-board showed an increase of twenty as the result of three overs. Every run was invaluable now, and the Ripton contingent made the pavilion re-echo as a fluky shot over mid-on's head sent up the hundred and fifty.

There are few things more exasperating to the fielding side than a last-wicket stand. It resembles in its effect the dragging-out of a book or play after the *dénouement* has been reached. At the fall of the ninth wicket the fieldsmen nearly always look on their outing as finished. Just a ball or two to the last man, and it will be their turn to bat. If the last man insists on keeping them out in the field, they resent it.

What made it especially irritating now was the knowledge that a straight yorker would solve the whole thing. But when Burgess bowled a yorker, it was not straight. And when he bowled a straight ball, it was not a yorker. A four and a three to de Freece, and a four bye sent up a hundred and sixty.

It was beginning to look as if this might go on for ever, when Ellerby, who had been missing the stumps by fractions of an inch, for the last ten minutes, did what Burgess had failed to do. He bowled a straight, medium-paced yorker, and de Freece, swiping at it with a bright smile, found his leg-stump knocked back. He had made twenty-eight. His record score, he explained to Mike, as they walked to the pavilion, for this or any ground.

The Ripton total was a hundred and sixty-six.

With the ground in its usual true, hard condition, Wrykyn would have gone in against a score of a hundred and sixty-six with the cheery intention of knocking off the runs for the loss of two or three wickets. It would have been a gentle canter for them.

But ordinary standards would not apply here. On a good wicket Wrykyn that season were a two hundred and fifty to three hundred side. On a bad wicket—-well, they had met the Incogniti on a bad wicket, and their total—-with Wyatt playing and making top score—-had worked out at a hundred and seven.

A grim determination to do their best, rather than confidence that their best, when done, would be anything record-breaking, was the spirit which animated the team when they opened their innings.

And in five minutes this had changed to a dull gloom.

The tragedy started with the very first ball. It hardly seemed that the innings had begun, when Morris was seen to leave the crease, and make for the pavilion.

"It's that googly man," said Burgess blankly.

"What's happened?" shouted a voice from the interior of the first eleven room.

"Morris is out."

"Good gracious! How?" asked Ellerby, emerging from the room with one pad on his leg and the other in his hand.

"L.-b.-w. First ball."

"My aunt! Who's in next? Not me?"

"No. Berridge. For goodness sake, Berry, stick a bat in the way, and not your legs. Watch that de Freece man like a hawk. He breaks like sin all over the shop. Hullo, Morris! Bad luck! Were you out, do you think?" A batsman who has been given l.-b.-w. is always asked this question on his return to the pavilion, and he answers it in nine cases out of ten in the negative. Morris was the tenth case. He thought it was all right, he said.

"Thought the thing was going to break, but it didn't."

"Hear that, Berry? He doesn't always break. You must look out for that," said Burgess helpfully. Morris sat down and began to take off his pads.

"That chap'll have Berry, if he doesn't look out," he said.

But Berridge survived the ordeal. He turned his first ball to leg for a single.

This brought Marsh to the batting end; and the second tragedy occurred.

It was evident from the way he shaped that Marsh was short of practice. His visit to the Infirmary had taken the edge off his batting. He scratched awkwardly at three balls without hitting them. The last of the over had him in two minds. He started to play forward, changed his stroke suddenly and tried to step back, and the next moment the bails had shot up like the *débris* of a small explosion, and the wicket-keeper was clapping his gloved hands gently and slowly in the introspective, dreamy way wicket-keepers have on these occasions.

A silence that could be felt brooded over the pavilion.

The voice of the scorer, addressing from his little wooden hut the melancholy youth who was working the telegraph-board, broke it.

"One for two. Last man duck."

Ellerby echoed the remark. He got up, and took off his blazer.

"This is all right," he said, "isn't it! I wonder if the man at the other end is a sort of young Rhodes too!"

Fortunately he was not. The star of the Ripton attack was evidently de Freece. The bowler at the other end looked fairly plain. He sent them down medium-pace, and on a good wicket would probably have been simple. But to-day there was danger in the most guileless-looking deliveries.

Berridge relieved the tension a little by playing safely through the over, and scoring a couple of twos off it. And when Ellerby not only survived the destructive de Freece's second over, but actually lifted a loose ball on to the roof of the scoring-hut, the cloud began perceptibly to lift. A no-ball in the same over sent up the first ten. Ten for two was not good; but it was considerably better than one for two.

With the score at thirty, Ellerby was missed in the slips off de Freece. He had been playing with slowly increasing confidence till then, but this seemed to throw him out of his stride. He played inside the next ball, and was all but bowled: and then, jumping out to drive, he was smartly stumped. The cloud began to settle again.

Bob was the next man in.

Ellerby took off his pads, and dropped into the chair next to Mike's. Mike was silent and thoughtful. He was in after Bob, and to be on the eve of batting does not make one conversational.

"You in next?" asked Ellerby.

Mike nodded.

"It's getting trickier every minute," said Ellerby. "The only thing is, if we can only stay in, we might have a chance. The wicket'll get better, and I don't believe they've any bowling at all bar de Freece. By George, Bob's out!... No, he isn't."

Bob had jumped out at one of de Freece's slows, as Ellerby had done, and had nearly met the same fate. The wicket-keeper, however, had fumbled the ball.

"That's the way I was had," said Ellerby. "That man's keeping such a jolly good length that you don't know whether to stay in your ground or go out at them. If only somebody would knock him off his length, I believe we might win yet."

The same idea apparently occurred to Burgess. He came to where Mike was sitting.

"I'm going to shove you down one, Jackson," he said. "I shall go in next myself and swipe, and try and knock that man de Freece off."

"All right," said Mike. He was not quite sure whether he was glad or sorry at the respite.

"It's a pity old Wyatt isn't here," said Ellerby. "This is just the sort of time when he might have come off."

"Bob's broken his egg," said Mike.

"Good man. Every little helps.... Oh, you silly ass, get *back*!"

Berridge had called Bob for a short run that was obviously no run. Third man was returning the ball as the batsmen crossed. The next moment the wicket-keeper had the bails off. Berridge was out by a yard.

"Forty-one for four," said Ellerby. "Help!"

Burgess began his campaign against de Freece by skying his first ball over cover's head to the boundary. A howl of delight went up from the school, which was repeated, *fortissimo*, when, more by accident than by accurate timing, the captain put on two more fours past extra-cover. The bowler's cheerful smile never varied.

Whether Burgess would have knocked de Freece off his length or not was a question that was destined to remain unsolved, for in the middle of the other bowler's over Bob hit a single; the batsmen crossed; and Burgess had his leg-stump uprooted while trying a gigantic pull-stroke.

The melancholy youth put up the figures, 54, 5, 12, on the board.

Mike, as he walked out of the pavilion to join Bob, was not conscious of any particular nervousness. It had been an ordeal having to wait and look on while wickets fell, but now that the time of inaction was at an end he felt curiously composed. When he had gone out to bat against the M.C.C. on the occasion of his first appearance for the school, he experienced a quaint sensation of unreality. He seemed to be watching his body walking to the wickets, as if it were some one else's. There was no sense of individuality.

But now his feelings were different. He was cool. He noticed small things—-mid-off chewing bits of grass, the bowler re-tying the scarf round his waist, little patches of brown where the turf had been worn away. He took guard with a clear picture of the positions of the fieldsmen photographed on his brain.

Fitness, which in a batsman exhibits itself mainly in an increased power of seeing the ball, is one of the most inexplicable things connected with cricket. It has nothing, or very little, to do with actual health. A man may come out of a sick-room with just that extra quickness in sighting the ball that makes all the difference; or he may be in perfect training and play inside straight half-volleys. Mike would not have said that he felt more than ordinarily well that day. Indeed, he was rather painfully conscious of having bolted his food at lunch. But something seemed to whisper to him, as he settled himself to face the bowler, that he was at the top of his batting form. A difficult wicket always brought out his latent powers as a bat. It was a standing mystery with the sporting Press how Joe Jackson managed to collect fifties and sixties on wickets that completely upset men who were, apparently, finer players. On days when the Olympians of the cricket world were bringing their averages down with ducks and singles, Joe would be in his element, watching the ball and pushing it through the slips as if there were no such thing as a tricky wicket. And Mike took after Joe.

A single off the fifth ball of the over opened his score and brought him to the opposite end. Bob played ball number six back to the bowler, and Mike took guard preparatory to facing de Freece.

CHAPTER XXVIII MIKE WINS HOME

The Ripton slow bowler took a long run, considering his pace. In the early part of an innings he often trapped the batsmen in this way, by leading them to expect a faster ball than he actually sent down. A queer little jump in the middle of the run increased the difficulty of watching him.

The smiting he had received from Burgess in the previous over had not had the effect of knocking de Freece off his length. The ball was too short to reach with comfort, and not short enough to take liberties with. It pitched slightly to leg, and whipped in quickly. Mike had faced half-left, and stepped back. The increased speed of the ball after it had touched the ground beat him. The ball hit his right pad.

"'S that?" shouted mid-on. Mid-on has a habit of appealing for l.-b.-w. in school matches.

De Freece said nothing. The Ripton bowler was as conscientious in the matter of appeals as a good bowler should be. He had seen that the ball had pitched off the leg-stump.

The umpire shook his head. Mid-on tried to look as if he had not spoken.

Mike prepared himself for the next ball with a glow of confidence. He felt that he knew where he was now. Till then he had not thought the wicket was so fast. The two balls he had played at the other end had told him nothing. They had been well pitched up, and he had smothered them. He knew what to do now. He had played on wickets of this pace at home against Saunders's bowling, and Saunders had shown him the right way to cope with them.

The next ball was of the same length, but this time off the off-stump. Mike jumped out, and hit it before it had time to break. It flew along the ground through the gap between cover and extra-cover, a comfortable three.

Bob played out the over with elaborate care.

Off the second ball of the other man's over Mike scored his first boundary. It was a long-hop on the off. He banged it behind point to the terrace-bank. The last ball of the over, a half-volley to leg, he lifted over the other boundary.

"Sixty up," said Ellerby, in the pavilion, as the umpire signalled another no-ball. "By George! I believe these chaps are going to knock off the runs. Young Jackson looks as if he was in for a century."

"You ass," said Berridge. "Don't say that, or he's certain to get out."

Berridge was one of those who are skilled in cricket superstitions.

But Mike did not get out. He took seven off de Freece's next over by means of two cuts and a drive. And, with Bob still exhibiting a stolid and rock-like defence, the score mounted to eighty, thence to ninety, and so, mainly by singles, to a hundred.

At a hundred and four, when the wicket had put on exactly fifty, Bob fell to a combination of de Freece and extra-cover. He had stuck like a limpet for an hour and a quarter, and made twenty-one.

Mike watched him go with much the same feelings as those of a man who turns away from the platform after seeing a friend off on a long railway journey. His departure upset the scheme of things. For himself he had no fear now. He might possibly get out off his next ball, but he felt set enough to stay at the wickets till nightfall. He had had narrow escapes from de Freece, but he was full of that conviction, which comes to all batsmen on occasion, that this was his day. He had made twenty-six, and the wicket was getting easier. He could feel the sting going out of the bowling every over.

Henfrey, the next man in, was a promising rather than an effective bat. He had an excellent style, but he was uncertain. (Two years later, when he captained the Wrykyn teams, he made a lot of runs.) But this season his batting had been spasmodic.

To-day he never looked like settling down. He survived an over from de Freece, and hit a fast change bowler who had been put on at the other end for a couple of fluky fours. Then Mike got the bowling for three consecutive overs, and raised the score to a hundred and twenty-six. A bye brought Henfrey to the batting end again, and de Freece's pet googly, which had not been much in evidence hitherto, led to his snicking an easy catch into short-slip's hands.

A hundred and twenty-seven for seven against a total of a hundred and sixty-six gives the impression that the batting side has the advantage. In the present case, however, it was Ripton who were really in the better position. Apparently, Wrykyn had three more wickets to fall. Practically they had only one, for neither Ashe, nor Grant, nor Devenish had any pretensions to be considered batsmen. Ashe was the school wicket-keeper. Grant and Devenish were bowlers. Between them the three could not be relied on for a dozen in a decent match.

Mike watched Ashe shape with a sinking heart. The wicket-keeper looked like a man who feels that his hour has come. Mike could see him licking his lips. There was nervousness written all over him.

He was not kept long in suspense. De Freece's first ball made a hideous wreck of his wicket.

"Over," said the umpire.

Mike felt that the school's one chance now lay in his keeping the bowling. But how was he to do this? It suddenly occurred to him that it was a delicate position that he was in. It was not often that he was troubled by an inconvenient modesty, but this happened now. Grant was a fellow he hardly knew, and a school prefect to boot. Could he go up to him and explain that he, Jackson, did not consider him competent to bat in this crisis? Would not this get about and be accounted to him for side? He had made forty, but even so....

Fortunately Grant solved the problem on his own account. He came up to Mike and spoke with an earnestness born of nerves. "For goodness sake," he whispered, "collar the bowling all you know, or we're done. I shall get outed first ball."

"All right," said Mike, and set his teeth. Forty to win! A large order. But it was going to be done. His whole existence seemed to concentrate itself on those forty runs.

CHAPTER XXVIII MIKE WINS HOME

The fast bowler, who was the last of several changes that had been tried at the other end, was well-meaning but erratic. The wicket was almost true again now, and it was possible to take liberties.

Mike took them.

A distant clapping from the pavilion, taken up a moment later all round the ground, and echoed by the Ripton fieldsmen, announced that he had reached his fifty.

The last ball of the over he mishit. It rolled in the direction of third man.

"Come on," shouted Grant.

Mike and the ball arrived at the opposite wicket almost simultaneously. Another fraction of a second, and he would have been run out.

MIKE AND THE BALL ARRIVED ALMOST SIMULTANEOUSLY

The last balls of the next two overs provided repetitions of this performance. But each time luck was with him, and his bat was across the crease before the bails were off. The telegraph-board showed a hundred and fifty.

The next over was doubly sensational. The original medium-paced bowler had gone on again in place of the fast man, and for the first five balls he could not find his length. During those five balls Mike raised the score to a hundred and sixty.

But the sixth was of a different kind. Faster than the rest and of a perfect length, it all but got through Mike's defence. As it was, he stopped it. But he did not score. The umpire called "Over!" and there was Grant at the batting end, with de Freece smiling pleasantly as he walked back to begin his run with the comfortable reflection that at last he had got somebody except Mike to bowl at.

That over was an experience Mike never forgot.

Grant pursued the Fabian policy of keeping his bat almost immovable and trusting to luck. Point and the slips crowded round. Mid-off and mid-on moved half-way down the pitch. Grant looked embarrassed, but determined. For four balls he baffled the attack, though once nearly caught by point a yard from the wicket. The fifth curled round his bat, and touched the off-stump. A bail fell silently to the ground.

Devenish came in to take the last ball of the over.

It was an awe-inspiring moment. A great stillness was over all the ground. Mike's knees trembled. Devenish's face was a delicate grey.

The only person unmoved seemed to be de Freece. His smile was even more amiable than usual as he began his run.

The next moment the crisis was past. The ball hit the very centre of Devenish's bat, and rolled back down the pitch.

The school broke into one great howl of joy. There were still seven runs between them and victory, but nobody appeared to recognise this fact as important. Mike had got the bowling, and the bowling was not de Freece's.

It seemed almost an anti-climax when a four to leg and two two's through the slips settled the thing.

Devenish was caught and bowled in de Freece's next over; but the Wrykyn total was one hundred and seventy-two.

"Good game," said Maclaine, meeting Burgess in the pavilion. "Who was the man who made all the runs? How many, by the way?"

"Eighty-three. It was young Jackson. Brother of the other one."

"That family! How many more of them are you going to have here?"

"He's the last. I say, rough luck on de Freece. He bowled rippingly."

Politeness to a beaten foe caused Burgess to change his usual "not bad."

"The funny part of it is," continued he, "that young Jackson was only playing as a sub."

"You've got a rum idea of what's funny," said Maclaine.

CHAPTER XXIX WYATT AGAIN

It was a morning in the middle of September. The Jacksons were breakfasting. Mr. Jackson was reading letters. The rest, including Gladys Maud, whose finely chiselled features were gradually disappearing behind a mask of bread-and-milk, had settled down to serious work. The usual catch-as-catch-can contest between Marjory and Phyllis for the jam (referee and time-keeper, Mrs. Jackson) had resulted, after both combatants had been cautioned by the referee, in a victory for Marjory, who had duly secured the stakes. The hour being nine-fifteen, and the official time for breakfast nine o'clock, Mike's place was still empty.

"I've had a letter from MacPherson," said Mr. Jackson.

MacPherson was the vigorous and persevering gentleman, referred to in a previous chapter, who kept a fatherly eye on the Buenos Ayres sheep.

"He seems very satisfied with Mike's friend Wyatt. At the moment of writing Wyatt is apparently incapacitated owing to a bullet in the shoulder, but expects to be fit again shortly. That young man seems to make things fairly lively wherever he is. I don't wonder he found a public school too restricted a sphere for his energies."

"Has he been fighting a duel?" asked Marjory, interested.

"Bushrangers," said Phyllis.

"There aren't any bushrangers in Buenos Ayres," said Ella.

"How do you know?" said Phyllis clinchingly.

"Bush-ray, bush-ray, bush-ray," began Gladys Maud, conversationally, through the bread-and-milk; but was headed off.

"He gives no details. Perhaps that letter on Mike's plate supplies them. I see it comes from Buenos Ayres."

"I wish Mike would come and open it," said Marjory. "Shall I go and hurry him up?"

The missing member of the family entered as she spoke.

"Buck up, Mike," she shouted. "There's a letter from Wyatt. He's been wounded in a duel."

"With a bushranger," added Phyllis.

"Bush-ray," explained Gladys Maud.

"Is there?" said Mike. "Sorry I'm late."

He opened the letter and began to read.

"What does he say?" inquired Marjory. "Who was the duel with?"

"How many bushrangers were there?" asked Phyllis.

Mike read on.

"Good old Wyatt! He's shot a man."

"Killed him?" asked Marjory excitedly.

"No. Only potted him in the leg. This is what he says. First page is mostly about the Ripton match and so on. Here you are. 'I'm dictating this to a sportsman of the name of Danvers, a good chap who can't help being ugly, so excuse bad writing. The fact is we've been having a bust-up here, and I've come out of it with a bullet in the shoulder, which has crocked me for the time being. It happened like this. An ass of a Gaucho had gone into the town and got jolly tight, and coming back, he wanted to ride through our place. The old woman who keeps the lodge wouldn't have it at any price. Gave him the absolute miss-in-baulk. So this rotter, instead of shifting off, proceeded to cut the fence, and go through that way. All the farms out here have their boundaries marked by wire fences, and it is supposed to be a deadly sin to cut these. Well, the lodge-keeper's son dashed off in search of help. A chap called Chester, an Old Wykehamist, and I were dipping sheep close by, so he came to us and told us what had happened. We nipped on to a couple of horses, pulled out our revolvers, and tooled after him. After a bit we overtook him, and that's when the trouble began. The johnny had dismounted when we arrived. I thought he was simply tightening his horse's girths. What he was really doing was getting a steady aim at us with his revolver. He fired as we came up, and dropped poor old Chester. I thought he was killed at first, but it turned out it was only his leg. I got going then. I emptied all the six chambers of my revolver, and missed him clean every time. In the meantime he got me in the right shoulder. Hurt like sin afterwards, though it was only a sort of dull shock at the moment. The next item of the programme was a forward move in force on the part of the enemy. The man had got his knife out now—-why he didn't shoot again I don't know—-and toddled over in our direction to finish us off. Chester was unconscious, and it was any money on the Gaucho, when I happened to catch sight of Chester's pistol, which had fallen just by where I came down. I picked it up, and loosed off. Missed the first shot, but got him with the second in the ankle at about two yards; and his day's work was done. That's the painful story. Danvers says he's getting writer's cramp, so I shall have to stop....'"

"By Jove!" said Mike.

"What a dreadful thing!" said Mrs. Jackson.

"Anyhow, it was practically a bushranger," said Phyllis.

"I told you it was a duel, and so it was," said Marjory.

"What a terrible experience for the poor boy!" said Mrs. Jackson.

"Much better than being in a beastly bank," said Mike, summing up. "I'm glad he's having such a ripping time. It must be almost as decent as Wrykyn out there.... I say, what's under that dish?"

CHAPTER XXX MR. JACKSON MAKES UP HIS MIND

Two years have elapsed and Mike is home again for the Easter holidays.

If Mike had been in time for breakfast that morning he might have gathered from the expression on his father's face, as Mr. Jackson opened the envelope containing his school report and read the contents, that the document in question was not exactly a paean of praise from beginning to end. But he was late, as usual. Mike always was late for breakfast in the holidays.

When he came down on this particular morning, the meal was nearly over. Mr. Jackson had disappeared, taking his correspondence with him; Mrs. Jackson had gone into the kitchen, and when Mike appeared the thing had resolved itself into a mere vulgar brawl between Phyllis and Ella for the jam, while Marjory, who had put her hair up a fortnight before, looked on in a detached sort of way, as if these juvenile gambols distressed her.

"Hullo, Mike," she said, jumping up as he entered; "here you are—-I've been keeping everything hot for you."

"Have you? Thanks awfully. I say—-" his eye wandered in mild surprise round the table. "I'm a bit late."

Marjory was bustling about, fetching and carrying for Mike, as she always did. She had adopted him at an early age, and did the thing thoroughly. She was fond of her other brothers, especially when they made centuries in first-class cricket, but Mike was her favourite. She would field out in the deep as a natural thing when Mike was batting at the net in the paddock, though for the others, even for Joe, who had played in all five Test Matches in the previous summer, she would do it only as a favour.

Phyllis and Ella finished their dispute and went out. Marjory sat on the table and watched Mike eat.

"Your report came this morning, Mike," she said.

The kidneys failed to retain Mike's undivided attention. He looked up interested. "What did it say?"

"I didn't see—-I only caught sight of the Wrykyn crest on the envelope. Father didn't say anything."

Mike seemed concerned. "I say, that looks rather rotten! I wonder if it was awfully bad. It's the first I've had from Appleby."

"It can't be any worse than the horrid ones Mr. Blake used to write when you were in his form."

"No, that's a comfort," said Mike philosophically. "Think there's any more tea in that pot?"

"I call it a shame," said Marjory; "they ought to be jolly glad to have you at Wrykyn just for cricket, instead of writing beastly reports that make father angry and don't do any good to anybody."

"Last summer he said he'd take me away if I got another one."

"He didn't mean it really, I *know* he didn't! He couldn't! You're the best bat Wrykyn's ever had."

"What ho!" interpolated Mike.

"You *are*. Everybody says you are. Why, you got your first the very first term you were there—-even Joe didn't do anything nearly so good as that. Saunders says you're simply bound to play for England in another year or two."

"Saunders is a jolly good chap. He bowled me a half-volley on the off the first ball I had in a school match. By the way, I wonder if he's out at the net now. Let's go and see."

Saunders was setting up the net when they arrived. Mike put on his pads and went to the wickets, while Marjory and the dogs retired as usual to the far hedge to retrieve.

She was kept busy. Saunders was a good sound bowler of the M.C.C. minor match type, and there had been a time when he had worried Mike considerably, but Mike had been in the Wrykyn team for three seasons now, and each season he had advanced tremendously in his batting. He had filled out in three years. He had always had the style, and now he had the strength as well. Saunders's bowling on a true wicket seemed simple to him. It was early in the Easter holidays, but already he was beginning to find his form. Saunders, who looked on Mike as his own special invention, was delighted.

"If you don't be worried by being too anxious now that you're captain, Master Mike," he said, "you'll make a century every match next term."

"I wish I wasn't; it's a beastly responsibility."

Henfrey, the Wrykyn cricket captain of the previous season, was not returning next term, and Mike was to reign in his stead. He liked the prospect, but it certainly carried with it a rather awe-inspiring responsibility. At night sometimes he would lie awake, appalled by the fear of losing his form, or making a hash of things by choosing the wrong men to play for the school and leaving the right men out. It is no light thing to captain a public school at cricket.

As he was walking towards the house, Phyllis met him. "Oh, I've been hunting for you, Mike; father wants you."

"What for?"

"I don't know."

"Where?"

"He's in the study. He seems—" added Phyllis, throwing in the information by way of a make-weight, "in a beastly wax."

Mike's jaw fell slightly. "I hope the dickens it's nothing to do with that bally report," was his muttered exclamation.

Mike's dealings with his father were as a rule of a most pleasant nature. Mr. Jackson was an understanding sort of man, who treated his sons as companions. From time to time, however, breezes were apt to ruffle the placid sea of good-fellowship. Mike's end-of-term report was an unfailing wind-raiser; indeed, on the arrival of Mr. Blake's sarcastic *résumé* of Mike's short-comings at the end of the previous term, there had been something not unlike a typhoon. It was on this occasion that Mr. Jackson had solemnly declared his intention of removing Mike from Wrykyn unless the critics became more flattering; and Mr. Jackson was a man of his word.

It was with a certain amount of apprehension, therefore, that Jackson entered the study.

"Come in, Mike," said his father, kicking the waste-paper basket; "I want to speak to you."

Mike, skilled in omens, scented a row in the offing. Only in moments of emotion was Mr. Jackson in the habit of booting the basket.

There followed an awkward silence, which Mike broke by remarking that he had carted a half-volley from Saunders over the on-side hedge that morning.

"It was just a bit short and off the leg stump, so I stepped out—may I bag the paper-knife for a jiffy? I'll just show——"

"Never mind about cricket now," said Mr. Jackson; "I want you to listen to this report."

"Oh, is that my report, father?" said Mike, with a sort of sickly interest, much as a dog about to be washed might evince in his tub.

"It is," replied Mr. Jackson in measured tones, "your report; what is more, it is without exception the worst report you have ever had."

"Oh, I say!" groaned the record-breaker.

"'His conduct,'" quoted Mr. Jackson, "'has been unsatisfactory in the extreme, both in and out of school.'"

"It wasn't anything really. I only happened——"

Remembering suddenly that what he had happened to do was to drop a cannon-ball (the school weight) on the form-room floor, not once, but on several occasions, he paused.

"'French bad; conduct disgraceful——'"

"Everybody rags in French."

"'Mathematics bad. Inattentive and idle.'"

"Nobody does much work in Math."

"'Latin poor. Greek, very poor.'"

"We were doing Thucydides, Book Two, last term—all speeches and doubtful readings, and cruxes and things—beastly hard! Everybody says so."

"Here are Mr. Appleby's remarks: 'The boy has genuine ability, which he declines to use in the smallest degree.'"

Mike moaned a moan of righteous indignation.

"'An abnormal proficiency at games has apparently destroyed all desire in him to realise the more serious issues of life.' There is more to the same effect."

Mr. Appleby was a master with very definite ideas as to what constituted a public-school master's duties. As a man he was distinctly pro-Mike. He understood cricket, and some of Mike's shots on the off gave him thrills of pure aesthetic joy; but as a master he always made it his habit to regard the manners and customs of the boys in his form with an unbiased eye, and to an unbiased eye Mike in a form-room was about as near the extreme edge as a boy could be, and Mr. Appleby said as much in a clear firm hand.

"You remember what I said to you about your report at Christmas, Mike?" said Mr. Jackson, folding the lethal document and replacing it in its envelope.

Mike said nothing; there was a sinking feeling in his interior.

"I shall abide by what I said."

Mike's heart thumped.

"You will not go back to Wrykyn next term."

Somewhere in the world the sun was shining, birds were twittering; somewhere in the world lambkins frisked and peasants sang blithely at their toil (flat, perhaps, but still blithely), but to Mike at that moment the sky was black, and an icy wind blew over the face of the earth.

The tragedy had happened, and there was an end of it. He made no attempt to appeal against the sentence. He knew it would be useless, his father, when he made up his mind, having all the unbending tenacity of the normally easy-going man.

Mr. Jackson was sorry for Mike. He understood him, and for that reason he said very little now.

"I am sending you to Sedleigh," was his next remark.

Sedleigh! Mike sat up with a jerk. He knew Sedleigh by name—one of those schools with about a hundred fellows which you never hear of except when they send up their gymnasium pair to Aldershot, or their Eight to Bisley. Mike's outlook on life was that of a cricketer, pure and simple. What had Sedleigh ever done? What were they ever likely to do? Whom did they play? What Old Sedleighan had ever done anything at cricket? Perhaps they didn't even *play* cricket!

"But it's an awful hole," he said blankly.

Mr. Jackson could read Mike's mind like a book. Mike's point of view was plain to him. He did not approve of it, but he knew that in Mike's place and at Mike's age he would have felt the same. He spoke drily to hide his sympathy.

"It is not a large school," he said, "and I don't suppose it could play Wrykyn at cricket, but it has one merit—boys work there. Young Barlitt won a Balliol scholarship from Sedleigh last year." Barlitt was the vicar's son, a silent, spectacled youth who did not enter very largely into Mike's world. They had met occasionally at tennis-parties, but not much conversation had ensued. Barlitt's mind was massive, but his topics of conversation were not Mike's.

"Mr. Barlitt speaks very highly of Sedleigh," added Mr. Jackson.

Mike said nothing, which was a good deal better than saying what he would have liked to have said.

CHAPTER XXXI SEDLEIGH

The train, which had been stopping everywhere for the last half-hour, pulled up again, and Mike, seeing the name of the station, got up, opened the door, and hurled a Gladstone bag out on to the platform in an emphatic and vindictive manner. Then he got out himself and looked about him.

"For the school, sir?" inquired the solitary porter, bustling up, as if he hoped by sheer energy to deceive the traveller into thinking that Sedleigh station was staffed by a great army of porters.

Mike nodded. A sombre nod. The nod Napoleon might have given if somebody had met him in 1812, and said, "So you're back from Moscow, eh?" Mike was feeling thoroughly jaundiced. The future seemed wholly gloomy. And, so far from attempting to make the best of things, he had set himself deliberately to look on the dark side. He thought, for instance, that he had never seen a more repulsive porter, or one more obviously incompetent than the man who had attached himself with a firm grasp to the handle of the bag as he strode off in the direction of the luggage-van. He disliked his voice, his appearance, and the colour of his hair. Also the boots he wore. He hated the station, and the man who took his ticket.

"Young gents at the school, sir," said the porter, perceiving from Mike's *distrait* air that the boy was a stranger to the place, "goes up in the 'bus mostly. It's waiting here, sir. Hi, George!"

"I'll walk, thanks," said Mike frigidly.

"It's a goodish step, sir."

"Here you are."

"Thank you, sir. I'll send up your luggage by the 'bus, sir. Which 'ouse was it you was going to?"

"Outwood's."

"Right, sir. It's straight on up this road to the school. You can't miss it, sir."

"Worse luck," said Mike.

He walked off up the road, sorrier for himself than ever. It was such absolutely rotten luck. About now, instead of being on his way to a place where they probably ran a diabolo team instead of a cricket eleven, and played hunt-the-slipper in winter, he would be on the point of arriving at Wrykyn. And as captain of cricket, at that. Which was the bitter part of it. He had never been in command. For the last two seasons he had been the star man, going in first, and heading the averages easily at the end of the season; and the three captains under whom he had played during his career as a Wrykynian, Burgess, Enderby, and Henfrey had always been sportsmen to him. But it was not the same thing. He had meant to do such a lot for Wrykyn cricket this term. He had had an entirely new system of coaching in his mind. Now it might never be used. He had handed it on in a letter to Strachan, who would be captain in his place; but probably Strachan would have some scheme of his own. There is nobody who could not edit a paper in the ideal way; and there is nobody who has not a theory of his own about cricket-coaching at school.

Wrykyn, too, would be weak this year, now that he was no longer there. Strachan was a good, free bat on his day, and, if he survived a few overs, might make a century in an hour, but he was not to be depended upon. There was no doubt that Mike's sudden withdrawal meant that Wrykyn would have a bad time that season. And it had been such a wretched athletic year for the school. The football fifteen had been hopeless, and had lost both the Ripton matches, the return by over sixty points. Sheen's victory in the light-weights at Aldershot had been their one success. And now, on top of all this, the captain of cricket was removed during the Easter holidays. Mike's heart bled for Wrykyn, and he found himself loathing Sedleigh and all its works with a great loathing.

The only thing he could find in its favour was the fact that it was set in a very pretty country. Of a different type from the Wrykyn country, but almost as good. For three miles Mike made his way through woods and past fields. Once he crossed a river. It was soon after this that he caught sight, from the top of a hill, of a group of buildings that wore an unmistakably school-like look.

This must be Sedleigh.

Ten minutes' walk brought him to the school gates, and a baker's boy directed him to Mr. Outwood's.

There were three houses in a row, separated from the school buildings by a cricket-field. Outwood's was the middle one of these.

Mike went to the front door, and knocked. At Wrykyn he had always charged in at the beginning of term at the boys' entrance, but this formal reporting of himself at Sedleigh suited his mood.

He inquired for Mr. Outwood, and was shown into a room lined with books. Presently the door opened, and the house-master appeared.

There was something pleasant and homely about Mr. Outwood. In appearance he reminded Mike of Smee in "Peter Pan." He had the same eyebrows and pince-nez and the same motherly look.

"Jackson?" he said mildly.

"Yes, sir."

"I am very glad to see you, very glad indeed. Perhaps you would like a cup of tea after your journey. I think you might like a cup of tea. You come from Crofton, in Shropshire, I understand, Jackson, near Brindleford? It is a part of the country which I have always wished to visit. I daresay you have frequently seen the Cluniac Priory of St. Ambrose at Brindleford?"

Mike, who would not have recognised a Cluniac Priory if you had handed him one on a tray, said he had not.

"Dear me! You have missed an opportunity which I should have been glad to have. I am preparing a book on Ruined Abbeys and Priories of England, and it has always been my wish to see the Cluniac Priory of St. Ambrose. A deeply interesting relic of the sixteenth century. Bishop Geoffrey, 1133-40——"

"Shall I go across to the boys' part, sir?"

"What? Yes. Oh, yes. Quite so. And perhaps you would like a cup of tea after your journey? No? Quite so. Quite so. You should make a point of visiting the remains of the Cluniac Priory in the summer holidays, Jackson. You will find the matron in her room. In many respects it is unique. The northern altar is in a state of really wonderful preservation. It consists of a solid block of masonry five feet long and two and a half wide, with chamfered plinth, standing quite free from the apse wall. It will well repay a visit. Good-bye for the present, Jackson, good-bye."

Mike wandered across to the other side of the house, his gloom visibly deepened. All alone in a strange school, where they probably played hopscotch, with a house-master who offered one cups of tea after one's journey and talked about chamfered plinths and apses. It was a little hard.

He strayed about, finding his bearings, and finally came to a room which he took to be the equivalent of the senior day-room at a Wrykyn house. Everywhere else he had found nothing but emptiness. Evidently he had come by an earlier train than was usual. But this room was occupied.

A very long, thin youth, with a solemn face and immaculate clothes, was leaning against the mantelpiece. As Mike entered, he fumbled in his top left waistcoat pocket, produced an eyeglass attached to a cord, and fixed it in his right eye. With the help of this aid to vision he inspected Mike in silence for a while, then, having flicked an invisible speck of dust from the left sleeve of his coat, he spoke.

"Hullo," he said.

He spoke in a tired voice.

"Hullo," said Mike.

"Take a seat," said the immaculate one. "If you don't mind dirtying your bags, that's to say. Personally, I don't see any prospect of ever sitting down in this place. It looks to me as if they meant to use these chairs as mustard-and-cress beds. A Nursery Garden in the Home. That sort of idea. My name," he added pensively, "is Smith. What's yours?"

CHAPTER XXXII PSMITH

"Jackson," said Mike.

"Are you the Bully, the Pride of the School, or the Boy who is Led Astray and takes to Drink in Chapter Sixteen?"

"The last, for choice," said Mike, "but I've only just arrived, so I don't know."

"The boy—-what will he become? Are you new here, too, then?"

"Yes! Why, are you new?"

"Do I look as if I belonged here? I'm the latest import. Sit down on yonder settee, and I will tell you the painful story of my life. By the way, before I start, there's just one thing. If you ever have occasion to write to me, would you mind sticking a P at the beginning of my name? P-s-m-i-t-h. See? There are too many Smiths, and I don't care for Smythe. My father's content to worry along in the old-fashioned way, but I've decided to strike out a fresh line. I shall found a new dynasty. The resolve came to me unexpectedly this morning, as I was buying a simple penn'orth of butterscotch out of the automatic machine at Paddington. I jotted it down on the back of an envelope. In conversation you may address me as Rupert (though I hope you won't), or simply Smith, the P not being sounded. Cp. the name Zbysco, in which the Z is given a similar miss-in-baulk. See?"

Mike said he saw. Psmith thanked him with a certain stately old-world courtesy.

"Let us start at the beginning," he resumed. "My infancy. When I was but a babe, my eldest sister was bribed with a shilling an hour by my nurse to keep an rye on me, and see that I did not raise Cain. At the end of the first day she struck for one-and six, and got it. We now pass to my boyhood. At an early age, I was sent to Eton, everybody predicting a bright career for me. But," said Psmith solemnly, fixing an owl-like gaze on Mike through the eye-glass, "it was not to be."

"No?" said Mike.

"No. I was superannuated last term."

"Bad luck."

"For Eton, yes. But what Eton loses, Sedleigh gains."

"But why Sedleigh, of all places?"

"This is the most painful part of my narrative. It seems that a certain scug in the next village to ours happened last year to collar a Balliol——-"

"Not Barlitt!" exclaimed Mike.

"That was the man. The son of the vicar. The vicar told the curate, who told our curate, who told our vicar, who told my father, who sent me off here to get a Balliol too. Do *you* know Barlitt?"

"His pater's vicar of our village. It was because his son got a Balliol that I was sent here."

"Do you come from Crofton?"

"Yes."

"I've lived at Lower Benford all my life. We are practically long-lost brothers. Cheer a little, will you?"

Mike felt as Robinson Crusoe felt when he met Friday. Here was a fellow human being in this desert place. He could almost have embraced Psmith. The very sound of the name Lower Benford was heartening. His dislike for his new school was not diminished, but now he felt that life there might at least be tolerable.

"Where were you before you came here?" asked Psmith. "You have heard my painful story. Now tell me yours."

"Wrykyn. My pater took me away because I got such a lot of bad reports."

"My reports from Eton were simply scurrilous. There's a libel action in every sentence. How do you like this place from what you've seen of it?"

"Rotten."

"I am with you, Comrade Jackson. You won't mind my calling you Comrade, will you? I've just become a Socialist. It's a great scheme. You ought to be one. You work for the equal distribution of property, and start by collaring all you can and sitting on it. We must stick together. We are companions in misfortune. Lost lambs. Sheep that have gone astray. Divided, we fall, together we may worry through. Have you seen Professor Radium yet? I should say Mr. Outwood. What do you think of him?"

"He doesn't seem a bad sort of chap. Bit off his nut. Jawed about apses and things."

"And thereby," said Psmith, "hangs a tale. I've been making inquiries of a stout sportsman in a sort of Salvation Army uniform, whom I met in the grounds—-he's the school sergeant or something, quite a solid man—-and I hear that Comrade Outwood's an archaeological cove. Goes about the country beating up old ruins and fossils and things. There's an Archaeological Society in the school, run by him. It goes out on half-holidays, prowling about, and is allowed to break bounds and generally steep itself to the eyebrows in reckless devilry. And, mark you, laddie, if you belong to the Archaeological Society you get off cricket. To get off cricket," said Psmith, dusting his right trouser-leg, "was the dream of my youth and the aspiration of my riper years. A noble game, but a bit too thick for me. At Eton I used to have to field out at the nets till the soles of my boots wore through. I suppose you are a blood at the game? Play for the school against Loamshire, and so on."

"I'm not going to play here, at any rate," said Mike.

He had made up his mind on this point in the train. There is a certain fascination about making the very worst of a bad job. Achilles knew his business when he sat in his tent. The determination not to play cricket for Sedleigh as he could not play for Wrykyn gave Mike a sort of pleasure. To stand by with folded arms and a sombre frown, as it were, was one way of treating the situation, and one not without its meed of comfort.

Psmith approved the resolve.

"Stout fellow," he said. "'Tis well. You and I, hand in hand, will search the countryside for ruined abbeys. We will snare the elusive fossil together. Above all, we will go out of bounds. We shall thus improve our minds, and have a jolly good time as well. I shouldn't wonder if one mightn't borrow a gun from some friendly native, and do a bit of rabbit-shooting here and there. From what I saw of Comrade Outwood during our brief interview, I shouldn't think he was one of the lynx-eyed contingent. With tact we ought to be able to slip away from the merry throng of fossil-chasers, and do a bit on our own account."

"Good idea," said Mike. "We will. A chap at Wrykyn, called Wyatt, used to break out at night and shoot at cats with an air-pistol."

"It would take a lot to make me do that. I am all against anything that interferes with my sleep. But rabbits in the daytime is a scheme. We'll nose about for a gun at the earliest opp. Meanwhile we'd better go up to Comrade Outwood, and get our names shoved down for the Society."

"I vote we get some tea first somewhere."

"Then let's beat up a study. I suppose they have studies here. Let's go and look."

They went upstairs. On the first floor there was a passage with doors on either side. Psmith opened the first of these.

"This'll do us well," he said.

It was a biggish room, looking out over the school grounds. There were a couple of deal tables, two empty bookcases, and a looking-glass, hung on a nail.

"Might have been made for us," said Psmith approvingly.

"I suppose it belongs to some rotter."

"Not now."

"You aren't going to collar it!"

"That," said Psmith, looking at himself earnestly in the mirror, and straightening his tie, "is the exact programme. We must stake out our claims. This is practical Socialism."

"But the real owner's bound to turn up some time or other."

"His misfortune, not ours. You can't expect two master-minds like us to pig it in that room downstairs. There are moments when one wants to be alone. It is imperative that we have a place to retire to after a fatiguing day. And now, if you want to be really useful, come and help me fetch up my box from downstairs. It's got an Etna and various things in it."

CHAPTER XXXIII STAKING OUT A CLAIM

Psmith, in the matter of decorating a study and preparing tea in it, was rather a critic than an executant. He was full of ideas, but he preferred to allow Mike to carry them out. It was he who suggested that the wooden bar which ran across the window was unnecessary, but it was Mike who wrenched it from its place. Similarly, it was Mike who abstracted the key from the door of the next study, though the idea was Psmith's.

"Privacy," said Psmith, as he watched Mike light the Etna, "is what we chiefly need in this age of publicity. If you leave a study door unlocked in these strenuous times, the first thing you know is, somebody comes right in, sits down, and begins to talk about himself. I think with a little care we ought to be able to make this room quite decently comfortable. That putrid calendar must come down, though. Do you think you could make a long arm, and haul it off the parent tin-tack? Thanks. We make progress. We make progress."

"We shall jolly well make it out of the window," said Mike, spooning up tea from a paper bag with a postcard, "if a sort of young Hackenschmidt turns up and claims the study. What are you going to do about it?"

"Don't let us worry about it. I have a presentiment that he will be an insignificant-looking little weed. How are you getting on with the evening meal?"

"Just ready. What would you give to be at Eton now? I'd give something to be at Wrykyn."

"These school reports," said Psmith sympathetically, "are the very dickens. Many a bright young lad has been soured by them. Hullo. What's this, I wonder."

A heavy body had plunged against the door, evidently without a suspicion that there would be any resistance. A rattling at the handle followed, and a voice outside said, "Dash the door!"

"Hackenschmidt!" said Mike.

"The weed," said Psmith. "You couldn't make a long arm, could you, and turn the key? We had better give this merchant audience. Remind me later to go on with my remarks on school reports. I had several bright things to say on the subject."

Mike unlocked the door, and flung it open. Framed in the entrance was a smallish, freckled boy, wearing a bowler hat and carrying a bag. On his face was an expression of mingled wrath and astonishment.

Psmith rose courteously from his chair, and moved forward with slow stateliness to do the honours.

"What the dickens," inquired the newcomer, "are you doing here?"

"WHAT THE DICKENS ARE YOU DOING HERE?"

"We were having a little tea," said Psmith, "to restore our tissues after our journey. Come in and join us. We keep open house, we Psmiths. Let me introduce you to Comrade Jackson. A stout fellow. Homely in appearance, perhaps, but one of us. I am Psmith. Your own name will doubtless come up in the course of general chit-chat over the tea-cups."

"My name's Spiller, and this is my study."

Psmith leaned against the mantelpiece, put up his eyeglass, and harangued Spiller in a philosophical vein.

"Of all sad words of tongue or pen," said he, "the saddest are these: 'It might have been.' Too late! That is the bitter cry. If you had torn yourself from the bosom of the Spiller family by an earlier train, all might have been well. But no. Your father held your hand and said huskily, 'Edwin, don't leave us!' Your mother clung to you weeping, and said, 'Edwin, stay!' Your sisters——"

"I want to know what——"

"Your sisters froze on to your knees like little octopuses (or octopi), and screamed, 'Don't go, Edwin!' And so," said Psmith, deeply affected by his recital, "you stayed on till the later train; and, on arrival, you find strange faces in the familiar room, a people that know not Spiller." Psmith went to the table, and cheered himself with a sip of tea. Spiller's sad case had moved him greatly.

The victim of Fate seemed in no way consoled.

"It's beastly cheek, that's what I call it. Are you new chaps?"

"The very latest thing," said Psmith.

"Well, it's beastly cheek."

Mike's outlook on life was of the solid, practical order. He went straight to the root of the matter.

"What are you going to do about it?" he asked.

Spiller evaded the question.

"It's beastly cheek," he repeated. "You can't go about the place bagging studies."

"But we do," said Psmith. "In this life, Comrade Spiller, we must be prepared for every emergency. We must distinguish between the unusual and the impossible. It is unusual for people to go about the place bagging studies, so you have rashly ordered your life on the assumption that it is impossible. Error! Ah, Spiller, Spiller, let this be a lesson to you."

"Look here, I tell you what it——"

"I was in a motor with a man once. I said to him: 'What would happen if you trod on that pedal thing instead of that other pedal thing?' He said, 'I couldn't. One's the foot-brake, and the other's the accelerator.' 'But suppose you did?' I said. 'I wouldn't,' he said. 'Now we'll let her rip.' So he stamped on the accelerator. Only it turned out to be the foot-brake after all, and we stopped dead, and skidded into a ditch. The advice I give to every young man starting life is: 'Never confuse the unusual and the impossible.' Take the present case. If you had only realised the possibility of somebody some day collaring your study, you might have thought out dozens of sound schemes for dealing with the matter. As it is, you are unprepared. The thing comes on you as a surprise. The cry goes round: 'Spiller has been taken unawares. He cannot cope with the situation.'"

"Can't I! I'll——"

"What *are* you going to do about it?" said Mike.

"All I know is, I'm going to have it. It was Simpson's last term, and Simpson's left, and I'm next on the house list, so, of course, it's my study."

"But what steps," said Psmith, "are you going to take? Spiller, the man of Logic, we know. But what of Spiller, the Man of Action? How do you intend to set about it? Force is useless. I was saying to Comrade Jackson before you came in, that I didn't mind betting you were an insignificant-looking little weed. And you *are* an insignificant-looking little weed."

"We'll see what Outwood says about it."

"Not an unsound scheme. By no means a scaly project. Comrade Jackson and myself were about to interview him upon another point. We may as well all go together."

The trio made their way to the Presence, Spiller pink and determined, Mike sullen, Psmith particularly debonair. He hummed lightly as he walked, and now and then pointed out to Spiller objects of interest by the wayside.

Mr. Outwood received them with the motherly warmth which was evidently the leading characteristic of his normal manner.

"Ah, Spiller," he said. "And Smith, and Jackson. I am glad to see that you have already made friends."

"Spiller's, sir," said Psmith, laying a hand patronisingly on the study-claimer's shoulder—a proceeding violently resented by Spiller—"is a character one cannot help but respect. His nature expands before one like some beautiful flower."

Mr. Outwood received this eulogy with rather a startled expression, and gazed at the object of the tribute in a surprised way.

"Er—quite so, Smith, quite so," he said at last. "I like to see boys in my house friendly towards one another."

"There is no vice in Spiller," pursued Psmith earnestly. "His heart is the heart of a little child."

"Please, sir," burst out this paragon of all the virtues, "I——"

"But it was not entirely with regard to Spiller that I wished to speak to you, sir, if you were not too busy."

"Not at all, Smith, not at all. Is there anything——"

"Please, sir—" began Spiller.

"I understand, sir," said Psmith, "that there is an Archaeological Society in the school."

Mr. Outwood's eyes sparkled behind their pince-nez. It was a disappointment to him that so few boys seemed to wish to belong to his chosen band. Cricket and football, games that left him cold, appeared to be the main interest in their lives. It was but rarely that he could induce new boys to join. His colleague, Mr. Downing, who presided over the School Fire Brigade, never had any difficulty in finding support. Boys came readily at his call. Mr. Outwood pondered wistfully on this at times, not knowing that the Fire Brigade owed its support to the fact that it provided its light-hearted members with perfectly unparalleled opportunities for ragging, while his own band, though small, were in the main earnest.

"Yes, Smith." he said. "Yes. We have a small Archaeological Society. I—-er—-in a measure look after it. Perhaps you would care to become a member?"

"Please, sir—-" said Spiller.

"One moment, Spiller. Do you want to join, Smith?"

"Intensely, sir. Archaeology fascinates me. A grand pursuit, sir."

"Undoubtedly, Smith. I am very pleased, very pleased indeed. I will put down your name at once."

"And Jackson's, sir."

"Jackson, too!" Mr. Outwood beamed. "I am delighted. Most delighted. This is capital. This enthusiasm is most capital."

"Spiller, sir," said Psmith sadly, "I have been unable to induce to join."

"Oh, he is one of our oldest members."

"Ah," said Psmith, tolerantly, "that accounts for it."

"Please, sir—-" said Spiller.

"One moment, Spiller. We shall have the first outing of the term on Saturday. We intend to inspect the Roman Camp at Embury Hill, two miles from the school."

"We shall be there, sir."

"Capital!"

"Please, sir—-" said Spiller.

"One moment, Spiller," said Psmith. "There is just one other matter, if you could spare the time, sir."

"Certainly, Smith. What is that?"

"Would there be any objection to Jackson and myself taking Simpson's old study?"

"By all means, Smith. A very good idea."

"Yes, sir. It would give us a place where we could work quietly in the evenings."

"Quite so. Quite so."

"Thank you very much, sir. We will move our things in."

"Thank you very much, sir," said Mike.

"Please, sir," shouted Spiller, "aren't I to have it? I'm next on the list, sir. I come next after Simpson. Can't I have it?"

"I'm afraid I have already promised it to Smith, Spiller. You should have spoken before."

"But, sir——-"

Psmith eyed the speaker pityingly.

"This tendency to delay, Spiller," he said, "is your besetting fault. Correct it, Edwin. Fight against it."

He turned to Mr. Outwood.

"We should, of course, sir, always be glad to see Spiller in our study. He would always find a cheery welcome waiting there for him. There is no formality between ourselves and Spiller."

"Quite so. An excellent arrangement, Smith. I like this spirit of comradeship in my house. Then you will be with us on Saturday?"

"On Saturday, sir."

"All this sort of thing, Spiller," said Psmith, as they closed the door, "is very, very trying for a man of culture. Look us up in our study one of these afternoons."

CHAPTER XXXIV GUERRILLA WARFARE

"There are few pleasures," said Psmith, as he resumed his favourite position against the mantelpiece and surveyed the commandeered study with the pride of a householder, "keener to the reflective mind than sitting under one's own roof-tree. This place would have been wasted on Spiller; he would not have appreciated it properly."

Mike was finishing his tea. "You're a jolly useful chap to have by you in a crisis, Smith," he said with approval. "We ought to have known each other before."

"The loss was mine," said Psmith courteously. "We will now, with your permission, face the future for awhile. I suppose you realise that we are now to a certain extent up against it. Spiller's hot Spanish blood is not going to sit tight and do nothing under a blow like this."

"What can he do? Outwood's given us the study."

"What would you have done if somebody had bagged your study?"

"Made it jolly hot for them!"

"So will Comrade Spiller. I take it that he will collect a gang and make an offensive movement against us directly he can. To all appearances we are in a fairly tight place. It all depends on how big Comrade Spiller's gang will be. I don't like rows, but I'm prepared to take on a reasonable number of bravoes in defence of the home."

Mike intimated that he was with him on the point. "The difficulty is, though," he said, "about when we leave this room. I mean, we're all right while we stick here, but we can't stay all night."

"That's just what I was about to point out when you put it with such admirable clearness. Here we are in a stronghold, they can only get at us through the door, and we can lock that."

"And jam a chair against it."

"*And*, as you rightly remark, jam a chair against it. But what of the nightfall? What of the time when we retire to our dormitory?"

"Or dormitories. I say, if we're in separate rooms we shall be in the cart."

Psmith eyed Mike with approval. "He thinks of everything! You're the man, Comrade Jackson, to conduct an affair of this kind—-such foresight! such resource! We must see to this at once; if they put us in different rooms we're done—-we shall be destroyed singly in the watches of the night."

"We'd better nip down to the matron right off."

"Not the matron—-Comrade Outwood is the man. We are as sons to him; there is nothing he can deny us. I'm afraid we are quite spoiling his afternoon by these interruptions, but we must rout him out once more."

As they got up, the door handle rattled again, and this time there followed a knocking.

"This must be an emissary of Comrade Spiller's," said Psmith. "Let us parley with the man."

Mike unlocked the door. A light-haired youth with a cheerful, rather vacant face and a receding chin strolled into the room, and stood giggling with his hands in his pockets.

"I just came up to have a look at you," he explained.

"If you move a little to the left," said Psmith, "you will catch the light and shade effects on Jackson's face better."

The new-comer giggled with renewed vigour. "Are you the chap with the eyeglass who jaws all the time?"

"I *do* wear an eyeglass," said Psmith; "as to the rest of the description——-"

"My name's Jellicoe."

"Mine is Psmith—-P-s-m-i-t-h—-one of the Shropshire Psmiths. The object on the skyline is Comrade Jackson."

"Old Spiller," giggled Jellicoe, "is cursing you like anything downstairs. You *are* chaps! Do you mean to say you simply bagged his study? He's making no end of a row about it."

"Spiller's fiery nature is a byword," said Psmith.

"What's he going to do?" asked Mike, in his practical way.

"He's going to get the chaps to turn you out."

"As I suspected," sighed Psmith, as one mourning over the frailty of human nature. "About how many horny-handed assistants should you say that he would be likely to bring? Will you, for instance, join the glad throng?"

"Me? No fear! I think Spiller's an ass."

"There's nothing like a common thought for binding people together. *I* think Spiller's an ass."

"How many *will* there be, then?" asked Mike.

"He might get about half a dozen, not more, because most of the chaps don't see why they should sweat themselves just because Spiller's study has been bagged."

"Sturdy common sense," said Psmith approvingly, "seems to be the chief virtue of the Sedleigh character."

"We shall be able to tackle a crowd like that," said Mike. "The only thing is we must get into the same dormitory."

"This is where Comrade Jellicoe's knowledge of the local geography will come in useful. Do you happen to know of any snug little room, with, say, about four beds in it? How many dormitories are there?"

"Five—-there's one with three beds in it, only it belongs to three chaps."

"I believe in the equal distribution of property. We will go to Comrade Outwood and stake out another claim."

Mr. Outwood received them even more beamingly than before. "Yes, Smith?" he said.

"We must apologise for disturbing you, sir——-"

"Not at all, Smith, not at all! I like the boys in my house to come to me when they wish for my advice or help."

"We were wondering, sir, if you would have any objection to Jackson, Jellicoe and myself sharing the dormitory with the three beds in it. A very warm friendship—-" explained Psmith, patting the gurgling Jellicoe kindly on the shoulder, "has sprung up between Jackson, Jellicoe and myself."

"You make friends easily, Smith. I like to see it—-I like to see it."

"And we can have the room, sir?"

"Certainly—-certainly! Tell the matron as you go down."

"And now," said Psmith, as they returned to the study, "we may say that we are in a fairly winning position. A vote of thanks to Comrade Jellicoe for his valuable assistance."

"You *are* a chap!" said Jellicoe.

The handle began to revolve again.

"That door," said Psmith, "is getting a perfect incubus! It cuts into one's leisure cruelly."

This time it was a small boy. "They told me to come up and tell you to come down," he said.

Psmith looked at him searchingly through his eyeglass.

"Who?"

"The senior day-room chaps."

"Spiller?"

"Spiller and Robinson and Stone, and some other chaps."

"They want us to speak to them?"

"They told me to come up and tell you to come down."

"Go and give Comrade Spiller our compliments and say that we can't come down, but shall be delighted to see him up here. Things," he said, as the messenger departed, "are beginning to move. Better leave the door open, I think; it will save trouble. Ah, come in, Comrade Spiller, what can we do for you?"

Spiller advanced into the study; the others waited outside, crowding in the doorway.

"Look here," said Spiller, "are you going to clear out of here or not?"

"After Mr. Outwood's kindly thought in giving us the room? You suggest a black and ungrateful action, Comrade Spiller."

"You'll get it hot, if you don't."

"We'll risk it," said Mike.

Jellicoe giggled in the background; the drama in the atmosphere appealed to him. His was a simple and appreciative mind.

"Come on, you chaps," cried Spiller suddenly.

There was an inward rush on the enemy's part, but Mike had been watching. He grabbed Spiller by the shoulders and ran him back against the advancing crowd. For a moment the doorway was blocked, then the weight and impetus of Mike and Spiller prevailed, the enemy gave back, and Mike, stepping into the room again, slammed the door and locked it.

"A neat piece of work," said Psmith approvingly, adjusting his tie at the looking-glass. "The preliminaries may now be considered over, the first shot has been fired. The dogs of war are now loose."

A heavy body crashed against the door.

"They'll have it down," said Jellicoe.

"We must act, Comrade Jackson! Might I trouble you just to turn that key quietly, and the handle, and then to stand by for the next attack."

There was a scrambling of feet in the passage outside, and then a repetition of the onslaught on the door. This time, however, the door, instead of resisting, swung open, and the human battering-ram staggered through into the study. Mike, turning after re-locking the door, was just in time to see Psmith, with a display of energy of which one would not have believed him capable, grip the invader scientifically by an arm and a leg.

Mike jumped to help, but it was needless; the captive was already on the window-sill. As Mike arrived, Psmith dropped him on to the flower-bed below.

Psmith closed the window gently and turned to Jellicoe. "Who was our guest?" he asked, dusting the knees of his trousers where they had pressed against the wall.

"Robinson. I say, you *are* a chap!"

"Robinson, was it? Well, we are always glad to see Comrade Robinson, always. I wonder if anybody else is thinking of calling?"

Apparently frontal attack had been abandoned. Whisperings could be heard in the corridor.

Somebody hammered on the door.

"Yes?" called Psmith patiently.

"You'd better come out, you know; you'll only get it hotter if you don't."

"Leave us, Spiller; we would be alone."

A bell rang in the distance.

"Tea," said Jellicoe; "we shall have to go now."

"They won't do anything till after tea, I shouldn't think," said Mike. "There's no harm in going out."

The passage was empty when they opened the door; the call to food was evidently a thing not to be treated lightly by the enemy.

In the dining-room the beleaguered garrison were the object of general attention. Everybody turned to look at them as they came in. It was plain that the study episode had been a topic of conversation. Spiller's face was crimson, and Robinson's coat-sleeve still bore traces of garden mould.

Mike felt rather conscious of the eyes, but Psmith was in his element. His demeanour throughout the meal was that of some whimsical monarch condescending for a freak to revel with his humble subjects.

Towards the end of the meal Psmith scribbled a note and passed it to Mike. It read: "Directly this is over, nip upstairs as quickly as you can."

Mike followed the advice; they were first out of the room. When they had been in the study a few moments, Jellicoe knocked at the door. "Lucky you two cut away so quick," he said. "They were going to try and get you into the senior day-room and scrag you there."

"This," said Psmith, leaning against the mantelpiece, "is exciting, but it can't go on. We have got for our sins to be in this place for a whole term, and if we are going to do the Hunted Fawn business all the time, life in the true sense of the word will become an impossibility. My nerves are so delicately attuned that the strain would simply reduce them to hash. We are not prepared to carry on a long campaign—-the thing must be settled at once."

"Shall we go down to the senior day-room, and have it out?" said Mike.

"No, we will play the fixture on our own ground. I think we may take it as tolerably certain that Comrade Spiller and his hired ruffians will try to corner us in the dormitory to-night. Well, of course, we could fake up some sort of barricade for the door, but then we should have all the trouble over again to-morrow and the day after that. Personally I don't propose to be chivvied about indefinitely like this, so I propose that we let them come into the dormitory, and see what happens. Is this meeting with me?"

"I think that's sound," said Mike. "We needn't drag Jellicoe into it."

"As a matter of fact—-if you don't mind—-" began that man of peace.

"Quite right," said Psmith; "this is not Comrade Jellicoe's scene at all; he has got to spend the term in the senior day-room, whereas we have our little wooden *châlet* to retire to in times of stress. Comrade Jellicoe must stand out of the game altogether. We shall be glad of his moral support, but otherwise, *ne pas*. And now, as there won't be anything doing till bedtime, I think I'll collar this table and write home and tell my people that all is well with their Rupert."

CHAPTER XXXV UNPLEASANTNESS IN THE SMALL HOURS

Jellicoe, that human encyclopaedia, consulted on the probable movements of the enemy, deposed that Spiller, retiring at ten, would make for Dormitory One in the same passage, where Robinson also had a bed. The rest of the opposing forces were distributed among other and more distant rooms. It was probable, therefore, that Dormitory One would be the rendezvous. As to the time when an attack might be expected, it was unlikely that it would occur before half-past eleven. Mr. Outwood went the round of the dormitories at eleven.

"And touching," said Psmith, "the matter of noise, must this business be conducted in a subdued and *sotto voce* manner, or may we let ourselves go a bit here and there?"

"I shouldn't think old Outwood's likely to hear you—-he sleeps miles away on the other side of the house. He never hears anything. We often rag half the night and nothing happens."

This appears to be a thoroughly nice, well-conducted establishment. What would my mother say if she could see her Rupert in the midst of these reckless youths!"

"All the better," said Mike; "we don't want anybody butting in and stopping the show before it's half started."

"Comrade Jackson's Berserk blood is up—-I can hear it sizzling. I quite agree these things are all very disturbing and painful, but it's as well to do them thoroughly when one's once in for them. Is there nobody else who might interfere with our gambols?"

"Barnes might," said Jellicoe, "only he won't."

"Who is Barnes?"

"Head of the house—-a rotter. He's in a funk of Stone and Robinson; they rag him; he'll simply sit tight."

"Then I think," said Psmith placidly, "we may look forward to a very pleasant evening. Shall we be moving?"

Mr. Outwood paid his visit at eleven, as predicted by Jellicoe, beaming vaguely into the darkness over a candle, and disappeared again, closing the door.

"How about that door?" said Mike. "Shall we leave it open for them?"

"Not so, but far otherwise. If it's shut we shall hear them at it when they come. Subject to your approval, Comrade Jackson, I have evolved the following plan of action. I always ask myself on these occasions, 'What would Napoleon have done?' I think Napoleon would have sat in a chair by his washhand-stand, which is close to the door; he would have posted you by your washhand-stand, and he would have instructed Comrade Jellicoe, directly he heard the door-handle turned, to give his celebrated imitation of a dormitory breathing heavily in its sleep. He would then——"

"I tell you what," said Mike, "how about tying a string at the top of the steps?"

"Yes, Napoleon would have done that, too. Hats off to Comrade Jackson, the man with the big brain!"

The floor of the dormitory was below the level of the door. There were three steps leading down to it. Psmith lit a candle and they examined the ground. The leg of a wardrobe and the leg of Jellicoe's bed made it possible for the string to be fastened in a satisfactory manner across the lower step. Psmith surveyed the result with approval.

"Dashed neat!" he said. "Practically the sunken road which dished the Cuirassiers at Waterloo. I seem to see Comrade Spiller coming one of the finest purlers in the world's history."

"If they've got a candle——"

"They won't have. If they have, stand by with your water-jug and douse it at once; then they'll charge forward and all will be well. If they have no candle, fling the water at a venture—fire into the brown! Lest we forget, I'll collar Comrade Jellicoe's jug now and keep it handy. A couple of sheets would also not be amiss—we will enmesh the enemy!"

"Right ho!" said Mike.

"These humane preparations being concluded," said Psmith, "we will retire to our posts and wait. Comrade Jellicoe, don't forget to breathe like an asthmatic sheep when you hear the door opened; they may wait at the top of the steps, listening."

"You *are* a chap!" said Jellicoe.

Waiting in the dark for something to happen is always a trying experience, especially if, as on this occasion, silence is essential. Mike found his thoughts wandering back to the vigil he had kept with Mr. Wain at Wrykyn on the night when Wyatt had come in through the window and found authority sitting on his bed, waiting for him. Mike was tired after his journey, and he had begun to doze when he was jerked back to wakefulness by the stealthy turning of the door-handle; the faintest rustle from Psmith's direction followed, and a slight giggle, succeeded by a series of deep breaths, showed that Jellicoe, too, had heard the noise.

There was a creaking sound.

It was pitch-dark in the dormitory, but Mike could follow the invaders' movements as clearly as if it had been broad daylight. They had opened the door and were listening. Jellicoe's breathing grew more asthmatic; he was flinging himself into his part with the whole-heartedness of the true artist.

The creak was followed by a sound of whispering, then another creak. The enemy had advanced to the top step.... Another creak.... The vanguard had reached the second step.... In another moment——-

CRASH!

And at that point the proceedings may be said to have formally opened.

A struggling mass bumped against Mike's shins as he rose from his chair; he emptied his jug on to this mass, and a yell of anguish showed that the contents had got to the right address.

Then a hand grabbed his ankle and he went down, a million sparks dancing before his eyes as a fist, flying out at a venture, caught him on the nose.

Mike had not been well-disposed towards the invaders before, but now he ran amok, hitting out right and left at random. His right missed, but his left went home hard on some portion of somebody's anatomy. A kick freed his ankle and he staggered to his feet. At the same moment a sudden increase in the general volume of noise spoke eloquently of good work that was being put in by Psmith.

Even at that crisis, Mike could not help feeling that if a row of this calibre did not draw Mr. Outwood from his bed, he must be an unusual kind of house-master.

He plunged forward again with outstretched arms, and stumbled and fell over one of the on-the-floor section of the opposing force. They seized each other earnestly and rolled across the room till Mike, contriving to secure his adversary's head, bumped it on the floor with such abandon that, with a muffled yell, the other let go, and for the second time he rose. As he did so he was conscious of a curious thudding sound that made itself heard through the other assorted noises of the battle.

All this time the fight had gone on in the blackest darkness, but now a light shone on the proceedings. Interested occupants of other dormitories, roused from their slumbers, had come to observe the sport. They were crowding in the doorway with a candle.

By the light of this Mike got a swift view of the theatre of war. The enemy appeared to number five. The warrior whose head Mike had bumped on the floor was Robinson, who was sitting up feeling his skull in a gingerly fashion. To Mike's right, almost touching him, was Stone. In the direction of the door, Psmith, wielding in his right hand the cord of a dressing-gown, was engaging the remaining three with a patient smile. They were clad in pyjamas, and appeared to be feeling the dressing-gown cord acutely.

The sudden light dazed both sides momentarily. The defence was the first to recover, Mike, with a swing, upsetting Stone, and Psmith, having seized and emptied Jellicoe's jug over Spiller, getting to work again with the cord in a manner that roused the utmost enthusiasm of the spectators.

Agility seemed to be the leading feature of Psmith's tactics. He was everywhere—-on Mike's bed, on his own, on Jellicoe's (drawing a passionate complaint from that non-combatant, on whose face he inadvertently trod), on the floor—-he ranged the room, sowing destruction.

PSMITH SEIZED AND EMPTIED JELLICOE'S JUG OVER SPILLER

The enemy were disheartened; they had started with the idea that this was to be a surprise attack, and it was disconcerting to find the garrison armed at all points. Gradually they edged to the door, and a final rush sent them through.

"Hold the door for a second," cried Psmith, and vanished. Mike was alone in the doorway.

It was a situation which exactly suited his frame of mind; he stood alone in direct opposition to the community into which Fate had pitchforked him so abruptly. He liked the feeling; for the first time since his father had given him his views upon school reports that morning in the Easter holidays, he felt satisfied with life. He hoped, outnumbered as he was, that the enemy would come on again and not give the thing up in disgust; he wanted more.

On an occasion like this there is rarely anything approaching concerted action on the part of the aggressors. When the attack came, it was not a combined attack; Stone, who was nearest to the door, made a sudden dash forward, and Mike hit him under the chin.

Stone drew back, and there was another interval for rest and reflection.

It was interrupted by the reappearance of Psmith, who strolled back along the passage swinging his dressing-gown cord as if it were some clouded cane.

"Sorry to keep you waiting, Comrade Jackson," he said politely. "Duty called me elsewhere. With the kindly aid of a guide who knows the lie of the land, I have been making a short tour of the dormitories. I have poured divers jugfuls of water over Comrade Spiller's bed, Comrade Robinson's bed, Comrade Stone's—-Spiller, Spiller, these are harsh words; where you pick them up I can't think—-not from me. Well, well, I suppose there must be an end to the pleasantest of functions. Good-night, good-night."

The door closed behind Mike and himself. For ten minutes shufflings and whisperings went on in the corridor, but nobody touched the handle.

Then there was a sound of retreating footsteps, and silence reigned.

On the following morning there was a notice on the house-board. It ran:

> **INDOOR GAMES**
>
> *Dormitory-raiders are informed that in future neither Mr. Psmith nor Mr. Jackson will be at home to visitors. This nuisance must now cease.*
>
> R. PSMITH.
> M. JACKSON.

CHAPTER XXXVI ADAIR

On the same morning Mike met Adair for the first time.

He was going across to school with Psmith and Jellicoe, when a group of three came out of the gate of the house next door.

"That's Adair," said Jellicoe, "in the middle."

His voice had assumed a tone almost of awe.

"Who's Adair?" asked Mike.

"Captain of cricket, and lots of other things."

Mike could only see the celebrity's back. He had broad shoulders and wiry, light hair, almost white. He walked well, as if he were used to running. Altogether a fit-looking sort of man. Even Mike's jaundiced eye saw that.

As a matter of fact, Adair deserved more than a casual glance. He was that rare type, the natural leader. Many boys and men, if accident, or the passage of time, places them in a position where they are expected to lead, can handle the job without disaster; but that is a very different thing from being a born leader. Adair was of the sort that comes to the top by sheer force of character and determination. He was not naturally clever at work, but he had gone at it with a dogged resolution which had carried him up the school, and landed him high in the Sixth. As a cricketer he was almost entirely self-taught. Nature had given him a good eye, and left the thing at that. Adair's doggedness had triumphed over her failure to do her work thoroughly. At the cost of more trouble than most people give to their life-work he had made himself into a bowler. He read the authorities, and watched first-class players, and thought the thing out on his own account, and he divided the art of bowling into three sections. First, and most important—-pitch. Second on the list—-break. Third—-pace. He set himself to acquire pitch. He acquired it. Bowling at his own pace and without any attempt at break, he could now drop the ball on an envelope seven times out of ten.

Break was a more uncertain quantity. Sometimes he could get it at the expense of pitch, sometimes at the expense of pace. Some days he could get all three, and then he was an uncommonly bad man to face on anything but a plumb wicket.

Running he had acquired in a similar manner. He had nothing approaching style, but he had twice won the mile and half-mile at the Sports off elegant runners, who knew all about stride and the correct timing of the sprints and all the rest of it.

Briefly, he was a worker. He had heart.

A boy of Adair's type is always a force in a school. In a big public school of six or seven hundred, his influence is felt less; but in a small school like Sedleigh he is like a tidal wave, sweeping all before him. There were two hundred boys at Sedleigh, and there was not one of them in all probability who had not, directly or indirectly, been influenced by Adair. As a small boy his sphere was not large, but the effects of his work began to be apparent even then. It is human nature to want to get something which somebody else obviously values very much; and when it was observed by members of his form that Adair was going to great trouble and inconvenience to secure a place in the form eleven or fifteen, they naturally began to think, too, that it was worth being in those teams. The consequence was that his form always played hard. This made other forms play hard. And the net result was that, when Adair succeeded to the captaincy of football and cricket in the same year, Sedleigh, as Mr. Downing, Adair's house-master and the nearest approach to a cricket-master that Sedleigh possessed, had a fondness for saying, was a keen school. As a whole, it both worked and played with energy.

All it wanted now was opportunity.

This Adair was determined to give it. He had that passionate fondness for his school which every boy is popularly supposed to have, but which really is implanted in about one in every thousand. The average public-school boy *likes* his school. He hopes it will lick Bedford at footer and Malvern at cricket, but he rather bets it won't. He is sorry to leave, and he likes going back at the end of the holidays, but as for any passionate, deep-seated love of the place, he would think it rather bad form than otherwise. If anybody came up to him, slapped him on the back, and cried, "Come along, Jenkins, my boy! Play up for the old school, Jenkins! The dear old school! The old place you love so!" he would feel seriously ill.

Adair was the exception.

To Adair, Sedleigh was almost a religion. Both his parents were dead; his guardian, with whom he spent the holidays, was a man with neuralgia at one end of him and gout at the other; and the only really pleasant times Adair had had, as far back as he could remember, he owed to Sedleigh. The place had grown on him, absorbed him. Where Mike, violently transplanted from Wrykyn, saw only a wretched little hole not to be mentioned in the same breath with Wrykyn, Adair, dreaming of the future, saw a colossal establishment, a public school among public schools, a lump of human radium, shooting out Blues and Balliol Scholars year after year without ceasing.

It would not be so till long after he was gone and forgotten, but he did not mind that. His devotion to Sedleigh was purely unselfish. He did not want fame. All he worked for was that the school should grow and grow, keener and better at games and more prosperous year by year, till it should take its rank among *the* schools, and to be an Old Sedleighan should be a badge passing its owner everywhere.

"He's captain of cricket and footer," said Jellicoe impressively. "He's in the shooting eight. He's won the mile and half two years running. He would have boxed at Aldershot last term, only he sprained his wrist. And he plays fives jolly well!"

"Sort of little tin god," said Mike, taking a violent dislike to Adair from that moment.

Mike's actual acquaintance with this all-round man dated from the dinner-hour that day. Mike was walking to the house with Psmith. Psmith was a little ruffled on account of a slight passage-of-arms he had had with his form-master during morning school.

"'There's a P before the Smith,' I said to him. 'Ah, P. Smith, I see,' replied the goat. 'Not Peasmith,' I replied, exercising wonderful self-restraint, 'just Psmith.' It took me ten minutes to drive the thing into the man's head; and when I *had* driven it in, he sent me out of the room for looking at him through my eye-glass. Comrade Jackson, I fear me we have fallen among bad men. I suspect that we are going to be much persecuted by scoundrels."

"Both you chaps play cricket, I suppose?"

They turned. It was Adair. Seeing him face to face, Mike was aware of a pair of very bright blue eyes and a square jaw. In any other place and mood he would have liked Adair at sight. His prejudice, however, against all things Sedleighan was too much for him. "I don't," he said shortly.

"Haven't you *ever* played?"

"My little sister and I sometimes play with a soft ball at home."

Adair looked sharply at him. A temper was evidently one of his numerous qualities.

"Oh," he said. "Well, perhaps you wouldn't mind turning out this afternoon and seeing what you can do with a hard ball—-if you can manage without your little sister."

"I should think the form at this place would be about on a level with hers. But I don't happen to be playing cricket, as I think I told you."

Adair's jaw grew squarer than ever. Mike was wearing a gloomy scowl.

Psmith joined suavely in the dialogue.

"My dear old comrades," he said, "don't let us brawl over this matter. This is a time for the honeyed word, the kindly eye, and the pleasant smile. Let me explain to Comrade Adair. Speaking for Comrade Jackson and myself, we should both be delighted to join in the mimic warfare of our National Game, as you suggest, only the fact is, we happen to be the Young Archaeologists. We gave in our names last night. When you are being carried back to the pavilion after your century against Loamshire—-do you play Loamshire?—-we shall be grubbing in the hard ground for ruined abbeys. The old choice between Pleasure and Duty, Comrade Adair. A Boy's Cross-Roads."

"Then you won't play?"

"No," said Mike.

"Archaeology," said Psmith, with a deprecatory wave of the hand, "will brook no divided allegiance from her devotees."

Adair turned, and walked on.

Scarcely had he gone, when another voice hailed them with precisely the same question.

"Both you fellows are going to play cricket, eh?"

It was a master. A short, wiry little man with a sharp nose and a general resemblance, both in manner and appearance, to an excitable bullfinch.

"I saw Adair speaking to you. I suppose you will both play. I like every new boy to begin at once. The more new blood we have, the better. We want keenness here. We are, above all, a keen school. I want every boy to be keen."

"We are, sir," said Psmith, with fervour.

"Excellent."

"On archaeology."

Mr. Downing—for it was no less a celebrity—started, as one who perceives a loathly caterpillar in his salad.

"Archaeology!"

"We gave in our names to Mr. Outwood last night, sir. Archaeology is a passion with us, sir. When we heard that there was a society here, we went singing about the house."

"I call it an unnatural pursuit for boys," said Mr. Downing vehemently. "I don't like it. I tell you I don't like it. It is not for me to interfere with one of my colleagues on the staff, but I tell you frankly that in my opinion it is an abominable waste of time for a boy. It gets him into idle, loafing habits."

"I never loaf, sir," said Psmith.

"I was not alluding to you in particular. I was referring to the principle of the thing. A boy ought to be playing cricket with other boys, not wandering at large about the country, probably smoking and going into low public-houses."

"A very wild lot, sir, I fear, the Archaeological Society here," sighed Psmith, shaking his head.

"If you choose to waste your time, I suppose I can't hinder you. But in my opinion it is foolery, nothing else."

He stumped off.

"Now *he's* cross," said Psmith, looking after him. "I'm afraid we're getting ourselves disliked here."

"Good job, too."

"At any rate, Comrade Outwood loves us. Let's go on and see what sort of a lunch that large-hearted fossil-fancier is going to give us."

CHAPTER XXXVII MIKE FINDS OCCUPATION

There was more than one moment during the first fortnight of term when Mike found himself regretting the attitude he had imposed upon himself with regard to Sedleighan cricket. He began to realise the eternal truth of the proverb about half a loaf and no bread. In the first flush of his resentment against his new surroundings he had refused to play cricket. And now he positively ached for a game. Any sort of a game. An innings for a Kindergarten *v.* the Second Eleven of a Home of Rest for Centenarians would have soothed him. There were times, when the sun shone, and he caught sight of white flannels on a green ground, and heard the "plonk" of bat striking ball, when he felt like rushing to Adair and shouting, "I *will* be good. I was in the Wrykyn team three years, and had an average of over fifty the last two seasons. Lead me to the nearest net, and let me feel a bat in my hands again."

But every time he shrank from such a climb down. It couldn't be done.

What made it worse was that he saw, after watching behind the nets once or twice, that Sedleigh cricket was not the childish burlesque of the game which he had been rash enough to assume that it must be. Numbers do not make good cricket. They only make the presence of good cricketers more likely, by the law of averages.

Mike soon saw that cricket was by no means an unknown art at Sedleigh. Adair, to begin with, was a very good bowler indeed. He was not a Burgess, but Burgess was the only Wrykyn bowler whom, in his three years' experience of the school, Mike would have placed above him. He was a long way better than Neville-Smith, and Wyatt, and Milton, and the others who had taken wickets for Wrykyn.

The batting was not so good, but there were some quite capable men. Barnes, the head of Outwood's, he who preferred not to interfere with Stone and Robinson, was a mild, rather timid-looking youth—-not unlike what Mr. Outwood must have been as a boy—-but he knew how to keep balls out of his wicket. He was a good bat of the old plodding type.

Stone and Robinson themselves, that swash-buckling pair, who now treated Mike and Psmith with cold but consistent politeness, were both fair batsmen, and Stone was a good slow bowler.

There were other exponents of the game, mostly in Downing's house.

Altogether, quite worthy colleagues even for a man who had been a star at Wrykyn.

One solitary overture Mike made during that first fortnight. He did not repeat the experiment. It was on a Thursday afternoon, after school. The day was warm, but freshened by an almost imperceptible breeze. The air was full of the scent of the cut grass which lay in little heaps behind the nets. This is the real cricket scent, which calls to one like the very voice of the game.

Mike, as he sat there watching, could stand it no longer.

He went up to Adair.

"May I have an innings at this net?" he asked. He was embarrassed and nervous, and was trying not to show it. The natural result was that his manner was offensively abrupt.

Adair was taking off his pads after his innings. He looked up. "This net," it may be observed, was the first eleven net.

"What?" he said.

Mike repeated his request. More abruptly this time, from increased embarrassment.

"This is the first eleven net," said Adair coldly. "Go in after Lodge over there."

"Over there" was the end net, where frenzied novices were bowling on a corrugated pitch to a red-haired youth with enormous feet, who looked as if he were taking his first lesson at the game.

Mike walked away without a word.

The Archaeological Society expeditions, even though they carried with them the privilege of listening to Psmith's views on life, proved but a poor substitute for cricket. Psmith, who had no counter-attraction shouting to him that he ought to be elsewhere, seemed to enjoy them hugely, but Mike almost cried sometimes from boredom. It was not always possible to slip away from the throng, for Mr. Outwood evidently looked upon them as among the very faithful, and kept them by his aide.

Mike on these occasions was silent and jumpy, his brow "sicklied o'er with the pale cast of care." But Psmith followed his leader with the pleased and indulgent air of a father whose infant son is showing him round the garden. Psmith's attitude towards archaeological research struck a new note in the history of that neglected science. He was amiable, but patronising. He patronised fossils, and he patronised ruins. If he had been confronted with the Great Pyramid, he would have patronised that.

He seemed to be consumed by a thirst for knowledge.

That this was not altogether a genuine thirst was proved on the third expedition. Mr. Outwood and his band were pecking away at the site of an old Roman camp. Psmith approached Mike.

"Having inspired confidence," he said, "by the docility of our demeanour, let us slip away, and brood apart for awhile. Roman camps, to be absolutely accurate, give me the pip. And I never want to see another putrid fossil in my life. Let us find some shady nook where a man may lie on his back for a bit."

Mike, over whom the proceedings connected with the Roman camp had long since begun to shed a blue depression, offered no opposition, and they strolled away down the hill.

Looking back, they saw that the archaeologists were still hard at it. Their departure had passed unnoticed.

"A fatiguing pursuit, this grubbing for mementoes of the past," said Psmith. "And, above all, dashed bad for the knees of the trousers. Mine are like some furrowed field. It's a great grief to a man of refinement, I can tell you, Comrade Jackson. Ah, this looks a likely spot."

They had passed through a gate into the field beyond. At the further end there was a brook, shaded by trees and running with a pleasant sound over pebbles.

"Thus far," said Psmith, hitching up the knees of his trousers, and sitting down, "and no farther. We will rest here awhile, and listen to the music of the brook. In fact, unless you have anything important to say, I rather think I'll go to sleep. In this busy life of ours these naps by the wayside are invaluable. Call me in about an hour." And Psmith, heaving the comfortable sigh of the worker who by toil has earned rest, lay down, with his head against a mossy tree-stump, and closed his eyes.

Mike sat on for a few minutes, listening to the water and making centuries in his mind, and then, finding this a little dull, he got up, jumped the brook, and began to explore the wood on the other side.

He had not gone many yards when a dog emerged suddenly from the undergrowth, and began to bark vigorously at him.

Mike liked dogs, and, on acquaintance, they always liked him. But when you meet a dog in some one else's wood, it is as well not to stop in order that you may get to understand each other. Mike began to thread his way back through the trees.

He was too late.

"Stop! What the dickens are you doing here?" shouted a voice behind him.

In the same situation a few years before, Mike would have carried on, and trusted to speed to save him. But now there seemed a lack of dignity in the action. He came back to where the man was standing.

"I'm sorry if I'm trespassing," he said. "I was just having a look round."

"The dickens you—-Why, you're Jackson!"

Mike looked at him. He was a short, broad young man with a fair moustache. Mike knew that he had seen him before somewhere, but he could not place him.

"I played against you, for the Free Foresters last summer. In passing, you seem to be a bit of a free forester yourself, dancing in among my nesting pheasants."

"I'm frightfully sorry."

"That's all right. Where do you spring from?"

"Of course—-I remember you now. You're Prendergast. You made fifty-eight not out."

"Thanks. I was afraid the only thing you would remember about me was that you took a century mostly off my bowling."

"You ought to have had me second ball, only cover dropped it."

"Don't rake up forgotten tragedies. How is it you're not at Wrykyn? What are you doing down here?"

"I've left Wrykyn."

Prendergast suddenly changed the conversation. When a fellow tells you that he has left school unexpectedly, it is not always tactful to inquire the reason. He began to talk about himself.

"I hang out down here. I do a little farming and a good deal of pottering about."

"Get any cricket?" asked Mike, turning to the subject next his heart.

"Only village. Very keen, but no great shakes. By the way, how are you off for cricket now? Have you ever got a spare afternoon?"

Mike's heart leaped.

"Any Wednesday or Saturday. Look here, I'll tell you how it is."

And he told how matters stood with him.

"So, you see," he concluded, "I'm supposed to be hunting for ruins and things"—-Mike's ideas on the subject of archaeology were vague—-"but I could always slip away. We all start out together, but I could nip back, get on to my bike—-I've got it down here—-and meet you anywhere you liked. By Jove, I'm simply dying for a game. I can hardly keep my hands off a bat."

"I'll give you all you want. What you'd better do is to ride straight to Lower Borlock—-that's the name of the place—-and I'll meet you on the ground. Any one will tell you where Lower Borlock is. It's just off the London road. There's a sign-post where you turn off. Can you come next Saturday?"

"Rather. I suppose you can fix me up with a bat and pads? I don't want to bring mine."

"I'll lend you everything. I say, you know, we can't give you a Wrykyn wicket. The Lower Borlock pitch isn't a shirt-front."

"I'll play on a rockery, if you want me to," said Mike.

"You're going to what?" asked Psmith, sleepily, on being awakened and told the news.

"I'm going to play cricket, for a village near here. I say, don't tell a soul, will you? I don't want it to get about, or I may get lugged in to play for the school."

"My lips are sealed. I think I'll come and watch you. Cricket I dislike, but watching cricket is one of the finest of Britain's manly sports. I'll borrow Jellicoe's bicycle."

That Saturday, Lower Borlock smote the men of Chidford hip and thigh. Their victory was due to a hurricane innings of seventy-five by a new-comer to the team, M. Jackson.

CHAPTER XXXVIII THE FIRE BRIGADE MEETING

Cricket is the great safety-valve. If you like the game, and are in a position to play it at least twice a week, life can never be entirely grey. As time went on, and his average for Lower Borlock reached the fifties and stayed there, Mike began, though he would not have admitted it, to enjoy himself. It was not Wrykyn, but it was a very decent substitute.

The only really considerable element making for discomfort now was Mr. Downing. By bad luck it was in his form that Mike had been placed on arrival; and Mr. Downing, never an easy form-master to get on with, proved more than usually difficult in his dealings with Mike.

They had taken a dislike to each other at their first meeting; and it grew with further acquaintance. To Mike, Mr. Downing was all that a master ought not to be, fussy, pompous, and openly influenced in his official dealings with his form by his own private likes and dislikes. To Mr. Downing, Mike was simply an unamiable loafer, who did nothing for the school and apparently had none of the instincts which should be implanted in the healthy boy. Mr. Downing was rather strong on the healthy boy.

The two lived in a state of simmering hostility, punctuated at intervals by crises, which usually resulted in Lower Borlock having to play some unskilled labourer in place of their star batsman, employed doing "over-time."

One of the most acute of these crises, and the most important, in that it was the direct cause of Mike's appearance in Sedleigh cricket, had to do with the third weekly meeting of the School Fire Brigade.

It may be remembered that this well-supported institution was under Mr. Downing's special care. It was, indeed, his pet hobby and the apple of his eye.

Just as you had to join the Archaeological Society to secure the esteem of Mr. Outwood, so to become a member of the Fire Brigade was a safe passport to the regard of Mr. Downing. To show a keenness for cricket was good, but to join the Fire Brigade was best of all. The Brigade was carefully organised. At its head was Mr. Downing, a sort of high priest; under him was a captain, and under the captain a vice-captain. These two officials were those sportive allies, Stone and Robinson, of Outwood's house, who, having perceived at a very early date the gorgeous opportunities for ragging which the Brigade offered to its members, had joined young and worked their way up.

Under them were the rank and file, about thirty in all, of whom perhaps seven were earnest workers, who looked on the Brigade in the right, or Downing, spirit. The rest were entirely frivolous.

The weekly meetings were always full of life and excitement.

At this point it is as well to introduce Sammy to the reader.

Sammy, short for Sampson, was a young bull-terrier belonging to Mr. Downing. If it is possible for a man to have two apples of his eye, Sammy was the other. He was a large, light-hearted dog with a white coat, an engaging expression, the tongue of an ant-eater, and a manner which was a happy blend of hurricane and circular saw. He had long legs, a tenor voice, and was apparently made of india-rubber.

Sammy was a great favourite in the school, and a particular friend of Mike's, the Wrykynian being always a firm ally of every dog he met after two minutes' acquaintance.

In passing, Jellicoe owned a clock-work rat, much in request during French lessons.

We will now proceed to the painful details.

The meetings of the Fire Brigade were held after school in Mr. Downing's form-room. The proceedings always began in the same way, by the reading of the minutes of the last meeting. After that the entertainment varied according to whether the members happened to be fertile or not in ideas for the disturbing of the peace.

To-day they were in very fair form.

As soon as Mr. Downing had closed the minute-book, Wilson, of the School House, held up his hand.

"Well, Wilson?"

"Please, sir, couldn't we have a uniform for the Brigade?"

"A uniform?" Mr. Downing pondered

"Red, with green stripes, sir,"

Red, with a thin green stripe, was the Sedleigh colour.

"Shall I put it to the vote, sir?" asked Stone.

"One moment, Stone."

"Those in favour of the motion move to the left, those against it to the right."

A scuffling of feet, a slamming of desk-lids and an upset blackboard, and the meeting had divided.

Mr. Downing rapped irritably on his desk.

"Sit down!" he said, "sit down! I won't have this noise and disturbance. Stone, sit down—-Wilson, get back to your place."

"Please, sir, the motion is carried by twenty-five votes to six."

"Please, sir, may I go and get measured this evening?"

"Please, sir——-"

"Si-*lence*! The idea of a uniform is, of course, out of the question."

"Oo-oo-oo-oo, sir-r-r!"

"Be *quiet!* Entirely out of the question. We cannot plunge into needless expense. Stone, listen to me. I cannot have this noise and disturbance! Another time when a point arises it must be settled by a show of hands. Well, Wilson?"

"Please, sir, may we have helmets?"

"Very useful as a protection against falling timbers, sir," said Robinson.

"I don't think my people would be pleased, sir, if they knew I was going out to fires without a helmet," said Stone.

The whole strength of the company: "Please, sir, may we have helmets?"

"Those in favour—-" began Stone.

Mr. Downing banged on his desk. "Silence! Silence!! Silence!!! Helmets are, of course, perfectly preposterous."

"Oo-oo-oo-oo, sir-r-r!"

"But, sir, the danger!"

"Please, sir, the falling timbers!"

The Fire Brigade had been in action once and once only in the memory of man, and that time it was a haystack which had burnt itself out just as the rescuers had succeeded in fastening the hose to the hydrant.

"Silence!"

"Then, please, sir, couldn't we have an honour cap? It wouldn't be expensive, and it would be just as good as a helmet for all the timbers that are likely to fall on our heads."

Mr. Downing smiled a wry smile.

"Our Wilson is facetious," he remarked frostily.

"Sir, no, sir! I wasn't facetious! Or couldn't we have footer-tops, like the first fifteen have? They——-"

"Wilson, leave the room!"

"Sir, *please*, sir!"

"This moment, Wilson. And," as he reached the door, "do me one hundred lines."

A pained "OO-oo-oo, sir-r-r," was cut off by the closing door.

Mr. Downing proceeded to improve the occasion. "I deplore this growing spirit of flippancy," he said. "I tell you I deplore it! It is not right! If this Fire Brigade is to be of solid use, there must be less of this flippancy. We must have keenness. I want you boys above all to be keen. I—-What is that noise?"

From the other side of the door proceeded a sound like water gurgling from a bottle, mingled with cries half-suppressed, as if somebody were being prevented from uttering them by a hand laid over his mouth. The sufferer appeared to have a high voice.

There was a tap at the door and Mike walked in. He was not alone. Those near enough to see, saw that he was accompanied by Jellicoe's clock-work rat, which moved rapidly over the floor in the direction of the opposite wall.

"May I fetch a book from my desk, sir?" asked Mike.

"Very well—-be quick, Jackson; we are busy."

CHAPTER XXXVIII THE FIRE BRIGADE MEETING

Being interrupted in one of his addresses to the Brigade irritated Mr. Downing.

The muffled cries grew more distinct.

"What—-is—-that—-noise?" shrilled Mr. Downing.

"Noise, sir?" asked Mike, puzzled.

"I think it's something outside the window, sir," said Stone helpfully.

"A bird, I think, sir," said Robinson.

"Don't be absurd!" snapped Mr. Downing. "It's outside the door. Wilson!"

"Yes, sir?" said a voice "off."

"Are you making that whining noise?"

"Whining noise, sir? No, sir, I'm not making a whining noise."

"What *sort* of noise, sir?" inquired Mike, as many Wrykynians had asked before him. It was a question invented by Wrykyn for use in just such a case as this.

"I do not propose," said Mr. Downing acidly, "to imitate the noise; you can all hear it perfectly plainly. It is a curious whining noise."

"They are mowing the cricket field, sir," said the invisible Wilson. "Perhaps that's it."

"It may be one of the desks squeaking, sir," put in Stone. "They do sometimes."

"Or somebody's boots, sir," added Robinson.

"Silence! Wilson?"

"Yes, sir?" bellowed the unseen one.

"Don't shout at me from the corridor like that. Come in."

"Yes, sir!"

As he spoke the muffled whining changed suddenly to a series of tenor shrieks, and the india-rubber form of Sammy bounded into the room like an excited kangaroo.

Willing hands had by this time deflected the clockwork rat from the wall to which it had been steering, and pointed it up the alley-way between the two rows of desks. Mr. Downing, rising from his place, was just in time to see Sammy with a last leap spring on his prey and begin worrying it.

Chaos reigned.

"A rat!" shouted Robinson.

The twenty-three members of the Brigade who were not earnest instantly dealt with the situation, each in the manner that seemed proper to him. Some leaped on to forms, others flung books, all shouted. It was a stirring, bustling scene.

Sammy had by this time disposed of the clock-work rat, and was now standing, like Marius, among the ruins barking triumphantly.

The banging on Mr. Downing's desk resembled thunder. It rose above all the other noises till in time they gave up the competition and died away.

Mr. Downing shot out orders, threats, and penalties with the rapidity of a Maxim gun.

"Stone, sit down! Donovan, if you do not sit down, you will be severely punished. Henderson, one hundred lines for gross disorder! Windham, the same! Go to your seat, Vincent. What are you doing, Broughton-Knight? I will not have this disgraceful noise and disorder! The meeting is at an end; go quietly from the room, all of you. Jackson and Wilson, remain. *Quietly*, I said, Durand! Don't shuffle your feet in that abominable way."

Crash!

"Wolferstan, I distinctly saw you upset that black-board with a movement of your hand—-one hundred lines. Go quietly from the room, everybody."

The meeting dispersed.

"Jackson and Wilson, come here. What's the meaning of this disgraceful conduct? Put that dog out of the room, Jackson."

Mike removed the yelling Sammy and shut the door on him.

"Well, Wilson?"

"Please, sir, I was playing with a clock-work rat——-"

"What business have you to be playing with clock-work rats?"

"Then I remembered," said Mike, "that I had left my Horace in my desk, so I came in——-"

"And by a fluke, sir," said Wilson, as one who tells of strange things, "the rat happened to be pointing in the same direction, so he came in, too."

"I met Sammy on the gravel outside and he followed me."

"I tried to collar him, but when you told me to come in, sir, I had to let him go, and he came in after the rat."

It was plain to Mr. Downing that the burden of sin was shared equally by both culprits. Wilson had supplied the rat, Mike the dog; but Mr. Downing liked Wilson and disliked Mike. Wilson was in the Fire Brigade, frivolous at times, it was true, but nevertheless a member. Also he kept wicket for the school. Mike was a member of the Archaeological Society, and had refused to play cricket.

Mr. Downing allowed these facts to influence him in passing sentence.

"One hundred lines, Wilson," he said. "You may go."

Wilson departed with the air of a man who has had a great deal of fun, and paid very little for it.

Mr. Downing turned to Mike. "You will stay in on Saturday afternoon, Jackson; it will interfere with your Archaeological studies, I fear, but it may teach you that we have no room at Sedleigh for boys who spend their time loafing about and making themselves a nuisance. We are a keen school; this is no place for boys who do nothing but waste their time. That will do, Jackson."

And Mr. Downing walked out of the room. In affairs of this kind a master has a habit of getting the last word.

CHAPTER XXXIX ACHILLES LEAVES HIS TENT

They say misfortunes never come singly. As Mike sat brooding over his wrongs in his study, after the Sammy incident, Jellicoe came into the room, and, without preamble, asked for the loan of a sovereign.

When one has been in the habit of confining one's lendings and borrowings to sixpences and shillings, a request for a sovereign comes as something of a blow.

"What on earth for?" asked Mike.

"I say, do you mind if I don't tell you? I don't want to tell anybody. The fact is, I'm in a beastly hole."

"Oh, sorry," said Mike. "As a matter of fact, I do happen to have a quid. You can freeze on to it, if you like. But it's about all I have got, so don't be shy about paying it back."

Jellicoe was profuse in his thanks, and disappeared in a cloud of gratitude.

Mike felt that Fate was treating him badly. Being kept in on Saturday meant that he would be unable to turn out for Little Borlock against Claythorpe, the return match. In the previous game he had scored ninety-eight, and there was a lob bowler in the Claythorpe ranks whom he was particularly anxious to meet again. Having to yield a sovereign to Jellicoe—-why on earth did the man want all that?—-meant that, unless a carefully worded letter to his brother Bob at Oxford had the desired effect, he would be practically penniless for weeks.

In a gloomy frame of mind he sat down to write to Bob, who was playing regularly for the 'Varsity this season, and only the previous week had made a century against Sussex, so might be expected to be in a sufficiently softened mood to advance the needful. (Which, it may be stated at once, he did, by return of post.)

Mike was struggling with the opening sentences of this letter—-he was never a very ready writer—-when Stone and Robinson burst into the room.

Mike put down his pen, and got up. He was in warlike mood, and welcomed the intrusion. If Stone and Robinson wanted battle, they should have it.

But the motives of the expedition were obviously friendly. Stone beamed. Robinson was laughing.

"You're a sportsman," said Robinson.

"What did he give you?" asked Stone.

They sat down, Robinson on the table, Stone in Psmith's deck-chair. Mike's heart warmed to them. The little disturbance in the dormitory was a thing of the past, done with, forgotten, contemporary with Julius Caesar. He felt that he, Stone and Robinson must learn to know and appreciate one another.

There was, as a matter of fact, nothing much wrong with Stone and Robinson. They were just ordinary raggers of the type found at every public school, small and large. They were absolutely free from brain. They had a certain amount of muscle, and a vast store of animal spirits. They looked on school life purely as a vehicle for ragging. The Stones and Robinsons are the swashbucklers of the school world. They go about, loud and boisterous, with a whole-hearted and cheerful indifference to other people's feelings, treading on the toes of their neighbour and shoving him off the pavement, and always with an eye wide open for any adventure. As to the kind of adventure, they are not particular so long as it promises excitement. Sometimes they go through their whole school career without accident. More often they run up against a snag in the shape of some serious-minded and muscular person who objects to having his toes trodden on and being shoved off the pavement, and then they usually sober down, to the mutual advantage of themselves and the rest of the community.

One's opinion of this type of youth varies according to one's point of view. Small boys whom they had occasion to kick, either from pure high spirits or as a punishment for some slip from the narrow path which the ideal small boy should tread, regarded Stone and Robinson as bullies of the genuine "Eric" and "St. Winifred's" brand. Masters were rather afraid of them. Adair had a smouldering dislike for them. They were useful at cricket, but apt not to take Sedleigh as seriously as he could have wished.

As for Mike, he now found them pleasant company, and began to get out the tea-things.

"Those Fire Brigade meetings," said Stone, "are a rag. You can do what you like, and you never get more than a hundred lines."

"Don't you!" said Mike. "I got Saturday afternoon."

"What!"

"Is Wilson in too?"

"No. He got a hundred lines."

Stone and Robinson were quite concerned.

"What a beastly swindle!"

"That's because you don't play cricket. Old Downing lets you do what you like if you join the Fire Brigade and play cricket."

"'We are, above all, a keen school,'" quoted Stone. "Don't you ever play?"

"I have played a bit," said Mike.

"Well, why don't you have a shot? We aren't such flyers here. If you know one end of a bat from the other, you could get into some sort of a team. Were you at school anywhere before you came here?"

"I was at Wrykyn."

"Why on earth did you leave?" asked Stone. "Were you sacked?"

"No. My pater took me away."

"Wrykyn?" said Robinson. "Are you any relation of the Jacksons there—-J. W. and the others?"

"Brother."

"What!"

"Well, didn't you play at all there?"

"Yes," said Mike, "I did. I was in the team three years, and I should have been captain this year, if I'd stopped on."

There was a profound and gratifying sensation. Stone gaped, and Robinson nearly dropped his tea-cup.

Stone broke the silence.

"But I mean to say—-look here! What I mean is, why aren't you playing? Why don't you play now?"

"I do. I play for a village near here. Place called Little Borlock. A man who played against Wrykyn for the Free Foresters captains them. He asked me if I'd like some games for them."

"But why not for the school?"

"Why should I? It's much better fun for the village. You don't get ordered about by Adair, for a start."

"Adair sticks on side," said Stone.

"Enough for six," agreed Robinson.

"By Jove," said Stone, "I've got an idea. My word, what a rag!"

"What's wrong now?" inquired Mike politely.

"Why, look here. To-morrow's Mid-term Service day. It's nowhere near the middle of the term, but they always have it in the fourth week. There's chapel at half-past nine till half-past ten. Then the rest of the day's a whole holiday. There are always house matches. We're playing Downing's. Why don't you play and let's smash them?"

"By Jove, yes," said Robinson. "Why don't you? They're always sticking on side because they've won the house cup three years running. I say, do you bat or bowl?"

"Bat. Why?"

Robinson rocked on the table.

"Why, old Downing fancies himself as a bowler. You *must* play, and knock the cover off him."

"Masters don't play in house matches, surely?"

"This isn't a real house match. Only a friendly. Downing always turns out on Mid-term Service day. I say, do play."

"Think of the rag."

"But the team's full," said Mike.

"The list isn't up yet. We'll nip across to Barnes' study, and make him alter it."

They dashed out of the room. From down the passage Mike heard yells of "*Barnes*!" the closing of a door, and a murmur of excited conversation. Then footsteps returning down the passage.

Barnes appeared, on his face the look of one who has seen visions.

"ARE YOU THE M. JACKSON, THEN, WHO HAD AN AVERAGE OF FIFTY-ONE POINT NOUGHT THREE LAST YEAR?"

p. 225

"I say," he said, "is it true? Or is Stone rotting? About Wrykyn, I mean."

"Yes, I was in the team."

Barnes was an enthusiastic cricketer. He studied his *Wisden*, and he had an immense respect for Wrykyn cricket.

"Are you the M. Jackson, then, who had an average of fifty-one point nought three last year?"

"Yes."

Barnes's manner became like that of a curate talking to a bishop.

"I say," he said, "then—-er—-will you play against Downing's to-morrow?"

"Rather," said Mike. "Thanks awfully. Have some tea?"

CHAPTER XL THE MATCH WITH DOWNING'S

It is the curious instinct which prompts most people to rub a thing in that makes the lot of the average convert an unhappy one. Only the very self-controlled can refrain from improving the occasion and scoring off the convert. Most leap at the opportunity.

It was so in Mike's case. Mike was not a genuine convert, but to Mr. Downing he had the outward aspect of one. When you have been impressing upon a non-cricketing boy for nearly a month that (*a*) the school is above all a keen school, (*b*) that all members of it should play cricket, and (*c*) that by not playing cricket he is ruining his chances in this world and imperilling them in the next; and when, quite unexpectedly, you come upon this boy dressed in cricket flannels, wearing cricket boots and carrying a cricket bag, it seems only natural to assume that you have converted him, that the seeds of your eloquence have fallen on fruitful soil and sprouted.

Mr. Downing assumed it.

He was walking to the field with Adair and another member of his team when he came upon Mike.

"What!" he cried. "Our Jackson clad in suit of mail and armed for the fray!"

This was Mr. Downing's No. 2 manner—the playful.

"This is indeed Saul among the prophets. Why this sudden enthusiasm for a game which I understood that you despised? Are our opponents so reduced?"

Psmith, who was with Mike, took charge of the affair with a languid grace which had maddened hundreds in its time, and which never failed to ruffle Mr. Downing.

"We are, above all, sir," he said, "a keen house. Drones are not welcomed by us. We are essentially versatile. Jackson, the archaeologist of yesterday, becomes the cricketer of to-day. It is the right spirit, sir," said Psmith earnestly. "I like to see it."

"Indeed, Smith? You are not playing yourself, I notice. Your enthusiasm has bounds."

"In our house, sir, competition is fierce, and the Selection Committee unfortunately passed me over."

There were a number of pitches dotted about over the field, for there was always a touch of the London Park about it on Mid-term Service day. Adair, as captain of cricket, had naturally selected the best for his own match. It was a good wicket, Mike saw. As a matter of fact the wickets at Sedleigh were nearly always good. Adair had infected the ground-man with some of his own keenness, with the result that that once-leisurely official now found himself sometimes, with a kind of mild surprise, working really hard. At the beginning of the previous season Sedleigh had played a scratch team from a neighbouring town on a wicket which, except for the creases, was absolutely undistinguishable from the surrounding turf, and behind the pavilion after the match Adair had spoken certain home truths to the ground-man. The latter's reformation had dated from that moment.

Barnes, timidly jubilant, came up to Mike with the news that he had won the toss, and the request that Mike would go in first with him.

In stories of the "Not Really a Duffer" type, where the nervous new boy, who has been found crying in the boot-room over the photograph of his sister, contrives to get an innings in a game, nobody suspects that he is really a prodigy till he hits the Bully's first ball out of the ground for six.

With Mike it was different. There was no pitying smile on Adair's face as he started his run preparatory to sending down the first ball. Mike, on the cricket field, could not have looked anything but a cricketer if he had turned out in a tweed suit and hobnail boots. Cricketer was written all over him—in his walk, in the way he took guard, in his stand at the wickets. Adair started to bowl with the feeling that this was somebody who had more than a little knowledge of how to deal with good bowling and punish bad.

Mike started cautiously. He was more than usually anxious to make runs today, and he meant to take no risks till he could afford to do so. He had seen Adair bowl at the nets, and he knew that he was good.

The first over was a maiden, six dangerous balls beautifully played. The fieldsmen changed over.

The general interest had now settled on the match between Outwood's and Downing's. The fact in Mike's case had gone round the field, and, as several of the other games had not yet begun, quite a large crowd had collected near the pavilion to watch. Mike's masterly treatment of the opening over had impressed the spectators, and there was a popular desire to see how he would deal with Mr. Downing's slows. It was generally anticipated that he would do something special with them.

Off the first ball of the master's over a leg-bye was run.

Mike took guard.

Mr. Downing was a bowler with a style of his own. He took two short steps, two long steps, gave a jump, took three more short steps, and ended with a combination of step and jump, during which the ball emerged from behind his back and started on its slow career to the wicket. The whole business had some of the dignity of the old-fashioned minuet, subtly blended with the careless vigour of a cake-walk. The ball, when delivered, was billed to break from leg, but the programme was subject to alterations.

If the spectators had expected Mike to begin any firework effects with the first ball, they were disappointed. He played the over through with a grace worthy of his brother Joe. The last ball he turned to leg for a single.

His treatment of Adair's next over was freer. He had got a sight of the ball now. Half-way through the over a beautiful square cut forced a passage through the crowd by the pavilion, and dashed up against the rails. He drove the sixth ball past cover for three.

The crowd was now reluctantly dispersing to its own games, but it stopped as Mr. Downing started his minuet-cake-walk, in the hope that it might see something more sensational.

This time the hope was fulfilled.

The ball was well up, slow, and off the wicket on the on-side. Perhaps if it had been allowed to pitch, it might have broken in and become quite dangerous. Mike went out at it, and hit it a couple of feet from the ground. The ball dropped with a thud and a spurting of dust in the road that ran along one side of the cricket field.

It was returned on the instalment system by helpers from other games, and the bowler began his manoeuvres again. A half-volley this time. Mike slammed it back, and mid-on, whose heart was obviously not in the thing, failed to stop it.

"Get to them, Jenkins," said Mr. Downing irritably, as the ball came back from the boundary. "Get to them."

"Sir, please, sir——"

"Don't talk in the field, Jenkins."

Having had a full-pitch hit for six and a half-volley for four, there was a strong probability that Mr. Downing would pitch his next ball short.

The expected happened. The third ball was a slow long-hop, and hit the road at about the same spot where the first had landed. A howl of untuneful applause rose from the watchers in the pavilion, and Mike, with the feeling that this sort of bowling was too good to be true, waited in position for number four.

There are moments when a sort of panic seizes a bowler. This happened now with Mr. Downing. He suddenly abandoned science and ran amok. His run lost its stateliness and increased its vigour. He charged up to the wicket as a wounded buffalo sometimes charges a gun. His whole idea now was to bowl fast.

When a slow bowler starts to bowl fast, it is usually as well to be batting, if you can manage it.

By the time the over was finished, Mike's score had been increased by sixteen, and the total of his side, in addition, by three wides.

And a shrill small voice, from the neighbourhood of the pavilion, uttered with painful distinctness the words, "Take him off!"

That was how the most sensational day's cricket began that Sedleigh had known.

A description of the details of the morning's play would be monotonous. It is enough to say that they ran on much the same lines as the third and fourth overs of the match. Mr. Downing bowled one more over, off which Mike helped himself to sixteen runs, and then retired moodily to cover-point, where, in Adair's fifth over, he missed Barnes—-the first occasion since the game began on which that mild batsman had attempted to score more than a single. Scared by this escape, Outwood's captain shrank back into his shell, sat on the splice like a limpet, and, offering no more chances, was not out at lunch time with a score of eleven.

Mike had then made a hundred and three.

"WHY DID YOU SAY YOU DIDN'T PLAY CRICKET?" HE ASKED

As Mike was taking off his pads in the pavilion, Adair came up.

"Why did you say you didn't play cricket?" he asked abruptly.

When one has been bowling the whole morning, and bowling well, without the slightest success, one is inclined to be abrupt.

Mike finished unfastening an obstinate strap. Then he looked up.

"I didn't say anything of the kind. I said I wasn't going to play here. There's a difference. As a matter of fact, I was in the Wrykyn team before I came here. Three years."

Adair was silent for a moment.

"Will you play for us against the Old Sedleighans to-morrow?" he said at length.

Mike tossed his pads into his bag and got up.

"No, thanks."

There was a silence.

"Above it, I suppose?"

"Not a bit. Not up to it. I shall want a lot of coaching at that end net of yours before I'm fit to play for Sedleigh."

There was another pause.

"Then you won't play?" asked Adair.

"I'm not keeping you, am I?" said Mike, politely.

It was remarkable what a number of members of Outwood's house appeared to cherish a personal grudge against Mr. Downing. It had been that master's somewhat injudicious practice for many years to treat his own house as a sort of Chosen People. Of all masters, the most unpopular is he who by the silent tribunal of a school is convicted of favouritism. And the dislike deepens if it is a house which he favours and not merely individuals. On occasions when boys in his own house and boys from other houses were accomplices and partners in wrong-doing, Mr. Downing distributed his thunderbolts unequally, and the school noticed it. The result was that not only he himself, but also—-which was rather unfair—-his house, too, had acquired a good deal of unpopularity.

The general consensus of opinion in Outwood's during the luncheon interval was that, having got Downing's up a tree, they would be fools not to make the most of the situation.

Barnes's remark that he supposed, unless anything happened and wickets began to fall a bit faster, they had better think of declaring somewhere about half-past three or four, was met with a storm of opposition.

"Declare!" said Robinson. "Great Scott, what on earth are you talking about?"

"Declare!" Stone's voice was almost a wail of indignation. "I never saw such a chump."

"They'll be rather sick if we don't, won't they?" suggested Barnes.

"Sick! I should think they would," said Stone. "That's just the gay idea. Can't you see that by a miracle we've got a chance of getting a jolly good bit of our own back against those Downing's ticks? What we've got to do is to jolly well keep them in the field all day if we can, and be jolly glad it's so beastly hot.

If they lose about a dozen pounds each through sweating about in the sun after Jackson's drives, perhaps they'll stick on less side about things in general in future. Besides, I want an innings against that bilge of old Downing's, if I can get it."

"So do I," said Robinson.

"If you declare, I swear I won't field. Nor will Robinson."

"Rather not."

"Well, I won't then," said Barnes unhappily. "Only you know they're rather sick already."

"Don't you worry about that," said Stone with a wide grin. "They'll be a lot sicker before we've finished."

And so it came about that that particular Mid-term Service-day match made history. Big scores had often been put up on Mid-term Service day. Games had frequently been one-sided. But it had never happened before in the annals of the school that one side, going in first early in the morning, had neither completed its innings nor declared it closed when stumps were drawn at 6.30. In no previous Sedleigh match, after a full day's play, had the pathetic words "Did not bat" been written against the whole of one of the contending teams.

These are the things which mark epochs.

Play was resumed at 2.15. For a quarter of an hour Mike was comparatively quiet. Adair, fortified by food and rest, was bowling really well, and his first half-dozen overs had to be watched carefully. But the wicket was too good to give him a chance, and Mike, playing himself in again, proceeded to get to business once more. Bowlers came and went. Adair pounded away at one end with brief intervals between the attacks. Mr. Downing took a couple more overs, in one of which a horse, passing in the road, nearly had its useful life cut suddenly short. Change-bowlers of various actions and paces, each weirder and more futile than the last, tried their luck. But still the first-wicket stand continued.

The bowling of a house team is all head and no body. The first pair probably have some idea of length and break. The first-change pair are poor. And the rest, the small change, are simply the sort of things one sees in dreams after a heavy supper, or when one is out without one's gun.

Time, mercifully, generally breaks up a big stand at cricket before the field has suffered too much, and that is what happened now. At four o'clock, when the score stood at two hundred and twenty for no wicket, Barnes, greatly daring, smote lustily at a rather wide half-volley and was caught at short-slip for thirty-three. He retired blushfully to the pavilion, amidst applause, and Stone came out.

As Mike had then made a hundred and eighty-seven, it was assumed by the field, that directly he had topped his second century, the closure would be applied and their ordeal finished. There was almost a sigh of relief when frantic cheering from the crowd told that the feat had been accomplished. The fieldsmen clapped in quite an indulgent sort of way, as who should say, "Capital, capital. And now let's start *our* innings." Some even began to edge towards the pavilion. But the next ball was bowled, and the next over, and the next after that, and still Barnes made no sign. (The conscience-stricken captain of Outwood's was, as a matter of fact, being practically held down by Robinson and other ruffians by force.)

A grey dismay settled on the field.

The bowling had now become almost unbelievably bad. Lobs were being tried, and Stone, nearly weeping with pure joy, was playing an innings of the How-to-brighten-cricket type. He had an unorthodox style, but an excellent eye, and the road at this period of the game became absolutely unsafe for pedestrians and traffic.

Mike's pace had become slower, as was only natural, but his score, too, was mounting steadily.

"This is foolery," snapped Mr. Downing, as the three hundred and fifty went up on the board. "Barnes!" he called.

There was no reply. A committee of three was at that moment engaged in sitting on Barnes's head in the first eleven changing-room, in order to correct a more than usually feverish attack of conscience.

"Barnes!"

"Please, sir," said Stone, some species of telepathy telling him what was detaining his captain. "I think Barnes must have left the field. He has probably gone over to the house to fetch something."

"This is absurd. You must declare your innings closed. The game has become a farce."

"Declare! Sir, we can't unless Barnes does. He might be awfully annoyed if we did anything like that without consulting him."

"Absurd."

"He's very touchy, sir."

"It is perfect foolery."

"I think Jenkins is just going to bowl, sir."

Mr. Downing walked moodily to his place.

In a neat wooden frame in the senior day-room at Outwood's, just above the mantelpiece, there was on view, a week later, a slip of paper. The writing on it was as follows:

OUTWOOD'S *v.* DOWNING'S

Outwood's. First innings.

J. P. Barnes, *c.* Hammond, *b.* Hassall...	33
M. Jackson, not out........................	277
W. J. Stone, not out.......................	124
Extras...............................	37

Total (for one wicket)......	471

Downing's did not bat.

CHAPTER XLI THE SINGULAR BEHAVIOUR OF JELLICOE

Outwood's rollicked considerably that night. Mike, if he had cared to take the part, could have been the Petted Hero. But a cordial invitation from the senior day-room to be the guest of the evening at about the biggest rag of the century had been refused on the plea of fatigue. One does not make two hundred and seventy-seven runs on a hot day without feeling the effects, even if one has scored mainly by the medium of boundaries; and Mike, as he lay back in Psmith's deck-chair, felt that all he wanted was to go to bed and stay there for a week. His hands and arms burned as if they were red-hot, and his eyes were so tired that he could not keep them open.

Psmith, leaning against the mantelpiece, discoursed in a desultory way on the day's happenings—the score off Mr. Downing, the undeniable annoyance of that battered bowler, and the probability of his venting his annoyance on Mike next day.

"In theory," said he, "the manly what-d'you-call-it of cricket and all that sort of thing ought to make him fall on your neck to-morrow and weep over you as a foeman worthy of his steel. But I am prepared to bet a reasonable sum that he will give no Jiu-jitsu exhibition of this kind. In fact, from what I have seen of our bright little friend, I should say that, in a small way, he will do his best to make it distinctly hot for you, here and there."

"I don't care," murmured Mike, shifting his aching limbs in the chair.

"In an ordinary way, I suppose, a man can put up with having his bowling hit a little. But your performance was cruelty to animals. Twenty-eight off one over, not to mention three wides, would have made Job foam at the mouth. You will probably get sacked. On the other hand, it's worth it. You have lit a candle this day which can never be blown out. You have shown the lads of the village how Comrade Downing's bowling ought to be treated. I don't suppose he'll ever take another wicket."

"He doesn't deserve to."

Psmith smoothed his hair at the glass and turned round again.

"The only blot on this day of mirth and good-will is," he said, "the singular conduct of our friend Jellicoe. When all the place was ringing with song and merriment, Comrade Jellicoe crept to my side, and, slipping his little hand in mine, touched me for three quid."

This interested Mike, fagged as he was.

"What! Three quid!"

"Three jingling, clinking sovereigns. He wanted four."

"But the man must be living at the rate of I don't know what. It was only yesterday that he borrowed a quid from *me*!"

"He must be saving money fast. There appear to be the makings of a financier about Comrade Jellicoe. Well, I hope, when he's collected enough for his needs, he'll pay me back a bit. I'm pretty well cleaned out."

"I got some from my brother at Oxford."

"Perhaps he's saving up to get married. We may be helping towards furnishing the home. There was a Siamese prince fellow at my dame's at Eton who had four wives when he arrived, and gathered in a fifth during his first summer holidays. It was done on the correspondence system. His Prime Minister fixed it up at the other end, and sent him the glad news on a picture post-card. I think an eye ought to be kept on Comrade Jellicoe."

Mike tumbled into bed that night like a log, but he could not sleep. He ached all over. Psmith chatted for a time on human affairs in general, and then dropped gently off. Jellicoe, who appeared to be wrapped in gloom, contributed nothing to the conversation.

After Psmith had gone to sleep, Mike lay for some time running over in his mind, as the best substitute for sleep, the various points of his innings that day. He felt very hot and uncomfortable.

Just as he was wondering whether it would not be a good idea to get up and have a cold bath, a voice spoke from the darkness at his side.

"Are you asleep, Jackson?"

"Who's that?"

"Me—-Jellicoe. I can't get to sleep."

"Nor can I. I'm stiff all over."

"I'll come over and sit on your bed."

There was a creaking, and then a weight descended in the neighbourhood of Mike's toes.

Jellicoe was apparently not in conversational mood. He uttered no word for quite three minutes. At the end of which time he gave a sound midway between a snort and a sigh.

"I say, Jackson!" he said.

"Yes?"

"Have you—-oh, nothing."

Silence again.

"Jackson."

"Hullo?"

"I say, what would your people say if you got sacked?"

"All sorts of things. Especially my pater. Why?"

"Oh, I don't know. So would mine."

"Everybody's would, I expect."

"Yes."

The bed creaked, as Jellicoe digested these great thoughts. Then he spoke again.

"It would be a jolly beastly thing to get sacked."

Mike was too tired to give his mind to the subject. He was not really listening. Jellicoe droned on in a depressed sort of way.

"You'd get home in the middle of the afternoon, I suppose, and you'd drive up to the house, and the servant would open the door, and you'd go in. They might all be out, and then you'd have to hang about, and wait; and presently you'd hear them come in, and you'd go out into the passage, and they'd say 'Hullo!'"

Jellicoe, in order to give verisimilitude, as it were, to an otherwise bald and unconvincing narrative, flung so much agitated surprise into the last word that it woke Mike from a troubled doze into which he had fallen.

"Hullo?" he said. "What's up?"

"Then you'd say. 'Hullo!' And then they'd say, 'What are you doing here? 'And you'd say——"

"What on earth are you talking about?"

"About what would happen."

"Happen when?"

"When you got home. After being sacked, you know."

"Who's been sacked?" Mike's mind was still under a cloud.

"Nobody. But if you were, I meant. And then I suppose there'd be an awful row and general sickness, and all that. And then you'd be sent into a bank, or to Australia, or something."

Mike dozed off again.

"My pater would be frightfully sick. My mater would be sick. My sister would be jolly sick, too. Have you got any sisters, Jackson? I say, Jackson!"

"Hullo! What's the matter? Who's that?"

"Me—-Jellicoe."

"What's up?"

"I asked you if you'd got any sisters."

"Any *what*?"

"Sisters."

"Whose sisters?"

"Yours. I asked if you'd got any."

"Any what?"

"Sisters."

"What about them?"

The conversation was becoming too intricate for Jellicoe. He changed the subject.

"I say, Jackson!"

"Well?"

"I say, you don't know any one who could lend me a pound, do you?"

"What!" cried Mike, sitting up in bed and staring through the darkness in the direction whence the numismatist's voice was proceeding. "Do *what*?"

"I say, look out. You'll wake Smith."

"Did you say you wanted some one to lend you a quid?"

"Yes," said Jellicoe eagerly. "Do you know any one?"

Mike's head throbbed. This thing was too much. The human brain could not be expected to cope with it. Here was a youth who had borrowed a pound from one friend the day before, and three pounds from another friend that very afternoon, already looking about him for further loans. Was it a hobby, or was he saving up to buy an aeroplane?

"What on earth do you want a pound for?"

"I don't want to tell anybody. But it's jolly serious. I shall get sacked if I don't get it."

Mike pondered.

Those who have followed Mike's career as set forth by the present historian will have realised by this time that he was a good long way from being perfect. As the Blue-Eyed Hero he would have been a rank failure. Except on the cricket field, where he was a natural genius, he was just ordinary. He resembled ninety per cent. of other members of English public schools. He had some virtues and a good many defects. He was as obstinate as a mule, though people whom he liked could do as they pleased with him. He was good-natured as a general thing, but on occasion his temper could be of the worst, and had, in his childhood, been the subject of much adverse comment among his aunts. He was rigidly truthful, where the issue concerned only himself. Where it was a case of saving a friend, he was prepared to act in a manner reminiscent of an American expert witness.

He had, in addition, one good quality without any defect to balance it. He was always ready to help people. And when he set himself to do this, he was never put off by discomfort or risk. He went at the thing with a singleness of purpose that asked no questions.

Bob's postal order, which had arrived that evening, was reposing in the breast-pocket of his coat.

It was a wrench, but, if the situation was so serious with Jellicoe, it had to be done.

Two minutes later the night was being made hideous by Jellicoe's almost tearful protestations of gratitude, and the postal order had moved from one side of the dormitory to the other.

CHAPTER XLII JELLICOE GOES ON THE SICK-LIST

Mike woke next morning with a confused memory of having listened to a great deal of incoherent conversation from Jellicoe, and a painfully vivid recollection of handing over the bulk of his worldly wealth to him. The thought depressed him, though it seemed to please Jellicoe, for the latter carolled in a gay undertone as he dressed, till Psmith, who had a sensitive ear, asked as a favour that these farm-yard imitations might cease until he was out of the room.

There were other things to make Mike low-spirited that morning. To begin with, he was in detention, which in itself is enough to spoil a day. It was a particularly fine day, which made the matter worse. In addition to this, he had never felt stiffer in his life. It seemed to him that the creaking of his joints as he walked must be audible to every one within a radius of several yards. Finally, there was the interview with Mr. Downing to come. That would probably be unpleasant. As Psmith had said, Mr. Downing was the sort of master who would be likely to make trouble. The great match had not been an ordinary match. Mr. Downing was a curious man in many ways, but he did not make a fuss on ordinary occasions when his bowling proved expensive. Yesterday's performance, however, stood in a class by itself. It stood forth without disguise as a deliberate rag. One side does not keep another in the field the whole day in a one-day match except as a grisly kind of practical joke. And Mr. Downing and his house realised this. The house's way of signifying its comprehension of the fact was to be cold and distant as far as the seniors were concerned, and abusive and pugnacious as regards the juniors. Young blood had been shed overnight, and more flowed during the eleven o'clock interval that morning to avenge the insult.

Mr. Downing's methods of retaliation would have to be, of necessity, more elusive; but Mike did not doubt that in some way or other his form-master would endeavour to get a bit of his own back.

As events turned out, he was perfectly right. When a master has got his knife into a boy, especially a master who allows himself to be influenced by his likes and dislikes, he is inclined to single him out in times of stress, and savage him as if he were the official representative of the evildoers. Just as, at sea, the skipper, when he has trouble with the crew, works it off on the boy.

Mr. Downing was in a sarcastic mood when he met Mike. That is to say, he began in a sarcastic strain. But this sort of thing is difficult to keep up. By the time he had reached his peroration, the rapier had given place to the bludgeon. For sarcasm to be effective, the user of it must be met half-way. His hearer must appear to be conscious of the sarcasm and moved by it. Mike, when masters waxed sarcastic towards him, always assumed an air of stolid stupidity, which was as a suit of mail against satire.

So Mr. Downing came down from the heights with a run, and began to express himself with a simple strength which it did his form good to listen to. Veterans who had been in the form for terms said afterwards that there had been nothing to touch it, in their experience of the orator, since the glorious day when Dunster, that prince of raggers, who had left at Christmas to go to a crammer's, had introduced three lively grass-snakes into the room during a Latin lesson.

"You are surrounded," concluded Mr. Downing, snapping his pencil in two in his emotion, "by an impenetrable mass of conceit and vanity and selfishness. It does not occur to you to admit your capabilities as a cricketer in an open, straightforward way and place them at the disposal of the school. No, that would not be dramatic enough for you. It would be too commonplace altogether. Far too commonplace!" Mr. Downing laughed bitterly. "No, you must conceal your capabilities. You must act a lie. You must—who is that shuffling his feet? I will not have it, I *will* have silence—you must hang back in order to make a more effective entrance, like some wretched actor who—I will *not* have this shuffling. I have spoken of this before. Macpherson, are you shuffling your feet?"

"Sir, no, sir."

"Please, sir."

"Well, Parsons?"

"I think it's the noise of the draught under the door, sir."

Instant departure of Parsons for the outer regions. And, in the excitement of this side-issue, the speaker lost his inspiration, and abruptly concluded his remarks by putting Mike on to translate in Cicero. Which Mike, who happened to have prepared the first half-page, did with much success.

The Old Boys' match was timed to begin shortly after eleven o'clock. During the interval most of the school walked across the field to look at the pitch. One or two of the Old Boys had already changed and were practising in front of the pavilion.

It was through one of these batsmen that an accident occurred which had a good deal of influence on Mike's affairs.

Mike had strolled out by himself. Half-way across the field Jellicoe joined him. Jellicoe was cheerful, and rather embarrassingly grateful. He was just in the middle of his harangue when the accident happened.

To their left, as they crossed the field, a long youth, with the faint beginnings of a moustache and a blazer that lit up the surrounding landscape like a glowing beacon, was lashing out recklessly at a friend's bowling. Already he had gone within an ace of slaying a small boy. As Mike and Jellicoe proceeded on their way, there was a shout of "Heads!"

The almost universal habit of batsmen of shouting "Heads!" at whatever height from the ground the ball may be, is not a little confusing. The average person, on hearing the shout, puts his hands over his skull, crouches down and trusts to luck. This is an excellent plan if the ball is falling, but is not much protection against a skimming drive along the ground.

When "Heads!" was called on the present occasion, Mike and Jellicoe instantly assumed the crouching attitude.

Jellicoe was the first to abandon it. He uttered a yell and sprang into the air. After which he sat down and began to nurse his ankle.

The bright-blazered youth walked up.

"Awfully sorry, you know, man. Hurt?"

Jellicoe was pressing the injured spot tenderly with his finger-tips, uttering sharp howls whenever, zeal outrunning discretion, he prodded himself too energetically.

"Silly ass, Dunster," he groaned, "slamming about like that."

"Awfully sorry. But I did yell."

"It's swelling up rather," said Mike. "You'd better get over to the house and have it looked at. Can you walk?"

Jellicoe tried, but sat down again with a loud "Ow!" At that moment the bell rang.

"I shall have to be going in," said Mike, "or I'd have helped you over."

"I'll give you a hand," said Dunster.

He helped the sufferer to his feet and they staggered off together, Jellicoe hopping, Dunster advancing with a sort of polka step. Mike watched them start and then turned to go in.

CHAPTER XLIII MIKE RECEIVES A COMMISSION

There is only one thing to be said in favour of detention on a fine summer's afternoon, and that is that it is very pleasant to come out of. The sun never seems so bright or the turf so green as during the first five minutes after one has come out of the detention-room. One feels as if one were entering a new and very delightful world. There is also a touch of the Rip van Winkle feeling. Everything seems to have gone on and left one behind. Mike, as he walked to the cricket field, felt very much behind the times.

Arriving on the field he found the Old Boys batting. He stopped and watched an over of Adair's. The fifth ball bowled a man. Mike made his way towards the pavilion.

Before he got there he heard his name called, and turning, found Psmith seated under a tree with the bright-blazered Dunster.

"Return of the exile," said Psmith. "A joyful occasion tinged with melancholy. Have a cherry?—take one or two. These little acts of unremembered kindness are what one needs after a couple of hours in extra pupil-room. Restore your tissues, Comrade Jackson, and when you have finished those, apply again."

"Is your name Jackson?" inquired Dunster, "because Jellicoe wants to see you."

"Alas, poor Jellicoe!" said Psmith. "He is now prone on his bed in the dormitory—there a sheer hulk lies poor Tom Jellicoe, the darling of the crew, faithful below he did his duty, but Comrade Dunster has broached him to. I have just been hearing the melancholy details."

"Old Smith and I," said Dunster, "were at a private school together. I'd no idea I should find him here."

"It was a wonderfully stirring sight when we met," said Psmith; "not unlike the meeting of Ulysses and the hound Argos, of whom you have doubtless read in the course of your dabblings in the classics. I was Ulysses; Dunster gave a life-like representation of the faithful dawg."

"You still jaw as much as ever, I notice," said the animal delineator, fondling the beginnings of his moustache.

"More," sighed Psmith, "more. Is anything irritating you?" he added, eyeing the other's manoeuvres with interest.

"You needn't be a funny ass, man," said Dunster, pained; "heaps of people tell me I ought to have it waxed."

"What it really wants is top-dressing with guano. Hullo! another man out. Adair's bowling better to-day than he did yesterday."

"I heard about yesterday," said Dunster. "It must have been a rag! Couldn't we work off some other rag on somebody before I go? I shall be stopping here till Monday in the village. Well hit, sir—-Adair's bowling is perfectly simple if you go out to it."

"Comrade Dunster went out to it first ball," said Psmith to Mike.

"Oh! chuck it, man; the sun was in my eyes. I hear Adair's got a match on with the M.C.C. at last."

"Has he?" said Psmith; "I hadn't heard. Archaeology claims so much of my time that I have little leisure for listening to cricket chit-chat."

"What was it Jellicoe wanted?" asked Mike; "was it anything important?"

"He seemed to think so—-he kept telling me to tell you to go and see him."

"I fear Comrade Jellicoe is a bit of a weak-minded blitherer——-"

"Did you ever hear of a rag we worked off on Jellicoe once?" asked Dunster. "The man has absolutely no sense of humour—-can't see when he's being rotted. Well it was like this—-Hullo! We're all out—-I shall have to be going out to field again, I suppose, dash it! I'll tell you when I see you again."

"I shall count the minutes," said Psmith.

Mike stretched himself; the sun was very soothing after his two hours in the detention-room; he felt disinclined for exertion.

"I don't suppose it's anything special about Jellicoe, do you?" he said. "I mean, it'll keep till tea-time; it's no catch having to sweat across to the house now."

"Don't dream of moving," said Psmith. "I have several rather profound observations on life to make and I can't make them without an audience. Soliloquy is a knack. Hamlet had got it, but probably only after years of patient practice. Personally, I need some one to listen when I talk. I like to feel that I am doing good. You stay where you are—-don't interrupt too much."

Mike tilted his hat over his eyes and abandoned Jellicoe.

It was not until the lock-up bell rang that he remembered him. He went over to the house and made his way to the dormitory, where he found the injured one in a parlous state, not so much physical as mental. The doctor had seen his ankle and reported that it would be on the active list in a couple of days. It was Jellicoe's mind that needed attention now.

Mike found him in a condition bordering on collapse.

"I say, you might have come before!" said Jellicoe.

"What's up? I didn't know there was such a hurry about it—-what did you want?"

"It's no good now," said Jellicoe gloomily; "it's too late, I shall get sacked."

"What on earth are you talking about? What's the row?"

"It's about that money."

"What about it?"

"I had to pay it to a man to-day, or he said he'd write to the Head—-then of course I should get sacked. I was going to take the money to him this afternoon, only I got crocked, so I couldn't move. I wanted to get hold of you to ask you to take it for me—-it's too late now!"

Mike's face fell. "Oh, hang it!" he said, "I'm awfully sorry. I'd no idea it was anything like that—-what a fool I was! Dunster did say he thought it was something important, only like an ass I thought it would do if I came over at lock-up."

"It doesn't matter," said Jellicoe miserably; "it can't be helped."

"Yes, it can," said Mike. "I know what I'll do—-it's all right. I'll get out of the house after lights-out."

Jellicoe sat up. "You can't! You'd get sacked if you were caught."

"Who would catch me? There was a chap at Wrykyn I knew who used to break out every night nearly and go and pot at cats with an air-pistol; it's as easy as anything."

The toad-under-the-harrow expression began to fade from Jellicoe's face. "I say, do you think you could, really?"

"Of course I can! It'll be rather a rag."

"I say, it's frightfully decent of you."

"What absolute rot!"

"But, look here, are you certain——-"

"I shall be all right. Where do you want me to go?"

"It's a place about a mile or two from here, called Lower Borlock."

"Lower Borlock?"

"Yes, do you know it?"

"Rather! I've been playing cricket for them all the term."

"I say, have you? Do you know a man called Barley?"

"Barley? Rather—-he runs the 'White Boar'."

"He's the chap I owe the money to."

"Old Barley!"

Mike knew the landlord of the "White Boar" well; he was the wag of the village team. Every village team, for some mysterious reason, has its comic man. In the Lower Borlock eleven Mr. Barley filled the post. He was a large, stout man, with a red and cheerful face, who looked exactly like the jovial inn-keeper of melodrama. He was the last man Mike would have expected to do the "money by Monday-week or I write to the headmaster" business.

But he reflected that he had only seen him in his leisure moments, when he might naturally be expected to unbend and be full of the milk of human kindness. Probably in business hours he was quite different. After all, pleasure is one thing and business another.

Besides, five pounds is a large sum of money, and if Jellicoe owed it, there was nothing strange in Mr. Barley's doing everything he could to recover it.

He wondered a little what Jellicoe could have been doing to run up a bill as big as that, but it did not occur to him to ask, which was unfortunate, as it might have saved him a good deal of inconvenience. It seemed to him that it was none of his business to inquire into Jellicoe's private affairs. He took the envelope containing the money without question.

"I shall bike there, I think," he said, "if I can get into the shed."

The school's bicycles were stored in a shed by the pavilion.

"You can manage that," said Jellicoe; "it's locked up at night, but I had a key made to fit it last summer, because I used to go out in the early morning sometimes before it was opened."

"Got it on you?"

"Smith's got it."

"I'll get it from him."

"I say!"

"Well?"

"Don't tell Smith why you want it, will you? I don't want anybody to know—-if a thing once starts getting about it's all over the place in no time."

"All right, I won't tell him."

"I say, thanks most awfully! I don't know what I should have done, I——-"

"Oh, chuck it!" said Mike.

CHAPTER XLIV AND FULFILS IT

Mike started on his ride to Lower Borlock with mixed feelings. It is pleasant to be out on a fine night in summer, but the pleasure is to a certain extent modified when one feels that to be detected will mean expulsion.

Mike did not want to be expelled, for many reasons. Now that he had grown used to the place he was enjoying himself at Sedleigh to a certain extent. He still harboured a feeling of resentment against the school in general and Adair in particular, but it was pleasant in Outwood's now that he had got to know some of the members of the house, and he liked playing cricket for Lower Borlock; also, he was fairly certain that his father would not let him go to Cambridge if he were expelled from Sedleigh. Mr. Jackson was easy-going with his family, but occasionally his foot came down like a steam-hammer, as witness the Wrykyn school report affair.

So Mike pedalled along rapidly, being wishful to get the job done without delay.

Psmith had yielded up the key, but his inquiries as to why it was needed had been embarrassing. Mike's statement that he wanted to get up early and have a ride had been received by Psmith, with whom early rising was not a hobby, with honest amazement and a flood of advice and warning on the subject.

"One of the Georges," said Psmith, "I forget which, once said that a certain number of hours' sleep a day—-I cannot recall for the moment how many—-made a man something, which for the time being has slipped my memory. However, there you are. I've given you the main idea of the thing; and a German doctor says that early rising causes insanity. Still, if you're bent on it——-" After which he had handed over the key.

Mike wished he could have taken Psmith into his confidence. Probably he would have volunteered to come, too; Mike would have been glad of a companion.

It did not take him long to reach Lower Borlock. The "White Boar" stood at the far end of the village, by the cricket field. He rode past the church—-standing out black and mysterious against the light sky—-and the rows of silent cottages, until he came to the inn.

The place was shut, of course, and all the lights were out—-it was some time past eleven.

The advantage an inn has over a private house, from the point of view of the person who wants to get into it when it has been locked up, is that a nocturnal visit is not so unexpected in the case of the former. Preparations have been made to meet such an emergency. Where with a private house you would probably have to wander round heaving rocks and end by climbing up a water-spout, when you want to get into an inn you simply ring the night-bell, which, communicating with the boots' room, has that hard-worked menial up and doing in no time.

After Mike had waited for a few minutes there was a rattling of chains and a shooting of bolts and the door opened.

"Yes, sir?" said the boots, appearing in his shirt-sleeves. "Why, 'ullo! Mr. Jackson, sir!"

Mike was well known to all dwellers in Lower Borlock, his scores being the chief topic of conversation when the day's labours were over.

"I want to see Mr. Barley, Jack."

"He's bin in bed this half-hour back, Mr. Jackson."

"I must see him. Can you get him down?"

The boots looked doubtful. "Roust the guv'nor outer bed?" he said.

Mike quite admitted the gravity of the task. The landlord of the "White Boar" was one of those men who need a beauty sleep.

"I wish you would—-it's a thing that can't wait. I've got some money to give to him."

"Oh, if it's *that*—-" said the boots.

Five minutes later mine host appeared in person, looking more than usually portly in a check dressing-gown and red bedroom slippers of the *Dreadnought* type.

"You can pop off, Jack."

Exit boots to his slumbers once more.

"Well, Mr. Jackson, what's it all about?"

"Jellicoe asked me to come and bring you the money."

"The money? What money?"

"What he owes you; the five pounds, of course."

"The five—-" Mr. Barley stared open-mouthed at Mike for a moment; then he broke into a roar of laughter which shook the sporting prints on the wall and drew barks from dogs in some distant part of the house. He staggered about laughing and coughing till Mike began to expect a fit of some kind. Then he collapsed into a chair, which creaked under him, and wiped his eyes.

"Oh dear!" he said, "oh dear! the five pounds!"

Mike was not always abreast of the rustic idea of humour, and now he felt particularly fogged. For the life of him he could not see what there was to amuse any one so much in the fact that a person who owed five pounds was ready to pay it back. It was an occasion for rejoicing, perhaps, but rather for a solemn, thankful, eyes-raised-to-heaven kind of rejoicing.

"What's up?" he asked.

"Five pounds!"

"You might tell us the joke."

Mr. Barley opened the letter, read it, and had another attack; when this was finished he handed the letter to Mike, who was waiting patiently by, hoping for light, and requested him to read it.

"Dear, dear!" chuckled Mr. Barley, "five pounds! They may teach you young gentlemen to talk Latin and Greek and what not at your school, but it 'ud do a lot more good if they'd teach you how many beans make five; it 'ud do a lot more good if they'd teach you to come in when it rained, it 'ud do——-"

Mike was reading the letter.

> "DEAR MR. BARLEY," it ran.—-"I send the £5, which I could not get before. I hope it is in time, because I don't want you to write to the headmaster. I am sorry Jane and John ate your wife's hat and the chicken and broke the vase."

There was some more to the same effect; it was signed "T. G. Jellicoe."

"What on earth's it all about?" said Mike, finishing this curious document.

Mr. Barley slapped his leg. "Why, Mr. Jellicoe keeps two dogs here; I keep 'em for him till the young gentlemen go home for their holidays. Aberdeen terriers, they are, and as sharp as mustard. Mischief! I believe you, but, love us! they don't do no harm! Bite up an old shoe sometimes and such sort of things. The other day, last Wednesday it were, about 'ar parse five, Jane—-she's the worst of the two, always up to it, she is—-she got hold of my old hat and had it in bits before you could say knife. John upset a china vase in one of the bedrooms chasing a mouse, and they got on the coffee-room table and ate half a cold chicken what had been left there. So I says to myself, 'I'll have a game with Mr. Jellicoe over this,' and I sits down and writes off saying the little dogs have eaten a valuable hat and a chicken and what not, and the damage'll be five pounds, and will he kindly remit same by Saturday night at the latest or I write to his headmaster. Love us!" Mr. Barley slapped his thigh, "he took it all in, every word—-and here's the five pounds in cash in this envelope here! I haven't had such a laugh since we got old Tom Raxley out of bed at twelve of a winter's night by telling him his house was a-fire."

It is not always easy to appreciate a joke of the practical order if one has been made even merely part victim of it. Mike, as he reflected that he had been dragged out of his house in the middle of the night, in contravention of all school rules and discipline, simply in order to satisfy Mr. Barley's sense of humour, was more inclined to be abusive than mirthful. Running risks is all very well when they are necessary, or if one chooses to run them for one's own amusement, but to be placed in a dangerous position, a position imperilling one's chance of going to the 'Varsity, is another matter altogether.

But it is impossible to abuse the Barley type of man. Barley's enjoyment of the whole thing was so honest and child-like. Probably it had given him the happiest quarter of an hour he had known for years, since, in fact, the affair of old Tom Raxley. It would have been cruel to damp the man.

CHAPTER XLIV AND FULFILS IT

So Mike laughed perfunctorily, took back the envelope with the five pounds, accepted a stone ginger beer and a plateful of biscuits, and rode off on his return journey.

Mention has been made above of the difference which exists between getting into an inn after lock-up and into a private house. Mike was to find this out for himself.

His first act on arriving at Sedleigh was to replace his bicycle in the shed. This he accomplished with success. It was pitch-dark in the shed, and as he wheeled his machine in, his foot touched something on the floor. Without waiting to discover what this might be, he leaned his bicycle against the wall, went out, and locked the door, after which he ran across to Outwood's.

Fortune had favoured his undertaking by decreeing that a stout drain-pipe should pass up the wall within a few inches of his and Psmith's study. On the first day of term, it may be remembered he had wrenched away the wooden bar which bisected the window-frame, thus rendering exit and entrance almost as simple as they had been for Wyatt during Mike's first term at Wrykyn.

He proceeded to scale this water-pipe.

He had got about half-way up when a voice from somewhere below cried, "Who's that?"

CHAPTER XLV PURSUIT

These things are Life's Little Difficulties. One can never tell precisely how one will act in a sudden emergency. The right thing for Mike to have done at this crisis was to have ignored the voice, carried on up the water-pipe, and through the study window, and gone to bed. It was extremely unlikely that anybody could have recognised him at night against the dark background of the house. The position then would have been that somebody in Mr. Outwood's house had been seen breaking in after lights-out; but it would have been very difficult for the authorities to have narrowed the search down any further than that. There were thirty-four boys in Outwood's, of whom about fourteen were much the same size and build as Mike.

The suddenness, however, of the call caused Mike to lose his head. He made the strategic error of sliding rapidly down the pipe, and running.

There were two gates to Mr. Outwood's front garden. The carriage drive ran in a semicircle, of which the house was the centre. It was from the right-hand gate, nearest to Mr. Downing's house, that the voice had come, and, as Mike came to the ground, he saw a stout figure galloping towards him from that direction. He bolted like a rabbit for the other gate. As he did so, his pursuer again gave tongue.

"Oo-oo-oo yer!" was the exact remark.

Whereby Mike recognised him as the school sergeant.

"Oo-oo-oo yer!" was that militant gentleman's habitual way of beginning a conversation.

With this knowledge, Mike felt easier in his mind. Sergeant Collard was a man of many fine qualities, (notably a talent for what he was wont to call "spott'n," a mysterious gift which he exercised on the rifle range), but he could not run. There had been a time in his hot youth when he had sprinted like an untamed mustang in pursuit of volatile Pathans in Indian hill wars, but Time, increasing his girth, had taken from him the taste for such exercise. When he moved now it was at a stately walk. The fact that he ran to-night showed how the excitement of the chase had entered into his blood.

"Oo-oo-oo yer!" he shouted again, as Mike, passing through the gate, turned into the road that led to the school. Mike's attentive ear noted that the bright speech was a shade more puffily delivered this time. He began to feel that this was not such bad fun after all. He would have liked to be in bed, but, if that was out of the question, this was certainly the next best thing.

He ran on, taking things easily, with the sergeant panting in his wake, till he reached the entrance to the school grounds. He dashed in and took cover behind a tree.

Presently the sergeant turned the corner, going badly and evidently cured of a good deal of the fever of the chase. Mike heard him toil on for a few yards and then stop. A sound of panting was borne to him.

Then the sound of footsteps returning, this time at a walk. They passed the gate and went on down the road.

The pursuer had given the thing up.

Mike waited for several minutes behind his tree. His programme now was simple. He would give Sergeant Collard about half an hour, in case the latter took it into his head to "guard home" by waiting at the gate. Then he would trot softly back, shoot up the water-pipe once more, and so to bed. It had just struck a quarter to something—-twelve, he supposed—-on the school clock. He would wait till a quarter past.

Meanwhile, there was nothing to be gained from lurking behind a tree. He left his cover, and started to stroll in the direction of the pavilion. Having arrived there, he sat on the steps, looking out on to the cricket field.

His thoughts were miles away, at Wrykyn, when he was recalled to Sedleigh by the sound of somebody running. Focussing his gaze, he saw a dim figure moving rapidly across the cricket field straight for him.

His first impression, that he had been seen and followed, disappeared as the runner, instead of making for the pavilion, turned aside, and stopped at the door of the bicycle shed. Like Mike, he was evidently possessed of a key, for Mike heard it grate in the lock. At this point he left the pavilion and hailed his fellow rambler by night in a cautious undertone.

The other appeared startled.

"Who the dickens is that?" he asked. "Is that you, Jackson?"

Mike recognised Adair's voice. The last person he would have expected to meet at midnight obviously on the point of going for a bicycle ride.

"What are you doing out here, Jackson?"

"What are you, if it comes to that?"

Adair was lighting his lamp.

"I'm going for the doctor. One of the chaps in our house is bad."

"Oh!"

"What are you doing out here?"

"Just been for a stroll."

"Hadn't you better be getting back?"

"Plenty of time."

"I suppose you think you're doing something tremendously brave and dashing?"

"Hadn't you better be going to the doctor?"

"If you want to know what I think——"

"I don't. So long."

Mike turned away, whistling between his teeth. After a moment's pause, Adair rode off. Mike saw his light pass across the field and through the gate. The school clock struck the quarter.

It seemed to Mike that Sergeant Collard, even if he had started to wait for him at the house, would not keep up the vigil for more than half an hour. He would be safe now in trying for home again.

He walked in that direction.

Now it happened that Mr. Downing, aroused from his first sleep by the news, conveyed to him by Adair, that MacPhee, one of the junior members of Adair's dormitory, was groaning and exhibiting other symptoms of acute illness, was disturbed in his mind. Most housemasters feel uneasy in the event of illness in their houses, and Mr. Downing was apt to get jumpy beyond the ordinary on such occasions. All that was wrong with MacPhee, as a matter of fact, was a very fair stomach-ache, the direct and legitimate result of eating six buns, half a cocoa-nut, three doughnuts, two ices, an apple, and a pound of cherries, and washing the lot down with tea. But Mr. Downing saw in his attack the beginnings of some deadly scourge which would sweep through and decimate the house. He had despatched Adair for the doctor, and, after spending a few minutes prowling restlessly about his room, was now standing at his front gate, waiting for Adair's return.

It came about, therefore, that Mike, sprinting lightly in the direction of home and safety, had his already shaken nerves further maltreated by being hailed, at a range of about two yards, with a cry of "Is that you, Adair?" The next moment Mr. Downing emerged from his gate.

Mike stood not upon the order of his going. He was off like an arrow—a flying figure of Guilt. Mr. Downing, after the first surprise, seemed to grasp the situation. Ejaculating at intervals the words, "Who is that? Stop! Who is that? Stop!" he dashed after the much-enduring Wrykynian at an extremely creditable rate of speed. Mr. Downing was by way of being a sprinter. He had won handicap events at College sports at Oxford, and, if Mike had not got such a good start, the race might have been over in the first fifty yards. As it was, that victim of Fate, going well, kept ahead. At the entrance to the school grounds he led by a dozen yards. The procession passed into the field, Mike heading as before for the pavilion.

As they raced across the soft turf, an idea occurred to Mike which he was accustomed in after years to attribute to genius, the one flash of it which had ever illumined his life.

It was this.

One of Mr. Downing's first acts, on starting the Fire Brigade at Sedleigh, had been to institute an alarm bell. It had been rubbed into the school officially—in speeches from the daïs—by the headmaster, and unofficially—in earnest private conversations—by Mr. Downing, that at the sound of this bell, at whatever hour of day or night, every member of the school must leave his house in the quickest possible way, and make for the open. The bell might mean that the school was on fire, or it might mean that one of the houses was on fire. In any case, the school had its orders—-to get out into the open at once.

Nor must it be supposed that the school was without practice at this feat. Every now and then a notice would be found posted up on the board to the effect that there would be fire drill during the dinner hour that day. Sometimes the performance was bright and interesting, as on the occasion when Mr. Downing, marshalling the brigade at his front gate, had said, "My house is supposed to be on fire. Now let's do a record!" which the Brigade, headed by Stone and Robinson, obligingly did. They fastened the hose to the hydrant, smashed a window on the ground floor (Mr. Downing having retired for a moment to talk with the headmaster), and poured a stream of water into the room. When Mr. Downing was at liberty to turn his attention to the matter, he found that the room selected was his private study, most of the light furniture of which was floating on a miniature lake. That episode had rather discouraged his passion for realism, and fire drill since then had taken the form, for the most part, of "practising escaping." This was done by means of canvas shoots, kept in the dormitories. At the sound of the bell the prefect of the dormitory would heave one end of the shoot out of window, the other end being fastened to the sill. He would then go down it himself, using his elbows as a brake. Then the second man would follow his example, and these two, standing below, would hold the end of the shoot so that the rest of the dormitory could fly rapidly down it without injury, except to their digestions.

After the first novelty of the thing had worn off, the school had taken a rooted dislike to fire drill. It was a matter for self-congratulation among them that Mr. Downing had never been able to induce the headmaster to allow the alarm bell to be sounded for fire drill at night. The headmaster, a man who had his views on the amount of sleep necessary for the growing boy, had drawn the line at night operations. "Sufficient unto the day" had been the gist of his reply. If the alarm bell were to ring at night when there was no fire, the school might mistake a genuine alarm of fire for a bogus one, and refuse to hurry themselves.

So Mr. Downing had had to be content with day drill.

The alarm bell hung in the archway leading into the school grounds. The end of the rope, when not in use, was fastened to a hook half-way up the wall.

Mike, as he raced over the cricket field, made up his mind in a flash that his only chance of getting out of this tangle was to shake his pursuer off for a space of time long enough to enable him to get to the rope and tug it. Then the school would come out. He would mix with them, and in the subsequent confusion get back to bed unnoticed.

The task was easier than it would have seemed at the beginning of the chase. Mr. Downing, owing to the two facts that he was not in the strictest training, and that it is only an Alfred Shrubb who can run for any length of time at top speed shouting "Who is that? Stop! Who is that? Stop!" was beginning to feel distressed. There were bellows to mend in the Downing camp. Mike perceived this, and forced the pace. He rounded the pavilion ten yards to the good. Then, heading for the gate, he put all he knew into one last sprint. Mr. Downing was not equal to the effort. He worked gamely for a few strides, then fell behind. When Mike reached the gate, a good forty yards separated them.

As far as Mike could judge—-he was not in a condition to make nice calculations—-he had about four seconds in which to get busy with that bell rope.

Probably nobody has ever crammed more energetic work into four seconds than he did then.

The night was as still as only an English summer night can be, and the first clang of the clapper sounded like a million iron girders falling from a height on to a sheet of tin. He tugged away furiously, with an eye on the now rapidly advancing and loudly shouting figure of the housemaster.

And from the darkened house beyond there came a gradually swelling hum, as if a vast hive of bees had been disturbed.

The school was awake.

CHAPTER XLVI THE DECORATION OF SAMMY

Psmith leaned against the mantelpiece in the senior day-room at Outwood's—-since Mike's innings against Downing's the Lost Lambs had been received as brothers by that centre of disorder, so that even Spiller was compelled to look on the hatchet as buried—-and gave his views on the events of the preceding night, or, rather, of that morning, for it was nearer one than twelve when peace had once more fallen on the school.

"Nothing that happens in this luny-bin," said Psmith, "has power to surprise me now. There was a time when I might have thought it a little unusual to have to leave the house through a canvas shoot at one o'clock in the morning, but I suppose it's quite the regular thing here. Old school tradition, &c. Men leave the school, and find that they've got so accustomed to jumping out of window that they look on it as a sort of affectation to go out by the door. I suppose none of you merchants can give me any idea when the next knockabout entertainment of this kind is likely to take place?"

"I wonder who rang that bell!" said Stone. "Jolly sporting idea."

"I believe it was Downing himself. If it was, I hope he's satisfied."

Jellicoe, who was appearing in society supported by a stick, looked meaningly at Mike, and giggled, receiving in answer a stony stare. Mike had informed Jellicoe of the details of his interview with Mr. Barley at the "White Boar," and Jellicoe, after a momentary splutter of wrath against the practical joker, was now in a particularly light-hearted mood. He hobbled about, giggling at nothing and at peace with all the world.

"It was a stirring scene," said Psmith. "The agility with which Comrade Jellicoe boosted himself down the shoot was a triumph of mind over matter. He seemed to forget his ankle. It was the nearest thing to a Boneless Acrobatic Wonder that I have ever seen."

"I was in a beastly funk, I can tell you."

Stone gurgled.

"So was I," he said, "for a bit. Then, when I saw that it was all a rag, I began to look about for ways of doing the thing really well. I emptied about six jugs of water on a gang of kids under my window."

"I rushed into Downing's, and ragged some of the beds," said Robinson.

"It was an invigorating time," said Psmith. "A sort of pageant. I was particularly struck with the way some of the bright lads caught hold of the idea. There was no skimping. Some of the kids, to my certain knowledge, went down the shoot a dozen times. There's nothing like doing a thing thoroughly. I saw them come down, rush upstairs, and be saved again, time after time. The thing became chronic with them. I should say Comrade Downing ought to be satisfied with the high state of efficiency to which he has brought us. At any rate I hope——-"

There was a sound of hurried footsteps outside the door, and Sharpe, a member of the senior day-room, burst excitedly in. He seemed amused.

"I say, have you chaps seen Sammy?"

"Seen who?" said Stone. "Sammy? Why?"

"You'll know in a second. He's just outside. Here, Sammy, Sammy, Sammy! Sam! Sam!"

A bark and a patter of feet outside.

"Come on, Sammy. Good dog."

There was a moment's silence. Then a great yell of laughter burst forth. Even Psmith's massive calm was shattered. As for Jellicoe, he sobbed in a corner.

Sammy's beautiful white coat was almost entirely concealed by a thick covering of bright red paint. His head, with the exception of the ears, was untouched, and his serious, friendly eyes seemed to emphasise the weirdness of his appearance. He stood in the doorway, barking and wagging his tail, plainly puzzled at his reception. He was a popular dog, and was always well received when he visited any of the houses, but he had never before met with enthusiasm like this.

"Good old Sammy!"

"What on earth's been happening to him?"

"Who did it?"

Sharpe, the introducer, had no views on the matter.

"I found him outside Downing's, with a crowd round him. Everybody seems to have seen him. I wonder who on earth has gone and mucked him up like that!"

Mike was the first to show any sympathy for the maltreated animal.

"Poor old Sammy," he said, kneeling on the floor beside the victim, and scratching him under the ear. "What a beastly shame! It'll take hours to wash all that off him, and he'll hate it."

"It seems to me," said Psmith, regarding Sammy dispassionately through his eyeglass, "that it's not a case for mere washing. They'll either have to skin him bodily, or leave the thing to time. Time, the Great Healer. In a year or two he'll fade to a delicate pink. I don't see why you shouldn't have a pink bull-terrier. It would lend a touch of distinction to the place. Crowds would come in excursion trains to see him. By charging a small fee you might make him self-supporting. I think I'll suggest it to Comrade Downing."

"There'll be a row about this," said Stone.

"Rows are rather sport when you're not mixed up in them," said Robinson, philosophically. "There'll be another if we don't start off for chapel soon. It's a quarter to."

There was a general move. Mike was the last to leave the room. As he was going, Jellicoe stopped him. Jellicoe was staying in that Sunday, owing to his ankle.

"I say," said Jellicoe, "I just wanted to thank you again about that——"

"Oh, that's all right."

"No, but it really was awfully decent of you. You might have got into a frightful row. Were you nearly caught?"

"Jolly nearly."

"It *was* you who rang the bell, wasn't it?"

"Yes, it was. But for goodness sake don't go gassing about it, or somebody will get to hear who oughtn't to, and I shall be sacked."

"All right. But, I say, you *are* a chap!"

"What's the matter now?"

"I mean about Sammy, you know. It's a jolly good score off old Downing. He'll be frightfully sick."

"Sammy!" cried Mike. "My good man, you don't think I did that, do you? What absolute rot! I never touched the poor brute."

"Oh, all right," said Jellicoe. "But I wasn't going to tell any one, of course."

"What do you mean?"

"You *are* a chap!" giggled Jellicoe.

Mike walked to chapel rather thoughtfully.

CHAPTER XLVII MR. DOWNING ON THE SCENT

There was just one moment, the moment in which, on going down to the junior day-room of his house to quell an unseemly disturbance, he was boisterously greeted by a vermilion bull terrier, when Mr. Downing was seized with a hideous fear lest he had lost his senses. Glaring down at the crimson animal that was pawing at his knees, he clutched at his reason for one second as a drowning man clutches at a lifebelt.

Then the happy laughter of the young onlookers reassured him.

"Who—-" he shouted, "WHO has done this?"

"Please, sir, we don't know," shrilled the chorus.

"Please, sir, he came in like that."

"Please, sir, we were sitting here when he suddenly ran in, all red."

A voice from the crowd: "Look at old Sammy!"

The situation was impossible. There was nothing to be done. He could not find out by verbal inquiry who had painted the dog. The possibility of Sammy being painted red during the night had never occurred to Mr. Downing, and now that the thing had happened he had no scheme of action. As Psmith would have said, he had confused the unusual with the impossible, and the result was that he was taken by surprise.

While he was pondering on this the situation was rendered still more difficult by Sammy, who, taking advantage of the door being open, escaped and rushed into the road, thus publishing his condition to all and sundry. You can hush up a painted dog while it confines itself to your own premises, but once it has mixed with the great public this becomes out of the question. Sammy's state advanced from a private trouble into a row. Mr. Downing's next move was in the same direction that Sammy had taken, only, instead of running about the road, he went straight to the headmaster.

The Head, who had had to leave his house in the small hours in his pyjamas and a dressing-gown, was not in the best of tempers. He had a cold in the head, and also a rooted conviction that Mr. Downing, in spite of his strict orders, had rung the bell himself on the previous night in order to test the efficiency of the school in saving themselves in the event of fire. He received the housemaster frostily, but thawed as the latter related the events which had led up to the ringing of the bell.

"Dear me!" he said, deeply interested. "One of the boys at the school, you think?"

"WHO——" HE SHOUTED, "WHO HAS DONE THIS?"

"I am certain of it," said Mr. Downing.

"Was he wearing a school cap?"

"He was bare-headed. A boy who breaks out of his house at night would hardly run the risk of wearing a distinguishing cap."

"No, no, I suppose not. A big boy, you say?"

"Very big."

"You did not see his face?"

"It was dark and he never looked back—-he was in front of me all the time."

"Dear me!"

"There is another matter——-"

"Yes?"

"This boy, whoever he was, had done something before he rang the bell—-he had painted my dog Sampson red."

The headmaster's eyes protruded from their sockets. "He—-he—-*what*, Mr. Downing?"

"He painted my dog red—-bright red." Mr. Downing was too angry to see anything humorous in the incident. Since the previous night he had been wounded in his tenderest feelings. His Fire Brigade system had been most shamefully abused by being turned into a mere instrument in the hands of a malefactor for escaping justice, and his dog had been held up to ridicule to all the world. He did not want to smile, he wanted revenge.

The headmaster, on the other hand, did want to smile. It was not his dog, he could look on the affair with an unbiased eye, and to him there was something ludicrous in a white dog suddenly appearing as a red dog.

"It is a scandalous thing!" said Mr. Downing.

"Quite so! Quite so!" said the headmaster hastily. "I shall punish the boy who did it most severely. I will speak to the school in the Hall after chapel."

Which he did, but without result. A cordial invitation to the criminal to come forward and be executed was received in wooden silence by the school, with the exception of Johnson III., of Outwood's, who, suddenly reminded of Sammy's appearance by the headmaster's words, broke into a wild screech of laughter, and was instantly awarded two hundred lines.

The school filed out of the Hall to their various lunches, and Mr. Downing was left with the conviction that, if he wanted the criminal discovered, he would have to discover him for himself.

The great thing in affairs of this kind is to get a good start, and Fate, feeling perhaps that it had been a little hard upon Mr. Downing, gave him a most magnificent start. Instead of having to hunt for a needle in a haystack, he found himself in a moment in the position of being set to find it in a mere truss of straw.

It was Mr. Outwood who helped him. Sergeant Collard had waylaid the archaeological expert on his way to chapel, and informed him that at close on twelve the night before he had observed a youth, unidentified, attempting to get into his house *via* the water-pipe. Mr. Outwood, whose thoughts were occupied with apses and plinths, not to mention cromlechs, at the time, thanked the sergeant with absent-minded politeness and passed on. Later he remembered the fact *à propos* of some reflections on the subject of burglars in mediaeval England, and passed it on to Mr. Downing as they walked back to lunch.

"Then the boy was in your house!" exclaimed Mr. Downing.

"Not actually in, as far as I understand. I gather from the sergeant that he interrupted him before——"

"I mean he must have been one of the boys in your house."

"But what was he doing out at that hour?"

"He had broken out."

"Impossible, I think. Oh yes, quite impossible! I went round the dormitories as usual at eleven o'clock last night, and all the boys were asleep—all of them."

Mr. Downing was not listening. He was in a state of suppressed excitement and exultation which made it hard for him to attend to his colleague's slow utterances. He had a clue! Now that the search had narrowed itself down to Outwood's house, the rest was comparatively easy. Perhaps Sergeant Collard had actually recognised the boy. Or reflection he dismissed this as unlikely, for the sergeant would scarcely have kept a thing like that to himself; but he might very well have seen more of him than he, Downing, had seen. It was only with an effort that he could keep himself from rushing to the sergeant then and there, and leaving the house lunch to look after itself. He resolved to go the moment that meal was at an end.

Sunday lunch at a public-school house is probably one of the longest functions in existence. It drags its slow length along like a languid snake, but it finishes in time. In due course Mr. Downing, after sitting still and eyeing with acute dislike everybody who asked for a second helping, found himself at liberty.

Regardless of the claims of digestion, he rushed forth on the trail.

Sergeant Collard lived with his wife and a family of unknown dimensions in the lodge at the school front gate. Dinner was just over when Mr. Downing arrived, as a blind man could have told.

The sergeant received his visitor with dignity, ejecting the family, who were torpid after roast beef and resented having to move, in order to ensure privacy.

Having requested his host to smoke, which the latter was about to do unasked, Mr. Downing stated his case.

"Mr. Outwood," he said, "tells me that last night, sergeant, you saw a boy endeavouring to enter his house."

The sergeant blew a cloud of smoke. "Oo-oo-oo, yer," he said; "I did, sir—spotted 'im, I did. Feeflee good at spottin', I am, sir. Dook of Connaught, he used to say, ''Ere comes Sergeant Collard,' he used to say, ''e's feeflee good at spottin'.'"

"What did you do?"

"Do? Oo-oo-oo! I shouts 'Oo-oo-oo yer, yer young monkey, what yer doin' there?'"

"Yes?"

"But 'e was off in a flash, and I doubles after 'im prompt."

"But you didn't catch him?"

"No, sir," admitted the sergeant reluctantly.

"Did you catch sight of his face, sergeant?"

"No, sir, 'e was doublin' away in the opposite direction."

"Did you notice anything at all about his appearance?"

"'E was a long young chap, sir, with a pair of legs on him—-feeflee fast 'e run, sir. Oo-oo-oo, feeflee!"

"You noticed nothing else?"

"'E wasn't wearing no cap of any sort, sir."

"Ah!"

"Bare-'eaded, sir," added the sergeant, rubbing the point in.

"It was undoubtedly the same boy, undoubtedly! I wish you could have caught a glimpse of his face, sergeant."

"So do I, sir."

"You would not be able to recognise him again if you saw him, you think?"

"Oo-oo-oo! Wouldn't go so far as to say that, sir, 'cos yer see, I'm feeflee good at spottin', but it was a dark night."

Mr. Downing rose to go.

"Well," he said, "the search is now considerably narrowed down, considerably! It is certain that the boy was one of the boys in Mr. Outwood's house."

"Young monkeys!" interjected the sergeant helpfully.

"Good-afternoon, sergeant."

"Good-afternoon to you, sir."

"Pray do not move, sergeant."

The sergeant had not shown the slightest inclination of doing anything of the kind.

"I will find my way out. Very hot to-day, is it not?"

"Feeflee warm, sir; weather's goin' to break—-workin' up for thunder."

"I hope not. The school plays the M.C.C. on Wednesday, and it would be a pity if rain were to spoil our first fixture with them. Good afternoon."

And Mr. Downing went out into the baking sunlight, while Sergeant Collard, having requested Mrs. Collard to take the children out for a walk at once, and furthermore to give young Ernie a clip side of the 'ead, if he persisted in making so much noise, put a handkerchief over his face, rested his feet on the table, and slept the sleep of the just.

CHAPTER XLVIII THE SLEUTH-HOUND

For the Doctor Watsons of this world, as opposed to the Sherlock Holmeses, success in the province of detective work must always be, to a very large extent, the result of luck. Sherlock Holmes can extract a clue from a wisp of straw or a flake of cigar-ash. But Doctor Watson has got to have it taken out for him, and dusted, and exhibited clearly, with a label attached.

The average man is a Doctor Watson. We are wont to scoff in a patronising manner at that humble follower of the great investigator, but, as a matter of fact, we should have been just as dull ourselves. We should not even have risen to the modest level of a Scotland Yard Bungler. We should simply have hung around, saying:

"My dear Holmes, how—?" and all the rest of it, just as the downtrodden medico did.

It is not often that the ordinary person has any need to see what he can do in the way of detection. He gets along very comfortably in the humdrum round of life without having to measure footprints and smile quiet, tight-lipped smiles. But if ever the emergency does arise, he thinks naturally of Sherlock Holmes, and his methods.

Mr. Downing had read all the Holmes stories with great attention, and had thought many times what an incompetent ass Doctor Watson was; but, now that he had started to handle his own first case, he was compelled to admit that there was a good deal to be said in extenuation of Watson's inability to unravel tangles. It certainly was uncommonly hard, he thought, as he paced the cricket field after leaving Sergeant Collard, to detect anybody, unless you knew who had really done the crime. As he brooded over the case in hand, his sympathy for Dr. Watson increased with every minute, and he began to feel a certain resentment against Sir Arthur Conan Doyle. It was all very well for Sir Arthur to be so shrewd and infallible about tracing a mystery to its source, but he knew perfectly well who had done the thing before he started!

Now that he began really to look into this matter of the alarm bell and the painting of Sammy, the conviction was creeping over him that the problem was more difficult than a casual observer might imagine. He had got as far as finding that his quarry of the previous night was a boy in Mr. Outwood's house, but how was he to get any farther? That was the thing. There were, of course, only a limited number of boys in Mr. Outwood's house as tall as the one he had pursued; but even if there had been only one other, it would have complicated matters. If you go to a boy and say, "Either you or Jones were out of your house last night at twelve o'clock," the boy does not reply, "Sir, I cannot tell a lie—-I was out of my house last night at twelve o'clock." He simply assumes the animated expression of a stuffed fish, and leaves the next move to you. It is practically Stalemate.

All these things passed through Mr. Downing's mind as he walked up and down the cricket field that afternoon.

What he wanted was a clue. But it is so hard for the novice to tell what is a clue and what isn't. Probably, if he only knew, there were clues lying all over the place, shouting to him to pick them up.

What with the oppressive heat of the day and the fatigue of hard thinking, Mr. Downing was working up for a brain-storm, when Fate once more intervened, this time in the shape of Riglett, a junior member of his house.

Riglett slunk up in the shamefaced way peculiar to some boys, even when they have done nothing wrong, and, having capped Mr. Downing with the air of one who has been caught in the act of doing something particularly shady, requested that he might be allowed to fetch his bicycle from the shed.

"Your bicycle?" snapped Mr. Downing. Much thinking had made him irritable. "What do you want with your bicycle?"

Riglett shuffled, stood first on his left foot, then on his right, blushed, and finally remarked, as if it were not so much a sound reason as a sort of feeble excuse for the low and blackguardly fact that he wanted his bicycle, that he had got leave for tea that afternoon.

Then Mr. Downing remembered. Riglett had an aunt resident about three miles from the school, whom he was accustomed to visit occasionally on Sunday afternoons during the term.

He felt for his bunch of keys, and made his way to the shed, Riglett shambling behind at an interval of two yards.

Mr. Downing unlocked the door, and there on the floor was the Clue!

A clue that even Dr. Watson could not have overlooked.

Mr. Downing saw it, but did not immediately recognise it for what it was. What he saw at first was not a Clue, but just a mess. He had a tidy soul and abhorred messes. And this was a particularly messy mess. The greater part of the flooring in the neighbourhood of the door was a sea of red paint. The tin from which it had flowed was lying on its side in the middle of the shed. The air was full of the pungent scent.

"Pah!" said Mr. Downing.

Then suddenly, beneath the disguise of the mess, he saw the clue. A foot-mark! No less. A crimson foot-mark on the grey concrete!

Riglett, who had been waiting patiently two yards away, now coughed plaintively. The sound recalled Mr. Downing to mundane matters.

"Get your bicycle, Riglett," he said, "and be careful where you tread. Somebody has upset a pot of paint on the floor."

CHAPTER XLVIII THE SLEUTH-HOUND

Riglett, walking delicately through dry places, extracted his bicycle from the rack, and presently departed to gladden the heart of his aunt, leaving Mr. Downing, his brain fizzing with the enthusiasm of the detective, to lock the door and resume his perambulation of the cricket field.

Give Dr. Watson a fair start, and he is a demon at the game. Mr. Downing's brain was now working with a rapidity and clearness which a professional sleuth might have envied.

Paint. Red paint. Obviously the same paint with which Sammy had been decorated. A foot-mark. Whose foot-mark? Plainly that of the criminal who had done the deed of decoration.

Yoicks!

There were two things, however, to be considered. Your careful detective must consider everything. In the first place, the paint might have been upset by the ground-man. It was the ground-man's paint. He had been giving a fresh coating to the wood-work in front of the pavilion scoring-box at the conclusion of yesterday's match. (A labour of love which was the direct outcome of the enthusiasm for work which Adair had instilled into him.) In that case the foot-mark might be his.

Note one: Interview the ground-man on this point.

In the second place Adair might have upset the tin and trodden in its contents when he went to get his bicycle in order to fetch the doctor for the suffering MacPhee. This was the more probable of the two contingencies, for it would have been dark in the shed when Adair went into it.

Note two Interview Adair as to whether he found, on returning to the house, that there was paint on his boots.

Things were moving.

He resolved to take Adair first. He could get the ground-man's address from him.

Passing by the trees under whose shade Mike and Psmith and Dunster had watched the match on the previous day, he came upon the Head of his house in a deck-chair reading a book. A summer Sunday afternoon is the time for reading in deck-chairs.

"Oh, Adair," he said. "No, don't get up. I merely wished to ask you if you found any paint on your boots when you returned to the house last night?"

"Paint, sir?" Adair was plainly puzzled. His book had been interesting, and had driven the Sammy incident out of his head.

"I see somebody has spilt some paint on the floor of the bicycle shed. You did not do that, I suppose, when you went to fetch your bicycle?"

"No, sir."

"It is spilt all over the floor. I wondered whether you had happened to tread in it. But you say you found no paint on your boots this morning?"

"No, sir, my bicycle is always quite near the door of the shed. I didn't go into the shed at all."

"I see. Quite so. Thank you, Adair. Oh, by the way, Adair, where does Markby live?"

"I forget the name of his cottage, sir, but I could show you in a second. It's one of those cottages just past the school gates, on the right as you turn out into the road. There are three in a row. His is the first you come to. There's a barn just before you get to them."

"Thank you. I shall be able to find them. I should like to speak to Markby for a moment on a small matter."

A sharp walk took him to the cottages Adair had mentioned. He rapped at the door of the first, and the ground-man came out in his shirt-sleeves, blinking as if he had just woke up, as was indeed the case.

"Oh, Markby!"

"Sir?"

"You remember that you were painting the scoring-box in the pavilion last night after the match?"

"Yes, sir. It wanted a lick of paint bad. The young gentlemen will scramble about and get through the window. Makes it look shabby, sir. So I thought I'd better give it a coating so as to look ship-shape when the Marylebone come down."

"Just so. An excellent idea. Tell me, Markby, what did you do with the pot of paint when you had finished?"

"Put it in the bicycle shed, sir."

"On the floor?"

"On the floor, sir? No. On the shelf at the far end, with the can of whitening what I use for marking out the wickets, sir."

"Of course, yes. Quite so. Just as I thought."

"Do you want it, sir?"

"No, thank you, Markby, no, thank you. The fact is, somebody who had no business to do so has moved the pot of paint from the shelf to the floor, with the result that it has been kicked over, and spilt. You had better get some more to-morrow. Thank you, Markby. That is all I wished to know."

Mr. Downing walked back to the school thoroughly excited. He was hot on the scent now. The only other possible theories had been tested and successfully exploded. The thing had become simple to a degree. All he had to do was to go to Mr. Outwood's house—the idea of searching a fellow-master's house did not appear to him at all a delicate task; somehow one grew unconsciously to feel that Mr. Outwood did not really exist as a man capable of resenting liberties—find the paint-splashed boot, ascertain its owner, and denounce him to the headmaster. Picture, Blue Fire and "God Save the King" by the full strength of the company. There could be no doubt that a paint-splashed boot must be in Mr. Outwood's house somewhere. A boy cannot tread in a pool of paint without showing some signs of having done so. It was Sunday, too, so that the boot would not yet have been cleaned. Yoicks! Also Tally-ho! This really was beginning to be something like business.

CHAPTER XLVIII THE SLEUTH-HOUND

Regardless of the heat, the sleuth-hound hurried across to Outwood's as fast as he could walk.

CHAPTER XLIX A CHECK

The only two members of the house not out in the grounds when he arrived were Mike and Psmith. They were standing on the gravel drive in front of the boys' entrance. Mike had a deck-chair in one hand and a book in the other. Psmith—-for even the greatest minds will sometimes unbend—-was playing diabolo. That is to say, he was trying without success to raise the spool from the ground.

"There's a kid in France," said Mike disparagingly, as the bobbin rolled off the string for the fourth time, "who can do it three thousand seven hundred and something times."

Psmith smoothed a crease out of his waistcoat and tried again. He had just succeeded in getting the thing to spin when Mr. Downing arrived. The sound of his footsteps disturbed Psmith and brought the effort to nothing.

"Enough of this spoolery," said he, flinging the sticks through the open window of the senior day-room. "I was an ass ever to try it. The philosophical mind needs complete repose in its hours of leisure. Hullo!"

He stared after the sleuth-hound, who had just entered the house.

"What the dickens," said Mike, "does he mean by barging in as if he'd bought the place?"

"Comrade Downing looks pleased with himself. What brings him round in this direction, I wonder! Still, no matter. The few articles which he may sneak from our study are of inconsiderable value. He is welcome to them. Do you feel inclined to wait awhile till I have fetched a chair and book?"

"I'll be going on. I shall be under the trees at the far end of the ground."

"'Tis well. I will be with you in about two ticks."

Mike walked on towards the field, and Psmith, strolling upstairs to fetch his novel, found Mr. Downing standing in the passage with the air of one who has lost his bearings.

"A warm afternoon, sir," murmured Psmith courteously, as he passed.

"Er—-Smith!"

"Sir?"

"I—-er—-wish to go round the dormitories."

It was Psmith's guiding rule in life never to be surprised at anything, so he merely inclined his head gracefully, and said nothing.

"I should be glad if you would fetch the keys and show me where the rooms are."

"With acute pleasure, sir," said Psmith. "Or shall I fetch Mr. Outwood, sir?"

"Do as I tell you, Smith," snapped Mr. Downing.

Psmith said no more, but went down to the matron's room. The matron being out, he abstracted the bunch of keys from her table and rejoined the master.

"Shall I lead the way, sir?" he asked.

Mr. Downing nodded.

"Here, sir," said Psmith, opening a door, "we have Barnes' dormitory. An airy room, constructed on the soundest hygienic principles. Each boy, I understand, has quite a considerable number of cubic feet of air all to himself. It is Mr. Outwood's boast that no boy has ever asked for a cubic foot of air in vain. He argues justly——"

He broke off abruptly and began to watch the other's manoeuvres in silence. Mr. Downing was peering rapidly beneath each bed in turn.

"Are you looking for Barnes, sir?" inquired Psmith politely. "I think he's out in the field."

Mr. Downing rose, having examined the last bed, crimson in the face with the exercise.

"Show me the next dormitory, Smith," he said, panting slightly.

"This," said Psmith, opening the next door and sinking his voice to an awed whisper, "is where *I* sleep!"

Mr. Downing glanced swiftly beneath the three beds. "Excuse me, sir," said Psmith, "but are we chasing anything?"

"Be good enough, Smith," said Mr. Downing with asperity, "to keep your remarks to yourself."

"I was only wondering, sir. Shall I show you the next in order?"

"Certainly."

They moved on up the passage.

Drawing blank at the last dormitory, Mr. Downing paused, baffled. Psmith waited patiently by. An idea struck the master.

"The studies, Smith," he cried.

"Aha!" said Psmith. "I beg your pardon, sir. The observation escaped me unawares. The frenzy of the chase is beginning to enter into my blood. Here we have——"

Mr. Downing stopped short.

"Is this impertinence studied, Smith?"

"Ferguson's study, sir? No, sir. That's further down the passage. This is Barnes'."

Mr. Downing looked at him closely. Psmith's face was wooden in its gravity. The master snorted suspiciously, then moved on.

"Whose is this?" he asked, rapping a door.

"This, sir, is mine and Jackson's."

"What! Have you a study? You are low down in the school for it."

"I think, sir, that Mr. Outwood gave it us rather as a testimonial to our general worth than to our proficiency in school-work."

Mr. Downing raked the room with a keen eye. The absence of bars from the window attracted his attention.

"Have you no bars to your windows here, such as there are in my house?"

"There appears to be no bar, sir," said Psmith, putting up his eyeglass.

Mr Downing was leaning out of the window.

"A lovely view, is it not, sir?" said Psmith. "The trees, the field, the distant hills——"

Mr. Downing suddenly started. His eye had been caught by the water-pipe at the side of the window. The boy whom Sergeant Collard had seen climbing the pipe must have been making for this study.

He spun round and met Psmith's blandly inquiring gaze. He looked at Psmith carefully for a moment. No. The boy he had chased last night had not been Psmith. That exquisite's figure and general appearance were unmistakable, even in the dusk.

"Whom did you say you shared this study with, Smith?"

"Jackson, sir. The cricketer."

"Never mind about his cricket, Smith," said Mr. Downing with irritation.

"No, sir."

"He is the only other occupant of the room?"

"Yes, sir."

"Nobody else comes into it?"

"If they do, they go out extremely quickly, sir."

"Ah! Thank you, Smith."

"Not at all, sir."

Mr. Downing pondered. Jackson! The boy bore him a grudge. The boy was precisely the sort of boy to revenge himself by painting the dog Sammy. And, gadzooks! The boy whom he had pursued last night had been just about Jackson's size and build!

Mr. Downing was as firmly convinced at that moment that Mike's had been the hand to wield the paint-brush as he had ever been of anything in his life.

"Smith!" he said excitedly.

"On the spot, sir," said Psmith affably.

"Where are Jackson's boots?"

There are moments when the giddy excitement of being right on the trail causes the amateur (or Watsonian) detective to be incautious. Such a moment came to Mr. Downing then. If he had been wise, he would have achieved his object, the getting a glimpse of Mike's boots, by a devious and snaky route. As it was, he rushed straight on.

"His boots, sir? He has them on. I noticed them as he went out just now."

"Where is the pair he wore yesterday?"

"Where are the boots of yester-year?" murmured Psmith to himself. "I should say at a venture, sir, that they would be in the basket downstairs. Edmund, our genial knife-and-boot boy, collects them, I believe, at early dawn."

"Would they have been cleaned yet?"

"If I know Edmund, sir—-no."

"Smith," said Mr. Downing, trembling with excitement, "go and bring that basket to me here."

Psmith's brain was working rapidly as he went downstairs. What exactly was at the back of the sleuth's mind, prompting these manoeuvres, he did not know. But that there was something, and that that something was directed in a hostile manner against Mike, probably in connection with last night's wild happenings, he was certain. Psmith had noticed, on leaving his bed at the sound of the alarm bell, that he and Jellicoe were alone in the room. That might mean that Mike had gone out through the door when the bell sounded, or it might mean that he had been out all the time. It began to look as if the latter solution were the correct one.

He staggered back with the basket, painfully conscious the while that it was creasing his waistcoat, and dumped it down on the study floor. Mr. Downing stooped eagerly over it. Psmith leaned against the wall, and straightened out the damaged garment.

"We have here, sir," he said, "a fair selection of our various bootings."

Mr. Downing looked up.

"You dropped none of the boots on your way up, Smith?"

"Not one, sir. It was a fine performance."

Mr. Downing uttered a grunt of satisfaction, and bent once more to his task. Boots flew about the room. Mr. Downing knelt on the floor beside the basket, and dug like a terrier at a rat-hole.

At last he made a dive, and, with an exclamation of triumph, rose to his feet. In his hand he held a boot.

"Put those back again, Smith," he said.

The ex-Etonian, wearing an expression such as a martyr might have worn on being told off for the stake, began to pick up the scattered footgear, whistling softly the tune of "I do all the dirty work," as he did so.

"That's the lot, sir," he said, rising.

"Ah. Now come across with me to the headmaster's house. Leave the basket here. You can carry it back when you return."

"Shall I put back that boot, sir?"

"Certainly not. I shall take this with me, of course."

"Shall I carry it, sir?"

Mr. Downing reflected.

"Yes, Smith," he said. "I think it would be best."

It occurred to him that the spectacle of a housemaster wandering abroad on the public highway, carrying a dirty boot, might be a trifle undignified. You never knew whom you might meet on Sunday afternoon.

Psmith took the boot, and doing so, understood what before had puzzled him.

Across the toe of the boot was a broad splash of red paint.

He knew nothing, of course, of the upset tin in the bicycle shed; but when a housemaster's dog has been painted red in the night, and when, on the following day, the housemaster goes about in search of a paint-splashed boot, one puts two and two together. Psmith looked at the name inside the boot. It was "Brown, boot-maker, Bridgnorth." Bridgnorth was only a few miles from his own home and Mike's. Undoubtedly it was Mike's boot.

"Can you tell me whose boot that is?" asked Mr. Downing.

Psmith looked at it again.

"No, sir. I can't say the little chap's familiar to me."

"Come with me, then."

Mr. Downing left the room. After a moment Psmith followed him.

The headmaster was in his garden. Thither Mr. Downing made his way, the boot-bearing Psmith in close attendance.

The Head listened to the amateur detective's statement with interest.

"Indeed?" he said, when Mr. Downing had finished.

"Indeed? Dear me! It certainly seems—-It is a curiously well-connected thread of evidence. You are certain that there was red paint on this boot you discovered in Mr. Outwood's house?"

"I have it with me. I brought it on purpose to show to you. Smith!"

"Sir?"

"You have the boot?"

"Ah," said the headmaster, putting on a pair of pince-nez, "now let me look at—-This, you say, is the—? Just so. Just so. Just.... But, er, Mr. Downing, it may be that I have not examined this boot with sufficient care, but—-Can *you* point out to me exactly where this paint is that you speak of?"

Mr. Downing stood staring at the boot with a wild, fixed stare. Of any suspicion of paint, red or otherwise, it was absolutely and entirely innocent.

CHAPTER L THE DESTROYER OF EVIDENCE

The boot became the centre of attraction, the cynosure of all eyes. Mr. Downing fixed it with the piercing stare of one who feels that his brain is tottering. The headmaster looked at it with a mildly puzzled expression. Psmith, putting up his eyeglass, gazed at it with a sort of affectionate interest, as if he were waiting for it to do a trick of some kind.

Mr. Downing was the first to break the silence.

"There was paint on this boot," he said vehemently. "I tell you there was a splash of red paint across the toe. Smith will bear me out in this. Smith, you saw the paint on this boot?"

"Paint, sir!"

"What! Do you mean to tell me that you did *not* see it?"

"No, sir. There was no paint on this boot."

"This is foolery. I saw it with my own eyes. It was a broad splash right across the toe."

The headmaster interposed.

"You must have made a mistake, Mr. Downing. There is certainly no trace of paint on this boot. These momentary optical delusions are, I fancy, not uncommon. Any doctor will tell you——"

"I had an aunt, sir," said Psmith chattily, "who was remarkably subject——"

"It is absurd. I cannot have been mistaken," said Mr. Downing. "I am positively certain the toe of this boot was red when I found it."

"It is undoubtedly black now, Mr. Downing."

"A sort of chameleon boot," murmured Psmith.

The goaded housemaster turned on him.

"What did you say, Smith?"

"Did I speak, sir?" said Psmith, with the start of one coming suddenly out of a trance.

Mr. Downing looked searchingly at him.

"You had better be careful, Smith."

"Yes, sir."

"I strongly suspect you of having something to do with this."

"Really, Mr. Downing," said the headmaster, "that is surely improbable. Smith could scarcely have cleaned the boot on his way to my house. On one occasion I inadvertently spilt some paint on a shoe of my own. I can assure you that it does not brush off. It needs a very systematic cleaning before all traces are removed."

"Exactly, sir," said Psmith. "My theory, if I may——?"

"Certainly, Smith."

Psmith bowed courteously and proceeded.

"My theory, sir, is that Mr. Downing was deceived by the light and shade effects on the toe of the boot. The afternoon sun, streaming in through the window, must have shone on the boot in such a manner as to give it a momentary and fictitious aspect of redness. If Mr. Downing recollects, he did not look long at the boot. The picture on the retina of the eye, consequently, had not time to fade. I remember thinking myself, at the moment, that the boot appeared to have a certain reddish tint. The mistake——"

"Bah!" said Mr. Downing shortly.

"Well, really," said the headmaster, "it seems to me that that is the only explanation that will square with the facts. A boot that is really smeared with red paint does not become black of itself in the course of a few minutes."

"You are very right, sir," said Psmith with benevolent approval. "May I go now, sir? I am in the middle of a singularly impressive passage of Cicero's speech De Senectute."

"I am sorry that you should leave your preparation till Sunday, Smith. It is a habit of which I altogether disapprove."

"I am reading it, sir," said Psmith, with simple dignity, "for pleasure. Shall I take the boot with me, sir?"

"If Mr. Downing does not want it?"

The housemaster passed the fraudulent piece of evidence to Psmith without a word, and the latter, having included both masters in a kindly smile, left the garden.

Pedestrians who had the good fortune to be passing along the road between the housemaster's house and Mr. Outwood's at that moment saw what, if they had but known it, was a most unusual sight, the spectacle of Psmith running. Psmith's usual mode of progression was a dignified walk. He believed in the contemplative style rather than the hustling.

On this occasion, however, reckless of possible injuries to the crease of his trousers, he raced down the road, and turning in at Outwood's gate, bounded upstairs like a highly trained professional athlete.

On arriving at the study, his first act was to remove a boot from the top of the pile in the basket, place it in the small cupboard under the bookshelf, and lock the cupboard. Then he flung himself into a chair and panted.

"Brain," he said to himself approvingly, "is what one chiefly needs in matters of this kind. Without brain, where are we? In the soup, every time. The next development will be when Comrade Downing thinks it over, and is struck with the brilliant idea that it's just possible that the boot he gave me to carry and the boot I did carry were not one boot but two boots. Meanwhile——"

He dragged up another chair for his feet and picked up his novel.

He had not been reading long when there was a footstep in the passage, and Mr. Downing appeared.

The possibility, in fact the probability, of Psmith having substituted another boot for the one with the incriminating splash of paint on it had occurred to him almost immediately on leaving the headmaster's garden. Psmith and Mike, he reflected, were friends. Psmith's impulse would be to do all that lay in his power to shield Mike. Feeling aggrieved with himself that he had not thought of this before, he, too, hurried over to Outwood's.

Mr. Downing was brisk and peremptory.

"I wish to look at these boots again," he said. Psmith, with a sigh, laid down his novel, and rose to assist him.

"Sit down, Smith," said the housemaster. "I can manage without your help."

Psmith sat down again, carefully tucking up the knees of his trousers, and watched him with silent interest through his eyeglass.

The scrutiny irritated Mr. Downing.

"Put that thing away, Smith," he said.

"That thing, sir?"

"Yes, that ridiculous glass. Put it away."

"Why, sir?"

"Why! Because I tell you to do so."

"I guessed that that was the reason, sir," sighed Psmith replacing the eyeglass in his waistcoat pocket. He rested his elbows on his knees, and his chin on his hands, and resumed his contemplative inspection of the boot-expert, who, after fidgeting for a few moments, lodged another complaint.

"Don't sit there staring at me, Smith."

"I was interested in what you were doing, sir."

"Never mind. Don't stare at me in that idiotic way."

"May I read, sir?" asked Psmith, patiently.

"Yes, read if you like."

"Thank you, sir."

Psmith took up his book again, and Mr. Downing, now thoroughly irritated, pursued his investigations in the boot-basket.

He went through it twice, but each time without success. After the second search, he stood up, and looked wildly round the room. He was as certain as he could be of anything that the missing piece of evidence was somewhere in the study. It was no use asking Psmith point-blank where it was, for Psmith's ability to parry dangerous questions with evasive answers was quite out of the common.

His eye roamed about the room. There was very little cover there, even for so small a fugitive as a number nine boot. The floor could be acquitted, on sight, of harbouring the quarry.

Then he caught sight of the cupboard, and something seemed to tell him that there was the place to look.

"Smith!" he said.

Psmith had been reading placidly all the while.

"Yes, sir?"

"What is in this cupboard?"

"That cupboard, sir?"

"Yes. This cupboard." Mr. Downing rapped the door irritably.

"Just a few odd trifles, sir. We do not often use it. A ball of string, perhaps. Possibly an old note-book. Nothing of value or interest."

"Open it."

"I think you will find that it is locked, sir."

"Unlock it."

"But where is the key, sir?"

"Have you not got the key?"

"If the key is not in the lock, sir, you may depend upon it that it will take a long search to find it."

"Where did you see it last?"

"It was in the lock yesterday morning. Jackson might have taken it."

"Where is Jackson?"

"Out in the field somewhere, sir."

Mr. Downing thought for a moment.

"I don't believe a word of it," he said shortly. "I have my reasons for thinking that you are deliberately keeping the contents of that cupboard from me. I shall break open the door."

Psmith got up.

"I'm afraid you mustn't do that, sir."

Mr. Downing stared, amazed.

"Are you aware whom you are talking to, Smith?" he inquired acidly.

"Yes, sir. And I know it's not Mr. Outwood, to whom that cupboard happens to belong. If you wish to break it open, you must get his permission. He is the sole lessee and proprietor of that cupboard. I am only the acting manager."

Mr. Downing paused. He also reflected. Mr. Outwood in the general rule did not count much in the scheme of things, but possibly there were limits to the treating of him as if he did not exist. To enter his house without his permission and search it to a certain extent was all very well. But when it came to breaking up his furniture, perhaps——!

On the other hand, there was the maddening thought that if he left the study in search of Mr. Outwood, in order to obtain his sanction for the house-breaking work which he proposed to carry through, Smith would be alone in the room. And he knew that, if Smith were left alone in the room, he would instantly remove the boot to some other hiding-place. He thoroughly disbelieved the story of the lost key. He was perfectly convinced that the missing boot was in the cupboard.

He stood chewing these thoughts for awhile, Psmith in the meantime standing in a graceful attitude in front of the cupboard, staring into vacancy.

Then he was seized with a happy idea. Why should he leave the room at all? If he sent Smith, then he himself could wait and make certain that the cupboard was not tampered with.

"Smith," he said, "go and find Mr. Outwood, and ask him to be good enough to come here for a moment."

CHAPTER LI MAINLY ABOUT BOOTS

"Be quick, Smith," he said, as the latter stood looking at him without making any movement in the direction of the door.

"*Quick*, sir?" said Psmith meditatively, as if he had been asked a conundrum.

"Go and find Mr. Outwood at once."

Psmith still made no move.

"Do you intend to disobey me, Smith?" Mr. Downing's voice was steely.

"Yes, sir."

"What!"

"Yes, sir."

There was one of those you-could-have-heard-a-pin-drop silences. Psmith was staring reflectively at the ceiling. Mr. Downing was looking as if at any moment he might say, "Thwarted to me face, ha, ha! And by a very stripling!"

It was Psmith, however, who resumed the conversation. His manner was almost too respectful; which made it all the more a pity that what he said did not keep up the standard of docility.

"I take my stand," he said, "on a technical point. I say to myself, 'Mr. Downing is a man I admire as a human being and respect as a master. In——-'"

"This impertinence is doing you no good, Smith."

Psmith waved a hand deprecatingly.

"If you will let me explain, sir. I was about to say that in any other place but Mr. Outwood's house, your word would be law. I would fly to do your bidding. If you pressed a button, I would do the rest. But in Mr. Outwood's house I cannot do anything except what pleases me or what is ordered by Mr. Outwood. I ought to have remembered that before. One cannot," he continued, as who should say, "Let us be reasonable," "one cannot, to take a parallel case, imagine the colonel commanding the garrison at a naval station going on board a battleship and ordering the crew to splice the jibboom spanker. It might be an admirable thing for the Empire that the jibboom spanker *should* be spliced at that particular juncture, but the crew would naturally decline to move in the matter until the order came from the commander of the ship. So in my case. If you will go to Mr. Outwood, and explain to him how matters stand, and come back and say to me, 'Psmith, Mr. Outwood wishes you to ask him to be good enough to come to this study,' then I shall be only too glad to go and find him. You see my difficulty, sir?"

"Go and fetch Mr. Outwood, Smith. I shall not tell you again."

Psmith flicked a speck of dust from his coat-sleeve.

"Very well, Smith."

"I can assure you, sir, at any rate, that if there is a boot in that cupboard now, there will be a boot there when you return."

Mr. Downing stalked out of the room.

"But," added Psmith pensively to himself, as the footsteps died away, "I did not promise that it would be the same boot."

He took the key from his pocket, unlocked the cupboard, and took out the boot. Then he selected from the basket a particularly battered specimen. Placing this in the cupboard, he re-locked the door.

His next act was to take from the shelf a piece of string. Attaching one end of this to the boot that he had taken from the cupboard, he went to the window. His first act was to fling the cupboard-key out into the bushes. Then he turned to the boot. On a level with the sill the water-pipe, up which Mike had started to climb the night before, was fastened to the wall by an iron band. He tied the other end of the string to this, and let the boot swing free. He noticed with approval, when it had stopped swinging, that it was hidden from above by the window-sill.

He returned to his place at the mantelpiece.

As an after-thought he took another boot from the basket, and thrust it up the chimney. A shower of soot fell into the grate, blackening his hand.

The bathroom was a few yards down the corridor. He went there, and washed off the soot.

When he returned, Mr. Downing was in the study, and with him Mr. Outwood, the latter looking dazed, as if he were not quite equal to the intellectual pressure of the situation.

"Where have you been, Smith?" asked Mr. Downing sharply.

"I have been washing my hands, sir."

"H'm!" said Mr. Downing suspiciously.

"Yes, I saw Smith go into the bathroom," said Mr. Outwood. "Smith, I cannot quite understand what it is Mr. Downing wishes me to do."

"My dear Outwood," snapped the sleuth, "I thought I had made it perfectly clear. Where is the difficulty?"

"I cannot understand why you should suspect Smith of keeping his boots in a cupboard, and," added Mr. Outwood with spirit, catching sight of a Good-Gracious-has-the-man-*no*-sense look on the other's face," why he should not do so if he wishes it."

"Exactly, sir," said Psmith, approvingly. "You have touched the spot."

"If I must explain again, my dear Outwood, will you kindly give me your attention for a moment. Last night a boy broke out of your house, and painted my dog Sampson red."

"He painted—!" said Mr. Outwood, round-eyed. "Why?"

"I don't know why. At any rate, he did. During the escapade one of his boots was splashed with the paint. It is that boot which I believe Smith to be concealing in this cupboard. Now, do you understand?"

Mr. Outwood looked amazedly at Smith, and Psmith shook his head sorrowfully at Mr. Outwood. Psmith'a expression said, as plainly as if he had spoken the words, "We must humour him."

"So with your permission, as Smith declares that he has lost the key, I propose to break open the door of this cupboard. Have you any objection?"

Mr. Outwood started.

"Objection? None at all, my dear fellow, none at all. Let me see, *what* is it you wish to do?"

"This," said Mr. Downing shortly.

There was a pair of dumb-bells on the floor, belonging to Mike. He never used them, but they always managed to get themselves packed with the rest of his belongings on the last day of the holidays. Mr. Downing seized one of these, and delivered two rapid blows at the cupboard-door. The wood splintered. A third blow smashed the flimsy lock. The cupboard, with any skeletons it might contain, was open for all to view.

Mr. Downing uttered a cry of triumph, and tore the boot from its resting-place.

"I told you," he said. "I told you."

"I wondered where that boot had got to," said Psmith. "I've been looking for it for days."

Mr. Downing was examining his find. He looked up with an exclamation of surprise and wrath.

"This boot has no paint on it," he said, glaring at Psmith. "This is not the boot."

"It certainly appears, sir," said Psmith sympathetically, "to be free from paint. There's a sort of reddish glow just there, if you look at it sideways," he added helpfully.

"Did you place that boot there, Smith?"

"I must have done. Then, when I lost the key——"

"Are you satisfied now, Downing?" interrupted Mr. Outwood with asperity, "or is there any more furniture you wish to break?"

The excitement of seeing his household goods smashed with a dumb-bell had made the archaeological student quite a swashbuckler for the moment. A little more, and one could imagine him giving Mr. Downing a good, hard knock.

The sleuth-hound stood still for a moment, baffled. But his brain was working with the rapidity of a buzz-saw. A chance remark of Mr. Outwood's set him fizzing off on the trail once more. Mr. Outwood had caught sight of the little pile of soot in the grate. He bent down to inspect it.

"Dear me," he said, "I must remember to have the chimneys swept. It should have been done before."

Mr. Downing's eye, rolling in a fine frenzy from heaven to earth, from earth to heaven, also focussed itself on the pile of soot; and a thrill went through him.

Soot in the fireplace! Smith washing his hands! ("You know my methods, my dear Watson. Apply them.")

Mr. Downing's mind at that moment contained one single thought; and that thought was "What ho for the chimney!"

He dived forward with a rush, nearly knocking Mr. Outwood off his feet, and thrust an arm up into the unknown. An avalanche of soot fell upon his hand and wrist, but he ignored it, for at the same instant his fingers had closed upon what he was seeking.

"Ah," he said. "I thought as much. You were not quite clever enough, after all, Smith."

"No, sir," said Psmith patiently. "We all make mistakes."

"You would have done better, Smith, not to have given me all this trouble. You have done yourself no good by it."

"It's been great fun, though, sir," argued Psmith.

"Fun!" Mr. Downing laughed grimly. "You may have reason to change your opinion of what constitutes——-"

His voice failed as his eye fell on the all-black toe of the boot. He looked up, and caught Psmith's benevolent gaze. He straightened himself and brushed a bead of perspiration from his face with the back of his hand. Unfortunately, he used the sooty hand, and the result was like some gruesome burlesque of a nigger minstrel.

"Did—-you—-put—-that—-boot—-there, Smith?" he asked slowly.

"Yes, sir."

"Then what did you *MEAN* by putting it there?" roared Mr. Downing.

"Animal spirits, sir," said Psmith.

"WHAT!"

"Animal spirits, sir."

What Mr. Downing would have replied to this one cannot tell, though one can guess roughly. For, just as he was opening his mouth, Mr. Outwood, catching sight of his Chirgwin-like countenance, intervened.

"My dear Downing," he said, "your face. It is positively covered with soot, positively. You must come and wash it. You are quite black. Really, you present a most curious appearance, most. Let me show you the way to my room."

In all times of storm and tribulation there comes a breaking-point, a point where the spirit definitely refuses to battle any longer against the slings and arrows of outrageous fortune. Mr. Downing could not bear up against this crowning blow. He went down beneath it. In the language of the Ring, he took the count. It was the knock-out.

"Soot!" he murmured weakly. "Soot!"

"Your face is covered, my dear fellow, quite covered."

"It certainly has a faintly sooty aspect, sir," said Psmith.

His voice roused the sufferer to one last flicker of spirit.

"You will hear more of this, Smith," he said. "I say you will hear more of it."

"DID—YOU—PUT—THAT—BOOT—THERE, SMITH?"

Then he allowed Mr. Outwood to lead him out to a place where there were towels, soap, and sponges.

When they had gone, Psmith went to the window, and hauled in the string. He felt the calm after-glow which comes to the general after a successfully conducted battle. It had been trying, of course, for a man of refinement, and it had cut into his afternoon, but on the whole it had been worth it.

The problem now was what to do with the painted boot. It would take a lot of cleaning, he saw, even if he could get hold of the necessary implements for cleaning it. And he rather doubted if he would be able to do so. Edmund, the boot-boy, worked in some mysterious cell, far from the madding crowd, at the back of the house. In the boot-cupboard downstairs there would probably be nothing likely to be of any use.

His fears were realised. The boot-cupboard was empty. It seemed to him that, for the time being, the best thing he could do would be to place the boot in safe hiding, until he should have thought out a scheme.

Having restored the basket to its proper place, accordingly, he went up to the study again, and placed the red-toed boot in the chimney, at about the same height where Mr. Downing had found the other. Nobody would think of looking there a second time, and it was improbable that Mr. Outwood really would have the chimneys swept, as he had said. The odds were that he had forgotten about it already.

Psmith went to the bathroom to wash his hands again, with the feeling that he had done a good day's work.

CHAPTER LII ON THE TRAIL AGAIN

The most massive minds are apt to forget things at times. The most adroit plotters make their little mistakes. Psmith was no exception to the rule. He made the mistake of not telling Mike of the afternoon's happenings.

It was not altogether forgetfulness. Psmith was one of those people who like to carry through their operations entirely by themselves. Where there is only one in a secret the secret is more liable to remain unrevealed. There was nothing, he thought, to be gained from telling Mike. He forgot what the consequences might be if he did not.

So Psmith kept his own counsel, with the result that Mike went over to school on the Monday morning in pumps.

Edmund, summoned from the hinterland of the house to give his opinion why only one of Mike's boots was to be found, had no views on the subject. He seemed to look on it as one of those things which no fellow can understand.

"'Ere's one of 'em, Mr. Jackson," he said, as if he hoped that Mike might be satisfied with a compromise.

"One? What's the good of that, Edmund, you chump? I can't go over to school in one boot."

Edmund turned this over in his mind, and then said, "No, sir," as much as to say, "I may have lost a boot, but, thank goodness, I can still understand sound reasoning."

"Well, what am I to do? Where is the other boot?"

"Don't know, Mr. Jackson," replied Edmund to both questions.

"Well, I mean—-Oh, dash it, there's the bell."

And Mike sprinted off in the pumps he stood in.

It is only a deviation from those ordinary rules of school life, which one observes naturally and without thinking, that enables one to realise how strong public-school prejudices really are. At a school, for instance, where the regulations say that coats only of black or dark blue are to be worn, a boy who appears one day in even the most respectable and unostentatious brown finds himself looked on with a mixture of awe and repulsion, which would be excessive if he had sand-bagged the headmaster. So in the case of boots. School rules decree that a boy shall go to his form-room in boots, There is no real reason why, if the day is fine, he should not wear shoes, should he prefer them. But, if he does, the thing creates a perfect sensation. Boys say, "Great Scott, what *have* you got on?" Masters say, "Jones, *what* are you wearing on your feet?" In the few minutes which elapse between the assembling of the form for call-over and the arrival of the form-master, some wag is sure either to stamp on the shoes, accompanying the act with some satirical remark, or else to pull one of them off, and inaugurate an impromptu game of football with it. There was once a boy who went to school one morning in elastic-sided boots....

Mike had always been coldly distant in his relations to the rest of his form, looking on them, with a few exceptions, as worms; and the form, since his innings against Downing's on the Friday, had regarded Mike with respect. So that he escaped the ragging he would have had to undergo at Wrykyn in similar circumstances. It was only Mr. Downing who gave trouble.

There is a sort of instinct which enables some masters to tell when a boy in their form is wearing shoes instead of boots, just as people who dislike cats always know when one is in a room with them. They cannot see it, but they feel it in their bones.

Mr. Downing was perhaps the most bigoted anti-shoeist in the whole list of English schoolmasters. He waged war remorselessly against shoes. Satire, abuse, lines, detention—every weapon was employed by him in dealing with their wearers. It had been the late Dunster's practice always to go over to school in shoes when, as he usually did, he felt shaky in the morning's lesson. Mr. Downing always detected him in the first five minutes, and that meant a lecture of anything from ten minutes to a quarter of an hour on Untidy Habits and Boys Who Looked like Loafers—which broke the back of the morning's work nicely. On one occasion, when a particularly tricky bit of Livy was on the bill of fare, Dunster had entered the form-room in heel-less Turkish bath-slippers, of a vivid crimson; and the subsequent proceedings, including his journey over to the house to change the heel-less atrocities, had seen him through very nearly to the quarter to eleven interval.

Mike, accordingly, had not been in his place for three minutes when Mr. Downing, stiffening like a pointer, called his name.

"Yes, sir?" said Mike.

"*What* are you wearing on your feet, Jackson?"

"Pumps, sir."

"You are wearing pumps? Are you not aware that PUMPS are not the proper things to come to school in? Why are you wearing *PUMPS*?"

The form, leaning back against the next row of desks, settled itself comfortably for the address from the throne.

"I have lost one of my boots, sir."

A kind of gulp escaped from Mr. Downing's lips. He stared at Mike for a moment in silence. Then, turning to Stone, he told him to start translating.

Stone, who had been expecting at least ten minutes' respite, was taken unawares. When he found the place in his book and began to construe, he floundered hopelessly. But, to his growing surprise and satisfaction, the form-master appeared to notice nothing wrong. He said "Yes, yes," mechanically, and finally "That will do," whereupon Stone resumed his seat with the feeling that the age of miracles had returned.

Mr. Downing's mind was in a whirl. His case was complete. Mike's appearance in shoes, with the explanation that he had lost a boot, completed the chain. As Columbus must have felt when his ship ran into harbour, and the first American interviewer, jumping on board, said, "Wal, sir, and what are your impressions of our glorious country?" so did Mr. Downing feel at that moment.

When the bell rang at a quarter to eleven, he gathered up his gown, and sped to the headmaster.

CHAPTER LIII THE KETTLE METHOD

It was during the interval that day that Stone and Robinson, discussing the subject of cricket over a bun and ginger-beer at the school shop, came to a momentous decision, to wit, that they were fed up with Adair administration and meant to strike. The immediate cause of revolt was early-morning fielding-practice, that searching test of cricket keenness. Mike himself, to whom cricket was the great and serious interest of life, had shirked early-morning fielding-practice in his first term at Wrykyn. And Stone and Robinson had but a lukewarm attachment to the game, compared with Mike's.

As a rule, Adair had contented himself with practice in the afternoon after school, which nobody objects to; and no strain, consequently, had been put upon Stone's and Robinson's allegiance. In view of the M.C.C. match on the Wednesday, however, he had now added to this an extra dose to be taken before breakfast. Stone and Robinson had left their comfortable beds that day at six o'clock, yawning and heavy-eyed, and had caught catches and fielded drives which, in the cool morning air, had stung like adders and bitten like serpents. Until the sun has really got to work, it is no joke taking a high catch. Stone's dislike of the experiment was only equalled by Robinson's. They were neither of them of the type which likes to undergo hardships for the common good. They played well enough when on the field, but neither cared greatly whether the school had a good season or not. They played the game entirely for their own sakes.

The result was that they went back to the house for breakfast with a never-again feeling, and at the earliest possible moment met to debate as to what was to be done about it. At all costs another experience like to-day's must be avoided.

"It's all rot," said Stone. "What on earth's the good of sweating about before breakfast? It only makes you tired."

"I shouldn't wonder," said Robinson, "if it wasn't bad for the heart. Rushing about on an empty stomach, I mean, and all that sort of thing."

"Personally," said Stone, gnawing his bun, "I don't intend to stick it."

"Nor do I."

"I mean, it's such absolute rot. If we aren't good enough to play for the team without having to get up overnight to catch catches, he'd better find somebody else."

"Yes."

At this moment Adair came into the shop.

"Fielding-practice again to-morrow," he said briskly, "at six."

"Before breakfast?" said Robinson.

"Rather. You two must buck up, you know. You were rotten to-day." And he passed on, leaving the two malcontents speechless.

Stone was the first to recover.

"I'm hanged if I turn out to-morrow," he said, as they left the shop. "He can do what he likes about it. Besides, what can he do, after all? Only kick us out of the team. And I don't mind that."

"Nor do I."

"I don't think he will kick us out, either. He can't play the M.C.C. with a scratch team. If he does, we'll go and play for that village Jackson plays for. We'll get Jackson to shove us into the team."

"All right," said Robinson. "Let's."

Their position was a strong one. A cricket captain may seem to be an autocrat of tremendous power, but in reality he has only one weapon, the keenness of those under him. With the majority, of course, the fear of being excluded or ejected from a team is a spur that drives. The majority, consequently, are easily handled. But when a cricket captain runs up against a boy who does not much care whether he plays for the team or not, then he finds himself in a difficult position, and, unless he is a man of action, practically helpless.

Stone and Robinson felt secure. Taking it all round, they felt that they would just as soon play for Lower Borlock as for the school. The bowling of the opposition would be weaker in the former case, and the chance of making runs greater. To a certain type of cricketer runs are runs, wherever and however made.

The result of all this was that Adair, turning out with the team next morning for fielding-practice, found himself two short. Barnes was among those present, but of the other two representatives of Outwood's house there were no signs.

Barnes, questioned on the subject, had no information to give, beyond the fact that he had not seen them about anywhere. Which was not a great help. Adair proceeded with the fielding-practice without further delay.

At breakfast that morning he was silent and apparently wrapped in thought. Mr. Downing, who sat at the top of the table with Adair on his right, was accustomed at the morning meal to blend nourishment of the body with that of the mind. As a rule he had ten minutes with the daily paper before the bell rang, and it was his practice to hand on the results of his reading to Adair and the other house-prefects, who, not having seen the paper, usually formed an interested and appreciative audience. To-day, however, though the house-prefects expressed varying degrees of excitement at the news that Tyldesley had made a century against Gloucestershire, and that a butter famine was expected in the United States, these world-shaking news-items seemed to leave Adair cold. He champed his bread and marmalade with an abstracted air.

He was wondering what to do in this matter of Stone and Robinson.

CHAPTER LIII THE KETTLE METHOD

Many captains might have passed the thing over. To take it for granted that the missing pair had overslept themselves would have been a safe and convenient way out of the difficulty. But Adair was not the sort of person who seeks for safe and convenient ways out of difficulties. He never shirked anything, physical or moral.

He resolved to interview the absentees.

It was not until after school that an opportunity offered itself. He went across to Outwood's and found the two non-starters in the senior day-room, engaged in the intellectual pursuit of kicking the wall and marking the height of each kick with chalk. Adair's entrance coincided with a record effort by Stone, which caused the kicker to overbalance and stagger backwards against the captain.

"Sorry," said Stone. "Hullo, Adair!"

"Don't mention it. Why weren't you two at fielding-practice this morning?"

Robinson, who left the lead to Stone in all matters, said nothing. Stone spoke.

"We didn't turn up," he said.

"I know you didn't. Why not?"

Stone had rehearsed this scene in his mind, and he spoke with the coolness which comes from rehearsal.

"We decided not to."

"Oh?"

"Yes. We came to the conclusion that we hadn't any use for early-morning fielding."

Adair's manner became ominously calm.

"You were rather fed-up, I suppose?"

"That's just the word."

"Sorry it bored you."

"It didn't. We didn't give it the chance to."

Robinson laughed appreciatively.

"What's the joke, Robinson?" asked Adair.

"There's no joke," said Robinson, with some haste. "I was only thinking of something."

"I'll give you something else to think about soon."

Stone intervened.

"It's no good making a row about it, Adair. You must see that you can't do anything. Of course, you can kick us out of the team, if you like, but we don't care if you do. Jackson will get us a game any Wednesday or Saturday for the village he plays for. So we're all right. And the school team aren't such a lot of flyers that you can afford to go chucking people out of it whenever you want to. See what I mean?"

"You and Jackson seem to have fixed it all up between you."

"What are you going to do? Kick us out?"

"No."

"Good. I thought you'd see it was no good making a beastly row. We'll play for the school all right. There's no earthly need for us to turn out for fielding-practice before breakfast."

"You don't think there is? You may be right. All the same, you're going to to-morrow morning."

"What!"

"Six sharp. Don't be late."

"Don't be an ass, Adair. We've told you we aren't going to."

"That's only your opinion. I think you are. I'll give you till five past six, as you seem to like lying in bed."

"You can turn out if you feel like it. You won't find me there."

"That'll be a disappointment. Nor Robinson?"

"No," said the junior partner in the firm; but he said it without any deep conviction. The atmosphere was growing a great deal too tense for his comfort.

"You've quite made up your minds?"

"Yes," said Stone.

"Right," said Adair quietly, and knocked him down.

He was up again in a moment. Adair had pushed the table back, and was standing in the middle of the open space.

"You cad," said Stone. "I wasn't ready."

"Well, you are now. Shall we go on?"

Stone dashed in without a word, and for a few moments the two might have seemed evenly matched to a not too intelligent spectator. But science tells, even in a confined space. Adair was smaller and lighter than Stone, but he was cooler and quicker, and he knew more about the game. His blow was always home a fraction of a second sooner than his opponent's. At the end of a minute Stone was on the floor again.

He got up slowly and stood leaning with one hand on the table.

"Suppose we say ten past six?" said Adair. "I'm not particular to a minute or two."

Stone made no reply.

"Will ten past six suit you for fielding-practice to-morrow?" said Adair.

"All right," said Stone.

"Thanks. How about you, Robinson?"

Robinson had been a petrified spectator of the Captain-Kettle-like manoeuvres of the cricket captain, and it did not take him long to make up his mind. He was not altogether a coward. In different circumstances he might have put up a respectable show. But it takes a more than ordinarily courageous person to embark on a fight which he knows must end in his destruction. Robinson knew that he was nothing like a match even for Stone, and Adair had disposed of Stone in a little over one minute. It seemed to Robinson that neither pleasure nor profit was likely to come from an encounter with Adair.

"All right," he said hastily, "I'll turn up."

"Good," said Adair. "I wonder if either of you chaps could tell me which is Jackson's study."

Stone was dabbing at his mouth with a handkerchief, a task which precluded anything in the shape of conversation; so Robinson replied that Mike's study was the first you came to on the right of the corridor at the top of the stairs.

"Thanks," said Adair. "You don't happen to know if he's in, I suppose?"

"He went up with Smith a quarter of an hour ago. I don't know if he's still there."

"I'll go and see," said Adair. "I should like a word with him if he isn't busy."

CHAPTER LIV ADAIR HAS A WORD WITH MIKE

Mike, all unconscious of the stirring proceedings which had been going on below stairs, was peacefully reading a letter he had received that morning from Strachan at Wrykyn, in which the successor to the cricket captaincy which should have been Mike's had a good deal to say in a lugubrious strain. In Mike's absence things had been going badly with Wrykyn. A broken arm, contracted in the course of some rash experiments with a day-boy's motor-bicycle, had deprived the team of the services of Dunstable, the only man who had shown any signs of being able to bowl a side out. Since this calamity, wrote Strachan, everything had gone wrong. The M.C.C., led by Mike's brother Reggie, the least of the three first-class-cricketing Jacksons, had smashed them by a hundred and fifty runs. Geddington had wiped them off the face of the earth. The Incogs, with a team recruited exclusively from the rabbit-hutch—not a well-known man on the side except Stacey, a veteran who had been playing for the club since Fuller Pilch's time—had got home by two wickets. In fact, it was Strachan's opinion that the Wrykyn team that summer was about the most hopeless gang of dead-beats that had ever made an exhibition of itself on the school grounds. The Ripton match, fortunately, was off, owing to an outbreak of mumps at that shrine of learning and athletics—the second outbreak of the malady in two terms. Which, said Strachan, was hard lines on Ripton, but a bit of jolly good luck for Wrykyn, as it had saved them from what would probably have been a record hammering, Ripton having eight of their last year's team left, including Dixon, the fast bowler, against whom Mike alone of the Wrykyn team had been able to make runs in the previous season. Altogether, Wrykyn had struck a bad patch.

Mike mourned over his suffering school. If only he could have been there to help. It might have made all the difference. In school cricket one good batsman, to go in first and knock the bowlers off their length, may take a weak team triumphantly through a season. In school cricket the importance of a good start for the first wicket is incalculable.

As he put Strachan's letter away in his pocket, all his old bitterness against Sedleigh, which had been ebbing during the past few days, returned with a rush.

He was conscious once more of that feeling of personal injury which had made him hate his new school on the first day of term.

And it was at this point, when his resentment was at its height, that Adair, the concrete representative of everything Sedleighan, entered the room.

There are moments in life's placid course when there has got to be the biggest kind of row. This was one of them.

Psmith, who was leaning against the mantelpiece, reading the serial story in a daily paper which he had abstracted from the senior day-room, made the intruder free of the study with a dignified wave of the hand, and went on reading. Mike remained in the deck-chair in which he was sitting, and contented himself with glaring at the newcomer.

Psmith was the first to speak.

"If you ask my candid opinion," he said, looking up from his paper, "I should say that young Lord Antony Trefusis was in the soup already. I seem to see the *consommé* splashing about his ankles. He's had a note telling him to be under the oak-tree in the Park at midnight. He's just off there at the end of this instalment. I bet Long Jack, the poacher, is waiting there with a sandbag. Care to see the paper, Comrade Adair? Or don't you take any interest in contemporary literature?"

"Thanks," said Adair. "I just wanted to speak to Jackson for a minute."

"Fate," said Psmith, "has led your footsteps to the right place. That is Comrade Jackson, the Pride of the School, sitting before you."

"What do you want?" said Mike.

He suspected that Adair had come to ask him once again to play for the school. The fact that the M.C.C. match was on the following day made this a probable solution of the reason for his visit. He could think of no other errand that was likely to have set the head of Downing's paying afternoon calls.

"I'll tell you in a minute. It won't take long."

"That," said Psmith approvingly, "is right. Speed is the key-note of the present age. Promptitude. Despatch. This is no time for loitering. We must be strenuous. We must hustle. We must Do It Now. We——"

"Buck up," said Mike.

"Certainly," said Adair. "I've just been talking to Stone and Robinson."

"An excellent way of passing an idle half-hour," said Psmith.

"We weren't exactly idle," said Adair grimly. "It didn't last long, but it was pretty lively while it did. Stone chucked it after the first round."

Mike got up out of his chair. He could not quite follow what all this was about, but there was no mistaking the truculence of Adair's manner. For some reason, which might possibly be made dear later, Adair was looking for trouble, and Mike in his present mood felt that it would be a privilege to see that he got it.

Psmith was regarding Adair through his eyeglass with pain and surprise.

"Surely," he said, "you do not mean us to understand that you have been *brawling* with Comrade Stone! This is bad hearing. I thought that you and he were like brothers. Such a bad example for Comrade Robinson, too. Leave us, Adair. We would brood. Oh, go thee, knave, I'll none of thee. Shakespeare."

Psmith turned away, and resting his elbows on the mantelpiece, gazed at himself mournfully in the looking-glass.

"I'm not the man I was," he sighed, after a prolonged inspection. "There are lines on my face, dark circles beneath my eyes. The fierce rush of life at Sedleigh is wasting me away."

"Stone and I had a discussion about early-morning fielding-practice," said Adair, turning to Mike.

Mike said nothing.

"I thought his fielding wanted working up a bit, so I told him to turn out at six to-morrow morning. He said he wouldn't, so we argued it out. He's going to all right. So is Robinson."

Mike remained silent.

"So are you," added Adair.

"I get thinner and thinner," said Psmith from the mantelpiece.

Mike looked at Adair, and Adair looked at Mike, after the manner of two dogs before they fly at one another. There was an electric silence in the study. Psmith peered with increased earnestness into the glass.

"Oh?" said Mike at last. "What makes you think that?"

"I don't think. I know."

"Any special reason for my turning out?"

"Yes."

"What's that?"

"You're going to play for the school against the M.C.C. to-morrow, and I want you to get some practice."

"I wonder how you got that idea!"

"Curious I should have done, isn't it?"

"Very. You aren't building on it much, are you?" said Mike politely.

"I am, rather," replied Adair with equal courtesy.

"I'm afraid you'll be disappointed."

"I don't think so."

"My eyes," said Psmith regretfully, "are a bit close together. However," he added philosophically, "it's too late to alter that now."

Mike drew a step closer to Adair.

"What makes you think I shall play against the M.C.C.?" he asked curiously.

"I'm going to make you."

Mike took another step forward. Adair moved to meet him.

"Would you care to try now?" said Mike.

For just one second the two drew themselves together preparatory to beginning the serious business of the interview, and in that second Psmith, turning from the glass, stepped between them.

"Get out of the light, Smith," said Mike.

Psmith waved him back with a deprecating gesture.

"My dear young friends," he said placidly, "if you *will* let your angry passions rise, against the direct advice of Doctor Watts, I suppose you must, But when you propose to claw each other in my study, in the midst of a hundred fragile and priceless ornaments, I lodge a protest. If you really feel that you want to scrap, for goodness sake do it where there's some room. I don't want all the study furniture smashed. I know a bank whereon the wild thyme grows, only a few yards down the road, where you can scrap all night if you want to. How would it be to move on there? Any objections? None? Then shift ho! and let's get it over."

CHAPTER LV CLEARING THE AIR

Psmith was one of those people who lend a dignity to everything they touch. Under his auspices the most unpromising ventures became somehow enveloped in an atmosphere of measured stateliness. On the present occasion, what would have been, without his guiding hand, a mere unscientific scramble, took on something of the impressive formality of the National Sporting Club.

"The rounds," he said, producing a watch, as they passed through a gate into a field a couple of hundred yards from the house gate, "will be of three minutes' duration, with a minute rest in between. A man who is down will have ten seconds in which to rise. Are you ready, Comrades Adair and Jackson? Very well, then. Time."

After which, it was a pity that the actual fight did not quite live up to its referee's introduction. Dramatically, there should have been cautious sparring for openings and a number of tensely contested rounds, as if it had been the final of a boxing competition. But school fights, when they do occur—-which is only once in a decade nowadays, unless you count junior school scuffles—-are the outcome of weeks of suppressed bad blood, and are consequently brief and furious. In a boxing competition, however much one may want to win, one does not dislike one's opponent. Up to the moment when "time" was called, one was probably warmly attached to him, and at the end of the last round one expects to resume that attitude of mind. In a fight each party, as a rule, hates the other.

So it happened that there was nothing formal or cautious about the present battle. All Adair wanted was to get at Mike, and all Mike wanted was to get at Adair. Directly Psmith called "time," they rushed together as if they meant to end the thing in half a minute.

It was this that saved Mike. In an ordinary contest with the gloves, with his opponent cool and boxing in his true form, he could not have lasted three rounds against Adair. The latter was a clever boxer, while Mike had never had a lesson in his life. If Adair had kept away and used his head, nothing could have prevented him winning.

As it was, however, he threw away his advantages, much as Tom Brown did at the beginning of his fight with Slogger Williams, and the result was the same as on that historic occasion. Mike had the greater strength, and, thirty seconds from the start, knocked his man clean off his feet with an unscientific but powerful right-hander.

This finished Adair's chances. He rose full of fight, but with all the science knocked out of him. He went in at Mike with both hands. The Irish blood in him, which for the ordinary events of life made him merely energetic and dashing, now rendered him reckless. He abandoned all attempt at guarding. It was the Frontal Attack in its most futile form, and as unsuccessful as a frontal attack is apt to be. There was a swift exchange of blows, in the course of which Mike's left elbow, coming into contact with his opponent's right fist, got a shock which kept it tingling for the rest of the day; and then Adair went down in a heap.

He got up slowly and with difficulty. For a moment he stood blinking vaguely. Then he lurched forward at Mike.

In the excitement of a fight—-which is, after all, about the most exciting thing that ever happens to one in the course of one's life—-it is difficult for the fighters to see what the spectators see. Where the spectators see an assault on an already beaten man, the fighter himself only sees a legitimate piece of self-defence against an opponent whose chances are equal to his own. Psmith saw, as anybody looking on would have seen, that Adair was done. Mike's blow had taken him within a fraction of an inch of the point of the jaw, and he was all but knocked out. Mike could not see this. All he understood was that his man was on his feet again and coming at him, so he hit out with all his strength; and this time Adair went down and stayed down.

"Brief," said Psmith, coming forward, "but exciting. We may take that, I think, to be the conclusion of the entertainment. I will now have a dash at picking up the slain. I shouldn't stop, if I were you. He'll be sitting up and taking notice soon, and if he sees you he may want to go on with the combat, which would do him no earthly good. If it's going to be continued in our next, there had better be a bit of an interval for alterations and repairs first."

"Is he hurt much, do you think?" asked Mike. He had seen knock-outs before in the ring, but this was the first time he had ever effected one on his own account, and Adair looked unpleasantly corpse-like.

"*He's* all right," said Psmith. "In a minute or two he'll be skipping about like a little lambkin. I'll look after him. You go away and pick flowers."

Mike put on his coat and walked back to the house. He was conscious of a perplexing whirl of new and strange emotions, chief among which was a curious feeling that he rather liked Adair. He found himself thinking that Adair was a good chap, that there was something to be said for his point of view, and that it was a pity he had knocked him about so much. At the same time, he felt an undeniable thrill of pride at having beaten him. The feat presented that interesting person, Mike Jackson, to him in a fresh and pleasing light, as one who had had a tough job to face and had carried it through. Jackson, the cricketer, he knew, but Jackson, the deliverer of knock-out blows, was strange to him, and he found this new acquaintance a man to be respected.

The fight, in fact, had the result which most fights have, if they are fought fairly and until one side has had enough. It revolutionised Mike's view of things. It shook him up, and drained the bad blood out of him. Where, before, he had seemed to himself to be acting with massive dignity, he now saw that he had simply been sulking like some wretched kid. There had appeared to him something rather fine in his policy of refusing to identify himself in any way with Sedleigh, a touch of the stone-walls-do-not-a-prison-make sort of thing. He now saw that his attitude was to be summed up in the words, "Sha'n't play."

It came upon Mike with painful clearness that he had been making an ass of himself.

He had come to this conclusion, after much earnest thought, when Psmith entered the study.

"How's Adair?" asked Mike.

"Sitting up and taking nourishment once more. We have been chatting. He's not a bad cove."

"He's all right," said Mike.

There was a pause. Psmith straightened his tie.

"Look here," he said, "I seldom interfere in terrestrial strife, but it seems to me that there's an opening here for a capable peace-maker, not afraid of work, and willing to give his services in exchange for a comfortable home. Comrade Adair's rather a stoutish fellow in his way. I'm not much on the 'Play up for the old school, Jones,' game, but every one to his taste. I shouldn't have thought anybody would get overwhelmingly attached to this abode of wrath, but Comrade Adair seems to have done it. He's all for giving Sedleigh a much-needed boost-up. It's not a bad idea in its way. I don't see why one shouldn't humour him. Apparently he's been sweating since early childhood to buck the school up. And as he's leaving at the end of the term, it mightn't be a scaly scheme to give him a bit of a send-off, if possible, by making the cricket season a bit of a banger. As a start, why not drop him a line to say that you'll play against the M.C.C. tomorrow?"

Mike did not reply at once. He was feeling better disposed towards Adair and Sedleigh than he had felt, but he was not sure that he was quite prepared to go as far as a complete climb-down.

"It wouldn't be a bad idea," continued Psmith. "There's nothing like giving a man a bit in every now and then. It broadens the soul and improves the action of the skin. What seems to have fed up Comrade Adair, to a certain extent, is that Stone apparently led him to understand that you had offered to give him and Robinson places in your village team. You didn't, of course?"

"Of course not," said Mike indignantly.

"I told him he didn't know the old *noblesse oblige* spirit of the Jacksons. I said that you would scorn to tarnish the Jackson escutcheon by not playing the game. My eloquence convinced him. However, to return to the point under discussion, why not?"

"I don't—What I mean to say—" began Mike.

"If your trouble is," said Psmith, "that you fear that you may be in unworthy company——"

"Don't be an ass."

"——Dismiss it. *I* am playing."

Mike stared.

"You're what? You?"

"I," said Psmith, breathing on a coat-button, and polishing it with his handkerchief.

"Can you play cricket?"

"You have discovered," said Psmith, "my secret sorrow."

"You're rotting."

"You wrong me, Comrade Jackson."

"Then why haven't you played?"

"Why haven't you?"

"Why didn't you come and play for Lower Borlock, I mean?"

"The last time I played in a village cricket match I was caught at point by a man in braces. It would have been madness to risk another such shock to my system. My nerves are so exquisitely balanced that a thing of that sort takes years off my life."

"No, but look here, Smith, bar rotting. Are you really any good at cricket?"

"Competent judges at Eton gave me to understand so. I was told that this year I should be a certainty for Lord's. But when the cricket season came, where was I? Gone. Gone like some beautiful flower that withers in the night."

"But you told me you didn't like cricket. You said you only liked watching it."

"Quite right. I do. But at schools where cricket is compulsory you have to overcome your private prejudices. And in time the thing becomes a habit. Imagine my feelings when I found that I was degenerating, little by little, into a slow left-hand bowler with a swerve. I fought against it, but it was useless, and after a while I gave up the struggle, and drifted with the stream. Last year, in a house match"—Psmith's voice took on a deeper tone of melancholy—"I took seven for thirteen in the second innings on a hard wicket. I did think, when I came here, that I had found a haven of rest, but it was not to be. I turn out to-morrow. What Comrade Outwood will say, when he finds that his keenest archaeological disciple has deserted, I hate to think. However——"

Mike felt as if a young and powerful earthquake had passed. The whole face of his world had undergone a quick change. Here was he, the recalcitrant, wavering on the point of playing for the school, and here was Psmith, the last person whom he would have expected to be a player, stating calmly that he had been in the running for a place in the Eton eleven.

Then in a flash Mike understood. He was not by nature intuitive, but he read Psmith's mind now. Since the term began, he and Psmith had been acting on precisely similar motives. Just as he had been disappointed of the captaincy of cricket at Wrykyn, so had Psmith been disappointed of his place in the Eton team at Lord's. And they had both worked it off, each in his own way—-Mike sullenly, Psmith whimsically, according to their respective natures—-on Sedleigh.

If Psmith, therefore, did not consider it too much of a climb-down to renounce his resolution not to play for Sedleigh, there was nothing to stop Mike doing so, as—-at the bottom of his heart—-he wanted to do.

"By Jove," he said, "if you're playing, I'll play. I'll write a note to Adair now. But, I say—-" he stopped—-"I'm hanged if I'm going to turn out and field before breakfast to-morrow."

"That's all right. You won't have to. Adair won't be there himself. He's not playing against the M.C.C. He's sprained his wrist."

CHAPTER LVI IN WHICH PEACE IS DECLARED

"Sprained his wrist?" said Mike. "How did he do that?"

"During the brawl. Apparently one of his efforts got home on your elbow instead of your expressive countenance, and whether it was that your elbow was particularly tough or his wrist particularly fragile, I don't know. Anyhow, it went. It's nothing bad, but it'll keep him out of the game to-morrow."

"I say, what beastly rough luck! I'd no idea. I'll go round."

"Not a bad scheme. Close the door gently after you, and if you see anybody downstairs who looks as if he were likely to be going over to the shop, ask him to get me a small pot of some rare old jam and tell the man to chalk it up to me. The jam Comrade Outwood supplies to us at tea is all right as a practical joke or as a food for those anxious to commit suicide, but useless to anybody who values life."

On arriving at Mr. Downing's and going to Adair's study, Mike found that his late antagonist was out. He left a note informing him of his willingness to play in the morrow's match. The lock-up bell rang as he went out of the house.

A spot of rain fell on his hand. A moment later there was a continuous patter, as the storm, which had been gathering all day, broke in earnest. Mike turned up his coat-collar, and ran back to Outwood's. "At this rate," he said to himself, "there won't be a match at all to-morrow."

When the weather decides, after behaving well for some weeks, to show what it can do in another direction, it does the thing thoroughly. When Mike woke the next morning the world was grey and dripping. Leaden-coloured clouds drifted over the sky, till there was not a trace of blue to be seen, and then the rain began again, in the gentle, determined way rain has when it means to make a day of it.

It was one of those bad days when one sits in the pavilion, damp and depressed, while figures in mackintoshes, with discoloured buckskin boots, crawl miserably about the field in couples.

Mike, shuffling across to school in a Burberry, met Adair at Downing's gate.

These moments are always difficult. Mike stopped—-he could hardly walk on as if nothing had happened—-and looked down at his feet.

"Coming across?" he said awkwardly.

"Right ho!" said Adair.

They walked on in silence.

"It's only about ten to, isn't it?" said Mike.

Adair fished out his watch, and examined it with an elaborate care born of nervousness.

"About nine to."

"Good. We've got plenty of time."

"Yes."

"I hate having to hurry over to school."

"So do I."

"I often do cut it rather fine, though."

"Yes. So do I."

"Beastly nuisance when one does."

"Beastly."

"It's only about a couple of minutes from the houses to the school, I should think, shouldn't you?"

"Not much more. Might be three."

"Yes. Three if one didn't hurry."

"Oh, yes, if one didn't hurry."

Another silence.

"Beastly day," said Adair.

"Rotten."

Silence again.

"I say," said Mike, scowling at his toes, "awfully sorry about your wrist."

"Oh, that's all right. It was my fault."

"Does it hurt?"

"Oh, no, rather not, thanks."

"I'd no idea you'd crocked yourself."

"Oh, no, that's all right. It was only right at the end. You'd have smashed me anyhow."

"Oh, rot."

"I bet you anything you like you would."

"I bet you I shouldn't.... Jolly hard luck, just before the match."

"Oh, no.... I say, thanks awfully for saying you'd play."

"Oh, rot.... Do you think we shall get a game?"

Adair inspected the sky carefully.

"I don't know. It looks pretty bad, doesn't it?"

"Rotten. I say, how long will your wrist keep you out of cricket?"

"Be all right in a week. Less, probably."

"Good."

"Now that you and Smith are going to play, we ought to have a jolly good season."

"Rummy, Smith turning out to be a cricketer."

"Yes. I should think he'd be a hot bowler, with his height."

"He must be jolly good if he was only just out of the Eton team last year."

"Yes."

"What's the time?" asked Mike.

Adair produced his watch once more.

"Five to."

"We've heaps of time."

"Yes, heaps."

"Let's stroll on a bit down the road, shall we?"

"Right ho!"

Mike cleared his throat.

"I say."

"Hullo?"

"I've been talking to Smith. He was telling me that you thought I'd promised to give Stone and Robinson places in the——-"

"Oh, no, that's all right. It was only for a bit. Smith told me you couldn't have done, and I saw that I was an ass to think you could have. It was Stone seeming so dead certain that he could play for Lower Borlock if I chucked him from the school team that gave me the idea."

"He never even asked me to get him a place."

"No, I know."

"Of course, I wouldn't have done it, even if he had."

"Of course not."

"I didn't want to play myself, but I wasn't going to do a rotten trick like getting other fellows away from the team."

"No, I know."

"It was rotten enough, really, not playing myself."

"Oh, no. Beastly rough luck having to leave Wrykyn just when you were going to be captain, and come to a small school like this."

The excitement of the past few days must have had a stimulating effect on Mike's mind—-shaken it up, as it were: for now, for the second time in two days, he displayed quite a creditable amount of intuition. He might have been misled by Adair's apparently deprecatory attitude towards Sedleigh, and blundered into a denunciation of the place. Adair had said "a small school like this" in the sort of voice which might have led his hearer to think that he was expected to say, "Yes, rotten little hole, isn't it?" or words to that effect. Mike, fortunately, perceived that the words were used purely from politeness, on the Chinese principle. When a Chinaman wishes to pay a compliment, he does so by belittling himself and his belongings.

He eluded the pitfall.

"What rot!" he said. "Sedleigh's one of the most sporting schools I've ever come across. Everybody's as keen as blazes. So they ought to be, after the way you've sweated."

Adair shuffled awkwardly.

"I've always been fairly keen on the place," he said. "But I don't suppose I've done anything much."

"You've loosened one of my front teeth," said Mike, with a grin, "if that's any comfort to you."

"I couldn't eat anything except porridge this morning. My jaw still aches."

For the first time during the conversation their eyes met, and the humorous side of the thing struck them simultaneously. They began to laugh.

"What fools we must have looked!" said Adair.

"*You* were all right. I must have looked rotten. I've never had the gloves on in my life. I'm jolly glad no one saw us except Smith, who doesn't count. Hullo, there's the bell. We'd better be moving on. What about this match? Not much chance of it from the look of the sky at present."

"It might clear before eleven. You'd better get changed, anyhow, at the interval, and hang about in case."

"All right. It's better than doing Thucydides with Downing. We've got math, till the interval, so I don't see anything of him all day; which won't hurt me."

"He isn't a bad sort of chap, when you get to know him," said Adair.

"I can't have done, then. I don't know which I'd least soon be, Downing or a black-beetle, except that if one was Downing one could tread on the black-beetle. Dash this rain. I got about half a pint down my neck just then. We sha'n't get a game to-day, of anything like it. As you're crocked, I'm not sure that I care much. You've been sweating for years to get the match on, and it would be rather rot playing it without you."

"I don't know that so much. I wish we could play, because I'm certain, with you and Smith, we'd walk into them. They probably aren't sending down much of a team, and really, now that you and Smith are turning out, we've got a jolly hot lot. There's quite decent batting all the way through, and the bowling isn't so bad. If only we could have given this M.C.C. lot a really good hammering, it might have been easier to get some good fixtures for next season. You see, it's all right for a school like Wrykyn, but with a small place like this you simply can't get the best teams to give you a match till you've done something to show that you aren't absolute rotters at the game. As for the schools, they're worse. They'd simply laugh at you. You were cricket secretary at Wrykyn last year. What would you have done if you'd had a challenge from Sedleigh? You'd either have laughed till you were sick, or else had a fit at the mere idea of the thing."

Mike stopped.

"By Jove, you've struck about the brightest scheme on record. I never thought of it before. Let's get a match on with Wrykyn."

"What! They wouldn't play us."

"Yes, they would. At least, I'm pretty sure they would. I had a letter from Strachan, the captain, yesterday, saying that the Ripton match had had to be scratched owing to illness. So they've got a vacant date. Shall I try them? I'll write to Strachan to-night, if you like. And they aren't strong this year. We'll smash them. What do you say?"

CHAPTER LVI IN WHICH PEACE IS DECLARED

Adair was as one who has seen a vision.
"By Jove," he said at last, "if we only could!"

CHAPTER LVII MR. DOWNING MOVES

The rain continued without a break all the morning. The two teams, after hanging about dismally, and whiling the time away with stump-cricket in the changing-rooms, lunched in the pavilion at one o'clock. After which the M.C.C. captain, approaching Adair, moved that this merry meeting be considered off and himself and his men permitted to catch the next train back to town. To which Adair, seeing that it was out of the question that there should be any cricket that afternoon, regretfully agreed, and the first Sedleigh *v.* M.C.C. match was accordingly scratched.

Mike and Psmith, wandering back to the house, were met by a damp junior from Downing's, with a message that Mr. Downing wished to see Mike as soon as he was changed.

"What's he want me for?" inquired Mike.

The messenger did not know. Mr. Downing, it seemed, had not confided in him. All he knew was that the housemaster was in the house, and would be glad if Mike would step across.

"A nuisance," said Psmith, "this incessant demand for you. That's the worst of being popular. If he wants you to stop to tea, edge away. A meal on rather a sumptuous scale will be prepared in the study against your return."

Mike changed quickly, and went off, leaving Psmith, who was fond of simple pleasures in his spare time, earnestly occupied with a puzzle which had been scattered through the land by a weekly paper. The prize for a solution was one thousand pounds, and Psmith had already informed Mike with some minuteness of his plans for the disposition of this sum. Meanwhile, he worked at it both in and out of school, generally with abusive comments on its inventor.

He was still fiddling away at it when Mike returned.

Mike, though Psmith was at first too absorbed to notice it, was agitated.

"I don't wish to be in any way harsh," said Psmith, without looking up, "but the man who invented this thing was a blighter of the worst type. You come and have a shot. For the moment I am baffled. The whisper flies round the clubs, 'Psmith is baffled.'"

"The man's an absolute drivelling ass," said Mike warmly.

"Me, do you mean?"

"What on earth would be the point of my doing it?"

"You'd gather in a thousand of the best. Give you a nice start in life."

"I'm not talking about your rotten puzzle."

"What are you talking about?"

"That ass Downing. I believe he's off his nut."

"Then your chat with Comrade Downing was not of the old-College-chums-meeting-unexpectedly-after-years'-separation type? What has he been doing to you?"

"He's off his nut."

"I know. But what did he do? How did the brainstorm burst? Did he jump at you from behind a door and bite a piece out of your leg, or did he say he was a tea-pot?"

Mike sat down.

"You remember that painting Sammy business?"

"As if it were yesterday," said Psmith. "Which it was, pretty nearly."

"He thinks I did it."

"Why? Have you ever shown any talent in the painting line?"

"The silly ass wanted me to confess that I'd done it. He as good as asked me to. Jawed a lot of rot about my finding it to my advantage later on if I behaved sensibly."

"Then what are you worrying about? Don't you know that when a master wants you to do the confessing-act, it simply means that he hasn't enough evidence to start in on you with? You're all right. The thing's a stand-off."

"Evidence!" said Mike, "My dear man, he's got enough evidence to sink a ship. He's absolutely sweating evidence at every pore. As far as I can see, he's been crawling about, doing the Sherlock Holmes business for all he's worth ever since the thing happened, and now he's dead certain that I painted Sammy."

"*Did* you, by the way?" asked Psmith.

"No," said Mike shortly, "I didn't. But after listening to Downing I almost began to wonder if I hadn't. The man's got stacks of evidence to prove that I did."

"Such as what?"

"It's mostly about my boots. But, dash it, you know all about that. Why, you were with him when he came and looked for them."

"It is true," said Psmith, "that Comrade Downing and I spent a very pleasant half-hour together inspecting boots, but how does he drag you into it?"

"He swears one of the boots was splashed with paint."

"Yes. He babbled to some extent on that point when I was entertaining him. But what makes him think that the boot, if any, was yours?"

"He's certain that somebody in this house got one of his boots splashed, and is hiding it somewhere. And I'm the only chap in the house who hasn't got a pair of boots to show, so he thinks it's me. I don't know where the dickens my other boot has gone. Edmund swears he hasn't seen it, and it's nowhere about. Of course I've got two pairs, but one's being soled. So I had to go over to school yesterday in pumps. That's how he spotted me."

Psmith sighed.

"Comrade Jackson," he said mournfully, "all this very sad affair shows the folly of acting from the best motives. In my simple zeal, meaning to save you unpleasantness, I have landed you, with a dull, sickening thud, right in the cart. Are you particular about dirtying your hands? If you aren't, just reach up that chimney a bit?"

Mike stared, "What the dickens are you talking about?"

"Go on. Get it over. Be a man, and reach up the chimney."

MIKE DROPPED THE SOOT-COVERED OBJECT IN THE FENDER

"I don't know what the game is," said Mike, kneeling beside the fender and groping, "but—*Hullo*!"

"Ah ha!" said Psmith moodily.

Mike dropped the soot-covered object in the fender, and glared at it.

"It's my boot!" he said at last.

"It *is*," said Psmith, "your boot. And what is that red stain across the toe? Is it blood? No, 'tis not blood. It is red paint."

Mike seemed unable to remove his eyes from the boot.

"How on earth did—By Jove! I remember now. I kicked up against something in the dark when I was putting my bicycle back that night. It must have been the paint-pot."

"Then you were out that night?"

"Rather. That's what makes it so jolly awkward. It's too long to tell you now——"

"Your stories are never too long for me," said Psmith. "Say on!"

"Well, it was like this." And Mike related the events which had led up to his midnight excursion. Psmith listened attentively.

"This," he said, when Mike had finished, "confirms my frequently stated opinion that Comrade Jellicoe is one of Nature's blitherers. So that's why he touched us for our hard-earned, was it?"

"Yes. Of course there was no need for him to have the money at all."

"And the result is that you are in something of a tight place. You're *absolutely* certain you didn't paint that dog? Didn't do it, by any chance, in a moment of absent-mindedness, and forgot all about it? No? No, I suppose not. I wonder who did!"

"It's beastly awkward. You see, Downing chased me that night. That was why I rang the alarm bell. So, you see, he's certain to think that the chap he chased, which was me, and the chap who painted Sammy, are the same. I shall get landed both ways."

Psmith pondered.

"It *is* a tightish place," he admitted.

"I wonder if we could get this boot clean," said Mike, inspecting it with disfavour.

"Not for a pretty considerable time."

"I suppose not. I say, I *am* in the cart. If I can't produce this boot, they're bound to guess why."

"What exactly," asked Psmith, "was the position of affairs between you and Comrade Downing when you left him? Had you definitely parted brass-rags? Or did you simply sort of drift apart with mutual courtesies?"

"Oh, he said I was ill-advised to continue that attitude, or some rot, and I said I didn't care, I hadn't painted his bally dog, and he said very well, then, he must take steps, and—well, that was about all."

"Sufficient, too," said Psmith, "quite sufficient. I take it, then, that he is now on the war-path, collecting a gang, so to speak."

"I suppose he's gone to the Old Man about it."

"Probably. A very worrying time our headmaster is having, taking it all round, in connection with this painful affair. What do you think his move will be?"

"I suppose he'll send for me, and try to get something out of me."

"*He'll* want you to confess, too. Masters are all whales on confession. The worst of it is, you can't prove an alibi, because at about the time the foul act was perpetrated, you were playing Round-and-round-the-mulberry-bush with Comrade Downing. This needs thought. You had better put the case in my hands, and go out and watch the dandelions growing. I will think over the matter."

"Well, I hope you'll be able to think of something. I can't."

"Possibly. You never know."

There was a tap at the door.

"See how we have trained them," said Psmith. "They now knock before entering. There was a time when they would have tried to smash in a panel. Come in."

A small boy, carrying a straw hat adorned with the school-house ribbon, answered the invitation.

"Oh, I say, Jackson," he said, "the headmaster sent me over to tell you he wants to see you."

"I told you so," said Mike to Psmith.

"Don't go," suggested Psmith. "Tell him to write."

Mike got up.

"All this is very trying," said Psmith. "I'm seeing nothing of you to-day." He turned to the small boy. "Tell Willie," he added, "that Mr. Jackson will be with him in a moment."

The emissary departed.

"*You're* all right," said Psmith encouragingly. "Just you keep on saying you're all right. Stout denial is the thing. Don't go in for any airy explanations. Simply stick to stout denial. You can't beat it."

With which expert advice, he allowed Mike to go on his way.

He had not been gone two minutes, when Psmith, who had leaned back in his chair, wrapped in thought, heaved himself up again. He stood for a moment straightening his tie at the looking-glass; then he picked up his hat and moved slowly out of the door and down the passage. Thence, at the same dignified rate of progress, out of the house and in at Downing's front gate.

The postman was at the door when he got there, apparently absorbed in conversation with the parlour-maid. Psmith stood by politely till the postman, who had just been told it was like his impudence, caught sight of him, and, having handed over the letters in an ultra-formal and professional manner, passed away.

"Is Mr. Downing at home?" inquired Psmith.

He was, it seemed. Psmith was shown into the dining-room on the left of the hall, and requested to wait. He was examining a portrait of Mr. Downing which hung on the wall, when the housemaster came in.

CHAPTER LVII MR. DOWNING MOVES

"An excellent likeness, sir," said Psmith, with a gesture of the hand towards the painting.

"Well, Smith," said Mr. Downing shortly, "what do you wish to see me about?"

"It was in connection with the regrettable painting of your dog, sir."

"Ha!" said Mr. Downing.

"I did it, sir," said Psmith, stopping and flicking a piece of fluff off his knee.

CHAPTER LVIII THE ARTIST CLAIMS HIS WORK

The line of action which Psmith had called Stout Denial is an excellent line to adopt, especially if you really are innocent, but it does not lead to anything in the shape of a bright and snappy dialogue between accuser and accused. Both Mike and the headmaster were oppressed by a feeling that the situation was difficult. The atmosphere was heavy, and conversation showed a tendency to flag. The headmaster had opened brightly enough, with a summary of the evidence which Mr. Downing had laid before him, but after that a massive silence had been the order of the day. There is nothing in this world quite so stolid and uncommunicative as a boy who has made up his mind to be stolid and uncommunicative; and the headmaster, as he sat and looked at Mike, who sat and looked past him at the bookshelves, felt awkward. It was a scene which needed either a dramatic interruption or a neat exit speech. As it happened, what it got was the dramatic interruption.

The headmaster was just saying, "I do not think you fully realise, Jackson, the extent to which appearances—-" —-which was practically going back to the beginning and starting again—-when there was a knock at the door. A voice without said, "Mr. Downing to see you, sir," and the chief witness for the prosecution burst in.

"I would not have interrupted you," said Mr. Downing, "but——-"

"Not at all, Mr. Downing. Is there anything I can——?"

"I have discovered—-I have been informed—-In short, it was not Jackson, who committed the—-who painted my dog."

Mike and the headmaster both looked at the speaker. Mike with a feeling of relief—-for Stout Denial, unsupported by any weighty evidence, is a wearing game to play—-the headmaster with astonishment.

"Not Jackson?" said the headmaster.

"No. It was a boy in the same house. Smith."

Psmith! Mike was more than surprised. He could not believe it. There is nothing which affords so clear an index to a boy's character as the type of rag which he considers humorous. Between what is a rag and what is merely a rotten trick there is a very definite line drawn. Masters, as a rule, do not realise this, but boys nearly always do. Mike could not imagine Psmith doing a rotten thing like covering a housemaster's dog with red paint, any more than he could imagine doing it himself. They had both been amused at the sight of Sammy after the operation, but anybody, except possibly the owner of the dog, would have thought it funny at first. After the first surprise, their feeling had been that it was a scuggish thing to have done and beastly rough luck on the poor brute. It was a kid's trick. As for Psmith having done it, Mike simply did not believe it.

"Smith!" said the headmaster. "What makes you think that?"

"Simply this," said Mr. Downing, with calm triumph, "that the boy himself came to me a few moments ago and confessed."

Mike was conscious of a feeling of acute depression. It did not make him in the least degree jubilant, or even thankful, to know that he himself was cleared of the charge. All he could think of was that Psmith was done for. This was bound to mean the sack. If Psmith had painted Sammy, it meant that Psmith had broken out of his house at night: and it was not likely that the rules about nocturnal wandering were less strict at Sedleigh than at any other school in the kingdom. Mike felt, if possible, worse than he had felt when Wyatt had been caught on a similar occasion. It seemed as if Fate had a special grudge against his best friends. He did not make friends very quickly or easily, though he had always had scores of acquaintances—-and with Wyatt and Psmith he had found himself at home from the first moment he had met them.

He sat there, with a curious feeling of having swallowed a heavy weight, hardly listening to what Mr. Downing was saying. Mr. Downing was talking rapidly to the headmaster, who was nodding from time to time.

Mike took advantage of a pause to get up. "May I go, sir?" he said.

"Certainly, Jackson, certainly," said the Head. "Oh, and er—-, if you are going back to your house, tell Smith that I should like to see him."

"Yes, sir."

He had reached the door, when again there was a knock.

"Come in," said the headmaster.

It was Adair.

"Yes, Adair?"

Adair was breathing rather heavily, as if he had been running.

"It was about Sammy—-Sampson, sir," he said, looking at Mr. Downing.

"Ah, we know—. Well, Adair, what did you wish to say?"

"It wasn't Jackson who did it, sir."

"No, no, Adair. So Mr. Downing——-"

"It was Dunster, sir."

Terrific sensation! The headmaster gave a sort of strangled yelp of astonishment. Mr. Downing leaped in his chair. Mike's eyes opened to their fullest extent.

"Adair!"

There was almost a wail in the headmaster's voice. The situation had suddenly become too much for him. His brain was swimming. That Mike, despite the evidence against him, should be innocent, was curious, perhaps, but not particularly startling. But that Adair should inform him, two minutes after Mr. Downing's announcement of Psmith's confession, that Psmith, too, was guiltless, and that the real criminal was Dunster—-it was this that made him feel that somebody, in the words of an American author, had played a mean trick on him, and substituted for his brain a side-order of cauliflower. Why Dunster, of all people? Dunster, who, he remembered dizzily, had left the school at Christmas. And why, if Dunster had really painted the dog, had Psmith asserted that he himself was the culprit? Why—-why anything? He concentrated his mind on Adair as the only person who could save him from impending brain-fever.

"Adair!"

"Yes, sir?"

"What—-*what* do you mean?"

"It *was* Dunster, sir. I got a letter from him only five minutes ago, in which he said that he had painted Sammy—-Sampson, the dog, sir, for a rag—-for a joke, and that, as he didn't want any one here to get into a row—-be punished for it, I'd better tell Mr. Downing at once. I tried to find Mr. Downing, but he wasn't in the house. Then I met Smith outside the house, and he told me that Mr. Downing had gone over to see you, sir."

"Smith told you?" said Mr. Downing.

"Yes, sir."

"Did you say anything to him about your having received this letter from Dunster?"

"I gave him the letter to read, sir."

"And what was his attitude when he had read it?"

"He laughed, sir."

"*Laughed!*" Mr. Downing's voice was thunderous.

"Yes, sir. He rolled about."

Mr. Downing snorted.

"But Adair," said the headmaster, "I do not understand how this thing could have been done by Dunster. He has left the school."

"He was down here for the Old Sedleighans' match, sir. He stopped the night in the village."

"And that was the night the—-it happened?"

"Yes, sir."

"I see. Well, I am glad to find that the blame cannot be attached to any boy in the school. I am sorry that it is even an Old Boy. It was a foolish, discreditable thing to have done, but it is not as bad as if any boy still at the school had broken out of his house at night to do it."

"The sergeant," said Mr. Downing, "told me that the boy he saw was attempting to enter Mr. Outwood's house."

"Another freak of Dunster's, I suppose," said the headmaster. "I shall write to him."

"If it was really Dunster who painted my dog," said Mr. Downing, "I cannot understand the part played by Smith in this affair. If he did not do it, what possible motive could he have had for coming to me of his own accord and deliberately confessing?"

"To be sure," said the headmaster, pressing a bell. "It is certainly a thing that calls for explanation. Barlow," he said, as the butler appeared, "kindly go across to Mr. Outwood's house and inform Smith that I should like to see him."

"If you please, sir, Mr. Smith is waiting in the hall."

"In the hall!"

"Yes, sir. He arrived soon after Mr. Adair, sir, saying that he would wait, as you would probably wish to see him shortly."

"H'm. Ask him to step up, Barlow."

"Yes, sir."

There followed one of the tensest "stage waits" of Mike's experience. It was not long, but, while it lasted, the silence was quite solid. Nobody seemed to have anything to say, and there was not even a clock in the room to break the stillness with its ticking. A very faint drip-drip of rain could be heard outside the window.

Presently there was a sound of footsteps on the stairs. The door was opened.

"Mr. Smith, sir."

The old Etonian entered as would the guest of the evening who is a few moments late for dinner. He was cheerful, but slightly deprecating. He gave the impression of one who, though sure of his welcome, feels that some slight apology is expected from him. He advanced into the room with a gentle half-smile which suggested good-will to all men.

"It is still raining," he observed. "You wished to see me, sir?"

"Sit down, Smith."

"Thank you, sir."

He dropped into a deep arm-chair (which both Adair and Mike had avoided in favour of less luxurious seats) with the confidential cosiness of a fashionable physician calling on a patient, between whom and himself time has broken down the barriers of restraint and formality.

Mr. Downing burst out, like a reservoir that has broken its banks.

"Smith."

Psmith turned his gaze politely in the housemaster's direction.

"Smith, you came to me a quarter of an hour ago and told me that it was you who had painted my dog Sampson."

"Yes, sir."

"It was absolutely untrue?"

"I am afraid so, sir."

"But, Smith——" began the headmaster.

Psmith bent forward encouragingly.

"——This is a most extraordinary affair. Have you no explanation to offer? What induced you to do such a thing?"

Psmith sighed softly.

"The craze for notoriety, sir," he replied sadly. "The curse of the present age."

"What!" cried the headmaster.

"It is remarkable," proceeded Psmith placidly, with the impersonal touch of one lecturing on generalities, "how frequently, when a murder has been committed, one finds men confessing that they have done it when it is out of the question that they should have committed it. It is one of the most interesting problems with which anthropologists are confronted. Human nature——"

The headmaster interrupted.

"Smith," he said, "I should like to see you alone for a moment. Mr. Downing might I trouble—? Adair, Jackson."

He made a motion towards the door.

When he and Psmith were alone, there was silence. Psmith leaned back comfortably in his chair. The headmaster tapped nervously with his foot on the floor.

"Er—Smith."

"Sir?"

The headmaster seemed to have some difficulty in proceeding. He paused again. Then he went on.

"Er—Smith, I do not for a moment wish to pain you, but have you—er, do you remember ever having had, as a child, let us say, any—er—severe illness? Any—er—*mental* illness?"

"No, sir."

"There is no—forgive me if I am touching on a sad subject—there is no—none of your near relatives have ever suffered in the way I—er—have described?"

"There isn't a lunatic on the list, sir," said Psmith cheerfully.

"Of course, Smith, of course," said the headmaster hurriedly, "I did not mean to suggest—quite so, quite so.... You think, then, that you confessed to an act which you had not committed purely from some sudden impulse which you cannot explain?"

"Strictly between ourselves, sir——"

Privately, the headmaster found Psmith's man-to-man attitude somewhat disconcerting, but he said nothing.

"Well, Smith?"

"I should not like it to go any further, sir."

"I will certainly respect any confidence——"

"I don't want anybody to know, sir. This is strictly between ourselves."

"I think you are sometimes apt to forget, Smith, the proper relations existing between boy and—Well, never mind that for the present. We can return to it later. For the moment, let me hear what you wish to say. I shall, of course, tell nobody, if you do not wish it."

"Well, it was like this, sir," said Psmith. "Jackson happened to tell me that you and Mr. Downing seemed to think he had painted Mr. Downing's dog, and there seemed some danger of his being expelled, so I thought it wouldn't be an unsound scheme if I were to go and say I had done it. That was the whole thing. Of course, Dunster writing created a certain amount of confusion."

There was a pause.

"It was a very wrong thing to do, Smith," said the headmaster, at last, "but.... You are a curious boy, Smith. Good-night."

He held out his hand.

"Good-night, sir," said Psmith.

"Not a bad old sort," said Psmith meditatively to himself, as he walked downstairs. "By no means a bad old sort. I must drop in from time to time and cultivate him."

Mike and Adair were waiting for him outside the front door.

"Well?" said Mike.

"You *are* the limit," said Adair. "What's he done?"

"Nothing. We had a very pleasant chat, and then I tore myself away."

"Do you mean to say he's not going to do a thing?"

"Not a thing."

"Well, you're a marvel," said Adair.

Psmith thanked him courteously. They walked on towards the houses.

"By the way, Adair," said Mike, as the latter started to turn in at Downing's, "I'll write to Strachan to-night about that match."

"What's that?" asked Psmith.

"Jackson's going to try and get Wrykyn to give us a game," said Adair. "They've got a vacant date. I hope the dickens they'll do it."

"Oh, I should think they're certain to," said Mike. "Good-night."

"And give Comrade Downing, when you see him," said Psmith, "my very best love. It is men like him who make this Merrie England of ours what it is."

"I say, Psmith," said Mike suddenly, "what really made you tell Downing you'd done it?"

"The craving for——"

"Oh, chuck it. You aren't talking to the Old Man now. I believe it was simply to get me out of a jolly tight corner."

Psmith's expression was one of pain.

"My dear Comrade Jackson," said he, "you wrong me. You make me writhe. I'm surprised at you. I never thought to hear those words from Michael Jackson."

"Well, I believe you did, all the same," said Mike obstinately. "And it was jolly good of you, too."

Psmith moaned.

CHAPTER LIX SEDLEIGH *v.* WRYKYN

The Wrykyn match was three-parts over, and things were going badly for Sedleigh. In a way one might have said that the game was over, and that Sedleigh had lost; for it was a one day match, and Wrykyn, who had led on the first innings, had only to play out time to make the game theirs.

Sedleigh were paying the penalty for allowing themselves to be influenced by nerves in the early part of the day. Nerves lose more school matches than good play ever won. There is a certain type of school batsman who is a gift to any bowler when he once lets his imagination run away with him. Sedleigh, with the exception of Adair, Psmith, and Mike, had entered upon this match in a state of the most azure funk. Ever since Mike had received Strachan's answer and Adair had announced on the notice-board that on Saturday, July the twentieth, Sedleigh would play Wrykyn, the team had been all on the jump. It was useless for Adair to tell them, as he did repeatedly, on Mike's authority, that Wrykyn were weak this season, and that on their present form Sedleigh ought to win easily. The team listened, but were not comforted. Wrykyn might be below their usual strength, but then Wrykyn cricket, as a rule, reached such a high standard that this probably meant little. However weak Wrykyn might be—-for them—-there was a very firm impression among the members of the Sedleigh first eleven that the other school was quite strong enough to knock the cover off *them*. Experience counts enormously in school matches. Sedleigh had never been proved. The teams they played were the sort of sides which the Wrykyn second eleven would play. Whereas Wrykyn, from time immemorial, had been beating Ripton teams and Free Foresters teams and M.C.C. teams packed with county men and sending men to Oxford and Cambridge who got their blues as freshmen.

Sedleigh had gone on to the field that morning a depressed side.

It was unfortunate that Adair had won the toss. He had had no choice but to take first innings. The weather had been bad for the last week, and the wicket was slow and treacherous. It was likely to get worse during the day, so Adair had chosen to bat first.

Taking into consideration the state of nerves the team was in, this in itself was a calamity. A school eleven are always at their worst and nerviest before lunch. Even on their own ground they find the surroundings lonely and unfamiliar. The subtlety of the bowlers becomes magnified. Unless the first pair make a really good start, a collapse almost invariably ensues.

To-day the start had been gruesome beyond words. Mike, the bulwark of the side, the man who had been brought up on Wrykyn bowling, and from whom, whatever might happen to the others, at least a fifty was expected—-Mike, going in first with Barnes and taking first over, had played inside one from Bruce, the Wrykyn slow bowler, and had been caught at short slip off his second ball.

That put the finishing-touch on the panic. Stone, Robinson, and the others, all quite decent punishing batsmen when their nerves allowed them to play their own game, crawled to the wickets, declined to hit out at anything, and were clean bowled, several of them, playing back to half-volleys. Adair did not suffer from panic, but his batting was not equal to his bowling, and he had fallen after hitting one four. Seven wickets were down for thirty when Psmith went in.

Psmith had always disclaimed any pretensions to batting skill, but he was undoubtedly the right man for a crisis like this. He had an enormous reach, and he used it. Three consecutive balls from Bruce he turned into full-tosses and swept to the leg-boundary, and, assisted by Barnes, who had been sitting on the splice in his usual manner, he raised the total to seventy-one before being yorked, with his score at thirty-five. Ten minutes later the innings was over, with Barnes not out sixteen, for seventy-nine.

Wrykyn had then gone in, lost Strachan for twenty before lunch, and finally completed their innings at a quarter to four for a hundred and thirty-one.

This was better than Sedleigh had expected. At least eight of the team had looked forward dismally to an afternoon's leather-hunting. But Adair and Psmith, helped by the wicket, had never been easy, especially Psmith, who had taken six wickets, his slows playing havoc with the tail.

It would be too much to say that Sedleigh had any hope of pulling the game out of the fire; but it was a comfort, they felt, at any rate, having another knock. As is usual at this stage of a match, their nervousness had vanished, and they felt capable of better things than in the first innings.

It was on Mike's suggestion that Psmith and himself went in first. Mike knew the limitations of the Wrykyn bowling, and he was convinced that, if they could knock Bruce off, it might be possible to rattle up a score sufficient to give them the game, always provided that Wrykyn collapsed in the second innings. And it seemed to Mike that the wicket would be so bad then that they easily might.

So he and Psmith had gone in at four o'clock to hit. And they had hit. The deficit had been wiped off, all but a dozen runs, when Psmith was bowled, and by that time Mike was set and in his best vein. He treated all the bowlers alike. And when Stone came in, restored to his proper frame of mind, and lashed out stoutly, and after him Robinson and the rest, it looked as if Sedleigh had a chance again. The score was a hundred and twenty when Mike, who had just reached his fifty, skied one to Strachan at cover. The time was twenty-five past five.

As Mike reached the pavilion, Adair declared the innings closed.

Wrykyn started batting at twenty-five minutes to six, with sixty-nine to make if they wished to make them, and an hour and ten minutes during which to keep up their wickets if they preferred to take things easy and go for a win on the first innings.

At first it looked as if they meant to knock off the runs, for Strachan forced the game from the first ball, which was Psmith's, and which he hit into the pavilion. But, at fifteen, Adair bowled him. And when, two runs later, Psmith got the next man stumped, and finished up his over with a c-and-b, Wrykyn decided that it was not good enough. Seventeen for three, with an hour all but five minutes to go, was getting too dangerous. So Drummond and Rigby, the next pair, proceeded to play with caution, and the collapse ceased.

This was the state of the game at the point at which this chapter opened. Seventeen for three had become twenty-four for three, and the hands of the clock stood at ten minutes past six. Changes of bowling had been tried, but there seemed no chance of getting past the batsmen's defence. They were playing all the good balls, and refused to hit at the bad.

A quarter past six struck, and then Psmith made a suggestion which altered the game completely.

"Why don't you have a shot this end?" he said to Adair, as they were crossing over. "There's a spot on the off which might help you a lot. You can break like blazes if only you land on it. It doesn't help my leg-breaks a bit, because they won't hit at them."

Barnes was on the point of beginning to bowl, when Adair took the ball from him. The captain of Outwood's retired to short leg with an air that suggested that he was glad to be relieved of his prominent post.

The next moment Drummond's off-stump was lying at an angle of forty-five. Adair was absolutely accurate as a bowler, and he had dropped his first ball right on the worn patch.

Two minutes later Drummond's successor was retiring to the pavilion, while the wicket-keeper straightened the stumps again.

There is nothing like a couple of unexpected wickets for altering the atmosphere of a game. Five minutes before, Sedleigh had been lethargic and without hope. Now there was a stir and buzz all round the ground. There were twenty-five minutes to go, and five wickets were down. Sedleigh was on top again.

The next man seemed to take an age coming out. As a matter of fact, he walked more rapidly than a batsman usually walks to the crease.

Adair's third ball dropped just short of the spot. The batsman, hitting out, was a shade too soon. The ball hummed through the air a couple of feet from the ground in the direction of mid-off, and Mike, diving to the right, got to it as he was falling, and chucked it up.

After that the thing was a walk-over. Psmith clean bowled a man in his next over; and the tail, demoralised by the sudden change in the game, collapsed uncompromisingly. Sedleigh won by thirty-five runs with eight minutes in hand.

CHAPTER LIX SEDLEIGH v. WRYKYN

Psmith and Mike sat in their study after lock-up, discussing things in general and the game in particular.

"I feel like a beastly renegade, playing against Wrykyn," said Mike. "Still, I'm glad we won. Adair's a jolly good sort, and it'll make him happy for weeks."

"When I last saw Comrade Adair," said Psmith, "he was going about in a sort of trance, beaming vaguely and wanting to stand people things at the shop."

"He bowled awfully well."

"Yes," said Psmith. "I say, I don't wish to cast a gloom over this joyful occasion in any way, but you say Wrykyn are going to give Sedleigh a fixture again next year?"

"Well?"

"Well, have you thought of the massacre which will ensue? You will have left, Adair will have left. Incidentally, I shall have left. Wrykyn will swamp them."

"I suppose they will. Still, the great thing, you see, is to get the thing started. That's what Adair was so keen on. Now Sedleigh has beaten Wrykyn, he's satisfied. They can get on fixtures with decent clubs, and work up to playing the big schools. You've got to start somehow. So it's all right, you see."

"And, besides," said Psmith, reflectively, "in an emergency they can always get Comrade Downing to bowl for them, what? Let us now sally out and see if we can't promote a rag of some sort in this abode of wrath. Comrade Outwood has gone over to dinner at the School House, and it would be a pity to waste a somewhat golden opportunity. Shall we stagger?"

They staggered.

Psmith in the City

to

Leslie Havergal Bradshaw

1. Mr Bickersdyke Walks behind the Bowler's Arm

Considering what a prominent figure Mr John Bickersdyke was to be in Mike Jackson's life, it was only appropriate that he should make a dramatic entry into it. This he did by walking behind the bowler's arm when Mike had scored ninety-eight, causing him thereby to be clean bowled by a long-hop.

It was the last day of the Ilsworth cricket week, and the house team were struggling hard on a damaged wicket. During the first two matches of the week all had been well. Warm sunshine, true wickets, tea in the shade of the trees. But on the Thursday night, as the team champed their dinner contentedly after defeating the Incogniti by two wickets, a pattering of rain made itself heard upon the windows. By bedtime it had settled to a steady downpour. On Friday morning, when the team of the local regiment arrived in their brake, the sun was shining once more in a watery, melancholy way, but play was not possible before lunch. After lunch the bowlers were in their element. The regiment, winning the toss, put together a hundred and thirty, due principally to a last wicket stand between two enormous corporals, who swiped at everything and had luck enough for two whole teams. The house team followed with seventy-eight, of which Psmith, by his usual golf methods, claimed thirty. Mike, who had gone in first as the star bat of the side, had been run out with great promptitude off the first ball of the innings, which his partner had hit in the immediate neighbourhood of point. At close of play the regiment had made five without loss. This, on the Saturday morning, helped by another shower of rain which made the wicket easier for the moment, they had increased to a hundred and forty-eight, leaving the house just two hundred to make on a pitch which looked as if it were made of linseed.

It was during this week that Mike had first made the acquaintance of Psmith's family. Mr Smith had moved from Shropshire, and taken Ilsworth Hall in a neighbouring county. This he had done, as far as could be ascertained, simply because he had a poor opinion of Shropshire cricket. And just at the moment cricket happened to be the pivot of his life.

'My father,' Psmith had confided to Mike, meeting him at the station in the family motor on the Monday, 'is a man of vast but volatile brain. He has not that calm, dispassionate outlook on life which marks your true philosopher, such as myself. I—'

'I say,' interrupted Mike, eyeing Psmith's movements with apprehension, 'you aren't going to drive, are you?'

'Who else? As I was saying, I am like some contented spectator of a Pageant. My pater wants to jump in and stage-manage. He is a man of hobbies. He never has more than one at a time, and he never has that long. But while he has it, it's all there. When I left the house this morning he was all for cricket. But by the time we get to the ground he may have chucked cricket and taken up the Territorial Army. Don't be surprised if you find the wicket being dug up into trenches, when we arrive, and the pro. moving in echelon towards the pavilion. No,' he added, as the car turned into the drive, and they caught a glimpse of white flannels and blazers in the distance, and heard the sound of bat meeting ball, 'cricket seems still to be topping the bill. Come along, and I'll show you your room. It's next to mine, so that, if brooding on Life in the still hours of the night, I hit on any great truth, I shall pop in and discuss it with you.'

While Mike was changing, Psmith sat on his bed, and continued to discourse.

'I suppose you're going to the 'Varsity?' he said.

'Rather,' said Mike, lacing his boots. 'You are, of course? Cambridge,

I hope. I'm going to King's.'

'Between ourselves,' confided Psmith, 'I'm dashed if I know what's going to happen to me. I am the thingummy of what's-its-name.'

'You look it,' said Mike, brushing his hair.

'Don't stand there cracking the glass,' said Psmith. 'I tell you I am practically a human three-shies-a-penny ball. My father is poising me lightly in his hand, preparatory to flinging me at one of the milky cocos of Life. Which one he'll aim at I don't know. The least thing fills him with a whirl of new views as to my future. Last week we were out shooting together, and he said that the life of the gentleman-farmer was the most manly and independent on earth, and that he had a good mind to start me on that. I pointed out that lack of early training had rendered me unable to distinguish between a threshing-machine and a mangel-wurzel, so he chucked that. He has now worked round to Commerce. It seems that a blighter of the name of Bickersdyke is coming here for the week-end next Saturday. As far as I can say without searching the Newgate Calendar, the man Bickersdyke's career seems to have been as follows. He was at school with my pater, went into the City, raked in a certain amount of doubloons—probably dishonestly—and is now a sort of Captain of Industry, manager of some bank or other, and about to stand for Parliament. The result of these excesses is that my pater's imagination has been fired, and at time of going to press he wants me to imitate Comrade Bickersdyke. However, there's plenty of time. That's one comfort. He's certain to change his mind again. Ready? Then suppose we filter forth into the arena?'

Out on the field Mike was introduced to the man of hobbies. Mr Smith, senior, was a long, earnest-looking man who might have been Psmith in a grey wig but for his obvious energy. He was as wholly on the move as Psmith was wholly statuesque. Where Psmith stood like some dignified piece of sculpture, musing on deep questions with a glassy eye, his father would be trying to be in four places at once. When Psmith presented Mike to him, he shook hands warmly with him and started a sentence, but broke off in the middle of both performances to dash wildly in the direction of the pavilion in an endeavour to catch an impossible catch some thirty yards away. The impetus so gained carried him on towards Bagley, the Ilsworth Hall ground-man, with whom a moment later he was carrying on an animated discussion as to whether he had or had not seen a dandelion on the field that morning. Two minutes afterwards he had skimmed away again. Mike, as he watched him, began to appreciate Psmith's reasons for feeling some doubt as to what would be his future walk in life.

At lunch that day Mike sat next to Mr Smith, and improved his acquaintance with him; and by the end of the week they were on excellent terms. Psmith's father had Psmith's gift of getting on well with people.

On this Saturday, as Mike buckled on his pads, Mr Smith bounded up, full of advice and encouragement.

'My boy,' he said, 'we rely on you. These others'—he indicated with a disparaging wave of the hand the rest of the team, who were visible through the window of the changing-room—'are all very well. Decent club bats. Good for a few on a billiard-table. But you're our hope on a wicket like this. I have studied cricket all my life'—till that summer it is improbable that Mr Smith had ever handled a bat—'and I know a first-class batsman when I see one. I've seen your brothers play. Pooh, you're better than any of them. That century of yours against the Green Jackets was a wonderful innings, wonderful. Now look here, my boy. I want you to be careful. We've a lot of runs to make, so we mustn't take any risks. Hit plenty of boundaries, of course, but be careful. Careful. Dash it, there's a youngster trying to climb up the elm. He'll break his neck. It's young Giles, my keeper's boy. Hi! Hi, there!'

He scudded out to avert the tragedy, leaving Mike to digest his expert advice on the art of batting on bad wickets.

Possibly it was the excellence of this advice which induced Mike to play what was, to date, the best innings of his life. There are moments when the batsman feels an almost super-human fitness. This came to Mike now. The sun had begun to shine strongly. It made the wicket more difficult, but it added a cheerful touch to the scene. Mike felt calm and masterful. The bowling had no terrors for him. He scored nine off his first over and seven off his second, half-way through which he lost his partner. He was to undergo a similar bereavement several times that afternoon, and at frequent intervals. However simple the bowling might seem to him, it had enough sting in it to worry the rest of the team considerably. Batsmen came and went at the other end with such rapidity that it seemed hardly worth while their troubling to come in at all. Every now and then one would give promise of better things by lifting the slow bowler into the pavilion or over the boundary, but it always happened that a similar stroke, a few balls later, ended in an easy catch. At five o'clock the Ilsworth score was eighty-one for seven wickets, last man nought, Mike not out fifty-nine. As most of the house team, including Mike, were dispersing to their homes or were due for visits at other houses that night, stumps were to be drawn at six. It was obvious that they could not hope to win. Number nine on the list, who was Bagley, the ground-man, went in with instructions to play for a draw, and minute advice from Mr Smith as to how he was to do it. Mike had now begun to score rapidly, and it was not to be expected that he could change his game; but Bagley, a dried-up little man of the type which bowls for five hours on a hot August day without exhibiting any symptoms of fatigue, put a much-bound bat stolidly in front of every ball he received; and the Hall's prospects of saving the game grew brighter.

At a quarter to six the professional left, caught at very silly point for eight. The score was a hundred and fifteen, of which Mike had made eighty-five.

A lengthy young man with yellow hair, who had done some good fast bowling for the Hall during the week, was the next man in. In previous matches he had hit furiously at everything, and against the Green Jackets had knocked up forty in twenty minutes while Mike was putting the finishing touches to his century. Now, however, with his host's warning ringing in his ears, he adopted the unspectacular, or Bagley, style of play. His manner of dealing with the ball was that of one playing croquet. He patted it gingerly back to the bowler when it was straight, and left it icily alone when it was off the wicket. Mike, still in the brilliant vein, clumped a half-volley past point to the boundary, and with highly scientific late cuts and glides brought his score to ninety-eight. With Mike's score at this, the total at a hundred and thirty, and the hands of the clock at five minutes to six, the yellow-haired croquet exponent fell, as Bagley had fallen, a victim to silly point, the ball being the last of the over.

Mr Smith, who always went in last for his side, and who so far had not received a single ball during the week, was down the pavilion steps and half-way to the wicket before the retiring batsman had taken half a dozen steps.

'Last over,' said the wicket-keeper to Mike. 'Any idea how many you've got? You must be near your century, I should think.'

'Ninety-eight,' said Mike. He always counted his runs.

'By Jove, as near as that? This is something like a finish.'

Mike left the first ball alone, and the second. They were too wide of the off-stump to be hit at safely. Then he felt a thrill as the third ball left the bowler's hand. It was a long-hop. He faced square to pull it.

And at that moment Mr John Bickersdyke walked into his life across the bowling-screen.

He crossed the bowler's arm just before the ball pitched. Mike lost sight of it for a fraction of a second, and hit wildly. The next moment his leg stump was askew; and the Hall had lost the match.

'I'm sorry,' he said to Mr Smith. 'Some silly idiot walked across the screen just as the ball was bowled.'

'What!' shouted Mr Smith. 'Who was the fool who walked behind the bowler's arm?' he yelled appealingly to Space.

'Here he comes, whoever he is,' said Mike.

A short, stout man in a straw hat and a flannel suit was walking towards them. As he came nearer Mike saw that he had a hard, thin-lipped mouth, half-hidden by a rather ragged moustache, and that behind a pair of gold spectacles were two pale and slightly protruding eyes, which, like his mouth, looked hard.

'How are you, Smith,' he said.

'Hullo, Bickersdyke.' There was a slight internal struggle, and then Mr Smith ceased to be the cricketer and became the host. He chatted amiably to the newcomer.

'You lost the game, I suppose,' said Mr Bickersdyke.

The cricketer in Mr Smith came to the top again, blended now, however, with the host. He was annoyed, but restrained in his annoyance.

'I say, Bickersdyke, you know, my dear fellow,' he said complainingly, 'you shouldn't have walked across the screen. You put Jackson off, and made him get bowled.'

'The screen?'

'That curious white object,' said Mike. 'It is not put up merely as an ornament. There's a sort of rough idea of giving the batsman a chance of seeing the ball, as well. It's a great help to him when people come charging across it just as the bowler bowls.'

Mr Bickersdyke turned a slightly deeper shade of purple, and was about to reply, when what sporting reporters call 'the veritable ovation' began.

Quite a large crowd had been watching the game, and they expressed their approval of Mike's performance.

There is only one thing for a batsman to do on these occasions. Mike ran into the pavilion, leaving Mr Bickersdyke standing.

2. Mike Hears Bad News

It seemed to Mike, when he got home, that there was a touch of gloom in the air. His sisters were as glad to see him as ever. There was a good deal of rejoicing going on among the female Jacksons because Joe had scored his first double century in first-class cricket. Double centuries are too common, nowadays, for the papers to take much notice of them; but, still, it is not everybody who can make them, and the occasion was one to be marked. Mike had read the news in the evening paper in the train, and had sent his brother a wire from the station, congratulating him. He had wondered whether he himself would ever achieve the feat in first-class cricket. He did not see why he should not. He looked forward through a long vista of years of county cricket. He had a birth qualification for the county in which Mr Smith had settled, and he had played for it once already at the beginning of the holidays. His *debut* had not been sensational, but it had been promising. The fact that two members of the team had made centuries, and a third seventy odd, had rather eclipsed his own twenty-nine not out; but it had been a faultless innings, and nearly all the papers had said that here was yet another Jackson, evidently well up to the family standard, who was bound to do big things in the future.

The touch of gloom was contributed by his brother Bob to a certain extent, and by his father more noticeably. Bob looked slightly thoughtful. Mr Jackson seemed thoroughly worried.

Mike approached Bob on the subject in the billiard-room after dinner.

Bob was practising cannons in rather a listless way.

'What's up, Bob?' asked Mike.

Bob laid down his cue.

'I'm hanged if I know,' said Bob. 'Something seems to be. Father's worried about something.'

'He looked as if he'd got the hump rather at dinner.'

'I only got here this afternoon, about three hours before you did. I had a bit of a talk with him before dinner. I can't make out what's up. He seemed awfully keen on my finding something to do now I've come down from Oxford. Wanted to know whether I couldn't get a tutoring job or a mastership at some school next term. I said I'd have a shot. I don't see what all the hurry's about, though. I was hoping he'd give me a bit of travelling on the Continent somewhere before I started in.'

'Rough luck,' said Mike. 'I wonder why it is. Jolly good about Joe, wasn't it? Let's have fifty up, shall we?'

Bob's remarks had given Mike no hint of impending disaster. It seemed strange, of course, that his father, who had always been so easy-going, should have developed a hustling Get On or Get Out spirit, and be urging Bob to Do It Now; but it never occurred to him that there could be any serious reason for it. After all, fellows had to start working some time or other. Probably his father had merely pointed this out to Bob, and Bob had made too much of it.

Half-way through the game Mr Jackson entered the room, and stood watching in silence.

'Want a game, father?' asked Mike.

'No, thanks, Mike. What is it? A hundred up?'

'Fifty.'

'Oh, then you'll be finished in a moment. When you are, I wish you'd just look into the study for a moment, Mike. I want to have a talk with you.'

'Rum,' said Mike, as the door closed. 'I wonder what's up?'

For a wonder his conscience was free. It was not as if a bad school-report might have arrived in his absence. His Sedleigh report had come at the beginning of the holidays, and had been, on the whole, fairly decent—nothing startling either way. Mr Downing, perhaps through remorse at having harried Mike to such an extent during the Sammy episode, had exercised a studied moderation in his remarks. He had let Mike down far more easily than he really deserved. So it could not be a report that was worrying Mr Jackson. And there was nothing else on his conscience.

Bob made a break of sixteen, and ran out. Mike replaced his cue, and walked to the study.

His father was sitting at the table. Except for the very important fact that this time he felt that he could plead Not Guilty on every possible charge, Mike was struck by the resemblance in the general arrangement of the scene to that painful ten minutes at the end of the previous holidays, when his father had announced his intention of taking him away from Wrykyn and sending him to Sedleigh. The resemblance was increased by the fact that, as Mike entered, Mr Jackson was kicking at the waste-paper basket—a thing which with him was an infallible sign of mental unrest.

'Sit down, Mike,' said Mr Jackson. 'How did you get on during the week?'

'Topping. Only once out under double figures. And then I was run out.
Got a century against the Green Jackets, seventy-one against the
Incogs, and today I made ninety-eight on a beast of a wicket, and only
got out because some silly goat of a chap—'

He broke off. Mr Jackson did not seem to be attending. There was a silence. Then Mr Jackson spoke with an obvious effort.

'Look here, Mike, we've always understood one another, haven't we?'

'Of course we have.'

'You know I wouldn't do anything to prevent you having a good time, if I could help it. I took you away from Wrykyn, I know, but that was a special case. It was necessary. But I understand perfectly how keen you are to go to Cambridge, and I wouldn't stand in the way for a minute, if I could help it.'

Mike looked at him blankly. This could only mean one thing. He was not to go to the 'Varsity. But why? What had happened? When he had left for the Smith's cricket week, his name had been down for King's, and the whole thing settled. What could have happened since then?

'But I can't help it,' continued Mr Jackson.

'Aren't I going up to Cambridge, father?' stammered Mike.

'I'm afraid not, Mike. I'd manage it if I possibly could. I'm just as anxious to see you get your Blue as you are to get it. But it's kinder to be quite frank. I can't afford to send you to Cambridge. I won't go into details which you would not understand; but I've lost a very large sum of money since I saw you last. So large that we shall have to economize in every way. I shall let this house and take a much smaller one. And you and Bob, I'm afraid, will have to start earning your living. I know it's a terrible disappointment to you, old chap.'

'Oh, that's all right,' said Mike thickly. There seemed to be something sticking in his throat, preventing him from speaking.

'If there was any possible way—'

'No, it's all right, father, really. I don't mind a bit. It's awfully rough luck on you losing all that.'

There was another silence. The clock ticked away energetically on the mantelpiece, as if glad to make itself heard at last. Outside, a plaintive snuffle made itself heard. John, the bull-dog, Mike's inseparable companion, who had followed him to the study, was getting tired of waiting on the mat. Mike got up and opened the door. John lumbered in.

The movement broke the tension.

'Thanks, Mike,' said Mr Jackson, as Mike started to leave the room, 'you're a sportsman.'

3. The New Era Begins

Details of what were in store for him were given to Mike next morning. During his absence at Ilsworth a vacancy had been got for him in that flourishing institution, the New Asiatic Bank; and he was to enter upon his duties, whatever they might be, on the Tuesday of the following week. It was short notice, but banks have a habit of swallowing their victims rather abruptly. Mike remembered the case of Wyatt, who had had just about the same amount of time in which to get used to the prospect of Commerce.

On the Monday morning a letter arrived from Psmith. Psmith was still perturbed. 'Commerce,' he wrote, 'continues to boom. My pater referred to Comrade Bickersdyke last night as a Merchant Prince. Comrade B. and I do not get on well together. Purely for his own good, I drew him aside yesterday and explained to him at great length the frightfulness of walking across the bowling-screen. He seemed restive, but I was firm. We parted rather with the Distant Stare than the Friendly Smile. But I shall persevere. In many ways the casual observer would say that he was hopeless. He is a poor performer at Bridge, as I was compelled to hint to him on Saturday night. His eyes have no animated sparkle of intelligence. And the cut of his clothes jars my sensitive soul to its foundations. I don't wish to speak ill of a man behind his back, but I must confide in you, as my Boyhood's Friend, that he wore a made-up tie at dinner. But no more of a painful subject. I am working away at him with a brave smile. Sometimes I think that I am succeeding. Then he seems to slip back again. However,' concluded the letter, ending on an optimistic note, 'I think that I shall make a man of him yet—some day.'

Mike re-read this letter in the train that took him to London. By this time Psmith would know that his was not the only case in which Commerce was booming. Mike had written to him by return, telling him of the disaster which had befallen the house of Jackson. Mike wished he could have told him in person, for Psmith had a way of treating unpleasant situations as if he were merely playing at them for his own amusement. Psmith's attitude towards the slings and arrows of outrageous Fortune was to regard them with a bland smile, as if they were part of an entertainment got up for his express benefit.

Arriving at Paddington, Mike stood on the platform, waiting for his box to emerge from the luggage-van, with mixed feelings of gloom and excitement. The gloom was in the larger quantities, perhaps, but the excitement was there, too. It was the first time in his life that he had been entirely dependent on himself. He had crossed the Rubicon. The occasion was too serious for him to feel the same helplessly furious feeling with which he had embarked on life at Sedleigh. It was possible to look on Sedleigh with quite a personal enmity. London was too big to be angry with. It took no notice of him. It did not care whether he was glad to be there or sorry, and there was no means of making it care. That is the peculiarity of London. There is a sort of cold unfriendliness about it. A city like New York makes the new arrival feel at home in half an hour; but London is a specialist in what Psmith in his letter had called the Distant Stare. You have to buy London's good-will.

Mike drove across the Park to Victoria, feeling very empty and small. He had settled on Dulwich as the spot to get lodgings, partly because, knowing nothing about London, he was under the impression that rooms anywhere inside the four-mile radius were very expensive, but principally because there was a school at Dulwich, and it would be a comfort being near a school. He might get a game of fives there sometimes, he thought, on a Saturday afternoon, and, in the summer, occasional cricket.

Wandering at a venture up the asphalt passage which leads from Dulwich station in the direction of the College, he came out into Acacia Road. There is something about Acacia Road which inevitably suggests furnished apartments. A child could tell at a glance that it was bristling with bed-sitting rooms.

Mike knocked at the first door over which a card hung.

There is probably no more depressing experience in the world than the process of engaging furnished apartments. Those who let furnished apartments seem to take no joy in the act. Like Pooh-Bah, they do it, but it revolts them.

In answer to Mike's knock, a female person opened the door. In appearance she resembled a pantomime 'dame', inclining towards the restrained melancholy of Mr Wilkie Bard rather than the joyous abandon of Mr George Robey. Her voice she had modelled on the gramophone. Her most recent occupation seemed to have been something with a good deal of yellow soap in it. As a matter of fact—there are no secrets between our readers and ourselves—she had been washing a shirt. A useful occupation, and an honourable, but one that tends to produce a certain homeliness in the appearance.

She wiped a pair of steaming hands on her apron, and regarded Mike with an eye which would have been markedly expressionless in a boiled fish.

'Was there anything?' she asked.

Mike felt that he was in for it now. He had not sufficient ease of manner to back gracefully away and disappear, so he said that there was something. In point of fact, he wanted a bed-sitting room.

'Orkup stays,' said the pantomime dame. Which Mike interpreted to mean, would he walk upstairs?

The procession moved up a dark flight of stairs until it came to a door. The pantomime dame opened this, and shuffled through. Mike stood in the doorway, and looked in.

3. The New Era Begins

It was a repulsive room. One of those characterless rooms which are only found in furnished apartments. To Mike, used to the comforts of his bedroom at home and the cheerful simplicity of a school dormitory, it seemed about the most dismal spot he had ever struck. A sort of Sargasso Sea among bedrooms.

He looked round in silence. Then he said: 'Yes.' There did not seem much else to say.

'It's a nice room,' said the pantomime dame. Which was a black lie. It was not a nice room. It never had been a nice room. And it did not seem at all probable that it ever would be a nice room. But it looked cheap. That was the great thing. Nobody could have the assurance to charge much for a room like that. A landlady with a conscience might even have gone to the length of paying people some small sum by way of compensation to them for sleeping in it.

'About what?' queried Mike. Cheapness was the great consideration. He understood that his salary at the bank would be about four pounds ten a month, to begin with, and his father was allowing him five pounds a month. One does not do things *en prince* on a hundred and fourteen pounds a year.

The pantomime dame became slightly more animated. Prefacing her remarks by a repetition of her statement that it was a nice room, she went on to say that she could 'do' it at seven and sixpence per week 'for him'—giving him to understand, presumably, that, if the Shah of Persia or Mr Carnegie ever applied for a night's rest, they would sigh in vain for such easy terms. And that included lights. Coals were to be looked on as an extra. 'Sixpence a scuttle.' Attendance was thrown in.

Having stated these terms, she dribbled a piece of fluff under the bed, after the manner of a professional Association footballer, and relapsed into her former moody silence.

Mike said he thought that would be all right. The pantomime dame exhibited no pleasure.

''Bout meals?' she said. 'You'll be wanting breakfast. Bacon, aigs, an' that, I suppose?'

Mike said he supposed so.

'That'll be extra,' she said. 'And dinner? A chop, or a nice steak?'

Mike bowed before this original flight of fancy. A chop or a nice steak seemed to be about what he might want.

'That'll be extra,' said the pantomime dame in her best Wilkie Bard manner.

Mike said yes, he supposed so. After which, having put down seven and sixpence, one week's rent in advance, he was presented with a grubby receipt and an enormous latchkey, and the *seance* was at an end. Mike wandered out of the house. A few steps took him to the railings that bounded the College grounds. It was late August, and the evenings had begun to close in. The cricket-field looked very cool and spacious in the dim light, with the school buildings looming vague and shadowy through the slight mist. The little gate by the railway bridge was not locked. He went in, and walked slowly across the turf towards the big clump of trees which marked the division between the cricket and football fields. It was all very pleasant and soothing after the pantomime dame and her stuffy bed-sitting room. He sat down on a bench beside the second eleven telegraph-board, and looked across the ground at the pavilion. For the first time that day he began to feel really home-sick. Up till now the excitement of a strange venture had borne him up; but the cricket-field and the pavilion reminded him so sharply of Wrykyn. They brought home to him with a cutting distinctness, the absolute finality of his break with the old order of things. Summers would come and go, matches would be played on this ground with all the glory of big scores and keen finishes; but he was done. 'He was a jolly good bat at school. Top of the Wrykyn averages two years. But didn't do anything after he left. Went into the city or something.' That was what they would say of him, if they didn't quite forget him.

The clock on the tower over the senior block chimed quarter after quarter, but Mike sat on, thinking. It was quite late when he got up, and began to walk back to Acacia Road. He felt cold and stiff and very miserable.

4. First Steps in a Business Career

The City received Mike with the same aloofness with which the more western portion of London had welcomed him on the previous day. Nobody seemed to look at him. He was permitted to alight at St Paul's and make his way up Queen Victoria Street without any demonstration. He followed the human stream till he reached the Mansion House, and eventually found himself at the massive building of the New Asiatic Bank, Limited.

The difficulty now was to know how to make an effective entrance. There was the bank, and here was he. How had he better set about breaking it to the authorities that he had positively arrived and was ready to start earning his four pound ten *per mensem*? Inside, the bank seemed to be in a state of some confusion. Men were moving about in an apparently irresolute manner. Nobody seemed actually to be working. As a matter of fact, the business of a bank does not start very early in the morning. Mike had arrived before things had really begun to move. As he stood near the doorway, one or two panting figures rushed up the steps, and flung themselves at a large book which stood on the counter near the door. Mike was to come to know this book well. In it, if you were an *employe* of the New Asiatic Bank, you had to inscribe your name every morning. It was removed at ten sharp to the accountant's room, and if you reached the bank a certain number of times in the year too late to sign, bang went your bonus.

After a while things began to settle down. The stir and confusion gradually ceased. All down the length of the bank, figures could be seen, seated on stools and writing hieroglyphics in large letters. A benevolent-looking man, with spectacles and a straggling grey beard, crossed the gangway close to where Mike was standing. Mike put the thing to him, as man to man.

'Could you tell me,' he said, 'what I'm supposed to do? I've just joined the bank.' The benevolent man stopped, and looked at him with a pair of mild blue eyes. 'I think, perhaps, that your best plan would be to see the manager,' he said. 'Yes, I should certainly do that. He will tell you what work you have to do. If you will permit me, I will show you the way.'

'It's awfully good of you,' said Mike. He felt very grateful. After his experience of London, it was a pleasant change to find someone who really seemed to care what happened to him. His heart warmed to the benevolent man.

'It feels strange to you, perhaps, at first, Mr—'

'Jackson.'

'Mr Jackson. My name is Waller. I have been in the City some time, but I can still recall my first day. But one shakes down. One shakes down quite quickly. Here is the manager's room. If you go in, he will tell you what to do.'

'Thanks awfully,' said Mike.

'Not at all.' He ambled off on the quest which Mike had interrupted, turning, as he went, to bestow a mild smile of encouragement on the new arrival. There was something about Mr Waller which reminded Mike pleasantly of the White Knight in 'Alice through the Looking-glass.'

Mike knocked at the managerial door, and went in.

Two men were sitting at the table. The one facing the door was writing when Mike went in. He continued to write all the time he was in the room. Conversation between other people in his presence had apparently no interest for him, nor was it able to disturb him in any way.

The other man was talking into a telephone. Mike waited till he had finished. Then he coughed. The man turned round. Mike had thought, as he looked at his back and heard his voice, that something about his appearance or his way of speaking was familiar. He was right. The man in the chair was Mr Bickersdyke, the cross-screen pedestrian.

These reunions are very awkward. Mike was frankly unequal to the situation. Psmith, in his place, would have opened the conversation, and relaxed the tension with some remark on the weather or the state of the crops. Mike merely stood wrapped in silence, as in a garment.

That the recognition was mutual was evident from Mr Bickersdyke's look. But apart from this, he gave no sign of having already had the pleasure of making Mike's acquaintance. He merely stared at him as if he were a blot on the arrangement of the furniture, and said, 'Well?'

The most difficult parts to play in real life as well as on the stage are those in which no 'business' is arranged for the performer. It was all very well for Mr Bickersdyke. He had been 'discovered sitting'. But Mike had had to enter, and he wished now that there was something he could do instead of merely standing and speaking.

'I've come,' was the best speech he could think of. It was not a good speech. It was too sinister. He felt that even as he said it. It was the sort of thing Mephistopheles would have said to Faust by way of opening conversation. And he was not sure, either, whether he ought not to have added, 'Sir.'

Apparently such subtleties of address were not necessary, for Mr Bickersdyke did not start up and shout, 'This language to me!' or anything of that kind. He merely said, 'Oh! And who are you?'

'Jackson,' said Mike. It was irritating, this assumption on Mr

Bickersdyke's part that they had never met before.

'Jackson? Ah, yes. You have joined the staff?'

Mike rather liked this way of putting it. It lent a certain dignity to the proceedings, making him feel like some important person for whose services there had been strenuous competition. He seemed to see the bank's directors being reassured by the chairman. ('I am happy to say, gentlemen, that our profits for the past year are 3,000,006-2-2 1/2 pounds—(cheers)—and'—impressively—'that we have finally succeeded in inducing Mr Mike Jackson—(sensation)—to—er—in fact, to join the staff!' (Frantic cheers, in which the chairman joined.)

'Yes,' he said.

Mr Bickersdyke pressed a bell on the table beside him, and picking up a pen, began to write. Of Mike he took no further notice, leaving that toy of Fate standing stranded in the middle of the room.

After a few moments one of the men in fancy dress, whom Mike had seen hanging about the gangway, and whom he afterwards found to be messengers, appeared. Mr Bickersdyke looked up.

'Ask Mr Bannister to step this way,' he said.

The messenger disappeared, and presently the door opened again to admit a shock-headed youth with paper cuff-protectors round his wrists.

'This is Mr Jackson, a new member of the staff. He will take your place in the postage department. You will go into the cash department, under Mr Waller. Kindly show him what he has to do.'

Mike followed Mr Bannister out. On the other side of the door the shock-headed one became communicative.

'Whew!' he said, mopping his brow. 'That's the sort of thing which gives me the pip. When William came and said old Bick wanted to see me, I said to him, "William, my boy, my number is up. This is the sack." I made certain that Rossiter had run me in for something. He's been waiting for a chance to do it for weeks, only I've been as good as gold and haven't given it him. I pity you going into the postage. There's one thing, though. If you can stick it for about a month, you'll get through all right. Men are always leaving for the East, and then you get shunted on into another department, and the next new man goes into the postage. That's the best of this place. It's not like one of those banks where you stay in London all your life. You only have three years here, and then you get your orders, and go to one of the branches in the East, where you're the dickens of a big pot straight away, with a big screw and a dozen native Johnnies under you. Bit of all right, that. I shan't get my orders for another two and a half years and more, worse luck. Still, it's something to look forward to.'

'Who's Rossiter?' asked Mike.

'The head of the postage department. Fussy little brute. Won't leave you alone. Always trying to catch you on the hop. There's one thing, though. The work in the postage is pretty simple. You can't make many mistakes, if you're careful. It's mostly entering letters and stamping them.'

They turned in at the door in the counter, and arrived at a desk which ran parallel to the gangway. There was a high rack running along it, on which were several ledgers. Tall, green-shaded electric lamps gave it rather a cosy look.

As they reached the desk, a little man with short, black whiskers buzzed out from behind a glass screen, where there was another desk.

'Where have you been, Bannister, where have you been? You must not leave your work in this way. There are several letters waiting to be entered. Where have you been?'

'Mr Bickersdyke sent for me,' said Bannister, with the calm triumph of one who trumps an ace.

'Oh! Ah! Oh! Yes, very well. I see. But get to work, get to work. Who is this?'

'This is a new man. He's taking my place. I've been moved on to the cash.'

'Oh! Ah! Is your name Smith?' asked Mr Rossiter, turning to Mike.

Mike corrected the rash guess, and gave his name. It struck him as a curious coincidence that he should be asked if his name were Smith, of all others. Not that it is an uncommon name.

'Mr Bickersdyke told me to expect a Mr Smith. Well, well, perhaps there are two new men. Mr Bickersdyke knows we are short-handed in this department. But, come along, Bannister, come along. Show Jackson what he has to do. We must get on. There is no time to waste.'

He buzzed back to his lair. Bannister grinned at Mike. He was a cheerful youth. His normal expression was a grin.

'That's a sample of Rossiter,' he said. 'You'd think from the fuss he's made that the business of the place was at a standstill till we got to work. Perfect rot! There's never anything to do here till after lunch, except checking the stamps and petty cash, and I've done that ages ago. There are three letters. You may as well enter them. It all looks like work. But you'll find the best way is to wait till you get a couple of dozen or so, and then work them off in a batch. But if you see Rossiter about, then start stamping something or writing something, or he'll run you in for neglecting your job. He's a nut. I'm jolly glad I'm under old Waller now. He's the pick of the bunch. The other heads of departments are all nuts, and Bickersdyke's the nuttiest of the lot. Now, look here. This is all you've got to do. I'll just show you, and then you can manage for yourself. I shall have to be shunting off to my own work in a minute.'

5. The Other Man

As Bannister had said, the work in the postage department was not intricate. There was nothing much to do except enter and stamp letters, and, at intervals, take them down to the post office at the end of the street. The nature of the work gave Mike plenty of time for reflection.

His thoughts became gloomy again. All this was very far removed from the life to which he had looked forward. There are some people who take naturally to a life of commerce. Mike was not of these. To him the restraint of the business was irksome. He had been used to an open-air life, and a life, in its way, of excitement. He gathered that he would not be free till five o'clock, and that on the following day he would come at ten and go at five, and the same every day, except Saturdays and Sundays, all the year round, with a ten days' holiday. The monotony of the prospect appalled him. He was not old enough to know what a narcotic is Habit, and that one can become attached to and interested in the most unpromising jobs. He worked away dismally at his letters till he had finished them. Then there was nothing to do except sit and wait for more.

He looked through the letters he had stamped, and re-read the addresses. Some of them were directed to people living in the country, one to a house which he knew quite well, near to his own home in Shropshire. It made him home-sick, conjuring up visions of shady gardens and country sounds and smells, and the silver Severn gleaming in the distance through the trees. About now, if he were not in this dismal place, he would be lying in the shade in the garden with a book, or wandering down to the river to boat or bathe. That envelope addressed to the man in Shropshire gave him the worst moment he had experienced that day.

The time crept slowly on to one o'clock. At two minutes past Mike awoke from a day-dream to find Mr Waller standing by his side. The cashier had his hat on.

'I wonder,' said Mr Waller, 'if you would care to come out to lunch. I generally go about this time, and Mr Rossiter, I know, does not go out till two. I thought perhaps that, being unused to the City, you might have some difficulty in finding your way about.'

'It's awfully good of you,' said Mike. 'I should like to.'

The other led the way through the streets and down obscure alleys till they came to a chop-house. Here one could have the doubtful pleasure of seeing one's chop in its various stages of evolution. Mr Waller ordered lunch with the care of one to whom lunch is no slight matter. Few workers in the City do regard lunch as a trivial affair. It is the keynote of their day. It is an oasis in a desert of ink and ledgers. Conversation in city office deals, in the morning, with what one is going to have for lunch, and in the afternoon with what one has had for lunch.

At intervals during the meal Mr Waller talked. Mike was content to listen. There was something soothing about the grey-bearded one.

'What sort of a man is Bickersdyke?' asked Mike.

'A very able man. A very able man indeed. I'm afraid he's not popular in the office. A little inclined, perhaps, to be hard on mistakes. I can remember the time when he was quite different. He and I were fellow clerks in Morton and Blatherwick's. He got on better than I did. A great fellow for getting on. They say he is to be the Unionist candidate for Kenningford when the time comes. A great worker, but perhaps not quite the sort of man to be generally popular in an office.'

'He's a blighter,' was Mike's verdict. Mr Waller made no comment. Mike was to learn later that the manager and the cashier, despite the fact that they had been together in less prosperous days—or possibly because of it—were not on very good terms. Mr Bickersdyke was a man of strong prejudices, and he disliked the cashier, whom he looked down upon as one who had climbed to a lower rung of the ladder than he himself had reached.

As the hands of the chop-house clock reached a quarter to two, Mr Waller rose, and led the way back to the office, where they parted for their respective desks. Gratitude for any good turn done to him was a leading characteristic of Mike's nature, and he felt genuinely grateful to the cashier for troubling to seek him out and be friendly to him.

His three-quarters-of-an-hour absence had led to the accumulation of a small pile of letters on his desk. He sat down and began to work them off. The addresses continued to exercise a fascination for him. He was miles away from the office, speculating on what sort of a man J. B. Garside, Esq, was, and whether he had a good time at his house in Worcestershire, when somebody tapped him on the shoulder.

He looked up.

Standing by his side, immaculately dressed as ever, with his eye-glass fixed and a gentle smile on his face, was Psmith.

Mike stared.

'Commerce,' said Psmith, as he drew off his lavender gloves, 'has claimed me for her own. Comrade of old, I, too, have joined this blighted institution.'

As he spoke, there was a whirring noise in the immediate neighbourhood, and Mr Rossiter buzzed out from his den with the *esprit* and animation of a clockwork toy.

'Who's here?' said Psmith with interest, removing his eye-glass, polishing it, and replacing it in his eye.

'Mr Jackson,' exclaimed Mr Rossiter. 'I really must ask you to be good enough to come in from your lunch at the proper time. It was fully seven minutes to two when you returned, and—'

'That little more,' sighed Psmith, 'and how much is it!'

'Who are you?' snapped Mr Rossiter, turning on him.

'I shall be delighted, Comrade—'

'Rossiter,' said Mike, aside.

'Comrade Rossiter. I shall be delighted to furnish you with particulars of my family history. As follows. Soon after the Norman Conquest, a certain Sieur de Psmith grew tired of work—a family failing, alas!—and settled down in this country to live peacefully for the remainder of his life on what he could extract from the local peasantry. He may be described as the founder of the family which ultimately culminated in Me. Passing on—'

Mr Rossiter refused to pass on.

'What are you doing here? What have you come for?'

'Work,' said Psmith, with simple dignity. 'I am now a member of the staff of this bank. Its interests are my interests. Psmith, the individual, ceases to exist, and there springs into being Psmith, the cog in the wheel of the New Asiatic Bank; Psmith, the link in the bank's chain; Psmith, the Worker. I shall not spare myself,' he proceeded earnestly. 'I shall toil with all the accumulated energy of one who, up till now, has only known what work is like from hearsay. Whose is that form sitting on the steps of the bank in the morning, waiting eagerly for the place to open? It is the form of Psmith, the Worker. Whose is that haggard, drawn face which bends over a ledger long after the other toilers have sped blithely westwards to dine at Lyons' Popular Cafe? It is the face of Psmith, the Worker.'

'I—' began Mr Rossiter.

'I tell you,' continued Psmith, waving aside the interruption and tapping the head of the department rhythmically in the region of the second waistcoat-button with a long finger, 'I tell *you*, Comrade Rossiter, that you have got hold of a good man. You and I together, not forgetting Comrade Jackson, the pet of the Smart Set, will toil early and late till we boost up this Postage Department into a shining model of what a Postage Department should be. What that is, at present, I do not exactly know. However. Excursion trains will be run from distant shires to see this Postage Department. American visitors to London will do it before going on to the Tower. And now,' he broke off, with a crisp, businesslike intonation, 'I must ask you to excuse me. Much as I have enjoyed this little chat, I fear it must now cease. The time has come to work. Our trade rivals are getting ahead of us. The whisper goes round, "Rossiter and Psmith are talking, not working," and other firms prepare to pinch our business. Let me Work.'

Two minutes later, Mr Rossiter was sitting at his desk with a dazed expression, while Psmith, perched gracefully on a stool, entered figures in a ledger.

6. Psmith Explains

For the space of about twenty-five minutes Psmith sat in silence, concentrated on his ledger, the picture of the model bank-clerk. Then he flung down his pen, slid from his stool with a satisfied sigh, and dusted his waistcoat. 'A commercial crisis,' he said, 'has passed. The job of work which Comrade Rossiter indicated for me has been completed with masterly skill. The period of anxiety is over. The bank ceases to totter. Are you busy, Comrade Jackson, or shall we chat awhile?'

Mike was not busy. He had worked off the last batch of letters, and there was nothing to do but to wait for the next, or—happy thought—to take the present batch down to the post, and so get out into the sunshine and fresh air for a short time. 'I rather think I'll nip down to the post-office,' said he, 'You couldn't come too, I suppose?'

'On the contrary,' said Psmith, 'I could, and will. A stroll will just restore those tissues which the gruelling work of the last half-hour has wasted away. It is a fearful strain, this commercial toil. Let us trickle towards the post office. I will leave my hat and gloves as a guarantee of good faith. The cry will go round, "Psmith has gone! Some rival institution has kidnapped him!" Then they will see my hat,'—he built up a foundation of ledgers, planted a long ruler in the middle, and hung his hat on it—'my gloves,'—he stuck two pens into the desk and hung a lavender glove on each—'and they will sink back swooning with relief. The awful suspense will be over. They will say, "No, he has not gone permanently. Psmith will return. When the fields are white with daisies he'll return." And now, Comrade Jackson, lead me to this picturesque little post-office of yours of which I have heard so much.'

Mike picked up the long basket into which he had thrown the letters after entering the addresses in his ledger, and they moved off down the aisle. No movement came from Mr Rossiter's lair. Its energetic occupant was hard at work. They could just see part of his hunched-up back.

'I wish Comrade Downing could see us now,' said Psmith. 'He always set us down as mere idlers. Triflers. Butterflies. It would be a wholesome corrective for him to watch us perspiring like this in the cause of Commerce.'

'You haven't told me yet what on earth you're doing here,' said Mike. 'I thought you were going to the 'Varsity. Why the dickens are you in a bank? Your pater hasn't lost his money, has he?'

'No. There is still a tolerable supply of doubloons in the old oak chest. Mine is a painful story.'

'It always is,' said Mike.

'You are very right, Comrade Jackson. I am the victim of Fate. Ah, so you put the little chaps in there, do you?' he said, as Mike, reaching the post-office, began to bundle the letters into the box. 'You seem to have grasped your duties with admirable promptitude. It is the same with me. I fancy we are both born men of Commerce. In a few years we shall be pinching Comrade Bickersdyke's job. And talking of Comrade B. brings me back to my painful story. But I shall never have time to tell it to you during our walk back. Let us drift aside into this tea-shop. We can order a buckwheat cake or a butter-nut, or something equally succulent, and carefully refraining from consuming these dainties, I will tell you all.'

'Right O!' said Mike.

'When last I saw you,' resumed Psmith, hanging Mike's basket on the hat-stand and ordering two portions of porridge, 'you may remember that a serious crisis in my affairs had arrived. My father inflamed with the idea of Commerce had invited Comrade Bickersdyke—'

'When did you know he was a manager here?' asked Mike.

'At an early date. I have my spies everywhere. However, my pater invited Comrade Bickersdyke to our house for the weekend. Things turned out rather unfortunately. Comrade B. resented my purely altruistic efforts to improve him mentally and morally. Indeed, on one occasion he went so far as to call me an impudent young cub, and to add that he wished he had me under him in his bank, where, he asserted, he would knock some of the nonsense out of me. All very painful. I tell you, Comrade Jackson, for the moment it reduced my delicately vibrating ganglions to a mere frazzle. Recovering myself, I made a few blithe remarks, and we then parted. I cannot say that we parted friends, but at any rate I bore him no ill-will. I was still determined to make him a credit to me. My feelings towards him were those of some kindly father to his prodigal son. But he, if I may say so, was fairly on the hop. And when my pater, after dinner the same night, played into his hands by mentioning that he thought I ought to plunge into a career of commerce, Comrade B. was, I gather, all over him. Offered to make a vacancy for me in the bank, and to take me on at once. My pater, feeling that this was the real hustle which he admired so much, had me in, stated his case, and said, in effect, "How do we go?" I intimated that Comrade Bickersdyke was my greatest chum on earth. So the thing was fixed up and here I am. But you are not getting on with your porridge, Comrade Jackson. Perhaps you don't care for porridge? Would you like a finnan haddock, instead? Or a piece of shortbread? You have only to say the word.'

'It seems to me,' said Mike gloomily, 'that we are in for a pretty rotten time of it in this bally bank. If Bickersdyke's got his knife into us, he can make it jolly warm for us. He's got his knife into me all right about that walking-across-the-screen business.'

'True,' said Psmith, 'to a certain extent. It is an undoubted fact that Comrade Bickersdyke will have a jolly good try at making life a nuisance to us; but, on the other hand, I propose, so far as in me lies, to make things moderately unrestful for him, here and there.'

'But you can't,' objected Mike. 'What I mean to say is, it isn't like a school. If you wanted to score off a master at school, you could always rag and so on. But here you can't. How can you rag a man who's sitting all day in a room of his own while you're sweating away at a desk at the other end of the building?'

'You put the case with admirable clearness, Comrade Jackson,' said Psmith approvingly. 'At the hard-headed, common-sense business you sneak the biscuit every time with ridiculous case. But you do not know all. I do not propose to do a thing in the bank except work. I shall be a model as far as work goes. I shall be flawless. I shall bound to do Comrade Rossiter's bidding like a highly trained performing dog. It is outside the bank, when I have staggered away dazed with toil, that I shall resume my attention to the education of Comrade Bickersdyke.'

'But, dash it all, how can you? You won't see him. He'll go off home, or to his club, or—'

Psmith tapped him earnestly on the chest.

'There, Comrade Jackson,' he said, 'you have hit the bull's-eye, rung the bell, and gathered in the cigar or cocoanut according to choice. He *will* go off to his club. And I shall do precisely the same.'

'How do you mean?'

'It is this way. My father, as you may have noticed during your stay at our stately home of England, is a man of a warm, impulsive character. He does not always do things as other people would do them. He has his own methods. Thus, he has sent me into the City to do the hard-working, bank-clerk act, but at the same time he is allowing me just as large an allowance as he would have given me if I had gone to the 'Varsity. Moreover, while I was still at Eton he put my name up for his clubs, the Senior Conservative among others. My pater belongs to four clubs altogether, and in course of time, when my name comes up for election, I shall do the same. Meanwhile, I belong to one, the Senior Conservative. It is a bigger club than the others, and your name comes up for election sooner. About the middle of last month a great yell of joy made the West End of London shake like a jelly. The three thousand members of the Senior Conservative had just learned that I had been elected.'

Psmith paused, and ate some porridge.

'I wonder why they call this porridge,' he observed with mild interest. 'It would be far more manly and straightforward of them to give it its real name. To resume. I have gleaned, from casual chit-chat with my father, that Comrade Bickersdyke also infests the Senior Conservative. You might think that that would make me, seeing how particular I am about whom I mix with, avoid the club. Error. I shall go there every day. If Comrade Bickersdyke wishes to emend any little traits in my character of which he may disapprove, he shall never say that I did not give him the opportunity. I shall mix freely with Comrade Bickersdyke at the Senior

Conservative Club. I shall be his constant companion. I shall, in short, haunt the man. By these strenuous means I shall, as it were, get a bit of my own back. And now,' said Psmith, rising, 'it might be as well, perhaps, to return to the bank and resume our commercial duties. I don't know how long you are supposed to be allowed for your little trips to and from the post-office, but, seeing that the distance is about thirty yards, I should say at a venture not more than half an hour. Which is exactly the space of time which has flitted by since we started out on this important expedition. Your devotion to porridge, Comrade Jackson, has led to our spending about twenty-five minutes in this hostelry.'

'Great Scott,' said Mike, 'there'll be a row.'

'Some slight temporary breeze, perhaps,' said Psmith. 'Annoying to men of culture and refinement, but not lasting. My only fear is lest we may have worried Comrade Rossiter at all. I regard Comrade Rossiter as an elder brother, and would not cause him a moment's heart-burning for worlds. However, we shall soon know,' he added, as they passed into the bank and walked up the aisle, 'for there is Comrade Rossiter waiting to receive us in person.'

The little head of the Postage Department was moving restlessly about in the neighbourhood of Psmith's and Mike's desk.

'Am I mistaken,' said Psmith to Mike, 'or is there the merest suspicion of a worried look on our chief's face? It seems to me that there is the slightest soupcon of shadow about that broad, calm brow.'

7. Going into Winter Quarters

There was.

Mr Rossiter had discovered Psmith's and Mike's absence about five minutes after they had left the building. Ever since then, he had been popping out of his lair at intervals of three minutes, to see whether they had returned. Constant disappointment in this respect had rendered him decidedly jumpy. When Psmith and Mike reached the desk, he was a kind of human soda-water bottle. He fizzed over with questions, reproofs, and warnings.

'What does it mean? What does it mean?' he cried. 'Where have you been?

Where have you been?'

'Poetry,' said Psmith approvingly.

'You have been absent from your places for over half an hour. Why? Why? Why? Where have you been? Where have you been? I cannot have this. It is preposterous. Where have you been? Suppose Mr Bickersdyke had happened to come round here. I should not have known what to say to him.'

'Never an easy man to chat with, Comrade Bickersdyke,' agreed Psmith.

'You must thoroughly understand that you are expected to remain in your places during business hours.'

'Of course,' said Psmith, 'that makes it a little hard for Comrade

Jackson to post letters, does it not?'

'Have you been posting letters?'

'We have,' said Psmith. 'You have wronged us. Seeing our absent places you jumped rashly to the conclusion that we were merely gadding about in pursuit of pleasure. Error. All the while we were furthering the bank's best interests by posting letters.'

'You had no business to leave your place. Jackson is on the posting desk.'

'You are very right,' said Psmith, 'and it shall not occur again. It was only because it was the first day, Comrade Jackson is not used to the stir and bustle of the City. His nerve failed him. He shrank from going to the post-office alone. So I volunteered to accompany him. And,' concluded Psmith, impressively, 'we won safely through. Every letter has been posted.'

'That need not have taken you half an hour.'

'True. And the actual work did not. It was carried through swiftly and surely. But the nerve-strain had left us shaken. Before resuming our more ordinary duties we had to refresh. A brief breathing-space, a little coffee and porridge, and here we are, fit for work once more.'

'If it occurs again, I shall report the matter to Mr Bickersdyke.'

'And rightly so,' said Psmith, earnestly. 'Quite rightly so. Discipline, discipline. That is the cry. There must be no shirking of painful duties. Sentiment must play no part in business. Rossiter, the man, may sympathise, but Rossiter, the Departmental head, must be adamant.'

Mr Rossiter pondered over this for a moment, then went off on a side-issue.

'What is the meaning of this foolery?' he asked, pointing to Psmith's gloves and hat. 'Suppose Mr Bickersdyke had come round and seen them, what should I have said?'

'You would have given him a message of cheer. You would have said, "All is well. Psmith has not left us. He will come back. And Comrade Bickersdyke, relieved, would have—"'

'You do not seem very busy, Mr Smith.'

Both Psmith and Mr Rossiter were startled.

Mr Rossiter jumped as if somebody had run a gimlet into him, and even
Psmith started slightly. They had not heard Mr Bickersdyke approaching.
Mike, who had been stolidly entering addresses in his ledger during the
latter part of the conversation, was also taken by surprise.

Psmith was the first to recover. Mr Rossiter was still too confused for speech, but Psmith took the situation in hand.

'Apparently no,' he said, swiftly removing his hat from the ruler. 'In reality, yes. Mr Rossiter and I were just scheming out a line of work for me as you came up. If you had arrived a moment later, you would have found me toiling.'

'H'm. I hope I should. We do not encourage idling in this bank.'

'Assuredly not,' said Psmith warmly. 'Most assuredly not. I would not have it otherwise. I am a worker. A bee, not a drone. A *Lusitania,* not a limpet. Perhaps I have not yet that grip on my duties which I shall soon acquire; but it is coming. It is coming. I see daylight.'

'H'm. I have only your word for it.' He turned to Mr Rossiter, who had now recovered himself, and was as nearly calm as it was in his nature to be. 'Do you find Mr Smith's work satisfactory, Mr Rossiter?'

Psmith waited resignedly for an outburst of complaint respecting the small matter that had been under discussion between the head of the department and himself; but to his surprise it did not come.

'Oh—ah—quite, quite, Mr Bickersdyke. I think he will very soon pick things up.'

Mr Bickersdyke turned away. He was a conscientious bank manager, and one can only suppose that Mr Rossiter's tribute to the earnestness of one of his *employes* was gratifying to him. But for that, one would have said that he was disappointed.

'Oh, Mr Bickersdyke,' said Psmith.

The manager stopped.

'Father sent his kind regards to you,' said Psmith benevolently.

Mr Bickersdyke walked off without comment.

'An uncommonly cheery, companionable feller,' murmured Psmith, as he turned to his work.

The first day anywhere, if one spends it in a sedentary fashion, always seemed unending; and Mike felt as if he had been sitting at his desk for weeks when the hour for departure came. A bank's day ends gradually, reluctantly, as it were. At about five there is a sort of stir, not unlike the stir in a theatre when the curtain is on the point of falling. Ledgers are closed with a bang. Men stand about and talk for a moment or two before going to the basement for their hats and coats. Then, at irregular intervals, forms pass down the central aisle and out through the swing doors. There is an air of relaxation over the place, though some departments are still working as hard as ever under a blaze of electric light. Somebody begins to sing, and an instant chorus of protests and maledictions rises from all sides. Gradually, however, the electric lights go out. The procession down the centre aisle becomes more regular; and eventually the place is left to darkness and the night watchman.

The postage department was one of the last to be freed from duty. This was due to the inconsiderateness of the other departments, which omitted to disgorge their letters till the last moment. Mike as he grew familiar with the work, and began to understand it, used to prowl round the other departments during the afternoon and wrest letters from them, usually receiving with them much abuse for being a nuisance and not leaving honest workers alone. Today, however, he had to sit on till nearly six, waiting for the final batch of correspondence.

Psmith, who had waited patiently with him, though his own work was finished, accompanied him down to the post office and back again to the bank to return the letter basket; and they left the office together.

'By the way,' said Psmith, 'what with the strenuous labours of the bank and the disturbing interviews with the powers that be, I have omitted to ask you where you are digging. Wherever it is, of course you must clear out. It is imperative, in this crisis, that we should be together. I have acquired a quite snug little flat in Clement's Inn. There is a spare bedroom. It shall be yours.'

'My dear chap,' said Mike, 'it's all rot. I can't sponge on you.'

'You pain me, Comrade Jackson. I was not suggesting such a thing. We are business men, hard-headed young bankers. I make you a business proposition. I offer you the post of confidential secretary and adviser to me in exchange for a comfortable home. The duties will be light. You will be required to refuse invitations to dinner from crowned heads, and to listen attentively to my views on Life. Apart from this, there is little to do. So that's settled.'

'It isn't,' said Mike. 'I—'

'You will enter upon your duties tonight. Where are you suspended at present?'

'Dulwich. But, look here—'

'A little more, and you'll get the sack. I tell you the thing is settled. Now, let us hail yon taximeter cab, and desire the stern-faced aristocrat on the box to drive us to Dulwich. We will then collect a few of your things in a bag, have the rest off by train, come back in the taxi, and go and bite a chop at the Carlton. This is a momentous day in our careers, Comrade Jackson. We must buoy ourselves up.'

Mike made no further objections. The thought of that bed-sitting room in Acacia Road and the pantomime dame rose up and killed them. After all, Psmith was not like any ordinary person. There would be no question of charity. Psmith had invited him to the flat in exactly the same spirit as he had invited him to his house for the cricket week.

'You know,' said Psmith, after a silence, as they flitted through the streets in the taximeter, 'one lives and learns. Were you so wrapped up in your work this afternoon that you did not hear my very entertaining little chat with Comrade Bickersdyke, or did it happen to come under your notice? It did? Then I wonder if you were struck by the singular conduct of Comrade Rossiter?'

'I thought it rather decent of him not to give you away to that blighter Bickersdyke.'

'Admirably put. It was precisely that that struck me. He had his opening, all ready made for him, but he refrained from depositing me in the soup. I tell you, Comrade Jackson, my rugged old heart was touched. I said to myself, "There must be good in Comrade Rossiter, after all. I must cultivate him." I shall make it my business to be kind to our Departmental head. He deserves the utmost consideration. His action shone like a good deed in a wicked world. Which it was, of course. From today onwards I take Comrade Rossiter under my wing. We seem to be getting into a tolerably benighted quarter. Are we anywhere near? "Through Darkest Dulwich in a Taximeter."'

The cab arrived at Dulwich station, and Mike stood up to direct the driver. They whirred down Acacia Road. Mike stopped the cab and got out. A brief and somewhat embarrassing interview with the pantomime dame, during which Mike was separated from a week's rent in lieu of notice, and he was in the cab again, bound for Clement's Inn.

His feelings that night differed considerably from the frame of mind in which he had gone to bed the night before. It was partly a very excellent dinner and partly the fact that Psmith's flat, though at present in some disorder, was obviously going to be extremely comfortable, that worked the change. But principally it was due to his having found an ally. The gnawing loneliness had gone. He did not look forward to a career of Commerce with any greater pleasure than before; but there was no doubt that with Psmith, it would be easier to get through the time after office hours. If all went well in the bank he might find that he had not drawn such a bad ticket after all.

8. The Friendly Native

'The first principle of warfare,' said Psmith at breakfast next morning, doling out bacon and eggs with the air of a medieval monarch distributing largesse, 'is to collect a gang, to rope in allies, to secure the cooperation of some friendly native. You may remember that at Sedleigh it was partly the sympathetic cooperation of that record blitherer, Comrade Jellicoe, which enabled us to nip the pro-Spiller movement in the bud. It is the same in the present crisis. What Comrade Jellicoe was to us at Sedleigh, Comrade Rossiter must be in the City. We must make an ally of that man. Once I know that he and I are as brothers, and that he will look with a lenient and benevolent eye on any little shortcomings in my work, I shall be able to devote my attention whole-heartedly to the moral reformation of Comrade Bickersdyke, that man of blood. I look on Comrade Bickersdyke as a bargee of the most pronounced type; and anything I can do towards making him a decent member of Society shall be done freely and ungrudgingly. A trifle more tea, Comrade Jackson?'

'No, thanks,' said Mike. 'I've done. By Jove, Smith, this flat of yours is all right.'

'Not bad,' assented Psmith, 'not bad. Free from squalor to a great extent. I have a number of little objects of *vertu* coming down shortly from the old homestead. Pictures, and so on. It will be by no means un-snug when they are up. Meanwhile, I can rough it. We are old campaigners, we Psmiths. Give us a roof, a few comfortable chairs, a sofa or two, half a dozen cushions, and decent meals, and we do not repine. Reverting once more to Comrade Rossiter—'

'Yes, what about him?' said Mike. 'You'll have a pretty tough job turning him into a friendly native, I should think. How do you mean to start?'

Psmith regarded him with a benevolent eye.

'There is but one way,' he said. 'Do you remember the case of Comrade Outwood, at Sedleigh? How did we corral him, and become to him practically as long-lost sons?'

'We got round him by joining the Archaeological Society.'

'Precisely,' said Psmith. 'Every man has his hobby. The thing is to find it out. In the case of comrade Rossiter, I should say that it would be either postage stamps, dried seaweed, or Hall Caine. I shall endeavour to find out today. A few casual questions, and the thing is done. Shall we be putting in an appearance at the busy hive now? If we are to continue in the running for the bonus stakes, it would be well to start soon.'

Mike's first duty at the bank that morning was to check the stamps and petty cash. While he was engaged on this task, he heard Psmith conversing affably with Mr Rossiter.

'Good morning,' said Psmith.

'Morning,' replied his chief, doing sleight-of-hand tricks with a bundle of letters which lay on his desk. 'Get on with your work, Psmith. We have a lot before us.'

'Undoubtedly. I am all impatience. I should say that in an institution like this, dealing as it does with distant portions of the globe, a philatelist would have excellent opportunities of increasing his collection. With me, stamp-collecting has always been a positive craze. I—'

'I have no time for nonsense of that sort myself,' said Mr Rossiter. 'I should advise you, if you mean to get on, to devote more time to your work and less to stamps.'

'I will start at once. Dried seaweed, again—'

'Get on with your work, Smith.'

Psmith retired to his desk.

'This,' he said to Mike, 'is undoubtedly something in the nature of a set-back. I have drawn blank. The papers bring out posters, "Psmith Baffled." I must try again. Meanwhile, to work. Work, the hobby of the philosopher and the poor man's friend.'

The morning dragged slowly on without incident. At twelve o'clock Mike had to go out and buy stamps, which he subsequently punched in the punching-machine in the basement, a not very exhilarating job in which he was assisted by one of the bank messengers, who discoursed learnedly on roses during the *seance*. Roses were his hobby. Mike began to see that Psmith had reason in his assumption that the way to every man's heart was through his hobby. Mike made a firm friend of William, the messenger, by displaying an interest and a certain knowledge of roses. At the same time the conversation had the bad effect of leading to an acute relapse in the matter of homesickness. The rose-garden at home had been one of Mike's favourite haunts on a summer afternoon. The contrast between it and the basement of the new Asiatic Bank, the atmosphere of which was far from being roselike, was too much for his feelings. He emerged from the depths, with his punched stamps, filled with bitterness against Fate.

He found Psmith still baffled.

'Hall Caine,' said Psmith regretfully, 'has also proved a frost. I wandered round to Comrade Rossiter's desk just now with a rather brainy excursus on "The Eternal City", and was received with the Impatient Frown rather than the Glad Eye. He was in the middle of adding up a rather tricky column of figures, and my remarks caused him to drop a stitch. So far from winning the man over, I have gone back. There now exists between Comrade Rossiter and myself a certain coldness. Further investigations will be postponed till after lunch.'

The postage department received visitors during the morning. Members of other departments came with letters, among them Bannister. Mr Rossiter was away in the manager's room at the time.

'How are you getting on?' said Bannister to Mike.

'Oh, all right,' said Mike.

'Had any trouble with Rossiter yet?'

'No, not much.'

'He hasn't run you in to Bickersdyke?'

'No.'

'Pardon my interrupting a conversation between old college chums,' said Psmith courteously, 'but I happened to overhear, as I toiled at my desk, the name of Comrade Rossiter.'

Bannister looked somewhat startled. Mike introduced them.

'This is Smith,' he said. 'Chap I was at school with. This is

Bannister, Smith, who used to be on here till I came.'

'In this department?' asked Psmith.

'Yes.'

'Then, Comrade Bannister, you are the very man I have been looking for. Your knowledge will be invaluable to us. I have no doubt that, during your stay in this excellently managed department, you had many opportunities of observing Comrade Rossiter?'

'I should jolly well think I had,' said Bannister with a laugh. 'He saw to that. He was always popping out and cursing me about something.'

'Comrade Rossiter's manners are a little restive,' agreed Psmith. 'What used you to talk to him about?'

'What used I to talk to him about?'

'Exactly. In those interviews to which you have alluded, how did you amuse, entertain Comrade Rossiter?'

'I didn't. He used to do all the talking there was.'

Psmith straightened his tie, and clicked his tongue, disappointed.

'This is unfortunate,' he said, smoothing his hair. 'You see, Comrade Bannister, it is this way. In the course of my professional duties, I find myself continually coming into contact with Comrade Rossiter.'

'I bet you do,' said Bannister.

'On these occasions I am frequently at a loss for entertaining conversation. He has no difficulty, as apparently happened in your case, in keeping up his end of the dialogue. The subject of my shortcomings provides him with ample material for speech. I, on the other hand, am dumb. I have nothing to say.'

'I should think that was a bit of a change for you, wasn't it?'

'Perhaps, so,' said Psmith, 'perhaps so. On the other hand, however restful it may be to myself, it does not enable me to secure Comrade Rossiter's interest and win his esteem.'

'What Smith wants to know,' said Mike, 'is whether Rossiter has any hobby of any kind. He thinks, if he has, he might work it to keep in with him.'

Psmith, who had been listening with an air of pleased interest, much as a father would listen to his child prattling for the benefit of a visitor, confirmed this statement.

'Comrade Jackson,' he said, 'has put the matter with his usual admirable clearness. That is the thing in a nutshell. Has Comrade Rossiter any hobby that you know of? Spillikins, brass-rubbing, the Near Eastern Question, or anything like that? I have tried him with postage-stamps (which you'd think, as head of a postage department, he ought to be interested in), and dried seaweed, Hall Caine, but I have the honour to report total failure. The man seems to have no pleasures. What does he do with himself when the day's toil is ended? That giant brain must occupy itself somehow.'

'I don't know,' said Bannister, 'unless it's football. I saw him once watching Chelsea. I was rather surprised.'

'Football,' said Psmith thoughtfully, 'football. By no means a scaly idea. I rather fancy, Comrade Bannister, that you have whanged the nail on the head. Is he strong on any particular team? I mean, have you ever heard him, in the intervals of business worries, stamping on his desk and yelling, "Buck up Cottagers!" or "Lay 'em out, Pensioners!" or anything like that? One moment.' Psmith held up his hand. 'I will get my Sherlock Holmes system to work. What was the other team in the modern gladiatorial contest at which you saw Comrade Rossiter?'

'Manchester United.'

'And Comrade Rossiter, I should say, was a Manchester man.'

'I believe he is.'

'Then I am prepared to bet a small sum that he is nuts on Manchester United. My dear Holmes, how—! Elementary, my dear fellow, quite elementary. But here comes the lad in person.'

Mr Rossiter turned in from the central aisle through the counter-door, and, observing the conversational group at the postage-desk, came bounding up. Bannister moved off.

'Really, Smith,' said Mr Rossiter, 'you always seem to be talking. I have overlooked the matter once, as I did not wish to get you into trouble so soon after joining; but, really, it cannot go on. I must take notice of it.'

Psmith held up his hand.

'The fault was mine,' he said, with manly frankness. 'Entirely mine.
Bannister came in a purely professional spirit to deposit a letter with
Comrade Jackson. I engaged him in conversation on the subject of the
Football League, and I was just trying to correct his view that
Newcastle United were the best team playing, when you arrived.'

'It is perfectly absurd,' said Mr Rossiter, 'that you should waste the bank's time in this way. The bank pays you to work, not to talk about professional football.'

'Just so, just so,' murmured Psmith.

'There is too much talking in this department.'

'I fear you are right.'

'It is nonsense.'

'My own view,' said Psmith, 'was that Manchester United were by far the finest team before the public.'

'Get on with your work, Smith.'

Mr Rossiter stumped off to his desk, where he sat as one in thought.

'Smith,' he said at the end of five minutes.

Psmith slid from his stool, and made his way deferentially towards him.

'Bannister's a fool,' snapped Mr Rossiter.

'So I thought,' said Psmith.

'A perfect fool. He always was.'

Psmith shook his head sorrowfully, as who should say, 'Exit Bannister.'

'There is no team playing today to touch Manchester United.'

'Precisely what I said to Comrade Bannister.'

'Of course. You know something about it.'

'The study of League football,' said Psmith, 'has been my relaxation for years.'

'But we have no time to discuss it now.'

'Assuredly not, sir. Work before everything.'

'Some other time, when—'

'—We are less busy. Precisely.'

Psmith moved back to his seat.

'I fear,' he said to Mike, as he resumed work, 'that as far as Comrade Rossiter's friendship and esteem are concerned, I have to a certain extent landed Comrade Bannister in the bouillon; but it was in a good cause. I fancy we have won through. Half an hour's thoughtful perusal of the "Footballers' Who's Who", just to find out some elementary facts about Manchester United, and I rather think the friendly Native is corralled. And now once more to work. Work, the hobby of the hustler and the deadbeat's dread.'

9. The Haunting of Mr Bickersdyke

Anything in the nature of a rash and hasty move was wholly foreign to Psmith's tactics. He had the patience which is the chief quality of the successful general. He was content to secure his base before making any offensive movement. It was a fortnight before he turned his attention to the education of Mr Bickersdyke. During that fortnight he conversed attractively, in the intervals of work, on the subject of League football in general and Manchester United in particular. The subject is not hard to master if one sets oneself earnestly to it; and Psmith spared no pains. The football editions of the evening papers are not reticent about those who play the game: and Psmith drank in every detail with the thoroughness of the conscientious student. By the end of the fortnight he knew what was the favourite breakfast-food of J. Turnbull; what Sandy Turnbull wore next his skin; and who, in the opinion of Meredith, was England's leading politician. These facts, imparted to and discussed with Mr Rossiter, made the progress of the *entente cordiale* rapid. It was on the eighth day that Mr Rossiter consented to lunch with the Old Etonian. On the tenth he played the host. By the end of the fortnight the flapping of the white wings of Peace over the Postage Department was setting up a positive draught. Mike, who had been introduced by Psmith as a distant relative of Moger, the goalkeeper, was included in the great peace.

'So that now,' said Psmith, reflectively polishing his eye-glass, 'I think that we may consider ourselves free to attend to Comrade Bickersdyke. Our bright little Mancunian friend would no more run us in now than if we were the brothers Turnbull. We are as inside forwards to him.'

The club to which Psmith and Mr Bickersdyke belonged was celebrated for the steadfastness of its political views, the excellence of its cuisine, and the curiously Gorgonzolaesque marble of its main staircase. It takes all sorts to make a world. It took about four thousand of all sorts to make the Senior Conservative Club. To be absolutely accurate, there were three thousand seven hundred and eighteen members.

To Mr Bickersdyke for the next week it seemed as if there was only one.

There was nothing crude or overdone about Psmith's methods. The ordinary man, having conceived the idea of haunting a fellow clubman, might have seized the first opportunity of engaging him in conversation. Not so Psmith. The first time he met Mr Bickersdyke in the club was on the stairs after dinner one night.

The great man, having received practical proof of the excellence of cuisine referred to above, was coming down the main staircase at peace with all men, when he was aware of a tall young man in the 'faultless evening dress' of which the female novelist is so fond, who was regarding him with a fixed stare through an eye-glass. The tall young man, having caught his eye, smiled faintly, nodded in a friendly but patronizing manner, and passed on up the staircase to the library. Mr Bickersdyke sped on in search of a waiter.

As Psmith sat in the library with a novel, the waiter entered, and approached him.

'Beg pardon, sir,' he said. 'Are you a member of this club?'

Psmith fumbled in his pocket and produced his eye-glass, through which he examined the waiter, button by button.

'I am Psmith,' he said simply.

'A member, sir?'

'*The* member,' said Psmith. 'Surely you participated in the general rejoicings which ensued when it was announced that I had been elected? But perhaps you were too busy working to pay any attention. If so, I respect you. I also am a worker. A toiler, not a flatfish. A sizzler, not a squab. Yes, I am a member. Will you tell Mr Bickersdyke that I am sorry, but I have been elected, and have paid my entrance fee and subscription.'

'Thank you, sir.'

The waiter went downstairs and found Mr Bickersdyke in the lower smoking-room.

'The gentleman says he is, sir.'

'H'm,' said the bank-manager. 'Coffee and Benedictine, and a cigar.'

'Yes, sir.'

On the following day Mr Bickersdyke met Psmith in the club three times, and on the day after that seven. Each time the latter's smile was friendly, but patronizing. Mr Bickersdyke began to grow restless.

On the fourth day Psmith made his first remark. The manager was reading the evening paper in a corner, when Psmith sinking gracefully into a chair beside him, caused him to look up.

'The rain keeps off,' said Psmith.

Mr Bickersdyke looked as if he wished his employee would imitate the rain, but he made no reply.

Psmith called a waiter.

'Would you mind bringing me a small cup of coffee?' he said. 'And for you,' he added to Mr Bickersdyke.

'Nothing,' growled the manager.

'And nothing for Mr Bickersdyke.'

The waiter retired. Mr Bickersdyke became absorbed in his paper.

'I see from my morning paper,' said Psmith, affably, 'that you are to address a meeting at the Kenningford Town Hall next week. I shall come and hear you. Our politics differ in some respects, I fear—I incline to the Socialist view—but nevertheless I shall listen to your remarks with great interest, great interest.'

The paper rustled, but no reply came from behind it.

'I heard from father this morning,' resumed Psmith.

Mr Bickersdyke lowered his paper and glared at him.

'I don't wish to hear about your father,' he snapped.

An expression of surprise and pain came over Psmith's face.

'What!' he cried. 'You don't mean to say that there is any coolness between my father and you? I am more grieved than I can say. Knowing, as I do, what a genuine respect my father has for your great talents, I can only think that there must have been some misunderstanding. Perhaps if you would allow me to act as a mediator—'

Mr Bickersdyke put down his paper and walked out of the room.

Psmith found him a quarter of an hour later in the card-room. He sat down beside his table, and began to observe the play with silent interest. Mr Bickersdyke, never a great performer at the best of times, was so unsettled by the scrutiny that in the deciding game of the rubber he revoked, thereby presenting his opponents with the rubber by a very handsome majority of points. Psmith clicked his tongue sympathetically.

Dignified reticence is not a leading characteristic of the bridge-player's manner at the Senior Conservative Club on occasions like this. Mr Bickersdyke's partner did not bear his calamity with manly resignation. He gave tongue on the instant. 'What on earth's', and 'Why on earth's' flowed from his mouth like molten lava. Mr Bickersdyke sat and fermented in silence. Psmith clicked his tongue sympathetically throughout.

Mr Bickersdyke lost that control over himself which every member of a club should possess. He turned on Psmith with a snort of frenzy.

'How can I keep my attention fixed on the game when you sit staring at me like a—like a—'

'I am sorry,' said Psmith gravely, 'if my stare falls short in any way of your ideal of what a stare should be; but I appeal to these gentlemen. Could I have watched the game more quietly?'

'Of course not,' said the bereaved partner warmly. 'Nobody could have any earthly objection to your behaviour. It was absolute carelessness. I should have thought that one might have expected one's partner at a club like this to exercise elementary—'

But Mr Bickersdyke had gone. He had melted silently away like the driven snow.

Psmith took his place at the table.

'A somewhat nervous excitable man, Mr Bickersdyke, I should say,' he observed.

'A somewhat dashed, blanked idiot,' emended the bank-manager's late partner. 'Thank goodness he lost as much as I did. That's some light consolation.'

Psmith arrived at the flat to find Mike still out. Mike had repaired to the Gaiety earlier in the evening to refresh his mind after the labours of the day. When he returned, Psmith was sitting in an armchair with his feet on the mantelpiece, musing placidly on Life.

'Well?' said Mike.

'Well? And how was the Gaiety? Good show?'

'Jolly good. What about Bickersdyke?'

Psmith looked sad.

'I cannot make Comrade Bickersdyke out,' he said. 'You would think that a man would be glad to see the son of a personal friend. On the contrary, I may be wronging Comrade B., but I should almost be inclined to say that my presence in the Senior Conservative Club tonight irritated him. There was no *bonhomie* in his manner. He seemed to me to be giving a spirited imitation of a man about to foam at the mouth. I did my best to entertain him. I chatted. His only reply was to leave the room. I followed him to the card-room, and watched his very remarkable and brainy tactics at bridge, and he accused me of causing him to revoke. A very curious personality, that of Comrade Bickersdyke. But let us dismiss him from our minds. Rumours have reached me,' said Psmith, 'that a very decent little supper may be obtained at a quaint, old-world eating-house called the Savoy. Will you accompany me thither on a tissue-restoring expedition? It would be rash not to probe these rumours to their foundation, and ascertain their exact truth.'

10. Mr Bickersdyke Addresses His Constituents

It was noted by the observant at the bank next morning that Mr Bickersdyke had something on his mind. William, the messenger, knew it, when he found his respectful salute ignored. Little Briggs, the accountant, knew it when his obsequious but cheerful 'Good morning' was acknowledged only by a 'Morn" which was almost an oath. Mr Bickersdyke passed up the aisle and into his room like an east wind. He sat down at his table and pressed the bell. Harold, William's brother and co-messenger, entered with the air of one ready to duck if any missile should be thrown at him. The reports of the manager's frame of mind had been circulated in the office, and Harold felt somewhat apprehensive. It was on an occasion very similar to this that George Barstead, formerly in the employ of the New Asiatic Bank in the capacity of messenger, had been rash enough to laugh at what he had taken for a joke of Mr Bickersdyke's, and had been instantly presented with the sack for gross impertinence.

'Ask Mr Smith—' began the manager. Then he paused. 'No, never mind,' he added.

Harold remained in the doorway, puzzled.

'Don't stand there gaping at me, man,' cried Mr Bickersdyke, 'Go away.'

Harold retired and informed his brother, William, that in his,

Harold's, opinion, Mr Bickersdyke was off his chump.

'Off his onion,' said William, soaring a trifle higher in poetic imagery.

'Barmy,' was the terse verdict of Samuel Jakes, the third messenger. 'Always said so.' And with that the New Asiatic Bank staff of messengers dismissed Mr Bickersdyke and proceeded to concentrate themselves on their duties, which consisted principally of hanging about and discussing the prophecies of that modern seer, Captain Coe.

What had made Mr Bickersdyke change his mind so abruptly was the sudden realization of the fact that he had no case against Psmith. In his capacity of manager of the bank he could not take official notice of Psmith's behaviour outside office hours, especially as Psmith had done nothing but stare at him. It would be impossible to make anybody understand the true inwardness of Psmith's stare. Theoretically, Mr Bickersdyke had the power to dismiss any subordinate of his whom he did not consider satisfactory, but it was a power that had to be exercised with discretion. The manager was accountable for his actions to the Board of Directors. If he dismissed Psmith, Psmith would certainly bring an action against the bank for wrongful dismissal, and on the evidence he would infallibly win it. Mr Bickersdyke did not welcome the prospect of having to explain to the Directors that he had let the shareholders of the bank in for a fine of whatever a discriminating jury cared to decide upon, simply because he had been stared at while playing bridge. His only hope was to catch Psmith doing his work badly.

He touched the bell again, and sent for Mr Rossiter.

The messenger found the head of the Postage Department in conversation with Psmith. Manchester United had been beaten by one goal to nil on the previous afternoon, and Psmith was informing Mr Rossiter that the referee was a robber, who had evidently been financially interested in the result of the game. The way he himself looked at it, said Psmith, was that the thing had been a moral victory for the United. Mr Rossiter said yes, he thought so too. And it was at this moment that Mr Bickersdyke sent for him to ask whether Psmith's work was satisfactory.

The head of the Postage Department gave his opinion without hesitation. Psmith's work was about the hottest proposition he had ever struck. Psmith's work—well, it stood alone. You couldn't compare it with anything. There are no degrees in perfection. Psmith's work was perfect, and there was an end to it.

He put it differently, but that was the gist of what he said.

Mr Bickersdyke observed he was glad to hear it, and smashed a nib by stabbing the desk with it.

It was on the evening following this that the bank-manager was due to address a meeting at the Kenningford Town Hall.

He was looking forward to the event with mixed feelings. He had stood for Parliament once before, several years back, in the North. He had been defeated by a couple of thousand votes, and he hoped that the episode had been forgotten. Not merely because his defeat had been heavy. There was another reason. On that occasion he had stood as a Liberal. He was standing for Kenningford as a Unionist. Of course, a man is at perfect liberty to change his views, if he wishes to do so, but the process is apt to give his opponents a chance of catching him (to use the inspired language of the music-halls) on the bend. Mr Bickersdyke was rather afraid that the light-hearted electors of Kenningford might avail themselves of this chance.

Kenningford, S.E., is undoubtedly by way of being a tough sort of place. Its inhabitants incline to a robust type of humour, which finds a verbal vent in catch phrases and expends itself physically in smashing shop-windows and kicking policemen. He feared that the meeting at the Town Hall might possibly be a trifle rowdy.

All political meetings are very much alike. Somebody gets up and introduces the speaker of the evening, and then the speaker of the evening says at great length what he thinks of the scandalous manner in which the Government is behaving or the iniquitous goings-on of the Opposition. From time to time confederates in the audience rise and ask carefully rehearsed questions, and are answered fully and satisfactorily by the orator. When a genuine heckler interrupts, the orator either ignores him, or says haughtily that he can find him arguments but cannot find him brains. Or, occasionally, when the question is an easy one, he answers it. A quietly conducted political meeting is one of England's most delightful indoor games. When the meeting is rowdy, the audience has more fun, but the speaker a good deal less.

Mr Bickersdyke's introducer was an elderly Scotch peer, an excellent man for the purpose in every respect, except that he possessed a very strong accent.

The audience welcomed that accent uproariously. The electors of Kenningford who really had any definite opinions on politics were fairly equally divided. There were about as many earnest Liberals as there were earnest Unionists. But besides these there was a strong contingent who did not care which side won. These looked on elections as Heaven-sent opportunities for making a great deal of noise. They attended meetings in order to extract amusement from them; and they voted, if they voted at all, quite irresponsibly. A funny story at the expense of one candidate told on the morning of the polling, was quite likely to send these brave fellows off in dozens filling in their papers for the victim's opponent.

There was a solid block of these gay spirits at the back of the hall. They received the Scotch peer with huge delight. He reminded them of Harry Lauder and they said so. They addressed him affectionately as 'Arry', throughout his speech, which was rather long. They implored him to be a pal and sing 'The Saftest of the Family'. Or, failing that, 'I love a lassie'. Finding they could not induce him to do this, they did it themselves. They sang it several times. When the peer, having finished his remarks on the subject of Mr Bickersdyke, at length sat down, they cheered for seven minutes, and demanded an encore.

The meeting was in excellent spirits when Mr Bickersdyke rose to address it.

The effort of doing justice to the last speaker had left the free and independent electors at the back of the hall slightly limp. The bank-manager's opening remarks were received without any demonstration.

Mr Bickersdyke spoke well. He had a penetrating, if harsh, voice, and he said what he had to say forcibly. Little by little the audience came under his spell. When, at the end of a well-turned sentence, he paused and took a sip of water, there was a round of applause, in which many of the admirers of Mr Harry Lauder joined.

He resumed his speech. The audience listened intently. Mr Bickersdyke, having said some nasty things about Free Trade and the Alien Immigrant, turned to the Needs of the Navy and the necessity of increasing the fleet at all costs.

'This is no time for half-measures,' he said. 'We must do our utmost.

We must burn our boats—'

'Excuse me,' said a gentle voice.

Mr Bickersdyke broke off. In the centre of the hall a tall figure had risen. Mr Bickersdyke found himself looking at a gleaming eye-glass which the speaker had just polished and inserted in his eye.

The ordinary heckler Mr Bickersdyke would have taken in his stride. He had got his audience, and simply by continuing and ignoring the interruption, he could have won through in safety. But the sudden appearance of Psmith unnerved him. He remained silent.

'How,' asked Psmith, 'do you propose to strengthen the Navy by burning boats?'

The inanity of the question enraged even the pleasure-seekers at the back.

'Order! Order!' cried the earnest contingent.

'Sit down, fice!' roared the pleasure-seekers.

Psmith sat down with a patient smile.

Mr Bickersdyke resumed his speech. But the fire had gone out of it. He had lost his audience. A moment before, he had grasped them and played on their minds (or what passed for minds down Kenningford way) as on a stringed instrument. Now he had lost his hold.

He spoke on rapidly, but he could not get into his stride. The trivial interruption had broken the spell. His words lacked grip. The dead silence in which the first part of his speech had been received, that silence which is a greater tribute to the speaker than any applause, had given place to a restless medley of little noises; here a cough; there a scraping of a boot along the floor, as its wearer moved uneasily in his seat; in another place a whispered conversation. The audience was bored.

Mr Bickersdyke left the Navy, and went on to more general topics. But he was not interesting. He quoted figures, saw a moment later that he had not quoted them accurately, and instead of carrying on boldly, went back and corrected himself.

'Gow up top!' said a voice at the back of the hall, and there was a general laugh.

Mr Bickersdyke galloped unsteadily on. He condemned the Government. He said they had betrayed their trust.

And then he told an anecdote.

'The Government, gentlemen,' he said, 'achieves nothing worth achieving, and every individual member of the Government takes all the credit for what is done to himself. Their methods remind me, gentlemen, of an amusing experience I had while fishing one summer in the Lake District.'

In a volume entitled 'Three Men in a Boat' there is a story of how the author and a friend go into a riverside inn and see a very large trout in a glass case. They make inquiries about it, have men assure them, one by one, that the trout was caught by themselves. In the end the trout turns out to be made of plaster of Paris.

Mr Bickersdyke told that story as an experience of his own while fishing one summer in the Lake District.

It went well. The meeting was amused. Mr Bickersdyke went on to draw a trenchant comparison between the lack of genuine merit in the trout and the lack of genuine merit in the achievements of His Majesty's Government.

There was applause.

When it had ceased, Psmith rose to his feet again.

'Excuse me,' he said.

11. Misunderstood

Mike had refused to accompany Psmith to the meeting that evening, saying that he got too many chances in the ordinary way of business of hearing Mr Bickersdyke speak, without going out of his way to make more. So Psmith had gone off to Kenningford alone, and Mike, feeling too lazy to sally out to any place of entertainment, had remained at the flat with a novel.

He was deep in this, when there was the sound of a key in the latch, and shortly afterwards Psmith entered the room. On Psmith's brow there was a look of pensive care, and also a slight discoloration. When he removed his overcoat, Mike saw that his collar was burst and hanging loose and that he had no tie. On his erstwhile speckless and gleaming shirt front were number of finger-impressions, of a boldness and clearness of outline which would have made a Bertillon expert leap with joy.

'Hullo!' said Mike dropping his book.

Psmith nodded in silence, went to his bedroom, and returned with a looking-glass. Propping this up on a table, he proceeded to examine himself with the utmost care. He shuddered slightly as his eye fell on the finger-marks; and without a word he went into his bathroom again. He emerged after an interval of ten minutes in sky-blue pyjamas, slippers, and an Old Etonian blazer. He lit a cigarette; and, sitting down, stared pensively into the fire.

'What the dickens have you been playing at?' demanded Mike.

Psmith heaved a sigh.

'That,' he replied, 'I could not say precisely. At one moment it seemed to be Rugby football, at another a jiu-jitsu *seance*. Later, it bore a resemblance to a pantomime rally. However, whatever it was, it was all very bright and interesting. A distinct experience.'

'Have you been scrapping?' asked Mike. 'What happened? Was there a row?'

'There was,' said Psmith, 'in a measure what might be described as a row. At least, when you find a perfect stranger attaching himself to your collar and pulling, you begin to suspect that something of that kind is on the bill.'

'Did they do that?'

Psmith nodded.

'A merchant in a moth-eaten bowler started warbling to a certain extent with me. It was all very trying for a man of culture. He was a man who had, I should say, discovered that alcohol was a food long before the doctors found it out. A good chap, possibly, but a little boisterous in his manner. Well, well.'

Psmith shook his head sadly.

'He got you one on the forehead,' said Mike, 'or somebody did. Tell us what happened. I wish the dickens I'd come with you. I'd no notion there would be a rag of any sort. What did happen?'

'Comrade Jackson,' said Psmith sorrowfully, 'how sad it is in this life of ours to be consistently misunderstood. You know, of course, how wrapped up I am in Comrade Bickersdyke's welfare. You know that all my efforts are directed towards making a decent man of him; that, in short, I am his truest friend. Does he show by so much as a word that he appreciates my labours? Not he. I believe that man is beginning to dislike me, Comrade Jackson.'

'What happened, anyhow? Never mind about Bickersdyke.'

'Perhaps it was mistaken zeal on my part.... Well, I will tell you all. Make a long arm for the shovel, Comrade Jackson, and pile on a few more coals. I thank you. Well, all went quite smoothly for a while. Comrade B. in quite good form. Got his second wind, and was going strong for the tape, when a regrettable incident occurred. He informed the meeting, that while up in the Lake country, fishing, he went to an inn and saw a remarkably large stuffed trout in a glass case. He made inquiries, and found that five separate and distinct people had caught—'

'Why, dash it all,' said Mike, 'that's a frightful chestnut.'

Psmith nodded.

'It certainly has appeared in print,' he said. 'In fact I should have said it was rather a well-known story. I was so interested in Comrade Bickersdyke's statement that the thing had happened to himself that, purely out of good-will towards him, I got up and told him that I thought it was my duty, as a friend, to let him know that a man named Jerome had pinched his story, put it in a book, and got money by it. Money, mark you, that should by rights have been Comrade Bickersdyke's. He didn't appear to care much about sifting the matter thoroughly. In fact, he seemed anxious to get on with his speech, and slur the matter over. But, tactlessly perhaps, I continued rather to harp on the thing. I said that the book in which the story had appeared was published in 1889. I asked him how long ago it was that he had been on his fishing tour, because it was important to know in order to bring the charge home against Jerome. Well, after a bit, I was amazed, and pained, too, to hear Comrade Bickersdyke urging certain bravoes in the audience to turn me out. If ever there was a case of biting the hand that fed him.... Well, well.... By this time the meeting had begun to take sides to some extent. What I might call my party, the Earnest Investigators, were whistling between their fingers, stamping on the floor, and shouting, "Chestnuts!" while the opposing party, the bravoes, seemed to be trying, as I say, to do jiu-jitsu tricks with me. It was a painful situation. I know the cultivated man of affairs should have passed the thing off with a short, careless laugh; but, owing to the above-mentioned alcohol-expert having got both hands under my collar, short, careless laughs were off. I was compelled, very reluctantly, to conclude the interview by tapping the bright boy on the jaw. He took the hint, and sat down on the floor. I thought no more of the matter, and was making my way thoughtfully to the exit, when a second man of wrath put the above on my forehead. You can't ignore a thing like that. I collected some of his waistcoat and one of his legs, and hove him with some vim into the middle distance. By this time a good many of the Earnest Investigators were beginning to join in; and it was just there that the affair began to have certain points of resemblance to a pantomime rally. Everybody seemed to be shouting a good deal and hitting everybody else. It was no place for a man of delicate culture, so I edged towards the door, and drifted out. There was a cab in the offing. I boarded it. And, having kicked a vigorous politician in the stomach, as he was endeavouring to climb in too, I drove off home.'

Psmith got up, looked at his forehead once more in the glass, sighed, and sat down again.

'All very disturbing,' he said.

'Great Scott,' said Mike, 'I wish I'd come. Why on earth didn't you tell me you were going to rag? I think you might as well have done. I wouldn't have missed it for worlds.'

Psmith regarded him with raised eyebrows.

'Rag!' he said. 'Comrade Jackson, I do not understand you. You surely do not think that I had any other object in doing what I did than to serve Comrade Bickersdyke? It's terrible how one's motives get distorted in this world of ours.'

'Well,' said Mike, with a grin, 'I know one person who'll jolly well distort your motives, as you call it, and that's Bickersdyke.'

Psmith looked thoughtful.

'True,' he said, 'true. There is that possibility. I tell you, Comrade Jackson, once more that my bright young life is being slowly blighted by the frightful way in which that man misunderstands me. It seems almost impossible to try to do him a good turn without having the action misconstrued.'

'What'll you say to him tomorrow?'

'I shall make no allusion to the painful affair. If I happen to meet him in the ordinary course of business routine, I shall pass some light, pleasant remark—on the weather, let us say, or the Bank rate—and continue my duties.'

'How about if he sends for you, and wants to do the light, pleasant remark business on his own?'

'In that case I shall not thwart him. If he invites me into his private room, I shall be his guest, and shall discuss, to the best of my ability, any topic which he may care to introduce. There shall be no constraint between Comrade Bickersdyke and myself.'

'No, I shouldn't think there would be. I wish I could come and hear you.'

'I wish you could,' said Psmith courteously.

'Still, it doesn't matter much to you. You don't care if you do get sacked.'

Psmith rose.

'In that way possibly, as you say, I am agreeably situated. If the New Asiatic Bank does not require Psmith's services, there are other spheres where a young man of spirit may carve a place for himself. No, what is worrying me, Comrade Jackson, is not the thought of the push. It is the growing fear that Comrade Bickersdyke and I will never thoroughly understand and appreciate one another. A deep gulf lies between us. I do what I can do to bridge it over, but he makes no response. On his side of the gulf building operations appear to be at an entire standstill. That is what is carving these lines of care on my forehead, Comrade Jackson. That is what is painting these purple circles beneath my eyes. Quite inadvertently to be disturbing Comrade Bickersdyke, annoying him, preventing him from enjoying life. How sad this is. Life bulges with these tragedies.'

Mike picked up the evening paper.

'Don't let it keep you awake at night,' he said. 'By the way, did you see that Manchester United were playing this afternoon? They won. You'd better sit down and sweat up some of the details. You'll want them tomorrow.'

'You are very right, Comrade Jackson,' said Psmith, reseating himself. 'So the Mancunians pushed the bulb into the meshes beyond the uprights no fewer than four times, did they? Bless the dear boys, what spirits they do enjoy, to be sure. Comrade Jackson, do not disturb me. I must concentrate myself. These are deep waters.'

12. In a Nutshell

Mr Bickersdyke sat in his private room at the New Asiatic Bank with a pile of newspapers before him. At least, the casual observer would have said that it was Mr Bickersdyke. In reality, however, it was an active volcano in the shape and clothes of the bank-manager. It was freely admitted in the office that morning that the manager had lowered all records with ease. The staff had known him to be in a bad temper before—frequently; but his frame of mind on all previous occasions had been, compared with his present frame of mind, that of a rather exceptionally good-natured lamb. Within ten minutes of his arrival the entire office was on the jump. The messengers were collected in a pallid group in the basement, discussing the affair in whispers and endeavouring to restore their nerve with about sixpenn'orth of the beverage known as 'unsweetened'. The heads of departments, to a man, had bowed before the storm. Within the space of seven minutes and a quarter Mr Bickersdyke had contrived to find some fault with each of them. Inward Bills was out at an A.B.C. shop snatching a hasty cup of coffee, to pull him together again. Outward Bills was sitting at his desk with the glazed stare of one who has been struck in the thorax by a thunderbolt. Mr Rossiter had been torn from Psmith in the middle of a highly technical discussion of the Manchester United match, just as he was showing—with the aid of a ball of paper—how he had once seen Meredith centre to Sandy Turnbull in a Cup match, and was now leaping about like a distracted grasshopper. Mr Waller, head of the Cash Department, had been summoned to the Presence, and after listening meekly to a rush of criticism, had retired to his desk with the air of a beaten spaniel.

Only one man of the many in the building seemed calm and happy—Psmith.

Psmith had resumed the chat about Manchester United, on Mr Rossiter's return from the lion's den, at the spot where it had been broken off; but, finding that the head of the Postage Department was in no mood for discussing football (or any thing else), he had postponed his remarks and placidly resumed his work.

Mr Bickersdyke picked up a paper, opened it, and began searching the columns. He had not far to look. It was a slack season for the newspapers, and his little trouble, which might have received a paragraph in a busy week, was set forth fully in three-quarters of a column.

The column was headed, 'Amusing Heckling'.

Mr Bickersdyke read a few lines, and crumpled the paper up with a snort.

The next he examined was an organ of his own shade of political opinion. It too, gave him nearly a column, headed 'Disgraceful Scene at Kenningford'. There was also a leaderette on the subject.

The leaderette said so exactly what Mr Bickersdyke thought himself that for a moment he was soothed. Then the thought of his grievance returned, and he pressed the bell.

'Send Mr Smith to me,' he said.

William, the messenger, proceeded to inform Psmith of the summons.

Psmith's face lit up.

'I am always glad to sweeten the monotony of toil with a chat with

Little Clarence,' he said. 'I shall be with him in a moment.'

He cleaned his pen very carefully, placed it beside his ledger, flicked a little dust off his coatsleeve, and made his way to the manager's room.

Mr Bickersdyke received him with the ominous restraint of a tiger crouching for its spring. Psmith stood beside the table with languid grace, suggestive of some favoured confidential secretary waiting for instructions.

A ponderous silence brooded over the room for some moments. Psmith broke it by remarking that the Bank Rate was unchanged. He mentioned this fact as if it afforded him a personal gratification.

Mr Bickersdyke spoke.

'Well, Mr Smith?' he said.

'You wished to see me about something, sir?' inquired Psmith, ingratiatingly.

'You know perfectly well what I wished to see you about. I want to hear your explanation of what occurred last night.'

'May I sit, sir?'

He dropped gracefully into a chair, without waiting for permission, and, having hitched up the knees of his trousers, beamed winningly at the manager.

'A deplorable affair,' he said, with a shake of his head. 'Extremely deplorable. We must not judge these rough, uneducated men too harshly, however. In a time of excitement the emotions of the lower classes are easily stirred. Where you or I would—'

Mr Bickersdyke interrupted.

'I do not wish for any more buffoonery, Mr Smith—'

Psmith raised a pained pair of eyebrows.

'Buffoonery, sir!'

'I cannot understand what made you act as you did last night, unless you are perfectly mad, as I am beginning to think.'

'But, surely, sir, there was nothing remarkable in my behaviour? When a merchant has attached himself to your collar, can you do less than smite him on the other cheek? I merely acted in self-defence. You saw for yourself—'

'You know what I am alluding to. Your behaviour during my speech.'

'An excellent speech,' murmured Psmith courteously.

'Well?' said Mr Bickersdyke.

'It was, perhaps, mistaken zeal on my part, sir, but you must remember that I acted purely from the best motives. It seemed to me—'

'That is enough, Mr Smith. I confess that I am absolutely at a loss to understand you—'

'It is too true, sir,' sighed Psmith.

'You seem,' continued Mr Bickersdyke, warming to his subject, and turning gradually a richer shade of purple, 'you seem to be determined to endeavour to annoy me.' ('No no,' from Psmith.) 'I can only assume that you are not in your right senses. You follow me about in my club—'

'Our club, sir,' murmured Psmith.

'Be good enough not to interrupt me, Mr Smith. You dog my footsteps in my club—'

'Purely accidental, sir. We happen to meet—that is all.'

'You attend meetings at which I am speaking, and behave in a perfectly imbecile manner.'

Psmith moaned slightly.

'It may seem humorous to you, but I can assure you it is extremely bad policy on your part. The New Asiatic Bank is no place for humour, and I think—'

'Excuse me, sir,' said Psmith.

The manager started at the familiar phrase. The plum-colour of his complexion deepened.

'I entirely agree with you, sir,' said Psmith, 'that this bank is no place for humour.'

'Very well, then. You—'

'And I am never humorous in it. I arrive punctually in the morning, and I work steadily and earnestly till my labours are completed. I think you will find, on inquiry, that Mr Rossiter is satisfied with my work.'

'That is neither here nor—'

'Surely, sir,' said Psmith, 'you are wrong? Surely your jurisdiction ceases after office hours? Any little misunderstanding we may have at the close of the day's work cannot affect you officially. You could not, for instance, dismiss me from the service of the bank if we were partners at bridge at the club and I happened to revoke.'

'I can dismiss you, let me tell you, Mr Smith, for studied insolence, whether in the office or not.'

'I bow to superior knowledge,' said Psmith politely, 'but I confess I doubt it. And,' he added, 'there is another point. May I continue to some extent?'

'If you have anything to say, say it.'

Psmith flung one leg over the other, and settled his collar.

'It is perhaps a delicate matter,' he said, 'but it is best to be frank. We should have no secrets. To put my point quite clearly, I must go back a little, to the time when you paid us that very welcome week-end visit at our house in August.'

'If you hope to make capital out of the fact that I have been a guest of your father—'

'Not at all,' said Psmith deprecatingly. 'Not at all. You do not take me. My point is this. I do not wish to revive painful memories, but it cannot be denied that there was, here and there, some slight bickering between us on that occasion. The fault,' said Psmith magnanimously, 'was possibly mine. I may have been too exacting, too capricious. Perhaps so. However, the fact remains that you conceived the happy notion of getting me into this bank, under the impression that, once I was in, you would be able to—if I may use the expression—give me beans. You said as much to me, if I remember. I hate to say it, but don't you think that if you give me the sack, although my work is satisfactory to the head of my department, you will be by way of admitting that you bit off rather more than you could chew? I merely make the suggestion.'

Mr Bickersdyke half rose from his chair.

'You—'

'Just so, just so, but—to return to the main point—don't you? The whole painful affair reminds me of the story of Agesilaus and the Petulant Pterodactyl, which as you have never heard, I will now proceed to relate. Agesilaus—'

Mr Bickersdyke made a curious clucking noise in his throat.

'I am boring you,' said Psmith, with ready tact. 'Suffice it to say that Comrade Agesilaus interfered with the pterodactyl, which was doing him no harm; and the intelligent creature, whose motto was "Nemo me impune lacessit", turned and bit him. Bit him good and hard, so that Agesilaus ever afterwards had a distaste for pterodactyls. His reluctance to disturb them became quite a byword. The Society papers of the period frequently commented upon it. Let us draw the parallel.'

Here Mr Bickersdyke, who had been clucking throughout this speech, essayed to speak; but Psmith hurried on.

'You are Agesilaus,' he said. 'I am the Petulant Pterodactyl. You, if I may say so, butted in of your own free will, and took me from a happy home, simply in order that you might get me into this place under you, and give me beans. But, curiously enough, the major portion of that vegetable seems to be coming to you. Of course, you can administer the push if you like; but, as I say, it will be by way of a confession that your scheme has sprung a leak. Personally,' said Psmith, as one friend to another, 'I should advise you to stick it out. You never know what may happen. At any moment I may fall from my present high standard of industry and excellence; and then you have me, so to speak, where the hair is crisp.'

He paused. Mr Bickersdyke's eyes, which even in their normal state protruded slightly, now looked as if they might fall out at any moment. His face had passed from the plum-coloured stage to something beyond. Every now and then he made the clucking noise, but except for that he was silent. Psmith, having waited for some time for something in the shape of comment or criticism on his remarks, now rose.

'It has been a great treat to me, this little chat,' he said affably, 'but I fear that I must no longer allow purely social enjoyments to interfere with my commercial pursuits. With your permission, I will rejoin my department, where my absence is doubtless already causing comment and possibly dismay. But we shall be meeting at the club shortly, I hope. Good-bye, sir, good-bye.'

He left the room, and walked dreamily back to the Postage Department, leaving the manager still staring glassily at nothing.

13. Mike is Moved On

This episode may be said to have concluded the first act of the commercial drama in which Mike and Psmith had been cast for leading parts. And, as usually happens after the end of an act, there was a lull for a while until things began to work up towards another climax. Mike, as day succeeded day, began to grow accustomed to the life of the bank, and to find that it had its pleasant side after all. Whenever a number of people are working at the same thing, even though that thing is not perhaps what they would have chosen as an object in life, if left to themselves, there is bound to exist an atmosphere of good-fellowship; something akin to, though a hundred times weaker than, the public school spirit. Such a community lacks the main motive of the public school spirit, which is pride in the school and its achievements. Nobody can be proud of the achievements of a bank. When the business of arranging a new Japanese loan was given to the New Asiatic Bank, its employees did not stand on stools, and cheer. On the contrary, they thought of the extra work it would involve; and they cursed a good deal, though there was no denying that it was a big thing for the bank—not unlike winning the Ashburton would be to a school. There is a cold impersonality about a bank. A school is a living thing.

Setting aside this important difference, there was a good deal of the public school about the New Asiatic Bank. The heads of departments were not quite so autocratic as masters, and one was treated more on a grown-up scale, as man to man; but, nevertheless, there remained a distinct flavour of a school republic. Most of the men in the bank, with the exception of certain hard-headed Scotch youths drafted in from other establishments in the City, were old public school men. Mike found two Old Wrykinians in the first week. Neither was well known to him. They had left in his second year in the team. But it was pleasant to have them about, and to feel that they had been educated at the right place.

As far as Mike's personal comfort went, the presence of these two Wrykinians was very much for the good. Both of them knew all about his cricket, and they spread the news. The New Asiatic Bank, like most London banks, was keen on sport, and happened to possess a cricket team which could make a good game with most of the second-rank clubs. The disappearance to the East of two of the best bats of the previous season caused Mike's advent to be hailed with a good deal of enthusiasm. Mike was a county man. He had only played once for his county, it was true, but that did not matter. He had passed the barrier which separates the second-class bat from the first-class, and the bank welcomed him with awe. County men did not come their way every day.

Mike did not like being in the bank, considered in the light of a career. But he bore no grudge against the inmates of the bank, such as he had borne against the inmates of Sedleigh. He had looked on the latter as bound up with the school, and, consequently, enemies. His fellow workers in the bank he regarded as companions in misfortune. They were all in the same boat together. There were men from Tonbridge, Dulwich, Bedford, St Paul's, and a dozen other schools. One or two of them he knew by repute from the pages of Wisden. Bannister, his cheerful predecessor in the Postage Department, was the Bannister, he recollected now, who had played for Geddington against Wrykyn in his second year in the Wrykyn team. Munroe, the big man in the Fixed Deposits, he remembered as leader of the Ripton pack. Every day brought fresh discoveries of this sort, and each made Mike more reconciled to his lot. They were a pleasant set of fellows in the New Asiatic Bank, and but for the dreary outlook which the future held—for Mike, unlike most of his follow workers, was not attracted by the idea of a life in the East—he would have been very fairly content.

The hostility of Mr Bickersdyke was a slight drawback. Psmith had developed a habit of taking Mike with him to the club of an evening; and this did not do anything towards wiping out of the manager's mind the recollection of his former passage of arms with the Old Wrykinian. The glass remaining Set Fair as far as Mr Rossiter's approval was concerned, Mike was enabled to keep off the managerial carpet to a great extent; but twice, when he posted letters without going through the preliminary formality of stamping them, Mr Bickersdyke had opportunities of which he availed himself. But for these incidents life was fairly enjoyable. Owing to Psmith's benevolent efforts, the Postage Department became quite a happy family, and ex-occupants of the postage desk, Bannister especially, were amazed at the change that had come over Mr Rossiter. He no longer darted from his lair like a pouncing panther. To report his subordinates to the manager seemed now to be a lost art with him. The sight of Psmith and Mr Rossiter proceeding high and disposedly to a mutual lunch became quite common, and ceased to excite remark.

'By kindness,' said Psmith to Mike, after one of these expeditions. 'By tact and kindness. That is how it is done. I do not despair of training Comrade Rossiter one of these days to jump through paper hoops.'

So that, altogether, Mike's life in the bank had become very fairly pleasant.

Out of office-hours he enjoyed himself hugely. London was strange to him, and with Psmith as a companion, he extracted a vast deal of entertainment from it. Psmith was not unacquainted with the West End, and he proved an excellent guide. At first Mike expostulated with unfailing regularity at the other's habit of paying for everything, but Psmith waved aside all objections with languid firmness.

'I need you, Comrade Jackson,' he said, when Mike lodged a protest on finding himself bound for the stalls for the second night in succession. 'We must stick together. As my confidential secretary and adviser, your place is by my side. Who knows but that between the acts tonight I may not be seized with some luminous thought? Could I utter this to my next-door neighbour or the programme-girl? Stand by me, Comrade Jackson, or we are undone.'

So Mike stood by him.

By this time Mike had grown so used to his work that he could tell to within five minutes when a rush would come; and he was able to spend a good deal of his time reading a surreptitious novel behind a pile of ledgers, or down in the tea-room. The New Asiatic Bank supplied tea to its employees. In quality it was bad, and the bread-and-butter associated with it was worse. But it had the merit of giving one an excuse for being away from one's desk. There were large printed notices all over the tea-room, which was in the basement, informing gentlemen that they were only allowed ten minutes for tea, but one took just as long as one thought the head of one's department would stand, from twenty-five minutes to an hour and a quarter.

This state of things was too good to last. Towards the beginning of the New Year a new man arrived, and Mike was moved on to another department.

14. Mr Waller Appears in a New Light

The department into which Mike was sent was the Cash, or, to be more exact, that section of it which was known as Paying Cashier. The important task of shooting doubloons across the counter did not belong to Mike himself, but to Mr Waller. Mike's work was less ostentatious, and was performed with pen, ink, and ledgers in the background. Occasionally, when Mr Waller was out at lunch, Mike had to act as substitute for him, and cash cheques; but Mr Waller always went out at a slack time, when few customers came in, and Mike seldom had any very startling sum to hand over.

He enjoyed being in the Cash Department. He liked Mr Waller. The work was easy; and when he did happen to make mistakes, they were corrected patiently by the grey-bearded one, and not used as levers for boosting him into the presence of Mr Bickersdyke, as they might have been in some departments. The cashier seemed to have taken a fancy to Mike; and Mike, as was usually the way with him when people went out of their way to be friendly, was at his best. Mike at his ease and unsuspicious of hostile intentions was a different person from Mike with his prickles out.

Psmith, meanwhile, was not enjoying himself. It was an unheard-of thing, he said, depriving a man of his confidential secretary without so much as asking his leave.

'It has caused me the greatest inconvenience,' he told Mike, drifting round in a melancholy way to the Cash Department during a slack spell one afternoon. 'I miss you at every turn. Your keen intelligence and ready sympathy were invaluable to me. Now where am I? In the cart. I evolved a slightly bright thought on life just now. There was nobody to tell it to except the new man. I told it him, and the fool gaped. I tell you, Comrade Jackson, I feel like some lion that has been robbed of its cub. I feel as Marshall would feel if they took Snelgrove away from him, or as Peace might if he awoke one morning to find Plenty gone. Comrade Rossiter does his best. We still talk brokenly about Manchester United—they got routed in the first round of the Cup yesterday and Comrade Rossiter is wearing black—but it is not the same. I try work, but that is no good either. From ledger to ledger they hurry me, to stifle my regret. And when they win a smile from me, they think that I forget. But I don't. I am a broken man. That new exhibit they've got in your place is about as near to the Extreme Edge as anything I've ever seen. One of Nature's blighters. Well, well, I must away. Comrade Rossiter awaits me.'

Mike's successor, a youth of the name of Bristow, was causing Psmith a great deal of pensive melancholy. His worst defect—which he could not help—was that he was not Mike. His others—which he could—were numerous. His clothes were cut in a way that harrowed Psmith's sensitive soul every time he looked at them. The fact that he wore detachable cuffs, which he took off on beginning work and stacked in a glistening pile on the desk in front of him, was no proof of innate viciousness of disposition, but it prejudiced the Old Etonian against him. It was part of Psmith's philosophy that a man who wore detachable cuffs had passed beyond the limit of human toleration. In addition, Bristow wore a small black moustache and a ring and that, as Psmith informed Mike, put the lid on it.

Mike would sometimes stroll round to the Postage Department to listen to the conversations between the two. Bristow was always friendliness itself. He habitually addressed Psmith as Smithy, a fact which entertained Mike greatly but did not seem to amuse Psmith to any overwhelming extent. On the other hand, when, as he generally did, he called Mike 'Mister Cricketer', the humour of the thing appeared to elude Mike, though the mode of address always drew from Psmith a pale, wan smile, as of a broken heart made cheerful against its own inclination.

The net result of the coming of Bristow was that Psmith spent most of his time, when not actually oppressed by a rush of work, in the precincts of the Cash Department, talking to Mike and Mr Waller. The latter did not seem to share the dislike common among the other heads of departments of seeing his subordinates receiving visitors. Unless the work was really heavy, in which case a mild remonstrance escaped him, he offered no objection to Mike being at home to Psmith. It was this tolerance which sometimes got him into trouble with Mr Bickersdyke. The manager did not often perambulate the office, but he did occasionally, and the interview which ensued upon his finding Hutchinson, the underling in the Cash Department at that time, with his stool tilted comfortably against the wall, reading the sporting news from a pink paper to a friend from the Outward Bills Department who lay luxuriously on the floor beside him, did not rank among Mr Waller's pleasantest memories. But Mr Waller was too soft-hearted to interfere with his assistants unless it was absolutely necessary. The truth of the matter was that the New Asiatic Bank was over-staffed. There were too many men for the work. The London branch of the bank was really only a nursery. New men were constantly wanted in the Eastern branches, so they had to be put into the London branch to learn the business, whether there was any work for them to do or not.

It was after one of these visits of Psmith's that Mr Waller displayed a new and unsuspected side to his character. Psmith had come round in a state of some depression to discuss Bristow, as usual. Bristow, it seemed, had come to the bank that morning in a fancy waistcoat of so emphatic a colour-scheme that Psmith stoutly refused to sit in the same department with it.

'What with Comrades Bristow and Bickersdyke combined,' said Psmith plaintively, 'the work is becoming too hard for me. The whisper is beginning to circulate, "Psmith's number is up—As a reformer he is merely among those present. He is losing his dash." But what can I do? I cannot keep an eye on both of them at the same time. The moment I concentrate myself on Comrade Bickersdyke for a brief spell, and seem to be doing him a bit of good, what happens? Why, Comrade Bristow sneaks off and buys a sort of woollen sunset. I saw the thing unexpectedly. I tell you I was shaken. It is the suddenness of that waistcoat which hits you. It's discouraging, this sort of thing. I try always to think well of my fellow man. As an energetic Socialist, I do my best to see the good that is in him, but it's hard. Comrade Bristow's the most striking argument against the equality of man I've ever come across.'

Mr Waller intervened at this point.

'I think you must really let Jackson go on with his work, Smith,' he said. 'There seems to be too much talking.'

'My besetting sin,' said Psmith sadly. 'Well, well, I will go back and do my best to face it, but it's a tough job.'

He tottered wearily away in the direction of the Postage Department.

'Oh, Jackson,' said Mr Waller, 'will you kindly take my place for a few minutes? I must go round and see the Inward Bills about something. I shall be back very soon.'

Mike was becoming accustomed to deputizing for the cashier for short spaces of time. It generally happened that he had to do so once or twice a day. Strictly speaking, perhaps, Mr Waller was wrong to leave such an important task as the actual cashing of cheques to an inexperienced person of Mike's standing; but the New Asiatic Bank differed from most banks in that there was not a great deal of cross-counter work. People came in fairly frequently to cash cheques of two or three pounds, but it was rare that any very large dealings took place.

Having completed his business with the Inward Bills, Mr Waller made his way back by a circuitous route, taking in the Postage desk.

He found Psmith with a pale, set face, inscribing figures in a ledger. The Old Etonian greeted him with the faint smile of a persecuted saint who is determined to be cheerful even at the stake.

'Comrade Bristow,' he said.

'Hullo, Smithy?' said the other, turning.

Psmith sadly directed Mr Waller's attention to the waistcoat, which was certainly definite in its colouring.

'Nothing,' said Psmith. 'I only wanted to look at you.'

'Funny ass,' said Bristow, resuming his work. Psmith glanced at Mr Waller, as who should say, 'See what I have to put up with. And yet I do not give way.'

'Oh—er—Smith,' said Mr Waller, 'when you were talking to Jackson just now—'

'Say no more,' said Psmith. 'It shall not occur again. Why should I dislocate the work of your department in my efforts to win a sympathetic word? I will bear Comrade Bristow like a man here. After all, there are worse things at the Zoo.'

'No, no,' said Mr Waller hastily, 'I did not mean that. By all means pay us a visit now and then, if it does not interfere with your own work. But I noticed just now that you spoke to Bristow as Comrade Bristow.'

'It is too true,' said Psmith. 'I must correct myself of the habit. He will be getting above himself.'

'And when you were speaking to Jackson, you spoke of yourself as a Socialist.'

'Socialism is the passion of my life,' said Psmith.

Mr Waller's face grew animated. He stammered in his eagerness.

'I am delighted,' he said. 'Really, I am delighted. I also—'

'A fellow worker in the Cause?' said Psmith.

'Er—exactly.'

Psmith extended his hand gravely. Mr Waller shook it with enthusiasm.

'I have never liked to speak of it to anybody in the office,' said Mr Waller, 'but I, too, am heart and soul in the movement.'

'Yours for the Revolution?' said Psmith.

'Just so. Just so. Exactly. I was wondering—the fact is, I am in the habit of speaking on Sundays in the open air, and—'

'Hyde Park?'

'No. No. Clapham Common. It is—er—handier for me where I live. Now, as you are interested in the movement, I was thinking that perhaps you might care to come and hear me speak next Sunday. Of course, if you have nothing better to do.'

'I should like to excessively,' said Psmith.

'Excellent. Bring Jackson with you, and both of you come to supper afterwards, if you will.'

'Thanks very much.'

'Perhaps you would speak yourself?'

'No,' said Psmith. 'No. I think not. My Socialism is rather of the practical sort. I seldom speak. But it would be a treat to listen to you. What—er—what type of oratory is yours?'

'Oh, well,' said Mr Waller, pulling nervously at his beard, 'of course I—. Well, I am perhaps a little bitter—'

'Yes, yes.'

'A little mordant and ironical.'

'You would be,' agreed Psmith. 'I shall look forward to Sunday with every fibre quivering. And Comrade Jackson shall be at my side.'

'Excellent,' said Mr Waller. 'I will go and tell him now.'

15. Stirring Times on the Common

'The first thing to do,' said Psmith, 'is to ascertain that such a place as Clapham Common really exists. One has heard of it, of course, but has its existence ever been proved? I think not. Having accomplished that, we must then try to find out how to get to it. I should say at a venture that it would necessitate a sea-voyage. On the other hand, Comrade Waller, who is a native of the spot, seems to find no difficulty in rolling to the office every morning. Therefore—you follow me, Jackson?—it must be in England. In that case, we will take a taximeter cab, and go out into the unknown, hand in hand, trusting to luck.'

'I expect you could get there by tram,' said Mike.

Psmith suppressed a slight shudder.

'I fear, Comrade Jackson,' he said, 'that the old noblesse oblige traditions of the Psmiths would not allow me to do that. No. We will stroll gently, after a light lunch, to Trafalgar Square, and hail a taxi.'

'Beastly expensive.'

'But with what an object! Can any expenditure be called excessive which enables us to hear Comrade Waller being mordant and ironical at the other end?'

'It's a rum business,' said Mike. 'I hope the dickens he won't mix us up in it. We should look frightful fools.'

'I may possibly say a few words,' said Psmith carelessly, 'if the spirit moves me. Who am I that I should deny people a simple pleasure?'

Mike looked alarmed.

'Look here,' he said, 'I say, if you *are* going to play the goat, for goodness' sake don't go lugging me into it. I've got heaps of troubles without that.'

Psmith waved the objection aside.

'You,' he said, 'will be one of the large, and, I hope, interested audience. Nothing more. But it is quite possible that the spirit may not move me. I may not feel inspired to speak. I am not one of those who love speaking for speaking's sake. If I have no message for the many-headed, I shall remain silent.'

'Then I hope the dickens you won't have,' said Mike. Of all things he hated most being conspicuous before a crowd—except at cricket, which was a different thing—and he had an uneasy feeling that Psmith would rather like it than otherwise.

'We shall see,' said Psmith absently. 'Of course, if in the vein, I might do something big in the way of oratory. I am a plain, blunt man, but I feel convinced that, given the opportunity, I should haul up my slacks to some effect. But—well, we shall see. We shall see.'

And with this ghastly state of doubt Mike had to be content.

It was with feelings of apprehension that he accompanied Psmith from the flat to Trafalgar Square in search of a cab which should convey them to Clapham Common.

They were to meet Mr Waller at the edge of the Common nearest the old town of Clapham. On the journey down Psmith was inclined to be *debonnaire*. Mike, on the other hand, was silent and apprehensive. He knew enough of Psmith to know that, if half an opportunity were offered him, he would extract entertainment from this affair after his own fashion; and then the odds were that he himself would be dragged into it. Perhaps—his scalp bristled at the mere idea—he would even be let in for a speech.

This grisly thought had hardly come into his head, when Psmith spoke.

'I'm not half sure,' he said thoughtfully, 'I sha'n't call on you for a speech, Comrade Jackson.'

'Look here, Psmith—' began Mike agitatedly.

'I don't know. I think your solid, incisive style would rather go down with the masses. However, we shall see, we shall see.'

Mike reached the Common in a state of nervous collapse.

Mr Waller was waiting for them by the railings near the pond. The apostle of the Revolution was clad soberly in black, except for a tie of vivid crimson. His eyes shone with the light of enthusiasm, vastly different from the mild glow of amiability which they exhibited for six days in every week. The man was transformed.

'Here you are,' he said. 'Here you are. Excellent. You are in good time. Comrades Wotherspoon and Prebble have already begun to speak. I shall commence now that you have come. This is the way. Over by these trees.'

They made their way towards a small clump of trees, near which a fair-sized crowd had already begun to collect. Evidently listening to the speakers was one of Clapham's fashionable Sunday amusements. Mr Waller talked and gesticulated incessantly as he walked. Psmith's demeanour was perhaps a shade patronizing, but he displayed interest. Mike proceeded to the meeting with the air of an about-to-be-washed dog. He was loathing the whole business with a heartiness worthy of a better cause. Somehow, he felt he was going to be made to look a fool before the afternoon was over. But he registered a vow that nothing should drag him on to the small platform which had been erected for the benefit of the speaker.

As they drew nearer, the voices of Comrades Wotherspoon and Prebble became more audible. They had been audible all the time, very much so, but now they grew in volume. Comrade Wotherspoon was a tall, thin man with side-whiskers and a high voice. He scattered his aitches as a fountain its sprays in a strong wind. He was very earnest. Comrade Prebble was earnest, too. Perhaps even more so than Comrade Wotherspoon. He was handicapped to some extent, however, by not having a palate. This gave to his profoundest thoughts a certain weirdness, as if they had been uttered in an unknown tongue. The crowd was thickest round his platform. The grown-up section plainly regarded him as a comedian, pure and simple, and roared with happy laughter when he urged them to march upon Park Lane and loot the same without mercy or scruple. The children were more doubtful. Several had broken down, and been led away in tears.

When Mr Waller got up to speak on platform number three, his audience consisted at first only of Psmith, Mike, and a fox-terrier. Gradually however, he attracted others. After wavering for a while, the crowd finally decided that he was worth hearing. He had a method of his own. Lacking the natural gifts which marked Comrade Prebble out as an entertainer, he made up for this by his activity. Where his colleagues stood comparatively still, Mr Waller behaved with the vivacity generally supposed to belong only to peas on shovels and cats on hot bricks. He crouched to denounce the House of Lords. He bounded from side to side while dissecting the methods of the plutocrats. During an impassioned onslaught on the monarchical system he stood on one leg and hopped. This was more the sort of thing the crowd had come to see. Comrade Wotherspoon found himself deserted, and even Comrade Prebble's shortcomings in the way of palate were insufficient to keep his flock together. The entire strength of the audience gathered in front of the third platform.

Mike, separated from Psmith by the movement of the crowd, listened with a growing depression. That feeling which attacks a sensitive person sometimes at the theatre when somebody is making himself ridiculous on the stage—the illogical feeling that it is he and not the actor who is floundering—had come over him in a wave. He liked Mr Waller, and it made his gorge rise to see him exposing himself to the jeers of a crowd. The fact that Mr Waller himself did not know that they were jeers, but mistook them for applause, made it no better. Mike felt vaguely furious.

His indignation began to take a more personal shape when the speaker, branching off from the main subject of Socialism, began to touch on temperance. There was no particular reason why Mr Waller should have introduced the subject of temperance, except that he happened to be an enthusiast. He linked it on to his remarks on Socialism by attributing the lethargy of the masses to their fondness for alcohol; and the crowd, which had been inclined rather to pat itself on the back during the assaults on Rank and Property, finding itself assailed in its turn, resented it. They were there to listen to speakers telling them that they were the finest fellows on earth, not pointing out their little failings to them. The feeling of the meeting became hostile. The jeers grew more frequent and less good-tempered.

'Comrade Waller means well,' said a voice in Mike's ear, 'but if he shoots it at them like this much more there'll be a bit of an imbroglio.'

'Look here, Smith,' said Mike quickly, 'can't we stop him? These chaps are getting fed up, and they look bargees enough to do anything. They'll be going for him or something soon.'

'How can we switch off the flow? I don't see. The man is wound up. He means to get it off his chest if it snows. I feel we are by way of being in the soup once more, Comrade Jackson. We can only sit tight and look on.'

The crowd was becoming more threatening every minute. A group of young men of the loafer class who stood near Mike were especially fertile in comment. Psmith's eyes were on the speaker; but Mike was watching this group closely. Suddenly he saw one of them, a thick-set youth wearing a cloth cap and no collar, stoop.

When he rose again there was a stone in his hand.

The sight acted on Mike like a spur. Vague rage against nobody in particular had been simmering in him for half an hour. Now it concentrated itself on the cloth-capped one.

Mr Waller paused momentarily before renewing his harangue. The man in the cloth cap raised his hand. There was a swirl in the crowd, and the first thing that Psmith saw as he turned was Mike seizing the would-be marksman round the neck and hurling him to the ground, after the manner of a forward at football tackling an opponent during a line-out from touch.

There is one thing which will always distract the attention of a crowd from any speaker, and that is a dispute between two of its units. Mr Waller's views on temperance were forgotten in an instant. The audience surged round Mike and his opponent.

The latter had scrambled to his feet now, and was looking round for his assailant.

'That's 'im, Bill!' cried eager voices, indicating Mike.

''E's the bloke wot 'it yer, Bill,' said others, more precise in detail.

Bill advanced on Mike in a sidelong, crab-like manner.

''Oo're you, I should like to know?' said Bill.

Mike, rightly holding that this was merely a rhetorical question and that Bill had no real thirst for information as to his family history, made no reply. Or, rather, the reply he made was not verbal. He waited till his questioner was within range, and then hit him in the eye. A reply far more satisfactory, if not to Bill himself, at any rate to the interested onlookers, than any flow of words.

A contented sigh went up from the crowd. Their Sunday afternoon was going to be spent just as they considered Sunday afternoons should be spent.

'Give us your coat,' said Psmith briskly, 'and try and get it over quick. Don't go in for any fancy sparring. Switch it on, all you know, from the start. I'll keep a thoughtful eye open to see that none of his friends and relations join in.'

Outwardly Psmith was unruffled, but inwardly he was not feeling so composed. An ordinary turn-up before an impartial crowd which could be relied upon to preserve the etiquette of these matters was one thing. As regards the actual little dispute with the cloth-capped Bill, he felt that he could rely on Mike to handle it satisfactorily. But there was no knowing how long the crowd would be content to remain mere spectators. There was no doubt which way its sympathies lay. Bill, now stripped of his coat and sketching out in a hoarse voice a scenario of what he intended to do—knocking Mike down and stamping him into the mud was one of the milder feats he promised to perform for the entertainment of an indulgent audience—was plainly the popular favourite.

Psmith, though he did not show it, was more than a little apprehensive.

Mike, having more to occupy his mind in the immediate present, was not anxious concerning the future. He had the great advantage over Psmith of having lost his temper. Psmith could look on the situation as a whole, and count the risks and possibilities. Mike could only see Bill shuffling towards him with his head down and shoulders bunched.

'Gow it, Bill!' said someone.

'Pliy up, the Arsenal!' urged a voice on the outskirts of the crowd.

A chorus of encouragement from kind friends in front: 'Step up, Bill!'

And Bill stepped.

16. Further Developments

Bill (surname unknown) was not one of your ultra-scientific fighters. He did not favour the American crouch and the artistic feint. He had a style wholly his own. It seemed to have been modelled partly on a tortoise and partly on a windmill. His head he appeared to be trying to conceal between his shoulders, and he whirled his arms alternately in circular sweeps.

Mike, on the other hand, stood upright and hit straight, with the result that he hurt his knuckles very much on his opponent's skull, without seeming to disturb the latter to any great extent. In the process he received one of the windmill swings on the left ear. The crowd, strong pro-Billites, raised a cheer.

This maddened Mike. He assumed the offensive. Bill, satisfied for the moment with his success, had stepped back, and was indulging in some fancy sparring, when Mike sprang upon him like a panther. They clinched, and Mike, who had got the under grip, hurled Bill forcibly against a stout man who looked like a publican. The two fell in a heap, Bill underneath.

At the same time Bill's friends joined in.

The first intimation Mike had of this was a violent blow across the shoulders with a walking-stick. Even if he had been wearing his overcoat, the blow would have hurt. As he was in his jacket it hurt more than anything he had ever experienced in his life. He leapt up with a yell, but Psmith was there before him. Mike saw his assailant lift the stick again, and then collapse as the old Etonian's right took him under the chin.

He darted to Psmith's side.

'This is no place for us,' observed the latter sadly. 'Shift ho, I think. Come on.'

They dashed simultaneously for the spot where the crowd was thinnest. The ring which had formed round Mike and Bill had broken up as the result of the intervention of Bill's allies, and at the spot for which they ran only two men were standing. And these had apparently made up their minds that neutrality was the best policy, for they made no movement to stop them. Psmith and Mike charged through the gap, and raced for the road.

The suddenness of the move gave them just the start they needed. Mike looked over his shoulder. The crowd, to a man, seemed to be following. Bill, excavated from beneath the publican, led the field. Lying a good second came a band of three, and after them the rest in a bunch.

16. Further Developments

They reached the road in this order.

Some fifty yards down the road was a stationary tram. In the ordinary course of things it would probably have moved on long before Psmith and Mike could have got to it; but the conductor, a man with sporting blood in him, seeing what appeared to be the finish of some Marathon Race, refrained from giving the signal, and moved out into the road to observe events more clearly, at the same time calling to the driver, who joined him. Passengers on the roof stood up to get a good view. There was some cheering.

Psmith and Mike reached the tram ten yards to the good; and, if it had been ready to start then, all would have been well. But Bill and his friends had arrived while the driver and conductor were both out in the road.

The affair now began to resemble the doings of Horatius on the bridge. Psmith and Mike turned to bay on the platform at the foot of the tram steps. Bill, leading by three yards, sprang on to it, grabbed Mike, and fell with him on to the road. Psmith, descending with a dignity somewhat lessened by the fact that his hat was on the side of his head, was in time to engage the runners-up.

Psmith, as pugilist, lacked something of the calm majesty which characterized him in the more peaceful moments of life, but he was undoubtedly effective. Nature had given him an enormous reach and a lightness on his feet remarkable in one of his size; and at some time in his career he appeared to have learned how to use his hands. The first of the three runners, the walking-stick manipulator, had the misfortune to charge straight into the old Etonian's left. It was a well-timed blow, and the force of it, added to the speed at which the victim was running, sent him on to the pavement, where he spun round and sat down. In the subsequent proceedings he took no part.

The other two attacked Psmith simultaneously, one on each side. In doing so, the one on the left tripped over Mike and Bill, who were still in the process of sorting themselves out, and fell, leaving Psmith free to attend to the other. He was a tall, weedy youth. His conspicuous features were a long nose and a light yellow waistcoat. Psmith hit him on the former with his left and on the latter with his right. The long youth emitted a gurgle, and collided with Bill, who had wrenched himself free from Mike and staggered to his feet. Bill, having received a second blow in the eye during the course of his interview on the road with Mike, was not feeling himself. Mistaking the other for an enemy, he proceeded to smite him in the parts about the jaw. He had just upset him, when a stern official voice observed, "Ere, now, what's all this?'

There is no more unfailing corrective to a scene of strife than the 'What's all this?' of the London policeman. Bill abandoned his intention of stamping on the prostrate one, and the latter, sitting up, blinked and was silent.

'What's all this?' asked the policeman again. Psmith, adjusting his hat at the correct angle again, undertook the explanations.

'A distressing scene, officer,' he said. 'A case of that unbridled brawling which is, alas, but too common in our London streets. These two, possibly till now the closest friends, fall out over some point, probably of the most trivial nature, and what happens? They brawl. They—'

'He 'it me,' said the long youth, dabbing at his face with a handkerchief and pointing an accusing finger at Psmith, who regarded him through his eyeglass with a look in which pity and censure were nicely blended.

Bill, meanwhile, circling round restlessly, in the apparent hope of getting past the Law and having another encounter with Mike, expressed himself in a stream of language which drew stern reproof from the shocked constable.

'You 'op it,' concluded the man in blue. 'That's what you do. You 'op it.'

'I should,' said Psmith kindly. 'The officer is speaking in your best interests. A man of taste and discernment, he knows what is best. His advice is good, and should be followed.'

The constable seemed to notice Psmith for the first time. He turned and stared at him. Psmith's praise had not had the effect of softening him. His look was one of suspicion.

'And what might *you* have been up to?' he inquired coldly. 'This man says you hit him.'

Psmith waved the matter aside.

'Purely in self-defence,' he said, 'purely in self-defence. What else could the man of spirit do? A mere tap to discourage an aggressive movement.'

The policeman stood silent, weighing matters in the balance. He produced a notebook and sucked his pencil. Then he called the conductor of the tram as a witness.

'A brainy and admirable step,' said Psmith, approvingly. 'This rugged, honest man, all unused to verbal subtleties, shall give us his plain account of what happened. After which, as I presume this tram—little as I know of the habits of trams—has got to go somewhere today, I would suggest that we all separated and moved on.'

He took two half-crowns from his pocket, and began to clink them meditatively together. A slight softening of the frigidity of the constable's manner became noticeable. There was a milder beam in the eyes which gazed into Psmith's.

Nor did the conductor seem altogether uninfluenced by the sight.

The conductor deposed that he had bin on the point of pushing on, seeing as how he'd hung abart long enough, when he see'd them two gents, the long 'un with the heye-glass (Psmith bowed) and t'other 'un, a-legging of it dahn the road towards him, with the other blokes pelting after 'em. He added that, when they reached the trem, the two gents had got aboard, and was then set upon by the blokes. And after that, he concluded, well, there was a bit of a scrap, and that's how it was.

'Lucidly and excellently put,' said Psmith. 'That is just how it was. Comrade Jackson, I fancy we leave the court without a stain on our characters. We win through. Er—constable, we have given you a great deal of trouble. Possibly—?'

'Thank you, sir.' There was a musical clinking. 'Now then, all of you, you 'op it. You're all bin poking your noses in 'ere long enough. Pop off. Get on with that tram, conductor.' Psmith and Mike settled themselves in a seat on the roof. When the conductor came along, Psmith gave him half a crown, and asked after his wife and the little ones at home. The conductor thanked goodness that he was a bachelor, punched the tickets, and retired.

'Subject for a historical picture,' said Psmith. 'Wounded leaving the field after the Battle of Clapham Common. How are your injuries, Comrade Jackson?'

'My back's hurting like blazes,' said Mike. 'And my ear's all sore where that chap got me. Anything the matter with you?'

'Physically,' said Psmith, 'no. Spiritually much. Do you realize, Comrade Jackson, the thing that has happened? I am riding in a tram. I, Psmith, have paid a penny for a ticket on a tram. If this should get about the clubs! I tell you, Comrade Jackson, no such crisis has ever occurred before in the course of my career.'

'You can always get off, you know,' said Mike.

'He thinks of everything,' said Psmith, admiringly. 'You have touched the spot with an unerring finger. Let us descend. I observe in the distance a cab. That looks to me more the sort of thing we want. Let us go and parley with the driver.'

17. Sunday Supper

The cab took them back to the flat, at considerable expense, and Psmith requested Mike to make tea, a performance in which he himself was interested purely as a spectator. He had views on the subject of tea-making which he liked to expound from an armchair or sofa, but he never got further than this. Mike, his back throbbing dully from the blow he had received, and feeling more than a little sore all over, prepared the Etna, fetched the milk, and finally produced the finished article.

Psmith sipped meditatively.

'How pleasant,' he said, 'after strife is rest. We shouldn't have appreciated this simple cup of tea had our sensibilities remained unstirred this afternoon. We can now sit at our ease, like warriors after the fray, till the time comes for setting out to Comrade Waller's once more.'

Mike looked up.

'What! You don't mean to say you're going to sweat out to Clapham again?'

'Undoubtedly. Comrade Waller is expecting us to supper.'

'What absolute rot! We can't fag back there.'

'Noblesse oblige. The cry has gone round the Waller household, "Jackson and Psmith are coming to supper," and we cannot disappoint them now. Already the fatted blanc-mange has been killed, and the table creaks beneath what's left of the midday beef. We must be there; besides, don't you want to see how the poor man is? Probably we shall find him in the act of emitting his last breath. I expect he was lynched by the enthusiastic mob.'

'Not much,' grinned Mike. 'They were too busy with us. All right, I'll come if you really want me to, but it's awful rot.'

One of the many things Mike could never understand in Psmith was his fondness for getting into atmospheres that were not his own. He would go out of his way to do this. Mike, like most boys of his age, was never really happy and at his ease except in the presence of those of his own years and class. Psmith, on the contrary, seemed to be bored by them, and infinitely preferred talking to somebody who lived in quite another world. Mike was not a snob. He simply had not the ability to be at his ease with people in another class from his own. He did not know what to talk to them about, unless they were cricket professionals. With them he was never at a loss.

But Psmith was different. He could get on with anyone. He seemed to have the gift of entering into their minds and seeing things from their point of view.

As regarded Mr Waller, Mike liked him personally, and was prepared, as we have seen, to undertake considerable risks in his defence; but he loathed with all his heart and soul the idea of supper at his house. He knew that he would have nothing to say. Whereas Psmith gave him the impression of looking forward to the thing as a treat.

* * * * *

The house where Mr Waller lived was one of a row of semi-detached villas on the north side of the Common. The door was opened to them by their host himself. So far from looking battered and emitting last breaths, he appeared particularly spruce. He had just returned from Church, and was still wearing his gloves and tall hat. He squeaked with surprise when he saw who were standing on the mat.

'Why, dear me, dear me,' he said. 'Here you are! I have been wondering what had happened to you. I was afraid that you might have been seriously hurt. I was afraid those ruffians might have injured you. When last I saw you, you were being—'

'Chivvied,' interposed Psmith, with dignified melancholy. 'Do not let us try to wrap the fact up in pleasant words. We were being chivvied. We were legging it with the infuriated mob at our heels. An ignominious position for a Shropshire Psmith, but, after all, Napoleon did the same.'

'But what happened? I could not see. I only know that quite suddenly the people seemed to stop listening to me, and all gathered round you and Jackson. And then I saw that Jackson was engaged in a fight with a young man.'

'Comrade Jackson, I imagine, having heard a great deal about all men being equal, was anxious to test the theory, and see whether Comrade Bill was as good a man as he was. The experiment was broken off prematurely, but I personally should be inclined to say that Comrade Jackson had a shade the better of the exchanges.'

Mr Waller looked with interest at Mike, who shuffled and felt awkward. He was hoping that Psmith would say nothing about the reason of his engaging Bill in combat. He had an uneasy feeling that Mr Waller's gratitude would be effusive and overpowering, and he did not wish to pose as the brave young hero. There are moments when one does not feel equal to the *role*.

Fortunately, before Mr Waller had time to ask any further questions, the supper-bell sounded, and they went into the dining-room.

Sunday supper, unless done on a large and informal scale, is probably the most depressing meal in existence. There is a chill discomfort in the round of beef, an icy severity about the open jam tart. The blancmange shivers miserably.

Spirituous liquor helps to counteract the influence of these things, and so does exhilarating conversation. Unfortunately, at Mr Waller's table there was neither. The cashier's views on temperance were not merely for the platform; they extended to the home. And the company was not of the exhilarating sort. Besides Psmith and Mike and their host, there were four people present—Comrade Prebble, the orator; a young man of the name of Richards; Mr Waller's niece, answering to the name of Ada, who was engaged to Mr Richards; and Edward.

Edward was Mr Waller's son. He was ten years old, wore a very tight Eton suit, and had the peculiarly loathsome expression which a snub nose sometimes gives to the young.

It would have been plain to the most casual observer that Mr Waller was fond and proud of his son. The cashier was a widower, and after five minutes' acquaintance with Edward, Mike felt strongly that Mrs Waller was the lucky one. Edward sat next to Mike, and showed a tendency to concentrate his conversation on him. Psmith, at the opposite end of the table, beamed in a fatherly manner upon the pair through his eyeglass.

Mike got on with small girls reasonably well. He preferred them at a distance, but, if cornered by them, could put up a fairly good show. Small boys, however, filled him with a sort of frozen horror. It was his view that a boy should not be exhibited publicly until he reached an age when he might be in the running for some sort of colours at a public school.

Edward was one of those well-informed small boys. He opened on Mike with the first mouthful.

'Do you know the principal exports of Marseilles?' he inquired.

'What?' said Mike coldly.

'Do you know the principal exports of Marseilles? I do.'

'Oh?' said Mike.

'Yes. Do you know the capital of Madagascar?'

Mike, as crimson as the beef he was attacking, said he did not.

'I do.'

'Oh?' said Mike.

'Who was the first king—'

'You mustn't worry Mr Jackson, Teddy,' said Mr Waller, with a touch of pride in his voice, as who should say 'There are not many boys of his age, I can tell you, who *could* worry you with questions like that.'

'No, no, he likes it,' said Psmith, unnecessarily. 'He likes it. I always hold that much may be learned by casual chit-chat across the dinner-table. I owe much of my own grasp of—'

'I bet *you* don't know what's the capital of Madagascar,' interrupted Mike rudely.

'I do,' said Edward. 'I can tell you the kings of Israel?' he added, turning to Mike. He seemed to have no curiosity as to the extent of Psmith's knowledge. Mike's appeared to fascinate him.

Mike helped himself to beetroot in moody silence.

His mouth was full when Comrade Prebble asked him a question. Comrade Prebble, as has been pointed out in an earlier part of the narrative, was a good chap, but had no roof to his mouth.

'I beg your pardon?' said Mike.

Comrade Prebble repeated his observation. Mike looked helplessly at Psmith, but Psmith's eyes were on his plate.

Mike felt he must venture on some answer.

'No,' he said decidedly.

Comrade Prebble seemed slightly taken aback. There was an awkward pause. Then Mr Waller, for whom his fellow Socialist's methods of conversation held no mysteries, interpreted.

'The mustard, Prebble? Yes, yes. Would you mind passing Prebble the mustard, Mr Jackson?'

'Oh, sorry,' gasped Mike, and, reaching out, upset the water-jug into the open jam-tart.

Through the black mist which rose before his eyes as he leaped to his feet and stammered apologies came the dispassionate voice of Master Edward Waller reminding him that mustard was first introduced into Peru by Cortez.

His host was all courtesy and consideration. He passed the matter off genially. But life can never be quite the same after you have upset a water-jug into an open jam-tart at the table of a comparative stranger. Mike's nerve had gone. He ate on, but he was a broken man.

At the other end of the table it became gradually apparent that things were not going on altogether as they should have done. There was a sort of bleakness in the atmosphere. Young Mr Richards was looking like a stuffed fish, and the face of Mr Waller's niece was cold and set.

'Why, come, come, Ada,' said Mr Waller, breezily, 'what's the matter? You're eating nothing. What's George been saying to you?' he added jocularly.

'Thank you, uncle Robert,' replied Ada precisely, 'there's nothing the matter. Nothing that Mr Richards can say to me can upset me.'

'Mr Richards!' echoed Mr Waller in astonishment. How was he to know that, during the walk back from church, the world had been transformed, George had become Mr Richards, and all was over?

'I assure you, Ada—' began that unfortunate young man. Ada turned a frigid shoulder towards him.

'Come, come,' said Mr Waller disturbed. 'What's all this? What's all this?'

His niece burst into tears and left the room.

If there is anything more embarrassing to a guest than a family row, we have yet to hear of it. Mike, scarlet to the extreme edges of his ears, concentrated himself on his plate. Comrade Prebble made a great many remarks, which were probably illuminating, if they could have been understood. Mr Waller looked, astonished, at Mr Richards. Mr Richards, pink but dogged, loosened his collar, but said nothing. Psmith, leaning forward, asked Master Edward Waller his opinion on the Licensing Bill.

'We happened to have a word or two,' said Mr Richards at length, 'on the way home from church on the subject of Women's Suffrage.'

'That fatal topic!' murmured Psmith.

'In Australia—' began Master Edward Waller.

'I was rayther—well, rayther facetious about it,' continued Mr Richards.

Psmith clicked his tongue sympathetically.

'In Australia—' said Edward.

'I went talking on, laughing and joking, when all of a sudden she flew out at me. How was I to know she was 'eart and soul in the movement? You never told me,' he added accusingly to his host.

'In Australia—' said Edward.

'I'll go and try and get her round. How was I to know?'

Mr Richards thrust back his chair and bounded from the room.

'Now, iawinyaw, iear oiler—' said Comrade Prebble judicially, but was interrupted.

'How very disturbing!' said Mr Waller. 'I am so sorry that this should have happened. Ada is such a touchy, sensitive girl. She—'

'In Australia,' said Edward in even tones, 'they've *got* Women's Suffrage already. Did *you* know that?' he said to Mike.

Mike made no answer. His eyes were fixed on his plate. A bead of perspiration began to roll down his forehead. If his feelings could have been ascertained at that moment, they would have been summed up in the words, 'Death, where is thy sting?'

18. Psmith Makes a Discovery

'Women,' said Psmith, helping himself to trifle, and speaking with the air of one launched upon his special subject, 'are, one must recollect, like—like—er, well, in fact, just so. Passing on lightly from that conclusion, let us turn for a moment to the Rights of Property, in connection with which Comrade Prebble and yourself had so much that was interesting to say this afternoon. Perhaps you'—he bowed in Comrade Prebble's direction—'would resume, for the benefit of Comrade Jackson—a novice in the Cause, but earnest—your very lucid—'

Comrade Prebble beamed, and took the floor. Mike began to realize that, till now, he had never known what boredom meant. There had been moments in his life which had been less interesting than other moments, but nothing to touch this for agony. Comrade Prebble's address streamed on like water rushing over a weir. Every now and then there was a word or two which was recognizable, but this happened so rarely that it amounted to little. Sometimes Mr Waller would interject a remark, but not often. He seemed to be of the opinion that Comrade Prebble's was the master mind and that to add anything to his views would be in the nature of painting the lily and gilding the refined gold. Mike himself said nothing. Psmith and Edward were equally silent. The former sat like one in a trance, thinking his own thoughts, while Edward, who, prospecting on the sideboard, had located a rich biscuit-mine, was too occupied for speech.

After about twenty minutes, during which Mike's discomfort changed to a dull resignation, Mr Waller suggested a move to the drawing-room, where Ada, he said, would play some hymns.

The prospect did not dazzle Mike, but any change, he thought, must be for the better. He had sat staring at the ruin of the blancmange so long that it had begun to hypnotize him. Also, the move had the excellent result of eliminating the snub-nosed Edward, who was sent to bed. His last words were in the form of a question, addressed to Mike, on the subject of the hypotenuse and the square upon the same.

'A remarkably intelligent boy,' said Psmith. 'You must let him come to tea at our flat one day. I may not be in myself—I have many duties which keep me away—but Comrade Jackson is sure to be there, and will be delighted to chat with him.'

On the way upstairs Mike tried to get Psmith to himself for a moment to suggest the advisability of an early departure; but Psmith was in close conversation with his host. Mike was left to Comrade Prebble, who, apparently, had only touched the fringe of his subject in his lecture in the dining-room.

When Mr Waller had predicted hymns in the drawing-room, he had been too sanguine (or too pessimistic). Of Ada, when they arrived, there were no signs. It seemed that she had gone straight to bed. Young Mr Richards was sitting on the sofa, moodily turning the leaves of a photograph album, which contained portraits of Master Edward Waller in geometrically progressing degrees of repulsiveness—here, in frocks, looking like a gargoyle; there, in sailor suit, looking like nothing on earth. The inspection of these was obviously deepening Mr Richards' gloom, but he proceeded doggedly with it.

Comrade Prebble backed the reluctant Mike into a corner, and, like the Ancient Mariner, held him with a glittering eye. Psmith and Mr Waller, in the opposite corner, were looking at something with their heads close together. Mike definitely abandoned all hope of a rescue from Psmith, and tried to buoy himself up with the reflection that this could not last for ever.

Hours seemed to pass, and then at last he heard Psmith's voice saying good-bye to his host.

He sprang to his feet. Comrade Prebble was in the middle of a sentence, but this was no time for polished courtesy. He felt that he must get away, and at once. 'I fear,' Psmith was saying, 'that we must tear ourselves away. We have greatly enjoyed our evening. You must look us up at our flat one day, and bring Comrade Prebble. If I am not in, Comrade Jackson is certain to be, and he will be more than delighted to hear Comrade Prebble speak further on the subject of which he is such a master.' Comrade Prebble was understood to say that he would certainly come. Mr Waller beamed. Mr Richards, still steeped in gloom, shook hands in silence.

Out in the road, with the front door shut behind them, Mike spoke his mind.

'Look here, Smith,' he said definitely, 'if being your confidential secretary and adviser is going to let me in for any more of that sort of thing, you can jolly well accept my resignation.'

'The orgy was not to your taste?' said Psmith sympathetically.

Mike laughed. One of those short, hollow, bitter laughs.

'I am at a loss, Comrade Jackson,' said Psmith, 'to understand your attitude. You fed sumptuously. You had fun with the crockery—that knockabout act of yours with the water-jug was alone worth the money—and you had the advantage of listening to the views of a master of his subject. What more do you want?'

'What on earth did you land me with that man Prebble for?'

'Land you! Why, you courted his society. I had practically to drag you away from him. When I got up to say good-bye, you were listening to him with bulging eyes. I never saw such a picture of rapt attention. Do you mean to tell me, Comrade Jackson, that your appearance belied you, that you were not interested? Well, well. How we misread our fellow creatures.'

'I think you might have come and lent a hand with Prebble. It was a bit thick.'

'I was too absorbed with Comrade Waller. We were talking of things of vital moment. However, the night is yet young. We will take this cab, wend our way to the West, seek a cafe, and cheer ourselves with light refreshments.'

Arrived at a cafe whose window appeared to be a sort of museum of every kind of German sausage, they took possession of a vacant table and ordered coffee. Mike soon found himself soothed by his bright surroundings, and gradually his impressions of blancmange, Edward, and Comrade Prebble faded from his mind. Psmith, meanwhile, was preserving an unusual silence, being deep in a large square book of the sort in which Press cuttings are pasted. As Psmith scanned its contents a curious smile lit up his face. His reflections seemed to be of an agreeable nature.

'Hullo,' said Mike, 'what have you got hold of there? Where did you get that?'

'Comrade Waller very kindly lent it to me. He showed it to me after supper, knowing how enthusiastically I was attached to the Cause. Had you been less tensely wrapped up in Comrade Prebble's conversation, I would have desired you to step across and join us. However, you now have your opportunity.'

'But what is it?' asked Mike.

'It is the record of the meetings of the Tulse Hill Parliament,' said Psmith impressively. 'A faithful record of all they said, all the votes of confidence they passed in the Government, and also all the nasty knocks they gave it from time to time.'

'What on earth's the Tulse Hill Parliament?'

'It is, alas,' said Psmith in a grave, sad voice, 'no more. In life it was beautiful, but now it has done the Tom Bowling act. It has gone aloft. We are dealing, Comrade Jackson, not with the live, vivid present, but with the far-off, rusty past. And yet, in a way, there is a touch of the live, vivid present mixed up in it.'

'I don't know what the dickens you're talking about,' said Mike. 'Let's have a look, anyway.'

Psmith handed him the volume, and, leaning back, sipped his coffee, and watched him. At first Mike's face was bored and blank, but suddenly an interested look came into it.

'Aha!' said Psmith.

'Who's Bickersdyke? Anything to do with our Bickersdyke?'

'No other than our genial friend himself.'

Mike turned the pages, reading a line or two on each.

'Hullo!' he said, chuckling. 'He lets himself go a bit, doesn't he!'

'He does,' acknowledged Psmith. 'A fiery, passionate nature, that of Comrade Bickersdyke.'

'He's simply cursing the Government here. Giving them frightful beans.'

Psmith nodded.

'I noticed the fact myself.'

'But what's it all about?'

'As far as I can glean from Comrade Waller,' said Psmith, 'about twenty years ago, when he and Comrade Bickersdyke worked hand-in-hand as fellow clerks at the New Asiatic, they were both members of the Tulse Hill Parliament, that powerful institution. At that time Comrade Bickersdyke was as fruity a Socialist as Comrade Waller is now. Only, apparently, as he began to get on a bit in the world, he altered his views to some extent as regards the iniquity of freezing on to a decent share of the doubloons. And that, you see, is where the dim and rusty past begins to get mixed up with the live, vivid present. If any tactless person were to publish those very able speeches made by Comrade Bickersdyke when a bulwark of the Tulse Hill Parliament, our revered chief would be more or less caught bending, if I may employ the expression, as regards his chances of getting in as Unionist candidate at Kenningford. You follow me, Watson? I rather fancy the light-hearted electors of Kenningford, from what I have seen of their rather acute sense of humour, would be, as it were, all over it. It would be very, very trying for Comrade Bickersdyke if these speeches of his were to get about.'

'You aren't going to—!'

'I shall do nothing rashly. I shall merely place this handsome volume among my treasured books. I shall add it to my "Books that have helped me" series. Because I fancy that, in an emergency, it may not be at all a bad thing to have about me. And now,' he concluded, 'as the hour is getting late, perhaps we had better be shoving off for home.'

19. The Illness of Edward

Life in a bank is at its pleasantest in the winter. When all the world outside is dark and damp and cold, the light and warmth of the place are comforting. There is a pleasant air of solidity about the interior of a bank. The green shaded lamps look cosy. And, the outside world offering so few attractions, the worker, perched on his stool, feels that he is not so badly off after all. It is when the days are long and the sun beats hot on the pavement, and everything shouts to him how splendid it is out in the country, that he begins to grow restless.

Mike, except for a fortnight at the beginning of his career in the New Asiatic Bank, had not had to stand the test of sunshine. At present, the weather being cold and dismal, he was almost entirely contented. Now that he had got into the swing of his work, the days passed very quickly; and with his life after office-hours he had no fault to find at all.

His life was very regular. He would arrive in the morning just in time to sign his name in the attendance-book before it was removed to the accountant's room. That was at ten o'clock. From ten to eleven he would potter. There was nothing going on at that time in his department, and Mr Waller seemed to take it for granted that he should stroll off to the Postage Department and talk to Psmith, who had generally some fresh grievance against the ring-wearing Bristow to air. From eleven to half past twelve he would put in a little gentle work. Lunch, unless there was a rush of business or Mr Waller happened to suffer from a spasm of conscientiousness, could be spun out from half past twelve to two. More work from two till half past three. From half past three till half past four tea in the tea-room, with a novel. And from half past four till five either a little more work or more pottering, according to whether there was any work to do or not. It was by no means an unpleasant mode of spending a late January day.

Then there was no doubt that it was an interesting little community, that of the New Asiatic Bank. The curiously amateurish nature of the institution lent a certain air of light-heartedness to the place. It was not like one of those banks whose London office is their main office, where stern business is everything and a man becomes a mere machine for getting through a certain amount of routine work. The employees of the New Asiatic Bank, having plenty of time on their hands, were able to retain their individuality. They had leisure to think of other things besides their work. Indeed, they had so much leisure that it is a wonder they thought of their work at all.

The place was full of quaint characters. There was West, who had been requested to leave Haileybury owing to his habit of borrowing horses and attending meets in the neighbourhood, the same being always out of bounds and necessitating a complete disregard of the rules respecting evening chapel and lock-up. He was a small, dried-up youth, with black hair plastered down on his head. He went about his duties in a costume which suggested the sportsman of the comic papers.

There was also Hignett, who added to the meagre salary allowed him by the bank by singing comic songs at the minor music halls. He confided to Mike his intention of leaving the bank as soon as he had made a name, and taking seriously to the business. He told him that he had knocked them at the Bedford the week before, and in support of the statement showed him a cutting from the Era, in which the writer said that 'Other acceptable turns were the Bounding Zouaves, Steingruber's Dogs, and Arthur Hignett.' Mike wished him luck.

And there was Raymond who dabbled in journalism and was the author of 'Straight Talks to Housewives' in *Trifles*, under the pseudonym of 'Lady Gussie'; Wragge, who believed that the earth was flat, and addressed meetings on the subject in Hyde Park on Sundays; and many others, all interesting to talk to of a morning when work was slack and time had to be filled in.

Mike found himself, by degrees, growing quite attached to the New
Asiatic Bank.

One morning, early in February, he noticed a curious change in Mr Waller. The head of the Cash Department was, as a rule, mildly cheerful on arrival, and apt (excessively, Mike thought, though he always listened with polite interest) to relate the most recent sayings and doings of his snub-nosed son, Edward. No action of this young prodigy was withheld from Mike. He had heard, on different occasions, how he had won a prize at his school for General Information (which Mike could well believe); how he had trapped young Mr Richards, now happily reconciled to Ada, with an ingenious verbal catch; and how he had made a sequence of diverting puns on the name of the new curate, during the course of that cleric's first Sunday afternoon visit.

On this particular day, however, the cashier was silent and absent-minded. He answered Mike's good-morning mechanically, and sitting down at his desk, stared blankly across the building. There was a curiously grey, tired look on his face.

Mike could not make it out. He did not like to ask if there was anything the matter. Mr Waller's face had the unreasonable effect on him of making him feel shy and awkward. Anything in the nature of sorrow always dried Mike up and robbed him of the power of speech. Being naturally sympathetic, he had raged inwardly in many a crisis at this devil of dumb awkwardness which possessed him and prevented him from putting his sympathy into words. He had always envied the cooing readiness of the hero on the stage when anyone was in trouble. He wondered whether he would ever acquire that knack of pouring out a limpid stream of soothing words on such occasions. At present he could get no farther than a scowl and an almost offensive gruffness.

The happy thought struck him of consulting Psmith. It was his hour for pottering, so he pottered round to the Postage Department, where he found the old Etonian eyeing with disfavour a new satin tie which Bristow was wearing that morning for the first time.

'I say, Smith,' he said, 'I want to speak to you for a second.'

Psmith rose. Mike led the way to a quiet corner of the Telegrams Department.

'I tell you, Comrade Jackson,' said Psmith, 'I am hard pressed. The fight is beginning to be too much for me. After a grim struggle, after days of unremitting toil, I succeeded yesterday in inducing the man Bristow to abandon that rainbow waistcoat of his. Today I enter the building, blythe and buoyant, worn, of course, from the long struggle, but seeing with aching eyes the dawn of another, better era, and there is Comrade Bristow in a satin tie. It's hard, Comrade Jackson, it's hard, I tell you.'

'Look here, Smith,' said Mike, 'I wish you'd go round to the Cash and find out what's up with old Waller. He's got the hump about something. He's sitting there looking absolutely fed up with things. I hope there's nothing up. He's not a bad sort. It would be rot if anything rotten's happened.'

Psmith began to display a gentle interest.

'So other people have troubles as well as myself,' he murmured musingly. 'I had almost forgotten that. Comrade Waller's misfortunes cannot but be trivial compared with mine, but possibly it will be as well to ascertain their nature. I will reel round and make inquiries.'

'Good man,' said Mike. 'I'll wait here.'

Psmith departed, and returned, ten minutes later, looking more serious than when he had left.

'His kid's ill, poor chap,' he said briefly. 'Pretty badly too, from what I can gather. Pneumonia. Waller was up all night. He oughtn't to be here at all today. He doesn't know what he's doing half the time. He's absolutely fagged out. Look here, you'd better nip back and do as much of the work as you can. I shouldn't talk to him much if I were you. Buck along.'

Mike went. Mr Waller was still sitting staring out across the aisle. There was something more than a little gruesome in the sight of him. He wore a crushed, beaten look, as if all the life and fight had gone out of him. A customer came to the desk to cash a cheque. The cashier shovelled the money to him under the bars with the air of one whose mind is elsewhere. Mike could guess what he was feeling, and what he was thinking about. The fact that the snub-nosed Edward was, without exception, the most repulsive small boy he had ever met in this world, where repulsive small boys crowd and jostle one another, did not interfere with his appreciation of the cashier's state of mind. Mike's was essentially a sympathetic character. He had the gift of intuitive understanding, where people of whom he was fond were concerned. It was this which drew to him those who had intelligence enough to see beyond his sometimes rather forbidding manner, and to realize that his blunt speech was largely due to shyness. In spite of his prejudice against Edward, he could put himself into Mr Waller's place, and see the thing from his point of view.

Psmith's injunction to him not to talk much was unnecessary. Mike, as always, was rendered utterly dumb by the sight of suffering. He sat at his desk, occupying himself as best he could with the driblets of work which came to him.

Mr Waller's silence and absentness continued unchanged. The habit of years had made his work mechanical. Probably few of the customers who came to cash cheques suspected that there was anything the matter with the man who paid them their money. After all, most people look on the cashier of a bank as a sort of human slot-machine. You put in your cheque, and out comes money. It is no affair of yours whether life is treating the machine well or ill that day.

The hours dragged slowly by till five o'clock struck, and the cashier, putting on his coat and hat, passed silently out through the swing doors. He walked listlessly. He was evidently tired out.

Mike shut his ledger with a vicious bang, and went across to find

Psmith. He was glad the day was over.

20. Concerning a Cheque

Things never happen quite as one expects them to. Mike came to the office next morning prepared for a repetition of the previous day. He was amazed to find the cashier not merely cheerful, but even exuberantly cheerful. Edward, it appeared, had rallied in the afternoon, and, when his father had got home, had been out of danger. He was now going along excellently, and had stumped Ada, who was nursing him, with a question about the Thirty Years' War, only a few minutes before his father had left to catch his train. The cashier was overflowing with happiness and goodwill towards his species. He greeted customers with bright remarks on the weather, and snappy views on the leading events of the day: the former tinged with optimism, the latter full of a gentle spirit of toleration. His attitude towards the latest actions of His Majesty's Government was that of one who felt that, after all, there was probably some good even in the vilest of his fellow creatures, if one could only find it.

Altogether, the cloud had lifted from the Cash Department. All was joy, jollity, and song.

'The attitude of Comrade Waller,' said Psmith, on being informed of the change, 'is reassuring. I may now think of my own troubles. Comrade Bristow has blown into the office today in patent leather boots with white kid uppers, as I believe the technical term is. Add to that the fact that he is still wearing the satin tie, the waistcoat, and the ring, and you will understand why I have definitely decided this morning to abandon all hope of his reform. Henceforth my services, for what they are worth, are at the disposal of Comrade Bickersdyke. My time from now onward is his. He shall have the full educative value of my exclusive attention. I give Comrade Bristow up. Made straight for the corner flag, you understand,' he added, as Mr Rossiter emerged from his lair, 'and centred, and Sandy Turnbull headed a beautiful goal. I was just telling Jackson about the match against Blackburn Rovers,' he said to Mr Rossiter.

'Just so, just so. But get on with your work, Smith. We are a little behind-hand. I think perhaps it would be as well not to leave it just yet.'

'I will leap at it at once,' said Psmith cordially.

Mike went back to his department.

The day passed quickly. Mr Waller, in the intervals of work, talked a good deal, mostly of Edward, his doings, his sayings, and his prospects. The only thing that seemed to worry Mr Waller was the problem of how to employ his son's almost superhuman talents to the best advantage. Most of the goals towards which the average man strives struck him as too unambitious for the prodigy.

By the end of the day Mike had had enough of Edward. He never wished to hear the name again.

We do not claim originality for the statement that things never happen quite as one expects them to. We repeat it now because of its profound truth. The Edward's pneumonia episode having ended satisfactorily (or, rather, being apparently certain to end satisfactorily, for the invalid, though out of danger, was still in bed), Mike looked forward to a series of days unbroken by any but the minor troubles of life. For these he was prepared. What he did not expect was any big calamity.

At the beginning of the day there were no signs of it. The sky was blue and free from all suggestions of approaching thunderbolts. Mr Waller, still chirpy, had nothing but good news of Edward. Mike went for his morning stroll round the office feeling that things had settled down and had made up their mind to run smoothly.

When he got back, barely half an hour later, the storm had burst.

There was no one in the department at the moment of his arrival; but a few minutes later he saw Mr Waller come out of the manager's room, and make his way down the aisle.

It was his walk which first gave any hint that something was wrong. It was the same limp, crushed walk which Mike had seen when Edward's safety still hung in the balance.

As Mr Waller came nearer, Mike saw that the cashier's face was deadly pale.

Mr Waller caught sight of him and quickened his pace.

'Jackson,' he said.

Mike came forward.

'Do you—remember—' he spoke slowly, and with an effort, 'do you remember a cheque coming through the day before yesterday for a hundred pounds, with Sir John Morrison's signature?'

'Yes. It came in the morning, rather late.'

Mike remembered the cheque perfectly well, owing to the amount. It was the only three-figure cheque which had come across the counter during the day. It had been presented just before the cashier had gone out to lunch. He recollected the man who had presented it, a tallish man with a beard. He had noticed him particularly because of the contrast between his manner and that of the cashier. The former had been so very cheery and breezy, the latter so dazed and silent.

'Why,' he said.

'It was a forgery,' muttered Mr Waller, sitting down heavily.

Mike could not take it in all at once. He was stunned. All he could understand was that a far worse thing had happened than anything he could have imagined.

'A forgery?' he said.

'A forgery. And a clumsy one. Oh it's hard. I should have seen it on any other day but that. I could not have missed it. They showed me the cheque in there just now. I could not believe that I had passed it. I don't remember doing it. My mind was far away. I don't remember the cheque or anything about it. Yet there it is.'

Once more Mike was tongue-tied. For the life of him he could not think of anything to say. Surely, he thought, he could find *something* in the shape of words to show his sympathy. But he could find nothing that would not sound horribly stilted and cold. He sat silent.

'Sir John is in there,' went on the cashier. 'He is furious. Mr Bickersdyke, too. They are both furious. I shall be dismissed. I shall lose my place. I shall be dismissed.' He was talking more to himself than to Mike. It was dreadful to see him sitting there, all limp and broken.

'I shall lose my place. Mr Bickersdyke has wanted to get rid of me for
a long time. He never liked me. I shall be dismissed. What can I do?
I'm an old man. I can't make another start. I am good for nothing.
Nobody will take an old man like me.'

His voice died away. There was a silence. Mike sat staring miserably in front of him.

Then, quite suddenly, an idea came to him. The whole pressure of the atmosphere seemed to lift. He saw a way out. It was a curious crooked way, but at that moment it stretched clear and broad before him. He felt lighthearted and excited, as if he were watching the development of some interesting play at the theatre.

He got up, smiling.

The cashier did not notice the movement. Somebody had come in to cash a cheque, and he was working mechanically.

Mike walked up the aisle to Mr Bickersdyke's room, and went in.

The manager was in his chair at the big table. Opposite him, facing slightly sideways, was a small, round, very red-faced man. Mr Bickersdyke was speaking as Mike entered.

'I can assure you, Sir John—' he was saying.

He looked up as the door opened.

'Well, Mr Jackson?'

Mike almost laughed. The situation was tickling him.

'Mr Waller has told me—' he began.

'I have already seen Mr Waller.'

'I know. He told me about the cheque. I came to explain.'

'Explain?'

'Yes. He didn't cash it at all.'

'I don't understand you, Mr Jackson.'

'I was at the counter when it was brought in,' said Mike. 'I cashed it.'

21. Psmith Makes Inquiries

Psmith, as was his habit of a morning when the fierce rush of his commercial duties had abated somewhat, was leaning gracefully against his desk, musing on many things, when he was aware that Bristow was standing before him.

Focusing his attention with some reluctance upon this blot on the horizon, he discovered that the exploiter of rainbow waistcoats and satin ties was addressing him.

'I say, Smithy,' said Bristow. He spoke in rather an awed voice.

'Say on, Comrade Bristow,' said Psmith graciously. 'You have our ear. You would seem to have something on your chest in addition to that Neapolitan ice garment which, I regret to see, you still flaunt. If it is one tithe as painful as that, you have my sympathy. Jerk it out, Comrade Bristow.'

'Jackson isn't half copping it from old Bick.'

'Isn't—? What exactly did you say?'

'He's getting it hot on the carpet.'

'You wish to indicate,' said Psmith, 'that there is some slight disturbance, some passing breeze between Comrades Jackson and Bickersdyke?'

Bristow chuckled.

'Breeze! Blooming hurricane, more like it. I was in Bick's room just now with a letter to sign, and I tell you, the fur was flying all over the bally shop. There was old Bick cursing for all he was worth, and a little red-faced buffer puffing out his cheeks in an armchair.'

'We all have our hobbies,' said Psmith.

'Jackson wasn't saying much. He jolly well hadn't a chance. Old Bick was shooting it out fourteen to the dozen.'

'I have been privileged,' said Psmith, 'to hear Comrade Bickersdyke speak both in his sanctum and in public. He has, as you suggest, a ready flow of speech. What, exactly was the cause of the turmoil?'

'I couldn't wait to hear. I was too jolly glad to get away. Old Bick looked at me as if he could eat me, snatched the letter out of my hand, signed it, and waved his hand at the door as a hint to hop it. Which I jolly well did. He had started jawing Jackson again before I was out of the room.'

'While applauding his hustle,' said Psmith, 'I fear that I must take official notice of this. Comrade Jackson is essentially a Sensitive Plant, highly strung, neurotic. I cannot have his nervous system jolted and disorganized in this manner, and his value as a confidential secretary and adviser impaired, even though it be only temporarily. I must look into this. I will go and see if the orgy is concluded. I will hear what Comrade Jackson has to say on the matter. I shall not act rashly, Comrade Bristow. If the man Bickersdyke is proved to have had good grounds for his outbreak, he shall escape uncensured. I may even look in on him and throw him a word of praise. But if I find, as I suspect, that he has wronged Comrade Jackson, I shall be forced to speak sharply to him.'

* * * * *

Mike had left the scene of battle by the time Psmith reached the Cash Department, and was sitting at his desk in a somewhat dazed condition, trying to clear his mind sufficiently to enable him to see exactly how matters stood as concerned himself. He felt confused and rattled. He had known, when he went to the manager's room to make his statement, that there would be trouble. But, then, trouble is such an elastic word. It embraces a hundred degrees of meaning. Mike had expected sentence of dismissal, and he had got it. So far he had nothing to complain of. But he had not expected it to come to him riding high on the crest of a great, frothing wave of verbal denunciation. Mr Bickersdyke, through constantly speaking in public, had developed the habit of fluent denunciation to a remarkable extent. He had thundered at Mike as if Mike had been his Majesty's Government or the Encroaching Alien, or something of that sort. And that kind of thing is a little overwhelming at short range. Mike's head was still spinning.

It continued to spin; but he never lost sight of the fact round which it revolved, namely, that he had been dismissed from the service of the bank. And for the first time he began to wonder what they would say about this at home.

Up till now the matter had seemed entirely a personal one. He had charged in to rescue the harassed cashier in precisely the same way as that in which he had dashed in to save him from Bill, the Stone-Flinging Scourge of Clapham Common. Mike's was one of those direct, honest minds which are apt to concentrate themselves on the crisis of the moment, and to leave the consequences out of the question entirely.

What would they say at home? That was the point.

Again, what could he do by way of earning a living? He did not know much about the City and its ways, but he knew enough to understand that summary dismissal from a bank is not the best recommendation one can put forward in applying for another job. And if he did not get another job in the City, what could he do? If it were only summer, he might get taken on somewhere as a cricket professional. Cricket was his line. He could earn his pay at that. But it was very far from being summer.

He had turned the problem over in his mind till his head ached, and had eaten in the process one-third of a wooden penholder, when Psmith arrived.

'It has reached me,' said Psmith, 'that you and Comrade Bickersdyke have been seen doing the Hackenschmidt-Gotch act on the floor. When my informant left, he tells me, Comrade B. had got a half-Nelson on you, and was biting pieces out of your ear. Is this so?'

Mike got up. Psmith was the man, he felt, to advise him in this crisis.

Psmith's was the mind to grapple with his Hard Case.

'Look here, Smith,' he said, 'I want to speak to you. I'm in a bit of a hole, and perhaps you can tell me what to do. Let's go out and have a cup of coffee, shall we? I can't tell you about it here.'

'An admirable suggestion,' said Psmith. 'Things in the Postage Department are tolerably quiescent at present. Naturally I shall be missed, if I go out. But my absence will not spell irretrievable ruin, as it would at a period of greater commercial activity. Comrades Rossiter and Bristow have studied my methods. They know how I like things to be done. They are fully competent to conduct the business of the department in my absence. Let us, as you say, scud forth. We will go to a Mecca. Why so-called I do not know, nor, indeed, do I ever hope to know. There we may obtain, at a price, a passable cup of coffee, and you shall tell me your painful story.'

The Mecca, except for the curious aroma which pervades all Meccas, was deserted. Psmith, moving a box of dominoes on to the next table, sat down.

'Dominoes,' he said, 'is one of the few manly sports which have never had great attractions for me. A cousin of mine, who secured his chess blue at Oxford, would, they tell me, have represented his University in the dominoes match also, had he not unfortunately dislocated the radius bone of his bazooka while training for it. Except for him, there has been little dominoes talent in the Psmith family. Let us merely talk. What of this slight brass-rag-parting to which I alluded just now? Tell me all.'

He listened gravely while Mike related the incidents which had led up to his confession and the results of the same. At the conclusion of the narrative he sipped his coffee in silence for a moment.

'This habit of taking on to your shoulders the harvest of other people's bloomers,' he said meditatively, 'is growing upon you, Comrade Jackson. You must check it. It is like dram-drinking. You begin in a small way by breaking school rules to extract Comrade Jellicoe (perhaps the supremest of all the blitherers I have ever met) from a hole. If you had stopped there, all might have been well. But the thing, once started, fascinated you. Now you have landed yourself with a splash in the very centre of the Oxo in order to do a good turn to Comrade Waller. You must drop it, Comrade Jackson. When you were free and without ties, it did not so much matter. But now that you are confidential secretary and adviser to a Shropshire Psmith, the thing must stop. Your secretarial duties must be paramount. Nothing must be allowed to interfere with them. Yes. The thing must stop before it goes too far.'

'It seems to me,' said Mike, 'that it has gone too far. I've got the sack. I don't know how much farther you want it to go.'

Psmith stirred his coffee before replying.

'True,' he said, 'things look perhaps a shade rocky just now, but all is not yet lost. You must recollect that Comrade Bickersdyke spoke in the heat of the moment. That generous temperament was stirred to its depths. He did not pick his words. But calm will succeed storm, and we may be able to do something yet. I have some little influence with Comrade Bickersdyke. Wrongly, perhaps,' added Psmith modestly, 'he thinks somewhat highly of my judgement. If he sees that I am opposed to this step, he may possibly reconsider it. What Psmith thinks today, is his motto, I shall think tomorrow. However, we shall see.'

'I bet we shall!' said Mike ruefully.

'There is, moreover,' continued Psmith, 'another aspect to the affair. When you were being put through it, in Comrade Bickersdyke's inimitably breezy manner, Sir John What's-his-name was, I am given to understand, present. Naturally, to pacify the aggrieved bart., Comrade B. had to lay it on regardless of expense. In America, as possibly you are aware, there is a regular post of mistake-clerk, whose duty it is to receive in the neck anything that happens to be coming along when customers make complaints. He is hauled into the presence of the foaming customer, cursed, and sacked. The customer goes away appeased. The mistake-clerk, if the harangue has been unusually energetic, applies for a rise of salary. Now, possibly, in your case—'

'In my case,' interrupted Mike, 'there was none of that rot. Bickersdyke wasn't putting it on. He meant every word. Why, dash it all, you know yourself he'd be only too glad to sack me, just to get some of his own back with me.'

Psmith's eyes opened in pained surprise.

'Get some of his own back!' he repeated.

'Are you insinuating, Comrade Jackson, that my relations with Comrade Bickersdyke are not of the most pleasant and agreeable nature possible? How do these ideas get about? I yield to nobody in my respect for our manager. I may have had occasion from time to time to correct him in some trifling matter, but surely he is not the man to let such a thing rankle? No! I prefer to think that Comrade Bickersdyke regards me as his friend and well-wisher, and will lend a courteous ear to any proposal I see fit to make. I hope shortly to be able to prove this to you. I will discuss this little affair of the cheque with him at our ease at the club, and I shall be surprised if we do not come to some arrangement.'

'Look here, Smith,' said Mike earnestly, 'for goodness' sake don't go playing the goat. There's no earthly need for you to get lugged into this business. Don't you worry about me. I shall be all right.'

'I think,' said Psmith, 'that you will—when I have chatted with
Comrade Bickersdyke.'

22. And Take Steps

On returning to the bank, Mike found Mr Waller in the grip of a peculiarly varied set of mixed feelings. Shortly after Mike's departure for the Mecca, the cashier had been summoned once more into the Presence, and had there been informed that, as apparently he had not been directly responsible for the gross piece of carelessness by which the bank had suffered so considerable a loss (here Sir John puffed out his cheeks like a meditative toad), the matter, as far as he was concerned, was at an end. On the other hand—! Here Mr Waller was hauled over the coals for Incredible Rashness in allowing a mere junior subordinate to handle important tasks like the paying out of money, and so on, till he felt raw all over. However, it was not dismissal. That was the great thing. And his principal sensation was one of relief.

Mingled with the relief were sympathy for Mike, gratitude to him for having given himself up so promptly, and a curiously dazed sensation, as if somebody had been hitting him on the head with a bolster.

All of which emotions, taken simultaneously, had the effect of rendering him completely dumb when he saw Mike. He felt that he did not know what to say to him. And as Mike, for his part, simply wanted to be let alone, and not compelled to talk, conversation was at something of a standstill in the Cash Department.

After five minutes, it occurred to Mr Waller that perhaps the best plan would be to interview Psmith. Psmith would know exactly how matters stood. He could not ask Mike point-blank whether he had been dismissed. But there was the probability that Psmith had been informed and would pass on the information.

Psmith received the cashier with a dignified kindliness.

'Oh, er, Smith,' said Mr Waller, 'I wanted just to ask you about
Jackson.'

Psmith bowed his head gravely.

'Exactly,' he said. 'Comrade Jackson. I think I may say that you have come to the right man. Comrade Jackson has placed himself in my hands, and I am dealing with his case. A somewhat tricky business, but I shall see him through.'

'Has he—?' Mr Waller hesitated.

'You were saying?' said Psmith.

'Does Mr Bickersdyke intend to dismiss him?'

'At present,' admitted Psmith, 'there is some idea of that description floating—nebulously, as it were—in Comrade Bickersdyke's mind. Indeed, from what I gather from my client, the push was actually administered, in so many words. But tush! And possibly bah! we know what happens on these occasions, do we not? You and I are students of human nature, and we know that a man of Comrade Bickersdyke's warm-hearted type is apt to say in the heat of the moment a great deal more than he really means. Men of his impulsive character cannot help expressing themselves in times of stress with a certain generous strength which those who do not understand them are inclined to take a little too seriously. I shall have a chat with Comrade Bickersdyke at the conclusion of the day's work, and I have no doubt that we shall both laugh heartily over this little episode.'

Mr Waller pulled at his beard, with an expression on his face that seemed to suggest that he was not quite so confident on this point. He was about to put his doubts into words when Mr Rossiter appeared, and Psmith, murmuring something about duty, turned again to his ledger. The cashier drifted back to his own department.

It was one of Psmith's theories of Life, which he was accustomed to propound to Mike in the small hours of the morning with his feet on the mantelpiece, that the secret of success lay in taking advantage of one's occasional slices of luck, in seizing, as it were, the happy moment. When Mike, who had had the passage to write out ten times at Wrykyn on one occasion as an imposition, reminded him that Shakespeare had once said something about there being a tide in the affairs of men, which, taken at the flood, &c., Psmith had acknowledged with an easy grace that possibly Shakespeare *had* got on to it first, and that it was but one more proof of how often great minds thought alike.

Though waiving his claim to the copyright of the maxim, he nevertheless had a high opinion of it, and frequently acted upon it in the conduct of his own life.

Thus, when approaching the Senior Conservative Club at five o'clock with the idea of finding Mr Bickersdyke there, he observed his quarry entering the Turkish Baths which stand some twenty yards from the club's front door, he acted on his maxim, and decided, instead of waiting for the manager to finish his bath before approaching him on the subject of Mike, to corner him in the Baths themselves.

He gave Mr Bickersdyke five minutes' start. Then, reckoning that by that time he would probably have settled down, he pushed open the door and went in himself. And, having paid his money, and left his boots with the boy at the threshold, he was rewarded by the sight of the manager emerging from a box at the far end of the room, clad in the mottled towels which the bather, irrespective of his personal taste in dress, is obliged to wear in a Turkish bath.

Psmith made for the same box. Mr Bickersdyke's clothes lay at the head of one of the sofas, but nobody else had staked out a claim. Psmith took possession of the sofa next to the manager's. Then, humming lightly, he undressed, and made his way downstairs to the Hot Rooms. He rather fancied himself in towels. There was something about them which seemed to suit his figure. They gave him, he though, rather a *debonnaire* look. He paused for a moment before the looking-glass to examine himself, with approval, then pushed open the door of the Hot Rooms and went in.

23. Mr Bickersdyke Makes a Concession

Mr Bickersdyke was reclining in an easy-chair in the first room, staring before him in the boiled-fish manner customary in a Turkish Bath. Psmith dropped into the next seat with a cheery 'Good evening.' The manager started as if some firm hand had driven a bradawl into him. He looked at Psmith with what was intended to be a dignified stare. But dignity is hard to achieve in a couple of parti-coloured towels. The stare did not differ to any great extent from the conventional boiled-fish look, alluded to above.

Psmith settled himself comfortably in his chair. 'Fancy finding you here,' he said pleasantly. 'We seem always to be meeting. To me,' he added, with a reassuring smile, 'it is a great pleasure. A very great pleasure indeed. We see too little of each other during office hours. Not that one must grumble at that. Work before everything. You have your duties, I mine. It is merely unfortunate that those duties are not such as to enable us to toil side by side, encouraging each other with word and gesture. However, it is idle to repine. We must make the most of these chance meetings when the work of the day is over.'

Mr Bickersdyke heaved himself up from his chair and took another at the opposite end of the room. Psmith joined him.

'There's something pleasantly mysterious, to my mind,' said he chattily, 'in a Turkish Bath. It seems to take one out of the hurry and bustle of the everyday world. It is a quiet backwater in the rushing river of Life. I like to sit and think in a Turkish Bath. Except, of course, when I have a congenial companion to talk to. As now. To me—'

Mr Bickersdyke rose, and went into the next room.

'To me,' continued Psmith, again following, and seating himself beside the manager, 'there is, too, something eerie in these places. There is a certain sinister air about the attendants. They glide rather than walk. They say little. Who knows what they may be planning and plotting? That drip-drip again. It may be merely water, but how are we to know that it is not blood? It would be so easy to do away with a man in a Turkish Bath. Nobody has seen him come in. Nobody can trace him if he disappears. These are uncomfortable thoughts, Mr Bickersdyke.'

Mr Bickersdyke seemed to think them so. He rose again, and returned to the first room.

'I have made you restless,' said Psmith, in a voice of self-reproach, when he had settled himself once more by the manager's side. 'I am sorry. I will not pursue the subject. Indeed, I believe that my fears are unnecessary. Statistics show, I understand, that large numbers of men emerge in safety every year from Turkish Baths. There was another matter of which I wished to speak to you. It is a somewhat delicate matter, and I am only encouraged to mention it to you by the fact that you are so close a friend of my father's.'

Mr Bickersdyke had picked up an early edition of an evening paper, left on the table at his side by a previous bather, and was to all appearances engrossed in it. Psmith, however, not discouraged, proceeded to touch upon the matter of Mike.

'There was,' he said, 'some little friction, I hear, in the office today in connection with a cheque.' The evening paper hid the manager's expressive face, but from the fact that the hands holding it tightened their grip Psmith deduced that Mr Bickersdyke's attention was not wholly concentrated on the City news. Moreover, his toes wriggled. And when a man's toes wriggle, he is interested in what you are saying.

'All these petty breezes,' continued Psmith sympathetically, 'must be very trying to a man in your position, a man who wishes to be left alone in order to devote his entire thought to the niceties of the higher Finance. It is as if Napoleon, while planning out some intricate scheme of campaign, were to be called upon in the midst of his meditations to bully a private for not cleaning his buttons. Naturally, you were annoyed. Your giant brain, wrenched temporarily from its proper groove, expended its force in one tremendous reprimand of Comrade Jackson. It was as if one had diverted some terrific electric current which should have been controlling a vast system of machinery, and turned it on to annihilate a black-beetle. In the present case, of course, the result is as might have been expected. Comrade Jackson, not realizing the position of affairs, went away with the absurd idea that all was over, that you meant all you said—briefly, that his number was up. I assured him that he was mistaken, but no! He persisted in declaring that all was over, that you had dismissed him from the bank.'

Mr Bickersdyke lowered the paper and glared bulbously at the old Etonian.

'Mr Jackson is perfectly right,' he snapped. 'Of course I dismissed him.'

'Yes, yes,' said Psmith, 'I have no doubt that at the moment you did work the rapid push. What I am endeavouring to point out is that Comrade Jackson is under the impression that the edict is permanent, that he can hope for no reprieve.'

'Nor can he.'

'You don't mean—'

'I mean what I say.'

'Ah, I quite understand,' said Psmith, as one who sees that he must make allowances. 'The incident is too recent. The storm has not yet had time to expend itself. You have not had leisure to think the matter over coolly. It is hard, of course, to be cool in a Turkish Bath. Your ganglions are still vibrating. Later, perhaps—'

'Once and for all,' growled Mr Bickersdyke, 'the thing is ended. Mr Jackson will leave the bank at the end of the month. We have no room for fools in the office.'

'You surprise me,' said Psmith. 'I should not have thought that the standard of intelligence in the bank was extremely high. With the exception of our two selves, I think that there are hardly any men of real intelligence on the staff. And comrade Jackson is improving every day. Being, as he is, under my constant supervision he is rapidly developing a stranglehold on his duties, which—'

'I have no wish to discuss the matter any further.'

'No, no. Quite so, quite so. Not another word. I am dumb.'

'There are limits you see, to the uses of impertinence, Mr Smith.'

Psmith started.

'You are not suggesting—! You do not mean that I—!'

'I have no more to say. I shall be glad if you will allow me to read my paper.'

Psmith waved a damp hand.

'I should be the last man,' he said stiffly, 'to force my conversation on another. I was under the impression that you enjoyed these little chats as keenly as I did. If I was wrong—'

He relapsed into a wounded silence. Mr Bickersdyke resumed his perusal of the evening paper, and presently, laying it down, rose and made his way to the room where muscular attendants were in waiting to perform that blend of Jiu-Jitsu and Catch-as-catch-can which is the most valuable and at the same time most painful part of a Turkish Bath.

It was not till he was resting on his sofa, swathed from head to foot in a sheet and smoking a cigarette, that he realized that Psmith was sharing his compartment.

He made the unpleasant discovery just as he had finished his first cigarette and lighted his second. He was blowing out the match when Psmith, accompanied by an attendant, appeared in the doorway, and proceeded to occupy the next sofa to himself. All that feeling of dreamy peace, which is the reward one receives for allowing oneself to be melted like wax and kneaded like bread, left him instantly. He felt hot and annoyed. To escape was out of the question. Once one has been scientifically wrapped up by the attendant and placed on one's sofa, one is a fixture. He lay scowling at the ceiling, resolved to combat all attempt at conversation with a stony silence.

Psmith, however, did not seem to desire conversation. He lay on his sofa motionless for a quarter of an hour, then reached out for a large book which lay on the table, and began to read.

When he did speak, he seemed to be speaking to himself. Every now and then he would murmur a few words, sometimes a single name. In spite of himself, Mr Bickersdyke found himself listening.

At first the murmurs conveyed nothing to him. Then suddenly a name caught his ear. Strowther was the name, and somehow it suggested something to him. He could not say precisely what. It seemed to touch some chord of memory. He knew no one of the name of Strowther. He was sure of that. And yet it was curiously familiar. An unusual name, too. He could not help feeling that at one time he must have known it quite well.

'Mr Strowther,' murmured Psmith, 'said that the hon. gentleman's remarks would have been nothing short of treason, if they had not been so obviously the mere babblings of an irresponsible lunatic. Cries of "Order, order," and a voice, "Sit down, fat-head!"'

For just one moment Mr Bickersdyke's memory poised motionless, like a hawk about to swoop. Then it darted at the mark. Everything came to him in a flash. The hands of the clock whizzed back. He was no longer Mr John Bickersdyke, manager of the London branch of the New Asiatic Bank, lying on a sofa in the Cumberland Street Turkish Baths. He was Jack Bickersdyke, clerk in the employ of Messrs Norton and Biggleswade, standing on a chair and shouting 'Order! order!' in the Masonic Room of the 'Red Lion' at Tulse Hill, while the members of the Tulse Hill Parliament, divided into two camps, yelled at one another, and young Tom Barlow, in his official capacity as Mister Speaker, waved his arms dumbly, and banged the table with his mallet in his efforts to restore calm.

He remembered the whole affair as if it had happened yesterday. It had been a speech of his own which had called forth the above expression of opinion from Strowther. He remembered Strowther now, a pale, spectacled clerk in Baxter and Abrahams, an inveterate upholder of the throne, the House of Lords and all constituted authority. Strowther had objected to the socialistic sentiments of his speech in connection with the Budget, and there had been a disturbance unparalleled even in the Tulse Hill Parliament, where disturbances were frequent and loud....

Psmith looked across at him with a bright smile. 'They report you verbatim,' he said. 'And rightly. A more able speech I have seldom read. I like the bit where you call the Royal Family "blood-suckers". Even then, it seems you knew how to express yourself fluently and well.'

Mr Bickersdyke sat up. The hands of the clock had moved again, and he was back in what Psmith had called the live, vivid present.

'What have you got there?' he demanded.

'It is a record,' said Psmith, 'of the meeting of an institution called the Tulse Hill Parliament. A bright, chatty little institution, too, if one may judge by these reports. You in particular, if I may say so, appear to have let yourself go with refreshing vim. Your political views have changed a great deal since those days, have they not? It is extremely interesting. A most fascinating study for political students. When I send these speeches of yours to the *Clarion*—'

Mr Bickersdyke bounded on his sofa.

'What!' he cried.

'I was saying,' said Psmith, 'that the *Clarion* will probably make a most interesting comparison between these speeches and those you have been making at Kenningford.'

'I—I—I forbid you to make any mention of these speeches.'

Psmith hesitated.

'It would be great fun seeing what the papers said,' he protested.

'Great fun!'

'It is true,' mused Psmith, 'that in a measure, it would dish you at the election. From what I saw of those light-hearted lads at Kenningford the other night, I should say they would be so amused that they would only just have enough strength left to stagger to the poll and vote for your opponent.'

Mr Bickersdyke broke out into a cold perspiration.

'I forbid you to send those speeches to the papers,' he cried.

Psmith reflected.

'You see,' he said at last, 'it is like this. The departure of Comrade Jackson, my confidential secretary and adviser, is certain to plunge me into a state of the deepest gloom. The only way I can see at present by which I can ensure even a momentary lightening of the inky cloud is the sending of these speeches to some bright paper like the *Clarion.* I feel certain that their comments would wring, at any rate, a sad, sweet smile from me. Possibly even a hearty laugh. I must, therefore, look on these very able speeches of yours in something of the light of an antidote. They will stand between me and black depression. Without them I am in the cart. With them I may possibly buoy myself up.'

Mr Bickersdyke shifted uneasily on his sofa. He glared at the floor. Then he eyed the ceiling as if it were a personal enemy of his. Finally he looked at Psmith. Psmith's eyes were closed in peaceful meditation.

'Very well,' said he at last. 'Jackson shall stop.'

Psmith came out of his thoughts with a start. 'You were observing—?' he said.

'I shall not dismiss Jackson,' said Mr Bickersdyke.

Psmith smiled winningly.

'Just as I had hoped,' he said. 'Your very justifiable anger melts before reflection. The storm subsides, and you are at leisure to examine the matter dispassionately. Doubts begin to creep in. Possibly, you say to yourself, I have been too hasty, too harsh. Justice must be tempered with mercy. I have caught Comrade Jackson bending, you add (still to yourself), but shall I press home my advantage too ruthlessly? No, you cry, I will abstain. And I applaud your action. I like to see this spirit of gentle toleration. It is bracing and comforting. As for these excellent speeches,' he added, 'I shall, of course, no longer have any need of their consolation. I can lay them aside. The sunlight can now enter and illumine my life through more ordinary channels. The cry goes round, "Psmith is himself again."'

Mr Bickersdyke said nothing. Unless a snort of fury may be counted as anything.

24. The Spirit of Unrest

During the following fortnight, two things happened which materially altered Mike's position in the bank.

The first was that Mr Bickersdyke was elected a member of Parliament. He got in by a small majority amidst scenes of disorder of a nature unusual even in Kenningford. Psmith, who went down on the polling-day to inspect the revels and came back with his hat smashed in, reported that, as far as he could see, the electors of Kenningford seemed to be in just that state of happy intoxication which might make them vote for Mr Bickersdyke by mistake. Also it had been discovered, on the eve of the poll, that the bank manager's opponent, in his youth, had been educated at a school in Germany, and had subsequently spent two years at Heidelberg University. These damaging revelations were having a marked effect on the warm-hearted patriots of Kenningford, who were now referring to the candidate in thick but earnest tones as 'the German Spy'.

'So that taking everything into consideration,' said Psmith, summing up, 'I fancy that Comrade Bickersdyke is home.'

And the papers next day proved that he was right.

'A hundred and fifty-seven,' said Psmith, as he read his paper at breakfast. 'Not what one would call a slashing victory. It is fortunate for Comrade Bickersdyke, I think, that I did not send those very able speeches of his to the *Clarion'*.

Till now Mike had been completely at a loss to understand why the manager had sent for him on the morning following the scene about the cheque, and informed him that he had reconsidered his decision to dismiss him. Mike could not help feeling that there was more in the matter than met the eye. Mr Bickersdyke had not spoken as if it gave him any pleasure to reprieve him. On the contrary, his manner was distinctly brusque. Mike was thoroughly puzzled. To Psmith's statement, that he had talked the matter over quietly with the manager and brought things to a satisfactory conclusion, he had paid little attention. But now he began to see light.

'Great Scott, Smith,' he said, 'did you tell him you'd send those speeches to the papers if he sacked me?'

Psmith looked at him through his eye-glass, and helped himself to another piece of toast.

'I am unable,' he said, 'to recall at this moment the exact terms of the very pleasant conversation I had with Comrade Bickersdyke on the occasion of our chance meeting in the Turkish Bath that afternoon; but, thinking things over quietly now that I have more leisure, I cannot help feeling that he may possibly have read some such intention into my words. You know how it is in these little chats, Comrade Jackson. One leaps to conclusions. Some casual word I happened to drop may have given him the idea you mention. At this distance of time it is impossible to say with any certainty. Suffice it that all has ended well. He *did* reconsider his resolve. I shall be only too happy if it turns out that the seed of the alteration in his views was sown by some careless word of mine. Perhaps we shall never know.'

Mike was beginning to mumble some awkward words of thanks, when Psmith resumed his discourse.

'Be that as it may, however,' he said, 'we cannot but perceive that Comrade Bickersdyke's election has altered our position to some extent. As you have pointed out, he may have been influenced in this recent affair by some chance remark of mine about those speeches. Now, however, they will cease to be of any value. Now that he is elected he has nothing to lose by their publication. I mention this by way of indicating that it is possible that, if another painful episode occurs, he may be more ruthless.'

'I see what you mean,' said Mike. 'If he catches me on the hop again, he'll simply go ahead and sack me.'

'That,' said Psmith, 'is more or less the position of affairs.'

The other event which altered Mike's life in the bank was his removal from Mr Waller's department to the Fixed Deposits. The work in the Fixed Deposits was less pleasant, and Mr Gregory, the head of the department was not of Mr Waller's type. Mr Gregory, before joining the home-staff of the New Asiatic Bank, had spent a number of years with a firm in the Far East, where he had acquired a liver and a habit of addressing those under him in a way that suggested the mate of a tramp steamer. Even on the days when his liver was not troubling him, he was truculent. And when, as usually happened, it did trouble him, he was a perfect fountain of abuse. Mike and he hated each other from the first. The work in the Fixed Deposits was not really difficult, when you got the hang of it, but there was a certain amount of confusion in it to a beginner; and Mike, in commercial matters, was as raw a beginner as ever began. In the two other departments through which he had passed, he had done tolerably well. As regarded his work in the Postage Department, stamping letters and taking them down to the post office was just about his form. It was the sort of work on which he could really get a grip. And in the Cash Department, Mr Waller's mild patience had helped him through. But with Mr Gregory it was different. Mike hated being shouted at. It confused him. And Mr Gregory invariably shouted. He always spoke as if he were competing against a high wind. With Mike he shouted more than usual. On his side, it must be admitted that Mike was something out of the common run of bank clerks. The whole system of banking was a horrid mystery to him. He did not understand why things were done, or how the various departments depended on and dovetailed into one another. Each department seemed to him something separate and distinct. Why they were all in the same building at all he never really gathered. He knew that it could not be purely from motives of sociability, in order that the clerks might have each other's company during slack spells. That much he suspected, but beyond that he was vague.

It naturally followed that, after having grown, little by little, under Mr Waller's easy-going rule, to enjoy life in the bank, he now suffered a reaction. Within a day of his arrival in the Fixed Deposits he was loathing the place as earnestly as he had loathed it on the first morning.

Psmith, who had taken his place in the Cash Department, reported that Mr Waller was inconsolable at his loss.

'I do my best to cheer him up,' he said, 'and he smiles bravely every now and then. But when he thinks I am not looking, his head droops and that wistful expression comes into his face. The sunshine has gone out of his life.'

It had just come into Mike's, and, more than anything else, was making him restless and discontented. That is to say, it was now late spring: the sun shone cheerfully on the City; and cricket was in the air. And that was the trouble.

In the dark days, when everything was fog and slush, Mike had been contented enough to spend his mornings and afternoons in the bank, and go about with Psmith at night. Under such conditions, London is the best place in which to be, and the warmth and light of the bank were pleasant.

But now things had changed. The place had become a prison. With all the energy of one who had been born and bred in the country, Mike hated having to stay indoors on days when all the air was full of approaching summer. There were mornings when it was almost more than he could do to push open the swing doors, and go out of the fresh air into the stuffy atmosphere of the bank.

The days passed slowly, and the cricket season began. Instead of being a relief, this made matters worse. The little cricket he could get only made him want more. It was as if a starving man had been given a handful of wafer biscuits.

If the summer had been wet, he might have been less restless. But, as it happened, it was unusually fine. After a week of cold weather at the beginning of May, a hot spell set in. May passed in a blaze of sunshine. Large scores were made all over the country.

Mike's name had been down for the M.C.C. for some years, and he had become a member during his last season at Wrykyn. Once or twice a week he managed to get up to Lord's for half an hour's practice at the nets; and on Saturdays the bank had matches, in which he generally managed to knock the cover off rather ordinary club bowling. But it was not enough for him.

June came, and with it more sunshine. The atmosphere of the bank seemed more oppressive than ever.

25. At the Telephone

If one looks closely into those actions which are apparently due to sudden impulse, one generally finds that the sudden impulse was merely the last of a long series of events which led up to the action. Alone, it would not have been powerful enough to effect anything. But, coming after the way has been paved for it, it is irresistible. The hooligan who bonnets a policeman is apparently the victim of a sudden impulse. In reality, however, the bonneting is due to weeks of daily encounters with the constable, at each of which meetings the dislike for his helmet and the idea of smashing it in grow a little larger, till finally they blossom into the deed itself.

This was what happened in Mike's case. Day by day, through the summer, as the City grew hotter and stuffier, his hatred of the bank became more and more the thought that occupied his mind. It only needed a moderately strong temptation to make him break out and take the consequences.

Psmith noticed his restlessness and endeavoured to soothe it.

'All is not well,' he said, 'with Comrade Jackson, the Sunshine of the Home. I note a certain wanness of the cheek. The peach-bloom of your complexion is no longer up to sample. Your eye is wild; your merry laugh no longer rings through the bank, causing nervous customers to leap into the air with startled exclamations. You have the manner of one whose only friend on earth is a yellow dog, and who has lost the dog. Why is this, Comrade Jackson?'

They were talking in the flat at Clement's Inn. The night was hot. Through the open windows the roar of the Strand sounded faintly. Mike walked to the window and looked out.

'I'm sick of all this rot,' he said shortly.

Psmith shot an inquiring glance at him, but said nothing. This restlessness of Mike's was causing him a good deal of inconvenience, which he bore in patient silence, hoping for better times. With Mike obviously discontented and out of tune with all the world, there was but little amusement to be extracted from the evenings now. Mike did his best to be cheerful, but he could not shake off the caged feeling which made him restless.

'What rot it all is!' went on Mike, sitting down again. 'What's the good of it all? You go and sweat all day at a desk, day after day, for about twopence a year. And when you're about eighty-five, you retire. It isn't living at all. It's simply being a bally vegetable.'

'You aren't hankering, by any chance, to be a pirate of the Spanish main, or anything like that, are you?' inquired Psmith.

'And all this rot about going out East,' continued Mike. 'What's the good of going out East?'

'I gather from casual chit-chat in the office that one becomes something of a blood when one goes out East,' said Psmith. 'Have a dozen native clerks under you, all looking up to you as the Last Word in magnificence, and end by marrying the Governor's daughter.'

'End by getting some foul sort of fever, more likely, and being booted out as no further use to the bank.'

'You look on the gloomy side, Comrade Jackson. I seem to see you sitting in an armchair, fanned by devoted coolies, telling some Eastern potentate that you can give him five minutes. I understand that being in a bank in the Far East is one of the world's softest jobs. Millions of natives hang on your lightest word. Enthusiastic rajahs draw you aside and press jewels into your hand as a token of respect and esteem. When on an elephant's back you pass, somebody beats on a booming brass gong! The Banker of Bhong! Isn't your generous young heart stirred to any extent by the prospect? I am given to understand—'

'I've a jolly good mind to chuck up the whole thing and become a pro. I've got a birth qualification for Surrey. It's about the only thing I could do any good at.'

Psmith's manner became fatherly.

'*You're* all right,' he said. 'The hot weather has given you that tired feeling. What you want is a change of air. We will pop down together hand in hand this week-end to some seaside resort. You shall build sand castles, while I lie on the beach and read the paper. In the evening we will listen to the band, or stroll on the esplanade, not so much because we want to, as to give the natives a treat. Possibly, if the weather continues warm, we may even paddle. A vastly exhilarating pastime, I am led to believe, and so strengthening for the ankles. And on Monday morning we will return, bronzed and bursting with health, to our toil once more.'

'I'm going to bed,' said Mike, rising.

Psmith watched him lounge from the room, and shook his head sadly. All was not well with his confidential secretary and adviser.

The next day, which was a Thursday, found Mike no more reconciled to the prospect of spending from ten till five in the company of Mr Gregory and the ledgers. He was silent at breakfast, and Psmith, seeing that things were still wrong, abstained from conversation. Mike propped the *Sportsman* up against the hot-water jug, and read the cricket news. His county, captained by brother Joe, had, as he had learned already from yesterday's evening paper, beaten Sussex by five wickets at Brighton. Today they were due to play Middlesex at Lord's. Mike thought that he would try to get off early, and go and see some of the first day's play.

25. At the Telephone

As events turned out, he got off a good deal earlier, and saw a good deal more of the first day's play than he had anticipated.

He had just finished the preliminary stages of the morning's work, which consisted mostly of washing his hands, changing his coat, and eating a section of a pen-holder, when William, the messenger, approached.

'You're wanted on the 'phone, Mr Jackson.'

The New Asiatic Bank, unlike the majority of London banks, was on the telephone, a fact which Psmith found a great convenience when securing seats at the theatre. Mike went to the box and took up the receiver.

'Hullo!' he said.

'Who's that?' said an agitated voice. 'Is that you, Mike? I'm Joe.'

'Hullo, Joe,' said Mike. 'What's up? I'm coming to see you this evening. I'm going to try and get off early.'

'Look here, Mike, are you busy at the bank just now?'

'Not at the moment. There's never anything much going on before eleven.'

'I mean, are you busy today? Could you possibly manage to get off and play for us against Middlesex?'

Mike nearly dropped the receiver.

'What?' he cried.

'There's been the dickens of a mix-up. We're one short, and you're our only hope. We can't possibly get another man in the time. We start in half an hour. Can you play?'

For the space of, perhaps, one minute, Mike thought.

'Well?' said Joe's voice.

The sudden vision of Lord's ground, all green and cool in the morning sunlight, was too much for Mike's resolution, sapped as it was by days of restlessness. The feeling surged over him that whatever happened afterwards, the joy of the match in perfect weather on a perfect wicket would make it worth while. What did it matter what happened afterwards?

'All right, Joe,' he said. 'I'll hop into a cab now, and go and get my things.'

'Good man,' said Joe, hugely relieved.

26. Breaking The News

Dashing away from the call-box, Mike nearly cannoned into Psmith, who was making his way pensively to the telephone with the object of ringing up the box office of the Haymarket Theatre.

'Sorry,' said Mike. 'Hullo, Smith.'

'Hullo indeed,' said Psmith, courteously. 'I rejoice, Comrade Jackson, to find you going about your commercial duties like a young bomb. How is it, people repeatedly ask me, that Comrade Jackson contrives to catch his employer's eye and win the friendly smile from the head of his department? My reply is that where others walk, Comrade Jackson runs. Where others stroll, Comrade Jackson legs it like a highly-trained mustang of the prairie. He does not loiter. He gets back to his department bathed in perspiration, in level time. He—'

'I say, Smith,' said Mike, 'you might do me a favour.'

'A thousand. Say on.'

'Just look in at the Fixed Deposits and tell old Gregory that I shan't be with him today, will you? I haven't time myself. I must rush!'

Psmith screwed his eyeglass into his eye, and examined Mike carefully.

'What exactly—?' be began.

'Tell the old ass I've popped off.'

'Just so, just so,' murmured Psmith, as one who assents to a thoroughly reasonable proposition. 'Tell him you have popped off. It shall be done. But it is within the bounds of possibility that Comrade Gregory may inquire further. Could you give me some inkling as to why you are popping?'

'My brother Joe has just rung me up from Lords. The county are playing Middlesex and they're one short. He wants me to roll up.'

Psmith shook his head sadly.

'I don't wish to interfere in any way,' he said, 'but I suppose you realize that, by acting thus, you are to some extent knocking the stuffing out of your chances of becoming manager of this bank? If you dash off now, I shouldn't count too much on that marrying the Governor's daughter scheme I sketched out for you last night. I doubt whether this is going to help you to hold the gorgeous East in fee, and all that sort of thing.'

'Oh, dash the gorgeous East.'

'By all means,' said Psmith obligingly. 'I just thought I'd mention it. I'll look in at Lord's this afternoon. I shall send my card up to you, and trust to your sympathetic cooperation to enable me to effect an entry into the pavilion on my face. My father is coming up to London today. I'll bring him along, too.'

'Right ho. Dash it, it's twenty to. So long. See you at Lord's.'

Psmith looked after his retreating form till it had vanished through the swing-door, and shrugged his shoulders resignedly, as if disclaiming all responsibility.

'He has gone without his hat,' he murmured. 'It seems to me that this is practically a case of running amok. And now to break the news to bereaved Comrade Gregory.'

He abandoned his intention of ringing up the Haymarket Theatre, and turning away from the call-box, walked meditatively down the aisle till he came to the Fixed Deposits Department, where the top of Mr Gregory's head was to be seen over the glass barrier, as he applied himself to his work.

Psmith, resting his elbows on the top of the barrier and holding his head between his hands, eyed the absorbed toiler for a moment in silence, then emitted a hollow groan.

Mr Gregory, who was ruling a line in a ledger—most of the work in the Fixed Deposits Department consisted of ruling lines in ledgers, sometimes in black ink, sometimes in red—started as if he had been stung, and made a complete mess of the ruled line. He lifted a fiery, bearded face, and met Psmith's eye, which shone with kindly sympathy.

He found words.

'What the dickens are you standing there for, mooing like a blanked cow?' he inquired.

'I was groaning,' explained Psmith with quiet dignity. 'And why was I groaning?' he continued. 'Because a shadow has fallen on the Fixed Deposits Department. Comrade Jackson, the Pride of the Office, has gone.'

Mr Gregory rose from his seat.

'I don't know who the dickens you are—' he began.

'I am Psmith,' said the old Etonian,

'Oh, you're Smith, are you?'

'With a preliminary P. Which, however, is not sounded.'

'And what's all this dashed nonsense about Jackson?'

'He is gone. Gone like the dew from the petal of a rose.'

'Gone! Where's he gone to?'

'Lord's.'

'What lord's?'

Psmith waved his hand gently.

'You misunderstand me. Comrade Jackson has not gone to mix with any member of our gay and thoughtless aristocracy. He has gone to Lord's cricket ground.'

Mr Gregory's beard bristled even more than was its wont.

'What!' he roared. 'Gone to watch a cricket match! Gone—!'

'Not to watch. To play. An urgent summons I need not say. Nothing but an urgent summons could have wrenched him from your very delightful society, I am sure.'

Mr Gregory glared.

'I don't want any of your impudence,' he said.

Psmith nodded gravely.

'We all have these curious likes and dislikes,' he said tolerantly. 'You do not like my impudence. Well, well, some people don't. And now, having broken the sad news, I will return to my own department.'

'Half a minute. You come with me and tell this yarn of yours to Mr

Bickersdyke.'

'You think it would interest, amuse him? Perhaps you are right. Let us buttonhole Comrade Bickersdyke.'

Mr Bickersdyke was disengaged. The head of the Fixed Deposits Department stumped into the room. Psmith followed at a more leisurely pace.

'Allow me,' he said with a winning smile, as Mr Gregory opened his mouth to speak, 'to take this opportunity of congratulating you on your success at the election. A narrow but well-deserved victory.'

There was nothing cordial in the manager's manner.

'What do you want?' he said.

'Myself, nothing,' said Psmith. 'But I understand that Mr Gregory has some communication to make.'

'Tell Mr Bickersdyke that story of yours,' said Mr Gregory.

'Surely,' said Psmith reprovingly, 'this is no time for anecdotes. Mr

Bickersdyke is busy. He—'

'Tell him what you told me about Jackson.'

Mr Bickersdyke looked up inquiringly.

'Jackson,' said Psmith, 'has been obliged to absent himself from work today owing to an urgent summons from his brother, who, I understand, has suffered a bereavement.'

'It's a lie,' roared Mr Gregory. 'You told me yourself he'd gone to play in a cricket match.'

'True. As I said, he received an urgent summons from his brother.'

'What about the bereavement, then?'

'The team was one short. His brother was very distressed about it. What could Comrade Jackson do? Could he refuse to help his brother when it was in his power? His generous nature is a byword. He did the only possible thing. He consented to play.'

Mr Bickersdyke spoke.

'Am I to understand,' he asked, with sinister calm, 'that Mr Jackson has left his work and gone off to play in a cricket match?'

'Something of that sort has, I believe, happened,' said Psmith. 'He knew, of course,' he added, bowing gracefully in Mr Gregory's direction, 'that he was leaving his work in thoroughly competent hands.'

'Thank you,' said Mr Bickersdyke. 'That will do. You will help Mr Gregory in his department for the time being, Mr Smith. I will arrange for somebody to take your place in your own department.'

'It will be a pleasure,' murmured Psmith.

'Show Mr Smith what he has to do, Mr Gregory,' said the manager.

They left the room.

'How curious, Comrade Gregory,' mused Psmith, as they went, 'are the workings of Fate! A moment back, and your life was a blank. Comrade Jackson, that prince of Fixed Depositors, had gone. How, you said to yourself despairingly, can his place be filled? Then the cloud broke, and the sun shone out again. *I* came to help you. What you lose on the swings, you make up on the roundabouts. Now show me what I have to do, and then let us make this department sizzle. You have drawn a good ticket, Comrade Gregory.'

27. At Lord's

Mike got to Lord's just as the umpires moved out into the field. He raced round to the pavilion. Joe met him on the stairs.

'It's all right,' he said. 'No hurry. We've won the toss. I've put you in fourth wicket.'

'Right ho,' said Mike. 'Glad we haven't to field just yet.'

'We oughtn't to have to field today if we don't chuck our wickets away.'

'Good wicket?'

'Like a billiard-table. I'm glad you were able to come. Have any difficulty in getting away?'

Joe Jackson's knowledge of the workings of a bank was of the slightest. He himself had never, since he left Oxford, been in a position where there were obstacles to getting off to play in first-class cricket. By profession he was agent to a sporting baronet whose hobby was the cricket of the county, and so, far from finding any difficulty in playing for the county, he was given to understand by his employer that that was his chief duty. It never occurred to him that Mike might find his bank less amenable in the matter of giving leave. His only fear, when he rang Mike up that morning, had been that this might be a particularly busy day at the New Asiatic Bank. If there was no special rush of work, he took it for granted that Mike would simply go to the manager, ask for leave to play in the match, and be given it with a beaming smile.

Mike did not answer the question, but asked one on his own account.

'How did you happen to be short?' he said.

'It was rotten luck. It was like this. We were altering our team after the Sussex match, to bring in Ballard, Keene, and Willis. They couldn't get down to Brighton, as the 'Varsity had a match, but there was nothing on for them in the last half of the week, so they'd promised to roll up.'

Ballard, Keene, and Willis were members of the Cambridge team, all very capable performers and much in demand by the county, when they could get away to play for it.

'Well?' said Mike.

'Well, we all came up by train from Brighton last night. But these three asses had arranged to motor down from Cambridge early today, and get here in time for the start. What happens? Why, Willis, who fancies himself as a chauffeur, undertakes to do the driving; and naturally, being an absolute rotter, goes and smashes up the whole concern just outside St Albans. The first thing I knew of it was when I got to Lord's at half past ten, and found a wire waiting for me to say that they were all three of them crocked, and couldn't possibly play. I tell you, it was a bit of a jar to get half an hour before the match started. Willis has sprained his ankle, apparently; Keene's damaged his wrist; and Ballard has smashed his collar-bone. I don't suppose they'll be able to play in the 'Varsity match. Rotten luck for Cambridge. Well, fortunately we'd had two reserve pros, with us at Brighton, who had come up to London with the team in case they might be wanted, so, with them, we were only one short. Then I thought of you. That's how it was.'

'I see,' said Mike. 'Who are the pros?'

'Davis and Brockley. Both bowlers. It weakens our batting a lot. Ballard or Willis might have got a stack of runs on this wicket. Still, we've got a certain amount of batting as it is. We oughtn't to do badly, if we're careful. You've been getting some practice, I suppose, this season?'

'In a sort of a way. Nets and so on. No matches of any importance.'

'Dash it, I wish you'd had a game or two in decent class cricket. Still, nets are better than nothing, I hope you'll be in form. We may want a pretty long knock from you, if things go wrong. These men seem to be settling down all right, thank goodness,' he added, looking out of the window at the county's first pair, Warrington and Mills, two professionals, who, as the result of ten minutes' play, had put up twenty.

'I'd better go and change,' said Mike, picking up his bag. 'You're in first wicket, I suppose?'

'Yes. And Reggie, second wicket.'

Reggie was another of Mike's brothers, not nearly so fine a player as

Joe, but a sound bat, who generally made runs if allowed to stay in.

Mike changed, and went out into the little balcony at the top of the pavilion. He had it to himself. There were not many spectators in the pavilion at this early stage of the game.

There are few more restful places, if one wishes to think, than the upper balconies of Lord's pavilion. Mike, watching the game making its leisurely progress on the turf below, set himself seriously to review the situation in all its aspects. The exhilaration of bursting the bonds had begun to fade, and he found himself able to look into the matter of his desertion and weigh up the consequences. There was no doubt that he had cut the painter once and for all. Even a friendly-disposed management could hardly overlook what he had done. And the management of the New Asiatic Bank was the very reverse of friendly. Mr Bickersdyke, he knew, would jump at this chance of getting rid of him. He realized that he must look on his career in the bank as a closed book. It was definitely over, and he must now think about the future.

It was not a time for half-measures. He could not go home. He must carry the thing through, now that he had begun, and find something definite to do, to support himself.

There seemed only one opening for him. What could he do, he asked himself. Just one thing. He could play cricket. It was by his cricket that he must live. He would have to become a professional. Could he get taken on? That was the question. It was impossible that he should play for his own county on his residential qualification. He could not appear as a professional in the same team in which his brothers were playing as amateurs. He must stake all on his birth qualification for Surrey.

On the other hand, had he the credentials which Surrey would want? He had a school reputation. But was that enough? He could not help feeling that it might not be.

Thinking it over more tensely than he had ever thought over anything in his whole life, he saw clearly that everything depended on what sort of show he made in this match which was now in progress. It was his big chance. If he succeeded, all would be well. He did not care to think what his position would be if he did not succeed.

A distant appeal and a sound of clapping from the crowd broke in on his thoughts. Mills was out, caught at the wicket. The telegraph-board gave the total as forty-eight. Not sensational. The success of the team depended largely on what sort of a start the two professionals made.

The clapping broke out again as Joe made his way down the steps. Joe, as an All England player, was a favourite with the crowd.

Mike watched him play an over in his strong, graceful style: then it suddenly occurred to him that he would like to know how matters had gone at the bank in his absence.

He went down to the telephone, rang up the bank, and asked for Psmith.

Presently the familiar voice made itself heard.

'Hullo, Smith.'

'Hullo. Is that Comrade Jackson? How are things progressing?'

'Fairly well. We're in first. We've lost one wicket, and the fifty's just up. I say, what's happened at the bank?'

'I broke the news to Comrade Gregory. A charming personality. I feel that we shall be friends.'

'Was he sick?'

'In a measure, yes. Indeed, I may say he practically foamed at the mouth. I explained the situation, but he was not to be appeased. He jerked me into the presence of Comrade Bickersdyke, with whom I had a brief but entertaining chat. He had not a great deal to say, but he listened attentively to my narrative, and eventually told me off to take your place in the Fixed Deposits. That melancholy task I am now performing to the best of my ability. I find the work a little trying. There is too much ledger-lugging to be done for my simple tastes. I have been hauling ledgers from the safe all the morning. The cry is beginning to go round, "Psmith is willing, but can his physique stand the strain?" In the excitement of the moment just now I dropped a somewhat massive tome on to Comrade Gregory's foot, unfortunately, I understand, the foot in which he has of late been suffering twinges of gout. I passed the thing off with ready tact, but I cannot deny that there was a certain temporary coolness, which, indeed, is not yet past. These things, Comrade Jackson, are the whirlpools in the quiet stream of commercial life.'

'Have I got the sack?'

'No official pronouncement has been made to me as yet on the subject, but I think I should advise you, if you are offered another job in the course of the day, to accept it. I cannot say that you are precisely the pet of the management just at present. However, I have ideas for your future, which I will divulge when we meet. I propose to slide coyly from the office at about four o'clock. I am meeting my father at that hour. We shall come straight on to Lord's.'

'Right ho,' said Mike. 'I'll be looking out for you.'

'Is there any little message I can give Comrade Gregory from you?'

'You can give him my love, if you like.'

'It shall be done. Good-bye.'

'Good-bye.'

Mike replaced the receiver, and went up to his balcony again.

As soon as his eye fell on the telegraph-board he saw with a start that things had been moving rapidly in his brief absence. The numbers of the batsmen on the board were three and five.

'Great Scott!' he cried. 'Why, I'm in next. What on earth's been happening?'

He put on his pads hurriedly, expecting every moment that a wicket would fall and find him unprepared. But the batsmen were still together when he rose, ready for the fray, and went downstairs to get news.

He found his brother Reggie in the dressing-room.

'What's happened?' he said. 'How were you out?'

'L.b.w.,' said Reggie. 'Goodness knows how it happened. My eyesight must be going. I mistimed the thing altogether.'

'How was Warrington out?'

'Caught in the slips.'

'By Jove!' said Mike. 'This is pretty rocky. Three for sixty-one. We shall get mopped.'

'Unless you and Joe do something. There's no earthly need to get out.

The wicket's as good as you want, and the bowling's nothing special.

Well played, Joe!'

A beautiful glide to leg by the greatest of the Jacksons had rolled up against the pavilion rails. The fieldsmen changed across for the next over.

'If only Peters stops a bit—' began Mike, and broke off. Peters' off stump was lying at an angle of forty-five degrees.

'Well, he hasn't,' said Reggie grimly. 'Silly ass, why did he hit at that one? All he'd got to do was to stay in with Joe. Now it's up to you. Do try and do something, or we'll be out under the hundred.'

Mike waited till the outcoming batsman had turned in at the professionals' gate. Then he walked down the steps and out into the open, feeling more nervous than he had felt since that far-off day when he had first gone in to bat for Wrykyn against the M.C.C. He found his thoughts flying back to that occasion. Today, as then, everything seemed very distant and unreal. The spectators were miles away. He had often been to Lord's as a spectator, but the place seemed entirely unfamiliar now. He felt as if he were in a strange land.

He was conscious of Joe leaving the crease to meet him on his way. He smiled feebly. 'Buck up,' said Joe in that robust way of his which was so heartening. 'Nothing in the bowling, and the wicket like a shirt-front. Play just as if you were at the nets. And for goodness' sake don't try to score all your runs in the first over. Stick in, and we've got them.'

Mike smiled again more feebly than before, and made a weird gurgling noise in his throat.

It had been the Middlesex fast bowler who had destroyed Peters. Mike was not sorry. He did not object to fast bowling. He took guard, and looked round him, taking careful note of the positions of the slips.

As usual, once he was at the wicket the paralysed feeling left him. He became conscious again of his power. Dash it all, what was there to be afraid of? He was a jolly good bat, and he would jolly well show them that he was, too.

The fast bowler, with a preliminary bound, began his run. Mike settled himself into position, his whole soul concentrated on the ball. Everything else was wiped from his mind.

28. Psmith Arranges his Future

It was exactly four o'clock when Psmith, sliding unostentatiously from his stool, flicked divers pieces of dust from the leg of his trousers, and sidled towards the basement, where he was wont to keep his hat during business hours. He was aware that it would be a matter of some delicacy to leave the bank at that hour. There was a certain quantity of work still to be done in the Fixed Deposits Department—work in which, by rights, as Mike's understudy, he should have lent a sympathetic and helping hand. 'But what of that?' he mused, thoughtfully smoothing his hat with his knuckles. 'Comrade Gregory is a man who takes such an enthusiastic pleasure in his duties that he will go singing about the office when he discovers that he has got a double lot of work to do.'

With this comforting thought, he started on his perilous journey to the open air. As he walked delicately, not courting observation, he reminded himself of the hero of 'Pilgrim's Progress'. On all sides of him lay fearsome beasts, lying in wait to pounce upon him. At any moment Mr Gregory's hoarse roar might shatter the comparative stillness, or the sinister note of Mr Bickersdyke make itself heard.

'However,' said Psmith philosophically, 'these are Life's Trials, and must be borne patiently.'

A roundabout route, via the Postage and Inwards Bills Departments, took him to the swing-doors. It was here that the danger became acute. The doors were well within view of the Fixed Deposits Department, and Mr Gregory had an eye compared with which that of an eagle was more or less bleared.

Psmith sauntered to the door and pushed it open in a gingerly manner.

As he did so a bellow rang through the office, causing a timid customer, who had come in to arrange about an overdraft, to lose his nerve completely and postpone his business till the following afternoon.

Psmith looked up. Mr Gregory was leaning over the barrier which divided his lair from the outer world, and gesticulating violently.

'Where are you going,' roared the head of the Fixed Deposits.

Psmith did not reply. With a benevolent smile and a gesture intended to signify all would come right in the future, he slid through the swing-doors, and began to move down the street at a somewhat swifter pace than was his habit.

Once round the corner he slackened his speed.

'This can't go on,' he said to himself. 'This life of commerce is too great a strain. One is practically a hunted hare. Either the heads of my department must refrain from View Halloos when they observe me going for a stroll, or I abandon Commerce for some less exacting walk in life.'

He removed his hat, and allowed the cool breeze to play upon his forehead. The episode had been disturbing.

He was to meet his father at the Mansion House. As he reached that land-mark he saw with approval that punctuality was a virtue of which he had not the sole monopoly in the Smith family. His father was waiting for him at the tryst.

'Certainly, my boy,' said Mr Smith senior, all activity in a moment, when Psmith had suggested going to Lord's. 'Excellent. We must be getting on. We must not miss a moment of the match. Bless my soul: I haven't seen a first-class match this season. Where's a cab? Hi, cabby! No, that one's got some one in it. There's another. Hi! Here, lunatic! Are you blind? Good, he's seen us. That's right. Here he comes. Lord's Cricket Ground, cabby, as quick as you can. Jump in, Rupert, my boy, jump in.'

Psmith rarely jumped. He entered the cab with something of the stateliness of an old Roman Emperor boarding his chariot, and settled himself comfortably in his seat. Mr Smith dived in like a rabbit.

A vendor of newspapers came to the cab thrusting an evening paper into the interior. Psmith bought it.

'Let's see how they're getting on,' he said, opening the paper. 'Where are we? Lunch scores. Lord's. Aha! Comrade Jackson is in form.'

'Jackson?' said Mr Smith, 'is that the same youngster you brought home last summer? The batsman? Is he playing today?'

'He was not out thirty at lunch-time. He would appear to be making something of a stand with his brother Joe, who has made sixty-one up to the moment of going to press. It's possible he may still be in when we get there. In which case we shall not be able to slide into the pavilion.'

'A grand bat, that boy. I said so last summer. Better than any of his brothers. He's in the bank with you, isn't he?'

'He was this morning. I doubt, however, whether he can be said to be still in that position.'

'Eh? what? How's that?'

'There was some slight friction between him and the management. They wished him to be glued to his stool; he preferred to play for the county. I think we may say that Comrade Jackson has secured the Order of the Boot.'

'What? Do you mean to say—?'

Psmith related briefly the history of Mike's departure.

Mr Smith listened with interest.

'Well,' he said at last, 'hang me if I blame the boy. It's a sin cooping up a fellow who can bat like that in a bank. I should have done the same myself in his place.'

Psmith smoothed his waistcoat.

'Do you know, father,' he said, 'this bank business is far from being much of a catch. Indeed, I should describe it definitely as a bit off. I have given it a fair trial, and I now denounce it unhesitatingly as a shade too thick.'

'What? Are you getting tired of it?'

'Not precisely tired. But, after considerable reflection, I have come to the conclusion that my talents lie elsewhere. At lugging ledgers I am among the also-rans—a mere cipher. I have been wanting to speak to you about this for some time. If you have no objection, I should like to go to the Bar.'

'The Bar? Well—'

'I fancy I should make a pretty considerable hit as a barrister.'

Mr Smith reflected. The idea had not occurred to him before. Now that it was suggested, his always easily-fired imagination took hold of it readily. There was a good deal to be said for the Bar as a career. Psmith knew his father, and he knew that the thing was practically as good as settled. It was a new idea, and as such was bound to be favourably received.

'What I should do, if I were you,' he went on, as if he were advising a friend on some course of action certain to bring him profit and pleasure, 'is to take me away from the bank at once. Don't wait. There is no time like the present. Let me hand in my resignation tomorrow. The blow to the management, especially to Comrade Bickersdyke, will be a painful one, but it is the truest kindness to administer it swiftly. Let me resign tomorrow, and devote my time to quiet study. Then I can pop up to Cambridge next term, and all will be well.'

'I'll think it over—' began Mr Smith.

'Let us hustle,' urged Psmith. 'Let us Do It Now. It is the only way. Have I your leave to shoot in my resignation to Comrade Bickersdyke tomorrow morning?'

Mr Smith hesitated for a moment, then made up his mind.

'Very well,' he said. 'I really think it is a good idea. There are great opportunities open to a barrister. I wish we had thought of it before.'

'I am not altogether sorry that we did not,' said Psmith. 'I have enjoyed the chances my commercial life has given me of associating with such a man as Comrade Bickersdyke. In many ways a master-mind. But perhaps it is as well to close the chapter. How it happened it is hard to say, but somehow I fancy I did not precisely hit it off with Comrade Bickersdyke. With Psmith, the worker, he had no fault to find; but it seemed to me sometimes, during our festive evenings together at the club, that all was not well. From little, almost imperceptible signs I have suspected now and then that he would just as soon have been without my company. One cannot explain these things. It must have been some incompatibility of temperament. Perhaps he will manage to bear up at my departure. But here we are,' he added, as the cab drew up. 'I wonder if Comrade Jackson is still going strong.'

They passed through the turnstile, and caught sight of the telegraph-board.

'By Jove!' said Psmith, 'he is. I don't know if he's number three or number six. I expect he's number six. In which case he has got ninety-eight. We're just in time to see his century.'

29. And Mike's

For nearly two hours Mike had been experiencing the keenest pleasure that it had ever fallen to his lot to feel. From the moment he took his first ball till the luncheon interval he had suffered the acutest discomfort. His nervousness had left him to a great extent, but he had never really settled down. Sometimes by luck, and sometimes by skill, he had kept the ball out of his wicket; but he was scratching, and he knew it. Not for a single over had he been comfortable. On several occasions he had edged balls to leg and through the slips in quite an inferior manner, and it was seldom that he managed to hit with the centre of the bat.

Nobody is more alive to the fact that he is not playing up to his true form than the batsman. Even though his score mounted little by little into the twenties, Mike was miserable. If this was the best he could do on a perfect wicket, he felt there was not much hope for him as a professional.

The poorness of his play was accentuated by the brilliance of Joe's. Joe combined science and vigour to a remarkable degree. He laid on the wood with a graceful robustness which drew much cheering from the crowd. Beside him Mike was oppressed by that leaden sense of moral inferiority which weighs on a man who has turned up to dinner in ordinary clothes when everybody else has dressed. He felt awkward and conspicuously out of place.

Then came lunch—and after lunch a glorious change.

Volumes might be written on the cricket lunch and the influence it has on the run of the game; how it undoes one man, and sends another back to the fray like a giant refreshed; how it turns the brilliant fast bowler into the sluggish medium, and the nervous bat into the masterful smiter.

On Mike its effect was magical. He lunched wisely and well, chewing his food with the concentration of a thirty-three-bites a mouthful crank, and drinking dry ginger-ale. As he walked out with Joe after the interval he knew that a change had taken place in him. His nerve had come back, and with it his form.

It sometimes happens at cricket that when one feels particularly fit one gets snapped in the slips in the first over, or clean bowled by a full toss; but neither of these things happened to Mike. He stayed in, and began to score. Now there were no edgings through the slips and snicks to leg. He was meeting the ball in the centre of the bat, and meeting it vigorously. Two boundaries in successive balls off the fast bowler, hard, clean drives past extra-cover, put him at peace with all the world. He was on top. He had found himself.

Joe, at the other end, resumed his brilliant career. His century and

Mike's fifty arrived in the same over. The bowling began to grow loose.

Joe, having reached his century, slowed down somewhat, and Mike took up the running. The score rose rapidly.

A leg-theory bowler kept down the pace of the run-getting for a time, but the bowlers at the other end continued to give away runs. Mike's score passed from sixty to seventy, from seventy to eighty, from eighty to ninety. When the Smiths, father and son, came on to the ground the total was ninety-eight. Joe had made a hundred and thirty-three.

* * * * *

Mike reached his century just as Psmith and his father took their seats. A square cut off the slow bowler was just too wide for point to get to. By the time third man had sprinted across and returned the ball the batsmen had run two.

Mr Smith was enthusiastic.

'I tell you,' he said to Psmith, who was clapping in a gently encouraging manner, 'the boy's a wonderful bat. I said so when he was down with us. I remember telling him so myself. "I've seen your brothers play," I said, "and you're better than any of them." I remember it distinctly. He'll be playing for England in another year or two. Fancy putting a cricketer like that into the City! It's a crime.'

'I gather,' said Psmith, 'that the family coffers had got a bit low. It was necessary for Comrade Jackson to do something by way of saving the Old Home.'

'He ought to be at the University. Look, he's got that man away to the boundary again. They'll never get him out.'

At six o'clock the partnership was broken, Joe running himself out in trying to snatch a single where no single was. He had made a hundred and eighty-nine.

Mike flung himself down on the turf with mixed feelings. He was sorry Joe was out, but he was very glad indeed of the chance of a rest. He was utterly fagged. A half-day match once a week is no training for first-class cricket. Joe, who had been playing all the season, was as tough as india-rubber, and trotted into the pavilion as fresh as if he had been having a brief spell at the nets. Mike, on the other hand, felt that he simply wanted to be dropped into a cold bath and left there indefinitely. There was only another half-hour's play, but he doubted if he could get through it.

He dragged himself up wearily as Joe's successor arrived at the wickets. He had crossed Joe before the latter's downfall, and it was his turn to take the bowling.

Something seemed to have gone out of him. He could not time the ball properly. The last ball of the over looked like a half-volley, and he hit out at it. But it was just short of a half-volley, and his stroke arrived too soon. The bowler, running in the direction of mid-on, brought off an easy c.-and-b.

Mike turned away towards the pavilion. He heard the gradually swelling applause in a sort of dream. It seemed to him hours before he reached the dressing-room.

He was sitting on a chair, wishing that somebody would come along and take off his pads, when Psmith's card was brought to him. A few moments later the old Etonian appeared in person.

'Hullo, Smith,' said Mike, 'By Jove! I'm done.'

'"How Little Willie Saved the Match,"' said Psmith. 'What you want is one of those gin and ginger-beers we hear so much about. Remove those pads, and let us flit downstairs in search of a couple. Well, Comrade Jackson, you have fought the good fight this day. My father sends his compliments. He is dining out, or he would have come up. He is going to look in at the flat latish.'

'How many did I get?' asked Mike. 'I was so jolly done I didn't think of looking.'

'A hundred and forty-eight of the best,' said Psmith. 'What will they say at the old homestead about this? Are you ready? Then let us test this fruity old ginger-beer of theirs.'

The two batsmen who had followed the big stand were apparently having a little stand all of their own. No more wickets fell before the drawing of stumps. Psmith waited for Mike while he changed, and carried him off in a cab to Simpson's, a restaurant which, as he justly observed, offered two great advantages, namely, that you need not dress, and, secondly, that you paid your half-crown, and were then at liberty to eat till you were helpless, if you felt so disposed, without extra charge.

Mike stopped short of this giddy height of mastication, but consumed enough to make him feel a great deal better. Psmith eyed his inroads on the menu with approval.

'There is nothing,' he said, 'like victualling up before an ordeal.'

'What's the ordeal?' said Mike.

'I propose to take you round to the club anon, where I trust we shall find Comrade Bickersdyke. We have much to say to one another.'

'Look here, I'm hanged—' began Mike.

'Yes, you must be there,' said Psmith. 'Your presence will serve to cheer Comrade B. up. Fate compels me to deal him a nasty blow, and he will want sympathy. I have got to break it to him that I am leaving the bank.'

'What, are you going to chuck it?'

Psmith inclined his head.

'The time,' he said, 'has come to part. It has served its turn. The startled whisper runs round the City. "Psmith has had sufficient."'

'What are you going to do?'

'I propose to enter the University of Cambridge, and there to study the intricacies of the Law, with a view to having a subsequent dash at becoming Lord Chancellor.'

'By Jove!' said Mike, 'you're lucky. I wish I were coming too.'

Psmith knocked the ash off his cigarette.

'Are you absolutely set on becoming a pro?' he asked.

'It depends on what you call set. It seems to me it's about all I can do.'

'I can offer you a not entirely scaly job,' said Smith, 'if you feel like taking it. In the course of conversation with my father during the match this afternoon, I gleaned the fact that he is anxious to secure your services as a species of agent. The vast Psmith estates, it seems, need a bright boy to keep an eye upon them. Are you prepared to accept the post?'

Mike stared.

'Me! Dash it all, how old do you think I am? I'm only nineteen.'

'I had suspected as much from the alabaster clearness of your unwrinkled brow. But my father does not wish you to enter upon your duties immediately. There would be a preliminary interval of three, possibly four, years at Cambridge, during which I presume, you would be learning divers facts concerning spuds, turmuts, and the like. At least,' said Psmith airily, 'I suppose so. Far be it from me to dictate the line of your researches.'

'Then I'm afraid it's off,' said Mike gloomily. 'My pater couldn't afford to send me to Cambridge.'

'That obstacle,' said Psmith, 'can be surmounted. You would, of course, accompany me to Cambridge, in the capacity, which you enjoy at the present moment, of my confidential secretary and adviser. Any expenses that might crop up would be defrayed from the Psmith family chest.'

Mike's eyes opened wide again.

'Do you mean,' he asked bluntly, 'that your pater would pay for me at the 'Varsity? No I say—dash it—I mean, I couldn't—'

'Do you suggest,' said Psmith, raising his eyebrows, 'that I should go to the University *without* a confidential secretary and adviser?'

'No, but I mean—' protested Mike.

'Then that's settled,' said Psmith. 'I knew you would not desert me in my hour of need, Comrade Jackson. "What will you do," asked my father, alarmed for my safety, "among these wild undergraduates? I fear for my Rupert." "Have no fear, father," I replied. "Comrade Jackson will be beside me." His face brightened immediately. "Comrade Jackson," he said, "is a man in whom I have the supremest confidence. If he is with you I shall sleep easy of nights." It was after that that the conversation drifted to the subject of agents.'

Psmith called for the bill and paid it in the affable manner of a monarch signing a charter. Mike sat silent, his mind in a whirl. He saw exactly what had happened. He could almost hear Psmith talking his father into agreeing with his scheme. He could think of nothing to say. As usually happened in any emotional crisis in his life, words absolutely deserted him. The thing was too big. Anything he could say would sound too feeble. When a friend has solved all your difficulties and smoothed out all the rough places which were looming in your path, you cannot thank him as if he had asked you to lunch. The occasion demanded some neat, polished speech; and neat, polished speeches were beyond Mike.

'I say, Psmith—' he began.

Psmith rose.

'Let us now,' he said, 'collect our hats and meander to the club, where, I have no doubt, we shall find Comrade Bickersdyke, all unconscious of impending misfortune, dreaming pleasantly over coffee and a cigar in the lower smoking-room.'

30. The Last Sad Farewells

As it happened, that was precisely what Mr Bickersdyke was doing. He was feeling thoroughly pleased with life. For nearly nine months Psmith had been to him a sort of spectre at the feast inspiring him with an ever-present feeling of discomfort which he had found impossible to shake off. And tonight he saw his way of getting rid of him.

At five minutes past four Mr Gregory, crimson and wrathful, had plunged into his room with a long statement of how Psmith, deputed to help in the life and thought of the Fixed Deposits Department, had left the building at four o'clock, when there was still another hour and a half's work to be done.

Moreover, Mr Gregory deposed, the errant one, seen sliding out of the swinging door, and summoned in a loud, clear voice to come back, had flatly disobeyed and had gone upon his ways 'Grinning at me,' said the aggrieved Mr Gregory, 'like a dashed ape.' A most unjust description of the sad, sweet smile which Psmith had bestowed upon him from the doorway.

Ever since that moment Mr Bickersdyke had felt that there was a silver lining to the cloud. Hitherto Psmith had left nothing to be desired in the manner in which he performed his work. His righteousness in the office had clothed him as in a suit of mail. But now he had slipped. To go off an hour and a half before the proper time, and to refuse to return when summoned by the head of his department—these were offences for which he could be dismissed without fuss. Mr Bickersdyke looked forward to tomorrow's interview with his employee.

Meanwhile, having enjoyed an excellent dinner, he was now, as Psmith had predicted, engaged with a cigar and a cup of coffee in the lower smoking-room of the Senior Conservative Club.

Psmith and Mike entered the room when he was about half through these luxuries.

Psmith's first action was to summon a waiter, and order a glass of neat brandy. 'Not for myself,' he explained to Mike. 'For Comrade Bickersdyke. He is about to sustain a nasty shock, and may need a restorative at a moment's notice. For all we know, his heart may not be strong. In any case, it is safest to have a pick-me-up handy.'

He paid the waiter, and advanced across the room, followed by Mike. In his hand, extended at arm's length, he bore the glass of brandy.

Mr Bickersdyke caught sight of the procession, and started. Psmith set the brandy down very carefully on the table, beside the manager's coffee cup, and, dropping into a chair, regarded him pityingly through his eyeglass. Mike, who felt embarrassed, took a seat some little way behind his companion. This was Psmith's affair, and he proposed to allow him to do the talking.

Mr Bickersdyke, except for a slight deepening of the colour of his complexion, gave no sign of having seen them. He puffed away at his cigar, his eyes fixed on the ceiling.

'An unpleasant task lies before us,' began Psmith in a low, sorrowful voice, 'and it must not be shirked. Have I your ear, Mr Bickersdyke?'

Addressed thus directly, the manager allowed his gaze to wander from the ceiling. He eyed Psmith for a moment like an elderly basilisk, then looked back at the ceiling again.

'I shall speak to you tomorrow,' he said.

Psmith heaved a heavy sigh.

'You will not see us tomorrow,' he said, pushing the brandy a little nearer.

Mr Bickersdyke's eyes left the ceiling once more.

'What do you mean?' he said.

'Drink this,' urged Psmith sympathetically, holding out the glass. 'Be brave,' he went on rapidly. 'Time softens the harshest blows. Shocks stun us for the moment, but we recover. Little by little we come to ourselves again. Life, which we had thought could hold no more pleasure for us, gradually shows itself not wholly grey.'

Mr Bickersdyke seemed about to make an observation at this point, but

Psmith, with a wave of the hand, hurried on.

'We find that the sun still shines, the birds still sing. Things which used to entertain us resume their attraction. Gradually we emerge from the soup, and begin—'

'If you have anything to say to me,' said the manager, 'I should be glad if you would say it, and go.'

'You prefer me not to break the bad news gently?' said Psmith. 'Perhaps you are wise. In a word, then,'—he picked up the brandy and held it out to him—'Comrade Jackson and myself are leaving the bank.'

'I am aware of that,' said Mr Bickersdyke drily.

Psmith put down the glass.

'You have been told already?' he said. 'That accounts for your calm. The shock has expended its force on you, and can do no more. You are stunned. I am sorry, but it had to be. You will say that it is madness for us to offer our resignations, that our grip on the work of the bank made a prosperous career in Commerce certain for us. It may be so. But somehow we feel that our talents lie elsewhere. To Comrade Jackson the management of the Psmith estates seems the job on which he can get the rapid half-Nelson. For my own part, I feel that my long suit is the Bar. I am a poor, unready speaker, but I intend to acquire a knowledge of the Law which shall outweigh this defect. Before leaving you, I should like to say—I may speak for you as well as myself, Comrade Jackson—?'

Mike uttered his first contribution to the conversation—a gurgle—and relapsed into silence again.

'I should like to say,' continued Psmith, 'how much Comrade Jackson and I have enjoyed our stay in the bank. The insight it has given us into your masterly handling of the intricate mechanism of the office has been a treat we would not have missed. But our place is elsewhere.'

He rose. Mike followed his example with alacrity. It occurred to Mr Bickersdyke, as they turned to go, that he had not yet been able to get in a word about their dismissal. They were drifting away with all the honours of war.

'Come back,' he cried.

Psmith paused and shook his head sadly.

'This is unmanly, Comrade Bickersdyke,' he said. 'I had not expected this. That you should be dazed by the shock was natural. But that you should beg us to reconsider our resolve and return to the bank is unworthy of you. Be a man. Bite the bullet. The first keen pang will pass. Time will soften the feeling of bereavement. You must be brave. Come, Comrade Jackson.'

Mike responded to the call without hesitation.

'We will now,' said Psmith, leading the way to the door, 'push back to the flat. My father will be round there soon.' He looked over his shoulder. Mr Bickersdyke appeared to be wrapped in thought.

'A painful business,' sighed Psmith. 'The man seems quite broken up. It had to be, however. The bank was no place for us. An excellent career in many respects, but unsuitable for you and me. It is hard on Comrade Bickersdyke, especially as he took such trouble to get me into it, but I think we may say that we are well out of the place.'

Mike's mind roamed into the future. Cambridge first, and then an open-air life of the sort he had always dreamed of. The Problem of Life seemed to him to be solved. He looked on down the years, and he could see no troubles there of any kind whatsoever. Reason suggested that there were probably one or two knocking about somewhere, but this was no time to think of them. He examined the future, and found it good.

'I should jolly well think,' he said simply, 'that we might.'

Psmith, Journalist

PREFACE

THE conditions of life in New York are so different from those of London that a story of this kind calls for a little explanation. There are several million inhabitants of New York. Not all of them eke out a precarious livelihood by murdering one another, but there is a definite section of the population which murders—not casually, on the spur of the moment, but on definitely commercial lines at so many dollars per murder. The "gangs" of New York exist in fact. I have not invented them. Most of the incidents in this story are based on actual happenings. The Rosenthal case, where four men, headed by a genial individual calling himself "Gyp the Blood" shot a fellow-citizen in cold blood in a spot as public and fashionable as Piccadilly Circus and escaped in a motor-car, made such a stir a few years ago that the noise of it was heard all over the world and not, as is generally the case with the doings of the gangs, in New York only. Rosenthal cases on a smaller and less sensational scale are frequent occurrences on Manhattan Island. It was the prominence of the victim rather than the unusual nature of the occurrence that excited the New York press. Most gang victims get a quarter of a column in small type.

P. G. WODEHOUSE

New York, 1915

CHAPTER I - "COSY MOMENTS"

The man in the street would not have known it, but a great crisis was imminent in New York journalism.

Everything seemed much as usual in the city. The cars ran blithely on Broadway. Newsboys shouted "Wux-try!" into the ears of nervous pedestrians with their usual Caruso-like vim. Society passed up and down Fifth Avenue in its automobiles, and was there a furrow of anxiety upon Society's brow? None. At a thousand street corners a thousand policemen preserved their air of massive superiority to the things of this world. Not one of them showed the least sign of perturbation. Nevertheless, the crisis was at hand. Mr. J. Fillken Wilberfloss, editor-in-chief of *Cosy Moments*, was about to leave his post and start on a ten weeks' holiday.

In New York one may find every class of paper which the imagination can conceive. Every grade of society is catered for. If an Esquimau came to New York, the first thing he would find on the bookstalls in all probability would be the *Blubber Magazine*, or some similar production written by Esquimaux for Esquimaux. Everybody reads in New York, and reads all the time. The New Yorker peruses his favourite paper while he is being jammed into a crowded compartment on the subway or leaping like an antelope into a moving Street car.

There was thus a public for *Cosy Moments*. *Cosy Moments*, as its name (an inspiration of Mr. Wilberfloss's own) is designed to imply, is a journal for the home. It is the sort of paper which the father of the family is expected to take home with him from his office and read aloud to the chicks before bed-time. It was founded by its proprietor, Mr. Benjamin White, as an antidote to yellow journalism. One is forced to admit that up to the present yellow journalism seems to be competing against it with a certain measure of success. Headlines are still of as generous a size as heretofore, and there is no tendency on the part of editors to scamp the details of the last murder-case.

Nevertheless, *Cosy Moments* thrives. It has its public.

Its contents are mildly interesting, if you like that sort of thing. There is a "Moments in the Nursery" page, conducted by Luella Granville Waterman, to which parents are invited to contribute the bright speeches of their offspring, and which bristles with little stories about the nursery canary, by Jane (aged six), and other works of rising young authors. There is a "Moments of Meditation" page, conducted by the Reverend Edwin T. Philpotts; a "Moments Among the Masters" page, consisting of assorted chunks looted from the literature of the past, when foreheads were bulgy and thoughts profound, by Mr. Wilberfloss himself; one or two other pages; a short story; answers to correspondents on domestic matters; and a "Moments of Mirth" page, conducted by an alleged humorist of the name of B. Henderson Asher, which is about the most painful production ever served up to a confiding public.

The guiding spirit of *Cosy Moments* was Mr. Wilberfloss. Circumstances had left the development of the paper mainly to him. For the past twelve months the proprietor had been away in Europe, taking the waters at Carlsbad, and the sole control of *Cosy Moments* had passed into the hands of Mr. Wilberfloss. Nor had he proved unworthy of the trust or unequal to the duties. In that year *Cosy Moments* had reached the highest possible level of domesticity. Anything not calculated to appeal to the home had been rigidly excluded. And as a result the circulation had increased steadily. Two extra pages had been added, "Moments Among the Shoppers" and "Moments with Society." And the advertisements had grown in volume. But the work had told upon the Editor. Work of that sort carries its penalties with it. Success means absorption, and absorption spells softening of the brain.

Whether it was the strain of digging into the literature of the past every week, or the effort of reading B. Henderson Asher's "Moments of Mirth" is uncertain. At any rate, his duties, combined with the heat of a New York summer, had sapped Mr. Wilberfloss's health to such an extent that the doctor had ordered him ten weeks' complete rest in the mountains. This Mr. Wilberfloss could, perhaps, have endured, if this had been all. There are worse places than the mountains of America in which to spend ten weeks of the tail-end of summer, when the sun has ceased to grill and the mosquitoes have relaxed their exertions. But it was not all. The doctor, a far-seeing man who went down to first causes, had absolutely declined to consent to Mr. Wilberfloss's suggestion that he should keep in touch with the paper during his vacation. He was adamant. He had seen copies of *Cosy Moments* once or twice, and he refused to permit a man in the editor's state of health to come in contact with Luella Granville Waterman's "Moments in the Nursery" and B. Henderson Asher's "Moments of Mirth." The medicine-man put his foot down firmly.

"You must not see so much as the cover of the paper for ten weeks," he said. "And I'm not so sure that it shouldn't be longer. You must forget that such a paper exists. You must dismiss the whole thing from your mind, live in the open, and develop a little flesh and muscle."

To Mr. Wilberfloss the sentence was almost equivalent to penal servitude. It was with tears in his voice that he was giving his final instructions to his sub-editor, in whose charge the paper would be left during his absence. He had taken a long time doing this. For two days he had been fussing in and out of the office, to the discontent of its inmates, more especially Billy Windsor, the sub-editor, who was now listening moodily to the last harangue of the series, with the air of one whose heart is not in the subject. Billy Windsor was a tall, wiry, loose-jointed young man, with unkempt hair and the general demeanour of a caged eagle. Looking at him, one could picture him astride of a bronco, rounding up cattle, or cooking his dinner at a camp-fire. Somehow he did not seem to fit into the *Cosy Moments* atmosphere.

"Well, I think that that is all, Mr. Windsor," chirruped the editor. He was a little man with a long neck and large *pince-nez*, and he always chirruped. "You understand the general lines on which I think the paper should be conducted?" The sub-editor nodded. Mr. Wilberfloss made him tired. Sometimes he made him more tired than at other times. At the present moment he filled him with an aching weariness. The editor meant well, and was full of zeal, but he had a habit of covering and recovering the ground. He possessed the art of saying the same obvious thing in a number of different ways to a degree which is found usually only in politicians. If Mr. Wilberfloss had been a politician, he would have been one of those dealers in glittering generalities who used to be fashionable in American politics.

"There is just one thing," he continued "Mrs. Julia Burdett Parslow is a little inclined—I may have mentioned this before—"

"You did," said the sub-editor.

Mr. Wilberfloss chirruped on, unchecked.

"A little inclined to be late with her 'Moments with Budding Girlhood'. If this should happen while I am away, just write her a letter, quite a pleasant letter, you understand, pointing out the necessity of being in good time. The machinery of a weekly paper, of course, cannot run smoothly unless contributors are in good time with their copy. She is a very sensible woman, and she will understand, I am sure, if you point it out to her."

The sub-editor nodded.

"And there is just one other thing. I wish you would correct a slight tendency I have noticed lately in Mr. Asher to be just a trifle—well, not precisely *risky*, but perhaps a shade *broad* in his humour."

"His what?" said Billy Windsor.

"Mr. Asher is a very sensible man, and he will be the first to acknowledge that his sense of humour has led him just a little beyond the bounds. You understand? Well, that is all, I think. Now I must really be going, or I shall miss my train. Good-bye, Mr. Windsor."

"Good-bye," said the sub-editor thankfully.

At the door Mr. Wilberfloss paused with the air of an exile bidding farewell to his native land, sighed, and trotted out.

Billy Windsor put his feet upon the table, and with a deep scowl resumed his task of reading the proofs of Luella Granville Waterman's "Moments in the Nursery."

CHAPTER II - BILLY WINDSOR

Billy Windsor had started life twenty-five years before this story opens on his father's ranch in Wyoming. From there he had gone to a local paper of the type whose Society column consists of such items as "Pawnee Jim Williams was to town yesterday with a bunch of other cheap skates. We take this opportunity of once more informing Jim that he is a liar and a skunk," and whose editor works with a revolver on his desk and another in his hip-pocket. Graduating from this, he had proceeded to a reporter's post on a daily paper in a Kentucky town, where there were blood feuds and other Southern devices for preventing life from becoming dull. All this time New York, the magnet, had been tugging at him. All reporters dream of reaching New York. At last, after four years on the Kentucky paper, he had come East, minus the lobe of one ear and plus a long scar that ran diagonally across his left shoulder, and had worked without much success as a free-lance. He was tough and ready for anything that might come his way, but these things are a great deal a matter of luck. The cub-reporter cannot make a name for himself unless he is favoured by fortune. Things had not come Billy Windsor's way. His work had been confined to turning in reports of fires and small street accidents, which the various papers to which he supplied them cut down to a couple of inches.

Billy had been in a bad way when he had happened upon the sub-editorship of *Cosy Moments*. He despised the work with all his heart, and the salary was infinitesimal. But it was regular, and for a while Billy felt that a regular salary was the greatest thing on earth. But he still dreamed of winning through to a post on one of the big New York dailies, where there was something doing and a man would have a chance of showing what was in him.

The unfortunate thing, however, was that *Cosy Moments* took up his time so completely. He had no chance of attracting the notice of big editors by his present work, and he had no leisure for doing any other.

All of which may go to explain why his normal aspect was that of a caged eagle.

To him, brooding over the outpourings of Luella Granville Waterman, there entered Pugsy Maloney, the office-boy, bearing a struggling cat.

"Say!" said Pugsy.

CHAPTER II - BILLY WINDSOR

He was a nonchalant youth, with a freckled, mask-like face, the expression of which never varied. He appeared unconscious of the cat. Its existence did not seem to occur to him.

"Well?" said Billy, looking up. "Hello, what have you got there?"

Master Maloney eyed the cat, as if he were seeing it for the first time.

"It's a kitty what I got in de street," he said.

"Don't hurt the poor brute. Put her down."

Master Maloney obediently dropped the cat, which sprang nimbly on to an upper shelf of the book-case.

"I wasn't hoitin' her," he said, without emotion. "Dere was two fellers in de street sickin' a dawg on to her. An' I comes up an' says, 'G'wan! What do youse t'ink you're doin', fussin' de poor dumb animal?' An' one of de guys, he says, 'G'wan! Who do youse t'ink youse is?' An' I says, 'I'm de guy what's goin' to swat youse one on de coco if youse don't quit fussin' de poor dumb animal.' So wit dat he makes a break at swattin' me one, but I swats him one, an' I swats de odder feller one, an' den I swats dem bote some more, an' I gets de kitty, an' I brings her in here, cos I t'inks maybe youse'll look after her."

And having finished this Homeric narrative, Master Maloney fixed an expressionless eye on the ceiling, and was silent.

Billy Windsor, like most men of the plains, combined the toughest of muscle with the softest of hearts. He was always ready at any moment to become the champion of the oppressed on the slightest provocation. His alliance with Pugsy Maloney had begun on the occasion when he had rescued that youth from the clutches of a large negro, who, probably from the soundest of motives, was endeavouring to slay him. Billy had not inquired into the rights and wrongs of the matter: he had merely sailed in and rescued the office-boy. And Pugsy, though he had made no verbal comment on the affair, had shown in many ways that he was not ungrateful.

"Bully for you, Pugsy!" he cried. "You're a little sport. Here"—he produced a dollar-bill—"go out and get some milk for the poor brute. She's probably starving. Keep the change."

"Sure thing," assented Master Maloney. He strolled slowly out, while Billy Windsor, mounting a chair, proceeded to chirrup and snap his fingers in the effort to establish the foundations of an *entente cordiale* with the rescued cat.

By the time that Pugsy returned, carrying a five-cent bottle of milk, the animal had vacated the book-shelf, and was sitting on the table, washing her face. The milk having been poured into the lid of a tobacco-tin, in lieu of a saucer, she suspended her operations and adjourned for refreshments. Billy, business being business, turned again to Luella Granville Waterman, but Pugsy, having no immediate duties on hand, concentrated himself on the cat.

"Say!" he said.

"Well?"

"Dat kitty."

"What about her?"

"Pipe de leather collar she's wearing."

Billy had noticed earlier in the proceedings that a narrow leather collar encircled the cat's neck. He had not paid any particular attention to it. "What about it?" he said.

"Guess I know where dat kitty belongs. Dey all have dose collars. I guess she's one of Bat Jarvis's kitties. He's got a lot of dem for fair, and every one wit one of dem collars round deir neck."

"Who's Bat Jarvis? Do you mean the gang-leader?"

"Sure. He's a cousin of mine," said Master Maloney with pride.

"Is he?" said Billy. "Nice sort of fellow to have in the family. So you think that's his cat?"

"Sure. He's got twenty-t'ree of dem, and dey all has dose collars."

"Are you on speaking terms with the gentleman?"

"Huh?"

"Do you know Bat Jarvis to speak to?"

"Sure. He's me cousin."

"Well, tell him I've got the cat, and that if he wants it he'd better come round to my place. You know where I live?"

"Sure."

"Fancy you being a cousin of Bat's, Pugsy. Why did you never tell us? Are you going to join the gang some day?"

"Nope. Nothin' doin'. I'm goin' to be a cow-boy."

"Good for you. Well, you tell him when you see him. And now, my lad, out you get, because if I'm interrupted any more I shan't get through to-night."

"Sure," said Master Maloney, retiring.

"Oh, and Pugsy . . ."

"Huh?"

"Go out and get a good big basket. I shall want one to carry this animal home in."

"Sure," said Master Maloney.

CHAPTER III - AT "THE GARDENIA"

"It would ill beseem me, Comrade Jackson," said Psmith, thoughtfully sipping his coffee, "to run down the metropolis of a great and friendly nation, but candour compels me to state that New York is in some respects a singularly blighted town."

"What's the matter with it?" asked Mike.

"Too decorous, Comrade Jackson. I came over here principally, it is true, to be at your side, should you be in any way persecuted by scoundrels. But at the same time I confess that at the back of my mind there lurked a hope that stirring adventures might come my way. I had heard so much of the place. Report had it that an earnest seeker after amusement might have a tolerably spacious rag in this modern Byzantium. I thought that a few weeks here might restore that keen edge to my nervous system which the languor of the past term had in a measure blunted. I wished my visit to be a tonic rather than a sedative. I anticipated that on my return the cry would go round Cambridge, 'Psmith has been to New York. He is full of oats. For he on honey-dew hath fed, and drunk the milk of Paradise. He is hot stuff. Rah!' But what do we find?"

He paused, and lit a cigarette.

"What do we find?" he asked again.

"I don't know," said Mike. "What?"

"A very judicious query, Comrade Jackson. What, indeed? We find a town very like London. A quiet, self-respecting town, admirable to the apostle of social reform, but disappointing to one who, like myself, arrives with a brush and a little bucket of red paint, all eager for a treat. I have been here a week, and I have not seen a single citizen clubbed by a policeman. No negroes dance cake-walks in the street. No cow-boy has let off his revolver at random in Broadway. The cables flash the message across the ocean, 'Psmith is losing his illusions.'"

Mike had come to America with a team of the M.C.C. which was touring the cricket-playing section of the United States. Psmith had accompanied him in a private capacity. It was the end of their first year at Cambridge, and Mike, with a century against Oxford to his credit, had been one of the first to be invited to join the tour. Psmith, who had played cricket in a rather desultory way at the University, had not risen to these heights. He had merely taken the opportunity of Mike's visit to the other side to accompany him. Cambridge had proved pleasant to

Psmith, but a trifle quiet. He had welcomed the chance of getting a change of scene.

So far the visit had failed to satisfy him. Mike, whose tastes in pleasure were simple, was delighted with everything. The cricket so far had been rather of the picnic order, but it was very pleasant; and there was no limit to the hospitality with which the visitors were treated. It was this more than anything which had caused Psmith's grave disapproval of things American. He was not a member of the team, so that the advantages of the hospitality did not reach him. He had all the disadvantages. He saw far too little of Mike. When he wished to consult his confidential secretary and adviser on some aspect of Life, that invaluable official was generally absent at dinner with the rest of the team. To-night was one of the rare occasions when Mike could get away. Psmith was becoming bored. New York is a better city than London to be alone in, but it is never pleasant to be alone in any big city.

As they sat discussing New York's shortcomings over their coffee, a young man passed them, carrying a basket, and seated himself at the next table. He was a tall, loose-jointed young man, with unkempt hair.

A waiter made an ingratiating gesture towards the basket, but the young man stopped him. "Not on your life, sonny," he said. "This stays right here." He placed it carefully on the floor beside his chair, and proceeded to order dinner.

Psmith watched him thoughtfully.

"I have a suspicion, Comrade Jackson," he said, "that this will prove to be a somewhat stout fellow. If possible, we will engage him in conversation. I wonder what he's got in the basket. I must get my Sherlock Holmes system to work. What is the most likely thing for a man to have in a basket? You would reply, in your unthinking way, 'sandwiches.' Error. A man with a basketful of sandwiches does not need to dine at restaurants. We must try again."

The young man at the next table had ordered a jug of milk to be accompanied by a saucer. These having arrived, he proceeded to lift the basket on to his lap, pour the milk into the saucer, and remove the lid from the basket. Instantly, with a yell which made the young man's table the centre of interest to all the diners, a large grey cat shot up like a rocket, and darted across the room. Psmith watched with silent interest.

It is hard to astonish the waiters at a New York restaurant, but when the cat performed this feat there was a squeal of surprise all round the room. Waiters rushed to and fro, futile but energetic. The cat, having secured a strong strategic position on the top of a large oil-painting which hung on the far wall, was expressing loud disapproval of the efforts of one of the waiters to drive it from its post with a walking-stick. The young man, seeing these manoeuvres, uttered a wrathful shout, and rushed to the rescue.

"Comrade Jackson," said Psmith, rising, "we must be in this."

When they arrived on the scene of hostilities, the young man had just possessed himself of the walking-stick, and was deep in a complex argument with the head-waiter on the ethics of the matter. The head-waiter, a stout impassive German, had taken his stand on a point of etiquette. "Id is," he said, "to bring gats into der grill-room vorbidden. No gendleman would gats into der grill-room bring. Der gendleman—"

The young man meanwhile was making enticing sounds, to which the cat was maintaining an attitude of reserved hostility. He turned furiously on the head-waiter.

"For goodness' sake," he cried, "can't you see the poor brute's scared stiff? Why don't you clear your gang of German comedians away, and give her a chance to come down?"

"Der gendleman—" argued the head-waiter.

Psmith stepped forward and touched him on the arm.

"May I have a word with you in private?"

"Zo?"

Psmith drew him away.

"You don't know who that is?" he whispered, nodding towards the young man.

"No gendleman he is," asserted the head-waiter. "Der gendleman would not der gat into—"

Psmith shook his head pityingly.

"These petty matters of etiquette are not for his Grace—but, hush, he wishes to preserve his incognito."

"Ingognito?"

"You understand. You are a man of the world, Comrade—may I call you Freddie? You understand, Comrade Freddie, that in a man in his Grace's position a few little eccentricities may be pardoned. You follow me, Frederick?"

The head-waiter's eye rested upon the young man with a new interest and respect.

"He is noble?" he inquired with awe.

"He is here strictly incognito, you understand," said Psmith warningly. The head-waiter nodded.

The young man meanwhile had broken down the cat's reserve, and was now standing with her in his arms, apparently anxious to fight all-comers in her defence. The head-waiter approached deferentially.

"Der gendleman," he said, indicating Psmith, who beamed in a friendly manner through his eye-glass, "haf everything exblained. All will now quite satisfactory be."

The young man looked inquiringly at Psmith, who winked encouragingly. The head-waiter bowed.

"Let me present Comrade Jackson," said Psmith, "the pet of our English Smart Set. I am Psmith, one of the Shropshire Psmiths. This is a great moment. Shall we be moving back? We were about to order a second instalment of coffee, to correct the effects of a fatiguing day. Perhaps you would care to join us?"

"Sure," said the alleged duke.

"This," said Psmith, when they were seated, and the head-waiter had ceased to hover, "is a great meeting. I was complaining with some acerbity to Comrade

Jackson, before you introduced your very interesting performing-animal speciality, that things in New York were too quiet, too decorous. I have an inkling, Comrade—"

"Windsor's my name."

"I have an inkling, Comrade Windsor, that we see eye to eye on the subject."

"I guess that's right. I was raised in the plains, and I lived in Kentucky a while. There's more doing there in a day than there is here in a month. Say, how did you fix it with the old man?"

"With Comrade Freddie? I have a certain amount of influence with him. He is content to order his movements in the main by my judgment. I assured him that all would be well, and he yielded." Psmith gazed with interest at the cat, which was lapping milk from the saucer. "Are you training that animal for a show of some kind, Comrade Windsor, or is it a domestic pet?"

"I've adopted her. The office-boy on our paper got her away from a dog this morning, and gave her to me."

"Your paper?"

"*Cosy Moments*," said Billy Windsor, with a touch of shame.

"*Cosy Moments*?" said Psmith reflectively. "I regret that the bright little sheet has not come my way up to the present. I must seize an early opportunity of perusing it."

"Don't you do it."

"You've no paternal pride in the little journal?"

"It's bad enough to hurt," said Billy Windsor disgustedly. "If you really want to see it, come along with me to my place, and I'll show you a copy."

"It will be a pleasure," said Psmith. "Comrade Jackson, have you any previous engagement for to-night?"

"I'm not doing anything," said Mike.

"Then let us stagger forth with Comrade Windsor. While he is loading up that basket, we will be collecting our hats. . . . I am not half sure, Comrade Jackson," he added, as they walked out, "that Comrade Windsor may not prove to be the genial spirit for whom I have been searching. If you could give me your undivided company, I should ask no more. But with you constantly away, mingling with the gay throng, it is imperative that I have some solid man to accompany me in my ramblings hither and thither. It is possible that Comrade Windsor may possess the qualifications necessary for the post. But here he comes. Let us foregather with him and observe him in private life before arriving at any premature decision."

CHAPTER IV - BAT JARVIS

Billy Windsor lived in a single room on East Fourteenth Street. Space in New York is valuable, and the average bachelor's apartments consist of one room with a bathroom opening off it. During the daytime this one room loses all traces of being used for sleeping purposes at night. Billy Windsor's room was very much like a public-school study. Along one wall ran a settee. At night this became a bed; but in the daytime it was a settee and nothing but a settee. There was no space for a great deal of furniture. There was one rocking-chair, two ordinary chairs, a table, a book-stand, a typewriter—nobody uses pens in New York—and on the walls a mixed collection of photographs, drawings, knives, and skins, relics of their owner's prairie days. Over the door was the head of a young bear.

Billy's first act on arriving in this sanctum was to release the cat, which, having moved restlessly about for some moments, finally came to the conclusion that there was no means of getting out, and settled itself on a corner of the settee. Psmith, sinking gracefully down beside it, stretched out his legs and lit a cigarette. Mike took one of the ordinary chairs; and Billy Windsor, planting himself in the rocker, began to rock rhythmically to and fro, a performance which he kept up untiringly all the time.

"A peaceful scene," observed Psmith. "Three great minds, keen, alert, restless during business hours, relax. All is calm and pleasant chit-chat. You have snug quarters up here, Comrade Windsor. I hold that there is nothing like one's own roof-tree. It is a great treat to one who, like myself, is located in one of these vast caravanserai—to be exact, the Astor—to pass a few moments in the quiet privacy of an apartment such as this."

"It's beastly expensive at the Astor," said Mike.

"The place has that drawback also. Anon, Comrade Jackson, I think we will hunt around for some such cubby-hole as this, built for two. Our nervous systems must be conserved."

"On Fourth Avenue," said Billy Windsor, "you can get quite good flats very cheap. Furnished, too. You should move there. It's not much of a neighbourhood. I don't know if you mind that?"

"Far from it, Comrade Windsor. It is my aim to see New York in all its phases. If a certain amount of harmless revelry can be whacked out of Fourth Avenue, we must dash there with the vim of highly-trained smell-dogs. Are you with me, Comrade Jackson?"

"All right," said Mike.

"And now, Comrade Windsor, it would be a pleasure to me to peruse that little journal of which you spoke. I have had so few opportunities of getting into touch with the literature of this great country."

Billy Windsor stretched out an arm and pulled a bundle of papers from the book-stand. He tossed them on to the settee by Psmith's side.

"There you are," he said, "if you really feel like it. Don't say I didn't warn you. If you've got the nerve, read on."

Psmith had picked up one of the papers when there came a shuffling of feet in the passage outside, followed by a knock upon the door. The next moment there appeared in the doorway a short, stout young man. There was an indescribable air of toughness about him, partly due to the fact that he wore his hair in a well-oiled fringe almost down to his eyebrows, which gave him the appearance of having no forehead at all. His eyes were small and set close together. His mouth was wide, his jaw prominent. Not, in short, the sort of man you would have picked out on sight as a model citizen.

His entrance was marked by a curious sibilant sound, which, on acquaintance, proved to be a whistled tune. During the interview which followed, except when he was speaking, the visitor whistled softly and unceasingly.

"Mr. Windsor?" he said to the company at large.

Psmith waved a hand towards the rocking-chair. "That," he said, "is Comrade Windsor. To your right is Comrade Jackson, England's favourite son. I am Psmith."

The visitor blinked furtively, and whistled another tune. As he looked round the room, his eye fell on the cat. His face lit up.

"Say!" he said, stepping forward, and touching the cat's collar, "mine, mister."

"Are you Bat Jarvis?" asked Windsor with interest.

"Sure," said the visitor, not without a touch of complacency, as of a monarch abandoning his incognito.

For Mr. Jarvis was a celebrity.

By profession he was a dealer in animals, birds, and snakes. He had a fancier's shop in Groome street, in the heart of the Bowery. This was on the ground-floor. His living abode was in the upper story of that house, and it was there that he kept the twenty-three cats whose necks were adorned with leather collars, and whose numbers had so recently been reduced to twenty-two. But it was not the fact that he possessed twenty-three cats with leather collars that made Mr. Jarvis a celebrity.

A man may win a purely local reputation, if only for eccentricity, by such means. But Mr. Jarvis's reputation was far from being purely local. Broadway knew him, and the Tenderloin. Tammany Hall knew him. Long Island City knew him. In the underworld of New York his name was a by-word. For Bat Jarvis was the leader of the famous Groome Street Gang, the most noted of all New York's collections of Apaches. More, he was the founder and originator of it. And, curiously enough, it had come into being from motives of sheer benevolence. In Groome Street in those days there had been a dance-hall, named the Shamrock and presided over by one Maginnis, an Irishman and a friend of Bat's. At the Shamrock nightly dances were given and well attended by the youth of the neighbourhood at ten cents a head. All might have been well, had it not been for certain other youths of the neighbourhood who did not dance and so had to seek other means of getting rid of their surplus energy. It was the practice of these light-hearted sportsmen to pay their ten cents for admittance, and once in, to make hay. And this habit, Mr. Maginnis found, was having a marked effect on his earnings. For genuine lovers of the dance fought shy of a place where at any moment Philistines might burst in and break heads and furniture. In this crisis the proprietor thought of his friend Bat Jarvis. Bat at that time had a solid reputation as a man of his hands. It is true that, as his detractors pointed out, he had killed no one—a defect which he had subsequently corrected; but his admirers based his claim to respect on his many meritorious performances with fists and with the black-jack. And Mr. Maginnis for one held him in the very highest esteem. To Bat accordingly he went, and laid his painful case before him. He offered him a handsome salary to be on hand at the nightly dances and check undue revelry by his own robust methods. Bat had accepted the offer. He had gone to Shamrock Hall; and with him, faithful adherents, had gone such stalwarts as Long Otto, Red Logan, Tommy Jefferson, and Pete Brodie. Shamrock Hall became a place of joy and order; and—more important still—the nucleus of the Groome Street Gang had been formed. The work progressed. Off-shoots of the main gang sprang up here and there about the East Side. Small thieves, pickpockets and the like, flocked to Mr. Jarvis as their tribal leader and protector and he protected them. For he, with his followers, were of use to the politicians. The New York gangs, and especially the Groome Street Gang, have brought to a fine art the gentle practice of "repeating"; which, broadly speaking, is the art of voting a number of different times at different polling-stations on election days. A man who can vote, say, ten times in a single day for you, and who controls a great number of followers who are also prepared, if they like you, to vote ten times in a single day for you, is worth cultivating. So the politicians passed the word to the police, and the police left the Groome Street Gang unmolested and they waxed fat and flourished.

Such was Bat Jarvis.

* * *

"Pipe de collar," said Mr. Jarvis, touching the cat's neck. "Mine, mister."

"Pugsy said it must be," said Billy Windsor. "We found two fellows setting a dog on to it, so we took it in for safety."

Mr. Jarvis nodded approval.

"There's a basket here, if you want it," said Billy.

"Nope. Here, kit."

Mr. Jarvis stooped, and, still whistling softly, lifted the cat. He looked round the company, met Psmith's eye-glass, was transfixed by it for a moment, and finally turned again to Billy Windsor.

"Say!" he said, and paused. "Obliged," he added.

He shifted the cat on to his left arm, and extended his right hand to Billy.

"Shake!" he said.

Billy did so.

Mr. Jarvis continued to stand and whistle for a few moments more.

"Say!" he said at length, fixing his roving gaze once more upon

Billy. "Obliged. Fond of de kit, I am."

Psmith nodded approvingly.

"And rightly," he said. "Rightly, Comrade Jarvis. She is not unworthy of your affection. A most companionable animal, full of the highest spirits. Her knockabout act in the restaurant would have satisfied the most jaded critic. No diner-out can afford to be without such a cat. Such a cat spells death to boredom."

Mr. Jarvis eyed him fixedly, as if pondering over his remarks. Then he turned to Billy again.

"Say!" he said. "Any time you're in bad. Glad to be of service.

You know the address. Groome Street. Bat Jarvis. Good night.

Obliged."

He paused and whistled a few more bars, then nodded to Psmith and

Mike, and left the room. They heard him shuffling downstairs.

"A blithe spirit," said Psmith. "Not garrulous, perhaps, but what of that? I am a man of few words myself. Comrade Jarvis's massive silences appeal to me. He seems to have taken a fancy to you, Comrade Windsor."

Billy Windsor laughed.

"I don't know that he's just the sort of side-partner I'd go out of my way to choose, from what I've heard about him. Still, if one got mixed up with any of that East-Side crowd, he would be a mighty useful friend to have. I guess there's no harm done by getting him grateful."

"Assuredly not," said Psmith. "We should not despise the humblest. And now, Comrade Windsor," he said, taking up the paper again, "let me concentrate myself tensely on this very entertaining little journal of yours. Comrade Jackson, here is one for you. For sound, clear-headed criticism," he added to Billy, "Comrade Jackson's name is a by-word in our English literary salons. His opinion will be both of interest and of profit to you, Comrade Windsor."

CHAPTER V - PLANNING IMPROVEMENTS

"By the way," said Psmith, "what is your exact position on this paper? Practically, we know well, you are its back-bone, its life-blood; but what is your technical position? When your proprietor is congratulating himself on having secured the ideal man for your job, what precise job does he congratulate himself on having secured the ideal man for?"

"I'm sub-editor."

"Merely sub? You deserve a more responsible post than that, Comrade Windsor. Where is your proprietor? I must buttonhole him and point out to him what a wealth of talent he is allowing to waste itself. You must have scope."

"He's in Europe. At Carlsbad, or somewhere. He never comes near the paper. He just sits tight and draws the profits. He lets the editor look after things. Just at present I'm acting as editor."

"Ah! then at last you have your big chance. You are free, untrammelled."

"You bet I'm not," said Billy Windsor. "Guess again. There's no room for developing free untrammelled ideas on this paper. When you've looked at it, you'll see that each page is run by some one. I'm simply the fellow who minds the shop."

Psmith clicked his tongue sympathetically. "It is like setting a gifted French chef to wash up dishes," he said. "A man of your undoubted powers, Comrade Windsor, should have more scope. That is the cry, 'more scope!' I must look into this matter. When I gaze at your broad, bulging forehead, when I see the clear light of intelligence in your eyes, and hear the grey matter splashing restlessly about in your cerebellum, I say to myself without hesitation, 'Comrade Windsor must have more scope.'" He looked at Mike, who was turning over the leaves of his copy of *Cosy Moments* in a sort of dull despair. "Well, Comrade Jackson, and what is your verdict?"

Mike looked at Billy Windsor. He wished to be polite, yet he could find nothing polite to say. Billy interpreted the look.

"Go on," he said. "Say it. It can't be worse than what I think."

"I expect some people would like it awfully," said Mike.

"They must, or they wouldn't buy it. I've never met any of them yet, though."

Psmith was deep in Lucia Granville Waterman's "Moments in the

Nursery." He turned to Billy Windsor.

"Luella Granville Waterman," he said, "is not by any chance your *nom-de-plume*, Comrade Windsor?"

"Not on your life. Don't think it."

"I am glad," said Psmith courteously. "For, speaking as man to man, I must confess that for sheer, concentrated bilge she gets away with the biscuit with almost insolent ease. Luella Granville Waterman must go."

"How do you mean?"

"She must go," repeated Psmith firmly. "Your first act, now that you have swiped the editorial chair, must be to sack her."

"But, say, I can't. The editor thinks a heap of her stuff."

"We cannot help his troubles. We must act for the good of the paper. Moreover, you said, I think, that he was away?"

"So he is. But he'll come back."

"Sufficient unto the day, Comrade Windsor. I have a suspicion that he will be the first to approve your action. His holiday will have cleared his brain. Make a note of improvement number one—the sacking of Luella Granville Waterman."

"I guess it'll be followed pretty quick by improvement number two—the sacking of William Windsor. I can't go monkeying about with the paper that way."

Psmith reflected for a moment.

"Has this job of yours any special attractions for you, Comrade Windsor?"

"I guess not."

"As I suspected. You yearn for scope. What exactly are your ambitions?"

"I want to get a job on one of the big dailies. I don't see how I'm going to fix it, though, at the present rate."

Psmith rose, and tapped him earnestly on the chest.

"Comrade Windsor, you have touched the spot. You are wasting the golden hours of your youth. You must move. You must hustle. You must make Windsor of *Cosy Moments* a name to conjure with. You must boost this sheet up till New York rings with your exploits. On the present lines that is impossible. You must strike out a line for yourself. You must show the world that even *Cosy Moments* cannot keep a good man down."

He resumed his seat.

"How do you mean?" said Billy Windsor.

Psmith turned to Mike.

"Comrade Jackson, if you were editing this paper, is there a single feature you would willingly retain?"

"I don't think there is," said Mike. "It's all pretty bad rot."

"My opinion in a nutshell," said Psmith, approvingly. "Comrade Jackson," he explained, turning to Billy, "has a secure reputation on the other side for the keenness and lucidity of his views upon literature. You may safely build upon him. In England when Comrade Jackson says 'Turn' we all turn. Now, my views on the matter are as follows. *Cosy Moments*, in my opinion (worthless, were it not backed by such a virtuoso as Comrade Jackson), needs more snap, more go. All these putrid pages must disappear. Letters must be despatched to-morrow morning, informing Luella Granville Waterman and the others (and in particular B. Henderson Asher, who from a cursory glance strikes me as an ideal candidate for a lethal chamber) that, unless they cease their contributions instantly, you will be compelled to place yourself under police protection. After that we can begin to move."

Billy Windsor sat and rocked himself in his chair without replying. He was trying to assimilate this idea. So far the grandeur of it had dazed him. It was too spacious, too revolutionary. Could it be done? It would undoubtedly mean the sack when Mr. J. Fillken Wilberfloss returned and found the apple of his eye torn asunder and, so to speak, deprived of its choicest pips. On the other hand . . . His brow suddenly cleared. After all, what was the sack? One crowded hour of glorious life is worth an age without a name, and he would have no name as long as he clung to his present position. The editor would be away ten weeks. He would have ten weeks in which to try himself out. Hope leaped within him. In ten weeks he could change *Cosy Moments* into a real live paper. He wondered that the idea had not occurred to him before. The trifling fact that the despised journal was the property of Mr. Benjamin White, and that he had no right whatever to tinker with it without that gentleman's approval, may have occurred to him, but, if it did, it occurred so momentarily that he did not notice it. In these crises one cannot think of everything.

"I'm on," he said, briefly.

Psmith smiled approvingly.

"That," he said, "is the right spirit. You will, I fancy, have little cause to regret your decision. Fortunately, if I may say so, I happen to have a certain amount of leisure just now. It is at your disposal. I have had little experience of journalistic work, but I foresee that I shall be a quick learner. I will become your sub-editor, without salary."

"Bully for you," said Billy Windsor.

"Comrade Jackson," continued Psmith, "is unhappily more fettered. The exigencies of his cricket tour will compel him constantly to be gadding about, now to Philadelphia, now to Saskatchewan, anon to Onehorseville, Ga. His services, therefore, cannot be relied upon continuously. From him, accordingly, we shall expect little but moral support. An occasional congratulatory telegram. Now and then a bright smile of approval. The bulk of the work will devolve upon our two selves."

"Let it devolve," said Billy Windsor, enthusiastically.

"Assuredly," said Psmith. "And now to decide upon our main scheme. You, of course, are the editor, and my suggestions are merely suggestions, subject to your approval. But, briefly, my idea is that *Cosy Moments* should become red-hot stuff. I could wish its tone to be such that the public will wonder why we do not print it on asbestos. We must chronicle all the live events of the day, murders, fires, and the like in a manner which will make our readers' spines thrill. Above all, we must be the guardians of the People's rights. We must be a search-light, showing up the dark spot in the souls of those who would endeavour in any way to do the PEOPLE in the eye. We must detect the wrong-doer, and deliver him such a series of resentful buffs that he will abandon his little games and become a model citizen. The details of the campaign we must think out after, but I fancy that, if we follow those main lines, we shall produce a bright, readable little sheet which will in a measure make this city sit up and take notice. Are you with me, Comrade Windsor?"

"Surest thing you know," said Billy with fervour.

CHAPTER VI - THE TENEMENTS

To alter the scheme of a weekly from cover to cover is not a task that is completed without work. The dismissal of *Cosy Moments*' entire staff of contributors left a gap in the paper which had to be filled, and owing to the nearness of press day there was no time to fill it before the issue of the next number. The editorial staff had to be satisfied with heading every page with the words "Look out! Look out!! Look out!!! See foot of page!!!!" printing in the space at the bottom the legend, "Next Week! See Editorial!" and compiling in conjunction a snappy editorial, setting forth the proposed changes. This was largely the work of Psmith.

"Comrade Jackson," he said to Mike, as they set forth one evening in search of their new flat, "I fancy I have found my metier. Commerce, many considered, was the line I should take; and doubtless, had I stuck to that walk in life, I should soon have become a financial magnate. But something seemed to whisper to me, even in the midst of my triumphs in the New Asiatic Bank, that there were other fields. For the moment it seems to me that I have found the job for which nature specially designed me. At last I have Scope. And without Scope, where are we? Wedged tightly in among the ribstons. There are some very fine passages in that editorial. The last paragraph, beginning '*Cosy Moments* cannot be muzzled,' in particular. I like it. It strikes the right note. It should stir the blood of a free and independent people till they sit in platoons on the doorstep of our office, waiting for the next number to appear."

"How about that next number?" asked Mike. "Are you and Windsor going to fill the whole paper yourselves?"

"By no means. It seems that Comrade Windsor knows certain stout fellows, reporters on other papers, who will be delighted to weigh in with stuff for a moderate fee."

"How about Luella What's-her-name and the others? How have they taken it?"

"Up to the present we have no means of ascertaining. The letters giving them the miss-in-baulk in no uncertain voice were only despatched yesterday. But it cannot affect us how they writhe beneath the blow. There is no reprieve."

Mike roared with laughter.

"It's the rummiest business I ever struck," he said. "I'm jolly glad it's not my paper. It's pretty lucky for you two lunatics that the proprietor's in Europe."

Psmith regarded him with pained surprise.

"I do not understand you, Comrade Jackson. Do you insinuate that we are not acting in the proprietor's best interests? When he sees the receipts, after we have handled the paper for a while, he will go singing about his hotel. His beaming smile will be a by-word in Carlsbad. Visitors will be shown it as one of the sights. His only doubt will be whether to send his money to the bank or keep it in tubs and roll in it. We are on to a big thing, Comrade Jackson. Wait till you see our first number."

"And how about the editor? I should think that first number would bring him back foaming at the mouth."

"I have ascertained from Comrade Windsor that there is nothing to fear from that quarter. By a singular stroke of good fortune Comrade Wilberfloss—his name is Wilberfloss—has been ordered complete rest during his holiday. The kindly medico, realising the fearful strain inflicted by reading *Cosy Moments* in its old form, specifically mentioned that the paper was to be withheld from him until he returned."

"And when he does return, what are you going to do?"

"By that time, doubtless, the paper will be in so flourishing a state that he will confess how wrong his own methods were and adopt ours without a murmur. In the meantime, Comrade Jackson, I would call your attention to the fact that we seem to have lost our way. In the exhilaration of this little chat, our footsteps have wandered. Where we are, goodness only knows. I can only say that I shouldn't care to have to live here."

"There's a name up on the other side of that lamp-post."

"Let us wend in that direction. Ah, Pleasant Street? I fancy that the master-mind who chose that name must have had the rudiments of a sense of humour."

It was indeed a repellent neighbourhood in which they had arrived. The New York slum stands in a class of its own. It is unique. The height of the houses and the narrowness of the streets seem to condense its unpleasantness. All the smells and noises, which are many and varied, are penned up in a sort of canyon, and gain in vehemence from the fact. The masses of dirty clothes hanging from the fire-escapes increase the depression. Nowhere in the city does one realise so fully the disadvantages of a lack of space. New York, being an island, has had no room to spread. It is a town of human sardines. In the poorer quarters the congestion is unbelievable.

Psmith and Mike picked their way through the groups of ragged children who covered the roadway. There seemed to be thousands of them.

"Poor kids!" said Mike. "It must be awful living in a hole like this."

Psmith said nothing. He was looking thoughtful. He glanced up at the grimy buildings on each side. On the lower floors one could see into dark, bare rooms. These were the star apartments of the tenement-houses, for they opened on to the street, and so got a little light and air. The imagination jibbed at the thought of the back rooms.

"I wonder who owns these places," said Psmith. "It seems to me that there's what you might call room for improvement. It wouldn't be a scaly idea to turn that *Cosy Moments* search-light we were talking about on to them."

They walked on a few steps.

"Look here," said Psmith, stopping. "This place makes me sick. I'm going in to have a look round. I expect some muscular householder will resent the intrusion and boot us out, but we'll risk it."

Followed by Mike, he turned in at one of the doors. A group of men leaning against the opposite wall looked at them without curiosity. Probably they took them for reporters hunting for a story. Reporters were the only tolerably well-dressed visitors Pleasant Street ever entertained.

It was almost pitch dark on the stairs. They had to feel their way up. Most of the doors were shut but one on the second floor was ajar. Through the opening they had a glimpse of a number of women sitting round on boxes. The floor was covered with little heaps of linen. All the women were sewing. Mike, stumbling in the darkness, almost fell against the door. None of the women looked up at the noise. Time was evidently money in Pleasant Street.

On the fourth floor there was an open door. The room was empty. It was a good representative Pleasant Street back room. The architect in this case had given rein to a passion for originality. He had constructed the room without a window of any sort whatsoever. There was a square opening in the door. Through this, it was to be presumed, the entire stock of air used by the occupants was supposed to come.

They stumbled downstairs again and out into the street. By contrast with the conditions indoors the street seemed spacious and breezy.

"This," said Psmith, as they walked on, "is where *Cosy Moments* gets busy at a singularly early date."

"What are you going to do?" asked Mike.

"I propose, Comrade Jackson," said Psmith, "if Comrade Windsor is agreeable, to make things as warm for the owner of this place as I jolly well know how. What he wants, of course," he proceeded in the tone of a family doctor prescribing for a patient, "is disembowelling. I fancy, however, that a mawkishly sentimental legislature will prevent our performing that national service. We must endeavour to do what we can by means of kindly criticism in the paper. And now, having settled that important point, let us try and get out of this place of wrath, and find Fourth Avenue."

CHAPTER VII - VISITORS AT THE OFFICE

On the following morning Mike had to leave with the team for Philadelphia. Psmith came down to the ferry to see him off, and hung about moodily until the time of departure.

"It is saddening me to a great extent, Comrade Jackson," he said, "this perpetual parting of the ways. When I think of the happy moments we have spent hand-in-hand across the seas, it fills me with a certain melancholy to have you flitting off in this manner without me. Yet there is another side to the picture. To me there is something singularly impressive in our unhesitating reply to the calls of Duty. Your Duty summons you to Philadelphia, to knock the cover off the local bowling. Mine retains me here, to play my part in the great work of making New York sit up. By the time you return, with a century or two, I trust, in your bag, the good work should, I fancy, be getting something of a move on. I will complete the arrangements with regard to the flat."

After leaving Pleasant Street they had found Fourth Avenue by a devious route, and had opened negotiations for a large flat near Thirtieth Street. It was immediately above a saloon, which was something of a drawback, but the landlord had assured them that the voices of the revellers did not penetrate to it.

* * *

When the ferry-boat had borne Mike off across the river, Psmith turned to stroll to the office of *Cosy Moments*. The day was fine, and on the whole, despite Mike's desertion, he felt pleased with life. Psmith's was a nature which required a certain amount of stimulus in the way of gentle excitement; and it seemed to him that the conduct of the remodelled *Cosy Moments* might supply this. He liked Billy Windsor, and looked forward to a not unenjoyable time till Mike should return.

The offices of *Cosy Moments* were in a large building in the street off Madison Avenue. They consisted of a sort of outer lair, where Pugsy Maloney spent his time reading tales of life in the prairies and heading off undesirable visitors; a small room, which would have belonged to the stenographer if *Cosy Moments* had possessed one; and a larger room beyond, which was the editorial sanctum.

As Psmith passed through the front door, Pugsy Maloney rose.

"Say!" said Master Maloney.

"Say on, Comrade Maloney," said Psmith.

"Dey're in dere."

"Who, precisely?"

"A whole bunch of dem."

Psmith inspected Master Maloney through his eye-glass. "Can you give me any particulars?" he asked patiently. "You are well-meaning, but vague, Comrade Maloney. Who are in there?"

"De whole bunch of dem. Dere's Mr. Asher and the Rev. Philpotts and a gazebo what calls himself Waterman and about 'steen more of dem."

A faint smile appeared upon Psmith's face.

"And is Comrade Windsor in there, too, in the middle of them?"

"Nope. Mr. Windsor's out to lunch."

"Comrade Windsor knows his business. Why did you let them in?"

"Sure, dey just butted in," said Master Maloney complainingly. "I was sittin' here, readin' me book, when de foist of de guys blew in. 'Boy,' says he, 'is de editor in?' 'Nope,' I says. 'I'll go in an' wait,' says he. 'Nuttin' doin',' says I. 'Nix on de goin' in act.' I might as well have saved me breat'. In he butts, and he's in der now. Well, in about t'ree minutes along comes another gazebo. 'Boy,' says he, 'is de editor in?' 'Nope,' I says. 'I'll wait,' says he lightin' out for de door. Wit dat I sees de proposition's too fierce for muh. I can't keep dese big husky guys out if dey's for buttin' in. So when de rest of de bunch comes along, I don't try to give dem de t'run down. I says, 'Well, gents,' I says, 'it's up to youse. De editor ain't in, but if youse wants to join de giddy t'rong, push t'roo inter de inner room. I can't be boddered.'"

"And what more *could* you have said?" agreed Psmith approvingly. "Tell me, Comrade Maloney, what was the general average aspect of these determined spirits?"

"Huh?"

"Did they seem to you to be gay, lighthearted? Did they carol snatches of song as they went? Or did they appear to be looking for some one with a hatchet?"

"Dey was hoppin'-mad, de whole bunch of dem."

"As I suspected. But we must not repine, Comrade Maloney. These trifling contretemps are the penalties we pay for our high journalistic aims. I will interview these merchants. I fancy that with the aid of the Diplomatic Smile and the Honeyed Word I may manage to pull through. It is as well, perhaps, that Comrade Windsor is out. The situation calls for the handling of a man of delicate culture and nice tact. Comrade Windsor would probably have endeavoured to clear the room with a chair. If he should arrive during the seance, Comrade Maloney, be so good as to inform him of the state of affairs, and tell him not to come in. Give him my compliments, and tell him to go out and watch the snowdrops growing in Madison Square Garden."

"Sure," said Master Maloney.

Then Psmith, having smoothed the nap of his hat and flicked a speck of dust from his coat-sleeve, walked to the door of the inner room and went in.

CHAPTER VIII - THE HONEYED WORD

Master Maloney's statement that "about 'steen visitors" had arrived in addition to Messrs. Asher, Waterman, and the Rev. Philpotts proved to have been due to a great extent to a somewhat feverish imagination. There were only five men in the room.

As Psmith entered, every eye was turned upon him. To an outside spectator he would have seemed rather like a very well-dressed Daniel introduced into a den of singularly irritable lions. Five pairs of eyes were smouldering with a long-nursed resentment. Five brows were corrugated with wrathful lines. Such, however, was the simple majesty of Psmith's demeanour that for a moment there was dead silence. Not a word was spoken as he paced, wrapped in thought, to the editorial chair. Stillness brooded over the room as he carefully dusted that piece of furniture, and, having done so to his satisfaction, hitched up the knees of his trousers and sank gracefully into a sitting position.

This accomplished, he looked up and started. He gazed round the room.

"Ha! I am observed!" he murmured.

The words broke the spell. Instantly, the five visitors burst simultaneously into speech.

"Are you the acting editor of this paper?"

"I wish to have a word with you, sir."

"Mr. Windsor, I presume?"

"Pardon me!"

"I should like a few moments' conversation."

The start was good and even; but the gentleman who said "Pardon me!" necessarily finished first with the rest nowhere.

Psmith turned to him, bowed, and fixed him with a benevolent gaze through his eye-glass.

"Are you Mr. Windsor, sir, may I ask?" inquired the favoured one.

The others paused for the reply.

"Alas! no," said Psmith with manly regret.

"Then who are you?"

"I am Psmith."

There was a pause.

"Where is Mr. Windsor?"

"He is, I fancy, champing about forty cents' worth of lunch at some neighbouring hostelry."

"When will he return?"

"Anon. But how much anon I fear I cannot say."

The visitors looked at each other.

"This is exceedingly annoying," said the man who had said "Pardon me!" "I came for the express purpose of seeing Mr. Windsor."

"So did I," chimed in the rest. "Same here. So did I."

Psmith bowed courteously.

"Comrade Windsor's loss is my gain. Is there anything I can do for you?"

"Are you on the editorial staff of this paper?"

"I am acting sub-editor. The work is not light," added Psmith gratuitously. "Sometimes the cry goes round, 'Can Psmith get through it all? Will his strength support his unquenchable spirit?' But I stagger on. I do not repine."

"Then maybe you can tell me what all this means?" said a small round gentleman who so far had done only chorus work.

"If it is in my power to do so, it shall be done, Comrade—I have not the pleasure of your name."

"My name is Waterman, sir. I am here on behalf of my wife, whose name you doubtless know."

"Correct me if I am wrong," said Psmith, "but I should say it, also, was Waterman."

"Luella Granville Waterman, sir," said the little man proudly. Psmith removed his eye-glass, polished it, and replaced it in his eye. He felt that he must run no risk of not seeing clearly the husband of one who, in his opinion, stood alone in literary circles as a purveyor of sheer bilge.

"My wife," continued the little man, producing an envelope and handing it to Psmith, "has received this extraordinary communication from a man signing himself W. Windsor. We are both at a loss to make head or tail of it."

Psmith was reading the letter.

"It seems reasonably clear to me," he said.

"It is an outrage. My wife has been a contributor to this journal from its foundation. Her work has given every satisfaction to Mr. Wilberfloss. And now, without the slightest warning, comes this peremptory dismissal from W. Windsor. Who is W. Windsor? Where is Mr. Wilberfloss?"

The chorus burst forth. It seemed that that was what they all wanted to know: Who was W. Windsor? Where was Mr. Wilberfloss?

"I am the Reverend Edwin T. Philpotts, sir," said a cadaverous-looking man with pale blue eyes and a melancholy face. "I have contributed 'Moments of Meditation' to this journal for a very considerable period of time."

"I have read your page with the keenest interest," said Psmith. "I may be wrong, but yours seems to me work which the world will not willingly let die."

The Reverend Edwin's frosty face thawed into a bleak smile.

"And yet," continued Psmith, "I gather that Comrade Windsor, on the other hand, actually wishes to hurry on its decease. It is these strange contradictions, these clashings of personal taste, which make up what we call life. Here we have, on the one hand—"

A man with a face like a walnut, who had hitherto lurked almost unseen behind a stout person in a serge suit, bobbed into the open, and spoke his piece.

"Where's this fellow Windsor? W. Windsor. That's the man we want to see. I've been working for this paper without a break, except when I had the mumps, for four years, and I've reason to know that my page was as widely read and appreciated as any in New York. And now up comes this Windsor fellow, if you please, and tells me in so many words the paper's got no use for me."

"These are life's tragedies," murmured Psmith.

"What's he mean by it? That's what I want to know. And that's what these gentlemen want to know—See here—"

"I am addressing—?" said Psmith.

"Asher's my name. B. Henderson Asher. I write 'Moments of Mirth.'"

A look almost of excitement came into Psmith's face, such a look as a visitor to a foreign land might wear when confronted with some great national monument. That he should be privileged to look upon the author of "Moments of Mirth" in the flesh, face to face, was almost too much.

"Comrade Asher," he said reverently, "may I shake your hand?"

The other extended his hand with some suspicion.

"Your 'Moments of Mirth,'" said Psmith, shaking it, "have frequently reconciled me to the toothache."

He reseated himself.

"Gentlemen," he said, "this is a painful case. The circumstances, as you will readily admit when you have heard all, are peculiar. You have asked me where Mr. Wilberfloss is. I do not know."

"You don't know!" exclaimed Mr. Waterman.

"I don't know. You don't know. They," said Psmith, indicating the rest with a wave of the hand, "don't know. Nobody knows. His locality is as hard to ascertain as that of a black cat in a coal-cellar on a moonless night. Shortly before I joined this journal, Mr. Wilberfloss, by his doctor's orders, started out on a holiday, leaving no address. No letters were to be forwarded. He was to enjoy complete rest. Where is he now? Who shall say? Possibly legging it down some rugged slope in the Rockies, with two bears and a wild cat in earnest pursuit. Possibly in the midst of some Florida everglade, making a noise like a piece of meat in order to snare crocodiles. Possibly in Canada, baiting moose-traps. We have no data."

Silent consternation prevailed among the audience. Finally the Rev.

Edwin T. Philpotts was struck with an idea.

"Where is Mr. White?" he asked.

The point was well received.

"Yes, where's Mr. Benjamin White?" chorused the rest.

Psmith shook his head.

"In Europe. I cannot say more."

The audience's consternation deepened.

"Then, do you mean to say," demanded Mr. Asher, "that this fellow Windsor's the boss here, that what he says goes?"

Psmith bowed.

"With your customary clear-headedness, Comrade Asher, you have got home on the bull's-eye first pop. Comrade Windsor is indeed the boss. A man of intensely masterful character, he will brook no opposition. I am powerless to sway him. Suggestions from myself as to the conduct of the paper would infuriate him. He believes that radical changes are necessary in the programme of *Cosy Moments*, and he means to put them through if it snows. Doubtless he would gladly consider your work if it fitted in with his ideas. A snappy account of a glove-fight, a spine-shaking word-picture of a railway smash, or something on those lines, would be welcomed. But—"

"I have never heard of such a thing," said Mr. Waterman indignantly.

Psmith sighed.

"Some time ago," he said, "—how long it seems!—I remember saying to a young friend of mine of the name of Spiller, 'Comrade Spiller, never confuse the unusual with the impossible.' It is my guiding rule in life. It is unusual for the substitute-editor of a weekly paper to do a Captain Kidd act and take entire command of the journal on his own account; but is it impossible? Alas no. Comrade Windsor has done it. That is where you, Comrade Asher, and you, gentlemen, have landed yourselves squarely in the broth. You have confused the unusual with the impossible."

"But what is to be done?" cried Mr. Asher.

"I fear that there is nothing to be done, except wait. The present *régime* is but an experiment. It may be that when Comrade Wilberfloss, having dodged the bears and eluded the wild cat, returns to his post at the helm of this journal, he may decide not to continue on the lines at present mapped out. He should be back in about ten weeks."

"Ten weeks!"

"I fancy that was to be the duration of his holiday. Till then my advice to you gentlemen is to wait. You may rely on me to keep a watchful eye upon your interests. When your thoughts tend to take a gloomy turn, say to yourselves, 'All is well. Psmith is keeping a watchful eye upon our interests.'"

"All the same, I should like to see this W. Windsor," said Mr. Asher.

Psmith shook his head.

"I shouldn't," he said. "I speak in your best interests. Comrade Windsor is a man of the fiercest passions. He cannot brook interference. Were you to question the wisdom of his plans, there is no knowing what might not happen. He would be the first to regret any violent action, when once he had cooled off, but would that be any consolation to his victim? I think not. Of course, if you wish it, I could arrange a meeting—"

Mr. Asher said no, he thought it didn't matter.

"I guess I can wait," he said.

"That," said Psmith approvingly, "is the right spirit. Wait. That is the watchword. And now," he added, rising, "I wonder if a bit of lunch somewhere might not be a good thing? We have had an interesting but fatiguing little chat. Our tissues require restoring. If you gentlemen would care to join me—"

Ten minutes later the company was seated in complete harmony round a table at the Knickerbocker. Psmith, with the dignified bonhomie of a seigneur of the old school, was ordering the wine; while B. Henderson Asher, brimming over with good-humour, was relating to an attentive circle an anecdote which should have appeared in his next instalment of "Moments of Mirth."

CHAPTER IX - FULL STEAM AHEAD

When Psmith returned to the office, he found Billy Windsor in the doorway, just parting from a thick-set young man, who seemed to be expressing his gratitude to the editor for some good turn. He was shaking him warmly by the hand.

Psmith stood aside to let him pass.

"An old college chum, Comrade Windsor?" he asked.

"That was Kid Brady."

"The name is unfamiliar to me. Another contributor?"

"He's from my part of the country—Wyoming. He wants to fight any one in the world at a hundred and thirty-three pounds."

"We all have our hobbies. Comrade Brady appears to have selected a somewhat exciting one. He would find stamp-collecting less exacting."

"It hasn't given him much excitement so far, poor chap," said Billy Windsor. "He's in the championship class, and here he has been pottering about New York for a month without being able to get a fight. It's always the way in this rotten East," continued Billy, warming up as was his custom when discussing a case of oppression and injustice. "It's all graft here. You've got to let half a dozen brutes dip into every dollar you earn, or you don't get a chance. If the kid had a manager, he'd get all the fights he wanted. And the manager would get nearly all the money. I've told him that we will back him up."

"You have hit it, Comrade Windsor," said Psmith with enthusiasm. "*Cosy Moments* shall be Comrade Brady's manager. We will give him a much-needed boost up in our columns. A sporting section is what the paper requires more than anything."

"If things go on as they've started, what it will require still more will be a fighting-editor. Pugsy tells me you had visitors while I was out."

"A few," said Psmith. "One or two very entertaining fellows. Comrades Asher, Philpotts, and others. I have just been giving them a bite of lunch at the Knickerbocker."

"Lunch!"

"A most pleasant little lunch. We are now as brothers. I fear I have made you perhaps a shade unpopular with our late contributors; but these things must be. We must clench our teeth and face them manfully. If I were you, I think I should not drop in at the house of Comrade Asher and the rest to take pot-luck for some little time to come. In order to soothe the squad I was compelled to curse you to some extent."

"Don't mind me."

"I think I may say I didn't."

"Say, look here, you must charge up the price of that lunch to the office. Necessary expenses, you know."

"I could not dream of doing such a thing, Comrade Windsor. The whole affair was a great treat to me. I have few pleasures. Comrade Asher alone was worth the money. I found his society intensely interesting. I have always believed in the Darwinian theory. Comrade Asher confirmed my views."

They went into the inner office. Psmith removed his hat and coat.

"And now once more to work," he said. "Psmith the *flaneur* of Fifth
Avenue ceases to exist. In his place we find Psmith the hard-headed
sub-editor. Be so good as to indicate a job of work for me,
Comrade Windsor. I am champing at my bit."

Billy Windsor sat down, and lit his pipe.

"What we want most," he said thoughtfully, "is some big topic. That's the only way to get a paper going. Look at *Everybody's Magazine*. They didn't amount to a row of beans till Lawson started his 'Frenzied Finance' articles. Directly they began, the whole country was squealing for copies. *Everybody's* put up their price from ten to fifteen cents, and now they lead the field."

"The country must squeal for *Cosy Moments*," said Psmith firmly. "I fancy I have a scheme which may not prove wholly scaly. Wandering yesterday with Comrade Jackson in a search for Fourth Avenue, I happened upon a spot called Pleasant Street. Do you know it?"

Billy Windsor nodded.

"I went down there once or twice when I was a reporter. It's a beastly place."

"It is a singularly beastly place. We went into one of the houses."

"They're pretty bad."

"Who owns them?"

"I don't know. Probably some millionaire. Those tenement houses are about as paying an investment as you can have."

"Hasn't anybody ever tried to do anything about them?"

"Not so far as I know. It's pretty difficult to get at these fellows, you see. But they're fierce, aren't they, those houses!"

"What," asked Psmith, "is the precise difficulty of getting at these merchants?"

"Well, it's this way. There are all sorts of laws about the places, but any one who wants can get round them as easy as falling off a log. The law says a tenement house is a building occupied by more than two families. Well, when there's a fuss, all the man has to do is to clear out all the families but two. Then, when the inspector fellow comes along, and says, let's say, 'Where's your running water on each floor? That's what the law says you've got to have, and here are these people having to go downstairs and out of doors to fetch their water supplies,' the landlord simply replies, 'Nothing doing. This isn't a tenement house at all. There are only two families here.' And when the fuss has blown over, back come the rest of the crowd, and things go on the same as before."

"I see," said Psmith. "A very cheery scheme."

"Then there's another thing. You can't get hold of the man who's really responsible, unless you're prepared to spend thousands ferreting out evidence. The land belongs in the first place to some corporation or other. They lease it to a lessee. When there's a fuss, they say they aren't responsible, it's up to the lessee. And he lies so low that you can't find out who he is. It's all just like the East. Everything in the East is as crooked as Pearl Street. If you want a square deal, you've got to come out Wyoming way."

"The main problem, then," said Psmith, "appears to be the discovery of the lessee, lad? Surely a powerful organ like *Cosy Moments*, with its vast ramifications, could bring off a thing like that?"

"I doubt it. We'll try, anyway. There's no knowing but what we may have luck."

"Precisely," said Psmith. "Full steam ahead, and trust to luck. The chances are that, if we go on long enough, we shall eventually arrive somewhere. After all, Columbus didn't know that America existed when he set out. All he knew was some highly interesting fact about an egg. What that was, I do not at the moment recall, but it bucked Columbus up like a tonic. It made him fizz ahead like a two-year-old. The facts which will nerve us to effort are two. In the first place, we know that there must be some one at the bottom of the business. Secondly, as there appears to be no law of libel whatsoever in this great and free country, we shall be enabled to haul up our slacks with a considerable absence of restraint."

"Sure," said Billy Windsor. "Which of us is going to write the first article?"

"You may leave it to me, Comrade Windsor. I am no hardened old journalist, I fear, but I have certain qualifications for the post. A young man once called at the office of a certain newspaper, and asked for a job. 'Have you any special line?' asked the editor. 'Yes,' said the bright lad, 'I am rather good at invective.' 'Any special kind of invective?' queried the man up top. 'No,' replied our hero, 'just general invective.' Such is my own case, Comrade Windsor. I am a very fair purveyor of good, general invective. And as my visit to Pleasant Street is of such recent date, I am tolerably full of my subject. Taking full advantage of the benevolent laws of this country governing libel, I fancy I will produce a screed which will make this anonymous lessee feel as if he had inadvertently seated himself upon a tin-tack. Give me pen and paper, Comrade Windsor, instruct Comrade Maloney to suspend his whistling till such time as I am better able to listen to it; and I think we have got a success."

CHAPTER X - GOING SOME

There was once an editor of a paper in the Far West who was sitting at his desk, musing pleasantly of life, when a bullet crashed through the window and embedded itself in the wall at the back of his head. A happy smile lit up the editor's face. "Ah," he said complacently, "I knew that Personal column of ours was going to be a success!"

What the bullet was to the Far West editor, the visit of Mr.

Francis Parker to the offices of *Cosy Moments* was to Billy Windsor.

It occurred in the third week of the new *régime* of the paper. *Cosy Moments*, under its new management, had bounded ahead like a motor-car when the throttle is opened. Incessant work had been the order of the day. Billy Windsor's hair had become more dishevelled than ever, and even Psmith had at moments lost a certain amount of his dignified calm. Sandwiched in between the painful case of Kid Brady and the matter of the tenements, which formed the star items of the paper's contents, was a mass of bright reading dealing with the events of the day. Billy Windsor's newspaper friends had turned in some fine, snappy stuff in their best Yellow Journal manner, relating to the more stirring happenings in the city. Psmith, who had constituted himself guardian of the literary and dramatic interests of the paper, had employed his gift of general invective to considerable effect, as was shown by a conversation between Master Maloney and a visitor one morning, heard through the open door.

"I wish to see the editor of this paper," said the visitor.

"Editor not in," said Master Maloney, untruthfully.

"Ha! Then when he returns I wish you to give him a message."

"Sure."

"I am Aubrey Bodkin, of the National Theatre. Give him my compliments, and tell him that Mr. Bodkin does not lightly forget."

An unsolicited testimonial which caused Psmith the keenest satisfaction.

The section of the paper devoted to Kid Brady was attractive to all those with sporting blood in them. Each week there appeared in the same place on the same page a portrait of the Kid, looking moody and important, in an attitude of self-defence, and under the portrait the legend, "Jimmy Garvin must meet this boy." Jimmy was the present holder of the light-weight title. He had won it a year before, and since then had confined himself to smoking cigars as long as walking-sticks and appearing nightly as the star in a music-hall sketch entitled "A Fight for Honour." His reminiscences were appearing weekly in a Sunday paper. It was this that gave Psmith the idea of publishing Kid Brady's autobiography in *Cosy Moments*, an idea which made the Kid his devoted adherent from then on. Like most pugilists, the Kid had a passion for bursting into print, and his life had been saddened up to the present by the refusal of the press to publish his reminiscences. To appear in print is the fighter's accolade. It signifies that he has arrived. Psmith extended the hospitality of page four of *Cosy Moments* to Kid Brady, and the latter leaped at the chance. He was grateful to Psmith for not editing his contributions. Other pugilists, contributing to other papers, groaned under the supervision of a member of the staff who cut out their best passages and altered the rest into Addisonian English. The readers of *Cosy Moments* got Kid Brady raw.

"Comrade Brady," said Psmith to Billy, "has a singularly pure and pleasing style. It is bound to appeal powerfully to the many-headed. Listen to this bit. Our hero is fighting Battling Jack Benson in that eminent artist's native town of Louisville, and the citizens have given their native son the Approving Hand, while receiving Comrade Brady with chilly silence. Here is the Kid on the subject: 'I looked around that house, and I seen I hadn't a friend in it. And then the gong goes, and I says to myself how I has one friend, my poor old mother way out in Wyoming, and I goes in and mixes it, and then I seen Benson losing his goat, so I ups with an awful half-scissor hook to the plexus, and in the next round I seen Benson has a chunk of yellow, and I gets in with a hay-maker and I picks up another sleep-producer from the floor and hands it him, and he takes the count all right.' . . Crisp, lucid, and to the point. That is what the public wants. If this does not bring Comrade Garvin up to the scratch, nothing will."

But the feature of the paper was the "Tenement" series. It was late summer now, and there was nothing much going on in New York. The public was consequently free to take notice. The sale of *Cosy Moments* proceeded briskly. As Psmith had predicted, the change of policy had the effect of improving the sales to a marked extent. Letters of complaint from old subscribers poured into the office daily. But, as Billy Windsor complacently remarked, they had paid their subscriptions, so that the money was safe whether they read the paper or not. And, meanwhile, a large new public had sprung up and was growing every week. Advertisements came trooping in. *Cosy Moments*, in short, was passing through an era of prosperity undreamed of in its history.

"Young blood," said Psmith nonchalantly, "young blood. That is the secret. A paper must keep up to date, or it falls behind its competitors in the race. Comrade Wilberfloss's methods were possibly sound, but too limited and archaic. They lacked ginger. We of the younger generation have our fingers more firmly on the public pulse. We read off the public's unspoken wishes as if by intuition. We know the game from A to Z."

At this moment Master Maloney entered, bearing in his hand a card.

"'Francis Parker'?" said Billy, taking it. "Don't know him."

"Nor I," said Psmith. "We make new friends daily."

"He's a guy with a tall-shaped hat," volunteered Master Maloney, "an' he's wearin' a dude suit an' shiny shoes."

"Comrade Parker," said Psmith approvingly, "has evidently not been blind to the importance of a visit to *Cosy Moments*. He has dressed himself in his best. He has felt, rightly, that this is no occasion for the old straw hat and the baggy flannels. I would not have it otherwise. It is the right spirit. Shall we give him audience, Comrade Windsor?"

"I wonder what he wants."

"That," said Psmith, "we shall ascertain more clearly after a personal interview. Comrade Maloney, show the gentleman in. We can give him three and a quarter minutes."

Pugsy withdrew.

Mr. Francis Parker proved to be a man who might have been any age between twenty-five and thirty-five. He had a smooth, clean-shaven face, and a cat-like way of moving. As Pugsy had stated in effect, he wore a tail-coat, trousers with a crease which brought a smile of kindly approval to Psmith's face, and patent-leather boots of pronounced shininess. Gloves and a tall hat, which he carried, completed an impressive picture.

He moved softly into the room.

"I wished to see the editor."

Psmith waved a hand towards Billy.

"The treat has not been denied you," he said. "Before you is Comrade Windsor, the Wyoming cracker-jack. He is our editor. I myself—I am Psmith—though but a subordinate, may also claim the title in a measure. Technically, I am but a sub-editor; but such is the mutual esteem in which Comrade Windsor and I hold each other that we may practically be said to be inseparable. We have no secrets from each other. You may address us both impartially. Will you sit for a space?"

He pushed a chair towards the visitor, who seated himself with the care inspired by a perfect trouser-crease. There was a momentary silence while he selected a spot on the table on which to place his hat.

"The style of the paper has changed greatly, has it not, during the past few weeks?" he said. "I have never been, shall I say, a constant reader of *Cosy Moments*, and I may be wrong. But is not its interest in current affairs a recent development?"

"You are very right," responded Psmith. "Comrade Windsor, a man of alert and restless temperament, felt that a change was essential if *Cosy Moments* was to lead public thought. Comrade Wilberfloss's methods were good in their way. I have no quarrel with Comrade Wilberfloss. But he did not lead public thought. He catered exclusively for children with water on the brain, and men and women with solid ivory skulls. Comrade Windsor, with a broader view, feels that there are other and larger publics. He refuses to content himself with ladling out a weekly dole of mental predigested breakfast food. He provides meat. He—"

"Then—excuse me—" said Mr. Parker, turning to Billy, "You, I take it, are responsible for this very vigorous attack on the tenement-house owners?"

"You can take it I am," said Billy.

Psmith interposed.

"We are both responsible, Comrade Parker. If any husky guy, as I fancy Master Maloney would phrase it, is anxious to aim a swift kick at the man behind those articles, he must distribute it evenly between Comrade Windsor and myself."

"I see." Mr. Parker paused. "They are—er—very outspoken articles," he added.

"Warm stuff," agreed Psmith. "Distinctly warm stuff."

"May I speak frankly?" said Mr. Parker.

"Assuredly, Comrade Parker. There must be no secrets, no restraint between us. We would not have you go away and say to yourself, 'Did I make my meaning clear? Was I too elusive?' Say on."

"I am speaking in your best interests."

"Who would doubt it, Comrade Parker. Nothing has buoyed us up more strongly during the hours of doubt through which we have passed than the knowledge that you wish us well."

Billy Windsor suddenly became militant. There was a feline smoothness about the visitor which had been jarring upon him ever since he first spoke. Billy was of the plains, the home of blunt speech, where you looked your man in the eye and said it quick. Mr. Parker was too bland for human consumption. He offended Billy's honest soul.

"See here," cried he, leaning forward, "what's it all about? Let's have it. If you've anything to say about those articles, say it right out. Never mind our best interests. We can look after them. Let's have what's worrying you."

Psmith waved a deprecating hand.

"Do not let us be abrupt on this happy occasion. To me it is enough simply to sit and chat with Comrade Parker, irrespective of the trend of his conversation. Still, as time is money, and this is our busy day, possibly it might be as well, sir, if you unburdened yourself as soon as convenient. Have you come to point out some flaw in those articles? Do they fall short in any way of your standard for such work?"

Mr. Parker's smooth face did not change its expression, but he came to the point.

"I should not go on with them if I were you," he said.

"Why?" demanded Billy.

"There are reasons why you should not," said Mr. Parker.

"And there are reasons why we should."

"Less powerful ones."

There proceeded from Billy a noise not describable in words. It was partly a snort, partly a growl. It resembled more than anything else the preliminary sniffing snarl a bull-dog emits before he joins battle. Billy's cow-boy blood was up. He was rapidly approaching the state of mind in which the men of the plains, finding speech unequal to the expression of their thoughts, reach for their guns.

Psmith intervened.

"We do not completely gather your meaning, Comrade Parker. I fear we must ask you to hand it to us with still more breezy frankness. Do you speak from purely friendly motives? Are you advising us to discontinue the articles merely because you fear that they will damage our literary reputation? Or are there other reasons why you feel that they should cease? Do you speak solely as a literary connoisseur? Is it the style or the subject-matter of which you disapprove?"

Mr. Parker leaned forward.

"The gentleman whom I represent—"

"Then this is no matter of your own personal taste? You are an emissary?"

"These articles are causing a certain inconvenience to the gentleman whom I represent. Or, rather, he feels that, if continued, they may do so."

"You mean," broke in Billy explosively, "that if we kick up enough fuss to make somebody start a commission to inquire into this rotten business, your friend who owns the private Hades we're trying to get improved, will have to get busy and lose some of his money by making the houses fit to live in? Is that it?"

"It is not so much the money, Mr. Windsor, though, of course, the expense would be considerable. My employer is a wealthy man."

"I bet he is," said Billy disgustedly. "I've no doubt he makes a mighty good pile out of Pleasant Street."

"It is not so much the money," repeated Mr. Parker, "as the publicity involved. I speak quite frankly. There are reasons why my employer would prefer not to come before the public just now as the owner of the Pleasant Street property. I need not go into those reasons. It is sufficient to say that they are strong ones."

"Well, he knows what to do, I guess. The moment he starts in to make those houses decent, the articles stop. It's up to him."

Psmith nodded.

"Comrade Windsor is correct. He has hit the mark and rung the bell. No conscientious judge would withhold from Comrade Windsor a cigar or a cocoanut, according as his private preference might dictate. That is the matter in a nutshell. Remove the reason for those very scholarly articles, and they cease."

Mr. Parker shook his head.

"I fear that is not feasible. The expense of reconstructing the houses makes that impossible."

"Then there's no use in talking," said Billy. "The articles will go on."

Mr. Parker coughed. A tentative cough, suggesting that the situation was now about to enter upon a more delicate phase. Billy and Psmith waited for him to begin. From their point of view the discussion was over. If it was to be reopened on fresh lines, it was for their visitor to effect that reopening.

"Now, I'm going to be frank, gentlemen," said he, as who should say, "We are all friends here. Let us be hearty." "I'm going to put my cards on the table, and see if we can't fix something up. Now, see here: We don't want unpleasantness. You aren't in this business for your healths, eh? You've got your living to make, just like everybody else, I guess. Well, see here. This is how it stands. To a certain extant, I don't mind admitting, seeing that we're being frank with one another, you two gentlemen have got us—that's to say, my employer—in a cleft stick. Frankly, those articles are beginning to attract attention, and if they go on there's going to be a lot of inconvenience for my employer. That's clear, I reckon. Well, now, here's a square proposition. How much do you want to stop those articles? That's straight. I've been frank with you, and I want you to be frank with me. What's your figure? Name it, and, if it's not too high, I guess we needn't quarrel."

He looked expectantly at Billy. Billy's eyes were bulging. He struggled for speech. He had got as far as "Say!" when Psmith interrupted him. Psmith, gazing sadly at Mr. Parker through his monocle, spoke quietly, with the restrained dignity of some old Roman senator dealing with the enemies of the Republic.

"Comrade Parker," he said, "I fear that you have allowed constant communication with the conscienceless commercialism of this worldly city to undermine your moral sense. It is useless to dangle rich bribes before our eyes. *Cosy Moments* cannot be muzzled. You doubtless mean well, according to your—if I may say so—somewhat murky lights, but we are not for sale, except at ten cents weekly. From the hills of Maine to the Everglades of Florida, from Sandy Hook to San Francisco, from Portland, Oregon, to Melonsquashville, Tennessee, one sentence is in every man's mouth. And what is that sentence? I give you three guesses. You give it up? It is this: '*Cosy Moments* cannot be muzzled!'"

Mr. Parker rose.

"There's nothing more to be done then," he said.

"Nothing," agreed Psmith, "except to make a noise like a hoop and roll away."

"And do it quick," yelled Billy, exploding like a fire-cracker.

Psmith bowed.

"Speed," he admitted, "would be no bad thing. Frankly—if I may borrow the expression—your square proposition has wounded us. I am a man of powerful self-restraint, one of those strong, silent men, and I can curb my emotions. But I fear that Comrade Windsor's generous temperament may at any moment prompt him to start throwing ink-pots. And in Wyoming his deadly aim with the ink-pot won him among the admiring cowboys the sobriquet of Crack-Shot Cuthbert. As man to man, Comrade Parker, I should advise you to bound swiftly away."

"I'm going," said Mr. Parker, picking up his hat. "And I'll give you a piece of advice, too. Those articles are going to be stopped, and if you've any sense between you, you'll stop them yourselves before you get hurt. That's all I've got to say, and that goes."

He went out, closing the door behind him with a bang that added emphasis to his words.

"To men of nicely poised nervous organisation such as ourselves, Comrade Windsor," said Psmith, smoothing his waistcoat thoughtfully, "these scenes are acutely painful. We wince before them. Our ganglions quiver like cinematographs. Gradually recovering command of ourselves, we review the situation. Did our visitor's final remarks convey anything definite to you? Were they the mere casual badinage of a parting guest, or was there something solid behind them?"

Billy Windsor was looking serious.

"I guess he meant it all right. He's evidently working for somebody pretty big, and that sort of man would have a pull with all kinds of Thugs. We shall have to watch out. Now that they find we can't be bought, they'll try the other way. They mean business sure enough. But, by George, let 'em! We're up against a big thing, and I'm going to see it through if they put every gang in New York on to us."

"Precisely, Comrade Windsor. *Cosy Moments*, as I have had occasion to observe before, cannot be muzzled."

"That's right," said Billy Windsor. "And," he added, with the contented look the Far West editor must have worn as the bullet came through the window, "we must have got them scared, or they wouldn't have shown their hand that way. I guess we're making a hit. *Cosy Moments* is going some now."

CHAPTER XI - THE MAN AT THE ASTOR

The duties of Master Pugsy Maloney at the offices of *Cosy Moments* were not heavy; and he was accustomed to occupy his large store of leisure by reading narratives dealing with life in the prairies, which he acquired at a neighbouring shop at cut rates in consideration of their being shop-soiled. It was while he was engrossed in one of these, on the morning following the visit of Mr. Parker, that the seedy-looking man made his appearance. He walked in from the street, and stood before Master Maloney.

"Hey, kid," he said.

Pugsy looked up with some hauteur. He resented being addressed as "kid" by perfect strangers.

"Editor in, Tommy?" inquired the man.

Pugsy by this time had taken a thorough dislike to him. To be called "kid" was bad. The subtle insult of "Tommy" was still worse.

"Nope," he said curtly, fixing his eyes again on his book. A movement on the part of the visitor attracted his attention. The seedy man was making for the door of the inner room. Pugsy instantly ceased to be the student and became the man of action. He sprang from his seat and wriggled in between the man and the door.

"Youse can't butt in dere," he said authoritatively. "Chase yerself."

The man eyed him with displeasure.

"Fresh kid!" he observed disapprovingly.

"Fade away," urged Master Maloney.

The visitor's reply was to extend a hand and grasp Pugsy's left ear between a long finger and thumb. Since time began, small boys in every country have had but one answer for this action. Pugsy made it. He emitted a piercing squeal in which pain, fear, and resentment strove for supremacy.

The noise penetrated into the editorial sanctum, losing only a small part of its strength on the way. Psmith, who was at work on a review of a book of poetry, looked up with patient sadness.

"If Comrade Maloney," he said, "is going to take to singing as well as whistling, I fear this journal must put up its shutters. Concentrated thought will be out of the question."

A second squeal rent the air. Billy Windsor jumped up.

"Somebody must be hurting the kid," he exclaimed.

He hurried to the door and flung it open. Psmith followed at a more leisurely pace. The seedy man, caught in the act, released Master Maloney, who stood rubbing his ear with resentment written on every feature.

On such occasions as this Billy was a man of few words. He made a dive for the seedy man; but the latter, who during the preceding moment had been eyeing the two editors as if he were committing their appearance to memory, sprang back, and was off down the stairs with the agility of a Marathon runner.

"He blows in," said Master Maloney, aggrieved, "and asks is de editor dere. I tells him no, 'cos youse said youse wasn't, and he nips me by the ear when I gets busy to stop him gettin' t'roo."

"Comrade Maloney," said Psmith, "you are a martyr. What would Horatius have done if somebody had nipped him by the ear when he was holding the bridge? The story does not consider the possibility. Yet it might have made all the difference. Did the gentleman state his business?"

"Nope. Just tried to butt t'roo."

"Another of these strong silent men. The world is full of us. These are the perils of the journalistic life. You will be safer and happier when you are rounding up cows on your mustang."

"I wonder what he wanted," said Billy, when they were back again in the inner room.

"Who can say, Comrade Windsor? Possibly our autographs. Possibly five minutes' chat on general subjects."

"I don't like the look of him," said Billy.

"Whereas what Comrade Maloney objected to was the feel of him. In what respect did his look jar upon you? His clothes were poorly cut, but such things, I know, leave you unmoved."

"It seems to me," said Billy thoughtfully, "as if he came just to get a sight of us."

"And he got it. Ah, Providence is good to the poor."

"Whoever's behind those tenements isn't going to stick at any odd trifle. We must watch out. That man was probably sent to mark us down for one of the gangs. Now they'll know what we look like, and they can get after us."

"These are the drawbacks to being public men, Comrade Windsor. We must bear them manfully, without wincing."

Billy turned again to his work.

"I'm not going to wince," he said, "so's you could notice it with a microscope. What I'm going to do is to buy a good big stick. And I'd advise you to do the same."

* * *

It was by Psmith's suggestion that the editorial staff of *Cosy Moments* dined that night in the roof-garden at the top of the Astor Hotel.

"The tired brain," he said, "needs to recuperate. To feed on such a night as this in some low-down hostelry on the level of the street, with German waiters breathing heavily down the back of one's neck and two fiddles and a piano whacking out 'Beautiful Eyes' about three feet from one's tympanum, would be false economy. Here, fanned by cool breezes and surrounded by fair women and brave men, one may do a bit of tissue-restoring. Moreover, there is little danger up here of being slugged by our moth-eaten acquaintance of this morning. A man with trousers like his would not be allowed in. We shall probably find him waiting for us at the main entrance with a sand-bag, when we leave, but, till then—"

He turned with gentle grace to his soup.

It was a warm night, and the roof-garden was full. From where they sat they could see the million twinkling lights of the city. Towards the end of the meal, Psmith's gaze concentrated itself on the advertisement of a certain brand of ginger-ale in Times Square. It is a mass of electric light arranged in the shape of a great bottle, and at regular intervals there proceed from the bottle's mouth flashes of flame representing ginger-ale. The thing began to exercise a hypnotic effect on Psmith. He came to himself with a start, to find Billy Windsor in conversation with a waiter.

"Yes, my name's Windsor," Billy was saying.

The waiter bowed and retired to one of the tables where a young man in evening clothes was seated. Psmith recollected having seen this solitary diner looking in their direction once or twice during dinner, but the fact had not impressed him.

"What is happening, Comrade Windsor?" he inquired. "I was musing with a certain tenseness at the moment, and the rush of events has left me behind."

"Man at that table wanted to know if my name was Windsor," said Billy.

"Ah?" said Psmith, interested; "and was it?"

"Here he comes. I wonder what he wants. I don't know the man from Adam."

The stranger was threading his way between the tables.

"Can I have a word with you, Mr. Windsor?" he said.

Billy looked at him curiously. Recent events had made him wary of strangers.

"Won't you sit down?" he said.

A waiter was bringing a chair. The young man seated himself.

"By the way," added Billy; "my friend, Mr. Smith."

"Pleased to meet you," said the other.

"I don't know your name," Billy hesitated.

"Never mind about my name," said the stranger. "It won't be needed. Is Mr. Smith on your paper? Excuse my asking."

Psmith bowed. "That's all right, then. I can go ahead." He bent forward.

"Neither of you gentlemen are hard of hearing, eh?"

"In the old prairie days," said Psmith, "Comrade Windsor was known to the Indians as Boola-Ba-Na-Gosh, which, as you doubtless know, signifies Big-Chief-Who-Can-Hear-A-Fly-Clear-Its-Throat. I too can hear as well as the next man. Why?"

"That's all right, then. I don't want to have to shout it. There's some things it's better not to yell."

He turned to Billy, who had been looking at him all the while with a combination of interest and suspicion. The man might or might not be friendly. In the meantime, there was no harm in being on one's guard. Billy's experience as a cub-reporter had given him the knowledge that is only given in its entirety to police and newspaper men: that there are two New Yorks. One is a modern, well-policed city, through which one may walk from end to end without encountering adventure. The other is a city as full of sinister intrigue, of whisperings and conspiracies, of battle, murder, and sudden death in dark by-ways, as any town of mediaeval Italy. Given certain conditions, anything may happen to any one in New York. And Billy realised that these conditions now prevailed in his own case. He had come into conflict with New York's underworld. Circumstances had placed him below the surface, where only his wits could help him.

"It's about that tenement business," said the stranger.

Billy bristled. "Well, what about it?" he demanded truculently.

The stranger raised a long and curiously delicately shaped hand. "Don't bite at me," he said. "This isn't my funeral. I've no kick coming. I'm a friend."

"Yet you don't tell us your name."

"Never mind my name. If you were in my line of business, you wouldn't be so durned stuck on this name thing. Call me Smith, if you like."

"You could select no nobler pseudonym," said Psmith cordially.

"Eh? Oh, I see. Well, make it Brown, then. Anything you please. It don't signify. See here, let's get back. About this tenement thing. You understand certain parties have got it in against you?"

"A charming conversationalist, one Comrade Parker, hinted at something of the sort," said Psmith, "in a recent interview. *Cosy Moments*, however, cannot be muzzled."

"Well?" said Billy.

"You're up against a big proposition."

"We can look after ourselves."

"Gum! you'll need to. The man behind is a big bug."

Billy leaned forward eagerly.

"Who is he?"

The other shrugged his shoulders.

"I don't know. You wouldn't expect a man like that to give himself away."

"Then how do you know he's a big bug?"

"Precisely," said Psmith. "On what system have you estimated the size of the gentleman's bughood?"

The stranger lit a cigar.

"By the number of dollars he was ready to put up to have you done in."

Billy's eyes snapped.

"Oh?" he said. "And which gang has he given the job to?"

"I wish I could tell you. He—his agent, that is—came to Bat

Jarvis."

"The cat-expert?" said Psmith. "A man of singularly winsome personality."

"Bat turned the job down."

"Why was that?" inquired Billy.

"He said he needed the money as much as the next man, but when he found out who he was supposed to lay for, he gave his job the frozen face. Said you were a friend of his and none of his fellows were going to put a finger on you. I don't know what you've been doing to Bat, but he's certainly Willie the Long-Lost Brother with you."

"A powerful argument in favour of kindness to animals!" said Psmith. "Comrade Windsor came into possession of one of Comrade Jarvis's celebrated stud of cats. What did he do? Instead of having the animal made into a nourishing soup, he restored it to its bereaved owner. Observe the sequel. He is now as a prize tortoiseshell to Comrade Jarvis."

"So Bat wouldn't stand for it?" said Billy.

"Not on his life. Turned it down without a blink. And he sent me along to find you and tell you so."

"We are much obliged to Comrade Jarvis," said Psmith.

"He told me to tell you to watch out, because another gang is dead sure to take on the job. But he said you were to know he wasn't mixed up in it. He also said that any time you were in bad, he'd do his best for you. You've certainly made the biggest kind of hit with Bat. I haven't seen him so worked up over a thing in years. Well, that's all, I reckon. Guess I'll be pushing along. I've a date to keep. Glad to have met you. Glad to have met you, Mr. Smith. Pardon me, you have an insect on your coat."

He flicked at Psmith's coat with a quick movement. Psmith thanked him gravely.

"Good night," concluded the stranger, moving off. For a few moments after he had gone, Psmith and Billy sat smoking in silence. They had plenty to think about.

"How's the time going?" asked Billy at length. Psmith felt for his watch, and looked at Billy with some sadness.

"I am sorry to say, Comrade Windsor—"

"Hullo," said Billy, "here's that man coming back again."

The stranger came up to their table, wearing a light overcoat over his dress clothes. From the pocket of this he produced a gold watch.

"Force of habit," he said apologetically, handing it to Psmith.

"You'll pardon me. Good night, gentlemen, again."

CHAPTER XII - A RED TAXIMETER

The Astor Hotel faces on to Times Square. A few paces to the right of the main entrance the Times Building towers to the sky; and at the foot of this the stream of traffic breaks, forming two channels. To the right of the building is Seventh Avenue, quiet, dark, and dull. To the left is Broadway, the Great White Way, the longest, straightest, brightest, wickedest street in the world.

Psmith and Billy, having left the Astor, started to walk down Broadway to Billy's lodgings in Fourteenth Street. The usual crowd was drifting slowly up and down in the glare of the white lights.

They had reached Herald Square, when a voice behind them exclaimed,

"Why, it's Mr. Windsor!"

They wheeled round. A flashily dressed man was standing with outstetched hand.

"I saw you come out of the Astor," he said cheerily. "I said to myself, 'I know that man.' Darned if I could put a name to you, though. So I just followed you along, and right here it came to me."

"It did, did it?" said Billy politely.

"It did, sir. I've never set eyes on you before, but I've seen so many photographs of you that I reckon we're old friends. I know your father very well, Mr. Windsor. He showed me the photographs. You may have heard him speak of me—Jack Lake? How is the old man? Seen him lately?"

"Not for some time. He was well when he last wrote."

"Good for him. He would be. Tough as a plank, old Joe Windsor. We always called him Joe."

"You'd have known him down in Missouri, of course?" said Billy.

"That's right. In Missouri. We were side-partners for years. Now, see here, Mr. Windsor, it's early yet. Won't you and your friend come along with me and have a smoke and a chat? I live right here in Thirty-Third Street. I'd be right glad for you to come."

"I don't doubt it," said Billy, "but I'm afraid you'll have to excuse us."

"In a hurry, are you?"

"Not in the least."

"Then come right along."

"No, thanks."

"Say, why not? It's only a step."

"Because we don't want to. Good night."

He turned, and started to walk away. The other stood for a moment, staring; then crossed the road.

Psmith broke the silence.

"Correct me if I am wrong, Comrade Windsor," he said tentatively, "but were you not a trifle—shall we say abrupt?—with the old family friend?"

Billy Windsor laughed.

"If my father's name was Joseph," he said, "instead of being William, the same as mine, and if he'd ever been in Missouri in his life, which he hasn't, and if I'd been photographed since I was a kid, which I haven't been, I might have gone along. As it was, I thought it better not to."

"These are deep waters, Comrade Windsor. Do you mean to intimate—?"

"If they can't do any better than that, we shan't have much to worry us. What do they take us for, I wonder? Farmers? Playing off a comic-supplement bluff like that on us!"

There was honest indignation in Billy's voice.

"You think, then, that if we had accepted Comrade Lake's invitation, and gone along for a smoke and a chat, the chat would not have been of the pleasantest nature?"

"We should have been put out of business."

"I have heard so much," said Psmith, thoughtfully, "of the lavish hospitality of the American."

"Taxi, sir?"

A red taximeter cab was crawling down the road at their side. Billy shook his head.

"Not that a taxi would be an unsound scheme," said Psmith.

"Not that particular one, if you don't mind."

"Something about it that offends your aesthetic taste?" queried

Psmith sympathetically.

"Something about it makes my aesthetic taste kick like a mule," said Billy.

"Ah, we highly strung literary men do have these curious prejudices. We cannot help it. We are the slaves of our temperaments. Let us walk, then. After all, the night is fine, and we are young and strong."

They had reached Twenty-Third Street when Billy stopped. "I don't know about walking," he said. "Suppose we take the Elevated?"

"Anything you wish, Comrade Windsor. I am in your hands."

They cut across into Sixth Avenue, and walked up the stairs to the station of the Elevated Railway. A train was just coming in.

"Has it escaped your notice, Comrade Windsor," said Psmith after a pause, "that, so far from speeding to your lodgings, we are going in precisely the opposite direction? We are in an up-town train."

"I noticed it," said Billy briefly.

"Are we going anywhere in particular?"

"This train goes as far as Hundred and Tenth Street. We'll go up to there."

"And then?"

"And then we'll come back."

"And after that, I suppose, we'll make a trip to Philadelphia, or Chicago, or somewhere? Well, well, I am in your hands, Comrade Windsor. The night is yet young. Take me where you will. It is only five cents a go, and we have money in our purses. We are two young men out for reckless dissipation. By all means let us have it."

At Hundred and Tenth Street they left the train, went down the stairs, and crossed the street. Half-way across Billy stopped.

"What now, Comrade Windsor?" inquired Psmith patiently. "Have you thought of some new form of entertainment?"

Billy was making for a spot some few yards down the road. Looking in that direction, Psmith saw his objective. In the shadow of the Elevated there was standing a taximeter cab.

"Taxi, sir?" said the driver, as they approached.

"We are giving you a great deal of trouble," said Billy. "You must be losing money over this job. All this while you might be getting fares down-town."

"These meetings, however," urged Psmith, "are very pleasant."

"I can save you worrying," said Billy. "My address is 84 East

Fourteenth Street. We are going back there now."

"Search me," said the driver, "I don't know what you're talking about."

"I thought perhaps you did," replied Billy. "Good night."

"These things are very disturbing," said Psmith, when they were in the train. "Dignity is impossible when one is compelled to be the Hunted Fawn. When did you begin to suspect that yonder merchant was doing the sleuth-hound act?"

"When I saw him in Broadway having a heart-to-heart talk with our friend from Missouri."

"He must be something of an expert at the game to have kept on our track."

"Not on your life. It's as easy as falling off a log. There are only certain places where you can get off an Elevated train. All he'd got to do was to get there before the train, and wait. I didn't expect to dodge him by taking the Elevated. I just wanted to make certain of his game."

The train pulled up at the Fourteenth Street station. In the roadway at the foot of the opposite staircase was a red taximeter cab.

CHAPTER XIII - REVIEWING THE SITUATION

Arriving at the bed-sitting-room, Billy proceeded to occupy the rocking-chair, and, as was his wont, began to rock himself rhythmically to and fro. Psmith seated himself gracefully on the couch-bed. There was a silence.

The events of the evening had been a revelation to Psmith. He had not realised before the extent of the ramifications of New York's underworld. That members of the gangs should crop up in the Astor roof-garden and in gorgeous raiment in the middle of Broadway was a surprise. When Billy Windsor had mentioned the gangs, he had formed a mental picture of low-browed hooligans, keeping carefully to their own quarter of the town. This picture had been correct, as far as it went, but it had not gone far enough. The bulk of the gangs of New York are of the hooligan class, and are rarely met with outside their natural boundaries. But each gang has its more prosperous members; gentlemen, who, like the man of the Astor roof-garden, support life by more delicate and genteel methods than the rest. The main body rely for their incomes, except at election-time, on such primitive feats as robbing intoxicated pedestrians. The aristocracy of the gangs soar higher.

It was a considerable time before Billy spoke.

"Say," he said, "this thing wants talking over."

"By all means, Comrade Windsor."

"It's this way. There's no doubt now that we're up against a mighty big proposition."

"Something of the sort would seem to be the case."

"It's like this. I'm going to see this through. It isn't only that I want to do a bit of good to the poor cusses in those tenements, though I'd do it for that alone. But, as far as I'm concerned, there's something to it besides that. If we win out, I'm going to get a job out of one of the big dailies. It'll give me just the chance I need. See what I mean? Well, it's different with you. I don't see that it's up to you to run the risk of getting yourself put out of business with a black-jack, and maybe shot. Once you get mixed up with the gangs there's no saying what's going to be doing. Well, I don't see why you shouldn't quit. All this has got nothing to do with you. You're over here on a vacation. You haven't got to make a living this side. You want to go about and have a good time, instead of getting mixed up with—"

He broke off.

"Well, that's what I wanted to say, anyway," he concluded.

Psmith looked at him reproachfully.

"Are you trying to *sack* me, Comrade Windsor?"

"How's that?"

"In various treatises on 'How to Succeed in Literature,'" said Psmith sadly, "which I have read from time to time, I have always found it stated that what the novice chiefly needed was an editor who believed in him. In you, Comrade Windsor, I fancied that I had found such an editor."

"What's all this about?" demanded Billy. "I'm making no kick about your work."

"I gathered from your remarks that you were anxious to receive my resignation."

"Well, I told you why. I didn't want you be black-jacked."

"Was that the only reason?"

"Sure."

"Then all is well," said Psmith, relieved. "For the moment I fancied that my literary talents had been weighed in the balance and adjudged below par. If that is all—why, these are the mere everyday risks of the young journalist's life. Without them we should be dull and dissatisfied. Our work would lose its fire. Men such as ourselves, Comrade Windsor, need a certain stimulus, a certain fillip, if they are to keep up their high standards. The knowledge that a low-browed gentleman is waiting round the corner with a sand-bag poised in air will just supply that stimulus. Also that fillip. It will give our output precisely the edge it requires."

"Then you'll stay in this thing? You'll stick to the work?"

"Like a conscientious leech, Comrade Windsor."

"Bully for you," said Billy.

It was not Psmith's habit, when he felt deeply on any subject, to exhibit his feelings; and this matter of the tenements had hit him harder than any one who did not know him intimately would have imagined. Mike would have understood him, but Billy Windsor was too recent an acquaintance. Psmith was one of those people who are content to accept most of the happenings of life in an airy spirit of tolerance. Life had been more or less of a game with him up till now. In his previous encounters with those with whom fate had brought him in contact there had been little at stake. The prize of victory had been merely a comfortable feeling of having had the best of a battle of wits; the penalty of defeat nothing worse than the discomfort of having failed to score. But this tenement business was different. Here he had touched the realities. There was something worth fighting for. His lot had been cast in pleasant places, and the sight of actual raw misery had come home to him with an added force from that circumstance. He was fully aware of the risks that he must run. The words of the man at the Astor, and still more the episodes of the family friend from Missouri and the taximeter cab, had shown him that this thing was on a different plane from anything that had happened to him before. It was a fight without the gloves, and to a finish at that. But he meant to see it through. Somehow or other those tenement houses had got to be cleaned up. If it meant trouble, as it undoubtedly did, that trouble would have to be faced.

CHAPTER XIII - REVIEWING THE SITUATION

"Now that Comrade Jarvis," he said, "showing a spirit of forbearance which, I am bound to say, does him credit, has declined the congenial task of fracturing our occiputs, who should you say, Comrade Windsor, would be the chosen substitute?"

Billy shook his head. "Now that Bat has turned up the job, it might be any one of three gangs. There are four main gangs, you know. Bat's is the biggest. But the smallest of them's large enough to put us away, if we give them the chance."

"I don't quite grasp the nice points of this matter. Do you mean that we have an entire gang on our trail in one solid mass, or will it be merely a section?"

"Well, a section, I guess, if it comes to that. Parker, or whoever fixed this thing up, would go to the main boss of the gang. If it was the Three Points, he'd go to Spider Reilly. If it was the Table Hill lot, he'd look up Dude Dawson. And so on."

"And what then?"

"And then the boss would talk it over with his own special partners. Every gang-leader has about a dozen of them. A sort of Inner Circle. They'd fix it up among themselves. The rest of the gang wouldn't know anything about it. The fewer in the game, you see, the fewer to split up the dollars."

"I see. Then things are not so black. All we have to do is to look out for about a dozen hooligans with a natural dignity in their bearing, the result of intimacy with the main boss. Carefully eluding these aristocrats, we shall win through. I fancy, Comrade Windsor, that all may yet be well. What steps do you propose to take by way of self-defence?"

"Keep out in the middle of the street, and not go off the Broadway after dark. You're pretty safe on Broadway. There's too much light for them there."

"Now that our sleuth-hound friend in the taximeter has ascertained your address, shall you change it?"

"It wouldn't do any good. They'd soon find where I'd gone to. How about yours?"

"I fancy I shall be tolerably all right. A particularly massive policeman is on duty at my very doors. So much for our private lives. But what of the day-time? Suppose these sandbag-specialists drop in at the office during business hours. Will Comrade Maloney's frank and manly statement that we are not in be sufficient to keep them out? I doubt it. All unused to the nice conventions of polite society, these rugged persons will charge through. In such circumstances good work will be hard to achieve. Your literary man must have complete quiet if he is to give the public of his best. But stay. An idea!"

"Well?"

"Comrade Brady. The Peerless Kid. The man *Cosy Moments* is running for the light-weight championship. We are his pugilistic sponsors. You may say that it is entirely owing to our efforts that he has obtained this match with—who exactly is the gentleman Comrade Brady fights at the Highfield Club on Friday night?"

"Cyclone Al. Wolmann, isn't it?"

"You are right. As I was saying, but for us the privilege of smiting Comrade Cyclone Al. Wolmann under the fifth rib on Friday night would almost certainly have been denied to him."

It almost seemed as if he were right. From the moment the paper had taken up his cause, Kid Brady's star had undoubtedly been in the ascendant. People began to talk about him as a likely man. Edgren, in the *Evening World*, had a paragraph about his chances for the light-weight title. Tad, in the *Journal*, drew a picture of him. Finally, the management of the Highfield Club had signed him for a ten-round bout with Mr. Wolmann. There were, therefore, reasons why *Cosy Moments* should feel a claim on the Kid's services.

"He should," continued Psmith, "if equipped in any degree with finer feelings, be bubbling over with gratitude towards us. 'But for *Cosy Moments*,' he should be saying to himself, 'where should I be? Among the also-rans.' I imagine that he will do any little thing we care to ask of him. I suggest that we approach Comrade Brady, explain the facts of the case, and offer him at a comfortable salary the post of fighting-editor of *Cosy Moments*. His duties will be to sit in the room opening out of ours, girded as to the loins and full of martial spirit, and apply some of those half-scissor hooks of his to the persons of any who overcome the opposition of Comrade Maloney. We, meanwhile, will enjoy that leisure and freedom from interruption which is so essential to the artist."

"It's not a bad idea," said Billy.

"It is about the soundest idea," said Psmith, "that has ever been struck. One of your newspaper friends shall supply us with tickets, and Friday night shall see us at the Highfield."

CHAPTER XIV - THE HIGHFIELD

Far up at the other end of the island, on the banks of the Harlem River, there stands the old warehouse which modern progress has converted into the Highfield Athletic and Gymnastic Club. The imagination, stimulated by the title, conjures up a sort of National Sporting Club, with pictures on the walls, padding on the chairs, and a sea of white shirt-fronts from roof to floor. But the Highfield differs in some respects from this fancy picture. Indeed, it would be hard to find a respect in which it does not differ. But these names are so misleading. The title under which the Highfield used to be known till a few years back was "Swifty Bob's." It was a good, honest title. You knew what to expect; and if you attended *séances* at Swifty Bob's you left your gold watch and your little savings at home. But a wave of anti-pugilistic feeling swept over the New York authorities. Promoters of boxing contests found themselves, to their acute disgust, raided by the police. The industry began to languish. People avoided places where at any moment the festivities might be marred by an inrush of large men in blue uniforms armed with locust-sticks.

And then some big-brained person suggested the club idea, which stands alone as an example of American dry humour. There are now no boxing contests in New York. Swifty Bob and his fellows would be shocked at the idea of such a thing. All that happens now is exhibition sparring bouts between members of the club. It is true that next day the papers very tactlessly report the friendly exhibition spar as if it had been quite a serious affair, but that is not the fault of Swifty Bob.

Kid Brady, the chosen of *Cosy Moments*, was billed for a "ten-round exhibition contest," to be the main event of the evening's entertainment. No decisions are permitted at these clubs. Unless a regrettable accident occurs, and one of the sparrers is knocked out, the verdict is left to the newspapers next day. It is not uncommon to find a man win easily in the *World*, draw in the *American*, and be badly beaten in the *Evening Mail*. The system leads to a certain amount of confusion, but it has the merit of offering consolation to a much-smitten warrior.

The best method of getting to the Highfield is by the Subway. To see the Subway in its most characteristic mood one must travel on it during the rush-hour, when its patrons are packed into the carriages in one solid jam by muscular guards and policemen, shoving in a manner reminiscent of a Rugby football scrum. When Psmith and Billy entered it on the Friday evening, it was comparatively empty. All the seats were occupied, but only a few of the straps and hardly any of the space reserved by law for the conductor alone.

Conversation on the Subway is impossible. The ingenious gentlemen who constructed it started with the object of making it noisy. Not ordinarily noisy, like a ton of coal falling on to a sheet of tin, but really noisy. So they fashioned the pillars of thin steel, and the sleepers of thin wood, and loosened all the nuts, and now a Subway train in motion suggests a prolonged dynamite explosion blended with the voice of some great cataract.

Psmith, forced into temporary silence by this combination of noises, started to make up for lost time on arriving in the street once more.

"A thoroughly unpleasant neighbourhood," he said, critically surveying the dark streets. "I fear me, Comrade Windsor, that we have been somewhat rash in venturing as far into the middle west as this. If ever there was a blighted locality where low-browed desperadoes might be expected to spring with whoops of joy from every corner, this blighted locality is that blighted locality. But we must carry on. In which direction, should you say, does this arena lie?"

It had begun to rain as they left Billy's lodgings. Psmith turned up the collar of his Burberry.

"We suffer much in the cause of Literature," he said. "Let us inquire of this genial soul if he knows where the Highfield is."

The pedestrian referred to proved to be going there himself. They went on together, Psmith courteously offering views on the weather and forecasts of the success of Kid Brady in the approaching contest.

Rattling on, he was alluding to the prominent part *Cosy Moments* had played in the affair, when a rough thrust from Windsor's elbow brought home to him his indiscretion.

He stopped suddenly, wishing he had not said as much. Their connection with that militant journal was not a thing even to be suggested to casual acquaintances, especially in such a particularly ill-lighted neighbourhood as that through which they were now passing.

Their companion, however, who seemed to be a man of small speech, made no comment. Psmith deftly turned the conversation back to the subject of the weather, and was deep in a comparison of the respective climates of England and the United States, when they turned a corner and found themselves opposite a gloomy, barn-like building, over the door of which it was just possible to decipher in the darkness the words "Highfield Athletic and Gymnastic Club."

The tickets which Billy Windsor had obtained from his newspaper friend were for one of the boxes. These proved to be sort of sheep-pens of unpolished wood, each with four hard chairs in it. The interior of the Highfield Athletic and Gymnastic Club was severely free from anything in the shape of luxury and ornament. Along the four walls were raised benches in tiers. On these were seated as tough-looking a collection of citizens as one might wish to see. On chairs at the ring-side were the reporters, with tickers at their sides, by means of which they tapped details of each round through to their down-town offices, where write-up reporters were waiting to read off and elaborate the messages. In the centre of the room, brilliantly lighted by half a dozen electric chandeliers, was the ring.

There were preliminary bouts before the main event. A burly gentleman in shirt-sleeves entered the ring, followed by two slim youths in fighting costume and a massive person in a red jersey, blue serge trousers, and yellow braces, who chewed gum with an abstracted air throughout the proceedings.

The burly gentleman gave tongue in a voice that cleft the air like a cannon-ball.

"Ex-hib-it-i-on four-round bout between Patsy Milligan and Tommy

Goodley, members of this club. Patsy on my right, Tommy on my left.

Gentlemen will kindly stop smokin'."

The audience did nothing of the sort. Possibly they did not apply the description to themselves. Possibly they considered the appeal a mere formula. Somewhere in the background a gong sounded, and Patsy, from the right, stepped briskly forward to meet Tommy, approaching from the left.

The contest was short but energetic. At intervals the combatants would cling affectionately to one another, and on these occasions the red-jerseyed man, still chewing gum and still wearing the same air of being lost in abstract thought, would split up the mass by the simple method of ploughing his way between the pair. Towards the end of the first round Thomas, eluding a left swing, put Patrick neatly to the floor, where the latter remained for the necessary ten seconds.

The remaining preliminaries proved disappointing. So much so that in the last of the series a soured sportsman on one of the benches near the roof began in satirical mood to whistle the "Merry Widow Waltz." It was here that the red-jerseyed thinker for the first and last time came out of his meditative trance. He leaned over the ropes, and spoke—without heat, but firmly.

"If that guy whistling back up yonder thinks he can do better than these boys, he can come right down into the ring."

The whistling ceased.

There was a distinct air of relief when the last preliminary was finished and preparations for the main bout began. It did not commence at once. There were formalities to be gone through, introductions and the like. The burly gentleman reappeared from nowhere, ushering into the ring a sheepishly-grinning youth in a flannel suit.

"In-ter-*doo*-cin' Young Leary," he bellowed impressively, "a noo member of this chub, who will box some good boy here in September."

He walked to the other side of the ring and repeated the remark. A raucous welcome was accorded to the new member.

Two other notable performers were introduced in a similar manner, and then the building became suddenly full of noise, for a tall youth in a bath-robe, attended by a little army of assistants, had entered the ring. One of the army carried a bright green bucket, on which were painted in white letters the words "Cyclone Al. Wolmann." A moment later there was another, though a far lesser, uproar, as

Kid Brady, his pleasant face wearing a self-conscious smirk, ducked under the ropes and sat down in the opposite corner.

"Ex-hib-it-i-on ten-round bout," thundered the burly gentleman, "between Cyclone. Al. Wolmann—"

Loud applause. Mr. Wolmann was one of the famous, a fighter with a reputation from New York to San Francisco. He was generally considered the most likely man to give the hitherto invincible Jimmy Garvin a hard battle for the lightweight championship.

"Oh, you Al.!" roared the crowd.

Mr. Wolmann bowed benevolently.

"—and Kid Brady, members of this—"

There was noticeably less applause for the Kid. He was an unknown. A few of those present had heard of his victories in the West, but these were but a small section of the crowd. When the faint applause had ceased, Psmith rose to his feet.

"Oh, you Kid!" he observed encouragingly.

"I should not like Comrade Brady," he said, reseating himself, "to think that he has no friend but his poor old mother, as, you will recollect, occurred on a previous occasion."

The burly gentleman, followed by the two armies of assistants, dropped down from the ring, and the gong sounded.

Mr. Wolmann sprang from his corner as if somebody had touched a spring. He seemed to be of the opinion that if you are a cyclone, it is never too soon to begin behaving like one. He danced round the Kid with an india-rubber agility. The *Cosy Moments* representative exhibited more stolidity. Except for the fact that he was in fighting attitude, with one gloved hand moving slowly in the neighbourhood of his stocky chest, and the other pawing the air on a line with his square jaw, one would have said that he did not realise the position of affairs. He wore the friendly smile of the good-natured guest who is led forward by his hostess to join in some round game.

Suddenly his opponent's long left shot out. The Kid, who had been strolling forward, received it under the chin, and continued to stroll forward as if nothing of note had happened. He gave the impression of being aware that Mr. Wolmann had committed a breach of good taste and of being resolved to pass it off with ready tact.

The Cyclone, having executed a backward leap, a forward leap, and a feint, landed heavily with both hands. The Kid's genial smile did not even quiver, but he continued to move forward. His opponent's left flashed out again, but this time, instead of ignoring the matter, the Kid replied with a heavy right swing; and Mr. Wolmann, leaping back, found himself against the ropes. By the time he had got out of that uncongenial position, two more of the Kid's swings had found their mark. Mr. Wolmann, somewhat perturbed, scuttered out into the middle of the ring, the Kid following in his self-contained, solid way.

The Cyclone now became still more cyclonic. He had a left arm which seemed to open out in joints like a telescope. Several times when the Kid appeared well out of distance there was a thud as a brown glove ripped in over his guard and jerked his head back. But always he kept boring in, delivering an occasional right to the body with the pleased smile of an infant destroying a Noah's Ark with a tack-hammer. Despite these efforts, however, he was plainly getting all the worst of it. Energetic Mr. Wolmann, relying on his long left, was putting in three blows to his one. When the gong sounded, ending the first round, the house was practically solid for the Cyclone. Whoops and yells rose from everywhere. The building rang with shouts of, "Oh, you Al.!"

Psmith turned sadly to Billy.

"It seems to me, Comrade Windsor," he said, "that this merry meeting looks like doing Comrade Brady no good. I should not be surprised at any moment to see his head bounce off on to the floor."

"Wait," said Billy. "He'll win yet."

"You think so?"

"Sure. He comes from Wyoming," said Billy with simple confidence.

Rounds two and three were a repetition of round one. The Cyclone raged almost unchecked about the ring. In one lightning rally in the third he brought his right across squarely on to the Kid's jaw. It was a blow which should have knocked any boxer out. The Kid merely staggered slightly and returned to business, still smiling.

"See!" roared Billy enthusiastically in Psmith's ear, above the uproar. "He doesn't mind it! He likes it! He comes from Wyoming!"

With the opening of round four there came a subtle change. The Cyclone's fury was expending itself. That long left shot out less sharply. Instead of being knocked back by it, the *Cosy Moments* champion now took the hits in his stride, and came shuffling in with his damaging body-blows. There were cheers and "Oh, you Al.'s!" at the sound of the gong, but there was an appealing note in them this time. The gallant sportsmen whose connection with boxing was confined to watching other men fight, and betting on what they considered a certainty, and who would have expired promptly if any one had tapped them sharply on their well-filled waistcoats, were beginning to fear that they might lose their money after all.

In the fifth round the thing became a certainty. Like the month of March, the Cyclone, who had come in like a lion, was going out like a lamb. A slight decrease in the pleasantness of the Kid's smile was noticeable. His expression began to resemble more nearly the gloomy importance of the *Cosy Moments* photographs. Yells of agony from panic-stricken speculators around the ring began to smite the rafters. The Cyclone, now but a gentle breeze, clutched repeatedly, hanging on like a leech till removed by the red-jerseyed referee.

Suddenly a grisly silence fell upon the house. It was broken by a cow-boy yell from Billy Windsor. For the Kid, battered, but obviously content, was standing in the middle of the ring, while on the ropes the Cyclone, drooping like a wet sock, was sliding slowly to the floor.

"*Cosy Moments* wins," said Psmith. "An omen, I fancy, Comrade Windsor."

CHAPTER XV - AN ADDITION TO THE STAFF

Penetrating into the Kid's dressing-room some moments later, the editorial staff found the winner of the ten-round exhibition bout between members of the club seated on a chair, having his right leg rubbed by a shock-headed man in a sweater, who had been one of his seconds during the conflict. The Kid beamed as they entered.

"Gents," he said, "come right in. Mighty glad to see you."

"It is a relief to me, Comrade Brady," said Psmith, "to find that you can see us. I had expected to find that Comrade Wolmann's purposeful buffs had completely closed your star-likes."

"Sure, I never felt them. He's a good quick boy, is Al., but," continued the Kid with powerful imagery, "he couldn't hit a hole in a block of ice-cream, not if he was to use a hammer."

"And yet at one period in the proceedings, Comrade Brady," said Psmith, "I fancied that your head would come unglued at the neck. But the fear was merely transient. When you began to administer those—am I correct in saying?—half-scissor hooks to the body, why, then I felt like some watcher of the skies when a new planet swims into his ken; or like stout Cortez when with eagle eyes he stared at the Pacific."

The Kid blinked.

"How's that?" he inquired.

"And why did I feel like that, Comrade Brady? I will tell you. Because my faith in you was justified. Because there before me stood the ideal fighting-editor of *Cosy Moments*. It is not a post that any weakling can fill. There charm of manner cannot qualify a man for the position. No one can hold down the job simply by having a kind heart or being good at farmyard imitations. No. We want a man of thews and sinews, a man who would rather be hit on the head with a half-brick than not. And you, Comrade Brady, are such a man."

The Kid turned appealingly to Billy.

"Say, this gets past me, Mr. Windsor. Put me wise."

"Can we have a couple of words with you alone, Kid?" said Billy.

"We want to talk over something with you."

"Sure. Sit down, gents. Jack'll be through in a minute."

Jack, who during this conversation had been concentrating himself on his subject's left leg, now announced that he guessed that would about do, and having advised the Kid not to stop and pick daisies, but to get into his clothes at once before he caught a chill, bade the company good night and retired.

Billy shut the door.

"Kid," he said, "you know those articles about the tenements we've been having in the paper?"

"Sure. I read 'em. They're to the good."

Psmith bowed.

"You stimulate us, Comrade Brady. This is praise from Sir Hubert

Stanley."

"It was about time some strong josher came and put it across to 'em," added the Kid.

"So we thought. Comrade Parker, however, totally disagreed with us."

"Parker?"

"That's what I'm coming to," said Billy. "The day before yesterday a man named Parker called at the office and tried to buy us off."

Billy's voice grew indignant at the recollection.

"You gave him the hook, I guess?" queried the interested Kid.

"To such an extent, Comrade Brady," said Psmith, "that he left breathing threatenings and slaughter. And it is for that reason that we have ventured to call upon you."

"It's this way," said Billy. "We're pretty sure by this time that whoever the man is this fellow Parker's working for has put one of the gangs on to us."

"You don't say!" exclaimed the Kid. "Gum! Mr. Windsor, they're tough propositions, those gangs."

"We've been followed in the streets, and once they put up a bluff to get us where they could do us in. So we've come along to you. We can look after ourselves out of the office, you see, but what we want is some one to help in case they try to rush us there."

"In brief, a fighting-editor," said Psmith. "At all costs we must have privacy. No writer can prune and polish his sentences to his satisfaction if he is compelled constantly to break off in order to eject boisterous hooligans. We therefore offer you the job of sitting in the outer room and intercepting these bravoes before they can reach us. The salary we leave to you. There are doubloons and to spare in the old oak chest. Take what you need and put the rest—if any—back. How does the offer strike you, Comrade Brady?"

"We don't want to get you in under false pretences, Kid," said Billy. "Of course, they may not come anywhere near the office. But still, if they did, there would be something doing. What do you feel about it?"

"Gents," said the Kid, "it's this way."

He stepped into his coat, and resumed.

"Now that I've made good by getting the decision over Al., they'll be giving me a chance of a big fight. Maybe with Jimmy Garvin. Well, if that happens, see what I mean? I'll have to be going away somewhere and getting into training. I shouldn't be able to come and sit with you. But, if you gents feel like it, I'd be mighty glad to come in till I'm wanted to go into training-camp."

"Great," said Billy; "that would suit us all the way up. If you'd do that, Kid, we'd be tickled to death."

"And touching salary—" put in Psmith.

"Shucks!" said the Kid with emphasis. "Nix on the salary thing. I wouldn't take a dime. If it hadn't a-been for you gents, I'd have been waiting still for a chance of lining up in the championship class. That's good enough for me. Any old thing you gents want me to do, I'll do it. And glad, too."

"Comrade Brady," said Psmith warmly, "you are, if I may say so, the goods. You are, beyond a doubt, supremely the stuff. We three, then, hand-in-hand, will face the foe; and if the foe has good, sound sense, he will keep right away. You appear to be ready. Shall we meander forth?"

The building was empty and the lights were out when they emerged from the dressing-room. They had to grope their way in darkness. It was still raining when they reached the street, and the only signs of life were a moist policeman and the distant glare of public-house lights down the road.

They turned off to the left, and, after walking some hundred yards, found themselves in a blind alley.

"Hullo!" said Billy. "Where have we come to?"

Psmith sighed.

"In my trusting way," he said, "I had imagined that either you or
Comrade Brady was in charge of this expedition and taking me by a
known route to the nearest Subway station. I did not think to ask.
I placed myself, without hesitation, wholly in your hands."

"I thought the Kid knew the way," said Billy.

"I was just taggin' along with you gents," protested the light-weight, "I thought you was taking me right. This is the first time I been up here."

"Next time we three go on a little jaunt anywhere," said Psmith resignedly, "it would be as well to take a map and a corps of guides with us. Otherwise we shall start for Broadway and finish up at Minneapolis."

They emerged from the blind alley and stood in the dark street, looking doubtfully up and down it.

"Aha!" said Psmith suddenly, "I perceive a native. Several natives, in fact. Quite a little covey of them. We will put our case before them, concealing nothing, and rely on their advice to take us to our goal."

A little knot of men was approaching from the left. In the darkness it was impossible to say how many of them there were. Psmith stepped forward, the Kid at his side.

"Excuse me, sir," he said to the leader, "but if you can spare me a moment of your valuable time—"

CHAPTER XV - AN ADDITION TO THE STAFF

There was a sudden shuffle of feet on the pavement, a quick movement on the part of the Kid, a chunky sound as of wood striking wood, and the man Psmith had been addressing fell to the ground in a heap.

As he fell, something dropped from his hand on to the pavement with a bump and a rattle. Stooping swiftly, the Kid picked it up, and handed it to Psmith. His fingers closed upon it. It was a short, wicked-looking little bludgeon, the black-jack of the New York tough.

"Get busy," advised the Kid briefly.

CHAPTER XVI - THE FIRST BATTLE

The promptitude and despatch with which the Kid had attended to the gentleman with the black-jack had not been without its effect on the followers of the stricken one. Physical courage is not an outstanding quality of the New York hooligan. His personal preference is for retreat when it is a question of unpleasantness with a stranger. And, in any case, even when warring among themselves, the gangs exhibit a lively distaste for the hard knocks of hand-to-hand fighting. Their chosen method of battling is to lie down on the ground and shoot. This is more suited to their physique, which is rarely great. The gangsman, as a rule, is stunted and slight of build.

The Kid's rapid work on the present occasion created a good deal of confusion. There was no doubt that much had been hoped for from speedy attack. Also, the generalship of the expedition had been in the hands of the fallen warrior. His removal from the sphere of active influence had left the party without a head. And, to add to their discomfiture, they could not account for the Kid. Psmith they knew, and Billy Windsor they knew, but who was this stranger with the square shoulders and the upper-cut that landed like a cannon-ball? Something approaching a panic prevailed among the gang.

It was not lessened by the behaviour of the intended victims. Billy Windsor, armed with the big stick which he had bought after the visit of Mr. Parker, was the first to join issue. He had been a few paces behind the others during the black-jack incident; but, dark as it was, he had seen enough to show him that the occasion was, as Psmith would have said, one for the Shrewd Blow rather than the Prolonged Parley. With a whoop of the purest Wyoming brand, he sprang forward into the confused mass of the enemy. A moment later Psmith and the Kid followed, and there raged over the body of the fallen leader a battle of Homeric type.

It was not a long affair. The rules and conditions governing the encounter offended the delicate sensibilities of the gang. Like artists who feel themselves trammelled by distasteful conventions, they were damped and could not do themselves justice. Their forte was long-range fighting with pistols. With that they felt *en rapport*. But this vulgar brawling in the darkness with muscular opponents who hit hard and often with sticks and hands was distasteful to them. They could not develop any enthusiasm for it. They carried pistols, but it was too dark and the combatants were too entangled to allow them to use these. Besides, this was not the dear, homely old Bowery, where a gentleman may fire a pistol without exciting vulgar comment. It was up-town, where curious crowds might collect at the first shot.

There was but one thing to be done. Reluctant as they might be to abandon their fallen leader, they must tear themselves away. Already they were suffering grievously from the stick, the black-jack, and the lightning blows of the Kid. For a moment they hung, wavering; then stampeded in half a dozen different directions, melting into the night whence they had come.

Billy, full of zeal, pursued one fugitive some fifty yards down the street, but his quarry, exhibiting a rare turn of speed, easily outstripped him.

He came back, panting, to find Psmith and the Kid examining the fallen leader of the departed ones with the aid of a match, which went out just as Billy arrived.

"It is our friend of the earlier part of the evening, Comrade Windsor," said Psmith. "The merchant with whom we hob-nobbed on our way to the Highfield. In a moment of imprudence I mentioned *Cosy Moments*. I fancy that this was his first intimation that we were in the offing. His visit to the Highfield was paid, I think, purely from sport-loving motives. He was not on our trail. He came merely to see if Comrade Brady was proficient with his hands. Subsequent events must have justified our fighting editor in his eyes. It seems to be a moot point whether he will ever recover consciousness."

"Mighty good thing if he doesn't," said Billy uncharitably.

"From one point of view, Comrade Windsor, yes. Such an event would undoubtedly be an excellent thing for the public good. But from our point of view, it would be as well if he were to sit up and take notice. We could ascertain from him who he is and which particular collection of horny-handeds he represents. Light another match, Comrade Brady."

The Kid did so. The head of it fell off and dropped upon the up-turned face. The hooligan stirred, shook himself, sat up, and began to mutter something in a foggy voice.

"He's still woozy," said the Kid.

"Still—what exactly, Comrade Brady?"

"In the air," explained the Kid. "Bats in the belfry. Dizzy. See what I mean? It's often like that when a feller puts one in with a bit of weight behind it just where that one landed. Gum! I remember when I fought Martin Kelly; I was only starting to learn the game then. Martin and me was mixing it good and hard all over the ring, when suddenly he puts over a stiff one right on the point. What do you think I done? Fall down and take the count? Not on your life. I just turns round and walks straight out of the ring to my dressing-room. Willie Harvey, who was seconding me, comes tearing in after me, and finds me getting into my clothes. 'What's doing, Kid?' he asks. 'I'm going fishin', Willie,' I says. 'It's a lovely day.' 'You've lost the fight,' he says. 'Fight?' says I. 'What fight?' See what I mean? I hadn't a notion of what had happened. It was a half an hour and more before I could remember a thing."

During this reminiscence, the man on the ground had contrived to clear his mind of the mistiness induced by the Kid's upper-cut. The first sign he showed of returning intelligence was a sudden dash for safety up the road. But he had not gone five yards when he sat down limply.

The Kid was inspired to further reminiscence. "Guess he's feeling pretty poor," he said. "It's no good him trying to run for a while after he's put his chin in the way of a real live one. I remember when Joe Peterson put me out, way back when I was new to the game—it was the same year I fought Martin Kelly. He had an awful punch, had old Joe, and he put me down and out in the eighth round. After the fight they found me on the fire-escape outside my dressing-room. 'Come in, Kid,' says they. 'It's all right, chaps,' I says, 'I'm dying.' Like that. 'It's all right, chaps, I'm dying.' Same with this guy. See what I mean?"

They formed a group about the fallen black-jack expert.

"Pardon us," said Psmith courteously, "for breaking in upon your reverie; but, if you could spare us a moment of your valuable time, there are one or two things which we should like to know."

"Sure thing," agreed the Kid.

"In the first place," continued Psmith, "would it be betraying professional secrets if you told us which particular bevy of energetic sandbaggers it is to which you are attached?"

"Gent," explained the Kid, "wants to know what's your gang."

The man on the ground muttered something that to Psmith and Billy was unintelligible.

"It would be a charity," said the former, "if some philanthropist would give this blighter elocution lessons. Can you interpret, Comrade Brady?"

"Says it's the Three Points," said the Kid.

"The Three Points? Let me see, is that Dude Dawson, Comrade
Windsor, or the other gentleman?"

"It's Spider Reilly. Dude Dawson runs the Table Hill crowd."

"Perhaps this *is* Spider Reilly?"

"Nope," said the Kid. "I know the Spider. This ain't him. This is some other mutt."

"Which other mutt in particular?" asked Psmith. "Try and find out, Comrade Brady. You seem to be able to understand what he says. To me, personally, his remarks sound like the output of a gramophone with a hot potato in its mouth."

"Says he's Jack Repetto," announced the interpreter.

There was another interruption at this moment. The bashful Mr. Repetto, plainly a man who was not happy in the society of strangers, made another attempt to withdraw. Reaching out a pair of lean hands, he pulled the Kid's legs from under him with a swift jerk, and, wriggling to his feet, started off again down the road. Once more, however, desire outran performance. He got as far as the nearest street-lamp, but no farther. The giddiness seemed to overcome him again, for he grasped the lamp-post, and, sliding slowly to the ground, sat there motionless.

CHAPTER XVI - THE FIRST BATTLE

The Kid, whose fall had jolted and bruised him, was inclined to be wrathful and vindictive. He was the first of the three to reach the elusive Mr. Repetto, and if that worthy had happened to be standing instead of sitting it might have gone hard with him. But the Kid was not the man to attack a fallen foe. He contented himself with brushing the dust off his person and addressing a richly abusive flow of remarks to Mr. Repetto.

Under the rays of the lamp it was possible to discern more closely the features of the black-jack exponent. There was a subtle but noticeable resemblance to those of Mr. Bat Jarvis. Apparently the latter's oiled forelock, worn low over the forehead, was more a concession to the general fashion prevailing in gang circles than an expression of personal taste. Mr. Repetto had it, too. In his case it was almost white, for the fallen warrior was an albino. His eyes, which were closed, had white lashes and were set as near together as Nature had been able to manage without actually running them into one another. His under-lip protruded and drooped. Looking at him, one felt instinctively that no judging committee of a beauty contest would hesitate a moment before him.

It soon became apparent that the light of the lamp, though bestowing the doubtful privilege of a clearer view of Mr. Repetto's face, held certain disadvantages. Scarcely had the staff of *Cosy Moments* reached the faint yellow pool of light, in the centre of which Mr. Repetto reclined, than, with a suddenness which caused them to leap into the air, there sounded from the darkness down the road the *crack-crack-crack* of a revolver. Instantly from the opposite direction came other shots. Three bullets flicked grooves in the roadway almost at Billy's feet. The Kid gave a sudden howl. Psmith's hat, suddenly imbued with life, sprang into the air and vanished, whirling into the night.

The thought did not come to them consciously at the moment, there being little time to think, but it was evident as soon as, diving out of the circle of light into the sheltering darkness, they crouched down and waited for the next move, that a somewhat skilful ambush had been effected. The other members of the gang, who had fled with such remarkable speed, had by no means been eliminated altogether from the game. While the questioning of Mr. Repetto had been in progress, they had crept back, unperceived except by Mr. Repetto himself. It being too dark for successful shooting, it had become Mr. Repetto's task to lure his captors into the light, which he had accomplished with considerable skill.

For some minutes the battle halted. There was dead silence. The circle of light was empty now. Mr. Repetto had vanished. A tentative shot from nowhere ripped through the air close to where Psmith lay flattened on the pavement. And then the pavement began to vibrate and give out a curious resonant sound. To Psmith it conveyed nothing, but to the opposing army it meant much. They knew it for what it was. Somewhere—it might be near or far—a policeman had heard the shots, and was signalling for help to other policemen along the line by beating on the flag-stones with his night-stick, the New York constable's substitute for the London police-whistle.

The noise grew, filling the still air. From somewhere down the road sounded the ring of running feet.

"De cops!" cried a voice. "Beat it!"

Next moment the night was full of clatter. The gang was "beating it."

Psmith rose to his feet and dusted his clothes ruefully. For the first time he realised the horrors of war. His hat had gone for ever. His trousers could never be the same again after their close acquaintance with the pavement.

The rescue party was coming up at the gallop.

The New York policeman may lack the quiet dignity of his London rival, but he is a hustler.

"What's doing?"

"Nothing now," said the disgusted voice of Billy Windsor from the shadows. "They've beaten it."

The circle of lamplight became as if by mutual consent a general rendezvous. Three grey-clad policemen, tough, clean-shaven men with keen eyes and square jaws, stood there, revolver in one hand, night-stick in the other. Psmith, hatless and dusty, joined them. Billy Windsor and the Kid, the latter bleeding freely from his left ear, the lobe of which had been chipped by a bullet, were the last to arrive.

"What's bin the rough house?" inquired one of the policemen, mildly interested.

"Do you know a sportsman of the name of Repetto?" inquired Psmith.

"Jack Repetto! Sure."

"He belongs to the Three Points," said another intelligent officer, as one naming some fashionable club.

"When next you see him," said Psmith, "I should be obliged if you would use your authority to make him buy me a new hat. I could do with another pair of trousers, too; but I will not press the trousers. A new hat, is, however, essential. Mine has a six-inch hole in it."

"Shot at you, did they?" said one of the policemen, as who should say, "Dash the lads, they're always up to some of their larks."

"Shot at us!" burst out the ruffled Kid. "What do you think's bin happening? Think an aeroplane ran into my ear and took half of it off? Think the noise was somebody opening bottles of pop? Think those guys that sneaked off down the road was just training for a Marathon?"

"Comrade Brady," said Psmith, "touches the spot. He—"

"Say, are you Kid Brady?" inquired one of the officers. For the first time the constabulary had begun to display any real animation.

"Reckoned I'd seen you somewhere!" said another. "You licked

Cyclone Al. all right, Kid, I hear."

"And who but a bone-head thought he wouldn't?" demanded the third warmly. "He could whip a dozen Cyclone Al.'s in the same evening with his eyes shut."

"He's the next champeen," admitted the first speaker.

"If he puts it over Jimmy Garvin," argued the second.

"Jimmy Garvin!" cried the third. "He can whip twenty Jimmy Garvins with his feet tied. I tell you—"

"I am loath," observed Psmith, "to interrupt this very impressive brain-barbecue, but, trivial as it may seem to you, to me there is a certain interest in this other little matter of my ruined hat. I know that it may strike you as hypersensitive of us to protest against being riddled with bullets, but—"

"Well, what's bin doin'?" inquired the Force. It was a nuisance, this perpetual harping on trifles when the deep question of the light-weight Championship of the World was under discussion, but the sooner it was attended to, the sooner it would be over.

Billy Windsor undertook to explain.

"The Three Points laid for us," he said. "Jack Repetto was bossing the crowd. I don't know who the rest were. The Kid put one over on to Jack Repetto's chin, and we were asking him a few questions when the rest came back, and started into shooting. Then we got to cover quick, and you came up and they beat it."

"That," said Psmith, nodding, "is a very fair *précis* of the evening's events. We should like you, if you will be so good, to corral this Comrade Repetto, and see that he buys me a new hat."

"We'll round Jack up," said one of the policemen indulgently.

"Do it nicely," urged Psmith. "Don't go hurting his feelings."

The second policeman gave it as his opinion that Jack was getting too gay. The third policeman conceded this. Jack, he said, had shown signs for some time past of asking for it in the neck. It was an error on Jack's part, he gave his hearers to understand, to assume that the lid was completely off the great city of New York.

"Too blamed fresh he's gettin'," the trio agreed. They could not have been more disapproving if they had been prefects at Haileybury and Mr. Repetto a first-termer who had been detected in the act of wearing his cap on the back of his head.

They seemed to think it was too bad of Jack.

"The wrath of the Law," said Psmith, "is very terrible. We will leave the matter, then, in your hands. In the meantime, we should be glad if you would direct us to the nearest Subway station. Just at the moment, the cheerful lights of the Great White Way are what I seem to chiefly need."

CHAPTER XVII - GUERILLA WARFARE

Thus ended the opening engagement of the campaign, seemingly in a victory for the *Cosy Moments* army. Billy Windsor, however, shook his head.

"We've got mighty little out of it," he said.

"The victory," said Psmith, "was not bloodless. Comrade Brady's ear, my hat—these are not slight casualties. On the other hand, surely we are one up? Surely we have gained ground? The elimination of Comrade Repetto from the scheme of things in itself is something. I know few men I would not rather meet in a lonely road than Comrade Repetto. He is one of Nature's sand-baggers. Probably the thing crept upon him slowly. He started, possibly, in a merely tentative way by slugging one of the family circle. His nurse, let us say, or his young brother. But, once started, he is unable to resist the craving. The thing grips him like dram-drinking. He sandbags now not because he really wants to, but because he cannot help himself. To me there is something consoling in the thought that Comrade Repetto will no longer be among those present."

"What makes you think that?"

"I should imagine that a benevolent Law will put him away in his little cell for at least a brief spell."

"Not on your life," said Billy. "He'll prove an alibi."

Psmith's eyeglass dropped out of his eye. He replaced it, and gazed, astonished, at Billy.

"An alibi? When three keen-eyed men actually caught him at it?"

"He can find thirty toughs to swear he was five miles away."

"And get the court to believe it?" said Psmith.

"Sure," said Billy disgustedly. "You don't catch them hurting a gangsman unless they're pushed against the wall. The politicians don't want the gangs in gaol, especially as the Aldermanic elections will be on in a few weeks. Did you ever hear of Monk Eastman?"

"I fancy not, Comrade Windsor. If I did, the name has escaped me.

Who was this cleric?"

"He was the first boss of the East Side gang, before Kid Twist took it on."

"Yes?"

"He was arrested dozens of times, but he always got off. Do you know what he said once, when they pulled him for thugging a fellow out in New Jersey?"

"I fear not, Comrade Windsor. Tell me all."

"He said, 'You're arresting me, huh? Say, you want to look where you're goin'; I cut some ice in this town. I made half the big politicians in New York!' That was what he said."

"His small-talk," said Psmith, "seems to have been bright and well-expressed. What happened then? Was he restored to his friends and his relations?"

"Sure, he was. What do you think? Well, Jack Repetto isn't Monk Eastman, but he's in with Spider Reilly, and the Spider's in with the men behind. Jack'll get off."

"It looks to me, Comrade Windsor," said Psmith thoughtfully, "as if my stay in this great city were going to cost me a small fortune in hats."

Billy's prophecy proved absolutely correct. The police were as good as their word. In due season they rounded up the impulsive Mr. Repetto, and he was haled before a magistrate. And then, what a beautiful exhibition of brotherly love and auld-lang-syne camaraderie was witnessed! One by one, smirking sheepishly, but giving out their evidence with unshaken earnestness, eleven greasy, wandering-eyed youths mounted the witness-stand and affirmed on oath that at the time mentioned dear old Jack had been making merry in their company in a genial and law-abiding fashion, many, many blocks below the scene of the regrettable assault. The magistrate discharged the prisoner, and the prisoner, meeting Billy and Psmith in the street outside, leered triumphantly at them.

Billy stepped up to him. "You may have wriggled out of this," he said furiously, "but if you don't get a move on and quit looking at me like that, I'll knock you over the Singer Building. Hump yourself."

Mr. Repetto humped himself.

So was victory turned into defeat, and Billy's jaw became squarer and his eye more full of the light of battle than ever. And there was need of a square jaw and a battle-lit eye, for now began a period of guerilla warfare such as no New York paper had ever had to fight against.

It was Wheeler, the gaunt manager of the business side of the journal, who first brought it to the notice of the editorial staff. Wheeler was a man for whom in business hours nothing existed but his job; and his job was to look after the distribution of the paper. As to the contents of the paper he was absolutely ignorant. He had been with *Cosy Moments* from its start, but he had never read a line of it. He handled it as if it were so much soap. The scholarly writings of Mr. Wilberfloss, the mirth-provoking sallies of Mr. B. Henderson Asher, the tender outpourings of Louella Granville Waterman—all these were things outside his ken. He was a distributor, and he distributed.

A few days after the restoration of Mr. Repetto to East Side Society, Mr. Wheeler came into the editorial room with information and desire for information. He endeavoured to satisfy the latter first.

"What's doing, anyway?" he asked. He then proceeded to his information. "Some one's got it in against the paper, sure," he said. "I don't know what it's all about. I ha'n't never read the thing. Don't see what any one could have against a paper with a name like *Cosy Moments*, anyway. The way things have been going last few days, seems it might be the organ of a blamed mining-camp what the boys have took a dislike to."

"What's been happening?" asked Billy with gleaming eyes.

"Why, nothing in the world to fuss about, only our carriers can't go out without being beaten up by gangs of toughs. Pat Harrigan's in the hospital now. Just been looking in on him. Pat's a feller who likes to fight. Rather fight he would than see a ball-game. But this was too much for him. Know what happened? Why, see here, just like this it was. Pat goes out with his cart. Passing through a low-down street on his way up-town he's held up by a bunch of toughs. He shows fight. Half a dozen of them attend to him, while the rest gets clean away with every copy of the paper there was in the cart. When the cop comes along, there's Pat in pieces on the ground and nobody in sight but a Dago chewing gum. Cop asks the Dago what's been doing, and the Dago says he's only just come round the corner and ha'n't seen nothing of anybody. What I want to know is, what's it all about? Who's got it in for us and why?"

Mr. Wheeler leaned back in his chair, while Billy, his hair rumpled more than ever and his eyes glowing, explained the situation. Mr. Wheeler listened absolutely unmoved, and, when the narrative had come to an end, gave it as his opinion that the editorial staff had sand. That was his sole comment. "It's up to you," he said, rising. "You know your business. Say, though, some one had better get busy right quick and do something to stop these guys rough-housing like this. If we get a few more carriers beat up the way Pat was, there'll be a strike. It's not as if they were all Irishmen. The most of them are Dagoes and such, and they don't want any more fight than they can get by beating their wives and kicking kids off the sidewalk. I'll do my best to get this paper distributed right and it's a shame if it ain't, because it's going big just now—but it's up to you. Good day, gents."

He went out. Psmith looked at Billy.

"As Comrade Wheeler remarks," he said, "it is up to us. What do you propose to do about it? This is a move of the enemy which I have not anticipated. I had fancied that their operations would be confined exclusively to our two selves. If they are going to strew the street with our carriers, we are somewhat in the soup."

Billy said nothing. He was chewing the stem of an unlighted pipe.

Psmith went on.

"It means, of course, that we must buck up to a certain extent. If the campaign is to be a long one, they have us where the hair is crisp. We cannot stand the strain. *Cosy Moments* cannot be muzzled, but it can undoubtedly be choked. What we want to do is to find out the name of the man behind the tenements as soon as ever we can and publish it; and, then, if we perish, fall yelling the name."

Billy admitted the soundness of this scheme, but wished to know how it was to be done.

"Comrade Windsor," said Psmith. "I have been thinking this thing over, and it seems to me that we are on the wrong track, or rather we aren't on any track at all; we are simply marking time. What we want to do is to go out and hustle round till we stir up something. Our line up to the present has been to sit at home and scream vigorously in the hope of some stout fellow hearing and rushing to help. In other words, we've been saying in the paper what an out-size in scugs the merchant must be who owns those tenements, in the hope that somebody else will agree with us and be sufficiently interested to get to work and find out who the blighter is. That's all wrong. What we must do now, Comrade Windsor, is put on our hats, such hats as Comrade Repetto has left us, and sally forth as sleuth-hounds on our own account."

"Yes, but how?" demanded Billy. "That's all right in theory, but how's it going to work in practice? The only thing that can corner the man is a commission."

"Far from it, Comrade Windsor. The job may be worked more simply. I don't know how often the rents are collected in these places, but I should say at a venture once a week. My idea is to hang negligently round till the rent-collector arrives, and when he has loomed up on the horizon, buttonhole him and ask him quite politely, as man to man, whether he is collecting those rents for himself or for somebody else, and if somebody else, who that somebody else is. Simple, I fancy? Yet brainy. Do you take me, Comrade Windsor?"

Billy sat up, excited. "I believe you've hit it."

Psmith shot his cuffs modestly.

CHAPTER XVIII - AN EPISODE BY THE WAY

It was Pugsy Maloney who, on the following morning, brought to the office the gist of what is related in this chapter. Pugsy's version was, however, brief and unadorned, as was the way with his narratives. Such things as first causes and piquant details he avoided, as tending to prolong the telling excessively, thus keeping him from perusal of his cowboy stories. The way Pugsy put it was as follows. He gave the thing out merely as an item of general interest, a bubble on the surface of the life of a great city. He did not know how nearly interested were his employers in any matter touching that gang which is known as the Three Points. Pugsy said: "Dere's trouble down where I live. Dude Dawson's mad at Spider Reilly, an' now de Table Hills are layin' for de T'ree Points. Sure." He had then retired to his outer fastness, yielding further details jerkily and with the distrait air of one whose mind is elsewhere.

Skilfully extracted and pieced together, these details formed themselves into the following typical narrative of East Side life in New York.

The really important gangs of New York are four. There are other less important institutions, but these are little more than mere friendly gatherings of old boyhood chums for purposes of mutual companionship. In time they may grow, as did Bat Jarvis's coterie, into formidable organisations, for the soil is undoubtedly propitious to such growth. But at present the amount of ice which good judges declare them to cut is but small. They "stick up" an occasional wayfarer for his "cush," and they carry "canisters" and sometimes fire them off, but these things do not signify the cutting of ice. In matters political there are only four gangs which count, the East Side, the Groome Street, the Three Points, and the Table Hill. Greatest of these by virtue of their numbers are the East Side and the Groome Street, the latter presided over at the time of this story by Mr. Bat Jarvis. These two are colossal, and, though they may fight each other, are immune from attack at the hands of lesser gangs. But between the other gangs, and especially between the Table Hill and the Three Points, which are much of a size, warfare rages as briskly as among the republics of South America. There has always been bad blood between the Table Hill and the Three Points, and until they wipe each other out after the manner of the Kilkenny cats, it is probable that there always will be. Little events, trifling in themselves, have always occurred to shatter friendly relations just when there has seemed a chance of their being formed. Thus, just as the

Table Hillites were beginning to forgive the Three Points for shooting the redoubtable Paul Horgan down at Coney Island, a Three Pointer injudiciously wiped out another of the rival gang near Canal Street. He pleaded self-defence, and in any case it was probably mere thoughtlessness, but nevertheless the Table Hillites were ruffled.

That had been a month or so back. During that month things had been simmering down, and peace was just preparing to brood when there occurred the incident to which Pugsy had alluded, the regrettable falling out of Dude Dawson and Spider Reilly at Mr. Maginnis's dancing saloon, Shamrock Hall, the same which Bat Jarvis had been called in to protect in the days before the Groome Street gang began to be.

Shamrock Hall, being under the eyes of the great Bat, was, of course, forbidden ground; and it was with no intention of spoiling the harmony of the evening that Mr. Dawson had looked in. He was there in a purely private and peaceful character.

As he sat smoking, sipping, and observing the revels, there settled at the next table Mr. Robert ("Nigger") Coston, an eminent member of the Three Points.

There being temporary peace between the two gangs, the great men exchanged a not unfriendly nod and, after a short pause, a word or two. Mr. Coston, alluding to an Italian who had just pirouetted past, remarked that there sure was some class to the way that wop hit it up. Mr. Dawson said Yup, there sure was. You would have said that all Nature smiled.

Alas! The next moment the sky was covered with black clouds and the storm broke. For Mr. Dawson, continuing in this vein of criticism, rather injudiciously gave it as his opinion that one of the lady dancers had two left feet.

For a moment Mr. Coston did not see which lady was alluded to.

"De goil in de pink skoit," said Mr. Dawson, facilitating the other's search by pointing with a much-chewed cigarette. It was at this moment that Nature's smile was shut off as if by a tap. For the lady in the pink skirt had been in receipt of Mr. Coston's respectful devotion for the past eight days.

From this point onwards the march of events was rapid.

Mr. Coston, rising, asked Mr. Dawson who he thought he, Mr. Dawson, was.

Mr. Dawson, extinguishing his cigarette and placing it behind his ear, replied that he was the fellow who could bite his, Mr. Coston's, head off.

Mr. Coston said: "Huh?"

Mr. Dawson said: "Sure."

Mr. Coston called Mr. Dawson a pie-faced rubber-necked four-flusher.

Mr. Dawson called Mr. Coston a coon.

And that was where the trouble really started.

It was secretly a great grief to Mr. Coston that his skin was of so swarthy a hue. To be permitted to address Mr. Coston face to face by his nickname was a sign of the closest friendship, to which only Spider Reilly, Jack Repetto, and one or two more of the gang could aspire. Others spoke of him as Nigger, or, more briefly, Nig—strictly behind his back. For Mr. Coston had a wide reputation as a fighter, and his particular mode of battling was to descend on his antagonist and bite him. Into this action he flung himself with the passionate abandonment of the artist. When he bit he bit. He did not nibble.

If a friend had called Mr. Coston "Nig" he would have been running grave risks. A stranger, and a leader of a rival gang, who addressed him as "coon" was more than asking for trouble. He was pleading for it.

Great men seldom waste time. Mr. Coston, leaning towards Mr. Dawson, promptly bit him on the cheek. Mr. Dawson bounded from his seat. Such was the excitement of the moment that, instead of drawing his "canister," he forgot that he had one on his person, and, seizing a mug which had held beer, bounced it vigorously on Mr. Coston's skull, which, being of solid wood, merely gave out a resonant note and remained unbroken.

So far the honours were comparatively even, with perhaps a slight balance in favour of Mr. Coston. But now occurred an incident which turned the scale, and made war between the gangs inevitable. In the far corner of the room, surrounded by a crowd of admiring friends, sat Spider Reilly, monarch of the Three Points. He had noticed that there was a slight disturbance at the other side of the hall, but had given it little attention till, the dancing ceasing suddenly and the floor emptying itself of its crowd, he had a plain view of Mr. Dawson and Mr. Coston squaring up at each other for the second round. We must assume that Mr. Reilly was not thinking what he did, for his action was contrary to all rules of gang-etiquette. In the street it would have been perfectly legitimate, even praiseworthy, but in a dance-hall belonging to a neutral power it was unpardonable.

What he did was to produce his "canister" and pick off the unsuspecting Mr. Dawson just as that exquisite was preparing to get in some more good work with the beer-mug. The leader of the Table Hillites fell with a crash, shot through the leg; and Spider Reilly, together with Mr. Coston and others of the Three Points, sped through the doorway for safety, fearing the wrath of Bat Jarvis, who, it was known, would countenance no such episodes at the dance-hall which he had undertaken to protect.

Mr. Dawson, meanwhile, was attended to and helped home. Willing informants gave him the name of his aggressor, and before morning the Table Hill camp was in ferment. Shooting broke out in three places, though there were no casualties. When the day dawned there existed between the two gangs a state of war more bitter than any in their record; for this time it was no question of obscure nonentities. Chieftain had assaulted chieftain; royal blood had been spilt.

* * *

"Comrade Windsor," said Psmith, when Master Maloney had spoken his last word, "we must take careful note of this little matter. I rather fancy that sooner or later we may be able to turn it to our profit. I am sorry for Dude Dawson, anyhow. Though I have never met him, I have a sort of instinctive respect for him. A man such as he would feel a bullet through his trouser-leg more than one of common clay who cared little how his clothes looked."

CHAPTER XIX - IN PLEASANT STREET

Careful inquiries, conducted incognito by Master Maloney among the denizens of Pleasant Street, brought the information that rents in the tenements were collected not weekly but monthly, a fact which must undoubtedly cause a troublesome hitch in the campaign. Rent-day, announced Pugsy, fell on the last day of the month.

"I rubbered around," he said, "and did de sleut' act, and I finds t'ings out. Dere's a feller comes round 'bout supper time dat day, an' den it's up to de fam'lies what lives in de tenements to dig down into deir jeans fer de stuff, or out dey goes dat same night."

"Evidently a hustler, our nameless friend," said Psmith.

"I got dat from a kid what knows anuder kid what lives dere," explained Master Maloney. "Say," he proceeded confidentially, "dat kid's in bad, sure he is. Dat second kid, de one what lives dere. He's a wop kid, an—"

"A what, Comrade Maloney?"

"A wop. A Dago. Why, don't you get next? Why, an Italian. Sure, dat's right. Well, dis kid, he is sure to de bad, 'cos his father come over from Italy to work on de Subway."

"I don't see why that puts him in bad," said Billy Windsor wonderingly.

"Nor I," agreed Psmith. "Your narratives, Comrade Maloney, always seem to me to suffer from a certain lack of construction. You start at the end, and then you go back to any portion of the story which happens to appeal to you at the moment, eventually winding up at the beginning. Why should the fact that this stripling's father has come over from Italy to work on the Subway be a misfortune?"

"Why, sure, because he got fired an' went an' swatted de foreman one on de coco, an' de magistrate gives him t'oity days."

"And then, Comrade Maloney? This thing is beginning to get clearer. You are like Sherlock Holmes. After you've explained a thing from start to finish—or, as you prefer to do, from finish to start—it becomes quite simple."

"Why, den dis kid's in bad for fair, 'cos der ain't nobody to pungle de bones."

"Pungle de what, Comrade Maloney?"

"De bones. De stuff. Dat's right. De dollars. He's all alone, dis kid, so when de rent-guy blows in, who's to slip him over de simoleons? It'll be outside for his, quick."

Billy warmed up at this tale of distress in his usual way. "Somebody ought to do something. It's a vile shame the kid being turned out like that."

"We will see to it, Comrade Windsor. *Cosy Moments* shall step in. We will combine business with pleasure, paying the stripling's rent and corralling the rent-collector at the same time. What is today? How long before the end of the month? Another week! A murrain on it, Comrade Windsor. Two murrains. This delay may undo us."

But the days went by without any further movement on the part of the enemy. A strange quiet seemed to be brooding over the other camp. As a matter of fact, the sudden outbreak of active hostilities with the Table Hill contingent had had the effect of taking the minds of Spider Reilly and his warriors off *Cosy Moments* and its affairs, much as the unexpected appearance of a mad bull would make a man forget that he had come out butterfly-hunting. Psmith and Billy could wait; they were not likely to take the offensive; but the Table Hillites demanded instant attention.

War had broken out, as was usual between the gangs, in a somewhat tentative fashion at first sight. There had been sniping and skirmishes by the wayside, but as yet no pitched battle. The two armies were sparring for an opening.

* * *

The end of the week arrived, and Psmith and Billy, conducted by Master Maloney, made their way to Pleasant Street. To get there it was necessary to pass through a section of the enemy's country; but the perilous passage was safely negotiated. The expedition reached its unsavoury goal intact.

The wop kid, whose name, it appeared, was Giuseppe Orloni, inhabited a small room at the very top of the building next to the one Psmith and Mike had visited on their first appearance in Pleasant Street. He was out when the party, led by Pugsy up dark stairs, arrived; and, on returning, seemed both surprised and alarmed to see visitors. Pugsy undertook to do the honours. Pugsy as interpreter was energetic but not wholly successful. He appeared to have a fixed idea that the Italian language was one easily mastered by the simple method of saying "da" instead of "the," and tacking on a final "a" to any word that seemed to him to need one.

"Say, kid," he began, "has da rent-a-man come yet-a?"

The black eyes of the wop kid clouded. He gesticulated, and said something in his native language.

"He hasn't got next," reported Master Maloney. "He can't git on to me curves. Dese wop kids is all boneheads. Say, kid, look-a here." He walked out of the room and closed the door; then, rapping on it smartly from the outside, re-entered and, assuming a look of extreme ferocity, stretched out his hand and thundered: "Unbelt-a! Slip-a me da stuff!"

The wop kid's puzzlement became pathetic.

"This," said Psmith, deeply interested, "is getting about as tense as anything I ever struck. Don't give in, Comrade Maloney. Who knows but that you may yet win through? I fancy the trouble is that your too perfect Italian accent is making the youth home-sick. Once more to the breach, Comrade Maloney."

Master Maloney made a gesture of disgust. "I'm t'roo. Dese Dagoes makes me tired. Dey don't know enough to go upstairs to take de Elevated. Beat it, you mutt," he observed with moody displeasure to the wop kid, accompanying the words with a gesture which conveyed its own meaning. The wop kid, plainly glad to get away, slipped out of the door like a shadow.

Pugsy shrugged his shoulders.

"Gents," he said resignedly, "it's up to youse."

"I fancy," said Psmith, "that this is one of those moments when it is necessary for me to unlimber my Sherlock Holmes system. As thus. If the rent collector *had* been here, it is certain, I think, that Comrade Spaghetti, or whatever you said his name was, wouldn't have been. That is to say, if the rent collector had called and found no money waiting for him, surely Comrade Spaghetti would have been out in the cold night instead of under his own roof-tree. Do you follow me, Comrade Maloney?"

"That's right," said Billy Windsor. "Of course."

"Elementary, my dear Watson, elementary," murmured Psmith.

"So all we have to do is to sit here and wait."

"All?" said Psmith sadly. "Surely it is enough. For of all the scaly localities I have struck this seems to me the scaliest. The architect of this Stately Home of America seems to have had a positive hatred for windows. His idea of ventilation was to leave a hole in the wall about the size of a lima bean and let the thing go at that. If our friend does not arrive shortly, I shall pull down the roof. Why, gadzooks! Not to mention stap my vitals! Isn't that a trap-door up there? Make a long-arm, Comrade Windsor."

Billy got on a chair and pulled the bolt. The trap-door opened downwards. It fell, disclosing a square of deep blue sky.

"Gum!" he said. "Fancy living in this atmosphere when you don't have to. Fancy these fellows keeping that shut all the time."

"I expect it is an acquired taste," said Psmith, "like Limburger cheese. They don't begin to appreciate air till it is thick enough to scoop chunks out of with a spoon. Then they get up on their hind legs and inflate their chests and say, 'This is fine! This beats ozone hollow!' Leave it open, Comrade Windsor. And now, as to the problem of dispensing with Comrade Maloney's services?"

"Sure," said Billy. "Beat it, Pugsy, my lad."

Pugsy looked up, indignant.

"Beat it?" he queried.

"While your shoe leather's good," said Billy. "This is no place for a minister's son. There may be a rough house in here any minute, and you would be in the way."

"I want to stop and pipe de fun," objected Master Maloney.

"Never mind. Cut off. We'll tell you all about it to-morrow."

Master Maloney prepared reluctantly to depart. As he did so there was a sound of a well-shod foot on the stairs, and a man in a snuff-coloured suit, wearing a brown Homburg hat and carrying a small notebook in one hand, walked briskly into the room. It was not necessary for Psmith to get his Sherlock Holmes system to work. His whole appearance proclaimed the new-comer to be the long-expected collector of rents.

CHAPTER XX - CORNERED

He stood in the doorway looking with some surprise at the group inside. He was a smallish, pale-faced man with protruding eyes and teeth which gave him a certain resemblance to a rabbit.

"Hello," he said.

"Welcome to New York," said Psmith.

Master Maloney, who had taken advantage of the interruption to edge farther into the room, now appeared to consider the question of his departure permanently shelved. He sidled to a corner and sat down on an empty soap-box with the air of a dramatic critic at the opening night of a new play. The scene looked good to him. It promised interesting developments. Master Maloney was an earnest student of the drama, as exhibited in the theatres of the East Side, and few had ever applauded the hero of "Escaped from Sing-Sing," or hissed the villain of "Nellie, the Beautiful Cloak-Model" with more fervour than he. He liked his drama to have plenty of action, and to his practised eye this one promised well. Psmith he looked upon as a quite amiable lunatic, from whom little was to be expected; but there was a set expression on Billy Windsor's face which suggested great things.

His pleasure was abruptly quenched. Billy Windsor, placing a firm hand on his collar, led him to the door and pushed him out, closing the door behind him.

The rent collector watched these things with a puzzled eye. He now turned to Psmith.

"Say, seen anything of the wops that live here?" he inquired.

"I am addressing—?" said Psmith courteously.

"My name's Gooch."

Psmith bowed.

"Touching these wops, Comrade Gooch," he said, "I fear there is little chance of your seeing them to-night, unless you wait some considerable time. With one of them—the son and heir of the family, I should say—we have just been having a highly interesting and informative chat. Comrade Maloney, who has just left us, acted as interpreter. The father, I am told, is in the dungeon below the castle moat for a brief spell for punching his foreman in the eye. The result? The rent is not forthcoming."

"Then it's outside for theirs," said Mr. Gooch definitely.

"It's a big shame," broke in Billy, "turning the kid out. Where's he to go?"

"That's up to him. Nothing to do with me. I'm only acting under orders from up top."

"Whose orders, Comrade Gooch?" inquired Psmith.

"The gent who owns this joint."

"Who is he?" said Billy.

Suspicion crept into the protruding eyes of the rent collector. He waxed wroth. "Say!" he demanded. "Who are you two guys, anyway, and what do you think you're doing here? That's what I'd like to know. What do you want with the name of the owner of this place? What business is it of yours?"

"The fact is, Comrade Gooch, we are newspaper men."

"I guessed you were," said Mr. Gooch with triumph. "You can't bluff me. Well, it's no good, boys. I've nothing for you. You'd better chase off and try something else."

He became more friendly.

"Say, though," he said, "I just guessed you were from some paper. I wish I could give you a story, but I can't. I guess it's this *Cosy Moments* business that's been and put your editor on to this joint, ain't it? Say, though, that's a queer thing, that paper. Why, only a few weeks ago it used to be a sort of take-home-and-read-to-the-kids affair. A friend of mine used to buy it regular. And then suddenly it comes out with a regular whoop, and started knocking these tenements and boosting Kid Brady, and all that. I can't understand it. All I know is that it's begun to get this place talked about. Why, you see for yourselves how it is. Here is your editor sending you down to get a story about it. But, say, those *Cosy Moments* guys are taking big risks. I tell you straight they are, and that goes. I happen to know a thing or two about what's going on on the other side, and I tell you there's going to be something doing if they don't cut it out quick. Mr.—" he stopped and chuckled, "Mr. Jones isn't the man to sit still and smile. He's going to get busy. Say, what paper do you boys come from?"

"*Cosy Moments*, Comrade Gooch," Psmith replied. "Immediately behind you, between you and the door, is Comrade Windsor, our editor. I am Psmith. I sub-edit."

For a moment the inwardness of the information did not seem to come home to Mr. Gooch. Then it hit him. He spun round. Billy Windsor was standing with his back against the door and a more than nasty look on his face.

"What's all this?" demanded Mr. Gooch.

"I will explain all," said Psmith soothingly. "In the first place, however, this matter of Comrade Spaghetti's rent. Sooner than see that friend of my boyhood slung out to do the wandering-child-in-the-snow act, I will brass up for him."

"Confound his rent. Let me out."

"Business before pleasure. How much is it? Twelve dollars? For the privilege of suffocating in this compact little Black Hole? By my halidom, Comrade Gooch, that gentleman whose name you are so shortly to tell us has a very fair idea of how to charge! But who am I that I should criticise? Here are the simoleons, as our young friend, Comrade Maloney, would call them. Push me over a receipt."

"Let me out."

"Anon, gossip, anon.—Shakespeare. First, the receipt."

Mr. Gooch scribbled a few words in his notebook and tore out the page. Psmith thanked him.

"I will see that it reaches Comrade Spaghetti," he said. "And now to a more important matter. Don't put away that notebook. Turn to a clean page, moisten your pencil, and write as follows. Are you ready? By the way, what is your Christian name? . . . Gooch, Gooch, this is no way to speak! Well, if you are sensitive on the point, we will waive the Christian name. It is my duty to tell you, however, that I suspect it to be Percy. Let us push on. Are you ready, once more? Pencil moistened? Very well, then. 'I'—comma—'being of sound mind and body'—comma—'and a bright little chap altogether'—comma—Why, you're not writing."

"Let me out," bellowed Mr. Gooch. "I'll summon you for assault and battery. Playing a fool game like this! Get away from that door."

"There has been no assault and battery yet, Comrade Gooch, but who shall predict how long so happy a state of things will last? Do not be deceived by our gay and smiling faces, Comrade Gooch. We mean business. Let me put the whole position of affairs before you; and I am sure a man of your perception will see that there is only one thing to be done."

He dusted the only chair in the room with infinite care and sat down. Billy Windsor, who had not spoken a word or moved an inch since the beginning of the interview, continued to stand and be silent. Mr. Gooch shuffled restlessly in the middle of the room.

"As you justly observed a moment ago," said Psmith, "the staff of *Cosy Moments* is taking big risks. We do not rely on your unsupported word for that. We have had practical demonstration of the fact from one J. Repetto, who tried some few nights ago to put us out of business. Well, it struck us both that we had better get hold of the name of the blighter who runs these tenements as quickly as possible, before Comrade Repetto's next night out. That is what we should like you to give us, Comrade Gooch. And we should like it in writing. And, on second thoughts, in ink. I have one of those patent non-leakable fountain pens in my pocket. The Old Journalist's Best Friend. Most of the ink has come out and is permeating the lining of my coat, but I think there is still sufficient for our needs. Remind me later, Comrade Gooch, to continue on the subject of fountain pens. I have much to say on the theme. Meanwhile, however, business, business. That is the cry."

He produced a pen and an old letter, the last page of which was blank, and began to write.

"How does this strike you?" he said. "'I'—(I have left a blank for the Christian name: you can write it in yourself later)—'I, blank Gooch, being a collector of rents in Pleasant Street, New York, do hereby swear'—hush, Comrade Gooch, there is no need to do it yet—'that the name of the owner of the Pleasant Street tenements, who is responsible for the perfectly foul conditions there, is—' And that is where you come in, Comrade Gooch. That is where we need your specialised knowledge. Who is he?"

Billy Windsor reached out and grabbed the rent collector by the collar. Having done this, he proceeded to shake him.

Billy was muscular, and his heart was so much in the business that Mr. Gooch behaved as if he had been caught in a high wind. It is probable that in another moment the desired information might have been shaken out of him, but before this could happen there was a banging at the door, followed by the entrance of Master Maloney. For the first time since Psmith had known him, Pugsy was openly excited.

"Say," he began, "youse had better beat it quick, you had. Dey's coming!"

"And now go back to the beginning, Comrade Maloney," said Psmith patiently, "which in the exuberance of the moment you have skipped. Who are coming?"

"Why, dem. De guys."

Psmith shook his head.

"Your habit of omitting essentials, Comrade Maloney, is going to undo you one of these days. When you get to that ranch of yours, you will probably start out to gallop after the cattle without remembering to mount your mustang. There are four million guys in New York. Which section is it that is coming?"

"Gum! I don't know how many dere is ob dem. I seen Spider Reilly an' Jack Repetto an'—"

"Say no more," said Psmith. "If Comrade Repetto is there, that is enough for me. I am going to get on the roof and pull it up after me."

Billy released Mr. Gooch, who fell, puffing, on to the low bed, which stood in one corner of the room.

"They must have spotted us as we were coming here," he said, "and followed us. Where did you see them, Pugsy?"

"On de Street just outside. Dere was a bunch of dem talkin' togedder, and I hears dem say you was in here. One of dem seen you come in, an dere ain't no ways out but de front, so dey ain't hurryin'! Dey just reckon to pike along upstairs, lookin' into each room till dey finds you. An dere's a bunch of dem goin' to wait on de Street in case youse beat it past down de stairs while de udder guys is rubberin' for youse. Say, gents, it's pretty fierce, dis proposition. What are youse goin' to do?"

Mr. Gooch, from the bed, laughed unpleasantly.

"I guess you ain't the only assault-and-battery artists in the business," he said. "Looks to me as if some one else was going to get shaken up some."

Billy looked at Psmith.

"Well?" he said. "What shall we do? Go down and try and rush through?"

Psmith shook his head.

"Not so, Comrade Windsor, but about as much otherwise as you can jolly well imagine."

"Well, what then?"

"We will stay here. Or rather we will hop nimbly up on to the roof through that skylight. Once there, we may engage these varlets on fairly equal terms. They can only get through one at a time. And while they are doing it I will give my celebrated imitation of Horatius. We had better be moving. Our luggage, fortunately, is small. Merely Comrade Gooch. If you will get through the skylight, I will pass him up to you."

Mr. Gooch, with much verbal embroidery, stated that he would not go. Psmith acted promptly. Gripping the struggling rent collector round the waist, and ignoring his frantic kicks as mere errors in taste, he lifted him to the trap-door, whence the head, shoulders and arms of Billy Windsor protruded into the room. Billy collected the collector, and then Psmith turned to Pugsy.

"Comrade Maloney."

"Huh?"

"Have I your ear?"

"Huh?"

"Are you listening till you feel that your ears are the size of footballs? Then drink this in. For weeks you have been praying for a chance to show your devotion to the great cause; or if you haven't, you ought to have been. That chance has come. You alone can save us. In a sense, of course, we do not need to be saved. They will find it hard to get at us, I fancy, on the roof. But it ill befits the dignity of the editorial staff of a great New York weekly to roost like pigeons for any length of time; and consequently it is up to you."

"Shall I go for de cops, Mr. Smith?"

"No, Comrade Maloney, I thank you. I have seen the cops in action, and they did not impress me. We do not want allies who will merely shake their heads at Comrade Repetto and the others, however sternly. We want some one who will swoop down upon these merry roisterers, and, as it were, soak to them good. Do you know where Dude Dawson lives?"

The light of intelligence began to shine in Master Maloney's face. His eye glistened with respectful approval. This was strategy of the right sort.

"Dude Dawson? Nope. But I can ask around."

"Do so, Comrade Maloney. And when found, tell him that his old college chum, Spider Reilly, is here. He will not be able to come himself, I fear, but he can send representatives."

"Sure."

"That's all, then. Go downstairs with a gay and jaunty air, as if you had no connection with the old firm at all. Whistle a few lively bars. Make careless gestures. Thus shall you win through. And now it would be no bad idea, I fancy, for me to join the rest of the brains of the paper up aloft. Off you go, Comrade Maloney. And, in passing, don't take a week about it. Leg it with all the speed you possess."

Pugsy vanished, and Psmith closed the door behind him. Inspection revealed the fact that it possessed no lock. As a barrier it was useless. He left it ajar, and, jumping up, gripped the edge of the opening in the roof and pulled himself through.

Billy Windsor was seated comfortably on Mr. Gooch's chest a few feet away. By his side was his big stick. Psmith possessed himself of this, and looked about him. The examination was satisfactory. The trap-door appeared to be the only means of access to the roof, and between their roof and that of the next house there was a broad gulf.

"Practically impregnable," he murmured. "Only one thing can dish us, Comrade Windsor; and that is if they have the sense to get on to the roof next door and start shooting. Even in that case, however, we have cover in the shape of the chimneys. I think we may fairly say that all is well. How are you getting along? Has the patient responded at all?"

"Not yet," said Billy. "But he's going to."

"He will be in your charge. I must devote myself exclusively to guarding the bridge. It is a pity that the trap has not got a bolt this side. If it had, the thing would be a perfect picnic. As it is, we must leave it open. But we mustn't expect everything."

Billy was about to speak, but Psmith suddenly held up his hand warningly. From the room below came a sound of feet.

For a moment the silence was tense. Then from Mr. Gooch's lips there escaped a screech.

"This way! They're up—"

The words were cut short as Billy banged his hand over the speaker's mouth. But the thing was done.

"On top de roof," cried a voice. "Dey've beaten it for de roof."

The chair rasped over the floor. Feet shuffled. And then, like a jack-in-the-box, there popped through the opening a head and shoulders.

CHAPTER XXI - THE BATTLE OF PLEASANT STREET

The new arrival was a young man with a shock of red hair, an ingrowing Roman nose, and a mouth from which force or the passage of time had removed three front teeth. He held on to the edges of the trap with his hands, and stared in a glassy manner into Psmith's face, which was within a foot of his own.

There was a momentary pause, broken by an oath from Mr. Gooch, who was still undergoing treatment in the background.

"Aha!" said Psmith genially. "Historic picture. 'Doctor Cook discovers the North Pole.'"

The red-headed young man blinked. The strong light of the open air was trying to his eyes.

"Youse had better come down," he observed coldly. "We've got youse."

"And," continued Psmith, unmoved, "is instantly handed a gum-drop by his faithful Esquimaux."

As he spoke, he brought the stick down on the knuckles which disfigured the edges of the trap. The intruder uttered a howl and dropped out of sight. In the room below there were whisperings and mutterings, growing gradually louder till something resembling coherent conversation came to Psmith's ears, as he knelt by the trap making meditative billiard-shots with the stick at a small pebble.

"Aw g'wan! Don't be a quitter!"

"Who's a quitter?"

"Youse is a quitter. Get on top de roof. He can't hoit youse."

"De guy's gotten a big stick." Psmith nodded appreciatively. "I and Roosevelt," he murmured.

A somewhat baffled silence on the part of the attacking force was followed by further conversation.

"Gum! some guy's got to go up." Murmur of assent from the audience.

A voice, in inspired tones: "Let Sam do it!"

This suggestion made a hit. There was no doubt about that. It was a success from the start. Quite a little chorus of voices expressed sincere approval of the very happy solution to what had seemed an insoluble problem. Psmith, listening from above, failed to detect in the choir of glad voices one that might belong to Sam himself. Probably gratification had rendered the chosen one dumb.

"Yes, let Sam do it!" cried the unseen chorus. The first speaker, unnecessarily, perhaps—for the motion had been carried almost unanimously—but possibly with the idea of convincing the one member of the party in whose bosom doubts might conceivably be harboured, went on to adduce reasons.

"Sam bein' a coon," he argued, "ain't goin' to git hoit by no stick. Youse can't hoit a coon by soakin' him on de coco, can you, Sam?"

Psmith waited with some interest for the reply, but it did not come. Possibly Sam did not wish to generalise on insufficient experience.

"*Solvitur ambulando*," said Psmith softly, turning the stick round in his fingers. "Comrade Windsor!"

"Hullo?"

"Is it possible to hurt a coloured gentleman by hitting him on the head with a stick?"

"If you hit him hard enough."

"I knew there was some way out of the difficulty," said Psmith with satisfaction. "How are you getting on up at your end of the table, Comrade Windsor?"

"Fine."

"Any result yet?"

"Not at present."

"Don't give up."

"Not me."

"The right spirit, Comrade Win—"

A report like a cannon in the room below interrupted him. It was merely a revolver shot, but in the confined space it was deafening. The bullet sang up into the sky.

"Never hit me!" said Psmith with dignified triumph.

The noise was succeeded by a shuffling of feet. Psmith grasped his stick more firmly. This was evidently the real attack. The revolver shot had been a mere demonstration of artillery to cover the infantry's advance.

Sure enough, the next moment a woolly head popped through the opening, and a pair of rolling eyes gleamed up at the old Etonian.

"Why, Sam!" said Psmith cordially, "this is well met! I remember *you*. Yes, indeed, I do. Wasn't you the feller with the open umbereller that I met one rainy morning on the Av-en-ue? What, are you coming up? Sam, I hate to do it, but—"

A yell rang out.

"What was that?" asked Billy Windsor over his shoulder.

"Your statement, Comrade Windsor, has been tested and proved correct."

By this time the affair had begun to draw a "gate." The noise of the revolver had proved a fine advertisement. The roof of the house next door began to fill up. Only a few of the occupants could get a clear view of the proceedings, for a large chimney-stack intervened. There was considerable speculation as to what was passing between Billy Windsor and Mr. Gooch. Psmith's share in the entertainment was more obvious. The early comers had seen his interview with Sam, and were relating it with gusto to their friends. Their attitude towards Psmith was that of a group of men watching a terrier at a rat-hole. They looked to him to provide entertainment for them, but they realised that the first move must be with the attackers. They were fair-minded men, and they did not expect Psmith to make any aggressive move.

Their indignation, when the proceedings began to grow slow, was directed entirely at the dilatory Three Pointers. With an aggrieved air, akin to that of a crowd at a cricket match when batsmen are playing for a draw, they began to "barrack." They hooted the Three Pointers. They begged them to go home and tuck themselves up in bed. The men on the roof were mostly Irishmen, and it offended them to see what should have been a spirited fight so grossly bungled.

"G'wan away home, ye quitters!" roared one.

"Call yersilves the Three Points, do ye? An' would ye know what *I* call ye? The Young Ladies' Seminary!" bellowed another with withering scorn.

A third member of the audience alluded to them as "stiffs."

"I fear, Comrade Windsor," said Psmith, "that our blithe friends below are beginning to grow a little unpopular with the many-headed. They must be up and doing if they wish to retain the esteem of Pleasant Street. Aha!"

Another and a longer explosion from below, and more bullets wasted themselves on air. Psmith sighed.

"They make me tired," he said. "This is no time for a *feu de joie*.

Action! That is the cry. Action! Get busy, you blighters!"

The Irish neighbours expressed the same sentiment in different and more forcible words. There was no doubt about it—as warriors, the Three Pointers had failed to give satisfaction.

A voice from the room called up to Psmith.

"Say!"

"You have our ear," said Psmith.

"What's that?"

"I said you had our ear."

"Are youse stiffs comin' down off out of dat roof?"

"Would you mind repeating that remark?"

"Are youse guys goin' to quit off out of dat roof?"

"Your grammar is perfectly beastly," said Psmith severely.

"Hey!"

"Well?"

"Are youse guys—?"

"No, my lad," said Psmith, "since you ask, we are not. And why?
Because the air up here is refreshing, the view pleasant, and we
are expecting at any moment an important communication from Comrade
Gooch."

"We're goin' to wait here till youse come down."

"If you wish it," said Psmith courteously, "by all means do. Who am I that I should dictate your movements? The most I aspire to is to check them when they take an upward direction."

There was silence below. The time began to pass slowly. The Irishmen on the other roof, now definitely abandoning hope of further entertainment, proceeded with hoots of scorn to climb down one by one into the recesses of their own house.

Suddenly from the street far below there came a fusillade of shots and a babel of shouts and counter-shouts. The roof of the house next door, which had been emptying itself slowly and reluctantly, filled again with a magical swiftness, and the low wall facing into the street became black with the backs of those craning over.

"What's that?" inquired Billy.

"I rather fancy," said Psmith, "that our allies of the Table Hill contingent must have arrived. I sent Comrade Maloney to explain matters to Dude Dawson, and it seems as if that golden-hearted sportsman had responded. There appear to be great doings in the street."

In the room below confusion had arisen. A scout, clattering upstairs, had brought the news of the Table Hillites' advent, and there was doubt as to the proper course to pursue. Certain voices urged going down to help the main body. Others pointed out that that would mean abandoning the siege of the roof. The scout who had brought the news was eloquent in favour of the first course.

"Gum!" he cried, "don't I keep tellin' youse dat de Table Hills is here? Sure, dere's a whole bunch of dem, and unless youse come on down dey'll bite de hull head off of us lot. Leave those stiffs on de roof. Let Sam wait here with his canister, and den dey can't get down, 'cos Sam'll pump dem full of lead while dey're beatin' it t'roo de trap-door. Sure."

Psmith nodded reflectively.

"There is certainly something in what the bright boy says," he murmured. "It seems to me the grand rescue scene in the third act has sprung a leak. This will want thinking over."

In the street the disturbance had now become terrific. Both sides were hard at it, and the Irishmen on the roof, rewarded at last for their long vigil, were yelling encouragement promiscuously and whooping with the unfettered ecstasy of men who are getting the treat of their lives without having paid a penny for it.

The behaviour of the New York policeman in affairs of this kind is based on principles of the soundest practical wisdom. The unthinking man would rush in and attempt to crush the combat in its earliest and fiercest stages. The New York policeman, knowing the importance of his own safety, and the insignificance of the gangsman's, permits the opposing forces to hammer each other into a certain distaste for battle, and then, when both sides have begun to have enough of it, rushes in himself and clubs everything in sight. It is an admirable process in its results, but it is sure rather than swift.

Proceedings in the affair below had not yet reached the police interference stage. The noise, what with the shots and yells from the street and the ear-piercing approval of the roof-audience, was just working up to a climax.

Psmith rose. He was tired of kneeling by the trap, and there was no likelihood of Sam making another attempt to climb through. He walked towards Billy.

As he did so, Billy got up and turned to him. His eyes were gleaming with excitement. His whole attitude was triumphant. In his hand he waved a strip of paper.

"I've got it," he cried.

"Excellent, Comrade Windsor," said Psmith. "Surely we must win through now. All we have to do is to get off this roof, and fate cannot touch us. Are two mammoth minds such as ours unequal to such a feat? It can hardly be. Let us ponder."

"Why not go down through the trap? They've all gone to the street."

Psmith shook his head.

"All," he replied, "save Sam. Sam was the subject of my late successful experiment, when I proved that coloured gentlemen's heads could be hurt with a stick. He is now waiting below, armed with a pistol, ready—even anxious—to pick us off as we climb through the trap. How would it be to drop Comrade Gooch through first, and so draw his fire? Comrade Gooch, I am sure, would be delighted to do a little thing like that for old friends of our standing or—but what's that!"

"What's the matter?"

"Is that a ladder that I see before me, its handle to my hand? It is! Comrade Windsor, we win through. *Cosy Moments*' editorial staff may be tree'd, but it cannot be put out of business. Comrade Windsor, take the other end of that ladder and follow me."

The ladder was lying against the farther wall. It was long, more than long enough for the purpose for which it was needed. Psmith and Billy rested it on the coping, and pushed it till the other end reached across the gulf to the roof of the house next door, Mr. Gooch eyeing them in silence the while.

Psmith turned to him.

"Comrade Gooch," he said, "do nothing to apprise our friend Sam of these proceedings. I speak in your best interests. Sam is in no mood to make nice distinctions between friend and foe. If you bring him up here, he will probably mistake you for a member of the staff of *Cosy Moments*, and loose off in your direction without waiting for explanations. I think you had better come with us. I will go first, Comrade Windsor, so that if the ladder breaks, the paper will lose merely a sub-editor, not an editor."

He went down on all-fours, and in this attitude wormed his way across to the opposite roof, whose occupants, engrossed in the fight in the street, in which the police had now joined, had their backs turned and did not observe him. Mr. Gooch, pallid and obviously ill-attuned to such feats, followed him; and finally Billy Windsor reached the other side.

"Neat," said Psmith complacently. "Uncommonly neat. Comrade Gooch reminded me of the untamed chamois of the Alps, leaping from crag to crag."

In the street there was now comparative silence. The police, with their clubs, had knocked the last remnant of fight out of the combatants. Shooting had definitely ceased.

"I think," said Psmith, "that we might now descend. If you have no other engagements, Comrade Windsor, I will take you to the Knickerbocker, and buy you a square meal. I would ask for the pleasure of your company also, Comrade Gooch, were it not that matters of private moment, relating to the policy of the paper, must be discussed at the table. Some other day, perhaps. We are infinitely obliged to you for your sympathetic co-operation in this little matter. And now good-bye. Comrade Windsor, let us debouch."

CHAPTER XXII - CONCERNING MR. WARING

Psmith pushed back his chair slightly, stretched out his legs, and lit a cigarette. The resources of the Knickerbocker Hotel had proved equal to supplying the fatigued staff of *Cosy Moments* with an excellent dinner, and Psmith had stoutly declined to talk business until the coffee arrived. This had been hard on Billy, who was bursting with his news. Beyond a hint that it was sensational he had not been permitted to go.

"More bright young careers than I care to think of," said Psmith, "have been ruined by the fatal practice of talking shop at dinner. But now that we are through, Comrade Windsor, by all means let us have it. What's the name which Comrade Gooch so eagerly divulged?"

Billy leaned forward excitedly.

"Stewart Waring," he whispered.

"Stewart who?" asked Psmith.

Billy stared.

"Great Scott, man!" he said, "haven't you heard of Stewart Waring?"

"The name seems vaguely familiar, like isinglass or Post-toasties.

I seem to know it, but it conveys nothing to me."

"Don't you ever read the papers?"

"I toy with my *American* of a morning, but my interest is confined mainly to the sporting page which reminds me that Comrade Brady has been matched against one Eddie Wood a month from to-day. Gratifying as it is to find one of the staff getting on in life, I fear this will cause us a certain amount of inconvenience. Comrade Brady will have to leave the office temporarily in order to go into training, and what shall we do then for a fighting editor? However, possibly we may not need one now. *Cosy Moments* should be able shortly to give its message to the world and ease up for a while. Which brings us back to the point. Who is Stewart Waring?"

"Stewart Waring is running for City Alderman. He's one of the biggest men in New York!"

"Do you mean in girth? If so, he seems to have selected the right career for himself."

"He's one of the bosses. He used to be Commissioner of Buildings for the city."

"Commissioner of Buildings? What exactly did that let him in for?"

"It let him in for a lot of graft."

"How was that?"

"Oh, he took it off the contractors. Shut his eyes and held out his hands when they ran up rotten buildings that a strong breeze would have knocked down, and places like that Pleasant Street hole without any ventilation."

"Why did he throw up the job?" inquired Psmith. "It seems to me that it was among the World's Softest. Certain drawbacks to it, perhaps, to the man with the Hair-Trigger Conscience; but I gather that Comrade Waring did not line up in that class. What was his trouble?"

"His trouble," said Billy, "was that he stood in with a contractor who was putting up a music-hall, and the contractor put it up with material about as strong as a heap of meringues, and it collapsed on the third night and killed half the audience."

"And then?"

"The papers raised a howl, and they got after the contractor, and the contractor gave Waring away. It killed him for the time being."

"I should have thought it would have had that excellent result permanently," said Psmith thoughtfully. "Do you mean to say he got back again after that?"

"He had to quit being Commissioner, of course, and leave the town for a time; but affairs move so fast here that a thing like that blows over. He made a bit of a pile out of the job, and could afford to lie low for a year or two."

"How long ago was that?"

"Five years. People don't remember a thing here that happened five years back unless they're reminded of it."

Psmith lit another cigarette.

"We will remind them," he said.

Billy nodded.

"Of course," he said, "one or two of the papers against him in this Aldermanic Election business tried to bring the thing up, but they didn't cut any ice. The other papers said it was a shame, hounding a man who was sorry for the past and who was trying to make good now; so they dropped it. Everybody thought that Waring was on the level now. He's been shooting off a lot of hot air lately about philanthropy and so on. Not that he has actually done a thing—not so much as given a supper to a dozen news-boys; but he's talked, and talk gets over if you keep it up long enough."

Psmith nodded adhesion to this dictum.

"So that naturally he wants to keep it dark about these tenements.

It'll smash him at the election when it gets known."

"Why is he so set on becoming an Alderman," inquired Psmith.

"There's a lot of graft to being an Alderman," explained Billy.

"I see. No wonder the poor gentleman was so energetic in his methods. What is our move now, Comrade Windsor?"

Billy stared.

"Why, publish the name, of course."

"But before then? How are we going to ensure the safety of our evidence? We stand or fall entirely by that slip of paper, because we've got the beggar's name in the writing of his own collector, and that's proof positive."

"That's all right," said Billy, patting his breast-pocket.

"Nobody's going to get it from me."

Psmith dipped his hand into his trouser-pocket.

"Comrade Windsor," he said, producing a piece of paper, "how do we go?"

He leaned back in his chair, surveying Billy blandly through his eye-glass. Billy's eyes were goggling. He looked from Psmith to the paper and from the paper to Psmith.

"What—what the—?" he stammered. "Why, it's it!"

Psmith nodded.

"How on earth did you get it?"

Psmith knocked the ash off his cigarette.

"Comrade Windsor," he said, "I do not wish to cavil or carp or rub it in in any way. I will merely remark that you pretty nearly landed us in the soup, and pass on to more congenial topics. Didn't you know we were followed to this place?"

"Followed!"

"By a merchant in what Comrade Maloney would call a tall-shaped hat. I spotted him at an early date, somewhere down by Twenty-ninth Street. When we dived into Sixth Avenue for a space at Thirty-third Street, did he dive, too? He did. And when we turned into Forty-second Street, there he was. I tell you, Comrade Windsor, leeches were aloof, and burrs non-adhesive compared with that tall-shaped-hatted blighter."

"Yes?"

"Do you remember, as you came to the entrance of this place, somebody knocking against you?"

"Yes, there was a pretty big crush in the entrance."

"There was; but not so big as all that. There was plenty of room for this merchant to pass if he had wished. Instead of which he butted into you. I happened to be waiting for just that, so I managed to attach myself to his wrist with some vim and give it a fairly hefty wrench. The paper was inside his hand."

Billy was leaning forward with a pale face.

"Jove!" he muttered.

"That about sums it up," said Psmith.

Billy snatched the paper from the table and extended it towards him.

"Here," he said feverishly, "you take it. Gum, I never thought I was such a mutt! I'm not fit to take charge of a toothpick. Fancy me not being on the watch for something of that sort. I guess I was so tickled with myself at the thought of having got the thing, that it never struck me they might try for it. But I'm through. No more for me. You're the man in charge now."

Psmith shook his head.

"These stately compliments," he said, "do my old heart good, but I fancy I know a better plan. It happened that I chanced to have my eye on the blighter in the tall-shaped hat, and so was enabled to land him among the ribstones; but who knows but that in the crowd on Broadway there may not lurk other, unidentified blighters in equally tall-shaped hats, one of whom may work the same sleight-of-hand speciality on me? It was not that you were not capable of taking care of that paper: it was simply that you didn't happen to spot the man. Now observe me closely, for what follows is an exhibition of Brain."

He paid the bill, and they went out into the entrance-hall of the hotel. Psmith, sitting down at a table, placed the paper in an envelope and addressed it to himself at the address of *Cosy Moments*. After which, he stamped the envelope and dropped it into the letter-box at the back of the hall.

"And now, Comrade Windsor," he said, "let us stroll gently homewards down the Great White Way. What matter though it be fairly stiff with low-browed bravoes in tall-shaped hats? They cannot harm us. From me, if they search me thoroughly, they may scoop a matter of eleven dollars, a watch, two stamps, and a packet of chewing-gum. Whether they would do any better with you I do not know. At any rate, they wouldn't get that paper; and that's the main thing."

"You're a genius," said Billy Windsor.

"You think so?" said Psmith diffidently. "Well, well, perhaps you are right, perhaps you are right. Did you notice the hired ruffian in the flannel suit who just passed? He wore a baffled look, I fancy. And hark! Wasn't that a muttered 'Failed!' I heard? Or was it the breeze moaning in the tree-tops? To-night is a cold, disappointing night for Hired Ruffians, Comrade Windsor."

CHAPTER XXIII - REDUCTIONS IN THE STAFF

The first member of the staff of *Cosy Moments* to arrive at the office on the following morning was Master Maloney. This sounds like the beginning of a "Plod and Punctuality," or "How Great Fortunes have been Made" story; but, as a matter of fact, Master Maloney was no early bird. Larks who rose in his neighbourhood, rose alone. He did not get up with them. He was supposed to be at the office at nine o'clock. It was a point of honour with him, a sort of daily declaration of independence, never to put in an appearance before nine-thirty. On this particular morning he was punctual to the minute, or half an hour late, whichever way you choose to look at it.

He had only whistled a few bars of "My Little Irish Rose," and had barely got into the first page of his story of life on the prairie when Kid Brady appeared. The Kid, as was his habit when not in training, was smoking a big black cigar. Master Maloney eyed him admiringly. The Kid, unknown to that gentleman himself, was Pugsy's ideal. He came from the Plains; and had, indeed, once actually been a cowboy; he was a coming champion; and he could smoke black cigars. It was, therefore, without his usual well-what-is-it-now? air that Pugsy laid down his book, and prepared to converse.

"Say, Mr. Smith or Mr. Windsor about, Pugsy?" asked the Kid.

"Naw, Mr. Brady, they ain't came yet," replied Master Maloney respectfully.

"Late, ain't they?"

"Sure. Mr. Windsor generally blows in before I do."

"Wonder what's keepin' them."

"P'raps, dey've bin put out of business," suggested Pugsy nonchalantly.

"How's that?"

Pugsy related the events of the previous day, relaxing something of his austere calm as he did so. When he came to the part where the Table Hill allies swooped down on the unsuspecting Three Pointers, he was almost animated.

"Say," said the Kid approvingly, "that Smith guy's got more grey matter under his thatch than you'd think to look at him. I—"

"Comrade Brady," said a voice in the doorway, "you do me proud."

"Why, say," said the Kid, turning, "I guess the laugh's on me. I didn't see you, Mr. Smith. Pugsy's been tellin' me how you sent him for the Table Hills yesterday. That was cute. It was mighty smart. But say, those guys are goin' some, ain't they now! Seems as if they was dead set on puttin' you out of business."

"Their manner yesterday, Comrade Brady, certainly suggested the presence of some sketchy outline of such an ideal in their minds. One Sam, in particular, an ebony-hued sportsman, threw himself into the task with great vim. I rather fancy he is waiting for us with his revolver to this moment. But why worry? Here we are, safe and sound, and Comrade Windsor may be expected to arrive at any moment. I see, Comrade Brady, that you have been matched against one Eddie Wood."

"It's about that I wanted to see you, Mr. Smith. Say, now that things have been and brushed up so, what with these gang guys layin' for you the way they're doin', I guess you'll be needin' me around here. Isn't that right? Say the word and I'll call off this Eddie Wood fight."

"Comrade Brady," said Psmith with some enthusiasm, "I call that a sporting offer. I'm very much obliged. But we mustn't stand in your way. If you eliminate this Comrade Wood, they will have to give you a chance against Jimmy Garvin, won't they?"

"I guess that's right, sir," said the Kid. "Eddie stayed nineteen rounds against Jimmy, and if I can put him away, it gets me into line with Jimmy, and he can't side-step me."

"Then go in and win, Comrade Brady. We shall miss you. It will be as if a ray of sunshine had been removed from the office. But you mustn't throw a chance away. We shall be all right, I think."

"I'll train at White Plains," said the Kid. "That ain't far from here, so I'll be pretty near in case I'm wanted. Hullo, who's here?"

He pointed to the door. A small boy was standing there, holding a note.

"Mr. Smith?"

"Sir to you," said Psmith courteously.

"P. Smith?"

"The same. This is your lucky day."

"Cop at Jefferson Market give me dis to take to youse."

"A cop in Jefferson Market?" repeated Psmith. "I did not know I had friends among the constabulary there. Why, it's from Comrade Windsor." He opened the envelope and read the letter. "Thanks," he said, giving the boy a quarter-dollar.

It was apparent the Kid was politely endeavouring to veil his curiosity. Master Maloney had no such scruples.

"What's in de letter, boss?" he inquired.

"The letter, Comrade Maloney, is from our Mr. Windsor, and relates in terse language the following facts, that our editor last night hit a policeman in the eye, and that he was sentenced this morning to thirty days on Blackwell's Island."

"He's de guy!" admitted Master Maloney approvingly.

"What's that?" said the Kid. "Mr. Windsor bin punchin' cops! What's he bin doin' that for?"

"He gives no clue. I must go and find out. Could you help Comrade

Maloney mind the shop for a few moments while I push round to Jefferson Market and make inquiries?"

"Sure. But say, fancy Mr. Windsor cuttin' loose that way!" said the Kid admiringly.

The Jefferson Market Police Court is a little way down town, near Washington Square. It did not take Psmith long to reach it, and by the judicious expenditure of a few dollars he was enabled to obtain an interview with Billy in a back room.

The chief editor of *Cosy Moments* was seated on a bench, looking upon the world through a pair of much blackened eyes. His general appearance was dishevelled. He had the air of a man who has been caught in the machinery.

"Hullo, Smith," he said. "You got my note all right then?"

Psmith looked at him, concerned.

"Comrade Windsor," he said, "what on earth has been happening to you?"

"Oh, that's all right," said Billy. "That's nothing."

"Nothing! You look as if you had been run over by a motor-car."

"The cops did that," said Billy, without any apparent resentment. "They always turn nasty if you put up a fight. I was a fool to do it, I suppose, but I got so mad. They knew perfectly well that I had nothing to do with any pool-room downstairs."

Psmith's eye-glass dropped from his eye.

"Pool-room, Comrade Windsor?"

"Yes. The house where I live was raided late last night. It seems that some gamblers have been running a pool-room on the ground floor. Why the cops should have thought I had anything to do with it, when I was sleeping peacefully upstairs, is more than I can understand. Anyway, at about three in the morning there was the dickens of a banging at my door. I got up to see what was doing, and found a couple of Policemen there. They told me to come along with them to the station. I asked what on earth for. I might have known it was no use arguing with a New York cop. They said they had been tipped off that there was a pool-room being run in the house, and that they were cleaning up the house, and if I wanted to say anything I'd better say it to the magistrate. I said, all right, I'd put on some clothes and come with them. They said they couldn't wait about while I put on clothes. I said I wasn't going to travel about New York in pyjamas, and started to get into my shirt. One of them gave me a shove in the ribs with his night-stick, and told me to come along quick. And that made me so mad I hit out." A chuckle escaped Billy. "He wasn't expecting it, and I got him fair. He went down over the bookcase. The other cop took a swipe at me with his club, but by that time I was so mad I'd have taken on Jim Jeffries, if he had shown up and got in my way. I just sailed in, and was beginning to make the man think that he had stumbled on Stanley Ketchel or Kid Brady or a dynamite explosion by mistake, when the other fellow loosed himself from the bookcase, and they started in on me together, and there was a general rough house, in the middle of which somebody seemed to let off about fifty thousand dollars' worth of fireworks all in a bunch; and I didn't remember anything more till I found myself in a cell, pretty nearly knocked to pieces. That's my little life-history. I guess I was a fool to cut loose that way, but I was so mad I didn't stop to think."

Psmith sighed.

"You have told me your painful story," he said. "Now hear mine. After parting with you last night, I went meditatively back to my Fourth Avenue address, and, with a courtly good night to the large policeman who, as I have mentioned in previous conversations, is stationed almost at my very door, I passed on into my room, and had soon sunk into a dreamless slumber. At about three o'clock in the morning I was aroused by a somewhat hefty banging on the door."

"What!"

"A banging at the door," repeated Psmith. "There, standing on the mat, were three policemen. From their remarks I gathered that certain bright spirits had been running a gambling establishment in the lower regions of the building—where, I think I told you, there is a saloon—and the Law was now about to clean up the place. Very cordially the honest fellows invited me to go with them. A conveyance, it seemed, waited in the street without. I pointed out, even as you appear to have done, that sea-green pyjamas with old rose frogs were not the costume in which a Shropshire Psmith should be seen abroad in one of the world's greatest cities; but they assured me—more by their manner than their words—that my misgivings were out of place, so I yielded. These men, I told myself, have lived longer in New York than I. They know what is done and what is not done. I will bow to their views. So I went with them, and after a very pleasant and cosy little ride in the patrol waggon, arrived at the police station. This morning I chatted a while with the courteous magistrate, convinced him by means of arguments and by silent evidence of my open, honest face and unwavering eye that I was not a professional gambler, and came away without a stain on my character."

Billy Windsor listened to this narrative with growing interest.

"Gum! it's them!" he cried.

"As Comrade Maloney would say," said Psmith, "meaning what,
Comrade Windsor?"

"Why, the fellows who are after that paper. They tipped the police off about the pool-rooms, knowing that we should be hauled off without having time to take anything with us. I'll bet anything you like they have been in and searched our rooms by now."

"As regards yours, Comrade Windsor, I cannot say. But it is an undoubted fact that mine, which I revisited before going to the office, in order to correct what seemed to me even on reflection certain drawbacks to my costume, looks as if two cyclones and a threshing machine had passed through it."

"They've searched it?"

"With a fine-toothed comb. Not one of my objects of vertu but has been displaced."

Billy Windsor slapped his knee.

"It was lucky you thought of sending that paper by post," he said. "We should have been done if you hadn't. But, say," he went on miserably, "this is awful. Things are just warming up for the final burst, and I'm out of it all."

"For thirty days," sighed Psmith. "What *Cosy Moments* really needs is a *sitz-redacteur*."

"A what?"

"A *sitz-redacteur*, Comrade Windsor, is a gentleman employed by German newspapers with a taste for *lèse majesté* to go to prison whenever required in place of the real editor. The real editor hints in his bright and snappy editorial, for instance, that the Kaiser's moustache reminds him of a bad dream. The police force swoops down en masse on the office of the journal, and are met by the *sitz-redacteur*, who goes with them peaceably, allowing the editor to remain and sketch out plans for his next week's article on the Crown Prince. We need a *sitz-redacteur* on *Cosy Moments* almost as much as a fighting editor; and we have neither."

"The Kid has had to leave then?"

"He wants to go into training at once. He very sportingly offered to cancel his match, but of course that would never do. Unless you consider Comrade Maloney equal to the job, I must look around me for some one else. I shall be too fully occupied with purely literary matters to be able to deal with chance callers. But I have a scheme."

"What's that?"

"It seems to me that we are allowing much excellent material to lie unused in the shape of Comrade Jarvis."

"Bat Jarvis."

"The same. The cat-specialist to whom you endeared yourself somewhat earlier in the proceedings by befriending one of his wandering animals. Little deeds of kindness, little acts of love, as you have doubtless heard, help, etc. Should we not give Comrade Jarvis an opportunity of proving the correctness of this statement? I think so. Shortly after you—if you will forgive me for touching on a painful subject—have been haled to your dungeon, I will push round to Comrade Jarvis's address, and sound him on the subject. Unfortunately, his affection is confined, I fancy, to you. Whether he will consent to put himself out on my behalf remains to be seen. However, there is no harm in trying. If nothing else comes of the visit, I shall at least have had the opportunity of chatting with one of our most prominent citizens."

A policeman appeared at the door.

"Say, pal," he remarked to Psmith, "you'll have to be fading away soon, I guess. Give you three minutes more. Say it quick."

He retired. Billy leaned forward to Psmith.

"I guess they won't give me much chance," he whispered, "but if you see me around in the next day or two, don't be surprised."

"I fail to follow you, Comrade Windsor."

"Men have escaped from Blackwell's Island before now. Not many, it's true; but it has been done."

Psmith shook his head.

"I shouldn't," he said. "They're bound to catch you, and then you will be immersed in the soup beyond hope of recovery. I shouldn't wonder if they put you in your little cell for a year or so."

"I don't care," said Billy stoutly. "I'd give a year later on to be round and about now."

"I shouldn't," urged Psmith. "All will be well with the paper. You have left a good man at the helm."

"I guess I shan't get a chance, but I'll try it if I do."

The door opened and the policeman reappeared.

"Time's up, I reckon."

"Well, good-bye, Comrade Windsor," said Psmith regretfully. "Abstain from undue worrying. It's a walk-over from now on, and there's no earthly need for you to be around the office. Once, I admit, this could not have been said. But now things have simplified themselves. Have no fear. This act is going to be a scream from start to finish."

CHAPTER XXIV - A GATHERING OF CAT-SPECIALISTS

Master Maloney raised his eyes for a moment from his book as Psmith re-entered the office.

"Dere's a guy in dere waitin' ter see youse," he said briefly, jerking his head in the direction of the inner room.

"A guy waiting to see me, Comrade Maloney? With or without a sand-bag?"

"Says his name's Jackson," said Master Maloney, turning a page.

Psmith moved quickly to the door of the inner room.

"Why, Comrade Jackson," he said, with the air of a father welcoming home the prodigal son, "this is the maddest, merriest day of all the glad New Year. Where did you come from?"

Mike, looking very brown and in excellent condition, put down the paper he was reading.

"Hullo, Psmith," he said. "I got back this morning. We're playing a game over in Brooklyn to-morrow."

"No engagements of any importance to-day?"

"Not a thing. Why?"

"Because I propose to take you to visit Comrade Jarvis, whom you will doubtless remember."

"Jarvis?" said Mike, puzzled. "I don't remember any Jarvis."

"Let your mind wander back a little through the jungle of the past.

Do you recollect paying a visit to Comrade Windsor's room—"

"By the way, where is Windsor?"

"In prison. Well, on that evening—"

"In prison?"

"For thirty days. For slugging a policeman. More of this, however, anon. Let us return to that evening. Don't you remember a certain gentleman with just about enough forehead to keep his front hair from getting all tangled up with his eyebrows?"

"Oh, the cat chap? *I* know."

"As you very justly observe, Comrade Jackson, the cat chap. For going straight to the mark and seizing on the salient point of a situation, I know of no one who can last two minutes against you. Comrade Jarvis may have other sides to his character—possibly many—but it is as a cat chap that I wish to approach him to-day."

"What's the idea? What are you going to see him for?"

"We," corrected Psmith. "I will explain all at a little luncheon at which I trust that you will be my guest. Already, such is the stress of this journalistic life, I hear my tissues crying out imperatively to be restored. An oyster and a glass of milk somewhere round the corner, Comrade Jackson? I think so, I think so."

* * *

"I was reading *Cosy Moments* in there," said Mike, as they lunched. "You certainly seem to have bucked it up rather. Kid Brady's reminiscences are hot stuff."

"Somewhat sizzling, Comrade Jackson," admitted Psmith. "They have, however, unfortunately cost us a fighting editor."

"How's that?"

"Such is the boost we have given Comrade Brady, that he is now never without a match. He has had to leave us to-day to go to White Plains to train for an encounter with a certain Mr. Wood, a four-ounce-glove juggler of established fame."

"I expect you need a fighting editor, don't you?"

"He is indispensable, Comrade Jackson, indispensable."

"No rotting. Has anybody cut up rough about the stuff you've printed?"

"Cut up rough? Gadzooks! I need merely say that one critical reader put a bullet through my hat—"

"Rot! Not really?"

"While others kept me tree'd on top of a roof for the space of nearly an hour. Assuredly they have cut up rough, Comrade Jackson."

"Great Scott! Tell us."

Psmith briefly recounted the adventures of the past few weeks.

"But, man," said Mike, when he had finished "why on earth don't you call in the police?"

"We have mentioned the matter to certain of the force. They appeared tolerably interested, but showed no tendency to leap excitedly to our assistance. The New York policeman, Comrade Jackson, like all great men, is somewhat peculiar. If you go to a New York policeman and exhibit a black eye, he will examine it and express some admiration for the abilities of the citizen responsible for the same. If you press the matter, he becomes bored, and says, 'Ain't youse satisfied with what youse got? G'wan!' His advice in such cases is good, and should be followed. No; since coming to this city I have developed a habit of taking care of myself, or employing private help. That is why I should like you, if you will, to come with me to call upon Comrade Jarvis. He is a person of considerable influence among that section of the populace which is endeavouring to smash in our occiputs. Indeed, I know of nobody who cuts a greater quantity of ice. If I can only enlist Comrade Jarvis's assistance, all will be well. If you are through with your refreshment, shall we be moving in his direction? By the way, it will probably be necessary in the course of our interview to allude to you as one of our most eminent living cat-fanciers. You do not object? Remember that you have in your English home seventy-four fine cats, mostly Angoras. Are you on to that? Then let us be going. Comrade Maloney has given me the address. It is a goodish step down on the East side. I should like to take a taxi, but it might seem ostentatious. Let us walk."

* * *

They found Mr. Jarvis in his Groome Street fancier's shop, engaged in the intellectual occupation of greasing a cat's paws with butter. He looked up as they entered, and began to breathe a melody with a certain coyness.

"Comrade Jarvis," said Psmith, "we meet again. You remember me?"

"Nope," said Mr. Jarvis, pausing for a moment in the middle of a bar, and then taking up the air where he had left off. Psmith was not discouraged.

"Ah," he said tolerantly, "the fierce rush of New York life. How it wipes from the retina of to-day the image impressed on it but yesterday. Are you with me, Comrade Jarvis?"

The cat-expert concentrated himself on the cat's paws without replying.

"A fine animal," said Psmith, adjusting his eyeglass. "To which particular family of the Felis Domestica does that belong? In colour it resembles a Neapolitan ice more than anything."

Mr. Jarvis's manner became unfriendly.

"Say, what do youse want? That's straight ain't it? If youse want to buy a boid or a snake why don't youse say so?"

"I stand corrected," said Psmith. "I should have remembered that time is money. I called in here partly on the strength of being a colleague and side-partner of Comrade Windsor—"

"Mr. Windsor! De gent what caught my cat?"

"The same—and partly in order that I might make two very eminent cat-fanciers acquainted. This," he said, with a wave of his hand in the direction of the silently protesting Mike, "is Comrade Jackson, possibly the best known of our English cat-fanciers. Comrade Jackson's stud of Angoras is celebrated wherever the King's English is spoken, and in Hoxton."

Mr. Jarvis rose, and, having inspected Mike with silent admiration for a while, extended a well-buttered hand towards him. Psmith looked on benevolently.

"What Comrade Jackson does not know about cats," he said, "is not knowledge. His information on Angoras alone would fill a volume."

"Say,"—Mr. Jarvis was evidently touching on a point which had weighed deeply upon him—"why's catnip called catnip?"

Mike looked at Psmith helplessly. It sounded like a riddle, but it was obvious that Mr. Jarvis's motive in putting the question was not frivolous. He really wished to know.

"The word, as Comrade Jackson was just about to observe," said Psmith, "is a corruption of cat-mint. Why it should be so corrupted I do not know. But what of that? The subject is too deep to be gone fully into at the moment. I should recommend you to read Comrade Jackson's little brochure on the matter. Passing lightly on from that—"

"Did youse ever have a cat dat ate beetles?" inquired Mr. Jarvis.

"There was a time when many of Comrade Jackson's felidae supported life almost entirely on beetles."

"Did they git thin?"

Mike felt that it was time, if he was to preserve his reputation, to assert himself.

"No," he replied firmly.

Mr. Jarvis looked astonished.

"English beetles," said Psmith, "don't make cats thin. Passing lightly—"

"I had a cat oncest," said Mr. Jarvis, ignoring the remark and sticking to his point, "dat ate beetles and got thin and used to tie itself into knots."

"A versatile animal," agreed Psmith.

"Say," Mr. Jarvis went on, now plainly on a subject near to his heart, "dem beetles is fierce. Sure. Can't keep de cats off of eatin' dem, I can't. First t'ing you know dey've swallowed dem, and den dey gits thin and ties theirselves into knots."

"You should put them into strait-waistcoats," said Psmith.

"Passing, however, lightly—"

"Say, ever have a cross-eyed cat?"

"Comrade Jackson's cats," said Psmith, "have happily been almost free from strabismus."

"Dey's lucky, cross-eyed cats is. You has a cross-eyed cat, and not'in' don't never go wrong. But, say, was dere ever a cat wit one blue eye and one yaller one in your bunch? Gum, it's fierce when it's like dat. It's a real skiddoo, is a cat wit one blue eye and one yaller one. Puts you in bad, surest t'ing you know. Oncest a guy give me a cat like dat, and first t'ing you know I'm in bad all round. It wasn't till I give him away to de cop on de corner and gets me one dat's cross-eyed dat I lifts de skiddoo off of me."

"And what happened to the cop?" inquired Psmith, interested.

"Oh, he got in bad, sure enough," said Mr. Jarvis without emotion. "One of de boys what he'd pinched and had sent to de Island once lays for him and puts one over him wit a black-jack. Sure. Dat's what comes of havin' a cat wit one blue eye and one yaller one."

Mr. Jarvis relapsed into silence. He seemed to be meditating on the inscrutable workings of Fate. Psmith took advantage of the pause to leave the cat topic and touch on matter of more vital import.

"Tense and exhilarating as is this discussion of the optical peculiarities of cats," he said, "there is another matter on which, if you will permit me, I should like to touch. I would hesitate to bore you with my own private troubles, but this is a matter which concerns Comrade Windsor as well as myself, and I know that your regard for Comrade Windsor is almost an obsession."

"How's that?"

"I should say," said Psmith, "that Comrade Windsor is a man to whom you give the glad hand."

"Sure. He's to the good, Mr. Windsor is. He caught me cat."

"He did. By the way, was that the one that used to tie itself into knots?"

"Nope. Dat was anudder."

"Ah! However, to resume. The fact is, Comrade Jarvis, we are much persecuted by scoundrels. How sad it is in this world! We look to every side. We look north, east, south, and west, and what do we see? Mainly scoundrels. I fancy you have heard a little about our troubles before this. In fact, I gather that the same scoundrels actually approached you with a view to engaging your services to do us in, but that you very handsomely refused the contract."

"Sure," said Mr. Jarvis, dimly comprehending.

"A guy comes to me and says he wants you and Mr. Windsor put through it, but I gives him de t'run down. 'Nuttin' done,' I says. 'Mr. Windsor caught me cat.'"

"So I was informed," said Psmith. "Well, failing you, they went to a gentleman of the name of Reilly."

"Spider Reilly?"

"You have hit it, Comrade Jarvis. Spider Reilly, the lessee and manager of the Three Points gang."

"Dose T'ree Points, dey're to de bad. Dey're fresh."

"It is too true, Comrade Jarvis."

"Say," went on Mr. Jarvis, waxing wrathful at the recollection, "what do youse t'ink dem fresh stiffs done de udder night. Started some rough woik in me own dance-joint."

"Shamrock Hall?" said Psmith.

"Dat's right. Shamrock Hall. Got gay, dey did, wit some of de Table Hillers. Say, I got it in for dem gazebos, sure I have. Surest t'ing you know."

Psmith beamed approval.

"That," he said, "is the right spirit. Nothing could be more admirable. We are bound together by our common desire to check the ever-growing spirit of freshness among the members of the Three Points. Add to that the fact that we are united by a sympathetic knowledge of the manners and customs of cats, and especially that Comrade Jackson, England's greatest fancier, is our mutual friend, and what more do we want? Nothing."

"Mr. Jackson's to de good," assented Mr. Jarvis, eyeing Mike in friendly fashion.

"We are all to de good," said Psmith. "Now the thing I wished to ask you is this. The office of the paper on which I work was until this morning securely guarded by Comrade Brady, whose name will be familiar to you."

"De Kid?"

"On the bull's-eye, as usual, Comrade Jarvis. Kid Brady, the coming lightweight champion of the world. Well, he has unfortunately been compelled to leave us, and the way into the office is consequently clear to any sand-bag specialist who cares to wander in. Matters connected with the paper have become so poignant during the last few days that an inrush of these same specialists is almost a certainty, unless—and this is where you come in."

"Me?"

"Will you take Comrade Brady's place for a few days?"

"How's that?"

"Will you come in and sit in the office for the next day or so and help hold the fort? I may mention that there is money attached to the job. We will pay for your services. How do we go, Comrade Jarvis?"

Mr. Jarvis reflected but a brief moment.

"Why, sure," he said. "Me fer dat. When do I start?"

"Excellent, Comrade Jarvis. Nothing could be better. I am obliged. I rather fancy that the gay band of Three Pointers who will undoubtedly visit the offices of *Cosy Moments* in the next few days, probably to-morrow, are due to run up against the surprise of their lives. Could you be there at ten to-morrow morning?"

"Sure t'ing. I'll bring me canister."

"I should," said Psmith. "In certain circumstances one canister is worth a flood of rhetoric. Till to-morrow, then, Comrade Jarvis. I am very much obliged to you."

* * *

"Not at all a bad hour's work," said Psmith complacently, as they turned out of Groome Street. "A vote of thanks to you, Comrade Jackson, for your invaluable assistance."

"It strikes me I didn't do much," said Mike with a grin.

"Apparently, no. In reality, yes. Your manner was exactly right. Reserved, yet not haughty. Just what an eminent cat-fancier's manner should be. I could see that you made a pronounced hit with Comrade Jarvis. By the way, if you are going to show up at the office to-morrow, perhaps it would be as well if you were to look up a few facts bearing on the feline world. There is no knowing what thirst for information a night's rest may not give Comrade Jarvis. I do not presume to dictate, but if you were to make yourself a thorough master of the subject of catnip, for instance, it might quite possibly come in useful."

CHAPTER XXV - TRAPPED

Mr. Jarvis was as good as his word. On the following morning, at ten o'clock to the minute, he made his appearance at the office of *Cosy Moments*, his forelock more than usually well oiled in honour of the occasion, and his right coat-pocket bulging in a manner that betrayed to the initiated eye the presence of the faithful "canister." With him, in addition to his revolver, he brought a long, thin young man who wore under his brown tweed coat a blue-and-red striped jersey. Whether he brought him as an ally in case of need or merely as a kindred soul with whom he might commune during his vigil, was not ascertained.

Pugsy, startled out of his wonted calm by the arrival of this distinguished company, observed the pair, as they passed through into the inner office, with protruding eyes, and sat speechless for a full five minutes. Psmith received the new-corners in the editorial sanctum with courteous warmth. Mr. Jarvis introduced his colleague.

"Thought I'd bring him along. Long Otto's his monaker."

"You did very rightly, Comrade Jarvis," Psmith assured him. "Your unerring instinct did not play you false when it told you that Comrade Otto would be as welcome as the flowers in May. With Comrade Otto I fancy we shall make a combination which will require a certain amount of tackling."

Mr. Jarvis confirmed this view. Long Otto, he affirmed, was no rube, but a scrapper from Biffville-on-the-Slosh. The hardiest hooligan would shrink from introducing rough-house proceedings into a room graced by the combined presence of Long Otto and himself.

"Then," said Psmith, "I can go about my professional duties with a light heart. I may possibly sing a bar or two. You will find cigars in that box. If you and Comrade Otto will select one apiece and group yourselves tastefully about the room in chairs, I will start in to hit up a slightly spicy editorial on the coming election."

Mr. Jarvis regarded the paraphernalia of literature on the table with interest. So did Long Otto, who, however, being a man of silent habit, made no comment. Throughout the seance and the events which followed it he confined himself to an occasional grunt. He seemed to lack other modes of expression. A charming chap, however.

"Is dis where youse writes up pieces fer de paper?" inquired Mr.

Jarvis, eyeing the table.

"It is," said Psmith. "In Comrade Windsor's pre-dungeon days he was wont to sit where I am sitting now, while I bivouacked over there at the smaller table. On busy mornings you could hear our brains buzzing in Madison Square Garden. But wait! A thought strikes me." He called for Pugsy.

"Comrade Maloney," he said, "if the Editorial Staff of this paper were to give you a day off, could you employ it to profit?"

"Surest t'ing you know," replied Pugsy with some fervour. "I'd take me goil to de Bronx Zoo."

"Your girl?" said Psmith inquiringly. "I had heard no inkling of this, Comrade Maloney. I had always imagined you one of those strong, rugged, blood-and-iron men who were above the softer emotions. Who is she?"

"Aw, she's a kid," said Pugsy. "Her pa runs a delicatessen shop down our street. She ain't a bad mutt," added the ardent swain. "I'm her steady."

"See that I have a card for the wedding, Comrade Maloney," said Psmith, "and in the meantime take her to the Bronx, as you suggest."

"Won't youse be wantin' me to-day."

"Not to-day. You need a holiday. Unflagging toil is sapping your physique. Go up and watch the animals, and remember me very kindly to the Peruvian Llama, whom friends have sometimes told me I resemble in appearance. And if two dollars would in any way add to the gaiety of the jaunt . . ."

"Sure t'ing. T'anks, boss."

"It occurred to me," said Psmith, when he had gone, "that the probable first move of any enterprising Three Pointer who invaded this office would be to knock Comrade Maloney on the head to prevent his announcing him. Comrade Maloney's services are too valuable to allow him to be exposed to unnecessary perils. Any visitors who call must find their way in for themselves. And now to work. Work, the what's-its-name of the thingummy and the thing-um-a-bob of the what d'you-call-it."

For about a quarter of an hour the only sound that broke the silence of the room was the scratching of Psmith's pen and the musical expectoration of Messrs. Otto and Jarvis. Finally Psmith leaned back in his chair with a satisfied expression, and spoke.

"While, as of course you know, Comrade Jarvis," he said, "there is no agony like the agony of literary composition, such toil has its compensations. The editorial I have just completed contains its measure of balm. Comrade Otto will bear me out in my statement that there is a subtle joy in the manufacture of the well-formed phrase. Am I not right, Comrade Otto?"

The long one gazed appealingly at Mr. Jarvis, who spoke for him.

"He's a bit shy on handin' out woids, is Otto," he said.

Psmith nodded.

"I understand. I am a man of few words myself. All great men are like that. Von Moltke, Comrade Otto, and myself. But what are words? Action is the thing. That is the cry. Action. If that is Comrade Otto's forte, so much the better, for I fancy that action rather than words is what we may be needing in the space of about a quarter of a minute. At least, if the footsteps I hear without are, as I suspect, those of our friends of the Three Points."

Jarvis and Long Otto turned towards the door. Psmith was right. Some one was moving stealthily in the outer office. Judging from the sound, more than one person.

"It is just as well," said Psmith softly, "that Comrade Maloney is not at his customary post. Now, in about a quarter of a minute, as I said—Aha!"

The handle of the door began to revolve slowly and quietly. The next moment three figures tumbled into the room. It was evident that they had not expected to find the door unlocked, and the absence of resistance when they applied their weight had had surprising effects. Two of the three did not pause in their career till they cannoned against the table. The third, who was holding the handle, was more fortunate.

Psmith rose with a kindly smile to welcome his guests.

"Why, surely!" he said in a pleased voice. "I thought I knew the face. Comrade Repetto, this is a treat. Have you come bringing me a new hat?"

The white-haired leader's face, as he spoke, was within a few inches of his own. Psmith's observant eye noted that the bruise still lingered on the chin where Kid Brady's upper-cut had landed at their previous meeting.

"I cannot offer you all seats," he went on, "unless you care to dispose yourselves upon the tables. I wonder if you know my friend, Mr. Bat Jarvis? And my friend, Mr. L. Otto? Let us all get acquainted on this merry occasion."

The three invaders had been aware of the presence of the great Bat and his colleague for some moments, and the meeting seemed to be causing them embarrassment. This may have been due to the fact that both Mr. Jarvis and Mr. Otto had produced and were toying meditatively with distinctly ugly-looking pistols.

Mr. Jarvis spoke.

"Well," he said, "what's doin'?"

Mr. Repetto, to whom the remark was directly addressed, appeared to have some difficulty in finding a reply. He shuffled his feet, and looked at the floor. His two companions seemed equally at a loss.

"Goin' to start any rough stuff?" inquired Mr. Jarvis casually.

"The cigars are on the table," said Psmith hospitably. "Draw up your chairs, and let's all be jolly. I will open the proceedings with a song."

In a rich baritone, with his eyeglass fixed the while on Mr.

Repetto, he proceeded to relieve himself of the first verse of

"I only know I love thee."

"Chorus, please," he added, as he finished. "Come along, Comrade Repetto. Why this shrinking coyness? Fling out your chest, and cut loose."

But Mr. Repetto's eye was fastened on Mr. Jarvis's revolver. The sight apparently had the effect of quenching his desire for song.

"'Lov' muh, ahnd ther world is—ah—mine!'" concluded Psmith.

He looked round the assembled company.

"Comrade Otto," he observed, "will now recite that pathetic little poem 'Baby's Sock is now a Blue-bag.' Pray, gentlemen, silence for Comrade Otto."

He looked inquiringly at the long youth, who remained mute. Psmith clicked his tongue regretfully.

"Comrade Jarvis," he said, "I fear that as a smoking-concert this is not going to be a success. I understand, however. Comrade Repetto and his colleagues have come here on business, and nothing will make them forget it. Typical New York men of affairs, they close their minds to all influences that might lure them from their business. Let us get on, then. What did you wish to see me about, Comrade Repetto?"

Mr. Repetto's reply was unintelligible.

Mr. Jarvis made a suggestion.

"Youse had better beat it," he said.

Long Otto grunted sympathy with this advice.

"And youse had better go back to Spider Reilly," continued Mr. Jarvis, "and tell him that there's nothin' doin' in the way of rough house wit dis gent here." He indicated Psmith, who bowed. "And you can tell de Spider," went on Bat with growing ferocity, "dat next time he gits gay and starts in to shoot guys in me dance-joint I'll bite de head off'n him. See? Does dat go? If he t'inks his little two-by-four gang can put it across de Groome Street, he can try. Dat's right. An' don't fergit dis gent here and me is pals, and any one dat starts anyt'ing wit dis gent is going to have to git busy wit me. Does dat go?"

Psmith coughed, and shot his cuffs.

"I do not know," he said, in the manner of a chairman addressing a meeting, "that I have anything to add to the very well-expressed remarks of my friend, Comrade Jarvis. He has, in my opinion, covered the ground very thoroughly and satisfactorily. It now only remains for me to pass a vote of thanks to Comrade Jarvis and to declare this meeting at an end."

"Beat it," said Mr. Jarvis, pointing to the door.

The delegation then withdrew.

"I am very much obliged," said Psmith, "for your courtly assistance, Comrade Jarvis. But for you I do not care to think with what a splash I might not have been immersed in the gumbo. Thank you, Comrade Jarvis. And you, Comrade Otto."

"Aw chee!" said Mr. Jarvis, handsomely dismissing the matter. Mr.

Otto kicked the leg of the table, and grunted.

* * *

For half an hour after the departure of the Three Pointers Psmith chatted amiably to his two assistants on matters of general interest. The exchange of ideas was somewhat one-sided, though Mr. Jarvis had one or two striking items of information to impart, notably some hints on the treatment of fits in kittens.

At the end of this period the conversation was once more interrupted by the sound of movements in the outer office.

"If dat's dose stiffs come back—" began Mr. Jarvis, reaching for his revolver.

"Stay your hand, Comrade Jarvis," said as a sharp knock sounded on the door. "I do not think it can be our late friends. Comrade Repetto's knowledge of the usages of polite society is too limited, I fancy, to prompt him to knock on doors. Come in."

The door opened. It was not Mr. Repetto or his colleagues, but another old friend. No other, in fact, than Mr. Francis Parker, he who had come as an embassy from the man up top in the very beginning of affairs, and had departed, wrathful, mouthing declarations of war. As on his previous visit, he wore the dude suit, the shiny shoes, and the tall-shaped hat.

"Welcome, Comrade Parker," said Psmith. "It is too long since we met. Comrade Jarvis I think you know. If I am right, that is to say, in supposing that it was you who approached him at an earlier stage in the proceedings with a view to engaging his sympathetic aid in the great work of putting Comrade Windsor and myself out of business. The gentleman on your left is Comrade Otto."

Mr. Parker was looking at Bat in bewilderment. It was plain that he had not expected to find Psmith entertaining such company.

"Did you come purely for friendly chit-chat, Comrade Parker," inquired Psmith, "or was there, woven into the social motives of your call, a desire to talk business of any kind?"

"My business is private. I didn't expect a crowd."

"Especially of ancient friends such as Comrade Jarvis. Well, well, you are breaking up a most interesting little symposium. Comrade Jarvis, I think I shall be forced to postpone our very entertaining discussion of fits in kittens till a more opportune moment. Meanwhile, as Comrade Parker wishes to talk over some private business—"

Bat Jarvis rose.

"I'll beat it," he said.

"Reluctantly, I hope, Comrade Jarvis. As reluctantly as I hint that I would be alone. If I might drop in some time at your private residence?"

"Sure," said Mr. Jarvis warmly.

"Excellent. Well, for the present, good-bye. And many thanks for your invaluable co-operation."

"Aw chee!" said Mr. Jarvis.

"And now, Comrade Parker," said Psmith, when the door had closed, "let her rip. What can I do for you?"

"You seem to be all to the merry with Bat Jarvis," observed Mr. Parker.

"The phrase exactly expresses it, Comrade Parker. I am as a tortoiseshell kitten to him. But, touching your business?"

Mr. Parker was silent for a moment.

"See here," he said at last, "aren't you going to be good? Say, what's the use of keeping on at this fool game? Why not quit it before you get hurt?"

Psmith smoothed his waistcoat reflectively.

"I may be wrong, Comrade Parker," he said, "but it seems to me that the chances of my getting hurt are not so great as you appear to imagine. The person who is in danger of getting hurt seems to me to be the gentleman whose name is on that paper which is now in my possession."

"Where is it?" demanded Mr. Parker quickly.

Psmith eyed him benevolently.

"If you will pardon the expression, Comrade Parker," he said,

"'Aha!' Meaning that I propose to keep that information to myself."

Mr. Parker shrugged his shoulders.

"You know your own business, I guess."

Psmith nodded.

"You are absolutely correct, Comrade Parker. I do. Now that *Cosy Moments* has our excellent friend Comrade Jarvis on its side, are you not to a certain extent among the Blenheim Oranges? I think so. I think so."

As he spoke there was a rap at the door. A small boy entered. In his hand was a scrap of paper.

"Guy asks me give dis to gazebo named Smiff," he said.

"There are many gazebos of that name, my lad. One of whom I am which, as Artemus Ward was wont to observe. Possibly the missive is for me."

He took the paper. It was dated from an address on the East Side.

"Dear Smith," it ran. "Come here as quick as you can, and bring some money. Explain when I see you."

It was signed "W. W."

So Billy Windsor had fulfilled his promise. He had escaped.

A feeling of regret for the futility of the thing was Psmith's first emotion. Billy could be of no possible help in the campaign at its present point. All the work that remained to be done could easily be carried through without his assistance. And by breaking out from the Island he had committed an offence which was bound to carry with it serious penalties. For the first time since his connection with *Cosy Moments* began Psmith was really disturbed.

He turned to Mr. Parker.

"Comrade Parker," he said, "I regret to state that this office is now closing for the day. But for this, I should be delighted to sit chatting with you. As it is—"

"Very well," said Mr. Parker. "Then you mean to go on with this business?"

"Though it snows, Comrade Parker."

They went out into the street, Psmith thoughtful and hardly realising the other's presence. By the side of the pavement a few yards down the road a taximeter-cab was standing. Psmith hailed it.

Mr. Parker was still beside him. It occurred to Psmith that it would not do to let him hear the address Billy Windsor had given in his note.

"Turn and go on down the street," he said to the driver.

He had taken his seat and was closing the door, when it was snatched from his grasp and Mr. Parker darted on to the seat opposite. The next moment the cab had started up the street instead of down and the hard muzzle of a revolver was pressing against Psmith's waistcoat.

"Now what?" said Mr. Parker smoothly, leaning back with the pistol resting easily on his knee.

CHAPTER XXVI - A FRIEND IN NEED

"The point is well taken," said Psmith thoughtfully.

"You think so?" said Mr. Parker.

"I am convinced of it."

"Good. But don't move. Put that hand back where it was."

"You think of everything, Comrade Parker."

He dropped his hand on to the seat, and remained silent for a few moments. The taxi-cab was buzzing along up Fifth Avenue now. Looking towards the window, Psmith saw that they were nearing the park. The great white mass of the Plaza Hotel showed up on the left.

"Did you ever stop at the Plaza, Comrade Parker?"

"No," said Mr. Parker shortly.

"Don't bite at me, Comrade Parker. Why be brusque on so joyous an
occasion? Better men than us have stopped at the Plaza. Ah, the
Park! How fresh the leaves, Comrade Parker, how green the herbage!
Fling your eye at yonder grassy knoll."

He raised his hand to point. Instantly the revolver was against his waistcoat, making an unwelcome crease in that immaculate garment.

"I told you to keep that hand where it was."

"You did, Comrade Parker, you did. The fault," said Psmith handsomely, "was entirely mine. Carried away by my love of nature, I forgot. It shall not occur again."

"It had better not," said Mr. Parker unpleasantly. "If it does, I'll blow a hole through you."

Psmith raised his eyebrows.

"That, Comrade Parker," he said, "is where you make your error. You would no more shoot me in the heart of the metropolis than, I trust, you would wear a made-up tie with evening dress. Your skin, however unhealthy to the eye of the casual observer, is doubtless precious to yourself, and you are not the man I take you for if you would risk it purely for the momentary pleasure of plugging me with a revolver. The cry goes round criminal circles in New York, 'Comrade Parker is not such a fool as he looks.' Think for a moment what would happen. The shot would ring out, and instantly bicycle-policemen would be pursuing this taxi-cab with the purposeful speed of greyhounds trying to win the Waterloo Cup. You would be headed off and stopped. Ha! What is this? Psmith, the People's Pet, weltering in his gore? Death to the assassin! I fear nothing could save you from the fury of the mob, Comrade Parker. I seem to see them meditatively plucking you limb from limb. 'She loves me!' Off comes an arm. 'She loves me not.' A leg joins the little heap of limbs on the ground. That is how it would be. And what would you have left out of it? Merely, as I say, the momentary pleasure of potting me. And it isn't as if such a feat could give you the thrill of successful marksmanship. Anybody could hit a man with a pistol at an inch and a quarter. I fear you have not thought this matter out with sufficient care, Comrade Parker. You said to yourself, 'Happy thought, I will kidnap Psmith!' and all your friends said, 'Parker is the man with the big brain!' But now, while it is true that I can't get out, you are moaning, 'What on earth shall I do with him, now that I have got him?'"

"You think so, do you?"

"I am convinced of it. Your face is contorted with the anguish of mental stress. Let this be a lesson to you, Comrade Parker, never to embark on any enterprise of which you do not see the end."

"I guess I see the end of this all right."

"You have the advantage of me then, Comrade Parker. It seems to me that we have nothing before us but to go on riding about New York till you feel that my society begins to pall."

"You figure you're clever, I guess."

"There are few brighter brains in this city, Comrade Parker. But why this sudden tribute?"

"You reckon you've thought it all out, eh?"

"There may be a flaw in my reasoning, but I confess I do not at the moment see where it lies. Have you detected one?"

"I guess so."

"Ah! And what is it?"

"You seem to think New York's the only place on the map."

"Meaning what, Comrade Parker?"

"It might be a fool trick to shoot you in the city as you say, but, you see, we aren't due to stay in the city. This cab is moving on."

"Like John Brown's soul," said Psmith, nodding. "I see. Then you propose to make quite a little tour in this cab?"

"You've got it."

"And when we are out in the open country, where there are no witnesses, things may begin to move."

"That's it."

"Then," said Psmith heartily, "till that moment arrives what we must do is to entertain each other with conversation. You can take no step of any sort for a full half-hour, possibly more, so let us give ourselves up to the merriment of the passing instant. Are you good at riddles, Comrade Parker? How much wood would a wood-chuck chuck, assuming for purposes of argument that it was in the power of a wood-chuck to chuck wood?"

Mr. Parker did not attempt to solve this problem. He was sitting in the same attitude of watchfulness, the revolver resting on his knee. He seemed mistrustful of Psmith's right hand, which was hanging limply at his side. It was from this quarter that he seemed to expect attack. The cab was bowling easily up the broad street, past rows on rows of high houses, all looking exactly the same. Occasionally, to the right, through a break in the line of buildings, a glimpse of the river could be seen.

Psmith resumed the conversation.

"You are not interested in wood-chucks, Comrade Parker? Well, well, many people are not. A passion for the flora and fauna of our forests is innate rather than acquired. Let us talk of something else. Tell me about your home-life, Comrade Parker. Are you married? Are there any little Parkers running about the house? When you return from this very pleasant excursion will baby voices crow gleefully, 'Fahzer's come home'?"

Mr. Parker said nothing.

"I see," said Psmith with ready sympathy. "I understand. Say no more. You are unmarried. She wouldn't have you. Alas, Comrade Parker! However, thus it is! We look around us, and what do we see? A solid phalanx of the girls we have loved and lost. Tell me about her, Comrade Parker. Was it your face or your manners at which she drew the line?"

Mr. Parker leaned forward with a scowl. Psmith did not move, but his right hand, as it hung, closed. Another moment and Mr. Parker's chin would be in just the right position for a swift upper-cut. . .

This fact appeared suddenly to dawn on Mr. Parker himself. He drew back quickly, and half raised the revolver. Psmith's hand resumed its normal attitude.

"Leaving more painful topics," said Psmith, "let us turn to another point. That note which the grubby stripling brought to me at the office purported to come from Comrade Windsor, and stated that he had escaped from Blackwell's Island, and was awaiting my arrival at some address in the Bowery. Would you mind telling me, purely to satisfy my curiosity, if that note was genuine? I have never made a close study of Comrade Windsor's handwriting, and in an unguarded moment I may have assumed too much."

Mr. Parker permitted himself a smile.

"I guess you aren't so clever after all," he said. "The note was a fake all right."

"And you had this cab waiting for me on the chance?"

Mr. Parker nodded.

"Sherlock Holmes was right," said Psmith regretfully. "You may remember that he advised Doctor Watson never to take the first cab, or the second. He should have gone further, and urged him not to take cabs at all. Walking is far healthier."

"You'll find it so," said Mr. Parker.

Psmith eyed him curiously.

"What *are* you going to do with me, Comrade Parker?" he asked.

Mr. Parker did not reply. Psmith's eye turned again to the window. They had covered much ground since last he had looked at the view. They were off Manhattan Island now, and the houses were beginning to thin out. Soon, travelling at their present rate, they must come into the open country. Psmith relapsed into silence. It was necessary for him to think. He had been talking in the hope of getting the other off his guard; but Mr. Parker was evidently too keenly on the look-out. The hand that held the revolver never wavered. The muzzle, pointing in an upward direction, was aimed at Psmith's waist. There was no doubt that a move on his part would be fatal. If the pistol went off, it must hit him. If it had been pointed at his head in the orthodox way he might have risked a sudden blow to knock it aside, but in the present circumstances that would be useless. There was nothing to do but wait.

The cab moved swiftly on. Now they had reached the open country. An occasional wooden shack was passed, but that was all. At any moment the climax of the drama might be reached. Psmith's muscles stiffened for a spring. There was little chance of its being effective, but at least it would be better to put up some kind of a fight. And he had a faint hope that the suddenness of his movement might upset the other's aim. He was bound to be hit somewhere. That was certain. But quickness might save him to some extent.

He braced his leg against the back of the cab. In another moment he would have sprung; but just then the smooth speed of the cab changed to a series of jarring bumps, each more emphatic than the last. It slowed down, then came to a halt. One of the tyres had burst.

There was a thud, as the chauffeur jumped down. They heard him fumbling in the tool-box. Presently the body of the machine was raised slightly as he got to work with the jack.

It was about a minute later that somebody in the road outside spoke.

"Had a breakdown?" inquired the voice. Psmith recognised it. It was the voice of Kid Brady.

CHAPTER XXVII - PSMITH CONCLUDES HIS RIDE

The Kid, as he had stated to Psmith at their last interview that he intended to do, had begun his training for his match with Eddie Wood, at White Plains, a village distant but a few miles from New York. It was his practice to open a course of training with a little gentle road-work; and it was while jogging along the highway a couple of miles from his training-camp, in company with the two thick-necked gentlemen who acted as his sparring-partners, that he had come upon the broken-down taxi-cab.

If this had happened after his training had begun in real earnest, he would have averted his eyes from the spectacle, however alluring, and continued on his way without a pause. But now, as he had not yet settled down to genuine hard work, he felt justified in turning aside and looking into the matter. The fact that the chauffeur, who seemed to be a taciturn man, lacking the conversational graces, manifestly objected to an audience, deterred him not at all. One cannot have everything in this world, and the Kid and his attendant thick-necks were content to watch the process of mending the tyre, without demanding the additional joy of sparkling small-talk from the man in charge of the operations.

"Guy's had a breakdown, sure," said the first of the thick-necks.

"Surest thing you know," agreed his colleague.

"Seems to me the tyre's punctured," said the Kid.

All three concentrated their gaze on the machine

"Kid's right," said thick-neck number one. "Guy's been an' bust a tyre."

"Surest thing you know," said thick-neck number two.

They observed the perspiring chauffeur in silence for a while.

"Wonder how he did that, now?" speculated the Kid.

"Guy ran over a nail, I guess," said thick-neck number one.

"Surest thing you know," said the other, who, while perhaps somewhat lacking in the matter of original thought, was a most useful fellow to have by one. A sort of Boswell.

"Did you run over a nail?" the Kid inquired of the chauffeur.

The chauffeur ignored the question.

"This is his busy day," said the first thick-neck with satire.

"Guy's too full of work to talk to us."

"Deaf, shouldn't wonder," surmised the Kid.

"Say, wonder what he's doin' with a taxi so far out of the city."

"Some guy tells him to drive him out here, I guess. Say, it'll cost him something, too. He'll have to strip off a few from his roll to pay for this."

Psmith, in the interior of the cab, glanced at Mr. Parker.

"You heard, Comrade Parker? He is right, I fancy. The bill—"

Mr. Parker dug viciously at him with the revolver.

"Keep quiet," he whispered, "or you'll get hurt."

Psmith suspended his remarks.

Outside, the conversation had begun again.

"Pretty rich guy inside," said the Kid, following up his companion's train of thought. "I'm goin' to rubber in at the window."

Psmith, meeting Mr. Parker's eye, smiled pleasantly. There was no answering smile on the other's face.

There came the sound of the Kid's feet grating on the road as he turned; and as he heard it Mr. Parker, that eminent tactician, for the first time lost his head. With a vague idea of screening Psmith from the eyes of the man in the road he half rose. For an instant the muzzle of the pistol ceased to point at Psmith's waistcoat. It was the very chance Psmith had been waiting for. His left hand shot out, grasped the other's wrist, and gave it a sharp wrench. The revolver went off with a deafening report, the bullet passing through the back of the cab; then fell to the floor, as the fingers lost their hold. The next moment Psmith's right fist, darting upwards, took Mr. Parker neatly under the angle of the jaw.

The effect was instantaneous. Psmith had risen from his seat as he delivered the blow, and it consequently got the full benefit of his weight, which was not small. Mr. Parker literally crumpled up. His head jerked back, then fell limply on his chest. He would have slipped to the floor had not Psmith pushed him on to the seat.

The interested face of the Kid appeared at the window. Behind him could be seen portions of the faces of the two thick-necks.

"Ah, Comrade Brady!" said Psmith genially. "I heard your voice, and was hoping you might look in for a chat."

"What's doin', Mr. Smith?" queried the excited Kid.

"Much, Comrade Brady, much. I will tell you all anon. Meanwhile, however, kindly knock that chauffeur down and sit on his head. He's a bad person."

"De guy's beat it," volunteered the first thick-neck.

"Surest thing you know," said the other.

"What's been doin', Mr. Smith?" asked the Kid.

"I'll tell you about it as we go, Comrade Brady," said Psmith, stepping into the road. "Riding in a taxi is pleasant provided it is not overdone. For the moment I have had sufficient. A bit of walking will do me good."

"What are you going to do with this guy, Mr. Smith?" asked the Kid, pointing to Parker, who had begun to stir slightly.

Psmith inspected the stricken one gravely.

"I have no use for him, Comrade Brady," he said. "Our ride together gave me as much of his society as I desire for to-day. Unless you or either of your friends are collecting Parkers, I propose that we leave him where he is. We may as well take the gun, however. In my opinion, Comrade Parker is not the proper man to have such a weapon. He is too prone to go firing it off in any direction at a moment's notice, causing inconvenience to all." He groped on the floor of the cab for the revolver. "Now, Comrade Brady," he said, straightening himself up, "I am at your disposal. Shall we be pushing on?"

* * *

It was late in the evening when Psmith returned to the metropolis, after a pleasant afternoon at the Brady training-camp. The Kid, having heard the details of the ride, offered once more to abandon his match with Eddie Wood, but Psmith would not hear of it. He was fairly satisfied that the opposition had fired their last shot, and that their next move would be to endeavour to come to terms. They could not hope to catch him off his guard a second time, and, as far as hired assault and battery were concerned, he was as safe in New York, now that Bat Jarvis had declared himself on his side, as he would have been in the middle of a desert. What Bat said was law on the East Side. No hooligan, however eager to make money, would dare to act against a *protégé* of the Groome Street leader.

The only flaw in Psmith's contentment was the absence of Billy Windsor. On this night of all nights the editorial staff of *Cosy Moments* should have been together to celebrate the successful outcome of their campaign. Psmith dined alone, his enjoyment of the rather special dinner which he felt justified in ordering in honour of the occasion somewhat diminished by the thought of Billy's hard case. He had seen Mr William Collier in *The Man from Mexico*, and that had given him an understanding of what a term of imprisonment on Blackwell's Island meant. Billy, during these lean days, must be supporting life on bread, bean soup, and water. Psmith, toying with the hors d'oeuvre, was somewhat saddened by the thought.

* * *

All was quiet at the office on the following day. Bat Jarvis, again accompanied by the faithful Otto, took up his position in the inner room, prepared to repel all invaders; but none arrived. No sounds broke the peace of the outer office except the whistling of Master Maloney.

Things were almost dull when the telephone bell rang. Psmith took down the receiver.

"Hullo?" he said.

"I'm Parker," said a moody voice.

Psmith uttered a cry of welcome.

"Why, Comrade Parker, this is splendid! How goes it? Did you get back all right yesterday? I was sorry to have to tear myself away, but I had other engagements. But why use the telephone? Why not come here in person? You know how welcome you are. Hire a taxi-cab and come right round."

Mr. Parker made no reply to the invitation.

"Mr. Waring would like to see you."

"Who, Comrade Parker?"

"Mr. Stewart Waring."

"The celebrated tenement house-owner?"

Silence from the other end of the wire. "Well," said Psmith, "what step does he propose to take towards it?"

"He tells me to say that he will be in his office at twelve o'clock to-morrow morning. His office is in the Morton Building, Nassau Street."

Psmith clicked his tongue regretfully.

"Then I do not see how we can meet," he said. "I shall be here."

"He wishes to see you at his office."

"I am sorry, Comrade Parker. It is impossible. I am very busy just now, as you may know, preparing the next number, the one in which we publish the name of the owner of the Pleasant Street Tenements. Otherwise, I should be delighted. Perhaps later, when the rush of work has diminished somewhat."

"Am I to tell Mr. Waring that you refuse?"

"If you are seeing him at any time and feel at a loss for something to say, perhaps you might mention it. Is there anything else I can do for you, Comrade Parker?"

"See here—"

"Nothing? Then good-bye. Look in when you're this way."

He hung up the receiver.

As he did so, he was aware of Master Maloney standing beside the table.

"Yes, Comrade Maloney?"

"Telegram," said Pugsy. "For Mr. Windsor."

Psmith ripped open the envelope.

The message ran:

"Returning to-day. Will be at office to-morrow morning," and it was signed "Wilberfloss."

"See who's here!" said Psmith softly.

CHAPTER XXVIII - STANDING ROOM ONLY

In the light of subsequent events it was perhaps the least bit unfortunate that Mr. Jarvis should have seen fit to bring with him to the office of *Cosy Moments* on the following morning two of his celebrated squad of cats, and that Long Otto, who, as usual, accompanied him, should have been fired by his example to the extent of introducing a large and rather boisterous yellow dog. They were not to be blamed, of course. They could not know that before the morning was over space in the office would be at a premium. Still, it was unfortunate.

Mr. Jarvis was slightly apologetic.

"T'ought I'd bring de kits along," he said. "Dey started in scrappin' yesterday when I was here, so to-day I says I'll keep my eye on dem."

Psmith inspected the menagerie without resentment.

"Assuredly, Comrade Jarvis," he said. "They add a pleasantly cosy and domestic touch to the scene. The only possible criticism I can find to make has to do with their probable brawling with the dog."

"Oh, dey won't scrap wit de dawg. Dey knows him."

"But is he aware of that? He looks to me a somewhat impulsive animal. Well, well, the matter's in your hands. If you will undertake to look after the refereeing of any pogrom that may arise, I say no more."

Mr. Jarvis's statement as to the friendly relations between the animals proved to be correct. The dog made no attempt to annihilate the cats. After an inquisitive journey round the room he lay down and went to sleep, and an era of peace set in. The cats had settled themselves comfortably, one on each of Mr. Jarvis's knees, and Long Otto, surveying the ceiling with his customary glassy stare, smoked a long cigar in silence. Bat breathed a tune, and scratched one of the cats under the ear. It was a soothing scene.

But it did not last. Ten minutes had barely elapsed when the yellow dog, sitting up with a start, uttered a whine. In the outer office could be heard a stir and movement. The next moment the door burst open and a little man dashed in. He had a peeled nose and showed other evidences of having been living in the open air. Behind him was a crowd of uncertain numbers. Psmith recognised the leaders of this crowd. They were the Reverend Edwin T. Philpotts and Mr. B. Henderson Asher.

"Why, Comrade Asher," he said, "this is indeed a Moment of Mirth. I have been wondering for weeks where you could have got to. And Comrade Philpotts! Am I wrong in saying that this is the maddest, merriest day of all the glad New Year?"

The rest of the crowd had entered the room.

"Comrade Waterman, too!" cried Psmith. "Why we have all met before. Except—"

He glanced inquiringly at the little man with the peeled nose.

"My name is Wilberfloss," said the other with austerity. "Will you be so good as to tell me where Mr. Windsor is?"

A murmur of approval from his followers.

"In one moment," said Psmith. "First, however, let me introduce two important members of our staff. On your right, Mr. Bat Jarvis. On your left, Mr. Long Otto. Both of Groome Street."

The two Bowery boys rose awkwardly. The cats fell in an avalanche to the floor. Long Otto, in his haste, trod on the dog, which began barking, a process which it kept up almost without a pause during the rest of the interview.

"Mr. Wilberfloss," said Psmith in an aside to Bat, "is widely known as a cat fancier in Brooklyn circles."

"Honest?" said Mr. Jarvis. He tapped Mr. Wilberfloss in friendly fashion on the chest. "Say," he asked, "did youse ever have a cat wit one blue and one yellow eye?"

Mr. Wilberfloss side-stepped and turned once more to Psmith, who was offering B. Henderson Asher a cigarette.

"Who are you?" he demanded.

"Who am *I*?" repeated Psmith in an astonished tone.

"Who are you?"

"I am Psmith," said the old Etonian reverently. "There is a preliminary P before the name. This, however, is silent. Like the tomb. Compare such words as ptarmigan, psalm, and phthisis."

"These gentlemen tell me you're acting editor. Who appointed you?"

Psmith reflected.

"It is rather a nice point," he said. "It might be claimed that I appointed myself. You may say, however, that Comrade Windsor appointed me."

"Ah! And where is Mr. Windsor?"

"In prison," said Psmith sorrowfully.

"In prison!"

Psmith nodded.

"It is too true. Such is the generous impulsiveness of Comrade Windsor's nature that he hit a policeman, was promptly gathered in, and is now serving a sentence of thirty days on Blackwell's Island."

Mr. Wilberfloss looked at Mr. Philpotts. Mr. Asher looked at Mr. Wilberfloss. Mr. Waterman started, and stumbled over a cat.

"I never heard of such a thing," said Mr. Wilberfloss.

A faint, sad smile played across Psmith's face.

"Do you remember, Comrade Waterman—I fancy it was to you that I made the remark—my commenting at our previous interview on the rashness of confusing the unusual with the improbable? Here we see Comrade Wilberfloss, big-brained though he is, falling into error."

"I shall dismiss Mr. Windsor immediately," said the big-brained one.

"From Blackwell's Island?" said Psmith. "I am sure you will earn his gratitude if you do. They live on bean soup there. Bean soup and bread, and not much of either."

He broke off, to turn his attention to Mr. Jarvis and Mr. Waterman, between whom bad blood seemed to have arisen. Mr. Jarvis, holding a cat in his arms, was glowering at Mr. Waterman, who had backed away and seemed nervous.

"What is the trouble, Comrade Jarvis?"

"Dat guy dere wit two left feet," said Bat querulously, "goes and treads on de kit. I—"

"I assure you it was a pure accident. The animal—"

Mr. Wilberfloss, eyeing Bat and the silent Otto with disgust, intervened.

"Who are these persons, Mr. Smith?" he inquired.

"Poisson yourself," rejoined Bat, justly incensed. "Who's de little guy wit de peeled breezer, Mr. Smith?"

Psmith waved his hands.

"Gentlemen, gentlemen," he said, "let us not descend to mere personalities. I thought I had introduced you. This, Comrade Jarvis, is Mr. Wilberfloss, the editor of this journal. These, Comrade Wilberfloss—Zam-buk would put your nose right in a day—are, respectively, Bat Jarvis and Long Otto, our acting fighting-editors, vice Kid Brady, absent on unavoidable business."

"Kid Brady!" shrilled Mr. Wilberfloss. "I insist that you give me a full explanation of this matter. I go away by my doctor's orders for ten weeks, leaving Mr. Windsor to conduct the paper on certain well-defined lines. I return yesterday, and, getting into communication with Mr. Philpotts, what do I find? Why, that in my absence the paper has been ruined."

"Ruined?" said Psmith. "On the contrary. Examine the returns, and you will see that the circulation has gone up every week. *Cosy Moments* was never so prosperous and flourishing. Comrade Otto, do you think you could use your personal influence with that dog to induce it to suspend its barking for a while? It is musical, but renders conversation difficult."

Long Otto raised a massive boot and aimed it at the animal, which, dodging with a yelp, cannoned against the second cat and had its nose scratched. Piercing shrieks cleft the air.

"I demand an explanation," roared Mr. Wilberfloss above the din.

"I think, Comrade Otto," said Psmith, "it would make things a little easier if you removed that dog."

He opened the door. The dog shot out. They could hear it being ejected from the outer office by Master Maloney. When there was silence, Psmith turned courteously to the editor.

"You were saying, Comrade Wilberfloss?"

"Who is this person Brady? With Mr. Philpotts I have been going carefully over the numbers which have been issued since my departure—"

"An intellectual treat," murmured Psmith.

"—and in each there is a picture of this young man in a costume which I will not particularise—"

"There is hardly enough of it to particularise."

"—together with a page of disgusting autobiographical matter."

Psmith held up his hand.

"I protest," he said. "We court criticism, but this is mere abuse. I appeal to these gentlemen to say whether this, for instance, is not bright and interesting."

He picked up the current number of *Cosy Moments*, and turned to the

Kid's page.

"This," he said. "Describing a certain ten-round unpleasantness with one Mexican Joe. 'Joe comes up for the second round and he gives me a nasty look, but I thinks of my mother and swats him one in the lower ribs. He hollers foul, but nix on that. Referee says, "Fight on." Joe gives me another nasty look. "All right, Kid," he says; "now I'll knock you up into the gallery." And with that he cuts loose with a right swing, but I falls into the clinch, and then—-!'"

"Bah!" exclaimed Mr. Wilberfloss.

"Go on, boss," urged Mr. Jarvis approvingly. "It's to de good, dat stuff."

"There!" said Psmith triumphantly. "You heard? Comrade Jarvis, one of the most firmly established critics east of Fifth Avenue, stamps Kid Brady's reminiscences with the hall-mark of his approval."

"I falls fer de Kid every time," assented Mr. Jarvis.

"Assuredly, Comrade Jarvis. You know a good thing when you see one. Why," he went on warmly, "there is stuff in these reminiscences which would stir the blood of a jelly-fish. Let me quote you another passage to show that they are not only enthralling, but helpful as well. Let me see, where is it? Ah, I have it. 'A bully good way of putting a guy out of business is this. You don't want to use it in the ring, because by Queensberry Rules it's a foul; but you will find it mighty useful if any thick-neck comes up to you in the street and tries to start anything. It's this way. While he's setting himself for a punch, just place the tips of the fingers of your left hand on the right side of his chest. Then bring down the heel of your left hand. There isn't a guy living that could stand up against that. The fingers give you a leverage to beat the band. The guy doubles up, and you upper-cut him with your right, and out he goes.' Now, I bet you never knew that before, Comrade Philpotts. Try it on your parishioners."

"*Cosy Moments*," said Mr. Wilberfloss irately, "is no medium for exploiting low prize-fighters."

"Low prize-fighters! Comrade Wilberfloss, you have been misinformed. The Kid is as decent a little chap as you'd meet anywhere. You do not seem to appreciate the philanthropic motives of the paper in adopting Comrade Brady's cause. Think of it, Comrade Wilberfloss. There was that unfortunate stripling with only two pleasures in life, to love his mother and to knock the heads off other youths whose weight coincided with his own; and misfortune, until we took him up, had barred him almost completely from the second pastime. Our editorial heart was melted. We adopted Comrade Brady. And look at him now! Matched against Eddie Wood! And Comrade Waterman will support me in my statement that a victory over Eddie Wood means that he gets a legitimate claim to meet Jimmy Garvin for the championship."

"It is abominable," burst forth Mr. Wilberfloss. "It is disgraceful. I never heard of such a thing. The paper is ruined."

"You keep reverting to that statement, Comrade Wilberfloss. Can nothing reassure you? The returns are excellent. Prosperity beams on us like a sun. The proprietor is more than satisfied."

"The proprietor?" gasped Mr. Wilberfloss. "Does *he* know how you have treated the paper?"

"He is cognisant of our every move."

"And he approves?"

"He more than approves."

Mr. Wilberfloss snorted.

"I don't believe it," he said.

The assembled ex-contributors backed up this statement with a united murmur. B. Henderson Asher snorted satirically.

"They don't believe it," sighed Psmith. "Nevertheless, it is true."

"It is not true," thundered Mr. Wilberfloss, hopping to avoid a perambulating cat. "Nothing will convince me of it. Mr. Benjamin White is not a maniac."

"I trust not," said Psmith. "I sincerely trust not. I have every reason to believe in his complete sanity. What makes you fancy that there is even a possibility of his being—er—?"

"Nobody but a lunatic would approve of seeing his paper ruined."

"Again!" said Psmith. "I fear that the notion that this journal is ruined has become an obsession with you, Comrade Wilberfloss. Once again I assure you that it is more than prosperous."

"If," said Mr. Wilberfloss, "you imagine that I intend to take your word in this matter, you are mistaken. I shall cable Mr. White to-day, and inquire whether these alterations in the paper meet with his approval."

"I shouldn't, Comrade Wilberfloss. Cables are expensive, and in these hard times a penny saved is a penny earned. Why worry Comrade White? He is so far away, so out of touch with our New York literary life. I think it is practically a certainty that he has not the slightest inkling of any changes in the paper."

Mr. Wilberfloss uttered a cry of triumph.

"I knew it," he said, "I knew it. I knew you would give up when it came to the point, and you were driven into a corner. Now, perhaps, you will admit that Mr. White has given no sanction for the alterations in the paper?"

A puzzled look crept into Psmith's face.

"I think, Comrade Wilberfloss," he said, "we are talking at cross-purposes. You keep harping on Comrade White and his views and tastes. One would almost imagine that you fancied that Comrade White was the proprietor of this paper."

Mr. Wilberfloss stared. B. Henderson Asher stared. Every one stared, except Mr. Jarvis, who, since the readings from the Kid's reminiscences had ceased, had lost interest in the discussion, and was now entertaining the cats with a ball of paper tied to a string.

"Fancied that Mr. White . . .?" repeated Mr. Wilberfloss. "I don't follow you. Who is, if he isn't?"

Psmith removed his monocle, polished it thoughtfully, and put it back in its place.

"I am," he said.

CHAPTER XXIX - THE KNOCK-OUT FOR MR. WARING

"You!" cried Mr. Wilberfloss.

"The same," said Psmith.

"You!" exclaimed Messrs. Waterman, Asher, and the Reverend Edwin Philpotts.

"On the spot!" said Psmith.

Mr. Wilberfloss groped for a chair and sat down.

"Am I going mad?" he demanded feebly.

"Not so, Comrade Wilberfloss," said Psmith encouragingly. "All is well. The cry goes round New York, 'Comrade Wilberfloss is to the good. He does not gibber.'"

"Do I understand you to say that you own this paper?"

"I do."

"Since when?"

"Roughly speaking, about a month."

Among his audience (still excepting Mr. Jarvis, who was tickling one of the cats and whistling a plaintive melody) there was a tendency toward awkward silence. To start bally-ragging a seeming nonentity and then to discover he is the proprietor of the paper to which you wish to contribute is like kicking an apparently empty hat and finding your rich uncle inside it. Mr. Wilberfloss in particular was disturbed. Editorships of the kind which he aspired to are not easy to get. If he were to be removed from *Cosy Moments* he would find it hard to place himself anywhere else. Editors, like manuscripts, are rejected from want of space.

"Very early in my connection with this journal," said Psmith, "I saw that I was on to a good thing. I had long been convinced that about the nearest approach to the perfect job in this world, where good jobs are so hard to acquire, was to own a paper. All you had to do, once you had secured your paper, was to sit back and watch the other fellows work, and from time to time forward big cheques to the bank. Nothing could be more nicely attuned to the tastes of a Shropshire Psmith. The glimpses I was enabled to get of the workings of this little journal gave me the impression that Comrade White was not attached with any paternal fervour to *Cosy Moments*. He regarded it, I deduced, not so much as a life-work as in the light of an investment. I assumed that Comrade White had his price, and wrote to my father, who was visiting Carlsbad at the moment, to ascertain what that price might be. He cabled it to me. It was reasonable. Now it so happens that an uncle of mine some years ago left me a considerable number of simoleons, and though I shall not be legally entitled actually to close in on the opulence for a matter of nine months or so, I anticipated that my father would have no objection to staking me to the necessary amount on the security of my little bit of money. My father has spent some time of late hurling me at various professions, and we had agreed some time ago that the Law was to be my long suit. Paper-owning, however, may be combined with being Lord Chancellor, and I knew he would have no objection to my being a Napoleon of the Press on this side. So we closed with Comrade White, and—"

There was a knock at the door, and Master Maloney entered with a card.

"Guy's waiting outside," he said.

"Mr. Stewart Waring," read Psmith. "Comrade Maloney, do you know what Mahomet did when the mountain would not come to him?"

"Search me," said the office-boy indifferently.

"He went to the mountain. It was a wise thing to do. As a general rule in life you can't beat it. Remember that, Comrade Maloney."

"Sure," said Pugsy. "Shall I send the guy in?"

"Surest thing you know, Comrade Maloney."

He turned to the assembled company.

"Gentlemen," he said, "you know how I hate to have to send you away, but would you mind withdrawing in good order? A somewhat delicate and private interview is in the offing. Comrade Jarvis, we will meet anon. Your services to the paper have been greatly appreciated. If I might drop in some afternoon and inspect the remainder of your zoo—?"

"Any time you're down Groome Street way. Glad."

"I will make a point of it. Comrade Wilberfloss, would you mind remaining? As editor of this journal, you should be present. If the rest of you would look in about this time to-morrow—Show Mr. Waring in, Comrade Maloney."

He took a seat.

"We are now, Comrade Wilberfloss," he said, "at a crisis in the affairs of this journal, but I fancy we shall win through."

The door opened, and Pugsy announced Mr. Waring.

The owner of the Pleasant Street Tenements was of what is usually called commanding presence. He was tall and broad, and more than a little stout. His face was clean-shaven and curiously expressionless. Bushy eyebrows topped a pair of cold grey eyes. He walked into the room with the air of one who is not wont to apologise for existing. There are some men who seem to fill any room in which they may be. Mr. Waring was one of these.

He set his hat down on the table without speaking. After which he looked at Mr. Wilberfloss, who shrank a little beneath his gaze.

Psmith had risen to greet him.

"Won't you sit down?" he said.

"I prefer to stand."

"Just as you wish. This is Liberty Hall."

Mr. Waring again glanced at Mr. Wilberfloss.

"What I have to say is private," he said.

"All is well," said Psmith reassuringly. "It is no stranger that you see before you, no mere irresponsible lounger who has butted in by chance. That is Comrade J. Fillken Wilberfloss, the editor of this journal."

"The editor? I understood—"

"I know what you would say. You have Comrade Windsor in your mind. He was merely acting as editor while the chief was away hunting sand-eels in the jungles of Texas. In his absence Comrade Windsor and I did our best to keep the old journal booming along, but it lacked the master-hand. But now all is well: Comrade Wilberfloss is once more doing stunts at the old stand. You may speak as freely before him as you would before well, let us say Comrade Parker."

"Who are you, then, if this gentleman is the editor?"

"I am the proprietor."

"I understood that a Mr. White was the proprietor."

"Not so," said Psmith. "There was a time when that was the case, but not now. Things move so swiftly in New York journalistic matters that a man may well be excused for not keeping abreast of the times, especially one who, like yourself, is interested in politics and house-ownership rather than in literature. Are you sure you won't sit down?"

Mr. Waring brought his hand down with a bang on the table, causing

Mr. Wilberfloss to leap a clear two inches from his chair.

"What are you doing it for?" he demanded explosively. "I tell you, you had better quit it. It isn't healthy."

Psmith shook his head.

"You are merely stating in other—and, if I may say so, inferior—words what Comrade Parker said to us. I did not object to giving up valuable time to listen to Comrade Parker. He is a fascinating conversationalist, and it was a privilege to hob-nob with him. But if you are merely intending to cover the ground covered by him, I fear I must remind you that this is one of our busy days. Have you no new light to fling upon the subject?"

Mr. Waring wiped his forehead. He was playing a lost game, and he was not the sort of man who plays lost games well. The Waring type is dangerous when it is winning, but it is apt to crumple up against strong defence.

His next words proved his demoralisation.

"I'll sue you for libel," said he.

Psmith looked at him admiringly.

"Say no more," he said, "for you will never beat that. For pure richness and whimsical humour it stands alone. During the past seven weeks you have been endeavouring in your cheery fashion to blot the editorial staff of this paper off the face of the earth in a variety of ingenious and entertaining ways; and now you propose to sue us for libel! I wish Comrade Windsor could have heard you say that. It would have hit him right."

Mr. Waring accepted the invitation he had refused before. He sat down.

"What are you going to do?" he said.

It was the white flag. The fight had gone out of him.

Psmith leaned back in his chair.

"I'll tell you," he said. "I've thought the whole thing out. The right plan would be to put the complete kybosh (if I may use the expression) on your chances of becoming an alderman. On the other hand, I have been studying the papers of late, and it seems to me that it doesn't much matter who gets elected. Of course the opposition papers may have allowed their zeal to run away with them, but even assuming that to be the case, the other candidates appear to be a pretty fair contingent of blighters. If I were a native of New York, perhaps I might take a more fervid interest in the matter, but as I am merely passing through your beautiful little city, it doesn't seem to me to make any very substantial difference who gets in. To be absolutely candid, my view of the thing is this. If the People are chumps enough to elect you, then they deserve you. I hope I don't hurt your feelings in any way. I am merely stating my own individual opinion."

Mr. Waring made no remark.

"The only thing that really interests me," resumed Psmith, "is the matter of these tenements. I shall shortly be leaving this country to resume the strangle-hold on Learning which I relinquished at the beginning of the Long Vacation. If I were to depart without bringing off improvements down Pleasant Street way, I shouldn't be able to enjoy my meals. The startled cry would go round Cambridge: 'Something is the matter with Psmith. He is off his feed. He should try Blenkinsop's Balm for the Bilious.' But no balm would do me any good. I should simply droop and fade slowly away like a neglected lily. And you wouldn't like that, Comrade Wilberfloss, would you?"

Mr. Wilberfloss, thus suddenly pulled into the conversation, again leaped in his seat.

"What I propose to do," continued Psmith, without waiting for an answer, "is to touch you for the good round sum of five thousand and three dollars."

Mr. Waring half rose.

"Five thousand dollars!"

"Five thousand and three dollars," said Psmith. "It may possibly have escaped your memory, but a certain minion of yours, one J. Repetto, utterly ruined a practically new hat of mine. If you think that I can afford to come to New York and scatter hats about as if they were mere dross, you are making the culminating error of a misspent life. Three dollars are what I need for a new one. The balance of your cheque, the five thousand, I propose to apply to making those tenements fit for a tolerably fastidious pig to live in."

"Five thousand!" cried Mr. Waring. "It's monstrous."

"It isn't," said Psmith. "It's more or less of a minimum. I have made inquiries. So out with the good old cheque-book, and let's all be jolly."

"I have no cheque-book with me."

"*I* have," said Psmith, producing one from a drawer. "Cross out the name of my bank, substitute yours, and fate cannot touch us."

Mr. Waring hesitated for a moment, then capitulated. Psmith watched, as he wrote, with an indulgent and fatherly eye.

"Finished?" he said. "Comrade Maloney."

"Youse hollering fer me?" asked that youth, appearing at the door.

"Bet your life I am, Comrade Maloney. Have you ever seen an untamed mustang of the prairie?"

"Nope. But I've read about dem."

"Well, run like one down to Wall Street with this cheque, and pay it in to my account at the International Bank."

Pugsy disappeared.

"Cheques," said Psmith, "have been known to be stopped. Who knows but what, on reflection, you might not have changed your mind?"

"What guarantee have I," asked Mr. Waring, "that these attacks on me in your paper will stop?"

"If you like," said Psmith, "I will write you a note to that effect. But it will not be necessary. I propose, with Comrade Wilberfloss's assistance, to restore *Cosy Moments* to its old style. Some days ago the editor of Comrade Windsor's late daily paper called up on the telephone and asked to speak to him. I explained the painful circumstances, and, later, went round and hob-nobbed with the great man. A very pleasant fellow. He asks to re-engage Comrade Windsor's services at a pretty sizeable salary, so, as far as our prison expert is concerned, all may be said to be well. He has got where he wanted. *Cosy Moments* may therefore ease up a bit. If, at about the beginning of next month, you should hear a deafening squeal of joy ring through this city, it will be the infants of New York and their parents receiving the news that *Cosy Moments* stands where it did. May I count on your services, Comrade Wilberfloss? Excellent. I see I may. Then perhaps you would not mind passing the word round among Comrades Asher, Waterman, and the rest of the squad, and telling them to burnish their brains and be ready to wade in at a moment's notice. I fear you will have a pretty tough job roping in the old subscribers again, but it can be done. I look to you, Comrade Wilberfloss. Are you on?"

Mr. Wilberfloss, wriggling in his chair, intimated that he was.

CONCLUSION

IT was a drizzly November evening. The streets of Cambridge were a compound of mud, mist, and melancholy. But in Psmith's rooms the fire burned brightly, the kettle droned, and all, as the proprietor had just observed, was joy, jollity, and song. Psmith, in pyjamas and a college blazer, was lying on the sofa. Mike, who had been playing football, was reclining in a comatose state in an armchair by the fire.

"How pleasant it would be," said Psmith dreamily, "if all our friends on the other side of the Atlantic could share this very peaceful moment with us! Or perhaps not quite all. Let us say, Comrade Windsor in the chair over there, Comrades Brady and Maloney on the table, and our old pal Wilberfloss sharing the floor with B. Henderson Asher, Bat Jarvis, and the cats. By the way, I think it would be a graceful act if you were to write to Comrade Jarvis from time to time telling him how your Angoras are getting on. He regards you as the World's Most Prominent Citizen. A line from you every now and then would sweeten the lad's existence."

Mike stirred sleepily in his chair.

"What?" he said drowsily.

"Never mind, Comrade Jackson. Let us pass lightly on. I am filled with a strange content to-night. I may be wrong, but it seems to me that all is singularly to de good, as Comrade Maloney would put it. Advices from Comrade Windsor inform me that that prince of blighters, Waring, was rejected by an intelligent electorate. Those keen, clear-sighted citizens refused to vote for him to an extent that you could notice without a microscope. Still, he has one consolation. He owns what, when the improvements are completed, will be the finest and most commodious tenement houses in New York. Millionaires will stop at them instead of going to the Plaza. Are you asleep, Comrade Jackson?"

"Um-m," said Mike.

"That is excellent. You could not be better employed. Keep listening. Comrade Windsor also stated—as indeed did the sporting papers—that Comrade Brady put it all over friend Eddie Wood, administering the sleep-producer in the eighth round. My authorities are silent as to whether or not the lethal blow was a half-scissor hook, but I presume such to have been the case. The Kid is now definitely matched against Comrade Garvin for the championship, and the experts seem to think that he should win. He is a stout fellow, is Comrade Brady, and I hope he wins through. He will probably come to England later on. When he does, we must show him round. I don't think you ever met him, did you, Comrade Jackson?"

"Ur-r," said Mike.

"Say no more," said Psmith. "I take you."

He reached out for a cigarette.

"These," he said, comfortably, "are the moments in life to which we look back with that wistful pleasure. What of my boyhood at Eton? Do I remember with the keenest joy the brain-tourneys in the old form-room, and the bally rot which used to take place on the Fourth of June? No. Burned deeply into my memory is a certain hot bath I took after one of the foulest cross-country runs that ever occurred outside Dante's Inferno. So with the present moment. This peaceful scene, Comrade Jackson, will remain with me when I have forgotten that such a person as Comrade Repetto ever existed. These are the real *Cosy Moments.* And while on that subject you will be glad to hear that the little sheet is going strong. The man Wilberfloss is a marvel in his way. He appears to have gathered in the majority of the old subscribers again. Hopping mad but a brief while ago, they now eat out of his hand. You've really no notion what a feeling of quiet pride it gives you owning a paper. I try not to show it, but I seem to myself to be looking down on the world from some lofty peak. Yesterday night, when I was looking down from the peak without a cap and gown, a proctor slid up. To-day I had to dig down into my jeans for a matter of two plunks. But what of it? Life must inevitably be dotted with these minor tragedies. I do not repine. The whisper goes round, 'Psmith bites the bullet, and wears a brave smile.' Comrade Jackson—"

A snore came from the chair.

Psmith sighed. But he did not repine. He bit the bullet. His eyes closed.

Five minutes later a slight snore came from the sofa, too.

The man behind *Cosy Moments* slept.

THE MAN WITH TWO LEFT FEET

and Other Stories

BILL THE BLOODHOUND

There's a divinity that shapes our ends. Consider the case of Henry Pifield Rice, detective.

I must explain Henry early, to avoid disappointment. If I simply said he was a detective, and let it go at that, I should be obtaining the reader's interest under false pretences. He was really only a sort of detective, a species of sleuth. At Stafford's International Investigation Bureau, in the Strand, where he was employed, they did not require him to solve mysteries which had baffled the police. He had never measured a footprint in his life, and what he did not know about bloodstains would have filled a library. The sort of job they gave Henry was to stand outside a restaurant in the rain, and note what time someone inside left it. In short, it is not 'Pifield Rice, Investigator. No. 1.—The Adventure of the Maharajah's Ruby' that I submit to your notice, but the unsensational doings of a quite commonplace young man, variously known to his comrades at the Bureau as 'Fathead', 'That blighter what's-his-name', and 'Here, you!'

Henry lived in a boarding-house in Guildford Street. One day a new girl came to the boarding-house, and sat next to Henry at meals. Her name was Alice Weston. She was small and quiet, and rather pretty. They got on splendidly. Their conversation, at first confined to the weather and the moving-pictures, rapidly became more intimate. Henry was surprised to find that she was on the stage, in the chorus. Previous chorus-girls at the boarding-house had been of a more pronounced type—good girls, but noisy, and apt to wear beauty-spots. Alice Weston was different.

'I'm rehearsing at present,' she said. 'I'm going out on tour next month in "The Girl From Brighton". What do you do, Mr Rice?'

Henry paused for a moment before replying. He knew how sensational he was going to be.

'I'm a detective.'

Usually, when he told girls his profession, squeaks of amazed admiration greeted him. Now he was chagrined to perceive in the brown eyes that met his distinct disapproval.

'What's the matter?' he said, a little anxiously, for even at this early stage in their acquaintance he was conscious of a strong desire to win her approval. 'Don't you like detectives?'

'I don't know. Somehow I shouldn't have thought you were one.'

This restored Henry's equanimity somewhat. Naturally a detective does not want to look like a detective and give the whole thing away right at the start.

'I think—you won't be offended?'

'Go on.'

'I've always looked on it as rather a *sneaky* job.'

'Sneaky!' moaned Henry.

'Well, creeping about, spying on people.'

Henry was appalled. She had defined his own trade to a nicety. There might be detectives whose work was above this reproach, but he was a confirmed creeper, and he knew it. It wasn't his fault. The boss told him to creep, and he crept. If he declined to creep, he would be sacked *instanter*. It was hard, and yet he felt the sting of her words, and in his bosom the first seeds of dissatisfaction with his occupation took root.

You might have thought that this frankness on the girl's part would have kept Henry from falling in love with her. Certainly the dignified thing would have been to change his seat at table, and take his meals next to someone who appreciated the romance of detective work a little more. But no, he remained where he was, and presently Cupid, who never shoots with a surer aim than through the steam of boarding-house hash, sniped him where he sat.

He proposed to Alice Weston. She refused him.

'It's not because I'm not fond of you. I think you're the nicest man I ever met.' A good deal of assiduous attention had enabled Henry to win this place in her affections. He had worked patiently and well before actually putting his fortune to the test. 'I'd marry you tomorrow if things were different. But I'm on the stage, and I mean to stick there. Most of the girls want to get off it, but not me. And one thing I'll never do is marry someone who isn't in the profession. My sister Genevieve did, and look what happened to her. She married a commercial traveller, and take it from me he travelled. She never saw him for more than five minutes in the year, except when he was selling gent's hosiery in the same town where she was doing her refined speciality, and then he'd just wave his hand and whiz by, and start travelling again. My husband has got to be close by, where I can see him. I'm sorry, Henry, but I know I'm right.'

It seemed final, but Henry did not wholly despair. He was a resolute young man. You have to be to wait outside restaurants in the rain for any length of time.

He had an inspiration. He sought out a dramatic agent.

'I want to go on the stage, in musical comedy.'

'Let's see you dance.'

'I can't dance.'

'Sing,' said the agent. 'Stop singing,' added the agent, hastily.

'You go away and have a nice cup of hot tea,' said the agent, soothingly, 'and you'll be as right as anything in the morning.'

Henry went away.

A few days later, at the Bureau, his fellow-detective Simmonds hailed him.

'Here, you! The boss wants you. Buck up!'

Mr Stafford was talking into the telephone. He replaced the receiver as Henry entered.

'Oh, Rice, here's a woman wants her husband shadowed while he's on the road. He's an actor. I'm sending you. Go to this address, and get photographs and all particulars. You'll have to catch the eleven o'clock train on Friday.'

'Yes, sir.'

'He's in "The Girl From Brighton" company. They open at Bristol.'

It sometimes seemed to Henry as if Fate did it on purpose. If the commission had had to do with any other company, it would have been well enough, for, professionally speaking, it was the most important with which he had ever been entrusted. If he had never met Alice Weston, and heard her views upon detective work, he would have been pleased and flattered. Things being as they were, it was Henry's considered opinion that Fate had slipped one over on him.

In the first place, what torture to be always near her, unable to reveal himself; to watch her while she disported herself in the company of other men. He would be disguised, and she would not recognize him; but he would recognize her, and his sufferings would be dreadful.

In the second place, to have to do his creeping about and spying practically in her presence—

Still, business was business.

At five minutes to eleven on the morning named he was at the station, a false beard and spectacles shielding his identity from the public eye. If you had asked him he would have said that he was a Scotch business man. As a matter of fact, he looked far more like a motor-car coming through a haystack.

The platform was crowded. Friends of the company had come to see the company off. Henry looked on discreetly from behind a stout porter, whose bulk formed a capital screen. In spite of himself, he was impressed. The stage at close quarters always thrilled him. He recognized celebrities. The fat man in the brown suit was Walter Jelliffe, the comedian and star of the company. He stared keenly at him through the spectacles. Others of the famous were scattered about. He saw Alice. She was talking to a man with a face like a hatchet, and smiling, too, as if she enjoyed it. Behind the matted foliage which he had inflicted on his face, Henry's teeth came together with a snap.

In the weeks that followed, as he dogged 'The Girl From Brighton' company from town to town, it would be difficult to say whether Henry was happy or unhappy. On the one hand, to realize that Alice was so near and yet so inaccessible was a constant source of misery; yet, on the other, he could not but admit that he was having the very dickens of a time, loafing round the country like this.

He was made for this sort of life, he considered. Fate had placed him in a London office, but what he really enjoyed was this unfettered travel. Some gipsy strain in him rendered even the obvious discomforts of theatrical touring agreeable. He liked catching trains; he liked invading strange hotels; above all, he revelled in the artistic pleasure of watching unsuspecting fellow-men as if they were so many ants.

That was really the best part of the whole thing. It was all very well for Alice to talk about creeping and spying, but, if you considered it without bias, there was nothing degrading about it at all. It was an art. It took brains and a genius for disguise to make a man a successful creeper and spyer. You couldn't simply say to yourself, 'I will creep.' If you attempted to do it in your own person, you would be detected instantly. You had to be an adept at masking your personality. You had to be one man at Bristol and another quite different man at Hull—especially if, like Henry, you were of a gregarious disposition, and liked the society of actors.

The stage had always fascinated Henry. To meet even minor members of the profession off the boards gave him a thrill. There was a resting juvenile, of fit-up calibre, at his boarding-house who could always get a shilling out of him simply by talking about how he had jumped in and saved the show at the hamlets which he had visited in the course of his wanderings. And on this 'Girl From Brighton' tour he was in constant touch with men who really amounted to something. Walter Jelliffe had been a celebrity when Henry was going to school; and Sidney Crane, the baritone, and others of the lengthy cast, were all players not unknown in London. Henry courted them assiduously.

It had not been hard to scrape acquaintance with them. The principals of the company always put up at the best hotel, and—his expenses being paid by his employer—so did Henry. It was the easiest thing possible to bridge with a well-timed whisky-and-soda the gulf between non-acquaintance and warm friendship. Walter Jelliffe, in particular, was peculiarly accessible. Every time Henry accosted him—as a different individual, of course—and renewed in a fresh disguise the friendship which he had enjoyed at the last town, Walter Jelliffe met him more than half-way.

It was in the sixth week of the tour that the comedian, promoting him from mere casual acquaintanceship, invited him to come up to his room and smoke a cigar.

Henry was pleased and flattered. Jelliffe was a personage, always surrounded by admirers, and the compliment was consequently of a high order.

He lit his cigar. Among his friends at the Green-Room Club it was unanimously held that Walter Jelliffe's cigars brought him within the scope of the law forbidding the carrying of concealed weapons; but Henry would have smoked the gift of such a man if it had been a cabbage-leaf. He puffed away contentedly. He was made up as an old Indian colonel that week, and he complimented his host on the aroma with a fine old-world courtesy.

Walter Jelliffe seemed gratified.

'Quite comfortable?' he asked.

'Quite, I thank you,' said Henry, fondling his silver moustache.

'That's right. And now tell me, old man, which of us is it you're trailing?'

Henry nearly swallowed his cigar.

'What do you mean?'

'Oh, come,' protested Jelliffe; 'there's no need to keep it up with me.

I know you're a detective. The question is, Who's the man you're after?

That's what we've all been wondering all this time.'

All! They had all been wondering! It was worse than Henry could have imagined. Till now he had pictured his position with regard to 'The Girl From Brighton' company rather as that of some scientist who, seeing but unseen, keeps a watchful eye on the denizens of a drop of water under his microscope. And they had all detected him—every one of them.

It was a stunning blow. If there was one thing on which Henry prided himself it was the impenetrability of his disguises. He might be slow; he might be on the stupid side; but he could disguise himself. He had a variety of disguises, each designed to befog the public more hopelessly than the last.

Going down the street, you would meet a typical commercial traveller, dapper and alert. Anon, you encountered a heavily bearded Australian. Later, maybe, it was a courteous old retired colonel who stopped you and inquired the way to Trafalgar Square. Still later, a rather flashy individual of the sporting type asked you for a match for his cigar. Would you have suspected for one instant that each of these widely differing personalities was in reality one man?

Certainly you would.

Henry did not know it, but he had achieved in the eyes of the small servant who answered the front-door bell at his boarding-house a well-established reputation as a humorist of the more practical kind. It was his habit to try his disguises on her. He would ring the bell, inquire for the landlady, and when Bella had gone, leap up the stairs to his room. Here he would remove the disguise, resume his normal appearance, and come downstairs again, humming a careless air. Bella, meanwhile, in the kitchen, would be confiding to her ally the cook that 'Mr Rice had jest come in, lookin' sort o' funny again'.

He sat and gaped at Walter Jelliffe. The comedian regarded him curiously.

'You look at least a hundred years old,' he said. 'What are you made up as? A piece of Gorgonzola?'

Henry glanced hastily at the mirror. Yes, he did look rather old. He must have overdone some of the lines on his forehead. He looked something between a youngish centenarian and a nonagenarian who had seen a good deal of trouble.

'If you knew how you were demoralizing the company,' Jelliffe went on, 'you would drop it. As steady and quiet a lot of boys as ever you met till you came along. Now they do nothing but bet on what disguise you're going to choose for the next town. I don't see why you need to change so often. You were all right as the Scotchman at Bristol. We were all saying how nice you looked. You should have stuck to that. But what do you do at Hull but roll in in a scrubby moustache and a tweed suit, looking rotten. However, all that is beside the point. It's a free country. If you like to spoil your beauty, I suppose there's no law against it. What I want to know is, who's the man? Whose track are you sniffing on, Bill? You'll pardon my calling you Bill. You're known as Bill the Bloodhound in the company. Who's the man?'

'Never mind,' said Henry.

He was aware, as he made it, that it was not a very able retort, but he was feeling too limp for satisfactory repartee. Criticisms in the Bureau, dealing with his alleged solidity of skull, he did not resent. He attributed them to man's natural desire to chaff his fellow-man. But to be unmasked by the general public in this way was another matter. It struck at the root of all things.

'But I do mind,' objected Jelliffe. 'It's most important. A lot of money hangs on it. We've got a sweepstake on in the company, the holder of the winning name to take the entire receipts. Come on. Who is he?'

Henry rose and made for the door. His feelings were too deep for words. Even a minor detective has his professional pride; and the knowledge that his espionage is being made the basis of sweepstakes by his quarry cuts this to the quick.

'Here, don't go! Where are you going?'

'Back to London,' said Henry, bitterly. 'It's a lot of good my staying here now, isn't it?'

'I should say it was—to me. Don't be in a hurry. You're thinking that, now we know all about you, your utility as a sleuth has waned to some extent. Is that it?'

'Well?'

'Well, why worry? What does it matter to you? You don't get paid by results, do you? Your boss said "Trail along." Well, do it, then. I should hate to lose you. I don't suppose you know it, but you've been the best mascot this tour that I've ever come across. Right from the start we've been playing to enormous business. I'd rather kill a black cat than lose you. Drop the disguises, and stay with us. Come behind all you want, and be sociable.'

A detective is only human. The less of a detective, the more human he is. Henry was not much of a detective, and his human traits were consequently highly developed. From a boy, he had never been able to resist curiosity. If a crowd collected in the street he always added himself to it, and he would have stopped to gape at a window with 'Watch this window' written on it, if he had been running for his life from wild bulls. He was, and always had been, intensely desirous of some day penetrating behind the scenes of a theatre.

And there was another thing. At last, if he accepted this invitation, he would be able to see and speak to Alice Weston, and interfere with the manoeuvres of the hatchet-faced man, on whom he had brooded with suspicion and jealousy since that first morning at the station. To see Alice! Perhaps, with eloquence, to talk her out of that ridiculous resolve of hers!

'Why, there's something in that,' he said.

'Rather! Well, that's settled. And now, touching that sweep, who *is* it?'

'I can't tell you that. You see, so far as that goes, I'm just where I was before. I can still watch—whoever it is I'm watching.'

'Dash it, so you can. I didn't think of that,' said Jelliffe, who possessed a sensitive conscience. 'Purely between ourselves, it isn't *me*, is it?'

Henry eyed him inscrutably. He could look inscrutable at times.

'Ah!' he said, and left quickly, with the feeling that, however poorly he had shown up during the actual interview, his exit had been good. He might have been a failure in the matter of disguise, but nobody could have put more quiet sinisterness into that 'Ah!' It did much to soothe him and ensure a peaceful night's rest.

On the following night, for the first time in his life, Henry found himself behind the scenes of a theatre, and instantly began to experience all the complex emotions which come to the layman in that situation. That is to say, he felt like a cat which has strayed into a strange hostile back-yard. He was in a new world, inhabited by weird creatures, who flitted about in an eerie semi-darkness, like brightly coloured animals in a cavern.

'The Girl From Brighton' was one of those exotic productions specially designed for the Tired Business Man. It relied for a large measure of its success on the size and appearance of its chorus, and on their constant change of costume. Henry, as a consequence, was the centre of a kaleidoscopic whirl of feminine loveliness, dressed to represent such varying flora and fauna as rabbits, Parisian students, colleens, Dutch peasants, and daffodils. Musical comedy is the Irish stew of the drama. Anything may be put into it, with the certainty that it will improve the general effect.

He scanned the throng for a sight of Alice. Often as he had seen the piece in the course of its six weeks' wandering in the wilderness he had never succeeded in recognizing her from the front of the house. Quite possibly, he thought, she might be on the stage already, hidden in a rose-tree or some other shrub, ready at the signal to burst forth upon the audience in short skirts; for in 'The Girl From Brighton' almost anything could turn suddenly into a chorus-girl.

Then he saw her, among the daffodils. She was not a particularly convincing daffodil, but she looked good to Henry. With wabbling knees he butted his way through the crowd and seized her hand enthusiastically.

'Why, Henry! Where did you come from?'

'I *am* glad to see you!'

'How did you get here?'

'I *am* glad to see you!'

At this point the stage-manager, bellowing from the prompt-box, urged Henry to desist. It is one of the mysteries of behind-the-scenes acoustics that a whisper from any minor member of the company can be heard all over the house, while the stage-manager can burst himself without annoying the audience.

Henry, awed by authority, relapsed into silence. From the unseen stage came the sound of someone singing a song about the moon. June was also mentioned. He recognized the song as one that had always bored him. He disliked the woman who was singing it—a Miss Clarice Weaver, who played the heroine of the piece to Sidney Crane's hero.

In his opinion he was not alone. Miss Weaver was not popular in the company. She had secured the role rather as a testimony of personal esteem from the management than because of any innate ability. She sang badly, acted indifferently, and was uncertain what to do with her hands. All these things might have been forgiven her, but she supplemented them by the crime known in stage circles as 'throwing her weight about'. That is to say, she was hard to please, and, when not pleased, apt to say so in no uncertain voice. To his personal friends Walter Jelliffe had frequently confided that, though not a rich man, he was in the market with a substantial reward for anyone who was man enough to drop a ton of iron on Miss Weaver.

Tonight the song annoyed Henry more than usual, for he knew that very soon the daffodils were due on the stage to clinch the verisimilitude of the scene by dancing the tango with the rabbits. He endeavoured to make the most of the time at his disposal.

'I *am* glad to see you!' he said.

'Sh-h!' said the stage-manager.

Henry was discouraged. Romeo could not have made love under these conditions. And then, just when he was pulling himself together to begin again, she was torn from him by the exigencies of the play.

He wandered moodily off into the dusty semi-darkness. He avoided the prompt-box, whence he could have caught a glimpse of her, being loath to meet the stage-manager just at present.

Walter Jelliffe came up to him, as he sat on a box and brooded on life.

'A little less of the double forte, old man,' he said. 'Miss Weaver has been kicking about the noise on the side. She wanted you thrown out, but I said you were my mascot, and I would die sooner than part with you. But I should go easy on the chest-notes, I think, all the same.'

Henry nodded moodily. He was depressed. He had the feeling, which comes so easily to the intruder behind the scenes, that nobody loved him.

The piece proceeded. From the front of the house roars of laughter indicated the presence on the stage of Walter Jelliffe, while now and then a lethargic silence suggested that Miss Clarice Weaver was in action. From time to time the empty space about him filled with girls dressed in accordance with the exuberant fancy of the producer of the piece. When this happened, Henry would leap from his seat and endeavour to locate Alice; but always, just as he thought he had done so, the hidden orchestra would burst into melody and the chorus would be called to the front.

It was not till late in the second act that he found an opportunity for further speech.

The plot of 'The Girl From Brighton' had by then reached a critical stage. The situation was as follows: The hero, having been disinherited by his wealthy and titled father for falling in love with the heroine, a poor shop-girl, has disguised himself (by wearing a different coloured necktie) and has come in pursuit of her to a well-known seaside resort, where, having disguised herself by changing her dress, she is serving as a waitress in the Rotunda, on the Esplanade. The family butler, disguised as a Bath-chair man, has followed the hero, and the wealthy and titled father, disguised as an Italian opera-singer, has come to the place for a reason which, though extremely sound, for the moment eludes the memory. Anyhow, he is there, and they all meet on the Esplanade. Each recognizes the other, but thinks he himself is unrecognized. *Exeunt* all, hurriedly, leaving the heroine alone on the stage.

It is a crisis in the heroine's life. She meets it bravely. She sings a song entitled 'My Honolulu Queen', with chorus of Japanese girls and Bulgarian officers.

Alice was one of the Japanese girls.

She was standing a little apart from the other Japanese girls. Henry was on her with a bound. Now was his time. He felt keyed up, full of persuasive words. In the interval which had elapsed since their last conversation yeasty emotions had been playing the dickens with his self-control. It is practically impossible for a novice, suddenly introduced behind the scenes of a musical comedy, not to fall in love with somebody; and, if he is already in love, his fervour is increased to a dangerous point.

Henry felt that it was now or never. He forgot that it was perfectly possible—indeed, the reasonable course—to wait till the performance was over, and renew his appeal to Alice to marry him on the way back to her hotel. He had the feeling that he had got just about a quarter of a minute. Quick action! That was Henry's slogan.

He seized her hand.

'Alice!'

'Sh-h!' hissed the stage-manager.

'Listen! I love you. I'm crazy about you. What does it matter whether
I'm on the stage or not? I love you.'

'Stop that row there!'

'Won't you marry me?'

She looked at him. It seemed to him that she hesitated.

'Cut it out!' bellowed the stage-manager, and Henry cut it out.

And at this moment, when his whole fate hung in the balance, there came from the stage that devastating high note which is the sign that the solo is over and that the chorus are now about to mobilize. As if drawn by some magnetic power, she suddenly receded from him, and went on to the stage.

A man in Henry's position and frame of mind is not responsible for his actions. He saw nothing but her; he was blind to the fact that important manoeuvres were in progress. All he understood was that she was going from him, and that he must stop her and get this thing settled.

He clutched at her. She was out of range, and getting farther away every instant.

He sprang forward.

The advice that should be given to every young man starting life is—if you happen to be behind the scenes at a theatre, never spring forward. The whole architecture of the place is designed to undo those who so spring. Hours before, the stage-carpenters have laid their traps, and in the semi-darkness you cannot but fall into them.

The trap into which Henry fell was a raised board. It was not a very highly-raised board. It was not so deep as a well, nor so wide as a church-door, but 'twas enough—it served. Stubbing it squarely with his toe, Henry shot forward, all arms and legs.

It is the instinct of Man, in such a situation, to grab at the nearest support. Henry grabbed at the Hotel Superba, the pride of the Esplanade. It was a thin wooden edifice, and it supported him for perhaps a tenth of a second. Then he staggered with it into the limelight, tripped over a Bulgarian officer who was inflating himself for a deep note, and finally fell in a complicated heap as exactly in the centre of the stage as if he had been a star of years' standing.

It went well; there was no question of that. Previous audiences had always been rather cold towards this particular song, but this one got on its feet and yelled for more. From all over the house came rapturous demands that Henry should go back and do it again.

But Henry was giving no encores. He rose to his feet, a little stunned, and automatically began to dust his clothes. The orchestra, unnerved by this unrehearsed infusion of new business, had stopped playing. Bulgarian officers and Japanese girls alike seemed unequal to the situation. They stood about, waiting for the next thing to break loose. From somewhere far away came faintly the voice of the stage-manager inventing new words, new combinations of words, and new throat noises.

And then Henry, massaging a stricken elbow, was aware of Miss Weaver at his side. Looking up, he caught Miss Weaver's eye.

A familiar stage-direction of melodrama reads, 'Exit cautious through gap in hedge'. It was Henry's first appearance on any stage, but he did it like a veteran.

'My dear fellow,' said Walter Jelliffe. The hour was midnight, and he was sitting in Henry's bedroom at the hotel. Leaving the theatre, Henry had gone to bed almost instinctively. Bed seemed the only haven for him. 'My dear fellow, don't apologize. You have put me under lasting obligations. In the first place, with your unerring sense of the stage, you saw just the spot where the piece needed livening up, and you livened it up. That was good; but far better was it that you also sent our Miss Weaver into violent hysterics, from which she emerged to hand in her notice. She leaves us tomorrow.'

Henry was appalled at the extent of the disaster for which he was responsible.

'What will you do?'

'Do! Why, it's what we have all been praying for—a miracle which should eject Miss Weaver. It needed a genius like you to come to bring it off. Sidney Crane's wife can play the part without rehearsal. She understudied it all last season in London. Crane has just been speaking to her on the phone, and she is catching the night express.'

Henry sat up in bed.

'What!'

'What's the trouble now?'

'Sidney Crane's wife?'

'What about her?'

A bleakness fell upon Henry's soul.

'She was the woman who was employing me. Now I shall be taken off the job and have to go back to London.'

'You don't mean that it was really Crane's wife?'

Jelliffe was regarding him with a kind of awe.

'Laddie,' he said, in a hushed voice, 'you almost scare me. There seems to be no limit to your powers as a mascot. You fill the house every night, you get rid of the Weaver woman, and now you tell me this. I drew Crane in the sweep, and I would have taken twopence for my chance of winning it.'

'I shall get a telegram from my boss tomorrow recalling me.'

'Don't go. Stick with me. Join the troupe.'

Henry stared.

'What do you mean? I can't sing or act.'

Jelliffe's voice thrilled with earnestness.

'My boy, I can go down the Strand and pick up a hundred fellows who can sing and act. I don't want them. I turn them away. But a seventh son of a seventh son like you, a human horseshoe like you, a king of mascots like you—they don't make them nowadays. They've lost the pattern. If you like to come with me I'll give you a contract for any number of years you suggest. I need you in my business.' He rose. 'Think it over, laddie, and let me know tomorrow. Look here upon this picture, and on that. As a sleuth you are poor. You couldn't detect a bass-drum in a telephone-booth. You have no future. You are merely among those present. But as a mascot—my boy, you're the only thing in sight. You can't help succeeding on the stage. You don't have to know how to act. Look at the dozens of good actors who are out of jobs. Why? Unlucky. No other reason. With your luck and a little experience you'll be a star before you know you've begun. Think it over, and let me know in the morning.'

Before Henry's eyes there rose a sudden vision of Alice: Alice no longer unattainable; Alice walking on his arm down the aisle; Alice mending his socks; Alice with her heavenly hands fingering his salary envelope.

'Don't go,' he said. 'Don't go. I'll let you know now.'

* * * * *

The scene is the Strand, hard by Bedford Street; the time, that restful hour of the afternoon when they of the gnarled faces and the bright clothing gather together in groups to tell each other how good they are.

Hark! A voice.

'Rather! Courtneidge and the Guv'nor keep on trying to get me, but I turn them down every time. "No," I said to Malone only yesterday, "not for me! I'm going with old Wally Jelliffe, the same as usual, and there isn't the money in the Mint that'll get me away." Malone got all worked up. He—'

It is the voice of Pifield Rice, actor.

EXTRICATING YOUNG GUSSIE

She sprang it on me before breakfast. There in seven words you have a complete character sketch of my Aunt Agatha. I could go on indefinitely about brutality and lack of consideration. I merely say that she routed me out of bed to listen to her painful story somewhere in the small hours. It can't have been half past eleven when Jeeves, my man, woke me out of the dreamless and broke the news:

'Mrs Gregson to see you, sir.'

I thought she must be walking in her sleep, but I crawled out of bed and got into a dressing-gown. I knew Aunt Agatha well enough to know that, if she had come to see me, she was going to see me. That's the sort of woman she is.

She was sitting bolt upright in a chair, staring into space. When I came in she looked at me in that darn critical way that always makes me feel as if I had gelatine where my spine ought to be. Aunt Agatha is one of those strong-minded women. I should think Queen Elizabeth must have been something like her. She bosses her husband, Spencer Gregson, a battered little chappie on the Stock Exchange. She bosses my cousin, Gussie Mannering-Phipps. She bosses her sister-in-law, Gussie's mother. And, worst of all, she bosses me. She has an eye like a man-eating fish, and she has got moral suasion down to a fine point.

I dare say there are fellows in the world—men of blood and iron, don't you know, and all that sort of thing—whom she couldn't intimidate; but if you're a chappie like me, fond of a quiet life, you simply curl into a ball when you see her coming, and hope for the best. My experience is that when Aunt Agatha wants you to do a thing you do it, or else you find yourself wondering why those fellows in the olden days made such a fuss when they had trouble with the Spanish Inquisition.

'Halloa, Aunt Agatha!' I said

'Bertie,' she said, 'you look a sight. You look perfectly dissipated.'

I was feeling like a badly wrapped brown-paper parcel. I'm never at my best in the early morning. I said so.

'Early morning! I had breakfast three hours ago, and have been walking in the park ever since, trying to compose my thoughts.'

If I ever breakfasted at half past eight I should walk on the

Embankment, trying to end it all in a watery grave.

'I am extremely worried, Bertie. That is why I have come to you.'

And then I saw she was going to start something, and I bleated weakly to Jeeves to bring me tea. But she had begun before I could get it.

'What are your immediate plans, Bertie?'

'Well, I rather thought of tottering out for a bite of lunch later on, and then possibly staggering round to the club, and after that, if I felt strong enough, I might trickle off to Walton Heath for a round of golf.'

I am not interested in your totterings and tricklings. I mean, have you any important engagements in the next week or so?'

I scented danger.

'Rather,' I said. 'Heaps! Millions! Booked solid!'

'What are they?'

'I—er—well, I don't quite know.'

'I thought as much. You have no engagements. Very well, then, I want you to start immediately for America.'

'America!'

Do not lose sight of the fact that all this was taking place on an empty stomach, shortly after the rising of the lark.

'Yes, America. I suppose even you have heard of America?'

'But why America?'

'Because that is where your Cousin Gussie is. He is in New York, and I can't get at him.'

'What's Gussie been doing?'

'Gussie is making a perfect idiot of himself.'

To one who knew young Gussie as well as I did, the words opened up a wide field for speculation.

'In what way?'

'He has lost his head over a creature.'

On past performances this rang true. Ever since he arrived at man's estate Gussie had been losing his head over creatures. He's that sort of chap. But, as the creatures never seemed to lose their heads over him, it had never amounted to much.

'I imagine you know perfectly well why Gussie went to America, Bertie.

You know how wickedly extravagant your Uncle Cuthbert was.'

She alluded to Gussie's governor, the late head of the family, and I am bound to say she spoke the truth. Nobody was fonder of old Uncle Cuthbert than I was, but everybody knows that, where money was concerned, he was the most complete chump in the annals of the nation. He had an expensive thirst. He never backed a horse that didn't get housemaid's knee in the middle of the race. He had a system of beating the bank at Monte Carlo which used to make the administration hang out the bunting and ring the joy-bells when he was sighted in the offing. Take him for all in all, dear old Uncle Cuthbert was as willing a spender as ever called the family lawyer a bloodsucking vampire because he wouldn't let Uncle Cuthbert cut down the timber to raise another thousand.

'He left your Aunt Julia very little money for a woman in her position. Beechwood requires a great deal of keeping up, and poor dear Spencer, though he does his best to help, has not unlimited resources. It was clearly understood why Gussie went to America. He is not clever, but he is very good-looking, and, though he has no title, the Mannering-Phippses are one of the best and oldest families in England. He had some excellent letters of introduction, and when he wrote home to say that he had met the most charming and beautiful girl in the world I felt quite happy. He continued to rave about her for several mails, and then this morning a letter has come from him in which he says, quite casually as a sort of afterthought, that he knows we are broadminded enough not to think any the worse of her because she is on the vaudeville stage.'

'Oh, I say!'

'It was like a thunderbolt. The girl's name, it seems, is Ray Denison, and according to Gussie she does something which he describes as a single on the big time. What this degraded performance may be I have not the least notion. As a further recommendation he states that she lifted them out of their seats at Mosenstein's last week. Who she may be, and how or why, and who or what Mr Mosenstein may be, I cannot tell you.'

'By jove,' I said, 'it's like a sort of thingummybob, isn't it? A sort of fate, what?'

'I fail to understand you.'

'Well, Aunt Julia, you know, don't you know? Heredity, and so forth. What's bred in the bone will come out in the wash, and all that kind of thing, you know.'

'Don't be absurd, Bertie.'

That was all very well, but it was a coincidence for all that. Nobody ever mentions it, and the family have been trying to forget it for twenty-five years, but it's a known fact that my Aunt Julia, Gussie's mother, was a vaudeville artist once, and a very good one, too, I'm told. She was playing in pantomime at Drury Lane when Uncle Cuthbert saw her first. It was before my time, of course, and long before I was old enough to take notice the family had made the best of it, and Aunt Agatha had pulled up her socks and put in a lot of educative work, and with a microscope you couldn't tell Aunt Julia from a genuine dyed-in-the-wool aristocrat. Women adapt themselves so quickly!

I have a pal who married Daisy Trimble of the Gaiety, and when I meet her now I feel like walking out of her presence backwards. But there the thing was, and you couldn't get away from it. Gussie had vaudeville blood in him, and it looked as if he were reverting to type, or whatever they call it.

'By Jove,' I said, for I am interested in this heredity stuff, 'perhaps the thing is going to be a regular family tradition, like you read about in books—a sort of Curse of the Mannering-Phippses, as it were. Perhaps each head of the family's going to marry into vaudeville for ever and ever. Unto the what-d'you-call-it generation, don't you know?'

'Please do not be quite idiotic, Bertie. There is one head of the family who is certainly not going to do it, and that is Gussie. And you are going to America to stop him.'

'Yes, but why me?'

'Why you? You are too vexing, Bertie. Have you no sort of feeling for the family? You are too lazy to try to be a credit to yourself, but at least you can exert yourself to prevent Gussie's disgracing us. You are going to America because you are Gussie's cousin, because you have always been his closest friend, because you are the only one of the family who has absolutely nothing to occupy his time except golf and night clubs.'

'I play a lot of auction.'

'And as you say, idiotic gambling in low dens. If you require another reason, you are going because I ask you as a personal favour.'

What she meant was that, if I refused, she would exert the full bent of her natural genius to make life a Hades for me. She held me with her glittering eye. I have never met anyone who can give a better imitation of the Ancient Mariner.

'So you will start at once, won't you, Bertie?'

I didn't hesitate.

'Rather!' I said. 'Of course I will'

Jeeves came in with the tea.

'Jeeves,' I said, 'we start for America on Saturday.'

'Very good, sir,' he said; 'which suit will you wear?'

New York is a large city conveniently situated on the edge of America, so that you step off the liner right on to it without an effort. You can't lose your way. You go out of a barn and down some stairs, and there you are, right in among it. The only possible objection any reasonable chappie could find to the place is that they loose you into it from the boat at such an ungodly hour.

I left Jeeves to get my baggage safely past an aggregation of suspicious-minded pirates who were digging for buried treasures among my new shirts, and drove to Gussie's hotel, where I requested the squad of gentlemanly clerks behind the desk to produce him.

That's where I got my first shock. He wasn't there. I pleaded with them to think again, and they thought again, but it was no good. No Augustus Mannering-Phipps on the premises.

I admit I was hard hit. There I was alone in a strange city and no signs of Gussie. What was the next step? I am never one of the master minds in the early morning; the old bean doesn't somehow seem to get into its stride till pretty late in the p.m.s, and I couldn't think what to do. However, some instinct took me through a door at the back of the lobby, and I found myself in a large room with an enormous picture stretching across the whole of one wall, and under the picture a counter, and behind the counter divers chappies in white, serving drinks. They have barmen, don't you know, in New York, not barmaids. Rum idea!

I put myself unreservedly into the hands of one of the white chappies. He was a friendly soul, and I told him the whole state of affairs. I asked him what he thought would meet the case.

He said that in a situation of that sort he usually prescribed a 'lightning whizzer', an invention of his own. He said this was what rabbits trained on when they were matched against grizzly bears, and there was only one instance on record of the bear having lasted three rounds. So I tried a couple, and, by Jove! the man was perfectly right. As I drained the second a great load seemed to fall from my heart, and I went out in quite a braced way to have a look at the city.

I was surprised to find the streets quite full. People were bustling along as if it were some reasonable hour and not the grey dawn. In the tramcars they were absolutely standing on each other's necks. Going to business or something, I take it. Wonderful johnnies!

The odd part of it was that after the first shock of seeing all this frightful energy the thing didn't seem so strange. I've spoken to fellows since who have been to New York, and they tell me they found it just the same. Apparently there's something in the air, either the ozone or the phosphates or something, which makes you sit up and take notice. A kind of zip, as it were. A sort of bally freedom, if you know what I mean, that gets into your blood and bucks you up, and makes you feel that—

God's in His Heaven: All's right with the world,

and you don't care if you've got odd socks on. I can't express it better than by saying that the thought uppermost in my mind, as I walked about the place they call Times Square, was that there were three thousand miles of deep water between me and my Aunt Agatha.

It's a funny thing about looking for things. If you hunt for a needle in a haystack you don't find it. If you don't give a darn whether you ever see the needle or not it runs into you the first time you lean against the stack. By the time I had strolled up and down once or twice, seeing the sights and letting the white chappie's corrective permeate my system, I was feeling that I wouldn't care if Gussie and I never met again, and I'm dashed if I didn't suddenly catch sight of the old lad, as large as life, just turning in at a doorway down the street.

I called after him, but he didn't hear me, so I legged it in pursuit and caught him going into an office on the first floor. The name on the door was Abe Riesbitter, Vaudeville Agent, and from the other side of the door came the sound of many voices.

He turned and stared at me.

'Bertie! What on earth are you doing? Where have you sprung from? When did you arrive?'

'Landed this morning. I went round to your hotel, but they said you weren't there. They had never heard of you.'

'I've changed my name. I call myself George Wilson.'

'Why on earth?'

'Well, you try calling yourself Augustus Mannering-Phipps over here, and see how it strikes you. You feel a perfect ass. I don't know what it is about America, but the broad fact is that it's not a place where you can call yourself Augustus Mannering-Phipps. And there's another reason. I'll tell you later. Bertie, I've fallen in love with the dearest girl in the world.'

The poor old nut looked at me in such a deuced cat-like way, standing with his mouth open, waiting to be congratulated, that I simply hadn't the heart to tell him that I knew all about that already, and had come over to the country for the express purpose of laying him a stymie.

So I congratulated him.

'Thanks awfully, old man,' he said. 'It's a bit premature, but I fancy it's going to be all right. Come along in here, and I'll tell you about it.'

'What do you want in this place? It looks a rummy spot.'

'Oh, that's part of the story. I'll tell you the whole thing.'

We opened the door marked 'Waiting Room'. I never saw such a crowded place in my life. The room was packed till the walls bulged.

Gussie explained.

'Pros,' he said, 'music-hall artistes, you know, waiting to see old Abe Riesbitter. This is September the first, vaudeville's opening day. The early fall,' said Gussie, who is a bit of a poet in his way, 'is vaudeville's springtime. All over the country, as August wanes, sparkling comediennes burst into bloom, the sap stirs in the veins of tramp cyclists, and last year's contortionists, waking from their summer sleep, tie themselves tentatively into knots. What I mean is, this is the beginning of the new season, and everybody's out hunting for bookings.'

'But what do you want here?'

'Oh, I've just got to see Abe about something. If you see a fat man with about fifty-seven chins come out of that door there grab him, for that'll be Abe. He's one of those fellows who advertise each step up they take in the world by growing another chin. I'm told that way back in the nineties he only had two. If you do grab Abe, remember that he knows me as George Wilson.'

'You said that you were going to explain that George Wilson business to me, Gussie, old man.'

'Well, it's this way—'

At this juncture dear old Gussie broke off short, rose from his seat, and sprang with indescribable vim at an extraordinarily stout chappie who had suddenly appeared. There was the deuce of a rush for him, but Gussie had got away to a good start, and the rest of the singers, dancers, jugglers, acrobats, and refined sketch teams seemed to recognize that he had won the trick, for they ebbed back into their places again, and Gussie and I went into the inner room.

Mr Riesbitter lit a cigar, and looked at us solemnly over his zareba of chins.

'Now, let me tell ya something,' he said to Gussie. 'You lizzun t' me.'

Gussie registered respectful attention. Mr Riesbitter mused for a moment and shelled the cuspidor with indirect fire over the edge of the desk.

'Lizzun t' me,' he said again. 'I seen you rehearse, as I promised Miss Denison I would. You ain't bad for an amateur. You gotta lot to learn, but it's in you. What it comes to is that I can fix you up in the four-a-day, if you'll take thirty-five per. I can't do better than that, and I wouldn't have done that if the little lady hadn't of kep' after me. Take it or leave it. What do you say?'

'I'll take it,' said Gussie, huskily. 'Thank you.'

In the passage outside, Gussie gurgled with joy and slapped me on the back. 'Bertie, old man, it's all right. I'm the happiest man in New York.'

'Now what?'

'Well, you see, as I was telling you when Abe came in, Ray's father used to be in the profession. He was before our time, but I remember hearing about him—Joe Danby. He used to be well known in London before he came over to America. Well, he's a fine old boy, but as obstinate as a mule, and he didn't like the idea of Ray marrying me because I wasn't in the profession. Wouldn't hear of it. Well, you remember at Oxford I could always sing a song pretty well; so Ray got hold of old Riesbitter and made him promise to come and hear me rehearse and get me bookings if he liked my work. She stands high with him. She coached me for weeks, the darling. And now, as you heard him say, he's booked me in the small time at thirty-five dollars a week.'

I steadied myself against the wall. The effects of the restoratives supplied by my pal at the hotel bar were beginning to work off, and I felt a little weak. Through a sort of mist I seemed to have a vision of Aunt Agatha hearing that the head of the Mannering-Phippses was about to appear on the vaudeville stage. Aunt Agatha's worship of the family name amounts to an obsession. The Mannering-Phippses were an old-established clan when William the Conqueror was a small boy going round with bare legs and a catapult. For centuries they have called kings by their first names and helped dukes with their weekly rent; and there's practically nothing a Mannering-Phipps can do that doesn't blot his escutcheon. So what Aunt Agatha would say—beyond saying that it was all my fault—when she learned the horrid news, it was beyond me to imagine.

'Come back to the hotel, Gussie,' I said. 'There's a sportsman there who mixes things he calls "lightning whizzers". Something tells me I need one now. And excuse me for one minute, Gussie. I want to send a cable.'

It was clear to me by now that Aunt Agatha had picked the wrong man for this job of disentangling Gussie from the clutches of the American vaudeville profession. What I needed was reinforcements. For a moment I thought of cabling Aunt Agatha to come over, but reason told me that this would be overdoing it. I wanted assistance, but not so badly as that. I hit what seemed to me the happy mean. I cabled to Gussie's mother and made it urgent.

'What were you cabling about?' asked Gussie, later.

'Oh just to say I had arrived safely, and all that sort of tosh,' I answered.

* * * * *

Gussie opened his vaudeville career on the following Monday at a rummy sort of place uptown where they had moving pictures some of the time and, in between, one or two vaudeville acts. It had taken a lot of careful handling to bring him up to scratch. He seemed to take my sympathy and assistance for granted, and I couldn't let him down. My only hope, which grew as I listened to him rehearsing, was that he would be such a frightful frost at his first appearance that he would never dare to perform again; and, as that would automatically squash the marriage, it seemed best to me to let the thing go on.

He wasn't taking any chances. On the Saturday and Sunday we practically lived in a beastly little music-room at the offices of the publishers whose songs he proposed to use. A little chappie with a hooked nose sucked a cigarette and played the piano all day. Nothing could tire that lad. He seemed to take a personal interest in the thing.

Gussie would cleat his throat and begin:

'There's a great big choo-choo waiting at the deepo.'

THE CHAPPIE (playing chords): 'Is that so? What's it waiting for?'

GUSSIE (rather rattled at the interruption): 'Waiting for me.'

THE CHAPPIE (surprised): For you?'

GUSSIE (sticking to it): 'Waiting for me-e-ee!'

THE CHAPPIE (sceptically): 'You don't say!'

GUSSIE: 'For I'm off to Tennessee.'

THE CHAPPIE (conceding a point): 'Now, I live at Yonkers.'

He did this all through the song. At first poor old Gussie asked him to stop, but the chappie said, No, it was always done. It helped to get pep into the thing. He appealed to me whether the thing didn't want a bit of pep, and I said it wanted all the pep it could get. And the chappie said to Gussie, 'There you are!' So Gussie had to stand it.

The other song that he intended to sing was one of those moon songs. He told me in a hushed voice that he was using it because it was one of the songs that the girl Ray sang when lifting them out of their seats at Mosenstein's and elsewhere. The fact seemed to give it sacred associations for him.

You will scarcely believe me, but the management expected Gussie to show up and start performing at one o'clock in the afternoon. I told him they couldn't be serious, as they must know that he would be rolling out for a bit of lunch at that hour, but Gussie said this was the usual thing in the four-a-day, and he didn't suppose he would ever get any lunch again until he landed on the big time. I was just condoling with him, when I found that he was taking it for granted that I should be there at one o'clock, too. My idea had been that I should look in at night, when—if he survived—he would be coming up for the fourth time; but I've never deserted a pal in distress, so I said good-bye to the little lunch I'd been planning at a rather decent tavern I'd discovered on Fifth Avenue, and trailed along. They were showing pictures when I reached my seat. It was one of those Western films, where the cowboy jumps on his horse and rides across country at a hundred and fifty miles an hour to escape the sheriff, not knowing, poor chump! that he might just as well stay where he is, the sheriff having a horse of his own which can do three hundred miles an hour without coughing. I was just going to close my eyes and try to forget till they put Gussie's name up when I discovered that I was sitting next to a deucedly pretty girl.

No, let me be honest. When I went in I had seen that there was a deucedly pretty girl sitting in that particular seat, so I had taken the next one. What happened now was that I began, as it were, to drink her in. I wished they would turn the lights up so that I could see her better. She was rather small, with great big eyes and a ripping smile. It was a shame to let all that run to seed, so to speak, in semi-darkness.

Suddenly the lights did go up, and the orchestra began to play a tune which, though I haven't much of an ear for music, seemed somehow familiar. The next instant out pranced old Gussie from the wings in a purple frock-coat and a brown top-hat, grinned feebly at the audience, tripped over his feet, blushed, and began to sing the Tennessee song.

It was rotten. The poor nut had got stage fright so badly that it practically eliminated his voice. He sounded like some far-off echo of the past 'yodelling' through a woollen blanket.

For the first time since I had heard that he was about to go into vaudeville I felt a faint hope creeping over me. I was sorry for the wretched chap, of course, but there was no denying that the thing had its bright side. No management on earth would go on paying thirty-five dollars a week for this sort of performance. This was going to be Gussie's first and only. He would have to leave the profession. The old boy would say, 'Unhand my daughter'. And, with decent luck, I saw myself leading Gussie on to the next England-bound liner and handing him over intact to Aunt Agatha.

He got through the song somehow and limped off amidst roars of silence from the audience. There was a brief respite, then out he came again.

He sang this time as if nobody loved him. As a song, it was not a very pathetic song, being all about coons spooning in June under the moon, and so on and so forth, but Gussie handled it in such a sad, crushed way that there was genuine anguish in every line. By the time he reached the refrain I was nearly in tears. It seemed such a rotten sort of world with all that kind of thing going on in it.

He started the refrain, and then the most frightful thing happened. The girl next to me got up in her seat, chucked her head back, and began to sing too. I say 'too', but it wasn't really too, because her first note stopped Gussie dead, as if he had been pole-axed.

I never felt so bally conspicuous in my life. I huddled down in my seat and wished I could turn my collar up. Everybody seemed to be looking at me.

In the midst of my agony I caught sight of Gussie. A complete change had taken place in the old lad. He was looking most frightfully bucked. I must say the girl was singing most awfully well, and it seemed to act on Gussie like a tonic. When she came to the end of the refrain, he took it up, and they sang it together, and the end of it was that he went off the popular hero. The audience yelled for more, and were only quieted when they turned down the lights and put on a film.

When I had recovered I tottered round to see Gussie. I found him sitting on a box behind the stage, looking like one who had seen visions.

'Isn't she a wonder, Bertie?' he said, devoutly. 'I hadn't a notion she was going to be there. She's playing at the Auditorium this week, and she can only just have had time to get back to her *matinee*. She risked being late, just to come and see me through. She's my good angel, Bertie. She saved me. If she hadn't helped me out I don't know what would have happened. I was so nervous I didn't know what I was doing. Now that I've got through the first show I shall be all right.'

I was glad I had sent that cable to his mother. I was going to need her. The thing had got beyond me.

* * * * *

During the next week I saw a lot of old Gussie, and was introduced to the girl. I also met her father, a formidable old boy with quick eyebrows and a sort of determined expression. On the following Wednesday Aunt Julia arrived. Mrs Mannering-Phipps, my aunt Julia, is, I think, the most dignified person I know. She lacks Aunt Agatha's punch, but in a quiet way she has always contrived to make me feel, from boyhood up, that I was a poor worm. Not that she harries me like Aunt Agatha. The difference between the two is that Aunt Agatha conveys the impression that she considers me personally responsible for all the sin and sorrow in the world, while Aunt Julia's manner seems to suggest that I am more to be pitied than censured.

If it wasn't that the thing was a matter of historical fact, I should be inclined to believe that Aunt Julia had never been on the vaudeville stage. She is like a stage duchess.

She always seems to me to be in a perpetual state of being about to desire the butler to instruct the head footman to serve lunch in the blue-room overlooking the west terrace. She exudes dignity. Yet, twenty-five years ago, so I've been told by old boys who were lads about town in those days, she was knocking them cold at the Tivoli in a double act called 'Fun in a Tea-Shop', in which she wore tights and sang a song with a chorus that began, 'Rumpty-tiddley-umpty-ay'.

There are some things a chappie's mind absolutely refuses to picture, and Aunt Julia singing 'Rumpty-tiddley-umpty-ay' is one of them.

She got straight to the point within five minutes of our meeting.

'What is this about Gussie? Why did you cable for me, Bertie?'

'It's rather a long story,' I said, 'and complicated. If you don't mind, I'll let you have it in a series of motion pictures. Suppose we look in at the Auditorium for a few minutes.'

The girl, Ray, had been re-engaged for a second week at the Auditorium, owing to the big success of her first week. Her act consisted of three songs. She did herself well in the matter of costume and scenery. She had a ripping voice. She looked most awfully pretty; and altogether the act was, broadly speaking, a pippin.

Aunt Julia didn't speak till we were in our seats. Then she gave a sort of sigh.

'It's twenty-five years since I was in a music-hall!'

She didn't say any more, but sat there with her eyes glued on the stage.

After about half an hour the johnnies who work the card-index system at the side of the stage put up the name of Ray Denison, and there was a good deal of applause.

'Watch this act, Aunt Julia,' I said.

She didn't seem to hear me.

'Twenty-five years! What did you say, Bertie?'

'Watch this act and tell me what you think of it.'

'Who is it? Ray. Oh!'

'Exhibit A,' I said. 'The girl Gussie's engaged to.'

The girl did her act, and the house rose at her. They didn't want to let her go. She had to come back again and again. When she had finally disappeared I turned to Aunt Julia.

'Well?' I said.

'I like her work. She's an artist.'

'We will now, if you don't mind, step a goodish way uptown.'

And we took the subway to where Gussie, the human film, was earning his thirty-five per. As luck would have it, we hadn't been in the place ten minutes when out he came.

'Exhibit B,' I said. 'Gussie.'

I don't quite know what I had expected her to do, but I certainly didn't expect her to sit there without a word. She did not move a muscle, but just stared at Gussie as he drooled on about the moon. I was sorry for the woman, for it must have been a shock to her to see her only son in a mauve frockcoat and a brown top-hat, but I thought it best to let her get a strangle-hold on the intricacies of the situation as quickly as possible. If I had tried to explain the affair without the aid of illustrations I should have talked all day and left her muddled up as to who was going to marry whom, and why.

I was astonished at the improvement in dear old Gussie. He had got back his voice and was putting the stuff over well. It reminded me of the night at Oxford when, then but a lad of eighteen, he sang 'Let's All Go Down the Strand' after a bump supper, standing the while up to his knees in the college fountain. He was putting just the same zip into the thing now.

When he had gone off Aunt Julia sat perfectly still for a long time, and then she turned to me. Her eyes shone queerly.

'What does this mean, Bertie?'

She spoke quite quietly, but her voice shook a bit.

'Gussie went into the business,' I said, 'because the girl's father wouldn't let him marry her unless he did. If you feel up to it perhaps you wouldn't mind tottering round to One Hundred and Thirty-third Street and having a chat with him. He's an old boy with eyebrows, and he's Exhibit C on my list. When I've put you in touch with him I rather fancy my share of the business is concluded, and it's up to you.'

The Danbys lived in one of those big apartments uptown which look as if they cost the earth and really cost about half as much as a hall-room down in the forties. We were shown into the sitting-room, and presently old Danby came in.

'Good afternoon, Mr Danby,' I began.

I had got as far as that when there was a kind of gasping cry at my elbow.

'Joe!' cried Aunt Julia, and staggered against the sofa.

For a moment old Danby stared at her, and then his mouth fell open and his eyebrows shot up like rockets.

'Julie!'

And then they had got hold of each other's hands and were shaking them till I wondered their arms didn't come unscrewed.

I'm not equal to this sort of thing at such short notice. The change in Aunt Julia made me feel quite dizzy. She had shed her *grande-dame* manner completely, and was blushing and smiling. I don't like to say such things of any aunt of mine, or I would go further and put it on record that she was giggling. And old Danby, who usually looked like a cross between a Roman emperor and Napoleon Bonaparte in a bad temper, was behaving like a small boy.

'Joe!'

'Julie!'

'Dear old Joe! Fancy meeting you again!'

'Wherever have you come from, Julie?'

Well, I didn't know what it was all about, but I felt a bit out of it.

I butted in:

'Aunt Julia wants to have a talk with you, Mr Danby.'

'I knew you in a second, Joe!'

'It's twenty-five years since I saw you, kid, and you don't look a day older.'

'Oh, Joe! I'm an old woman!'

'What are you doing over here? I suppose'—old Danby's cheerfulness waned a trifle—'I suppose your husband is with you?'

'My husband died a long, long while ago, Joe.'

Old Danby shook his head.

'You never ought to have married out of the profession, Julie. I'm not saying a word against the late—I can't remember his name; never could—but you shouldn't have done it, an artist like you. Shall I ever forget the way you used to knock them with "Rumpty-tiddley-umpty-ay"?'

'Ah! how wonderful you were in that act, Joe.' Aunt Julia sighed. 'Do you remember the back-fall you used to do down the steps? I always have said that you did the best back-fall in the profession.'

'I couldn't do it now!'

'Do you remember how we put it across at the Canterbury, Joe? Think of it! The Canterbury's a moving-picture house now, and the old Mogul runs French revues.'

'I'm glad I'm not there to see them.'

'Joe, tell me, why did you leave England?'

'Well, I—I wanted a change. No I'll tell you the truth, kid. I wanted you, Julie. You went off and married that—whatever that stage-door johnny's name was—and it broke me all up.'

Aunt Julia was staring at him. She is what they call a well-preserved woman. It's easy to see that, twenty-five years ago, she must have been something quite extraordinary to look at. Even now she's almost beautiful. She has very large brown eyes, a mass of soft grey hair, and the complexion of a girl of seventeen.

'Joe, you aren't going to tell me you were fond of me yourself!'

'Of course I was fond of you. Why did I let you have all the fat in "Fun in a Tea-Shop"? Why did I hang about upstage while you sang "Rumpty-tiddley-umpty-ay"? Do you remember my giving you a bag of buns when we were on the road at Bristol?'

'Yes, but—'

'Do you remember my giving you the ham sandwiches at Portsmouth?'

'Joe!'

'Do you remember my giving you a seed-cake at Birmingham? What did you think all that meant, if not that I loved you? Why, I was working up by degrees to telling you straight out when you suddenly went off and married that cane-sucking dude. That's why I wouldn't let my daughter marry this young chap, Wilson, unless he went into the profession. She's an artist—'

'She certainly is, Joe.'

'You've seen her? Where?'

'At the Auditorium just now. But, Joe, you mustn't stand in the way of her marrying the man she's in love with. He's an artist, too.'

'In the small time.'

'You were in the small time once, Joe. You mustn't look down on him because he's a beginner. I know you feel that your daughter is marrying beneath her, but—'

'How on earth do you know anything about young Wilson?

'He's my son.'

'Your son?'

'Yes, Joe. And I've just been watching him work. Oh, Joe, you can't think how proud I was of him! He's got it in him. It's fate. He's my son and he's in the profession! Joe, you don't know what I've been through for his sake. They made a lady of me. I never worked so hard in my life as I did to become a real lady. They kept telling me I had got to put it across, no matter what it cost, so that he wouldn't be ashamed of me. The study was something terrible. I had to watch myself every minute for years, and I never knew when I might fluff my lines or fall down on some bit of business. But I did it, because I didn't want him to be ashamed of me, though all the time I was just aching to be back where I belonged.'

Old Danby made a jump at her, and took her by the shoulders.

'Come back where you belong, Julie!' he cried. 'Your husband's dead, your son's a pro. Come back! It's twenty-five years ago, but I haven't changed. I want you still. I've always wanted you. You've got to come back, kid, where you belong.'

Aunt Julia gave a sort of gulp and looked at him.

'Joe!' she said in a kind of whisper.

'You're here, kid,' said Old Danby, huskily. 'You've come back.... Twenty-five years!... You've come back and you're going to stay!'

She pitched forward into his arms, and he caught her.

'Oh, Joe! Joe! Joe!' she said. 'Hold me. Don't let me go. Take care of me.'

And I edged for the door and slipped from the room. I felt weak. The old bean will stand a certain amount, but this was too much. I groped my way out into the street and wailed for a taxi.

Gussie called on me at the hotel that night. He curveted into the room as if he had bought it and the rest of the city.

'Bertie,' he said, 'I feel as if I were dreaming.'

'I wish I could feel like that, old top,' I said, and I took another glance at a cable that had arrived half an hour ago from Aunt Agatha. I had been looking at it at intervals ever since.

'Ray and I got back to her flat this evening. Who do you think was there? The mater! She was sitting hand in hand with old Danby.'

'Yes?'

'He was sitting hand in hand with her.'

'Really?'

'They are going to be married.'

'Exactly.'

'Ray and I are going to be married.'

'I suppose so.'

'Bertie, old man, I feel immense. I look round me, and everything seems to be absolutely corking. The change in the mater is marvellous. She is twenty-five years younger. She and old Danby are talking of reviving "Fun in a Tea-Shop", and going out on the road with it.'

I got up.

'Gussie, old top,' I said, 'leave me for a while. I would be alone. I think I've got brain fever or something.'

'Sorry, old man; perhaps New York doesn't agree with you. When do you expect to go back to England?'

I looked again at Aunt Agatha's cable.

'With luck,' I said, 'in about ten years.'

When he was gone I took up the cable and read it again.

'What is happening?' it read. 'Shall I come over?'

I sucked a pencil for a while, and then I wrote the reply.

It was not an easy cable to word, but I managed it.

'No,' I wrote, 'stay where you are. Profession overcrowded.'

WILTON'S HOLIDAY

When Jack Wilton first came to Marois Bay, none of us dreamed that he was a man with a hidden sorrow in his life. There was something about the man which made the idea absurd, or would have made it absurd if he himself had not been the authority for the story. He looked so thoroughly pleased with life and with himself. He was one of those men whom you instinctively label in your mind as 'strong'. He was so healthy, so fit, and had such a confident, yet sympathetic, look about him that you felt directly you saw him that here was the one person you would have selected as the recipient of that hard-luck story of yours. You felt that his kindly strength would have been something to lean on.

As a matter of fact, it was by trying to lean on it that Spencer Clay got hold of the facts of the case; and when young Clay got hold of anything, Marois Bay at large had it hot and fresh a few hours later; for Spencer was one of those slack-jawed youths who are constitutionally incapable of preserving a secret.

Within two hours, then, of Clay's chat with Wilton, everyone in the place knew that, jolly and hearty as the new-comer might seem, there was that gnawing at his heart which made his outward cheeriness simply heroic.

Clay, it seems, who is the worst specimen of self-pitier, had gone to Wilton, in whom, as a new-comer, he naturally saw a fine fresh repository for his tales of woe, and had opened with a long yarn of some misfortune or other. I forget which it was; it might have been any one of a dozen or so which he had constantly in stock, and it is immaterial which it was. The point is that, having heard him out very politely and patiently, Wilton came back at him with a story which silenced even Clay. Spencer was equal to most things, but even he could not go on whining about how he had foozled his putting and been snubbed at the bridge-table, or whatever it was that he was pitying himself about just then, when a man was telling him the story of a wrecked life.

'He told me not to let it go any further,' said Clay to everyone he met, 'but of course it doesn't matter telling you. It is a thing he doesn't like to have known. He told me because he said there was something about me that seemed to extract confidences—a kind of strength, he said. You wouldn't think it to look at him, but his life is an absolute blank. Absolutely ruined, don't you know. He told me the whole thing so simply and frankly that it broke me all up. It seems that he was engaged to be married a few years ago, and on the wedding morning—absolutely on the wedding morning—the girl was taken suddenly ill, and—'

'And died?'

'And died. Died in his arms. Absolutely in his arms, old top.'

'What a terrible thing!'

'Absolutely. He's never got over it. You won't let it go any further, will you old man?'

And off sped Spencer, to tell the tale to someone else.

* * * * *

Everyone was terribly sorry for Wilton. He was such a good fellow, such a sportsman, and, above all, so young, that one hated the thought that, laugh as he might, beneath his laughter there lay the pain of that awful memory. He seemed so happy, too. It was only in moments of confidence, in those heart-to-heart talks when men reveal their deeper feelings, that he ever gave a hint that all was not well with him. As, for example, when Ellerton, who is always in love with someone, backed him into a corner one evening and began to tell him the story of his latest affair, he had hardly begun when such a look of pain came over Wilton's face that he ceased instantly. He said afterwards that the sudden realization of the horrible break he was making hit him like a bullet, and the manner in which he turned the conversation practically without pausing from love to a discussion of the best method of getting out of the bunker at the seventh hole was, in the circumstances, a triumph of tact.

Marois Bay is a quiet place even in the summer, and the Wilton tragedy was naturally the subject of much talk. It is a sobering thing to get a glimpse of the underlying sadness of life like that, and there was a disposition at first on the part of the community to behave in his presence in a manner reminiscent of pall-bearers at a funeral. But things soon adjusted themselves. He was outwardly so cheerful that it seemed ridiculous for the rest of us to step softly and speak with hushed voices. After all, when you came to examine it, the thing was his affair, and it was for him to dictate the lines on which it should be treated. If he elected to hide his pain under a bright smile and a laugh like that of a hyena with a more than usually keen sense of humour, our line was obviously to follow his lead.

We did so; and by degrees the fact that his life was permanently blighted became almost a legend. At the back of our minds we were aware of it, but it did not obtrude itself into the affairs of every day. It was only when someone, forgetting, as Ellerton had done, tried to enlist his sympathy for some misfortune of his own that the look of pain in his eyes and the sudden tightening of his lips reminded us that he still remembered.

Matters had been at this stage for perhaps two weeks when Mary Campbell arrived.

Sex attraction is so purely a question of the taste of the individual that the wise man never argues about it. He accepts its vagaries as part of the human mystery, and leaves it at that. To me there was no charm whatever about Mary Campbell. It may have been that, at the moment, I was in love with Grace Bates, Heloise Miller, and Clarice Wembley—for at Marois Bay, in the summer, a man who is worth his salt is more than equal to three love affairs simultaneously—but anyway, she left me cold. Not one thrill could she awake in me. She was small and, to my mind, insignificant. Some men said that she had fine eyes. They seemed to me just ordinary eyes. And her hair was just ordinary hair. In fact, ordinary was the word that described her.

But from the first it was plain that she seemed wonderful with Wilton, which was all the more remarkable, seeing that he was the one man of us all who could have got any girl in Marois Bay that he wanted. When a man is six foot high, is a combination of Hercules and Apollo, and plays tennis, golf, and the banjo with almost superhuman vim, his path with the girls of a summer seaside resort is pretty smooth. But, when you add to all these things a tragedy like Wilton's, he can only be described as having a walk-over.

Girls love a tragedy. At least, most girls do. It makes a man interesting to them. Grace Bates was always going on about how interesting Wilton was. So was Heloise Miller. So was Clarice Wembley. But it was not until Mary Campbell came that he displayed any real enthusiasm at all for the feminine element of Marois Bay. We put it down to the fact that he could not forget, but the real reason, I now know, was that he considered that girls were a nuisance on the links and in the tennis-court. I suppose a plus two golfer and a Wildingesque tennis-player, such as Wilton was, does feel like that. Personally, I think that girls add to the fun of the thing. But then, my handicap is twelve, and, though I have been playing tennis for many years, I doubt if I have got my first serve—the fast one—over the net more than half a dozen times.

But Mary Campbell overcame Wilton's prejudices in twenty-four hours. He seemed to feel lonely on the links without her, and he positively egged her to be his partner in the doubles. What Mary thought of him we did not know. She was one of those inscrutable girls.

And so things went on. If it had not been that I knew Wilton's story, I should have classed the thing as one of those summer love-affairs to which the Marois Bay air is so peculiarly conducive. The only reason why anyone comes away from a summer at Marois Bay unbetrothed is because there are so many girls that he falls in love with that his holiday is up before he can, so to speak, concentrate.

But in Wilton's case this was out of the question. A man does not get over the sort of blow he had had, not, at any rate, for many years: and we had gathered that his tragedy was comparatively recent.

I doubt if I was ever more astonished in my life than the night when he confided in me. Why he should have chosen me as a confidant I cannot say. I am inclined to think that I happened to be alone with him at the psychological moment when a man must confide in somebody or burst; and Wilton chose the lesser evil.

I was strolling along the shore after dinner, smoking a cigar and thinking of Grace Bates, Heloise Miller, and Clarice Wembley, when I happened upon him. It was a beautiful night, and we sat down and drank it in for a while. The first intimation I had that all was not well with him was when he suddenly emitted a hollow groan.

The next moment he had begun to confide.

'I'm in the deuce of a hole,' he said. 'What would you do in my position?'

'Yes?' I said.

'I proposed to Mary Campbell this evening.'

'Congratulations.'

'Thanks. She refused me.'

'Refused you!'

'Yes—because of Amy.'

It seemed to me that the narrative required footnotes.

'Who is Amy?' I said.

'Amy is the girl—'

'Which girl?'

'The girl who died, you know. Mary had got hold of the whole story. In fact, it was the tremendous sympathy she showed that encouraged me to propose. If it hadn't been for that, I shouldn't have had the nerve. I'm not fit to black her shoes.'

Odd, the poor opinion a man always has—when he is in love—of his personal attractions. There were times when I thought of Grace Bates, Heloise Miller, and Clarice Wembley, when I felt like one of the beasts that perish. But then, I'm nothing to write home about, whereas the smallest gleam of intelligence should have told Wilton that he was a kind of Ouida guardsman.

'This evening I managed somehow to do it. She was tremendously nice about it—said she was very fond of me and all that—but it was quite out of the question because of Amy.'

'I don't follow this. What did she mean?'

'It's perfectly clear, if you bear in mind that Mary is the most sensitive, spiritual, highly strung girl that ever drew breath,' said Wilton, a little coldly. 'Her position is this: she feels that, because of Amy, she can never have my love completely; between us there would always be Amy's memory. It would be the same as if she married a widower.'

'Well, widowers marry.'

'They don't marry girls like Mary.'

I couldn't help feeling that this was a bit of luck for the widowers; but I didn't say so. One has always got to remember that opinions differ about girls. One man's peach, so to speak, is another man's poison. I have met men who didn't like Grace Bates, men who, if Heloise Miller or Clarice Wembley had given them their photographs, would have used them to cut the pages of a novel.

'Amy stands between us,' said Wilton.

I breathed a sympathetic snort. I couldn't think of anything noticeably suitable to say.

'Stands between us,' repeated Wilton. 'And the damn silly part of the whole thing is that there isn't any Amy. I invented her.'

'You—what!'

'Invented her. Made her up. No, I'm not mad. I had a reason. Let me see, you come from London, don't you?'

'Yes.'

'Then you haven't any friends. It's different with me. I live in a small country town, and everyone's my friend. I don't know what it is about me, but for some reason, ever since I can remember, I've been looked on as the strong man of my town, the man who's *all right*. Am I making myself clear?'

'Not quite.'

'Well, what I am trying to get at is this. Either because I'm a strong sort of fellow to look at, and have obviously never been sick in my life, or because I can't help looking pretty cheerful, the whole of Bridley-in-the-Wold seems to take it for granted that I can't possibly have any troubles of my own, and that I am consequently fair game for anyone who has any sort of worry. I have the sympathetic manner, and they come to me to be cheered up. If a fellow's in love, he makes a bee-line for me, and tells me all about it. If anyone has had a bereavement, I am the rock on which he leans for support. Well, I'm a patient sort of man, and, as far as Bridley-in-the-Wold is concerned, I am willing to play the part. But a strong man does need an occasional holiday, and I made up my mind that I would get it. Directly I got here I saw that the same old game was going to start. Spencer Clay swooped down on me at once. I'm as big a draw with the Spencer Clay type of maudlin idiot as catnip is with a cat. Well, I could stand it at home, but I was hanged if I was going to have my holiday spoiled. So I invented Amy. Now do you see?'

'Certainly I see. And I perceive something else which you appear to have overlooked. If Amy doesn't exist—or, rather, never did exist—she cannot stand between you and Miss Campbell. Tell her what you have told me, and all will be well.'

He shook his head.

'You don't know Mary. She would never forgive me. You don't know what sympathy, what angelic sympathy, she has poured out on me about Amy. I can't possibly tell her the whole thing was a fraud. It would make her feel so foolish.'

'You must risk it. At the worst, you lose nothing.'

He brightened a little.

'No, that's true,' he said. 'I've half a mind to do it.'

'Make it a whole mind,' I said, 'and you win out.'

I was wrong. Sometimes I am. The trouble was, apparently, that I didn't know Mary. I am sure Grace Bates, Heloise Miller, or Clarice Wembley would not have acted as she did. They might have been a trifle stunned at first, but they would soon have come round, and all would have been joy. But with Mary, no. What took place at the interview I do not know; but it was swiftly perceived by Marois Bay that the Wilton-Campbell alliance was off. They no longer walked together, golfed together, and played tennis on the same side of the net. They did not even speak to each other.

* * * * *

The rest of the story I can speak of only from hearsay. How it became public property, I do not know. But there was a confiding strain in Wilton, and I imagine he confided in someone, who confided in someone else. At any rate, it is recorded in Marois Bay's unwritten archives, from which I now extract it.

* * * * *

For some days after the breaking-off of diplomatic relations, Wilton seemed too pulverized to resume the offensive. He mooned about the links by himself, playing a shocking game, and generally comported himself like a man who has looked for the escape of gas with a lighted candle. In affairs of love the strongest men generally behave with the most spineless lack of resolution. Wilton weighed thirteen stone, and his muscles were like steel cables; but he could not have shown less pluck in this crisis in his life if he had been a poached egg. It was pitiful to see him.

Mary, in these days, simply couldn't see that he was on the earth. She looked round him, above him, and through him, but never at him; which was rotten from Wilton's point of view, for he had developed a sort of wistful expression—I am convinced that he practised it before the mirror after his bath—which should have worked wonders, if only he could have got action with it. But she avoided his eye as if he had been a creditor whom she was trying to slide past on the street.

She irritated me. To let the breach widen in this way was absurd. Wilton, when I said as much to him, said that it was due to her wonderful sensitiveness and highly strungness, and that it was just one more proof to him of the loftiness of her soul and her shrinking horror of any form of deceit. In fact, he gave me the impression that, though the affair was rending his vitals, he took a mournful pleasure in contemplating her perfection.

Now one afternoon Wilton took his misery for a long walk along the seashore. He tramped over the sand for some considerable time, and finally pulled up in a little cove, backed by high cliffs and dotted with rocks. The shore around Marois Bay is full of them.

By this time the afternoon sun had begun to be too warm for comfort, and it struck Wilton that he could be a great deal more comfortable nursing his wounded heart with his back against one of the rocks than tramping any farther over the sand. Most of the Marois Bay scenery is simply made as a setting for the nursing of a wounded heart. The cliffs are a sombre indigo, sinister and forbidding; and even on the finest days the sea has a curious sullen look. You have only to get away from the crowd near the bathing-machines and reach one of these small coves and get your book against a rock and your pipe well alight, and you can simply wallow in misery. I have done it myself. The day when Heloise Miller went golfing with Teddy Bingley I spent the whole afternoon in one of these retreats. It is true that, after twenty minutes of contemplating the breakers, I fell asleep; but that is bound to happen.

It happened to Wilton. For perhaps half an hour he brooded, and then his pipe fell from his mouth and he dropped off into a peaceful slumber. And time went by.

It was a touch of cramp that finally woke him. He jumped up with a yell, and stood there massaging his calf. And he had hardly got rid of the pain, when a startled exclamation broke the primeval stillness; and there, on the other side of the rock, was Mary Campbell.

Now, if Wilton had had any inductive reasoning in his composition at all, he would have been tremendously elated. A girl does not creep out to a distant cove at Marois Bay unless she is unhappy; and if Mary Campbell was unhappy she must be unhappy about him; and if she was unhappy about him all he had to do was to show a bit of determination and get the whole thing straightened out. But Wilton, whom grief had reduced to the mental level of an oyster, did not reason this out; and the sight of her deprived him of practically all his faculties, including speech. He just stood there and yammered.

'Did you follow me here, Mr Wilton?' said Mary, very coldly.

He shook his head. Eventually he managed to say that he had come there by chance, and had fallen asleep under the rock. As this was exactly what Mary had done, she could not reasonably complain. So that concluded the conversation for the time being. She walked away in the direction of Marois Bay without another word, and presently he lost sight of her round a bend in the cliffs.

His position now was exceedingly unpleasant. If she had such a distaste for his presence, common decency made it imperative that he should give her a good start on the homeward journey. He could not tramp along a couple of yards in the rear all the way. So he had to remain where he was till she had got well off the mark. And as he was wearing a thin flannel suit, and the sun had gone in, and a chilly breeze had sprung up, his mental troubles were practically swamped in physical discomfort.

Just as he had decided that he could now make a move, he was surprised to see her coming back.

Wilton really was elated at this. The construction he put on it was that she had relented and was coming back to fling her arms round his neck. He was just bracing himself for the clash, when he caught her eye, and it was as cold and unfriendly as the sea.

'I must go round the other way,' she said. 'The water has come up too far on that side.'

And she walked past him to the other end of the cove.

The prospect of another wait chilled Wilton to the marrow. The wind had now grown simply freezing, and it came through his thin suit and roamed about all over him in a manner that caused him exquisite discomfort. He began to jump to keep himself warm.

He was leaping heavenwards for the hundredth time, when, chancing to glance to one side, he perceived Mary again returning. By this time his physical misery had so completely overcome the softer emotions in his bosom that his only feeling now was one of thorough irritation. It was not fair, he felt, that she should jockey at the start in this way and keep him hanging about here catching cold. He looked at her, when she came within range, quite balefully.

'It is impossible,' she said, 'to get round that way either.'

One grows so accustomed in this world to everything going smoothly, that the idea of actual danger had not yet come home to her. From where she stood in the middle of the cove, the sea looked so distant that the fact that it had closed the only ways of getting out was at the moment merely annoying. She felt much the same as she would have felt if she had arrived at a station to catch a train and had been told that the train was not running.

She therefore seated herself on a rock, and contemplated the ocean. Wilton walked up and down. Neither showed any disposition to exercise that gift of speech which places Man in a class of his own, above the ox, the ass, the common wart-hog, and the rest of the lower animals. It was only when a wave swished over the base of her rock that Mary broke the silence.

'The tide is coming *in*' she faltered.

She looked at the sea with such altered feelings that it seemed a different sea altogether.

There was plenty of it to look at. It filled the entire mouth of the little bay, swirling up the sand and lashing among the rocks in a fashion which made one thought stand out above all the others in her mind—the recollection that she could not swim.

'Mr Wilton!'

Wilton bowed coldly.

'Mr Wilton, the tide. It's coming IN.'

Wilton glanced superciliously at the sea.

'So,' he said, 'I perceive.'

'But what shall we do?'

Wilton shrugged his shoulders. He was feeling at war with Nature and Humanity combined. The wind had shifted a few points to the east, and was exploring his anatomy with the skill of a qualified surgeon.

'We shall drown,' cried Miss Campbell. 'We shall drown. We shall drown.

We shall drown.'

All Wilton's resentment left him. Until he heard that pitiful wail his only thoughts had been for himself.

'Mary!' he said, with a wealth of tenderness in his voice.

She came to him as a little child comes to its mother, and he put his arm around her.

'Oh, Jack!'

'My darling!'

'I'm frightened!'

'My precious!'

It is in moments of peril, when the chill breath of fear blows upon our souls, clearing them of pettiness, that we find ourselves.

She looked about her wildly.

'Could we climb the cliffs?'

'I doubt it.'

'If we called for help—'

'We could do that.'

They raised their voices, but the only answer was the crashing of the waves and the cry of the sea-birds. The water was swirling at their feet, and they drew back to the shelter of the cliffs. There they stood in silence, watching.

'Mary,' said Wilton in a low voice, 'tell me one thing.'

'Yes, Jack?'

'Have you forgiven me?'

'Forgiven you! How can you ask at a moment like this? I love you with all my heart and soul.'

He kissed her, and a strange look of peace came over his face.

'I am happy.'

'I, too.'

A fleck of foam touched her face, and she shivered.

'It was worth it,' he said quietly. 'If all misunderstandings are cleared away and nothing can come between us again, it is a small price to pay—unpleasant as it will be when it comes.'

'Perhaps—perhaps it will not be very unpleasant. They say that drowning is an easy death.'

'I didn't mean drowning, dearest. I meant a cold in the head.'

'A cold in the head!'

He nodded gravely.

'I don't see how it can be avoided. You know how chilly it gets these late summer nights. It will be a long time before we can get away.'

She laughed a shrill, unnatural laugh.

'You are talking like this to keep my courage up. You know in your heart that there is no hope for us. Nothing can save us now. The water will come creeping—creeping—'

'Let it creep! It can't get past that rock there.'

'What do you mean?'

'It can't. The tide doesn't come up any farther. I know, because I was caught here last week.'

For a moment she looked at him without speaking. Then she uttered a cry in which relief, surprise, and indignation were so nicely blended that it would have been impossible to say which predominated.

He was eyeing the approaching waters with an indulgent smile.

'Why didn't you tell me?' she cried.

'I did tell you.'

'You know what I mean. Why did you let me go on thinking we were in danger, when—'

'We *were* in danger. We shall probably get pneumonia.'

'Isch!'

'There! You're sneezing already.'

'I am not sneezing. That was an exclamation of disgust.'

'It sounded like a sneeze. It must have been, for you've every reason to sneeze, but why you should utter exclamations of disgust I cannot imagine.'

'I'm disgusted with you—with your meanness. You deliberately tricked me into saying—'

'Saying—'

She was silent.

'What you said was that you loved me with all your heart and soul. You can't get away from that, and it's good enough for me.'

'Well, it's not true any longer.'

'Yes, it is,' said Wilton, comfortably; 'bless it.'

'It is not. I'm going right away now, and I shall never speak to you again.'

She moved away from him, and prepared to sit down.

'There's a jelly-fish just where you're going to sit,' said Wilton.

'I don't care.'

'It will. I speak from experience, as one on whom you have sat so often.'

'I'm not amused.'

'Have patience. I can be funnier than that.'

'Please don't talk to me.'

'Very well.'

She seated herself with her back to him. Dignity demanded reprisals, so he seated himself with his back to her; and the futile ocean raged towards them, and the wind grew chillier every minute.

Time passed. Darkness fell. The little bay became a black cavern, dotted here and there with white, where the breeze whipped the surface of the water.

Wilton sighed. It was lonely sitting there all by himself. How much jollier it would have been if—

A hand touched his shoulder, and a voice spoke—meekly.

'Jack, dear, it—it's awfully cold. Don't you think if we were to—snuggle up—'

He reached out and folded her in an embrace which would have aroused the professional enthusiasm of Hackenschmidt and drawn guttural congratulations from Zbysco. She creaked, but did not crack, beneath the strain.

'That's much nicer,' she said, softly. 'Jack, I don't think the tide's started even to think of going down yet.'

'I hope not,' said Wilton.

THE MIXER

I. He Meets a Shy Gentleman

Looking back, I always consider that my career as a dog proper really started when I was bought for the sum of half a crown by the Shy Man. That event marked the end of my puppyhood. The knowledge that I was worth actual cash to somebody filled me with a sense of new responsibilities. It sobered me. Besides, it was only after that half-crown changed hands that I went out into the great world; and, however interesting life may be in an East End public-house, it is only when you go out into the world that you really broaden your mind and begin to see things.

Within its limitations, my life had been singularly full and vivid. I was born, as I say, in a public-house in the East End, and, however lacking a public-house may be in refinement and the true culture, it certainly provides plenty of excitement. Before I was six weeks old I had upset three policemen by getting between their legs when they came round to the side-door, thinking they had heard suspicious noises; and I can still recall the interesting sensation of being chased seventeen times round the yard with a broom-handle after a well-planned and completely successful raid on the larder. These and other happenings of a like nature soothed for the moment but could not cure the restlessness which has always been so marked a trait in my character. I have always been restless, unable to settle down in one place and anxious to get on to the next thing. This may be due to a gipsy strain in my ancestry—one of my uncles travelled with a circus—or it may be the Artistic Temperament, acquired from a grandfather who, before dying of a surfeit of paste in the property-room of the Bristol Coliseum, which he was visiting in the course of a professional tour, had an established reputation on the music-hall stage as one of Professor Pond's Performing Poodles.

I owe the fullness and variety of my life to this restlessness of mine, for I have repeatedly left comfortable homes in order to follow some perfect stranger who looked as if he were on his way to somewhere interesting. Sometimes I think I must have cat blood in me.

The Shy Man came into our yard one afternoon in April, while I was sleeping with mother in the sun on an old sweater which we had borrowed from Fred, one of the barmen. I heard mother growl, but I didn't take any notice. Mother is what they call a good watch-dog, and she growls at everybody except master. At first, when she used to do it, I would get up and bark my head off, but not now. Life's too short to bark at everybody who comes into our yard. It is behind the public-house, and they keep empty bottles and things there, so people are always coming and going.

Besides, I was tired. I had had a very busy morning, helping the men bring in a lot of cases of beer, and running into the saloon to talk to Fred and generally looking after things. So I was just dozing off again, when I heard a voice say, 'Well, he's ugly enough!' Then I knew that they were talking about me.

I have never disguised it from myself, and nobody has ever disguised it from me, that I am not a handsome dog. Even mother never thought me beautiful. She was no Gladys Cooper herself, but she never hesitated to criticize my appearance. In fact, I have yet to meet anyone who did. The first thing strangers say about me is, 'What an ugly dog!'

I don't know what I am. I have a bulldog kind of a face, but the rest of me is terrier. I have a long tail which sticks straight up in the air. My hair is wiry. My eyes are brown. I am jet black, with a white chest. I once overheard Fred saying that I was a Gorgonzola cheese-hound, and I have generally found Fred reliable in his statements.

When I found that I was under discussion, I opened my eyes. Master was standing there, looking down at me, and by his side the man who had just said I was ugly enough. The man was a thin man, about the age of a barman and smaller than a policeman. He had patched brown shoes and black trousers.

'But he's got a sweet nature,' said master.

This was true, luckily for me. Mother always said, 'A dog without influence or private means, if he is to make his way in the world, must have either good looks or amiability.' But, according to her, I overdid it. 'A dog,' she used to say, 'can have a good heart, without chumming with every Tom, Dick, and Harry he meets. Your behaviour is sometimes quite un-doglike.' Mother prided herself on being a one-man dog. She kept herself to herself, and wouldn't kiss anybody except master—not even Fred.

Now, I'm a mixer. I can't help it. It's my nature. I like men. I like the taste of their boots, the smell of their legs, and the sound of their voices. It may be weak of me, but a man has only to speak to me and a sort of thrill goes right down my spine and sets my tail wagging.

I wagged it now. The man looked at me rather distantly. He didn't pat me. I suspected—what I afterwards found to be the case—that he was shy, so I jumped up at him to put him at his ease. Mother growled again. I felt that she did not approve.

'Why, he's took quite a fancy to you already,' said master.

The man didn't say a word. He seemed to be brooding on something. He was one of those silent men. He reminded me of Joe, the old dog down the street at the grocer's shop, who lies at the door all day, blinking and not speaking to anybody.

Master began to talk about me. It surprised me, the way he praised me. I hadn't a suspicion he admired me so much. From what he said you would have thought I had won prizes and ribbons at the Crystal Palace. But the man didn't seem to be impressed. He kept on saying nothing.

When master had finished telling him what a wonderful dog I was till I blushed, the man spoke.

'Less of it,' he said. 'Half a crown is my bid, and if he was an angel from on high you couldn't get another ha'penny out of me. What about it?'

A thrill went down my spine and out at my tail, for of course I saw now what was happening. The man wanted to buy me and take me away. I looked at master hopefully.

'He's more like a son to me than a dog,' said master, sort of wistful.

'It's his face that makes you feel that way,' said the man, unsympathetically. 'If you had a son that's just how he would look. Half a crown is my offer, and I'm in a hurry.'

'All right,' said master, with a sigh, 'though it's giving him away, a valuable dog like that. Where's your half-crown?'

The man got a bit of rope and tied it round my neck.

I could hear mother barking advice and telling me to be a credit to the family, but I was too excited to listen.

'Good-bye, mother,' I said. 'Good-bye, master. Good-bye, Fred. Good-bye everybody. I'm off to see life. The Shy Man has bought me for half a crown. Wow!'

I kept running round in circles and shouting, till the man gave me a kick and told me to stop it.

So I did.

I don't know where we went, but it was a long way. I had never been off our street before in my life and I didn't know the whole world was half as big as that. We walked on and on, and the man jerked at my rope whenever I wanted to stop and look at anything. He wouldn't even let me pass the time of the day with dogs we met.

When we had gone about a hundred miles and were just going to turn in at a dark doorway, a policeman suddenly stopped the man. I could feel by the way the man pulled at my rope and tried to hurry on that he didn't want to speak to the policeman. The more I saw of the man the more I saw how shy he was.

'Hi!' said the policeman, and we had to stop.

'I've got a message for you, old pal,' said the policeman. 'It's from the Board of Health. They told me to tell you you needed a change of air. See?'

'All right!' said the man.

'And take it as soon as you like. Else you'll find you'll get it given you. See?'

I looked at the man with a good deal of respect. He was evidently someone very important, if they worried so about his health.

'I'm going down to the country tonight,' said the man.

The policeman seemed pleased.

'That's a bit of luck for the country,' he said. 'Don't go changing your mind.'

And we walked on, and went in at the dark doorway, and climbed about a million stairs and went into a room that smelt of rats. The man sat down and swore a little, and I sat and looked at him.

Presently I couldn't keep it in any longer.

'Do we live here?' I said. 'Is it true we're going to the country? Wasn't that policeman a good sort? Don't you like policemen? I knew lots of policemen at the public-house. Are there any other dogs here? What is there for dinner? What's in that cupboard? When are you going to take me out for another run? May I go out and see if I can find a cat?'

'Stop that yelping,' he said.

'When we go to the country, where shall we live? Are you going to be a caretaker at a house? Fred's father is a caretaker at a big house in Kent. I've heard Fred talk about it. You didn't meet Fred when you came to the public-house, did you? You would like Fred. I like Fred. Mother likes Fred. We all like Fred.'

I was going on to tell him a lot more about Fred, who had always been one of my warmest friends, when he suddenly got hold of a stick and walloped me with it.

'You keep quiet when you're told,' he said.

He really was the shyest man I had ever met. It seemed to hurt him to be spoken to. However, he was the boss, and I had to humour him, so I didn't say any more.

We went down to the country that night, just as the man had told the policeman we would. I was all worked up, for I had heard so much about the country from Fred that I had always wanted to go there. Fred used to go off on a motor-bicycle sometimes to spend the night with his father in Kent, and once he brought back a squirrel with him, which I thought was for me to eat, but mother said no. 'The first thing a dog has to learn,' mother used often to say, 'is that the whole world wasn't created for him to eat.'

It was quite dark when we got to the country, but the man seemed to know where to go. He pulled at my rope, and we began to walk along a road with no people in it at all. We walked on and on, but it was all so new to me that I forgot how tired I was. I could feel my mind broadening with every step I took.

Every now and then we would pass a very big house, which looked as if it was empty, but I knew that there was a caretaker inside, because of Fred's father. These big houses belong to very rich people, but they don't want to live in them till the summer, so they put in caretakers, and the caretakers have a dog to keep off burglars. I wondered if that was what I had been brought here for.

'Are you going to be a caretaker?' I asked the man.

'Shut up,' he said.

So I shut up.

After we had been walking a long time, we came to a cottage. A man came out. My man seemed to know him, for he called him Bill. I was quite surprised to see the man was not at all shy with Bill. They seemed very friendly.

'Is that him?' said Bill, looking at me.

'Bought him this afternoon,' said the man.

'Well,' said Bill, 'he's ugly enough. He looks fierce. If you want a dog, he's the sort of dog you want. But what do you want one for? It seems to me it's a lot of trouble to take, when there's no need of any trouble at all. Why not do what I've always wanted to do? What's wrong with just fixing the dog, same as it's always done, and walking in and helping yourself?'

'I'll tell you what's wrong,' said the man. 'To start with, you can't get at the dog to fix him except by day, when they let him out. At night he's shut up inside the house. And suppose you do fix him during the day what happens then? Either the bloke gets another before night, or else he sits up all night with a gun. It isn't like as if these blokes was ordinary blokes. They're down here to look after the house. That's their job, and they don't take any chances.'

It was the longest speech I had ever heard the man make, and it seemed to impress Bill. He was quite humble.

'I didn't think of that,' he said. 'We'd best start in to train this tyke at once.'

Mother often used to say, when I went on about wanting to go out into the world and see life, 'You'll be sorry when you do. The world isn't all bones and liver.' And I hadn't been living with the man and Bill in their cottage long before I found out how right she was.

It was the man's shyness that made all the trouble. It seemed as if he hated to be taken notice of.

It started on my very first night at the cottage. I had fallen asleep in the kitchen, tired out after all the excitement of the day and the long walks I had had, when something woke me with a start. It was somebody scratching at the window, trying to get in.

Well, I ask you, I ask any dog, what would you have done in my place? Ever since I was old enough to listen, mother had told me over and over again what I must do in a case like this. It is the A B C of a dog's education. 'If you are in a room and you hear anyone trying to get in,' mother used to say, 'bark. It may be someone who has business there, or it may not. Bark first, and inquire afterwards. Dogs were made to be heard and not seen.'

I lifted my head and yelled. I have a good, deep voice, due to a hound strain in my pedigree, and at the public-house, when there was a full moon, I have often had people leaning out of the windows and saying things all down the street. I took a deep breath and let it go.

'Man!' I shouted. 'Bill! Man! Come quick! Here's a burglar getting in!'

Then somebody struck a light, and it was the man himself. He had come in through the window.

He picked up a stick, and he walloped me. I couldn't understand it. I couldn't see where I had done the wrong thing. But he was the boss, so there was nothing to be said.

If you'll believe me, that same thing happened every night. Every single night! And sometimes twice or three times before morning. And every time I would bark my loudest and the man would strike a light and wallop me. The thing was baffling. I couldn't possibly have mistaken what mother had said to me. She said it too often for that. Bark! Bark! Bark! It was the main plank of her whole system of education. And yet, here I was, getting walloped every night for doing it.

I thought it out till my head ached, and finally I got it right. I began to see that mother's outlook was narrow. No doubt, living with a man like master at the public-house, a man without a trace of shyness in his composition, barking was all right. But circumstances alter cases. I belonged to a man who was a mass of nerves, who got the jumps if you spoke to him. What I had to do was to forget the training I had had from mother, sound as it no doubt was as a general thing, and to adapt myself to the needs of the particular man who had happened to buy me. I had tried mother's way, and all it had brought me was walloping, so now I would think for myself.

So next night, when I heard the window go, I lay there without a word, though it went against all my better feelings. I didn't even growl. Someone came in and moved about in the dark, with a lantern, but, though I smelt that it was the man, I didn't ask him a single question. And presently the man lit a light and came over to me and gave me a pat, which was a thing he had never done before.

'Good dog!' he said. 'Now you can have this.'

And he let me lick out the saucepan in which the dinner had been cooked.

After that, we got on fine. Whenever I heard anyone at the window I just kept curled up and took no notice, and every time I got a bone or something good. It was easy, once you had got the hang of things.'

It was about a week after that the man took me out one morning, and we walked a long way till we turned in at some big gates and went along a very smooth road till we came to a great house, standing all by itself in the middle of a whole lot of country. There was a big lawn in front of it, and all round there were fields and trees, and at the back a great wood.

The man rang a bell, and the door opened, and an old man came out.

'Well?' he said, not very cordially.

'I thought you might want to buy a good watch-dog,' said the man.

'Well, that's queer, your saying that,' said the caretaker. 'It's a coincidence. That's exactly what I do want to buy. I was just thinking of going along and trying to get one. My old dog picked up something this morning that he oughtn't to have, and he's dead, poor feller.'

'Poor feller,' said the man. 'Found an old bone with phosphorus on it,
I guess.'

'What do you want for this one?'

'Five shillings.'

'Is he a good watch-dog?'

'He's a grand watch-dog.'

'He looks fierce enough.'

'Ah!'

So the caretaker gave the man his five shillings, and the man went off and left me.

At first the newness of everything and the unaccustomed smells and getting to know the caretaker, who was a nice old man, prevented my missing the man, but as the day went on and I began to realize that he had gone and would never come back, I got very depressed. I pattered all over the house, whining. It was a most interesting house, bigger than I thought a house could possibly be, but it couldn't cheer me up. You may think it strange that I should pine for the man, after all the wallopings he had given me, and it is odd, when you come to think of it. But dogs are dogs, and they are built like that. By the time it was evening I was thoroughly miserable. I found a shoe and an old clothes-brush in one of the rooms, but could eat nothing. I just sat and moped.

It's a funny thing, but it seems as if it always happened that just when you are feeling most miserable, something nice happens. As I sat there, there came from outside the sound of a motor-bicycle, and somebody shouted.

It was dear old Fred, my old pal Fred, the best old boy that ever stepped. I recognized his voice in a second, and I was scratching at the door before the old man had time to get up out of his chair.

Well, well, well! That was a pleasant surprise! I ran five times round the lawn without stopping, and then I came back and jumped up at him.

'What are you doing down here, Fred?' I said. 'Is this caretaker your father? Have you seen the rabbits in the wood? How long are you going to stop? How's mother? I like the country. Have you come all the way from the public-house? I'm living here now. Your father gave five shillings for me. That's twice as much as I was worth when I saw you last.'

'Why, it's young Nigger!' That was what they called me at the saloon.

'What are you doing here? Where did you get this dog, father?'

'A man sold him to me this morning. Poor old Bob got poisoned. This one ought to be just as good a watch-dog. He barks loud enough.'

'He should be. His mother is the best watch-dog in London. This cheese-hound used to belong to the boss. Funny him getting down here.'

We went into the house and had supper. And after supper we sat and talked. Fred was only down for the night, he said, because the boss wanted him back next day.

'And I'd sooner have my job, than yours, dad,' he said. 'Of all the lonely places! I wonder you aren't scared of burglars.'

'I've my shot-gun, and there's the dog. I might be scared if it wasn't for him, but he kind of gives me confidence. Old Bob was the same. Dogs are a comfort in the country.'

'Get many tramps here?'

'I've only seen one in two months, and that's the feller who sold me the dog here.'

As they were talking about the man, I asked Fred if he knew him. They might have met at the public-house, when the man was buying me from the boss.

'You would like him,' I said. 'I wish you could have met.'

They both looked at me.

'What's he growling at?' asked Fred. 'Think he heard something?'

The old man laughed.

'He wasn't growling. He was talking in his sleep. You're nervous, Fred.

It comes of living in the city.'

'Well, I am. I like this place in the daytime, but it gives me the pip at night. It's so quiet. How you can stand it here all the time, I can't understand. Two nights of it would have me seeing things.'

His father laughed.

'If you feel like that, Fred, you had better take the gun to bed with you. I shall be quite happy without it.'

'I will,' said Fred. 'I'll take six if you've got them.'

And after that they went upstairs. I had a basket in the hall, which had belonged to Bob, the dog who had got poisoned. It was a comfortable basket, but I was so excited at having met Fred again that I couldn't sleep. Besides, there was a smell of mice somewhere, and I had to move around, trying to place it.

I was just sniffing at a place in the wall, when I heard a scratching noise. At first I thought it was the mice working in a different place, but, when I listened, I found that the sound came from the window. Somebody was doing something to it from outside.

If it had been mother, she would have lifted the roof off right there, and so should I, if it hadn't been for what the man had taught me. I didn't think it possible that this could be the man come back, for he had gone away and said nothing about ever seeing me again. But I didn't bark. I stopped where I was and listened. And presently the window came open, and somebody began to climb in.

I gave a good sniff, and I knew it was the man.

I was so delighted that for a moment I nearly forgot myself and shouted with joy, but I remembered in time how shy he was, and stopped myself. But I ran to him and jumped up quite quietly, and he told me to lie down. I was disappointed that he didn't seem more pleased to see me. I lay down.

It was very dark, but he had brought a lantern with him, and I could see him moving about the room, picking things up and putting them in a bag which he had brought with him. Every now and then he would stop and listen, and then he would start moving round again. He was very quick about it, but very quiet. It was plain that he didn't want Fred or his father to come down and find him.

I kept thinking about this peculiarity of his while I watched him. I suppose, being chummy myself, I find it hard to understand that everybody else in the world isn't chummy too. Of course, my experience at the public-house had taught me that men are just as different from each other as dogs. If I chewed master's shoe, for instance, he used to kick me; but if I chewed Fred's, Fred would tickle me under the ear. And, similarly, some men are shy and some men are mixers. I quite appreciated that, but I couldn't help feeling that the man carried shyness to a point where it became morbid. And he didn't give himself a chance to cure himself of it. That was the point. Imagine a man hating to meet people so much that he never visited their houses till the middle of the night, when they were in bed and asleep.

It was silly. Shyness has always been something so outside my nature that I suppose I have never really been able to look at it sympathetically. I have always held the view that you can get over it if you make an effort. The trouble with the man was that he wouldn't make an effort. He went out of his way to avoid meeting people.

I was fond of the man. He was the sort of person you never get to know very well, but we had been together for quite a while, and I wouldn't have been a dog if I hadn't got attached to him.

As I sat and watched him creep about the room, it suddenly came to me that here was a chance of doing him a real good turn in spite of himself. Fred was upstairs, and Fred, as I knew by experience, was the easiest man to get along with in the world. Nobody could be shy with Fred. I felt that if only I could bring him and the man together, they would get along splendidly, and it would teach the man not to be silly and avoid people. It would help to give him the confidence which he needed. I had seen him with Bill, and I knew that he could be perfectly natural and easy when he liked.

It was true that the man might object at first, but after a while he would see that I had acted simply for his good, and would be grateful.

The difficulty was, how to get Fred down without scaring the man. I knew that if I shouted he wouldn't wait, but would be out of the window and away before Fred could get there. What I had to do was to go to Fred's room, explain the whole situation quietly to him, and ask him to come down and make himself pleasant.

The man was far too busy to pay any attention to me. He was kneeling in a corner with his back to me, putting something in his bag. I seized the opportunity to steal softly from the room.

Fred's door was shut, and I could hear him snoring. I scratched gently, and then harder, till I heard the snores stop. He got out of bed and opened the door.

'Don't make a noise,' I whispered. 'Come on downstairs. I want you to meet a friend of mine.'

At first he was quite peevish.

'What's the idea,' he said, 'coming and spoiling a man's beauty-sleep?

Get out.'

He actually started to go back into the room.

'No, honestly, Fred,' I said, 'I'm not fooling you. There is a man downstairs. He got in through the window. I want you to meet him. He's very shy, and I think it will do him good to have a chat with you.'

'What are you whining about?' Fred began, and then he broke off suddenly and listened. We could both hear the man's footsteps as he moved about.

Fred jumped back into the room. He came out, carrying something. He didn't say any more but started to go downstairs, very quiet, and I went after him.

There was the man, still putting things in his bag. I was just going to introduce Fred, when Fred, the silly ass, gave a great yell.

I could have bitten him.

'What did you want to do that for, you chump?' I said 'I told you he was shy. Now you've scared him.'

He certainly had. The man was out of the window quicker than you would have believed possible. He just flew out. I called after him that it was only Fred and me, but at that moment a gun went off with a tremendous bang, so he couldn't have heard me.

I was pretty sick about it. The whole thing had gone wrong. Fred seemed to have lost his head entirely. He was behaving like a perfect ass. Naturally the man had been frightened with him carrying on in that way. I jumped out of the window to see if I could find the man and explain, but he was gone. Fred jumped out after me, and nearly squashed me.

It was pitch dark out there. I couldn't see a thing. But I knew the man could not have gone far, or I should have heard him. I started to sniff round on the chance of picking up his trail. It wasn't long before I struck it.

Fred's father had come down now, and they were running about. The old man had a light. I followed the trail, and it ended at a large cedar-tree, not far from the house. I stood underneath it and looked up, but of course I could not see anything.

'Are you up there?' I shouted. 'There's nothing to be scared at. It was only Fred. He's an old pal of mine. He works at the place where you bought me. His gun went off by accident. He won't hurt you.'

There wasn't a sound. I began to think I must have made a mistake.

'He's got away,' I heard Fred say to his father, and just as he said it I caught a faint sound of someone moving in the branches above me.

'No he hasn't!' I shouted. 'He's up this tree.'

'I believe the dog's found him, dad!'

'Yes, he's up here. Come along and meet him.'

Fred came to the foot of the tree.

'You up there,' he said, 'come along down.'

Not a sound from the tree.

'It's all right,' I explained, 'he *is* up there, but he's very shy. Ask him again.'

'All right,' said Fred. 'Stay there if you want to. But I'm going to shoot off this gun into the branches just for fun.'

And then the man started to come down. As soon as he touched the ground I jumped up at him.

'This is fine!' I said 'Here's my friend Fred. You'll like him.'

But it wasn't any good. They didn't get along together at all. They hardly spoke. The man went into the house, and Fred went after him, carrying his gun. And when they got into the house it was just the same. The man sat in one chair, and Fred sat in another, and after a long time some men came in a motor-car, and the man went away with them. He didn't say good-bye to me.

When he had gone, Fred and his father made a great fuss of me. I couldn't understand it. Men are so odd. The man wasn't a bit pleased that I had brought him and Fred together, but Fred seemed as if he couldn't do enough for me for having introduced him to the man. However, Fred's father produced some cold ham—my favourite dish—and gave me quite a lot of it, so I stopped worrying over the thing. As mother used to say, 'Don't bother your head about what doesn't concern you. The only thing a dog need concern himself with is the bill-of-fare. Eat your bun, and don't make yourself busy about other people's affairs.' Mother's was in some ways a narrow outlook, but she had a great fund of sterling common sense.

II. He Moves in Society

It was one of those things which are really nobody's fault. It was not the chauffeur's fault, and it was not mine. I was having a friendly turn-up with a pal of mine on the side-walk; he ran across the road; I ran after him; and the car came round the corner and hit me. It must have been going pretty slow, or I should have been killed. As it was, I just had the breath knocked out of me. You know how you feel when the butcher catches you just as you are edging out of the shop with a bit of meat. It was like that.

I wasn't taking much interest in things for awhile, but when I did I found that I was the centre of a group of three—the chauffeur, a small boy, and the small boy's nurse.

The small boy was very well-dressed, and looked delicate. He was crying.

'Poor doggie,' he said, 'poor doggie.'

'It wasn't my fault, Master Peter,' said the chauffeur respectfully.

'He run out into the road before I seen him.'

'That's right,' I put in, for I didn't want to get the man into trouble.

'Oh, he's not dead,' said the small boy. 'He barked.'

'He growled,' said the nurse. 'Come away, Master Peter. He might bite you.'

Women are trying sometimes. It is almost as if they deliberately misunderstood.

'I won't come away. I'm going to take him home with me and send for the doctor to come and see him. He's going to be my dog.'

This sounded all right. Goodness knows I am no snob, and can rough it when required, but I do like comfort when it comes my way, and it seemed to me that this was where I got it. And I liked the boy. He was the right sort.

The nurse, a very unpleasant woman, had to make objections.

'Master Peter! You can't take him home, a great, rough, fierce, common dog! What would your mother say?'

'I'm going to take him home,' repeated the child, with a determination which I heartily admired, 'and he's going to be my dog. I shall call him Fido.'

There's always a catch in these good things. Fido is a name I particularly detest. All dogs do. There was a dog called that that I knew once, and he used to get awfully sick when we shouted it out after him in the street. No doubt there have been respectable dogs called Fido, but to my mind it is a name like Aubrey or Clarence. You may be able to live it down, but you start handicapped. However, one must take the rough with the smooth, and I was prepared to yield the point.

'If you wait, Master Peter, your father will buy you a beautiful, lovely dog….'

'I don't want a beautiful, lovely dog. I want this dog.'

The slur did not wound me. I have no illusions about my looks. Mine is an honest, but not a beautiful, face.

'It's no use talking,' said the chauffeur, grinning. 'He means to have him. Shove him in, and let's be getting back, or they'll be thinking His Nibs has been kidnapped.'

So I was carried to the car. I could have walked, but I had an idea that I had better not. I had made my hit as a crippled dog, and a crippled dog I intended to remain till things got more settled down.

The chauffeur started the car off again. What with the shock I had had and the luxury of riding in a motor-car, I was a little distrait, and I could not say how far we went. But it must have been miles and miles, for it seemed a long time afterwards that we stopped at the biggest house I have ever seen. There were smooth lawns and flower-beds, and men in overalls, and fountains and trees, and, away to the right, kennels with about a million dogs in them, all pushing their noses through the bars and shouting. They all wanted to know who I was and what prizes I had won, and then I realized that I was moving in high society.

I let the small boy pick me up and carry me into the house, though it was all he could do, poor kid, for I was some weight. He staggered up the steps and along a great hall, and then let me flop on the carpet of the most beautiful room you ever saw. The carpet was a yard thick.

There was a woman sitting in a chair, and as soon as she saw me she gave a shriek.

'I told Master Peter you would not be pleased, m'lady,' said the nurse, who seemed to have taken a positive dislike to me, 'but he would bring the nasty brute home.'

'He's not a nasty brute, mother. He's my dog, and his name's Fido. John ran over him in the car, and I brought him home to live with us. I love him.'

This seemed to make an impression. Peter's mother looked as if she were weakening.

'But, Peter, dear, I don't know what your father will say. He's so particular about dogs. All his dogs are prize-winners, pedigree dogs. This is such a mongrel.'

'A nasty, rough, ugly, common dog, m'lady,' said the nurse, sticking her oar in in an absolutely uncalled-for way.

Just then a man came into the room.

'What on earth?' he said, catching sight of me.

'It's a dog Peter has brought home. He says he wants to keep him.'

'I'm going to keep him,' corrected Peter firmly.

I do like a child that knows his own mind. I was getting fonder of Peter every minute. I reached up and licked his hand.

'See! He knows he's my dog, don't you, Fido? He licked me.'

'But, Peter, he looks so fierce.' This, unfortunately, is true. I do look fierce. It is rather a misfortune for a perfectly peaceful dog. 'I'm sure it's not safe your having him.'

'He's my dog, and his name's Fido. I am going to tell cook to give him a bone.'

His mother looked at his father, who gave rather a nasty laugh.

'My dear Helen,' he said, 'ever since Peter was born, ten years ago, he has not asked for a single thing, to the best of my recollection, which he has not got. Let us be consistent. I don't approve of this caricature of a dog, but if Peter wants him, I suppose he must have him.'

'Very well. But the first sign of viciousness he shows, he shall be shot. He makes me nervous.'

So they left it at that, and I went off with Peter to get my bone.

After lunch, he took me to the kennels to introduce me to the other dogs. I had to go, but I knew it would not be pleasant, and it wasn't. Any dog will tell you what these prize-ribbon dogs are like. Their heads are so swelled they have to go into their kennels backwards.

It was just as I had expected. There were mastiffs, terriers, poodles, spaniels, bulldogs, sheepdogs, and every other kind of dog you can imagine, all prize-winners at a hundred shows, and every single dog in the place just shoved his head back and laughed himself sick. I never felt so small in my life, and I was glad when it was over and Peter took me off to the stables.

I was just feeling that I never wanted to see another dog in my life, when a terrier ran out, shouting. As soon as he saw me, he came up inquiringly, walking very stiff-legged, as terriers do when they see a stranger.

'Well,' I said, 'and what particular sort of a prize-winner are you? Tell me all about the ribbons they gave you at the Crystal Palace, and let's get it over.'

He laughed in a way that did me good.

'Guess again!' he said. 'Did you take me for one of the nuts in the kennels? My name's Jack, and I belong to one of the grooms.'

'What!' I cried. 'You aren't Champion Bowlegs Royal or anything of that sort! I'm glad to meet you.'

So we rubbed noses as friendly as you please. It was a treat meeting one of one's own sort. I had had enough of those high-toned dogs who look at you as if you were something the garbage-man had forgotten to take away.

'So you've been talking to the swells, have you?' said Jack.

'He would take me,' I said, pointing to Peter.

'Oh, you're his latest, are you? Then you're all right—while it lasts.'

'How do you mean, while it lasts?'

'Well, I'll tell you what happened to me. Young Peter took a great fancy to me once. Couldn't do enough for me for a while. Then he got tired of me, and out I went. You see, the trouble is that while he's a perfectly good kid, he has always had everything he wanted since he was born, and he gets tired of things pretty easy. It was a toy railway that finished me. Directly he got that, I might not have been on the earth. It was lucky for me that Dick, my present old man, happened to want a dog to keep down the rats, or goodness knows what might not have happened to me. They aren't keen on dogs here unless they've pulled down enough blue ribbons to sink a ship, and mongrels like you and me—no offence—don't last long. I expect you noticed that the grown-ups didn't exactly cheer when you arrived?'

'They weren't chummy.'

'Well take it from me, your only chance is to make them chummy. If you do something to please them, they might let you stay on, even though Peter was tired of you.'

'What sort of thing?'

'That's for you to think out. I couldn't find one. I might tell you to save Peter from drowning. You don't need a pedigree to do that. But you can't drag the kid to the lake and push him in. That's the trouble. A dog gets so few opportunities. But, take it from me, if you don't do something within two weeks to make yourself solid with the adults, you can make your will. In two weeks Peter will have forgotten all about you. It's not his fault. It's the way he has been brought up. His father has all the money on earth, and Peter's the only child. You can't blame him. All I say is, look out for yourself. Well, I'm glad to have met you. Drop in again when you can. I can give you some good ratting, and I have a bone or two put away. So long.'

* * * * *

It worried me badly what Jack had said. I couldn't get it out of my mind. If it hadn't been for that, I should have had a great time, for Peter certainly made a lot of fuss of me. He treated me as if I were the only friend he had.

And, in a way, I was. When you are the only son of a man who has all the money in the world, it seems that you aren't allowed to be like an ordinary kid. They coop you up, as if you were something precious that would be contaminated by contact with other children. In all the time that I was at the house I never met another child. Peter had everything in the world, except someone of his own age to go round with; and that made him different from any of the kids I had known.

He liked talking to me. I was the only person round who really understood him. He would talk by the hour and I would listen with my tongue hanging out and nod now and then.

It was worth listening to, what he used to tell me. He told me the most surprising things. I didn't know, for instance, that there were any Red Indians in England but he said there was a chief named Big Cloud who lived in the rhododendron bushes by the lake. I never found him, though I went carefully through them one day. He also said that there were pirates on the island in the lake. I never saw them either.

What he liked telling me about best was the city of gold and precious stones which you came to if you walked far enough through the woods at the back of the stables. He was always meaning to go off there some day, and, from the way he described it, I didn't blame him. It was certainly a pretty good city. It was just right for dogs, too, he said, having bones and liver and sweet cakes there and everything else a dog could want. It used to make my mouth water to listen to him.

We were never apart. I was with him all day, and I slept on the mat in his room at night. But all the time I couldn't get out of my mind what Jack had said. I nearly did once, for it seemed to me that I was so necessary to Peter that nothing could separate us; but just as I was feeling safe his father gave him a toy aeroplane, which flew when you wound it up. The day he got it, I might not have been on the earth. I trailed along, but he hadn't a word to say to me.

Well, something went wrong with the aeroplane the second day, and it wouldn't fly, and then I was in solid again; but I had done some hard thinking and I knew just where I stood. I was the newest toy, that's what I was, and something newer might come along at any moment, and then it would be the finish for me. The only thing for me was to do something to impress the adults, just as Jack had said.

Goodness knows I tried. But everything I did turned out wrong. There seemed to be a fate about it. One morning, for example, I was trotting round the house early, and I met a fellow I could have sworn was a burglar. He wasn't one of the family, and he wasn't one of the servants, and he was hanging round the house in a most suspicious way. I chased him up a tree, and it wasn't till the family came down to breakfast, two hours later, that I found that he was a guest who had arrived overnight, and had come out early to enjoy the freshness of the morning and the sun shining on the lake, he being that sort of man. That didn't help me much.

Next, I got in wrong with the boss, Peter's father. I don't know why. I met him out in the park with another man, both carrying bundles of sticks and looking very serious and earnest. Just as I reached him, the boss lifted one of the sticks and hit a small white ball with it. He had never seemed to want to play with me before, and I took it as a great compliment. I raced after the ball, which he had hit quite a long way, picked it up in my mouth, and brought it back to him. I laid it at his feet, and smiled up at him.

'Hit it again,' I said.

He wasn't pleased at all. He said all sorts of things and tried to kick me, and that night, when he thought I was not listening, I heard him telling his wife that I was a pest and would have to be got rid of. That made me think.

And then I put the lid on it. With the best intentions in the world I got myself into such a mess that I thought the end had come.

It happened one afternoon in the drawing-room. There were visitors that day—women; and women seem fatal to me. I was in the background, trying not to be seen, for, though I had been brought in by Peter, the family never liked my coming into the drawing-room. I was hoping for a piece of cake and not paying much attention to the conversation, which was all about somebody called Toto, whom I had not met. Peter's mother said Toto was a sweet little darling, he was; and one of the visitors said Toto had not been at all himself that day and she was quite worried. And a good lot more about how all that Toto would ever take for dinner was a little white meat of chicken, chopped up fine. It was not very interesting, and I had allowed my attention to wander.

And just then, peeping round the corner of my chair to see if there were any signs of cake, what should I see but a great beastly brute of a rat. It was standing right beside the visitor, drinking milk out of a saucer, if you please!

I may have my faults, but procrastination in the presence of rats is not one of them. I didn't hesitate for a second. Here was my chance. If there is one thing women hate, it is a rat. Mother always used to say, 'If you want to succeed in life, please the women. They are the real bosses. The men don't count.' By eliminating this rodent I should earn the gratitude and esteem of Peter's mother, and, if I did that, it did not matter what Peter's father thought of me.

I sprang.

The rat hadn't a chance to get away. I was right on to him. I got hold of his neck, gave him a couple of shakes, and chucked him across the room. Then I ran across to finish him off.

Just as I reached him, he sat up and barked at me. I was never so taken aback in my life. I pulled up short and stared at him.

'I'm sure I beg your pardon, sir,' I said apologetically. 'I thought you were a rat.'

And then everything broke loose. Somebody got me by the collar, somebody else hit me on the head with a parasol, and somebody else kicked me in the ribs. Everybody talked and shouted at the same time.

'Poor darling Toto!' cried the visitor, snatching up the little animal.

'Did the great savage brute try to murder you!'

'So absolutely unprovoked!'

'He just flew at the poor little thing!'

It was no good my trying to explain. Any dog in my place would have made the same mistake. The creature was a toy-dog of one of those extraordinary breeds—a prize-winner and champion, and so on, of course, and worth his weight in gold. I would have done better to bite the visitor than Toto. That much I gathered from the general run of the conversation, and then, having discovered that the door was shut, I edged under the sofa. I was embarrassed.

'That settles it!' said Peter's mother. 'The dog is not safe. He must be shot.'

Peter gave a yell at this, but for once he didn't swing the voting an inch.

'Be quiet, Peter,' said his mother. 'It is not safe for you to have such a dog. He may be mad.'

Women are very unreasonable.

Toto, of course, wouldn't say a word to explain how the mistake arose. He was sitting on the visitor's lap, shrieking about what he would have done to me if they hadn't separated us.

Somebody felt cautiously under the sofa. I recognized the shoes of Weeks, the butler. I suppose they had rung for him to come and take me, and I could see that he wasn't half liking it. I was sorry for Weeks, who was a friend of mine, so I licked his hand, and that seemed to cheer him up a whole lot.

'I have him now, madam,' I heard him say.

'Take him to the stables and tie him up, Weeks, and tell one of the men to bring his gun and shoot him. He is not safe.'

A few minutes later I was in an empty stall, tied up to the manger.

It was all over. It had been pleasant while it lasted, but I had reached the end of my tether now. I don't think I was frightened, but a sense of pathos stole over me. I had meant so well. It seemed as if good intentions went for nothing in this world. I had tried so hard to please everybody, and this was the result—tied up in a dark stable, waiting for the end.

The shadows lengthened in the stable-yard, and still nobody came. I began to wonder if they had forgotten me, and presently, in spite of myself, a faint hope began to spring up inside me that this might mean that I was not to be shot after all. Perhaps Toto at the eleventh hour had explained everything.

And then footsteps sounded outside, and the hope died away. I shut my eyes.

Somebody put his arms round my neck, and my nose touched a warm cheek. I opened my eyes. It was not the man with the gun come to shoot me. It was Peter. He was breathing very hard, and he had been crying.

'Quiet!' he whispered.

He began to untie the rope.

'You must keep quite quiet, or they will hear us, and then we shall be stopped. I'm going to take you into the woods, and we'll walk and walk until we come to the city I told you about that's all gold and diamonds, and we'll live there for the rest of our lives, and no one will be able to hurt us. But you must keep very quiet.'

He went to the stable-gate and looked out. Then he gave a little whistle to me to come after him. And we started out to find the city.

The woods were a long way away, down a hill of long grass and across a stream; and we went very carefully, keeping in the shadows and running across the open spaces. And every now and then we would stop and look back, but there was nobody to be seen. The sun was setting, and everything was very cool and quiet.

Presently we came to the stream and crossed it by a little wooden bridge, and then we were in the woods, where nobody could see us.

I had never been in the woods before, and everything was very new and exciting to me. There were squirrels and rabbits and birds, more than I had ever seen in my life, and little things that buzzed and flew and tickled my ears. I wanted to rush about and look at everything, but Peter called to me, and I came to heel. He knew where we were going, and I didn't, so I let him lead.

We went very slowly. The wood got thicker and thicker the farther we got into it. There were bushes that were difficult to push through, and long branches, covered with thorns, that reached out at you and tore at you when you tried to get away. And soon it was quite dark, so dark that I could see nothing, not even Peter, though he was so close. We went slower and slower, and the darkness was full of queer noises. From time to time Peter would stop, and I would run to him and put my nose in his hand. At first he patted me, but after a while he did not pat me any more, but just gave me his hand to lick, as if it was too much for him to lift it. I think he was getting very tired. He was quite a small boy and not strong, and we had walked a long way.

It seemed to be getting darker and darker. I could hear the sound of Peter's footsteps, and they seemed to drag as he forced his way through the bushes. And then, quite suddenly, he sat down without any warning, and when I ran up I heard him crying.

I suppose there are lots of dogs who would have known exactly the right thing to do, but I could not think of anything except to put my nose against his cheek and whine. He put his arm round my neck, and for a long time we stayed like that, saying nothing. It seemed to comfort him, for after a time he stopped crying.

I did not bother him by asking about the wonderful city where we were going, for he was so tired. But I could not help wondering if we were near it. There was not a sign of any city, nothing but darkness and odd noises and the wind singing in the trees. Curious little animals, such as I had never smelt before, came creeping out of the bushes to look at us. I would have chased them, but Peter's arm was round my neck and I could not leave him. But when something that smelt like a rabbit came so near that I could have reached out a paw and touched it, I turned my head and snapped; and then they all scurried back into the bushes and there were no more noises.

There was a long silence. Then Peter gave a great gulp.

'I'm not frightened,' he said. 'I'm not!'

I shoved my head closer against his chest. There was another silence for a long time.

'I'm going to pretend we have been captured by brigands,' said Peter at last. 'Are you listening? There were three of them, great big men with beards, and they crept up behind me and snatched me up and took me out here to their lair. This is their lair. One was called Dick, the others' names were Ted and Alfred. They took hold of me and brought me all the way through the wood till we got here, and then they went off, meaning to come back soon. And while they were away, you missed me and tracked me through the woods till you found me here. And then the brigands came back, and they didn't know you were here, and you kept quite quiet till Dick was quite near, and then you jumped out and bit him and he ran away. And then you bit Ted and you bit Alfred, and they ran away too. And so we were left all alone, and I was quite safe because you were here to look after me. And then—And then—'

His voice died away, and the arm that was round my neck went limp, and I could hear by his breathing that he was asleep. His head was resting on my back, but I didn't move. I wriggled a little closer to make him as comfortable as I could, and then I went to sleep myself.

I didn't sleep very well. I had funny dreams all the time, thinking these little animals were creeping up close enough out of the bushes for me to get a snap at them without disturbing Peter.

If I woke once, I woke a dozen times, but there was never anything there. The wind sang in the trees and the bushes rustled, and far away in the distance the frogs were calling.

And then I woke once more with the feeling that this time something really was coming through the bushes. I lifted my head as far as I could, and listened. For a little while nothing happened, and then, straight in front of me, I saw lights. And there was a sound of trampling in the undergrowth.

It was no time to think about not waking Peter. This was something definite, something that had to be attended to quick. I was up with a jump, yelling. Peter rolled off my back and woke up, and he sat there listening, while I stood with my front paws on him and shouted at the men. I was bristling all over. I didn't know who they were or what they wanted, but the way I looked at it was that anything could happen in those woods at that time of night, and, if anybody was coming along to start something, he had got to reckon with me.

Somebody called, 'Peter! Are you there, Peter?'

There was a crashing in the bushes, the lights came nearer and nearer, and then somebody said 'Here he is!' and there was a lot of shouting. I stood where I was, ready to spring if necessary, for I was taking no chances.

'Who are you?' I shouted. 'What do you want?' A light flashed in my eyes.

'Why, it's that dog!'

Somebody came into the light, and I saw it was the boss. He was looking very anxious and scared, and he scooped Peter up off the ground and hugged him tight.

Peter was only half awake. He looked up at the boss drowsily, and began to talk about brigands, and Dick and Ted and Alfred, the same as he had said to me. There wasn't a sound till he had finished. Then the boss spoke.

'Kidnappers! I thought as much. And the dog drove them away!'

For the first time in our acquaintance he actually patted me.

'Good old man!' he said.

'He's my dog,' said Peter sleepily, 'and he isn't to be shot.'

'He certainly isn't, my boy,' said the boss. 'From now on he's the honoured guest. He shall wear a gold collar and order what he wants for dinner. And now let's be getting home. It's time you were in bed.'

* * * * *

Mother used to say, 'If you're a good dog, you will be happy. If you're not, you won't,' but it seems to me that in this world it is all a matter of luck. When I did everything I could to please people, they wanted to shoot me; and when I did nothing except run away, they brought me back and treated me better than the most valuable prize-winner in the kennels. It was puzzling at first, but one day I heard the boss talking to a friend who had come down from the city.

The friend looked at me and said, 'What an ugly mongrel! Why on earth do you have him about? I thought you were so particular about your dogs?'

And the boss replied, 'He may be a mongrel, but he can have anything he wants in this house. Didn't you hear how he saved Peter from being kidnapped?'

And out it all came about the brigands.

'The kid called them brigands,' said the boss. 'I suppose that's how it would strike a child of that age. But he kept mentioning the name Dick, and that put the police on the scent. It seems there's a kidnapper well known to the police all over the country as Dick the Snatcher. It was almost certainly that scoundrel and his gang. How they spirited the child away, goodness knows, but they managed it, and the dog tracked them and scared them off. We found him and Peter together in the woods. It was a narrow escape, and we have to thank this animal here for it.'

What could I say? It was no more use trying to put them right than it had been when I mistook Toto for a rat. Peter had gone to sleep that night pretending about the brigands to pass the time, and when he awoke he still believed in them. He was that sort of child. There was nothing that I could do about it.

Round the corner, as the boss was speaking, I saw the kennel-man coming with a plate in his hand. It smelt fine, and he was headed straight for me.

He put the plate down before me. It was liver, which I love.

'Yes,' went on the boss, 'if it hadn't been for him, Peter would have been kidnapped and scared half to death, and I should be poorer, I suppose, by whatever the scoundrels had chosen to hold me up for.'

I am an honest dog, and hate to obtain credit under false pretences, but—liver is liver. I let it go at that.

CROWNED HEADS

Katie had never been more surprised in her life than when the serious young man with the brown eyes and the Charles Dana Gibson profile spirited her away from his friend and Genevieve. Till that moment she had looked on herself as playing a sort of 'villager and retainer' part to the brown-eyed young man's hero and Genevieve's heroine. She knew she was not pretty, though somebody (unidentified) had once said that she had nice eyes; whereas Genevieve was notoriously a beauty, incessantly pestered, so report had it, by musical comedy managers to go on the stage.

Genevieve was tall and blonde, a destroyer of masculine peace of mind. She said 'harf' and 'rahther', and might easily have been taken for an English duchess instead of a cloak-model at Macey's. You would have said, in short, that, in the matter of personable young men, Genevieve would have swept the board. Yet, here was this one deliberately selecting her, Katie, for his companion. It was almost a miracle.

He had managed it with the utmost dexterity at the merry-go-round. With winning politeness he had assisted Genevieve on her wooden steed, and then, as the machinery began to work, had grasped Katie's arm and led her at a rapid walk out into the sunlight. Katie's last glimpse of Genevieve had been the sight of her amazed and offended face as it whizzed round the corner, while the steam melodeon drowned protests with a spirited plunge into 'Alexander's Ragtime Band'.

Katie felt shy. This young man was a perfect stranger. It was true she had had a formal introduction to him, but only from Genevieve, who had scraped acquaintance with him exactly two minutes previously. It had happened on the ferry-boat on the way to Palisades Park. Genevieve's bright eye, roving among the throng on the lower deck, had singled out this young man and his companion as suitable cavaliers for the expedition. The young man pleased her, and his friend, with the broken nose and the face like a good-natured bulldog, was obviously suitable for Katie.

Etiquette is not rigid on New York ferry-boats. Without fuss or delay she proceeded to make their acquaintance—to Katie's concern, for she could never get used to Genevieve's short way with strangers. The quiet life she had led had made her almost prudish, and there were times when Genevieve's conduct shocked her. Of course, she knew there was no harm in Genevieve. As the latter herself had once put it, 'The feller that tries to get gay with me is going to get a call-down that'll make him holler for his winter overcoat.' But all the same she could not approve. And the net result of her disapproval was to make her shy and silent as she walked by this young man's side.

The young man seemed to divine her thoughts.

'Say, I'm on the level,' he observed. 'You want to get that. Right on the square. See?'

'Oh, yes,' said Katie, relieved but yet embarrassed. It was awkward to have one's thoughts read like this.

'You ain't like your friend. Don't think I don't see that.'

'Genevieve's a sweet girl,' said Katie, loyally.

'A darned sight too sweet. Somebody ought to tell her mother.'

'Why did you speak to her if you did not like her?'

'Wanted to get to know you,' said the young man simply.

They walked on in silence. Katie's heart was beating with a rapidity that forbade speech. Nothing like this very direct young man had ever happened to her before. She had grown so accustomed to regarding herself as something too insignificant and unattractive for the notice of the lordly male that she was overwhelmed. She had a vague feeling that there was a mistake somewhere. It surely could not be she who was proving so alluring to this fairy prince. The novelty of the situation frightened her.

'Come here often?' asked her companion.

'I've never been here before.'

'Often go to Coney?'

'I've never been.'

He regarded her with astonishment.

'You've never been to Coney Island! Why, you don't know what this sort of thing is till you've taken in Coney. This place isn't on the map with Coney. Do you mean to say you've never seen Luna Park, or Dreamland, or Steeplechase, or the diving ducks? Haven't you had a look at the Mardi Gras stunts? Why, Coney during Mardi Gras is the greatest thing on earth. It's a knockout. Just about a million boys and girls having the best time that ever was. Say, I guess you don't go out much, do you?'

'Not much.'

'If it's not a rude question, what do you do? I been trying to place you all along. Now I reckon your friend works in a store, don't she?'

'Yes. She's a cloak-model. She has a lovely figure, hasn't she?'

'Didn't notice it. I guess so, if she's what you say. It's what they pay her for, ain't it? Do you work in a store, too?'

'Not exactly. I keep a little shop.'

'All by yourself?'

'I do all the work now. It was my father's shop, but he's dead. It began by being my grandfather's. He started it. But he's so old now that, of course, he can't work any longer, so I look after things.'

'Say, you're a wonder! What sort of a shop?'

'It's only a little second-hand bookshop. There really isn't much to do.'

'Where is it?'

'Sixth Avenue. Near Washington Square.'

'What name?'

'Bennett.'

'That's your name, then?'

'Yes.'

'Anything besides Bennett?'

'My name's Kate.'

The young man nodded.

'I'd make a pretty good district attorney,' he said, disarming possible resentment at this cross-examination. 'I guess you're wondering if I'm ever going to stop asking you questions. Well, what would you like to do?'

'Don't you think we ought to go back and find your friend and Genevieve? They will be wondering where we are.'

'Let 'em,' said the young man briefly. 'I've had all I want of Jenny.'

'I can't understand why you don't like her.'

'I like you. Shall we have some ice-cream, or would you rather go on the Scenic Railway?'

Katie decided on the more peaceful pleasure. They resumed their walk, socially licking two cones. Out of the corner of her eyes Katie cast swift glances at her friend's face. He was a very grave young man. There was something important as well as handsome about him. Once, as they made their way through the crowds, she saw a couple of boys look almost reverently at him. She wondered who he could be, but was too shy to inquire. She had got over her nervousness to a great extent, but there were still limits to what she felt herself equal to saying. It did not strike her that it was only fair that she should ask a few questions in return for those which he had put. She had always repressed herself, and she did so now. She was content to be with him without finding out his name and history.

He supplied the former just before he finally consented to let her go.

They were standing looking over the river. The sun had spent its force, and it was cool and pleasant in the breeze which was coming up the Hudson. Katie was conscious of a vague feeling that was almost melancholy. It had been a lovely afternoon, and she was sorry that it was over.

The young man shuffled his feet on the loose stones.

'I'm mighty glad I met you,' he said. 'Say, I'm coming to see you. On Sixth Avenue. Don't mind, do you?'

He did not wait for a reply.

'Brady's my name. Ted Brady, Glencoe Athletic Club,' he paused. 'I'm on the level,' he added, and paused again. 'I like you a whole lot. There's your friend, Genevieve. Better go after her, hadn't you? Good-bye.' And he was gone, walking swiftly through the crowd about the bandstand.

Katie went back to Genevieve, and Genevieve was simply horrid. Cold and haughty, a beautiful iceberg of dudgeon, she refused to speak a single word during the whole long journey back to Sixth Avenue. And Katie, whose tender heart would at other times have been tortured by this hostility, leant back in her seat, and was happy. Her mind was far away from Genevieve's frozen gloom, living over again the wonderful happenings of the afternoon.

Yes, it had been a wonderful afternoon, but trouble was waiting for her in Sixth Avenue. Trouble was never absent for very long from Katie's unselfish life. Arriving at the little bookshop, she found Mr Murdoch, the glazier, preparing for departure. Mr Murdoch came in on Mondays, Wednesdays, and Fridays to play draughts with her grandfather, who was paralysed from the waist, and unable to leave the house except when Katie took him for his outing in Washington Square each morning in his bath-chair.

Mr Murdoch welcomed Katie with joy.

'I was wondering whenever you would come back, Katie. I'm afraid the old man's a little upset.'

'Not ill?'

'Not ill. Upset. And it was my fault, too. Thinking he'd be interested, I read him a piece from the paper where I seen about these English Suffragettes, and he just went up in the air. I guess he'll be all right now you've come back. I was a fool to read it, I reckon. I kind of forgot for the moment.'

'Please don't worry yourself about it, Mr Murdoch. He'll be all right soon. I'll go to him.'

In the inner room the old man was sitting. His face was flushed, and he gesticulated from time to time.

'I won't have it,' he cried as Katie entered. 'I tell you I won't have it. If Parliament can't do anything, I'll send Parliament about its business.'

'Here I am, grandpapa,' said Katie quickly. 'I've had the greatest time. It was lovely up there. I—'

'I tell you it's got to stop. I've spoken about it before. I won't have it.'

'I expect they're doing their best. It's your being so far away that makes it hard for them. But I do think you might write them a very sharp letter.'

'I will. I will. Get out the paper. Are you ready?' He stopped, and looked piteously at Katie. 'I don't know what to say. I don't know how to begin.'

Katie scribbled a few lines.

'How would this do? "His Majesty informs his Government that he is greatly surprised and indignant that no notice has been taken of his previous communications. If this goes on, he will be reluctantly compelled to put the matter in other hands."'

She read it glibly as she had written it. The formula had been a favourite one of her late father, when roused to fall upon offending patrons of the bookshop.

The old man beamed. His resentment was gone. He was soothed and happy.

'That'll wake 'em up,' he said. 'I won't have these goings on while I'm king, and if they don't like it, they know what to do. You're a good girl, Katie.'

He chuckled.

'I beat Lord Murdoch five games to nothing,' he said.

It was now nearly two years since the morning when old Matthew Bennett had announced to an audience consisting of Katie and a smoky blue cat, which had wandered in from Washington Square to take pot-luck, that he was the King of England.

This was a long time for any one delusion of the old man's to last. Usually they came and went with a rapidity which made it hard for Katie, for all her tact, to keep abreast of them. She was not likely to forget the time when he went to bed President Roosevelt and woke up the Prophet Elijah. It was the only occasion in all the years they had passed together when she had felt like giving way and indulging in the fit of hysterics which most girls of her age would have had as a matter of course.

She had handled that crisis, and she handled the present one with equal smoothness. When her grandfather made his announcement, which he did rather as one stating a generally recognized fact than as if the information were in any way sensational, she neither screamed nor swooned, nor did she rush to the neighbours for advice. She merely gave the old man his breakfast, not forgetting to set aside a suitable portion for the smoky cat, and then went round to notify Mr Murdoch of what had happened.

Mr Murdoch, excellent man, received the news without any fuss or excitement at all, and promised to look in on Schwartz, the stout saloon-keeper, who was Mr Bennett's companion and antagonist at draughts on Tuesdays, Thursdays, and Saturdays, and, as he expressed it, put him wise.

Life ran comfortably in the new groove. Old Mr Bennett continued to play draughts and pore over his second-hand classics. Every morning he took his outing in Washington Square where, from his invalid's chair, he surveyed somnolent Italians and roller-skating children with his old air of kindly approval. Katie, whom circumstances had taught to be thankful for small mercies, was perfectly happy in the shadow of the throne. She liked her work; she liked looking after her grandfather; and now that Ted Brady had come into her life, she really began to look on herself as an exceptionally lucky girl, a spoilt favourite of Fortune.

For Ted Brady had called, as he said he would, and from the very first he had made plain in his grave, direct way the objects of his visits. There was no subtlety about Ted, no finesse. He was as frank as a music-hall love song.

On his first visit, having handed Katie a large bunch of roses with the stolidity of a messenger boy handing over a parcel, he had proceeded, by way of establishing his *bona fides*, to tell her all about himself. He supplied the facts in no settled order, just as they happened to occur to him in the long silences with which his speech was punctuated. Small facts jostled large facts. He spoke of his morals and his fox-terrier in the same breath.

'I'm on the level. Ask anyone who knows me. They'll tell you that. Say, I got the cutest little dog you ever seen. Do you like dogs? I've never been a fellow that's got himself mixed up with girls. I don't like 'em as a general thing. A fellow's got too much to do keeping himself in training, if his club expects him to do things. I belong to the Glencoe Athletic. I ran the hundred yards dash in evens last sports there was. They expect me to do it at the Glencoe, so I've never got myself mixed up with girls. Till I seen you that afternoon I reckon I'd hardly looked at a girl, honest. They didn't seem to kind of make any hit with me. And then I seen you, and I says to myself, "That's the one." It sort of came over me in a flash. I fell for you directly I seen you. And I'm on the level. Don't forget that.'

And more in the same strain, leaning on the counter and looking into Katie's eyes with a devotion that added emphasis to his measured speech.

Next day he came again, and kissed her respectfully but firmly, making a sort of shuffling dive across the counter. Breaking away, he fumbled in his pocket and produced a ring, which he proceeded to place on her finger with the serious air which accompanied all his actions.

'That looks pretty good to me,' he said, as he stepped back and eyed it.

It struck Katie, when he had gone, how differently different men did things. Genevieve had often related stories of men who had proposed to her, and according to Genevieve, they always got excited and emotional, and sometimes cried. Ted Brady had fitted her with the ring more like a glover's assistant than anything else, and he had hardly spoken a word from beginning to end. He had seemed to take her acquiescence for granted. And yet there had been nothing flat or disappointing about the proceedings. She had been thrilled throughout. It is to be supposed that Mr Brady had the force of character which does not require the aid of speech.

It was not till she took the news of her engagement to old Mr Bennett that it was borne in upon Katie that Fate did not intend to be so wholly benevolent to her as she supposed.

That her grandfather could offer any opposition had not occurred to her as a possibility. She took his approval for granted. Never, as long as she could remember, had he been anything but kind to her. And the only possible objections to marriage from a grandfather's point of view—badness of character, insufficient means, or inferiority of social position—were in this case gloriously absent.

She could not see how anyone, however hypercritical, could find a flaw in Ted. His character was spotless. He was comfortably off. And so far from being in any way inferior socially, it was he who condescended. For Ted, she had discovered from conversation with Mr Murdoch, the glazier, was no ordinary young man. He was a celebrity. So much so that for a moment, when told the news of the engagement, Mr Murdoch, startled out of his usual tact, had exhibited frank surprise that the great Ted Brady should not have aimed higher.

'You're sure you've got the name right, Katie?' he had said. 'It's really Ted Brady? No mistake about the first name? Well-built, good-looking young chap with brown eyes? Well, this beats me. Not,' he went on hurriedly, 'that any young fellow mightn't think himself lucky to get a wife like you, Katie, but Ted Brady! Why, there isn't a girl in this part of the town, or in Harlem or the Bronx, for that matter, who wouldn't give her eyes to be in your place. Why, Ted Brady is the big noise. He's the star of the Glencoe.'

'He told me he belonged to the Glencoe Athletic.'

'Don't you believe it. It belongs to him. Why, the way that boy runs and jumps is the real limit. There's only Billy Burton, of the Irish-American, that can touch him. You've certainly got the pick of the bunch, Katie.'

He stared at her admiringly, as if for the first time realizing her true worth. For Mr Murdoch was a great patron of sport.

With these facts in her possession Katie had approached the interview with her grandfather with a good deal of confidence.

The old man listened to her recital of Mr Brady's qualities in silence.

Then he shook his head.

'It can't be, Katie. I couldn't have it.'

'Grandpapa!'

'You're forgetting, my dear.'

'Forgetting?'

'Who ever heard of such a thing? The grand-daughter of the King of England marrying a commoner! It wouldn't do at all.'

Consternation, surprise, and misery kept Katie dumb. She had learned in a hard school to be prepared for sudden blows from the hand of fate, but this one was so entirely unforeseen that it found her unprepared, and she was crushed by it. She knew her grandfather's obstinacy too well to argue against the decision.

'Oh, no, not at all,' he repeated. 'Oh, no, it wouldn't do.'

Katie said nothing; she was beyond speech. She stood there wide-eyed and silent among the ruins of her little air-castle. The old man patted her hand affectionately. He was pleased at her docility. It was the right attitude, becoming in one of her high rank.

'I am very sorry, my dear, but—oh, no! oh, no! oh, no—' His voice trailed away into an unintelligible mutter. He was a very old man, and he was not always able to concentrate his thoughts on a subject for any length of time.

So little did Ted Brady realize at first the true complexity of the situation that he was inclined, when he heard of the news, to treat the crisis in the jaunty, dashing, love-laughs-at-locksmith fashion so popular with young men of spirit when thwarted in their loves by the interference of parents and guardians.

It took Katie some time to convince him that, just because he had the licence in his pocket, he could not snatch her up on his saddle-bow and carry her off to the nearest clergyman after the manner of young Lochinvar.

In the first flush of his resentment at restraint he saw no reason why he should differentiate between old Mr Bennett and the conventional banns-forbidding father of the novelettes with which he was accustomed to sweeten his hours of idleness. To him, till Katie explained the intricacies of the position, Mr Bennett was simply the proud millionaire who would not hear of his daughter marrying the artist.

'But, Ted, dear, you don't understand,' Katie said. 'We simply couldn't do that. There's no one but me to look after him, poor old man. How could I run away like that and get married? What would become of him?'

'You wouldn't be away long,' urged Mr Brady, a man of many parts, but not a rapid thinker. 'The minister would have us fixed up inside of half an hour. Then we'd look in at Mouquin's for a steak and fried, just to make a sort of wedding breakfast. And then back we'd come, hand-in-hand, and say, "Well, here we are. Now what?"'

'He would never forgive me.'

'That,' said Ted judicially, 'would be up to him.'

'It would kill him. Don't you see, we know that it's all nonsense, this idea of his; but he really thinks he is the king, and he's so old that the shock of my disobeying him would be too much. Honest, Ted, dear, I couldn't.'

Gloom unutterable darkened Ted Brady's always serious countenance. The difficulties of the situation were beginning to come home to him.

'Maybe if I went and saw him—' he suggested at last.

'You *could*,' said Katie doubtfully.

Ted tightened his belt with an air of determination, and bit resolutely on the chewing-gum which was his inseparable companion.

'I will,' he said.

'You'll be nice to him, Ted?'

He nodded. He was the man of action, not words.

It was perhaps ten minutes before he came out of the inner room in which Mr Bennett passed his days. When he did, there was no light of jubilation on his face. His brow was darker than ever.

Katie looked at him anxiously. He returned the look with a sombre shake of the head.

'Nothing doing,' he said shortly. He paused. 'Unless,' he added, 'you count it anything that he's made me an earl.'

In the next two weeks several brains busied themselves with the situation. Genevieve, reconciled to Katie after a decent interval of wounded dignity, said she supposed there was a way out, if one could only think of it, but it certainly got past her. The only approach to a plan of action was suggested by the broken-nosed individual who had been Ted's companion that day at Palisades Park, a gentleman of some eminence in the boxing world, who rejoiced in the name of the Tennessee Bear-Cat.

What they ought to do, in the Bear-Cat's opinion, was to get the old man out into Washington Square one morning. He of Tennessee would then sasshay up in a flip manner and make a break. Ted, waiting close by, would resent his insolence. There would be words, followed by blows.

'See what I mean?' pursued the Bear-Cat. 'There's you and me mixing it. I'll square the cop on the beat to leave us be; he's a friend of mine. Pretty soon you land me one on the plexus, and I take th' count. Then there's you hauling me up by th' collar to the old gentleman, and me saying I quits and apologizing. See what I mean?'

The whole, presumably, to conclude with warm expressions of gratitude and esteem from Mr Bennett, and an instant withdrawal of the veto.

Ted himself approved of the scheme. He said it was a cracker-jaw, and he wondered how one so notoriously ivory-skulled as the other could have had such an idea. The Bear-Cat said modestly that he had 'em sometimes. And it is probable that all would have been well, had it not been necessary to tell the plan to Katie, who was horrified at the very idea, spoke warmly of the danger to her grandfather's nervous system, and said she did not think the Bear-Cat could be a nice friend for Ted. And matters relapsed into their old state of hopelessness.

And then, one day, Katie forced herself to tell Ted that she thought it would be better if they did not see each other for a time. She said that these meetings were only a source of pain to both of them. It would really be better if he did not come round for—well, quite some time.

It had not been easy for her to say it. The decision was the outcome of many wakeful nights. She had asked herself the question whether it was fair for her to keep Ted chained to her in this hopeless fashion, when, left to himself and away from her, he might so easily find some other girl to make him happy.

So Ted went, reluctantly, and the little shop on Sixth Avenue knew him no more. And Katie spent her time looking after old Mr Bennett (who had completely forgotten the affair by now, and sometimes wondered why Katie was not so cheerful as she had been), and—for, though unselfish, she was human—hating those unknown girls whom in her mind's eye she could see clustering round Ted, smiling at him, making much of him, and driving the bare recollection of her out of his mind.

The summer passed. July came and went, making New York an oven. August followed, and one wondered why one had complained of July's tepid advances.

It was on the evening of September the eleventh that Katie, having closed the little shop, sat in the dusk on the steps, as many thousands of her fellow-townsmen and townswomen were doing, turning her face to the first breeze which New York had known for two months. The hot spell had broken abruptly that afternoon, and the city was drinking in the coolness as a flower drinks water.

From round the corner, where the yellow cross of the Judson Hotel shone down on Washington Square, came the shouts of children, and the strains, mellowed by distance, of the indefatigable barrel-organ which had played the same tunes in the same place since the spring.

Katie closed her eyes, and listened. It was very peaceful this evening, so peaceful that for an instant she forgot even to think of Ted. And it was just during this instant that she heard his voice.

'That you, kid?'

He was standing before her, his hands in his pockets, one foot on the pavement, the other in the road; and if he was agitated, his voice did not show it.

'Ted!'

'That's me. Can I see the old man for a minute, Katie?'

This time it did seem to her that she could detect a slight ring of excitement.

'It's no use, Ted. Honest.'

'No harm in going in and passing the time of day, is there? I've got something I want to say to him.'

'What?'

'Tell you later, maybe. Is he in his room?'

He stepped past her, and went in. As he went, he caught her arm and pressed it, but he did not stop. She saw him go into the inner room and heard through the door as he closed it behind him, the murmur of voices. And almost immediately, it seemed to her, her name was called. It was her grandfather's voice which called, high and excited. The door opened, and Ted appeared.

'Come here a minute, Katie, will you?' he said. 'You're wanted.'

The old man was leaning forward in his chair. He was in a state of extraordinary excitement. He quivered and jumped. Ted, standing by the wall, looked as stolid as ever; but his eyes glittered.

'Katie,' cried the old man, 'this is a most remarkable piece of news.

This gentleman has just been telling me—extraordinary. He—'

He broke off, and looked at Ted, as he had looked at Katie when he had tried to write the letter to the Parliament of England.

Ted's eye, as it met Katie's, was almost defiant.

'I want to marry you,' he said.

'Yes, yes,' broke in Mr Bennett, impatiently, 'but—'

'And I'm a king.'

'Yes, yes, that's it, that's it, Katie. This gentleman is a king.'

Once more Ted's eye met Katie's, and this time there was an imploring look in it.

'That's right,' he said, slowly. 'I've just been telling your grandfather I'm the King of Coney Island.'

'That's it. Of Coney Island.'

'So there's no objection now to us getting married, kid—Your Royal

Highness. It's a royal alliance, see?'

'A royal alliance,' echoed Mr Bennett.

Out in the street, Ted held Katie's hand, and grinned a little sheepishly.

'You're mighty quiet, kid,' he said. 'It looks as if it don't make much of a hit with you, the notion of being married to me.'

'Oh, Ted! But—'

He squeezed her hand.

'I know what you're thinking. I guess it was raw work pulling a tale like that on the old man. I hated to do it, but gee! when a fellow's up against it like I was, he's apt to grab most any chance that comes along. Why, say, kid, it kind of looked to me as if it was sort of *meant*. Coming just now, like it did, just when it was wanted, and just when it didn't seem possible it could happen. Why, a week ago I was nigh on two hundred votes behind Billy Burton. The Irish-American put him up, and everybody thought he'd be King at the Mardi Gras. And then suddenly they came pouring in for me, till at the finish I had Billy looking like a regular has-been.

'It's funny the way the voting jumps about every year in this Coney election. It was just Providence, and it didn't seem right to let it go by. So I went in to the old man, and told him. Say, I tell you I was just sweating when I got ready to hand it to him. It was an outside chance he'd remember all about what the Mardi Gras at Coney was, and just what being a king at it amounted to. Then I remembered you telling me you'd never been to Coney, so I figured your grandfather wouldn't be what you'd call well fixed in his information about it, so I took the chance.

'I tried him out first. I tried him with Brooklyn. Why, say, from the way he took it, he'd either never heard of the place, or else he'd forgotten what it was. I guess he don't remember much, poor old fellow. Then I mentioned Yonkers. He asked me what Yonkers were. Then I reckoned it was safe to bring on Coney, and he fell for it right away. I felt mean, but it had to be done.'

He caught her up, and swung her into the air with a perfectly impassive face. Then, having kissed her, he lowered her gently to the ground again. The action seemed to have relieved his feelings, for when he spoke again it was plain that his conscience no longer troubled him.

'And say,' he said, 'come to think of it, I don't see where there's so much call for me to feel mean. I'm not so far short of being a regular king. Coney's just as big as some of those kingdoms you read about on the other side; and, from what you see in the papers about the goings-on there, it looks to me that, having a whole week on the throne like I'm going to have, amounts to a pretty steady job as kings go.'

AT GEISENHEIMER'S

As I walked to Geisenheimer's that night I was feeling blue and restless, tired of New York, tired of dancing, tired of everything. Broadway was full of people hurrying to the theatres. Cars rattled by. All the electric lights in the world were blazing down on the Great White Way. And it all seemed stale and dreary to me.

Geisenheimer's was full as usual. All the tables were occupied, and there were several couples already on the dancing-floor in the centre. The band was playing 'Michigan':

I want to go back, I want to go back
To the place where I was born.
Far away from harm
With a milk-pail on my arm.

I suppose the fellow who wrote that would have called for the police if anyone had ever really tried to get him on to a farm, but he has certainly put something into the tune which makes you think he meant what he said. It's a homesick tune, that.

I was just looking round for an empty table, when a man jumped up and came towards me, registering joy as if I had been his long-lost sister.

He was from the country. I could see that. It was written all over him, from his face to his shoes.

He came up with his hand out, beaming.

'Why, Miss Roxborough!'

'Why not?' I said.

'Don't you remember me?'

I didn't.

'My name is Ferris.'

'It's a nice name, but it means nothing in my young life.'

'I was introduced to you last time I came here. We danced together.'

This seemed to bear the stamp of truth. If he was introduced to me, he probably danced with me. It's what I'm at Geisenheimer's for.

'When was it?'

'A year ago last April.'

You can't beat these rural charmers. They think New York is folded up and put away in camphor when they leave, and only taken out again when they pay their next visit. The notion that anything could possibly have happened since he was last in our midst to blur the memory of that happy evening had not occurred to Mr Ferris. I suppose he was so accustomed to dating things from 'when I was in New York' that he thought everybody else must do the same.

'Why, sure, I remember you,' I said. 'Algernon Clarence, isn't it?'

'Not Algernon Clarence. My name's Charlie.'

'My mistake. And what's the great scheme, Mr Ferris? Do you want to dance with me again?'

He did. So we started. Mine not to reason why, mine but to do and die, as the poem says. If an elephant had come into Geisenheimer's and asked me to dance I'd have had to do it. And I'm not saying that Mr Ferris wasn't the next thing to it. He was one of those earnest, persevering dancers—the kind that have taken twelve correspondence lessons.

I guess I was about due that night to meet someone from the country. There still come days in the spring when the country seems to get a stranglehold on me and start in pulling. This particular day had been one of them. I got up in the morning and looked out of the window, and the breeze just wrapped me round and began whispering about pigs and chickens. And when I went out on Fifth Avenue there seemed to be flowers everywhere. I headed for the Park, and there was the grass all green, and the trees coming out, and a sort of something in the air—why, say, if there hadn't have been a big policeman keeping an eye on me, I'd have flung myself down and bitten chunks out of the turf.

And as soon as I got to Geisenheimer's they played that 'Michigan' thing.

Why, Charlie from Squeedunk's 'entrance' couldn't have been better worked up if he'd been a star in a Broadway show. The stage was just waiting for him.

But somebody's always taking the joy out of life. I ought to have remembered that the most metropolitan thing in the metropolis is a rustic who's putting in a week there. We weren't thinking on the same plane, Charlie and me. The way I had been feeling all day, what I wanted to talk about was last season's crops. The subject he fancied was this season's chorus-girls. Our souls didn't touch by a mile and a half.

'This is the life!' he said.

There's always a point when that sort of man says that.

'I suppose you come here quite a lot?' he said.

'Pretty often.'

I didn't tell him that I came there every night, and that I came because I was paid for it. If you're a professional dancer at Geisenheimer's, you aren't supposed to advertise the fact. The management thinks that if you did it might send the public away thinking too hard when they saw you win the Great Contest for the Love-r-ly Silver Cup which they offer later in the evening. Say, that Love-r-ly Cup's a joke. I win it on Mondays, Wednesdays, and Fridays, and Mabel Francis wins it on Tuesdays, Thursdays, and Saturdays. It's all perfectly fair and square, of course. It's purely a matter of merit who wins the Love-r-ly Cup. Anybody could win it. Only somehow they don't. And the coincidence of the fact that Mabel and I always do has kind of got on the management's nerves, and they don't like us to tell people we're employed there. They prefer us to blush unseen.

'It's a great place,' said Mr Ferris, 'and New York's a great place.

I'd like to live in New York.'

'The loss is ours. Why don't you?'

'Some city! But dad's dead now, and I've got the drugstore, you know.'

He spoke as if I ought to remember reading about it in the papers.

'And I'm making good with it, what's more. I've got push and ideas.

Say, I got married since I saw you last.'

'You did, did you?' I said. 'Then what are you doing, may I ask, dancing on Broadway like a gay bachelor? I suppose you have left your wife at Hicks' Corners, singing "Where is my wandering boy tonight"?'

'Not Hicks' Corners. Ashley, Maine. That's where I live. My wife comes from Rodney.... Pardon me, I'm afraid I stepped on your foot.'

'My fault,' I said; 'I lost step. Well, I wonder you aren't ashamed even to think of your wife, when you've left her all alone out there while you come whooping it up in New York. Haven't you got any conscience?'

'But I haven't left her. She's here.'

'In New York?'

'In this restaurant. That's her up there.'

I looked up at the balcony. There was a face hanging over the red plush rail. It looked to me as if it had some hidden sorrow. I'd noticed it before, when we were dancing around, and I had wondered what the trouble was. Now I began to see.

'Why aren't you dancing with her and giving her a good time, then?' I said.

'Oh, she's having a good time.'

'She doesn't look it. She looks as if she would like to be down here, treading the measure.'

'She doesn't dance much.'

'Don't you have dances at Ashley?'

'It's different at home. She dances well enough for Ashley, but—well, this isn't Ashley.'

'I see. But you're not like that?'

He gave a kind of smirk.

'Oh, I've been in New York before.'

I could have bitten him, the sawn-off little rube! It made me mad. He was ashamed to dance in public with his wife—didn't think her good enough for him. So he had dumped her in a chair, given her a lemonade, and told her to be good, and then gone off to have a good time. They could have had me arrested for what I was thinking just then.

The band began to play something else.

'This is the life!' said Mr Ferris. 'Let's do it again.'

'Let somebody else do it,' I said. 'I'm tired. I'll introduce you to some friends of mine.'

So I took him off, and whisked him on to some girls I knew at one of the tables.

'Shake hands with my friend Mr Ferris,' I said. 'He wants to show you the latest steps. He does most of them on your feet.'

I could have betted on Charlie, the Debonair Pride of Ashley. Guess what he said? He said, 'This is the life!'

And I left him, and went up to the balcony.

She was leaning with her elbows on the red plush, looking down on the dancing-floor. They had just started another tune, and hubby was moving around with one of the girls I'd introduced him to. She didn't have to prove to me that she came from the country. I knew it. She was a little bit of a thing, old-fashioned looking. She was dressed in grey, with white muslin collar and cuffs, and her hair done simple. She had a black hat.

I kind of hovered for awhile. It isn't the best thing I do, being shy; as a general thing I'm more or less there with the nerve; but somehow I sort of hesitated to charge in.

Then I braced up, and made for the vacant chair.

'I'll sit here, if you don't mind,' I said.

She turned in a startled way. I could see she was wondering who I was, and what right I had there, but wasn't certain whether it might not be city etiquette for strangers to come and dump themselves down and start chatting. 'I've just been dancing with your husband,' I said, to ease things along.

'I saw you.'

She fixed me with a pair of big brown eyes. I took one look at them, and then I had to tell myself that it might be pleasant, and a relief to my feelings, to take something solid and heavy and drop it over the rail on to hubby, but the management wouldn't like it. That was how I felt about him just then. The poor kid was doing everything with those eyes except crying. She looked like a dog that's been kicked.

She looked away, and fiddled with the string of the electric light. There was a hatpin lying on the table. She picked it up, and began to dig at the red plush.

'Ah, come on sis,' I said; 'tell me all about it.'

'I don't know what you mean.'

'You can't fool me. Tell me your troubles.'

'I don't know you.'

'You don't have to know a person to tell her your troubles. I sometimes tell mine to the cat that camps out on the wall opposite my room. What did you want to leave the country for, with summer coming on?'

She didn't answer, but I could see it coming, so I sat still and waited. And presently she seemed to make up her mind that, even if it was no business of mine, it would be a relief to talk about it.

'We're on our honeymoon. Charlie wanted to come to New York. I didn't want to, but he was set on it. He's been here before.'

'So he told me.'

'He's wild about New York.'

'But you're not.'

'I hate it.'

'Why?'

She dug away at the red plush with the hatpin, picking out little bits and dropping them over the edge. I could see she was bracing herself to put me wise to the whole trouble. There's a time comes when things aren't going right, and you've had all you can stand, when you have got to tell somebody about it, no matter who it is.

'I hate New York,' she said getting it out at last with a rush. 'I'm scared of it. It—it isn't fair Charlie bringing me here. I didn't want to come. I knew what would happen. I felt it all along.'

'What do you think will happen, then?'

She must have picked away at least an inch of the red plush before she answered. It's lucky Jimmy, the balcony waiter, didn't see her; it would have broken his heart; he's as proud of that red plush as if he had paid for it himself.

'When I first went to live at Rodney,' she said, 'two years ago—we moved there from Illinois—there was a man there named Tyson—Jack Tyson. He lived all alone and didn't seem to want to know anyone. I couldn't understand it till somebody told me all about him. I can understand it now. Jack Tyson married a Rodney girl, and they came to New York for their honeymoon, just like us. And when they got there I guess she got to comparing him with the fellows she saw, and comparing the city with Rodney, and when she got home she just couldn't settle down.'

'Well?'

'After they had been back in Rodney for a little while she ran away.

Back to the city, I guess.'

'I suppose he got a divorce?'

'No, he didn't. He still thinks she may come back to him.'

'He still thinks she will come back?' I said. 'After she has been away three years!'

'Yes. He keeps her things just the same as she left them when she went away, everything just the same.'

'But isn't he angry with her for what she did? If I was a man and a girl treated me that way, I'd be apt to murder her if she tried to show up again.'

'He wouldn't. Nor would I, if—if anything like that happened to me; I'd wait and wait, and go on hoping all the time. And I'd go down to the station to meet the train every afternoon, just like Jack Tyson.'

Something splashed on the tablecloth. It made me jump.

'For goodness' sake,' I said, 'what's your trouble? Brace up. I know it's a sad story, but it's not your funeral.'

'It is. It is. The same thing's going to happen to me.'

'Take a hold on yourself. Don't cry like that.'

'I can't help it. Oh! I knew it would happen. It's happening right now. Look—look at him.'

I glanced over the rail, and I saw what she meant. There was her Charlie, dancing about all over the floor as if he had just discovered that he hadn't lived till then. I saw him say something to the girl he was dancing with. I wasn't near enough to hear it, but I bet it was 'This is the life!' If I had been his wife, in the same position as this kid, I guess I'd have felt as bad as she did, for if ever a man exhibited all the symptoms of incurable Newyorkitis, it was this Charlie Ferris.

'I'm not like these New York girls,' she choked. 'I can't be smart. I don't want to be. I just want to live at home and be happy. I knew it would happen if we came to the city. He doesn't think me good enough for him. He looks down on me.'

'Pull yourself together.'

'And I do love him so!'

Goodness knows what I should have said if I could have thought of anything to say. But just then the music stopped, and somebody on the floor below began to speak.

'Ladeez 'n' gemmen,' he said, 'there will now take place our great Numbah Contest. This gen-u-ine sporting contest—'

It was Izzy Baermann making his nightly speech, introducing the Love-r-ly Cup; and it meant that, for me, duty called. From where I sat I could see Izzy looking about the room, and I knew he was looking for me. It's the management's nightmare that one of these evenings Mabel or I won't show up, and somebody else will get away with the Love-r-ly Cup.

'Sorry I've got to go,' I said. 'I have to be in this.'

And then suddenly I had the great idea. It came to me like a flash, I looked at her, crying there, and I looked over the rail at Charlie the Boy Wonder, and I knew that this was where I got a stranglehold on my place in the Hall of Fame, along with the great thinkers of the age.

'Come on,' I said. 'Come along. Stop crying and powder your nose and get a move on. You're going to dance this.'

'But Charlie doesn't want to dance with me.'

'It may have escaped your notice,' I said, 'but your Charlie is not the only man in New York, or even in this restaurant. I'm going to dance with Charlie myself, and I'll introduce you to someone who can go through the movements. Listen!'

'The lady of each couple'—this was Izzy, getting it off his diaphragm—'will receive a ticket containing a num-bah. The dance will then proceed, and the num-bahs will be eliminated one by one, those called out by the judge kindly returning to their seats as their num-bah is called. The num-bah finally remaining is the winning num-bah. The contest is a genuine sporting contest, decided purely by the skill of the holders of the various num-bahs.' (Izzy stopped blushing at the age of six.) 'Will ladies now kindly step forward and receive their num-bahs. The winner, the holder of the num-bah left on the floor when the other num-bahs have been eliminated' (I could see Izzy getting more and more uneasy, wondering where on earth I'd got to), 'will receive this Love-r-ly Silver Cup, presented by the management. Ladies will now kindly step forward and receive their num-bahs.'

I turned to Mrs Charlie. 'There,' I said, 'don't you want to win a

Love-r-ly Silver Cup?'

'But I couldn't.'

'You never know your luck.'

'But it isn't luck. Didn't you hear him say it's a contest decided purely by skill?'

'Well, try your skill, then.' I felt as if I could have shaken her. 'For goodness' sake,' I said, 'show a little grit. Aren't you going to stir a finger to keep your Charlie? Suppose you win, think what it will mean. He will look up to you for the rest of your life. When he starts talking about New York, all you will have to say is, "New York? Ah, yes, that was the town I won that Love-r-ly Silver Cup in, was it not?" and he'll drop as if you had hit him behind the ear with a sandbag. Pull yourself together and try.'

I saw those brown eyes of hers flash, and she said, 'I'll try.'

'Good for you,' I said. 'Now you get those tears dried, and fix yourself up, and I'll go down and get the tickets.'

Izzy was mighty relieved when I bore down on him.

'Gee!' he said, 'I thought you had run away, or was sick or something.

Here's your ticket.'

'I want two, Izzy. One's for a friend of mine. And I say, Izzy, I'd take it as a personal favour if you would let her stop on the floor as one of the last two couples. There's a reason. She's a kid from the country, and she wants to make a hit.'

'Sure, that'll be all right. Here are the tickets. Yours is thirty-six, hers is ten.' He lowered his voice. 'Don't go mixing them.'

I went back to the balcony. On the way I got hold of Charlie.

'We're dancing this together,' I said.

He grinned all across his face.

I found Mrs Charlie looking as if she had never shed a tear in her life. She certainly had pluck, that kid.

'Come on,' I said. 'Stick to your ticket like wax and watch your step.'

I guess you've seen these sporting contests at Geisenheimer's. Or, if you haven't seen them at Geisenheimer's, you've seen them somewhere else. They're all the same.

When we began, the floor was so crowded that there was hardly elbow-room. Don't tell me there aren't any optimists nowadays. Everyone was looking as if they were wondering whether to have the Love-r-ly Cup in the sitting-room or the bedroom. You never saw such a hopeful gang in your life.

Presently Izzy gave tongue. The management expects him to be humorous on these occasions, so he did his best.

'Num-bahs, seven, eleven, and twenty-one will kindly rejoin their sorrowing friends.'

This gave us a little more elbow-room, and the band started again.

A few minutes later, Izzy once more: 'Num-bahs thirteen, sixteen, and seventeen—good-bye.'

Off we went again.

'Num-bah twelve, we hate to part with you, but—back to your table!'

A plump girl in a red hat, who had been dancing with a kind smile, as if she were doing it to amuse the children, left the floor.

'Num-bahs six, fifteen, and twenty, thumbs down!'

And pretty soon the only couples left were Charlie and me, Mrs Charlie and the fellow I'd introduced her to, and a bald-headed man and a girl in a white hat. He was one of your stick-at-it performers. He had been dancing all the evening. I had noticed him from the balcony. He looked like a hard-boiled egg from up there.

He was a trier all right, that fellow, and had things been otherwise, so to speak, I'd have been glad to see him win. But it was not to be. Ah, no!

'Num-bah nineteen, you're getting all flushed. Take a rest.'

So there it was, a straight contest between me and Charlie and Mrs Charlie and her man. Every nerve in my system was tingling with suspense and excitement, was it not? It was not.

Charlie, as I've already hinted, was not a dancer who took much of his attention off his feet while in action. He was there to do his durnedest, not to inspect objects of interest by the wayside. The correspondence college he'd attended doesn't guarantee to teach you to do two things at once. It won't bind itself to teach you to look round the room while you're dancing. So Charlie hadn't the least suspicion of the state of the drama. He was breathing heavily down my neck in a determined sort of way, with his eyes glued to the floor. All he knew was that the competition had thinned out a bit, and the honour of Ashley, Maine, was in his hands.

You know how the public begins to sit up and take notice when these dance-contests have been narrowed down to two couples. There are evenings when I quite forget myself, when I'm one of the last two left in, and get all excited. There's a sort of hum in the air, and, as you go round the room, people at the tables start applauding. Why, if you didn't know about the inner workings of the thing, you'd be all of a twitter.

It didn't take my practised ear long to discover that it wasn't me and Charlie that the great public was cheering for. We would go round the floor without getting a hand, and every time Mrs Charlie and her guy got to a corner there was a noise like election night. She sure had made a hit.

I took a look at her across the floor, and I didn't wonder. She was a different kid from what she'd been upstairs. I never saw anybody look so happy and pleased with herself. Her eyes were like lamps, and her cheeks all pink, and she was going at it like a champion. I knew what had made a hit with the people. It was the look of her. She made you think of fresh milk and new-laid eggs and birds singing. To see her was like getting away to the country in August. It's funny about people who live in the city. They chuck out their chests, and talk about little old New York being good enough for them, and there's a street in heaven they call Broadway, and all the rest of it; but it seems to me that what they really live for is that three weeks in the summer when they get away into the country. I knew exactly why they were cheering so hard for Mrs Charlie. She made them think of their holidays which were coming along, when they would go and board at the farm and drink out of the old oaken bucket, and call the cows by their first names.

Gee! I felt just like that myself. All day the country had been tugging at me, and now it tugged worse than ever.

I could have smelled the new-mown hay if it wasn't that when you're in Geisenheimer's you have to smell Geisenheimer's, because it leaves no chance for competition.

'Keep working,' I said to Charlie. 'It looks to me as if we are going back in the betting.'

'Uh, huh!' he says, too busy to blink.

'Do some of those fancy steps of yours. We need them in our business.'

And the way that boy worked—it was astonishing!

Out of the corner of my eye I could see Izzy Baermann, and he wasn't looking happy. He was nerving himself for one of those quick referee's decisions—the sort you make and then duck under the ropes, and run five miles, to avoid the incensed populace. It was this kind of thing happening every now and then that prevented his job being perfect. Mabel Francis told me that one night when Izzy declared her the winner of the great sporting contest, it was such raw work that she thought there'd have been a riot. It looked pretty much as if he was afraid the same thing was going to happen now. There wasn't a doubt which of us two couples was the one that the customers wanted to see win that Love-r-ly Silver Cup. It was a walk-over for Mrs Charlie, and Charlie and I were simply among those present.

But Izzy had his duty to do, and drew a salary for doing it, so he moistened his lips, looked round to see that his strategic railways weren't blocked, swallowed twice, and said in a husky voice:

'Num-bah ten, please re-tiah!'

I stopped at once.

'Come along,' said I to Charlie. 'That's our exit cue.'

And we walked off the floor amidst applause.

'Well,' says Charlie, taking out his handkerchief and attending to his brow, which was like the village blacksmith's, 'we didn't do so bad, did we? We didn't do so bad, I guess! We—'

And he looked up at the balcony, expecting to see the dear little wife, draped over the rail, worshipping him; when, just as his eye is moving up, it gets caught by the sight of her a whole heap lower down than he had expected—on the floor, in fact.

She wasn't doing much in the worshipping line just at that moment. She was too busy.

It was a regular triumphal progress for the kid. She and her partner were doing one or two rounds now for exhibition purposes, like the winning couple always do at Geisenheimer's, and the room was fairly rising at them. You'd have thought from the way they were clapping that they had been betting all their spare cash on her.

Charlie gets her well focused, then he lets his jaw drop, till he pretty near bumped it against the floor.

'But—but—but—' he begins.

'I know,' I said. 'It begins to look as if she could dance well enough for the city after all. It begins to look as if she had sort of put one over on somebody, don't it? It begins to look as if it were a pity you didn't think of dancing with her yourself.'

'I—I—I—'

'You come along and have a nice cold drink,' I said, 'and you'll soon pick up.'

He tottered after me to a table, looking as if he had been hit by a street-car. He had got his.

I was so busy looking after Charlie, flapping the towel and working on him with the oxygen, that, if you'll believe me, it wasn't for quite a time that I thought of glancing around to see how the thing had struck Izzy Baermann.

If you can imagine a fond father whose only son has hit him with a brick, jumped on his stomach, and then gone off with all his money, you have a pretty good notion of how poor old Izzy looked. He was staring at me across the room, and talking to himself and jerking his hands about. Whether he thought he was talking to me, or whether he was rehearsing the scene where he broke it to the boss that a mere stranger had got away with his Love-r-ly Silver Cup, I don't know. Whichever it was, he was being mighty eloquent.

I gave him a nod, as much as to say that it would all come right in the future, and then I turned to Charlie again. He was beginning to pick up.

'She won the cup!' he said in a dazed voice, looking at me as if I could do something about it.

'You bet she did!'

'But—well, what do you know about that?'

I saw that the moment had come to put it straight to him. 'I'll tell you what I know about it,' I said. 'If you take my advice, you'll hustle that kid straight back to Ashley—or wherever it is that you said you poison the natives by making up the wrong prescriptions—before she gets New York into her system. When I was talking to her upstairs, she was telling me about a fellow in her village who got it in the neck just the same as you're apt to do.'

He started. 'She was telling you about Jack Tyson?'

'That was his name—Jack Tyson. He lost his wife through letting her have too much New York. Don't you think it's funny she should have mentioned him if she hadn't had some idea that she might act just the same as his wife did?'

He turned quite green.

'You don't think she would do that?'

'Well, if you'd heard her—She couldn't talk of anything except this Tyson, and what his wife did to him. She talked of it sort of sad, kind of regretful, as if she was sorry, but felt that it had to be. I could see she had been thinking about it a whole lot.'

Charlie stiffened in his seat, and then began to melt with pure fright. He took up his empty glass with a shaking hand and drank a long drink out of it. It didn't take much observation to see that he had had the jolt he wanted, and was going to be a whole heap less jaunty and metropolitan from now on. In fact, the way he looked, I should say he had finished with metropolitan jauntiness for the rest of his life.

'I'll take her home tomorrow,' he said. 'But—will she come?'

'That's up to you. If you can persuade her—Here she is now. I should start at once.'

Mrs Charlie, carrying the cup, came to the table. I was wondering what would be the first thing she would say. If it had been Charlie, of course he'd have said, 'This is the life!' but I looked for something snappier from her. If I had been in her place there were at least ten things I could have thought of to say, each nastier than the other.

She sat down and put the cup on the table. Then she gave the cup a long look. Then she drew a deep breath. Then she looked at Charlie.

'Oh, Charlie, dear,' she said, 'I do wish I'd been dancing with you!'

Well, I'm not sure that that wasn't just as good as anything I would have said. Charlie got right off the mark. After what I had told him, he wasn't wasting any time.

'Darling,' he said, humbly, 'you're a wonder! What will they say about this at home?' He did pause here for a moment, for it took nerve to say it; but then he went right on. 'Mary, how would it be if we went home right away—first train tomorrow, and showed it to them?'

'Oh, Charlie!' she said.

His face lit up as if somebody had pulled a switch.

'You will? You don't want to stop on? You aren't wild about New York?'

'If there was a train,' she said, 'I'd start tonight. But I thought you loved the city so, Charlie?'

He gave a kind of shiver. 'I never want to see it again in my life!' he said.

'You'll excuse me,' I said, getting up, 'I think there's a friend of mine wants to speak to me.'

And I crossed over to where Izzy had been standing for the last five minutes, making signals to me with his eyebrows.

You couldn't have called Izzy coherent at first. He certainly had trouble with his vocal chords, poor fellow. There was one of those African explorer men used to come to Geisenheimer's a lot when he was home from roaming the trackless desert, and he used to tell me about tribes he had met who didn't use real words at all, but talked to one another in clicks and gurgles. He imitated some of their chatter one night to amuse me, and, believe me, Izzy Baermann started talking the same language now. Only he didn't do it to amuse me.

He was like one of those gramophone records when it's getting into its stride.

'Be calm, Isadore,' I said. 'Something is troubling you. Tell me all about it.'

He clicked some more, and then he got it out.

'Say, are you crazy? What did you do it for? Didn't I tell you as plain as I could; didn't I say it twenty times, when you came for the tickets, that yours was thirty-six?'

'Didn't you say my friend's was thirty-six?'

'Are you deaf? I said hers was ten.'

'Then,' I said handsomely, 'say no more. The mistake was mine. It begins to look as if I must have got them mixed.'

He did a few Swedish exercises.

'Say no more? That's good! That's great! You've got nerve. I'll say that.'

'It was a lucky mistake, Izzy. It saved your life. The people would have lynched you if you had given me the cup. They were solid for her.'

'What's the boss going to say when I tell him?'

'Never mind what the boss will say. Haven't you any romance in your system, Izzy? Look at those two sitting there with their heads together. Isn't it worth a silver cup to have made them happy for life? They are on their honeymoon, Isadore. Tell the boss exactly how it happened, and say that I thought it was up to Geisenheimer's to give them a wedding-present.'

He clicked for a spell.

'Ah!' he said. 'Ah! now you've done it! Now you've given yourself away! You did it on purpose. You mixed those tickets on purpose. I thought as much. Say, who do you think you are, doing this sort of thing? Don't you know that professional dancers are three for ten cents? I could go out right now and whistle, and get a dozen girls for your job. The boss'll sack you just one minute after I tell him.'

'No, he won't, Izzy, because I'm going to resign.'

'You'd better!'

'That's what I think. I'm sick of this place, Izzy. I'm sick of dancing. I'm sick of New York. I'm sick of everything. I'm going back to the country. I thought I had got the pigs and chickens clear out of my system, but I hadn't. I've suspected it for a long, long time, and tonight I know it. Tell the boss, with my love, that I'm sorry, but it had to be done. And if he wants to talk back, he must do it by letter: Mrs John Tyson, Rodney, Maine, is the address.'

THE MAKING OF MAC'S

Mac's Restaurant—nobody calls it MacFarland's—is a mystery. It is off the beaten track. It is not smart. It does not advertise. It provides nothing nearer to an orchestra than a solitary piano, yet, with all these things against it, it is a success. In theatrical circles especially it holds a position which might turn the white lights of many a supper-palace green with envy.

This is mysterious. You do not expect Soho to compete with and even eclipse Piccadilly in this way. And when Soho does so compete, there is generally romance of some kind somewhere in the background.

Somebody happened to mention to me casually that Henry, the old waiter, had been at Mac's since its foundation.

'Me?' said Henry, questioned during a slack spell in the afternoon.

'Rather!'

'Then can you tell me what it was that first gave the place the impetus which started it on its upward course? What causes should you say were responsible for its phenomenal prosperity? What—'

'What gave it a leg-up? Is that what you're trying to get at?'

'Exactly. What gave it a leg-up? Can you tell me?'

'Me?' said Henry. 'Rather!'

And he told me this chapter from the unwritten history of the London whose day begins when Nature's finishes.

* * * * *

Old Mr MacFarland (*said Henry*) started the place fifteen years ago. He was a widower with one son and what you might call half a daughter. That's to say, he had adopted her. Katie was her name, and she was the child of a dead friend of his. The son's name was Andy. A little freckled nipper he was when I first knew him—one of those silent kids that don't say much and have as much obstinacy in them as if they were mules. Many's the time, in them days, I've clumped him on the head and told him to do something; and he didn't run yelling to his pa, same as most kids would have done, but just said nothing and went on not doing whatever it was I had told him to do. That was the sort of disposition Andy had, and it grew on him. Why, when he came back from Oxford College the time the old man sent for him—what I'm going to tell you about soon—he had a jaw on him like the ram of a battleship. Katie was the kid for my money. I liked Katie. We all liked Katie.

Old MacFarland started out with two big advantages. One was Jules, and the other was me. Jules came from Paris, and he was the greatest cook you ever seen. And me—well, I was just come from ten years as waiter at the Guelph, and I won't conceal it from you that I gave the place a tone. I gave Soho something to think about over its chop, believe me. It was a come-down in the world for me, maybe, after the Guelph, but what I said to myself was that, when you get a tip in Soho, it may be only tuppence, but you keep it; whereas at the Guelph about ninety-nine hundredths of it goes to helping to maintain some blooming head waiter in the style to which he has been accustomed. It was through my kind of harping on that fact that me and the Guelph parted company. The head waiter complained to the management the day I called him a fat-headed vampire.

Well, what with me and what with Jules, MacFarland's—it wasn't Mac's in them days—began to get a move on. Old MacFarland, who knew a good man when he saw one and always treated me more like a brother than anything else, used to say to me, 'Henry, if this keeps up, I'll be able to send the boy to Oxford College'; until one day he changed it to, 'Henry, I'm going to send the boy to Oxford College'; and next year, sure enough, off he went.

Katie was sixteen then, and she had just been given the cashier job, as a treat. She wanted to do something to help the old man, so he put her on a high chair behind a wire cage with a hole in it, and she gave the customers their change. And let me tell you, mister, that a man that wasn't satisfied after he'd had me serve him a dinner cooked by Jules and then had a chat with Katie through the wire cage would have groused at Paradise. For she was pretty, was Katie, and getting prettier every day. I spoke to the boss about it. I said it was putting temptation in the girl's way to set her up there right in the public eye, as it were. And he told me to hop it. So I hopped it.

Katie was wild about dancing. Nobody knew it till later, but all this while, it turned out, she was attending regular one of them schools. That was where she went to in the afternoons, when we all thought she was visiting girl friends. It all come out after, but she fooled us then. Girls are like monkeys when it comes to artfulness. She called me Uncle Bill, because she said the name Henry always reminded her of cold mutton. If it had been young Andy that had said it I'd have clumped him one; but he never said anything like that. Come to think of it, he never said anything much at all. He just thought a heap without opening his face.

So young Andy went off to college, and I said to him, 'Now then, you young devil, you be a credit to us, or I'll fetch you a clip when you come home.' And Katie said, 'Oh, Andy, I *shall* miss you.' And Andy didn't say nothing to me, and he didn't say nothing to Katie, but he gave her a look, and later in the day I found her crying, and she said she'd got toothache, and I went round the corner to the chemist's and brought her something for it.

It was in the middle of Andy's second year at college that the old man had the stroke which put him out of business. He went down under it as if he'd been hit with an axe, and the doctor tells him he'll never be able to leave his bed again.

So they sent for Andy, and he quit his college, and come back to London to look after the restaurant.

I was sorry for the kid. I told him so in a fatherly kind of way. And he just looked at me and says, 'Thanks very much, Henry.'

'What must be must be,' I says. 'Maybe, it's all for the best. Maybe it's better you're here than in among all those young devils in your Oxford school what might be leading you astray.'

'If you would think less of me and more of your work, Henry,' he says, 'perhaps that gentleman over there wouldn't have to shout sixteen times for the waiter.'

Which, on looking into it, I found to be the case, and he went away without giving me no tip, which shows what you lose in a hard world by being sympathetic.

I'm bound to say that young Andy showed us all jolly quick that he hadn't come home just to be an ornament about the place. There was exactly one boss in the restaurant, and it was him. It come a little hard at first to have to be respectful to a kid whose head you had spent many a happy hour clumping for his own good in the past; but he pretty soon showed me I could do it if I tried, and I done it. As for Jules and the two young fellers that had been taken on to help me owing to increase of business, they would jump through hoops and roll over if he just looked at them. He was a boy who liked his own way, was Andy, and, believe me, at MacFarland's Restaurant he got it.

And then, when things had settled down into a steady jog, Katie took the bit in her teeth.

She done it quite quiet and unexpected one afternoon when there was only me and her and Andy in the place. And I don't think either of them knew I was there, for I was taking an easy on a chair at the back, reading an evening paper.

She said, kind of quiet, 'Oh, Andy.'

'Yes, darling,' he said.

And that was the first I knew that there was anything between them.

'Andy, I've something to tell you.'

'What is it?'

She kind of hesitated.

'Andy, dear, I shan't be able to help any more in the restaurant.'

He looked at her, sort of surprised.

'What do you mean?'

'I'm—I'm going on the stage.'

I put down my paper. What do you mean? Did I listen? Of course I listened. What do you take me for?

From where I sat I could see young Andy's face, and I didn't need any more to tell me there was going to be trouble. That jaw of his was right out. I forgot to tell you that the old man had died, poor old feller, maybe six months before, so that now Andy was the real boss instead of just acting boss; and what's more, in the nature of things, he was, in a manner of speaking, Katie's guardian, with power to tell her what she could do and what she couldn't. And I felt that Katie wasn't going to have any smooth passage with this stage business which she was giving him. Andy didn't hold with the stage—not with any girl he was fond of being on it anyway. And when Andy didn't like a thing he said so.

He said so now.

'You aren't going to do anything of the sort.'

'Don't be horrid about it, Andy dear. I've got a big chance. Why should you be horrid about it?'

'I'm not going to argue about it. You don't go.'

'But it's such a big chance. And I've been working for it for years.'

'How do you mean working for it?'

And then it came out about this dancing-school she'd been attending regular.

When she'd finished telling him about it, he just shoved out his jaw another inch.

'You aren't going on the stage.'

'But it's such a chance. I saw Mr Mandelbaum yesterday, and he saw me dance, and he was very pleased, and said he would give me a solo dance to do in this new piece he's putting on.'

'You aren't going on the stage.'

What I always say is, you can't beat tact. If you're smooth and tactful you can get folks to do anything you want; but if you just shove your jaw out at them, and order them about, why, then they get their backs up and sauce you. I knew Katie well enough to know that she would do anything for Andy, if he asked her properly; but she wasn't going to stand this sort of thing. But you couldn't drive that into the head of a feller like young Andy with a steam-hammer.

She flared up, quick, as if she couldn't hold herself in no longer.

'I certainly am,' she said.

'You know what it means?'

'What does it mean?'

'The end of—everything.'

She kind of blinked as if he'd hit her, then she chucks her chin up.

'Very well,' she says. 'Good-bye.'

'Good-bye,' says Andy, the pig-headed young mule; and she walks out one way and he walks out another.

* * * * *

I don't follow the drama much as a general rule, but seeing that it was now, so to speak, in the family, I did keep an eye open for the newspaper notices of 'The Rose Girl', which was the name of the piece which Mr Mandelbaum was letting Katie do a solo dance in; and while some of them cussed the play considerable, they all gave Katie a nice word. One feller said that she was like cold water on the morning after, which is high praise coming from a newspaper man.

There wasn't a doubt about it. She was a success. You see, she was something new, and London always sits up and takes notice when you give it that.

There were pictures of her in the papers, and one evening paper had a piece about 'How I Preserve My Youth' signed by her. I cut it out and showed it to Andy.

He gave it a look. Then he gave me a look, and I didn't like his eye.

'Well?' he says.

'Pardon,' I says.

'What about it?' he says.

'I don't know,' I says.

'Get back to your work,' he says.

So I got back.

It was that same night that the queer thing happened.

We didn't do much in the supper line at MacFarland's as a rule in them days, but we kept open, of course, in case Soho should take it into its head to treat itself to a welsh rabbit before going to bed; so all hands was on deck, ready for the call if it should come, at half past eleven that night; but we weren't what you might term sanguine.

Well, just on the half-hour, up drives a taxicab, and in comes a party of four. There was a nut, another nut, a girl, and another girl. And the second girl was Katie.

'Hallo, Uncle Bill!' she says.

'Good evening, madam,' I says dignified, being on duty.

'Oh, stop it, Uncle Bill,' she says. 'Say "Hallo!" to a pal, and smile prettily, or I'll tell them about the time you went to the White City.'

Well, there's some bygones that are best left bygones, and the night at the White City what she was alluding to was one of them. I still maintain, as I always shall maintain, that the constable had no right to—but, there, it's a story that wouldn't interest you. And, anyway, I was glad to see Katie again, so I give her a smile.

'Not so much of it,' I says. 'Not so much of it. I'm glad to see you,

Katie.'

'Three cheers! Jimmy, I want to introduce you to my friend, Uncle Bill.

Ted, this is Uncle Bill. Violet, this is Uncle Bill.'

It wasn't my place to fetch her one on the side of the head, but I'd of liked to have; for she was acting like she'd never used to act when I knew her—all tough and bold. Then it come to me that she was nervous. And natural, too, seeing young Andy might pop out any moment.

And sure enough out he popped from the back room at that very instant. Katie looked at him, and he looked at Katie, and I seen his face get kind of hard; but he didn't say a word. And presently he went out again.

I heard Katie breathe sort of deep.

'He's looking well, Uncle Bill, ain't he?' she says to me, very soft.

'Pretty fair,' I says. 'Well, kid, I been reading the pieces in the papers. You've knocked 'em.'

'Ah, don't Bill,' she says, as if I'd hurt her. And me meaning only to say the civil thing. Girls are rum.

When the party had paid their bill and give me a tip which made me
think I was back at the Guelph again—only there weren't any Dick
Turpin of a head waiter standing by for his share—they hopped it. But
Katie hung back and had a word with me.

'He *was* looking well, wasn't he, Uncle Bill?'

'Rather!'

'Does—does he ever speak of me?'

'I ain't heard him.'

'I suppose he's still pretty angry with me, isn't he, Uncle Bill?
You're sure you've never heard him speak of me?'

So, to cheer her up, I tells her about the piece in the paper I showed him; but it didn't seem to cheer her up any. And she goes out.

The very next night in she come again for supper, but with different nuts and different girls. There was six of them this time, counting her. And they'd hardly sat down at their table, when in come the fellers she had called Jimmy and Ted with two girls. And they sat eating of their suppers and chaffing one another across the floor, all as pleasant and sociable as you please.

'I say, Katie,' I heard one of the nuts say, 'you were right. He's worth the price of admission.'

I don't know who they meant, but they all laughed. And every now and again I'd hear them praising the food, which I don't wonder at, for Jules had certainly done himself proud. All artistic temperament, these Frenchmen are. The moment I told him we had company, so to speak, he blossomed like a flower does when you put it in water.

'Ah, see, at last!' he says, trying to grab me and kiss me. 'Our fame has gone abroad in the world which amuses himself, ain't it? For a good supper connexion I have always prayed, and he has arrived.'

Well, it did begin to look as if he was right. Ten high-class supper-folk in an evening was pretty hot stuff for MacFarland's. I'm bound to say I got excited myself. I can't deny that I missed the Guelph at times.

On the fifth night, when the place was fairly packed and looked for all the world like Oddy's or Romano's, and me and the two young fellers helping me was working double tides, I suddenly understood, and I went up to Katie and, bending over her very respectful with a bottle, I whispers, 'Hot stuff, kid. This is a jolly fine boom you're working for the old place.' And by the way she smiled back at me, I seen I had guessed right.

Andy was hanging round, keeping an eye on things, as he always done, and I says to him, when I was passing, 'She's doing us proud, bucking up the old place, ain't she?' And he says, 'Get on with your work.' And I got on.

Katie hung back at the door, when she was on her way out, and had a word with me.

'Has he said anything about me, Uncle Bill?'

'Not a word,' I says.

And she goes out.

You've probably noticed about London, mister, that a flock of sheep isn't in it with the nuts, the way they all troop on each other's heels to supper-places. One month they're all going to one place, next month to another. Someone in the push starts the cry that he's found a new place, and off they all go to try it. The trouble with most of the places is that once they've got the custom they think it's going to keep on coming and all they've got to do is to lean back and watch it come. Popularity comes in at the door, and good food and good service flies out at the window. We wasn't going to have any of that at MacFarland's. Even if it hadn't been that Andy would have come down like half a ton of bricks on the first sign of slackness, Jules and me both of us had our professional reputations to keep up. I didn't give myself no airs when I seen things coming our way. I worked all the harder, and I seen to it that the four young fellers under me—there was four now—didn't lose no time fetching of the orders.

The consequence was that the difference between us and most popular restaurants was that we kept our popularity. We fed them well, and we served them well; and once the thing had started rolling it didn't stop. Soho isn't so very far away from the centre of things, when you come to look at it, and they didn't mind the extra step, seeing that there was something good at the end of it. So we got our popularity, and we kept our popularity; and we've got it to this day. That's how MacFarland's came to be what it is, mister.

* * * * *

With the air of one who has told a well-rounded tale, Henry ceased, and observed that it was wonderful the way Mr Woodward, of Chelsea, preserved his skill in spite of his advanced years.

I stared at him.

'But, heavens, man!' I cried, 'you surely don't think you've finished? What about Katie and Andy? What happened to them? Did they ever come together again?'

'Oh, ah,' said Henry, 'I was forgetting!'

And he resumed.

* * * * *

As time went on, I begin to get pretty fed up with young Andy. He was making a fortune as fast as any feller could out of the sudden boom in the supper-custom, and he knowing perfectly well that if it hadn't of been for Katie there wouldn't of been any supper-custom at all; and you'd of thought that anyone claiming to be a human being would have had the gratitood to forgive and forget and go over and say a civil word to Katie when she come in. But no, he just hung round looking black at all of them; and one night he goes and fairly does it.

The place was full that night, and Katie was there, and the piano going, and everybody enjoying themselves, when the young feller at the piano struck up the tune what Katie danced to in the show. Catchy tune it was. 'Lum-tum-tum, tiddle-iddle-um.' Something like that it went. Well, the young feller struck up with it, and everybody begin clapping and hammering on the tables and hollering to Katie to get up and dance; which she done, in an open space in the middle, and she hadn't hardly started when along come young Andy.

He goes up to her, all jaw, and I seen something that wanted dusting on the table next to 'em, so I went up and began dusting it, so by good luck I happened to hear the whole thing.

He says to her, very quiet, 'You can't do that here. What do you think this place is?'

And she says to him, 'Oh, Andy!'

'I'm very much obliged to you,' he says, 'for all the trouble you seem to be taking, but it isn't necessary. MacFarland's got on very well before your well-meant efforts to turn it into a bear-garden.'

And him coining the money from the supper-custom! Sometimes I think gratitood's a thing of the past and this world not fit for a self-respecting rattlesnake to live in.

'Andy!' she says.

'That's all. We needn't argue about it. If you want to come here and have supper, I can't stop you. But I'm not going to have the place turned into a night-club.'

I don't know when I've heard anything like it. If it hadn't of been that I hadn't of got the nerve, I'd have give him a look.

Katie didn't say another word, but just went back to her table.

But the episode, as they say, wasn't conclooded. As soon as the party she was with seen that she was through dancing, they begin to kick up a row; and one young nut with about an inch and a quarter of forehead and the same amount of chin kicked it up especial.

'No, I say! I say, you know!' he hollered. 'That's too bad, you know.

Encore! Don't stop. Encore!'

Andy goes up to him.

'I must ask you, please, not to make so much noise,' he says, quite respectful. 'You are disturbing people.'

'Disturbing be damned! Why shouldn't she—'

'One moment. You can make all the noise you please out in the street, but as long as you stay in here you'll be quiet. Do you understand?'

Up jumps the nut. He'd had quite enough to drink. I know, because I'd been serving him.

'Who the devil are you?' he says.

'Sit down,' says Andy.

And the young feller took a smack at him. And the next moment Andy had him by the collar and was chucking him out in a way that would have done credit to a real professional down Whitechapel way. He dumped him on the pavement as neat as you please.

That broke up the party.

You can never tell with restaurants. What kills one makes another. I've no doubt that if we had chucked out a good customer from the Guelph that would have been the end of the place. But it only seemed to do MacFarland's good. I guess it gave just that touch to the place which made the nuts think that this was real Bohemia. Come to think of it, it does give a kind of charm to a place, if you feel that at any moment the feller at the next table to you may be gathered up by the slack of his trousers and slung into the street.

Anyhow, that's the way our supper-custom seemed to look at it; and after that you had to book a table in advance if you wanted to eat with us. They fairly flocked to the place.

But Katie didn't. She didn't flock. She stayed away. And no wonder, after Andy behaving so bad. I'd of spoke to him about it, only he wasn't the kind of feller you do speak to about things.

One day I says to him to cheer him up, 'What price this restaurant now,

Mr Andy?'

'Curse the restaurant,' he says.

And him with all that supper-custom! It's a rum world!

Mister, have you ever had a real shock—something that came out of nowhere and just knocked you flat? I have, and I'm going to tell you about it.

When a man gets to be my age, and has a job of work which keeps him busy till it's time for him to go to bed, he gets into the habit of not doing much worrying about anything that ain't shoved right under his nose. That's why, about now, Katie had kind of slipped my mind. It wasn't that I wasn't fond of the kid, but I'd got so much to think about, what with having four young fellers under me and things being in such a rush at the restaurant that, if I thought of her at all, I just took it for granted that she was getting along all right, and didn't bother. To be sure we hadn't seen nothing of her at MacFarland's since the night when Andy bounced her pal with the small size in foreheads, but that didn't worry me. If I'd been her, I'd have stopped away the same as she done, seeing that young Andy still had his hump. I took it for granted, as I'm telling you, that she was all right, and that the reason we didn't see nothing of her was that she was taking her patronage elsewhere.

And then, one evening, which happened to be my evening off, I got a letter, and for ten minutes after I read it I was knocked flat.

You get to believe in fate when you get to be my age, and fate certainly had taken a hand in this game. If it hadn't of been my evening off, don't you see, I wouldn't have got home till one o'clock or past that in the morning, being on duty. Whereas, seeing it was my evening off, I was back at half past eight.

I was living at the same boarding-house in Bloomsbury what I'd lived at for the past ten years, and when I got there I find her letter shoved half under my door.

I can tell you every word of it. This is how it went:

Darling Uncle Bill,

Don't be too sorry when you read this. It is nobody's fault, but I am just tired of everything, and I want to end it all. You have been such a dear to me always that I want you to be good to me now. I should not like Andy to know the truth, so I want you to make it seem as if it had happened naturally. You will do this for me, won't you? It will be quite easy. By the time you get this, it will be one, and it will all be over, and you can just come up and open the window and let the gas out and then everyone will think I just died naturally. It will be quite easy. I am leaving the door unlocked so that you can get in. I am in the room just above yours. I took it yesterday, so as to be near you. Good-bye, Uncle Bill. You will do it for me, won't you? I don't want Andy to know what it really was.

KATIE

That was it, mister, and I tell you it floored me. And then it come to me, kind of as a new idea, that I'd best do something pretty soon, and up the stairs I went quick.

There she was, on the bed, with her eyes closed, and the gas just beginning to get bad.

As I come in, she jumped up, and stood staring at me. I went to the tap, and turned the flow off, and then I gives her a look.

'Now then,' I says.

'How did you get here?'

'Never mind how I got here. What have you got to say for yourself?'

She just began to cry, same as she used to when she was a kid and someone had hurt her.

'Here,' I says, 'let's get along out of here, and go where there's some air to breathe. Don't you take on so. You come along out and tell me all about it.'

She started to walk to where I was, and suddenly I seen she was limping. So I gave her a hand down to my room, and set her on a chair.

'Now then,' I says again.

'Don't be angry with me, Uncle Bill,' she says.

And she looks at me so pitiful that I goes up to her and puts my arm round her and pats her on the back.

'Don't you worry, dearie,' I says, 'nobody ain't going to be angry with you. But, for goodness' sake,' I says, 'tell a man why in the name of goodness you ever took and acted so foolish.'

'I wanted to end it all.'

'But why?'

She burst out a-crying again, like a kid.

'Didn't you read about it in the paper, Uncle Bill?'

'Read about what in the paper?'

'My accident. I broke my ankle at rehearsal ever so long ago, practising my new dance. The doctors say it will never be right again. I shall never be able to dance any more. I shall always limp. I shan't even be able to walk properly. And when I thought of that … and Andy … and everything … I….'

I got on to my feet.

'Well, well, well,' I says. 'Well, well, well! I don't know as I blame you. But don't you do it. It's a mug's game. Look here, if I leave you alone for half an hour, you won't go trying it on again? Promise.'

'Very well, Uncle Bill. Where are you going?'

'Oh, just out. I'll be back soon. You sit there and rest yourself.'

It didn't take me ten minutes to get to the restaurant in a cab. I found Andy in the back room.

'What's the matter, Henry?' he says.

'Take a look at this,' I says.

There's always this risk, mister, in being the Andy type of feller what must have his own way and goes straight ahead and has it; and that is that when trouble does come to him, it comes with a rush. It sometimes seems to me that in this life we've all got to have trouble sooner or later, and some of us gets it bit by bit, spread out thin, so to speak, and a few of us gets it in a lump—*biff*! And that was what happened to Andy, and what I knew was going to happen when I showed him that letter. I nearly says to him, 'Brace up, young feller, because this is where you get it.'

I don't often go to the theatre, but when I do I like one of those plays with some ginger in them which the papers generally cuss. The papers say that real human beings don't carry on in that way. Take it from me, mister, they do. I seen a feller on the stage read a letter once which didn't just suit him; and he gasped and rolled his eyes and tried to say something and couldn't, and had to get a hold on a chair to keep him from falling. There was a piece in the paper saying that this was all wrong, and that he wouldn't of done them things in real life. Believe me, the paper was wrong. There wasn't a thing that feller did that Andy didn't do when he read that letter.

'God!' he says. 'Is she … She isn't…. Were you in time?' he says.

And he looks at me, and I seen that he had got it in the neck, right enough.

'If you mean is she dead,' I says, 'no, she ain't dead.'

'Thank God!'

'Not yet,' I says.

And the next moment we was out of that room and in the cab and moving quick.

He was never much of a talker, wasn't Andy, and he didn't chat in that cab. He didn't say a word till we was going up the stairs.

'Where?' he says.

'Here,' I says.

And I opens the door.

Katie was standing looking out of the window. She turned as the door opened, and then she saw Andy. Her lips parted, as if she was going to say something, but she didn't say nothing. And Andy, he didn't say nothing, neither. He just looked, and she just looked.

And then he sort of stumbles across the room, and goes down on his knees, and gets his arms around her.

'Oh, my kid' he says.

* * * * *

And I seen I wasn't wanted, so I shut the door, and I hopped it. I went and saw the last half of a music-hall. But, I don't know, it didn't kind of have no fascination for me. You've got to give your mind to it to appreciate good music-hall turns.

ONE TOUCH OF NATURE

The feelings of Mr J. Wilmot Birdsey, as he stood wedged in the crowd that moved inch by inch towards the gates of the Chelsea Football Ground, rather resembled those of a starving man who has just been given a meal but realizes that he is not likely to get another for many days. He was full and happy. He bubbled over with the joy of living and a warm affection for his fellow-man. At the back of his mind there lurked the black shadow of future privations, but for the moment he did not allow it to disturb him. On this maddest, merriest day of all the glad New Year he was content to revel in the present and allow the future to take care of itself.

Mr Birdsey had been doing something which he had not done since he left New York five years ago. He had been watching a game of baseball.

New York lost a great baseball fan when Hugo Percy de Wynter Framlinghame, sixth Earl of Carricksteed, married Mae Elinor, only daughter of Mr and Mrs J. Wilmot Birdsey of East Seventy-Third Street; for scarcely had that internationally important event taken place when Mrs Birdsey, announcing that for the future the home would be in England as near as possible to dear Mae and dear Hugo, scooped J. Wilmot out of his comfortable morris chair as if he had been a clam, corked him up in a swift taxicab, and decanted him into a Deck B stateroom on the *Olympic*. And there he was, an exile.

Mr Birdsey submitted to the worst bit of kidnapping since the days of the old press gang with that delightful amiability which made him so popular among his fellows and such a cypher in his home. At an early date in his married life his position had been clearly defined beyond possibility of mistake. It was his business to make money, and, when called upon, to jump through hoops and sham dead at the bidding of his wife and daughter Mae. These duties he had been performing conscientiously for a matter of twenty years.

It was only occasionally that his humble role jarred upon him, for he loved his wife and idolized his daughter. The international alliance had been one of these occasions. He had no objection to Hugo Percy, sixth Earl of Carricksteed. The crushing blow had been the sentence of exile. He loved baseball with a love passing the love of women, and the prospect of never seeing a game again in his life appalled him.

And then, one morning, like a voice from another world, had come the news that the White Sox and the Giants were to give an exhibition in London at the Chelsea Football Ground. He had counted the days like a child before Christmas.

There had been obstacles to overcome before he could attend the game, but he had overcome them, and had been seated in the front row when the two teams lined up before King George.

And now he was moving slowly from the ground with the rest of the spectators. Fate had been very good to him. It had given him a great game, even unto two home-runs. But its crowning benevolence had been to allot the seats on either side of him to two men of his own mettle, two god-like beings who knew every move on the board, and howled like wolves when they did not see eye to eye with the umpire. Long before the ninth innings he was feeling towards them the affection of a shipwrecked mariner who meets a couple of boyhood's chums on a desert island.

As he shouldered his way towards the gate he was aware of these two men, one on either side of him. He looked at them fondly, trying to make up his mind which of them he liked best. It was sad to think that they must soon go out of his life again for ever.

He came to a sudden resolution. He would postpone the parting. He would ask them to dinner. Over the best that the Savoy Hotel could provide they would fight the afternoon's battle over again. He did not know who they were or anything about them, but what did that matter? They were brother-fans. That was enough for him.

The man on his right was young, clean-shaven, and of a somewhat vulturine cast of countenance. His face was cold and impassive now, almost forbiddingly so; but only half an hour before it had been a battle-field of conflicting emotions, and his hat still showed the dent where he had banged it against the edge of his seat on the occasion of Mr Daly's home-run. A worthy guest!

The man on Mr Birdsey's left belonged to another species of fan. Though there had been times during the game when he had howled, for the most part he had watched in silence so hungrily tense that a less experienced observer than Mr Birdsey might have attributed his immobility to boredom. But one glance at his set jaw and gleaming eyes told him that here also was a man and a brother.

This man's eyes were still gleaming, and under their curiously deep tan his bearded cheeks were pale. He was staring straight in front of him with an unseeing gaze.

Mr Birdsey tapped the young man on the shoulder.

'Some game!' he said.

The young man looked at him and smiled.

'You bet,' he said.

'I haven't seen a ball-game in five years.'

'The last one I saw was two years ago next June.'

'Come and have some dinner at my hotel and talk it over,' said Mr Birdsey impulsively.

'Sure!' said the young man.

Mr Birdsey turned and tapped the shoulder of the man on his left.

The result was a little unexpected. The man gave a start that was almost a leap, and the pallor of his face became a sickly white. His eyes, as he swung round, met Mr Birdsey's for an instant before they dropped, and there was panic fear in them. His breath whistled softly through clenched teeth.

Mr Birdsey was taken aback. The cordiality of the clean-shaven young man had not prepared him for the possibility of such a reception. He felt chilled. He was on the point of apologizing with some murmur about a mistake, when the man reassured him by smiling. It was rather a painful smile, but it was enough for Mr Birdsey. This man might be of a nervous temperament, but his heart was in the right place.

He, too, smiled. He was a small, stout, red-faced little man, and he possessed a smile that rarely failed to set strangers at their ease. Many strenuous years on the New York Stock Exchange had not destroyed a certain childlike amiability in Mr Birdsey, and it shone out when he smiled at you.

'I'm afraid I startled you,' he said soothingly. 'I wanted to ask you if you would let a perfect stranger, who also happens to be an exile, offer you dinner tonight.'

The man winced. 'Exile?'

'An exiled fan. Don't you feel that the Polo Grounds are a good long way away? This gentleman is joining me. I have a suite at the Savoy Hotel, and I thought we might all have a quiet little dinner there and talk about the game. I haven't seen a ball-game in five years.'

'Nor have I.'

'Then you must come. You really must. We fans ought to stick to one another in a strange land. Do come.'

'Thank you,' said the bearded man; 'I will.'

When three men, all strangers, sit down to dinner together, conversation, even if they happen to have a mutual passion for baseball, is apt to be for a while a little difficult. The first fine frenzy in which Mr Birdsey had issued his invitations had begun to ebb by the time the soup was served, and he was conscious of a feeling of embarrassment.

There was some subtle hitch in the orderly progress of affairs. He sensed it in the air. Both of his guests were disposed to silence, and the clean-shaven young man had developed a trick of staring at the man with the beard, which was obviously distressing that sensitive person.

'Wine,' murmured Mr Birdsey to the waiter. 'Wine, wine!'

He spoke with the earnestness of a general calling up his reserves for the grand attack. The success of this little dinner mattered enormously to him. There were circumstances which were going to make it an oasis in his life. He wanted it to be an occasion to which, in grey days to come, he could look back and be consoled. He could not let it be a failure.

He was about to speak when the young man anticipated him. Leaning forward, he addressed the bearded man, who was crumbling bread with an absent look in his eyes.

'Surely we have met before?' he said. 'I'm sure I remember your face.'

The effect of these words on the other was as curious as the effect of Mr Birdsey's tap on the shoulder had been. He looked up like a hunted animal.

He shook his head without speaking.

'Curious,' said the young man. 'I could have sworn to it, and I am positive that it was somewhere in New York. Do you come from New York?'

'Yes.'

'It seems to me,' said Mr Birdsey, 'that we ought to introduce ourselves. Funny it didn't strike any of us before. My name is Birdsey, J. Wilmot Birdsey. I come from New York.'

'My name is Waterall,' said the young man. 'I come from New York.'

The bearded man hesitated.

'My name is Johnson. I—used to live in New York.'

'Where do you live now, Mr Johnson?' asked Waterall.

The bearded man hesitated again. 'Algiers,' he said.

Mr Birdsey was inspired to help matters along with small-talk.

'Algiers,' he said. 'I have never been there, but I understand that it is quite a place. Are you in business there, Mr Johnson?'

'I live there for my health.'

'Have you been there some time?' inquired Waterall.

'Five years.'

'Then it must have been in New York that I saw you, for I have never been to Algiers, and I'm certain I have seen you somewhere. I'm afraid you will think me a bore for sticking to the point like this, but the fact is, the one thing I pride myself on is my memory for faces. It's a hobby of mine. If I think I remember a face, and can't place it, I worry myself into insomnia. It's partly sheer vanity, and partly because in my job a good memory for faces is a mighty fine asset. It has helped me a hundred times.'

Mr Birdsey was an intelligent man, and he could see that Waterall's table-talk was for some reason getting upon Johnson's nerves. Like a good host, he endeavoured to cut in and make things smooth.

'I've heard great accounts of Algiers,' he said helpfully. 'A friend of mine was there in his yacht last year. It must be a delightful spot.'

'It's a hell on earth,' snapped Johnson, and slew the conversation on the spot.

Through a grim silence an angel in human form fluttered in—a waiter bearing a bottle. The pop of the cork was more than music to Mr Birdsey's ears. It was the booming of the guns of the relieving army.

The first glass, as first glasses will, thawed the bearded man, to the extent of inducing him to try and pick up the fragments of the conversation which he had shattered.

'I am afraid you will have thought me abrupt, Mr Birdsey,' he said awkwardly; 'but then you haven't lived in Algiers for five years, and I have.'

Mr Birdsey chirruped sympathetically.

'I liked it at first. It looked mighty good to me. But five years of it, and nothing else to look forward to till you die....'

He stopped, and emptied his glass. Mr Birdsey was still perturbed. True, conversation was proceeding in a sort of way, but it had taken a distinctly gloomy turn. Slightly flushed with the excellent champagne which he had selected for this important dinner, he endeavoured to lighten it.

'I wonder,' he said, 'which of us three fans had the greatest difficulty in getting to the bleachers today. I guess none of us found it too easy.'

The young man shook his head.

'Don't count on me to contribute a romantic story to this Arabian Night's Entertainment. My difficulty would have been to stop away. My name's Waterall, and I'm the London correspondent of the *New York Chronicle*. I had to be there this afternoon in the way of business.'

Mr Birdsey giggled self-consciously, but not without a certain impish pride.

'The laugh will be on me when you hear my confession. My daughter married an English earl, and my wife brought me over here to mix with his crowd. There was a big dinner-party tonight, at which the whole gang were to be present, and it was as much as my life was worth to side-step it. But when you get the Giants and the White Sox playing ball within fifty miles of you—Well, I packed a grip and sneaked out the back way, and got to the station and caught the fast train to London. And what is going on back there at this moment I don't like to think. About now,' said Mr Birdsey, looking at his watch, 'I guess they'll be pronging the *hors d'oeuvres* and gazing at the empty chair. It was a shame to do it, but, for the love of Mike, what else could I have done?'

He looked at the bearded man.

'Did you have any adventures, Mr Johnson?'

'No. I—I just came.'

The young man Waterall leaned forward. His manner was quiet, but his eyes were glittering.

'Wasn't that enough of an adventure for you?' he said.

Their eyes met across the table. Seated between them, Mr Birdsey looked from one to the other, vaguely disturbed. Something was happening, a drama was going on, and he had not the key to it.

Johnson's face was pale, and the tablecloth crumpled into a crooked ridge under his fingers, but his voice was steady as he replied:

'I don't understand.'

'Will you understand if I give you your right name, Mr Benyon?'

'What's all this?' said Mr Birdsey feebly.

Waterall turned to him, the vulturine cast of his face more noticeable than ever. Mr Birdsey was conscious of a sudden distaste for this young man.

'It's quite simple, Mr Birdsey. If you have not been entertaining angels unawares, you have at least been giving a dinner to a celebrity. I told you I was sure I had seen this gentleman before. I have just remembered where, and when. This is Mr John Benyon, and I last saw him five years ago when I was a reporter in New York, and covered his trial.'

'His trial?'

'He robbed the New Asiatic Bank of a hundred thousand dollars, jumped his bail, and was never heard of again.'

'For the love of Mike!'

Mr Birdsey stared at his guest with eyes that grew momently wider. He was amazed to find that deep down in him there was an unmistakable feeling of elation. He had made up his mind, when he left home that morning, that this was to be a day of days. Well, nobody could call this an anti-climax.

'So that's why you have been living in Algiers?'

Benyon did not reply. Outside, the Strand traffic sent a faint murmur into the warm, comfortable room.

Waterall spoke. 'What on earth induced you, Benyon, to run the risk of coming to London, where every second man you meet is a New Yorker, I can't understand. The chances were two to one that you would be recognized. You made a pretty big splash with that little affair of yours five years ago.'

Benyon raised his head. His hands were trembling.

'I'll tell you,' he said with a kind of savage force, which hurt kindly little Mr Birdsey like a blow. 'It was because I was a dead man, and saw a chance of coming to life for a day; because I was sick of the damned tomb I've been living in for five centuries; because I've been aching for New York ever since I've left it—and here was a chance of being back there for a few hours. I knew there was a risk. I took a chance on it. Well?'

Mr Birdsey's heart was almost too full for words. He had found him at last, the Super-Fan, the man who would go through fire and water for a sight of a game of baseball. Till that moment he had been regarding himself as the nearest approach to that dizzy eminence. He had braved great perils to see this game. Even in this moment his mind would not wholly detach itself from speculation as to what his wife would say to him when he slunk back into the fold. But what had he risked compared with this man Benyon? Mr Birdsey glowed. He could not restrain his sympathy and admiration. True, the man was a criminal. He had robbed a bank of a hundred thousand dollars. But, after all, what was that? They would probably have wasted the money in foolishness. And, anyway, a bank which couldn't take care of its money deserved to lose it.

Mr Birdsey felt almost a righteous glow of indignation against the New Asiatic Bank.

He broke the silence which had followed Benyon's words with a peculiarly immoral remark:

'Well, it's lucky it's only us that's recognized you,' he said.

Waterall stared. 'Are you proposing that we should hush this thing up,

Mr Birdsey?' he said coldly.

'Oh, well—'

Waterall rose and went to the telephone.

'What are you going to do?'

'Call up Scotland Yard, of course. What did you think?'

Undoubtedly the young man was doing his duty as a citizen, yet it is to be recorded that Mr Birdsey eyed him with unmixed horror.

'You can't! You mustn't!' he cried.

'I certainly shall.'

'But—but—this fellow came all that way to see the ball-game.'

It seemed incredible to Mr Birdsey that this aspect of the affair should not be the one to strike everybody to the exclusion of all other aspects.

'You can't give him up. It's too raw.'

'He's a convicted criminal.'

'He's a fan. Why, say, he's *the* fan.'

Waterall shrugged his shoulders, and walked to the telephone. Benyon spoke.

'One moment.'

Waterall turned, and found himself looking into the muzzle of a small pistol. He laughed.

'I expected that. Wave it about all you want'

Benyon rested his shaking hand on the edge of the table.

'I'll shoot if you move.'

'You won't. You haven't the nerve. There's nothing to you. You're just a cheap crook, and that's all. You wouldn't find the nerve to pull that trigger in a million years.'

He took off the receiver.

'Give me Scotland Yard,' he said.

He had turned his back to Benyon. Benyon sat motionless. Then, with a thud, the pistol fell to the ground. The next moment Benyon had broken down. His face was buried in his arms, and he was a wreck of a man, sobbing like a hurt child.

Mr Birdsey was profoundly distressed. He sat tingling and helpless.

This was a nightmare.

Waterall's level voice spoke at the telephone.

'Is this Scotland Yard? I am Waterall, of the *New York Chronicle*. Is Inspector Jarvis there? Ask him to come to the phone.... Is that you, Jarvis? This is Waterall. I'm speaking from the Savoy, Mr Birdsey's rooms. Birdsey. Listen, Jarvis. There's a man here that's wanted by the American police. Send someone here and get him. Benyon. Robbed the New Asiatic Bank in New York. Yes, you've a warrant out for him, five years old.... All right.'

He hung up the receiver. Benyon sprang to his feet. He stood, shaking, a pitiable sight. Mr Birdsey had risen with him. They stood looking at Waterall.

'You—skunk!' said Mr Birdsey.

'I'm an American citizen,' said Waterall, 'and I happen to have some idea of a citizen's duties. What is more, I'm a newspaper man, and I have some idea of my duty to my paper. Call me what you like, you won't alter that.'

Mr Birdsey snorted.

'You're suffering from ingrowing sentimentality, Mr Birdsey. That's what's the matter with you. Just because this man has escaped justice for five years, you think he ought to be considered quit of the whole thing.'

'But—but—'

'I don't.'

He took out his cigarette case. He was feeling a great deal more strung-up and nervous than he would have had the others suspect. He had had a moment of very swift thinking before he had decided to treat that ugly little pistol in a spirit of contempt. Its production had given him a decided shock, and now he was suffering from reaction. As a consequence, because his nerves were strained, he lit his cigarette very languidly, very carefully, and with an offensive superiority which was to Mr Birdsey the last straw.

These things are matters of an instant. Only an infinitesimal fraction of time elapsed between the spectacle of Mr Birdsey, indignant but inactive, and Mr Birdsey berserk, seeing red, frankly and undisguisedly running amok. The transformation took place in the space of time required for the lighting of a match.

Even as the match gave out its flame, Mr Birdsey sprang.

Aeons before, when the young blood ran swiftly in his veins and life was all before him, Mr Birdsey had played football. Once a footballer, always a potential footballer, even to the grave. Time had removed the flying tackle as a factor in Mr Birdsey's life. Wrath brought it back. He dived at young Mr Waterall's neatly trousered legs as he had dived at other legs, less neatly trousered, thirty years ago. They crashed to the floor together; and with the crash came Mr Birdsey's shout:

'Run! Run, you fool! Run!'

And, even as he clung to his man, breathless, bruised, feeling as if all the world had dissolved in one vast explosion of dynamite, the door opened, banged to, and feet fled down the passage.

Mr Birdsey disentangled himself, and rose painfully. The shock had brought him to himself. He was no longer berserk. He was a middle-aged gentleman of high respectability who had been behaving in a very peculiar way.

Waterall, flushed and dishevelled, glared at him speechlessly. He gulped. 'Are you crazy?'

Mr Birdsey tested gingerly the mechanism of a leg which lay under suspicion of being broken. Relieved, he put his foot to the ground again. He shook his head at Waterall. He was slightly crumpled, but he achieved a manner of dignified reproof.

'You shouldn't have done it, young man. It was raw work. Oh, yes, I know all about that duty-of-a-citizen stuff. It doesn't go. There are exceptions to every rule, and this was one of them. When a man risks his liberty to come and root at a ball-game, you've got to hand it to him. He isn't a crook. He's a fan. And we exiled fans have got to stick together.'

Waterall was quivering with fury, disappointment, and the peculiar unpleasantness of being treated by an elderly gentleman like a sack of coals. He stammered with rage.

'You damned old fool, do you realize what you've done? The police will be here in another minute.'

'Let them come.'

'But what am I to say to them? What explanation can I give? What story can I tell them? Can't you see what a hole you've put me in?'

Something seemed to click inside Mr Birdsey's soul. It was the berserk mood vanishing and reason leaping back on to her throne. He was able now to think calmly, and what he thought about filled him with a sudden gloom.

'Young man,' he said, 'don't worry yourself. You've got a cinch. You've only got to hand a story to the police. Any old tale will do for them. I'm the man with the really difficult job—I've got to square myself with my wife!'

BLACK FOR LUCK

He was black, but comely. Obviously in reduced circumstances, he had nevertheless contrived to retain a certain smartness, a certain air—what the French call the *tournure*. Nor had poverty killed in him the aristocrat's instinct of personal cleanliness; for even as Elizabeth caught sight of him he began to wash himself.

At the sound of her step he looked up. He did not move, but there was suspicion in his attitude. The muscles of his back contracted, his eyes glowed like yellow lamps against black velvet, his tail switched a little, warningly.

Elizabeth looked at him. He looked at Elizabeth. There was a pause, while he summed her up. Then he stalked towards her, and, suddenly lowering his head, drove it vigorously against her dress. He permitted her to pick him up and carry him into the hall-way, where Francis, the janitor, stood.

'Francis,' said Elizabeth, 'does this cat belong to anyone here?'

'No, miss. That cat's a stray, that cat is. I been trying to locate that cat's owner for days.'

Francis spent his time trying to locate things. It was the one recreation of his eventless life. Sometimes it was a noise, sometimes a lost letter, sometimes a piece of ice which had gone astray in the dumb-waiter—whatever it was, Francis tried to locate it.

'Has he been round here long, then?'

'I seen him snooping about a considerable time.'

'I shall keep him.'

'Black cats bring luck,' said Francis sententiously.

'I certainly shan't object to that,' said Elizabeth. She was feeling that morning that a little luck would be a pleasing novelty. Things had not been going very well with her of late. It was not so much that the usual proportion of her manuscripts had come back with editorial compliments from the magazine to which they had been sent—she accepted that as part of the game; what she did consider scurvy treatment at the hands of fate was the fact that her own pet magazine, the one to which she had been accustomed to fly for refuge, almost sure of a welcome—when coldly treated by all the others—had suddenly expired with a low gurgle for want of public support. It was like losing a kind and open-handed relative, and it made the addition of a black cat to the household almost a necessity.

In her flat, the door closed, she watched her new ally with some anxiety. He had behaved admirably on the journey upstairs, but she would not have been surprised, though it would have pained her, if he had now proceeded to try to escape through the ceiling. Cats were so emotional. However, he remained calm, and, after padding silently about the room for awhile, raised his head and uttered a crooning cry.

'That's right,' said Elizabeth, cordially. 'If you don't see what you want, ask for it. The place is yours.'

She went to the ice-box, and produced milk and sardines. There was nothing finicky or affected about her guest. He was a good trencherman, and he did not care who knew it. He concentrated himself on the restoration of his tissues with the purposeful air of one whose last meal is a dim memory. Elizabeth, brooding over him like a Providence, wrinkled her forehead in thought.

'Joseph,' she said at last, brightening; 'that's your name. Now settle down, and start being a mascot.'

Joseph settled down amazingly. By the end of the second day he was conveying the impression that he was the real owner of the apartment, and that it was due to his good nature that Elizabeth was allowed the run of the place. Like most of his species, he was an autocrat. He waited a day to ascertain which was Elizabeth's favourite chair, then appropriated it for his own. If Elizabeth closed a door while he was in a room, he wanted it opened so that he might go out; if she closed it while he was outside, he wanted it opened so that he might come in; if she left it open, he fussed about the draught. But the best of us have our faults, and Elizabeth adored him in spite of his.

It was astonishing what a difference he made in her life. She was a friendly soul, and until Joseph's arrival she had had to depend for company mainly on the footsteps of the man in the flat across the way. Moreover, the building was an old one, and it creaked at night. There was a loose board in the passage which made burglar noises in the dark behind you when you stepped on it on the way to bed; and there were funny scratching sounds which made you jump and hold your breath. Joseph soon put a stop to all that. With Joseph around, a loose board became a loose board, nothing more, and a scratching noise just a plain scratching noise.

And then one afternoon he disappeared.

Having searched the flat without finding him, Elizabeth went to the window, with the intention of making a bird's-eye survey of the street. She was not hopeful, for she had just come from the street, and there had been no sign of him then.

Outside the window was a broad ledge, running the width of the building. It terminated on the left, in a shallow balcony belonging to the flat whose front door faced hers—the flat of the young man whose footsteps she sometimes heard. She knew he was a young man, because Francis had told her so. His name, James Renshaw Boyd, she had learned from the same source.

On this shallow balcony, licking his fur with the tip of a crimson tongue and generally behaving as if he were in his own backyard, sat Joseph.

'Jo-seph!' cried Elizabeth—surprise, joy, and reproach combining to give her voice an almost melodramatic quiver.

He looked at her coldly. Worse, he looked at her as if she had been an utter stranger. Bulging with her meat and drink, he cut her dead; and, having done so, turned and walked into the next flat.

Elizabeth was a girl of spirit. Joseph might look at her as if she were a saucerful of tainted milk, but he was her cat, and she meant to get him back. She went out and rang the bell of Mr James Renshaw Boyd's flat.

The door was opened by a shirt-sleeved young man. He was by no means an unsightly young man. Indeed, of his type—the rough-haired, clean-shaven, square-jawed type—he was a distinctly good-looking young man. Even though she was regarding him at the moment purely in the light of a machine for returning strayed cats, Elizabeth noticed that.

She smiled upon him. It was not the fault of this nice-looking young man that his sitting-room window was open; or that Joseph was an ungrateful little beast who should have no fish that night.

'Would you mind letting me have my cat, please?' she said pleasantly.

'He has gone into your sitting-room through the window.'

He looked faintly surprised.

'Your cat?'

'My black cat, Joseph. He is in your sitting-room.'

'I'm afraid you have come to the wrong place. I've just left my sitting-room, and the only cat there is my black cat, Reginald.'

'But I saw Joseph go in only a minute ago.'

'That was Reginald.'

For the first time, as one who examining a fair shrub abruptly discovers that it is a stinging-nettle, Elizabeth realized the truth. This was no innocent young man who stood before her, but the blackest criminal known to criminologists—a stealer of other people's cats. Her manner shot down to zero.

'May I ask how long you have had your Reginald?'

'Since four o'clock this afternoon.'

'Did he come in through the window?'

'Why, yes. Now you mention it, he did.'

'I must ask you to be good enough to give me back my cat,' said Elizabeth, icily.

He regarded her defensively.

'Assuming,' he said, 'purely for the purposes of academic argument, that your Joseph is my Reginald, couldn't we come to an agreement of some sort? Let me buy you another cat. A dozen cats.'

'I don't want a dozen cats. I want Joseph.'

'Fine, fat, soft cats,' he went on persuasively. 'Lovely, affectionate Persians and Angoras, and—'

'Of course, if you intend to steal Joseph—'

'These are harsh words. Any lawyer will tell you that there are special statutes regarding cats. To retain a stray cat is not a tort or a misdemeanour. In the celebrated test-case of Wiggins *v.* Bluebody it was established—'

'Will you please give me back my cat?'

She stood facing him, her chin in the air and her eyes shining, and the young man suddenly fell a victim to conscience.

'Look here,' he said, 'I'll throw myself on your mercy. I admit the cat is your cat, and that I have no right to it, and that I am just a common sneak-thief. But consider. I had just come back from the first rehearsal of my first play; and as I walked in at the door that cat walked in at the window. I'm as superstitious as a coon, and I felt that to give him up would be equivalent to killing the play before ever it was produced. I know it will sound absurd to you. *You* have no idiotic superstitions. You are sane and practical. But, in the circumstances, if you *could* see your way to waiving your rights—'

Before the wistfulness of his eye Elizabeth capitulated. She felt quite overcome by the revulsion of feeling which swept through her. How she had misjudged him! She had taken him for an ordinary soulless purloiner of cats, a snapper-up of cats at random and without reason; and all the time he had been reluctantly compelled to the act by this deep and praiseworthy motive. All the unselfishness and love of sacrifice innate in good women stirred within her.

'Why, of *course* you mustn't let him go! It would mean awful bad luck.'

'But how about you—'

'Never mind about me. Think of all the people who are dependent on your play being a success.'

The young man blinked.

'This is overwhelming,' he said.

'I had no notion why you wanted him. He was nothing to me—at least, nothing much—that is to say—well, I suppose I was rather fond of him—but he was not—not—'

'Vital?'

'That's just the word I wanted. He was just company, you know.'

'Haven't you many friends?'

'I haven't any friends.'

'You haven't any friends! That settles it. You must take him back.'

'I couldn't think of it.'

'Of course you must take him back at once.'

'I really couldn't.'

'You must.'

'I won't.'

'But, good gracious, how do you suppose I should feel, knowing that you were all alone and that I had sneaked your—your ewe lamb, as it were?'

'And how do you suppose I should feel if your play failed simply for lack of a black cat?'

He started, and ran his fingers through his rough hair in an overwrought manner.

'Solomon couldn't have solved this problem,' he said. 'How would it be—it seems the only possible way out—if you were to retain a sort of managerial right in him? Couldn't you sometimes step across and chat with him—and me, incidentally—over here? I'm very nearly as lonesome as you are. Chicago is my home. I hardly know a soul in New York.'

Her solitary life in the big city had forced upon Elizabeth the ability to form instantaneous judgements on the men she met. She flashed a glance at the young man and decided in his favour.

'It's very kind of you,' she said. 'I should love to. I want to hear all about your play. I write myself, you know, in a very small way, so a successful playwright is Someone to me.'

'I wish I were a successful playwright.'

'Well, you are having the first play you have ever written produced on

Broadway. That's pretty wonderful.'

"M—yes,' said the young man. It seemed to Elizabeth that he spoke doubtfully, and this modesty consolidated the favourable impression she had formed.

* * * * *

The gods are just. For every ill which they inflict they also supply a compensation. It seems good to them that individuals in big cities shall be lonely, but they have so arranged that, if one of these individuals does at last contrive to seek out and form a friendship with another, that friendship shall grow more swiftly than the tepid acquaintanceships of those on whom the icy touch of loneliness has never fallen. Within a week Elizabeth was feeling that she had known this James Renshaw Boyd all her life.

And yet there was a tantalizing incompleteness about his personal reminiscences. Elizabeth was one of those persons who like to begin a friendship with a full statement of their position, their previous life, and the causes which led up to their being in this particular spot at this particular time. At their next meeting, before he had had time to say much on his own account, she had told him of her life in the small Canadian town where she had passed the early part of her life; of the rich and unexpected aunt who had sent her to college for no particular reason that anyone could ascertain except that she enjoyed being unexpected; of the legacy from this same aunt, far smaller than might have been hoped for, but sufficient to send a grateful Elizabeth to New York, to try her luck there; of editors, magazines, manuscripts refused or accepted, plots for stories; of life in general, as lived down where the Arch spans Fifth Avenue and the lighted cross of the Judson shines by night on Washington Square.

Ceasing eventually, she waited for him to begin; and he did not begin—not, that is to say, in the sense the word conveyed to Elizabeth. He spoke briefly of college, still more briefly of Chicago—which city he appeared to regard with a distaste that made Lot's attitude towards the Cities of the Plain almost kindly by comparison. Then, as if he had fulfilled the demands of the most exacting inquisitor in the matter of personal reminiscence, he began to speak of the play.

The only facts concerning him to which Elizabeth could really have sworn with a clear conscience at the end of the second week of their acquaintance were that he was very poor, and that this play meant everything to him.

The statement that it meant everything to him insinuated itself so frequently into his conversation that it weighed on Elizabeth's mind like a burden, and by degrees she found herself giving the play place of honour in her thoughts over and above her own little ventures. With this stupendous thing hanging in the balance, it seemed almost wicked of her to devote a moment to wondering whether the editor of an evening paper, who had half promised to give her the entrancing post of Adviser to the Lovelorn on his journal, would fulfil that half-promise.

At an early stage in their friendship the young man had told her the plot of the piece; and if he had not unfortunately forgotten several important episodes and had to leap back to them across a gulf of one or two acts, and if he had referred to his characters by name instead of by such descriptions as 'the fellow who's in love with the girl—not what's-his-name but the other chap'—she would no doubt have got that mental half-Nelson on it which is such a help towards the proper understanding of a four-act comedy. As it was, his precis had left her a little vague; but she said it was perfectly splendid, and he said did she really think so. And she said yes, she did, and they were both happy.

Rehearsals seemed to prey on his spirits a good deal. He attended them with the pathetic regularity of the young dramatist, but they appeared to bring him little balm. Elizabeth generally found him steeped in gloom, and then she would postpone the recital, to which she had been looking forward, of whatever little triumph she might have happened to win, and devote herself to the task of cheering him up. If women were wonderful in no other way, they would be wonderful for their genius for listening to shop instead of talking it.

Elizabeth was feeling more than a little proud of the way in which her judgement of this young man was being justified. Life in Bohemian New York had left her decidedly wary of strange young men, not formally introduced; her faith in human nature had had to undergo much straining. Wolves in sheep's clothing were common objects of the wayside in her unprotected life; and perhaps her chief reason for appreciating this friendship was the feeling of safety which it gave her.

Their relations, she told herself, were so splendidly unsentimental. There was no need for that silent defensiveness which had come to seem almost an inevitable accompaniment to dealings with the opposite sex. James Boyd, she felt, she could trust; and it was wonderful how soothing the reflexion was.

And that was why, when the thing happened, it so shocked and frightened her.

It had been one of their quiet evenings. Of late they had fallen into the habit of sitting for long periods together without speaking. But it had differed from other quiet evenings through the fact that Elizabeth's silence hid a slight but well-defined feeling of injury. Usually she sat happy with her thoughts, but tonight she was ruffled. She had a grievance.

That afternoon the editor of the evening paper, whose angelic status not even a bald head and an absence of wings and harp could conceal, had definitely informed her that the man who had conducted the column hitherto having resigned, the post of Heloise Milton, official adviser to readers troubled with affairs of the heart, was hers; and he looked to her to justify the daring experiment of letting a woman handle so responsible a job. Imagine how Napoleon felt after Austerlitz, picture Colonel Goethale contemplating the last spadeful of dirt from the Panama Canal, try to visualize a suburban householder who sees a flower emerging from the soil in which he has inserted a packet of guaranteed seeds, and you will have some faint conception how Elizabeth felt as those golden words proceeded from that editor's lips. For the moment Ambition was sated. The years, rolling by, might perchance open out other vistas; but for the moment she was content.

Into James Boyd's apartment she had walked, stepping on fleecy clouds of rapture, to tell him the great news.

She told him the great news.

He said, 'Ah!'

There are many ways of saying 'Ah!' You can put joy, amazement, rapture into it; you can also make it sound as if it were a reply to a remark on the weather. James Boyd made it sound just like that. His hair was rumpled, his brow contracted, and his manner absent. The impression he gave Elizabeth was that he had barely heard her. The next moment he was deep in a recital of the misdemeanours of the actors now rehearsing for his four-act comedy. The star had done this, the leading woman that, the juvenile something else. For the first time Elizabeth listened unsympathetically.

The time came when speech failed James Boyd, and he sat back in his chair, brooding. Elizabeth, cross and wounded, sat in hers, nursing Joseph. And so, in a dim light, time flowed by.

Just how it happened she never knew. One moment, peace; the next chaos. One moment stillness; the next, Joseph hurtling through the air, all claws and expletives, and herself caught in a clasp which shook the breath from her.

One can dimly reconstruct James's train of thought. He is in despair; things are going badly at the theatre, and life has lost its savour. His eye, as he sits, is caught by Elizabeth's profile. It is a pretty—above all, a soothing—profile. An almost painful sentimentality sweeps over James Boyd. There she sits, his only friend in this cruel city. If you argue that there is no necessity to spring at your only friend and nearly choke her, you argue soundly; the point is well taken. But James Boyd was beyond the reach of sound argument. Much rehearsing had frayed his nerves to ribbons. One may say that he was not responsible for his actions.

That is the case for James. Elizabeth, naturally, was not in a position to take a wide and understanding view of it. All she knew was that James had played her false, abused her trust in him. For a moment, such was the shock of the surprise, she was not conscious of indignation—or, indeed, of any sensation except the purely physical one of semi-strangulation. Then, flushed, and more bitterly angry than she could ever have imagined herself capable of being, she began to struggle. She tore herself away from him. Coming on top of her grievance, this thing filled her with a sudden, very vivid hatred of James. At the back of her anger, feeding it, was the humiliating thought that it was all her own fault, that by her presence there she had invited this.

She groped her way to the door. Something was writhing and struggling inside her, blinding her eyes, and robbing her of speech. She was only conscious of a desire to be alone, to be back and safe in her own home. She was aware that he was speaking, but the words did not reach her. She found the door, and pulled it open. She felt a hand on her arm, but she shook it off. And then she was back behind her own door, alone and at liberty to contemplate at leisure the ruins of that little temple of friendship which she had built up so carefully and in which she had been so happy.

The broad fact that she would never forgive him was for a while her only coherent thought. To this succeeded the determination that she would never forgive herself. And having thus placed beyond the pale the only two friends she had in New York, she was free to devote herself without hindrance to the task of feeling thoroughly lonely and wretched.

The shadows deepened. Across the street a sort of bubbling explosion, followed by a jerky glare that shot athwart the room, announced the lighting of the big arc-lamp on the opposite side-walk. She resented it, being in the mood for undiluted gloom; but she had not the energy to pull down the shade and shut it out. She sat where she was, thinking thoughts that hurt.

The door of the apartment opposite opened. There was a single ring at her bell. She did not answer it. There came another. She sat where she was, motionless. The door closed again.

* * * * *

The days dragged by. Elizabeth lost count of time. Each day had its duties, which ended when you went to bed; that was all she knew—except that life had become very grey and very lonely, far lonelier even than in the time when James Boyd was nothing to her but an occasional sound of footsteps.

Of James she saw nothing. It is not difficult to avoid anyone in New York, even when you live just across the way.

* * * * *

It was Elizabeth's first act each morning, immediately on awaking, to open her front door and gather in whatever lay outside it. Sometimes there would be mail; and always, unless Francis, as he sometimes did, got mixed and absent-minded, the morning milk and the morning paper.

One morning, some two weeks after that evening of which she tried not to think, Elizabeth, opening the door, found immediately outside it a folded scrap of paper. She unfolded it.

I am just off to the theatre. Won't you wish me luck? I feel sure it is going to be a hit. Joseph is purring like a dynamo.—J.R.B.

In the early morning the brain works sluggishly. For an instant Elizabeth stood looking at the words uncomprehendingly; then, with a leaping of the heart, their meaning came home to her. He must have left this at her door on the previous night. The play had been produced! And somewhere in the folded interior of the morning paper at her feet must be the opinion of 'One in Authority' concerning it!

Dramatic criticisms have this peculiarity, that if you are looking for them, they burrow and hide like rabbits. They dodge behind murders; they duck behind baseball scores; they lie up snugly behind the Wall Street news. It was a full minute before Elizabeth found what she sought, and the first words she read smote her like a blow.

In that vein of delightful facetiousness which so endears him to all followers and perpetrators of the drama, the 'One in Authority' rent and tore James Boyd's play. He knocked James Boyd's play down, and kicked it; he jumped on it with large feet; he poured cold water on it, and chopped it into little bits. He merrily disembowelled James Boyd's play.

Elizabeth quivered from head to foot. She caught at the door-post to steady herself. In a flash all her resentment had gone, wiped away and annihilated like a mist before the sun. She loved him, and she knew now that she had always loved him.

It took her two seconds to realize that the 'One in Authority' was a miserable incompetent, incapable of recognizing merit when it was displayed before him. It took her five minutes to dress. It took her a minute to run downstairs and out to the news-stand on the corner of the street. Here, with a lavishness which charmed and exhilarated the proprietor, she bought all the other papers which he could supply.

Moments of tragedy are best described briefly. Each of the papers noticed the play, and each of them damned it with uncompromising heartiness. The criticisms varied only in tone. One cursed with relish and gusto; another with a certain pity; a third with a kind of wounded superiority, as of one compelled against his will to speak of something unspeakable; but the meaning of all was the same. James Boyd's play was a hideous failure.

Back to the house sped Elizabeth, leaving the organs of a free people to be gathered up, smoothed, and replaced on the stand by the now more than ever charmed proprietor. Up the stairs she sped, and arriving breathlessly at James's door rang the bell.

Heavy footsteps came down the passage; crushed, disheartened footsteps; footsteps that sent a chill to Elizabeth's heart. The door opened. James Boyd stood before her, heavy-eyed and haggard. In his eyes was despair, and on his chin the blue growth of beard of the man from whom the mailed fist of Fate has smitten the energy to perform his morning shave.

Behind him, littering the floor, were the morning papers; and at the sight of them Elizabeth broke down.

'Oh, Jimmy, darling!' she cried; and the next moment she was in his arms, and for a space time stood still.

How long afterwards it was she never knew; but eventually James Boyd spoke.

'If you'll marry me,' he said hoarsely, 'I don't care a hang.'

'Jimmy, darling!' said Elizabeth, 'of course I will.'

Past them, as they stood there, a black streak shot silently, and disappeared out of the door. Joseph was leaving the sinking ship.

'Let him go, the fraud,' said Elizabeth bitterly. 'I shall never believe in black cats again.'

But James was not of this opinion.

'Joseph has brought me all the luck I need.'

'But the play meant everything to you.'

'It did then.'

Elizabeth hesitated.

'Jimmy, dear, it's all right, you know. I know you will make a fortune out of your next play, and I've heaps for us both to live on till you make good. We can manage splendidly on my salary from the *Evening Chronicle*.'

'What! Have you got a job on a New York paper?'

'Yes, I told you about it. I am doing Heloise Milton. Why, what's the matter?'

He groaned hollowly.

'And I was thinking that you would come back to Chicago with me!'

'But I will. Of course I will. What did you think I meant to do?'

'What! Give up a real job in New York!' He blinked. 'This isn't really happening. I'm dreaming.'

'But, Jimmy, are you sure you can get work in Chicago? Wouldn't it be better to stay on here, where all the managers are, and—'

He shook his head.

'I think it's time I told you about myself,' he said. 'Am I sure I can get work in Chicago? I am, worse luck. Darling, have you in your more material moments ever toyed with a Boyd's Premier Breakfast-Sausage or kept body and soul together with a slice off a Boyd's Excelsior Home-Cured Ham? My father makes them, and the tragedy of my life is that he wants me to help him at it. This was my position. I loathed the family business as much as dad loved it. I had a notion—a fool notion, as it has turned out—that I could make good in the literary line. I've scribbled in a sort of way ever since I was in college. When the time came for me to join the firm, I put it to dad straight. I said, "Give me a chance, one good, square chance, to see if the divine fire is really there, or if somebody has just turned on the alarm as a practical joke." And we made a bargain. I had written this play, and we made it a test-case. We fixed it up that dad should put up the money to give it a Broadway production. If it succeeded, all right; I'm the young Gus Thomas, and may go ahead in the literary game. If it's a fizzle, off goes my coat, and I abandon pipe-dreams of literary triumphs and start in as the guy who put the Co. in Boyd & Co. Well, events have proved that I *am* the guy, and now I'm going to keep my part of the bargain just as squarely as dad kept his. I know quite well that if I refused to play fair and chose to stick on here in New York and try again, dad would go on staking me. That's the sort of man he is. But I wouldn't do it for a million Broadway successes. I've had my chance, and I've foozled; and now I'm going back to make him happy by being a real live member of the firm. And the queer thing about it is that last night I hated the idea, and this morning, now that I've got you, I almost look forward to it.'

He gave a little shiver.

'And yet—I don't know. There's something rather gruesome still to my near-artist soul in living in luxury on murdered piggies. Have you ever seen them persuading a pig to play the stellar role in a Boyd Premier Breakfast-Sausage? It's pretty ghastly. They string them up by their hind legs, and—b-r-r-r-r!'

'Never mind,' said Elizabeth soothingly. 'Perhaps they don't mind it really.'

'Well, I don't know,' said James Boyd, doubtfully. 'I've watched them at it, and I'm bound to say they didn't seem any too well pleased.'

'Try not to think of it.'

'Very well,' said James dutifully.

There came a sudden shout from the floor above, and on the heels of it a shock-haired youth in pyjamas burst into the apartment.

'Now what?' said James. 'By the way, Miss Herrold, my fiancee; Mr Briggs—Paul Axworthy Briggs, sometimes known as the Boy Novelist. What's troubling you, Paul?'

Mr Briggs was stammering with excitement.

'Jimmy,' cried the Boy Novelist, 'what do you think has happened! A black cat has just come into my apartment. I heard him mewing outside the door, and opened it, and he streaked in. And I started my new novel last night! Say, you *do* believe this thing of black cats bringing luck, don't you?'

'Luck! My lad, grapple that cat to your soul with hoops of steel. He's the greatest little luck-bringer in New York. He was boarding with me till this morning.'

'Then—by Jove! I nearly forgot to ask—your play was a hit? I haven't seen the papers yet'

'Well, when you see them, don't read the notices. It was the worst frost Broadway has seen since Columbus's time.'

'But—I don't understand.'

'Don't worry. You don't have to. Go back and fill that cat with fish, or she'll be leaving you. I suppose you left the door open?'

'My God!' said the Boy Novelist, paling, and dashed for the door.

'Do you think Joseph *will* bring him luck?' said Elizabeth, thoughtfully.

'It depends what sort of luck you mean. Joseph seems to work in devious ways. If I know Joseph's methods, Briggs's new novel will be rejected by every publisher in the city; and then, when he is sitting in his apartment, wondering which of his razors to end himself with, there will be a ring at the bell, and in will come the most beautiful girl in the world, and then—well, then, take it from me, he will be all right.'

'He won't mind about the novel?'

'Not in the least.'

'Not even if it means that he will have to go away and kill pigs and things.'

'About the pig business, dear. I've noticed a slight tendency in you to let yourself get rather morbid about it. I know they string them up by the hind-legs, and all that sort of thing; but you must remember that a pig looks at these things from a different standpoint. My belief is that the pigs like it. Try not to think of it.'

'Very well,' said Elizabeth, dutifully.

THE ROMANCE OF AN UGLY POLICEMAN

Crossing the Thames by Chelsea Bridge, the wanderer through London finds himself in pleasant Battersea. Rounding the Park, where the female of the species wanders with its young by the ornamental water where the wild-fowl are, he comes upon a vast road. One side of this is given up to Nature, the other to Intellect. On the right, green trees stretch into the middle distance; on the left, endless blocks of residential flats. It is Battersea Park Road, the home of the cliff-dwellers.

Police-constable Plimmer's beat embraced the first quarter of a mile of the cliffs. It was his duty to pace in the measured fashion of the London policeman along the front of them, turn to the right, turn to the left, and come back along the road which ran behind them. In this way he was enabled to keep the king's peace over no fewer than four blocks of mansions.

It did not require a deal of keeping. Battersea may have its tough citizens, but they do not live in Battersea Park Road. Battersea Park Road's speciality is Brain, not Crime. Authors, musicians, newspaper men, actors, and artists are the inhabitants of these mansions. A child could control them. They assault and batter nothing but pianos; they steal nothing but ideas; they murder nobody except Chopin and Beethoven. Not through these shall an ambitious young constable achieve promotion.

At this conclusion Edward Plimmer arrived within forty-eight hours of his installation. He recognized the flats for what they were—just so many layers of big-brained blamelessness. And there was not even the chance of a burglary. No burglar wastes his time burgling authors. Constable Plimmer reconciled his mind to the fact that his term in Battersea must be looked on as something in the nature of a vacation.

He was not altogether sorry. At first, indeed, he found the new atmosphere soothing. His last beat had been in the heart of tempestuous Whitechapel, where his arms had ached from the incessant hauling of wiry inebriates to the station, and his shins had revolted at the kicks showered upon them by haughty spirits impatient of restraint. Also, one Saturday night, three friends of a gentleman whom he was trying to induce not to murder his wife had so wrought upon him that, when he came out of hospital, his already homely appearance was further marred by a nose which resembled the gnarled root of a tree. All these things had taken from the charm of Whitechapel, and the cloistral peace of Battersea Park Road was grateful and comforting.

And just when the unbroken calm had begun to lose its attraction and dreams of action were once more troubling him, a new interest entered his life; and with its coming he ceased to wish to be removed from Battersea. He fell in love.

It happened at the back of York Mansions. Anything that ever happened, happened there; for it is at the back of these blocks of flats that the real life is. At the front you never see anything, except an occasional tousle-headed young man smoking a pipe; but at the back, where the cooks come out to parley with the tradesmen, there is at certain hours of the day quite a respectable activity. Pointed dialogues about yesterday's eggs and the toughness of Saturday's meat are conducted *fortissimo* between cheerful youths in the road and satirical young women in print dresses, who come out of their kitchen doors on to little balconies. The whole thing has a pleasing Romeo and Juliet touch. Romeo rattles up in his cart. 'Sixty-four!' he cries. 'Sixty-fower, sixty-fower, sixty-fow—' The kitchen door opens, and Juliet emerges. She eyes Romeo without any great show of affection. 'Are you Perkins and Blissett?' she inquires coldly. Romeo admits it. 'Two of them yesterday's eggs was bad.' Romeo protests. He defends his eggs. They were fresh from the hen; he stood over her while she laid them. Juliet listens frigidly. 'I *don't* think,' she says. 'Well, half of sugar, one marmalade, and two of breakfast bacon,' she adds, and ends the argument. There is a rattling as of a steamer weighing anchor; the goods go up in the tradesman's lift; Juliet collects them, and exits, banging the door. The little drama is over.

Such is life at the back of York Mansions—a busy, throbbing thing.

The peace of afternoon had fallen upon the world one day towards the end of Constable Plimmer's second week of the simple life, when his attention was attracted by a whistle. It was followed by a musical 'Hi!'

Constable Plimmer looked up. On the kitchen balcony of a second-floor flat a girl was standing. As he took her in with a slow and exhaustive gaze, he was aware of strange thrills. There was something about this girl which excited Constable Plimmer. I do not say that she was a beauty; I do not claim that you or I would have raved about her; I merely say that Constable Plimmer thought she was All Right.

'Miss?' he said.

'Got the time about you?' said the girl. 'All the clocks have stopped.'

'The time,' said Constable Plimmer, consulting his watch, 'wants exactly ten minutes to four.'

'Thanks.'

'Not at all, miss.'

The girl was inclined for conversation. It was that gracious hour of the day when you have cleared lunch and haven't got to think of dinner yet, and have a bit of time to draw a breath or two. She leaned over the balcony and smiled pleasantly.

'If you want to know the time, ask a pleeceman,' she said. 'You been on this beat long?'

'Just short of two weeks, miss.'

'I been here three days.'

'I hope you like it, miss.'

'So-so. The milkman's a nice boy.'

Constable Plimmer did not reply. He was busy silently hating the milkman. He knew him—one of those good-looking blighters; one of those oiled and curled perishers; one of those blooming fascinators who go about the world making things hard for ugly, honest men with loving hearts. Oh, yes, he knew the milkman.

'He's a rare one with his jokes,' said the girl.

Constable Plimmer went on not replying. He was perfectly aware that the milkman was a rare one with his jokes. He had heard him. The way girls fell for anyone with the gift of the gab—that was what embittered Constable Plimmer.

'He—' she giggled. 'He calls me Little Pansy-Face.'

'If you'll excuse me, miss,' said Constable Plimmer coldly, 'I'll have to be getting along on my beat.'

Little Pansy-Face! And you couldn't arrest him for it! What a world!

Constable Plimmer paced upon his way, a blue-clad volcano.

It is a terrible thing to be obsessed by a milkman. To Constable Plimmer's disordered imagination it seemed that, dating from this interview, the world became one solid milkman. Wherever he went, he seemed to run into this milkman. If he was in the front road, this milkman—Alf Brooks, it appeared, was his loathsome name—came rattling past with his jingling cans as if he were Apollo driving his chariot. If he was round at the back, there was Alf, his damned tenor doing duets with the balconies. And all this in defiance of the known law of natural history that milkmen do not come out after five in the morning. This irritated Constable Plimmer. You talk of a man 'going home with the milk' when you mean that he sneaks in in the small hours of the morning. If all milkmen were like Alf Brooks the phrase was meaningless.

He brooded. The unfairness of Fate was souring him. A man expects trouble in his affairs of the heart from soldiers and sailors, and to be cut out by even a postman is to fall before a worthy foe; but milkmen—no! Only grocers' assistants and telegraph-boys were intended by Providence to fear milkmen.

Yet here was Alf Brooks, contrary to all rules, the established pet of the mansions. Bright eyes shone from balconies when his 'Milk—oo—oo' sounded. Golden voices giggled delightedly at his bellowed chaff. And Ellen Brown, whom he called Little Pansy-Face, was definitely in love with him.

They were keeping company. They were walking out. This crushing truth

Edward Plimmer learned from Ellen herself.

She had slipped out to mail a letter at the pillar-box on the corner, and she reached it just as the policeman arrived there in the course of his patrol.

Nervousness impelled Constable Plimmer to be arch.

"Ullo, 'ullo, 'ullo,' he said. 'Posting love-letters?'

'What, me? This is to the Police Commissioner, telling him you're no good.'

'I'll give it to him. Him and me are taking supper tonight.'

Nature had never intended Constable Plimmer to be playful. He was at his worst when he rollicked. He snatched at the letter with what was meant to be a debonair gaiety, and only succeeded in looking like an angry gorilla. The girl uttered a startled squeak.

The letter was addressed to Mr A. Brooks.

Playfulness, after this, was at a discount. The girl was frightened and angry, and he was scowling with mingled jealousy and dismay.

'Ho!' he said. 'Ho! Mr A. Brooks!'

Ellen Brown was a nice girl, but she had a temper, and there were moments when her manners lacked rather noticeably the repose which stamps the caste of Vere de Vere.

'Well, what about it?' she cried. 'Can't one write to the young gentleman one's keeping company with, without having to get permission from every—' She paused to marshal her forces from the assault. 'Without having to get permission from every great, ugly, red-faced copper with big feet and a broken nose in London?'

Constable Plimmer's wrath faded into a dull unhappiness. Yes, she was right. That was the correct description. That was how an impartial Scotland Yard would be compelled to describe him, if ever he got lost. 'Missing. A great, ugly, red-faced copper with big feet and a broken nose.' They would never find him otherwise.

'Perhaps you object to my walking out with Alf? Perhaps you've got something against him? I suppose you're jealous!'

She threw in the last suggestion entirely in a sporting spirit. She loved battle, and she had a feeling that this one was going to finish far too quickly. To prolong it, she gave him this opening. There were a dozen ways in which he might answer, each more insulting than the last; and then, when he had finished, she could begin again. These little encounters, she held, sharpened the wits, stimulated the circulation, and kept one out in the open air.

'Yes,' said Constable Plimmer.

It was the one reply she was not expecting. For direct abuse, for sarcasm, for dignity, for almost any speech beginning, 'What! Jealous of you. Why—' she was prepared. But this was incredible. It disabled her, as the wild thrust of an unskilled fencer will disable a master of the rapier. She searched in her mind and found that she had nothing to say.

There was a tense moment in which she found him, looking her in the eyes, strangely less ugly than she had supposed, and then he was gone, rolling along on his beat with that air which all policemen must achieve, of having no feelings at all, and—as long as it behaves itself—no interest in the human race.

Ellen posted her letter. She dropped it into the box thoughtfully, and thoughtfully returned to the flat. She looked over her shoulder, but Constable Plimmer was out of sight.

Peaceful Battersea began to vex Constable Plimmer. To a man crossed in love, action is the one anodyne; and Battersea gave no scope for action. He dreamed now of the old Whitechapel days as a man dreams of the joys of his childhood. He reflected bitterly that a fellow never knows when he is well off in this world. Any one of those myriad drunk and disorderlies would have been as balm to him now. He was like a man who has run through a fortune and in poverty eats the bread of regret. Amazedly he recollected that in those happy days he had grumbled at his lot. He remembered confiding to a friend in the station-house, as he rubbed with liniment the spot on his right shin where the well-shod foot of a joyous costermonger had got home, that this sort of thing—meaning militant costermongers—was 'a bit too thick'. A bit too thick! Why, he would pay one to kick him now. And as for the three loyal friends of the would-be wife-murderer who had broken his nose, if he saw them coming round the corner he would welcome them as brothers.

And Battersea Park Road dozed on—calm, intellectual, law-abiding.

A friend of his told him that there had once been a murder in one of these flats. He did not believe it. If any of these white-corpuscled clams ever swatted a fly, it was much as they could do. The thing was ridiculous on the face of it. If they were capable of murder, they would have murdered Alf Brooks.

He stood in the road, and looked up at the placid buildings resentfully.

'Grr-rr-rr!' he growled, and kicked the side-walk.

And, even as he spoke, on the balcony of a second-floor flat there appeared a woman, an elderly, sharp-faced woman, who waved her arms and screamed, 'Policeman! Officer! Come up here! Come up here at once!'

Up the stone stairs went Constable Plimmer at the run. His mind was alert and questioning. Murder? Hardly murder, perhaps. If it had been that, the woman would have said so. She did not look the sort of woman who would be reticent about a thing like that. Well, anyway, it was something; and Edward Plimmer had been long enough in Battersea to be thankful for small favours. An intoxicated husband would be better than nothing. At least he would be something that a fellow could get his hands on to and throw about a bit.

The sharp-faced woman was waiting for him at the door. He followed her into the flat.

'What is it, ma'am?'

'Theft! Our cook has been stealing!'

She seemed sufficiently excited about it, but Constable Plimmer felt only depression and disappointment. A stout admirer of the sex, he hated arresting women. Moreover, to a man in the mood to tackle anarchists with bombs, to be confronted with petty theft is galling. But duty was duty. He produced his notebook.

'She is in her room. I locked her in. I know she has taken my brooch.

We have missed money. You must search her.'

'Can't do that, ma'am. Female searcher at the station.'

'Well, you can search her box.'

A little, bald, nervous man in spectacles appeared as if out of a trap. As a matter of fact, he had been there all the time, standing by the bookcase; but he was one of those men you do not notice till they move and speak.

'Er—Jane.'

'Well, Henry?'

The little man seemed to swallow something.

'I—I think that you may possibly be wronging Ellen. It is just possible, as regards the money—' He smiled in a ghastly manner and turned to the policeman. 'Er—officer, I ought to tell you that my wife—ah—holds the purse-strings of our little home; and it is just possible that in an absent-minded moment *I* may have—'

'Do you mean to tell me, Henry, that *you* have been taking my money?'

'My dear, it is just possible that in the abs—'

'How often?'

He wavered perceptibly. Conscience was beginning to lose its grip.

'Oh, not often.'

'How often? More than once?'

Conscience had shot its bolt. The little man gave up the Struggle.

'No, no, not more than once. Certainly not more than once.'

'You ought not to have done it at all. We will talk about that later. It doesn't alter the fact that Ellen is a thief. I have missed money half a dozen times. Besides that, there's the brooch. Step this way, officer.'

Constable Plimmer stepped that way—his face a mask. He knew who was waiting for them behind the locked door at the end of the passage. But it was his duty to look as if he were stuffed, and he did so.

* * * * *

She was sitting on her bed, dressed for the street. It was her afternoon out, the sharp-faced woman had informed Constable Plimmer, attributing the fact that she had discovered the loss of the brooch in time to stop her a direct interposition of Providence. She was pale, and there was a hunted look in her eyes.

'You wicked girl, where is my brooch?'

She held it out without a word. She had been holding it in her hand.

'You see, officer!'

'I wasn't stealing of it. I 'adn't but borrowed it. I was going to put it back.'

'Stuff and nonsense! Borrow it, indeed! What for?'

'I—I wanted to look nice.'

The woman gave a short laugh. Constable Plimmer's face was a mere block of wood, expressionless.

'And what about the money I've been missing? I suppose you'll say you only borrowed that?'

'I never took no money.'

'Well, it's gone, and money doesn't go by itself. Take her to the police-station, officer.'

Constable Plimmer raised heavy eyes.

'You make a charge, ma'am?'

'Bless the man! Of course I make a charge. What did you think I asked you to step in for?'

'Will you come along, miss?' said Constable Plimmer.

* * * * *

Out in the street the sun shone gaily down on peaceful Battersea. It was the hour when children walk abroad with their nurses; and from the green depths of the Park came the sound of happy voices. A cat stretched itself in the sunshine and eyed the two as they passed with lazy content.

They walked in silence. Constable Plimmer was a man with a rigid sense of what was and what was not fitting behaviour in a policeman on duty: he aimed always at a machine-like impersonality. There were times when it came hard, but he did his best. He strode on, his chin up and his eyes averted. And beside him—

Well, she was not crying. That was something.

Round the corner, beautiful in light flannel, gay at both ends with a new straw hat and the yellowest shoes in South-West London, scented, curled, a prince among young men, stood Alf Brooks. He was feeling piqued. When he said three o'clock, he meant three o'clock. It was now three-fifteen, and she had not appeared. Alf Brooks swore an impatient oath, and the thought crossed his mind, as it had sometimes crossed it before, that Ellen Brown was not the only girl in the world.

'Give her another five min—'

Ellen Brown, with escort, at that moment turned the corner.

Rage was the first emotion which the spectacle aroused in Alf Brooks. Girls who kept a fellow waiting about while they fooled around with policemen were no girls for him. They could understand once and for all that he was a man who could pick and choose.

And then an electric shock set the world dancing mistily before his eyes. This policeman was wearing his belt; he was on duty. And Ellen's face was not the face of a girl strolling with the Force for pleasure.

His heart stopped, and then began to race. His cheeks flushed a dusky crimson. His jaw fell, and a prickly warmth glowed in the parts about his spine.

'Goo'!'

His fingers sought his collar.

'Crumbs!'

He was hot all over.

'Goo' Lor'! She's been pinched!'

He tugged at his collar. It was choking him.

Alf Brooks did not show up well in the first real crisis which life had forced upon him. That must be admitted. Later, when it was over, and he had leisure for self-examination, he admitted it to himself. But even then he excused himself by asking Space in a blustering manner what else he could ha' done. And if the question did not bring much balm to his soul at the first time of asking, it proved won-wonderfully soothing on constant repetition. He repeated it at intervals for the next two days, and by the end of that time his cure was complete. On the third morning his 'Milk—oo—oo' had regained its customary carefree ring, and he was feeling that he had acted in difficult circumstances in the only possible manner.

Consider. He was Alf Brooks, well known and respected in the neighbourhood; a singer in the choir on Sundays; owner of a milk-walk in the most fashionable part of Battersea; to all practical purposes a public man. Was he to recognize, in broad daylight and in open street, a girl who walked with a policeman because she had to, a malefactor, a girl who had been pinched?

Ellen, Constable Plimmer woodenly at her side, came towards him. She was ten yards off—seven—five—three—Alf Brooks tilted his hat over his eyes and walked past her, unseeing, a stranger.

He hurried on. He was conscious of a curious feeling that somebody was just going to kick him, but he dared not look round.

* * * * *

Constable Plimmer eyed the middle distance with an earnest gaze. His face was redder than ever. Beneath his blue tunic strange emotions were at work. Something seemed to be filling his throat. He tried to swallow it.

He stopped in his stride. The girl glanced up at him in a kind of dull, questioning way. Their eyes met for the first time that afternoon, and it seemed to Constable Plimmer that whatever it was that was interfering with the inside of his throat had grown larger, and more unmanageable.

There was the misery of the stricken animal in her gaze. He had seen women look like that in Whitechapel. The woman to whom, indirectly, he owed his broken nose had looked like that. As his hand had fallen on the collar of the man who was kicking her to death, he had seen her eyes. They were Ellen's eyes, as she stood there now—tortured, crushed, yet uncomplaining.

Constable Plimmer looked at Ellen, and Ellen looked at Constable Plimmer. Down the street some children were playing with a dog. In one of the flats a woman began to sing.

'Hop it,' said Constable Plimmer.

He spoke gruffly. He found speech difficult.

The girl started.

'What say?'

'Hop it. Get along. Run away.'

'What do you mean?'

Constable Plimmer scowled. His face was scarlet. His jaw protruded like a granite break-water.

'Go on,' he growled. 'Hop it. Tell him it was all a joke. I'll explain at the station.'

Understanding seemed to come to her slowly.

'Do you mean I'm to go?'

'Yes.'

'What do you mean? You aren't going to take me to the station?'

'No.'

She stared at him. Then, suddenly, she broke down,

'He wouldn't look at me. He was ashamed of me. He pretended not to see me.'

She leaned against the wall, her back shaking.

'Well, run after him, and tell him it was all—'

'No, no, no.'

Constable Plimmer looked morosely at the side-walk. He kicked it.

She turned. Her eyes were red, but she was no longer crying. Her chin had a brave tilt.

'I couldn't—not after what he did. Let's go along. I—I don't care.'

She looked at him curiously.

'Were you really going to have let me go?'

Constable Plimmer nodded. He was aware of her eyes searching his face, but he did not meet them.

'Why?'

He did not answer.

'What would have happened to you, if you had have done?'

Constable Plimmer's scowl was of the stuff of which nightmares are made. He kicked the unoffending side-walk with an increased viciousness.

'Dismissed the Force,' he said curtly.

'And sent to prison, too, I shouldn't wonder.'

'Maybe.'

He heard her draw a deep breath, and silence fell upon them again. The dog down the road had stopped barking. The woman in the flat had stopped singing. They were curiously alone.

'Would you have done all that for me?' she said.

'Yes.'

'Why?'

'Because I don't think you ever did it. Stole that money, I mean. Nor the brooch, neither.'

'Was that all?'

'What do you mean—all?'

'Was that the only reason?'

He swung round on her, almost threateningly.

'No,' he said hoarsely. 'No, it wasn't, and you know it wasn't. Well, if you want it, you can have it. It was because I love you. There! Now I've said it, and now you can go on and laugh at me as much as you want.'

'I'm not laughing,' she said soberly.

'You think I'm a fool!'

'No, I don't.'

'I'm nothing to you. *He's* the fellow you're stuck on.'

She gave a little shudder.

'No.'

'What do you mean?'

'I've changed.' She paused. 'I think I shall have changed more by the time I come out.'

'Come out?'

'Come out of prison.'

'You're not going to prison.'

'Yes, I am.'

'I won't take you.'

'Yes, you will. Think I'm going to let you get yourself in trouble like that, to get me out of a fix? Not much.'

'You hop it, like a good girl.'

'Not me.'

He stood looking at her like a puzzled bear.

'They can't eat me.'

'They'll cut off all of your hair.'

'D'you like my hair?'

'Yes.'

'Well, it'll grow again.'

'Don't stand talking. Hop it.'

'I won't. Where's the station?'

'Next street.'

'Well, come along, then.'

* * * * *

The blue glass lamp of the police-station came into sight, and for an instant she stopped. Then she was walking on again, her chin tilted. But her voice shook a little as she spoke.

'Nearly there. Next stop, Battersea. All change! I say, mister—I don't know your name.'

'Plimmer's my name, miss. Edward Plimmer.'

'I wonder if—I mean it'll be pretty lonely where I'm going—I wonder if—What I mean is, it would be rather a lark, when I come out, if I was to find a pal waiting for me to say "Hallo".'

Constable Plimmer braced his ample feet against the stones, and turned purple.

'Miss,' he said, 'I'll be there, if I have to sit up all night. The first thing you'll see when they open the doors is a great, ugly, red-faced copper with big feet and a broken nose. And if you'll say "Hallo" to him when he says "Hallo" to you, he'll be as pleased as Punch and as proud as a duke. And, miss'—he clenched his hands till the nails hurt the leathern flesh—'and, miss, there's just one thing more I'd like to say. You'll be having a good deal of time to yourself for awhile; you'll be able to do a good bit of thinking without anyone to disturb you; and what I'd like you to give your mind to, if you don't object, is just to think whether you can't forget that narrow-chested, God-forsaken blighter who treated you so mean, and get half-way fond of someone who knows jolly well you're the only girl there is.'

She looked past him at the lamp which hung, blue and forbidding, over the station door.

'How long'll I get?' she said. 'What will they give me? Thirty days?'

He nodded.

'It won't take me as long as that,' she said. 'I say, what do people call you?—people who are fond of you, I mean?—Eddie or Ted?'

A SEA OF TROUBLES

Mr Meggs's mind was made up. He was going to commit suicide.

There had been moments, in the interval which had elapsed between the first inception of the idea and his present state of fixed determination, when he had wavered. In these moments he had debated, with Hamlet, the question whether it was nobler in the mind to suffer, or to take arms against a sea of troubles and by opposing end them. But all that was over now. He was resolved.

Mr Meggs's point, the main plank, as it were, in his suicidal platform, was that with him it was beside the question whether or not it was nobler to suffer in the mind. The mind hardly entered into it at all. What he had to decide was whether it was worth while putting up any longer with the perfectly infernal pain in his stomach. For Mr Meggs was a martyr to indigestion. As he was also devoted to the pleasures of the table, life had become for him one long battle, in which, whatever happened, he always got the worst of it.

He was sick of it. He looked back down the vista of the years, and found therein no hope for the future. One after the other all the patent medicines in creation had failed him. Smith's Supreme Digestive Pellets—he had given them a more than fair trial. Blenkinsop's Liquid Life-Giver—he had drunk enough of it to float a ship. Perkins's Premier Pain-Preventer, strongly recommended by the sword-swallowing lady at Barnum and Bailey's—he had wallowed in it. And so on down the list. His interior organism had simply sneered at the lot of them.

'Death, where is thy sting?' thought Mr Meggs, and forthwith began to make his preparations.

Those who have studied the matter say that the tendency to commit suicide is greatest among those who have passed their fifty-fifth year, and that the rate is twice as great for unoccupied males as for occupied males. Unhappy Mr Meggs, accordingly, got it, so to speak, with both barrels. He was fifty-six, and he was perhaps the most unoccupied adult to be found in the length and breadth of the United Kingdom. He toiled not, neither did he spin. Twenty years before, an unexpected legacy had placed him in a position to indulge a natural taste for idleness to the utmost. He was at that time, as regards his professional life, a clerk in a rather obscure shipping firm. Out of office hours he had a mild fondness for letters, which took the form of meaning to read right through the hundred best books one day, but actually contenting himself with the daily paper and an occasional magazine.

Such was Mr Meggs at thirty-six. The necessity for working for a living and a salary too small to permit of self-indulgence among the more expensive and deleterious dishes on the bill of fare had up to that time kept his digestion within reasonable bounds. Sometimes he had twinges; more often he had none.

Then came the legacy, and with it Mr Meggs let himself go. He left London and retired to his native village, where, with a French cook and a series of secretaries to whom he dictated at long intervals occasional paragraphs of a book on British Butterflies on which he imagined himself to be at work, he passed the next twenty years. He could afford to do himself well, and he did himself extremely well. Nobody urged him to take exercise, so he took no exercise. Nobody warned him of the perils of lobster and welsh rabbits to a man of sedentary habits, for it was nobody's business to warn him. On the contrary, people rather encouraged the lobster side of his character, for he was a hospitable soul and liked to have his friends dine with him. The result was that Nature, as is her wont, laid for him, and got him. It seemed to Mr Meggs that he woke one morning to find himself a chronic dyspeptic. That was one of the hardships of his position, to his mind. The thing seemed to hit him suddenly out of a blue sky. One moment, all appeared to be peace and joy; the next, a lively and irritable wild-cat with red-hot claws seemed somehow to have introduced itself into his interior.

So Mr Meggs decided to end it.

In this crisis of his life the old methodical habits of his youth returned to him. A man cannot be a clerk in even an obscure firm of shippers for a great length of time without acquiring system, and Mr Meggs made his preparations calmly and with a forethought worthy of a better cause.

And so we find him, one glorious June morning, seated at his desk, ready for the end.

Outside, the sun beat down upon the orderly streets of the village. Dogs dozed in the warm dust. Men who had to work went about their toil moistly, their minds far away in shady public-houses.

But Mr Meggs, in his study, was cool both in mind and body.

Before him, on the desk, lay six little slips of paper. They were bank-notes, and they represented, with the exception of a few pounds, his entire worldly wealth. Beside them were six letters, six envelopes, and six postage stamps. Mr Meggs surveyed them calmly.

He would not have admitted it, but he had had a lot of fun writing those letters. The deliberation as to who should be his heirs had occupied him pleasantly for several days, and, indeed, had taken his mind off his internal pains at times so thoroughly that he had frequently surprised himself in an almost cheerful mood. Yes, he would have denied it, but it had been great sport sitting in his arm-chair, thinking whom he should pick out from England's teeming millions to make happy with his money. All sorts of schemes had passed through his mind. He had a sense of power which the mere possession of the money had never given him. He began to understand why millionaires make freak wills. At one time he had toyed with the idea of selecting someone at random from the London Directory and bestowing on him all he had to bequeath. He had only abandoned the scheme when it occurred to him that he himself would not be in a position to witness the recipient's stunned delight. And what was the good of starting a thing like that, if you were not to be in at the finish?

Sentiment succeeded whimsicality. His old friends of the office—those were the men to benefit. What good fellows they had been! Some were dead, but he still kept intermittently in touch with half a dozen of them. And—an important point—he knew their present addresses.

This point was important, because Mr Meggs had decided not to leave a will, but to send the money direct to the beneficiaries. He knew what wills were. Even in quite straightforward circumstances they often made trouble. There had been some slight complication about his own legacy twenty years ago. Somebody had contested the will, and before the thing was satisfactorily settled the lawyers had got away with about twenty per cent of the whole. No, no wills. If he made one, and then killed himself, it might be upset on a plea of insanity. He knew of no relative who might consider himself entitled to the money, but there was the chance that some remote cousin existed; and then the comrades of his youth might fail to collect after all.

He declined to run the risk. Quietly and by degrees he had sold out the stocks and shares in which his fortune was invested, and deposited the money in his London bank. Six piles of large notes, dividing the total into six equal parts; six letters couched in a strain of reminiscent pathos and manly resignation; six envelopes, legibly addressed; six postage-stamps; and that part of his preparations was complete. He licked the stamps and placed them on the envelopes; took the notes and inserted them in the letters; folded the letters and thrust them into the envelopes; sealed the envelopes; and unlocking the drawer of his desk produced a small, black, ugly-looking bottle.

He opened the bottle and poured the contents into a medicine-glass.

It had not been without considerable thought that Mr Meggs had decided upon the method of his suicide. The knife, the pistol, the rope—they had all presented their charms to him. He had further examined the merits of drowning and of leaping to destruction from a height.

There were flaws in each. Either they were painful, or else they were messy. Mr Meggs had a tidy soul, and he revolted from the thought of spoiling his figure, as he would most certainly do if he drowned himself; or the carpet, as he would if he used the pistol; or the pavement—and possibly some innocent pedestrian, as must infallibly occur should he leap off the Monument. The knife was out of the question. Instinct told him that it would hurt like the very dickens.

No; poison was the thing. Easy to take, quick to work, and on the whole rather agreeable than otherwise.

Mr Meggs hid the glass behind the inkpot and rang the bell.

'Has Miss Pillenger arrived?' he inquired of the servant.

'She has just come, sir.'

'Tell her that I am waiting for her here.'

Jane Pillenger was an institution. Her official position was that of private secretary and typist to Mr Meggs. That is to say, on the rare occasions when Mr Meggs's conscience overcame his indolence to the extent of forcing him to resume work on his British Butterflies, it was to Miss Pillenger that he addressed the few rambling and incoherent remarks which constituted his idea of a regular hard, slogging spell of literary composition. When he sank back in his chair, speechless and exhausted like a Marathon runner who has started his sprint a mile or two too soon, it was Miss Pillenger's task to unscramble her shorthand notes, type them neatly, and place them in their special drawer in the desk.

Miss Pillenger was a wary spinster of austere views, uncertain age, and a deep-rooted suspicion of men—a suspicion which, to do an abused sex justice, they had done nothing to foster. Men had always been almost coldly correct in their dealings with Miss Pillenger. In her twenty years of experience as a typist and secretary she had never had to refuse with scorn and indignation so much as a box of chocolates from any of her employers. Nevertheless, she continued to be icily on her guard. The clenched fist of her dignity was always drawn back, ready to swing on the first male who dared to step beyond the bounds of professional civility.

Such was Miss Pillenger. She was the last of a long line of unprotected English girlhood which had been compelled by straitened circumstances to listen for hire to the appallingly dreary nonsense which Mr Meggs had to impart on the subject of British Butterflies. Girls had come, and girls had gone, blondes, ex-blondes, brunettes, ex-brunettes, near-blondes, near-brunettes; they had come buoyant, full of hope and life, tempted by the lavish salary which Mr Meggs had found himself after a while compelled to pay; and they had dropped off, one after another, like exhausted bivalves, unable to endure the crushing boredom of life in the village which had given Mr Meggs to the world. For Mr Meggs's home-town was no City of Pleasure. Remove the Vicar's magic-lantern and the try-your-weight machine opposite the post office, and you practically eliminated the temptations to tread the primrose path. The only young men in the place were silent, gaping youths, at whom lunacy commissioners looked sharply and suspiciously when they met. The tango was unknown, and the one-step. The only form of dance extant—and that only at the rarest intervals—was a sort of polka not unlike the movements of a slightly inebriated boxing kangaroo. Mr Meggs's secretaries and typists gave the town one startled, horrified glance, and stampeded for London like frightened ponies.

Not so Miss Pillenger. She remained. She was a business woman, and it was enough for her that she received a good salary. For five pounds a week she would have undertaken a post as secretary and typist to a Polar Expedition. For six years she had been with Mr Meggs, and doubtless she looked forward to being with him at least six years more.

Perhaps it was the pathos of this thought which touched Mr Meggs, as she sailed, notebook in hand, through the doorway of the study. Here, he told himself, was a confiding girl, all unconscious of impending doom, relying on him as a daughter relies on her father. He was glad that he had not forgotten Miss Pillenger when he was making his preparations.

He had certainly not forgotten Miss Pillenger. On his desk beside the letters lay a little pile of notes, amounting in all to five hundred pounds—her legacy.

Miss Pillenger was always business-like. She sat down in her chair, opened her notebook, moistened her pencil, and waited expectantly for Mr Meggs to clear his throat and begin work on the butterflies. She was surprised when, instead of frowning, as was his invariable practice when bracing himself for composition, he bestowed upon her a sweet, slow smile.

All that was maidenly and defensive in Miss Pillenger leaped to arms under that smile. It ran in and out among her nerve-centres. It had been long in arriving, this moment of crisis, but here it undoubtedly was at last. After twenty years an employer was going to court disaster by trying to flirt with her.

Mr Meggs went on smiling. You cannot classify smiles. Nothing lends itself so much to a variety of interpretations as a smile. Mr Meggs thought he was smiling the sad, tender smile of a man who, knowing himself to be on the brink of the tomb, bids farewell to a faithful employee. Miss Pillenger's view was that he was smiling like an abandoned old rip who ought to have been ashamed of himself.

'No, Miss Pillenger,' said Mr Meggs, 'I shall not work this morning. I shall want you, if you will be so good, to post these six letters for me.'

Miss Pillenger took the letters. Mr Meggs surveyed her tenderly.

'Miss Pillenger, you have been with me a long time now. Six years, is it not? Six years. Well, well. I don't think I have ever made you a little present, have I?'

'You give me a good salary.'

'Yes, but I want to give you something more. Six years is a long time. I have come to regard you with a different feeling from that which the ordinary employer feels for his secretary. You and I have worked together for six long years. Surely I may be permitted to give you some token of my appreciation of your fidelity.' He took the pile of notes. 'These are for you, Miss Pillenger.'

He rose and handed them to her. He eyed her for a moment with all the sentimentality of a man whose digestion has been out of order for over two decades. The pathos of the situation swept him away. He bent over Miss Pillenger, and kissed her on the forehead.

Smiles excepted, there is nothing so hard to classify as a kiss. Mr Meggs's notion was that he kissed Miss Pillenger much as some great general, wounded unto death, might have kissed his mother, his sister, or some particularly sympathetic aunt; Miss Pillenger's view, differing substantially from this, may be outlined in her own words.

'Ah!' she cried, as, dealing Mr Meggs's conveniently placed jaw a blow which, had it landed an inch lower down, might have knocked him out, she sprang to her feet. 'How dare you! I've been waiting for this Mr Meggs. I have seen it in your eye. I have expected it. Let me tell you that I am not at all the sort of girl with whom it is safe to behave like that. I can protect myself. I am only a working-girl—'

Mr Meggs, who had fallen back against the desk as a stricken pugilist falls on the ropes, pulled himself together to protest.

'Miss Pillenger,' he cried, aghast, 'you misunderstand me. I had no intention—'

'Misunderstand you? Bah! I am only a working-girl—'

'Nothing was farther from my mind—'

'Indeed! Nothing was farther from your mind! You give me money, you shower your vile kisses on me, but nothing was farther from your mind than the obvious interpretation of such behaviour!' Before coming to Mr Meggs, Miss Pillenger had been secretary to an Indiana novelist. She had learned style from the master. 'Now that you have gone too far, you are frightened at what you have done. You well may be, Mr Meggs. I am only a working-girl—'

'Miss Pillenger, I implore you—'

'Silence! I am only a working-girl—'

A wave of mad fury swept over Mr Meggs. The shock of the blow and still more of the frightful ingratitude of this horrible woman nearly made him foam at the mouth.

'Don't keep on saying you're only a working-girl,' he bellowed. 'You'll drive me mad. Go. Go away from me. Get out. Go anywhere, but leave me alone!'

Miss Pillenger was not entirely sorry to obey the request. Mr Meggs's sudden fury had startled and frightened her. So long as she could end the scene victorious, she was anxious to withdraw.

'Yes, I will go,' she said, with dignity, as she opened the door. 'Now that you have revealed yourself in your true colours, Mr Meggs, this house is no fit place for a wor—'

She caught her employer's eye, and vanished hastily.

Mr Meggs paced the room in a ferment. He had been shaken to his core by the scene. He boiled with indignation. That his kind thoughts should have been so misinterpreted—it was too much. Of all ungrateful worlds, this world was the most—

He stopped suddenly in his stride, partly because his shin had struck a chair, partly because an idea had struck his mind.

Hopping madly, he added one more parallel between himself and Hamlet by soliloquizing aloud.

'I'll be hanged if I commit suicide,' he yelled.

And as he spoke the words a curious peace fell on him, as on a man who has awakened from a nightmare. He sat down at the desk. What an idiot he had been ever to contemplate self-destruction. What could have induced him to do it? By his own hand to remove himself, merely in order that a pack of ungrateful brutes might wallow in his money—it was the scheme of a perfect fool.

He wouldn't commit suicide. Not if he knew it. He would stick on and laugh at them. And if he did have an occasional pain inside, what of that? Napoleon had them, and look at him. He would be blowed if he committed suicide.

With the fire of a new resolve lighting up his eyes, he turned to seize the six letters and rifle them of their contents.

They were gone.

It took Mr Meggs perhaps thirty seconds to recollect where they had gone to, and then it all came back to him. He had given them to the demon Pillenger, and, if he did not overtake her and get them back, she would mail them.

Of all the mixed thoughts which seethed in Mr Meggs's mind at that moment, easily the most prominent was the reflection that from his front door to the post office was a walk of less than five minutes.

* * * * *

Miss Pillenger walked down the sleepy street in the June sunshine, boiling, as Mr Meggs had done, with indignation. She, too, had been shaken to the core. It was her intention to fulfil her duty by posting the letters which had been entrusted to her, and then to quit for ever the service of one who, for six years a model employer, had at last forgotten himself and showed his true nature.

Her meditations were interrupted by a hoarse shout in her rear; and, turning, she perceived the model employer running rapidly towards her. His face was scarlet, his eyes wild, and he wore no hat.

Miss Pillenger's mind worked swiftly. She took in the situation in a flash. Unrequited, guilty love had sapped Mr Meggs's reason, and she was to be the victim of his fury. She had read of scores of similar cases in the newspapers. How little she had ever imagined that she would be the heroine of one of these dramas of passion.

She looked for one brief instant up and down the street. Nobody was in sight. With a loud cry she began to run.

'Stop!'

It was the fierce voice of her pursuer. Miss Pillenger increased to third speed. As she did so, she had a vision of headlines.

'Stop!' roared Mr Meggs.

'UNREQUITED PASSION MADE THIS MAN MURDERER,' thought Miss Pillenger.

'Stop!'

'CRAZED WITH LOVE HE SLAYS BEAUTIFUL BLONDE,' flashed out in letters of crimson on the back of Miss Pillenger's mind.

'Stop!'

'SPURNED, HE STABS HER THRICE.'

To touch the ground at intervals of twenty yards or so—that was the ideal she strove after. She addressed herself to it with all the strength of her powerful mind.

In London, New York, Paris, and other cities where life is brisk, the spectacle of a hatless gentleman with a purple face pursuing his secretary through the streets at a rapid gallop would, of course, have excited little, if any, remark. But in

Mr Meggs's home-town events were of rarer occurrence. The last milestone in the history of his native place had been the visit, two years before, of Bingley's Stupendous Circus, which had paraded along the main street on its way to the next town, while zealous members of its staff visited the back premises of the houses and removed all the washing from the lines. Since then deep peace had reigned.

Gradually, therefore, as the chase warmed up, citizens of all shapes and sizes began to assemble. Miss Pillenger's screams and the general appearance of Mr Meggs gave food for thought. Having brooded over the situation, they decided at length to take a hand, with the result that as Mr Meggs's grasp fell upon Miss Pillenger the grasp of several of his fellow-townsmen fell upon him.

'Save me!' said Miss Pillenger.

Mr Meggs pointed speechlessly to the letters, which she still grasped in her right hand. He had taken practically no exercise for twenty years, and the pace had told upon him.

Constable Gooch, guardian of the town's welfare, tightened his hold on Mr Meggs's arm, and desired explanations.

'He—he was going to murder me,' said Miss Pillenger.

'Kill him,' advised an austere bystander.

'What do you mean you were going to murder the lady?' inquired Constable Gooch.

Mr Meggs found speech.

'I—I—I—I only wanted those letters.'

'What for?'

'They're mine.'

'You charge her with stealing 'em?'

'He gave them me to post with his own hands,' cried Miss Pillenger.

'I know I did, but I want them back.'

By this time the constable, though age had to some extent dimmed his sight, had recognized beneath the perspiration, features which, though they were distorted, were nevertheless those of one whom he respected as a leading citizen.

'Why, Mr Meggs!' he said.

This identification by one in authority calmed, if it a little disappointed, the crowd. What it was they did not know, but, it was apparently not a murder, and they began to drift off.

'Why don't you give Mr Meggs his letters when he asks you, ma'am?' said the constable.

Miss Pillenger drew herself up haughtily.

'Here are your letters, Mr Meggs, I hope we shall never meet again.'

Mr Meggs nodded. That was his view, too.

All things work together for good. The following morning Mr Meggs awoke from a dreamless sleep with a feeling that some curious change had taken place in him. He was abominably stiff, and to move his limbs was pain, but down in the centre of his being there was a novel sensation of lightness. He could have declared that he was happy.

Wincing, he dragged himself out of bed and limped to the window. He threw it open. It was a perfect morning. A cool breeze smote his face, bringing with it pleasant scents and the soothing sound of God's creatures beginning a new day.

An astounding thought struck him.

'Why, I feel well!'

Then another.

'It must be the exercise I took yesterday. By George, I'll do it regularly.'

He drank in the air luxuriously. Inside him, the wild-cat gave him a sudden claw, but it was a half-hearted effort, the effort of one who knows that he is beaten. Mr Meggs was so absorbed in his thoughts that he did not even notice it.

'London,' he was saying to himself. 'One of these physical culture places.... Comparatively young man.... Put myself in their hands.... Mild, regular exercise....'

He limped to the bathroom.

THE MAN WITH TWO LEFT FEET

Students of the folk-lore of the United States of America are no doubt familiar with the quaint old story of Clarence MacFadden. Clarence MacFadden, it seems, was 'wishful to dance, but his feet wasn't gaited that way. So he sought a professor and asked him his price, and said he was willing to pay. The professor' (the legend goes on) 'looked down with alarm at his feet and marked their enormous expanse; and he tacked on a five to his regular price for teaching MacFadden to dance.'

I have often been struck by the close similarity between the case of Clarence and that of Henry Wallace Mills. One difference alone presents itself. It would seem to have been mere vanity and ambition that stimulated the former; whereas the motive force which drove Henry Mills to defy Nature and attempt dancing was the purer one of love. He did it to please his wife. Had he never gone to Ye Bonnie Briar-Bush Farm, that popular holiday resort, and there met Minnie Hill, he would doubtless have continued to spend in peaceful reading the hours not given over to work at the New York bank at which he was employed as paying-cashier. For Henry was a voracious reader. His idea of a pleasant evening was to get back to his little flat, take off his coat, put on his slippers, light a pipe, and go on from the point where he had left off the night before in his perusal of the BIS-CAL volume of the *Encyclopaedia Britannica*—making notes as he read in a stout notebook. He read the BIS-CAL volume because, after many days, he had finished the A-AND, AND-AUS, and the AUS-BIS. There was something admirable—and yet a little horrible—about Henry's method of study. He went after Learning with the cold and dispassionate relentlessness of a stoat pursuing a rabbit. The ordinary man who is paying instalments on the *Encyclopaedia Britannica* is apt to get over-excited and to skip impatiently to Volume XXVIII (VET-ZYM) to see how it all comes out in the end. Not so Henry. His was not a frivolous mind. He intended to read the *Encyclopaedia* through, and he was not going to spoil his pleasure by peeping ahead.

It would seem to be an inexorable law of Nature that no man shall shine at both ends. If he has a high forehead and a thirst for wisdom, his fox-trotting (if any) shall be as the staggerings of the drunken; while, if he is a good dancer, he is nearly always petrified from the ears upward. No better examples of this law could have been found than Henry Mills and his fellow-cashier, Sidney Mercer.

In New York banks paying-cashiers, like bears, tigers, lions, and other fauna, are always shut up in a cage in pairs, and are consequently dependent on each other for entertainment and social intercourse when business is slack. Henry Mills and Sidney simply could not find a subject in common. Sidney knew absolutely nothing of even such elementary things as Abana, Aberration, Abraham, or Acrogenae; while Henry, on his side, was scarcely aware that there had been any developments in the dance since the polka. It was a relief to Henry when Sidney threw up his job to join the chorus of a musical comedy, and was succeeded by a man who, though full of limitations, could at least converse intelligently on Bowls.

Such, then, was Henry Wallace Mills. He was in the middle thirties, temperate, studious, a moderate smoker, and—one would have said—a bachelor of the bachelors, armour-plated against Cupid's well-meant but obsolete artillery. Sometimes Sidney Mercer's successor in the teller's cage, a sentimental young man, would broach the topic of Woman and Marriage. He would ask Henry if he ever intended to get married. On such occasions Henry would look at him in a manner which was a blend of scorn, amusement, and indignation; and would reply with a single word:

'Me!'

It was the way he said it that impressed you.

But Henry had yet to experience the unmanning atmosphere of a lonely summer resort. He had only just reached the position in the bank where he was permitted to take his annual vacation in the summer. Hitherto he had always been released from his cage during the winter months, and had spent his ten days of freedom at his flat, with a book in his hand and his feet on the radiator. But the summer after Sidney Mercer's departure they unleashed him in August.

It was meltingly warm in the city. Something in Henry cried out for the country. For a month before the beginning of his vacation he devoted much of the time that should have been given to the *Encyclopaedia Britannica* in reading summer-resort literature. He decided at length upon Ye Bonnie Briar-Bush Farm because the advertisements spoke so well of it.

Ye Bonnie Briar-Bush Farm was a rather battered frame building many miles from anywhere. Its attractions included a Lovers' Leap, a Grotto, golf-links—a five-hole course where the enthusiast found unusual hazards in the shape of a number of goats tethered at intervals between the holes—and a silvery lake, only portions of which were used as a dumping-ground for tin cans and wooden boxes. It was all new and strange to Henry and caused him an odd exhilaration. Something of gaiety and reckless abandon began to creep into his veins. He had a curious feeling that in these romantic surroundings some adventure ought to happen to him.

At this juncture Minnie Hill arrived. She was a small, slim girl, thinner and paler than she should have been, with large eyes that seemed to Henry pathetic and stirred his chivalry. He began to think a good deal about Minnie Hill.

And then one evening he met her on the shores of the silvery lake. He was standing there, slapping at things that looked like mosquitoes, but could not have been, for the advertisements expressly stated that none were ever found in the neighbourhood of Ye Bonnie Briar-Bush Farm, when along she came. She walked slowly, as if she were tired. A strange thrill, half of pity, half of something else, ran through Henry. He looked at her. She looked at him.

'Good evening,' he said.

They were the first words he had spoken to her. She never contributed to the dialogue of the dining-room, and he had been too shy to seek her out in the open.

She said 'Good evening,' too, tying the score. And there was silence for a moment.

Commiseration overcame Henry's shyness.

'You're looking tired,' he said.

'I feel tired.' She paused. 'I overdid it in the city.'

'It?'

'Dancing.'

'Oh, dancing. Did you dance much?'

'Yes; a great deal.'

'Ah!'

A promising, even a dashing start. But how to continue? For the first time Henry regretted the steady determination of his methods with the *Encyclopaedia*. How pleasant if he could have been in a position to talk easily of Dancing. Then memory reminded him that, though he had not yet got up to Dancing, it was only a few weeks before that he had been reading of the Ballet.

'I don't dance myself,' he said, 'but I am fond of reading about it. Did you know that the word "ballet" incorporated three distinct modern words, "ballet", "ball", and "ballad", and that ballet-dancing was originally accompanied by singing?'

It hit her. It had her weak. She looked at him with awe in her eyes.

One might almost say that she gaped at Henry.

'I hardly know anything,' she said.

'The first descriptive ballet seen in London, England,' said Henry, quietly, 'was "The Tavern Bilkers", which was played at Drury Lane in—in seventeen—something.'

'Was it?'

'And the earliest modern ballet on record was that given by—by someone to celebrate the marriage of the Duke of Milan in 1489.'

There was no doubt or hesitation about the date this time. It was grappled to his memory by hoops of steel owing to the singular coincidence of it being also his telephone number. He gave it out with a roll, and the girl's eyes widened.

'What an awful lot you know!'

'Oh, no,' said Henry, modestly. 'I read a great deal.'

'It must be splendid to know a lot,' she said, wistfully. 'I've never had time for reading. I've always wanted to. I think you're wonderful!'

Henry's soul was expanding like a flower and purring like a well-tickled cat. Never in his life had he been admired by a woman. The sensation was intoxicating.

Silence fell upon them. They started to walk back to the farm, warned by the distant ringing of a bell that supper was about to materialize. It was not a musical bell, but distance and the magic of this unusual moment lent it charm. The sun was setting. It threw a crimson carpet across the silvery lake. The air was very still. The creatures, unclassified by science, who might have been mistaken for mosquitoes had their presence been possible at Ye Bonnie Briar-Bush Farm, were biting harder than ever. But Henry heeded them not. He did not even slap at them. They drank their fill of his blood and went away to put their friends on to this good thing; but for Henry they did not exist. Strange things were happening to him. And, lying awake that night in bed, he recognized the truth. He was in love.

After that, for the remainder of his stay, they were always together. They walked in the woods, they sat by the silvery lake. He poured out the treasures of his learning for her, and she looked at him with reverent eyes, uttering from time to time a soft 'Yes' or a musical 'Gee!'

In due season Henry went back to New York.

'You're dead wrong about love, Mills,' said his sentimental fellow-cashier, shortly after his return. 'You ought to get married.'

'I'm going to,' replied Henry, briskly. 'Week tomorrow.'

Which stunned the other so thoroughly that he gave a customer who entered at that moment fifteen dollars for a ten-dollar cheque, and had to do some excited telephoning after the bank had closed.

Henry's first year as a married man was the happiest of his life. He had always heard this period described as the most perilous of matrimony. He had braced himself for clashings of tastes, painful adjustments of character, sudden and unavoidable quarrels. Nothing of the kind happened. From the very beginning they settled down in perfect harmony. She merged with his life as smoothly as one river joins another. He did not even have to alter his habits. Every morning he had his breakfast at eight, smoked a cigarette, and walked to the Underground. At five he left the bank, and at six he arrived home, for it was his practice to walk the first two miles of the way, breathing deeply and regularly. Then dinner. Then the quiet evening. Sometimes the moving-pictures, but generally the quiet evening, he reading the *Encyclopaedia*—aloud now—Minnie darning his socks, but never ceasing to listen.

Each day brought the same sense of grateful amazement that he should be so wonderfully happy, so extraordinarily peaceful. Everything was as perfect as it could be. Minnie was looking a different girl. She had lost her drawn look. She was filling out.

Sometimes he would suspend his reading for a moment, and look across at her. At first he would see only her soft hair, as she bent over her sewing. Then, wondering at the silence, she would look up, and he would meet her big eyes. And then Henry would gurgle with happiness, and demand of himself, silently:

'Can you beat it!'

It was the anniversary of their wedding. They celebrated it in fitting style. They dined at a crowded and exhilarating Italian restaurant on a street off Seventh Avenue, where red wine was included in the bill, and excitable people, probably extremely clever, sat round at small tables and talked all together at the top of their voices. After dinner they saw a musical comedy. And then—the great event of the night—they went on to supper at a glittering restaurant near Times Square.

There was something about supper at an expensive restaurant which had always appealed to Henry's imagination. Earnest devourer as he was of the solids of literature, he had tasted from time to time its lighter face—those novels which begin with the hero supping in the midst of the glittering throng and having his attention attracted to a distinguished-looking elderly man with a grey imperial who is entering with a girl so strikingly beautiful that the revellers turn, as she passes, to look after her. And then, as he sits and smokes, a waiter comes up to the hero and, with a soft '*Pardon, m'sieu!*' hands him a note.

The atmosphere of Geisenheimer's suggested all that sort of thing to Henry. They had finished supper, and he was smoking a cigar—his second that day. He leaned back in his chair and surveyed the scene. He felt braced up, adventurous. He had that feeling, which comes to all quiet men who like to sit at home and read, that this was the sort of atmosphere in which he really belonged. The brightness of it all—the dazzling lights, the music, the hubbub, in which the deep-throated gurgle of the wine-agent surprised while drinking soup blended with the shriller note of the chorus-girl calling to her mate—these things got Henry. He was thirty-six next birthday, but he felt a youngish twenty-one.

A voice spoke at his side. Henry looked up, to perceive Sidney Mercer.

The passage of a year, which had turned Henry into a married man, had turned Sidney Mercer into something so magnificent that the spectacle for a moment deprived Henry of speech. Faultless evening dress clung with loving closeness to Sidney's lissom form. Gleaming shoes of perfect patent leather covered his feet. His light hair was brushed back into a smooth sleekness on which the electric lights shone like stars on some beautiful pool. His practically chinless face beamed amiably over a spotless collar.

Henry wore blue serge.

'What are you doing here, Henry, old top?' said the vision. 'I didn't know you ever came among the bright lights.'

His eyes wandered off to Minnie. There was admiration in them, for Minnie was looking her prettiest.

'Wife,' said Henry, recovering speech. And to Minnie: 'Mr Mercer. Old friend.'

'So you're married? Wish you luck. How's the bank?'

Henry said the bank was doing as well as could be expected.

'You still on the stage?'

Mr Mercer shook his head importantly.

'Got better job. Professional dancer at this show. Rolling in money. Why aren't you dancing?'

The words struck a jarring note. The lights and the music until that moment had had a subtle psychological effect on Henry, enabling him to hypnotize himself into a feeling that it was not inability to dance that kept him in his seat, but that he had had so much of that sort of thing that he really preferred to sit quietly and look on for a change. Sidney's question changed all that. It made him face the truth.

'I don't dance.'

'For the love of Mike! I bet Mrs Mills does. Would you care for a turn,

Mrs Mills?'

'No, thank you, really.'

But remorse was now at work on Henry. He perceived that he had been standing in the way of Minnie's pleasure. Of course she wanted to dance. All women did. She was only refusing for his sake.

'Nonsense, Min. Go to it.'

Minnie looked doubtful.

'Of course you must dance, Min. I shall be all right. I'll sit here and smoke.'

The next moment Minnie and Sidney were treading the complicated measure; and simultaneously Henry ceased to be a youngish twenty-one and was even conscious of a fleeting doubt as to whether he was really only thirty-five.

Boil the whole question of old age down, and what it amounts to is that a man is young as long as he can dance without getting lumbago, and, if he cannot dance, he is never young at all. This was the truth that forced itself upon Henry Wallace Mills, as he sat watching his wife moving over the floor in the arms of Sidney Mercer. Even he could see that Minnie danced well. He thrilled at the sight of her gracefulness; and for the first time since his marriage he became introspective. It had never struck him before how much younger Minnie was than himself. When she had signed the paper at the City Hall on the occasion of the purchase of the marriage licence, she had given her age, he remembered now, as twenty-six. It had made no impression on him at the time. Now, however, he perceived clearly that between twenty-six and thirty-five there was a gap of nine years; and a chill sensation came upon him of being old and stodgy. How dull it must be for poor little Minnie to be cooped up night after night with such an old fogy? Other men took their wives out and gave them a good time, dancing half the night with them. All he could do was to sit at home and read Minnie dull stuff from the *Encyclopaedia*. What a life for the poor child! Suddenly, he felt acutely jealous of the rubber-jointed Sidney Mercer, a man whom hitherto he had always heartily despised.

The music stopped. They came back to the table, Minnie with a pink glow on her face that made her younger than ever; Sidney, the insufferable ass, grinning and smirking and pretending to be eighteen. They looked like a couple of children—Henry, catching sight of himself in a mirror, was surprised to find that his hair was not white.

Half an hour later, in the cab going home, Minnie, half asleep, was aroused by a sudden stiffening of the arm that encircled her waist and a sudden snort close to her ear.

It was Henry Wallace Mills resolving that he would learn to dance.

Being of a literary turn of mind and also economical, Henry's first step towards his new ambition was to buy a fifty-cent book entitled *The ABC of Modern Dancing*, by 'Tango'. It would, he felt—not without reason—be simpler and less expensive if he should learn the steps by the aid of this treatise than by the more customary method of taking lessons. But quite early in the proceedings he was faced by complications. In the first place, it was his intention to keep what he was doing a secret from Minnie, in order to be able to give her a pleasant surprise on her birthday, which would be coming round in a few weeks. In the second place, *The ABC of Modern Dancing* proved on investigation far more complex than its title suggested.

These two facts were the ruin of the literary method, for, while it was possible to study the text and the plates at the bank, the home was the only place in which he could attempt to put the instructions into practice. You cannot move the right foot along dotted line A B and bring the left foot round curve C D in a paying-cashier's cage in a bank, nor, if you are at all sensitive to public opinion, on the pavement going home. And while he was trying to do it in the parlour of the flat one night when he imagined that Minnie was in the kitchen cooking supper, she came in unexpectedly to ask how he wanted the steak cooked. He explained that he had had a sudden touch of cramp, but the incident shook his nerve.

After this he decided that he must have lessons.

Complications did not cease with this resolve. Indeed, they became more acute. It was not that there was any difficulty about finding an instructor. The papers were full of their advertisements. He selected a Mme Gavarni because she lived in a convenient spot. Her house was in a side street, with a station within easy reach. The real problem was when to find time for the lessons. His life was run on such a regular schedule that he could hardly alter so important a moment in it as the hour of his arrival home without exciting comment. Only deceit could provide a solution.

'Min, dear,' he said at breakfast.

'Yes, Henry?'

Henry turned mauve. He had never lied to her before.

'I'm not getting enough exercise.'

'Why you look so well.'

'I get a kind of heavy feeling sometimes. I think I'll put on another mile or so to my walk on my way home. So—so I'll be back a little later in future.'

'Very well, dear.'

It made him feel like a particularly low type of criminal, but, by abandoning his walk, he was now in a position to devote an hour a day to the lessons; and Mme Gavarni had said that that would be ample.

'Sure, Bill,' she had said. She was a breezy old lady with a military moustache and an unconventional manner with her clientele. 'You come to me an hour a day, and, if you haven't two left feet, we'll make you the pet of society in a month.'

'Is that so?'

'It sure is. I never had a failure yet with a pupe, except one. And that wasn't my fault.'

'Had he two left feet?'

'Hadn't any feet at all. Fell off of a roof after the second lesson, and had to have 'em cut off him. At that, I could have learned him to tango with wooden legs, only he got kind of discouraged. Well, see you Monday, Bill. Be good.'

And the kindly old soul, retrieving her chewing gum from the panel of the door where she had placed it to facilitate conversation, dismissed him.

And now began what, in later years, Henry unhesitatingly considered the most miserable period of his existence. There may be times when a man who is past his first youth feels more unhappy and ridiculous than when he is taking a course of lessons in the modern dance, but it is not easy to think of them. Physically, his new experience caused Henry acute pain. Muscles whose existence he had never suspected came into being for—apparently—the sole purpose of aching. Mentally he suffered even more.

This was partly due to the peculiar method of instruction in vogue at Mme Gavarni's, and partly to the fact that, when it came to the actual lessons, a sudden niece was produced from a back room to give them. She was a blonde young lady with laughing blue eyes, and Henry never clasped her trim waist without feeling a black-hearted traitor to his absent Minnie. Conscience racked him. Add to this the sensation of being a strange, jointless creature with abnormally large hands and feet, and the fact that it was Mme Gavarni's custom to stand in a corner of the room during the hour of tuition, chewing gum and making comments, and it is not surprising that Henry became wan and thin.

Mme Gavarni had the trying habit of endeavouring to stimulate Henry by frequently comparing his performance and progress with that of a cripple whom she claimed to have taught at some previous time.

She and the niece would have spirited arguments in his presence as to whether or not the cripple had one-stepped better after his third lesson than Henry after his fifth. The niece said no. As well, perhaps, but not better. Mme Gavarni said that the niece was forgetting the way the cripple had slid his feet. The niece said yes, that was so, maybe she was. Henry said nothing. He merely perspired.

He made progress slowly. This could not be blamed upon his instructress, however. She did all that one woman could to speed him up. Sometimes she would even pursue him into the street in order to show him on the side-walk a means of doing away with some of his numerous errors of *technique*, the elimination of which would help to make him definitely the cripple's superior. The misery of embracing her indoors was as nothing to the misery of embracing her on the sidewalk.

Nevertheless, having paid for his course of lessons in advance, and being a determined man, he did make progress. One day, to his surprise, he found his feet going through the motions without any definite exercise of will-power on his part—almost as if they were endowed with an intelligence of their own. It was the turning-point. It filled him with a singular pride such as he had not felt since his first rise of salary at the bank.

Mme Gavarni was moved to dignified praise.

'Some speed, kid!' she observed. 'Some speed!'

Henry blushed modestly. It was the accolade.

Every day, as his skill at the dance became more manifest, Henry found occasion to bless the moment when he had decided to take lessons. He shuddered sometimes at the narrowness of his escape from disaster. Every day now it became more apparent to him, as he watched Minnie, that she was chafing at the monotony of her life. That fatal supper had wrecked the peace of their little home. Or perhaps it had merely precipitated the wreck. Sooner or later, he told himself, she was bound to have wearied of the dullness of her lot. At any rate, dating from shortly after that disturbing night, a lack of ease and spontaneity seemed to creep into their relations. A blight settled on the home.

Little by little Minnie and he were growing almost formal towards each other. She had lost her taste for being read to in the evenings and had developed a habit of pleading a headache and going early to bed. Sometimes, catching her eye when she was not expecting it, he surprised an enigmatic look in it. It was a look, however, which he was able to read. It meant that she was bored.

It might have been expected that this state of affairs would have distressed Henry. It gave him, on the contrary, a pleasurable thrill. It made him feel that it had been worth it, going through the torments of learning to dance. The more bored she was now the greater her delight when he revealed himself dramatically. If she had been contented with the life which he could offer her as a non-dancer, what was the sense of losing weight and money in order to learn the steps? He enjoyed the silent, uneasy evenings which had supplanted those cheery ones of the first year of their marriage. The more uncomfortable they were now, the more they would appreciate their happiness later on. Henry belonged to the large circle of human beings who consider that there is acuter pleasure in being suddenly cured of toothache than in never having toothache at all.

He merely chuckled inwardly, therefore, when, on the morning of her birthday, having presented her with a purse which he knew she had long coveted, he found himself thanked in a perfunctory and mechanical way.

'I'm glad you like it,' he said.

Minnie looked at the purse without enthusiasm.

'It's just what I wanted,' she said, listlessly.

'Well, I must be going. I'll get the tickets for the theatre while I'm in town.'

Minnie hesitated for a moment.

'I don't believe I want to go to the theatre much tonight, Henry.'

'Nonsense. We must have a party on your birthday. We'll go to the theatre and then we'll have supper at Geisenheimer's again. I may be working after hours at the bank today, so I guess I won't come home. I'll meet you at that Italian place at six.'

'Very well. You'll miss your walk, then?'

'Yes. It doesn't matter for once.'

'No. You're still going on with your walks, then?'

'Oh, yes, yes.'

'Three miles every day?'

'Never miss it. It keeps me well.'

'Yes.'

'Good-bye, darling.'

'Good-bye.'

Yes, there was a distinct chill in the atmosphere. Thank goodness, thought Henry, as he walked to the station, it would be different tomorrow morning. He had rather the feeling of a young knight who has done perilous deeds in secret for his lady, and is about at last to receive credit for them.

Geisenheimer's was as brilliant and noisy as it had been before when Henry reached it that night, escorting a reluctant Minnie. After a silent dinner and a theatrical performance during which neither had exchanged more than a word between the acts, she had wished to abandon the idea of supper and go home. But a squad of police could not have kept Henry from Geisenheimer's. His hour had come. He had thought of this moment for weeks, and he visualized every detail of his big scene. At first they would sit at their table in silent discomfort. Then Sidney Mercer would come up, as before, to ask Minnie to dance. And then—then—Henry would rise and, abandoning all concealment, exclaim grandly: 'No! I am going to dance with my wife!' Stunned amazement of Minnie, followed by wild joy. Utter rout and discomfiture of that pin-head, Mercer. And then, when they returned to their table, he breathing easily and regularly as a trained dancer in perfect condition should, she tottering a little with the sudden rapture of it all, they would sit with their heads close together and start a new life. That was the scenario which Henry had drafted.

It worked out—up to a certain point—as smoothly as ever it had done in his dreams. The only hitch which he had feared—to wit, the non-appearance of Sidney Mercer, did not occur. It would spoil the scene a little, he had felt, if Sidney Mercer did not present himself to play the role of foil; but he need have had no fears on this point. Sidney had the gift, not uncommon in the chinless, smooth-baked type of man, of being able to see a pretty girl come into the restaurant even when his back was towards the door. They had hardly seated themselves when he was beside their table bleating greetings.

'Why, Henry! Always here!'

'Wife's birthday.'

'Many happy returns of the day, Mrs Mills. We've just time for one turn before the waiter comes with your order. Come along.'

The band was staggering into a fresh tune, a tune that Henry knew well. Many a time had Mme Gavarni hammered it out of an aged and unwilling piano in order that he might dance with her blue-eyed niece. He rose.

'No!' he exclaimed grandly. 'I am going to dance with my wife!'

He had not under-estimated the sensation which he had looked forward to causing. Minnie looked at him with round eyes. Sidney Mercer was obviously startled.

'I thought you couldn't dance.'

'You never can tell,' said Henry, lightly. 'It looks easy enough.

Anyway, I'll try.'

'Henry!' cried Minnie, as he clasped her.

He had supposed that she would say something like that, but hardly in that kind of voice. There is a way of saying 'Henry!' which conveys surprised admiration and remorseful devotion; but she had not said it in that way. There had been a note of horror in her voice. Henry's was a simple mind, and the obvious solution, that Minnie thought that he had drunk too much red wine at the Italian restaurant, did not occur to him.

He was, indeed, at the moment too busy to analyse vocal inflections. They were on the floor now, and it was beginning to creep upon him like a chill wind that the scenario which he had mapped out was subject to unforeseen alterations.

At first all had been well. They had been almost alone on the floor, and he had begun moving his feet along dotted line A B with the smooth vim which had characterized the last few of his course of lessons. And then, as if by magic, he was in the midst of a crowd—a mad, jigging crowd that seemed to have no sense of direction, no ability whatever to keep out of his way. For a moment the tuition of weeks stood by him. Then, a shock, a stifled cry from Minnie, and the first collision had occurred. And with that all the knowledge which he had so painfully acquired passed from Henry's mind, leaving it an agitated blank. This was a situation for which his slidings round an empty room had not prepared him. Stage-fright at its worst came upon him. Somebody charged him in the back and asked querulously where he thought he was going. As he turned with a half-formed notion of apologizing, somebody else rammed him from the other side. He had a momentary feeling as if he were going down the Niagara Rapids in a barrel, and then he was lying on the floor with Minnie on top of him. Somebody tripped over his head.

He sat up. Somebody helped him to his feet. He was aware of Sidney

Mercer at his side.

'Do it again,' said Sidney, all grin and sleek immaculateness. 'It went down big, but lots of them didn't see it.'

The place was full of demon laughter.

* * * * *

'Min!' said Henry.

They were in the parlour of their little flat. Her back was towards him, and he could not see her face. She did not answer. She preserved the silence which she had maintained since they had left the restaurant. Not once during the journey home had she spoken.

The clock on the mantelpiece ticked on. Outside an Elevated train rumbled by. Voices came from the street.

'Min, I'm sorry.'

Silence.

'I thought I could do it. Oh, Lord!' Misery was in every note of Henry's voice. 'I've been taking lessons every day since that night we went to that place first. It's no good—I guess it's like the old woman said. I've got two left feet, and it's no use my ever trying to do it. I kept it secret from you, what I was doing. I wanted it to be a wonderful surprise for you on your birthday. I knew how sick and tired you were getting of being married to a man who never took you out, because he couldn't dance. I thought it was up to me to learn, and give you a good time, like other men's wives. I—'

'Henry!'

She had turned, and with a dull amazement he saw that her whole face had altered. Her eyes were shining with a radiant happiness.

'Henry! Was *that* why you went to that house—to take dancing lessons?'

He stared at her without speaking. She came to him, laughing.

'So that was why you pretended you were still doing your walks?'

'You knew!'

'I saw you come out of that house. I was just going to the station at the end of the street, and I saw you. There was a girl with you, a girl with yellow hair. You hugged her!'

Henry licked his dry lips.

'Min,' he said huskily. 'You won't believe it, but she was trying to teach me the Jelly Roll.'

She held him by the lapels of his coat.

'Of course I believe it. I understand it all now. I thought at the time that you were just saying good-bye to her! Oh, Henry, why ever didn't you tell me what you were doing? Oh, yes, I know you wanted it to be a surprise for me on my birthday, but you must have seen there was something wrong. You must have seen that I thought something. Surely you noticed how I've been these last weeks?'

'I thought it was just that you were finding it dull.'

'Dull! Here, with you!'

'It was after you danced that night with Sidney Mercer. I thought the whole thing out. You're so much younger than I, Min. It didn't seem right for you to have to spend your life being read to by a fellow like me.'

'But I loved it!'

'You had to dance. Every girl has to. Women can't do without it.'

'This one can. Henry, listen! You remember how ill and worn out I was when you met me first at that farm? Do you know why it was? It was because I had been slaving away for years at one of those places where you go in and pay five cents to dance with the lady instructresses. I was a lady instructress. Henry! Just think what I went through! Every day having to drag a million heavy men with large feet round a big room. I tell you, you are a professional compared with some of them! They trod on my feet and leaned their two hundred pounds on me and nearly killed me. Now perhaps you can understand why I'm not crazy about dancing! Believe me, Henry, the kindest thing you can do to me is to tell me I must never dance again.'

'You—you—' he gulped. 'Do you really mean that you can—can stand the sort of life we're living here? You really don't find it dull?'

'Dull!'

She ran to the bookshelf, and came back with a large volume.

'Read to me, Henry, dear. Read me something now. It seems ages and ages since you used to. Read me something out of the *Encyclopaedia*!'

Henry was looking at the book in his hand. In the midst of a joy that almost overwhelmed him, his orderly mind was conscious of something wrong.

'But this is the MED-MUM volume, darling.'

'Is it? Well, that'll be all right. Read me all about "Mum".'

'But we're only in the CAL-CHA—' He wavered. 'Oh, well—I' he went on, recklessly. 'I don't care. Do you?'

'No. Sit down here, dear, and I'll sit on the floor.'

Henry cleared his throat.

'"Milicz, or Militsch (d. 1374), Bohemian divine, was the most influential among those preachers and writers in Moravia and Bohemia who, during the fourteenth century, in a certain sense paved the way for the reforming activity of Huss."'

He looked down. Minnie's soft hair was resting against his knee. He put out a hand and stroked it. She turned and looked up, and he met her big eyes.

'Can you beat it?' said Henry, silently, to himself.

MY MAN JEEVES

LEAVE IT TO JEEVES

Jeeves—my man, you know—is really a most extraordinary chap. So capable. Honestly, I shouldn't know what to do without him. On broader lines he's like those chappies who sit peering sadly over the marble battlements at the Pennsylvania Station in the place marked "Inquiries." You know the Johnnies I mean. You go up to them and say: "When's the next train for Melonsquashville, Tennessee?" and they reply, without stopping to think, "Two-forty-three, track ten, change at San Francisco." And they're right every time. Well, Jeeves gives you just the same impression of omniscience.

As an instance of what I mean, I remember meeting Monty Byng in Bond Street one morning, looking the last word in a grey check suit, and I felt I should never be happy till I had one like it. I dug the address of the tailors out of him, and had them working on the thing inside the hour.

"Jeeves," I said that evening. "I'm getting a check suit like that one of Mr. Byng's."

"Injudicious, sir," he said firmly. "It will not become you."

"What absolute rot! It's the soundest thing I've struck for years."

"Unsuitable for you, sir."

Well, the long and the short of it was that the confounded thing came home, and I put it on, and when I caught sight of myself in the glass I nearly swooned. Jeeves was perfectly right. I looked a cross between a music-hall comedian and a cheap bookie. Yet Monty had looked fine in absolutely the same stuff. These things are just Life's mysteries, and that's all there is to it.

But it isn't only that Jeeves's judgment about clothes is infallible, though, of course, that's really the main thing. The man knows everything. There was the matter of that tip on the "Lincolnshire." I forget now how I got it, but it had the aspect of being the real, red-hot tabasco.

"Jeeves," I said, for I'm fond of the man, and like to do him a good turn when I can, "if you want to make a bit of money have something on Wonderchild for the 'Lincolnshire.'"

He shook his head.

"I'd rather not, sir."

"But it's the straight goods. I'm going to put my shirt on him."

"I do not recommend it, sir. The animal is not intended to win. Second place is what the stable is after."

Perfect piffle, I thought, of course. How the deuce could Jeeves know anything about it? Still, you know what happened. Wonderchild led till he was breathing on the wire, and then Banana Fritter came along and nosed him out. I went straight home and rang for Jeeves.

"After this," I said, "not another step for me without your advice. From now on consider yourself the brains of the establishment."

"Very good, sir. I shall endeavour to give satisfaction."

And he has, by Jove! I'm a bit short on brain myself; the old bean would appear to have been constructed more for ornament than for use, don't you know; but give me five minutes to talk the thing over with Jeeves, and I'm game to advise any one about anything. And that's why, when Bruce Corcoran came to me with his troubles, my first act was to ring the bell and put it up to the lad with the bulging forehead.

"Leave it to Jeeves," I said.

I first got to know Corky when I came to New York. He was a pal of my cousin Gussie, who was in with a lot of people down Washington Square way. I don't know if I ever told you about it, but the reason why I left England was because I was sent over by my Aunt Agatha to try to stop young Gussie marrying a girl on the vaudeville stage, and I got the whole thing so mixed up that I decided that it would be a sound scheme for me to stop on in America for a bit instead of going back and having long cosy chats about the thing with aunt. So I sent Jeeves out to find a decent apartment, and settled down for a bit of exile. I'm bound to say that New York's a topping place to be exiled in. Everybody was awfully good to me, and there seemed to be plenty of things going on, and I'm a wealthy bird, so everything was fine. Chappies introduced me to other chappies, and so on and so forth, and it wasn't long before I knew squads of the right sort, some who rolled in dollars in houses up by the Park, and others who lived with the gas turned down mostly around Washington Square—artists and writers and so forth. Brainy coves.

Corky was one of the artists. A portrait-painter, he called himself, but he hadn't painted any portraits. He was sitting on the side-lines with a blanket over his shoulders, waiting for a chance to get into the game. You see, the catch about portrait-painting—I've looked into the thing a bit—is that you can't start painting portraits till people come along and ask you to, and they won't come and ask you to until you've painted a lot first. This makes it kind of difficult for a chappie. Corky managed to get along by drawing an occasional picture for the comic papers—he had rather a gift for funny stuff when he got a good idea—and doing bedsteads and chairs and things for the advertisements. His principal source of income, however, was derived from biting the ear of a rich uncle—one Alexander Worple, who was in the jute business. I'm a bit foggy as to what jute is, but it's apparently something the populace is pretty keen on, for Mr. Worple had made quite an indecently large stack out of it.

Now, a great many fellows think that having a rich uncle is a pretty soft snap: but, according to Corky, such is not the case. Corky's uncle was a robust sort of cove, who looked like living for ever. He was fifty-one, and it seemed as if he might go to par. It was not this, however, that distressed poor old Corky, for he was not bigoted and had no objection to the man going on living. What Corky kicked at was the way the above Worple used to harry him.

Corky's uncle, you see, didn't want him to be an artist. He didn't think he had any talent in that direction. He was always urging him to chuck Art and go into the jute business and start at the bottom and work his way up. Jute had apparently become a sort of obsession with him. He seemed to attach almost a spiritual importance to it. And what Corky said was that, while he didn't know what they did at the bottom of the jute business, instinct told him that it was something too beastly for words. Corky, moreover, believed in his future as an artist. Some day, he said, he was going to make a hit. Meanwhile, by using the utmost tact and persuasiveness, he was inducing his uncle to cough up very grudgingly a small quarterly allowance.

He wouldn't have got this if his uncle hadn't had a hobby. Mr. Worple was peculiar in this respect. As a rule, from what I've observed, the American captain of industry doesn't do anything out of business hours. When he has put the cat out and locked up the office for the night, he just relapses into a state of coma from which he emerges only to start being a captain of industry again. But Mr. Worple in his spare time was what is known as an ornithologist. He had written a book called *American Birds*, and was writing another, to be called *More American Birds*. When he had finished that, the presumption was that he would begin a third, and keep on till the supply of American birds gave out. Corky used to go to him about once every three months and let him talk about American birds. Apparently you could do what you liked with old Worple if you gave him his head first on his pet subject, so these little chats used to make Corky's allowance all right for the time being. But it was pretty rotten for the poor chap. There was the frightful suspense, you see, and, apart from that, birds, except when broiled and in the society of a cold bottle, bored him stiff.

To complete the character-study of Mr. Worple, he was a man of extremely uncertain temper, and his general tendency was to think that Corky was a poor chump and that whatever step he took in any direction on his own account, was just another proof of his innate idiocy. I should imagine Jeeves feels very much the same about me.

So when Corky trickled into my apartment one afternoon, shooing a girl in front of him, and said, "Bertie, I want you to meet my fiancée, Miss Singer," the aspect of the matter which hit me first was precisely the one which he had come to consult me about. The very first words I spoke were, "Corky, how about your uncle?"

The poor chap gave one of those mirthless laughs. He was looking anxious and worried, like a man who has done the murder all right but can't think what the deuce to do with the body.

"We're so scared, Mr. Wooster," said the girl. "We were hoping that you might suggest a way of breaking it to him."

Muriel Singer was one of those very quiet, appealing girls who have a way of looking at you with their big eyes as if they thought you were the greatest thing on earth and wondered that you hadn't got on to it yet yourself. She sat there in a sort of shrinking way, looking at me as if she were saying to herself, "Oh, I do hope this great strong man isn't going to hurt me." She gave a fellow a protective kind of feeling, made him want to stroke her hand and say, "There, there, little one!" or words to that effect. She made me feel that there was nothing I wouldn't do for her. She was rather like one of those innocent-tasting American drinks which creep imperceptibly into your system so that, before you know what you're doing, you're starting out to reform the world by force if necessary and pausing on your way to tell the large man in the corner that, if he looks at you like that, you will knock his head off. What I mean is, she made me feel alert and dashing, like a jolly old knight-errant or something of that kind. I felt that I was with her in this thing to the limit.

"I don't see why your uncle shouldn't be most awfully bucked," I said to Corky. "He will think Miss Singer the ideal wife for you."

Corky declined to cheer up.

"You don't know him. Even if he did like Muriel he wouldn't admit it. That's the sort of pig-headed guy he is. It would be a matter of principle with him to kick. All he would consider would be that I had gone and taken an important step without asking his advice, and he would raise Cain automatically. He's always done it."

I strained the old bean to meet this emergency.

"You want to work it so that he makes Miss Singer's acquaintance without knowing that you know her. Then you come along——"

"But how can I work it that way?"

I saw his point. That was the catch.

"There's only one thing to do," I said.

"What's that?"

"Leave it to Jeeves."

And I rang the bell.

"Sir?" said Jeeves, kind of manifesting himself. One of the rummy things about Jeeves is that, unless you watch like a hawk, you very seldom see him come into a room. He's like one of those weird chappies in India who dissolve themselves into thin air and nip through space in a sort of disembodied way and assemble the parts again just where they want them. I've got a cousin who's what they call a Theosophist, and he says he's often nearly worked the thing himself, but couldn't quite bring it off, probably owing to having fed in his boyhood on the flesh of animals slain in anger and pie.

The moment I saw the man standing there, registering respectful attention, a weight seemed to roll off my mind. I felt like a lost child who spots his father in the offing. There was something about him that gave me confidence.

Jeeves is a tallish man, with one of those dark, shrewd faces. His eye gleams with the light of pure intelligence.

"Jeeves, we want your advice."

"Very good, sir."

I boiled down Corky's painful case into a few well-chosen words.

"So you see what it amount to, Jeeves. We want you to suggest some way by which Mr. Worple can make Miss Singer's acquaintance without getting on to the fact that Mr. Corcoran already knows her. Understand?"

"Perfectly, sir."

"Well, try to think of something."

"I have thought of something already, sir."

"You have!"

"The scheme I would suggest cannot fail of success, but it has what may seem to you a drawback, sir, in that it requires a certain financial outlay."

"He means," I translated to Corky, "that he has got a pippin of an idea, but it's going to cost a bit."

Naturally the poor chap's face dropped, for this seemed to dish the whole thing. But I was still under the influence of the girl's melting gaze, and I saw that this was where I started in as a knight-errant.

"You can count on me for all that sort of thing, Corky," I said. "Only too glad. Carry on, Jeeves."

"I would suggest, sir, that Mr. Corcoran take advantage of Mr. Worple's attachment to ornithology."

"How on earth did you know that he was fond of birds?"

"It is the way these New York apartments are constructed, sir. Quite unlike our London houses. The partitions between the rooms are of the flimsiest nature. With no wish to overhear, I have sometimes heard Mr. Corcoran expressing himself with a generous strength on the subject I have mentioned."

"Oh! Well?"

"Why should not the young lady write a small volume, to be entitled—let us say—*The Children's Book of American Birds*, and dedicate it to Mr. Worple! A limited edition could be published at your expense, sir, and a great deal of the book would, of course, be given over to eulogistic remarks concerning Mr. Worple's own larger treatise on the same subject. I should recommend the dispatching of a presentation copy to Mr. Worple, immediately on publication, accompanied by a letter in which the young lady asks to be allowed to make the acquaintance of one to whom she owes so much. This would, I fancy, produce the desired result, but as I say, the expense involved would be considerable."

I felt like the proprietor of a performing dog on the vaudeville stage when the tyke has just pulled off his trick without a hitch. I had betted on Jeeves all along, and I had known that he wouldn't let me down. It beats me sometimes why a man with his genius is satisfied to hang around pressing my clothes and what-not. If I had half Jeeves's brain, I should have a stab, at being Prime Minister or something.

"Jeeves," I said, "that is absolutely ripping! One of your very best efforts."

"Thank you, sir."

The girl made an objection.

"But I'm sure I couldn't write a book about anything. I can't even write good letters."

"Muriel's talents," said Corky, with a little cough "lie more in the direction of the drama, Bertie. I didn't mention it before, but one of our reasons for being a trifle nervous as to how Uncle Alexander will receive the news is that Muriel is in the chorus of that show *Choose your Exit* at the Manhattan. It's absurdly unreasonable, but we both feel that that fact might increase Uncle Alexander's natural tendency to kick like a steer."

I saw what he meant. Goodness knows there was fuss enough in our family when I tried to marry into musical comedy a few years ago. And the recollection of my Aunt Agatha's attitude in the matter of Gussie and the vaudeville girl was still fresh in my mind. I don't know why it is—one of these psychology sharps could explain it, I suppose—but uncles and aunts, as a class, are always dead against the drama, legitimate or otherwise. They don't seem able to stick it at any price.

But Jeeves had a solution, of course.

"I fancy it would be a simple matter, sir, to find some impecunious author who would be glad to do the actual composition of the volume for a small fee. It is only necessary that the young lady's name should appear on the title page."

"That's true," said Corky. "Sam Patterson would do it for a hundred dollars. He writes a novelette, three short stories, and ten thousand words of a serial for one of the all-fiction magazines under different names every month. A little thing like this would be nothing to him. I'll get after him right away."

"Fine!"

"Will that be all, sir?" said Jeeves. "Very good, sir. Thank you, sir."

I always used to think that publishers had to be devilish intelligent fellows, loaded down with the grey matter; but I've got their number now. All a publisher has to do is to write cheques at intervals, while a lot of deserving and industrious chappies rally round and do the real work. I know, because I've been one myself. I simply sat tight in the old apartment with a fountain-pen, and in due season a topping, shiny book came along.

I happened to be down at Corky's place when the first copies of *The Children's Book of American Birds* bobbed up. Muriel Singer was there, and we were talking of things in general when there was a bang at the door and the parcel was delivered.

It was certainly some book. It had a red cover with a fowl of some species on it, and underneath the girl's name in gold letters. I opened a copy at random.

"Often of a spring morning," it said at the top of page twenty-one, "as you wander through the fields, you will hear the sweet-toned, carelessly flowing warble of the purple finch linnet. When you are older you must read all about him in Mr. Alexander Worple's wonderful book—*American Birds*."

You see. A boost for the uncle right away. And only a few pages later there he was in the limelight again in connection with the yellow-billed cuckoo. It was great stuff. The more I read, the more I admired the chap who had written it and Jeeves's genius in putting us on to the wheeze. I didn't see how the uncle could fail to drop. You can't call a chap the world's greatest authority on the yellow-billed cuckoo without rousing a certain disposition towards chumminess in him.

"It's a cert!" I said.

"An absolute cinch!" said Corky.

And a day or two later he meandered up the Avenue to my apartment to tell me that all was well. The uncle had written Muriel a letter so dripping with the milk of human kindness that if he hadn't known Mr. Worple's handwriting Corky would have refused to believe him the author of it. Any time it suited Miss Singer to call, said the uncle, he would be delighted to make her acquaintance.

Shortly after this I had to go out of town. Divers sound sportsmen had invited me to pay visits to their country places, and it wasn't for several months that I settled down in the city again. I had been wondering a lot, of course, about Corky, whether it all turned out right, and so forth, and my first evening in New York, happening to pop into a quiet sort of little restaurant which I go to when I don't feel inclined for the bright lights, I found Muriel Singer there, sitting by herself at a table near the door. Corky, I took it, was out telephoning. I went up and passed the time of day.

"Well, well, well, what?" I said.

"Why, Mr. Wooster! How do you do?"

"Corky around?"

"I beg your pardon?"

"You're waiting for Corky, aren't you?"

"Oh, I didn't understand. No, I'm not waiting for him."

It seemed to me that there was a sort of something in her voice, a kind of thingummy, you know.

"I say, you haven't had a row with Corky, have you?"

"A row?"

"A spat, don't you know—little misunderstanding—faults on both sides—er—and all that sort of thing."

"Why, whatever makes you think that?"

"Oh, well, as it were, what? What I mean is—I thought you usually dined with him before you went to the theatre."

"I've left the stage now."

Suddenly the whole thing dawned on me. I had forgotten what a long time I had been away.

"Why, of course, I see now! You're married!"

"Yes."

"How perfectly topping! I wish you all kinds of happiness."

"Thank you, so much. Oh Alexander," she said, looking past me, "this is a friend of mine—Mr. Wooster."

I spun round. A chappie with a lot of stiff grey hair and a red sort of healthy face was standing there. Rather a formidable Johnnie, he looked, though quite peaceful at the moment.

"I want you to meet my husband, Mr. Wooster. Mr. Wooster is a friend of Bruce's, Alexander."

The old boy grasped my hand warmly, and that was all that kept me from hitting the floor in a heap. The place was rocking. Absolutely.

"So you know my nephew, Mr. Wooster," I heard him say. "I wish you would try to knock a little sense into him and make him quit this playing at painting. But I have an idea that he is steadying down. I noticed it first that night he came to dinner with us, my dear, to be introduced to you. He seemed altogether quieter and more serious. Something seemed to have sobered him. Perhaps you will give us the pleasure of your company at dinner to-night, Mr. Wooster? Or have you dined?"

I said I had. What I needed then was air, not dinner. I felt that I wanted to get into the open and think this thing out.

When I reached my apartment I heard Jeeves moving about in his lair. I called him.

"Jeeves," I said, "now is the time for all good men to come to the aid of the party. A stiff b.-and-s. first of all, and then I've a bit of news for you."

He came back with a tray and a long glass.

"Better have one yourself, Jeeves. You'll need it."

"Later on, perhaps, thank you, sir."

"All right. Please yourself. But you're going to get a shock. You remember my friend, Mr. Corcoran?"

"Yes, sir."

"And the girl who was to slide gracefully into his uncle's esteem by writing the book on birds?"

"Perfectly, sir."

"Well, she's slid. She's married the uncle."

He took it without blinking. You can't rattle Jeeves.

"That was always a development to be feared, sir."

"You don't mean to tell me that you were expecting it?"

"It crossed my mind as a possibility."

"Did it, by Jove! Well, I think, you might have warned us!"

"I hardly liked to take the liberty, sir."

Of course, as I saw after I had had a bite to eat and was in a calmer frame of mind, what had happened wasn't my fault, if you come down to it. I couldn't be expected to foresee that the scheme, in itself a cracker-jack, would skid into the ditch as it had done; but all the same I'm bound to admit that I didn't relish the idea of meeting Corky again until time, the great healer, had been able to get in a bit of soothing work. I cut Washington Square out absolutely for the next few months. I gave it the complete miss-in-baulk. And then, just when I was beginning to think I might safely pop down in that direction and gather up the dropped threads, so to speak, time, instead of working the healing wheeze, went and pulled the most awful bone and put the lid on it. Opening the paper one morning, I read that Mrs. Alexander Worple had presented her husband with a son and heir.

I was so darned sorry for poor old Corky that I hadn't the heart to touch my breakfast. I told Jeeves to drink it himself. I was bowled over. Absolutely. It was the limit.

I hardly knew what to do. I wanted, of course, to rush down to Washington Square and grip the poor blighter silently by the hand; and then, thinking it over, I hadn't the nerve. Absent treatment seemed the touch. I gave it him in waves.

But after a month or so I began to hesitate again. It struck me that it was playing it a bit low-down on the poor chap, avoiding him like this just when he probably wanted his pals to surge round him most. I pictured him sitting in his lonely studio with no company but his bitter thoughts, and the pathos of it got me to such an extent that I bounded straight into a taxi and told the driver to go all out for the studio.

I rushed in, and there was Corky, hunched up at the easel, painting away, while on the model throne sat a severe-looking female of middle age, holding a baby.

A fellow has to be ready for that sort of thing.

"Oh, ah!" I said, and started to back out.

Corky looked over his shoulder.

"Halloa, Bertie. Don't go. We're just finishing for the day. That will be all this afternoon," he said to the nurse, who got up with the baby and decanted it into a perambulator which was standing in the fairway.

"At the same hour to-morrow, Mr. Corcoran?"

"Yes, please."

"Good afternoon."

"Good afternoon."

Corky stood there, looking at the door, and then he turned to me and began to get it off his chest. Fortunately, he seemed to take it for granted that I knew all about what had happened, so it wasn't as awkward as it might have been.

"It's my uncle's idea," he said. "Muriel doesn't know about it yet. The portrait's to be a surprise for her on her birthday. The nurse takes the kid out ostensibly to get a breather, and they beat it down here. If you want an instance of the irony of fate, Bertie, get acquainted with this. Here's the first commission I have ever had to paint a portrait, and the sitter is that human poached egg that has butted in and bounced me out of my inheritance. Can you beat it! I call it rubbing the thing in to expect me to spend my afternoons gazing into the ugly face of a little brat who to all intents and purposes has hit me behind the ear with a blackjack and swiped all I possess. I can't refuse to paint the portrait because if I did my uncle would stop my allowance; yet every time I look up and catch that kid's vacant eye, I suffer agonies. I tell you, Bertie, sometimes when he gives me a patronizing glance and then turns away and is sick, as if it revolted him to look at me, I come within an ace of occupying the entire front page of the evening papers as the latest murder sensation. There are moments when I can almost see the headlines: 'Promising Young Artist Beans Baby With Axe.'"

I patted his shoulder silently. My sympathy for the poor old scout was too deep for words.

I kept away from the studio for some time after that, because it didn't seem right to me to intrude on the poor chappie's sorrow. Besides, I'm bound to say that nurse intimidated me. She reminded me so infernally of Aunt Agatha. She was the same gimlet-eyed type.

But one afternoon Corky called me on the 'phone.

"Bertie."

"Halloa?"

"Are you doing anything this afternoon?"

"Nothing special."

"You couldn't come down here, could you?"

"What's the trouble? Anything up?"

"I've finished the portrait."

"Good boy! Stout work!"

"Yes." His voice sounded rather doubtful. "The fact is, Bertie, it doesn't look quite right to me. There's something about it—My uncle's coming in half an hour to inspect it, and—I don't know why it is, but I kind of feel I'd like your moral support!"

I began to see that I was letting myself in for something. The sympathetic co-operation of Jeeves seemed to me to be indicated.

"You think he'll cut up rough?"

"He may."

I threw my mind back to the red-faced chappie I had met at the restaurant, and tried to picture him cutting up rough. It was only too easy. I spoke to Corky firmly on the telephone.

"I'll come," I said.

"Good!"

"But only if I may bring Jeeves!"

"Why Jeeves? What's Jeeves got to do with it? Who wants Jeeves? Jeeves is the fool who suggested the scheme that has led——"

"Listen, Corky, old top! If you think I am going to face that uncle of yours without Jeeves's support, you're mistaken. I'd sooner go into a den of wild beasts and bite a lion on the back of the neck."

"Oh, all right," said Corky. Not cordially, but he said it; so I rang for Jeeves, and explained the situation.

"Very good, sir," said Jeeves.

That's the sort of chap he is. You can't rattle him.

We found Corky near the door, looking at the picture, with one hand up in a defensive sort of way, as if he thought it might swing on him.

"Stand right where you are, Bertie," he said, without moving. "Now, tell me honestly, how does it strike you?"

The light from the big window fell right on the picture. I took a good look at it. Then I shifted a bit nearer and took another look. Then I went back to where I had been at first, because it hadn't seemed quite so bad from there.

"Well?" said Corky, anxiously.

I hesitated a bit.

"Of course, old man, I only saw the kid once, and then only for a moment, but—but it *was* an ugly sort of kid, wasn't it, if I remember rightly?"

"As ugly as that?"

I looked again, and honesty compelled me to be frank.

"I don't see how it could have been, old chap."

Poor old Corky ran his fingers through his hair in a temperamental sort of way. He groaned.

"You're right quite, Bertie. Something's gone wrong with the darned thing. My private impression is that, without knowing it, I've worked that stunt that Sargent and those fellows pull—painting the soul of the sitter. I've got through the mere outward appearance, and have put the child's soul on canvas."

"But could a child of that age have a soul like that? I don't see how he could have managed it in the time. What do you think, Jeeves?"

"I doubt it, sir."

"It—it sorts of leers at you, doesn't it?"

"You've noticed that, too?" said Corky.

"I don't see how one could help noticing."

"All I tried to do was to give the little brute a cheerful expression. But, as it worked out, he looks positively dissipated."

"Just what I was going to suggest, old man. He looks as if he were in the middle of a colossal spree, and enjoying every minute of it. Don't you think so, Jeeves?"

"He has a decidedly inebriated air, sir."

Corky was starting to say something when the door opened, and the uncle came in.

For about three seconds all was joy, jollity, and goodwill. The old boy shook hands with me, slapped Corky on the back, said that he didn't think he had ever seen such a fine day, and whacked his leg with his stick. Jeeves had projected himself into the background, and he didn't notice him.

"Well, Bruce, my boy; so the portrait is really finished, is it—really finished? Well, bring it out. Let's have a look at it. This will be a wonderful surprise for your aunt. Where is it? Let's——"

And then he got it—suddenly, when he wasn't set for the punch; and he rocked back on his heels.

"Oosh!" he exclaimed. And for perhaps a minute there was one of the scaliest silences I've ever run up against.

"Is this a practical joke?" he said at last, in a way that set about sixteen draughts cutting through the room at once.

I thought it was up to me to rally round old Corky.

"You want to stand a bit farther away from it," I said.

"You're perfectly right!" he snorted. "I do! I want to stand so far away from it that I can't see the thing with a telescope!" He turned on Corky like an untamed tiger of the jungle who has just located a chunk of meat. "And this—this—is what you have been wasting your time and my money for all these years! A painter! I wouldn't let you paint a house of mine! I gave you this commission, thinking that you were a competent worker, and this—this—this extract from a comic coloured supplement is the result!" He swung towards the door, lashing his tail and growling to himself. "This ends it! If you wish to continue this foolery of pretending to be an artist because you want an excuse for idleness, please yourself. But let me tell you this. Unless you report at my office on Monday morning, prepared to abandon all this idiocy and start in at the bottom of the business to work your way up, as you should have done half a dozen years ago, not another cent—not another cent—not another—Boosh!"

Then the door closed, and he was no longer with us. And I crawled out of the bombproof shelter.

"Corky, old top!" I whispered faintly.

Corky was standing staring at the picture. His face was set. There was a hunted look in his eye.

"Well, that finishes it!" he muttered brokenly.

"What are you going to do?"

"Do? What can I do? I can't stick on here if he cuts off supplies. You heard what he said. I shall have to go to the office on Monday."

I couldn't think of a thing to say. I knew exactly how he felt about the office. I don't know when I've been so infernally uncomfortable. It was like hanging round trying to make conversation to a pal who's just been sentenced to twenty years in quod.

And then a soothing voice broke the silence.

"If I might make a suggestion, sir!"

It was Jeeves. He had slid from the shadows and was gazing gravely at the picture. Upon my word, I can't give you a better idea of the shattering effect of Corky's uncle Alexander when in action than by saying that he had absolutely made me forget for the moment that Jeeves was there.

"I wonder if I have ever happened to mention to you, sir, a Mr. Digby Thistleton, with whom I was once in service? Perhaps you have met him? He was a financier. He is now Lord Bridgnorth. It was a favourite saying of his that there is always a way. The first time I heard him use the expression was after the failure of a patent depilatory which he promoted."

"Jeeves," I said, "what on earth are you talking about?"

"I mentioned Mr. Thistleton, sir, because his was in some respects a parallel case to the present one. His depilatory failed, but he did not despair. He put it on the market again under the name of Hair-o, guaranteed to produce a full crop of hair in a few months. It was advertised, if you remember, sir, by a humorous picture of a billiard-ball, before and after taking, and made such a substantial fortune that Mr. Thistleton was soon afterwards elevated to the peerage for services to his Party. It seems to me that, if Mr. Corcoran looks into the matter, he will find, like Mr. Thistleton, that there is always a way. Mr. Worple himself suggested the solution of the difficulty. In the heat of the moment he compared the portrait to an extract from a coloured comic supplement. I consider the suggestion a very valuable one, sir. Mr. Corcoran's portrait may not have pleased Mr. Worple as a likeness of his only child, but I have no doubt that editors would gladly consider it as a foundation for a series of humorous drawings. If Mr. Corcoran will allow me to make the suggestion, his talent has always been for the humorous. There is something about this picture—something bold and vigorous, which arrests the attention. I feel sure it would be highly popular."

Corky was glaring at the picture, and making a sort of dry, sucking noise with his mouth. He seemed completely overwrought.

And then suddenly he began to laugh in a wild way.

"Corky, old man!" I said, massaging him tenderly. I feared the poor blighter was hysterical.

He began to stagger about all over the floor.

"He's right! The man's absolutely right! Jeeves, you're a life-saver! You've hit on the greatest idea of the age! Report at the office on Monday! Start at the bottom of the business! I'll buy the business if I feel like it. I know the man who runs the comic section of the *Sunday Star*. He'll eat this thing. He was telling me only the other day how hard it was to get a good new series. He'll give me anything I ask for a real winner like this. I've got a gold-mine. Where's my hat? I've got an income for life! Where's that confounded hat? Lend me a fiver, Bertie. I want to take a taxi down to Park Row!"

Jeeves smiled paternally. Or, rather, he had a kind of paternal muscular spasm about the mouth, which is the nearest he ever gets to smiling.

"If I might make the suggestion, Mr. Corcoran—for a title of the series which you have in mind—'The Adventures of Baby Blobbs.'"

Corky and I looked at the picture, then at each other in an awed way. Jeeves was right. There could be no other title.

"Jeeves," I said. It was a few weeks later, and I had just finished looking at the comic section of the *Sunday Star*. "I'm an optimist. I always have been. The older I get, the more I agree with Shakespeare and those poet Johnnies about it always being darkest before the dawn and there's a silver lining and what you lose on the swings you make up on the roundabouts. Look at Mr. Corcoran, for instance. There was a fellow, one would have said, clear up to the eyebrows in the soup. To all appearances he had got it right in the neck. Yet look at him now. Have you seen these pictures?"

"I took the liberty of glancing at them before bringing them to you, sir. Extremely diverting."

"They have made a big hit, you know."

"I anticipated it, sir."

I leaned back against the pillows.

"You know, Jeeves, you're a genius. You ought to be drawing a commission on these things."

"I have nothing to complain of in that respect, sir. Mr. Corcoran has been most generous. I am putting out the brown suit, sir."

"No, I think I'll wear the blue with the faint red stripe."

"Not the blue with the faint red stripe, sir."

"But I rather fancy myself in it."

"Not the blue with the faint red stripe, sir."

"Oh, all right, have it your own way."

"Very good, sir. Thank you, sir."

Of course, I know it's as bad as being henpecked; but then Jeeves is always right. You've got to consider that, you know. What?

JEEVES AND THE UNBIDDEN GUEST

I'm not absolutely certain of my facts, but I rather fancy it's Shakespeare—or, if not, it's some equally brainy lad—who says that it's always just when a chappie is feeling particularly top-hole, and more than usually braced with things in general that Fate sneaks up behind him with a bit of lead piping. There's no doubt the man's right. It's absolutely that way with me. Take, for instance, the fairly rummy matter of Lady Malvern and her son Wilmot. A moment before they turned up, I was just thinking how thoroughly all right everything was.

It was one of those topping mornings, and I had just climbed out from under the cold shower, feeling like a two-year-old. As a matter of fact, I was especially bucked just then because the day before I had asserted myself with Jeeves—absolutely asserted myself, don't you know. You see, the way things had been going on I was rapidly becoming a dashed serf. The man had jolly well oppressed me. I didn't so much mind when he made me give up one of my new suits, because, Jeeves's judgment about suits is sound. But I as near as a toucher rebelled when he wouldn't let me wear a pair of cloth-topped boots which I loved like a couple of brothers. And when he tried to tread on me like a worm in the matter of a hat, I jolly well put my foot down and showed him who was who. It's a long story, and I haven't time to tell you now, but the point is that he wanted me to wear the Longacre—as worn by John Drew—when I had set my heart on the Country Gentleman—as worn by another famous actor chappie—and the end of the matter was that, after a rather painful scene, I bought the Country Gentleman. So that's how things stood on this particular morning, and I was feeling kind of manly and independent.

Well, I was in the bathroom, wondering what there was going to be for breakfast while I massaged the good old spine with a rough towel and sang slightly, when there was a tap at the door. I stopped singing and opened the door an inch.

"What ho without there!"

"Lady Malvern wishes to see you, sir," said Jeeves.

"Eh?"

"Lady Malvern, sir. She is waiting in the sitting-room."

"Pull yourself together, Jeeves, my man," I said, rather severely, for I bar practical jokes before breakfast. "You know perfectly well there's no one waiting for me in the sitting-room. How could there be when it's barely ten o'clock yet?"

"I gathered from her ladyship, sir, that she had landed from an ocean liner at an early hour this morning."

This made the thing a bit more plausible. I remembered that when I had arrived in America about a year before, the proceedings had begun at some ghastly hour like six, and that I had been shot out on to a foreign shore considerably before eight.

"Who the deuce is Lady Malvern, Jeeves?"

"Her ladyship did not confide in me, sir."

"Is she alone?"

"Her ladyship is accompanied by a Lord Pershore, sir. I fancy that his lordship would be her ladyship's son."

"Oh, well, put out rich raiment of sorts, and I'll be dressing."

"Our heather-mixture lounge is in readiness, sir."

"Then lead me to it."

While I was dressing I kept trying to think who on earth Lady Malvern could be. It wasn't till I had climbed through the top of my shirt and was reaching out for the studs that I remembered.

"I've placed her, Jeeves. She's a pal of my Aunt Agatha."

"Indeed, sir?"

"Yes. I met her at lunch one Sunday before I left London. A very vicious specimen. Writes books. She wrote a book on social conditions in India when she came back from the Durbar."

"Yes, sir? Pardon me, sir, but not that tie!"

"Eh?"

"Not that tie with the heather-mixture lounge, sir!"

It was a shock to me. I thought I had quelled the fellow. It was rather a solemn moment. What I mean is, if I weakened now, all my good work the night before would be thrown away. I braced myself.

"What's wrong with this tie? I've seen you give it a nasty look before. Speak out like a man! What's the matter with it?"

"Too ornate, sir."

"Nonsense! A cheerful pink. Nothing more."

"Unsuitable, sir."

"Jeeves, this is the tie I wear!"

"Very good, sir."

Dashed unpleasant. I could see that the man was wounded. But I was firm. I tied the tie, got into the coat and waistcoat, and went into the sitting-room.

"Halloa! Halloa! Halloa!" I said. "What?"

"Ah! How do you do, Mr. Wooster? You have never met my son, Wilmot, I think? Motty, darling, this is Mr. Wooster."

Lady Malvern was a hearty, happy, healthy, overpowering sort of dashed female, not so very tall but making up for it by measuring about six feet from the O.P. to the Prompt Side. She fitted into my biggest arm-chair as if it had been built round her by someone who knew they were wearing arm-chairs tight about the hips that season. She had bright, bulging eyes and a lot of yellow hair, and when she spoke she showed about fifty-seven front teeth. She was one of those women who kind of numb a fellow's faculties. She made me feel as if I were ten years old and had been brought into the drawing-room in my Sunday clothes to say how-d'you-do. Altogether by no means the sort of thing a chappie would wish to find in his sitting-room before breakfast.

Motty, the son, was about twenty-three, tall and thin and meek-looking. He had the same yellow hair as his mother, but he wore it plastered down and parted in the middle. His eyes bulged, too, but they weren't bright. They were a dull grey with pink rims. His chin gave up the struggle about half-way down, and he didn't appear to have any eyelashes. A mild, furtive, sheepish sort of blighter, in short.

"Awfully glad to see you," I said. "So you've popped over, eh? Making a long stay in America?"

"About a month. Your aunt gave me your address and told me to be sure and call on you."

I was glad to hear this, as it showed that Aunt Agatha was beginning to come round a bit. There had been some unpleasantness a year before, when she had sent me over to New York to disentangle my Cousin Gussie from the clutches of a girl on the music-hall stage. When I tell you that by the time I had finished my operations, Gussie had not only married the girl but had gone on the stage himself, and was doing well, you'll understand that Aunt Agatha was upset to no small extent. I simply hadn't dared go back and face her, and it was a relief to find that time had healed the wound and all that sort of thing enough to make her tell her pals to look me up. What I mean is, much as I liked America, I didn't want to have England barred to me for the rest of my natural; and, believe me, England is a jolly sight too small for anyone to live in with Aunt Agatha, if she's really on the war-path. So I braced on hearing these kind words and smiled genially on the assemblage.

"Your aunt said that you would do anything that was in your power to be of assistance to us."

"Rather? Oh, rather! Absolutely!"

"Thank you so much. I want you to put dear Motty up for a little while."

I didn't get this for a moment.

"Put him up? For my clubs?"

"No, no! Darling Motty is essentially a home bird. Aren't you, Motty darling?"

Motty, who was sucking the knob of his stick, uncorked himself.

"Yes, mother," he said, and corked himself up again.

"I should not like him to belong to clubs. I mean put him up here. Have him to live with you while I am away."

These frightful words trickled out of her like honey. The woman simply didn't seem to understand the ghastly nature of her proposal. I gave Motty the swift east-to-west. He was sitting with his mouth nuzzling the stick, blinking at the wall. The thought of having this planted on me for an indefinite period appalled me. Absolutely appalled me, don't you know. I was just starting to say that the shot wasn't on the board at any price, and that the first sign Motty gave of trying to nestle into my little home I would yell for the police, when she went on, rolling placidly over me, as it were.

There was something about this woman that sapped a chappie's will-power.

"I am leaving New York by the midday train, as I have to pay a visit to Sing-Sing prison. I am extremely interested in prison conditions in America. After that I work my way gradually across to the coast, visiting the points of interest on the journey. You see, Mr. Wooster, I am in America principally on business. No doubt you read my book, *India and the Indians*? My publishers are anxious for me to write a companion volume on the United States. I shall not be able to spend more than a month in the country, as I have to get back for the season, but a month should be ample. I was less than a month in India, and my dear friend Sir Roger Cremorne wrote his *America from Within* after a stay of only two weeks. I should love to take dear Motty with me, but the poor boy gets so sick when he travels by train. I shall have to pick him up on my return."

From where I sat I could see Jeeves in the dining-room, laying the breakfast-table. I wished I could have had a minute with him alone. I felt certain that he would have been able to think of some way of putting a stop to this woman.

"It will be such a relief to know that Motty is safe with you, Mr. Wooster. I know what the temptations of a great city are. Hitherto dear Motty has been sheltered from them. He has lived quietly with me in the country. I know that you will look after him carefully, Mr. Wooster. He will give very little trouble." She talked about the poor blighter as if he wasn't there. Not that Motty seemed to mind. He had stopped chewing his walking-stick and was sitting there with his mouth open. "He is a vegetarian and a teetotaller and is devoted to reading. Give him a nice book and he will be quite contented." She got up. "Thank you so much, Mr. Wooster! I don't know what I should have done without your help. Come, Motty! We have just time to see a few of the sights before my train goes. But I shall have to rely on you for most of my information about New York, darling. Be sure to keep your eyes open and take notes of your impressions! It will be such a help. Good-bye, Mr. Wooster. I will send Motty back early in the afternoon."

They went out, and I howled for Jeeves.

"Jeeves! What about it?"

"Sir?"

"What's to be done? You heard it all, didn't you? You were in the dining-room most of the time. That pill is coming to stay here."

"Pill, sir?"

"The excrescence."

"I beg your pardon, sir?"

I looked at Jeeves sharply. This sort of thing wasn't like him. It was as if he were deliberately trying to give me the pip. Then I understood. The man was really upset about that tie. He was trying to get his own back.

"Lord Pershore will be staying here from to-night, Jeeves," I said coldly.

"Very good, sir. Breakfast is ready, sir."

I could have sobbed into the bacon and eggs. That there wasn't any sympathy to be got out of Jeeves was what put the lid on it. For a moment I almost weakened and told him to destroy the hat and tie if he didn't like them, but I pulled my-myself together again. I was dashed if I was going to let Jeeves treat me like a bally one-man chain-gang!

But, what with brooding on Jeeves and brooding on Motty, I was in a pretty reduced sort of state. The more I examined the situation, the more blighted it became. There was nothing I could do. If I slung Motty out, he would report to his mother, and she would pass it on to Aunt Agatha, and I didn't like to think what would happen then. Sooner or later, I should be wanting to go back to England, and I didn't want to get there and find Aunt Agatha waiting on the quay for me with a stuffed eelskin. There was absolutely nothing for it but to put the fellow up and make the best of it.

About midday Motty's luggage arrived, and soon afterward a large parcel of what I took to be nice books. I brightened up a little when I saw it. It was one of those massive parcels and looked as if it had enough in it to keep the chappie busy for a year. I felt a trifle more cheerful, and I got my Country Gentleman hat and stuck it on my head, and gave the pink tie a twist, and reeled out to take a bite of lunch with one or two of the lads at a neighbouring hostelry; and what with excellent browsing and sluicing and cheery conversation and what-not, the afternoon passed quite happily. By dinner-time I had almost forgotten blighted Motty's existence.

I dined at the club and looked in at a show afterward, and it wasn't till fairly late that I got back to the flat. There were no signs of Motty, and I took it that he had gone to bed.

It seemed rummy to me, though, that the parcel of nice books was still there with the string and paper on it. It looked as if Motty, after seeing mother off at the station, had decided to call it a day.

Jeeves came in with the nightly whisky-and-soda. I could tell by the chappie's manner that he was still upset.

"Lord Pershore gone to bed, Jeeves?" I asked, with reserved hauteur and what-not.

"No, sir. His lordship has not yet returned."

"Not returned? What do you mean?"

"His lordship came in shortly after six-thirty, and, having dressed, went out again."

At this moment there was a noise outside the front door, a sort of scrabbling noise, as if somebody were trying to paw his way through the woodwork. Then a sort of thud.

"Better go and see what that is, Jeeves."

"Very good, sir."

He went out and came back again.

"If you would not mind stepping this way, sir, I think we might be able to carry him in."

"Carry him in?"

"His lordship is lying on the mat, sir."

I went to the front door. The man was right. There was Motty huddled up outside on the floor. He was moaning a bit.

"He's had some sort of dashed fit," I said. I took another look. "Jeeves! Someone's been feeding him meat!"

"Sir?"

"He's a vegetarian, you know. He must have been digging into a steak or something. Call up a doctor!"

"I hardly think it will be necessary, sir. If you would take his lordship's legs, while I——"

"Great Scot, Jeeves! You don't think—he can't be——"

"I am inclined to think so, sir."

And, by Jove, he was right! Once on the right track, you couldn't mistake it. Motty was under the surface.

It was the deuce of a shock.

"You never can tell, Jeeves!"

"Very seldom, sir."

"Remove the eye of authority and where are you?"

"Precisely, sir."

"Where is my wandering boy to-night and all that sort of thing, what?"

"It would seem so, sir."

"Well, we had better bring him in, eh?"

"Yes, sir."

So we lugged him in, and Jeeves put him to bed, and I lit a cigarette and sat down to think the thing over. I had a kind of foreboding. It seemed to me that I had let myself in for something pretty rocky.

Next morning, after I had sucked down a thoughtful cup of tea, I went into Motty's room to investigate. I expected to find the fellow a wreck, but there he was, sitting up in bed, quite chirpy, reading Gingery stories.

"What ho!" I said.

"What ho!" said Motty.

"What ho! What ho!"

"What ho! What ho! What ho!"

After that it seemed rather difficult to go on with the conversation.

"How are you feeling this morning?" I asked.

"Topping!" replied Motty, blithely and with abandon. "I say, you know, that fellow of yours—Jeeves, you know—is a corker. I had a most frightful headache when I woke up, and he brought me a sort of rummy dark drink, and it put me right again at once. Said it was his own invention. I must see more of that lad. He seems to me distinctly one of the ones!"

I couldn't believe that this was the same blighter who had sat and sucked his stick the day before.

"You ate something that disagreed with you last night, didn't you?" I said, by way of giving him a chance to slide out of it if he wanted to. But he wouldn't have it, at any price.

"No!" he replied firmly. "I didn't do anything of the kind. I drank too much! Much too much. Lots and lots too much! And, what's more, I'm going to do it again! I'm going to do it every night. If ever you see me sober, old top," he said, with a kind of holy exaltation, "tap me on the shoulder and say, 'Tut! Tut!' and I'll apologize and remedy the defect."

"But I say, you know, what about me?"

"What about you?"

"Well, I'm so to speak, as it were, kind of responsible for you. What I mean to say is, if you go doing this sort of thing I'm apt to get in the soup somewhat."

"I can't help your troubles," said Motty firmly. "Listen to me, old thing: this is the first time in my life that I've had a real chance to yield to the temptations of a great city. What's the use of a great city having temptations if fellows don't yield to them? Makes it so bally discouraging for a great city. Besides, mother told me to keep my eyes open and collect impressions."

I sat on the edge of the bed. I felt dizzy.

"I know just how you feel, old dear," said Motty consolingly. "And, if my principles would permit it, I would simmer down for your sake. But duty first! This is the first time I've been let out alone, and I mean to make the most of it. We're only young once. Why interfere with life's morning? Young man, rejoice in thy youth! Tra-la! What ho!"

Put like that, it did seem reasonable.

"All my bally life, dear boy," Motty went on, "I've been cooped up in the ancestral home at Much Middlefold, in Shropshire, and till you've been cooped up in Much Middlefold you don't know what cooping is! The only time we get any excitement is when one of the choir-boys is caught sucking chocolate during the sermon. When that happens, we talk about it for days. I've got about a month of New York, and I mean to store up a few happy memories for the long winter evenings. This is my only chance to collect a past, and I'm going to do it. Now tell me, old sport, as man to man, how does one get in touch with that very decent chappie Jeeves? Does one ring a bell or shout a bit? I should like to discuss the subject of a good stiff b.-and-s. with him!"

I had had a sort of vague idea, don't you know, that if I stuck close to Motty and went about the place with him, I might act as a bit of a damper on the gaiety. What I mean is, I thought that if, when he was being the life and soul of the party, he were to catch my reproving eye he might ease up a trifle on the revelry. So the next night I took him along to supper with me. It was the last time. I'm a quiet, peaceful sort of chappie who has lived all his life in London, and I can't stand the pace these swift sportsmen from the rural districts set. What I mean to say is this, I'm all for rational enjoyment and so forth, but I think a chappie makes himself conspicuous when he throws soft-boiled eggs at the electric fan. And decent mirth and all that sort of thing are all right, but I do bar dancing on tables and having to dash all over the place dodging waiters, managers, and chuckers-out, just when you want to sit still and digest.

Directly I managed to tear myself away that night and get home, I made up my mind that this was jolly well the last time that I went about with Motty. The only time I met him late at night after that was once when I passed the door of a fairly low-down sort of restaurant and had to step aside to dodge him as he sailed through the air *en route* for the opposite pavement, with a muscular sort of looking chappie peering out after him with a kind of gloomy satisfaction.

In a way, I couldn't help sympathizing with the fellow. He had about four weeks to have the good time that ought to have been spread over about ten years, and I didn't wonder at his wanting to be pretty busy. I should have been just the same in his place. Still, there was no denying that it was a bit thick. If it hadn't been for the thought of Lady Malvern and Aunt Agatha in the background, I should have regarded Motty's rapid work with an indulgent smile. But I couldn't get rid of the feeling that, sooner or later, I was the lad who was scheduled to get it behind the ear. And what with brooding on this prospect, and sitting up in the old flat waiting for the familiar footstep, and putting it to bed when it got there, and stealing into the sick-chamber next morning to contemplate the wreckage, I was beginning to lose weight. Absolutely becoming the good old shadow, I give you my honest word. Starting at sudden noises and what-not.

And no sympathy from Jeeves. That was what cut me to the quick. The man was still thoroughly pipped about the hat and tie, and simply wouldn't rally round. One morning I wanted comforting so much that I sank the pride of the Woosters and appealed to the fellow direct.

"Jeeves," I said, "this is getting a bit thick!"

"Sir?" Business and cold respectfulness.

"You know what I mean. This lad seems to have chucked all the principles of a well-spent boyhood. He has got it up his nose!"

"Yes, sir."

"Well, I shall get blamed, don't you know. You know what my Aunt Agatha is!"

"Yes, sir."

"Very well, then."

I waited a moment, but he wouldn't unbend.

"Jeeves," I said, "haven't you any scheme up your sleeve for coping with this blighter?"

"No, sir."

And he shimmered off to his lair. Obstinate devil! So dashed absurd, don't you know. It wasn't as if there was anything wrong with that Country Gentleman hat. It was a remarkably priceless effort, and much admired by the lads. But, just because he preferred the Longacre, he left me flat.

It was shortly after this that young Motty got the idea of bringing pals back in the small hours to continue the gay revels in the home. This was where I began to crack under the strain. You see, the part of town where I was living wasn't the right place for that sort of thing. I knew lots of chappies down Washington Square way who started the evening at about 2 a.m.—artists and writers and what-not, who frolicked considerably till checked by the arrival of the morning milk. That was all right. They like that sort of thing down there. The neighbours can't get to sleep unless there's someone dancing Hawaiian dances over their heads. But on Fifty-seventh Street the atmosphere wasn't right, and when Motty turned up at three in the morning with a collection of hearty lads, who only stopped singing their college song when they started singing "The Old Oaken Bucket," there was a marked peevishness among the old settlers in the flats. The management was extremely terse over the telephone at breakfast-time, and took a lot of soothing.

The next night I came home early, after a lonely dinner at a place which I'd chosen because there didn't seem any chance of meeting Motty there. The sitting-room was quite dark, and I was just moving to switch on the light, when there was a sort of explosion and something collared hold of my trouser-leg. Living with Motty had reduced me to such an extent that I was simply unable to cope with this thing. I jumped backward with a loud yell of anguish, and tumbled out into the hall just as Jeeves came out of his den to see what the matter was.

"Did you call, sir?"

"Jeeves! There's something in there that grabs you by the leg!"

"That would be Rollo, sir."

"Eh?"

"I would have warned you of his presence, but I did not hear you come in. His temper is a little uncertain at present, as he has not yet settled down."

"Who the deuce is Rollo?"

"His lordship's bull-terrier, sir. His lordship won him in a raffle, and tied him to the leg of the table. If you will allow me, sir, I will go in and switch on the light."

There really is nobody like Jeeves. He walked straight into the sitting-room, the biggest feat since Daniel and the lions' den, without a quiver. What's more, his magnetism or whatever they call it was such that the dashed animal, instead of pinning him by the leg, calmed down as if he had had a bromide, and rolled over on his back with all his paws in the air. If Jeeves had been his rich uncle he couldn't have been more chummy. Yet directly he caught sight of me again, he got all worked up and seemed to have only one idea in life—to start chewing me where he had left off.

"Rollo is not used to you yet, sir," said Jeeves, regarding the bally quadruped in an admiring sort of way. "He is an excellent watchdog."

"I don't want a watchdog to keep me out of my rooms."

"No, sir."

"Well, what am I to do?"

"No doubt in time the animal will learn to discriminate, sir. He will learn to distinguish your peculiar scent."

"What do you mean—my peculiar scent? Correct the impression that I intend to hang about in the hall while life slips by, in the hope that one of these days that dashed animal will decide that I smell all right." I thought for a bit. "Jeeves!"

"Sir?"

"I'm going away—to-morrow morning by the first train. I shall go and stop with Mr. Todd in the country."

"Do you wish me to accompany you, sir?"

"No."

"Very good, sir."

"I don't know when I shall be back. Forward my letters."

"Yes, sir."

As a matter of fact, I was back within the week. Rocky Todd, the pal I went to stay with, is a rummy sort of a chap who lives all alone in the wilds of Long Island, and likes it; but a little of that sort of thing goes a long way with me. Dear old Rocky is one of the best, but after a few days in his cottage in the woods, miles away from anywhere, New York, even with Motty on the premises, began to look pretty good to me. The days down on Long Island have forty-eight hours in them; you can't get to sleep at night because of the bellowing of the crickets; and you have to walk two miles for a drink and six for an evening paper. I thanked Rocky for his kind hospitality, and caught the only train they have down in those parts. It landed me in New York about dinner-time. I went straight to the old flat. Jeeves came out of his lair. I looked round cautiously for Rollo.

"Where's that dog, Jeeves? Have you got him tied up?"

"The animal is no longer here, sir. His lordship gave him to the porter, who sold him. His lordship took a prejudice against the animal on account of being bitten by him in the calf of the leg."

I don't think I've ever been so bucked by a bit of news. I felt I had misjudged Rollo. Evidently, when you got to know him better, he had a lot of intelligence in him.

"Ripping!" I said. "Is Lord Pershore in, Jeeves?"

"No, sir."

"Do you expect him back to dinner?"

"No, sir."

"Where is he?"

"In prison, sir."

Have you ever trodden on a rake and had the handle jump up and hit you? That's how I felt then.

"In prison!"

"Yes, sir."

"You don't mean—in prison?"

"Yes, sir."

I lowered myself into a chair.

"Why?" I said.

"He assaulted a constable, sir."

"Lord Pershore assaulted a constable!"

"Yes, sir."

I digested this.

"But, Jeeves, I say! This is frightful!"

"Sir?"

"What will Lady Malvern say when she finds out?"

"I do not fancy that her ladyship will find out, sir."

"But she'll come back and want to know where he is."

"I rather fancy, sir, that his lordship's bit of time will have run out by then."

"But supposing it hasn't?"

"In that event, sir, it may be judicious to prevaricate a little."

"How?"

"If I might make the suggestion, sir, I should inform her ladyship that his lordship has left for a short visit to Boston."

"Why Boston?"

"Very interesting and respectable centre, sir."

"Jeeves, I believe you've hit it."

"I fancy so, sir."

"Why, this is really the best thing that could have happened. If this hadn't turned up to prevent him, young Motty would have been in a sanatorium by the time Lady Malvern got back."

"Exactly, sir."

The more I looked at it in that way, the sounder this prison wheeze seemed to me. There was no doubt in the world that prison was just what the doctor ordered for Motty. It was the only thing that could have pulled him up. I was sorry for the poor blighter, but, after all, I reflected, a chappie who had lived all his life with Lady Malvern, in a small village in the interior of Shropshire, wouldn't have much to kick at in a prison. Altogether, I began to feel absolutely braced again. Life became like what the poet Johnnie says—one grand, sweet song. Things went on so comfortably and peacefully for a couple of weeks that I give you my word that I'd almost forgotten such a person as Motty existed. The only flaw in the scheme of things was that Jeeves was still pained and distant. It wasn't anything he said or did, mind you, but there was a rummy something about him all the time. Once when I was tying the pink tie I caught sight of him in the looking-glass. There was a kind of grieved look in his eye.

And then Lady Malvern came back, a good bit ahead of schedule. I hadn't been expecting her for days. I'd forgotten how time had been slipping along. She turned up one morning while I was still in bed sipping tea and thinking of this and that. Jeeves flowed in with the announcement that he had just loosed her into the sitting-room. I draped a few garments round me and went in.

There she was, sitting in the same arm-chair, looking as massive as ever. The only difference was that she didn't uncover the teeth, as she had done the first time.

"Good morning," I said. "So you've got back, what?"

"I have got back."

There was something sort of bleak about her tone, rather as if she had swallowed an east wind. This I took to be due to the fact that she probably hadn't breakfasted. It's only after a bit of breakfast that I'm able to regard the world with that sunny cheeriness which makes a fellow the universal favourite. I'm never much of a lad till I've engulfed an egg or two and a beaker of coffee.

"I suppose you haven't breakfasted?"

"I have not yet breakfasted."

"Won't you have an egg or something? Or a sausage or something? Or something?"

"No, thank you."

She spoke as if she belonged to an anti-sausage society or a league for the suppression of eggs. There was a bit of a silence.

"I called on you last night," she said, "but you were out."

"Awfully sorry! Had a pleasant trip?"

"Extremely, thank you."

"See everything? Niag'ra Falls, Yellowstone Park, and the jolly old Grand Canyon, and what-not?"

"I saw a great deal."

There was another slightly *frappé* silence. Jeeves floated silently into the dining-room and began to lay the breakfast-table.

"I hope Wilmot was not in your way, Mr. Wooster?"

I had been wondering when she was going to mention Motty.

"Rather not! Great pals! Hit it off splendidly."

"You were his constant companion, then?"

"Absolutely! We were always together. Saw all the sights, don't you know. We'd take in the Museum of Art in the morning, and have a bit of lunch at some good vegetarian place, and then toddle along to a sacred concert in the afternoon, and home to an early dinner. We usually played dominoes after dinner. And then the early bed and the refreshing sleep. We had a great time. I was awfully sorry when he went away to Boston."

"Oh! Wilmot is in Boston?"

"Yes. I ought to have let you know, but of course we didn't know where you were. You were dodging all over the place like a snipe—I mean, don't you know, dodging all over the place, and we couldn't get at you. Yes, Motty went off to Boston."

"You're sure he went to Boston?"

"Oh, absolutely." I called out to Jeeves, who was now messing about in the next room with forks and so forth: "Jeeves, Lord Pershore didn't change his mind about going to Boston, did he?"

"No, sir."

"I thought I was right. Yes, Motty went to Boston."

"Then how do you account, Mr. Wooster, for the fact that when I went yesterday afternoon to Blackwell's Island prison, to secure material for my book, I saw poor, dear Wilmot there, dressed in a striped suit, seated beside a pile of stones with a hammer in his hands?"

I tried to think of something to say, but nothing came. A chappie has to be a lot broader about the forehead than I am to handle a jolt like this. I strained the old bean till it creaked, but between the collar and the hair parting nothing stirred. I was dumb. Which was lucky, because I wouldn't have had a chance to get any persiflage out of my system. Lady Malvern collared the conversation. She had been bottling it up, and now it came out with a rush:

"So this is how you have looked after my poor, dear boy, Mr. Wooster! So this is how you have abused my trust! I left him in your charge, thinking that I could rely on you to shield him from evil. He came to you innocent, unversed in the ways of the world, confiding, unused to the temptations of a large city, and you led him astray!"

I hadn't any remarks to make. All I could think of was the picture of Aunt Agatha drinking all this in and reaching out to sharpen the hatchet against my return.

"You deliberately——"

Far away in the misty distance a soft voice spoke:

"If I might explain, your ladyship."

Jeeves had projected himself in from the dining-room and materialized on the rug. Lady Malvern tried to freeze him with a look, but you can't do that sort of thing to Jeeves. He is look-proof.

"I fancy, your ladyship, that you have misunderstood Mr. Wooster, and that he may have given you the impression that he was in New York when his lordship—was removed. When Mr. Wooster informed your ladyship that his lordship had gone to Boston, he was relying on the version I had given him of his lordship's movements. Mr. Wooster was away, visiting a friend in the country, at the time, and knew nothing of the matter till your ladyship informed him."

Lady Malvern gave a kind of grunt. It didn't rattle Jeeves.

"I feared Mr. Wooster might be disturbed if he knew the truth, as he is so attached to his lordship and has taken such pains to look after him, so I took the liberty of telling him that his lordship had gone away for a visit. It might have been hard for Mr. Wooster to believe that his lordship had gone to prison voluntarily and from the best motives, but your ladyship, knowing him better, will readily understand."

"What!" Lady Malvern goggled at him. "Did you say that Lord Pershore went to prison voluntarily?"

"If I might explain, your ladyship. I think that your ladyship's parting words made a deep impression on his lordship. I have frequently heard him speak to Mr. Wooster of his desire to do something to follow your ladyship's instructions and collect material for your ladyship's book on America. Mr. Wooster will bear me out when I say that his lordship was frequently extremely depressed at the thought that he was doing so little to help."

"Absolutely, by Jove! Quite pipped about it!" I said.

"The idea of making a personal examination into the prison system of the country—from within—occurred to his lordship very suddenly one night. He embraced it eagerly. There was no restraining him."

Lady Malvern looked at Jeeves, then at me, then at Jeeves again. I could see her struggling with the thing.

"Surely, your ladyship," said Jeeves, "it is more reasonable to suppose that a gentleman of his lordship's character went to prison of his own volition than that he committed some breach of the law which necessitated his arrest?"

Lady Malvern blinked. Then she got up.

"Mr. Wooster," she said, "I apologize. I have done you an injustice. I should have known Wilmot better. I should have had more faith in his pure, fine spirit."

"Absolutely!" I said.

"Your breakfast is ready, sir," said Jeeves.

I sat down and dallied in a dazed sort of way with a poached egg.

"Jeeves," I said, "you are certainly a life-saver!"

"Thank you, sir."

"Nothing would have convinced my Aunt Agatha that I hadn't lured that blighter into riotous living."

"I fancy you are right, sir."

I champed my egg for a bit. I was most awfully moved, don't you know, by the way Jeeves had rallied round. Something seemed to tell me that this was an occasion that called for rich rewards. For a moment I hesitated. Then I made up my mind.

"Jeeves!"

"Sir?"

"That pink tie!"

"Yes, sir?"

"Burn it!"

"Thank you, sir."

"And, Jeeves!"

"Yes, sir?"

"Take a taxi and get me that Longacre hat, as worn by John Drew!"

"Thank you very much, sir."

I felt most awfully braced. I felt as if the clouds had rolled away and all was as it used to be. I felt like one of those chappies in the novels who calls off the fight with his wife in the last chapter and decides to forget and forgive. I felt I wanted to do all sorts of other things to show Jeeves that I appreciated him.

"Jeeves," I said, "it isn't enough. Is there anything else you would like?"

"Yes, sir. If I may make the suggestion—fifty dollars."

"Fifty dollars?"

"It will enable me to pay a debt of honour, sir. I owe it to his lordship."

"You owe Lord Pershore fifty dollars?"

"Yes, sir. I happened to meet him in the street the night his lordship was arrested. I had been thinking a good deal about the most suitable method of inducing him to abandon his mode of living, sir. His lordship was a little over-excited at the time and I fancy that he mistook me for a friend of his. At any rate when I took the liberty of wagering him fifty dollars that he would not punch a passing policeman in the eye, he accepted the bet very cordially and won it."

I produced my pocket-book and counted out a hundred.

"Take this, Jeeves," I said; "fifty isn't enough. Do you know, Jeeves, you're—well, you absolutely stand alone!"

"I endeavour to give satisfaction, sir," said Jeeves.

JEEVES AND THE HARD-BOILED EGG

Sometimes of a morning, as I've sat in bed sucking down the early cup of tea and watched my man Jeeves flitting about the room and putting out the raiment for the day, I've wondered what the deuce I should do if the fellow ever took it into his head to leave me. It's not so bad now I'm in New York, but in London the anxiety was frightful. There used to be all sorts of attempts on the part of low blighters to sneak him away from me. Young Reggie Foljambe to my certain knowledge offered him double what I was giving him, and Alistair Bingham-Reeves, who's got a valet who had been known to press his trousers sideways, used to look at him, when he came to see me, with a kind of glittering hungry eye which disturbed me deucedly. Bally pirates!

The thing, you see, is that Jeeves is so dashed competent. You can spot it even in the way he shoves studs into a shirt.

I rely on him absolutely in every crisis, and he never lets me down. And, what's more, he can always be counted on to extend himself on behalf of any pal of mine who happens to be to all appearances knee-deep in the bouillon. Take the rather rummy case, for instance, of dear old Bicky and his uncle, the hard-boiled egg.

It happened after I had been in America for a few months. I got back to the flat latish one night, and when Jeeves brought me the final drink he said:

"Mr. Bickersteth called to see you this evening, sir, while you were out."

"Oh?" I said.

"Twice, sir. He appeared a trifle agitated."

"What, pipped?"

"He gave that impression, sir."

I sipped the whisky. I was sorry if Bicky was in trouble, but, as a matter of fact, I was rather glad to have something I could discuss freely with Jeeves just then, because things had been a bit strained between us for some time, and it had been rather difficult to hit on anything to talk about that wasn't apt to take a personal turn. You see, I had decided—rightly or wrongly—to grow a moustache and this had cut Jeeves to the quick. He couldn't stick the thing at any price, and I had been living ever since in an atmosphere of bally disapproval till I was getting jolly well fed up with it. What I mean is, while there's no doubt that in certain matters of dress Jeeves's judgment is absolutely sound and should be followed, it seemed to me that it was getting a bit too thick if he was going to edit my face as well as my costume. No one can call me an unreasonable chappie, and many's the time I've given in like a lamb when Jeeves has voted against one of my pet suits or ties; but when it comes to a valet's staking out a claim on your upper lip you've simply got to have a bit of the good old bulldog pluck and defy the blighter.

"He said that he would call again later, sir."

"Something must be up, Jeeves."

"Yes, sir."

I gave the moustache a thoughtful twirl. It seemed to hurt Jeeves a good deal, so I chucked it.

"I see by the paper, sir, that Mr. Bickersteth's uncle is arriving on the *Carmantic*."

"Yes?"

"His Grace the Duke of Chiswick, sir."

This was news to me, that Bicky's uncle was a duke. Rum, how little one knows about one's pals! I had met Bicky for the first time at a species of beano or jamboree down in Washington Square, not long after my arrival in New York. I suppose I was a bit homesick at the time, and I rather took to Bicky when I found that he was an Englishman and had, in fact, been up at Oxford with me. Besides, he was a frightful chump, so we naturally drifted together; and while we were taking a quiet snort in a corner that wasn't all cluttered up with artists and sculptors and what-not, he furthermore endeared himself to me by a most extraordinarily gifted imitation of a bull-terrier chasing a cat up a tree. But, though we had subsequently become extremely pally, all I really knew about him was that he was generally hard up, and had an uncle who relieved the strain a bit from time to time by sending him monthly remittances.

"If the Duke of Chiswick is his uncle," I said, "why hasn't he a title? Why isn't he Lord What-Not?"

"Mr. Bickersteth is the son of his grace's late sister, sir, who married Captain Rollo Bickersteth of the Coldstream Guards."

Jeeves knows everything.

"Is Mr. Bickersteth's father dead, too?"

"Yes, sir."

"Leave any money?"

"No, sir."

I began to understand why poor old Bicky was always more or less on the rocks. To the casual and irreflective observer, if you know what I mean, it may sound a pretty good wheeze having a duke for an uncle, but the trouble about old Chiswick was that, though an extremely wealthy old buster, owning half London and about five counties up north, he was notoriously the most prudent spender in England. He was what American chappies would call a hard-boiled egg. If Bicky's people hadn't left him anything and he depended on what he could prise out of the old duke, he was in a pretty bad way. Not that that explained why he was hunting me like this, because he was a chap who never borrowed money. He said he wanted to keep his pals, so never bit any one's ear on principle.

At this juncture the door bell rang. Jeeves floated out to answer it.

"Yes, sir. Mr. Wooster has just returned," I heard him say. And Bicky came trickling in, looking pretty sorry for himself.

"Halloa, Bicky!" I said. "Jeeves told me you had been trying to get me. Jeeves, bring another glass, and let the revels commence. What's the trouble, Bicky?"

"I'm in a hole, Bertie. I want your advice."

"Say on, old lad!"

"My uncle's turning up to-morrow, Bertie."

"So Jeeves told me."

"The Duke of Chiswick, you know."

"So Jeeves told me."

Bicky seemed a bit surprised.

"Jeeves seems to know everything."

"Rather rummily, that's exactly what I was thinking just now myself."

"Well, I wish," said Bicky gloomily, "that he knew a way to get me out of the hole I'm in."

Jeeves shimmered in with the glass, and stuck it competently on the table.

"Mr. Bickersteth is in a bit of a hole, Jeeves," I said, "and wants you to rally round."

"Very good, sir."

Bicky looked a bit doubtful.

"Well, of course, you know, Bertie, this thing is by way of being a bit private and all that."

"I shouldn't worry about that, old top. I bet Jeeves knows all about it already. Don't you, Jeeves?"

"Yes, sir."

"Eh!" said Bicky, rattled.

"I am open to correction, sir, but is not your dilemma due to the fact that you are at a loss to explain to his grace why you are in New York instead of in Colorado?"

Bicky rocked like a jelly in a high wind.

"How the deuce do you know anything about it?"

"I chanced to meet his grace's butler before we left England. He informed me that he happened to overhear his grace speaking to you on the matter, sir, as he passed the library door."

Bicky gave a hollow sort of laugh.

"Well, as everybody seems to know all about it, there's no need to try to keep it dark. The old boy turfed me out, Bertie, because he said I was a brainless nincompoop. The idea was that he would give me a remittance on condition that I dashed out to some blighted locality of the name of Colorado and learned farming or ranching, or whatever they call it, at some bally ranch or farm or whatever it's called. I didn't fancy the idea a bit. I should have had to ride horses and pursue cows, and so forth. I hate horses. They bite at you. I was all against the scheme. At the same time, don't you know, I had to have that remittance."

"I get you absolutely, dear boy."

"Well, when I got to New York it looked a decent sort of place to me, so I thought it would be a pretty sound notion to stop here. So I cabled to my uncle telling him that I had dropped into a good business wheeze in the city and wanted to chuck the ranch idea. He wrote back that it was all right, and here I've been ever since. He thinks I'm doing well at something or other over here. I never dreamed, don't you know, that he would ever come out here. What on earth am I to do?"

"Jeeves," I said, "what on earth is Mr. Bickersteth to do?"

"You see," said Bicky, "I had a wireless from him to say that he was coming to stay with me—to save hotel bills, I suppose. I've always given him the impression that I was living in pretty good style. I can't have him to stay at my boarding-house."

"Thought of anything, Jeeves?" I said.

"To what extent, sir, if the question is not a delicate one, are you prepared to assist Mr. Bickersteth?"

"I'll do anything I can for you, of course, Bicky, old man."

"Then, if I might make the suggestion, sir, you might lend Mr. Bickersteth——"

"No, by Jove!" said Bicky firmly. "I never have touched you, Bertie, and I'm not going to start now. I may be a chump, but it's my boast that I don't owe a penny to a single soul—not counting tradesmen, of course."

"I was about to suggest, sir, that you might lend Mr. Bickersteth this flat. Mr. Bickersteth could give his grace the impression that he was the owner of it. With your permission I could convey the notion that I was in Mr. Bickersteth's employment, and not in yours. You would be residing here temporarily as Mr. Bickersteth's guest. His grace would occupy the second spare bedroom. I fancy that you would find this answer satisfactorily, sir."

Bicky had stopped rocking himself and was staring at Jeeves in an awed sort of way.

"I would advocate the dispatching of a wireless message to his grace on board the vessel, notifying him of the change of address. Mr. Bickersteth could meet his grace at the dock and proceed directly here. Will that meet the situation, sir?"

"Absolutely."

"Thank you, sir."

Bicky followed him with his eye till the door closed.

"How does he do it, Bertie?" he said. "I'll tell you what I think it is. I believe it's something to do with the shape of his head. Have you ever noticed his head, Bertie, old man? It sort of sticks out at the back!"

I hopped out of bed early next morning, so as to be among those present when the old boy should arrive. I knew from experience that these ocean liners fetch up at the dock at a deucedly ungodly hour. It wasn't much after nine by the time I'd dressed and had my morning tea and was leaning out of the window, watching the street for Bicky and his uncle. It was one of those jolly, peaceful mornings that make a chappie wish he'd got a soul or something, and I was just brooding on life in general when I became aware of the dickens of a spate in progress down below. A taxi had driven up, and an old boy in a top hat had got out and was kicking up a frightful row about the fare. As far as I could make out, he was trying to get the cab chappie to switch from New York to London prices, and the cab chappie had apparently never heard of London before, and didn't seem to think a lot of it now. The old boy said that in London the trip would have set him back eightpence; and the cabby said he should worry. I called to Jeeves.

"The duke has arrived, Jeeves."

"Yes, sir?"

"That'll be him at the door now."

Jeeves made a long arm and opened the front door, and the old boy crawled in, looking licked to a splinter.

"How do you do, sir?" I said, bustling up and being the ray of sunshine. "Your nephew went down to the dock to meet you, but you must have missed him. My name's Wooster, don't you know. Great pal of Bicky's, and all that sort of thing. I'm staying with him, you know. Would you like a cup of tea? Jeeves, bring a cup of tea."

Old Chiswick had sunk into an arm-chair and was looking about the room.

"Does this luxurious flat belong to my nephew Francis?"

"Absolutely."

"It must be terribly expensive."

"Pretty well, of course. Everything costs a lot over here, you know."

He moaned. Jeeves filtered in with the tea. Old Chiswick took a stab at it to restore his tissues, and nodded.

"A terrible country, Mr. Wooster! A terrible country! Nearly eight shillings for a short cab-drive! Iniquitous!" He took another look round the room. It seemed to fascinate him. "Have you any idea how much my nephew pays for this flat, Mr. Wooster?"

"About two hundred dollars a month, I believe."

"What! Forty pounds a month!"

I began to see that, unless I made the thing a bit more plausible, the scheme might turn out a frost. I could guess what the old boy was thinking. He was trying to square all this prosperity with what he knew of poor old Bicky. And one had to admit that it took a lot of squaring, for dear old Bicky, though a stout fellow and absolutely unrivalled as an imitator of bull-terriers and cats, was in many ways one of the most pronounced fatheads that ever pulled on a suit of gent's underwear.

"I suppose it seems rummy to you," I said, "but the fact is New York often bucks chappies up and makes them show a flash of speed that you wouldn't have imagined them capable of. It sort of develops them. Something in the air, don't you know. I imagine that Bicky in the past, when you knew him, may have been something of a chump, but it's quite different now. Devilish efficient sort of chappie, and looked on in commercial circles as quite the nib!"

"I am amazed! What is the nature of my nephew's business, Mr. Wooster?"

"Oh, just business, don't you know. The same sort of thing Carnegie and Rockefeller and all these coves do, you know." I slid for the door. "Awfully sorry to leave you, but I've got to meet some of the lads elsewhere."

Coming out of the lift I met Bicky bustling in from the street.

"Halloa, Bertie! I missed him. Has he turned up?"

"He's upstairs now, having some tea."

"What does he think of it all?"

"He's absolutely rattled."

"Ripping! I'll be toddling up, then. Toodle-oo, Bertie, old man. See you later."

"Pip-pip, Bicky, dear boy."

He trotted off, full of merriment and good cheer, and I went off to the club to sit in the window and watch the traffic coming up one way and going down the other.

It was latish in the evening when I looked in at the flat to dress for dinner.

"Where's everybody, Jeeves?" I said, finding no little feet pattering about the place. "Gone out?"

"His grace desired to see some of the sights of the city, sir. Mr. Bickersteth is acting as his escort. I fancy their immediate objective was Grant's Tomb."

"I suppose Mr. Bickersteth is a bit braced at the way things are going—what?"

"Sir?"

"I say, I take it that Mr. Bickersteth is tolerably full of beans."

"Not altogether, sir."

"What's his trouble now?"

"The scheme which I took the liberty of suggesting to Mr. Bickersteth and yourself has, unfortunately, not answered entirely satisfactorily, sir."

"Surely the duke believes that Mr. Bickersteth is doing well in business, and all that sort of thing?"

"Exactly, sir. With the result that he has decided to cancel Mr. Bickersteth's monthly allowance, on the ground that, as Mr. Bickersteth is doing so well on his own account, he no longer requires pecuniary assistance."

"Great Scot, Jeeves! This is awful."

"Somewhat disturbing, sir."

"I never expected anything like this!"

"I confess I scarcely anticipated the contingency myself, sir."

"I suppose it bowled the poor blighter over absolutely?"

"Mr. Bickersteth appeared somewhat taken aback, sir."

My heart bled for Bicky.

"We must do something, Jeeves."

"Yes, sir."

"Can you think of anything?"

"Not at the moment, sir."

"There must be something we can do."

"It was a maxim of one of my former employers, sir—as I believe I mentioned to you once before—the present Lord Bridgnorth, that there is always a way. I remember his lordship using the expression on the occasion—he was then a business gentleman and had not yet received his title—when a patent hair-restorer which he chanced to be promoting failed to attract the public. He put it on the market under another name as a depilatory, and amassed a substantial fortune. I have generally found his lordship's aphorism based on sound foundations. No doubt we shall be able to discover some solution of Mr. Bickersteth's difficulty, sir."

"Well, have a stab at it, Jeeves!"

"I will spare no pains, sir."

I went and dressed sadly. It will show you pretty well how pipped I was when I tell you that I near as a toucher put on a white tie with a dinner-jacket. I sallied out for a bit of food more to pass the time than because I wanted it. It seemed brutal to be wading into the bill of fare with poor old Bicky headed for the breadline.

When I got back old Chiswick had gone to bed, but Bicky was there, hunched up in an arm-chair, brooding pretty tensely, with a cigarette hanging out of the corner of his mouth and a more or less glassy stare in his eyes. He had the aspect of one who had been soaked with what the newspaper chappies call "some blunt instrument."

"This is a bit thick, old thing—what!" I said.

He picked up his glass and drained it feverishly, overlooking the fact that it hadn't anything in it.

"I'm done, Bertie!" he said.

He had another go at the glass. It didn't seem to do him any good.

"If only this had happened a week later, Bertie! My next month's money was due to roll in on Saturday. I could have worked a wheeze I've been reading about in the magazine advertisements. It seems that you can make a dashed amount of money if you can only collect a few dollars and start a chicken-farm. Jolly sound scheme, Bertie! Say you buy a hen—call it one hen for the sake of argument. It lays an egg every day of the week. You sell the eggs seven for twenty-five cents. Keep of hen costs nothing. Profit practically twenty-five cents on every seven eggs. Or look at it another way: Suppose you have a dozen eggs. Each of the hens has a dozen chickens. The chickens grow up and have more chickens. Why, in no time you'd have the place covered knee-deep in hens, all laying eggs, at twenty-five cents for every seven. You'd make a fortune. Jolly life, too, keeping hens!" He had begun to get quite worked up at the thought of it, but he slopped back in his chair at this juncture with a good deal of gloom. "But, of course, it's no good," he said, "because I haven't the cash."

"You've only to say the word, you know, Bicky, old top."

"Thanks awfully, Bertie, but I'm not going to sponge on you."

That's always the way in this world. The chappies you'd like to lend money to won't let you, whereas the chappies you don't want to lend it to will do everything except actually stand you on your head and lift the specie out of your pockets. As a lad who has always rolled tolerably free in the right stuff, I've had lots of experience of the second class. Many's the time, back in London, I've hurried along Piccadilly and felt the hot breath of the toucher on the back of my neck and heard his sharp, excited yapping as he closed in on me. I've simply spent my life scattering largesse to blighters I didn't care a hang for; yet here was I now, dripping doubloons and pieces of eight and longing to hand them over, and Bicky, poor fish, absolutely on his uppers, not taking any at any price.

"Well, there's only one hope, then."

"What's that?"

"Jeeves."

"Sir?"

There was Jeeves, standing behind me, full of zeal. In this matter of shimmering into rooms the chappie is rummy to a degree. You're sitting in the old armchair, thinking of this and that, and then suddenly you look up, and there he is. He moves from point to point with as little uproar as a jelly fish. The thing startled poor old Bicky considerably. He rose from his seat like a rocketing pheasant. I'm used to Jeeves now, but often in the days when he first came to me I've bitten my tongue freely on finding him unexpectedly in my midst.

"Did you call, sir?"

"Oh, there you are, Jeeves!"

"Precisely, sir."

"Jeeves, Mr. Bickersteth is still up the pole. Any ideas?"

"Why, yes, sir. Since we had our recent conversation I fancy I have found what may prove a solution. I do not wish to appear to be taking a liberty, sir, but I think that we have overlooked his grace's potentialities as a source of revenue."

Bicky laughed, what I have sometimes seen described as a hollow, mocking laugh, a sort of bitter cackle from the back of the throat, rather like a gargle.

"I do not allude, sir," explained Jeeves, "to the possibility of inducing his grace to part with money. I am taking the liberty of regarding his grace in the light of an at present—if I may say so—useless property, which is capable of being developed."

Bicky looked at me in a helpless kind of way. I'm bound to say I didn't get it myself.

"Couldn't you make it a bit easier, Jeeves!"

"In a nutshell, sir, what I mean is this: His grace is, in a sense, a prominent personage. The inhabitants of this country, as no doubt you are aware, sir, are peculiarly addicted to shaking hands with prominent personages. It occurred to me that Mr. Bickersteth or yourself might know of persons who would be willing to pay a small fee—let us say two dollars or three—for the privilege of an introduction, including handshake, to his grace."

Bicky didn't seem to think much of it.

"Do you mean to say that anyone would be mug enough to part with solid cash just to shake hands with my uncle?"

"I have an aunt, sir, who paid five shillings to a young fellow for bringing a moving-picture actor to tea at her house one Sunday. It gave her social standing among the neighbours."

Bicky wavered.

"If you think it could be done——"

"I feel convinced of it, sir."

"What do you think, Bertie?"

"I'm for it, old boy, absolutely. A very brainy wheeze."

"Thank you, sir. Will there be anything further? Good night, sir."

And he floated out, leaving us to discuss details.

Until we started this business of floating old Chiswick as a money-making proposition I had never realized what a perfectly foul time those Stock Exchange chappies must have when the public isn't biting freely. Nowadays I read that bit they put in the financial reports about "The market opened quietly" with a sympathetic eye, for, by Jove, it certainly opened quietly for us! You'd hardly believe how difficult it was to interest the public and make them take a flutter on the old boy. By the end of the week the only name we had on our list was a delicatessen-store keeper down in Bicky's part of the town, and as he wanted us to take it out in sliced ham instead of cash that didn't help much. There was a gleam of light when the brother of Bicky's pawnbroker offered ten dollars, money down, for an introduction to old Chiswick, but the deal fell through, owing to its turning out that the chap was an anarchist and intended to kick the old boy instead of shaking hands with him. At that, it took me the deuce of a time to persuade Bicky not to grab the cash and let things take their course. He seemed to regard the pawnbroker's brother rather as a sportsman and benefactor of his species than otherwise.

The whole thing, I'm inclined to think, would have been off if it hadn't been for Jeeves. There is no doubt that Jeeves is in a class of his own. In the matter of brain and resource I don't think I have ever met a chappie so supremely like mother made. He trickled into my room one morning with a good old cup of tea, and intimated that there was something doing.

"Might I speak to you with regard to that matter of his grace, sir?"

"It's all off. We've decided to chuck it."

"Sir?"

"It won't work. We can't get anybody to come."

"I fancy I can arrange that aspect of the matter, sir."

"Do you mean to say you've managed to get anybody?"

"Yes, sir. Eighty-seven gentlemen from Birdsburg, sir."

I sat up in bed and spilt the tea.

"Birdsburg?"

"Birdsburg, Missouri, sir."

"How did you get them?"

"I happened last night, sir, as you had intimated that you would be absent from home, to attend a theatrical performance, and entered into conversation between the acts with the occupant of the adjoining seat. I had observed that he was wearing a somewhat ornate decoration in his buttonhole, sir—a large blue button with the words 'Boost for Birdsburg' upon it in red letters, scarcely a judicious addition to a gentleman's evening costume. To my surprise I noticed that the auditorium was full of persons similarly decorated. I ventured to inquire the explanation, and was informed that these gentlemen, forming a party of eighty-seven, are a convention from a town of the name if Birdsburg, in the State of Missouri. Their visit, I gathered, was purely of a social and pleasurable nature, and my informant spoke at some length of the entertainments arranged for their stay in the city. It was when he related with a considerable amount of satisfaction and pride, that a deputation of their number had been introduced to and had shaken hands with a well-known prizefighter, that it occurred to me to broach the subject of his grace. To make a long story short, sir, I have arranged, subject to your approval, that the entire convention shall be presented to his grace to-morrow afternoon."

I was amazed. This chappie was a Napoleon.

"Eighty-seven, Jeeves. At how much a head?"

"I was obliged to agree to a reduction for quantity, sir. The terms finally arrived at were one hundred and fifty dollars for the party."

I thought a bit.

"Payable in advance?"

"No, sir. I endeavoured to obtain payment in advance, but was not successful."

"Well, any way, when we get it I'll make it up to five hundred. Bicky'll never know. Do you suspect Mr. Bickersteth would suspect anything, Jeeves, if I made it up to five hundred?"

"I fancy not, sir. Mr. Bickersteth is an agreeable gentleman, but not bright."

"All right, then. After breakfast run down to the bank and get me some money."

"Yes, sir."

"You know, you're a bit of a marvel, Jeeves."

"Thank you, sir."

"Right-o!"

"Very good, sir."

When I took dear old Bicky aside in the course of the morning and told him what had happened he nearly broke down. He tottered into the sitting-room and buttonholed old Chiswick, who was reading the comic section of the morning paper with a kind of grim resolution.

"Uncle," he said, "are you doing anything special to-morrow afternoon? I mean to say, I've asked a few of my pals in to meet you, don't you know."

The old boy cocked a speculative eye at him.

"There will be no reporters among them?"

"Reporters? Rather not! Why?"

"I refuse to be badgered by reporters. There were a number of adhesive young men who endeavoured to elicit from me my views on America while the boat was approaching the dock. I will not be subjected to this persecution again."

"That'll be absolutely all right, uncle. There won't be a newspaper-man in the place."

"In that case I shall be glad to make the acquaintance of your friends."

"You'll shake hands with them and so forth?"

"I shall naturally order my behaviour according to the accepted rules of civilized intercourse."

Bicky thanked him heartily and came off to lunch with me at the club, where he babbled freely of hens, incubators, and other rotten things.

After mature consideration we had decided to unleash the Birdsburg contingent on the old boy ten at a time. Jeeves brought his theatre pal round to see us, and we arranged the whole thing with him. A very decent chappie, but rather inclined to collar the conversation and turn it in the direction of his home-town's new water-supply system. We settled that, as an hour was about all he would be likely to stand, each gang should consider itself entitled to seven minutes of the duke's society by Jeeves's stop-watch, and that when their time was up Jeeves should slide into the room and cough meaningly. Then we parted with what I believe are called mutual expressions of goodwill, the Birdsburg chappie extending a cordial invitation to us all to pop out some day and take a look at the new water-supply system, for which we thanked him.

Next day the deputation rolled in. The first shift consisted of the cove we had met and nine others almost exactly like him in every respect. They all looked deuced keen and businesslike, as if from youth up they had been working in the office and catching the boss's eye and what-not. They shook hands with the old boy with a good deal of apparent satisfaction—all except one chappie, who seemed to be brooding about something—and then they stood off and became chatty.

"What message have you for Birdsburg, Duke?" asked our pal.

The old boy seemed a bit rattled.

"I have never been to Birdsburg."

The chappie seemed pained.

"You should pay it a visit," he said. "The most rapidly-growing city in the country. Boost for Birdsburg!"

"Boost for Birdsburg!" said the other chappies reverently.

The chappie who had been brooding suddenly gave tongue.

"Say!"

He was a stout sort of well-fed cove with one of those determined chins and a cold eye.

The assemblage looked at him.

"As a matter of business," said the chappie—"mind you, I'm not questioning anybody's good faith, but, as a matter of strict business—I think this gentleman here ought to put himself on record before witnesses as stating that he really is a duke."

"What do you mean, sir?" cried the old boy, getting purple.

"No offence, simply business. I'm not saying anything, mind you, but there's one thing that seems kind of funny to me. This gentleman here says his name's Mr. Bickersteth, as I understand it. Well, if you're the Duke of Chiswick, why isn't he Lord Percy Something? I've read English novels, and I know all about it."

"This is monstrous!"

"Now don't get hot under the collar. I'm only asking. I've a right to know. You're going to take our money, so it's only fair that we should see that we get our money's worth."

The water-supply cove chipped in:

"You're quite right, Simms. I overlooked that when making the agreement. You see, gentlemen, as business men we've a right to reasonable guarantees of good faith. We are paying Mr. Bickersteth here a hundred and fifty dollars for this reception, and we naturally want to know——"

Old Chiswick gave Bicky a searching look; then he turned to the water-supply chappie. He was frightfully calm.

"I can assure you that I know nothing of this," he said, quite politely. "I should be grateful if you would explain."

"Well, we arranged with Mr. Bickersteth that eighty-seven citizens of Birdsburg should have the privilege of meeting and shaking hands with you for a financial consideration mutually arranged, and what my friend Simms here means—and I'm with him—is that we have only Mr. Bickersteth's word for it—and he is a stranger to us—that you are the Duke of Chiswick at all."

Old Chiswick gulped.

"Allow me to assure you, sir," he said, in a rummy kind of voice, "that I am the Duke of Chiswick."

"Then that's all right," said the chappie heartily. "That was all we wanted to know. Let the thing go on."

"I am sorry to say," said old Chiswick, "that it cannot go on. I am feeling a little tired. I fear I must ask to be excused."

"But there are seventy-seven of the boys waiting round the corner at this moment, Duke, to be introduced to you."

"I fear I must disappoint them."

"But in that case the deal would have to be off."

"That is a matter for you and my nephew to discuss."

The chappie seemed troubled.

"You really won't meet the rest of them?"

"No!"

"Well, then, I guess we'll be going."

They went out, and there was a pretty solid silence. Then old Chiswick turned to Bicky:

"Well?"

Bicky didn't seem to have anything to say.

"Was it true what that man said?"

"Yes, uncle."

"What do you mean by playing this trick?"

Bicky seemed pretty well knocked out, so I put in a word.

"I think you'd better explain the whole thing, Bicky, old top."

Bicky's Adam's-apple jumped about a bit; then he started:

"You see, you had cut off my allowance, uncle, and I wanted a bit of money to start a chicken farm. I mean to say it's an absolute cert if you once get a bit of capital. You buy a hen, and it lays an egg every day of the week, and you sell the eggs, say, seven for twenty-five cents.

"Keep of hens cost nothing. Profit practically——"

"What is all this nonsense about hens? You led me to suppose you were a substantial business man."

"Old Bicky rather exaggerated, sir," I said, helping the chappie out. "The fact is, the poor old lad is absolutely dependent on that remittance of yours, and when you cut it off, don't you know, he was pretty solidly in the soup, and had to think of some way of closing in on a bit of the ready pretty quick. That's why we thought of this handshaking scheme."

Old Chiswick foamed at the mouth.

"So you have lied to me! You have deliberately deceived me as to your financial status!"

"Poor old Bicky didn't want to go to that ranch," I explained. "He doesn't like cows and horses, but he rather thinks he would be hot stuff among the hens. All he wants is a bit of capital. Don't you think it would be rather a wheeze if you were to——"

"After what has happened? After this—this deceit and foolery? Not a penny!"

"But——"

"Not a penny!"

There was a respectful cough in the background.

"If I might make a suggestion, sir?"

Jeeves was standing on the horizon, looking devilish brainy.

"Go ahead, Jeeves!" I said.

"I would merely suggest, sir, that if Mr. Bickersteth is in need of a little ready money, and is at a loss to obtain it elsewhere, he might secure the sum he requires by describing the occurrences of this afternoon for the Sunday issue of one of the more spirited and enterprising newspapers."

"By Jove!" I said.

"By George!" said Bicky.

"Great heavens!" said old Chiswick.

"Very good, sir," said Jeeves.

Bicky turned to old Chiswick with a gleaming eye.

"Jeeves is right. I'll do it! The *Chronicle* would jump at it. They eat that sort of stuff."

Old Chiswick gave a kind of moaning howl.

"I absolutely forbid you, Francis, to do this thing!"

"That's all very well," said Bicky, wonderfully braced, "but if I can't get the money any other way——"

"Wait! Er—wait, my boy! You are so impetuous! We might arrange something."

"I won't go to that bally ranch."

"No, no! No, no, my boy! I would not suggest it. I would not for a moment suggest it. I—I think——"

He seemed to have a bit of a struggle with himself. "I—I think that, on the whole, it would be best if you returned with me to England. I—I might—in fact, I think I see my way to doing—to—I might be able to utilize your services in some secretarial position."

"I shouldn't mind that."

"I should not be able to offer you a salary, but, as you know, in English political life the unpaid secretary is a recognized figure——"

"The only figure I'll recognize," said Bicky firmly, "is five hundred quid a year, paid quarterly."

"My dear boy!"

"Absolutely!"

"But your recompense, my dear Francis, would consist in the unrivalled opportunities you would have, as my secretary, to gain experience, to accustom yourself to the intricacies of political life, to—in fact, you would be in an exceedingly advantageous position."

"Five hundred a year!" said Bicky, rolling it round his tongue. "Why, that would be nothing to what I could make if I started a chicken farm. It stands to reason. Suppose you have a dozen hens. Each of the hens has a dozen chickens. After a bit the chickens grow up and have a dozen chickens each themselves, and then they all start laying eggs! There's a fortune in it. You can get anything you like for eggs in America. Chappies keep them on ice for years and years, and don't sell them till they fetch about a dollar a whirl. You don't think I'm going to chuck a future like this for anything under five hundred o' goblins a year—what?"

A look of anguish passed over old Chiswick's face, then he seemed to be resigned to it. "Very well, my boy," he said.

"What-o!" said Bicky. "All right, then."

"Jeeves," I said. Bicky had taken the old boy off to dinner to celebrate, and we were alone. "Jeeves, this has been one of your best efforts."

"Thank you, sir."

"It beats me how you do it."

"Yes, sir."

"The only trouble is you haven't got much out of it—what!"

"I fancy Mr. Bickersteth intends—I judge from his remarks—to signify his appreciation of anything I have been fortunate enough to do to assist him, at some later date when he is in a more favourable position to do so."

"It isn't enough, Jeeves!"

"Sir?"

It was a wrench, but I felt it was the only possible thing to be done.
"Bring my shaving things."
A gleam of hope shone in the chappie's eye, mixed with doubt.
"You mean, sir?"
"And shave off my moustache."
There was a moment's silence. I could see the fellow was deeply moved.
"Thank you very much indeed, sir," he said, in a low voice, and popped off.

ABSENT TREATMENT

I want to tell you all about dear old Bobbie Cardew. It's a most interesting story. I can't put in any literary style and all that; but I don't have to, don't you know, because it goes on its Moral Lesson. If you're a man you mustn't miss it, because it'll be a warning to you; and if you're a woman you won't want to, because it's all about how a girl made a man feel pretty well fed up with things.

If you're a recent acquaintance of Bobbie's, you'll probably be surprised to hear that there was a time when he was more remarkable for the weakness of his memory than anything else. Dozens of fellows, who have only met Bobbie since the change took place, have been surprised when I told them that. Yet it's true. Believe *me*.

In the days when I first knew him Bobbie Cardew was about the most pronounced young rotter inside the four-mile radius. People have called me a silly ass, but I was never in the same class with Bobbie. When it came to being a silly ass, he was a plus-four man, while my handicap was about six. Why, if I wanted him to dine with me, I used to post him a letter at the beginning of the week, and then the day before send him a telegram and a phone-call on the day itself, and—half an hour before the time we'd fixed—a messenger in a taxi, whose business it was to see that he got in and that the chauffeur had the address all correct. By doing this I generally managed to get him, unless he had left town before my messenger arrived.

The funny thing was that he wasn't altogether a fool in other ways. Deep down in him there was a kind of stratum of sense. I had known him, once or twice, show an almost human intelligence. But to reach that stratum, mind you, you needed dynamite.

At least, that's what I thought. But there was another way which hadn't occurred to me. Marriage, I mean. Marriage, the dynamite of the soul; that was what hit Bobbie. He married. Have you ever seen a bull-pup chasing a bee? The pup sees the bee. It looks good to him. But he still doesn't know what's at the end of it till he gets there. It was like that with Bobbie. He fell in love, got married—with a sort of whoop, as if it were the greatest fun in the world—and then began to find out things.

She wasn't the sort of girl you would have expected Bobbie to rave about. And yet, I don't know. What I mean is, she worked for her living; and to a fellow who has never done a hand's turn in his life there's undoubtedly a sort of fascination, a kind of romance, about a girl who works for her living.

Her name was Anthony. Mary Anthony. She was about five feet six; she had a ton and a half of red-gold hair, grey eyes, and one of those determined chins. She was a hospital nurse. When Bobbie smashed himself up at polo, she was told off by the authorities to smooth his brow and rally round with cooling unguents and all that; and the old boy hadn't been up and about again for more than a week before they popped off to the registrar's and fixed it up. Quite the romance.

Bobbie broke the news to me at the club one evening, and next day he introduced me to her. I admired her. I've never worked myself—my name's Pepper, by the way. Almost forgot to mention it. Reggie Pepper. My uncle Edward was Pepper, Wells, and Co., the Colliery people. He left me a sizable chunk of bullion—I say I've never worked myself, but I admire any one who earns a living under difficulties, especially a girl. And this girl had had a rather unusually tough time of it, being an orphan and all that, and having had to do everything off her own bat for years.

Mary and I got along together splendidly. We don't now, but we'll come to that later. I'm speaking of the past. She seemed to think Bobbie the greatest thing on earth, judging by the way she looked at him when she thought I wasn't noticing. And Bobbie seemed to think the same about her. So that I came to the conclusion that, if only dear old Bobbie didn't forget to go to the wedding, they had a sporting chance of being quite happy.

Well, let's brisk up a bit here, and jump a year. The story doesn't really start till then.

They took a flat and settled down. I was in and out of the place quite a good deal. I kept my eyes open, and everything seemed to me to be running along as smoothly as you could want. If this was marriage, I thought, I couldn't see why fellows were so frightened of it. There were a lot of worse things that could happen to a man.

But we now come to the incident of the quiet Dinner, and it's just here that love's young dream hits a snag, and things begin to occur.

I happened to meet Bobbie in Piccadilly, and he asked me to come back to dinner at the flat. And, like a fool, instead of bolting and putting myself under police protection, I went.

When we got to the flat, there was Mrs. Bobbie looking—well, I tell you, it staggered me. Her gold hair was all piled up in waves and crinkles and things, with a what-d'-you-call-it of diamonds in it. And she was wearing the most perfectly ripping dress. I couldn't begin to describe it. I can only say it was the limit. It struck me that if this was how she was in the habit of looking every night when they were dining quietly at home together, it was no wonder that Bobbie liked domesticity.

"Here's old Reggie, dear," said Bobbie. "I've brought him home to have a bit of dinner. I'll phone down to the kitchen and ask them to send it up now—what?"

She stared at him as if she had never seen him before. Then she turned scarlet. Then she turned as white as a sheet. Then she gave a little laugh. It was most interesting to watch. Made me wish I was up a tree about eight hundred miles away. Then she recovered herself.

"I am so glad you were able to come, Mr. Pepper," she said, smiling at me.

And after that she was all right. At least, you would have said so. She talked a lot at dinner, and chaffed Bobbie, and played us ragtime on the piano afterwards, as if she hadn't a care in the world. Quite a jolly little party it was—not. I'm no lynx-eyed sleuth, and all that sort of thing, but I had seen her face at the beginning, and I knew that she was working the whole time and working hard, to keep herself in hand, and that she would have given that diamond what's-its-name in her hair and everything else she possessed to have one good scream—just one. I've sat through some pretty thick evenings in my time, but that one had the rest beaten in a canter. At the very earliest moment I grabbed my hat and got away.

Having seen what I did, I wasn't particularly surprised to meet Bobbie at the club next day looking about as merry and bright as a lonely gum-drop at an Eskimo tea-party.

He started in straightway. He seemed glad to have someone to talk to about it.

"Do you know how long I've been married?" he said.

I didn't exactly.

"About a year, isn't it?"

"Not *about* a year," he said sadly. "Exactly a year—yesterday!"

Then I understood. I saw light—a regular flash of light.

"Yesterday was——?"

"The anniversary of the wedding. I'd arranged to take Mary to the Savoy, and on to Covent Garden. She particularly wanted to hear Caruso. I had the ticket for the box in my pocket. Do you know, all through dinner I had a kind of rummy idea that there was something I'd forgotten, but I couldn't think what?"

"Till your wife mentioned it?"

He nodded——

"She—mentioned it," he said thoughtfully.

I didn't ask for details. Women with hair and chins like Mary's may be angels most of the time, but, when they take off their wings for a bit, they aren't half-hearted about it.

"To be absolutely frank, old top," said poor old Bobbie, in a broken sort of way, "my stock's pretty low at home."

There didn't seem much to be done. I just lit a cigarette and sat there. He didn't want to talk. Presently he went out. I stood at the window of our upper smoking-room, which looks out on to Piccadilly, and watched him. He walked slowly along for a few yards, stopped, then walked on again, and finally turned into a jeweller's. Which was an instance of what I meant when I said that deep down in him there was a certain stratum of sense.

It was from now on that I began to be really interested in this problem of Bobbie's married life. Of course, one's always mildly interested in one's friends' marriages, hoping they'll turn out well and all that; but this was different. The average man isn't like Bobbie, and the average girl isn't like Mary. It was that old business of the immovable mass and the irresistible force. There was Bobbie, ambling gently through life, a dear old chap in a hundred ways, but undoubtedly a chump of the first water.

And there was Mary, determined that he shouldn't be a chump. And Nature, mind you, on Bobbie's side. When Nature makes a chump like dear old Bobbie, she's proud of him, and doesn't want her handiwork disturbed. She gives him a sort of natural armour to protect him against outside interference. And that armour is shortness of memory. Shortness of memory keeps a man a chump, when, but for it, he might cease to be one. Take my case, for instance. I'm a chump. Well, if I had remembered half the things people have tried to teach me during my life, my size in hats would be about number nine. But I didn't. I forgot them. And it was just the same with Bobbie.

For about a week, perhaps a bit more, the recollection of that quiet little domestic evening bucked him up like a tonic. Elephants, I read somewhere, are champions at the memory business, but they were fools to Bobbie during that week. But, bless you, the shock wasn't nearly big enough. It had dinted the armour, but it hadn't made a hole in it. Pretty soon he was back at the old game.

It was pathetic, don't you know. The poor girl loved him, and she was frightened. It was the thin edge of the wedge, you see, and she knew it. A man who forgets what day he was married, when he's been married one year, will forget, at about the end of the fourth, that he's married at all. If she meant to get him in hand at all, she had got to do it now, before he began to drift away.

I saw that clearly enough, and I tried to make Bobbie see it, when he was by way of pouring out his troubles to me one afternoon. I can't remember what it was that he had forgotten the day before, but it was something she had asked him to bring home for her—it may have been a book.

"It's such a little thing to make a fuss about," said Bobbie. "And she knows that it's simply because I've got such an infernal memory about everything. I can't remember anything. Never could."

He talked on for a while, and, just as he was going, he pulled out a couple of sovereigns.

"Oh, by the way," he said.

"What's this for?" I asked, though I knew.

"I owe it you."

"How's that?" I said.

"Why, that bet on Tuesday. In the billiard-room. Murray and Brown were playing a hundred up, and I gave you two to one that Brown would win, and Murray beat him by twenty odd."

"So you do remember some things?" I said.

He got quite excited. Said that if I thought he was the sort of rotter who forgot to pay when he lost a bet, it was pretty rotten of me after knowing him all these years, and a lot more like that.

"Subside, laddie," I said.

Then I spoke to him like a father.

"What you've got to do, my old college chum," I said, "is to pull yourself together, and jolly quick, too. As things are shaping, you're due for a nasty knock before you know what's hit you. You've got to make an effort. Don't say you can't. This two quid business shows that, even if your memory is rocky, you can remember some things. What you've got to do is to see that wedding anniversaries and so on are included in the list. It may be a brainstrain, but you can't get out of it."

"I suppose you're right," said Bobbie. "But it beats me why she thinks such a lot of these rotten little dates. What's it matter if I forgot what day we were married on or what day she was born on or what day the cat had the measles? She knows I love her just as much as if I were a memorizing freak at the halls."

"That's not enough for a woman," I said. "They want to be shown. Bear that in mind, and you're all right. Forget it, and there'll be trouble."

He chewed the knob of his stick.

"Women are frightfully rummy," he said gloomily.

"You should have thought of that before you married one," I said.

I don't see that I could have done any more. I had put the whole thing in a nutshell for him. You would have thought he'd have seen the point, and that it would have made him brace up and get a hold on himself. But no. Off he went again in the same old way. I gave up arguing with him. I had a good deal of time on my hands, but not enough to amount to anything when it was a question of reforming dear old Bobbie by argument. If you see a man asking for trouble, and insisting on getting it, the only thing to do is to stand by and wait till it comes to him. After that you may get a chance. But till then there's nothing to be done. But I thought a lot about him.

Bobbie didn't get into the soup all at once. Weeks went by, and months, and still nothing happened. Now and then he'd come into the club with a kind of cloud on his shining morning face, and I'd know that there had been doings in the home; but it wasn't till well on in the spring that he got the thunderbolt just where he had been asking for it—in the thorax.

I was smoking a quiet cigarette one morning in the window looking out over Piccadilly, and watching the buses and motors going up one way and down the other—most interesting it is; I often do it—when in rushed Bobbie, with his eyes bulging and his face the colour of an oyster, waving a piece of paper in his hand.

"Reggie," he said. "Reggie, old top, she's gone!"

"Gone!" I said. "Who?"

"Mary, of course! Gone! Left me! Gone!"

"Where?" I said.

Silly question? Perhaps you're right. Anyhow, dear old Bobbie nearly foamed at the mouth.

"Where? How should I know where? Here, read this."

He pushed the paper into my hand. It was a letter.

"Go on," said Bobbie. "Read it."

So I did. It certainly was quite a letter. There was not much of it, but it was all to the point. This is what it said:

"MY DEAR BOBBIE,—I am going away. When you care enough about me to remember to wish me many happy returns on my birthday, I will come back. My address will be Box 341, *London Morning News*."

I read it twice, then I said, "Well, why don't you?"

"Why don't I what?"

"Why don't you wish her many happy returns? It doesn't seem much to ask."

"But she says on her birthday."

"Well, when is her birthday?"

"Can't you understand?" said Bobbie. "I've forgotten."

"Forgotten!" I said.

"Yes," said Bobbie. "Forgotten."

"How do you mean, forgotten?" I said. "Forgotten whether it's the twentieth or the twenty-first, or what? How near do you get to it?"

"I know it came somewhere between the first of January and the thirty-first of December. That's how near I get to it."

"Think."

"Think? What's the use of saying 'Think'? Think I haven't thought? I've been knocking sparks out of my brain ever since I opened that letter."

"And you can't remember?"

"No."

I rang the bell and ordered restoratives.

"Well, Bobbie," I said, "it's a pretty hard case to spring on an untrained amateur like me. Suppose someone had come to Sherlock Holmes and said, 'Mr. Holmes, here's a case for you. When is my wife's birthday?' Wouldn't that have given Sherlock a jolt? However, I know enough about the game to understand that a fellow can't shoot off his deductive theories unless you start him with a clue, so rouse yourself out of that pop-eyed trance and come across with two or three. For instance, can't you remember the last time she had a birthday? What sort of weather was it? That might fix the month."

Bobbie shook his head.

"It was just ordinary weather, as near as I can recollect."

"Warm?"

"Warmish."

"Or cold?"

"Well, fairly cold, perhaps. I can't remember."

I ordered two more of the same. They seemed indicated in the Young Detective's Manual. "You're a great help, Bobbie," I said. "An invaluable assistant. One of those indispensable adjuncts without which no home is complete."

Bobbie seemed to be thinking.

"I've got it," he said suddenly. "Look here. I gave her a present on her last birthday. All we have to do is to go to the shop, hunt up the date when it was bought, and the thing's done."

"Absolutely. What did you give her?"

He sagged.

"I can't remember," he said.

Getting ideas is like golf. Some days you're right off, others it's as easy as falling off a log. I don't suppose dear old Bobbie had ever had two ideas in the same morning before in his life; but now he did it without an effort. He just loosed another dry Martini into the undergrowth, and before you could turn round it had flushed quite a brain-wave.

Do you know those little books called *When were you Born*? There's one for each month. They tell you your character, your talents, your strong points, and your weak points at fourpence halfpenny a go. Bobbie's idea was to buy the whole twelve, and go through them till we found out which month hit off Mary's character. That would give us the month, and narrow it down a whole lot.

A pretty hot idea for a non-thinker like dear old Bobbie. We sallied out at once. He took half and I took half, and we settled down to work. As I say, it sounded good. But when we came to go into the thing, we saw that there was a flaw. There was plenty of information all right, but there wasn't a single month that didn't have something that exactly hit off Mary. For instance, in the December book it said, "December people are apt to keep their own secrets. They are extensive travellers." Well, Mary had certainly kept her secret, and she had travelled quite extensively enough for Bobbie's needs. Then, October people were "born with original ideas" and "loved moving." You couldn't have summed up Mary's little jaunt more neatly. February people had "wonderful memories"—Mary's speciality.

We took a bit of a rest, then had another go at the thing.

Bobbie was all for May, because the book said that women born in that month were "inclined to be capricious, which is always a barrier to a happy married life"; but I plumped for February, because February women "are unusually determined to have their own way, are very earnest, and expect a full return in their companion or mates." Which he owned was about as like Mary as anything could be.

In the end he tore the books up, stamped on them, burnt them, and went home.

It was wonderful what a change the next few days made in dear old Bobbie. Have you ever seen that picture, "The Soul's Awakening"? It represents a flapper of sorts gazing in a startled sort of way into the middle distance with a look in her eyes that seems to say, "Surely that is George's step I hear on the mat! Can this be love?" Well, Bobbie had a soul's awakening too. I don't suppose he had ever troubled to think in his life before—not really *think*. But now he was wearing his brain to the bone. It was painful in a way, of course, to see a fellow human being so thoroughly in the soup, but I felt strongly that it was all for the best. I could see as plainly as possible that all these brainstorms were improving Bobbie out of knowledge. When it was all over he might possibly become a rotter again of a sort, but it would only be a pale reflection of the rotter he had been. It bore out the idea I had always had that what he needed was a real good jolt.

I saw a great deal of him these days. I was his best friend, and he came to me for sympathy. I gave it him, too, with both hands, but I never failed to hand him the Moral Lesson when I had him weak.

One day he came to me as I was sitting in the club, and I could see that he had had an idea. He looked happier than he had done in weeks.

"Reggie," he said, "I'm on the trail. This time I'm convinced that I shall pull it off. I've remembered something of vital importance."

"Yes?" I said.

"I remember distinctly," he said, "that on Mary's last birthday we went together to the Coliseum. How does that hit you?"

"It's a fine bit of memorizing," I said; "but how does it help?"

"Why, they change the programme every week there."

"Ah!" I said. "Now you are talking."

"And the week we went one of the turns was Professor Some One's Terpsichorean Cats. I recollect them distinctly. Now, are we narrowing it down, or aren't we? Reggie, I'm going round to the Coliseum this minute, and I'm going to dig the date of those Terpsichorean Cats out of them, if I have to use a crowbar."

So that got him within six days; for the management treated us like brothers; brought out the archives, and ran agile fingers over the pages till they treed the cats in the middle of May.

"I told you it was May," said Bobbie. "Maybe you'll listen to me another time."

"If you've any sense," I said, "there won't be another time."

And Bobbie said that there wouldn't.

Once you get your money on the run, it parts as if it enjoyed doing it. I had just got off to sleep that night when my telephone-bell rang. It was Bobbie, of course. He didn't apologize.

"Reggie," he said, "I've got it now for certain. It's just come to me. We saw those Terpsichorean Cats at a matinee, old man."

"Yes?" I said.

"Well, don't you see that that brings it down to two days? It must have been either Wednesday the seventh or Saturday the tenth."

"Yes," I said, "if they didn't have daily matinees at the Coliseum."

I heard him give a sort of howl.

"Bobbie," I said. My feet were freezing, but I was fond of him.

"Well?"

"I've remembered something too. It's this. The day you went to the Coliseum I lunched with you both at the Ritz. You had forgotten to bring any money with you, so you wrote a cheque."

"But I'm always writing cheques."

"You are. But this was for a tenner, and made out to the hotel. Hunt up your cheque-book and see how many cheques for ten pounds payable to the Ritz Hotel you wrote out between May the fifth and May the tenth."

He gave a kind of gulp.

"Reggie," he said, "you're a genius. I've always said so. I believe you've got it. Hold the line."

Presently he came back again.

"Halloa!" he said.

"I'm here," I said.

"It was the eighth. Reggie, old man, I——"

"Topping," I said. "Good night."

It was working along into the small hours now, but I thought I might as well make a night of it and finish the thing up, so I rang up an hotel near the Strand.

"Put me through to Mrs. Cardew," I said.

"It's late," said the man at the other end.

"And getting later every minute," I said. "Buck along, laddie."

I waited patiently. I had missed my beauty-sleep, and my feet had frozen hard, but I was past regrets.

"What is the matter?" said Mary's voice.

"My feet are cold," I said. "But I didn't call you up to tell you that particularly. I've just been chatting with Bobbie, Mrs. Cardew."

"Oh! is that Mr. Pepper?"

"Yes. He's remembered it, Mrs. Cardew."

She gave a sort of scream. I've often thought how interesting it must be to be one of those Exchange girls. The things they must hear, don't you know. Bobbie's howl and gulp and Mrs. Bobbie's scream and all about my feet and all that. Most interesting it must be.

"He's remembered it!" she gasped. "Did you tell him?"

"No."

Well, I hadn't.

"Mr. Pepper."

"Yes?"

"Was he—has he been—was he very worried?"

I chuckled. This was where I was billed to be the life and soul of the party.

"Worried! He was about the most worried man between here and Edinburgh. He has been worrying as if he was paid to do it by the nation. He has started out to worry after breakfast, and——"

Oh, well, you can never tell with women. My idea was that we should pass the rest of the night slapping each other on the back across the wire, and telling each other what bally brainy conspirators we were, don't you know, and all that. But I'd got just as far as this, when she bit at me. Absolutely! I heard the snap. And then she said "Oh!" in that choked kind of way. And when a woman says "Oh!" like that, it means all the bad words she'd love to say if she only knew them.

And then she began.

"What brutes men are! What horrid brutes! How you could stand by and see poor dear Bobbie worrying himself into a fever, when a word from you would have put everything right, I can't——"

"But——"

"And you call yourself his friend! His friend!" (Metallic laugh, most unpleasant.) "It shows how one can be deceived. I used to think you a kind-hearted man."

"But, I say, when I suggested the thing, you thought it perfectly——"

"I thought it hateful, abominable."

"But you said it was absolutely top——"

"I said nothing of the kind. And if I did, I didn't mean it. I don't wish to be unjust, Mr. Pepper, but I must say that to me there seems to be something positively fiendish in a man who can go out of his way to separate a husband from his wife, simply in order to amuse himself by gloating over his agony——"

"But——!"

"When one single word would have——"

"But you made me promise not to——" I bleated.

"And if I did, do you suppose I didn't expect you to have the sense to break your promise?"

I had finished. I had no further observations to make. I hung up the receiver, and crawled into bed.

I still see Bobbie when he comes to the club, but I do not visit the old homestead. He is friendly, but he stops short of issuing invitations. I ran across Mary at the Academy last week, and her eyes went through me like a couple of bullets through a pat of butter. And as they came out the other side, and I limped off to piece myself together again, there occurred to me the simple epitaph which, when I am no more, I intend to have inscribed on my tombstone. It was this: "He was a man who acted from the best motives. There is one born every minute."

HELPING FREDDIE

I don't want to bore you, don't you know, and all that sort of rot, but I must tell you about dear old Freddie Meadowes. I'm not a flier at literary style, and all that, but I'll get some writer chappie to give the thing a wash and brush up when I've finished, so that'll be all right.

Dear old Freddie, don't you know, has been a dear old pal of mine for years and years; so when I went into the club one morning and found him sitting alone in a dark corner, staring glassily at nothing, and generally looking like the last rose of summer, you can understand I was quite disturbed about it. As a rule, the old rotter is the life and soul of our set. Quite the little lump of fun, and all that sort of thing.

Jimmy Pinkerton was with me at the time. Jimmy's a fellow who writes plays—a deuced brainy sort of fellow—and between us we set to work to question the poor pop-eyed chappie, until finally we got at what the matter was.

As we might have guessed, it was a girl. He had had a quarrel with Angela West, the girl he was engaged to, and she had broken off the engagement. What the row had been about he didn't say, but apparently she was pretty well fed up. She wouldn't let him come near her, refused to talk on the phone, and sent back his letters unopened.

I was sorry for poor old Freddie. I knew what it felt like. I was once in love myself with a girl called Elizabeth Shoolbred, and the fact that she couldn't stand me at any price will be recorded in my autobiography. I knew the thing for Freddie.

"Change of scene is what you want, old scout," I said. "Come with me to Marvis Bay. I've taken a cottage there. Jimmy's coming down on the twenty-fourth. We'll be a cosy party."

"He's absolutely right," said Jimmy. "Change of scene's the thing. I knew a man. Girl refused him. Man went abroad. Two months later girl wired him, 'Come back. Muriel.' Man started to write out a reply; suddenly found that he couldn't remember girl's surname; so never answered at all."

But Freddie wouldn't be comforted. He just went on looking as if he had swallowed his last sixpence. However, I got him to promise to come to Marvis Bay with me. He said he might as well be there as anywhere.

Do you know Marvis Bay? It's in Dorsetshire. It isn't what you'd call a fiercely exciting spot, but it has its good points. You spend the day there bathing and sitting on the sands, and in the evening you stroll out on the shore with the gnats. At nine o'clock you rub ointment on the wounds and go to bed.

It seemed to suit poor old Freddie. Once the moon was up and the breeze sighing in the trees, you couldn't drag him from that beach with a rope. He became quite a popular pet with the gnats. They'd hang round waiting for him to come out, and would give perfectly good strollers the miss-in-baulk just so as to be in good condition for him.

Yes, it was a peaceful sort of life, but by the end of the first week I began to wish that Jimmy Pinkerton had arranged to come down earlier: for as a companion Freddie, poor old chap, wasn't anything to write home to mother about. When he wasn't chewing a pipe and scowling at the carpet, he was sitting at the piano, playing "The Rosary" with one finger. He couldn't play anything except "The Rosary," and he couldn't play much of that. Somewhere round about the third bar a fuse would blow out, and he'd have to start all over again.

He was playing it as usual one morning when I came in from bathing.

"Reggie," he said, in a hollow voice, looking up, "I've seen her."

"Seen her?" I said. "What, Miss West?"

"I was down at the post office, getting the letters, and we met in the doorway. She cut me!"

He started "The Rosary" again, and side-slipped in the second bar.

"Reggie," he said, "you ought never to have brought me here. I must go away."

"Go away?" I said. "Don't talk such rot. This is the best thing that could have happened. This is where you come out strong."

"She cut me."

"Never mind. Be a sportsman. Have another dash at her."

"She looked clean through me!"

"Of course she did. But don't mind that. Put this thing in my hands. I'll see you through. Now, what you want," I said, "is to place her under some obligation to you. What you want is to get her timidly thanking you. What you want——"

"But what's she going to thank me timidly for?"

I thought for a moment.

"Look out for a chance and save her from drowning," I said.

"I can't swim," said Freddie.

That was Freddie all over, don't you know. A dear old chap in a thousand ways, but no help to a fellow, if you know what I mean.

He cranked up the piano once more and I sprinted for the open.

I strolled out on to the sands and began to think this thing over. There was no doubt that the brain-work had got to be done by me. Dear old Freddie had his strong qualities. He was top-hole at polo, and in happier days I've heard him give an imitation of cats fighting in a backyard that would have surprised you. But apart from that he wasn't a man of enterprise.

Well, don't you know, I was rounding some rocks, with my brain whirring like a dynamo, when I caught sight of a blue dress, and, by Jove, it was the girl. I had never met her, but Freddie had sixteen photographs of her sprinkled round his bedroom, and I knew I couldn't be mistaken. She was sitting on the sand, helping a small, fat child build a castle. On a chair close by was an elderly lady reading a novel. I heard the girl call her "aunt." So, doing the Sherlock Holmes business, I deduced that the fat child was her cousin. It struck me that if Freddie had been there he would probably have tried to work up some sentiment about the kid on the strength of it. Personally I couldn't manage it. I don't think I ever saw a child who made me feel less sentimental. He was one of those round, bulging kids.

After he had finished the castle he seemed to get bored with life, and began to whimper. The girl took him off to where a fellow was selling sweets at a stall. And I walked on.

Now, fellows, if you ask them, will tell you that I'm a chump. Well, I don't mind. I admit it. I *am* a chump. All the Peppers have been chumps. But what I do say is that every now and then, when you'd least expect it, I get a pretty hot brain-wave; and that's what happened now. I doubt if the idea that came to me then would have occurred to a single one of any dozen of the brainiest chappies you care to name.

It came to me on my return journey. I was walking back along the shore, when I saw the fat kid meditatively smacking a jelly-fish with a spade. The girl wasn't with him. In fact, there didn't seem to be any one in sight. I was just going to pass on when I got the brain-wave. I thought the whole thing out in a flash, don't you know. From what I had seen of the two, the girl was evidently fond of this kid, and, anyhow, he was her cousin, so what I said to myself was this: If I kidnap this young heavy-weight for the moment, and if, when the girl has got frightfully anxious about where he can have got to, dear old Freddie suddenly appears leading the infant by the hand and telling a story to the effect that he has found him wandering at large about the country and practically saved his life, why, the girl's gratitude is bound to make her chuck hostilities and be friends again. So I gathered in the kid and made off with him. All the way home I pictured that scene of reconciliation. I could see it so vividly, don't you know, that, by George, it gave me quite a choky feeling in my throat.

Freddie, dear old chap, was rather slow at getting on to the fine points of the idea. When I appeared, carrying the kid, and dumped him down in our sitting-room, he didn't absolutely effervesce with joy, if you know what I mean. The kid had started to bellow by this time, and poor old Freddie seemed to find it rather trying.

"Stop it!" he said. "Do you think nobody's got any troubles except you? What the deuce is all this, Reggie?"

The kid came back at him with a yell that made the window rattle. I raced to the kitchen and fetched a jar of honey. It was the right stuff. The kid stopped bellowing and began to smear his face with the stuff.

"Well?" said Freddie, when silence had set in. I explained the idea. After a while it began to strike him.

"You're not such a fool as you look, sometimes, Reggie," he said handsomely. "I'm bound to say this seems pretty good."

And he disentangled the kid from the honey-jar and took him out, to scour the beach for Angela.

I don't know when I've felt so happy. I was so fond of dear old Freddie that to know that he was soon going to be his old bright self again made me feel as if somebody had left me about a million pounds. I was leaning back in a chair on the veranda, smoking peacefully, when down the road I saw the old boy returning, and, by George, the kid was still with him. And Freddie looked as if he hadn't a friend in the world.

"Hello!" I said. "Couldn't you find her?"

"Yes, I found her," he replied, with one of those bitter, hollow laughs.

"Well, then——?"

Freddie sank into a chair and groaned.

"This isn't her cousin, you idiot!" he said.

"He's no relation at all. He's just a kid she happened to meet on the beach. She had never seen him before in her life."

"What! Who is he, then?"

"I don't know. Oh, Lord, I've had a time! Thank goodness you'll probably spend the next few years of your life in Dartmoor for kidnapping. That's my only consolation. I'll come and jeer at you through the bars."

"Tell me all, old boy," I said.

It took him a good long time to tell the story, for he broke off in the middle of nearly every sentence to call me names, but I gathered gradually what had happened. She had listened like an iceberg while he told the story he had prepared, and then—well, she didn't actually call him a liar, but she gave him to understand in a general sort of way that if he and Dr. Cook ever happened to meet, and started swapping stories, it would be about the biggest duel on record. And then he had crawled away with the kid, licked to a splinter.

"And mind, this is your affair," he concluded. "I'm not mixed up in it at all. If you want to escape your sentence, you'd better go and find the kid's parents and return him before the police come for you."

By Jove, you know, till I started to tramp the place with this infernal kid, I never had a notion it would have been so deuced difficult to restore a child to its anxious parents. It's a mystery to me how kidnappers ever get caught. I searched Marvis Bay like a bloodhound, but nobody came forward to claim the infant. You'd have thought, from the lack of interest in him, that he was stopping there all by himself in a cottage of his own. It wasn't till, by an inspiration, I thought to ask the sweet-stall man that I found out that his name was Medwin, and that his parents lived at a place called Ocean Rest, in Beach Road.

I shot off there like an arrow and knocked at the door. Nobody answered. I knocked again. I could hear movements inside, but nobody came. I was just going to get to work on that knocker in such a way that the idea would filter through into these people's heads that I wasn't standing there just for the fun of the thing, when a voice from somewhere above shouted, "Hi!"

I looked up and saw a round, pink face, with grey whiskers east and west of it, staring down from an upper window.

"Hi!" it shouted again.

"What the deuce do you mean by 'Hi'?" I said.

"You can't come in," said the face. "Hello, is that Tootles?"

"My name is not Tootles, and I don't want to come in," I said. "Are you Mr. Medwin? I've brought back your son."

"I see him. Peep-bo, Tootles! Dadda can see 'oo!"

The face disappeared with a jerk. I could hear voices. The face reappeared.

"Hi!"

I churned the gravel madly.

"Do you live here?" said the face.

"I'm staying here for a few weeks."

"What's your name?"

"Pepper. But——"

"Pepper? Any relation to Edward Pepper, the colliery owner?"

"My uncle. But——"

"I used to know him well. Dear old Edward Pepper! I wish I was with him now."

"I wish you were," I said.

He beamed down at me.

"This is most fortunate," he said. "We were wondering what we were to do with Tootles. You see, we have the mumps here. My daughter Bootles has just developed mumps. Tootles must not be exposed to the risk of infection. We could not think what we were to do with him. It was most fortunate your finding him. He strayed from his nurse. I would hesitate to trust him to the care of a stranger, but you are different. Any nephew of Edward Pepper's has my implicit confidence. You must take Tootles to your house. It will be an ideal arrangement. I have written to my brother in London to come and fetch him. He may be here in a few days."

"May!"

"He is a busy man, of course; but he should certainly be here within a week. Till then Tootles can stop with you. It is an excellent plan. Very much obliged to you. Your wife will like Tootles."

"I haven't got a wife," I yelled; but the window had closed with a bang, as if the man with the whiskers had found a germ trying to escape, don't you know, and had headed it off just in time.

I breathed a deep breath and wiped my forehead.

The window flew up again.

"Hi!"

A package weighing about a ton hit me on the head and burst like a bomb.

"Did you catch it?" said the face, reappearing. "Dear me, you missed it! Never mind. You can get it at the grocer's. Ask for Bailey's Granulated Breakfast Chips. Tootles takes them for breakfast with a little milk. Be certain to get Bailey's."

My spirit was broken, if you know what I mean. I accepted the situation. Taking Tootles by the hand, I walked slowly away. Napoleon's retreat from Moscow was a picnic by the side of it.

As we turned up the road we met Freddie's Angela.

The sight of her had a marked effect on the kid Tootles. He pointed at her and said, "Wah!"

The girl stopped and smiled. I loosed the kid, and he ran to her.

"Well, baby?" she said, bending down to him. "So father found you again, did he? Your little son and I made friends on the beach this morning," she said to me.

This was the limit. Coming on top of that interview with the whiskered lunatic it so utterly unnerved me, don't you know, that she had nodded good-bye and was half-way down the road before I caught up with my breath enough to deny the charge of being the infant's father.

I hadn't expected dear old Freddie to sing with joy when he found out what had happened, but I did think he might have shown a little more manly fortitude. He leaped up, glared at the kid, and clutched his head. He didn't speak for a long time, but, on the other hand, when he began he did not leave off for a long time. He was quite emotional, dear old boy. It beat me where he could have picked up such expressions.

"Well," he said, when he had finished, "say something! Heavens! man, why don't you say something?"

"You don't give me a chance, old top," I said soothingly.

"What are you going to do about it?"

"What can we do about it?"

"We can't spend our time acting as nurses to this—this exhibit."

He got up.

"I'm going back to London," he said.

"Freddie!" I cried. "Freddie, old man!" My voice shook. "Would you desert a pal at a time like this?"

"I would. This is your business, and you've got to manage it."

"Freddie," I said, "you've got to stand by me. You must. Do you realize that this child has to be undressed, and bathed, and dressed again? You wouldn't leave me to do all that single-handed? Freddie, old scout, we were at school together. Your mother likes me. You owe me a tenner."

He sat down again.

"Oh, well," he said resignedly.

"Besides, old top," I said, "I did it all for your sake, don't you know?"

He looked at me in a curious way.

"Reggie," he said, in a strained voice, "one moment. I'll stand a good deal, but I won't stand for being expected to be grateful."

Looking back at it, I see that what saved me from Colney Hatch in that crisis was my bright idea of buying up most of the contents of the local sweet-shop. By serving out sweets to the kid practically incessantly we managed to get through the rest of that day pretty satisfactorily. At eight o'clock he fell asleep in a chair, and, having undressed him by unbuttoning every button in sight and, where there were no buttons, pulling till something gave, we carried him up to bed.

Freddie stood looking at the pile of clothes on the floor and I knew what he was thinking. To get the kid undressed had been simple—a mere matter of muscle. But how were we to get him into his clothes again? I stirred the pile with my foot. There was a long linen arrangement which might have been anything. Also a strip of pink flannel which was like nothing on earth. We looked at each other and smiled wanly.

But in the morning I remembered that there were children at the next bungalow but one. We went there before breakfast and borrowed their nurse. Women are wonderful, by George they are! She had that kid dressed and looking fit for anything in about eight minutes. I showered wealth on her, and she promised to come in morning and evening. I sat down to breakfast almost cheerful again. It was the first bit of silver lining there had been to the cloud up to date.

"And after all," I said, "there's lots to be said for having a child about the house, if you know what I mean. Kind of cosy and domestic—what!"

Just then the kid upset the milk over Freddie's trousers, and when he had come back after changing his clothes he began to talk about what a much-maligned man King Herod was. The more he saw of Tootles, he said, the less he wondered at those impulsive views of his on infanticide.

Two days later Jimmy Pinkerton came down. Jimmy took one look at the kid, who happened to be howling at the moment, and picked up his portmanteau.

"For me," he said, "the hotel. I can't write dialogue with that sort of thing going on. Whose work is this? Which of you adopted this little treasure?"

I told him about Mr. Medwin and the mumps. Jimmy seemed interested.

"I might work this up for the stage," he said. "It wouldn't make a bad situation for act two of a farce."

"Farce!" snarled poor old Freddie.

"Rather. Curtain of act one on hero, a well-meaning, half-baked sort of idiot just like—that is to say, a well-meaning, half-baked sort of idiot, kidnapping the child. Second act, his adventures with it. I'll rough it out to-night. Come along and show me the hotel, Reggie."

As we went I told him the rest of the story—the Angela part. He laid down his portmanteau and looked at me like an owl through his glasses.

"What!" he said. "Why, hang it, this is a play, ready-made. It's the old 'Tiny Hand' business. Always safe stuff. Parted lovers. Lisping child. Reconciliation over the little cradle. It's big. Child, centre. Girl L.C.; Freddie, up stage, by the piano. Can Freddie play the piano?"

"He can play a little of 'The Rosary' with one finger."

Jimmy shook his head.

"No; we shall have to cut out the soft music. But the rest's all right. Look here." He squatted in the sand. "This stone is the girl. This bit of seaweed's the child. This nutshell is Freddie. Dialogue leading up to child's line. Child speaks like, 'Boofer lady, does 'oo love dadda?' Business of outstretched hands. Hold picture for a moment. Freddie crosses L., takes girl's hand. Business of swallowing lump in throat. Then big speech. 'Ah, Marie,' or whatever her name is—Jane—Agnes—Angela? Very well. 'Ah, Angela, has not this gone on too long? A little child rebukes us! Angela!' And so on. Freddie must work up his own part. I'm just giving you the general outline. And we must get a good line for the child. 'Boofer lady, does 'oo love dadda?' isn't definite enough. We want something more—ah! 'Kiss Freddie,' that's it. Short, crisp, and has the punch."

"But, Jimmy, old top," I said, "the only objection is, don't you know, that there's no way of getting the girl to the cottage. She cuts Freddie. She wouldn't come within a mile of him."

Jimmy frowned.

"That's awkward," he said. "Well, we shall have to make it an exterior set instead of an interior. We can easily corner her on the beach somewhere, when we're ready. Meanwhile, we must get the kid letter-perfect. First rehearsal for lines and business eleven sharp to-morrow."

Poor old Freddie was in such a gloomy state of mind that we decided not to tell him the idea till we had finished coaching the kid. He wasn't in the mood to have a thing like that hanging over him. So we concentrated on Tootles. And pretty early in the proceedings we saw that the only way to get Tootles worked up to the spirit of the thing was to introduce sweets of some sort as a sub-motive, so to speak.

"The chief difficulty," said Jimmy Pinkerton at the end of the first rehearsal, "is to establish a connection in the kid's mind between his line and the sweets. Once he has grasped the basic fact that those two words, clearly spoken, result automatically in acid-drops, we have got a success."

I've often thought, don't you know, how interesting it must be to be one of those animal-trainer Johnnies: to stimulate the dawning intelligence, and that sort of thing. Well, this was every bit as exciting. Some days success seemed to be staring us in the eye, and the kid got the line out as if he'd been an old professional. And then he'd go all to pieces again. And time was flying.

"We must hurry up, Jimmy," I said. "The kid's uncle may arrive any day now and take him away."

"And we haven't an understudy," said Jimmy. "There's something in that. We must work! My goodness, that kid's a bad study. I've known deaf-mutes who would have learned the part quicker."

I will say this for the kid, though: he was a trier. Failure didn't discourage him. Whenever there was any kind of sweet near he had a dash at his line, and kept on saying something till he got what he was after. His only fault was his uncertainty. Personally, I would have been prepared to risk it, and start the performance at the first opportunity, but Jimmy said no.

"We're not nearly ready," said Jimmy. "To-day, for instance, he said 'Kick Freddie.' That's not going to win any girl's heart. And she might do it, too. No; we must postpone production awhile yet."

But, by George, we didn't. The curtain went up the very next afternoon.

It was nobody's fault—certainly not mine. It was just Fate. Freddie had settled down at the piano, and I was leading the kid out of the house to exercise it, when, just as we'd got out to the veranda, along came the girl Angela on her way to the beach. The kid set up his usual yell at the sight of her, and she stopped at the foot of the steps.

"Hello, baby!" she said. "Good morning," she said to me. "May I come up?"

She didn't wait for an answer. She just came. She seemed to be that sort of girl. She came up on the veranda and started fussing over the kid. And six feet away, mind you, Freddie smiting the piano in the sitting-room. It was a dash disturbing situation, don't you know. At any minute Freddie might take it into his head to come out on to the veranda, and we hadn't even begun to rehearse him in his part.

I tried to break up the scene.

"We were just going down to the beach," I said.

"Yes?" said the girl. She listened for a moment. "So you're having your piano tuned?" she said. "My aunt has been trying to find a tuner for ours. Do you mind if I go in and tell this man to come on to us when he's finished here?"

"Er—not yet!" I said. "Not yet, if you don't mind. He can't bear to be disturbed when he's working. It's the artistic temperament. I'll tell him later."

"Very well," she said, getting up to go. "Ask him to call at Pine Bungalow. West is the name. Oh, he seems to have stopped. I suppose he will be out in a minute now. I'll wait."

"Don't you think—shouldn't we be going on to the beach?" I said.

She had started talking to the kid and didn't hear. She was feeling in her pocket for something.

"The beach," I babbled.

"See what I've brought for you, baby," she said. And, by George, don't you know, she held up in front of the kid's bulging eyes a chunk of toffee about the size of the Automobile Club.

That finished it. We had just been having a long rehearsal, and the kid was all worked up in his part. He got it right first time.

"Kiss Fweddie!" he shouted.

And the front door opened, and Freddie came out on to the veranda, for all the world as if he had been taking a cue.

He looked at the girl, and the girl looked at him. I looked at the ground, and the kid looked at the toffee.

"Kiss Fweddie!" he yelled. "Kiss Fweddie!"

The girl was still holding up the toffee, and the kid did what Jimmy Pinkerton would have called "business of outstretched hands" towards it.

"Kiss Fweddie!" he shrieked.

"What does this mean?" said the girl, turning to me.

"You'd better give it to him, don't you know," I said. "He'll go on till you do."

She gave the kid his toffee, and he subsided. Poor old Freddie still stood there gaping, without a word.

"What does it mean?" said the girl again. Her face was pink, and her eyes were sparkling in the sort of way, don't you know, that makes a fellow feel as if he hadn't any bones in him, if you know what I mean. Did you ever tread on your partner's dress at a dance and tear it, and see her smile at you like an angel and say: "*Please* don't apologize. It's nothing," and then suddenly meet her clear blue eyes and feel as if you had stepped on the teeth of a rake and had the handle jump up and hit you in the face? Well, that's how Freddie's Angela looked.

"*Well?*" she said, and her teeth gave a little click.

I gulped. Then I said it was nothing. Then I said it was nothing much. Then I said, "Oh, well, it was this way." And, after a few brief remarks about Jimmy Pinkerton, I told her all about it. And all the while Idiot Freddie stood there gaping, without a word.

And the girl didn't speak, either. She just stood listening.

And then she began to laugh. I never heard a girl laugh so much. She leaned against the side of the veranda and shrieked. And all the while Freddie, the World's Champion Chump, stood there, saying nothing.

Well I sidled towards the steps. I had said all I had to say, and it seemed to me that about here the stage-direction "exit" was written in my part. I gave poor old Freddie up in despair. If only he had said a word, it might have been all right. But there he stood, speechless. What can a fellow do with a fellow like that?

Just out of sight of the house I met Jimmy Pinkerton.

"Hello, Reggie!" he said. "I was just coming to you. Where's the kid? We must have a big rehearsal to-day."

"No good," I said sadly. "It's all over. The thing's finished. Poor dear old Freddie has made an ass of himself and killed the whole show."

"Tell me," said Jimmy.

I told him.

"Fluffed in his lines, did he?" said Jimmy, nodding thoughtfully. "It's always the way with these amateurs. We must go back at once. Things look bad, but it may not be too late," he said as we started. "Even now a few well-chosen words from a man of the world, and——"

"Great Scot!" I cried. "Look!"

In front of the cottage stood six children, a nurse, and the fellow from the grocer's staring. From the windows of the houses opposite projected about four hundred heads of both sexes, staring. Down the road came galloping five more children, a dog, three men, and a boy, about to stare. And on our porch, as unconscious of the spectators as if they had been alone in the Sahara, stood Freddie and Angela, clasped in each other's arms.

Dear old Freddie may have been fluffy in his lines, but, by George, his business had certainly gone with a bang!

RALLYING ROUND OLD GEORGE

I think one of the rummiest affairs I was ever mixed up with, in the course of a lifetime devoted to butting into other people's business, was that affair of George Lattaker at Monte Carlo. I wouldn't bore you, don't you know, for the world, but I think you ought to hear about it.

We had come to Monte Carlo on the yacht *Circe*, belonging to an old sportsman of the name of Marshall. Among those present were myself, my man Voules, a Mrs. Vanderley, her daughter Stella, Mrs. Vanderley's maid Pilbeam and George.

George was a dear old pal of mine. In fact, it was I who had worked him into the party. You see, George was due to meet his Uncle Augustus, who was scheduled, George having just reached his twenty-fifth birthday, to hand over to him a legacy left by one of George's aunts, for which he had been trustee. The aunt had died when George was quite a kid. It was a date that George had been looking forward to; for, though he had a sort of income—an income, after-all, is only an income, whereas a chunk of o' goblins is a pile. George's uncle was in Monte Carlo, and had written George that he would come to London and unbelt; but it struck me that a far better plan was for George to go to his uncle at Monte Carlo instead. Kill two birds with one stone, don't you know. Fix up his affairs and have a pleasant holiday simultaneously. So George had tagged along, and at the time when the trouble started we were anchored in Monaco Harbour, and Uncle Augustus was due next day.

Looking back, I may say that, so far as I was mixed up in it, the thing began at seven o'clock in the morning, when I was aroused from a dreamless sleep by the dickens of a scrap in progress outside my state-room door. The chief ingredients were a female voice that sobbed and said: "Oh, Harold!" and a male voice "raised in anger," as they say, which after considerable difficulty, I identified as Voules's. I hardly recognized it. In his official capacity Voules talks exactly like you'd expect a statue to talk, if it could. In private, however, he evidently relaxed to some extent, and to have that sort of thing going on in my midst at that hour was too much for me.

"Voules!" I yelled.

Spion Kop ceased with a jerk. There was silence, then sobs diminishing in the distance, and finally a tap at the door. Voules entered with that impressive, my-lord-the-carriage-waits look which is what I pay him for. You wouldn't have believed he had a drop of any sort of emotion in him.

"Voules," I said, "are you under the delusion that I'm going to be Queen of the May? You've called me early all right. It's only just seven."

"I understood you to summon me, sir."

"I summoned you to find out why you were making that infernal noise outside."

"I owe you an apology, sir. I am afraid that in the heat of the moment I raised my voice."

"It's a wonder you didn't raise the roof. Who was that with you?"

"Miss Pilbeam, sir; Mrs. Vanderley's maid."

"What was all the trouble about?"

"I was breaking our engagement, sir."

I couldn't help gaping. Somehow one didn't associate Voules with engagements. Then it struck me that I'd no right to butt in on his secret sorrows, so I switched the conversation.

"I think I'll get up," I said.

"Yes, sir."

"I can't wait to breakfast with the rest. Can you get me some right away?"

"Yes, sir."

So I had a solitary breakfast and went up on deck to smoke. It was a lovely morning. Blue sea, gleaming Casino, cloudless sky, and all the rest of the hippodrome. Presently the others began to trickle up. Stella Vanderley was one of the first. I thought she looked a bit pale and tired. She said she hadn't slept well. That accounted for it. Unless you get your eight hours, where are you?

"Seen George?" I asked.

I couldn't help thinking the name seemed to freeze her a bit. Which was queer, because all the voyage she and George had been particularly close pals. In fact, at any moment I expected George to come to me and slip his little hand in mine, and whisper: "I've done it, old scout; she loves muh!"

"I have not seen Mr. Lattaker," she said.

I didn't pursue the subject. George's stock was apparently low that a.m.

The next item in the day's programme occurred a few minutes later when the morning papers arrived.

Mrs. Vanderley opened hers and gave a scream.

"The poor, dear Prince!" she said.

"What a shocking thing!" said old Marshall.

"I knew him in Vienna," said Mrs. Vanderley. "He waltzed divinely."

Then I got at mine and saw what they were talking about. The paper was full of it. It seemed that late the night before His Serene Highness the Prince of Saxburg-Leignitz (I always wonder why they call these chaps "Serene") had been murderously assaulted in a dark street on his way back from the Casino to his yacht. Apparently he had developed the habit of going about without an escort, and some rough-neck, taking advantage of this, had laid for him and slugged him with considerable vim. The Prince had been found lying pretty well beaten up and insensible in the street by a passing pedestrian, and had been taken back to his yacht, where he still lay unconscious.

"This is going to do somebody no good," I said. "What do you get for slugging a Serene Highness? I wonder if they'll catch the fellow?"

"'Later,'" read old Marshall, "'the pedestrian who discovered His Serene Highness proves to have been Mr. Denman Sturgis, the eminent private investigator. Mr. Sturgis has offered his services to the police, and is understood to be in possession of a most important clue.' That's the fellow who had charge of that kidnapping case in Chicago. If anyone can catch the man, he can."

About five minutes later, just as the rest of them were going to move off to breakfast, a boat hailed us and came alongside. A tall, thin man came up the gangway. He looked round the group, and fixed on old Marshall as the probable owner of the yacht.

"Good morning," he said. "I believe you have a Mr. Lattaker on board—Mr. George Lattaker?"

"Yes," said Marshall. "He's down below. Want to see him? Whom shall I say?"

"He would not know my name. I should like to see him for a moment on somewhat urgent business."

"Take a seat. He'll be up in a moment. Reggie, my boy, go and hurry him up."

I went down to George's state-room.

"George, old man!" I shouted.

No answer. I opened the door and went in. The room was empty. What's more, the bunk hadn't been slept in. I don't know when I've been more surprised. I went on deck.

"He isn't there," I said.

"Not there!" said old Marshall. "Where is he, then? Perhaps he's gone for a stroll ashore. But he'll be back soon for breakfast. You'd better wait for him. Have you breakfasted? No? Then will you join us?"

The man said he would, and just then the gong went and they trooped down, leaving me alone on deck.

I sat smoking and thinking, and then smoking a bit more, when I thought I heard somebody call my name in a sort of hoarse whisper. I looked over my shoulder, and, by Jove, there at the top of the gangway in evening dress, dusty to the eyebrows and without a hat, was dear old George.

"Great Scot!" I cried.

"'Sh!" he whispered. "Anyone about?"

"They're all down at breakfast."

He gave a sigh of relief, sank into my chair, and closed his eyes. I regarded him with pity. The poor old boy looked a wreck.

"I say!" I said, touching him on the shoulder.

He leaped out of the chair with a smothered yell.

"Did you do that? What did you do it for? What's the sense of it? How do you suppose you can ever make yourself popular if you go about touching people on the shoulder? My nerves are sticking a yard out of my body this morning, Reggie!"

"Yes, old boy?"

"I did a murder last night."

"What?"

"It's the sort of thing that might happen to anybody. Directly Stella Vanderley broke off our engagement I——"

"Broke off your engagement? How long were you engaged?"

"About two minutes. It may have been less. I hadn't a stop-watch. I proposed to her at ten last night in the saloon. She accepted me. I was just going to kiss her when we heard someone coming. I went out. Coming along the corridor was that infernal what's-her-name—Mrs. Vanderley's maid—Pilbeam. Have you ever been accepted by the girl you love, Reggie?"

"Never. I've been refused dozens——"

"Then you won't understand how I felt. I was off my head with joy. I hardly knew what I was doing. I just felt I had to kiss the nearest thing handy. I couldn't wait. It might have been the ship's cat. It wasn't. It was Pilbeam."

"You kissed her?"

"I kissed her. And just at that moment the door of the saloon opened and out came Stella."

"Great Scott!"

"Exactly what I said. It flashed across me that to Stella, dear girl, not knowing the circumstances, the thing might seem a little odd. It did. She broke off the engagement, and I got out the dinghy and rowed off. I was mad. I didn't care what became of me. I simply wanted to forget. I went ashore. I—It's just on the cards that I may have drowned my sorrows a bit. Anyhow, I don't remember a thing, except that I can recollect having the deuce of a scrap with somebody in a dark street and somebody falling, and myself falling, and myself legging it for all I was worth. I woke up this morning in the Casino gardens. I've lost my hat."

I dived for the paper.

"Read," I said. "It's all there."

He read.

"Good heavens!" he said.

"You didn't do a thing to His Serene Nibs, did you?"

"Reggie, this is awful."

"Cheer up. They say he'll recover."

"That doesn't matter."

"It does to him."

He read the paper again.

"It says they've a clue."

"They always say that."

"But—My hat!"

"Eh?"

"My hat. I must have dropped it during the scrap. This man, Denman Sturgis, must have found it. It had my name in it!"

"George," I said, "you mustn't waste time. Oh!"

He jumped a foot in the air.

"Don't do it!" he said, irritably. "Don't bark like that. What's the matter?"

"The man!"

"What man?"

"A tall, thin man with an eye like a gimlet. He arrived just before you did. He's down in the saloon now, having breakfast. He said he wanted to see you on business, and wouldn't give his name. I didn't like the look of him from the first. It's this fellow Sturgis. It must be."

"No!"

"I feel it. I'm sure of it."

"Had he a hat?"

"Of course he had a hat."

"Fool! I mean mine. Was he carrying a hat?"

"By Jove, he *was* carrying a parcel. George, old scout, you must get a move on. You must light out if you want to spend the rest of your life out of prison. Slugging a Serene Highness is *lèse-majesté*. It's worse than hitting a policeman. You haven't got a moment to waste."

"But I haven't any money. Reggie, old man, lend me a tenner or something. I must get over the frontier into Italy at once. I'll wire my uncle to meet me in——"

"Look out," I cried; "there's someone coming!"

He dived out of sight just as Voules came up the companion-way, carrying a letter on a tray.

"What's the matter!" I said. "What do you want?"

"I beg your pardon, sir. I thought I heard Mr. Lattaker's voice. A letter has arrived for him."

"He isn't here."

"No, sir. Shall I remove the letter?"

"No; give it to me. I'll give it to him when he comes."

"Very good, sir."

"Oh, Voules! Are they all still at breakfast? The gentleman who came to see Mr. Lattaker? Still hard at it?"

"He is at present occupied with a kippered herring, sir."

"Ah! That's all, Voules."

"Thank you, sir."

He retired. I called to George, and he came out.

"Who was it?"

"Only Voules. He brought a letter for you. They're all at breakfast still. The sleuth's eating kippers."

"That'll hold him for a bit. Full of bones." He began to read his letter. He gave a kind of grunt of surprise at the first paragraph.

"Well, I'm hanged!" he said, as he finished.

"Reggie, this is a queer thing."

"What's that?"

He handed me the letter, and directly I started in on it I saw why he had grunted. This is how it ran:

"My dear George—I shall be seeing you to-morrow, I hope; but I think it is better, before we meet, to prepare you for a curious situation that has arisen in connection with the legacy which your father inherited from your Aunt Emily, and which you are expecting me, as trustee, to hand over to you, now that you have reached your twenty-fifth birthday. You have doubtless heard your father speak of your twin-brother Alfred, who was lost or kidnapped—which, was never ascertained—when you were both babies. When no news was received of him for so many years, it was supposed that he was dead. Yesterday, however, I received a letter purporting that he had been living all this time in Buenos Ayres as the adopted son of a wealthy South American, and has only recently discovered his identity. He states that he is on his way to meet me, and will arrive any day now. Of course, like other claimants, he may prove to be an impostor, but meanwhile his intervention will, I fear, cause a certain delay before I can hand over your money to you. It will be necessary to go into a thorough examination of credentials, etc., and this will take some time. But I will go fully into the matter with you when we meet.—Your affectionate uncle,

"Augustus Arbutt."

I read it through twice, and the second time I had one of those ideas I do sometimes get, though admittedly a chump of the premier class. I have seldom had such a thoroughly corking brain-wave.

"Why, old top," I said, "this lets you out."

"Lets me out of half the darned money, if that's what you mean. If this chap's not an imposter—and there's no earthly reason to suppose he is, though I've never heard my father say a word about him—we shall have to split the money. Aunt Emily's will left the money to my father, or, failing him, his 'offspring.' I thought that meant me, but apparently there are a crowd of us. I call it rotten work, springing unexpected offspring on a fellow at the eleventh hour like this."

"Why, you chump," I said, "it's going to save you. This lets you out of your spectacular dash across the frontier. All you've got to do is to stay here and be your brother Alfred. It came to me in a flash."

He looked at me in a kind of dazed way.

"You ought to be in some sort of a home, Reggie."

"Ass!" I cried. "Don't you understand? Have you ever heard of twin-brothers who weren't exactly alike? Who's to say you aren't Alfred if you swear you are? Your uncle will be there to back you up that you have a brother Alfred."

"And Alfred will be there to call me a liar."

"He won't. It's not as if you had to keep it up for the rest of your life. It's only for an hour or two, till we can get this detective off the yacht. We sail for England to-morrow morning."

At last the thing seemed to sink into him. His face brightened.

"Why, I really do believe it would work," he said.

"Of course it would work. If they want proof, show them your mole. I'll swear George hadn't one."

"And as Alfred I should get a chance of talking to Stella and making things all right for George. Reggie, old top, you're a genius."

"No, no."

"You *are*."

"Well, it's only sometimes. I can't keep it up."

And just then there was a gentle cough behind us. We spun round.

"What the devil are you doing here, Voules," I said.

"I beg your pardon, sir. I have heard all."

I looked at George. George looked at me.

"Voules is all right," I said. "Decent Voules! Voules wouldn't give us away, would you, Voules?"

"Yes, sir."

"You would?"

"Yes, sir."

"But, Voules, old man," I said, "be sensible. What would you gain by it?"

"Financially, sir, nothing."

"Whereas, by keeping quiet"—I tapped him on the chest—"by holding your tongue, Voules, by saying nothing about it to anybody, Voules, old fellow, you might gain a considerable sum."

"Am I to understand, sir, that, because you are rich and I am poor, you think that you can buy my self-respect?"

"Oh, come!" I said.

"How much?" said Voules.

So we switched to terms. You wouldn't believe the way the man haggled. You'd have thought a decent, faithful servant would have been delighted to oblige one in a little matter like that for a fiver. But not Voules. By no means. It was a hundred down, and the promise of another hundred when we had got safely away, before he was satisfied. But we fixed it up at last, and poor old George got down to his state-room and changed his clothes.

He'd hardly gone when the breakfast-party came on deck.

"Did you meet him?" I asked.

"Meet whom?" said old Marshall.

"George's twin-brother Alfred."

"I didn't know George had a brother."

"Nor did he till yesterday. It's a long story. He was kidnapped in infancy, and everyone thought he was dead. George had a letter from his uncle about him yesterday. I shouldn't wonder if that's where George has gone, to see his uncle and find out about it. In the meantime, Alfred has arrived. He's down in George's state-room now, having a brush-up. It'll amaze you, the likeness between them. You'll think it *is* George at first. Look! Here he comes."

And up came George, brushed and clean, in an ordinary yachting suit.

They were rattled. There was no doubt about that. They stood looking at him, as if they thought there was a catch somewhere, but weren't quite certain where it was. I introduced him, and still they looked doubtful.

"Mr. Pepper tells me my brother is not on board," said George.

"It's an amazing likeness," said old Marshall.

"Is my brother like me?" asked George amiably.

"No one could tell you apart," I said.

"I suppose twins always are alike," said George. "But if it ever came to a question of identification, there would be one way of distinguishing us. Do you know George well, Mr. Pepper?"

"He's a dear old pal of mine."

"You've been swimming with him perhaps?"

"Every day last August."

"Well, then, you would have noticed it if he had had a mole like this on the back of his neck, wouldn't you?" He turned his back and stooped and showed the mole. His collar hid it at ordinary times. I had seen it often when we were bathing together.

"Has George a mole like that?" he asked.

"No," I said. "Oh, no."

"You would have noticed it if he had?"

"Yes," I said. "Oh, yes."

"I'm glad of that," said George. "It would be a nuisance not to be able to prove one's own identity."

That seemed to satisfy them all. They couldn't get away from it. It seemed to me that from now on the thing was a walk-over. And I think George felt the same, for, when old Marshall asked him if he had had breakfast, he said he had not, went below, and pitched in as if he hadn't a care in the world.

Everything went right till lunch-time. George sat in the shade on the foredeck talking to Stella most of the time. When the gong went and the rest had started to go below, he drew me back. He was beaming.

"It's all right," he said. "What did I tell you?"

"What did you tell me?"

"Why, about Stella. Didn't I say that Alfred would fix things for George? I told her she looked worried, and got her to tell me what the trouble was. And then——"

"You must have shown a flash of speed if you got her to confide in you after knowing you for about two hours."

"Perhaps I did," said George modestly, "I had no notion, till I became him, what a persuasive sort of chap my brother Alfred was. Anyway, she told me all about it, and I started in to show her that George was a pretty good sort of fellow on the whole, who oughtn't to be turned down for what was evidently merely temporary insanity. She saw my point."

"And it's all right?"

"Absolutely, if only we can produce George. How much longer does that infernal sleuth intend to stay here? He seems to have taken root."

"I fancy he thinks that you're bound to come back sooner or later, and is waiting for you."

"He's an absolute nuisance," said George.

We were moving towards the companion way, to go below for lunch, when a boat hailed us. We went to the side and looked over.

"It's my uncle," said George.

A stout man came up the gangway.

"Halloa, George!" he said. "Get my letter?"

"I think you are mistaking me for my brother," said George. "My name is Alfred Lattaker."

"What's that?"

"I am George's brother Alfred. Are you my Uncle Augustus?"

The stout man stared at him.

"You're very like George," he said.

"So everyone tells me."

"And you're really Alfred?"

"I am."

"I'd like to talk business with you for a moment."

He cocked his eye at me. I sidled off and went below.

At the foot of the companion-steps I met Voules.

"I beg your pardon, sir," said Voules. "If it would be convenient I should be glad to have the afternoon off."

I'm bound to say I rather liked his manner. Absolutely normal. Not a trace of the fellow-conspirator about it. I gave him the afternoon off.

I had lunch—George didn't show up—and as I was going out I was waylaid by the girl Pilbeam. She had been crying.

"I beg your pardon, sir, but did Mr. Voules ask you for the afternoon?"

I didn't see what business if was of hers, but she seemed all worked up about it, so I told her.

"Yes, I have given him the afternoon off."

She broke down—absolutely collapsed. Devilish unpleasant it was. I'm hopeless in a situation like this. After I'd said, "There, there!" which didn't seem to help much, I hadn't any remarks to make.

"He s-said he was going to the tables to gamble away all his savings and then shoot himself, because he had nothing left to live for."

I suddenly remembered the scrap in the small hours outside my state-room door. I hate mysteries. I meant to get to the bottom of this. I couldn't have a really first-class valet like Voules going about the place shooting himself up. Evidently the girl Pilbeam was at the bottom of the thing. I questioned her. She sobbed.

I questioned her more. I was firm. And eventually she yielded up the facts. Voules had seen George kiss her the night before; that was the trouble.

Things began to piece themselves together. I went up to interview George. There was going to be another job for persuasive Alfred. Voules's mind had got to be eased as Stella's had been. I couldn't afford to lose a fellow with his genius for preserving a trouser-crease.

I found George on the foredeck. What is it Shakespeare or somebody says about some fellow's face being sicklied o'er with the pale cast of care? George's was like that. He looked green.

"Finished with your uncle?" I said.

He grinned a ghostly grin.

"There isn't any uncle," he said. "There isn't any Alfred. And there isn't any money."

"Explain yourself, old top," I said.

"It won't take long. The old crook has spent every penny of the trust money. He's been at it for years, ever since I was a kid. When the time came to cough up, and I was due to see that he did it, he went to the tables in the hope of a run of luck, and lost the last remnant of the stuff. He had to find a way of holding me for a while and postponing the squaring of accounts while he got away, and he invented this twin-brother business. He knew I should find out sooner or later, but meanwhile he would be able to get off to South America, which he has done. He's on his way now."

"You let him go?"

"What could I do? I can't afford to make a fuss with that man Sturgis around. I can't prove there's no Alfred when my only chance of avoiding prison is to be Alfred."

"Well, you've made things right for yourself with Stella Vanderley, anyway," I said, to cheer him up.

"What's the good of that now? I've hardly any money and no prospects. How can I marry her?"

I pondered.

"It looks to me, old top," I said at last, "as if things were in a bit of a mess."

"You've guessed it," said poor old George.

I spent the afternoon musing on Life. If you come to think of it, what a queer thing Life is! So unlike anything else, don't you know, if you see what I mean. At any moment you may be strolling peacefully along, and all the time Life's waiting around the corner to fetch you one. You can't tell when you may be going to get it. It's all dashed puzzling. Here was poor old George, as well-meaning a fellow as ever stepped, getting swatted all over the ring by the hand of Fate. Why? That's what I asked myself. Just Life, don't you know. That's all there was about it.

It was close on six o'clock when our third visitor of the day arrived. We were sitting on the afterdeck in the cool of the evening—old Marshall, Denman Sturgis, Mrs. Vanderley, Stella, George, and I—when he came up. We had been talking of George, and old Marshall was suggesting the advisability of sending out search-parties. He was worried. So was Stella Vanderley. So, for that matter, were George and I, only not for the same reason.

We were just arguing the thing out when the visitor appeared. He was a well-built, stiff sort of fellow. He spoke with a German accent.

"Mr. Marshall?" he said. "I am Count Fritz von Cöslin, equerry to His Serene Highness"—he clicked his heels together and saluted—"the Prince of Saxburg-Leignitz."

Mrs. Vanderley jumped up.

"Why, Count," she said, "what ages since we met in Vienna! You remember?"

"Could I ever forget? And the charming Miss Stella, she is well, I suppose not?"

"Stella, you remember Count Fritz?"

Stella shook hands with him.

"And how is the poor, dear Prince?" asked Mrs. Vanderley. "What a terrible thing to have happened!"

"I rejoice to say that my high-born master is better. He has regained consciousness and is sitting up and taking nourishment."

"That's good," said old Marshall.

"In a spoon only," sighed the Count. "Mr. Marshall, with your permission I should like a word with Mr. Sturgis."

"Mr. Who?"

The gimlet-eyed sportsman came forward.

"I am Denman Sturgis, at your service."

"The deuce you are! What are you doing here?"

"Mr. Sturgis," explained the Count, "graciously volunteered his services——"

"I know. But what's he doing here?"

"I am waiting for Mr. George Lattaker, Mr. Marshall."

"Eh?"

"You have not found him?" asked the Count anxiously.

"Not yet, Count; but I hope to do so shortly. I know what he looks like now. This gentleman is his twin-brother. They are doubles."

"You are sure this gentleman is not Mr. George Lattaker?"

George put his foot down firmly on the suggestion.

"Don't go mixing me up with my brother," he said. "I am Alfred. You can tell me by my mole."

He exhibited the mole. He was taking no risks.

The Count clicked his tongue regretfully.

"I am sorry," he said.

George didn't offer to console him,

"Don't worry," said Sturgis. "He won't escape me. I shall find him."

"Do, Mr. Sturgis, do. And quickly. Find swiftly that noble young man."

"What?" shouted George.

"That noble young man, George Lattaker, who, at the risk of his life, saved my high-born master from the assassin."

George sat down suddenly.

"I don't understand," he said feebly.

"We were wrong, Mr. Sturgis," went on the Count. "We leaped to the conclusion—was it not so?—that the owner of the hat you found was also the assailant of my high-born master. We were wrong. I have heard the story from His Serene Highness's own lips. He was passing down a dark street when a ruffian in a mask sprang out upon him. Doubtless he had been followed from the Casino, where he had been winning heavily. My high-born master was taken by surprise. He was felled. But before he lost consciousness he perceived a young man in evening dress, wearing the hat you found, running swiftly towards him. The hero engaged the assassin in combat, and my high-born master remembers no more. His Serene Highness asks repeatedly, 'Where is my brave preserver?' His gratitude is princely. He seeks for this young man to reward him. Ah, you should be proud of your brother, sir!"

"Thanks," said George limply.

"And you, Mr. Sturgis, you must redouble your efforts. You must search the land; you must scour the sea to find George Lattaker."

"He needn't take all that trouble," said a voice from the gangway.

It was Voules. His face was flushed, his hat was on the back of his head, and he was smoking a fat cigar.

"I'll tell you where to find George Lattaker!" he shouted.

He glared at George, who was staring at him.

"Yes, look at me," he yelled. "Look at me. You won't be the first this afternoon who's stared at the mysterious stranger who won for two hours without a break. I'll be even with you now, Mr. Blooming Lattaker. I'll learn you to break a poor man's heart. Mr. Marshall and gents, this morning I was on deck, and I over'eard 'im plotting to put up a game on you. They'd spotted that gent there as a detective, and they arranged that blooming Lattaker was to pass himself off as his own twin-brother. And if you wanted proof, blooming Pepper tells him to show them his mole and he'd swear George hadn't one. Those were his very words. That man there is George Lattaker, Hesquire, and let him deny it if he can."

George got up.

"I haven't the least desire to deny it, Voules."

"Mr. Voules, if *you* please."

"It's true," said George, turning to the Count. "The fact is, I had rather a foggy recollection of what happened last night. I only remembered knocking some one down, and, like you, I jumped to the conclusion that I must have assaulted His Serene Highness."

"Then you are really George Lattaker?" asked the Count.

"I am."

"'Ere, what does all this mean?" demanded Voules.

"Merely that I saved the life of His Serene Highness the Prince of Saxburg-Leignitz, Mr. Voules."

"It's a swindle!" began Voules, when there was a sudden rush and the girl Pilbeam cannoned into the crowd, sending me into old Marshall's chair, and flung herself into the arms of Voules.

"Oh, Harold!" she cried. "I thought you were dead. I thought you'd shot yourself."

He sort of braced himself together to fling her off, and then he seemed to think better of it and fell into the clinch.

It was all dashed romantic, don't you know, but there *are* limits.

"Voules, you're sacked," I said.

"Who cares?" he said. "Think I was going to stop on now I'm a gentleman of property? Come along, Emma, my dear. Give a month's notice and get your 'at, and I'll take you to dinner at Ciro's."

"And you, Mr. Lattaker," said the Count, "may I conduct you to the presence of my high-born master? He wishes to show his gratitude to his preserver."

"You may," said George. "May I have my hat, Mr. Sturgis?"

There's just one bit more. After dinner that night I came up for a smoke, and, strolling on to the foredeck, almost bumped into George and Stella. They seemed to be having an argument.

"I'm not sure," she was saying, "that I believe that a man can be so happy that he wants to kiss the nearest thing in sight, as you put it."

"Don't you?" said George. "Well, as it happens, I'm feeling just that way now."

I coughed and he turned round.

"Halloa, Reggie!" he said.

"Halloa, George!" I said. "Lovely night."

"Beautiful," said Stella.

"The moon," I said.

"Ripping," said George.

"Lovely," said Stella.

"And look at the reflection of the stars on the——"

George caught my eye. "Pop off," he said.

I popped.

DOING CLARENCE A BIT OF GOOD

Have you ever thought about—and, when I say thought about, I mean really carefully considered the question of—the coolness, the cheek, or, if you prefer it, the gall with which Woman, as a sex, fairly bursts? *I* have, by Jove! But then I've had it thrust on my notice, by George, in a way I should imagine has happened to pretty few fellows. And the limit was reached by that business of the Yeardsley "Venus."

To make you understand the full what-d'you-call-it of the situation, I shall have to explain just how matters stood between Mrs. Yeardsley and myself.

When I first knew her she was Elizabeth Shoolbred. Old Worcestershire family; pots of money; pretty as a picture. Her brother Bill was at Oxford with me.

I loved Elizabeth Shoolbred. I loved her, don't you know. And there was a time, for about a week, when we were engaged to be married. But just as I was beginning to take a serious view of life and study furniture catalogues and feel pretty solemn when the restaurant orchestra played "The Wedding Glide," I'm hanged if she didn't break it off, and a month later she was married to a fellow of the name of Yeardsley—Clarence Yeardsley, an artist.

What with golf, and billiards, and a bit of racing, and fellows at the club rallying round and kind of taking me out of myself, as it were, I got over it, and came to look on the affair as a closed page in the book of my life, if you know what I mean. It didn't seem likely to me that we should meet again, as she and Clarence had settled down in the country somewhere and never came to London, and I'm bound to own that, by the time I got her letter, the wound had pretty well healed, and I was to a certain extent sitting up and taking nourishment. In fact, to be absolutely honest, I was jolly thankful the thing had ended as it had done.

This letter I'm telling you about arrived one morning out of a blue sky, as it were. It ran like this:

"MY DEAR OLD REGGIE,—What ages it seems since I saw anything of you. How are you? We have settled down here in the most perfect old house, with a lovely garden, in the middle of delightful country. Couldn't you run down here for a few days? Clarence and I would be so glad to see you. Bill is here, and is most anxious to meet you again. He was speaking of you only this morning. *Do* come. Wire your train, and I will send the car to meet you.

—Yours most sincerely,

ELIZABETH YEARDSLEY.

"P.S.—We can give you new milk and fresh eggs. Think of that!

"P.P.S.—Bill says our billiard-table is one of the best he has ever played on.

"P.P.S.S.—We are only half a mile from a golf course. Bill says it is better than St. Andrews.

"P.P.S.S.S.—You *must* come!"

Well, a fellow comes down to breakfast one morning, with a bit of a head on, and finds a letter like that from a girl who might quite easily have blighted his life! It rattled me rather, I must confess.

However, that bit about the golf settled me. I knew Bill knew what he was talking about, and, if he said the course was so topping, it must be something special. So I went.

Old Bill met me at the station with the car. I hadn't come across him for some months, and I was glad to see him again. And he apparently was glad to see me.

"Thank goodness you've come," he said, as we drove off. "I was just about at my last grip."

"What's the trouble, old scout?" I asked.

"If I had the artistic what's-its-name," he went on, "if the mere mention of pictures didn't give me the pip, I dare say it wouldn't be so bad. As it is, it's rotten!"

"Pictures?"

"Pictures. Nothing else is mentioned in this household. Clarence is an artist. So is his father. And you know yourself what Elizabeth is like when one gives her her head?"

I remembered then—it hadn't come back to me before—that most of my time with Elizabeth had been spent in picture-galleries. During the period when I had let her do just what she wanted to do with me, I had had to follow her like a dog through gallery after gallery, though pictures are poison to me, just as they are to old Bill. Somehow it had never struck me that she would still be going on in this way after marrying an artist. I should have thought that by this time the mere sight of a picture would have fed her up. Not so, however, according to old Bill.

"They talk pictures at every meal," he said. "I tell you, it makes a chap feel out of it. How long are you down for?"

"A few days."

"Take my tip, and let me send you a wire from London. I go there to-morrow. I promised to play against the Scottish. The idea was that I was to come back after the match. But you couldn't get me back with a lasso."

I tried to point out the silver lining.

"But, Bill, old scout, your sister says there's a most corking links near here."

He turned and stared at me, and nearly ran us into the bank.

"You don't mean honestly she said that?"

"She said you said it was better than St. Andrews."

"So I did. Was that all she said I said?"

"Well, wasn't it enough?"

"She didn't happen to mention that I added the words, 'I don't think'?"

"No, she forgot to tell me that."

"It's the worst course in Great Britain."

I felt rather stunned, don't you know. Whether it's a bad habit to have got into or not, I can't say, but I simply can't do without my daily allowance of golf when I'm not in London.

I took another whirl at the silver lining.

"We'll have to take it out in billiards," I said. "I'm glad the table's good."

"It depends what you call good. It's half-size, and there's a seven-inch cut just out of baulk where Clarence's cue slipped. Elizabeth has mended it with pink silk. Very smart and dressy it looks, but it doesn't improve the thing as a billiard-table."

"But she said you said——"

"Must have been pulling your leg."

We turned in at the drive gates of a good-sized house standing well back from the road. It looked black and sinister in the dusk, and I couldn't help feeling, you know, like one of those Johnnies you read about in stories who are lured to lonely houses for rummy purposes and hear a shriek just as they get there. Elizabeth knew me well enough to know that a specially good golf course was a safe draw to me. And she had deliberately played on her knowledge. What was the game? That was what I wanted to know. And then a sudden thought struck me which brought me out in a cold perspiration. She had some girl down here and was going to have a stab at marrying me off. I've often heard that young married women are all over that sort of thing. Certainly she had said there was nobody at the house but Clarence and herself and Bill and Clarence's father, but a woman who could take the name of St. Andrews in vain as she had done wouldn't be likely to stick at a trifle.

"Bill, old scout," I said, "there aren't any frightful girls or any rot of that sort stopping here, are there?"

"Wish there were," he said. "No such luck."

As we pulled up at the front door, it opened, and a woman's figure appeared.

"Have you got him, Bill?" she said, which in my present frame of mind struck me as a jolly creepy way of putting it. The sort of thing Lady Macbeth might have said to Macbeth, don't you know.

"Do you mean me?" I said.

She came down into the light. It was Elizabeth, looking just the same as in the old days.

"Is that you, Reggie? I'm so glad you were able to come. I was afraid you might have forgotten all about it. You know what you are. Come along in and have some tea."

Have you ever been turned down by a girl who afterwards married and then been introduced to her husband? If so you'll understand how I felt when Clarence burst on me. You know the feeling. First of all, when you hear about the marriage, you say to yourself, "I wonder what he's like." Then you meet him, and think,

"There must be some mistake. She can't have preferred *this* to me!" That's what I thought, when I set eyes on Clarence.

He was a little thin, nervous-looking chappie of about thirty-five. His hair was getting grey at the temples and straggly on top. He wore pince-nez, and he had a drooping moustache. I'm no Bombardier Wells myself, but in front of Clarence I felt quite a nut. And Elizabeth, mind you, is one of those tall, splendid girls who look like princesses. Honestly, I believe women do it out of pure cussedness.

"How do you do, Mr. Pepper? Hark! Can you hear a mewing cat?" said Clarence. All in one breath, don't you know.

"Eh?" I said.

"A mewing cat. I feel sure I hear a mewing cat. Listen!"

While we were listening the door opened, and a white-haired old gentleman came in. He was built on the same lines as Clarence, but was an earlier model. I took him correctly, to be Mr. Yeardsley, senior. Elizabeth introduced us.

"Father," said Clarence, "did you meet a mewing cat outside? I feel positive I heard a cat mewing."

"No," said the father, shaking his head; "no mewing cat."

"I can't bear mewing cats," said Clarence. "A mewing cat gets on my nerves!"

"A mewing cat is so trying," said Elizabeth.

"*I* dislike mewing cats," said old Mr. Yeardsley.

That was all about mewing cats for the moment. They seemed to think they had covered the ground satisfactorily, and they went back to pictures.

We talked pictures steadily till it was time to dress for dinner. At least, they did. I just sort of sat around. Presently the subject of picture-robberies came up. Somebody mentioned the "Monna Lisa," and then I happened to remember seeing something in the evening paper, as I was coming down in the train, about some fellow somewhere having had a valuable painting pinched by burglars the night before. It was the first time I had had a chance of breaking into the conversation with any effect, and I meant to make the most of it. The paper was in the pocket of my overcoat in the hall. I went and fetched it.

"Here it is," I said. "A Romney belonging to Sir Bellamy Palmer——"

They all shouted "What!" exactly at the same time, like a chorus. Elizabeth grabbed the paper.

"Let me look! Yes. 'Late last night burglars entered the residence of Sir Bellamy Palmer, Dryden Park, Midford, Hants——'"

"Why, that's near here," I said. "I passed through Midford——"

"Dryden Park is only two miles from this house," said Elizabeth. I noticed her eyes were sparkling.

"Only two miles!" she said. "It might have been us! It might have been the 'Venus'!"

Old Mr. Yeardsley bounded in his chair.

"The 'Venus'!" he cried.

They all seemed wonderfully excited. My little contribution to the evening's chat had made quite a hit.

Why I didn't notice it before I don't know, but it was not till Elizabeth showed it to me after dinner that I had my first look at the Yeardsley "Venus." When she led me up to it, and switched on the light, it seemed impossible that I could have sat right through dinner without noticing it. But then, at meals, my attention is pretty well riveted on the foodstuffs. Anyway, it was not till Elizabeth showed it to me that I was aware of its existence.

She and I were alone in the drawing-room after dinner. Old Yeardsley was writing letters in the morning-room, while Bill and Clarence were rollicking on the half-size billiard table with the pink silk tapestry effects. All, in fact, was joy, jollity, and song, so to speak, when Elizabeth, who had been sitting wrapped in thought for a bit, bent towards me and said, "Reggie."

And the moment she said it I knew something was going to happen. You know that pre-what-d'you-call-it you get sometimes? Well, I got it then.

"What-o?" I said nervously.

"Reggie," she said, "I want to ask a great favour of you."

"Yes?"

She stooped down and put a log on the fire, and went on, with her back to me:

"Do you remember, Reggie, once saying you would do anything in the world for me?"

There! That's what I meant when I said that about the cheek of Woman as a sex. What I mean is, after what had happened, you'd have thought she would have preferred to let the dead past bury its dead, and all that sort of thing, what?

Mind you, I *had* said I would do anything in the world for her. I admit that. But it was a distinctly pre-Clarence remark. He hadn't appeared on the scene then, and it stands to reason that a fellow who may have been a perfect knight-errant to a girl when he was engaged to her, doesn't feel nearly so keen on spreading himself in that direction when she has given him the miss-in-baulk, and gone and married a man who reason and instinct both tell him is a decided blighter.

I couldn't think of anything to say but "Oh, yes."

"There's something you can do for me now, which will make me everlastingly grateful."

"Yes," I said.

"Do you know, Reggie," she said suddenly, "that only a few months ago Clarence was very fond of cats?"

"Eh! Well, he still seems—er—*interested* in them, what?"

"Now they get on his nerves. Everything gets on his nerves."

"Some fellows swear by that stuff you see advertised all over the——"

"No, that wouldn't help him. He doesn't need to take anything. He wants to get rid of something."

"I don't quite fellow. Get rid of something?"

"The 'Venus,'" said Elizabeth.

She looked up and caught my bulging eye.

"You saw the 'Venus,'" she said.

"Not that I remember."

"Well, come into the dining-room."

We went into the dining-room, and she switched on the lights.

"There," she said.

On the wall close to the door—that may have been why I hadn't noticed it before; I had sat with my back to it—was a large oil-painting. It was what you'd call a classical picture, I suppose. What I mean is—well, you know what I mean. All I can say is that it's funny I *hadn't* noticed it.

"Is that the 'Venus'?" I said.

She nodded.

"How would you like to have to look at that every time you sat down to a meal?"

"Well, I don't know. I don't think it would affect me much. I'd worry through all right."

She jerked her head impatiently.

"But you're not an artist," she said. "Clarence is."

And then I began to see daylight. What exactly was the trouble I didn't understand, but it was evidently something to do with the good old Artistic Temperament, and I could believe anything about that. It explains everything. It's like the Unwritten Law, don't you know, which you plead in America if you've done anything they want to send you to chokey for and you don't want to go. What I mean is, if you're absolutely off your rocker, but don't find it convenient to be scooped into the luny-bin, you simply explain that, when you said you were a teapot, it was just your Artistic Temperament, and they apologize and go away. So I stood by to hear just how the A.T. had affected Clarence, the Cat's Friend, ready for anything.

And, believe me, it had hit Clarence badly.

It was this way. It seemed that old Yeardsley was an amateur artist and that this "Venus" was his masterpiece. He said so, and he ought to have known. Well, when Clarence married, he had given it to him, as a wedding present, and had hung it where it stood with his own hands. All right so far, what? But mark the sequel. Temperamental Clarence, being a professional artist and consequently some streets ahead of the dad at the game, saw flaws in the "Venus." He couldn't stand it at any price. He didn't like the drawing. He didn't like the expression of the face. He didn't like the colouring. In fact, it made him feel quite ill to look at it. Yet, being devoted to his father and wanting to do anything rather than give him pain, he had not been able to bring himself to store the thing in the cellar, and the strain of confronting the picture three times a day had begun to tell on him to such an extent that Elizabeth felt something had to be done.

"Now you see," she said.

"In a way," I said. "But don't you think it's making rather heavy weather over a trifle?"

"Oh, can't you understand? Look!" Her voice dropped as if she was in church, and she switched on another light. It shone on the picture next to old Yeardsley's. "There!" she said. "Clarence painted that!"

She looked at me expectantly, as if she were waiting for me to swoon, or yell, or something. I took a steady look at Clarence's effort. It was another Classical picture. It seemed to me very much like the other one.

Some sort of art criticism was evidently expected of me, so I made a dash at it.

"Er—'Venus'?" I said.

Mark you, Sherlock Holmes would have made the same mistake. On the evidence, I mean.

"No. 'Jocund Spring,'" she snapped. She switched off the light. "I see you don't understand even now. You never had any taste about pictures. When we used to go to the galleries together, you would far rather have been at your club."

This was so absolutely true, that I had no remark to make. She came up to me, and put her hand on my arm.

"I'm sorry, Reggie. I didn't mean to be cross. Only I do want to make you understand that Clarence is *suffering*. Suppose—suppose—well, let us take the case of a great musician. Suppose a great musician had to sit and listen to a cheap vulgar tune—the same tune—day after day, day after day, wouldn't you expect his nerves to break! Well, it's just like that with Clarence. Now you see?"

"Yes, but——"

"But what? Surely I've put it plainly enough?"

"Yes. But what I mean is, where do I come in? What do you want me to do?"

"I want you to steal the 'Venus.'"

I looked at her.

"You want me to——?"

"Steal it. Reggie!" Her eyes were shining with excitement. "Don't you see? It's Providence. When I asked you to come here, I had just got the idea. I knew I could rely on you. And then by a miracle this robbery of the Romney takes place at a house not two miles away. It removes the last chance of the poor old man suspecting anything and having his feelings hurt. Why, it's the most wonderful compliment to him. Think! One night thieves steal a splendid Romney; the next the same gang take his 'Venus.' It will be the proudest moment of his life. Do it to-night, Reggie. I'll give you a sharp knife. You simply cut the canvas out of the frame, and it's done."

"But one moment," I said. "I'd be delighted to be of any use to you, but in a purely family affair like this, wouldn't it be better—in fact, how about tackling old Bill on the subject?"

"I have asked Bill already. Yesterday. He refused."

"But if I'm caught?"

"You can't be. All you have to do is to take the picture, open one of the windows, leave it open, and go back to your room."

It sounded simple enough.

"And as to the picture itself—when I've got it?"

"Burn it. I'll see that you have a good fire in your room."

"But——"

She looked at me. She always did have the most wonderful eyes.

"Reggie," she said; nothing more. Just "Reggie."

She looked at me.

"Well, after all, if you see what I mean—The days that are no more, don't you know. Auld Lang Syne, and all that sort of thing. You follow me?"

"All right," I said. "I'll do it."

I don't know if you happen to be one of those Johnnies who are steeped in crime, and so forth, and think nothing of pinching diamond necklaces. If you're not, you'll understand that I felt a lot less keen on the job I'd taken on when I sat in my room, waiting to get busy, than I had done when I promised to tackle it in the dining-room. On paper it all seemed easy enough, but I couldn't help feeling there was a catch somewhere, and I've never known time pass slower. The kick-off was scheduled for one o'clock in the morning, when the household might be expected to be pretty sound asleep, but at a quarter to I couldn't stand it any longer. I lit the lantern I had taken from Bill's bicycle, took a grip of my knife, and slunk downstairs.

The first thing I did on getting to the dining-room was to open the window. I had half a mind to smash it, so as to give an extra bit of local colour to the affair, but decided not to on account of the noise. I had put my lantern on the table, and was just reaching out for it, when something happened. What it was for the moment I couldn't have said. It might have been an explosion of some sort or an earthquake. Some solid object caught me a frightful whack on the chin. Sparks and things occurred inside my head and the next thing I remember is feeling something wet and cold splash into my face, and hearing a voice that sounded like old Bill's say, "Feeling better now?"

I sat up. The lights were on, and I was on the floor, with old Bill kneeling beside me with a soda siphon.

"What happened?" I said.

"I'm awfully sorry, old man," he said. "I hadn't a notion it was you. I came in here, and saw a lantern on the table, and the window open and a chap with a knife in his hand, so I didn't stop to make inquiries. I just let go at his jaw for all I was worth. What on earth do you think you're doing? Were you walking in your sleep?"

"It was Elizabeth," I said. "Why, you know all about it. She said she had told you."

"You don't mean——"

"The picture. You refused to take it on, so she asked me."

"Reggie, old man," he said. "I'll never believe what they say about repentance again. It's a fool's trick and upsets everything. If I hadn't repented, and thought it was rather rough on Elizabeth not to do a little thing like that for her, and come down here to do it after all, you wouldn't have stopped that sleep-producer with your chin. I'm sorry."

"Me, too," I said, giving my head another shake to make certain it was still on.

"Are you feeling better now?"

"Better than I was. But that's not saying much."

"Would you like some more soda-water? No? Well, how about getting this job finished and going to bed? And let's be quick about it too. You made a noise like a ton of bricks when you went down just now, and it's on the cards some of the servants may have heard. Toss you who carves."

"Heads."

"Tails it is," he said, uncovering the coin. "Up you get. I'll hold the light. Don't spike yourself on that sword of yours."

It was as easy a job as Elizabeth had said. Just four quick cuts, and the thing came out of its frame like an oyster. I rolled it up. Old Bill had put the lantern on the floor and was at the sideboard, collecting whisky, soda, and glasses.

"We've got a long evening before us," he said. "You can't burn a picture of that size in one chunk. You'd set the chimney on fire. Let's do the thing comfortably. Clarence can't grudge us the stuff. We've done him a bit of good this trip. To-morrow'll be the maddest, merriest day of Clarence's glad New Year. On we go."

We went up to my room, and sat smoking and yarning away and sipping our drinks, and every now and then cutting a slice off the picture and shoving it in the fire till it was all gone. And what with the cosiness of it and the cheerful blaze, and the comfortable feeling of doing good by stealth, I don't know when I've had a jollier time since the days when we used to brew in my study at school.

We had just put the last slice on when Bill sat up suddenly, and gripped my arm.

"I heard something," he said.

I listened, and, by Jove, I heard something, too. My room was just over the dining-room, and the sound came up to us quite distinctly. Stealthy footsteps, by George! And then a chair falling over.

"There's somebody in the dining-room," I whispered.

There's a certain type of chap who takes a pleasure in positively chivvying trouble. Old Bill's like that. If I had been alone, it would have taken me about three seconds to persuade myself that I hadn't really heard anything after all. I'm a peaceful sort of cove, and believe in living and letting live, and so forth. To old Bill, however, a visit from burglars was pure jam. He was out of his chair in one jump.

"Come on," he said. "Bring the poker."

I brought the tongs as well. I felt like it. Old Bill collared the knife. We crept downstairs.

"We'll fling the door open and make a rush," said Bill.

"Supposing they shoot, old scout?"

"Burglars never shoot," said Bill.

Which was comforting provided the burglars knew it.

Old Bill took a grip of the handle, turned it quickly, and in he went. And then we pulled up sharp, staring.

The room was in darkness except for a feeble splash of light at the near end. Standing on a chair in front of Clarence's "Jocund Spring," holding a candle in one hand and reaching up with a knife in the other, was old Mr. Yeardsley, in bedroom slippers and a grey dressing-gown. He had made a final cut just as we rushed in. Turning at the sound, he stopped, and he and the chair and the candle and the picture came down in a heap together. The candle went out.

"What on earth?" said Bill.

I felt the same. I picked up the candle and lit it, and then a most fearful thing happened. The old man picked himself up, and suddenly collapsed into a chair and began to cry like a child. Of course, I could see it was only the Artistic Temperament, but still, believe me, it was devilish unpleasant. I looked at old Bill. Old Bill looked at me. We shut the door quick, and after that we didn't know what to do. I saw Bill look at the sideboard, and I knew what he was looking for. But we had taken the siphon upstairs, and his ideas of first-aid stopped short at squirting soda-water. We just waited, and presently old Yeardsley switched off, sat up, and began talking with a rush.

"Clarence, my boy, I was tempted. It was that burglary at Dryden Park. It tempted me. It made it all so simple. I knew you would put it down to the same gang, Clarence, my boy. I——"

It seemed to dawn upon him at this point that Clarence was not among those present.

"Clarence?" he said hesitatingly.

"He's in bed," I said.

"In bed! Then he doesn't know? Even now—Young men, I throw myself on your mercy. Don't be hard on me. Listen." He grabbed at Bill, who sidestepped. "I can explain everything—everything."

He gave a gulp.

"You are not artists, you two young men, but I will try to make you understand, make you realise what this picture means to me. I was two years painting it. It is my child. I watched it grow. I loved it. It was part of my life. Nothing would have induced me to sell it. And then Clarence married, and in a mad moment I gave my treasure to him. You cannot understand, you two young men, what agonies I suffered. The thing was done. It was irrevocable. I saw how Clarence valued the picture. I knew that I could never bring myself to ask him for it back. And yet I was lost without it. What could I do? Till this evening I could see no hope. Then came this story of the theft of the Romney from a house quite close to this, and I saw my way. Clarence would never suspect. He would put the robbery down to the same band of criminals who stole the Romney. Once the idea had come, I could not drive it out. I fought against it, but to no avail. At last I yielded, and crept down here to carry out my plan. You found me." He grabbed again, at me this time, and got me by the arm. He had a grip like a lobster. "Young man," he said, "you would not betray me? You would not tell Clarence?"

I was feeling most frightfully sorry for the poor old chap by this time, don't you know, but I thought it would be kindest to give it him straight instead of breaking it by degrees.

"I won't say a word to Clarence, Mr. Yeardsley," I said. "I quite understand your feelings. The Artistic Temperament, and all that sort of thing. I mean—what? *I* know. But I'm afraid—Well, look!"

I went to the door and switched on the electric light, and there, staring him in the face, were the two empty frames. He stood goggling at them in silence. Then he gave a sort of wheezy grunt.

"The gang! The burglars! They *have* been here, and they have taken Clarence's picture!" He paused. "It might have been mine! My Venus!" he whispered It was getting most fearfully painful, you know, but he had to know the truth.

"I'm awfully sorry, you know," I said. "But it *was*."

He started, poor old chap.

"Eh? What do you mean?"

"They *did* take your Venus."

"But I have it here."

I shook my head.

"That's Clarence's 'Jocund Spring,'" I said.

He jumped at it and straightened it out.

"What! What are you talking about? Do you think I don't know my own picture—my child—my Venus. See! My own signature in the corner. Can you read, boy? Look: 'Matthew Yeardsley.' This is *my* picture!"

And—well, by Jove, it *was*, don't you know!

Well, we got him off to bed, him and his infernal Venus, and we settled down to take a steady look at the position of affairs. Bill said it was my fault for getting hold of the wrong picture, and I said it was Bill's fault for fetching me such a crack on the jaw that I couldn't be expected to see what I was getting hold of, and then there was a pretty massive silence for a bit.

"Reggie," said Bill at last, "how exactly do you feel about facing Clarence and Elizabeth at breakfast?"

"Old scout," I said. "I was thinking much the same myself."

"Reggie," said Bill, "I happen to know there's a milk-train leaving Midford at three-fifteen. It isn't what you'd call a flier. It gets to London at about half-past nine. Well—er—in the circumstances, how about it?"

THE AUNT AND THE SLUGGARD

Now that it's all over, I may as well admit that there was a time during the rather funny affair of Rockmetteller Todd when I thought that Jeeves was going to let me down. The man had the appearance of being baffled.

Jeeves is my man, you know. Officially he pulls in his weekly wages for pressing my clothes and all that sort of thing; but actually he's more like what the poet Johnnie called some bird of his acquaintance who was apt to rally round him in times of need—a guide, don't you know; philosopher, if I remember rightly, and—I rather fancy—friend. I rely on him at every turn.

So naturally, when Rocky Todd told me about his aunt, I didn't hesitate. Jeeves was in on the thing from the start.

The affair of Rocky Todd broke loose early one morning of spring. I was in bed, restoring the good old tissues with about nine hours of the dreamless, when the door flew open and somebody prodded me in the lower ribs and began to shake the bedclothes. After blinking a bit and generally pulling myself together, I located Rocky, and my first impression was that it was some horrid dream.

Rocky, you see, lived down on Long Island somewhere, miles away from New York; and not only that, but he had told me himself more than once that he never got up before twelve, and seldom earlier than one. Constitutionally the laziest young devil in America, he had hit on a walk in life which enabled him to go the limit in that direction. He was a poet. At least, he wrote poems when he did anything; but most of his time, as far as I could make out, he spent in a sort of trance. He told me once that he could sit on a fence, watching a worm and wondering what on earth it was up to, for hours at a stretch.

He had his scheme of life worked out to a fine point. About once a month he would take three days writing a few poems; the other three hundred and twenty-nine days of the year he rested. I didn't know there was enough money in poetry to support a chappie, even in the way in which Rocky lived; but it seems that, if you stick to exhortations to young men to lead the strenuous life and don't shove in any rhymes, American editors fight for the stuff. Rocky showed me one of his things once. It began:

Be!
Be!
 The past is dead.
 To-morrow is not born.
  Be to-day!
To-day!
 Be with every nerve,
   With every muscle,
   With every drop of your red blood!
Be!

It was printed opposite the frontispiece of a magazine with a sort of scroll round it, and a picture in the middle of a fairly-nude chappie, with bulging muscles, giving the rising sun the glad eye. Rocky said they gave him a hundred dollars for it, and he stayed in bed till four in the afternoon for over a month.

As regarded the future he was pretty solid, owing to the fact that he had a moneyed aunt tucked away somewhere in Illinois; and, as he had been named Rockmetteller after her, and was her only nephew, his position was pretty sound. He told me that when he did come into the money he meant to do no work at all, except perhaps an occasional poem recommending the young man with life opening out before him, with all its splendid possibilities, to light a pipe and shove his feet upon the mantelpiece.

And this was the man who was prodding me in the ribs in the grey dawn!

"Read this, Bertie!" I could just see that he was waving a letter or something equally foul in my face. "Wake up and read this!"

I can't read before I've had my morning tea and a cigarette. I groped for the bell.

Jeeves came in looking as fresh as a dewy violet. It's a mystery to me how he does it.

"Tea, Jeeves."

"Very good, sir."

He flowed silently out of the room—he always gives you the impression of being some liquid substance when he moves; and I found that Rocky was surging round with his beastly letter again.

"What is it?" I said. "What on earth's the matter?"

"Read it!"

"I can't. I haven't had my tea."

"Well, listen then."

"Who's it from?"

"My aunt."

At this point I fell asleep again. I woke to hear him saying:

"So what on earth am I to do?"

Jeeves trickled in with the tray, like some silent stream meandering over its mossy bed; and I saw daylight.

"Read it again, Rocky, old top," I said. "I want Jeeves to hear it. Mr. Todd's aunt has written him a rather rummy letter, Jeeves, and we want your advice."

"Very good, sir."

He stood in the middle of the room, registering devotion to the cause, and Rocky started again:

"MY DEAR ROCKMETTELLER.—I have been thinking things over for a long while, and I have come to the conclusion that I have been very thoughtless to wait so long before doing what I have made up my mind to do now."

"What do you make of that, Jeeves?"

"It seems a little obscure at present, sir, but no doubt it becomes cleared at a later point in the communication."

"It becomes as clear as mud!" said Rocky.

"Proceed, old scout," I said, champing my bread and butter.

"You know how all my life I have longed to visit New York and see for myself the wonderful gay life of which I have read so much. I fear that now it will be impossible for me to fulfil my dream. I am old and worn out. I seem to have no strength left in me."

"Sad, Jeeves, what?"

"Extremely, sir."

"Sad nothing!" said Rocky. "It's sheer laziness. I went to see her last Christmas and she was bursting with health. Her doctor told me himself that there was nothing wrong with her whatever. But she will insist that she's a hopeless invalid, so he has to agree with her. She's got a fixed idea that the trip to New York would kill her; so, though it's been her ambition all her life to come here, she stays where she is."

"Rather like the chappie whose heart was 'in the Highlands a-chasing of the deer,' Jeeves?"

"The cases are in some respects parallel, sir."

"Carry on, Rocky, dear boy."

"So I have decided that, if I cannot enjoy all the marvels of the city myself, I can at least enjoy them through you. I suddenly thought of this yesterday after reading a beautiful poem in the Sunday paper about a young man who had longed all his life for a certain thing and won it in the end only when he was too old to enjoy it. It was very sad, and it touched me."

"A thing," interpolated Rocky bitterly, "that I've not been able to do in ten years."

"As you know, you will have my money when I am gone; but until now I have never been able to see my way to giving you an allowance. I have now decided to do so—on one condition. I have written to a firm of lawyers in New York, giving them instructions to pay you quite a substantial sum each month. My one condition is that you live in New York and enjoy yourself as I have always wished to do. I want you to be my representative, to spend this money for me as I should do myself. I want you to plunge into the gay, prismatic life of New York. I want you to be the life and soul of brilliant supper parties.

"Above all, I want you—indeed, I insist on this—to write me letters at least once a week giving me a full description of all you are doing and all that is going on in the city, so that I may enjoy at second-hand what my wretched health prevents my enjoying for myself. Remember that I shall expect full details, and that no detail is too trivial to interest.—Your affectionate Aunt,

"ISABEL ROCKMETTELLER."

"What about it?" said Rocky.

"What about it?" I said.

"Yes. What on earth am I going to do?"

It was only then that I really got on to the extremely rummy attitude of the chappie, in view of the fact that a quite unexpected mess of the right stuff had suddenly descended on him from a blue sky. To my mind it was an occasion for the beaming smile and the joyous whoop; yet here the man was, looking and talking as if Fate had swung on his solar plexus. It amazed me.

"Aren't you bucked?" I said.

"Bucked!"

"If I were in your place I should be frightfully braced. I consider this pretty soft for you."

He gave a kind of yelp, stared at me for a moment, and then began to talk of New York in a way that reminded me of Jimmy Mundy, the reformer chappie. Jimmy had just come to New York on a hit-the-trail campaign, and I had popped in at the Garden a couple of days before, for half an hour or so, to hear him. He had certainly told New York some pretty straight things about itself, having apparently taken a dislike to the place, but, by Jove, you know, dear old Rocky made him look like a publicity agent for the old metrop.!

"Pretty soft!" he cried. "To have to come and live in New York! To have to leave my little cottage and take a stuffy, smelly, over-heated hole of an apartment in this Heaven-forsaken, festering Gehenna. To have to mix night after night with a mob who think that life is a sort of St. Vitus's dance, and imagine that they're having a good time because they're making enough noise for six and drinking too much for ten. I loathe New York, Bertie. I wouldn't come near the place if I hadn't got to see editors occasionally. There's a blight on it. It's got moral delirium tremens. It's the limit. The very thought of staying more than a day in it makes me sick. And you call this thing pretty soft for me!"

I felt rather like Lot's friends must have done when they dropped in for a quiet chat and their genial host began to criticise the Cities of the Plain. I had no idea old Rocky could be so eloquent.

"It would kill me to have to live in New York," he went on. "To have to share the air with six million people! To have to wear stiff collars and decent clothes all the time! To——" He started. "Good Lord! I suppose I should have to dress for dinner in the evenings. What a ghastly notion!"

I was shocked, absolutely shocked.

"My dear chap!" I said reproachfully.

"Do you dress for dinner every night, Bertie?"

"Jeeves," I said coldly. The man was still standing like a statue by the door. "How many suits of evening clothes have I?"

"We have three suits full of evening dress, sir; two dinner jackets——"

"Three."

"For practical purposes two only, sir. If you remember we cannot wear the third. We have also seven white waistcoats."

"And shirts?"

"Four dozen, sir."

"And white ties?"

"The first two shallow shelves in the chest of drawers are completely filled with our white ties, sir."

I turned to Rocky.

"You see?"

The chappie writhed like an electric fan.

"I won't do it! I can't do it! I'll be hanged if I'll do it! How on earth can I dress up like that? Do you realize that most days I don't get out of my pyjamas till five in the afternoon, and then I just put on an old sweater?"

I saw Jeeves wince, poor chap! This sort of revelation shocked his finest feelings.

"Then, what are you going to do about it?" I said.

"That's what I want to know."

"You might write and explain to your aunt."

"I might—if I wanted her to get round to her lawyer's in two rapid leaps and cut me out of her will."

I saw his point.

"What do you suggest, Jeeves?" I said.

Jeeves cleared his throat respectfully.

"The crux of the matter would appear to be, sir, that Mr. Todd is obliged by the conditions under which the money is delivered into his possession to write Miss Rockmetteller long and detailed letters relating to his movements, and the only method by which this can be accomplished, if Mr. Todd adheres to his expressed intention of remaining in the country, is for Mr. Todd to induce some second party to gather the actual experiences which Miss Rockmetteller wishes reported to her, and to convey these to him in the shape of a careful report, on which it would be possible for him, with the aid of his imagination, to base the suggested correspondence."

Having got which off the old diaphragm, Jeeves was silent. Rocky looked at me in a helpless sort of way. He hasn't been brought up on Jeeves as I have, and he isn't on to his curves.

"Could he put it a little clearer, Bertie?" he said. "I thought at the start it was going to make sense, but it kind of flickered. What's the idea?"

"My dear old man, perfectly simple. I knew we could stand on Jeeves. All you've got to do is to get somebody to go round the town for you and take a few notes, and then you work the notes up into letters. That's it, isn't it, Jeeves?"

"Precisely, sir."

The light of hope gleamed in Rocky's eyes. He looked at Jeeves in a startled way, dazed by the man's vast intellect.

"But who would do it?" he said. "It would have to be a pretty smart sort of man, a man who would notice things."

"Jeeves!" I said. "Let Jeeves do it."

"But would he?"

"You would do it, wouldn't you, Jeeves?"

For the first time in our long connection I observed Jeeves almost smile. The corner of his mouth curved quite a quarter of an inch, and for a moment his eye ceased to look like a meditative fish's.

"I should be delighted to oblige, sir. As a matter of fact, I have already visited some of New York's places of interest on my evening out, and it would be most enjoyable to make a practice of the pursuit."

"Fine! I know exactly what your aunt wants to hear about, Rocky. She wants an earful of cabaret stuff. The place you ought to go to first, Jeeves, is Reigelheimer's. It's on Forty-second Street. Anybody will show you the way."

Jeeves shook his head.

"Pardon me, sir. People are no longer going to Reigelheimer's. The place at the moment is Frolics on the Roof."

"You see?" I said to Rocky. "Leave it to Jeeves. He knows."

It isn't often that you find an entire group of your fellow-humans happy in this world; but our little circle was certainly an example of the fact that it can be done. We were all full of beans. Everything went absolutely right from the start.

Jeeves was happy, partly because he loves to exercise his giant brain, and partly because he was having a corking time among the bright lights. I saw him one night at the Midnight Revels. He was sitting at a table on the edge of the dancing floor, doing himself remarkably well with a fat cigar and a bottle of the best. I'd never imagined he could look so nearly human. His face wore an expression of austere benevolence, and he was making notes in a small book.

As for the rest of us, I was feeling pretty good, because I was fond of old Rocky and glad to be able to do him a good turn. Rocky was perfectly contented, because he was still able to sit on fences in his pyjamas and watch worms. And, as for the aunt, she seemed tickled to death. She was getting Broadway at pretty long range, but it seemed to be hitting her just right. I read one of her letters to Rocky, and it was full of life.

But then Rocky's letters, based on Jeeves's notes, were enough to buck anybody up. It was rummy when you came to think of it. There was I, loving the life, while the mere mention of it gave Rocky a tired feeling; yet here is a letter I wrote to a pal of mine in London:

"DEAR FREDDIE,—Well, here I am in New York. It's not a bad place. I'm not having a bad time. Everything's pretty all right. The cabarets aren't bad. Don't know when I shall be back. How's everybody? Cheer-o!—Yours,

"BERTIE.

"PS.—Seen old Ted lately?"

Not that I cared about Ted; but if I hadn't dragged him in I couldn't have got the confounded thing on to the second page.

Now here's old Rocky on exactly the same subject:

"DEAREST AUNT ISABEL,—How can I ever thank you enough for giving me the opportunity to live in this astounding city! New York seems more wonderful every day.

"Fifth Avenue is at its best, of course, just now. The dresses are magnificent!"

Wads of stuff about the dresses. I didn't know Jeeves was such an authority.

"I was out with some of the crowd at the Midnight Revels the other night. We took in a show first, after a little dinner at a new place on Forty-third Street. We were quite a gay party. Georgie Cohan looked in about midnight and got off a good one about Willie Collier. Fred Stone could only stay a minute, but Doug. Fairbanks did all sorts of stunts and made us roar. Diamond Jim Brady was there, as usual, and Laurette Taylor showed up with a party. The show at the Revels is quite good. I am enclosing a programme.

"Last night a few of us went round to Frolics on the Roof——"

And so on and so forth, yards of it. I suppose it's the artistic temperament or something. What I mean is, it's easier for a chappie who's used to writing poems and that sort of tosh to put a bit of a punch into a letter than it is for a chappie like me. Anyway, there's no doubt that Rocky's correspondence was hot stuff. I called Jeeves in and congratulated him.

"Jeeves, you're a wonder!"

"Thank you, sir."

"How you notice everything at these places beats me. I couldn't tell you a thing about them, except that I've had a good time."

"It's just a knack, sir."

"Well, Mr. Todd's letters ought to brace Miss Rockmetteller all right, what?"

"Undoubtedly, sir," agreed Jeeves.

And, by Jove, they did! They certainly did, by George! What I mean to say is, I was sitting in the apartment one afternoon, about a month after the thing had started, smoking a cigarette and resting the old bean, when the door opened and the voice of Jeeves burst the silence like a bomb.

It wasn't that he spoke loud. He has one of those soft, soothing voices that slide through the atmosphere like the note of a far-off sheep. It was what he said made me leap like a young gazelle.

"Miss Rockmetteller!"

And in came a large, solid female.

The situation floored me. I'm not denying it. Hamlet must have felt much as I did when his father's ghost bobbed up in the fairway. I'd come to look on Rocky's aunt as such a permanency at her own home that it didn't seem possible that she could really be here in New York. I stared at her. Then I looked at Jeeves. He was standing there in an attitude of dignified detachment, the chump, when, if ever he should have been rallying round the young master, it was now.

Rocky's aunt looked less like an invalid than any one I've ever seen, except my Aunt Agatha. She had a good deal of Aunt Agatha about her, as a matter of fact. She looked as if she might be deucedly dangerous if put upon; and something seemed to tell me that she would certainly regard herself as put upon if she ever found out the game which poor old Rocky had been pulling on her.

"Good afternoon," I managed to say.

"How do you do?" she said. "Mr. Cohan?"

"Er—no."

"Mr. Fred Stone?"

"Not absolutely. As a matter of fact, my name's Wooster—Bertie Wooster."

She seemed disappointed. The fine old name of Wooster appeared to mean nothing in her life.

"Isn't Rockmetteller home?" she said. "Where is he?"

She had me with the first shot. I couldn't think of anything to say. I couldn't tell her that Rocky was down in the country, watching worms.

There was the faintest flutter of sound in the background. It was the respectful cough with which Jeeves announces that he is about to speak without having been spoken to.

"If you remember, sir, Mr. Todd went out in the automobile with a party in the afternoon."

"So he did, Jeeves; so he did," I said, looking at my watch. "Did he say when he would be back?"

"He gave me to understand, sir, that he would be somewhat late in returning."

He vanished; and the aunt took the chair which I'd forgotten to offer her. She looked at me in rather a rummy way. It was a nasty look. It made me feel as if I were something the dog had brought in and intended to bury later on, when he had time. My own Aunt Agatha, back in England, has looked at me in exactly the same way many a time, and it never fails to make my spine curl.

"You seem very much at home here, young man. Are you a great friend of Rockmetteller's?"

"Oh, yes, rather!"

She frowned as if she had expected better things of old Rocky.

"Well, you need to be," she said, "the way you treat his flat as your own!"

I give you my word, this quite unforeseen slam simply robbed me of the power of speech. I'd been looking on myself in the light of the dashing host, and suddenly to be treated as an intruder jarred me. It wasn't, mark you, as if she had spoken in a way to suggest that she considered my presence in the place as an ordinary social call. She obviously looked on me as a cross between a burglar and the plumber's man come to fix the leak in the bathroom. It hurt her—my being there.

At this juncture, with the conversation showing every sign of being about to die in awful agonies, an idea came to me. Tea—the good old stand-by.

"Would you care for a cup of tea?" I said.

"Tea?"

She spoke as if she had never heard of the stuff.

"Nothing like a cup after a journey," I said. "Bucks you up! Puts a bit of zip into you. What I mean is, restores you, and so on, don't you know. I'll go and tell Jeeves."

I tottered down the passage to Jeeves's lair. The man was reading the evening paper as if he hadn't a care in the world.

"Jeeves," I said, "we want some tea."

"Very good, sir."

"I say, Jeeves, this is a bit thick, what?"

I wanted sympathy, don't you know—sympathy and kindness. The old nerve centres had had the deuce of a shock.

"She's got the idea this place belongs to Mr. Todd. What on earth put that into her head?"

Jeeves filled the kettle with a restrained dignity.

"No doubt because of Mr. Todd's letters, sir," he said. "It was my suggestion, sir, if you remember, that they should be addressed from this apartment in order that Mr. Todd should appear to possess a good central residence in the city."

I remembered. We had thought it a brainy scheme at the time.

"Well, it's bally awkward, you know, Jeeves. She looks on me as an intruder. By Jove! I suppose she thinks I'm someone who hangs about here, touching Mr. Todd for free meals and borrowing his shirts."

"Yes, sir."

"It's pretty rotten, you know."

"Most disturbing, sir."

"And there's another thing: What are we to do about Mr. Todd? We've got to get him up here as soon as ever we can. When you have brought the tea you had better go out and send him a telegram, telling him to come up by the next train."

"I have already done so, sir. I took the liberty of writing the message and dispatching it by the lift attendant."

"By Jove, you think of everything, Jeeves!"

"Thank you, sir. A little buttered toast with the tea? Just so, sir. Thank you."

I went back to the sitting-room. She hadn't moved an inch. She was still bolt upright on the edge of her chair, gripping her umbrella like a hammer-thrower. She gave me another of those looks as I came in. There was no doubt about it; for some reason she had taken a dislike to me. I suppose because I wasn't George M. Cohan. It was a bit hard on a chap.

"This is a surprise, what?" I said, after about five minutes' restful silence, trying to crank the conversation up again.

"What is a surprise?"

"Your coming here, don't you know, and so on."

She raised her eyebrows and drank me in a bit more through her glasses.

"Why is it surprising that I should visit my only nephew?" she said.

Put like that, of course, it did seem reasonable.

"Oh, rather," I said. "Of course! Certainly. What I mean is——"

Jeeves projected himself into the room with the tea. I was jolly glad to see him. There's nothing like having a bit of business arranged for one when one isn't certain of one's lines. With the teapot to fool about with I felt happier.

"Tea, tea, tea—what? What?" I said.

It wasn't what I had meant to say. My idea had been to be a good deal more formal, and so on. Still, it covered the situation. I poured her out a cup. She sipped it and put the cup down with a shudder.

"Do you mean to say, young man," she said frostily, "that you expect me to drink this stuff?"

"Rather! Bucks you up, you know."

"What do you mean by the expression 'Bucks you up'?"

"Well, makes you full of beans, you know. Makes you fizz."

"I don't understand a word you say. You're English, aren't you?"

I admitted it. She didn't say a word. And somehow she did it in a way that made it worse than if she had spoken for hours. Somehow it was brought home to me that she didn't like Englishmen, and that if she had had to meet an Englishman, I was the one she'd have chosen last.

Conversation languished again after that.

Then I tried again. I was becoming more convinced every moment that you can't make a real lively *salon* with a couple of people, especially if one of them lets it go a word at a time.

"Are you comfortable at your hotel?" I said.

"At which hotel?"

"The hotel you're staying at."

"I am not staying at an hotel."

"Stopping with friends—what?"

"I am naturally stopping with my nephew."

I didn't get it for the moment; then it hit me.

"What! Here?" I gurgled.

"Certainly! Where else should I go?"

The full horror of the situation rolled over me like a wave. I couldn't see what on earth I was to do. I couldn't explain that this wasn't Rocky's flat without giving the poor old chap away hopelessly, because she would then ask me where he did live, and then he would be right in the soup. I was trying to induce the old bean to recover from the shock and produce some results when she spoke again.

"Will you kindly tell my nephew's man-servant to prepare my room? I wish to lie down."

"Your nephew's man-servant?"

"The man you call Jeeves. If Rockmetteller has gone for an automobile ride, there is no need for you to wait for him. He will naturally wish to be alone with me when he returns."

I found myself tottering out of the room. The thing was too much for me. I crept into Jeeves's den.

"Jeeves!" I whispered.

"Sir?"

"Mix me a b.-and-s., Jeeves. I feel weak."

"Very good, sir."

"This is getting thicker every minute, Jeeves."

"Sir?"

"She thinks you're Mr. Todd's man. She thinks the whole place is his, and everything in it. I don't see what you're to do, except stay on and keep it up. We can't say anything or she'll get on to the whole thing, and I don't want to let Mr. Todd down. By the way, Jeeves, she wants you to prepare her bed."

He looked wounded.

"It is hardly my place, sir——"

"I know—I know. But do it as a personal favour to me. If you come to that, it's hardly my place to be flung out of the flat like this and have to go to an hotel, what?"

"Is it your intention to go to an hotel, sir? What will you do for clothes?"

"Good Lord! I hadn't thought of that. Can you put a few things in a bag when she isn't looking, and sneak them down to me at the St. Aurea?"

"I will endeavour to do so, sir."

"Well, I don't think there's anything more, is there? Tell Mr. Todd where I am when he gets here."

"Very good, sir."

I looked round the place. The moment of parting had come. I felt sad. The whole thing reminded me of one of those melodramas where they drive chappies out of the old homestead into the snow.

"Good-bye, Jeeves," I said.

"Good-bye, sir."

And I staggered out.

You know, I rather think I agree with those poet-and-philosopher Johnnies who insist that a fellow ought to be devilish pleased if he has a bit of trouble. All that stuff about being refined by suffering, you know. Suffering does give a chap a sort of broader and more sympathetic outlook. It helps you to understand other people's misfortunes if you've been through the same thing yourself.

As I stood in my lonely bedroom at the hotel, trying to tie my white tie myself, it struck me for the first time that there must be whole squads of chappies in the world who had to get along without a man to look after them. I'd always thought of Jeeves as a kind of natural phenomenon; but, by Jove! of course, when you come to think of it, there must be quite a lot of fellows who have to press their own clothes themselves and haven't got anybody to bring them tea in the morning, and so on. It was rather a solemn thought, don't you know. I mean to say, ever since then I've been able to appreciate the frightful privations the poor have to stick.

I got dressed somehow. Jeeves hadn't forgotten a thing in his packing. Everything was there, down to the final stud. I'm not sure this didn't make me feel worse. It kind of deepened the pathos. It was like what somebody or other wrote about the touch of a vanished hand.

I had a bit of dinner somewhere and went to a show of some kind; but nothing seemed to make any difference. I simply hadn't the heart to go on to supper anywhere. I just sucked down a whisky-and-soda in the hotel smoking-room and went straight up to bed. I don't know when I've felt so rotten. Somehow I found myself moving about the room softly, as if there had been a death in the family. If I had anybody to talk to I should have talked in a whisper; in fact, when the telephone-bell rang I answered in such a sad, hushed voice that the fellow at the other end of the wire said "Halloa!" five times, thinking he hadn't got me.

It was Rocky. The poor old scout was deeply agitated.

"Bertie! Is that you, Bertie! Oh, gosh? I'm having a time!"

"Where are you speaking from?"

"The Midnight Revels. We've been here an hour, and I think we're a fixture for the night. I've told Aunt Isabel I've gone out to call up a friend to join us. She's glued to a chair, with this-is-the-life written all over her, taking it in through the pores. She loves it, and I'm nearly crazy."

"Tell me all, old top," I said.

"A little more of this," he said, "and I shall sneak quietly off to the river and end it all. Do you mean to say you go through this sort of thing every night, Bertie, and enjoy it? It's simply infernal! I was just snatching a wink of sleep behind the bill of fare just now when about a million yelling girls swooped down, with toy balloons. There are two orchestras here, each trying to see if it can't play louder than the other. I'm a mental and physical wreck. When your telegram arrived I was just lying down for a quiet pipe, with a sense of absolute peace stealing over me. I had to get dressed and sprint two miles to catch the train. It nearly gave me heart-failure; and on top of that I almost got brain fever inventing lies to tell Aunt Isabel. And then I had to cram myself into these confounded evening clothes of yours."

I gave a sharp wail of agony. It hadn't struck me till then that Rocky was depending on my wardrobe to see him through.

"You'll ruin them!"

"I hope so," said Rocky, in the most unpleasant way. His troubles seemed to have had the worst effect on his character. "I should like to get back at them somehow; they've given me a bad enough time. They're about three sizes too small, and something's apt to give at any moment. I wish to goodness it would, and give me a chance to breathe. I haven't breathed since half-past seven. Thank Heaven, Jeeves managed to get out and buy me a collar that fitted, or I should be a strangled corpse by now! It was touch and go till the stud broke. Bertie, this is pure Hades! Aunt Isabel keeps on urging me to dance. How on earth can I dance when I don't know a soul to dance with? And how the deuce could I, even if I knew every girl in the place? It's taking big chances even to move in these trousers. I had to tell her I've hurt my ankle. She keeps asking me when Cohan and Stone are going to turn up; and it's simply a question of time before she discovers that Stone is sitting two tables away. Something's got to be done, Bertie! You've got to think up some way of getting me out of this mess. It was you who got me into it."

"Me! What do you mean?"

"Well, Jeeves, then. It's all the same. It was you who suggested leaving it to Jeeves. It was those letters I wrote from his notes that did the mischief. I made them too good! My aunt's just been telling me about it. She says she had resigned herself to ending her life where she was, and then my letters began to arrive, describing the joys of New York; and they stimulated her to such an extent that she pulled herself together and made the trip. She seems to think she's had some miraculous kind of faith cure. I tell you I can't stand it, Bertie! It's got to end!"

"Can't Jeeves think of anything?"

"No. He just hangs round saying: 'Most disturbing, sir!' A fat lot of help that is!"

"Well, old lad," I said, "after all, it's far worse for me than it is for you. You've got a comfortable home and Jeeves. And you're saving a lot of money."

"Saving money? What do you mean—saving money?"

"Why, the allowance your aunt was giving you. I suppose she's paying all the expenses now, isn't she?"

"Certainly she is; but she's stopped the allowance. She wrote the lawyers tonight. She says that, now she's in New York, there is no necessity for it to go on, as we shall always be together, and it's simpler for her to look after that end of it. I tell you, Bertie, I've examined the darned cloud with a microscope, and if it's got a silver lining it's some little dissembler!"

"But, Rocky, old top, it's too bally awful! You've no notion of what I'm going through in this beastly hotel, without Jeeves. I must get back to the flat."

"Don't come near the flat."

"But it's my own flat."

"I can't help that. Aunt Isabel doesn't like you. She asked me what you did for a living. And when I told her you didn't do anything she said she thought as much, and that you were a typical specimen of a useless and decaying aristocracy. So if you think you have made a hit, forget it. Now I must be going back, or she'll be coming out here after me. Good-bye."

Next morning Jeeves came round. It was all so home-like when he floated noiselessly into the room that I nearly broke down.

"Good morning, sir," he said. "I have brought a few more of your personal belongings."

He began to unstrap the suit-case he was carrying.

"Did you have any trouble sneaking them away?"

"It was not easy, sir. I had to watch my chance. Miss Rockmetteller is a remarkably alert lady."

"You know, Jeeves, say what you like—this is a bit thick, isn't it?"

"The situation is certainly one that has never before come under my notice, sir. I have brought the heather-mixture suit, as the climatic conditions are congenial.

To-morrow, if not prevented, I will endeavour to add the brown lounge with the faint green twill."

"It can't go on—this sort of thing—Jeeves."

"We must hope for the best, sir."

"Can't you think of anything to do?"

"I have been giving the matter considerable thought, sir, but so far without success. I am placing three silk shirts—the dove-coloured, the light blue, and the mauve—in the first long drawer, sir."

"You don't mean to say you can't think of anything, Jeeves?"

"For the moment, sir, no. You will find a dozen handkerchiefs and the tan socks in the upper drawer on the left." He strapped the suit-case and put it on a chair. "A curious lady, Miss Rockmetteller, sir."

"You understate it, Jeeves."

He gazed meditatively out of the window.

"In many ways, sir, Miss Rockmetteller reminds me of an aunt of mine who resides in the south-east portion of London. Their temperaments are much alike. My aunt has the same taste for the pleasures of the great city. It is a passion with her to ride in hansom cabs, sir. Whenever the family take their eyes off her she escapes from the house and spends the day riding about in cabs. On several occasions she has broken into the children's savings bank to secure the means to enable her to gratify this desire."

"I love to have these little chats with you about your female relatives, Jeeves," I said coldly, for I felt that the man had let me down, and I was fed up with him. "But I don't see what all this has got to do with my trouble."

"I beg your pardon, sir. I am leaving a small assortment of neckties on the mantelpiece, sir, for you to select according to your preference. I should recommend the blue with the red domino pattern, sir."

Then he streamed imperceptibly toward the door and flowed silently out.

I've often heard that chappies, after some great shock or loss, have a habit, after they've been on the floor for a while wondering what hit them, of picking themselves up and piecing themselves together, and sort of taking a whirl at beginning a new life. Time, the great healer, and Nature, adjusting itself, and so on and so forth. There's a lot in it. I know, because in my own case, after a day or two of what you might call prostration, I began to recover. The frightful loss of Jeeves made any thought of pleasure more or less a mockery, but at least I found that I was able to have a dash at enjoying life again. What I mean is, I braced up to the extent of going round the cabarets once more, so as to try to forget, if only for the moment.

New York's a small place when it comes to the part of it that wakes up just as the rest is going to bed, and it wasn't long before my tracks began to cross old Rocky's. I saw him once at Peale's, and again at Frolics on the roof. There wasn't anybody with him either time except the aunt, and, though he was trying to look as if he had struck the ideal life, it wasn't difficult for me, knowing the circumstances, to see that beneath the mask the poor chap was suffering. My heart bled for the fellow. At least, what there was of it that wasn't bleeding for myself bled for him. He had the air of one who was about to crack under the strain.

It seemed to me that the aunt was looking slightly upset also. I took it that she was beginning to wonder when the celebrities were going to surge round, and what had suddenly become of all those wild, careless spirits Rocky used to mix with in his letters. I didn't blame her. I had only read a couple of his letters, but they certainly gave the impression that poor old Rocky was by way of being the hub of New York night life, and that, if by any chance he failed to show up at a cabaret, the management said: "What's the use?" and put up the shutters.

The next two nights I didn't come across them, but the night after that I was sitting by myself at the Maison Pierre when somebody tapped me on the shoulder-blade, and I found Rocky standing beside me, with a sort of mixed expression of wistfulness and apoplexy on his face. How the chappie had contrived to wear my evening clothes so many times without disaster was a mystery to me. He confided later that early in the proceedings he had slit the waistcoat up the back and that that had helped a bit.

For a moment I had the idea that he had managed to get away from his aunt for the evening; but, looking past him, I saw that she was in again. She was at a table over by the wall, looking at me as if I were something the management ought to be complained to about.

"Bertie, old scout," said Rocky, in a quiet, sort of crushed voice, "we've always been pals, haven't we? I mean, you know I'd do you a good turn if you asked me?"

"My dear old lad," I said. The man had moved me.

"Then, for Heaven's sake, come over and sit at our table for the rest of the evening."

Well, you know, there are limits to the sacred claims of friendship.

"My dear chap," I said, "you know I'd do anything in reason; but——"

"You must come, Bertie. You've got to. Something's got to be done to divert her mind. She's brooding about something. She's been like that for the last two days. I think she's beginning to suspect. She can't understand why we never seem to meet anyone I know at these joints. A few nights ago I happened to run into two newspaper men I used to know fairly well. That kept me going for a while. I introduced them to Aunt Isabel as David Belasco and Jim Corbett, and it went well. But the effect has worn off now, and she's beginning to wonder again. Something's got to be done, or she will find out everything, and if she does I'd take a nickel for my chance of getting a cent from her later on. So, for the love of Mike, come across to our table and help things along."

I went along. One has to rally round a pal in distress. Aunt Isabel was sitting bolt upright, as usual. It certainly did seem as if she had lost a bit of the zest with which she had started out to explore Broadway. She looked as if she had been thinking a good deal about rather unpleasant things.

"You've met Bertie Wooster, Aunt Isabel?" said Rocky.

"I have."

There was something in her eye that seemed to say:

"Out of a city of six million people, why did you pick on me?"

"Take a seat, Bertie. What'll you have?" said Rocky.

And so the merry party began. It was one of those jolly, happy, bread-crumbling parties where you cough twice before you speak, and then decide not to say it after all. After we had had an hour of this wild dissipation, Aunt Isabel said she wanted to go home. In the light of what Rocky had been telling me, this struck me as sinister. I had gathered that at the beginning of her visit she had had to be dragged home with ropes.

It must have hit Rocky the same way, for he gave me a pleading look.

"You'll come along, won't you, Bertie, and have a drink at the flat?"

I had a feeling that this wasn't in the contract, but there wasn't anything to be done. It seemed brutal to leave the poor chap alone with the woman, so I went along.

Right from the start, from the moment we stepped into the taxi, the feeling began to grow that something was about to break loose. A massive silence prevailed in the corner where the aunt sat, and, though Rocky, balancing himself on the little seat in front, did his best to supply dialogue, we weren't a chatty party.

I had a glimpse of Jeeves as we went into the flat, sitting in his lair, and I wished I could have called to him to rally round. Something told me that I was about to need him.

The stuff was on the table in the sitting-room. Rocky took up the decanter.

"Say when, Bertie."

"Stop!" barked the aunt, and he dropped it.

I caught Rocky's eye as he stooped to pick up the ruins. It was the eye of one who sees it coming.

"Leave it there, Rockmetteller!" said Aunt Isabel; and Rocky left it there.

"The time has come to speak," she said. "I cannot stand idly by and see a young man going to perdition!"

Poor old Rocky gave a sort of gurgle, a kind of sound rather like the whisky had made running out of the decanter on to my carpet.

"Eh?" he said, blinking.

The aunt proceeded.

"The fault," she said, "was mine. I had not then seen the light. But now my eyes are open. I see the hideous mistake I have made. I shudder at the thought of the wrong I did you, Rockmetteller, by urging you into contact with this wicked city."

I saw Rocky grope feebly for the table. His fingers touched it, and a look of relief came into the poor chappie's face. I understood his feelings.

"But when I wrote you that letter, Rockmetteller, instructing you to go to the city and live its life, I had not had the privilege of hearing Mr. Mundy speak on the subject of New York."

"Jimmy Mundy!" I cried.

You know how it is sometimes when everything seems all mixed up and you suddenly get a clue. When she mentioned Jimmy Mundy I began to understand more or less what had happened. I'd seen it happen before. I remember, back in England, the man I had before Jeeves sneaked off to a meeting on his evening out and came back and denounced me in front of a crowd of chappies I was giving a bit of supper to as a moral leper.

The aunt gave me a withering up and down.

"Yes; Jimmy Mundy!" she said. "I am surprised at a man of your stamp having heard of him. There is no music, there are no drunken, dancing men, no shameless, flaunting women at his meetings; so for you they would have no attraction. But for others, less dead in sin, he has his message. He has come to save New York from itself; to force it—in his picturesque phrase—to hit the trail. It was three days ago, Rockmetteller, that I first heard him. It was an accident that took me to his meeting. How often in this life a mere accident may shape our whole future!

"You had been called away by that telephone message from Mr. Belasco; so you could not take me to the Hippodrome, as we had arranged. I asked your manservant, Jeeves, to take me there. The man has very little intelligence. He seems to have misunderstood me. I am thankful that he did. He took me to what I subsequently learned was Madison Square Garden, where Mr. Mundy is holding his meetings. He escorted me to a seat and then left me. And it was not till the meeting had begun that I discovered the mistake which had been made. My seat was in the middle of a row. I could not leave without inconveniencing a great many people, so I remained."

She gulped.

"Rockmetteller, I have never been so thankful for anything else. Mr. Mundy was wonderful! He was like some prophet of old, scourging the sins of the people. He leaped about in a frenzy of inspiration till I feared he would do himself an injury. Sometimes he expressed himself in a somewhat odd manner, but every word carried conviction. He showed me New York in its true colours. He showed me the vanity and wickedness of sitting in gilded haunts of vice, eating lobster when decent people should be in bed.

"He said that the tango and the fox-trot were devices of the devil to drag people down into the Bottomless Pit. He said that there was more sin in ten minutes with a negro banjo orchestra than in all the ancient revels of Nineveh and Babylon. And when he stood on one leg and pointed right at where I was sitting and shouted, 'This means you!' I could have sunk through the floor. I came away a changed woman. Surely you must have noticed the change in me, Rockmetteller? You must have seen that I was no longer the careless, thoughtless person who had urged you to dance in those places of wickedness?"

Rocky was holding on to the table as if it was his only friend.

"Y-yes," he stammered; "I—I thought something was wrong."

"Wrong? Something was right! Everything was right! Rockmetteller, it is not too late for you to be saved. You have only sipped of the evil cup. You have not drained it. It will be hard at first, but you will find that you can do it if you fight with a stout heart against the glamour and fascination of this dreadful city. Won't you, for my sake, try, Rockmetteller? Won't you go back to the country to-morrow and begin the struggle? Little by little, if you use your will——"

I can't help thinking it must have been that word "will" that roused dear old Rocky like a trumpet call. It must have brought home to him the realisation that a miracle had come off and saved him from being cut out of Aunt Isabel's. At any rate, as she said it he perked up, let go of the table, and faced her with gleaming eyes.

"Do you want me to go back to the country, Aunt Isabel?"

"Yes."

"Not to live in the country?"

"Yes, Rockmetteller."

"Stay in the country all the time, do you mean? Never come to New York?"

"Yes, Rockmetteller; I mean just that. It is the only way. Only there can you be safe from temptation. Will you do it, Rockmetteller? Will you—for my sake?"

Rocky grabbed the table again. He seemed to draw a lot of encouragement from that table.

"I will!" he said.

"Jeeves," I said. It was next day, and I was back in the old flat, lying in the old arm-chair, with my feet upon the good old table. I had just come from seeing dear old Rocky off to his country cottage, and an hour before he had seen his aunt off to whatever hamlet it was that she was the curse of; so we were alone at last. "Jeeves, there's no place like home—what?"

"Very true, sir."

"The jolly old roof-tree, and all that sort of thing—what?"

"Precisely, sir."

I lit another cigarette.

"Jeeves."

"Sir?"

"Do you know, at one point in the business I really thought you were baffled."

"Indeed, sir?"

"When did you get the idea of taking Miss Rockmetteller to the meeting? It was pure genius!"

"Thank you, sir. It came to me a little suddenly, one morning when I was thinking of my aunt, sir."

"Your aunt? The hansom cab one?"

"Yes, sir. I recollected that, whenever we observed one of her attacks coming on, we used to send for the clergyman of the parish. We always found that if he talked to her a while of higher things it diverted her mind from hansom cabs. It occurred to me that the same treatment might prove efficacious in the case of Miss Rockmetteller."

I was stunned by the man's resource.

"It's brain," I said; "pure brain! What do you do to get like that, Jeeves? I believe you must eat a lot of fish, or something. Do you eat a lot of fish, Jeeves?"

"No, sir."

"Oh, well, then, it's just a gift, I take it; and if you aren't born that way there's no use worrying."

"Precisely, sir," said Jeeves. "If I might make the suggestion, sir, I should not continue to wear your present tie. The green shade gives you a slightly bilious air. I should strongly advocate the blue with the red domino pattern instead, sir."

"All right, Jeeves." I said humbly. "You know!"

THE END

RIGHT HO, JEEVES

To

**RAYMOND NEEDHAM, K.C.
WITH AFFECTION AND
ADMIRATION**

-1-

"Jeeves," I said, "may I speak frankly?"

"Certainly, sir."

"What I have to say may wound you."

"Not at all, sir."

"Well, then——"

No—wait. Hold the line a minute. I've gone off the rails.

I don't know if you have had the same experience, but the snag I always come up against when I'm telling a story is this dashed difficult problem of where to begin it. It's a thing you don't want to go wrong over, because one false step and you're sunk. I mean, if you fool about too long at the start, trying to establish atmosphere, as they call it, and all that sort of rot, you fail to grip and the customers walk out on you.

Get off the mark, on the other hand, like a scalded cat, and your public is at a loss. It simply raises its eyebrows, and can't make out what you're talking about.

And in opening my report of the complex case of Gussie Fink-Nottle, Madeline Bassett, my Cousin Angela, my Aunt Dahlia, my Uncle Thomas, young Tuppy Glossop and the cook, Anatole, with the above spot of dialogue, I see that I have made the second of these two floaters.

I shall have to hark back a bit. And taking it for all in all and weighing this against that, I suppose the affair may be said to have had its inception, if inception is the word I want, with that visit of mine to Cannes. If I hadn't gone to Cannes, I shouldn't have met the Bassett or bought that white mess jacket, and Angela wouldn't have met her shark, and Aunt Dahlia wouldn't have played baccarat.

Yes, most decidedly, Cannes was the *point d'appui.*

Right ho, then. Let me marshal my facts.

I went to Cannes—leaving Jeeves behind, he having intimated that he did not wish to miss Ascot—round about the beginning of June. With me travelled my Aunt Dahlia and her daughter Angela. Tuppy Glossop, Angela's betrothed, was to have been of the party, but at the last moment couldn't get away. Uncle Tom, Aunt Dahlia's husband, remained at home, because he can't stick the South of France at any price.

So there you have the layout—Aunt Dahlia, Cousin Angela and self off to Cannes round about the beginning of June.

All pretty clear so far, what?

We stayed at Cannes about two months, and except for the fact that Aunt Dahlia lost her shirt at baccarat and Angela nearly got inhaled by a shark while aquaplaning, a pleasant time was had by all.

On July the twenty-fifth, looking bronzed and fit, I accompanied aunt and child back to London. At seven p.m. on July the twenty-sixth we alighted at Victoria. And at seven-twenty or thereabouts we parted with mutual expressions of esteem—they to shove off in Aunt Dahlia's car to Brinkley Court, her place in Worcestershire, where they were expecting to entertain Tuppy in a day or two; I to go to the flat, drop my luggage, clean up a bit, and put on the soup and fish preparatory to pushing round to the Drones for a bite of dinner.

And it was while I was at the flat, towelling the torso after a much-needed rinse, that Jeeves, as we chatted of this and that—picking up the threads, as it were—suddenly brought the name of Gussie Fink-Nottle into the conversation.

As I recall it, the dialogue ran something as follows:

SELF: Well, Jeeves, here we are, what?

JEEVES: Yes, sir.

SELF: I mean to say, home again.

JEEVES: Precisely, sir.

SELF: Seems ages since I went away.

JEEVES: Yes, sir.

SELF: Have a good time at Ascot?

JEEVES: Most agreeable, sir.

SELF: Win anything?

JEEVES: Quite a satisfactory sum, thank you, sir.

SELF: Good. Well, Jeeves, what news on the Rialto? Anybody been phoning or calling or anything during my abs.?

JEEVES: Mr. Fink-Nottle, sir, has been a frequent caller.

I stared. Indeed, it would not be too much to say that I gaped.

"Mr. Fink-Nottle?"

"Yes, sir."

"You don't mean Mr. Fink-Nottle?"

"Yes, sir."

"But Mr. Fink-Nottle's not in London?"

"Yes, sir."

"Well, I'm blowed."

And I'll tell you why I was blowed. I found it scarcely possible to give credence to his statement. This Fink-Nottle, you see, was one of those freaks you come across from time to time during life's journey who can't stand London. He lived year in and year out, covered with moss, in a remote village down in Lincolnshire, never coming up even for the Eton and Harrow match. And when I asked him once if he didn't find the time hang a bit heavy on his hands, he said, no, because he had a pond in his garden and studied the habits of newts.

I couldn't imagine what could have brought the chap up to the great city. I would have been prepared to bet that as long as the supply of newts didn't give out, nothing could have shifted him from that village of his.

"Are you sure?"

"Yes, sir."

"You got the name correctly? Fink-Nottle?"

"Yes, sir."

"Well, it's the most extraordinary thing. It must be five years since he was in London. He makes no secret of the fact that the place gives him the pip. Until now, he has always stayed glued to the country, completely surrounded by newts."

"Sir?"

"Newts, Jeeves. Mr. Fink-Nottle has a strong newt complex. You must have heard of newts. Those little sort of lizard things that charge about in ponds."

"Oh, yes, sir. The aquatic members of the family Salamandridae which constitute the genus Molge."

"That's right. Well, Gussie has always been a slave to them. He used to keep them at school."

"I believe young gentlemen frequently do, sir."

"He kept them in his study in a kind of glass-tank arrangement, and pretty niffy the whole thing was, I recall. I suppose one ought to have been able to see what the end would be even then, but you know what boys are. Careless, heedless, busy about our own affairs, we scarcely gave this kink in Gussie's character a thought. We may have exchanged an occasional remark about it taking all sorts to make a world, but nothing more. You can guess the sequel. The trouble spread,"

"Indeed, sir?"

"Absolutely, Jeeves. The craving grew upon him. The newts got him. Arrived at man's estate, he retired to the depths of the country and gave his life up to these dumb chums. I suppose he used to tell himself that he could take them or leave them alone, and then found—too late—that he couldn't."

"It is often the way, sir."

"Too true, Jeeves. At any rate, for the last five years he has been living at this place of his down in Lincolnshire, as confirmed a species-shunning hermit as ever put fresh water in the tank every second day and refused to see a soul. That's why I was so amazed when you told me he had suddenly risen to the surface like this. I still can't believe it. I am inclined to think that there must be some mistake, and that this bird who has been calling here is some different variety of Fink-Nottle. The chap I know wears horn-rimmed spectacles and has a face like a fish. How does that check up with your data?"

"The gentleman who came to the flat wore horn-rimmed spectacles, sir."

"And looked like something on a slab?"

"Possibly there was a certain suggestion of the piscine, sir."

"Then it must be Gussie, I suppose. But what on earth can have brought him up to London?"

"I am in a position to explain that, sir. Mr. Fink-Nottle confided to me his motive in visiting the metropolis. He came because the young lady is here."

"Young lady?"

"Yes, sir."

"You don't mean he's in love?"

"Yes, sir."

"Well, I'm dashed. I'm really dashed. I positively am dashed, Jeeves."

And I was too. I mean to say, a joke's a joke, but there are limits.

Then I found my mind turning to another aspect of this rummy affair. Conceding the fact that Gussie Fink-Nottle, against all the ruling of the form book, might have fallen in love, why should he have been haunting my flat like this? No doubt the occasion was one of those when a fellow needs a friend, but I couldn't see what had made him pick on me.

It wasn't as if he and I were in any way bosom. We had seen a lot of each other at one time, of course, but in the last two years I hadn't had so much as a post card from him.

I put all this to Jeeves:

"Odd, his coming to me. Still, if he did, he did. No argument about that. It must have been a nasty jar for the poor perisher when he found I wasn't here."

"No, sir. Mr. Fink-Nottle did not call to see you, sir."

"Pull yourself together, Jeeves. You've just told me that this is what he has been doing, and assiduously, at that."

"It was I with whom he was desirous of establishing communication, sir."

"You? But I didn't know you had ever met him."

"I had not had that pleasure until he called here, sir. But it appears that Mr. Sipperley, a fellow student of whom Mr. Fink-Nottle had been at the university, recommended him to place his affairs in my hands."

The mystery had conked. I saw all. As I dare say you know, Jeeves's reputation as a counsellor has long been established among the cognoscenti, and the first move of any of my little circle on discovering themselves in any form of soup is always to roll round and put the thing up to him. And when he's got A out of a bad spot, A puts B on to him. And then, when he has fixed up B, B sends C along. And so on, if you get my drift, and so forth.

That's how these big consulting practices like Jeeves's grow. Old Sippy, I knew, had been deeply impressed by the man's efforts on his behalf at the time when he was trying to get engaged to Elizabeth Moon, so it was not to be wondered at that he should have advised Gussie to apply. Pure routine, you might say.

"Oh, you're acting for him, are you?"

"Yes, sir."

"Now I follow. Now I understand. And what is Gussie's trouble?"

"Oddly enough, sir, precisely the same as that of Mr. Sipperley when I was enabled to be of assistance to him. No doubt you recall Mr. Sipperley's predicament, sir. Deeply attached to Miss Moon, he suffered from a rooted diffidence which made it impossible for him to speak."

I nodded.

"I remember. Yes, I recall the Sipperley case. He couldn't bring himself to the scratch. A marked coldness of the feet, was there not? I recollect you saying he was letting—what was it?—letting something do something. Cats entered into it, if I am not mistaken."

"Letting 'I dare not' wait upon 'I would', sir."

"That's right. But how about the cats?"

"Like the poor cat i' the adage, sir."

"Exactly. It beats me how you think up these things. And Gussie, you say, is in the same posish?"

"Yes, sir. Each time he endeavours to formulate a proposal of marriage, his courage fails him."

"And yet, if he wants this female to be his wife, he's got to say so, what? I mean, only civil to mention it."

"Precisely, sir."

I mused.

"Well, I suppose this was inevitable, Jeeves. I wouldn't have thought that this Fink-Nottle would ever have fallen a victim to the divine *p*, but, if he has, no wonder he finds the going sticky."

"Yes, sir."

"Look at the life he's led."

"Yes, sir."

"I don't suppose he has spoken to a girl for years. What a lesson this is to us, Jeeves, not to shut ourselves up in country houses and stare into glass tanks. You can't be the dominant male if you do that sort of thing. In this life, you can choose between two courses. You can either shut yourself up in a country house and stare into tanks, or you can be a dasher with the sex. You can't do both."

"No, sir."

I mused once more. Gussie and I, as I say, had rather lost touch, but all the same I was exercised about the poor fish, as I am about all my pals, close or distant, who find themselves treading upon Life's banana skins. It seemed to me that he was up against it.

I threw my mind back to the last time I had seen him. About two years ago, it had been. I had looked in at his place while on a motor trip, and he had put me right off my feed by bringing a couple of green things with legs to the luncheon table, crooning over them like a young mother and eventually losing one of them in the salad. That picture, rising before my eyes, didn't give me much confidence in the unfortunate goof's ability to woo and win, I must say. Especially if the girl he had earmarked was one of these tough modern thugs, all lipstick and cool, hard, sardonic eyes, as she probably was.

"Tell me, Jeeves," I said, wishing to know the worst, "what sort of a girl is this girl of Gussie's?"

"I have not met the young lady, sir. Mr. Fink-Nottle speaks highly of her attractions."

"Seemed to like her, did he?"

"Yes, sir."

"Did he mention her name? Perhaps I know her."

"She is a Miss Bassett, sir. Miss Madeline Bassett."

"What?"

"Yes, sir."

I was deeply intrigued.

"Egad, Jeeves! Fancy that. It's a small world, isn't it, what?"

"The young lady is an acquaintance of yours, sir?"

"I know her well. Your news has relieved my mind, Jeeves. It makes the whole thing begin to seem far more like a practical working proposition."

"Indeed, sir?"

"Absolutely. I confess that until you supplied this information I was feeling profoundly dubious about poor old Gussie's chances of inducing any spinster of any parish to join him in the saunter down the aisle. You will agree with me that he is not everybody's money."

"There may be something in what you say, sir."

"Cleopatra wouldn't have liked him."

"Possibly not, sir."

"And I doubt if he would go any too well with Tallulah Bankhead."

"No, sir."

"But when you tell me that the object of his affections is Miss Bassett, why, then, Jeeves, hope begins to dawn a bit. He's just the sort of chap a girl like Madeline Bassett might scoop in with relish."

This Bassett, I must explain, had been a fellow visitor of ours at Cannes; and as she and Angela had struck up one of those effervescent friendships which girls do strike up, I had seen quite a bit of her. Indeed, in my moodier moments it sometimes seemed to me that I could not move a step without stubbing my toe on the woman.

And what made it all so painful and distressing was that the more we met, the less did I seem able to find to say to her.

You know how it is with some girls. They seem to take the stuffing right out of you. I mean to say, there is something about their personality that paralyses the vocal cords and reduces the contents of the brain to cauliflower. It was like that with this Bassett and me; so much so that I have known occasions when for minutes at a stretch Bertram Wooster might have been observed fumbling with the tie, shuffling the feet, and behaving in all other respects in her presence like the complete dumb brick. When, therefore, she took her departure some two weeks before we did, you may readily imagine that, in Bertram's opinion, it was not a day too soon.

It was not her beauty, mark you, that thus numbed me. She was a pretty enough girl in a droopy, blonde, saucer-eyed way, but not the sort of breath-taker that takes the breath.

No, what caused this disintegration in a usually fairly fluent prattler with the sex was her whole mental attitude. I don't want to wrong anybody, so I won't go so far as to say that she actually wrote poetry, but her conversation, to my mind, was of a nature calculated to excite the liveliest suspicions. Well, I mean to say, when a girl suddenly asks you out of a blue sky if you don't sometimes feel that the stars are God's daisy-chain, you begin to think a bit.

As regards the fusing of her soul and mine, therefore, there was nothing doing. But with Gussie, the posish was entirely different. The thing that had stymied me—viz. that this girl was obviously all loaded down with ideals and sentiment and what not—was quite in order as far as he was concerned.

Gussie had always been one of those dreamy, soulful birds—you can't shut yourself up in the country and live only for newts, if you're not—and I could see no reason why, if he could somehow be induced to get the low, burning words off his chest, he and the Bassett shouldn't hit it off like ham and eggs.

"She's just the type for him," I said.

"I am most gratified to hear it, sir."

"And he's just the type for her. In fine, a good thing and one to be pushed along with the utmost energy. Strain every nerve, Jeeves."

"Very good, sir," replied the honest fellow. "I will attend to the matter at once."

Now up to this point, as you will doubtless agree, what you might call a perfect harmony had prevailed. Friendly gossip between employer and employed, and everything as sweet as a nut. But at this juncture, I regret to say, there was an unpleasant switch. The atmosphere suddenly changed, the storm clouds began to gather, and before we knew where we were, the jarring note had come bounding on the scene. I have known this to happen before in the Wooster home.

The first intimation I had that things were about to hot up was a pained and disapproving cough from the neighbourhood of the carpet. For, during the above exchanges, I should explain, while I, having dried the frame, had been dressing in a leisurely manner, donning here a sock, there a shoe, and gradually climbing into the vest, the shirt, the tie, and the knee-length, Jeeves had been down on the lower level, unpacking my effects.

He now rose, holding a white object. And at the sight of it, I realized that another of our domestic crises had arrived, another of those unfortunate clashes of will between two strong men, and that Bertram, unless he remembered his fighting ancestors and stood up for his rights, was about to be put upon.

I don't know if you were at Cannes this summer. If you were, you will recall that anybody with any pretensions to being the life and soul of the party was accustomed to attend binges at the Casino in the ordinary evening-wear trouserings topped to the north by a white mess-jacket with brass buttons. And ever since I had stepped aboard the Blue Train at Cannes station, I had been wondering on and off how mine would go with Jeeves.

In the matter of evening costume, you see, Jeeves is hidebound and reactionary. I had had trouble with him before about soft-bosomed shirts. And while these mess-jackets had, as I say, been all the rage—*tout ce qu'il y a de chic*—on the Côte d'Azur, I had never concealed it from myself, even when treading the measure at the Palm Beach Casino in the one I had hastened to buy, that there might be something of an upheaval about it on my return.

I prepared to be firm.

"Yes, Jeeves?" I said. And though my voice was suave, a close observer in a position to watch my eyes would have noticed a steely glint. Nobody has a greater respect for Jeeves's intellect than I have, but this disposition of his to dictate to the hand that fed him had got, I felt, to be checked. This mess-jacket was very near to my heart, and I jolly well intended to fight for it with all the vim of grand old Sieur de Wooster at the Battle of Agincourt.

"Yes, Jeeves?" I said. "Something on your mind, Jeeves?"

"I fear that you inadvertently left Cannes in the possession of a coat belonging to some other gentleman, sir."

I switched on the steely a bit more.

"No, Jeeves," I said, in a level tone, "the object under advisement is mine. I bought it out there."

"You wore it, sir?"

"Every night."

"But surely you are not proposing to wear it in England, sir?"

I saw that we had arrived at the nub.

"Yes, Jeeves."

"But, sir——"

"You were saying, Jeeves?"

"It is quite unsuitable, sir."

"I do not agree with you, Jeeves. I anticipate a great popular success for this jacket. It is my intention to spring it on the public tomorrow at Pongo Twistleton's birthday party, where I confidently expect it to be one long scream from start to finish. No argument, Jeeves. No discussion. Whatever fantastic objection you may have taken to it, I wear this jacket."

"Very good, sir."

He went on with his unpacking. I said no more on the subject. I had won the victory, and we Woosters do not triumph over a beaten foe. Presently, having completed my toilet, I bade the man a cheery farewell and in generous mood suggested that, as I was dining out, why didn't he take the evening off and go to some improving picture or something. Sort of olive branch, if you see what I mean.

He didn't seem to think much of it.

"Thank you, sir, I will remain in."

I surveyed him narrowly.

"Is this dudgeon, Jeeves?"

"No, sir, I am obliged to remain on the premises. Mr. Fink-Nottle informed me he would be calling to see me this evening."

"Oh, Gussie's coming, is he? Well, give him my love."

"Very good, sir."

"Yes, sir."

"And a whisky and soda, and so forth."

"Very good, sir."

"Right ho, Jeeves."

I then set off for the Drones.

At the Drones I ran into Pongo Twistleton, and he talked so much about his forthcoming merry-making of his, of which good reports had already reached me through my correspondents, that it was nearing eleven when I got home again.

And scarcely had I opened the door when I heard voices in the sitting-room, and scarcely had I entered the sitting-room when I found that these proceeded from Jeeves and what appeared at first sight to be the Devil.

A closer scrutiny informed me that it was Gussie Fink-Nottle, dressed as Mephistopheles.

-2-

"What-ho, Gussie," I said.

You couldn't have told it from my manner, but I was feeling more than a bit nonplussed. The spectacle before me was enough to nonplus anyone. I mean to say, this Fink-Nottle, as I remembered him, was the sort of shy, shrinking goop who might have been expected to shake like an aspen if invited to so much as a social Saturday afternoon at the vicarage. And yet here he was, if one could credit one's senses, about to take part in a fancy-dress ball, a form of entertainment notoriously a testing experience for the toughest.

And he was attending that fancy-dress ball, mark you—not, like every other well-bred Englishman, as a Pierrot, but as Mephistopheles—this involving, as I need scarcely stress, not only scarlet tights but a pretty frightful false beard.

Rummy, you'll admit. However, one masks one's feelings. I betrayed no vulgar astonishment, but, as I say, what-hoed with civil nonchalance.

He grinned through the fungus—rather sheepishly, I thought.

"Oh, hullo, Bertie."

"Long time since I saw you. Have a spot?"

"No, thanks. I must be off in a minute. I just came round to ask Jeeves how he thought I looked. How do you think I look, Bertie?"

Well, the answer to that, of course, was "perfectly foul". But we Woosters are men of tact and have a nice sense of the obligations of a host. We do not tell old friends beneath our roof-tree that they are an offence to the eyesight. I evaded the question.

"I hear you're in London," I said carelessly.

"Oh, yes."

"Must be years since you came up."

"Oh, yes."

"And now you're off for an evening's pleasure."

He shuddered a bit. He had, I noticed, a hunted air.

"Pleasure!"

"Aren't you looking forward to this rout or revel?"

"Oh, I suppose it'll be all right," he said, in a toneless voice. "Anyway, I ought to be off, I suppose. The thing starts round about eleven. I told my cab to wait.... Will you see if it's there, Jeeves?"

"Very good, sir."

There was something of a pause after the door had closed. A certain constraint. I mixed myself a beaker, while Gussie, a glutton for punishment, stared at himself in the mirror. Finally I decided that it would be best to let him know that I was abreast of his affairs. It might be that it would ease his mind to confide in a sympathetic man of experience. I have generally found, with those under the influence, that what they want more than anything is the listening ear.

"Well, Gussie, old leper," I said, "I've been hearing all about you."

"Eh?"

"This little trouble of yours. Jeeves has told me everything."

He didn't seem any too braced. It's always difficult to be sure, of course, when a chap has dug himself in behind a Mephistopheles beard, but I fancy he flushed a trifle.

"I wish Jeeves wouldn't go gassing all over the place. It was supposed to be confidential."

I could not permit this tone.

"Dishing up the dirt to the young master can scarcely be described as gassing all over the place," I said, with a touch of rebuke. "Anyway, there it is. I know all. And I should like to begin," I said, sinking my personal opinion that the female in question was a sloppy pest in my desire to buck and encourage, "by saying that Madeline Bassett is a charming girl. A winner, and just the sort for you."

"You don't know her?"

"Certainly I know her. What beats me is how you ever got in touch. Where did you meet?"

"She was staying at a place near mine in Lincolnshire the week before last."

"Yes, but even so. I didn't know you called on the neighbours."

"I don't. I met her out for a walk with her dog. The dog had got a thorn in its foot, and when she tried to take it out, it snapped at her. So, of course, I had to rally round."

"You extracted the thorn?"

"Yes."

"And fell in love at first sight?"

"Yes."

"Well, dash it, with a thing like that to give you a send-off, why didn't you cash in immediately?"

"I hadn't the nerve."

"What happened?"

"We talked for a bit."

"What about?"

"Oh, birds."

"Birds? What birds?"

"The birds that happened to be hanging round. And the scenery, and all that sort of thing. And she said she was going to London, and asked me to look her up if I was ever there."

"And even after that you didn't so much as press her hand?"

"Of course not."

Well, I mean, it looked as though there was no more to be said. If a chap is such a rabbit that he can't get action when he's handed the thing on a plate, his case would appear to be pretty hopeless. Nevertheless, I reminded myself that this non-starter and I had been at school together. One must make an effort for an old school friend.

"Ah, well," I said, "we must see what can be done. Things may brighten. At any rate, you will be glad to learn that I am behind you in this enterprise. You have Bertram Wooster in your corner, Gussie."

"Thanks, old man. And Jeeves, of course, which is the thing that really matters."

I don't mind admitting that I winced. He meant no harm, I suppose, but I'm bound to say that this tactless speech nettled me not a little. People are always nettling me like that. Giving me to understand, I mean to say, that in their opinion Bertram Wooster is a mere cipher and that the only member of the household with brains and resources is Jeeves.

It jars on me.

And tonight it jarred on me more than usual, because I was feeling pretty dashed fed with Jeeves. Over that matter of the mess jacket, I mean. True, I had forced him to climb down, quelling him, as described, with the quiet strength of my personality, but I was still a trifle shirty at his having brought the thing up at all. It seemed to me that what Jeeves wanted was the iron hand.

"And what is he doing about it?" I inquired stiffly.

"He's been giving the position of affairs a lot of thought."

"He has, has he?"

"It's on his advice that I'm going to this dance."

"Why?"

"She is going to be there. In fact, it was she who sent me the ticket of invitation. And Jeeves considered——"

"And why not as a Pierrot?" I said, taking up the point which had struck me before. "Why this break with a grand old tradition?"

"He particularly wanted me to go as Mephistopheles."

I started.

"He did, did he? He specifically recommended that definite costume?"

"Yes."

"Ha!"

"Eh?"

"Nothing. Just 'Ha!'"

And I'll tell you why I said "Ha!" Here was Jeeves making heavy weather about me wearing a perfectly ordinary white mess jacket, a garment not only *tout ce qu'il y a de chic*, but absolutely *de rigueur*, and in the same breath, as you might say, inciting Gussie Fink-Nottle to be a blot on the London scene in scarlet tights. Ironical, what? One looks askance at this sort of in-and-out running.

"What has he got against Pierrots?"

"I don't think he objects to Pierrots as Pierrots. But in my case he thought a Pierrot wouldn't be adequate."

"I don't follow that."

"He said that the costume of Pierrot, while pleasing to the eye, lacked the authority of the Mephistopheles costume."

"I still don't get it."

"Well, it's a matter of psychology, he said."

There was a time when a remark like that would have had me snookered. But long association with Jeeves has developed the Wooster vocabulary considerably. Jeeves has always been a whale for the psychology of the individual, and I now follow him like a bloodhound when he snaps it out of the bag.

"Oh, psychology?"

"Yes. Jeeves is a great believer in the moral effect of clothes. He thinks I might be emboldened in a striking costume like this. He said a Pirate Chief would be just as good. In fact, a Pirate Chief was his first suggestion, but I objected to the boots."

I saw his point. There is enough sadness in life without having fellows like Gussie Fink-Nottle going about in sea boots.

"And are you emboldened?"

"Well, to be absolutely accurate, Bertie, old man, no."

A gust of compassion shook me. After all, though we had lost touch a bit of recent years, this man and I had once thrown inked darts at each other.

"Gussie," I said, "take an old friend's advice, and don't go within a mile of this binge."

"But it's my last chance of seeing her. She's off tomorrow to stay with some people in the country. Besides, you don't know."

"Don't know what?"

"That this idea of Jeeves's won't work. I feel a most frightful chump now, yes, but who can say whether that will not pass off when I get into a mob of other people in fancy dress. I had the same experience as a child, one year during the Christmas festivities. They dressed me up as a rabbit, and the shame was indescribable. Yet when I got to the party and found myself surrounded by scores of other children, many in costumes even ghastlier than my own, I perked up amazingly, joined freely in the revels, and was able to eat so hearty a supper that I was sick twice in the cab coming home. What I mean is, you can't tell in cold blood."

I weighed this. It was specious, of course.

"And you can't get away from it that, fundamentally, Jeeves's idea is sound. In a striking costume like Mephistopheles, I might quite easily pull off something pretty impressive. Colour does make a difference. Look at newts. During the courting season the male newt is brilliantly coloured. It helps him a lot."

"But you aren't a male newt."

"I wish I were. Do you know how a male newt proposes, Bertie? He just stands in front of the female newt vibrating his tail and bending his body in a semi-circle. I could do that on my head. No, you wouldn't find me grousing if I were a male newt."

"But if you were a male newt, Madeline Bassett wouldn't look at you. Not with the eye of love, I mean."

"She would, if she were a female newt."

"But she isn't a female newt."

"No, but suppose she was."

"Well, if she was, you wouldn't be in love with her."

"Yes, I would, if I were a male newt."

A slight throbbing about the temples told me that this discussion had reached saturation point.

"Well, anyway," I said, "coming down to hard facts and cutting out all this visionary stuff about vibrating tails and what not, the salient point that emerges is that you are booked to appear at a fancy-dress ball. And I tell you out of my riper knowledge of fancy-dress balls, Gussie, that you won't enjoy yourself."

"It isn't a question of enjoying yourself."

"I wouldn't go."

"I must go. I keep telling you she's off to the country tomorrow."

I gave it up.

"So be it," I said. "Have it your own way.... Yes, Jeeves?"

"Mr. Fink-Nottle's cab, sir."

"Ah? The cab, eh?... Your cab, Gussie."

"Oh, the cab? Oh, right. Of course, yes, rather.... Thanks, Jeeves ... Well, so long, Bertie."

And giving me the sort of weak smile Roman gladiators used to give the Emperor before entering the arena, Gussie trickled off. And I turned to Jeeves. The moment had arrived for putting him in his place, and I was all for it.

It was a little difficult to know how to begin, of course. I mean to say, while firmly resolved to tick him off, I didn't want to gash his feelings too deeply. Even when displaying the iron hand, we Woosters like to keep the thing fairly matey.

However, on consideration, I saw that there was nothing to be gained by trying to lead up to it gently. It is never any use beating about the b.

"Jeeves," I said, "may I speak frankly?"

"Certainly, sir."

"What I have to say may wound you."

"Not at all, sir."

"Well, then, I have been having a chat with Mr. Fink-Nottle, and he has been telling me about this Mephistopheles scheme of yours."

"Yes, sir?"

"Now let me get it straight. If I follow your reasoning correctly, you think that, stimulated by being upholstered throughout in scarlet tights, Mr. Fink-Nottle, on encountering the adored object, will vibrate his tail and generally let himself go with a whoop."

"I am of opinion that he will lose much of his normal diffidence, sir."

"I don't agree with you, Jeeves."

"No, sir?"

"No. In fact, not to put too fine a point upon it, I consider that of all the dashed silly, drivelling ideas I ever heard in my puff this is the most blithering and futile. It won't work. Not a chance. All you have done is to subject Mr. Fink-Nottle to the nameless horrors of a fancy-dress ball for nothing. And this is not the first time this sort of thing has happened. To be quite candid, Jeeves, I have frequently noticed before now a tendency or disposition on your part to become—what's the word?"

"I could not say, sir."

"Eloquent? No, it's not eloquent. Elusive? No, it's not elusive. It's on the tip of my tongue. Begins with an 'e' and means being a jolly sight too clever."

"Elaborate, sir?"

"That is the exact word I was after. Too elaborate, Jeeves—that is what you are frequently prone to become. Your methods are not simple, not straightforward. You cloud the issue with a lot of fancy stuff that is not of the essence. All that Gussie needs is the elder-brotherly advice of a seasoned man of the world. So what I suggest is that from now onward you leave this case to me."

"Very good, sir."

"You lay off and devote yourself to your duties about the home."

"Very good, sir."

"I shall no doubt think of something quite simple and straightforward yet perfectly effective ere long. I will make a point of seeing Gussie tomorrow."

"Very good, sir."

"Right ho, Jeeves."

But on the morrow all those telegrams started coming in, and I confess that for twenty-four hours I didn't give the poor chap a thought, having problems of my own to contend with.

-3-

The first of the telegram arrived shortly after noon, and Jeeves brought it in with the before-luncheon snifter. It was from my Aunt Dahlia, operating from Market Snodsbury, a small town of sorts a mile or two along the main road as you leave her country seat.

It ran as follows:

Come at once. Travers.

And when I say it puzzled me like the dickens, I am understating it; if anything. As mysterious a communication, I considered, as was ever flashed over the wires. I studied it in a profound reverie for the best part of two dry Martinis and a dividend. I read it backwards. I read it forwards. As a matter of fact, I have a sort of recollection of even smelling it. But it still baffled me.

Consider the facts, I mean. It was only a few hours since this aunt and I had parted, after being in constant association for nearly two months. And yet here she was—with my farewell kiss still lingering on her cheek, so to speak—pleading for another reunion. Bertram Wooster is not accustomed to this gluttonous appetite for his society. Ask anyone who knows me, and they will tell you that after two months of my company, what the normal person feels is that that will about do for the present. Indeed, I have known people who couldn't stick it out for more than a few days.

Before sitting down to the well-cooked, therefore, I sent this reply:

Perplexed. Explain. Bertie.

To this I received an answer during the after-luncheon sleep:

What on earth is there to be perplexed about, ass? Come at once. Travers.

Three cigarettes and a couple of turns about the room, and I had my response ready:

How do you mean come at once? Regards. Bertie.

I append the comeback:

I mean come at once, you maddening half-wit. What did you think I meant? Come at once or expect an aunt's curse first post tomorrow. Love. Travers.

I then dispatched the following message, wishing to get everything quite clear:

When you say "Come" do you mean "Come to Brinkley Court"? And when you say "At once" do you mean "At once"? Fogged. At a loss. All the best. Bertie.

I sent this one off on my way to the Drones, where I spent a restful afternoon throwing cards into a top-hat with some of the better element. Returning in the evening hush, I found the answer waiting for me:

Yes, yes, yes, yes, yes, yes, yes. It doesn't matter whether you understand or not. You just come at once, as I tell you, and for heaven's sake stop this back-chat. Do you think I am made of money that I can afford to send you telegrams every ten minutes. Stop being a fathead and come immediately. Love. Travers.

It was at this point that I felt the need of getting a second opinion. I pressed the bell.

"Jeeves," I said, "a V-shaped rumminess has manifested itself from the direction of Worcestershire. Read these," I said, handing him the papers in the case.

He scanned them.

"What do you make of it, Jeeves?"

"I think Mrs. Travers wishes you to come at once, sir."

"You gather that too, do you?"

"Yes, sir."

"I put the same construction on the thing. But why, Jeeves? Dash it all, she's just had nearly two months of me."

"Yes, sir."

"And many people consider the medium dose for an adult two days."

"Yes, sir. I appreciate the point you raise. Nevertheless, Mrs. Travers appears very insistent. I think it would be well to acquiesce in her wishes."

"Pop down, you mean?"

"Yes, sir."

"Well, I certainly can't go at once. I've an important conference on at the Drones tonight. Pongo Twistleton's birthday party, you remember."

"Yes, sir."

There was a slight pause. We were both recalling the little unpleasantness that had arisen. I felt obliged to allude to it.

"You're all wrong about that mess jacket, Jeeves."

"These things are matters of opinion, sir."

"When I wore it at the Casino at Cannes, beautiful women nudged one another and whispered: 'Who is he?'"

"The code at Continental casinos is notoriously lax, sir."

"And when I described it to Pongo last night, he was fascinated."

"Indeed, sir?"

"So were all the rest of those present. One and all admitted that I had got hold of a good thing. Not a dissentient voice."

"Indeed, sir?"

"I am convinced that you will eventually learn to love this mess-jacket, Jeeves."

"I fear not, sir."

I gave it up. It is never any use trying to reason with Jeeves on these occasions. "Pig-headed" is the word that springs to the lips. One sighs and passes on.

"Well, anyway, returning to the agenda, I can't go down to Brinkley Court or anywhere else yet awhile. That's final. I'll tell you what, Jeeves. Give me form and pencil, and I'll wire her that I'll be with her some time next week or the week after. Dash it all, she ought to be able to hold out without me for a few days. It only requires will power."

"Yes, sir."

"Right ho, then. I'll wire 'Expect me tomorrow fortnight' or words to some such effect. That ought to meet the case. Then if you will toddle round the corner and send it off, that will be that."

"Very good, sir."

And so the long day wore on till it was time for me to dress for Pongo's party.

Pongo had assured me, while chatting of the affair on the previous night, that this birthday binge of his was to be on a scale calculated to stagger humanity, and I must say I have participated in less fruity functions. It was well after four when I got home, and by that time I was about ready to turn in. I can just remember groping for the bed and crawling into it, and it seemed to me that the lemon had scarcely touched the pillow before I was aroused by the sound of the door opening.

I was barely ticking over, but I contrived to raise an eyelid.

"Is that my tea, Jeeves?"

"No, sir. It is Mrs. Travers."

And a moment later there was a sound like a mighty rushing wind, and the relative had crossed the threshold at fifty m.p.h. under her own steam.

-4-

It has been well said of Bertram Wooster that, while no one views his flesh and blood with a keener and more remorselessly critical eye, he is nevertheless a man who delights in giving credit where credit is due. And if you have followed these memoirs of mine with the proper care, you will be aware that I have frequently had occasion to emphasise the fact that Aunt Dahlia is all right.

She is the one, if you remember, who married old Tom Travers *en secondes noces*, as I believe the expression is, the year Bluebottle won the Cambridgeshire, and once induced me to write an article on What the Well-Dressed Man is Wearing for that paper she runs—*Milady's Boudoir.* She is a large, genial soul, with whom it is a pleasure to hob-nob. In her spiritual make-up there is none of that subtle gosh-awfulness which renders such an exhibit as, say, my Aunt Agatha the curse of the Home Counties and a menace to one and all. I have the highest esteem for Aunt Dahlia, and have never wavered in my cordial appreciation of her humanity, sporting qualities and general good-eggishness.

This being so, you may conceive of my astonishment at finding her at my bedside at such an hour. I mean to say, I've stayed at her place many a time and oft, and she knows my habits. She is well aware that until I have had my cup of tea in the morning, I do not receive. This crashing in at a moment when she knew that solitude and repose were of the essence was scarcely, I could not but feel, the good old form.

Besides, what business had she being in London at all? That was what I asked myself. When a conscientious housewife has returned to her home after an absence of seven weeks, one does not expect her to start racing off again the day after her arrival. One feels that she ought to be sticking round, ministering to her husband, conferring with the cook, feeding the cat, combing and brushing the Pomeranian—in a word, staying put. I was more than a little bleary-eyed, but I endeavoured, as far as the fact that my eyelids were more or less glued together would permit, to give her an austere and censorious look.

She didn't seem to get it.

"Wake up, Bertie, you old ass!" she cried, in a voice that hit me between the eyebrows and went out at the back of my head.

If Aunt Dahlia has a fault, it is that she is apt to address a *vis-à-vis* as if he were somebody half a mile away whom she had observed riding over hounds. A throwback, no doubt, to the time when she counted the day lost that was not spent in chivvying some unfortunate fox over the countryside.

I gave her another of the austere and censorious, and this time it registered. All the effect it had, however, was to cause her to descend to personalities.

"Don't blink at me in that obscene way," she said. "I wonder, Bertie," she proceeded, gazing at me as I should imagine Gussie would have gazed at some newt that was not up to sample, "if you have the faintest conception how perfectly loathsome you look? A cross between an orgy scene in the movies and some low form of pond life. I suppose you were out on the tiles last night?"

"I attended a social function, yes," I said coldly. "Pongo Twistleton's birthday party. I couldn't let Pongo down. *Noblesse oblige.*"

"Well, get up and dress."

I felt I could not have heard her aright.

"Get up and dress?"

"Yes."

I turned on the pillow with a little moan, and at this juncture Jeeves entered with the vital oolong. I clutched at it like a drowning man at a straw hat. A deep sip or two, and I felt—I won't say restored, because a birthday party like Pongo Twistleton's isn't a thing you get restored after with a mere mouthful of tea, but sufficiently the old Bertram to be able to bend the mind on this awful thing which had come upon me.

And the more I bent same, the less could I grasp the trend of the scenario.

"What is this, Aunt Dahlia?" I inquired.

"It looks to me like tea," was her response. "But you know best. You're drinking it."

If I hadn't been afraid of spilling the healing brew, I have little doubt that I should have given an impatient gesture. I know I felt like it.

"Not the contents of this cup. All this. Your barging in and telling me to get up and dress, and all that rot."

"I've barged in, as you call it, because my telegrams seemed to produce no effect. And I told you to get up and dress because I want you to get up and dress. I've come to take you back with me. I like your crust, wiring that you would come next year or whenever it was. You're coming now. I've got a job for you."

"But I don't want a job."

"What you want, my lad, and what you're going to get are two very different things. There is man's work for you to do at Brinkley Court. Be ready to the last button in twenty minutes."

"But I can't possibly be ready to any buttons in twenty minutes. I'm feeling awful."

She seemed to consider.

"Yes," she said. "I suppose it's only humane to give you a day or two to recover. All right, then, I shall expect you on the thirtieth at the latest."

"But, dash it, what is all this? How do you mean, a job? Why a job? What sort of a job?"

"I'll tell you if you'll only stop talking for a minute. It's quite an easy, pleasant job. You will enjoy it. Have you ever heard of Market Snodsbury Grammar School?"

"Never."

"It's a grammar school at Market Snodsbury."

I told her a little frigidly that I had divined as much.

"Well, how was I to know that a man with a mind like yours would grasp it so quickly?" she protested. "All right, then. Market Snodsbury Grammar School is, as you have guessed, the grammar school at Market Snodsbury. I'm one of the governors."

"You mean one of the governesses."

"I don't mean one of the governesses. Listen, ass. There was a board of governors at Eton, wasn't there? Very well. So there is at Market Snodsbury Grammar School, and I'm a member of it. And they left the arrangements for the summer prize-giving to me. This prize-giving takes place on the last—or thirty-first—day of this month. Have you got that clear?"

I took another oz. of the life-saving and inclined my head. Even after a Pongo Twistleton birthday party, I was capable of grasping simple facts like these.

"I follow you, yes. I see the point you are trying to make, certainly. Market ... Snodsbury ... Grammar School ... Board of governors ... Prize-giving.... Quite. But what's it got to do with me?"

"You're going to give away the prizes."

I goggled. Her words did not appear to make sense. They seemed the mere aimless vapouring of an aunt who has been sitting out in the sun without a hat.

"Me?"

"You."

I goggled again.

"You don't mean me?"

"I mean you in person."

I goggled a third time.

"You're pulling my leg."

"I am not pulling your leg. Nothing would induce me to touch your beastly leg. The vicar was to have officiated, but when I got home I found a letter from him saying that he had strained a fetlock and must scratch his nomination. You can imagine the state I was in. I telephoned all over the place. Nobody would take it on. And then suddenly I thought of you."

I decided to check all this rot at the outset. Nobody is more eager to oblige deserving aunts than Bertram Wooster, but there are limits, and sharply defined limits, at that.

"So you think I'm going to strew prizes at this bally Dotheboys Hall of yours?"

"I do."

"And make a speech?"

"Exactly."

I laughed derisively.

"For goodness' sake, don't start gargling now. This is serious."

"I was laughing."

"Oh, were you? Well, I'm glad to see you taking it in this merry spirit."

"Derisively," I explained. "I won't do it. That's final. I simply will not do it."

"You will do it, young Bertie, or never darken my doors again. And you know what that means. No more of Anatole's dinners for you."

A strong shudder shook me. She was alluding to her *chef*, that superb artist. A monarch of his profession, unsurpassed—nay, unequalled—at dishing up the raw material so that it melted in the mouth of the ultimate consumer, Anatole had always been a magnet that drew me to Brinkley Court with my tongue hanging out. Many of my happiest moments had been those which I had spent champing this great man's roasts and ragouts, and the prospect of being barred from digging into them in the future was a numbing one.

"No, I say, dash it!"

"I thought that would rattle you. Greedy young pig."

"Greedy young pigs have nothing to do with it," I said with a touch of hauteur. "One is not a greedy young pig because one appreciates the cooking of a genius."

"Well, I will say I like it myself," conceded the relative. "But not another bite of it do you get, if you refuse to do this simple, easy, pleasant job. No, not so much as another sniff. So put that in your twelve-inch cigarette-holder and smoke it."

I began to feel like some wild thing caught in a snare.

"But why do you want me? I mean, what am I? Ask yourself that."

"I often have."

"I mean to say, I'm not the type. You have to have some terrific nib to give away prizes. I seem to remember, when I was at school, it was generally a prime minister or somebody."

"Ah, but that was at Eton. At Market Snodsbury we aren't nearly so choosy. Anybody in spats impresses us."

"Why don't you get Uncle Tom?"

"Uncle Tom!"

"Well, why not? He's got spats."

"Bertie," she said, "I will tell you why not Uncle Tom. You remember me losing all that money at baccarat at Cannes? Well, very shortly I shall have to sidle up to Tom and break the news to him. If, right after that, I ask him to put on lavender gloves and a topper and distribute the prizes at Market Snodsbury Grammar School, there will be a divorce in the family. He would pin a note to the pincushion and be off like a rabbit. No, my lad, you're for it, so you may as well make the best of it."

"But, Aunt Dahlia, listen to reason. I assure you, you've got hold of the wrong man. I'm hopeless at a game like that. Ask Jeeves about the time I got lugged in to address a girls' school. I made the most colossal ass of myself."

"And I confidently anticipate that you will make an equally colossal ass of yourself on the thirty-first of this month. That's why I want you. The way I look at it is that, as the thing is bound to be a frost, anyway, one may as well get a hearty laugh out of it. I shall enjoy seeing you distribute those prizes, Bertie. Well, I won't keep you, as, no doubt, you want to do your Swedish exercises. I shall expect you in a day or two."

And with these heartless words she beetled off, leaving me a prey to the gloomiest emotions. What with the natural reaction after Pongo's party and this stunning blow, it is not too much to say that the soul was seared.

And I was still writhing in the depths, when the door opened and Jeeves appeared.

"Mr. Fink-Nottle to see you, sir," he announced.

-5-

I gave him one of my looks.

"Jeeves," I said, "I had scarcely expected this of you. You are aware that I was up to an advanced hour last night. You know that I have barely had my tea. You cannot be ignorant of the effect of that hearty voice of Aunt Dahlia's on a man with a headache. And yet you come bringing me Fink-Nottles. Is this a time for Fink or any other kind of Nottle?"

"But did you not give me to understand, sir, that you wished to see Mr. Fink-Nottle to advise him on his affairs?"

This, I admit, opened up a new line of thought. In the stress of my emotions, I had clean forgotten about having taken Gussie's interests in hand. It altered things. One can't give the raspberry to a client. I mean, you didn't find Sherlock Holmes refusing to see clients just because he had been out late the night before at Doctor Watson's birthday party. I could have wished that the man had selected some more suitable hour for approaching me, but as he appeared to be a sort of human lark, leaving his watery nest at daybreak, I supposed I had better give him an audience.

"True," I said. "All right. Bung him in."

"Very good, sir."

"But before doing so, bring me one of those pick-me-ups of yours."

"Very good, sir."

And presently he returned with the vital essence.

I have had occasion, I fancy, to speak before now of these pick-me-ups of Jeeves's and their effect on a fellow who is hanging to life by a thread on the morning after. What they consist of, I couldn't tell you. He says some kind of sauce, the yolk of a raw egg and a dash of red pepper, but nothing will convince me that the thing doesn't go much deeper than that. Be that as it may, however, the results of swallowing one are amazing.

For perhaps the split part of a second nothing happens. It is as though all Nature waited breathless. Then, suddenly, it is as if the Last Trump had sounded and Judgment Day set in with unusual severity.

Bonfires burst out all in parts of the frame. The abdomen becomes heavily charged with molten lava. A great wind seems to blow through the world, and the subject is aware of something resembling a steam hammer striking the back of the head. During this phase, the ears ring loudly, the eyeballs rotate and there is a tingling about the brow.

And then, just as you are feeling that you ought to ring up your lawyer and see that your affairs are in order before it is too late, the whole situation seems to clarify. The wind drops. The ears cease to ring. Birds twitter. Brass bands start playing. The sun comes up over the horizon with a jerk.

And a moment later all you are conscious of is a great peace.

As I drained the glass now, new life seemed to burgeon within me. I remember Jeeves, who, however much he may go off the rails at times in the matter of dress clothes and in his advice to those in love, has always had a neat turn of phrase, once speaking of someone rising on stepping-stones of his dead self to higher things. It was that way with me now. I felt that the Bertram Wooster who lay propped up against the pillows had become a better, stronger, finer Bertram.

"Thank you, Jeeves," I said.

"Not at all, sir."

"That touched the exact spot. I am now able to cope with life's problems."

"I am gratified to hear it, sir."

"What madness not to have had one of those before tackling Aunt Dahlia! However, too late to worry about that now. Tell me of Gussie. How did he make out at the fancy-dress ball?"

"He did not arrive at the fancy-dress ball, sir."

I looked at him a bit austerely.

"Jeeves," I said, "I admit that after that pick-me-up of yours I feel better, but don't try me too high. Don't stand by my sick bed talking absolute rot. We shot Gussie into a cab and he started forth, headed for wherever this fancy-dress ball was. He must have arrived."

"No, sir. As I gather from Mr. Fink-Nottle, he entered the cab convinced in his mind that the entertainment to which he had been invited was to be held at No. 17, Suffolk Square, whereas the actual rendezvous was No. 71, Norfolk Terrace. These aberrations of memory are not uncommon with those who, like Mr. Fink-Nottle, belong essentially to what one might call the dreamer-type."

"One might also call it the fatheaded type."

"Yes, sir."

"Well?"

"On reaching No. 17, Suffolk Square, Mr. Fink-Nottle endeavoured to produce money to pay the fare."

"What stopped him?"

"The fact that he had no money, sir. He discovered that he had left it, together with his ticket of invitation, on the mantelpiece of his bedchamber in the house of his uncle, where he was residing. Bidding the cabman to wait, accordingly, he rang the door-bell, and when the butler appeared, requested him to pay the cab, adding that it was all right, as he was one of the guests invited to the dance. The butler then disclaimed all knowledge of a dance on the premises."

"And declined to unbelt?"

"Yes, sir."

"Upon which——"

"Mr. Fink-Nottle directed the cabman to drive him back to his uncle's residence."

"Well, why wasn't that the happy ending? All he had to do was go in, collect cash and ticket, and there he would have been, on velvet."

"I should have mentioned, sir, that Mr. Fink-Nottle had also left his latchkey on the mantelpiece of his bedchamber."

"He could have rung the bell."

"He did ring the bell, sir, for some fifteen minutes. At the expiration of that period he recalled that he had given permission to the caretaker—the house was officially closed and all the staff on holiday—to visit his sailor son at Portsmouth."

"Golly, Jeeves!"

"Yes, sir."

"These dreamer types do live, don't they?"

"Yes, sir."

"What happened then?"

"Mr. Fink-Nottle appears to have realized at this point that his position as regards the cabman had become equivocal. The figures on the clock had already reached a substantial sum, and he was not in a position to meet his obligations."

"He could have explained."

"You cannot explain to cabmen, sir. On endeavouring to do so, he found the fellow sceptical of his bona fides."

"I should have legged it."

"That is the policy which appears to have commended itself to Mr. Fink-Nottle. He darted rapidly away, and the cabman, endeavouring to detain him, snatched at his overcoat. Mr. Fink-Nottle contrived to extricate himself from the coat, and it would seem that his appearance in the masquerade costume beneath it came as something of a shock to the cabman. Mr. Fink-Nottle informs me that he heard a species of whistling gasp, and, looking round, observed the man crouching against the railings with his hands over his face. Mr. Fink-Nottle thinks he was praying. No doubt an uneducated, superstitious fellow, sir. Possibly a drinker."

"Well, if he hadn't been one before, I'll bet he started being one shortly afterwards. I expect he could scarcely wait for the pubs to open."

"Very possibly, in the circumstances he might have found a restorative agreeable, sir."

"And so, in the circumstances, might Gussie too, I should think. What on earth did he do after that? London late at night—or even in the daytime, for that matter—is no place for a man in scarlet tights."

"No, sir."

"He invites comment."

"Yes, sir."

"I can see the poor old bird ducking down side-streets, skulking in alley-ways, diving into dust-bins."

"I gathered from Mr. Fink-Nottle's remarks, sir, that something very much on those lines was what occurred. Eventually, after a trying night, he found his way to Mr. Sipperley's residence, where he was able to secure lodging and a change of costume in the morning."

I nestled against the pillows, the brow a bit drawn. It is all very well to try to do old school friends a spot of good, but I could not but feel that in espousing the cause of a lunkhead capable of mucking things up as Gussie had done, I had taken on a contract almost too big for human consumption. It seemed to me that what Gussie needed was not so much the advice of a seasoned man of the world as a padded cell in Colney Hatch and a couple of good keepers to see that he did not set the place on fire.

Indeed, for an instant I had half a mind to withdraw from the case and hand it back to Jeeves. But the pride of the Woosters restrained me. When we Woosters put our hands to the plough, we do not readily sheathe the sword. Besides, after that business of the mess-jacket, anything resembling weakness would have been fatal.

"I suppose you realize, Jeeves," I said, for though one dislikes to rub it in, these things have to be pointed out, "that all this was your fault?"

"Sir?"

"It's no good saying 'Sir?' You know it was. If you had not insisted on his going to that dance—a mad project, as I spotted from the first—this would not have happened."

"Yes, sir, but I confess I did not anticipate——"

"Always anticipate everything, Jeeves," I said, a little sternly. "It is the only way. Even if you had allowed him to wear a Pierrot costume, things would not have panned out as they did. A Pierrot costume has pockets. However," I went on more kindly, "we need not go into that now. If all this has shown you what comes of going about the place in scarlet tights, that is something gained. Gussie waits without, you say?"

"Yes, sir."

"Then shoot him in, and I will see what I can do for him."

-6-

Gussie, on arrival, proved to be still showing traces of his grim experience. The face was pale, the eyes gooseberry-like, the ears drooping, and the whole aspect that of a man who has passed through the furnace and been caught in the machinery. I hitched myself up a bit higher on the pillows and gazed at him narrowly. It was a moment, I could see, when first aid was required, and I prepared to get down to cases.

"Well, Gussie."

"Hullo, Bertie."

"What ho."

"What ho."

These civilities concluded, I felt that the moment had come to touch delicately on the past.

"I hear you've been through it a bit."

"Yes."

"Thanks to Jeeves."

"It wasn't Jeeves's fault."

"Entirely Jeeves's fault."

"I don't see that. I forgot my money and latchkey——"

"And now you'd better forget Jeeves. For you will be interested to hear, Gussie," I said, deeming it best to put him in touch with the position of affairs right away, "that he is no longer handling your little problem."

This seemed to slip it across him properly. The jaws fell, the ears drooped more limply. He had been looking like a dead fish. He now looked like a deader fish, one of last year's, cast up on some lonely beach and left there at the mercy of the wind and tides.

"What!"

"Yes."

"You don't mean that Jeeves isn't going to——"

"No."

"But, dash it——"

I was kind, but firm.

"You will be much better off without him. Surely your terrible experiences of that awful night have told you that Jeeves needs a rest. The keenest of thinkers strikes a bad patch occasionally. That is what has happened to Jeeves. I have seen it coming on for some time. He has lost his form. He wants his plugs decarbonized. No doubt this is a shock to you. I suppose you came here this morning to seek his advice?"

"Of course I did."

"On what point?"

"Madeline Bassett has gone to stay with these people in the country, and I want to know what he thinks I ought to do."

"Well, as I say, Jeeves is off the case."

"But, Bertie, dash it——"

"Jeeves," I said with a certain asperity, "is no longer on the case. I am now in sole charge."

"But what on earth can you do?"

I curbed my resentment. We Woosters are fair-minded. We can make allowances for men who have been parading London all night in scarlet tights.

"That," I said quietly, "we shall see. Sit down and let us confer. I am bound to say the thing seems quite simple to me. You say this girl has gone to visit friends in the country. It would appear obvious that you must go there too, and flock round her like a poultice. Elementary."

"But I can't plant myself on a lot of perfect strangers."

"Don't you know these people?"

"Of course I don't. I don't know anybody."

I pursed the lips. This did seem to complicate matters somewhat.

"All that I know is that their name is Travers, and it's a place called Brinkley Court down in Worcestershire."

I unpursed my lips.

"Gussie," I said, smiling paternally, "it was a lucky day for you when Bertram Wooster interested himself in your affairs. As I foresaw from the start, I can fix everything. This afternoon you shall go to Brinkley Court, an honoured guest."

He quivered like a *mousse.* I suppose it must always be rather a thrilling experience for the novice to watch me taking hold.

"But, Bertie, you don't mean you know these Traverses?"

"They are my Aunt Dahlia."

"My gosh!"

"You see now," I pointed out, "how lucky you were to get me behind you. You go to Jeeves, and what does he do? He dresses you up in scarlet tights and one of the foulest false beards of my experience, and sends you off to fancy-dress balls. Result, agony of spirit and no progress. I then take over and put you on the right lines. Could Jeeves have got you into Brinkley Court? Not a chance. Aunt Dahlia isn't his aunt. I merely mention these things."

"By Jove, Bertie, I don't know how to thank you."

"My dear chap!"

"But, I say."

"Now what?"

"What do I do when I get there?"

"If you knew Brinkley Court, you would not ask that question. In those romantic surroundings you can't miss. Great lovers through the ages have fixed up the preliminary formalities at Brinkley. The place is simply ill with atmosphere. You will stroll with the girl in the shady walks. You will sit with her on the shady lawns. You will row on the lake with her. And gradually you will find yourself working up to a point where——"

"By Jove, I believe you're right."

"Of course, I'm right. I've got engaged three times at Brinkley. No business resulted, but the fact remains. And I went there without the foggiest idea of indulging in the tender pash. I hadn't the slightest intention of proposing to anybody. Yet no sooner had I entered those romantic grounds than I found myself reaching out for the nearest girl in sight and slapping my soul down in front of her. It's something in the air."

"I see exactly what you mean. That's just what I want to be able to do—work up to it. And in London—curse the place—everything's in such a rush that you don't get a chance."

"Quite. You see a girl alone for about five minutes a day, and if you want to ask her to be your wife, you've got to charge into it as if you were trying to grab the gold ring on a merry-go-round."

"That's right. London rattles one. I shall be a different man altogether in the country. What a bit of luck this Travers woman turning out to be your aunt."

"I don't know what you mean, turning out to be my aunt. She has been my aunt all along."

"I mean, how extraordinary that it should be your aunt that Madeline's going to stay with."

"Not at all. She and my Cousin Angela are close friends. At Cannes she was with us all the time."

"Oh, you met Madeline at Cannes, did you? By Jove, Bertie," said the poor lizard devoutly, "I wish I could have seen her at Cannes. How wonderful she must have looked in beach pyjamas! Oh, Bertie——"

"Quite," I said, a little distantly. Even when restored by one of Jeeves's depth bombs, one doesn't want this sort of thing after a hard night. I touched the bell and, when Jeeves appeared, requested him to bring me telegraph form and pencil. I then wrote a well-worded communication to Aunt Dahlia, informing her that I was sending my friend, Augustus Fink-Nottle, down to Brinkley today to enjoy her hospitality, and handed it to Gussie.

"Push that in at the first post office you pass," I said. "She will find it waiting for her on her return."

Gussie popped along, flapping the telegram and looking like a close-up of Joan Crawford, and I turned to Jeeves and gave him a précis of my operations.

"Simple, you observe, Jeeves. Nothing elaborate."

"No, sir."

"Nothing far-fetched. Nothing strained or bizarre. Just Nature's remedy."

"Yes, sir."

"This is the attack as it should have been delivered. What do you call it when two people of opposite sexes are bunged together in close association in a secluded spot, meeting each other every day and seeing a lot of each other?"

"Is 'propinquity' the word you wish, sir?"

"It is. I stake everything on propinquity, Jeeves. Propinquity, in my opinion, is what will do the trick. At the moment, as you are aware, Gussie is a mere jelly when in the presence. But ask yourself how he will feel in a week or so, after he and she have been helping themselves to sausages out of the same dish day after day at the breakfast sideboard. Cutting the same ham, ladling out communal kidneys and bacon—why——"

I broke off abruptly. I had had one of my ideas.

"Golly, Jeeves!"

"Sir?"

"Here's an instance of how you have to think of everything. You heard me mention sausages, kidneys and bacon and ham."

"Yes, sir."

"Well, there must be nothing of that. Fatal. The wrong note entirely. Give me that telegraph form and pencil. I must warn Gussie without delay. What he's got to do is to create in this girl's mind the impression that he is pining away for love of her. This cannot be done by wolfing sausages."

"No, sir."

"Very well, then."

And, taking form and *p.*, I drafted the following:

Fink-Nottle

Brinkley Court,

Market Snodsbury

Worcestershire

Lay off the sausages. Avoid the ham. Bertie.

"Send that off, Jeeves, instanter."

"Very good, sir."

I sank back on the pillows.

"Well, Jeeves," I said, "you see how I am taking hold. You notice the grip I am getting on this case. No doubt you realize now that it would pay you to study my methods."

"No doubt, sir."

"And even now you aren't on to the full depths of the extraordinary sagacity I've shown. Do you know what brought Aunt Dahlia up here this morning? She came to tell me I'd got to distribute the prizes at some beastly seminary she's a governor of down at Market Snodsbury."

"Indeed, sir? I fear you will scarcely find that a congenial task."

"Ah, but I'm not going to do it. I'm going to shove it off on to Gussie."

"Sir?"

"I propose, Jeeves, to wire to Aunt Dahlia saying that I can't get down, and suggesting that she unleashes him on these young Borstal inmates of hers in my stead."

"But if Mr. Fink-Nottle should decline, sir?"

"Decline? Can you see him declining? Just conjure up the picture in your mind, Jeeves. Scene, the drawing-room at Brinkley; Gussie wedged into a corner, with Aunt Dahlia standing over him making hunting noises. I put it to you, Jeeves, can you see him declining?"

"Not readily, sir. I agree. Mrs. Travers is a forceful personality."

"He won't have a hope of declining. His only way out would be to slide off. And he can't slide off, because he wants to be with Miss Bassett. No, Gussie will have to toe the line, and I shall be saved from a job at which I confess the soul shuddered. Getting up on a platform and delivering a short, manly speech to a lot of foul school-kids! Golly, Jeeves. I've been through that sort of thing once, what? You remember that time at the girls' school?"

"Very vividly, sir."

"What an ass I made of myself!"

"Certainly I have seen you to better advantage, sir."

"I think you might bring me just one more of those dynamite specials of yours, Jeeves. This narrow squeak has made me come over all faint."

I suppose it must have taken Aunt Dahlia three hours or so to get back to Brinkley, because it wasn't till well after lunch that her telegram arrived. It read like a telegram that had been dispatched in a white-hot surge of emotion some two minutes after she had read mine.

As follows:

Am taking legal advice to ascertain whether strangling an idiot nephew counts as murder. If it doesn't look out for yourself. Consider your conduct frozen limit. What do you mean by planting your loathsome friends on me like this? Do you think Brinkley Court is a leper colony or what is it? Who is this Spink-Bottle? Love. Travers.

I had expected some such initial reaction. I replied in temperate vein:

Not Bottle. Nottle. Regards. Bertie.

Almost immediately after she had dispatched the above heart cry, Gussie must have arrived, for it wasn't twenty minutes later when I received the following:

Cipher telegram signed by you has reached me here. Runs "Lay off the sausages. Avoid the ham." Wire key immediately. Fink-Nottle.

I replied:

Also kidneys. Cheerio. Bertie.

I had staked all on Gussie making a favourable impression on his hostess, basing my confidence on the fact that he was one of those timid, obsequious, teacup-passing, thin-bread-and-butter-offering yes-men whom women of my Aunt Dahlia's type nearly always like at first sight. That I had not overrated my acumen was proved by her next in order, which, I was pleased to note, assayed a markedly larger percentage of the milk of human kindness.

As follows:

Well, this friend of yours has got here, and I must say that for a friend of yours he seems less sub-human than I had expected. A bit of a pop-eyed bleater, but on the whole clean and civil, and certainly most informative about newts. Am considering arranging series of lectures for him in neighbourhood. All the same I like your nerve using my house as a summer-hotel resort and shall have much to say to you on subject when you come down. Expect you thirtieth. Bring spats. Love. Travers.

To this I riposted:

On consulting engagement book find impossible come Brinkley Court. Deeply regret. Toodle-oo. Bertie.

Hers in reply stuck a sinister note:

Oh, so it's like that, is it? You and your engagement book, indeed. Deeply regret my foot. Let me tell you, my lad, that you will regret it a jolly sight more deeply if you don't come down. If you imagine for one moment that you are going to get out of distributing those prizes, you are very much mistaken. Deeply regret Brinkley Court hundred miles from London, as unable hit you with a brick. Love. Travers.

I then put my fortune to the test, to win or lose it all. It was not a moment for petty economies. I let myself go regardless of expense:

No, but dash it, listen. Honestly, you don't want me. Get Fink-Nottle distribute prizes. A born distributor, who will do you credit. Confidently anticipate Augustus Fink-Nottle as Master of Revels on thirty-first inst. would make genuine sensation. Do not miss this great chance, which may never occur again. Tinkerty-tonk. Bertie.

There was an hour of breathless suspense, and then the joyful tidings arrived:

Well, all right. Something in what you say, I suppose. Consider you treacherous worm and contemptible, spineless cowardly custard, but have booked Spink-Bottle. Stay where you are, then, and I hope you get run over by an omnibus. Love. Travers.

The relief, as you may well imagine, was stupendous. A great weight seemed to have rolled off my mind. It was as if somebody had been pouring Jeeves's pick-me-ups into me through a funnel. I sang as I dressed for dinner that night. At the Drones I was so gay and cheery that there were several complaints. And when I got home and turned into the old bed, I fell asleep like a little child within five minutes of inserting the person between the sheets. It seemed to me that the whole distressing affair might now be considered definitely closed.

Conceive my astonishment, therefore, when waking on the morrow and sitting up to dig into the morning tea-cup, I beheld on the tray another telegram.

My heart sank. Could Aunt Dahlia have slept on it and changed her mind? Could Gussie, unable to face the ordeal confronting him, have legged it during the night down a water-pipe? With these speculations racing through the bean, I tore open the envelope And as I noted contents I uttered a startled yip.

"Sir?" said Jeeves, pausing at the door.

I read the thing again. Yes, I had got the gist all right. No, I had not been deceived in the substance.

"Jeeves," I said, "do you know what?"

"No, sir."

"You know my cousin Angela?"

"Yes, sir."

"You know young Tuppy Glossop?"

"Yes, sir."

"They've broken off their engagement."

"I am sorry to hear that, sir."

"I have here a communication from Aunt Dahlia, specifically stating this. I wonder what the row was about."

"I could not say, sir."

"Of course you couldn't. Don't be an ass, Jeeves."

"No, sir."

I brooded. I was deeply moved.

"Well, this means that we shall have to go down to Brinkley today. Aunt Dahlia is obviously all of a twitter, and my place is by her side. You had better pack this morning, and catch that 12.45 train with the luggage. I have a lunch engagement, so will follow in the car."

"Very good, sir."

I brooded some more.

"I must say this has come as a great shock to me, Jeeves."

"No doubt, sir."

"A very great shock. Angela and Tuppy.... Tut, tut! Why, they seemed like the paper on the wall. Life is full of sadness, Jeeves."

"Yes, sir."

"Still, there it is."

"Undoubtedly, sir."

"Right ho, then. Switch on the bath."

"Very good, sir."

-7-

I meditated pretty freely as I drove down to Brinkley in the old two-seater that afternoon. The news of this rift or rupture of Angela's and Tuppy's had disturbed me greatly.

The projected match, you see, was one on which I had always looked with kindly approval. Too often, when a chap of your acquaintance is planning to marry a girl you know, you find yourself knitting the brow a bit and chewing the lower lip dubiously, feeling that he or she, or both, should be warned while there is yet time.

But I have never felt anything of this nature about Tuppy and Angela. Tuppy, when not making an ass of himself, is a soundish sort of egg. So is Angela a soundish sort of egg. And, as far as being in love was concerned, it had always seemed to me that you wouldn't have been far out in describing them as two hearts that beat as one.

True, they had had their little tiffs, notably on the occasion when Tuppy—with what he said was fearless honesty and I considered thorough goofiness—had told Angela that her new hat made her look like a Pekingese. But in every romance you have to budget for the occasional dust-up, and after that incident I had supposed that he had learned his lesson and that from then on life would be one grand, sweet song.

And now this wholly unforeseen severing of diplomatic relations had popped up through a trap.

I gave the thing the cream of the Wooster brain all the way down, but it continued to beat me what could have caused the outbreak of hostilities, and I bunged my foot sedulously on the accelerator in order to get to Aunt Dahlia with the greatest possible speed and learn the inside history straight from the horse's mouth. And what with all six cylinders hitting nicely, I made good time and found myself closeted with the relative shortly before the hour of the evening cocktail.

She seemed glad to see me. In fact, she actually said she was glad to see me—a statement no other aunt on the list would have committed herself to, the customary reaction of these near and dear ones to the spectacle of Bertram arriving for a visit being a sort of sick horror.

"Decent of you to rally round, Bertie," she said.

"My place was by your side, Aunt Dahlia," I responded.

I could see at a g. that the unfortunate affair had got in amongst her in no uncertain manner. Her usually cheerful map was clouded, and the genial smile conspic. by its a. I pressed her hand sympathetically, to indicate that my heart bled for her.

"Bad show this, my dear old flesh and blood," I said. "I'm afraid you've been having a sticky time. You must be worried."

She snorted emotionally. She looked like an aunt who has just bitten into a bad oyster.

"Worried is right. I haven't had a peaceful moment since I got back from Cannes. Ever since I put my foot across this blasted threshold," said Aunt Dahlia, returning for the nonce to the hearty *argot* of the hunting field, "everything's been at sixes and sevens. First there was that mix-up about the prize-giving."

She paused at this point and gave me a look. "I had been meaning to speak freely to you about your behaviour in that matter, Bertie," she said. "I had some good things all stored up. But, as you've rallied round like this, I suppose I shall have to let you off. And, anyway, it is probably all for the best that you evaded your obligations in that sickeningly craven way. I have an idea that this Spink-Bottle of yours is going to be good. If only he can keep off newts."

"Has he been talking about newts?"

"He has. Fixing me with a glittering eye, like the Ancient Mariner. But if that was the worst I had to bear, I wouldn't mind. What I'm worrying about is what Tom says when he starts talking."

"Uncle Tom?"

"I wish there was something else you could call him except 'Uncle Tom'," said Aunt Dahlia a little testily. "Every time you do it, I expect to see him turn black and start playing the banjo. Yes, Uncle Tom, if you must have it. I shall have to tell him soon about losing all that money at baccarat, and, when I do, he will go up like a rocket."

"Still, no doubt Time, the great healer——"

"Time, the great healer, be blowed. I've got to get a cheque for five hundred pounds out of him for *Milady's Boudoir* by August the third at the latest."

I was concerned. Apart from a nephew's natural interest in an aunt's refined weekly paper, I had always had a soft spot in my heart for *Milady's Boudoir* ever since I contributed that article to it on What the Well-Dressed Man is Wearing. Sentimental, possibly, but we old journalists do have these feelings.

"Is the *Boudoir* on the rocks?"

"It will be if Tom doesn't cough up. It needs help till it has turned the corner."

"But wasn't it turning the corner two years ago?"

"It was. And it's still at it. Till you've run a weekly paper for women, you don't know what corners are."

"And you think the chances of getting into uncle—into my uncle by marriage's ribs are slight?"

"I'll tell you, Bertie. Up till now, when these subsidies were required, I have always been able to come to Tom in the gay, confident spirit of an only child touching an indulgent father for chocolate cream. But he's just had a demand from the income-tax people for an additional fifty-eight pounds, one and threepence, and all he's been talking about since I got back has been ruin and the sinister trend of socialistic legislation and what will become of us all."

I could readily believe it. This Tom has a peculiarity I've noticed in other very oofy men. Nick him for the paltriest sum, and he lets out a squawk you can hear at Land's End. He has the stuff in gobs, but he hates giving up.

"If it wasn't for Anatole's cooking, I doubt if he would bother to carry on. Thank God for Anatole, I say."

I bowed my head reverently.

"Good old Anatole," I said.

"Amen," said Aunt Dahlia.

Then the look of holy ecstasy, which is always the result of letting the mind dwell, however briefly, on Anatole's cooking, died out of her face.

"But don't let me wander from the subject," she resumed. "I was telling you of the way hell's foundations have been quivering since I got home. First the prize-giving, then Tom, and now, on top of everything else, this infernal quarrel between Angela and young Glossop."

I nodded gravely. "I was frightfully sorry to hear of that. Terrible shock. What was the row about?"

"Sharks."

"Eh?"

"Sharks. Or, rather, one individual shark. The brute that went for the poor child when she was aquaplaning at Cannes. You remember Angela's shark?"

Certainly I remembered Angela's shark. A man of sensibility does not forget about a cousin nearly being chewed by monsters of the deep. The episode was still green in my memory.

In a nutshell, what had occurred was this: You know how you aquaplane. A motor-boat nips on ahead, trailing a rope. You stand on a board, holding the rope, and the boat tows you along. And every now and then you lose your grip on the rope and plunge into the sea and have to swim to your board again.

A silly process it has always seemed to me, though many find it diverting.

Well, on the occasion referred to, Angela had just regained her board after taking a toss, when a great beastly shark came along and cannoned into it, flinging her into the salty once more. It took her quite a bit of time to get on again and make the motor-boat chap realize what was up and haul her to safety, and during that interval you can readily picture her embarrassment.

According to Angela, the finny denizen kept snapping at her ankles virtually without cessation, so that by the time help arrived, she was feeling more like a salted almond at a public dinner than anything human. Very shaken the poor child had been, I recall, and had talked of nothing else for weeks.

"I remember the whole incident vividly," I said. "But how did that start the trouble?"

"She was telling him the story last night."

"Well?"

"Her eyes shining and her little hands clasped in girlish excitement."

"No doubt."

"And instead of giving her the understanding and sympathy to which she was entitled, what do you think this blasted Glossop did? He sat listening like a lump of dough, as if she had been talking about the weather, and when she had finished, he took his cigarette holder out of his mouth and said, 'I expect it was only a floating log'!"

"He didn't!"

"He did. And when Angela described how the thing had jumped and snapped at her, he took his cigarette holder out of his mouth again, and said, 'Ah! Probably a flatfish. Quite harmless. No doubt it was just trying to play.' Well, I mean! What would you have done if you had been Angela? She has pride, sensibility, all the natural feelings of a good woman. She told him he was an ass and a fool and an idiot, and didn't know what he was talking about."

I must say I saw the girl's viewpoint. It's only about once in a lifetime that anything sensational ever happens to one, and when it does, you don't want people taking all the colour out of it. I remember at school having to read that stuff where that chap, Othello, tells the girl what a hell of a time he'd been having among the cannibals and what not. Well, imagine his feelings if, after he had described some particularly sticky passage with a cannibal chief and was waiting for the awestruck "Oh-h! Not really?", she had said that the whole thing had no doubt been greatly exaggerated and that the man had probably really been a prominent local vegetarian.

Yes, I saw Angela's point of view.

"But don't tell me that when he saw how shirty she was about it, the chump didn't back down?"

"He didn't. He argued. And one thing led to another until, by easy stages, they had arrived at the point where she was saying that she didn't know if he was aware of it, but if he didn't knock off starchy foods and do exercises every morning, he would be getting as fat as a pig, and he was talking about this modern habit of girls putting make-up on their faces, of which he had always disapproved. This continued for a while, and then there was a loud pop and the air was full of mangled fragments of their engagement. I'm distracted about it. Thank goodness you've come, Bertie."

"Nothing could have kept me away," I replied, touched. "I felt you needed me."

"Yes."

"Quite."

"Or, rather," she said, "not you, of course, but Jeeves. The minute all this happened, I thought of him. The situation obviously cries out for Jeeves. If ever in the whole history of human affairs there was a moment when that lofty brain was required about the home, this is it."

I think, if I had been standing up, I would have staggered. In fact, I'm pretty sure I would. But it isn't so dashed easy to stagger when you're sitting in an armchair. Only my face, therefore, showed how deeply I had been stung by these words.

Until she spoke them, I had been all sweetness and light—the sympathetic nephew prepared to strain every nerve to do his bit. I now froze, and the face became hard and set.

"Jeeves!" I said, between clenched teeth.

"Oom beroofen," said Aunt Dahlia.

I saw that she had got the wrong angle.

"I was not sneezing. I was saying 'Jeeves!'"

"And well you may. What a man! I'm going to put the whole thing up to him. There's nobody like Jeeves."

My frigidity became more marked.

"I venture to take issue with you, Aunt Dahlia."

"You take what?"

"Issue."

"You do, do you?"

"I emphatically do. Jeeves is hopeless."

"What?"

"Quite hopeless. He has lost his grip completely. Only a couple of days ago I was compelled to take him off a case because his handling of it was so footling. And, anyway, I resent this assumption, if assumption is the word I want, that Jeeves is the only fellow with brain. I object to the way everybody puts things up to him without consulting me and letting me have a stab at them first."

She seemed about to speak, but I checked her with a gesture.

"It is true that in the past I have sometimes seen fit to seek Jeeves's advice. It is possible that in the future I may seek it again. But I claim the right to have a pop at these problems, as they arise, in person, without having everybody behave as if Jeeves was the only onion in the hash. I sometimes feel that Jeeves, though admittedly not unsuccessful in the past, has been lucky rather than gifted."

"Have you and Jeeves had a row?"

"Nothing of the kind."

"You seem to have it in for him."

"Not at all."

And yet I must admit that there was a modicum of truth in what she said. I had been feeling pretty austere about the man all day, and I'll tell you why.

You remember that he caught that 12.45 train with the luggage, while I remained on in order to keep a luncheon engagement. Well, just before I started out to the tryst, I was pottering about the flat, and suddenly—I don't know what put the suspicion into my head, possibly the fellow's manner had been furtive—something seemed to whisper to me to go and have a look in the wardrobe.

And it was as I had suspected. There was the mess-jacket still on its hanger. The hound hadn't packed it.

Well, as anybody at the Drones will tell you, Bertram Wooster is a pretty hard chap to outgeneral. I shoved the thing in a brown-paper parcel and put it in the back of the car, and it was on a chair in the hall now. But that didn't alter the fact that Jeeves had attempted to do the dirty on me, and I suppose a certain what-d'you-call-it had crept into my manner during the above remarks.

"There has been no breach," I said. "You might describe it as a passing coolness, but no more. We did not happen to see eye to eye with regard to my white mess-jacket with the brass buttons and I was compelled to assert my personality. But——"

"Well, it doesn't matter, anyway. The thing that matters is that you are talking piffle, you poor fish. Jeeves lost his grip? Absurd. Why, I saw him for a moment when he arrived, and his eyes were absolutely glittering with intelligence. I said to myself 'Trust Jeeves,' and I intend to."

"You would be far better advised to let me see what I can accomplish, Aunt Dahlia."

"For heaven's sake, don't you start butting in. You'll only make matters worse."

"On the contrary, it may interest you to know that while driving here I concentrated deeply on this trouble of Angela's and was successful in formulating a plan, based on the psychology of the individual, which I am proposing to put into effect at an early moment."

"Oh, my God!"

"My knowledge of human nature tells me it will work."

"Bertie," said Aunt Dahlia, and her manner struck me as febrile, "lay off, lay off! For pity's sake, lay off. I know these plans of yours. I suppose you want to shove Angela into the lake and push young Glossop in after her to save her life, or something like that."

"Nothing of the kind."

"It's the sort of thing you would do."

"My scheme is far more subtle. Let me outline it for you."

"No, thanks."

"I say to myself——"

"But not to me."

"Do listen for a second."

"I won't."

"Right ho, then. I am dumb."

"And have been from a child."

I perceived that little good could result from continuing the discussion. I waved a hand and shrugged a shoulder.

"Very well, Aunt Dahlia," I said, with dignity, "if you don't want to be in on the ground floor, that is your affair. But you are missing an intellectual treat. And, anyway, no matter how much you may behave like the deaf adder of Scripture which, as you are doubtless aware, the more one piped, the less it danced, or words to that effect, I shall carry on as planned. I am extremely fond of Angela, and I shall spare no effort to bring the sunshine back into her heart."

"Bertie, you abysmal chump, I appeal to you once more. Will you please lay off? You'll only make things ten times as bad as they are already."

I remember reading in one of those historical novels once about a chap—a buck he would have been, no doubt, or a macaroni or some such bird as that—who, when people said the wrong thing, merely laughed down from lazy eyelids and flicked a speck of dust from the irreproachable Mechlin lace at his wrists. This was practically what I did now. At least, I straightened my tie and smiled one of those inscrutable smiles of mine. I then withdrew and went out for a saunter in the garden.

And the first chap I ran into was young Tuppy. His brow was furrowed, and he was moodily bunging stones at a flowerpot.

-8-

I think I have told you before about young Tuppy Glossop. He was the fellow, if you remember, who, callously ignoring the fact that we had been friends since boyhood, betted me one night at the Drones that I could swing myself across the swimming bath by the rings—a childish feat for one of my lissomeness—and then, having seen me well on the way, looped back the last ring, thus rendering it necessary for me to drop into the deep end in formal evening costume.

To say that I had not resented this foul deed, which seemed to me deserving of the title of the crime of the century, would be paltering with the truth. I had resented it profoundly, chafing not a little at the time and continuing to chafe for some weeks.

But you know how it is with these things. The wound heals. The agony abates.

I am not saying, mind you, that had the opportunity presented itself of dropping a wet sponge on Tuppy from some high spot or of putting an eel in his bed or finding some other form of self-expression of a like nature, I would not have embraced it eagerly; but that let me out. I mean to say, grievously injured though I had been, it gave me no pleasure to feel that the fellow's bally life was being ruined by the loss of a girl whom, despite all that had passed, I was convinced he still loved like the dickens.

On the contrary, I was heart and soul in favour of healing the breach and rendering everything hotsy-totsy once more between these two young sundered blighters. You will have gleaned that from my remarks to Aunt Dahlia, and if you had been present at this moment and had seen the kindly commiserating look I gave Tuppy, you would have gleaned it still more.

It was one of those searching, melting looks, and was accompanied by the hearty clasp of the right hand and the gentle laying of the left on the collar-bone.

"Well, Tuppy, old man," I said. "How are you, old man?"

My commiseration deepened as I spoke the words, for there had been no lighting up of the eye, no answering pressure of the palm, no sign whatever, in short, of any disposition on his part to do Spring dances at the sight of an old friend. The man seemed sandbagged. Melancholy, as I remember Jeeves saying once about Pongo Twistleton when he was trying to knock off smoking, had marked him for her own. Not that I was surprised, of course. In the circs., no doubt, a certain moodiness was only natural.

I released the hand, ceased to knead the shoulder, and, producing the old case, offered him a cigarette.

He took it dully.

"Are you here, Bertie?" he asked.

"Yes, I'm here."

"Just passing through, or come to stay?"

I thought for a moment. I might have told him that I had arrived at Brinkley Court with the express intention of bringing Angela and himself together once more, of knitting up the severed threads, and so on and so forth; and for perhaps half the time required for the lighting of a gasper I had almost decided to do so. Then, I reflected, better, on the whole, perhaps not. To broadcast the fact that I proposed to take him and Angela and play on them as on a couple of stringed instruments might have been injudicious. Chaps don't always like being played on as on a stringed instrument.

"It all depends," I said. "I may remain. I may push on. My plans are uncertain."

He nodded listlessly, rather in the manner of a man who did not give a damn what I did, and stood gazing out over the sunlit garden. In build and appearance, Tuppy somewhat resembles a bulldog, and his aspect now was that of one of these fine animals who has just been refused a slice of cake. It was not difficult for a man of my discernment to read what was in his mind, and it occasioned me no surprise, therefore, when his next words had to do with the subject marked with a cross on the agenda paper.

"You've heard of this business of mine, I suppose? Me and Angela?"

"I have, indeed, Tuppy, old man."

"We've bust up."

"I know. Some little friction, I gather, *in re* Angela's shark."

"Yes. I said it must have been a flatfish."

"So my informant told me."

"Who did you hear it from?"

"Aunt Dahlia."

"I suppose she cursed me properly?"

"Oh, no."

"Beyond referring to you in one passage as 'this blasted Glossop', she was, I thought, singularly temperate in her language for a woman who at one time hunted regularly with the Quorn. All the same, I could see, if you don't mind me saying so, old man, that she felt you might have behaved with a little more tact."

"Tact!"

"And I must admit I rather agreed with her. Was it nice, Tuppy, was it quite kind to take the bloom off Angela's shark like that? You must remember that Angela's shark is very dear to her. Could you not see what a sock on the jaw it would be for the poor child to hear it described by the man to whom she had given her heart as a flatfish?"

I saw that he was struggling with some powerful emotion.

"And what about my side of the thing?" he demanded, in a voice choked with feeling.

"Your side?"

"You don't suppose," said Tuppy, with rising vehemence, "that I would have exposed this dashed synthetic shark for the flatfish it undoubtedly was if there had not been causes that led up to it. What induced me to speak as I did was the fact that Angela, the little squirt, had just been most offensive, and I seized the opportunity to get a bit of my own back."

"Offensive?"

"Exceedingly offensive. Purely on the strength of my having let fall some casual remark—simply by way of saying something and keeping the conversation going—to the effect that I wondered what Anatole was going to give us for dinner, she said that I was too material and ought not always to be thinking of food. Material, my elbow! As a matter of fact, I'm particularly spiritual."

"Quite."

"I don't see any harm in wondering what Anatole was going to give us for dinner. Do you?"

"Of course not. A mere ordinary tribute of respect to a great artist."

"Exactly."

"All the same——"

"Well?"

"I was only going to say that it seems a pity that the frail craft of love should come a stinker like this when a few manly words of contrition——"

He stared at me.

"You aren't suggesting that I should climb down?"

"It would be the fine, big thing, old egg."

"I wouldn't dream of climbing down."

"But, Tuppy——"

"No. I wouldn't do it."

"But you love her, don't you?"

This touched the spot. He quivered noticeably, and his mouth twisted. Quite the tortured soul.

"I'm not saying I don't love the little blighter," he said, obviously moved. "I love her passionately. But that doesn't alter the fact that I consider that what she needs most in this world is a swift kick in the pants."

A Wooster could scarcely pass this. "Tuppy, old man!"

"It's no good saying 'Tuppy, old man'."

"Well, I do say 'Tuppy, old man'. Your tone shocks me. One raises the eyebrows. Where is the fine, old, chivalrous spirit of the Glossops."

"That's all right about the fine, old, chivalrous spirit of the Glossops. Where is the sweet, gentle, womanly spirit of the Angelas? Telling a fellow he was getting a double chin!"

"Did she do that?"

"She did."

"Oh, well, girls will be girls. Forget it, Tuppy. Go to her and make it up."

He shook his head.

"No. It is too late. Remarks have been passed about my tummy which it is impossible to overlook."

"But, Tummy—Tuppy, I mean—be fair. You once told her her new hat made her look like a Pekingese."

"It did make her look like a Pekingese. That was not vulgar abuse. It was sound, constructive criticism, with no motive behind it but the kindly desire to keep her from making an exhibition of herself in public. Wantonly to accuse a man of puffing when he goes up a flight of stairs is something very different."

I began to see that the situation would require all my address and ingenuity. If the wedding bells were ever to ring out in the little church of Market Snodsbury, Bertram had plainly got to put in some shrewdish work. I had gathered, during my conversation with Aunt Dahlia, that there had been a certain amount of frank speech between the two contracting parties, but I had not realized till now that matters had gone so far.

The pathos of the thing gave me the pip. Tuppy had admitted in so many words that love still animated the Glossop bosom, and I was convinced that, even after all that occurred, Angela had not ceased to love him. At the moment, no doubt, she might be wishing that she could hit him with a bottle, but deep down in her I was prepared to bet that there still lingered all the old affection and tenderness. Only injured pride was keeping these two apart, and I felt that if Tuppy would make the first move, all would be well.

I had another whack at it.

"She's broken-hearted about this rift, Tuppy."

"How do you know? Have you seen her?"

"No, but I'll bet she is."

"She doesn't look it."

"Wearing the mask, no doubt. Jeeves does that when I assert my authority."

"She wrinkles her nose at me as if I were a drain that had got out of order."

"Merely the mask. I feel convinced she loves you still, and that a kindly word from you is all that is required."

I could see that this had moved him. He plainly wavered. He did a sort of twiddly on the turf with his foot. And, when he spoke, one spotted the tremolo in the voice:

"You really think that?"

"Absolutely."

"H'm."

"If you were to go to her——"

He shook his head.

"I can't do that. It would be fatal. Bing, instantly, would go my prestige. I know girls. Grovel, and the best of them get uppish." He mused. "The only way to work the thing would be by tipping her off in some indirect way that I am prepared to open negotiations. Should I sigh a bit when we meet, do you think?"

"She would think you were puffing."

"That's true."

I lit another cigarette and gave my mind to the matter. And first crack out of the box, as is so often the way with the Woosters, I got an idea. I remembered the counsel I had given Gussie in the matter of the sausages and ham.

"I've got it, Tuppy. There is one infallible method of indicating to a girl that you love her, and it works just as well when you've had a row and want to make it up. Don't eat any dinner tonight. You can see how impressive that would be. She knows how devoted you are to food."

He started violently.

"I am not devoted to food!"

"No, no."

"I am not devoted to food at all."

"Quite. All I meant——"

"This rot about me being devoted to food," said Tuppy warmly, "has got to stop. I am young and healthy and have a good appetite, but that's not the same as being devoted to food. I admire Anatole as a master of his craft, and am always willing to consider anything he may put before me, but when you say I am devoted to food——"

"Quite, quite. All I meant was that if she sees you push away your dinner untasted, she will realize that your heart is aching, and will probably be the first to suggest blowing the all clear."

Tuppy was frowning thoughtfully.

"Push my dinner away, eh?"

"Yes."

"Push away a dinner cooked by Anatole?"

"Yes."

"Push it away untasted?"

"Yes."

"Let us get this straight. Tonight, at dinner, when the butler offers me a *ris de veau à la financiere*, or whatever it may be, hot from Anatole's hands, you wish me to push it away untasted?"

"Yes."

He chewed his lip. One could sense the struggle going on within. And then suddenly a sort of glow came into his face. The old martyrs probably used to look like that.

"All right."

"You'll do it?"

"I will."

"Fine."

"Of course, it will be agony."

I pointed out the silver lining.

"Only for the moment. You could slip down tonight, after everyone is in bed, and raid the larder."

He brightened.

"That's right. I could, couldn't I?"

"I expect there would be something cold there."

"There is something cold there," said Tuppy, with growing cheerfulness. "A steak-and-kidney pie. We had it for lunch today. One of Anatole's ripest. The thing I admire about that man," said Tuppy reverently, "the thing that I admire so enormously about Anatole is that, though a Frenchman, he does not, like so many of these *chefs*, confine himself exclusively to French dishes, but is always willing and ready to weigh in with some good old simple English fare such as this steak-and-kidney pie to which I have alluded. A masterly pie, Bertie, and it wasn't more than half finished. It will do me nicely."

"And at dinner you will push, as arranged?"

"Absolutely as arranged."

"Fine."

"It's an excellent idea. One of Jeeves's best. You can tell him from me, when you see him, that I'm much obliged."

The cigarette fell from my fingers. It was as though somebody had slapped Bertram Wooster across the face with a wet dish-rag.

"You aren't suggesting that you think this scheme I have been sketching out is Jeeves's?"

"Of course it is. It's no good trying to kid me, Bertie. You wouldn't have thought of a wheeze like that in a million years."

There was a pause. I drew myself up to my full height; then, seeing that he wasn't looking at me, lowered myself again.

"Come, Glossop," I said coldly, "we had better be going. It is time we were dressing for dinner."

-9-

Tuppy's fatheaded words were still rankling in my bosom as I went up to my room. They continued rankling as I shed the form-fitting, and had not ceased to rankle when, clad in the old dressing-gown, I made my way along the corridor to the *salle de bain.*

It is not too much to say that I was piqued to the tonsils.

I mean to say, one does not court praise. The adulation of the multitude means very little to one. But, all the same, when one has taken the trouble to whack out a highly juicy scheme to benefit an in-the-soup friend in his hour of travail, it's pretty foul to find him giving the credit to one's personal attendant, particularly if that personal attendant is a man who goes about the place not packing mess-jackets.

But after I had been splashing about in the porcelain for a bit, composure began to return. I have always found that in moments of heart-bowed-downness there is nothing that calms the bruised spirit like a good go at the soap and water. I don't say I actually sang in the tub, but there were times when it was a mere spin of the coin whether I would do so or not.

The spiritual anguish induced by that tactless speech had become noticeably lessened.

The discovery of a toy duck in the soap dish, presumably the property of some former juvenile visitor, contributed not a little to this new and happier frame of mind. What with one thing and another, I hadn't played with toy ducks in my bath for years, and I found the novel experience most invigorating. For the benefit of those interested, I may mention that if you shove the thing under the surface with the sponge and then let it go, it shoots out of the water in a manner calculated to divert the most careworn. Ten minutes of this and I was enabled to return to the bedchamber much more the old merry Bertram.

Jeeves was there, laying out the dinner disguise. He greeted the young master with his customary suavity.

"Good evening, sir."

I responded in the same affable key.

"Good evening, Jeeves."

"I trust you had a pleasant drive, sir."

"Very pleasant, thank you, Jeeves. Hand me a sock or two, will you?"

He did so, and I commenced to don,

"Well, Jeeves," I said, reaching for the underlinen, "here we are again at Brinkley Court in the county of Worcestershire."

"Yes, sir."

"A nice mess things seem to have gone and got themselves into in this rustic joint."

"Yes, sir."

"The rift between Tuppy Glossop and my cousin Angela would appear to be serious."

"Yes, sir. Opinion in the servants' hall is inclined to take a grave view of the situation."

"And the thought that springs to your mind, no doubt, is that I shall have my work cut out to fix things up?"

"Yes, sir."

"You are wrong, Jeeves. I have the thing well in hand."

"You surprise me, sir."

"I thought I should. Yes, Jeeves, I pondered on the matter most of the way down here, and with the happiest results. I have just been in conference with Mr. Glossop, and everything is taped out."

"Indeed, sir? Might I inquire——"

"You know my methods, Jeeves. Apply them. Have you," I asked, slipping into the shirt and starting to adjust the cravat, "been gnawing on the thing at all?"

"Oh, yes, sir. I have always been much attached to Miss Angela, and I felt that it would afford me great pleasure were I to be able to be of service to her."

"A laudable sentiment. But I suppose you drew blank?"

"No, sir. I was rewarded with an idea."

"What was it?"

"It occurred to me that a reconciliation might be effected between Mr. Glossop and Miss Angela by appealing to that instinct which prompts gentlemen in time of peril to hasten to the rescue of——"

I had to let go of the cravat in order to raise a hand. I was shocked.

"Don't tell me you were contemplating descending to that old he-saved-her-from-drowning gag? I am surprised, Jeeves. Surprised and pained. When I was discussing the matter with Aunt Dahlia on my arrival, she said in a sniffy sort of way that she supposed I was going to shove my Cousin Angela into the lake and push Tuppy in to haul her out, and I let her see pretty clearly that I considered the suggestion an insult to my intelligence. And now, if your words have the meaning I read into them, you are mooting precisely the same drivelling scheme. Really, Jeeves!"

"No, sir. Not that. But the thought did cross my mind, as I walked in the grounds and passed the building where the fire-bell hangs, that a sudden alarm of fire in the night might result in Mr. Glossop endeavouring to assist Miss Angela to safety."

I shivered.

"Rotten, Jeeves."

"Well, sir——"

"No good. Not a bit like it."

"I fancy, sir——"

"No, Jeeves. No more. Enough has been said. Let us drop the subj."

I finished tying the tie in silence. My emotions were too deep for speech. I knew, of course, that this man had for the time being lost his grip, but I had never suspected that he had gone absolutely to pieces like this. Remembering some of the swift ones he had pulled in the past, I shrank with horror from the spectacle of his present ineptitude. Or is it ineptness? I mean this frightful disposition of his to stick straws in his hair and talk like a perfect ass. It was the old, old story, I supposed. A man's brain whizzes along for years exceeding the speed limit, and something suddenly goes wrong with the steering-gear and it skids and comes a smeller in the ditch.

"A bit elaborate," I said, trying to put the thing in as kindly a light as possible. "Your old failing. You can see that it's a bit elaborate?"

"Possibly the plan I suggested might be considered open to that criticism, sir, but *faute de mieux*——"

"I don't get you, Jeeves."

"A French expression, sir, signifying 'for want of anything better'."

A moment before, I had been feeling for this wreck of a once fine thinker nothing but a gentle pity. These words jarred the Wooster pride, inducing asperity.

"I understand perfectly well what *faute de mieux* means, Jeeves. I did not recently spend two months among our Gallic neighbours for nothing. Besides, I remember that one from school. What caused my bewilderment was that you should be employing the expression, well knowing that there is no bally *faute de mieux* about it at all. Where do you get that *faute-de-mieux* stuff? Didn't I tell you I had everything taped out?"

"Yes, sir, but——"

"What do you mean—but?"

"Well, sir——"

"Push on, Jeeves. I am ready, even anxious, to hear your views."

"Well, sir, if I may take the liberty of reminding you of it, your plans in the past have not always been uniformly successful."

There was a silence—rather a throbbing one—during which I put on my waistcoat in a marked manner. Not till I had got the buckle at the back satisfactorily adjusted did I speak.

"It is true, Jeeves," I said formally, "that once or twice in the past I may have missed the bus. This, however, I attribute purely to bad luck."

"Indeed, sir?"

"On the present occasion I shall not fail, and I'll tell you why I shall not fail. Because my scheme is rooted in human nature."

"Indeed, sir?"

"It is simple. Not elaborate. And, furthermore, based on the psychology of the individual."

"Indeed, sir?"

"Jeeves," I said, "don't keep saying 'Indeed, sir?' No doubt nothing is further from your mind than to convey such a suggestion, but you have a way of stressing the 'in' and then coming down with a thud on the 'deed' which makes it virtually tantamount to 'Oh, yeah?' Correct this, Jeeves."

"Very good, sir."

"I tell you I have everything nicely lined up. Would you care to hear what steps I have taken?"

"Very much, sir."

"Then listen. Tonight at dinner I have recommended Tuppy to lay off the food."

"Sir?"

"Tut, Jeeves, surely you can follow the idea, even though it is one that would never have occurred to yourself. Have you forgotten that telegram I sent to Gussie Fink-Nottle, steering him away from the sausages and ham? This is the same thing. Pushing the food away untasted is a universally recognized sign of love. It cannot fail to bring home the gravy. You must see that?"

"Well, sir——"

I frowned.

"I don't want to seem always to be criticizing your methods of voice production, Jeeves," I said, "but I must inform you that that 'Well, sir' of yours is in many respects fully as unpleasant as your 'Indeed, sir?' Like the latter, it seems to be tinged with a definite scepticism. It suggests a lack of faith in my vision. The impression I retain after hearing you shoot it at me a couple of times is that you consider me to be talking through the back of my neck, and that only a feudal sense of what is fitting restrains you from substituting for it the words 'Says you!'"

"Oh, no, sir."

"Well, that's what it sounds like. Why don't you think this scheme will work?"

"I fear Miss Angela will merely attribute Mr. Glossop's abstinence to indigestion, sir."

I hadn't thought of that, and I must confess it shook me for a moment. Then I recovered myself. I saw what was at the bottom of all this. Mortified by the consciousness of his own ineptness—or ineptitude—the fellow was simply trying to hamper and obstruct. I decided to knock the stuffing out of him without further preamble.

"Oh?" I said. "You do, do you? Well, be that as it may, it doesn't alter the fact that you've put out the wrong coat. Be so good, Jeeves," I said, indicating with a gesture the gent's ordinary dinner jacket or *smoking*, as we call it on the Côte d'Azur, which was suspended from the hanger on the knob of the wardrobe, "as to shove that bally black thing in the cupboard and bring out my white mess-jacket with the brass buttons."

He looked at me in a meaning manner. And when I say a meaning manner, I mean there was a respectful but at the same time uppish glint in his eye and a sort of muscular spasm flickered across his face which wasn't quite a quiet smile and yet wasn't quite not a quiet smile. Also the soft cough.

"I regret to say, sir, that I inadvertently omitted to pack the garment to which you refer."

The vision of that parcel in the hall seemed to rise before my eyes, and I exchanged a merry wink with it. I may even have hummed a bar or two. I'm not quite sure.

"I know you did, Jeeves," I said, laughing down from lazy eyelids and nicking a speck of dust from the irreproachable Mechlin lace at my wrists. "But I didn't. You will find it on a chair in the hall in a brown-paper parcel."

The information that his low manoeuvres had been rendered null and void and that the thing was on the strength after all, must have been the nastiest of jars, but there was no play of expression on his finely chiselled to indicate it. There very seldom is on Jeeves's f-c. In moments of discomfort, as I had told Tuppy, he wears a mask, preserving throughout the quiet stolidity of a stuffed moose.

"You might just slide down and fetch it, will you?"

"Very good, sir."

"Right ho, Jeeves."

And presently I was sauntering towards the drawing-room with me good old j. nestling snugly abaft the shoulder blades.

And Dahlia was in the drawing-room. She glanced up at my entrance.

"Hullo, eyesore," she said. "What do you think you're made up as?"

I did not get the purport.

"The jacket, you mean?" I queried, groping.

"I do. You look like one of the chorus of male guests at Abernethy Towers in Act 2 of a touring musical comedy."

"You do not admire this jacket?"

"I do not."

"You did at Cannes."

"Well, this isn't Cannes."

"But, dash it——"

"Oh, never mind. Let it go. If you want to give my butler a laugh, what does it matter? What does anything matter now?"

There was a death-where-is-thy-sting-fullness about her manner which I found distasteful. It isn't often that I score off Jeeves in the devastating fashion just described, and when I do I like to see happy, smiling faces about me.

"Tails up, Aunt Dahlia," I urged buoyantly.

"Tails up be dashed," was her sombre response. "I've just been talking to Tom."

"Telling him?"

"No, listening to him. I haven't had the nerve to tell him yet."

"Is he still upset about that income-tax money?"

"Upset is right. He says that Civilisation is in the melting-pot and that all thinking men can read the writing on the wall."

"What wall?"

"Old Testament, ass. Belshazzar's feast."

"Oh, that, yes. I've often wondered how that gag was worked. With mirrors, I expect."

"I wish I could use mirrors to break it to Tom about this baccarat business."

I had a word of comfort to offer here. I had been turning the thing over in my mind since our last meeting, and I thought I saw where she had got twisted. Where she made her error, it seemed to me, was in feeling she had got to tell Uncle Tom. To my way of thinking, the matter was one on which it would be better to continue to exercise a quiet reserve.

"I don't see why you need mention that you lost that money at baccarat."

"What do you suggest, then? Letting *Milady's Boudoir* join Civilisation in the melting-pot. Because that is what it will infallibly do unless I get a cheque by next week. The printers have been showing a nasty spirit for months."

"You don't follow. Listen. It's an understood thing, I take it, that Uncle Tom foots the *Boudoir* bills. If the bally sheet has been turning the corner for two years, he must have got used to forking out by this time. Well, simply ask him for the money to pay the printers."

"I did. Just before I went to Cannes."

"Wouldn't he give it to you?"

"Certainly he gave it to me. He brassed up like an officer and a gentleman. That was the money I lost at baccarat."

"Oh? I didn't know that."

"There isn't much you do know."

A nephew's love made me overlook the slur.

"Tut!" I said.

"What did you say?"

"I said 'Tut!'"

"Say it once again, and I'll biff you where you stand. I've enough to endure without being tutted at."

"Quite."

"Any tutting that's required, I'll attend to myself. And the same applies to clicking the tongue, if you were thinking of doing that."

"Far from it."

"Good."

I stood awhile in thought. I was concerned to the core. My heart, if you remember, had already bled once for Aunt Dahlia this evening. It now bled again. I knew how deeply attached she was to this paper of hers. Seeing it go down the drain would be for her like watching a loved child sink for the third time in some pond or mere.

And there was no question that, unless carefully prepared for the touch, Uncle Tom would see a hundred *Milady's Boudoirs* go phut rather than take the rap.

Then I saw how the thing could be handled. This aunt, I perceived, must fall into line with my other clients. Tuppy Glossop was knocking off dinner to melt Angela. Gussie Fink-Nottle was knocking off dinner to impress the Bassett. Aunt Dahlia must knock off dinner to soften Uncle Tom. For the beauty of this scheme of mine was that there was no limit to the number of entrants. Come one, come all, the more the merrier, and satisfaction guaranteed in every case.

"I've got it," I said. "There is only one course to pursue. Eat less meat."

She looked at me in a pleading sort of way. I wouldn't swear that her eyes were wet with unshed tears, but I rather think they were, certainly she clasped her hands in piteous appeal.

"Must you drivel, Bertie? Won't you stop it just this once? Just for tonight, to please Aunt Dahlia?"

"I'm not drivelling."

"I dare say that to a man of your high standards it doesn't come under the head of drivel, but——"

I saw what had happened. I hadn't made myself quite clear.

"It's all right," I said. "Have no misgivings. This is the real Tabasco. When I said 'Eat less meat', what I meant was that you must refuse your oats at dinner tonight. Just sit there, looking blistered, and wave away each course as it comes with a weary gesture of resignation. You see what will happen. Uncle Tom will notice your loss of appetite, and I am prepared to bet that at the conclusion of the meal he will come to you and say 'Dahlia, darling'—I take it he calls you 'Dahlia'—'Dahlia darling,' he will say, 'I noticed at dinner tonight that you were a bit off your feed. Is anything the matter, Dahlia, darling?' 'Why, yes, Tom, darling,' you will reply. 'It is kind of you to ask, darling. The fact is, darling, I am terribly worried.' 'My darling,' he will say——"

Aunt Dahlia interrupted at this point to observe that these Traverses seemed to be a pretty soppy couple of blighters, to judge by their dialogue. She also wished to know when I was going to get to the point.

I gave her a look.

"'My darling,' he will say tenderly, 'is there anything I can do?' To which your reply will be that there jolly well is—viz. reach for his cheque-book and start writing."

I was watching her closely as I spoke, and was pleased to note respect suddenly dawn in her eyes.

"But, Bertie, this is positively bright."

"I told you Jeeves wasn't the only fellow with brain."

"I believe it would work."

"It's bound to work. I've recommended it to Tuppy."

"Young Glossop?"

"In order to soften Angela."

"Splendid!"

"And to Gussie Fink-Nottle, who wants to make a hit with the Bassett."

"Well, well, well! What a busy little brain it is."

"Always working, Aunt Dahlia, always working."

"You're not the chump I took you for, Bertie."

"When did you ever take me for a chump?"

"Oh, some time last summer. I forget what gave me the idea. Yes, Bertie, this scheme is bright. I suppose, as a matter of fact, Jeeves suggested it."

"Jeeves did not suggest it. I resent these implications. Jeeves had nothing to do with it whatsoever."

"Well, all right, no need to get excited about it. Yes, I think it will work. Tom's devoted to me."

"Who wouldn't be?"

"I'll do it."

And then the rest of the party trickled in, and we toddled down to dinner.

Conditions being as they were at Brinkley Court—I mean to say, the place being loaded down above the Plimsoll mark with aching hearts and standing room only as regarded tortured souls—I hadn't expected the evening meal to be particularly effervescent. Nor was it. Silent. Sombre. The whole thing more than a bit like Christmas dinner on Devil's Island.

I was glad when it was over.

What with having, on top of her other troubles, to rein herself back from the trough, Aunt Dahlia was a total loss as far as anything in the shape of brilliant badinage was concerned. The fact that he was fifty quid in the red and expecting Civilisation to take a toss at any moment had caused Uncle Tom, who always looked a bit like a pterodactyl with a secret sorrow, to take on a deeper melancholy. The Bassett was a silent bread crumbler. Angela might have been hewn from the living rock. Tuppy had the air of a condemned murderer refusing to make the usual hearty breakfast before tooling off to the execution shed.

And as for Gussie Fink-Nottle, many an experienced undertaker would have been deceived by his appearance and started embalming him on sight.

This was the first glimpse I had had of Gussie since we parted at my flat, and I must say his demeanour disappointed me. I had been expecting something a great deal more sparkling.

At my flat, on the occasion alluded to, he had, if you recall, practically given me a signed guarantee that all he needed to touch him off was a rural setting. Yet in this aspect now I could detect no indication whatsoever that he was about to round into mid-season form. He still looked like a cat in an adage, and it did not take me long to realise that my very first act on escaping from this morgue must be to draw him aside and give him a pep talk.

If ever a chap wanted the clarion note, it looked as if it was this Fink-Nottle.

In the general exodus of mourners, however, I lost sight of him, and, owing to the fact that Aunt Dahlia roped me in for a game of backgammon, it was not immediately that I was able to institute a search. But after we had been playing for a while, the butler came in and asked her if she would speak to Anatole, so I managed to get away. And some ten minutes later, having failed to find scent in the house, I started to throw out the drag-net through the grounds, and flushed him in the rose garden.

He was smelling a rose at the moment in a limp sort of way, but removed the beak as I approached.

"Well, Gussie," I said.

I had beamed genially upon him as I spoke, such being my customary policy on meeting an old pal; but instead of beaming back genially, he gave me a most unpleasant look. His attitude perplexed me. It was as if he were not glad to see Bertram. For a moment he stood letting this unpleasant look play upon me, as it were, and then he spoke.

"You and your 'Well, Gussie'!"

He said this between clenched teeth, always an unmatey thing to do, and I found myself more fogged than ever.

"How do you mean—me and my 'Well, Gussie'?"

"I like your nerve, coming bounding about the place, saying 'Well, Gussie.' That's about all the 'Well, Gussie' I shall require from you, Wooster. And it's no good looking like that. You know what I mean. That damned prize-giving! It was a dastardly act to crawl out as you did and shove it off on to me. I will not mince my words. It was the act of a hound and a stinker."

Now, though, as I have shown, I had devoted most of the time on the journey down to meditating upon the case of Angela and Tuppy, I had not neglected to give a thought or two to what I was going to say when I encountered Gussie. I had foreseen that there might be some little temporary unpleasantness when we met, and when a difficult interview is in the offing Bertram Wooster likes to have his story ready.

So now I was able to reply with a manly, disarming frankness. The sudden introduction of the topic had given me a bit of a jolt, it is true, for in the stress of recent happenings I had rather let that prize-giving business slide to the back of my mind; but I had speedily recovered and, as I say, was able to reply with a manly d.f.

"But, my dear chap," I said, "I took it for granted that you would understand that that was all part of my schemes."

He said something about my schemes which I did not catch.

"Absolutely. 'Crawling out' is entirely the wrong way to put it. You don't suppose I didn't want to distribute those prizes, do you? Left to myself, there is nothing I would find a greater treat. But I saw that the square, generous thing to do was to step aside and let you take it on, so I did so. I felt that your need was greater than mine. You don't mean to say you aren't looking forward to it?"

He uttered a coarse expression which I wouldn't have thought he would have known. It just shows that you can bury yourself in the country and still somehow acquire a vocabulary. No doubt one picks up things from the neighbours—the vicar, the local doctor, the man who brings the milk, and so on.

"But, dash it," I said, "can't you see what this is going to do for you? It will send your stock up with a jump. There you will be, up on that platform, a romantic, impressive figure, the star of the whole proceedings, the what-d'you-call-it of all eyes. Madeline Bassett will be all over you. She will see you in a totally new light."

"She will, will she?"

"Certainly she will. Augustus Fink-Nottle, the newts' friend, she knows. She is acquainted with Augustus Fink-Nottle, the dogs' chiropodist. But Augustus Fink-Nottle, the orator—that'll knock her sideways, or I know nothing of the female heart. Girls go potty over a public man. If ever anyone did anyone else a kindness, it was I when I gave this extraordinary attractive assignment to you."

He seemed impressed by my eloquence. Couldn't have helped himself, of course. The fire faded from behind his horn-rimmed spectacles, and in its place appeared the old fish-like goggle.

"'Myes," he said meditatively. "Have you ever made a speech, Bertie?"

"Dozens of times. It's pie. Nothing to it. Why, I once addressed a girls' school."

"You weren't nervous?"

"Not a bit."

"How did you go?"

"They hung on my lips. I held them in the hollow of my hand."

"They didn't throw eggs, or anything?"

"Not a thing."

He expelled a deep breath, and for a space stood staring in silence at a passing slug.

"Well," he said, at length, "it may be all right. Possibly I am letting the thing prey on my mind too much. I may be wrong in supposing it the fate that is worse than death. But I'll tell you this much: the prospect of that prize-giving on the thirty-first of this month has been turning my existence into a nightmare. I haven't been able to sleep or think or eat ... By the way, that reminds me. You never explained that cipher telegram about the sausages and ham."

"It wasn't a cipher telegram. I wanted you to go light on the food, so that she would realize you were in love."

He laughed hollowly.

"I see. Well, I've been doing that, all right."

"Yes, I was noticing at dinner. Splendid."

"I don't see what's splendid about it. It's not going to get me anywhere. I shall never be able to ask her to marry me. I couldn't find nerve to do that if I lived on wafer biscuits for the rest of my life."

"But, dash it, Gussie. In these romantic surroundings. I should have thought the whispering trees alone——"

"I don't care what you would have thought. I can't do it."

"Oh, come!"

"I can't. She seems so aloof, so remote."

"She doesn't."

"Yes, she does. Especially when you see her sideways. Have you seen her sideways, Bertie? That cold, pure profile. It just takes all the heart out of one."

"It doesn't."

"I tell you it does. I catch sight of it, and the words freeze on my lips."

He spoke with a sort of dull despair, and so manifest was his lack of ginger and the spirit that wins to success that for an instant, I confess, I felt a bit stymied. It seemed hopeless to go on trying to steam up such a human jellyfish. Then I saw the way. With that extraordinary quickness of mine, I realized exactly what must be done if this Fink-Nottle was to be enabled to push his nose past the judges' box.

"She must be softened up," I said.

"Be what?"

"Softened up. Sweetened. Worked on. Preliminary spadework must be put in. Here, Gussie, is the procedure I propose to adopt: I shall now return to the house and lug this Bassett out for a stroll. I shall talk to her of hearts that yearn, intimating that there is one actually on the premises. I shall pitch it strong, sparing no effort. You, meanwhile, will lurk on the outskirts, and in about a quarter of an hour you will come along and carry on from there. By that time, her emotions having been stirred, you ought to be able to do the rest on your head. It will be like leaping on to a moving bus."

I remember when I was a kid at school having to learn a poem of sorts about a fellow named Pig-something—a sculptor he would have been, no doubt—who made a statue of a girl, and what should happen one morning but that the bally thing suddenly came to life. A pretty nasty shock for the chap, of course, but the point I'm working round to is that there were a couple of lines that went, if I remember correctly:

She starts. She moves. She seems to feel The stir of life along her keel.

And what I'm driving at is that you couldn't get a better description of what happened to Gussie as I spoke these heartening words. His brow cleared, his eyes brightened, he lost that fishy look, and he gazed at the slug, which was still on the long, long trail with something approaching bonhomie. A marked improvement.

"I see what you mean. You will sort of pave the way, as it were."

"That's right. Spadework."

"It's a terrific idea, Bertie. It will make all the difference."

"Quite. But don't forget that after that it will be up to you. You will have to haul up your slacks and give her the old oil, or my efforts will have been in vain."

Something of his former Gawd-help-us-ness seemed to return to him. He gasped a bit.

"That's true. What the dickens shall I say?"

I restrained my impatience with an effort. The man had been at school with me.

"Dash it, there are hundreds of things you can say. Talk about the sunset."

"The sunset?"

"Certainly. Half the married men you meet began by talking about the sunset."

"But what can I say about the sunset?"

"Well, Jeeves got off a good one the other day. I met him airing the dog in the park one evening, and he said, 'Now fades the glimmering landscape on the sight, sir, and all the air a solemn stillness holds.' You might use that."

"What sort of landscape?"

"Glimmering. *G* for 'gastritis,' *l* for 'lizard'——"

"Oh, glimmering? Yes, that's not bad. Glimmering landscape ... solemn stillness.... Yes, I call that pretty good."

"You could then say that you have often thought that the stars are God's daisy chain."

"But I haven't."

"I dare say not. But she has. Hand her that one, and I don't see how she can help feeling that you're a twin soul."

"God's daisy chain?"

"God's daisy chain. And then you go on about how twilight always makes you sad. I know you're going to say it doesn't, but on this occasion it has jolly well got to."

"Why?"

"That's just what she will ask, and you will then have got her going. Because you will reply that it is because yours is such a lonely life. It wouldn't be a bad idea to give her a brief description of a typical home evening at your Lincolnshire residence, showing how you pace the meadows with a heavy tread."

"I generally sit indoors and listen to the wireless."

"No, you don't. You pace the meadows with a heavy tread, wishing that you had someone to love you. And then you speak of the day when she came into your life."

"Like a fairy princess."

"Absolutely," I said with approval. I hadn't expected such a hot one from such a quarter. "Like a fairy princess. Nice work, Gussie."

"And then?"

"Well, after that it's easy. You say you have something you want to say to her, and then you snap into it. I don't see how it can fail. If I were you, I should do it in this rose garden. It is well established that there is no sounder move than to steer the adored object into rose gardens in the gloaming. And you had better have a couple of quick ones first."

"Quick ones?"

"Snifters."

"Drinks, do you mean? But I don't drink."

"What?"

"I've never touched a drop in my life."

This made me a bit dubious, I must confess. On these occasions it is generally conceded that a moderate skinful is of the essence.

However, if the facts were as he had stated, I supposed there was nothing to be done about it.

"Well, you'll have to make out as best you can on ginger pop."

"I always drink orange juice."

"Orange juice, then. Tell me, Gussie, to settle a bet, do you really like that muck?"

"Very much."

"Then there is no more to be said. Now, let's just have a run through, to see that you've got the lay-out straight. Start off with the glimmering landscape."

"Stars God's daisy chain."

"Twilight makes you feel sad."

"Because mine lonely life."

"Describe life."

"Talk about the day I met her."

"Add fairy-princess gag. Say there's something you want to say to her. Heave a couple of sighs. Grab her hand. And give her the works. Right."

And confident that he had grasped the scenario and that everything might now be expected to proceed through the proper channels, I picked up the feet and hastened back to the house.

It was not until I had reached the drawing-room and was enabled to take a square look at the Bassett that I found the debonair gaiety with which I had embarked on this affair beginning to wane a trifle. Beholding her at close range like this, I suddenly became cognisant of what I was in for. The thought of strolling with this rummy specimen undeniably gave me a most unpleasant sinking feeling. I could not but remember how often, when in her company at Cannes, I had gazed dumbly at her, wishing that some kindly motorist in a racing car would ease the situation by coming along and ramming her amidships. As I have already made abundantly clear, this girl was not one of my most congenial buddies.

However, a Wooster's word is his bond. Woosters may quail, but they do not edge out. Only the keenest ear could have detected the tremor in the voice as I asked her if she would care to come out for half an hour.

"Lovely evening," I said.

"Yes, lovely, isn't it?"

"Lovely. Reminds me of Cannes."

"How lovely the evenings were there!"

"Lovely," I said.

"Lovely," said the Bassett.

"Lovely," I agreed.

That completed the weather and news bulletin for the French Riviera. Another minute, and we were out in the great open spaces, she cooing a bit about the scenery, and self replying, "Oh, rather, quite," and wondering how best to approach the matter in hand.

-10-

How different it all would have been, I could not but reflect, if this girl had been the sort of girl one chirrups cheerily to over the telephone and takes for spins in the old two-seater. In that case, I would simply have said, "Listen," and she would have said, "What?" and I would have said, "You know Gussie Fink-Nottle," and she would have said, "Yes," and I would have said, "He loves you," and she would have said either, "What, that mutt? Well, thank heaven for one good laugh today," or else, in more passionate vein, "Hot dog! Tell me more."

I mean to say, in either event the whole thing over and done with in under a minute.

But with the Bassett something less snappy and a good deal more glutinous was obviously indicated. What with all this daylight-saving stuff, we had hit the great open spaces at a moment when twilight had not yet begun to cheese it in favour of the shades of night. There was a fag-end of sunset still functioning. Stars were beginning to peep out, bats were fooling round, the garden was full of the aroma of those niffy white flowers which only start to put in their heavy work at the end of the day—in short, the glimmering landscape was fading on the sight and all the air held a solemn stillness, and it was plain that this was having the worst effect on her. Her eyes were enlarged, and her whole map a good deal too suggestive of the soul's awakening for comfort.

Her aspect was that of a girl who was expecting something fairly fruity from Bertram.

In these circs., conversation inevitably flagged a bit. I am never at my best when the situation seems to call for a certain soupiness, and I've heard other members of the Drones say the same thing about themselves. I remember Pongo Twistleton telling me that he was out in a gondola with a girl by moonlight once, and the only time he spoke was to tell her that old story about the chap who was so good at swimming that they made him a traffic cop in Venice.

Fell rather flat, he assured me, and it wasn't much later when the girl said she thought it was getting a little chilly and how about pushing back to the hotel.

So now, as I say, the talk rather hung fire. It had been all very well for me to promise Gussie that I would cut loose to this girl about aching hearts, but you want a cue for that sort of thing. And when, toddling along, we reached the edge of the lake and she finally spoke, conceive my chagrin when I discovered that what she was talking about was stars.

Not a bit of good to me.

"Oh, look," she said. She was a confirmed Oh-looker. I had noticed this at Cannes, where she had drawn my attention in this manner on various occasions to such diverse objects as a French actress, a Provençal filling station, the sunset over the Estorels, Michael Arlen, a man selling coloured spectacles, the deep velvet blue of the Mediterranean, and the late mayor of New York in a striped one-piece bathing suit. "Oh, look at that sweet little star up there all by itself."

I saw the one she meant, a little chap operating in a detached sort of way above a spinney.

"Yes," I said.

"I wonder if it feels lonely."

"Oh, I shouldn't think so."

"A fairy must have been crying."

"Eh?"

"Don't you remember? 'Every time a fairy sheds a tear, a wee bit star is born in the Milky Way.' Have you ever thought that, Mr. Wooster?"

I never had. Most improbable, I considered, and it didn't seem to me to check up with her statement that the stars were God's daisy chain. I mean, you can't have it both ways.

However, I was in no mood to dissect and criticize. I saw that I had been wrong in supposing that the stars were not germane to the issue. Quite a decent cue they had provided, and I leaped on it Promptly: "Talking of shedding tears——"

But she was now on the subject of rabbits, several of which were messing about in the park to our right.

"Oh, look. The little bunnies!"

"Talking of shedding tears——"

"Don't you love this time of the evening, Mr. Wooster, when the sun has gone to bed and all the bunnies come out to have their little suppers? When I was a child, I used to think that rabbits were gnomes, and that if I held my breath and stayed quite still, I should see the fairy queen."

Indicating with a reserved gesture that this was just the sort of loony thing I should have expected her to think as a child, I returned to the point.

"Talking of shedding tears," I said firmly, "it may interest you to know that there is an aching heart in Brinkley Court."

This held her. She cheesed the rabbit theme. Her face, which had been aglow with what I supposed was a pretty animation, clouded. She unshipped a sigh that sounded like the wind going out of a rubber duck.

"Ah, yes. Life is very sad, isn't it?"

"It is for some people. This aching heart, for instance."

"Those wistful eyes of hers! Drenched irises. And they used to dance like elves of delight. And all through a foolish misunderstanding about a shark. What a tragedy misunderstandings are. That pretty romance broken and over just because Mr. Glossop would insist that it was a flatfish."

I saw that she had got the wires crossed.

"I'm not talking about Angela."

"But her heart is aching."

"I know it's aching. But so is somebody else's."

She looked at me, perplexed.

"Somebody else? Mr. Glossop's, you mean?"

"No, I don't."

"Mrs. Travers's?"

The exquisite code of politeness of the Woosters prevented me clipping her one on the ear-hole, but I would have given a shilling to be able to do it. There seemed to me something deliberately fat-headed in the way she persisted in missing the gist.

"No, not Aunt Dahlia's, either."

"I'm sure she is dreadfully upset."

"Quite. But this heart I'm talking about isn't aching because of Tuppy's row with Angela. It's aching for a different reason altogether. I mean to say—dash it, you know why hearts ache!"

She seemed to shimmy a bit. Her voice, when she spoke, was whispery: "You mean—for love?"

"Absolutely. Right on the bull's-eye. For love."

"Oh, Mr. Wooster!"

"I take it you believe in love at first sight?"

"I do, indeed."

"Well, that's what happened to this aching heart. It fell in love at first sight, and ever since it's been eating itself out, as I believe the expression is."

There was a silence. She had turned away and was watching a duck out on the lake. It was tucking into weeds, a thing I've never been able to understand anyone wanting to do. Though I suppose, if you face it squarely, they're no worse than spinach. She stood drinking it in for a bit, and then it suddenly stood on its head and disappeared, and this seemed to break the spell.

"Oh, Mr. Wooster!" she said again, and from the tone of her voice, I could see that I had got her going.

"For you, I mean to say," I proceeded, starting to put in the fancy touches. I dare say you have noticed on these occasions that the difficulty is to plant the main idea, to get the general outline of the thing well fixed. The rest is mere detail work. I don't say I became glib at this juncture, but I certainly became a dashed glibber than I had been.

"It's having the dickens of a time. Can't eat, can't sleep—all for love of you. And what makes it all so particularly rotten is that it—this aching heart—can't bring itself up to the scratch and tell you the position of affairs, because your profile has gone and given it cold feet. Just as it is about to speak, it catches sight of you sideways, and words fail it. Silly, of course, but there it is."

I heard her give a gulp, and I saw that her eyes had become moistish. Drenched irises, if you care to put it that way.

"Lend you a handkerchief?"

"No, thank you. I'm quite all right."

It was more than I could say for myself. My efforts had left me weak. I don't know if you suffer in the same way, but with me the act of talking anything in the nature of real mashed potatoes always induces a sort of prickly sensation and a hideous feeling of shame, together with a marked starting of the pores.

I remember at my Aunt Agatha's place in Hertfordshire once being put on the spot and forced to enact the role of King Edward III saying goodbye to that girl of his, Fair Rosamund, at some sort of pageant in aid of the Distressed Daughters of the Clergy. It involved some rather warmish medieval dialogue, I recall, racy of the days when they called a spade a spade, and by the time the whistle blew, I'll bet no Daughter of the Clergy was half as distressed as I was. Not a dry stitch.

My reaction now was very similar. It was a highly liquid Bertram who, hearing his *vis-à-vis* give a couple of hiccups and start to speak bent an attentive ear.

"Please don't say any more, Mr. Wooster."

Well, I wasn't going to, of course.

"I understand."

I was glad to hear this.

"Yes, I understand. I won't be so silly as to pretend not to know what you mean. I suspected this at Cannes, when you used to stand and stare at me without speaking a word, but with whole volumes in your eyes."

If Angela's shark had bitten me in the leg, I couldn't have leaped more convulsively. So tensely had I been concentrating on Gussie's interests that it hadn't so much as crossed my mind that another and an unfortunate construction could be placed on those words of mine. The persp., already bedewing my brow, became a regular Niagara.

My whole fate hung upon a woman's word. I mean to say, I couldn't back out. If a girl thinks a man is proposing to her, and on that understanding books him up, he can't explain to her that she has got hold of entirely the wrong end of the stick and that he hadn't the smallest intention of suggesting anything of the kind. He must simply let it ride. And the thought of being engaged to a girl who talked openly about fairies being born because stars blew their noses, or whatever it was, frankly appalled me.

She was carrying on with her remarks, and as I listened I clenched my fists till I shouldn't wonder if the knuckles didn't stand out white under the strain. It seemed as if she would never get to the nub.

"Yes, all through those days at Cannes I could see what you were trying to say. A girl always knows. And then you followed me down here, and there was that same dumb, yearning look in your eyes when we met this evening. And then you were so insistent that I should come out and walk with you in the twilight. And now you stammer out those halting words. No, this does not come as a surprise. But I am sorry——"

The word was like one of Jeeves's pick-me-ups. Just as if a glassful of meat sauce, red pepper, and the yolk of an egg—though, as I say, I am convinced that these are not the sole ingredients—had been shot into me, I expanded like some lovely flower blossoming in the sunshine. It was all right, after all. My guardian angel had not been asleep at the switch.

"—but I am afraid it is impossible."

She paused.

"Impossible," she repeated.

I had been so busy feeling saved from the scaffold that I didn't get on to it for a moment that an early reply was desired.

"Oh, right ho," I said hastily.

"I'm sorry."

"Quite all right."

"Sorrier than I can say."

"Don't give it another thought."

"We can still be friends."

"Oh, rather."

"Then shall we just say no more about it; keep what has happened as a tender little secret between ourselves?"

"Absolutely."

"We will. Like something lovely and fragrant laid away in lavender."

"In lavender—right."

There was a longish pause. She was gazing at me in a divinely pitying sort of way, much as if I had been a snail she had happened accidentally to bring her short French vamp down on, and I longed to tell her that it was all right, and that Bertram, so far from being the victim of despair, had never felt fizzier in his life. But, of course, one can't do that sort of thing. I simply said nothing, and stood there looking brave.

"I wish I could," she murmured.

"Could?" I said, for my attensh had been wandering.

"Feel towards you as you would like me to feel."

"Oh, ah."

"But I can't. I'm sorry."

"Absolutely O.K. Faults on both sides, no doubt."

"Because I am fond of you, Mr.—no, I think I must call you Bertie. May I?"

"Oh, rather."

"Because we are real friends."

"Quite."

"I do like you, Bertie. And if things were different—I wonder——"

"Eh?"

"After all, we are real friends.... We have this common memory.... You have a right to know.... I don't want you to think——Life is such a muddle, isn't it?"

To many men, no doubt, these broken utterances would have appeared mere drooling and would have been dismissed as such. But the Woosters are quicker-witted than the ordinary and can read between the lines. I suddenly divined what it was that she was trying to get off the chest.

"You mean there's someone else?"

She nodded.

"You're in love with some other bloke?"

She nodded.

"Engaged, what?"

This time she shook the pumpkin.

"No, not engaged."

Well, that was something, of course. Nevertheless, from the way she spoke, it certainly looked as if poor old Gussie might as well scratch his name off the entry list, and I didn't at all like the prospect of having to break the bad news to him. I had studied the man closely, and it was my conviction that this would about be his finish.

Gussie, you see, wasn't like some of my pals—the name of Bingo Little is one that springs to the lips—who, if turned down by a girl, would simply say, "Well, bung-oh!" and toddle off quite happily to find another. He was so manifestly a bird who, having failed to score in the first chukker, would turn the thing up and spend the rest of his life brooding over his newts and growing long grey whiskers, like one of those chaps you read about in novels, who live in the great white house you can just see over there through the trees and shut themselves off from the world and have pained faces.

"I'm afraid he doesn't care for me in that way. At least, he has said nothing. You understand that I am only telling you this because——"

"Oh, rather."

"It's odd that you should have asked me if I believed in love at first sight." She half closed her eyes. "'Who ever loved that loved not at first sight?'" she said in a rummy voice that brought back to me—I don't know why—the picture of my Aunt Agatha, as Boadicea, reciting at that pageant I was speaking of. "It's a silly little story. I was staying with some friends in the country, and I had gone for a walk with my dog, and the poor wee mite got a nasty thorn in his little foot and I didn't know what to do. And then suddenly this man came along——"

Harking back once again to that pageant, in sketching out for you my emotions on that occasion, I showed you only the darker side of the picture. There was, I should now mention, a splendid aftermath when, having climbed out of my suit of chain mail and sneaked off to the local pub, I entered the saloon bar and requested mine host to start pouring. A moment later, a tankard of their special home-brewed was in my hand, and the ecstasy of that first gollup is still green in my memory. The recollection of the agony through which I had passed was just what was needed to make it perfect.

It was the same now. When I realized, listening to her words, that she must be referring to Gussie—I mean to say, there couldn't have been a whole platoon of men taking thorns out of her dog that day; the animal wasn't a pin-cushion—and became aware that Gussie, who an instant before had, to all appearances, gone so far back in the betting as not to be worth a quotation, was the big winner after all, a positive thrill permeated the frame and there escaped my lips a "Wow!" so crisp and hearty that the Bassett leaped a liberal inch and a half from terra firma.

"I beg your pardon?" she said.

I waved a jaunty hand.

"Nothing," I said. "Nothing. Just remembered there's a letter I have to write to-night without fail. If you don't mind, I think I'll be going in. Here," I said, "comes Gussie Fink-Nottle. He will look after you."

And, as I spoke, Gussie came sidling out from behind a tree.

I passed away and left them to it. As regards these two, everything was beyond a question absolutely in order. All Gussie had to do was keep his head down and not press. Already, I felt, as I legged it back to the house, the happy ending must have begun to function. I mean to say, when you leave a girl and a man, each of whom has admitted in set terms that she and he loves him and her, in close juxta-position in the twilight, there doesn't seem much more to do but start pricing fish slices.

Something attempted, something done, seemed to me to have earned two-penn'orth of wassail in the smoking-room.

I proceeded thither.

-11-

The makings were neatly laid out on a side-table, and to pour into a glass an inch or so of the raw spirit and shoosh some soda-water on top of it was with me the work of a moment. This done, I retired to an arm-chair and put my feet up, sipping the mixture with carefree enjoyment, rather like Caesar having one in his tent the day he overcame the Nervii.

As I let the mind dwell on what must even now be taking place in that peaceful garden, I felt bucked and uplifted. Though never for an instant faltering in my opinion that Augustus Fink-Nottle was Nature's final word in cloth-headed guffins, I liked the man, wished him well, and could not have felt more deeply involved in the success of his wooing if I, and not he, had been under the ether.

The thought that by this time he might quite easily have completed the preliminary *pourparlers* and be deep in an informal discussion of honeymoon plans was very pleasant to me.

Of course, considering the sort of girl Madeline Bassett was—stars and rabbits and all that, I mean—you might say that a sober sadness would have been more fitting. But in these matters you have got to realize that tastes differ. The impulse of right-thinking men might be to run a mile when they saw the Bassett, but for some reason she appealed to the deeps in Gussie, so that was that.

I had reached this point in my meditations, when I was aroused by the sound of the door opening. Somebody came in and started moving like a leopard toward the side-table and, lowering the feet, I perceived that it was Tuppy Glossop.

The sight of him gave me a momentary twinge of remorse, reminding me, as it did, that in the excitement of getting Gussie fixed up I had rather forgotten about this other client. It is often that way when you're trying to run two cases at once.

However, Gussie now being off my mind, I was prepared to devote my whole attention to the Glossop problem.

I had been much pleased by the way he had carried out the task assigned him at the dinner-table. No easy one, I can assure you, for the browsing and sluicing had been of the highest quality, and there had been one dish in particular—I allude to the *nonnettes de poulet Agnès Sorel*—which might well have broken down the most iron resolution. But he had passed it up like a professional fasting man, and I was proud of him.

"Oh, hullo, Tuppy," I said, "I wanted to see you."

He turned, snifter in hand, and it was easy to see that his privations had tried him sorely. He was looking like a wolf on the steppes of Russia which has seen its peasant shin up a high tree.

"Yes?" he said, rather unpleasantly. "Well, here I am."

"Well?"

"How do you mean——well?"

"Make your report."

"What report?"

"Have you nothing to tell me about Angela?"

"Only that she's a blister."

I was concerned.

"Hasn't she come clustering round you yet?"

"She has not."

"Very odd."

"Why odd?"

"She must have noted your lack of appetite."

He barked raspingly, as if he were having trouble with the tonsils of the soul.

"Lack of appetite! I'm as hollow as the Grand Canyon."

"Courage, Tuppy! Think of Gandhi."

"What about Gandhi?"

"He hasn't had a square meal for years."

"Nor have I. Or I could swear I hadn't. Gandhi, my left foot."

I saw that it might be best to let the Gandhi *motif* slide. I went back to where we had started.

"She's probably looking for you now."

"Who is? Angela?"

"Yes. She must have noticed your supreme sacrifice."

"I don't suppose she noticed it at all, the little fathead. I'll bet it didn't register in any way whatsoever."

"Come, Tuppy," I urged, "this is morbid. Don't take this gloomy view. She must at least have spotted that you refused those *nonnettes de poulet Agnès Sorel.* It was a sensational renunciation and stuck out like a sore thumb. And the *cèpes à la Rossini*——"

A hoarse cry broke from his twisted lips:

"Will you stop it, Bertie! Do you think I am made of marble? Isn't it bad enough to have sat watching one of Anatole's supremest dinners flit by, course after course, without having you making a song about it? Don't remind me of those *nonnettes.* I can't stand it."

I endeavoured to hearten and console.

"Be brave, Tuppy. Fix your thoughts on that cold steak-and-kidney pie in the larder. As the Good Book says, it cometh in the morning."

"Yes, in the morning. And it's now about half-past nine at night. You would bring that pie up, wouldn't you? Just when I was trying to keep my mind off it."

I saw what he meant. Hours must pass before he could dig into that pie. I dropped the subject, and we sat for a pretty good time in silence. Then he rose and began to pace the room in an overwrought sort of way, like a zoo lion who has heard the dinner-gong go and is hoping the keeper won't forget him in the general distribution. I averted my gaze tactfully, but I could hear him kicking chairs and things. It was plain that the man's soul was in travail and his blood pressure high.

Presently he returned to his seat, and I saw that he was looking at me intently. There was that about his demeanour that led me to think that he had something to communicate.

Nor was I wrong. He tapped me significantly on the knee and spoke:

"Bertie."

"Hullo?"

"Shall I tell you something?"

"Certainly, old bird," I said cordially. "I was just beginning to feel that the scene could do with a bit more dialogue."

"This business of Angela and me."

"Yes?"

"I've been putting in a lot of solid thinking about it."

"Oh, yes?"

"I have analysed the situation pitilessly, and one thing stands out as clear as dammit. There has been dirty work afoot."

"I don't get you."

"All right. Let me review the facts. Up to the time she went to Cannes Angela loved me. She was all over me. I was the blue-eyed boy in every sense of the term. You'll admit that?"

"Indisputably."

"And directly she came back we had this bust-up."

"Quite."

"About nothing."

"Oh, dash it, old man, nothing? You were a bit tactless, what, about her shark."

"I was frank and candid about her shark. And that's my point. Do you seriously believe that a trifling disagreement about sharks would make a girl hand a man his hat, if her heart were really his?"

"Certainly."

It beats me why he couldn't see it. But then poor old Tuppy has never been very hot on the finer shades. He's one of those large, tough, football-playing blokes who lack the more delicate sensibilities, as I've heard Jeeves call them. Excellent at blocking a punt or walking across an opponent's face in cleated boots, but not so good when it comes to understanding the highly-strung female temperament. It simply wouldn't occur to him that a girl might be prepared to give up her life's happiness rather than waive her shark.

"Rot! It was just a pretext."

"What was?"

"This shark business. She wanted to get rid of me, and grabbed at the first excuse."

"No, no."

"I tell you she did."

"But what on earth would she want to get rid of you for?"

"Exactly. That's the very question I asked myself. And here's the answer: Because she has fallen in love with somebody else. It sticks out a mile. There's no other possible solution. She goes to Cannes all for me, she comes back all off me. Obviously during those two months, she must have transferred her affections to some foul blister she met out there."

"No, no."

"Don't keep saying 'No, no'. She must have done. Well, I'll tell you one thing, and you can take this as official. If ever I find this slimy, slithery snake in the grass, he had better make all the necessary arrangements at his favourite nursing-home without delay, because I am going to be very rough with him. I propose, if and when found, to take him by his beastly neck, shake him till he froths, and pull him inside out and make him swallow himself."

With which words he biffed off; and I, having given him a minute or two to get out of the way, rose and made for the drawing-room. The tendency of females to roost in drawing-rooms after dinner being well marked, I expected to find Angela there. It was my intention to have a word with Angela.

To Tuppy's theory that some insinuating bird had stolen the girl's heart from him at Cannes I had given, as I have indicated, little credence, considering it the mere unbalanced apple sauce of a bereaved man. It was, of course, the shark, and nothing but the shark, that had caused love's young dream to go temporarily off the boil, and I was convinced that a word or two with the cousin at this juncture would set everything right.

For, frankly, I thought it incredible that a girl of her natural sweetness and tender-heartedness should not have been moved to her foundations by what she had seen at dinner that night. Even Seppings, Aunt Dahlia's butler, a cold, unemotional man, had gasped and practically reeled when Tuppy waved aside those *nonnettes de poulet Agnès Sorel*, while the footman, standing by with the potatoes, had stared like one seeing a vision. I simply refused to consider the possibility of the significance of the thing having been lost on a nice girl like Angela. I fully expected to find her in the drawing-room with her heart bleeding freely, all ripe for an immediate reconciliation.

In the drawing-room, however, when I entered, only Aunt Dahlia met the eye. It seemed to me that she gave me rather a jaundiced look as I hove in sight, but this, having so recently beheld Tuppy in his agony, I attributed to the fact that she, like him, had been going light on the menu. You can't expect an empty aunt to beam like a full aunt.

"Oh, it's you, is it?" she said.

Well, it was, of course.

"Where's Angela?" I asked.

"Gone to bed."

"Already?"

"She said she had a headache."

"H'm."

I wasn't so sure that I liked the sound of that so much. A girl who has observed the sundered lover sensationally off his feed does not go to bed with headaches if love has been reborn in her heart. She sticks around and gives him the swift, remorseful glance from beneath the drooping eyelashes and generally endeavours to convey to him that, if he wants to get together across a round table and try to find a formula, she is all for it too. Yes, I am bound to say I found that going-to-bed stuff a bit disquieting.

"Gone to bed, eh?" I murmured musingly.

"What did you want her for?"

"I thought she might like a stroll and a chat."

"Are you going for a stroll?" said Aunt Dahlia, with a sudden show of interest. "Where?"

"Oh, hither and thither."

"Then I wonder if you would mind doing something for me."

"Give it a name."

"It won't take you long. You know that path that runs past the greenhouses into the kitchen garden. If you go along it, you come to a pond."

"That's right."

"Well, will you get a good, stout piece of rope or cord and go down that path till you come to the pond——"

"To the pond. Right."

"—and look about you till you find a nice, heavy stone. Or a fairly large brick would do."

"I see," I said, though I didn't, being still fogged. "Stone or brick. Yes. And then?"

"Then," said the relative, "I want you, like a good boy, to fasten the rope to the brick and tie it around your damned neck and jump into the pond and drown yourself. In a few days I will send and have you fished up and buried because I shall need to dance on your grave."

I was more fogged than ever. And not only fogged—wounded and resentful. I remember reading a book where a girl "suddenly fled from the room, afraid to stay for fear dreadful things would come tumbling from her lips; determined that she would not remain another day in this house to be insulted and misunderstood." I felt much about the same.

Then I reminded myself that one has got to make allowances for a woman with only about half a spoonful of soup inside her, and I checked the red-hot crack that rose to the lips.

"What," I said gently, "is this all about? You seem pipped with Bertram."

"Pipped!"

"Noticeably pipped. Why this ill-concealed animus?"

A sudden flame shot from her eyes, singeing my hair.

"Who was the ass, who was the chump, who was the dithering idiot who talked me, against my better judgment, into going without my dinner? I might have guessed——"

I saw that I had divined correctly the cause of her strange mood.

"It's all right. Aunt Dahlia. I know just how you're feeling. A bit on the hollow side, what? But the agony will pass. If I were you, I'd sneak down and raid the larder after the household have gone to bed. I am told there's a pretty good steak-and-kidney pie there which will repay inspection. Have faith, Aunt Dahlia," I urged. "Pretty soon Uncle Tom will be along, full of sympathy and anxious inquiries."

"Will he? Do you know where he is now?"

"I haven't seen him."

"He is in the study with his face buried in his hands, muttering about civilization and melting pots."

"Eh? Why?"

"Because it has just been my painful duty to inform him that Anatole has given notice."

I own that I reeled.

"What?"

"Given notice. As the result of that drivelling scheme of yours. What did you expect a sensitive, temperamental French cook to do, if you went about urging everybody to refuse all food? I hear that when the first two courses came back to the kitchen practically untouched, his feelings were so hurt that he cried like a child. And when the rest of the dinner followed, he came to the conclusion that the whole thing was a studied and calculated insult, and decided to hand in his portfolio."

"Golly!"

"You may well say 'Golly!' Anatole, God's gift to the gastric juices, gone like the dew off the petal of a rose, all through your idiocy. Perhaps you understand now why I want you to go and jump in that pond. I might have known that some hideous disaster would strike this house like a thunderbolt if once you wriggled your way into it and started trying to be clever."

Harsh words, of course, as from aunt to nephew, but I bore her no resentment. No doubt, if you looked at it from a certain angle, Bertram might be considered to have made something of a floater.

"I am sorry."

"What's the good of being sorry?"

"I acted for what I deemed the best."

"Another time try acting for the worst. Then we may possibly escape with a mere flesh wound."

"Uncle Tom's not feeling too bucked about it all, you say?"

"He's groaning like a lost soul. And any chance I ever had of getting that money out of him has gone."

I stroked the chin thoughtfully. There was, I had to admit, reason in what she said. None knew better than I how terrible a blow the passing of Anatole would be to Uncle Tom.

I have stated earlier in this chronicle that this curious object of the seashore with whom Aunt Dahlia has linked her lot is a bloke who habitually looks like a pterodactyl that has suffered, and the reason he does so is that all those years he spent in making millions in the Far East put his digestion on the blink, and the only cook that has ever been discovered capable of pushing food into him without starting something like Old Home Week in Moscow under the third waistcoat button is this uniquely gifted Anatole. Deprived of Anatole's services, all he was likely to give the wife of his b. was a dirty look. Yes, unquestionably, things seemed to have struck a somewhat rocky patch, and I must admit that I found myself, at moment of going to press, a little destitute of constructive ideas.

Confident, however, that these would come ere long, I kept the stiff upper lip.

"Bad," I conceded. "Quite bad, beyond a doubt. Certainly a nasty jar for one and all. But have no fear, Aunt Dahlia, I will fix everything."

I have alluded earlier to the difficulty of staggering when you're sitting down, showing that it is a feat of which I, personally, am not capable. Aunt Dahlia, to my amazement, now did it apparently without an effort. She was well wedged into a deep arm-chair, but, nevertheless, she staggered like billy-o. A sort of spasm of horror and apprehension contorted her face.

"If you dare to try any more of your lunatic schemes——"

I saw that it would be fruitless to try to reason with her. Quite plainly, she was not in the vein. Contenting myself, accordingly, with a gesture of loving sympathy, I left the room. Whether she did or did not throw a handsomely bound volume of the Works of Alfred, Lord Tennyson, at me, I am not in a position to say. I had seen it lying on the table beside her, and as I closed the door I remember receiving the impression that some blunt instrument had crashed against the woodwork, but I was feeling too pre-occupied to note and observe.

I blame myself for not having taken into consideration the possible effects of a sudden abstinence on the part of virtually the whole strength of the company on one of Anatole's impulsive Provençal temperament. These Gauls, I should have remembered, can't take it. Their tendency to fly off the handle at the slightest provocation is well known. No doubt the man had put his whole soul into those *nonnettes de poulet*, and to see them come homing back to him must have gashed him like a knife.

However, spilt milk blows nobody any good, and it is useless to dwell upon it. The task now confronting Bertram was to put matters right, and I was pacing the lawn, pondering to this end, when I suddenly heard a groan so lost-soulish that I thought it must have proceeded from Uncle Tom, escaped from captivity and come to groan in the garden.

Looking about me, however, I could discern no uncles. Puzzled, I was about to resume my meditations, when the sound came again. And peering into the shadows I observed a dim form seated on one of the rustic benches which so liberally dotted this pleasance and another dim form standing beside same. A second and more penetrating glance and I had assembled the facts.

These dim forms were, in the order named, Gussie Fink-Nottle and Jeeves. And what Gussie was doing, groaning all over the place like this, was more than I could understand.

Because, I mean to say, there was no possibility of error. He wasn't singing. As I approached, he gave an encore, and it was beyond question a groan. Moreover, I could now see him clearly, and his whole aspect was definitely sand-bagged.

"Good evening, sir," said Jeeves. "Mr. Fink-Nottle is not feeling well."

Nor was I. Gussie had begun to make a low, bubbling noise, and I could no longer disguise it from myself that something must have gone seriously wrong with the works. I mean, I know marriage is a pretty solemn business and the realization that he is in for it frequently churns a chap up a bit, but I had never come across a case of a newly-engaged man taking it on the chin so completely as this.

Gussie looked up. His eye was dull. He clutched the thatch.

"Goodbye, Bertie," he said, rising.

I seemed to spot an error.

"You mean 'Hullo,' don't you?"

"No, I don't. I mean goodbye. I'm off."

"Off where?"

"To the kitchen garden. To drown myself."

"Don't be an ass."

"I'm not an ass.... Am I an ass, Jeeves?"

"Possibly a little injudicious, sir."

"Drowning myself, you mean?"

"Yes, sir."

"You think, on the whole, not drown myself?"

"I should not advocate it, sir."

"Very well, Jeeves. I accept your ruling. After all, it would be unpleasant for Mrs. Travers to find a swollen body floating in her pond."

"Yes, sir."

"And she has been very kind to me."

"Yes, sir."

"And you have been very kind to me, Jeeves."

"Thank you, sir."

"So have you, Bertie. Very kind. Everybody has been very kind to me. Very, very kind. Very kind indeed. I have no complaints to make. All right, I'll go for a walk instead."

I followed him with bulging eyes as he tottered off into the dark.

"Jeeves," I said, and I am free to admit that in my emotion I bleated like a lamb drawing itself to the attention of the parent sheep, "what the dickens is all this?"

"Mr. Fink-Nottle is not quite himself, sir. He has passed through a trying experience."

I endeavoured to put together a brief synopsis of previous events.

"I left him out here with Miss Bassett."

"Yes, sir."

"I had softened her up."

"Yes, sir."

"He knew exactly what he had to do. I had coached him thoroughly in lines and business."

"Yes, sir. So Mr. Fink-Nottle informed me."

"Well, then——"

"I regret to say, sir, that there was a slight hitch."

"You mean, something went wrong?"

"Yes, sir."

I could not fathom. The brain seemed to be tottering on its throne.

"But how could anything go wrong? She loves him, Jeeves."

"Indeed, sir?"

"She definitely told me so. All he had to do was propose."

"Yes sir."

"Well, didn't he?"

"No, sir."

"Then what the dickens did he talk about?"

"Newts, sir."

"Newts?"

"Yes, sir."

"Newts?"

"Yes, sir."

"But why did he want to talk about newts?"

"He did not want to talk about newts, sir. As I gather from Mr. Fink-Nottle, nothing could have been more alien to his plans."

I simply couldn't grasp the trend.

"But you can't force a man to talk about newts."

"Mr. Fink-Nottle was the victim of a sudden unfortunate spasm of nervousness, sir. Upon finding himself alone with the young lady, he admits to having lost his morale. In such circumstances, gentlemen frequently talk at random, saying the first thing that chances to enter their heads. This, in Mr. Fink-Nottle's case, would seem to have been the newt, its treatment in sickness and in health."

The scales fell from my eyes. I understood. I had had the same sort of thing happen to me in moments of crisis. I remember once detaining a dentist with the drill at one of my lower bicuspids and holding him up for nearly ten minutes with a story about a Scotchman, an Irishman, and a Jew. Purely automatic. The more he tried to jab, the more I said "Hoots, mon," "Begorrah," and "Oy, oy". When one loses one's nerve, one simply babbles.

I could put myself in Gussie's place. I could envisage the scene. There he and the Bassett were, alone together in the evening stillness. No doubt, as I had advised, he had shot the works about sunsets and fairy princesses, and so forth, and then had arrived at the point where he had to say that bit about having something to say to her. At this, I take it, she lowered her eyes and said, "Oh, yes?"

He then, I should imagine, said it was something very important; to which her response would, one assumes, have been something on the lines of "Really?" or "Indeed?" or possibly just the sharp intake of the breath. And then their eyes met, just as mine met the dentist's, and something suddenly seemed to catch him in the pit of the stomach and everything went black and he heard his voice starting to drool about newts. Yes, I could follow the psychology.

Nevertheless, I found myself blaming Gussie. On discovering that he was stressing the newt note in this manner, he ought, of course, to have tuned out, even if it had meant sitting there saying nothing. No matter how much of a twitter he was in, he should have had sense enough to see that he was throwing a spanner into the works. No girl, when she has been led to expect that a man is about to pour forth his soul in a fervour of passion, likes to find him suddenly shelving the whole topic in favour of an address on aquatic Salamandridae.

"Bad, Jeeves."

"Yes, sir."

"And how long did this nuisance continue?"

"For some not inconsiderable time, I gather, sir. According to Mr. Fink-Nottle, he supplied Miss Bassett with very full and complete information not only with respect to the common newt, but also the crested and palmated varieties. He described to her how newts, during the breeding season, live in the water, subsisting upon tadpoles, insect larvae, and crustaceans; how, later, they make their way to the land and eat slugs and worms; and how the newly born newt has three pairs of long, plumlike, external gills. And he was just observing that newts differ from salamanders in the shape of the tail, which is compressed, and that a marked sexual dimorphism prevails in most species, when the young lady rose and said that she thought she would go back to the house."

"And then——"

"She went, sir."

I stood musing. More and more, it was beginning to be borne in upon me what a particularly difficult chap Gussie was to help. He seemed to so marked an extent to lack snap and finish. With infinite toil, you manoeuvred him into a position where all he had to do was charge ahead, and he didn't charge ahead, but went off sideways, missing the objective completely.

"Difficult, Jeeves."

"Yes, sir."

In happier circs., of course, I would have canvassed his views on the matter. But after what had occurred in connection with that mess-jacket, my lips were sealed.

"Well, I must think it over."

"Yes, sir."

"Burnish the brain a bit and endeavour to find the way out."

"Yes, sir."

"Well, good night, Jeeves."

"Good night, sir."

He shimmered off, leaving a pensive Bertram Wooster standing motionless in the shadows. It seemed to me that it was hard to know what to do for the best.

-12-

I don't know if it has happened you to at all, but a thing I've noticed with myself is that, when I'm confronted by a problem which seems for the moment to stump and baffle, a good sleep will often bring the solution in the morning.

It was so on the present occasion.

The nibs who study these matters claim, I believe, that this has got something to do with the subconscious mind, and very possibly they may be right. I wouldn't have said off-hand that I had a subconscious mind, but I suppose I must without knowing it, and no doubt it was there, sweating away diligently at the old stand, all the while the corporeal Wooster was getting his eight hours.

For directly I opened my eyes on the morrow, I saw daylight. Well, I don't mean that exactly, because naturally I did. What I mean is that I found I had the thing all mapped out. The good old subconscious m. had delivered the goods, and I perceived exactly what steps must be taken in order to put Augustus Fink-Nottle among the practising Romeos.

I should like you, if you can spare me a moment of your valuable time, to throw your mind back to that conversation he and I had had in the garden on the previous evening. Not the glimmering landscape bit, I don't mean that, but the concluding passages of it. Having done so, you will recall that when he informed me that he never touched alcoholic liquor, I shook the head a bit, feeling that this must inevitably weaken him as a force where proposing to girls was concerned.

And events had shown that my fears were well founded.

Put to the test, with nothing but orange juice inside him, he had proved a complete bust. In a situation calling for words of molten passion of a nature calculated to go through Madeline Bassett like a red-hot gimlet through half a pound of butter, he had said not a syllable that could bring a blush to the cheek of modesty, merely delivering a well-phrased but, in the circumstances, quite misplaced lecture on newts.

A romantic girl is not to be won by such tactics. Obviously, before attempting to proceed further, Augustus Fink-Nottle must be induced to throw off the shackling inhibitions of the past and fuel up. It must be a primed, confident Fink-Nottle who squared up to the Bassett for Round No. 2.

Only so could the *Morning Post* make its ten bob, or whatever it is, for printing the announcement of the forthcoming nuptials.

Having arrived at this conclusion I found the rest easy, and by the time Jeeves brought me my tea I had evolved a plan complete in every detail. This I was about to place before him—indeed, I had got as far as the preliminary "I say, Jeeves"—when we were interrupted by the arrival of Tuppy.

He came listlessly into the room, and I was pained to observe that a night's rest had effected no improvement in the unhappy wreck's appearance. Indeed, I should have said, if anything, that he was looking rather more moth-eaten than when I had seen him last. If you can visualize a bulldog which has just been kicked in the ribs and had its dinner sneaked by the cat, you will have Hildebrand Glossop as he now stood before me.

"Stap my vitals, Tuppy, old corpse," I said, concerned, "you're looking pretty blue round the rims."

Jeeves slid from the presence in that tactful, eel-like way of his, and I motioned the remains to take a seat.

"What's the matter?" I said.

He came to anchor on the bed, and for awhile sat picking at the coverlet in silence.

"I've been through hell, Bertie."

"Through where?"

"Hell."

"Oh, hell? And what took you there?"

Once more he became silent, staring before him with sombre eyes. Following his gaze, I saw that he was looking at an enlarged photograph of my Uncle Tom in some sort of Masonic uniform which stood on the mantelpiece. I've tried to reason with Aunt Dahlia about this photograph for years, placing before her two alternative suggestions: (a) To burn the beastly thing; or (b) if she must preserve it, to shove me in another room when I come to stay. But she declines to accede. She says it's good for me. A useful discipline, she maintains, teaching me that there is a darker side to life and that we were not put into this world for pleasure only.

"Turn it to the wall, if it hurts you, Tuppy," I said gently.

"Eh?"

"That photograph of Uncle Tom as the bandmaster."

"I didn't come here to talk about photographs. I came for sympathy."

"And you shall have it. What's the trouble? Worrying about Angela, I suppose? Well, have no fear. I have another well-laid plan for encompassing that young shrimp. I'll guarantee that she will be weeping on your neck before yonder sun has set."

He barked sharply.

"A fat chance!"

"Tup, Tushy!"

"Eh?"

"I mean 'Tush, Tuppy.' I tell you I will do it. I was just going to describe this plan of mine to Jeeves when you came in. Care to hear it?"

"I don't want to hear any of your beastly plans. Plans are no good. She's gone and fallen in love with this other bloke, and now hates my gizzard."

"Rot."

"It isn't rot."

"I tell you, Tuppy, as one who can read the female heart, that this Angela loves you still."

"Well, it didn't look much like it in the larder last night."

"Oh, you went to the larder last night?"

"I did."

"And Angela was there?"

"She was. And your aunt. Also your uncle."

I saw that I should require foot-notes. All this was new stuff to me. I had stayed at Brinkley Court quite a lot in my time, but I had no idea the larder was such a social vortex. More like a snack bar on a race-course than anything else, it seemed to have become.

"Tell me the whole story in your own words," I said, "omitting no detail, however apparently slight, for one never knows how important the most trivial detail may be."

He inspected the photograph for a moment with growing gloom.

"All right," he said. "This is what happened. You know my views about that steak-and-kidney pie."

"Quite."

"Well, round about one a.m. I thought the time was ripe. I stole from my room and went downstairs. The pie seemed to beckon me."

I nodded. I knew how pies do.

"I got to the larder. I fished it out. I set it on the table. I found knife and fork. I collected salt, mustard, and pepper. There were some cold potatoes. I added those. And I was about to pitch in when I heard a sound behind me, and there was your aunt at the door. In a blue-and-yellow dressing gown."

"Embarrassing."

"Most."

"I suppose you didn't know where to look."

"I looked at Angela."

"She came in with my aunt?"

"No. With your uncle, a minute or two later. He was wearing mauve pyjamas and carried a pistol. Have you ever seen your uncle in pyjamas and a pistol?"

"Never."

"You haven't missed much."

"Tell me, Tuppy," I asked, for I was anxious to ascertain this, "about Angela. Was there any momentary softening in her gaze as she fixed it on you?"

"She didn't fix it on me. She fixed it on the pie."

"Did she say anything?"

"Not right away. Your uncle was the first to speak. He said to your aunt, 'God bless my soul, Dahlia, what are you doing here?' To which she replied, 'Well, if it comes to that, my merry somnambulist, what are you?' Your uncle then said that he thought there must be burglars in the house, as he had heard noises."

I nodded again. I could follow the trend. Ever since the scullery window was found open the year Shining Light was disqualified in the Cesarewitch for boring, Uncle Tom has had a marked complex about burglars. I can still recall my emotions when, paying my first visit after he had bars put on all the windows and attempting to thrust the head out in order to get a sniff of country air, I nearly fractured my skull on a sort of iron grille, as worn by the tougher kinds of mediaeval prison.

"'What sort of noises?' said your aunt. 'Funny noises,' said your uncle. Whereupon Angela—with a nasty, steely tinkle in her voice, the little buzzard—observed, 'I expect it was Mr. Glossop eating.' And then she did give me a look. It was the sort of wondering, revolted look a very spiritual woman would give a fat man gulping soup in a restaurant. The kind of look that makes a fellow feel he's forty-six round the waist and has great rolls of superfluous flesh pouring down over the back of his collar. And, still speaking in the same unpleasant tone, she added, 'I ought to have told you, father, that Mr. Glossop always likes to have a good meal three or four times during the night. It helps to keep him going till breakfast. He has the most amazing appetite. See, he has practically finished a large steak-and-kidney pie already'."

As he spoke these words, a feverish animation swept over Tuppy. His eyes glittered with a strange light, and he thumped the bed violently with his fist, nearly catching me a juicy one on the leg.

"That was what hurt, Bertie. That was what stung. I hadn't so much as started on that pie. But that's a woman all over."

"The eternal feminine."

"She continued her remarks. 'You've no idea,' she said, 'how Mr. Glossop loves food. He just lives for it. He always eats six or seven meals a day, and then starts in again after bedtime. I think it's rather wonderful.' Your aunt seemed interested, and said it reminded her of a boa constrictor. Angela said, didn't she mean a python? And then they argued as to which of the two it was. Your uncle, meanwhile, poking about with that damned pistol of his till human life wasn't safe in the vicinity. And the pie lying there on the table, and me unable to touch it. You begin to understand why I said I had been through hell."

"Quite. Can't have been at all pleasant."

"Presently your aunt and Angela settled their discussion, deciding that Angela was right and that it was a python that I reminded them of. And shortly after that we all pushed back to bed, Angela warning me in a motherly voice not to take the stairs too quickly. After seven or eight solid meals, she said, a man of my build ought to be very careful, because of the danger of apoplectic fits. She said it was the same with dogs. When they became very fat and overfed, you had to see that they didn't hurry upstairs, as it made them puff and pant, and that was bad for their hearts. She asked your aunt if she remembered the late spaniel, Ambrose; and your aunt said, 'Poor old Ambrose, you couldn't keep him away from the garbage pail'; and Angela said, 'Exactly, so do please be careful, Mr. Glossop.' And you tell me she loves me still!"

I did my best to encourage.

"Girlish banter, what?"

"Girlish banter be dashed. She's right off me. Once her ideal, I am now less than the dust beneath her chariot wheels. She became infatuated with this chap, whoever he was, at Cannes, and now she can't stand the sight of me."

I raised my eyebrows.

"My dear Tuppy, you are not showing your usual good sense in this Angela-chap-at-Cannes matter. If you will forgive me saying so, you have got an *idée fixe.*"

"A what?"

"An *idée fixe.* You know. One of those things fellows get. Like Uncle Tom's delusion that everybody who is known even slightly to the police is lurking in the garden, waiting for a chance to break into the house. You keep talking about this chap at Cannes, and there never was a chap at Cannes, and I'll tell you why I'm so sure about this. During those two months on the Riviera, it so happens that Angela and I were practically inseparable. If there had been somebody nosing round her, I should have spotted it in a second."

He started. I could see that this had impressed him.

"Oh, she was with you all the time at Cannes, was she?"

"I don't suppose she said two words to anybody else, except, of course, idle conv. at the crowded dinner table or a chance remark in a throng at the Casino."

"I see. You mean that anything in the shape of mixed bathing and moonlight strolls she conducted solely in your company?"

"That's right. It was quite a joke in the hotel."

"You must have enjoyed that."

"Oh, rather. I've always been devoted to Angela."

"Oh, yes?"

"When we were kids, she used to call herself my little sweetheart."

"She did?"

"Absolutely."

"I see."

He sat plunged in thought, while I, glad to have set his mind at rest, proceeded with my tea. And presently there came the banging of a gong from the hall below, and he started like a war horse at the sound of the bugle.

"Breakfast!" he said, and was off to a flying start, leaving me to brood and ponder. And the more I brooded and pondered, the more did it seem to me that everything now looked pretty smooth. Tuppy, I could see, despite that painful scene in the larder, still loved Angela with all the old fervour.

This meant that I could rely on that plan to which I had referred to bring home the bacon. And as I had found the way to straighten out the Gussie-Bassett difficulty, there seemed nothing more to worry about.

It was with an uplifted heart that I addressed Jeeves as he came in to remove the tea tray.

-13-

"Jeeves," I said.

"Sir?"

"I've just been having a chat with young Tuppy, Jeeves. Did you happen to notice that he wasn't looking very roguish this morning?"

"Yes, sir. It seemed to me that Mr. Glossop's face was sicklied o'er with the pale cast of thought."

"Quite. He met my cousin Angela in the larder last night, and a rather painful interview ensued."

"I am sorry, sir."

"Not half so sorry as he was. She found him closeted with a steak-and-kidney pie, and appears to have been a bit caustic about fat men who lived for food alone."

"Most disturbing, sir."

"Very. In fact, many people would say that things had gone so far between these two nothing now could bridge the chasm. A girl who could make cracks about human pythons who ate nine or ten meals a day and ought to be careful not to hurry upstairs because of the danger of apoplectic fits is a girl, many people would say, in whose heart love is dead. Wouldn't people say that, Jeeves?"

"Undeniably, sir."

"They would be wrong."

"You think so, sir?"

"I am convinced of it. I know these females. You can't go by what they say."

"You feel that Miss Angela's strictures should not be taken too much *au pied de la lettre*, sir?"

"Eh?"

"In English, we should say 'literally'."

"Literally. That's exactly what I mean. You know what girls are. A tiff occurs, and they shoot their heads off. But underneath it all the old love still remains. Am I correct?"

"Quite correct, sir. The poet Scott——"

"Right ho, Jeeves."

"Very good, sir."

"And in order to bring that old love whizzing to the surface once more, all that is required is the proper treatment."

"By 'proper treatment,' sir, you mean——"

"Clever handling, Jeeves. A spot of the good old snaky work. I see what must be done to jerk my Cousin Angela back to normalcy. I'll tell you, shall I?"

"If you would be so kind, sir."

I lit a cigarette, and eyed him keenly through the smoke. He waited respectfully for me to unleash the words of wisdom. I must say for Jeeves that—till, as he is so apt to do, he starts shoving his oar in and cavilling and obstructing—he makes a very good audience. I don't know if he is actually agog, but he looks agog, and that's the great thing.

"Suppose you were strolling through the illimitable jungle, Jeeves, and happened to meet a tiger cub."

"The contingency is a remote one, sir."

"Never mind. Let us suppose it."

"Very good, sir."

"Let us now suppose that you sloshed that tiger cub, and let us suppose further that word reached its mother that it was being put upon. What would you expect the attitude of that mother to be? In what frame of mind do you consider that that tigress would approach you?"

"I should anticipate a certain show of annoyance, sir."

"And rightly. Due to what is known as the maternal instinct, what?"

"Yes, sir."

"Very good, Jeeves. We will now suppose that there has recently been some little coolness between this tiger cub and this tigress. For some days, let us say, they have not been on speaking terms. Do you think that that would make any difference to the vim with which the latter would leap to the former's aid?"

"No, sir."

"Exactly. Here, then, in brief, is my plan, Jeeves. I am going to draw my Cousin Angela aside to a secluded spot and roast Tuppy properly."

"Roast, sir?"

"Knock. Slam. Tick-off. Abuse. Denounce. I shall be very terse about Tuppy, giving it as my opinion that in all essentials he is more like a wart hog than an ex-member of a fine old English public school. What will ensue? Hearing him attacked, my Cousin Angela's womanly heart will be as sick as mud. The maternal tigress in her will awake. No matter what differences they may have had, she will remember only that he is the man she loves, and will leap to his defence. And from that to falling into his arms and burying the dead past will be but a step. How do you react to that?"

"The idea is an ingenious one, sir."

"We Woosters are ingenious, Jeeves, exceedingly ingenious."

"Yes, sir."

"As a matter of fact, I am not speaking without a knowledge of the form book. I have tested this theory."

"Indeed, sir?"

"Yes, in person. And it works. I was standing on the Eden rock at Antibes last month, idly watching the bathers disport themselves in the water, and a girl I knew slightly pointed at a male diver and asked me if I didn't think his legs were about the silliest-looking pair of props ever issued to human being. I replied that I did, indeed, and for the space of perhaps two minutes was extraordinarily witty and satirical about this bird's underpinning. At the end of that period, I suddenly felt as if I had been caught up in the tail of a cyclone.

"Beginning with a *critique* of my own limbs, which she said, justly enough, were nothing to write home about, this girl went on to dissect my manners, morals, intellect, general physique, and method of eating asparagus with such acerbity that by the time she had finished the best you could say of Bertram was that, so far as was known, he had never actually committed murder or set fire to an orphan asylum. Subsequent investigation proved that she was engaged to the fellow with the legs and had had a slight disagreement with him the evening before on the subject of whether she should or should not have made an original call of two spades, having seven, but without the ace. That night I saw them dining together with every indication of relish, their differences made up and the lovelight once more in their eyes. That shows you, Jeeves."

"Yes, sir."

"I expect precisely similar results from my Cousin Angela when I start roasting Tuppy. By lunchtime, I should imagine, the engagement will be on again and the diamond-and-platinum ring glittering as of yore on her third finger. Or is it the fourth?"

"Scarcely by luncheon time, sir. Miss Angela's maid informs me that Miss Angela drove off in her car early this morning with the intention of spending the day with friends in the vicinity."

"Well, within half an hour of whatever time she comes back, then. These are mere straws, Jeeves. Do not let us chop them."

"No, sir."

"The point is that, as far as Tuppy and Angela are concerned, we may say with confidence that everything will shortly be hotsy-totsy once more. And what an agreeable thought that is, Jeeves."

"Very true, sir."

"If there is one thing that gives me the pip, it is two loving hearts being estranged."

"I can readily appreciate the fact, sir."

I placed the stub of my gasper in the ash tray and lit another, to indicate that that completed Chap. I.

"Right ho, then. So much for the western front. We now turn to the eastern."

"Sir?"

"I speak in parables, Jeeves. What I mean is, we now approach the matter of Gussie and Miss Bassett."

"Yes, sir."

"Here, Jeeves, more direct methods are required. In handling the case of Augustus Fink-Nottle, we must keep always in mind the fact that we are dealing with a poop."

"A sensitive plant would, perhaps, be a kinder expression, sir."

"No, Jeeves, a poop. And with poops one has to employ the strong, forceful, straightforward policy. Psychology doesn't get you anywhere. You, if I may remind you without wounding your feelings, fell into the error of mucking about with psychology in connection with this Fink-Nottle, and the result was a washout. You attempted to push him over the line by rigging him out in a Mephistopheles costume and sending him off to a fancy-dress ball, your view being that scarlet tights would embolden him. Futile."

"The matter was never actually put to the test, sir."

"No. Because he didn't get to the ball. And that strengthens my argument. A man who can set out in a cab for a fancy-dress ball and not get there is manifestly a poop of no common order. I don't think I have ever known anybody else who was such a dashed silly ass that he couldn't even get to a fancy-dress ball. Have you, Jeeves?"

"No, sir."

"But don't forget this, because it is the point I wish, above all, to make: Even if Gussie had got to that ball; even if those scarlet tights, taken in conjunction with his horn-rimmed spectacles, hadn't given the girl a fit of some kind; even if she had rallied from the shock and he had been able to dance and generally hobnob with her; even then your efforts would have been fruitless, because, Mephistopheles costume or no Mephistopheles costume, Augustus Fink-Nottle would never have been able to summon up the courage to ask her to be his. All that would have resulted would have been that she would have got that lecture on newts a few days earlier. And why, Jeeves? Shall I tell you why?"

"Yes, sir."

"Because he would have been attempting the hopeless task of trying to do the thing on orange juice."

"Sir?"

"Gussie is an orange-juice addict. He drinks nothing else."

"I was not aware of that, sir."

"I have it from his own lips. Whether from some hereditary taint, or because he promised his mother he wouldn't, or simply because he doesn't like the taste of the stuff, Gussie Fink-Nottle has never in the whole course of his career pushed so much as the simplest gin and tonic over the larynx. And he expects—this poop expects, Jeeves—this wabbling, shrinking, diffident rabbit in human shape expects under these conditions to propose to the girl he loves. One hardly knows whether to smile or weep, what?"

"You consider total abstinence a handicap to a gentleman who wishes to make a proposal of marriage, sir?"

The question amazed me.

"Why, dash it," I said, astounded, "you must know it is. Use your intelligence, Jeeves. Reflect what proposing means. It means that a decent, self-respecting chap has got to listen to himself saying things which, if spoken on the silver screen, would cause him to dash to the box-office and demand his money back. Let him attempt to do it on orange juice, and what ensues? Shame seals his lips, or, if it doesn't do that, makes him lose his morale and start to babble. Gussie, for example, as we have seen, babbles of syncopated newts."

"Palmated newts, sir."

"Palmated or syncopated, it doesn't matter which. The point is that he babbles and is going to babble again, if he has another try at it. Unless—and this is where I want you to follow me very closely, Jeeves—unless steps are taken at once through the proper channels. Only active measures, promptly applied, can provide this poor, pusillanimous poop with the proper pep. And that is why, Jeeves, I intend tomorrow to secure a bottle of gin and lace his luncheon orange juice with it liberally."

"Sir?"

I clicked the tongue.

"I have already had occasion, Jeeves," I said rebukingly, "to comment on the way you say 'Well, sir' and 'Indeed, sir?' I take this opportunity of informing you that I object equally strongly to your 'Sir?' pure and simple. The word seems to suggest that in your opinion I have made a statement or mooted a scheme so bizarre that your brain reels at it. In the present instance, there is absolutely nothing to say 'Sir?' about. The plan I have put forward is entirely reasonable and icily logical, and should excite no sirring whatsoever. Or don't you think so?"

"Well, sir——"

"Jeeves!"

"I beg your pardon, sir. The expression escaped me inadvertently. What I intended to say, since you press me, was that the action which you propose does seem to me somewhat injudicious."

"Injudicious? I don't follow you, Jeeves."

"A certain amount of risk would enter into it, in my opinion, sir. It is not always a simple matter to gauge the effect of alcohol on a subject unaccustomed to such stimulant. I have known it to have distressing results in the case of parrots."

"Parrots?"

"I was thinking of an incident of my earlier life, sir, before I entered your employment. I was in the service of the late Lord Brancaster at the time, a gentleman who owned a parrot to which he was greatly devoted, and one day the bird chanced to be lethargic, and his lordship, with the kindly intention of restoring it to its customary animation, offered it a portion of seed cake steeped in the '84 port. The bird accepted the morsel gratefully and consumed it with every indication of satisfaction. Almost immediately afterwards, however, its manner became markedly feverish. Having bitten his lordship in the thumb and sung part of a sea-chanty, it fell to the bottom of the cage and remained there for a considerable period of time with its legs in the air, unable to move. I merely mention this, sir, in order to——"

I put my finger on the flaw. I had spotted it all along.

"But Gussie isn't a parrot."

"No, sir, but——"

"It is high time, in my opinion, that this question of what young Gussie really is was threshed out and cleared up. He seems to think he is a male newt, and you now appear to suggest that he is a parrot. The truth of the matter being that he is just a plain, ordinary poop and needs a snootful as badly as ever man did. So no more discussion, Jeeves. My mind is made up. There is only one way of handling this difficult case, and that is the way I have outlined."

"Very good, sir."

"Right ho, Jeeves. So much for that, then. Now here's something else: You noticed that I said I was going to put this project through tomorrow, and no doubt you wondered why I said tomorrow. Why did I, Jeeves?"

"Because you feel that if it were done when 'tis done, then 'twere well it were done quickly, sir?"

"Partly, Jeeves, but not altogether. My chief reason for fixing the date as specified is that tomorrow, though you have doubtless forgotten, is the day of the distribution of prizes at Market Snodsbury Grammar School, at which, as you know, Gussie is to be the male star and master of the revels. So you see we shall, by lacing that juice, not only embolden him to propose to Miss Bassett, but also put him so into shape that he will hold that Market Snodsbury audience spellbound."

"In fact, you will be killing two birds with one stone, sir."

"Exactly. A very neat way of putting it. And now here is a minor point. On second thoughts, I think the best plan will be for you, not me, to lace the juice."

"Sir?"

"Jeeves!"

"I beg your pardon, sir."

"And I'll tell you why that will be the best plan. Because you are in a position to obtain ready access to the stuff. It is served to Gussie daily, I have noticed, in an individual jug. This jug will presumably be lying about the kitchen or somewhere before lunch tomorrow. It will be the simplest of tasks for you to slip a few fingers of gin in it."

"No doubt, sir, but——"

"Don't say 'but,' Jeeves."

"I fear, sir——"

"'I fear, sir' is just as bad."

"What I am endeavouring to say, sir, is that I am sorry, but I am afraid I must enter an unequivocal *nolle prosequi.*"

"Do what?"

"The expression is a legal one, sir, signifying the resolve not to proceed with a matter. In other words, eager though I am to carry out your instructions, sir, as a general rule, on this occasion I must respectfully decline to co-operate."

"You won't do it, you mean?"

"Precisely, sir."

I was stunned. I began to understand how a general must feel when he has ordered a regiment to charge and has been told that it isn't in the mood.

"Jeeves," I said, "I had not expected this of you."

"No, sir?"

"No, indeed. Naturally, I realize that lacing Gussie's orange juice is not one of those regular duties for which you receive the monthly stipend, and if you care to stand on the strict letter of the contract, I suppose there is nothing to be done about it. But you will permit me to observe that this is scarcely the feudal spirit."

"I am sorry, sir."

"It is quite all right, Jeeves, quite all right. I am not angry, only a little hurt."

"Very good, sir."

"Right ho, Jeeves."

-14-

Investigation proved that the friends Angela had gone to spend the day with were some stately-home owners of the name of Stretchley-Budd, hanging out in a joint called Kingham Manor, about eight miles distant in the direction of Pershore. I didn't know these birds, but their fascination must have been considerable, for she tore herself away from them only just in time to get back and dress for dinner. It was, accordingly, not until coffee had been consumed that I was able to get matters moving. I found her in the drawing-room and at once proceeded to put things in train.

It was with very different feelings from those which had animated the bosom when approaching the Bassett twenty-four hours before in the same manner in this same drawing-room that I headed for where she sat. As I had told Tuppy, I have always been devoted to Angela, and there is nothing I like better than a ramble in her company.

And I could see by the look of her now how sorely in need she was of my aid and comfort.

Frankly, I was shocked by the unfortunate young prune's appearance. At Cannes she had been a happy, smiling English girl of the best type, full of beans and buck. Her face now was pale and drawn, like that of a hockey centre-forward at a girls' school who, in addition to getting a fruity one on the shin, has just been penalized for "sticks". In any normal gathering, her demeanour would have excited instant remark, but the standard of gloom at Brinkley Court had become so high that it passed unnoticed. Indeed, I shouldn't wonder if Uncle Tom, crouched in his corner waiting for the end, didn't think she was looking indecently cheerful.

I got down to the agenda in my debonair way.

"What ho, Angela, old girl."

"Hullo, Bertie, darling."

"Glad you're back at last. I missed you."

"Did you, darling?"

"I did, indeed. Care to come for a saunter?"

"I'd love it."

"Fine. I have much to say to you that is not for the public ear."

I think at this moment poor old Tuppy must have got a sudden touch of cramp. He had been sitting hard by, staring at the ceiling, and he now gave a sharp leap like a gaffed salmon and upset a small table containing a vase, a bowl of potpourri, two china dogs, and a copy of Omar Khayyám bound in limp leather.

Aunt Dahlia uttered a startled hunting cry. Uncle Tom, who probably imagined from the noise that this was civilization crashing at last, helped things along by breaking a coffee-cup.

Tuppy said he was sorry. Aunt Dahlia, with a deathbed groan, said it didn't matter. And Angela, having stared haughtily for a moment like a princess of the old régime confronted by some notable example of gaucherie on the part of some particularly foul member of the underworld, accompanied me across the threshold. And presently I had deposited her and self on one of the rustic benches in the garden, and was ready to snap into the business of the evening.

I considered it best, however, before doing so, to ease things along with a little informal chitchat. You don't want to rush a delicate job like the one I had in hand. And so for a while we spoke of neutral topics. She said that what had kept her so long at the Stretchley-Budds was that Hilda Stretchley-Budd had made her stop on and help with the arrangements for their servants' ball tomorrow night, a task which she couldn't very well decline, as all the Brinkley Court domestic staff were to be present. I said that a jolly night's revelry might be just what was needed to cheer Anatole up and take his mind off things. To which she replied that Anatole wasn't going. On being urged to do so by Aunt Dahlia, she said, he had merely shaken his head sadly and gone on talking of returning to Provence, where he was appreciated.

It was after the sombre silence induced by this statement that Angela said the grass was wet and she thought she would go in.

This, of course, was entirely foreign to my policy.

"No, don't do that. I haven't had a chance to talk to you since you arrived."

"I shall ruin my shoes."

"Put your feet up on my lap."

"All right. And you can tickle my ankles."

"Quite."

Matters were accordingly arranged on these lines, and for some minutes we continued chatting in desultory fashion. Then the conversation petered out. I made a few observations *in re* the scenic effects, featuring the twilight hush, the peeping stars, and the soft glimmer of the waters of the lake, and she said yes. Something rustled in the bushes in front of us, and I advanced the theory that it was possibly a weasel, and she said it might be. But it was plain that the girl was distraite, and I considered it best to waste no more time.

"Well, old thing," I said, "I've heard all about your little dust-up So those wedding bells are not going to ring out, what?"

"No."

"Definitely over, is it?"

"Yes."

"Well, if you want my opinion, I think that's a bit of goose for you, Angela, old girl. I think you're extremely well out of it. It's a mystery to me how you stood this Glossop so long. Take him for all in all, he ranks very low down among the wines and spirits. A washout, I should describe him as. A frightful oik, and a mass of side to boot. I'd pity the girl who was linked for life to a bargee like Tuppy Glossop."

And I emitted a hard laugh—one of the sneering kind.

"I always thought you were such friends," said Angela.

I let go another hard one, with a bit more top spin on it than the first time:

"Friends? Absolutely not. One was civil, of course, when one met the fellow, but it would be absurd to say one was a friend of his. A club acquaintance, and a mere one at that. And then one was at school with the man."

"At Eton?"

"Good heavens, no. We wouldn't have a fellow like that at Eton. At a kid's school before I went there. A grubby little brute he was, I recollect. Covered with ink and mire generally, washing only on alternate Thursdays. In short, a notable outsider, shunned by all."

I paused. I was more than a bit perturbed. Apart from the agony of having to talk in this fashion of one who, except when he was looping back rings and causing me to plunge into swimming baths in correct evening costume, had always been a very dear and esteemed crony, I didn't seem to be getting anywhere. Business was not resulting. Staring into the bushes without a yip, she appeared to be bearing these slurs and innuendos of mine with an easy calm.

I had another pop at it:

"'Uncouth' about sums it up. I doubt if I've ever seen an uncouther kid than this Glossop. Ask anyone who knew him in those days to describe him in a word, and the word they will use is 'uncouth'. And he's just the same today. It's the old story. The boy is the father of the man."

She appeared not to have heard.

"The boy," I repeated, not wishing her to miss that one, "is the father of the man."

"What are you talking about?"

"I'm talking about this Glossop."

"I thought you said something about somebody's father."

"I said the boy was the father of the man."

"What boy?"

"The boy Glossop."

"He hasn't got a father."

"I never said he had. I said he was the father of the boy—or, rather, of the man."

"What man?"

I saw that the conversation had reached a point where, unless care was taken, we should be muddled.

"The point I am trying to make," I said, "is that the boy Glossop is the father of the man Glossop. In other words, each loathsome fault and blemish that led the boy Glossop to be frowned upon by his fellows is present in the man Glossop, and causes him—I am speaking now of the man Glossop—to be a hissing and a by-word at places like the Drones, where a certain standard of decency is demanded from the inmates. Ask anyone at the Drones, and they will tell you that it was a black day for the dear old club when this chap Glossop somehow wriggled into the list of members. Here you will find a man who dislikes his face; there one who could stand his face if it wasn't for his habits. But the universal consensus of opinion is that the fellow is a bounder and a tick, and that the moment he showed signs of wanting to get into the place he should have been met with a firm *nolle prosequi* and heartily blackballed."

I had to pause again here, partly in order to take in a spot of breath, and partly to wrestle with the almost physical torture of saying these frightful things about poor old Tuppy.

"There are some chaps," I resumed, forcing myself once more to the nauseous task, "who, in spite of looking as if they had slept in their clothes, can get by quite nicely because they are amiable and suave. There are others who, for all that they excite adverse comment by being fat and uncouth, find themselves on the credit side of the ledger owing to their wit and sparkling humour. But this Glossop, I regret to say, falls into neither class. In addition to looking like one of those things that come out of hollow trees, he is universally admitted to be a dumb brick of the first water. No soul. No conversation. In short, any girl who, having been rash enough to get engaged to him, has managed at the eleventh hour to slide out is justly entitled to consider herself dashed lucky."

I paused once more, and cocked an eye at Angela to see how the treatment was taking. All the while I had been speaking, she had sat gazing silently into the bushes, but it seemed to me incredible that she should not now turn on me like a tigress, according to specifications. It beat me why she hadn't done it already. It seemed to me that a mere tithe of what I had said, if said to a tigress about a tiger of which she was fond, would have made her—the tigress, I mean—hit the ceiling.

And the next moment you could have knocked me down with a toothpick.

"Yes," she said, nodding thoughtfully, "you're quite right."

"Eh?"

"That's exactly what I've been thinking myself."

"What!"

"'Dumb brick.' It just describes him. One of the six silliest asses in England, I should think he must be."

I did not speak. I was endeavouring to adjust the faculties, which were in urgent need of a bit of first-aid treatment.

I mean to say, all this had come as a complete surprise. In formulating the well-laid plan which I had just been putting into effect, the one contingency I had not budgeted for was that she might adhere to the sentiments which I expressed. I had braced myself for a gush of stormy emotion. I was expecting the tearful ticking off, the girlish recriminations and all the rest of the bag of tricks along those lines.

But this cordial agreement with my remarks I had not foreseen, and it gave me what you might call pause for thought.

She proceeded to develop her theme, speaking in ringing, enthusiastic tones, as if she loved the topic. Jeeves could tell you the word I want. I think it's "ecstatic", unless that's the sort of rash you get on your face and have to use ointment for. But if that is the right word, then that's what her manner was as she ventilated the subject of poor old Tuppy. If you had been able to go simply by the sound of her voice, she might have been a court poet cutting loose about an Oriental monarch, or Gussie Fink-Nottle describing his last consignment of newts.

"It's so nice, Bertie, talking to somebody who really takes a sensible view about this man Glossop. Mother says he's a good chap, which is simply absurd. Anybody can see that he's absolutely impossible. He's conceited and opinionative and argues all the time, even when he knows perfectly well that he's talking through his hat, and he smokes too much and eats too much and drinks too much, and I don't like the colour of his hair. Not that he'll have any hair in a year or two, because he's pretty thin on the top already, and before he knows where he is he'll be as bald as an egg, and he's the last man who can afford to go bald. And I think it's simply disgusting, the way he gorges all the time. Do you know, I found him in the larder at one o'clock this morning, absolutely wallowing in a steak-and-kidney pie? There was hardly any of it left. And you remember what an enormous dinner he had. Quite disgusting, I call it. But I can't stop out here all night, talking about men who aren't worth wasting a word on and haven't even enough sense to tell sharks from flatfish. I'm going in."

And gathering about her slim shoulders the shawl which she had put on as a protection against the evening dew, she buzzed off, leaving me alone in the silent night.

Well, as a matter of fact, not absolutely alone, because a few moments later there was a sort of upheaval in the bushes in front of me, and Tuppy emerged.

-15-

I gave him the eye. The evening had begun to draw in a bit by now and the visibility, in consequence, was not so hot, but there still remained ample light to enable me to see him clearly. And what I saw convinced me that I should be a lot easier in my mind with a stout rustic bench between us. I rose, accordingly, modelling my style on that of a rocketing pheasant, and proceeded to deposit myself on the other side of the object named.

My prompt agility was not without its effect. He seemed somewhat taken aback. He came to a halt, and, for about the space of time required to allow a bead of persp. to trickle from the top of the brow to the tip of the nose, stood gazing at me in silence.

"So!" he said at length, and it came as a complete surprise to me that fellows ever really do say "So!" I had always thought it was just a thing you read in books. Like "Quotha!" I mean to say, or "Odds bodikins!" or even "Eh, ba goom!"

Still, there it was. Quaint or not quaint, bizarre or not bizarre, he had said "So!" and it was up to me to cope with the situation on those lines.

It would have been a duller man than Bertram Wooster who had failed to note that the dear old chap was a bit steamed up. Whether his eyes were actually shooting forth flame, I couldn't tell you, but there appeared to me to be a distinct incandescence. For the rest, his fists were clenched, his ears quivering, and the muscles of his jaw rotating rhythmically, as if he were making an early supper off something.

His hair was full of twigs, and there was a beetle hanging to the side of his head which would have interested Gussie Fink-Nottle. To this, however, I paid scant attention. There is a time for studying beetles and a time for not studying beetles.

"So!" he said again.

Now, those who know Bertram Wooster best will tell you that he is always at his shrewdest and most level-headed in moments of peril. Who was it who, when gripped by the arm of the law on boat-race night not so many years ago and hauled off to Vine Street police station, assumed in a flash the identity of Eustace H. Plimsoll, of The Laburnums, Alleyn Road, West Dulwich, thus saving the grand old name of Wooster from being dragged in the mire and avoiding wide publicity of the wrong sort? Who was it ...

But I need not labour the point. My record speaks for itself. Three times pinched, but never once sentenced under the correct label. Ask anyone at the Drones about this.

So now, in a situation threatening to become every moment more scaly, I did not lose my head. I preserved the old sang-froid. Smiling a genial and affectionate smile, and hoping that it wasn't too dark for it to register, I spoke with a jolly cordiality:

"Why, hallo, Tuppy. You here?"

He said, yes, he was here.

"Been here long?"

"I have."

"Fine. I wanted to see you."

"Well, here I am. Come out from behind that bench."

"No, thanks, old man. I like leaning on it. It seems to rest the spine."

"In about two seconds," said Tuppy, "I'm going to kick your spine up through the top of your head."

I raised the eyebrows. Not much good, of course, in that light, but it seemed to help the general composition.

"Is this Hildebrand Glossop speaking?" I said.

He replied that it was, adding that if I wanted to make sure I might move a few feet over in his direction. He also called me an opprobrious name.

I raised the eyebrows again.

"Come, come, Tuppy, don't let us let this little chat become acrid. Is 'acrid' the word I want?"

"I couldn't say," he replied, beginning to sidle round the bench.

I saw that anything I might wish to say must be said quickly. Already he had sidled some six feet. And though, by dint of sidling, too, I had managed to keep the bench between us, who could predict how long this happy state of affairs would last?

I came to the point, therefore.

"I think I know what's on your mind, Tuppy," I said. "If you were in those bushes during my conversation with the recent Angela, I dare say you heard what I was saying about you."

"I did."

"I see. Well, we won't go into the ethics of the thing. Eavesdropping, some people might call it, and I can imagine stern critics drawing in the breath to some extent. Considering it—I don't want to hurt your feelings, Tuppy—but considering it un-English. A bit un-English, Tuppy, old man, you must admit."

"I'm Scotch."

"Really?" I said. "I never knew that before. Rummy how you don't suspect a man of being Scotch unless he's Mac-something and says 'Och, aye' and things like that. I wonder," I went on, feeling that an academic discussion on some neutral topic might ease the tension, "if you can tell me something that has puzzled me a good deal. What exactly is it that they put into haggis? I've often wondered about that."

From the fact that his only response to the question was to leap over the bench and make a grab at me, I gathered that his mind was not on haggis.

"However," I said, leaping over the bench in my turn, "that is a side issue. If, to come back to it, you were in those bushes and heard what I was saying about you——"

He began to move round the bench in a nor'-nor'-easterly direction. I followed his example, setting a course sou'-sou'-west.

"No doubt you were surprised at the way I was talking."

"Not a bit."

"What? Did nothing strike you as odd in the tone of my remarks?"

"It was just the sort of stuff I should have expected a treacherous, sneaking hound like you to say."

"My dear chap," I protested, "this is not your usual form. A bit slow in the up-take, surely? I should have thought you would have spotted right away that it was all part of a well-laid plan."

"I'll get you in a jiffy," said Tuppy, recovering his balance after a swift clutch at my neck. And so probable did this seem that I delayed no longer, but hastened to place all the facts before him.

Speaking rapidly and keeping moving, I related my emotions on receipt of Aunt Dahlia's telegram, my instant rush to the scene of the disaster, my meditations in the car, and the eventual framing of this well-laid plan of mine. I spoke clearly and well, and it was with considerable concern, consequently, that I heard him observe—between clenched teeth, which made it worse—that he didn't believe a damned word of it.

"But, Tuppy," I said, "why not? To me the thing rings true to the last drop. What makes you sceptical? Confide in me, Tuppy."

He halted and stood taking a breather. Tuppy, pungently though Angela might have argued to the contrary, isn't really fat. During the winter months you will find him constantly booting the football with merry shouts, and in the summer the tennis racket is seldom out of his hand.

But at the recently concluded evening meal, feeling, no doubt, that after that painful scene in the larder there was nothing to be gained by further abstinence, he had rather let himself go and, as it were, made up leeway; and after really immersing himself in one of Anatole's dinners, a man of his sturdy build tends to lose elasticity a bit. During the exposition of my plans for his happiness a certain animation had crept into this round-and-round-the mulberry-bush jamboree of ours—so much so, indeed, that for the last few minutes we might have been a rather oversized greyhound and a somewhat slimmer electric hare doing their stuff on a circular track for the entertainment of the many-headed.

This, it appeared, had taken it out of him a bit, and I was not displeased. I was feeling the strain myself, and welcomed a lull.

"It absolutely beats me why you don't believe it," I said. "You know we've been pals for years. You must be aware that, except at the moment when you caused me to do a nose dive into the Drones' swimming bath, an incident which I long since decided to put out of my mind and let the dead past bury its dead about, if you follow what I mean—except on that one occasion, as I say, I have always regarded you with the utmost esteem. Why, then, if not for the motives I have outlined, should I knock you to Angela? Answer me that. Be very careful."

"What do you mean, be very careful?"

Well, as a matter of fact, I didn't quite know myself. It was what the magistrate had said to me on the occasion when I stood in the dock as Eustace Plimsoll, of The Laburnums: and as it had impressed me a good deal at the time, I just bunged it in now by way of giving the conversation a tone.

"All right. Never mind about being careful, then. Just answer me that question. Why, if I had not your interests sincerely at heart, should I have ticked you off, as stated?"

A sharp spasm shook him from base to apex. The beetle, which, during the recent exchanges, had been clinging to his head, hoping for the best, gave it up at this and resigned office. It shot off and was swallowed in the night.

"Ah!" I said. "Your beetle," I explained. "No doubt you were unaware of it, but all this while there has been a beetle of sorts parked on the side of your head. You have now dislodged it."

He snorted.

"Beetles!"

"Not beetles. One beetle only."

"I like your crust!" cried Tuppy, vibrating like one of Gussie's newts during the courting season. "Talking of beetles, when all the time you know you're a treacherous, sneaking hound."

It was a debatable point, of course, why treacherous, sneaking hounds should be considered ineligible to talk about beetles, and I dare say a good cross-examining counsel would have made quite a lot of it.

But I let it go.

"That's the second time you've called me that. And," I said firmly, "I insist on an explanation. I have told you that I acted throughout from the best and kindliest motives in roasting you to Angela. It cut me to the quick to have to speak like that, and only the recollection of our lifelong friendship would have made me do it. And now you say you don't believe me and call me names for which I am not sure I couldn't have you up before a beak and jury and mulct you in very substantial damages. I should have to consult my solicitor, of course, but it would surprise me very much if an action did not lie. Be reasonable, Tuppy. Suggest another motive I could have had. Just one."

"I will. Do you think I don't know? You're in love with Angela yourself."

"What?"

"And you knocked me in order to poison her mind against me and finally remove me from your path."

I had never heard anything so absolutely loopy in my life. Why, dash it, I've known Angela since she was so high. You don't fall in love with close relations you've known since they were so high. Besides, isn't there something in the book of rules about a man may not marry his cousin? Or am I thinking of grandmothers?

"Tuppy, my dear old ass," I cried, "this is pure banana oil! You've come unscrewed."

"Oh, yes?"

"Me in love with Angela? Ha-ha!"

"You can't get out of it with ha-ha's. She called you 'darling'."

"I know. And I disapproved. This habit of the younger g. of scattering 'darlings' about like birdseed is one that I deprecate. Lax, is how I should describe it."

"You tickled her ankles."

"In a purely cousinly spirit. It didn't mean a thing. Why, dash it, you must know that in the deeper and truer sense I wouldn't touch Angela with a barge pole."

"Oh? And why not? Not good enough for you?"

"You misunderstand me," I hastened to reply. "When I say I wouldn't touch Angela with a barge pole, I intend merely to convey that my feelings towards her are those of distant, though cordial, esteem. In other words, you may rest assured that between this young prune and myself there never has been and never could be any sentiment warmer and stronger than that of ordinary friendship."

"I believe it was you who tipped her off that I was in the larder last night, so that she could find me there with that pie, thus damaging my prestige."

"My dear Tuppy! A Wooster?" I was shocked. "You think a Wooster would do that?"

He breathed heavily.

"Listen," he said. "It's no good your standing there arguing. You can't get away from the facts. Somebody stole her from me at Cannes. You told me yourself that she was with you all the time at Cannes and hardly saw anybody else. You gloated over the mixed bathing, and those moonlight walks you had together——"

"Not gloated. Just mentioned them."

"So now you understand why, as soon as I can get you clear of this damned bench, I am going to tear you limb from limb. Why they have these bally benches in gardens," said Tuppy discontentedly, "is more than I can see. They only get in the way."

He ceased, and, grabbing out, missed me by a hair's breadth.

It was a moment for swift thinking, and it is at such moments, as I have already indicated, that Bertram Wooster is at his best. I suddenly remembered the recent misunderstanding with the Bassett, and with a flash of clear vision saw that this was where it was going to come in handy.

"You've got it all wrong, Tuppy," I said, moving to the left. "True, I saw a lot of Angela, but my dealings with her were on a basis from start to finish of the purest and most wholesome camaraderie. I can prove it. During that sojourn in Cannes my affections were engaged elsewhere."

"What?"

"Engaged elsewhere. My affections. During that sojourn."

I had struck the right note. He stopped sidling. His clutching hand fell to his side.

"Is that true?"

"Quite official."

"Who was she?"

"My dear Tuppy, does one bandy a woman's name?"

"One does if one doesn't want one's ruddy head pulled off."

I saw that it was a special case.

"Madeline Bassett," I said.

"Who?"

"Madeline Bassett."

He seemed stunned.

"You stand there and tell me you were in love with that Bassett disaster?"

"I wouldn't call her 'that Bassett disaster', Tuppy. Not respectful."

"Dash being respectful. I want the facts. You deliberately assert that you loved that weird Gawd-help-us?"

"I don't see why you should call her a weird Gawd-help-us, either. A very charming and beautiful girl. Odd in some of her views perhaps—one does not quite see eye to eye with her in the matter of stars and rabbits—but not a weird Gawd-help-us."

"Anyway, you stick to it that you were in love with her?"

"I do."

"It sounds thin to me, Wooster, very thin."

I saw that it would be necessary to apply the finishing touch.

"I must ask you to treat this as entirely confidential, Glossop, but I may as well inform you that it is not twenty-four hours since she turned me down."

"Turned you down?"

"Like a bedspread. In this very garden."

"Twenty-four hours?"

"Call it twenty-five. So you will readily see that I can't be the chap, if any, who stole Angela from you at Cannes."

And I was on the brink of adding that I wouldn't touch Angela with a barge pole, when I remembered I had said it already and it hadn't gone frightfully well. I desisted, therefore.

My manly frankness seemed to be producing good results. The homicidal glare was dying out of Tuppy's eyes. He had the aspect of a hired assassin who had paused to think things over.

"I see," he said, at length. "All right, then. Sorry you were troubled."

"Don't mention it, old man," I responded courteously.

For the first time since the bushes had begun to pour forth Glossops, Bertram Wooster could be said to have breathed freely. I don't say I actually came out from behind the bench, but I did let go of it, and with something of the relief which those three chaps in the Old Testament must have experienced after sliding out of the burning fiery furnace, I even groped tentatively for my cigarette case.

The next moment a sudden snort made me take my fingers off it as if it had bitten me. I was distressed to note in the old friend a return of the recent frenzy.

"What the hell did you mean by telling her that I used to be covered with ink when I was a kid?"

"My dear Tuppy——"

"I was almost finickingly careful about my personal cleanliness as a boy. You could have eaten your dinner off me."

"Quite. But——"

"And all that stuff about having no soul. I'm crawling with soul. And being looked on as an outsider at the Drones——"

"But, my dear old chap, I explained that. It was all part of my ruse or scheme."

"It was, was it? Well, in future do me a favour and leave me out of your foul ruses."

"Just as you say, old boy."

"All right, then. That's understood."

He relapsed into silence, standing with folded arms, staring before him rather like a strong, silent man in a novel when he's just been given the bird by the girl and is thinking of looking in at the Rocky Mountains and bumping off a few bears. His manifest pippedness excited my compash, and I ventured a kindly word.

"I don't suppose you know what *au pied de la lettre* means, Tuppy, but that's how I don't think you ought to take all that stuff Angela was saying just now too much."

He seemed interested.

"What the devil," he asked, "are you talking about?"

I saw that I should have to make myself clearer.

"Don't take all that guff of hers too literally, old man. You know what girls are like."

"I do," he said, with another snort that came straight up from his insteps. "And I wish I'd never met one."

"I mean to say, it's obvious that she must have spotted you in those bushes and was simply talking to score off you. There you were, I mean, if you follow the psychology, and she saw you, and in that impulsive way girls have, she seized the opportunity of ribbing you a bit—just told you a few home truths, I mean to say."

"Home truths?"

"That's right."

He snorted once more, causing me to feel rather like royalty receiving a twenty-one gun salute from the fleet. I can't remember ever having met a better right-and-left-hand snorter.

"What do you mean, 'home truths'? I'm not fat."

"No, no."

"And what's wrong with the colour of my hair?"

"Quite in order, Tuppy, old man. The hair, I mean."

"And I'm not a bit thin on the top.... What the dickens are you grinning about?"

"Not grinning. Just smiling slightly. I was conjuring up a sort of vision, if you know what I mean, of you as seen through Angela's eyes. Fat in the middle and thin on the top. Rather funny."

"You think it funny, do you?"

"Not a bit."

"You'd better not."

"Quite."

It seemed to me that the conversation was becoming difficult again. I wished it could be terminated. And so it was. For at this moment something came shimmering through the laurels in the quiet evenfall, and I perceived that it was Angela.

She was looking sweet and saintlike, and she had a plate of sandwiches in her hand. Ham, I was to discover later.

"If you see Mr. Glossop anywhere, Bertie," she said, her eyes resting dreamily on Tuppy's facade, "I wish you would give him these. I'm so afraid he may be hungry, poor fellow. It's nearly ten o'clock, and he hasn't eaten a morsel since dinner. I'll just leave them on this bench."

She pushed off, and it seemed to me that I might as well go with her. Nothing to keep me here, I mean. We moved towards the house, and presently from behind us there sounded in the night the splintering crash of a well-kicked plate of ham sandwiches, accompanied by the muffled oaths of a strong man in his wrath.

"How still and peaceful everything is," said Angela.

-16-

Sunshine was gilding the grounds of Brinkley Court and the ear detected a marked twittering of birds in the ivy outside the window when I woke next morning to a new day. But there was no corresponding sunshine in Bertram Wooster's soul and no answering twitter in his heart as he sat up in bed, sipping his cup of strengthening tea. It could not be denied that to Bertram, reviewing the happenings of the previous night, the Tuppy-Angela situation seemed more or less to have slipped a cog. With every desire to look for the silver lining, I could not but feel that the rift between these two haughty spirits had now reached such impressive proportions that the task of bridging same would be beyond even my powers.

I am a shrewd observer, and there had been something in Tuppy's manner as he booted that plate of ham sandwiches that seemed to tell me that he would not lightly forgive.

In these circs., I deemed it best to shelve their problem for the nonce and turn the mind to the matter of Gussie, which presented a brighter picture.

With regard to Gussie, everything was in train. Jeeves's morbid scruples about lacing the chap's orange juice had put me to a good deal of trouble, but I had surmounted every obstacle in the old Wooster way. I had secured an abundance of the necessary spirit, and it was now lying in its flask in the drawer of the dressing-table. I had also ascertained that the jug, duly filled, would be standing on a shelf in the butler's pantry round about the hour of one. To remove it from that shelf, sneak it up to my room, and return it, laced, in good time for the midday meal would be a task calling, no doubt, for address, but in no sense an exacting one.

It was with something of the emotions of one preparing a treat for a deserving child that I finished my tea and rolled over for that extra spot of sleep which just makes all the difference when there is man's work to be done and the brain must be kept clear for it.

And when I came downstairs an hour or so later, I knew how right I had been to formulate this scheme for Gussie's bucking up. I ran into him on the lawn, and I could see at a glance that if ever there was a man who needed a snappy stimulant, it was he. All nature, as I have indicated, was smiling, but not Augustus Fink-Nottle. He was walking round in circles, muttering something about not proposing to detain us long, but on this auspicious occasion feeling compelled to say a few words.

"Ah, Gussie," I said, arresting him as he was about to start another lap. "A lovely morning, is it not?"

Even if I had not been aware of it already, I could have divined from the abruptness with which he damned the lovely morning that he was not in merry mood. I addressed myself to the task of bringing the roses back to his cheeks.

"I've got good news for you, Gussie."

He looked at me with a sudden sharp interest.

"Has Market Snodsbury Grammar School burned down?"

"Not that I know of."

"Have mumps broken out? Is the place closed on account of measles?"

"No, no."

"Then what do you mean you've got good news?"

I endeavoured to soothe.

"You mustn't take it so hard, Gussie. Why worry about a laughably simple job like distributing prizes at a school?"

"Laughably simple, eh? Do you realize I've been sweating for days and haven't been able to think of a thing to say yet, except that I won't detain them long. You bet I won't detain them long. I've been timing my speech, and it lasts five seconds. What the devil am I to say, Bertie? What do you say when you're distributing prizes?"

I considered. Once, at my private school, I had won a prize for Scripture knowledge, so I suppose I ought to have been full of inside stuff. But memory eluded me.

Then something emerged from the mists.

"You say the race is not always to the swift."

"Why?"

"Well, it's a good gag. It generally gets a hand."

"I mean, why isn't it? Why isn't the race to the swift?"

"Ah, there you have me. But the nibs say it isn't."

"But what does it mean?"

"I take it it's supposed to console the chaps who haven't won prizes."

"What's the good of that to me? I'm not worrying about them. It's the ones that have won prizes that I'm worrying about, the little blighters who will come up on the platform. Suppose they make faces at me."

"They won't."

"How do you know they won't? It's probably the first thing they'll think of. And even if they don't—Bertie, shall I tell you something?"

"What?"

"I've a good mind to take that tip of yours and have a drink."

I smiled. He little knew, about summed up what I was thinking.

"Oh, you'll be all right," I said.

He became fevered again.

"How do you know I'll be all right? I'm sure to blow up in my lines."

"Tush!"

"Or drop a prize."

"Tut!"

"Or something. I can feel it in my bones. As sure as I'm standing here, something is going to happen this afternoon which will make everybody laugh themselves sick at me. I can hear them now. Like hyenas.... Bertie!"

"Hullo?"

"Do you remember that kids' school we went to before Eton?"

"Quite. It was there I won my Scripture prize."

"Never mind about your Scripture prize. I'm not talking about your Scripture prize. Do you recollect the Bosher incident?"

I did, indeed. It was one of the high spots of my youth.

"Major-General Sir Wilfred Bosher came to distribute the prizes at that school," proceeded Gussie in a dull, toneless voice. "He dropped a book. He stooped to pick it up. And, as he stooped, his trousers split up the back."

"How we roared!"

Gussie's face twisted.

"We did, little swine that we were. Instead of remaining silent and exhibiting a decent sympathy for a gallant officer at a peculiarly embarrassing moment, we howled and yelled with mirth. I loudest of any. That is what will happen to me this afternoon, Bertie. It will be a judgment on me for laughing like that at Major-General Sir Wilfred Bosher."

"No, no, Gussie, old man. Your trousers won't split."

"How do you know they won't? Better men than I have split their trousers. General Bosher was a D.S.O., with a fine record of service on the north-western frontier of India, and his trousers split. I shall be a mockery and a scorn. I know it. And you, fully cognizant of what I am in for, come babbling about good news. What news could possibly be good to me at this moment except the information that bubonic plague had broken out among the scholars of Market Snodsbury Grammar School, and that they were all confined to their beds with spots?"

The moment had come for me to speak. I laid a hand gently on his shoulder. He brushed it off. I laid it on again. He brushed it off once more. I was endeavouring to lay it on for the third time, when he moved aside and desired, with a certain petulance, to be informed if I thought I was a ruddy osteopath.

I found his manner trying, but one has to make allowances. I was telling myself that I should be seeing a very different Gussie after lunch.

"When I said I had good news, old man, I meant about Madeline Bassett."

The febrile gleam died out of his eyes, to be replaced by a look of infinite sadness.

"You can't have good news about her. I've dished myself there completely."

"Not at all. I am convinced that if you take another whack at her, all will be well."

And, keeping it snappy, I related what had passed between the Bassett and myself on the previous night.

"So all you have to do is play a return date, and you cannot fail to swing the voting. You are her dream man."

He shook his head.

"No."

"What?"

"No use."

"What do you mean?"

"Not a bit of good trying."

"But I tell you she said in so many words——"

"It doesn't make any difference. She may have loved me once. Last night will have killed all that."

"Of course it won't."

"It will. She despises me now."

"Not a bit of it. She knows you simply got cold feet."

"And I should get cold feet if I tried again. It's no good, Bertie. I'm hopeless, and there's an end of it. Fate made me the sort of chap who can't say 'bo' to a goose."

"It isn't a question of saying 'bo' to a goose. The point doesn't arise at all. It is simply a matter of——"

"I know, I know. But it's no good. I can't do it. The whole thing is off. I am not going to risk a repetition of last night's fiasco. You talk in a light way of taking another whack at her, but you don't know what it means. You have not been through the experience of starting to ask the girl you love to marry you and then suddenly finding yourself talking about the plumlike external gills of the newly-born newt. It's not a thing you can do twice. No, I accept my destiny. It's all over. And now, Bertie, like a good chap, shove off. I want to compose my speech. I can't compose my speech with you mucking around. If you are going to continue to muck around, at least give me a couple of stories. The little hell hounds are sure to expect a story or two."

"Do you know the one about——"

"No good. I don't want any of your off-colour stuff from the Drones' smoking-room. I need something clean. Something that will be a help to them in their after lives. Not that I care a damn about their after lives, except that I hope they'll all choke."

"I heard a story the other day. I can't quite remember it, but it was about a chap who snored and disturbed the neighbours, and it ended, 'It was his adenoids that adenoid them.'"

He made a weary gesture.

"You expect me to work that in, do you, into a speech to be delivered to an audience of boys, every one of whom is probably riddled with adenoids? Damn it, they'd rush the platform. Leave me, Bertie. Push off. That's all I ask you to do. Push off.... Ladies and gentlemen," said Gussie, in a low, soliloquizing sort of way, "I do not propose to detain this auspicious occasion long——"

It was a thoughtful Wooster who walked away and left him at it. More than ever I was congratulating myself on having had the sterling good sense to make all my arrangements so that I could press a button and set things moving at an instant's notice.

Until now, you see, I had rather entertained a sort of hope that when I had revealed to him the Bassett's mental attitude, Nature would have done the rest, bracing him up to such an extent that artificial stimulants would not be required. Because, naturally, a chap doesn't want to have to sprint about country houses lugging jugs of orange juice, unless it is absolutely essential.

But now I saw that I must carry on as planned. The total absence of pep, ginger, and the right spirit which the man had displayed during these conversational exchanges convinced me that the strongest measures would be necessary. Immediately upon leaving him, therefore, I proceeded to the pantry, waited till the butler had removed himself elsewhere, and nipped in and secured the vital jug. A few moments later, after a wary passage of the stairs, I was in my room. And the first thing I saw there was Jeeves, fooling about with trousers.

He gave the jug a look which—wrongly, as it was to turn out—I diagnosed as censorious. I drew myself up a bit. I intended to have no rot from the fellow.

"Yes, Jeeves?"

"Sir?"

"You have the air of one about to make a remark, Jeeves."

"Oh, no, sir. I note that you are in possession of Mr. Fink-Nottle's orange juice. I was merely about to observe that in my opinion it would be injudicious to add spirit to it."

"That is a remark, Jeeves, and it is precisely——"

"Because I have already attended to the matter, sir."

"What?"

"Yes, sir. I decided, after all, to acquiesce in your wishes."

I stared at the man, astounded. I was deeply moved. Well, I mean, wouldn't any chap who had been going about thinking that the old feudal spirit was dead and then suddenly found it wasn't have been deeply moved?

"Jeeves," I said, "I am touched."

"Thank you, sir."

"Touched and gratified."

"Thank you very much, sir."

"But what caused this change of heart?"

"I chanced to encounter Mr. Fink-Nottle in the garden, sir, while you were still in bed, and we had a brief conversation."

"And you came away feeling that he needed a bracer?"

"Very much so, sir. His attitude struck me as defeatist."

I nodded.

"I felt the same. 'Defeatist' sums it up to a nicety. Did you tell him his attitude struck you as defeatist?"

"Yes, sir."

"But it didn't do any good?"

"No, sir."

"Very well, then, Jeeves. We must act. How much gin did you put in the jug?"

"A liberal tumblerful, sir."

"Would that be a normal dose for an adult defeatist, do you think?"

"I fancy it should prove adequate, sir."

"I wonder. We must not spoil the ship for a ha'porth of tar. I think I'll add just another fluid ounce or so."

"I would not advocate it, sir. In the case of Lord Brancaster's parrot——"

"You are falling into your old error, Jeeves, of thinking that Gussie is a parrot. Fight against this. I shall add the oz."

"Very good, sir."

"And, by the way, Jeeves, Mr. Fink-Nottle is in the market for bright, clean stories to use in his speech. Do you know any?"

"I know a story about two Irishmen, sir."

"Pat and Mike?"

"Yes, sir."

"Who were walking along Broadway?"

"Yes, sir."

"Just what he wants. Any more?"

"No, sir."

"Well, every little helps. You had better go and tell it to him."

"Very good, sir."

He passed from the room, and I unscrewed the flask and tilted into the jug a generous modicum of its contents. And scarcely had I done so, when there came to my ears the sound of footsteps without. I had only just time to shove the jug behind the photograph of Uncle Tom on the mantelpiece before the door opened and in came Gussie, curveting like a circus horse.

"What-ho, Bertie," he said. "What-ho, what-ho, what-ho, and again what-ho. What a beautiful world this is, Bertie. One of the nicest I ever met."

I stared at him, speechless. We Woosters are as quick as lightning, and I saw at once that something had happened.

I mean to say, I told you about him walking round in circles. I recorded what passed between us on the lawn. And if I portrayed the scene with anything like adequate skill, the picture you will have retained of this Fink-Nottle will have been that of a nervous wreck, sagging at the knees, green about the gills, and picking feverishly at the lapels of his coat in an ecstasy of craven fear. In a word, defeatist. Gussie, during that interview, had, in fine, exhibited all the earmarks of one licked to a custard.

Vastly different was the Gussie who stood before me now. Self-confidence seemed to ooze from the fellow's every pore. His face was flushed, there was a jovial light in his eyes, the lips were parted in a swashbuckling smile. And when with a genial hand he sloshed me on the back before I could sidestep, it was as if I had been kicked by a mule.

"Well, Bertie," he proceeded, as blithely as a linnet without a thing on his mind, "you will be glad to hear that you were right. Your theory has been tested and proved correct. I feel like a fighting cock."

My brain ceased to reel. I saw all.

"Have you been having a drink?"

"I have. As you advised. Unpleasant stuff. Like medicine. Burns your throat, too, and makes one as thirsty as the dickens. How anyone can mop it up, as you do, for pleasure, beats me. Still, I would be the last to deny that it tunes up the system. I could bite a tiger."

"What did you have?"

"Whisky. At least, that was the label on the decanter, and I have no reason to suppose that a woman like your aunt—staunch, true-blue, British—would deliberately deceive the public. If she labels her decanters Whisky, then I consider that we know where we are."

"A whisky and soda, eh? You couldn't have done better."

"Soda?" said Gussie thoughtfully. "I knew there was something I had forgotten."

"Didn't you put any soda in it?"

"It never occurred to me. I just nipped into the dining-room and drank out of the decanter."

"How much?"

"Oh, about ten swallows. Twelve, maybe. Or fourteen. Say sixteen medium-sized gulps. Gosh, I'm thirsty."

He moved over to the wash-stand and drank deeply out of the water bottle. I cast a covert glance at Uncle Tom's photograph behind his back. For the first time since it had come into my life, I was glad that it was so large. It hid its secret well. If Gussie had caught sight of that jug of orange juice, he would unquestionably have been on to it like a knife.

"Well, I'm glad you're feeling braced," I said.

He moved buoyantly from the wash-hand stand, and endeavoured to slosh me on the back again. Foiled by my nimble footwork, he staggered to the bed and sat down upon it.

"Braced? Did I say I could bite a tiger?"

"You did."

"Make it two tigers. I could chew holes in a steel door. What an ass you must have thought me out there in the garden. I see now you were laughing in your sleeve."

"No, no."

"Yes," insisted Gussie. "That very sleeve," he said, pointing. "And I don't blame you. I can't imagine why I made all that fuss about a potty job like distributing prizes at a rotten little country grammar school. Can you imagine, Bertie?"

"Exactly. Nor can I imagine. There's simply nothing to it. I just shin up on the platform, drop a few gracious words, hand the little blighters their prizes, and hop down again, admired by all. Not a suggestion of split trousers from start to finish.

I mean, why should anybody split his trousers? I can't imagine. Can you imagine?"

"No."

"Nor can I imagine. I shall be a riot. I know just the sort of stuff that's needed—simple, manly, optimistic stuff straight from the shoulder. This shoulder," said Gussie, tapping. "Why I was so nervous this morning I can't imagine. For anything simpler than distributing a few footling books to a bunch of grimy-faced kids I can't imagine. Still, for some reason I can't imagine, I was feeling a little nervous, but now I feel fine, Bertie—fine, fine, fine—and I say this to you as an old friend. Because that's what you are, old man, when all the smoke has cleared away—an old friend. I don't think I've ever met an older friend. How long have you been an old friend of mine, Bertie?"

"Oh, years and years."

"Imagine! Though, of course, there must have been a time when you were a new friend.... Hullo, the luncheon gong. Come on, old friend."

And, rising from the bed like a performing flea, he made for the door.

I followed rather pensively. What had occurred was, of course, so much velvet, as you might say. I mean, I had wanted a braced Fink-Nottle— indeed, all my plans had had a braced Fink-Nottle as their end and aim —but I found myself wondering a little whether the Fink-Nottle now sliding down the banister wasn't, perhaps, a shade too braced. His demeanour seemed to me that of a man who might quite easily throw bread about at lunch.

Fortunately, however, the settled gloom of those round him exercised a restraining effect upon him at the table. It would have needed a far more plastered man to have been rollicking at such a gathering. I had told the Bassett that there were aching hearts in Brinkley Court, and it now looked probable that there would shortly be aching tummies. Anatole, I learned, had retired to his bed with a fit of the vapours, and the meal now before us had been cooked by the kitchen maid—as C3 a performer as ever wielded a skillet.

This, coming on top of their other troubles, induced in the company a pretty unanimous silence—a solemn stillness, as you might say—which even Gussie did not seem prepared to break. Except, therefore, for one short snatch of song on his part, nothing untoward marked the occasion, and presently we rose, with instructions from Aunt Dahlia to put on festal raiment and be at Market Snodsbury not later than 3.30. This leaving me ample time to smoke a gasper or two in a shady bower beside the lake, I did so, repairing to my room round about the hour of three.

Jeeves was on the job, adding the final polish to the old topper, and I was about to apprise him of the latest developments in the matter of Gussie, when he forestalled me by observing that the latter had only just concluded an agreeable visit to the Wooster bedchamber.

"I found Mr. Fink-Nottle seated here when I arrived to lay out your clothes, sir."

"Indeed, Jeeves? Gussie was in here, was he?"

"Yes, sir. He left only a few moments ago. He is driving to the school with Mr. and Mrs. Travers in the large car."

"Did you give him your story of the two Irishmen?"

"Yes, sir. He laughed heartily."

"Good. Had you any other contributions for him?"

"I ventured to suggest that he might mention to the young gentlemen that education is a drawing out, not a putting in. The late Lord Brancaster was much addicted to presenting prizes at schools, and he invariably employed this dictum."

"And how did he react to that?"

"He laughed heartily, sir."

"This surprised you, no doubt? This practically incessant merriment, I mean."

"Yes, sir."

"You thought it odd in one who, when you last saw him, was well up in Group A of the defeatists."

"Yes, sir."

"There is a ready explanation, Jeeves. Since you last saw him, Gussie has been on a bender. He's as tight as an owl."

"Indeed, sir?"

"Absolutely. His nerve cracked under the strain, and he sneaked into the dining-room and started mopping the stuff up like a vacuum cleaner. Whisky would seem to be what he filled the radiator with. I gather that he used up most of the decanter. Golly, Jeeves, it's lucky he didn't get at that laced orange juice on top of that, what?"

"Extremely, sir."

I eyed the jug. Uncle Tom's photograph had fallen into the fender, and it was standing there right out in the open, where Gussie couldn't have helped seeing it. Mercifully, it was empty now.

"It was a most prudent act on your part, if I may say so, sir, to dispose of the orange juice."

I stared at the man.

"What? Didn't you?"

"No, sir."

"Jeeves, let us get this clear. Was it not you who threw away that o.j.?"

"No, sir. I assumed, when I entered the room and found the pitcher empty, that you had done so."

We looked at each other, awed. Two minds with but a single thought.

"I very much fear, sir——"

"So do I, Jeeves."

"It would seem almost certain——"

"Quite certain. Weigh the facts. Sift the evidence. The jug was standing on the mantelpiece, for all eyes to behold. Gussie had been complaining of thirst. You found him in here, laughing heartily. I think that there can be little doubt, Jeeves, that the entire contents of that jug are at this moment reposing on top of the existing cargo in that already brilliantly lit man's interior. Disturbing, Jeeves."

"Most disturbing, sir."

"Let us face the position, forcing ourselves to be calm. You inserted in that jug—shall we say a tumblerful of the right stuff?"

"Fully a tumblerful, sir."

"And I added of my plenty about the same amount."

"Yes, sir."

"And in two shakes of a duck's tail Gussie, with all that lapping about inside him, will be distributing the prizes at Market Snodsbury Grammar School before an audience of all that is fairest and most refined in the county."

"Yes, sir."

"It seems to me, Jeeves, that the ceremony may be one fraught with considerable interest."

"Yes, sir."

"What, in your opinion, will the harvest be?"

"One finds it difficult to hazard a conjecture, sir."

"You mean imagination boggles?"

"Yes, sir."

I inspected my imagination. He was right. It boggled.

-17-

"And yet, Jeeves," I said, twiddling a thoughtful steering wheel, "there is always the bright side."

Some twenty minutes had elapsed, and having picked the honest fellow up outside the front door, I was driving in the two-seater to the picturesque town of Market Snodsbury. Since we had parted—he to go to his lair and fetch his hat, I to remain in my room and complete the formal costume—I had been doing some close thinking.

The results of this I now proceeded to hand on to him.

"However dark the prospect may be, Jeeves, however murkily the storm clouds may seem to gather, a keen eye can usually discern the blue bird. It is bad, no doubt, that Gussie should be going, some ten minutes from now, to distribute prizes in a state of advanced intoxication, but we must never forget that these things cut both ways."

"You imply, sir——"

"Precisely. I am thinking of him in his capacity of wooer. All this ought to have put him in rare shape for offering his hand in marriage. I shall be vastly surprised if it won't turn him into a sort of caveman. Have you ever seen James Cagney in the movies?"

"Yes, sir."

"Something on those lines."

I heard him cough, and sniped him with a sideways glance. He was wearing that informative look of his.

"Then you have not heard, sir?"

"Eh?"

"You are not aware that a marriage has been arranged and will shortly take place between Mr. Fink-Nottle and Miss Bassett?"

"What?"

"Yes, sir."

"When did this happen?"

"Shortly after Mr. Fink-Nottle had left your room, sir."

"Ah! In the post-orange-juice era?"

"Yes, sir."

"But are you sure of your facts? How do you know?"

"My informant was Mr. Fink-Nottle himself, sir. He appeared anxious to confide in me. His story was somewhat incoherent, but I had no difficulty in apprehending its substance. Prefacing his remarks with the statement that this was a beautiful world, he laughed heartily and said that he had become formally engaged."

"No details?"

"No, sir."

"But one can picture the scene."

"Yes, sir."

"I mean, imagination doesn't boggle."

"No, sir."

And it didn't. I could see exactly what must have happened. Insert a liberal dose of mixed spirits in a normally abstemious man, and he becomes a force. He does not stand around, twiddling his fingers and stammering. He acts. I had no doubt that Gussie must have reached for the Bassett and clasped her to him like a stevedore handling a sack of coals. And one could readily envisage the effect of that sort of thing on a girl of romantic mind.

"Well, well, well, Jeeves."

"Yes, sir."

"This is splendid news."

"Yes, sir."

"You see now how right I was."

"Yes, sir."

"It must have been rather an eye-opener for you, watching me handle this case."

"Yes, sir."

"The simple, direct method never fails."

"No, sir."

"Whereas the elaborate does."

"Yes, sir."

"Right ho, Jeeves."

We had arrived at the main entrance of Market Snodsbury Grammar School. I parked the car, and went in, well content. True, the Tuppy-Angela problem still remained unsolved and Aunt Dahlia's five hundred quid seemed as far off as ever, but it was gratifying to feel that good old Gussie's troubles were over, at any rate.

The Grammar School at Market Snodsbury had, I understood, been built somewhere in the year 1416, and, as with so many of these ancient foundations, there still seemed to brood over its Great Hall, where the afternoon's festivities were to take place, not a little of the fug of the centuries. It was the hottest day of the summer, and though somebody had opened a tentative window or two, the atmosphere remained distinctive and individual.

In this hall the youth of Market Snodsbury had been eating its daily lunch for a matter of five hundred years, and the flavour lingered. The air was sort of heavy and languorous, if you know what I mean, with the scent of Young England and boiled beef and carrots.

Aunt Dahlia, who was sitting with a bevy of the local nibs in the second row, sighted me as I entered and waved to me to join her, but I was too smart for that. I wedged myself in among the standees at the back, leaning up against a chap who, from the aroma, might have been a corn chandler or something on that order. The essence of strategy on these occasions is to be as near the door as possible.

The hall was gaily decorated with flags and coloured paper, and the eye was further refreshed by the spectacle of a mixed drove of boys, parents, and what not, the former running a good deal to shiny faces and Eton collars, the latter stressing the black-satin note rather when female, and looking as if their coats were too tight, if male. And presently there was some applause—sporadic, Jeeves has since told me it was—and I saw Gussie being steered by a bearded bloke in a gown to a seat in the middle of the platform.

And I confess that as I beheld him and felt that there but for the grace of God went Bertram Wooster, a shudder ran through the frame. It all reminded me so vividly of the time I had addressed that girls' school.

Of course, looking at it dispassionately, you may say that for horror and peril there is no comparison between an almost human audience like the one before me and a mob of small girls with pigtails down their backs, and this, I concede, is true. Nevertheless, the spectacle was enough to make me feel like a fellow watching a pal going over Niagara Falls in a barrel, and the thought of what I had escaped caused everything for a moment to go black and swim before my eyes.

When I was able to see clearly once more, I perceived that Gussie was now seated. He had his hands on his knees, with his elbows out at right angles, like a nigger minstrel of the old school about to ask Mr. Bones why a chicken crosses the road, and he was staring before him with a smile so fixed and pebble-beached that I should have thought that anybody could have guessed that there sat one in whom the old familiar juice was plashing up against the back of the front teeth.

In fact, I saw Aunt Dahlia, who, having assisted at so many hunting dinners in her time, is second to none as a judge of the symptoms, give a start and gaze long and earnestly. And she was just saying something to Uncle Tom on her left when the bearded bloke stepped to the footlights and started making a speech. From the fact that he spoke as if he had a hot potato in his mouth without getting the raspberry from the lads in the ringside seats, I deduced that he must be the head master.

With his arrival in the spotlight, a sort of perspiring resignation seemed to settle on the audience. Personally, I snuggled up against the chandler and let my attention wander. The speech was on the subject of the doings of the school during the past term, and this part of a prize-giving is always apt rather to fail to grip the visiting stranger. I mean, you know how it is. You're told that J.B. Brewster has won an Exhibition for Classics at Cat's, Cambridge, and you feel that it's one of those stories where you can't see how funny it is unless you really know the fellow. And the same applies to G. Bullett being awarded the Lady Jane Wix Scholarship at the Birmingham College of Veterinary Science.

In fact, I and the corn chandler, who was looking a bit fagged I thought, as if he had had a hard morning chandling the corn, were beginning to doze lightly when things suddenly brisked up, bringing Gussie into the picture for the first time.

"Today," said the bearded bloke, "we are all happy to welcome as the guest of the afternoon Mr. Fitz-Wattle——"

At the beginning of the address, Gussie had subsided into a sort of daydream, with his mouth hanging open. About half-way through, faint signs of life had begun to show. And for the last few minutes he had been trying to cross one leg over the other and failing and having another shot and failing again. But only now did he exhibit any real animation. He sat up with a jerk.

"Fink-Nottle," he said, opening his eyes.

"Fitz-Nottle."

"Fink-Nottle."

"I should say Fink-Nottle."

"Of course you should, you silly ass," said Gussie genially. "All right, get on with it."

And closing his eyes, he began trying to cross his legs again.

I could see that this little spot of friction had rattled the bearded bloke a bit. He stood for a moment fumbling at the fungus with a hesitating hand. But they make these head masters of tough stuff. The weakness passed. He came back nicely and carried on.

"We are all happy, I say, to welcome as the guest of the afternoon Mr. Fink-Nottle, who has kindly consented to award the prizes. This task, as you know, is one that should have devolved upon that well-beloved and vigorous member of our board of governors, the Rev. William Plomer, and we are all, I am sure, very sorry that illness at the last moment should have prevented him from being here today. But, if I may borrow a familiar metaphor from the—if I may employ a homely metaphor familiar to you all—what we lose on the swings we gain on the roundabouts."

He paused, and beamed rather freely, to show that this was comedy. I could have told the man it was no use. Not a ripple. The corn chandler leaned against me and muttered "Whoddidesay?" but that was all.

It's always a nasty jar to wait for the laugh and find that the gag hasn't got across. The bearded bloke was visibly discomposed. At that, however, I think he would have got by, had he not, at this juncture, unfortunately stirred Gussie up again.

"In other words, though deprived of Mr. Plomer, we have with us this afternoon Mr. Fink-Nottle. I am sure that Mr. Fink-Nottle's name is one that needs no introduction to you. It is, I venture to assert, a name that is familiar to us all."

"Not to you," said Gussie.

And the next moment I saw what Jeeves had meant when he had described him as laughing heartily. "Heartily" was absolutely the *mot juste.* It sounded like a gas explosion.

"You didn't seem to know it so dashed well, what, what?" said Gussie. And, reminded apparently by the word "what" of the word "Wattle," he repeated the latter some sixteen times with a rising inflection.

"Wattle, Wattle, Wattle," he concluded. "Right-ho. Push on."

But the bearded bloke had shot his bolt. He stood there, licked at last; and, watching him closely, I could see that he was now at the crossroads. I could spot what he was thinking as clearly as if he had confided it to my personal ear. He wanted to sit down and call it a day, I mean, but the thought that gave him pause was that, if he did, he must then either uncork Gussie or take the Fink-Nottle speech as read and get straight on to the actual prize-giving.

It was a dashed tricky thing, of course, to have to decide on the spur of the moment. I was reading in the paper the other day about those birds who are trying to split the atom, the nub being that they haven't the foggiest as to what will happen if they do. It may be all right. On the other hand, it may not be all right. And pretty silly a chap would feel, no doubt, if, having split the atom, he suddenly found the house going up in smoke and himself torn limb from limb.

So with the bearded bloke. Whether he was abreast of the inside facts in Gussie's case, I don't know, but it was obvious to him by this time that he had run into something pretty hot. Trial gallops had shown that Gussie had his own way of doing things. Those interruptions had been enough to prove to the perspicacious that here, seated on the platform at the big binge of the season, was one who, if pushed forward to make a speech, might let himself go in a rather epoch-making manner.

On the other hand, chain him up and put a green-baize cloth over him, and where were you? The proceeding would be over about half an hour too soon.

It was, as I say, a difficult problem to have to solve, and, left to himself, I don't know what conclusion he would have come to. Personally, I think he would have played it safe. As it happened, however, the thing was taken out of his hands, for at this moment, Gussie, having stretched his arms and yawned a bit, switched on that pebble-beached smile again and tacked down to the edge of the platform.

"Speech," he said affably.

He then stood with his thumbs in the armholes of his waistcoat, waiting for the applause to die down.

It was some time before this happened, for he had got a very fine hand indeed. I suppose it wasn't often that the boys of Market Snodsbury Grammar School came across a man public-spirited enough to call their head master a silly ass, and they showed their appreciation in no uncertain manner. Gussie may have been one over the eight, but as far as the majority of those present were concerned he was sitting on top of the world.

"Boys," said Gussie, "I mean ladies and gentlemen and boys, I do not detain you long, but I suppose on this occasion to feel compelled to say a few auspicious words; Ladies—and boys and gentlemen—we have all listened with interest to the remarks of our friend here who forgot to shave this morning—I don't know his name, but then he didn't know mine—Fitz-Wattle, I mean, absolutely absurd—which squares things up a bit—and we are all sorry that the Reverend What-ever-he-was-called should be dying of adenoids, but after all, here today, gone tomorrow, and all flesh is as grass, and what not, but that wasn't what I wanted to say. What I wanted to say was this—and I say it confidently—without fear of contradiction—I say, in short, I am happy to be here on this auspicious occasion and I take much pleasure in kindly awarding the prizes, consisting of the handsome books you see laid out on that table. As Shakespeare says, there are sermons in books, stones in the running brooks, or, rather, the other way about, and there you have it in a nutshell."

It went well, and I wasn't surprised. I couldn't quite follow some of it, but anybody could see that it was real ripe stuff, and I was amazed that even the course of treatment he had been taking could have rendered so normally tongue-tied a dumb brick as Gussie capable of it.

It just shows, what any member of Parliament will tell you, that if you want real oratory, the preliminary noggin is essential. Unless pie-eyed, you cannot hope to grip.

"Gentlemen," said Gussie, "I mean ladies and gentlemen and, of course, boys, what a beautiful world this is. A beautiful world, full of happiness on every side. Let me tell you a little story. Two Irishmen, Pat and Mike, were walking along Broadway, and one said to the other, 'Begorrah, the race is not always to the swift,' and the other replied, 'Faith and begob, education is a drawing out, not a putting in.'"

I must say it seemed to me the rottenest story I had ever heard, and I was surprised that Jeeves should have considered it worth while shoving into a speech. However, when I taxed him with this later, he said that Gussie had altered the plot a good deal, and I dare say that accounts for it.

At any rate, that was the *conte* as Gussie told it, and when I say that it got a very fair laugh, you will understand what a popular favourite he had become with the multitude. There might be a bearded bloke or so on the platform and a small section in the second row who were wishing the speaker would conclude his remarks and resume his seat, but the audience as a whole was for him solidly.

There was applause, and a voice cried: "Hear, hear!"

"Yes," said Gussie, "it is a beautiful world. The sky is blue, the birds are singing, there is optimism everywhere. And why not, boys and ladies and gentlemen? I'm happy, you're happy, we're all happy, even the meanest Irishman that walks along Broadway. Though, as I say, there were two of them—Pat and Mike, one drawing out, the other putting in. I should like you boys, taking the time from me, to give three cheers for this beautiful world. All together now."

Presently the dust settled down and the plaster stopped falling from the ceiling, and he went on.

"People who say it isn't a beautiful world don't know what they are talking about. Driving here in the car today to award the kind prizes, I was reluctantly compelled to tick off my host on this very point. Old Tom Travers. You will see him sitting there in the second row next to the large lady in beige."

He pointed helpfully, and the hundred or so Market Snods-buryians who craned their necks in the direction indicated were able to observe Uncle Tom blushing prettily.

"I ticked him off properly, the poor fish. He expressed the opinion that the world was in a deplorable state. I said, 'Don't talk rot, old Tom Travers.' 'I am not accustomed to talk rot,' he said. 'Then, for a beginner,' I said, 'you do it dashed well.' And I think you will admit, boys and ladies and gentlemen, that that was telling him."

The audience seemed to agree with him. The point went big. The voice that had said, "Hear, hear" said "Hear, hear" again, and my corn chandler hammered the floor vigorously with a large-size walking stick.

"Well, boys," resumed Gussie, having shot his cuffs and smirked horribly, "this is the end of the summer term, and many of you, no doubt, are leaving the school. And I don't blame you, because there's a froust in here you could cut with a knife. You are going out into the great world. Soon many of you will be walking along Broadway. And what I want to impress upon you is that, however much you may suffer from adenoids, you must all use every effort to prevent yourselves becoming pessimists and talking rot like old Tom Travers. There in the second row. The fellow with a face rather like a walnut."

He paused to allow those wishing to do so to refresh themselves with another look at Uncle Tom, and I found myself musing in some little perplexity. Long association with the members of the Drones has put me pretty well in touch with the various ways in which an overdose of the blushful Hippocrene can take the individual, but I had never seen anyone react quite as Gussie was doing.

There was a snap about his work which I had never witnessed before, even in Barmy Fotheringay-Phipps on New Year's Eve.

Jeeves, when I discussed the matter with him later, said it was something to do with inhibitions, if I caught the word correctly, and the suppression of, I think he said, the ego. What he meant, I gathered, was that, owing to the fact that Gussie had just completed a five years' stretch of blameless seclusion among the newts, all the goofiness which ought to have been spread out thin over those five years and had been bottled up during that period came to the surface on this occasion in a lump—or, if you prefer to put it that way, like a tidal wave.

There may be something in this. Jeeves generally knows.

Anyway, be that as it may, I was dashed glad I had had the shrewdness to keep out of that second row. It might be unworthy of the prestige of a Wooster to squash in among the proletariat in the standing-room-only section, but at least, I felt, I was out of the danger zone. So thoroughly had Gussie got it up his nose by now that it seemed to me that had he sighted me he might have become personal about even an old school friend.

"If there's one thing in the world I can't stand," proceeded Gussie, "it's a pessimist. Be optimists, boys. You all know the difference between an optimist and a pessimist. An optimist is a man who—well, take the case of two Irishmen walking along Broadway. One is an optimist and one is a pessimist, just as one's name is Pat and the other's Mike.... Why, hullo, Bertie; I didn't know you were here."

Too late, I endeavoured to go to earth behind the chandler, only to discover that there was no chandler there. Some appointment, suddenly remembered—possibly a promise to his wife that he would be home to tea—had caused him to ooze away while my attention was elsewhere, leaving me right out in the open.

Between me and Gussie, who was now pointing in an offensive manner, there was nothing but a sea of interested faces looking up at me.

"Now, there," boomed Gussie, continuing to point, "is an instance of what I mean. Boys and ladies and gentlemen, take a good look at that object standing up there at the back—morning coat, trousers as worn, quiet grey tie, and carnation in buttonhole—you can't miss him. Bertie Wooster, that is, and as foul a pessimist as ever bit a tiger. I tell you I despise that man. And why do I despise him? Because, boys and ladies and gentlemen, he is a pessimist. His attitude is defeatist. When I told him I was going to address you this afternoon, he tried to dissuade me. And do you know why he tried to dissuade me? Because he said my trousers would split up the back."

The cheers that greeted this were the loudest yet. Anything about splitting trousers went straight to the simple hearts of the young scholars of Market Snodsbury Grammar School. Two in the row in front of me turned purple, and a small lad with freckles seated beside them asked me for my autograph.

"Let me tell you a story about Bertie Wooster."

A Wooster can stand a good deal, but he cannot stand having his name bandied in a public place. Picking my feet up softly, I was in the very process of executing a quiet sneak for the door, when I perceived that the bearded bloke had at last decided to apply the closure.

Why he hadn't done so before is beyond me. Spell-bound, I take it. And, of course, when a chap is going like a breeze with the public, as Gussie had been, it's not so dashed easy to chip in. However, the prospect of hearing another of Gussie's anecdotes seemed to have done the trick. Rising rather as I had risen from my bench at the beginning of that painful scene with Tuppy in the twilight, he made a leap for the table, snatched up a book and came bearing down on the speaker.

He touched Gussie on the arm, and Gussie, turning sharply and seeing a large bloke with a beard apparently about to bean him with a book, sprang back in an attitude of self-defence.

"Perhaps, as time is getting on, Mr. Fink-Nottle, we had better——"

"Oh, ah," said Gussie, getting the trend. He relaxed. "The prizes, eh? Of course, yes. Right-ho. Yes, might as well be shoving along with it. What's this one?"

"Spelling and dictation—P.K. Purvis," announced the bearded bloke.

"Spelling and dictation—P.K. Purvis," echoed Gussie, as if he were calling coals. "Forward, P.K. Purvis."

Now that the whistle had been blown on his speech, it seemed to me that there was no longer any need for the strategic retreat which I had been planning. I had no wish to tear myself away unless I had to. I mean, I had told Jeeves that this binge would be fraught with interest, and it was fraught with interest. There was a fascination about Gussie's methods which gripped and made one reluctant to pass the thing up provided personal innuendoes were steered clear of. I decided, accordingly, to remain, and presently there was a musical squeaking and P.K. Purvis climbed the platform.

The spelling-and-dictation champ was about three foot six in his squeaking shoes, with a pink face and sandy hair. Gussie patted his hair. He seemed to have taken an immediate fancy to the lad.

"You P.K. Purvis?"

"Sir, yes, sir."

"It's a beautiful world, P.K. Purvis."

"Sir, yes, sir."

"Ah, you've noticed it, have you? Good. You married, by any chance?"

"Sir, no, sir."

"Get married, P.K. Purvis," said Gussie earnestly. "It's the only life ... Well, here's your book. Looks rather bilge to me from a glance at the title page, but, such as it is, here you are."

P.K. Purvis squeaked off amidst sporadic applause, but one could not fail to note that the sporadic was followed by a rather strained silence. It was evident that Gussie was striking something of a new note in Market Snodsbury scholastic circles. Looks were exchanged between parent and parent. The bearded bloke had the air of one who has drained the bitter cup. As for Aunt Dahlia, her demeanour now told only too clearly that her last doubts had been resolved and her verdict was in. I saw her whisper to the Bassett, who sat on her right, and the Bassett nodded sadly and looked like a fairy about to shed a tear and add another star to the Milky Way.

Gussie, after the departure of P.K. Purvis, had fallen into a sort of daydream and was standing with his mouth open and his hands in his pockets. Becoming abruptly aware that a fat kid in knickerbockers was at his elbow, he started violently.

"Hullo!" he said, visibly shaken. "Who are you?"

"This," said the bearded bloke, "is R.V. Smethurst."

"What's he doing here?" asked Gussie suspiciously.

"You are presenting him with the drawing prize, Mr. Fink-Nottle."

This apparently struck Gussie as a reasonable explanation. His face cleared.

"That's right, too," he said.... "Well, here it is, cocky. You off?" he said, as the kid prepared to withdraw.

"Sir, yes, sir."

"Wait, R.V. Smethurst. Not so fast. Before you go, there is a question I wish to ask you."

But the beard bloke's aim now seemed to be to rush the ceremonies a bit. He hustled R.V. Smethurst off stage rather like a chucker-out in a pub regretfully ejecting an old and respected customer, and starting paging G.G. Simmons. A moment later the latter was up and coming, and conceive my emotion when it was announced that the subject on which he had clicked was Scripture knowledge. One of us, I mean to say.

G.G. Simmons was an unpleasant, perky-looking stripling, mostly front teeth and spectacles, but I gave him a big hand. We Scripture-knowledge sharks stick together.

Gussie, I was sorry to see, didn't like him. There was in his manner, as he regarded G.G. Simmons, none of the chumminess which had marked it during his interview with P.K. Purvis or, in a somewhat lesser degree, with R.V. Smethurst. He was cold and distant.

"Well, G.G. Simmons."

"Sir, yes, sir."

"What do you mean—sir, yes, sir? Dashed silly thing to say. So you've won the Scripture-knowledge prize, have you?"

"Sir, yes, sir."

"Yes," said Gussie, "you look just the sort of little tick who would. And yet," he said, pausing and eyeing the child keenly, "how are we to know that this has all been open and above board? Let me test you, G.G. Simmons. What was What's-His-Name—the chap who begat Thingummy? Can you answer me that, Simmons?"

"Sir, no, sir."

Gussie turned to the bearded bloke.

"Fishy," he said. "Very fishy. This boy appears to be totally lacking in Scripture knowledge."

The bearded bloke passed a hand across his forehead.

"I can assure you, Mr. Fink-Nottle, that every care was taken to ensure a correct marking and that Simmons outdistanced his competitors by a wide margin."

"Well, if you say so," said Gussie doubtfully. "All right, G.G. Simmons, take your prize."

"Sir, thank you, sir."

"But let me tell you that there's nothing to stick on side about in winning a prize for Scripture knowledge. Bertie Wooster——"

I don't know when I've had a nastier shock. I had been going on the assumption that, now that they had stopped him making his speech, Gussie's fangs had been drawn, as you might say. To duck my head down and resume my edging toward the door was with me the work of a moment.

"Bertie Wooster won the Scripture-knowledge prize at a kids' school we were at together, and you know what he's like. But, of course, Bertie frankly cheated. He succeeded in scrounging that Scripture-knowledge trophy over the heads of better men by means of some of the rawest and most brazen swindling methods ever witnessed even at a school where such things were common. If that man's pockets, as he entered the examination-room, were not stuffed to bursting-point with lists of the kings of Judah——"

I heard no more. A moment later I was out in God's air, fumbling with a fevered foot at the self-starter of the old car.

The engine raced. The clutch slid into position. I tooted and drove off.

My ganglions were still vibrating as I ran the car into the stables of Brinkley Court, and it was a much shaken Bertram who tottered up to his room to change into something loose. Having donned flannels, I lay down on the bed for a bit, and I suppose I must have dozed off, for the next thing I remember is finding Jeeves at my side.

I sat up. "My tea, Jeeves?"

"No, sir. It is nearly dinner-time."

The mists cleared away.

"I must have been asleep."

"Yes, sir."

"Nature taking its toll of the exhausted frame."

"Yes, sir."

"And enough to make it."

"Yes, sir."

"And now it's nearly dinner-time, you say? All right. I am in no mood for dinner, but I suppose you had better lay out the clothes."

"It will not be necessary, sir. The company will not be dressing tonight. A cold collation has been set out in the dining-room."

"Why's that?"

"It was Mrs. Travers's wish that this should be done in order to minimize the work for the staff, who are attending a dance at Sir Percival Stretchley-Budd's residence tonight."

"Of course, yes. I remember. My Cousin Angela told me. Tonight's the night, what? You going, Jeeves?"

"No, sir. I am not very fond of this form of entertainment in the rural districts, sir."

"I know what you mean. These country binges are all the same. A piano, one fiddle, and a floor like sandpaper. Is Anatole going? Angela hinted not."

"Miss Angela was correct, sir. Monsieur Anatole is in bed."

"Temperamental blighters, these Frenchmen."

"Yes, sir."

There was a pause.

"Well, Jeeves," I said, "it was certainly one of those afternoons, what?"

"Yes, sir."

"I cannot recall one more packed with incident. And I left before the finish."

"Yes, sir. I observed your departure."

"You couldn't blame me for withdrawing."

"No, sir. Mr. Fink-Nottle had undoubtedly become embarrassingly personal."

"Was there much more of it after I went?"

"No, sir. The proceedings terminated very shortly. Mr. Fink-Nottle's remarks with reference to Master G.G. Simmons brought about an early closure."

"But he had finished his remarks about G.G. Simmons."

"Only temporarily, sir. He resumed them immediately after your departure. If you recollect, sir, he had already proclaimed himself suspicious of Master Simmons's bona fides, and he now proceeded to deliver a violent verbal attack upon the young gentleman, asserting that it was impossible for him to have won the Scripture-knowledge prize without systematic cheating on an impressive scale. He went so far as to suggest that Master Simmons was well known to the police."

"Golly, Jeeves!"

"Yes, sir. The words did create a considerable sensation. The reaction of those present to this accusation I should describe as mixed. The young students appeared pleased and applauded vigorously, but Master Simmons's mother rose from her seat and addressed Mr. Fink-Nottle in terms of strong protest."

"Did Gussie seem taken aback? Did he recede from his position?"

"No, sir. He said that he could see it all now, and hinted at a guilty liaison between Master Simmons's mother and the head master, accusing the latter of having cooked the marks, as his expression was, in order to gain favour with the former."

"You don't mean that?"

"Yes, sir."

"Egad, Jeeves! And then——"

"They sang the national anthem, sir."

"Surely not?"

"Yes, sir."

"At a moment like that?"

"Yes, sir."

"Well, you were there and you know, of course, but I should have thought the last thing Gussie and this woman would have done in the circs. would have been to start singing duets."

"You misunderstand me, sir. It was the entire company who sang. The head master turned to the organist and said something to him in a low tone. Upon which the latter began to play the national anthem, and the proceedings terminated."

"I see. About time, too."

"Yes, sir. Mrs. Simmons's attitude had become unquestionably menacing."

I pondered. What I had heard was, of course, of a nature to excite pity and terror, not to mention alarm and despondency, and it would be paltering with the truth to say that I was pleased about it. On the other hand, it was all over now, and it seemed to me that the thing to do was not to mourn over the past but to fix the mind on the bright future. I mean to say, Gussie might have lowered the existing Worcestershire record for goofiness and definitely forfeited all chance of becoming Market Snodsbury's favourite son, but you couldn't get away from the fact that he had proposed to Madeline Bassett, and you had to admit that she had accepted him.

I put this to Jeeves.

"A frightful exhibition," I said, "and one which will very possibly ring down history's pages. But we must not forget, Jeeves, that Gussie, though now doubtless looked upon in the neighbourhood as the world's worst freak, is all right otherwise."

"No, sir."

I did not get quite this.

"When you say 'No, sir,' do you mean 'Yes, sir'?"

"No, sir. I mean 'No, sir.'"

"He is not all right otherwise?"

"No, sir."

"But he's betrothed."

"No longer, sir. Miss Bassett has severed the engagement."

"You don't mean that?"

"Yes, sir."

I wonder if you have noticed a rather peculiar thing about this chronicle. I allude to the fact that at one time or another practically everybody playing a part in it has had occasion to bury his or her face in his or her hands. I have participated in some pretty glutinous affairs in my time, but I think that never before or since have I been mixed up with such a solid body of brow clutchers.

Uncle Tom did it, if you remember. So did Gussie. So did Tuppy. So, probably, though I have no data, did Anatole, and I wouldn't put it past the Bassett. And Aunt Dahlia, I have no doubt, would have done it, too, but for the risk of disarranging the carefully fixed coiffure.

Well, what I am trying to say is that at this juncture I did it myself. Up went the hands and down went the head, and in another jiffy I was clutching as energetically as the best of them.

And it was while I was still massaging the coconut and wondering what the next move was that something barged up against the door like the delivery of a ton of coals.

"I think this may very possibly be Mr. Fink-Nottle himself, sir," said Jeeves.

His intuition, however, had led him astray. It was not Gussie but Tuppy. He came in and stood breathing asthmatically. It was plain that he was deeply stirred.

-18-

I eyed him narrowly. I didn't like his looks. Mark you, I don't say I ever had, much, because Nature, when planning this sterling fellow, shoved in a lot more lower jaw than was absolutely necessary and made the eyes a bit too keen and piercing for one who was neither an Empire builder nor a traffic policeman. But on the present occasion, in addition to offending the aesthetic sense, this Glossop seemed to me to be wearing a distinct air of menace, and I found myself wishing that Jeeves wasn't always so dashed tactful. I mean, it's all very well to remove yourself like an eel sliding into mud when the employer has a visitor, but there are moments—and it looked to me as if this was going to be one of them—when the truer tact is to stick round and stand ready to lend a hand in the free-for-all.

For Jeeves was no longer with us. I hadn't seen him go, and I hadn't heard him go, but he had gone. As far as the eye could reach, one noted nobody but Tuppy. And in Tuppy's demeanour, as I say, there was a certain something that tended to disquiet. He looked to me very much like a man who had come to reopen that matter of my tickling Angela's ankles.

However, his opening remark told me that I had been alarming myself unduly. It was of a pacific nature, and came as a great relief.

"Bertie," he said, "I owe you an apology. I have come to make it."

My relief on hearing these words, containing as they did no reference of any sort to tickled ankles, was, as I say, great. But I don't think it was any greater than my surprise. Months had passed since that painful episode at the Drones, and until now he hadn't given a sign of remorse and contrition. Indeed, word had reached me through private sources that he frequently told the story at dinners and other gatherings and, when doing so, laughed his silly head off.

I found it hard to understand, accordingly, what could have caused him to abase himself at this later date. Presumably he had been given the elbow by his better self, but why?

Still, there it was.

"My dear chap," I said, gentlemanly to the gills, "don't mention it."

"What's the sense of saying, 'Don't mention it'? I have mentioned it."

"I mean, don't mention it any more. Don't give the matter another thought. We all of us forget ourselves sometimes and do things which, in our calmer moments, we regret. No doubt you were a bit tight at the time."

"What the devil do you think you're talking about?"

I didn't like his tone. Brusque.

"Correct me if I am wrong," I said, with a certain stiffness, "but I assumed that you were apologizing for your foul conduct in looping back the last ring that night in the Drones, causing me to plunge into the swimming b. in the full soup and fish."

"Ass! Not that, at all."

"Then what?"

"This Bassett business."

"What Bassett business?"

"Bertie," said Tuppy, "when you told me last night that you were in love with Madeline Bassett, I gave you the impression that I believed you, but I didn't. The thing seemed too incredible. However, since then I have made inquiries, and the facts appear to square with your statement. I have now come to apologize for doubting you."

"Made inquiries?"

"I asked her if you had proposed to her, and she said, yes, you had."

"Tuppy! You didn't?"

"I did."

"Have you no delicacy, no proper feeling?"

"No."

"Oh? Well, right-ho, of course, but I think you ought to have."

"Delicacy be dashed. I wanted to be certain that it was not you who stole Angela from me. I now know it wasn't."

So long as he knew that, I didn't so much mind him having no delicacy.

"Ah," I said. "Well, that's fine. Hold that thought."

"I have found out who it was."

"What?"

He stood brooding for a moment. His eyes were smouldering with a dull fire. His jaw stuck out like the back of Jeeves's head.

"Bertie," he said, "do you remember what I swore I would do to the chap who stole Angela from me?"

"As nearly as I recall, you planned to pull him inside out——"

"—and make him swallow himself. Correct. The programme still holds good."

"But, Tuppy, I keep assuring you, as a competent eyewitness, that nobody snitched Angela from you during that Cannes trip."

"No. But they did after she got back."

"What?"

"Don't keep saying, 'What?' You heard."

"But she hasn't seen anybody since she got back."

"Oh, no? How about that newt bloke?"

"Gussie?"

"Precisely. The serpent Fink-Nottle."

This seemed to me absolute gibbering.

"But Gussie loves the Bassett."

"You can't all love this blighted Bassett. What astonishes me is that anyone can do it. He loves Angela, I tell you. And she loves him."

"But Angela handed you your hat before Gussie ever got here."

"No, she didn't. Couple of hours after."

"He couldn't have fallen in love with her in a couple of hours."

"Why not? I fell in love with her in a couple of minutes. I worshipped her immediately we met, the popeyed little excrescence."

"But, dash it——"

"Don't argue, Bertie. The facts are all docketed. She loves this newt-nuzzling blister."

"Quite absurd, laddie—quite absurd."

"Oh?" He ground a heel into the carpet—a thing I've often read about, but had never seen done before. "Then perhaps you will explain how it is that she happens to come to be engaged to him?"

You could have knocked me down with a f.

"Engaged to him?"

"She told me herself."

"She was kidding you."

"She was not kidding me. Shortly after the conclusion of this afternoon's binge at Market Snodsbury Grammar School he asked her to marry him, and she appears to have right-hoed without a murmur."

"There must be some mistake."

"There was. The snake Fink-Nottle made it, and by now I bet he realizes it. I've been chasing him since 5.30."

"Chasing him?"

"All over the place. I want to pull his head off."

"I see. Quite."

"You haven't seen him, by any chance?"

"No."

"Well, if you do, say goodbye to him quickly and put in your order for lilies.... Oh, Jeeves."

"Sir?"

I hadn't heard the door open, but the man was on the spot once more. My private belief, as I think I have mentioned before, is that Jeeves doesn't have to open doors. He's like one of those birds in India who bung their astral bodies about—the chaps, I mean, who having gone into thin air in Bombay, reassemble the parts and appear two minutes later in Calcutta. Only some such theory will account for the fact that he's not there one moment and is there the next. He just seems to float from Spot A to Spot B like some form of gas.

"Have you seen Mr. Fink-Nottle, Jeeves?"

"No, sir."

"I'm going to murder him."

"Very good, sir."

Tuppy withdrew, banging the door behind him, and I put Jeeves abreast.

"Jeeves," I said, "do you know what? Mr. Fink-Nottle is engaged to my Cousin Angela."

"Indeed, sir?"

"Well, how about it? Do you grasp the psychology? Does it make sense? Only a few hours ago he was engaged to Miss Bassett."

"Gentlemen who have been discarded by one young lady are often apt to attach themselves without delay to another, sir. It is what is known as a gesture."

I began to grasp.

"I see what you mean. Defiant stuff."

"Yes, sir."

"A sort of 'Oh, right-ho, please yourself, but if you don't want me, there are plenty who do.'"

"Precisely, sir. My Cousin George——"

"Never mind about your Cousin George, Jeeves."

"Very good, sir."

"Keep him for the long winter evenings, what?"

"Just as you wish, sir."

"And, anyway, I bet your Cousin George wasn't a shrinking, non-goose-bo-ing jellyfish like Gussie. That is what astounds me, Jeeves—that it should be Gussie who has been putting in all this heavy gesture-making stuff."

"You must remember, sir, that Mr. Fink-Nottle is in a somewhat inflamed cerebral condition."

"That's true. A bit above par at the moment, as it were?"

"Exactly, sir."

"Well, I'll tell you one thing—he'll be in a jolly sight more inflamed cerebral condition if Tuppy gets hold of him.... What's the time?"

"Just on eight o'clock, sir."

"Then Tuppy has been chasing him for two hours and a half. We must save the unfortunate blighter, Jeeves."

"Yes, sir."

"A human life is a human life, what?"

"Exceedingly true, sir."

"The first thing, then, is to find him. After that we can discuss plans and schemes. Go forth, Jeeves, and scour the neighbourhood."

"It will not be necessary, sir. If you will glance behind you, you will see Mr. Fink-Nottle coming out from beneath your bed."

And, by Jove, he was absolutely right.

There was Gussie, emerging as stated. He was covered with fluff and looked like a tortoise popping forth for a bit of a breather.

"Gussie!" I said.

"Jeeves," said Gussie.

"Sir?" said Jeeves.

"Is that door locked, Jeeves?"

"No, sir, but I will attend to the matter immediately."

Gussie sat down on the bed, and I thought for a moment that he was going to be in the mode by burying his face in his hands. However, he merely brushed a dead spider from his brow.

"Have you locked the door, Jeeves?"

"Yes, sir."

"Because you can never tell that that ghastly Glossop may not take it into his head to come——"

The word "back" froze on his lips. He hadn't got any further than a *b*-ish sound, when the handle of the door began to twist and rattle. He sprang from the bed, and for an instant stood looking exactly like a picture my Aunt Agatha has in her dining-room—The Stag at Bay—Landseer. Then he made a dive for the cupboard and was inside it before one really got on to it that he had started leaping. I have seen fellows late for the 9.15 move less nippily.

I shot a glance at Jeeves. He allowed his right eyebrow to flicker slightly, which is as near as he ever gets to a display of the emotions.

"Hullo?" I yipped.

"Let me in, blast you!" responded Tuppy's voice from without. "Who locked this door?"

I consulted Jeeves once more in the language of the eyebrow. He raised one of his. I raised one of mine. He raised his other. I raised my other. Then we both raised both. Finally, there seeming no other policy to pursue, I flung wide the gates and Tuppy came shooting in.

"Now what?" I said, as nonchalantly as I could manage.

"Why was the door locked?" demanded Tuppy.

I was in pretty good eyebrow-raising form by now, so I gave him a touch of it.

"Is one to have no privacy, Glossop?" I said coldly. "I instructed Jeeves to lock the door because I was about to disrobe."

"A likely story!" said Tuppy, and I'm not sure he didn't add "Forsooth!" "You needn't try to make me believe that you're afraid people are going to run excursion trains to see you in your underwear. You locked that door because you've got the snake Fink-Nottle concealed in here. I suspected it the moment I'd left, and I decided to come back and investigate. I'm going to search this room from end to end. I believe he's in that cupboard.... What's in this cupboard?"

"Just clothes," I said, having another stab at the nonchalant, though extremely dubious as to whether it would come off. "The usual wardrobe of the English gentleman paying a country-house visit."

"You're lying!"

Well, I wouldn't have been if he had only waited a minute before speaking, because the words were hardly out of his mouth before Gussie was out of the cupboard. I have commented on the speed with which he had gone in. It was as nothing to the speed with which he emerged. There was a sort of whir and blur, and he was no longer with us.

I think Tuppy was surprised. In fact, I'm sure he was. Despite the confidence with which he had stated his view that the cupboard contained Fink-Nottles, it plainly disconcerted him to have the chap fizzing out at him like this. He gargled sharply, and jumped back about five feet. The next moment, however, he had recovered his poise and was galloping down the corridor in pursuit. It only needed Aunt Dahlia after them, shouting "Yoicks!" or whatever is customary on these occasions, to complete the resemblance to a brisk run with the Quorn.

I sank into a handy chair. I am not a man whom it is easy to discourage, but it seemed to me that things had at last begun to get too complex for Bertram.

"Jeeves," I said, "all this is a bit thick."

"Yes, sir."

"The head rather swims."

"Yes, sir."

"I think you had better leave me, Jeeves. I shall need to devote the very closest thought to the situation which has arisen."

"Very good, sir."

The door closed. I lit a cigarette and began to ponder.

-19-

Most chaps in my position, I imagine, would have pondered all the rest of the evening without getting a bite, but we Woosters have an uncanny knack of going straight to the heart of things, and I don't suppose it was much more than ten minutes after I had started pondering before I saw what had to be done.

What was needed to straighten matters out, I perceived, was a heart-to- heart talk with Angela. She had caused all the trouble by her mutton- headed behaviour in saying "Yes" instead of "No" when Gussie, in the grip of mixed drinks and cerebral excitement, had suggested teaming up. She must obviously be properly ticked off and made to return him to store. A quarter of an hour later, I had tracked her down to the summer-house in which she was taking a cooler and was seating myself by her side.

"Angela," I said, and if my voice was stern, well, whose wouldn't have been, "this is all perfect drivel."

She seemed to come out of a reverie. She looked at me inquiringly.

"I'm sorry, Bertie, I didn't hear. What were you talking drivel about?"

"I was not talking drivel."

"Oh, sorry, I thought you said you were."

"Is it likely that I would come out here in order to talk drivel?"

"Very likely."

I thought it best to haul off and approach the matter from another angle.

"I've just been seeing Tuppy."

"Oh?"

"And Gussie Fink-Nottle."

"Oh, yes?"

"It appears that you have gone and got engaged to the latter."

"Quite right."

"Well, that's what I meant when I said it was all perfect drivel. You can't possibly love a chap like Gussie."

"Why not?"

"You simply can't."

Well, I mean to say, of course she couldn't. Nobody could love a freak like Gussie except a similar freak like the Bassett. The shot wasn't on the board. A splendid chap, of course, in many ways—courteous, amiable, and just the fellow to tell you what to do till the doctor came, if you had a sick newt on your hands—but quite obviously not of Mendelssohn's March timber. I have no doubt that you could have flung bricks by the hour in England's most densely populated districts without endangering the safety of a single girl capable of becoming Mrs. Augustus Fink-Nottle without an anaesthetic.

I put this to her, and she was forced to admit the justice of it.

"All right, then. Perhaps I don't."

"Then what," I said keenly, "did you want to go and get engaged to him for, you unreasonable young fathead?"

"I thought it would be fun."

"Fun!"

"And so it has been. I've had a lot of fun out of it. You should have seen Tuppy's face when I told him."

A sudden bright light shone upon me.

"Ha! A gesture!"

"What?"

"You got engaged to Gussie just to score off Tuppy?"

"I did."

"Well, then, that was what I was saying. It was a gesture."

"Yes, I suppose you could call it that."

"And I'll tell you something else I'll call it—viz. a dashed low trick. I'm surprised at you, young Angela."

"I don't see why."

I curled the lip about half an inch. "Being a female, you wouldn't. You gentler sexes are like that. You pull off the rawest stuff without a pang. You pride yourselves on it. Look at Jael, the wife of Heber."

"Where did you ever hear of Jael, the wife of Heber?"

"Possibly you are not aware that I once won a Scripture-knowledge prize at school?"

"Oh, yes. I remember Augustus mentioning it in his speech."

"Quite," I said, a little hurriedly. I had no wish to be reminded of Augustus's speech. "Well, as I say, look at Jael, the wife of Heber. Dug spikes into the guest's coconut while he was asleep, and then went swanking about the place like a Girl Guide. No wonder they say, 'Oh, woman, woman!'"

"Who?"

"The chaps who do. Coo, what a sex! But you aren't proposing to keep this up, of course?"

"Keep what up?"

"This rot of being engaged to Gussie."

"I certainly am."

"Just to make Tuppy look silly."

"Do you think he looks silly?"

"I do."

"So he ought to."

I began to get the idea that I wasn't making real headway. I remember when I won that Scripture-knowledge prize, having to go into the facts about Balaam's ass. I can't quite recall what they were, but I still retain a sort of general impression of something digging its feet in and putting its ears back and refusing to co-operate; and it seemed to me that this was what Angela was doing now. She and Balaam's ass were, so to speak, sisters under the skin. There's a word beginning with r——"re" something——"recal" something—No, it's gone. But what I am driving at is that is what this Angela was showing herself.

"Silly young geezer," I said.

She pinkened.

"I'm not a silly young geezer."

"You are a silly young geezer. And, what's more, you know it."

"I don't know anything of the kind."

"Here you are, wrecking Tuppy's life, wrecking Gussie's life, all for the sake of a cheap score."

"Well, it's no business of yours."

I sat on this promptly:

"No business of mine when I see two lives I used to go to school with wrecked? Ha! Besides, you know you're potty about Tuppy."

"I'm not!"

"Is that so? If I had a quid for every time I've seen you gaze at him with the lovelight in your eyes——"

She gazed at me, but without the lovelight.

"Oh, for goodness sake, go away and boil your head, Bertie!"

I drew myself up.

"That," I replied, with dignity, "is just what I am going to go away and boil. At least, I mean, I shall now leave you. I have said my say."

"Good."

"But permit me to add——"

"I won't."

"Very good," I said coldly. "In that case, tinkerty tonk."

And I meant it to sting.

"Moody" and "discouraged" were about the two adjectives you would have selected to describe me as I left the summer-house. It would be idle to deny that I had expected better results from this little chat.

I was surprised at Angela. Odd how you never realize that every girl is at heart a vicious specimen until something goes wrong with her love affair. This cousin and I had been meeting freely since the days when I wore sailor suits and she hadn't any front teeth, yet only now was I beginning to get on to her hidden depths. A simple, jolly, kindly young pimple she had always struck me as—the sort you could more or less rely on not to hurt a fly. But here she was now laughing heartlessly—at least, I seemed to remember hearing her laugh heartlessly—like something cold and callous out of a sophisticated talkie, and fairly spitting on her hands in her determination to bring Tuppy's grey hairs in sorrow to the grave.

I've said it before, and I'll say it again—girls are rummy. Old Pop Kipling never said a truer word than when he made that crack about the f. of the s. being more d. than the m.

It seemed to me in the circs. that there was but one thing to do—that is head for the dining-room and take a slash at the cold collation of which Jeeves had spoken. I felt in urgent need of sustenance, for the recent interview had pulled me down a bit. There is no gainsaying the fact that this naked-emotion stuff reduces a chap's vitality and puts him in the vein for a good whack at the beef and ham.

To the dining-room, accordingly, I repaired, and had barely crossed the threshold when I perceived Aunt Dahlia at the sideboard, tucking into salmon mayonnaise.

The spectacle drew from me a quick "Oh, ah," for I was somewhat embarrassed. The last time this relative and I had enjoyed a *tête-à-tête,* it will be remembered, she had sketched out plans for drowning me in the kitchen-garden pond, and I was not quite sure what my present standing with her was.

I was relieved to find her in genial mood. Nothing could have exceeded the cordiality with which she waved her fork.

"Hallo, Bertie, you old ass," was her very matey greeting. "I thought I shouldn't find you far away from the food. Try some of this salmon. Excellent."

"Anatole's?" I queried.

"No. He's still in bed. But the kitchen maid has struck an inspired streak. It suddenly seems to have come home to her that she isn't catering for a covey of buzzards in the Sahara Desert, and she has put out something quite fit for human consumption. There is good in the girl, after all, and I hope she enjoys herself at the dance."

I ladled out a portion of salmon, and we fell into pleasant conversation, chatting of this servants' ball at the Stretchley-Budds and speculating idly, I recall, as to what Seppings, the butler, would look like, doing the rumba.

It was not till I had cleaned up the first platter and was embarking on a second that the subject of Gussie came up. Considering what had passed at Market Snodsbury that afternoon, it was one which I had been expecting her to touch on earlier. When she did touch on it, I could see that she had not yet been informed of Angela's engagement.

"I say, Bertie," she said, meditatively chewing fruit salad. "This Spink-Bottle."

"Nottle."

"Bottle," insisted the aunt firmly. "After that exhibition of his this afternoon, Bottle, and nothing but Bottle, is how I shall always think of him. However, what I was going to say was that, if you see him, I wish you would tell him that he has made an old woman very, very happy. Except for the time when the curate tripped over a loose shoelace and fell down the pulpit steps, I don't think I have ever had a more wonderful moment than when good old Bottle suddenly started ticking Tom off from the platform. In fact, I thought his whole performance in the most perfect taste."

I could not but demur.

"Those references to myself——"

"Those were what I liked next best. I thought they were fine. Is it true that you cheated when you won that Scripture-knowledge prize?"

"Certainly not. My victory was the outcome of the most strenuous and unremitting efforts."

"And how about this pessimism we hear of? Are you a pessimist, Bertie?"

I could have told her that what was occurring in this house was rapidly making me one, but I said no, I wasn't.

"That's right. Never be a pessimist. Everything is for the best in this best of all possible worlds. It's a long lane that has no turning. It s always darkest before the dawn. Have patience and all will come right. The sun will shine, although the day's a grey one.... Try some of this salad."

I followed her advice, but even as I plied the spoon my thoughts were elsewhere. I was perplexed. It may have been the fact that I had recently been hobnobbing with so many bowed-down hearts that made this cheeriness of hers seem so bizarre, but bizarre was certainly what I found it.

"I thought you might have been a trifle peeved," I said.

"Peeved?"

"By Gussie's manoeuvres on the platform this afternoon. I confess that I had rather expected the tapping foot and the drawn brow."

"Nonsense. What was there to be peeved about? I took the whole thing as a great compliment, proud to feel that any drink from my cellars could have produced such a majestic jag. It restores one's faith in post-war whisky. Besides, I couldn't be peeved at anything tonight. I am like a little child clapping its hands and dancing in the sunshine. For though it has been some time getting a move on, Bertie, the sun has at last broken through the clouds. Ring out those joy bells. Anatole has withdrawn his notice."

"What? Oh, very hearty congratulations."

"Thanks. Yes, I worked on him like a beaver after I got back this afternoon, and finally, vowing he would ne'er consent, he consented. He stays on, praises be, and the way I look at it now is that God's in His heaven and all's right with——"

She broke off. The door had opened, and we were plus a butler.

"Hullo, Seppings," said Aunt Dahlia. "I thought you had gone."

"Not yet, madam."

"Well, I hope you will all have a good time."

"Thank you, madam."

"Was there something you wanted to see me about?"

"Yes, madam. It is with reference to Monsieur Anatole. Is it by your wish, madam, that Mr. Fink-Nottle is making faces at Monsieur Anatole through the skylight of his bedroom?"

-20-

There was one of those long silences. Pregnant, I believe, is what they're generally called. Aunt looked at butler. Butler looked at aunt. I looked at both of them. An eerie stillness seemed to envelop the room like a linseed poultice. I happened to be biting on a slice of apple in my fruit salad at the moment, and it sounded as if Carnera had jumped off the top of the Eiffel Tower on to a cucumber frame.

Aunt Dahlia steadied herself against the sideboard, and spoke in a low, husky voice:

"Faces?"

"Yes, madam."

"Through the skylight?"

"Yes, madam."

"You mean he's sitting on the roof?"

"Yes, madam. It has upset Monsieur Anatole very much."

I suppose it was that word "upset" that touched Aunt Dahlia off. Experience had taught her what happened when Anatole got upset. I had always known her as a woman who was quite active on her pins, but I had never suspected her of being capable of the magnificent burst of speed which she now showed. Pausing merely to get a rich hunting-field expletive off her chest, she was out of the room and making for the stairs before I could swallow a sliver of—I think—banana. And feeling, as I had felt when I got that telegram of hers about Angela and Tuppy, that my place was by her side, I put down my plate and hastened after her, Seppings following at a loping gallop.

I say that my place was by her side, but it was not so dashed easy to get there, for she was setting a cracking pace. At the top of the first flight she must have led by a matter of half a dozen lengths, and was still shaking off my challenge when she rounded into the second. At the next landing, however, the gruelling going appeared to tell on her, for she slackened off a trifle and showed symptoms of roaring, and by the time we were in the straight we were running practically neck and neck. Our entry into Anatole's room was as close a finish as you could have wished to see.

Result:

1. *Aunt Dahlia.*

2. *Bertram.*

3. *Seppings.*

Won by a short head. Half a staircase separated second and third.

The first thing that met the eye on entering was Anatole. This wizard of the cooking-stove is a tubby little man with a moustache of the outsize or soup-strainer type, and you can generally take a line through it as to the state of his emotions. When all is well, it turns up at the ends like a sergeant-major's. When the soul is bruised, it droops.

It was drooping now, striking a sinister note. And if any shadow of doubt had remained as to how he was feeling, the way he was carrying on would have dispelled it. He was standing by the bed in pink pyjamas, waving his fists at the skylight. Through the glass, Gussie was staring down. His eyes were bulging and his mouth was open, giving him so striking a resemblance to some rare fish in an aquarium that one's primary impulse was to offer him an ant's egg.

Watching this fist-waving cook and this goggling guest, I must say that my sympathies were completely with the former. I considered him thoroughly justified in waving all the fists he wanted to.

Review the facts, I mean to say. There he had been, lying in bed, thinking idly of whatever French cooks do think about when in bed, and he had suddenly become aware of that frightful face at the window. A thing to jar the most phlegmatic. I know I should hate to be lying in bed and have Gussie popping up like that. A chap's bedroom—you can't get away from it—is his castle, and he has every right to look askance if gargoyles come glaring in at him.

While I stood musing thus, Aunt Dahlia, in her practical way, was coming straight to the point:

"What's all this?"

Anatole did a sort of Swedish exercise, starting at the base of the spine, carrying on through the shoulder-blades and finishing up among the back hair.

Then he told her.

In the chats I have had with this wonder man, I have always found his English fluent, but a bit on the mixed side. If you remember, he was with Mrs. Bingo Little for a time before coming to Brinkley, and no doubt he picked up a good deal from Bingo. Before that, he had been a couple of years with an American family at Nice and had studied under their chauffeur, one of the Maloneys of Brooklyn. So, what with Bingo and what with Maloney, he is, as I say, fluent but a bit mixed.

He spoke, in part, as follows:

"Hot dog! You ask me what is it? Listen. Make some attention a little. Me, I have hit the hay, but I do not sleep so good, and presently I wake and up I look, and there is one who make faces against me through the dashed window. Is that a pretty affair? Is that convenient? If you think I like it, you jolly well mistake yourself. I am so mad as a wet hen. And why not? I am somebody, isn't it? This is a bedroom, what-what, not a house for some apes? Then for what do blighters sit on my window so cool as a few cucumbers, making some faces?"

"Quite," I said. Dashed reasonable, was my verdict.

He threw another look up at Gussie, and did Exercise 2—the one where you clutch the moustache, give it a tug and then start catching flies.

"Wait yet a little. I am not finish. I say I see this type on my window, making a few faces. But what then? Does he buzz off when I shout a cry, and leave me peaceable? Not on your life. He remain planted there, not giving any damns, and sit regarding me like a cat watching a duck. He make faces against me and again he make faces against me, and the more I command that he should get to hell out of here, the more he do not get to hell out of here. He cry something towards me, and I demand what is his desire, but he do not explain. Oh, no, that arrives never. He does but shrug his head. What damn silliness! Is this amusing for me? You think I like it? I am not content with such folly. I think the poor mutt's loony. *Je me fiche de ce type infect. C'est idiot de faire comme ça l'oiseau.... Allez-vous-en, louffier....* Tell the boob to go away. He is mad as some March hatters."

I must say I thought he was making out a jolly good case, and evidently Aunt Dahlia felt the same. She laid a quivering hand on his shoulder.

"I will, Monsieur Anatole, I will," she said, and I couldn't have believed that robust voice capable of sinking to such an absolute coo. More like a turtle dove calling to its mate than anything else. "It's quite all right."

She had said the wrong thing. He did Exercise 3.

"All right? *Nom d'un nom d'un nom*! The hell you say it's all right! Of what use to pull stuff like that? Wait one half-moment. Not yet quite so quick, my old sport. It is by no means all right. See yet again a little. It is some very different dishes of fish. I can take a few smooths with a rough, it is true, but I do not find it agreeable when one play larks against me on my windows. That cannot do. A nice thing, no. I am a serious man. I do not wish a few larks on my windows. I enjoy larks on my windows worse as any. It is very little all right. If such rannygazoo is to arrive, I do not remain any longer in this house no more. I buzz off and do not stay planted."

Sinister words, I had to admit, and I was not surprised that Aunt Dahlia, hearing them, should have uttered a cry like the wail of a master of hounds seeing a fox shot. Anatole had begun to wave his fists again at Gussie, and she now joined him. Seppings, who was puffing respectfully in the background, didn't actually wave his fists, but he gave Gussie a pretty austere look. It was plain to the thoughtful observer that this Fink-Nottle, in getting on to that skylight, had done a mistaken thing. He couldn't have been more unpopular in the home of G.G. Simmons.

"Go away, you crazy loon!" cried Aunt Dahlia, in that ringing voice of hers which had once caused nervous members of the Quorn to lose stirrups and take tosses from the saddle.

Gussie's reply was to waggle his eyebrows. I could read the message he was trying to convey.

"I think he means," I said—reasonable old Bertram, always trying to throw oil on the troubled w's——"that if he does he will fall down the side of the house and break his neck."

"Well, why not?" said Aunt Dahlia.

I could see her point, of course, but it seemed to me that there might be a nearer solution. This skylight happened to be the only window in the house which Uncle Tom had not festooned with his bally bars. I suppose he felt that if a burglar had the nerve to climb up as far as this, he deserved what was coming to him.

"If you opened the skylight, he could jump in."

The idea got across.

"Seppings, how does this skylight open?"

"With a pole, madam."

"Then get a pole. Get two poles. Ten."

And presently Gussie was mixing with the company, Like one of those chaps you read about in the papers, the wretched man seemed deeply conscious of his position.

I must say Aunt Dahlia's bearing and demeanour did nothing to assist toward a restored composure. Of the amiability which she had exhibited when discussing this unhappy chump's activities with me over the fruit salad, no trace remained, and I was not surprised that speech more or less froze on the Fink-Nottle lips. It isn't often that Aunt Dahlia, normally as genial a bird as ever encouraged a gaggle of hounds to get their noses down to it, lets her angry passions rise, but when she does, strong men climb trees and pull them up after them.

"Well?" she said.

In answer to this, all that Gussie could produce was a sort of strangled hiccough.

"Well?"

Aunt Dahlia's face grew darker. Hunting, if indulged in regularly over a period of years, is a pastime that seldom fails to lend a fairly deepish tinge to the patient's complexion, and her best friends could not have denied that even at normal times the relative's map tended a little toward the crushed strawberry. But never had I seen it take on so pronounced a richness as now. She looked like a tomato struggling for self-expression.

"Well?"

Gussie tried hard. And for a moment it seemed as if something was going to come through. But in the end it turned out nothing more than a sort of death-rattle.

"Oh, take him away, Bertie, and put ice on his head," said Aunt Dahlia, giving the thing up. And she turned to tackle what looked like the rather man's size job of soothing Anatole, who was now carrying on a muttered conversation with himself in a rapid sort of way.

Seeming to feel that the situation was one to which he could not do justice in Bingo-cum-Maloney Anglo-American, he had fallen back on his native tongue. Words like "*marmiton de Domange,*" "*pignouf,*" "*hurluberlu*" and "*roustisseur*" were fluttering from him like bats out of a barn. Lost on me, of course, because, though I sweated a bit at the Gallic language during that Cannes visit, I'm still more or less in the Esker-vous-avez stage. I regretted this, for they sounded good.

I assisted Gussie down the stairs. A cooler thinker than Aunt Dahlia, I had already guessed the hidden springs and motives which had led him to the roof. Where she had seen only a cockeyed reveller indulging himself in a drunken prank or whimsy, I had spotted the hunted fawn.

"Was Tuppy after you?" I asked sympathetically.

What I believe is called a *frisson* shook him.

"He nearly got me on the top landing. I shinned out through a passage window and scrambled along a sort of ledge."

"That baffled him, what?"

"Yes. But then I found I had stuck. The roof sloped down in all directions. I couldn't go back. I had to go on, crawling along this ledge. And then I found myself looking down the skylight. Who was that chap?"

"That was Anatole, Aunt Dahlia's chef."

"French?"

"To the core."

"That explains why I couldn't make him understand. What asses these Frenchmen are. They don't seem able to grasp the simplest thing. You'd have thought if a chap saw a chap on a skylight, the chap would realize the chap wanted to be let in. But no, he just stood there."

"Waving a few fists."

"Yes. Silly idiot. Still, here I am."

"Here you are, yes—for the moment."

"Eh?"

"I was thinking that Tuppy is probably lurking somewhere."

He leaped like a lamb in springtime.

"What shall I do?"

I considered this.

"Sneak back to your room and barricade the door. That is the manly policy."

"Suppose that's where he's lurking?"

"In that case, move elsewhere."

But on arrival at the room, it transpired that Tuppy, if anywhere, was infesting some other portion of the house. Gussie shot in, and I heard the key turn. And feeling that there was no more that I could do in that quarter, I returned to the dining-room for further fruit salad and a quiet think. And I had barely filled my plate when the door opened and Aunt Dahlia came in. She sank into a chair, looking a bit shopworn.

"Give me a drink, Bertie."

"What sort?"

"Any sort, so long as it's strong."

Approach Bertram Wooster along these lines, and you catch him at his best. St. Bernard dogs doing the square thing by Alpine travellers could not have bustled about more assiduously. I filled the order, and for some moments nothing was to be heard but the sloshing sound of an aunt restoring her tissues.

"Shove it down, Aunt Dahlia," I said sympathetically. "These things take it out of one, don't they? You've had a toughish time, no doubt, soothing Anatole," I proceeded, helping myself to anchovy paste on toast. "Everything pretty smooth now, I trust?"

She gazed at me in a long, lingering sort of way, her brow wrinkled as if in thought.

"Attila," she said at length. "That's the name. Attila, the Hun."

"Eh?"

"I was trying to think who you reminded me of. Somebody who went about strewing ruin and desolation and breaking up homes which, until he came along, had been happy and peaceful. Attila is the man. It's amazing." she said, drinking me in once more. "To look at you, one would think you were just an ordinary sort of amiable idiot—certifiable, perhaps, but quite harmless. Yet, in reality, you are worse a scourge than the Black Death. I tell you, Bertie, when I contemplate you I seem to come up against all the underlying sorrow and horror of life with such a thud that I feel as if I had walked into a lamp post."

Pained and surprised, I would have spoken, but the stuff I had thought was anchovy paste had turned out to be something far more gooey and adhesive. It seemed to wrap itself round the tongue and impede utterance like a gag. And while I was still endeavouring to clear the vocal cords for action, she went on:

"Do you realize what you started when you sent that Spink-Bottle man down here? As regards his getting blotto and turning the prize-giving ceremonies at Market Snodsbury Grammar School into a sort of two-reel comic film, I will say nothing, for frankly I enjoyed it. But when he comes leering at Anatole through skylights, just after I had with infinite pains and tact induced him to withdraw his notice, and makes him so temperamental that he won't hear of staying on after tomorrow——"

The paste stuff gave way. I was able to speak:

"What?"

"Yes, Anatole goes tomorrow, and I suppose poor old Tom will have indigestion for the rest of his life. And that is not all. I have just seen Angela, and she tells me she is engaged to this Bottle."

"Temporarily, yes," I had to admit.

"Temporarily be blowed. She's definitely engaged to him and talks with a sort of hideous coolness of getting married in October. So there it is. If the prophet Job were to walk into the room at this moment, I could sit swapping hard-luck stories with him till bedtime. Not that Job was in my class."

"He had boils."

"Well, what are boils?"

"Dashed painful, I understand."

"Nonsense. I'd take all the boils on the market in exchange for my troubles. Can't you realize the position? I've lost the best cook to England. My husband, poor soul, will probably die of dyspepsia. And my only daughter, for whom I had dreamed such a wonderful future, is engaged to be married to an inebriated newt fancier. And you talk about boils!"

I corrected her on a small point:

"I don't absolutely talk about boils. I merely mentioned that Job had them. Yes, I agree with you, Aunt Dahlia, that things are not looking too oojah-cum-spiff at the moment, but be of good cheer. A Wooster is seldom baffled for more than the nonce."

"You rather expect to be coming along shortly with another of your schemes?"

"At any minute."

She sighed resignedly.

"I thought as much. Well, it needed but this. I don't see how things could possibly be worse than they are, but no doubt you will succeed in making them so. Your genius and insight will find the way. Carry on, Bertie. Yes, carry on. I am past caring now. I shall even find a faint interest in seeing into what darker and profounder abysses of hell you can plunge this home. Go to it, lad.... What's that stuff you're eating?"

"I find it a little difficult to classify. Some sort of paste on toast. Rather like glue flavoured with beef extract."

"Gimme," said Aunt Dahlia listlessly.

"Be careful how you chew," I advised. "It sticketh closer than a brother.... Yes, Jeeves?"

The man had materialized on the carpet. Absolutely noiseless, as usual.

"A note for you, sir."

"A note for me, Jeeves?"

"A note for you, sir."

"From whom, Jeeves?"

"From Miss Bassett, sir."

"From whom, Jeeves?"

"From Miss Bassett, sir."

"From Miss Bassett, Jeeves?"

"From Miss Bassett, sir."

At this point, Aunt Dahlia, who had taken one nibble at her whatever-it-was-on-toast and laid it down, begged us—a little fretfully, I thought—for heaven's sake to cut out the cross-talk vaudeville stuff, as she had enough to bear already without having to listen to us doing our imitation of the Two Macs. Always willing to oblige, I dismissed Jeeves with a nod, and he flickered for a moment and was gone. Many a spectre would have been less slippy.

"But what," I mused, toying with the envelope, "can this female be writing to me about?"

"Why not open the damn thing and see?"

"A very excellent idea," I said, and did so.

"And if you are interested in my movements," proceeded Aunt Dahlia, heading for the door, "I propose to go to my room, do some Yogi deep breathing, and try to forget."

"Quite," I said absently, skimming p. l. And then, as I turned over, a sharp howl broke from my lips, causing Aunt Dahlia to shy like a startled mustang.

"Don't do it!" she exclaimed, quivering in every limb.

"Yes, but dash it——"

"What a pest you are, you miserable object," she sighed. "I remember years ago, when you were in your cradle, being left alone with you one day and you nearly swallowed your rubber comforter and started turning purple. And I, ass that I was, took it out and saved your life. Let me tell you, young Bertie, it will go very hard with you if you ever swallow a rubber comforter again when only I am by to aid."

"But, dash it!" I cried. "Do you know what's happened? Madeline Bassett says she's going to marry me!"

"I hope it keeps fine for you," said the relative, and passed from the room looking like something out of an Edgar Allan Poe story.

-21-

I don't suppose I was looking so dashed unlike something out of an Edgar Allan Poe story myself, for, as you can readily imagine, the news item which I have just recorded had got in amongst me properly. If the Bassett, in the belief that the Wooster heart had long been hers and was waiting ready to be scooped in on demand, had decided to take up her option, I should, as a man of honour and sensibility, have no choice but to come across and kick in. The matter was obviously not one that could be straightened out with a curt *nolle prosequi.* All the evidence, therefore, seemed to point to the fact that the doom had come upon me and, what was more, had come to stay.

And yet, though it would be idle to pretend that my grip on the situation was quite the grip I would have liked it to be, I did not despair of arriving at a solution. A lesser man, caught in this awful snare, would no doubt have thrown in the towel at once and ceased to struggle; but the whole point about the Woosters is that they are not lesser men.

By way of a start, I read the note again. Not that I had any hope that a second perusal would enable me to place a different construction on its contents, but it helped to fill in while the brain was limbering up. I then, to assist thought, had another go at the fruit salad, and in addition ate a slice of sponge cake. And it was as I passed on to the cheese that the machinery started working. I saw what had to be done.

To the question which had been exercising the mind—viz., can Bertram cope?—I was now able to reply with a confident "Absolutely."

The great wheeze on these occasions of dirty work at the crossroads is not to lose your head but to keep cool and try to find the ringleaders. Once find the ringleaders, and you know where you are.

The ringleader here was plainly the Bassett. It was she who had started the whole imbroglio by chucking Gussie, and it was clear that before anything could be done to solve and clarify, she must be induced to revise her views and take him on again. This would put Angela back into circulation, and that would cause Tuppy to simmer down a bit, and then we could begin to get somewhere.

I decided that as soon as I had had another morsel of cheese I would seek this Bassett out and be pretty eloquent.

And at this moment in she came. I might have foreseen that she would be turning up shortly. I mean to say, hearts may ache, but if they know that there is a cold collation set out in the dining-room, they are pretty sure to come popping in sooner or later.

Her eyes, as she entered the room, were fixed on the salmon mayonnaise, and she would no doubt have made a bee-line for it and started getting hers, had I not, in the emotion of seeing her, dropped a glass of the best with which I was endeavouring to bring about a calmer frame of mind. The noise caused her to turn, and for an instant embarrassment supervened. A slight flush mantled the cheek, and the eyes popped a bit.

"Oh!" she said.

I have always found that there is nothing that helps to ease you over one of these awkward moments like a spot of stage business. Find something to do with your hands, and it's half the battle. I grabbed a plate and hastened forward.

"A touch of salmon?"

"Thank you."

"With a suspicion of salad?"

"If you please."

"And to drink? Name the poison."

"I think I would like a little orange juice."

She gave a gulp. Not at the orange juice, I don't mean, because she hadn't got it yet, but at all the tender associations those two words provoked. It was as if someone had mentioned spaghetti to the relict of an Italian organ-grinder. Her face flushed a deeper shade, she registered anguish, and I saw that it was no longer within the sphere of practical politics to try to confine the conversation to neutral topics like cold boiled salmon.

So did she, I imagine, for when I, as a preliminary to getting down to brass tacks, said "Er," she said "Er," too, simultaneously, the brace of "Ers" clashing in mid-air.

"I'm sorry."

"I beg your pardon."

"You were saying——"

"You were saying——"

"No, please go on."

"Oh, right-ho."

I straightened the tie, my habit when in this girl's society, and had at it:

"With reference to yours of even date——"

She flushed again, and took a rather strained forkful of salmon.

"You got my note?"

"Yes, I got your note."

"I gave it to Jeeves to give it to you."

"Yes, he gave it to me. That's how I got it."

There was another silence. And as she was plainly shrinking from talking turkey, I was reluctantly compelled to do so. I mean, somebody had got to. Too dashed silly, a male and female in our position simply standing eating salmon and cheese at one another without a word.

"Yes, I got it all right."

"I see. You got it."

"Yes, I got it. I've just been reading it. And what I was rather wanting to ask you, if we happened to run into each other, was—well, what about it?"

"What about it?"

"That's what I say: What about it?"

"But it was quite clear."

"Oh, quite. Perfectly clear. Very well expressed and all that. But—I mean—Well, I mean, deeply sensible of the honour, and so forth—but—— Well, dash it!"

She had polished off her salmon, and now put the plate down.

"Fruit salad?"

"No, thank you."

"Spot of pie?"

"No, thanks."

"One of those glue things on toast?"

"No, thank you."

She took a cheese straw. I found a cold egg which I had overlooked. Then I said "I mean to say" just as she said "I think I know", and there was another collision.

"I beg your pardon."

"I'm sorry."

"Do go on."

"No, you go on."

I waved my cold egg courteously, to indicate that she had the floor, and she started again:

"I think I know what you are trying to say. You are surprised."

"Yes."

"You are thinking of——"

"Exactly."

"—Mr. Fink-Nottle."

"The very man."

"You find what I have done hard to understand."

"Absolutely."

"I don't wonder."

"I do."

"And yet it is quite simple."

She took another cheese straw. She seemed to like cheese straws.

"Quite simple, really. I want to make you happy."

"Dashed decent of you."

"I am going to devote the rest of my life to making you happy."

"A very matey scheme."

"I can at least do that. But—may I be quite frank with you, Bertie?"

"Oh, rather."

"Then I must tell you this. I am fond of you. I will marry you. I will do my best to make you a good wife. But my affection for you can never be the flame-like passion I felt for Augustus."

"Just the very point I was working round to. There, as you say, is the snag. Why not chuck the whole idea of hitching up with me? Wash it out altogether. I mean, if you love old Gussie——"

"No longer."

"Oh, come."

"No. What happened this afternoon has killed my love. A smear of ugliness has been drawn across a thing of beauty, and I can never feel towards him as I did."

I saw what she meant, of course. Gussie had bunged his heart at her feet; she had picked it up, and, almost immediately after doing so, had discovered that he had been stewed to the eyebrows all the time. The shock must have been severe. No girl likes to feel that a chap has got to be thoroughly plastered before he can ask her to marry him. It wounds the pride.

Nevertheless, I persevered.

"But have you considered," I said, "that you may have got a wrong line on Gussie's performance this afternoon? Admitted that all the evidence points to a more sinister theory, what price him simply having got a touch of the sun? Chaps do get touches of the sun, you know, especially when the weather's hot."

She looked at me, and I saw that she was putting in a bit of the old drenched-irises stuff.

"It was like you to say that, Bertie. I respect you for it."

"Oh, no."

"Yes. You have a splendid, chivalrous soul."

"Not a bit."

"Yes, you have. You remind me of Cyrano."

"Who?"

"Cyrano de Bergerac."

"The chap with the nose?"

"Yes."

I can't say I was any too pleased. I felt the old beak furtively. It was a bit on the prominent side, perhaps, but, dash it, not in the Cyrano class. It began to look as if the next thing this girl would do would be to compare me to Schnozzle Durante.

"He loved, but pleaded another's cause."

"Oh, I see what you mean now."

"I like you for that, Bertie. It was fine of you—fine and big. But it is no use. There are things which kill love. I can never forget Augustus, but my love for him is dead. I will be your wife."

Well, one has to be civil.

"Right ho," I said. "Thanks awfully."

Then the dialogue sort of poofed out once more, and we stood eating cheese straws and cold eggs respectively in silence. There seemed to exist some little uncertainty as to what the next move was.

Fortunately, before embarrassment could do much more supervening, Angela came in, and this broke up the meeting. Then Bassett announced our engagement, and Angela kissed her and said she hoped she would be very, very happy, and the Bassett kissed her and said she hoped she would be very, very happy with Gussie, and Angela said she was sure she would, because Augustus was such a dear, and the Bassett kissed her again, and Angela kissed her again and, in a word, the whole thing got so bally feminine that I was glad to edge away.

I would have been glad to do so, of course, in any case, for if ever there was a moment when it was up to Bertram to think, and think hard, this moment was that moment.

It was, it seemed to me, the end. Not even on the occasion, some years earlier, when I had inadvertently become betrothed to Tuppy's frightful Cousin Honoria, had I experienced a deeper sense of being waist high in the gumbo and about to sink without trace. I wandered out into the garden, smoking a tortured gasper, with the iron well embedded in the soul. And I had fallen into a sort of trance, trying to picture what it would be like having the Bassett on the premises for the rest of my life and at the same time, if you follow me, trying not to picture what it would be like, when I charged into something which might have been a tree, but was not—being, in point of fact, Jeeves.

"I beg your pardon, sir," he said. "I should have moved to one side."

I did not reply. I stood looking at him in silence. For the sight of him had opened up a new line of thought.

This Jeeves, now, I reflected. I had formed the opinion that he had lost his grip and was no longer the force he had been, but was it not possible, I asked myself, that I might be mistaken? Start him off exploring avenues and might he not discover one through which I would be enabled to sneak off to safety, leaving no hard feelings behind? I found myself answering that it was quite on the cards that he might.

After all, his head still bulged out at the back as of old. One noted in the eyes the same intelligent glitter.

Mind you, after what had passed between us in the matter of that white mess-jacket with the brass buttons, I was not prepared absolutely to hand over to the man. I would, of course, merely take him into consultation. But, recalling some of his earlier triumphs—the Sipperley Case, the Episode of My Aunt Agatha and the Dog McIntosh, and the smoothly handled Affair of Uncle George and The Barmaid's Niece were a few that sprang to my mind—I felt justified at least in offering him the opportunity of coming to the aid of the young master in his hour of peril.

But before proceeding further, there was one thing that had got to be understood between us, and understood clearly.

"Jeeves," I said, "a word with you."

"Sir?"

"I am up against it a bit, Jeeves."

"I am sorry to hear that, sir. Can I be of any assistance?"

"Quite possibly you can, if you have not lost your grip. Tell me frankly, Jeeves, are you in pretty good shape mentally?"

"Yes, sir."

"Still eating plenty of fish?"

"Yes, sir."

"Then it may be all right. But there is just one point before I begin. In the past, when you have contrived to extricate self or some pal from some little difficulty, you have frequently shown a disposition to take advantage of my gratitude to gain some private end. Those purple socks, for instance. Also the plus fours and the Old Etonian spats. Choosing your moment with subtle cunning, you came to me when I was weakened by relief and got me to get rid of them. And what I am saying now is that if you are successful on the present occasion there must be no rot of that description about that mess-jacket of mine."

"Very good, sir."

"You will not come to me when all is over and ask me to jettison the jacket?"

"Certainly not, sir."

"On that understanding then, I will carry on. Jeeves, I'm engaged."

"I hope you will be very happy, sir."

"Don't be an ass. I'm engaged to Miss Bassett."

"Indeed, sir? I was not aware——"

"Nor was I. It came as a complete surprise. However, there it is. The official intimation was in that note you brought me."

"Odd, sir."

"What is?"

"Odd, sir, that the contents of that note should have been as you describe. It seemed to me that Miss Bassett, when she handed me the communication, was far from being in a happy frame of mind."

"She is far from being in a happy frame of mind. You don't suppose she really wants to marry me, do you? Pshaw, Jeeves! Can't you see that this is simply another of those bally gestures which are rapidly rendering Brinkley Court a hell for man and beast? Dash all gestures, is my view."

"Yes, sir."

"Well, what's to be done?"

"You feel that Miss Bassett, despite what has occurred, still retains a fondness for Mr. Fink-Nottle, sir?"

"She's pining for him."

"In that case, sir, surely the best plan would be to bring about a reconciliation between them."

"How? You see. You stand silent and twiddle the fingers. You are stumped."

"No, sir. If I twiddled my fingers, it was merely to assist thought."

"Then continue twiddling."

"It will not be necessary, sir."

"You don't mean you've got a bite already?"

"Yes, sir."

"You astound me, Jeeves. Let's have it."

"The device which I have in mind is one that I have already mentioned to you, sir."

"When did you ever mention any device to me?"

"If you will throw your mind back to the evening of our arrival, sir. You were good enough to inquire of me if I had any plan to put forward with a view to bringing Miss Angela and Mr. Glossop together, and I ventured to suggest——"

"Good Lord! Not the old fire-alarm thing?"

"Precisely, sir."

"You're still sticking to that?"

"Yes, sir."

It shows how much the ghastly blow I had received had shaken me when I say that, instead of dismissing the proposal with a curt "Tchah!" or anything like that, I found myself speculating as to whether there might not be something in it, after all.

When he had first mooted this fire-alarm scheme of his, I had sat upon it, if you remember, with the maximum of promptitude and vigour. "Rotten" was the adjective I had employed to describe it, and you may recall that I mused a bit sadly, considering the idea conclusive proof of the general breakdown of a once fine mind. But now it somehow began to look as if it might have possibilities. The fact of the matter was that I had about reached the stage where I was prepared to try anything once, however goofy.

"Just run through that wheeze again, Jeeves," I said thoughtfully. "I remember thinking it cuckoo, but it may be that I missed some of the finer shades."

"Your criticism of it at the time, sir, was that it was too elaborate, but I do not think it is so in reality. As I see it, sir, the occupants of the house, hearing the fire bell ring, will suppose that a conflagration has broken out."

I nodded. One could follow the train of thought.

"Yes, that seems reasonable."

"Whereupon Mr. Glossop will hasten to save Miss Angela, while Mr. Fink-Nottle performs the same office for Miss Bassett."

"Is that based on psychology?"

"Yes, sir. Possibly you may recollect that it was an axiom of the late Sir Arthur Conan Doyle's fictional detective, Sherlock Holmes, that the instinct of everyone, upon an alarm of fire, is to save the object dearest to them."

"It seems to me that there is a grave danger of seeing Tuppy come out carrying a steak-and-kidney pie, but resume, Jeeves, resume. You think that this would clean everything up?"

"The relations of the two young couples could scarcely continue distant after such an occurrence, sir."

"Perhaps you're right. But, dash it, if we go ringing fire bells in the night watches, shan't we scare half the domestic staff into fits? There is one of the housemaids—Jane, I believe—who already skips like the high hills if I so much as come on her unexpectedly round a corner."

"A neurotic girl, sir, I agree. I have noticed her. But by acting promptly we should avoid such a contingency. The entire staff, with the exception of Monsieur Anatole, will be at the ball at Kingham Manor tonight."

"Of course. That just shows the condition this thing has reduced me to. Forget my own name next. Well, then, let's just try to envisage. Bong goes the bell. Gussie rushes and grabs the Bassett.... Wait. Why shouldn't she simply walk downstairs?"

"You are overlooking the effect of sudden alarm on the feminine temperament, sir."

"That's true."

"Miss Bassett's impulse, I would imagine, sir, would be to leap from her window."

"Well, that's worse. We don't want her spread out in a sort of *purée* on the lawn. It seems to me that the flaw in this scheme of yours, Jeeves, is that it's going to litter the garden with mangled corpses."

"No, sir. You will recall that Mr. Travers's fear of burglars has caused him to have stout bars fixed to all the windows."

"Of course, yes. Well, it sounds all right," I said, though still a bit doubtfully. "Quite possibly it may come off. But I have a feeling that it will slip up somewhere. However, I am in no position to cavil at even a 100 to 1 shot. I will adopt this policy of yours, Jeeves, though, as I say, with misgivings. At what hour would you suggest bonging the bell?"

"Not before midnight, sir."

"That is to say, some time after midnight."

"Yes, sir."

"Right-ho, then. At 12.30 on the dot, I will bong."

"Very good, sir."

-22-

I Don't know why it is, but there's something about the rural districts after dark that always has a rummy effect on me. In London I can stay out till all hours and come home with the milk without a tremor, but put me in the garden of a country house after the strength of the company has gone to roost and the place is shut up, and a sort of goose-fleshy feeling steals over me. The night wind stirs the tree-tops, twigs crack, bushes rustle, and before I know where I am, the morale has gone phut and I'm expecting the family ghost to come sneaking up behind me, making groaning noises. Dashed unpleasant, the whole thing, and if you think it improves matters to know that you are shortly about to ring the loudest fire bell in England and start an all-hands-to-the-pumps panic in that quiet, darkened house, you err.

I knew all about the Brinkley Court fire bell. The dickens of a row it makes. Uncle Tom, in addition to not liking burglars, is a bloke who has always objected to the idea of being cooked in his sleep, so when he bought the place he saw to it that the fire bell should be something that might give you heart failure, but which you couldn't possibly mistake for the drowsy chirping of a sparrow in the ivy.

When I was a kid and spent my holidays at Brinkley, we used to have fire drills after closing time, and many is the night I've had it jerk me out of the dreamless like the Last Trump.

I confess that the recollection of what this bell could do when it buckled down to it gave me pause as I stood that night at 12.30 p.m. prompt beside the outhouse where it was located. The sight of the rope against the whitewashed wall and the thought of the bloodsome uproar which was about to smash the peace of the night into hash served to deepen that rummy feeling to which I have alluded.

Moreover, now that I had had time to meditate upon it, I was more than ever defeatist about this scheme of Jeeves's.

Jeeves seemed to take it for granted that Gussie and Tuppy, faced with a hideous fate, would have no thought beyond saving the Bassett and Angela.

I could not bring myself to share his sunny confidence.

I mean to say, I know how moments when they're faced with a hideous fate affect chaps. I remember Freddie Widgeon, one of the most chivalrous birds in the Drones, telling me how there was an alarm of fire once at a seaside hotel where he was staying and, so far from rushing about saving women, he was down the escape within ten seconds of the kick-off, his mind concerned with but one thing—viz., the personal well-being of F. Widgeon.

As far as any idea of doing the delicately nurtured a bit of good went, he tells me, he was prepared to stand underneath and catch them in blankets, but no more.

Why, then, should this not be so with Augustus Fink-Nottle and Hildebrand Glossop?

Such were my thoughts as I stood toying with the rope, and I believe I should have turned the whole thing up, had it not been that at this juncture there floated into my mind a picture of the Bassett hearing that bell for the first time. Coming as a wholly new experience, it would probably startle her into a decline.

And so agreeable was this reflection that I waited no longer, but seized the rope, braced the feet and snapped into it.

Well, as I say, I hadn't been expecting that bell to hush things up to any great extent. Nor did it. The last time I had heard it, I had been in my room on the other side of the house, and even so it had hoiked me out of bed as if something had exploded under me. Standing close to it like this, I got the full force and meaning of the thing, and I've never heard anything like it in my puff.

I rather enjoy a bit of noise, as a general rule. I remember Cats-meat Potter-Pirbright bringing a police rattle into the Drones one night and loosing it off behind my chair, and I just lay back and closed my eyes with a pleasant smile, like someone in a box at the opera. And the same applies to the time when my Aunt Agatha's son, young Thos., put a match to the parcel of Guy Fawkes Day fireworks to see what would happen.

But the Brinkley Court fire bell was too much for me. I gave about half a dozen tugs, and then, feeling that enough was enough, sauntered round to the front lawn to ascertain what solid results had been achieved.

Brinkley Court had given of its best. A glance told me that we were playing to capacity. The eye, roving to and fro, noted here Uncle Tom in a purple dressing gown, there Aunt Dahlia in the old blue and yellow. It also fell upon Anatole, Tuppy, Gussie, Angela, the Bassett and Jeeves, in the order named. There they all were, present and correct.

But—and this was what caused me immediate concern—I could detect no sign whatever that there had been any rescue work going on.

What I had been hoping, of course, was to see Tuppy bending solicitously over Angela in one corner, while Gussie fanned the Bassett with a towel in the other. Instead of which, the Bassett was one of the group which included Aunt Dahlia and Uncle Tom and seemed to be busy trying to make Anatole see the bright side, while Angela and Gussie were, respectively, leaning against the sundial with a peeved look and sitting on the grass rubbing a barked shin. Tuppy was walking up and down the path, all by himself.

A disturbing picture, you will admit. It was with a rather imperious gesture that I summoned Jeeves to my side.

"Well, Jeeves?"

"Sir?"

I eyed him sternly. "Sir?" forsooth!

"It's no good saying 'Sir?' Jeeves. Look round you. See for yourself. Your scheme has proved a bust."

"Certainly it would appear that matters have not arranged themselves quite as we anticipated, sir."

"We?"

"As I had anticipated, sir."

"That's more like it. Didn't I tell you it would be a flop?"

"I remember that you did seem dubious, sir."

"Dubious is no word for it, Jeeves. I hadn't a scrap of faith in the idea from the start. When you first mooted it, I said it was rotten, and I was right. I'm not blaming you, Jeeves. It is not your fault that you have sprained your brain. But after this—forgive me if I hurt your feelings, Jeeves——I shall know better than to allow you to handle any but the simplest and most elementary problems. It is best to be candid about this, don't you think? Kindest to be frank and straightforward?"

"Certainly, sir."

"I mean, the surgeon's knife, what?"

"Precisely, sir."

"I consider——"

"If you will pardon me for interrupting you, sir, I fancy Mrs. Travers is endeavouring to attract your attention."

And at this moment a ringing "Hoy!" which could have proceeded only from the relative in question, assured me that his view was correct.

"Just step this way a moment, Attila, if you don't mind," boomed that well-known—and under certain conditions, well-loved—voice, and I moved over.

I was not feeling unmixedly at my ease. For the first time it was beginning to steal upon me that I had not prepared a really good story in support of my questionable behaviour in ringing fire bells at such an hour, and I have known Aunt Dahlia to express herself with a hearty freedom upon far smaller provocation.

She exhibited, however, no signs of violence. More a sort of frozen calm, if you know what I mean. You could see that she was a woman who had suffered.

"Well, Bertie, dear," she said, "here we all are."

"Quite," I replied guardedly.

"Nobody missing, is there?"

"I don't think so."

"Splendid. So much healthier for us out in the open like this than frowsting in bed. I had just dropped off when you did your bell-ringing act. For it was you, my sweet child, who rang that bell, was knot?"

"I did ring the bell, yes."

"Any particular reason, or just a whim?"

"I thought there was a fire."

"What gave you that impression, dear?"

"I thought I saw flames."

"Where, darling? Tell Aunt Dahlia."

"In one of the windows."

"I see. So we have all been dragged out of bed and scared rigid because you have been seeing things."

Here Uncle Tom made a noise like a cork coming out of a bottle, and Anatole, whose moustache had hit a new low, said something about "some apes" and, if I am not mistaken, a "*rogommier*"—whatever that is.

"I admit I was mistaken. I am sorry."

"Don't apologize, ducky. Can't you see how pleased we all are? What were you doing out here, anyway?"

"Just taking a stroll."

"I see. And are you proposing to continue your stroll?"

"No, I think I'll go in now."

"That's fine. Because I was thinking of going in, too, and I don't believe I could sleep knowing you were out here giving rein to that powerful imagination of yours. The next thing that would happen would be that you would think you saw a pink elephant sitting on the drawing-room window-sill and start throwing bricks at it.... Well, come on, Tom, the entertainment seems to be over.... But wait. The newt king wishes a word with us.... Yes, Mr. Fink-Nottle?"

Gussie, as he joined our little group, seemed upset about something.

"I say!"

"Say on, Augustus."

"I say, what are we going to do?"

"Speaking for myself, I intend to return to bed."

"But the door's shut."

"What door?"

"The front door. Somebody must have shut it."

"Then I shall open it."

"But it won't open."

"Then I shall try another door."

"But all the other doors are shut."

"What? Who shut them?"

"I don't know."

I advanced a theory!

"The wind?"

Aunt Dahlia's eyes met mine.

"Don't try me too high," she begged. "Not now, precious." And, indeed, even as I spoke, it did strike me that the night was pretty still.

Uncle Tom said we must get in through a window. Aunt Dahlia sighed a bit.

"How? Could Lloyd George do it, could Winston do it, could Baldwin do it? No. Not since you had those bars of yours put on."

"Well, well, well. God bless my soul, ring the bell, then."

"The fire bell?"

"The door bell."

"To what end, Thomas? There's nobody in the house. The servants are all at Kingham."

"But, confound it all, we can't stop out here all night."

"Can't we? You just watch us. There is nothing—literally nothing—which a country house party can't do with Attila here operating on the premises. Seppings presumably took the back-door key with him. We must just amuse ourselves till he comes back."

Tuppy made a suggestion:

"Why not take out one of the cars and drive over to Kingham and get the key from Seppings?"

It went well. No question about that. For the first time, a smile lit up Aunt Dahlia's drawn face. Uncle Tom grunted approvingly. Anatole said something in Provençal that sounded complimentary. And I thought I detected even on Angela's map a slight softening.

"A very excellent idea," said Aunt Dahlia. "One of the best. Nip round to the garage at once."

After Tuppy had gone, some extremely flattering things were said about his intelligence and resource, and there was a disposition to draw rather invidious comparisons between him and Bertram. Painful for me, of course, but the ordeal didn't last long, for it couldn't have been more than five minutes before he was with us again.

Tuppy seemed perturbed.

"I say, it's all off."

"Why?"

"The garage is locked."

"Unlock it."

"I haven't the key."

"Shout, then, and wake Waterbury."

"Who's Waterbury?"

"The chauffeur, ass. He sleeps over the garage."

"But he's gone to the dance at Kingham."

It was the final wallop. Until this moment, Aunt Dahlia had been able to preserve her frozen calm. The dam now burst. The years rolled away from her, and she was once more the Dahlia Wooster of the old yoicks-and-tantivy days—the emotional, free-speaking girl who had so often risen in her stirrups to yell derogatory personalities at people who were heading hounds.

"Curse all dancing chauffeurs! What on earth does a chauffeur want to dance for? I mistrusted that man from the start. Something told me he was a dancer. Well, this finishes it. We're out here till breakfast-time. If those blasted servants come back before eight o'clock, I shall be vastly surprised. You won't get Seppings away from a dance till you throw him out. I know him. The jazz'll go to his head, and he'll stand clapping and demanding encores till his hands blister. Damn all dancing butlers! What is Brinkley Court? A respectable English country house or a crimson dancing school? One might as well be living in the middle of the

Russian Ballet. Well, all right. If we must stay out here, we must. We shall all be frozen stiff, except"—here she directed at me not one of her friendliest glances—
—"except dear old Attila, who is, I observe, well and warmly clad. We will resign ourselves to the prospect of freezing to death like the Babes in the Wood, merely expressing a dying wish that our old pal Attila will see that we are covered with leaves. No doubt he will also toll that fire bell of his as a mark of respect—And what might you want, my good man?"

She broke off, and stood glaring at Jeeves. During the latter portion of her address, he had been standing by in a respectful manner, endeavouring to catch the speaker's eye.

"If I might make a suggestion, madam."

I am not saying that in the course of our long association I have always found myself able to view Jeeves with approval. There are aspects of his character which have frequently caused coldnesses to arise between us. He is one of those fellows who, if you give them a thingummy, take a what-d'you-call-it. His work is often raw, and he has been known to allude to me as "mentally negligible". More than once, as I have shown, it has been my painful task to squelch in him a tendency to get uppish and treat the young master as a serf or peon.

These are grave defects.

But one thing I have never failed to hand the man. He is magnetic. There is about him something that seems to soothe and hypnotize. To the best of my knowledge, he has never encountered a charging rhinoceros, but should this contingency occur, I have no doubt that the animal, meeting his eye, would check itself in mid-stride, roll over and lie purring with its legs in the air.

At any rate he calmed down Aunt Dahlia, the nearest thing to a charging rhinoceros, in under five seconds. He just stood there looking respectful, and though I didn't time the thing—not having a stop-watch on me—I should say it wasn't more than three seconds and a quarter before her whole manner underwent an astounding change for the better. She melted before one's eyes.

"Jeeves! You haven't got an idea?"

"Yes, madam."

"That great brain of yours has really clicked as ever in the hour of need?"

"Yes, madam."

"Jeeves," said Aunt Dahlia in a shaking voice, "I am sorry I spoke so abruptly. I was not myself. I might have known that you would not come simply trying to make conversation. Tell us this idea of yours, Jeeves. Join our little group of thinkers and let us hear what you have to say. Make yourself at home, Jeeves, and give us the good word. Can you really get us out of this mess?"

"Yes, madam, if one of the gentlemen would be willing to ride a bicycle."

"A bicycle?"

"There is a bicycle in the gardener's shed in the kitchen garden, madam. Possibly one of the gentlemen might feel disposed to ride over to Kingham Manor and procure the back-door key from Mr. Seppings."

"Splendid, Jeeves!"

"Thank you, madam."

"Wonderful!"

"Thank you, madam."

"Attila!" said Aunt Dahlia, turning and speaking in a quiet, authoritative manner.

I had been expecting it. From the very moment those ill-judged words had passed the fellow's lips, I had had a presentiment that a determined effort would be made to elect me as the goat, and I braced myself to resist and obstruct.

And as I was about to do so, while I was in the very act of summoning up all my eloquence to protest that I didn't know how to ride a bike and couldn't possibly learn in the brief time at my disposal, I'm dashed if the man didn't go and nip me in the bud.

"Yes, madam, Mr. Wooster would perform the task admirably. He is an expert cyclist. He has often boasted to me of his triumphs on the wheel."

I hadn't. I hadn't done anything of the sort. It's simply monstrous how one's words get twisted. All I had ever done was to mention to him—casually, just as an interesting item of information, one day in New York when we were watching the six-day bicycle race—that at the age of fourteen, while spending my holidays with a vicar of sorts who had been told off to teach me Latin, I had won the Choir Boys' Handicap at the local school treat.

A different thing from boasting of one's triumphs on the wheel.

I mean, he was a man of the world and must have known that the form of school treats is never of the hottest. And, if I'm not mistaken, I had specifically told him that on the occasion referred to I had received half a lap start and that Willie Punting, the odds-on favourite to whom the race was expected to be a gift, had been forced to retire, owing to having pinched his elder brother's machine without asking the elder brother, and the elder brother coming along just as the pistol went and giving him one on the side of the head and taking it away from him, thus rendering him a scratched-at-the-post non-starter. Yet, from the way he talked, you would have thought I was one of those chaps in sweaters with medals all over them, whose photographs bob up from time to time in the illustrated press on the occasion of their having ridden from Hyde Park Corner to Glasgow in three seconds under the hour, or whatever it is.

And as if this were not bad enough, Tuppy had to shove his oar in.

"That's right," said Tuppy. "Bertie has always been a great cyclist. I remember at Oxford he used to take all his clothes off on bump-supper nights and ride around the quad, singing comic songs. Jolly fast he used to go too."

"Then he can go jolly fast now," said Aunt Dahlia with animation. "He can't go too fast for me. He may also sing comic songs, if he likes.... And if you wish to take your clothes off, Bertie, my lamb, by all means do so. But whether clothed or in the nude, whether singing comic songs or not singing comic songs, get a move on."

I found speech:

"But I haven't ridden for years."

"Then it's high time you began again."

"I've probably forgotten how to ride."

"You'll soon get the knack after you've taken a toss or two. Trial and error. The only way."

"But it's miles to Kingham."

"So the sooner you're off, the better."

"But——"

"Bertie, dear."

"But, dash it——"

"Bertie, darling."

"Yes, but dash it——"

"Bertie, my sweet."

And so it was arranged. Presently I was moving sombrely off through the darkness, Jeeves at my side, Aunt Dahlia calling after me something about trying to imagine myself the man who brought the good news from Ghent to Aix. The first I had heard of the chap.

"So, Jeeves," I said, as we reached the shed, and my voice was cold and bitter, "this is what your great scheme has accomplished! Tuppy, Angela, Gussie and the Bassett not on speaking terms, and self faced with an eight-mile ride——"

"Nine, I believe, sir."

"—a nine-mile ride, and another nine-mile ride back."

"I am sorry, sir."

"No good being sorry now. Where is this foul bone-shaker?"

"I will bring it out, sir."

He did so. I eyed it sourly.

"Where's the lamp?"

"I fear there is no lamp, sir."

"No lamp?"

"No, sir."

"But I may come a fearful stinker without a lamp. Suppose I barge into something."

I broke off and eyed him frigidly.

"You smile, Jeeves. The thought amuses you?"

"I beg your pardon, sir. I was thinking of a tale my Uncle Cyril used to tell me as a child. An absurd little story, sir, though I confess that I have always found it droll. According to my Uncle Cyril, two men named Nicholls and Jackson set out to ride to Brighton on a tandem bicycle, and were so unfortunate as to come into collision with a brewer's van. And when the rescue party arrived on the scene of the accident, it was discovered that they had been hurled together with such force that it was impossible to sort them out at all adequately. The keenest eye could not discern which portion of the fragments was Nicholls and which Jackson. So they collected as much as they could, and called it Nixon. I remember laughing very much at that story when I was a child, sir."

I had to pause a moment to master my feelings.

"You did, eh?"

"Yes, sir."

"You thought it funny?"

"Yes, sir."

"And your Uncle Cyril thought it funny?"

"Yes, sir."

"Golly, what a family! Next time you meet your Uncle Cyril, Jeeves, you can tell him from me that his sense of humour is morbid and unpleasant."

"He is dead, sir."

"Thank heaven for that.... Well, give me the blasted machine."

"Very good, sir."

"Are the tyres inflated?"

"Yes, sir."

"The nuts firm, the brakes in order, the sprockets running true with the differential gear?"

"Yes, sir."

"Right ho, Jeeves."

In Tuppy's statement that, when at the University of Oxford, I had been known to ride a bicycle in the nude about the quadrangle of our mutual college, there had been, I cannot deny, a certain amount of substance. Correct, however, though his facts were, so far as they went, he had not told all. What he had omitted to mention was that I had invariably been well oiled at the time, and when in that condition a chap is capable of feats at which in cooler moments his reason would rebel.

Stimulated by the juice, I believe, men have even been known to ride alligators.

As I started now to pedal out into the great world, I was icily sober, and the old skill, in consequence, had deserted me entirely. I found myself wobbling badly, and all the stories I had ever heard of nasty bicycle accidents came back to me with a rush, headed by Jeeves's Uncle Cyril's cheery little anecdote about Nicholls and Jackson.

Pounding wearily through the darkness, I found myself at a loss to fathom the mentality of men like Jeeves's Uncle Cyril. What on earth he could see funny in a disaster which had apparently involved the complete extinction of a human creature—or, at any rate, of half a human creature and half another human creature—was more than I could understand. To me, the thing was one of the most poignant tragedies that had ever been brought to my attention, and I have no doubt that I should have continued to brood over it for quite a time, had my thoughts not been diverted by the sudden necessity of zigzagging sharply in order to avoid a pig in the fairway.

For a moment it looked like being real Nicholls-and-Jackson stuff, but, fortunately, a quick zig on my part, coinciding with an adroit zag on the part of the pig, enabled me to win through, and I continued my ride safe, but with the heart fluttering like a captive bird.

The effect of this narrow squeak upon me was to shake the nerve to the utmost. The fact that pigs were abroad in the night seemed to bring home to me the perilous nature of my enterprise. It set me thinking of all the other things that could happen to a man out and about on a velocipede without a lamp after lighting-up time. In particular, I recalled the statement of a pal of mine that in certain sections of the rural districts goats were accustomed to stray across the road to the extent of their chains, thereby forming about as sound a booby trap as one could well wish.

He mentioned, I remember, the case of a friend of his whose machine got entangled with a goat chain and who was dragged seven miles—like skijoring in Switzerland—so that he was never the same man again. And there was one chap who ran into an elephant, left over from a travelling circus.

Indeed, taking it for all in all, it seemed to me that, with the possible exception of being bitten by sharks, there was virtually no front-page disaster that could not happen to a fellow, once he had allowed his dear ones to override his better judgment and shove him out into the great unknown on a push-bike, and I am not ashamed to confess that, taking it by and large, the amount of quailing I did from this point on was pretty considerable.

However, in respect to goats and elephants, I must say things panned out unexpectedly well.

Oddly enough, I encountered neither. But when you have said that you have said everything, for in every other way the conditions could scarcely have been fouler.

Apart from the ceaseless anxiety of having to keep an eye skinned for elephants, I found myself much depressed by barking dogs, and once I received a most unpleasant shock when, alighting to consult a signpost, I saw sitting on top of it an owl that looked exactly like my Aunt Agatha. So agitated, indeed, had my frame of mind become by this time that I thought at first it was Aunt Agatha, and only when reason and reflection told me how alien to her habits it would be to climb signposts and sit on them, could I pull myself together and overcome the weakness.

In short, what with all this mental disturbance added to the more purely physical anguish in the billowy portions and the calves and ankles, the Bertram Wooster who eventually toppled off at the door of Kingham Manor was a very different Bertram from the gay and insouciant *boulevardier* of Bond Street and Piccadilly.

Even to one unaware of the inside facts, it would have been evident that Kingham Manor was throwing its weight about a bit tonight. Lights shone in the windows, music was in the air, and as I drew nearer my ear detected the sibilant shuffling of the feet of butlers, footmen, chauffeurs, parlourmaids, housemaids, tweenies and, I have no doubt, cooks, who were busily treading the measure. I suppose you couldn't sum it up much better than by saying that there was a sound of revelry by night.

The orgy was taking place in one of the ground-floor rooms which had French windows opening on to the drive, and it was to these French windows that I now made my way. An orchestra was playing something with a good deal of zip to it, and under happier conditions I dare say my feet would have started twitching in time to the melody. But I had sterner work before me than to stand hoofing it by myself on gravel drives.

I wanted that back-door key, and I wanted it instanter.

Scanning the throng within, I found it difficult for a while to spot Seppings. Presently, however, he hove in view, doing fearfully lissom things in mid-floor. I "Hi-Seppings!"-ed a couple of times, but his mind was too much on his job to be diverted, and it was only when the swirl of the dance had brought him within prodding distance of my forefinger that a quick one to the lower ribs enabled me to claim his attention.

The unexpected buffet caused him to trip over his partner's feet, and it was with marked austerity that he turned. As he recognized Bertram, however, coldness melted, to be replaced by astonishment.

"Mr. Wooster!"

I was in no mood for bandying words.

"Less of the 'Mr. Wooster' and more back-door keys," I said curtly. "Give me the key of the back door, Seppings."

He did not seem to grasp the gist.

"The key of the back door, sir?"

"Precisely. The Brinkley Court back-door key."

"But it is at the Court, sir."

I clicked the tongue, annoyed.

"Don't be frivolous, my dear old butler," I said. "I haven't ridden nine miles on a push-bike to listen to you trying to be funny. You've got it in your trousers pocket."

"No, sir. I left it with Mr. Jeeves."

"You did—what?"

"Yes, sir. Before I came away. Mr. Jeeves said that he wished to walk in the garden before retiring for the night. He was to place the key on the kitchen window-sill."

I stared at the man dumbly. His eye was clear, his hand steady. He had none of the appearance of a butler who has had a couple.

"You mean that all this while the key has been in Jeeves's possession?"??

"Yes, sir."

I could speak no more. Emotion had overmastered my voice. I was at a loss and not abreast; but of one thing, it seemed to me, there could be no doubt. For some reason, not to be fathomed now, but most certainly to be gone well into as soon as I had pushed this infernal sewing-machine of mine over those nine miles of lonely, country road and got within striking distance of him, Jeeves had been doing the dirty. Knowing that at any given moment he could have solved the whole situation, he had kept Aunt Dahlia and others roosting out on the front lawn *en déshabille* and, worse still, had stood calmly by and watched his young employer set out on a wholly unnecessary eighteen-mile bicycle ride.

I could scarcely believe such a thing of him. Of his Uncle Cyril, yes. With that distorted sense of humour of his, Uncle Cyril might quite conceivably have been capable of such conduct. But that it should be Jeeves—

I leaped into the saddle and, stifling the cry of agony which rose to the lips as the bruised person touched the hard leather, set out on the homeward journey.

-23-

I remember Jeeves saying on one occasion—I forgot how the subject had arisen—he may simply have thrown the observation out, as he does sometimes, for me to take or leave—that hell hath no fury like a woman scorned. And until tonight I had always felt that there was a lot in it. I had never scorned a woman myself, but Pongo Twistleton once scorned an aunt of his, flatly refusing to meet her son Gerald at Paddington and give him lunch and see him off to school at Waterloo, and he never heard the end of it. Letters were written, he tells me, which had to be seen to be believed. Also two very strong telegrams and a bitter picture post card with a view of the Little Chilbury War Memorial on it.

Until tonight, therefore, as I say, I had never questioned the accuracy of the statement. Scorned women first and the rest nowhere, was how it had always seemed to me.

But tonight I revised my views. If you want to know what hell can really do in the way of furies, look for the chap who has been hornswoggled into taking a long and unnecessary bicycle ride in the dark without a lamp.

Mark that word "unnecessary". That was the part of it that really jabbed the iron into the soul. I mean, if it was a case of riding to the doctor's to save the child with croup, or going off to the local pub to fetch supplies in the event of the cellar having run dry, no one would leap to the handlebars more readily than I. Young Lochinvar, absolutely. But this business of being put through it merely to gratify one's personal attendant's diseased sense of the amusing was a bit too thick, and I chafed from start to finish.

So, what I mean to say, although the providence which watches over good men saw to it that I was enabled to complete the homeward journey unscathed except in the billowy portions, removing from my path all goats, elephants, and even owls that looked like my Aunt Agatha, it was a frowning and jaundiced Bertram who finally came to anchor at the Brinkley Court front door. And when I saw a dark figure emerging from the porch to meet me, I prepared to let myself go and uncork all that was fizzing in the mind.

"Jeeves!" I said.

"It is I, Bertie."

The voice which spoke sounded like warm treacle, and even if I had not recognized it immediately as that of the Bassett, I should have known that it did not proceed from the man I was yearning to confront. For this figure before me was wearing a simple tweed dress and had employed my first name in its remarks. And Jeeves, whatever his moral defects, would never go about in skirts calling me Bertie.

The last person, of course, whom I would have wished to meet after a long evening in the saddle, but I vouchsafed a courteous "What ho!"

There was a pause, during which I massaged the calves. Mine, of course, I mean.

"You got in, then?" I said, in allusion to the change of costume.

"Oh, yes. About a quarter of an hour after you left Jeeves went searching about and found the back-door key on the kitchen window-sill."

"Ha!"

"What?"

"Nothing."

"I thought you said something."

"No, nothing."

And I continued to do so. For at this juncture, as had so often happened when this girl and I were closeted, the conversation once more went blue on us. The night breeze whispered, but not the Bassett. A bird twittered, but not so much as a chirp escaped Bertram. It was perfectly amazing, the way her mere presence seemed to wipe speech from my lips—and mine, for that matter, from hers. It began to look as if our married life together would be rather like twenty years among the Trappist monks.

"Seen Jeeves anywhere?" I asked, eventually coming through.

"Yes, in the dining-room."

"The dining-room?"

"Waiting on everybody. They are having eggs and bacon and champagne.... What did you say?"

I had said nothing—merely snorted. There was something about the thought of these people carelessly revelling at a time when, for all they knew, I was probably being dragged about the countryside by goats or chewed by elephants, that struck home at me like a poisoned dart. It was the sort of thing you read about as having happened just before the French Revolution—the haughty nobles in their castles callously digging in and quaffing while the unfortunate blighters outside were suffering frightful privations.

The voice of the Bassett cut in on these mordant reflections:

"Bertie."

"Hullo!"

Silence.

"Hullo!" I said again.

No response. Whole thing rather like one of those telephone conversations where you sit at your end of the wire saying: "Hullo! Hullo!" unaware that the party of the second part has gone off to tea.

Eventually, however, she came to the surface again:

"Bertie, I have something to say to you."

"What?"

"I have something to say to you."

"I know. I said 'What?'"

"Oh, I thought you didn't hear what I said."

"Yes, I heard what you said, all right, but not what you were going to say."

"Oh, I see."

"Right-ho."

So that was straightened out. Nevertheless, instead of proceeding she took time off once more. She stood twisting the fingers and scratching the gravel with her foot. When finally she spoke, it was to deliver an impressive boost:

"Bertie, do you read Tennyson?"

"Not if I can help."

"You remind me so much of those Knights of the Round Table in the 'Idylls of the King'."

Of course I had heard of them—Lancelot, Galahad and all that lot, but I didn't see where the resemblance came in. It seemed to me that she must be thinking of a couple of other fellows.

"How do you mean?"

"You have such a great heart, such a fine soul. You are so generous, so unselfish, so chivalrous. I have always felt that about you—that you are one of the few really chivalrous men I have ever met."

Well, dashed difficult, of course, to know what to say when someone is giving you the old oil on a scale like that. I muttered an "Oh, yes?" or something on those lines, and rubbed the billowy portions in some embarrassment. And there was another silence, broken only by a sharp howl as I rubbed a bit too hard.

"Bertie."

"Hullo?"

I heard her give a sort of gulp.

"Bertie, will you be chivalrous now?"

"Rather. Only too pleased. How do you mean?"

"I am going to try you to the utmost. I am going to test you as few men have ever been tested. I am going——"

I didn't like the sound of this.

"Well," I said doubtfully, "always glad to oblige, you know, but I've just had the dickens of a bicycle ride, and I'm a bit stiff and sore, especially in the—as I say, a bit stiff and sore. If it's anything to be fetched from upstairs——"

"No, no, you don't understand."

"I don't, quite, no."

"Oh, it's so difficult.... How can I say it?... Can't you guess?"

"No. I'm dashed if I can."

"Bertie—let me go!"

"But I haven't got hold of you."

"Release me!"

"Re——"

And then I suddenly got it. I suppose it was fatigue that had made me so slow to apprehend the nub.

"What?"

I staggered, and the left pedal came up and caught me on the shin. But such was the ecstasy in the soul that I didn't utter a cry.

"Release you?"

"Yes."

I didn't want any confusion on the point.

"You mean you want to call it all off? You're going to hitch up with Gussie, after all?"

"Only if you are fine and big enough to consent."

"Oh, I am."

"I gave you my promise."

"Dash promises."

"Then you really——"

"Absolutely."

"Oh, Bertie!"

She seemed to sway like a sapling. It is saplings that sway, I believe.

"A very parfait knight!" I heard her murmur, and there not being much to say after that, I excused myself on the ground that I had got about two pecks of dust down my back and would like to go and get my maid to put me into something loose.

"You go back to Gussie," I said, "and tell him that all is well."

She gave a sort of hiccup and, darting forward, kissed me on the forehead. Unpleasant, of course, but, as Anatole would say, I can take a few smooths with a rough. The next moment she was legging it for the dining-room, while I, having bunged the bicycle into a bush, made for the stairs.

I need not dwell upon my buckedness. It can be readily imagined. Talk about chaps with the noose round their necks and the hangman about to let her go and somebody galloping up on a foaming horse, waving the reprieve—not in it. Absolutely not in it at all. I don't know that I can give you a better idea of the state of my feelings than by saying that as I started to cross the hall I was conscious of so profound a benevolence toward all created things that I found myself thinking kindly thoughts even of Jeeves.

I was about to mount the stairs when a sudden "What ho!" from my rear caused me to turn. Tuppy was standing in the hall. He had apparently been down to the cellar for reinforcements, for there were a couple of bottles under his arm.

"Hullo, Bertie," he said. "You back?" He laughed amusedly. "You look like the Wreck of the Hesperus. Get run over by a steam-roller or something?"

At any other time I might have found his coarse badinage hard to bear. But such was my uplifted mood that I waved it aside and slipped him the good news.

"Tuppy, old man, the Bassett's going to marry Gussie Fink-Nottle."

"Tough luck on both of them, what?"

"But don't you understand? Don't you see what this means? It means that Angela is once more out of pawn, and you have only to play your cards properly——"

He bellowed rollickingly. I saw now that he was in the pink. As a matter of fact, I had noticed something of the sort directly I met him, but had attributed it to alcoholic stimulant.

"Good Lord! You're right behind the times, Bertie. Only to be expected, of course, if you will go riding bicycles half the night. Angela and I made it up hours ago."

"What?"

"Certainly. Nothing but a passing tiff. All you need in these matters is a little give and take, a bit of reasonableness on both sides. We got together and talked things over. She withdrew my double chin. I conceded her shark. Perfectly simple. All done in a couple of minutes."

"But——"

"Sorry, Bertie. Can't stop chatting with you all night. There is a rather impressive beano in progress in the dining-room, and they are waiting for supplies."

Endorsement was given to this statement by a sudden shout from the apartment named. I recognized—as who would not—Aunt Dahlia's voice:

"Glossop!"

"Hullo?"

"Hurry up with that stuff."

"Coming, coming."

"Well, come, then. Yoicks! Hard for-rard!"

"Tallyho, not to mention tantivy. Your aunt," said Tuppy, "is a bit above herself. I don't know all the facts of the case, but it appears that Anatole gave notice and has now consented to stay on, and also your uncle has given her a cheque for that paper of hers. I didn't get the details, but she is much braced. See you later. I must rush."

To say that Bertram was now definitely nonplussed would be but to state the simple truth. I could make nothing of this. I had left Brinkley Court a stricken home, with hearts bleeding wherever you looked, and I had returned to find it a sort of earthly paradise. It baffled me.

I bathed bewilderedly. The toy duck was still in the soap-dish, but I was too preoccupied to give it a thought. Still at a loss, I returned to my room, and there was Jeeves. And it is proof of my fogged condish that my first words to him were words not of reproach and stern recrimination but of inquiry:

"I say, Jeeves!"

"Good evening, sir. I was informed that you had returned. I trust you had an enjoyable ride."

At any other moment, a crack like that would have woken the fiend in Bertram Wooster. I barely noticed it. I was intent on getting to the bottom of this mystery.

"But I say, Jeeves, what?"

"Sir?"

"What does all this mean?"

"You refer, sir——"

"Of course I refer. You know what I'm talking about. What has been happening here since I left? The place is positively stiff with happy endings."

"Yes, sir. I am glad to say that my efforts have been rewarded."

"What do you mean, your efforts? You aren't going to try to make out that that rotten fire bell scheme of yours had anything to do with it?"

"Yes, sir."

"Don't be an ass, Jeeves. It flopped."

"Not altogether, sir. I fear, sir, that I was not entirely frank with regard to my suggestion of ringing the fire bell. I had not really anticipated that it would in itself produce the desired results. I had intended it merely as a preliminary to what I might describe as the real business of the evening."

"You gibber, Jeeves."

"No, sir. It was essential that the ladies and gentlemen should be brought from the house, in order that, once out of doors, I could ensure that they remained there for the necessary period of time."

"How do you mean?"

"My plan was based on psychology, sir."

"How?"

"It is a recognized fact, sir, that there is nothing that so satisfactorily unites individuals who have been so unfortunate as to quarrel amongst themselves as a strong mutual dislike for some definite person. In my own family, if I may give a homely illustration, it was a generally accepted axiom that in times of domestic disagreement it was necessary only to invite my Aunt Annie for a visit to heal all breaches between the other members of the household. In the mutual animosity excited by Aunt Annie, those who had become estranged were reconciled almost immediately. Remembering this, it occurred to me that were you, sir, to be established as the person responsible for the ladies and gentlemen being forced to spend the night in the garden, everybody would take so strong a dislike to you that in this common sympathy they would sooner or later come together."

I would have spoken, but he continued:

"And such proved to be the case. All, as you see, sir, is now well. After your departure on the bicycle, the various estranged parties agreed so heartily in their abuse of you that the ice, if I may use the expression, was broken, and it was not long before Mr. Glossop was walking beneath the trees with Miss Angela, telling her anecdotes of your career at the university in exchange for hers regarding your childhood; while Mr. Fink-Nottle, leaning against the sundial, held Miss Bassett enthralled with stories of your schooldays. Mrs. Travers, meanwhile, was telling Monsieur Anatole——"

I found speech.

"Oh?" I said. "I see. And now, I suppose, as the result of this dashed psychology of yours, Aunt Dahlia is so sore with me that it will be years before I can dare to show my face here again—years, Jeeves, during which, night after night, Anatole will be cooking those dinners of his——"

"No, sir. It was to prevent any such contingency that I suggested that you should bicycle to Kingham Manor. When I informed the ladies and gentlemen that I had found the key, and it was borne in upon them that you were having that long ride for nothing, their animosity vanished immediately, to be replaced by cordial amusement. There was much laughter."

"There was, eh?"

"Yes, sir. I fear you may possibly have to submit to a certain amount of good-natured chaff, but nothing more. All, if I may say so, is forgiven, sir."

"Oh?"

"Yes, sir."

I mused awhile.

"You certainly seem to have fixed things."

"Yes, sir."

"Tuppy and Angela are once more betrothed. Also Gussie and the Bassett; Uncle Tom appears to have coughed up that money for *Milady's Boudoir.* And Anatole is staying on."

"Yes, sir."

"I suppose you might say that all's well that ends well."

"Very apt, sir."

I mused again.

"All the same, your methods are a bit rough, Jeeves."

"One cannot make an omelette without breaking eggs, sir."

I started.

"Omelette! Do you think you could get me one?"

"Certainly, sir."

"Together with half a bot. of something?"

"Undoubtedly, sir."

"Do so, Jeeves, and with all speed."

I climbed into bed and sank back against the pillows. I must say that my generous wrath had ebbed a bit. I was aching the whole length of my body, particularly toward the middle, but against this you had to set the fact that I was no longer engaged to Madeline Bassett. In a good cause one is prepared to suffer. Yes, looking at the thing from every angle, I saw that Jeeves had done well, and it was with an approving beam that I welcomed him as he returned with the needful.

He did not check up with this beam. A bit grave, he seemed to me to be looking, and I probed the matter with a kindly query:

"Something on your mind, Jeeves?"

"Yes, sir. I should have mentioned it earlier, but in the evening's disturbance it escaped my memory, I fear I have been remiss, sir."

"Yes, Jeeves?" I said, champing contentedly.

"In the matter of your mess-jacket, sir."

A nameless fear shot through me, causing me to swallow a mouthful of omelette the wrong way.

"I am sorry to say, sir, that while I was ironing it this afternoon I was careless enough to leave the hot instrument upon it. I very much fear that it will be impossible for you to wear it again, sir."

One of those old pregnant silences filled the room.

"I am extremely sorry, sir."

For a moment, I confess, that generous wrath of mine came bounding back, hitching up its muscles and snorting a bit through the nose, but, as we say on the Riviera, *à quoi sert-il*? There was nothing to be gained by g.w. now.

We Woosters can bite the bullet. I nodded moodily and speared another slab of omelette.

"Right ho, Jeeves."

"Very good, sir."

Make Way for Lucia - The Complete Mapp & Lucia - Queen Lucia, Miss Mapp including 'The Male Impersonator', Lucia in London, Mapp and Lucia, Lucia's Progress (also known as The Worshipful Lucia), & Trouble for Lucia
E F Benson
Benediction Classics, 2012
1052 pages
ISBN: 978-1-78139-148-8

Available from www.amazon.com, www.amazon.co.uk

Make way for Lucia is a series of novels written by E.F Benson. They feature hilarious incidents in the lives of upper-middle class people in the 1920s and '30s. The characters vie for social standing in an extremely snobby world. In the series the two main characters - sophisticated Lucia and frumpy Miss Mapp compete with each other and have to extricate themselves from a series of social disasters in comical style. The novels are: Queen Lucia (1920) Miss Mapp (1922) The Male Impersonator (a short story) Lucia in London (1927) Mapp and Lucia (1931) Lucia's Progress (1935) (published in the U.S. as The Worshipful Lucia) Trouble for Lucia (1939)

Famous Novels -(unabridged) Lost Horizon, Knight Without Armour, Goodbye, Mr. Chips, Random Harvest, The Story of Dr Wassell, & So Well Remembered
James Hilton
Oxford City Press, 2012
830 pages
ISBN: 978-1-78139-202-7

Available from www.amazon.com, www.amazon.co.uk

James Hilton was an eminent novelist, many of his stories critiquing English culture. His first novel was published when he was just 20, and several of his books were international best sellers and successfully adapted for film. This is a compilation brings together Hilton's most famous novels, all unabridged: Lost Horizon, Knight Without Armour , Goodbye, Mr. Chips, Random Harvest, The Story of Dr Wassell and So Well Remembered.

The Pat Hobby Stories
F. Scott Fitzgerald
Benediction Classics, 2011
120 pages
ISBN: 978-1-84902-367-2

Available from www.amazon.com, www.amazon.co.uk

The Pat Hobby Stories are a collection of 17 comedic short stories written by F. Scott Fitzgerald. They first appeared in Esquire magazine between January 1940 and May 1941, but in 1962 they were collected into a single book and published posthumously. Pat Hobby is a once successful screenwriter in Hollywood, but now an alcoholic and broke, who spends his time hanging around the studio, hoping for work. The stories generally revolve around him hatching a plan to earn money or glory in some way, but they usually end in further humiliation. The introduction to the book states, "while it would be unfair to judge this book as a novel, it would be less than fair to consider it as anything but a full-length portrait. It was as such that Fitzgerald worked on it, and would have wanted it presented in book form, after its original magazine publication. He thought of it as a comedy."

Eve's Diary, Complete with original cover design and over 50 illustrations
Mark Twain
Benediction Classics, 2011
116 pages
ISBN 978-1-84902-286-6

Available from www.amazon.com, www.amazon.co.uk

Eve's Diary, by Mark Twain, is a beautiful book with pictures of Eve exploring the delights of Eden on every other page, with the text on the adjacent page. The book is written in Eve's voice and gives her description of the events in Eden and her relationship with Adam, as if she wrote a diary. Shelley Fisher Fishkin, a Twain scholar at Stanford University, said the book was "infused with his appreciation for the women he was close to." This is perhaps because Twain wrote it shortly after his wife, Olivia, died. This book comes fully illustrated with over fifty delightful illustrations and the original cover design.

Also from Benediction Books ...

Wandering Between Two Worlds: Essays on Faith and Art
Anita Mathias
Benediction Books, 2007
152 pages
ISBN: 0955373700

Available from www.amazon.com, www.amazon.co.uk

In these wide-ranging lyrical essays, Anita Mathias writes, in lush, lovely prose, of her naughty Catholic childhood in Jamshedpur, India; her large, eccentric family in Mangalore, a sea-coast town converted by the Portuguese in the sixteenth century; her rebellion and atheism as a teenager in her Himalayan boarding school, run by German missionary nuns, St. Mary's Convent, Nainital; and her abrupt religious conversion after which she entered Mother Teresa's convent in Calcutta as a novice. Later rich, elegant essays explore the dualities of her life as a writer, mother, and Christian in the United States-- Domesticity and Art, Writing and Prayer, and the experience of being "an alien and stranger" as an immigrant in America, sensing the need for roots.

About the Author

Anita Mathias is the author of *Wandering Between Two Worlds: Essays on Faith and Art*. She has a B.A. and M.A. in English from Somerville College, Oxford University, and an M.A. in Creative Writing from the Ohio State University, USA. Anita won a National Endowment of the Arts fellowship in Creative Non-fiction in 1997. She lives in Oxford, England with her husband, Roy, and her daughters, Zoe and Irene.

Anita's website:
http://www.anitamathias.com, and
Anita's blog Dreaming Beneath the Spires:
http://dreamingbeneaththespires.blogspot.com

The Church That Had Too Much
Anita Mathias
Benediction Books, 2010
52 pages
ISBN: 9781849026567

Available from www.amazon.com, www.amazon.co.uk

The Church That Had Too Much was very well-intentioned. She wanted to love God, she wanted to love people, but she was both hampered by her muchness and the abundance of her possessions, and beset by ambition, power struggles and snobbery. Read about the surprising way The Church That Had Too Much began to resolve her problems in this deceptively simple and enchanting fable.

About the Author

Anita Mathias is the author of *Wandering Between Two Worlds: Essays on Faith and Art*. She has a B.A. and M.A. in English from Somerville College, Oxford University, and an M.A. in Creative Writing from the Ohio State University, USA. Anita won a National Endowment of the Arts fellowship in Creative Non-fiction in 1997. She lives in Oxford, England with her husband, Roy, and her daughters, Zoe and Irene.

Anita's website:
    http://www.anitamathias.com, and
Anita's blog Dreaming Beneath the Spires:
    http://dreamingbeneaththespires.blogspot.com

www.ingramcontent.com/pod-product-compliance
Lightning Source LLC
Chambersburg PA
CBHW081129300726
48982CB00005B/895

* 9 7 8 1 7 8 1 3 9 2 9 1 1 *